The Chronicle Series
S.J. Garrett

Books by S.J. Garrett

CHRONICLE SERIES
Chronicle of Destiny
Chronicle of Summer

ETERNITY SERIES
Ghost Eyes

DESCENDANTS SERIES
Shadow on the Sea

3RD DISTRICT SERIES
The Shaughnessy File
The Carmichael File
The Dease File
The Lucino File
The Taber File

SINGLES
Until The Dawn Breaks

Chronicle of Destiny and Chronicle of Summer

Copyright © 2017 S.J. Garrett

Published by Line By Lion Publications, LLC, 318 Louis Coleman Jr. Drive, Louisville, KY 40212

Cover art by Stacy J. Garrett Photography

ISBN 9781948807-081

Chronicle of Destiny
Book One of The Chronicle Series

Part One
~Tariah~

Prologue

Dear reader,

I was born in a normal city, at the edges of a normal country, on the normal world of Lucksphere. I was a normal girl, with normal Magi powers, and I had a normal life. My parents were normal, one an Air Magi and the other a Water Magi. They had grown up normal, in normal cities, inside normal countries, on this normal world.

But during my thirteenth year of life, all that normality changed. I woke one morning and discovered that I was destined to die.

You see, my body had changed overnight. My skin had developed lines. Far from normal, these brown lines patterned me in a wide array of swirls and loops. They covered me from my face and down over my body and all the way to my toes. They swept down only the right half of my face and then expanded across the entirety of the front of my body, and then down only the outside of my left leg.

I was marked as a Chronicle. I was a member of the most hated race on the world. I didn't even know why they were hated! When people spoke of Chronicles, they spoke of Dragons and evil pacts. And yet, Dragons themselves were not so frowned on. In fact, Dragons scorned Magi as bigots and murderers.

I knew nothing about Chronicles, yet during my thirteenth summer, I became one. Before I started developing a figure, I developed lines.

It was law. All Chronicles were to be put to death instantly upon discovery. Children had been murdered for centuries just because they were different. My parents . . . let me live. They loved me no matter what I was. But how would I hide? The answer came from an unlikely source. There was a SunKin Faerie within our city who took pity on me. She sensed my awakening and came to my home. She used her magic to make my lines invisible.

There was a price to be paid. I could not let myself become passionate about anything. In temper, in amusement, or in love, I had to remain dispassionate about it all. If I ever grew passionate, my Chronicle body would respond and all her magic would disappear. Even the Kin cannot stop a Chronicle's power forever.

So. There I was. Thirteen years old, still waiting to grow breasts, and I was doomed to death if I ever let my emotions show. I could never fall in love, could never marry. Tell me honestly. Which is better? To be doomed to choke on my own emotions, or to die?

Well, I did not die. I continued to grow and age. I choked on my emotions, never let loose the feelings that welled so often inside me. In some ways, in my efforts to stay alive, I think I forgot how to truly live.

Then, in the summer of my twentieth year, it all changed. And that is the summer where my story begins.

Tariah M. Chronis

Chapter One

The sun was devilishly hot. Even the Magi with Air powers could not keep cool enough breezes blowing to prevent the sun from trying to bake them all. Any storm that was summoned to block the sun only managed to make the air humid and increase the discomfort of all. Even the SunKin, the Faeries and Elves who existed on the light of the sun, were feeling the effects.

Tariah Chronis lifted her visor for a moment long enough to squint at the distance, then lowered it again. It was the only thing keeping her silver eyes from straining in the bright light glaring off every reflective object. Thanks to the full desert clothes that were considered casual summer wear of the citizens of Symphony, she wasn't completely melting either.

She glanced down at the thought. 'Full clothes' was really a misnomer. By the standards of other cities, she might be considered barely dressed at all. On top, she wore a piece of cloth crossed over her breasts and tied both behind her neck and around her chest. On the bottom she wore a pair of cloth shorts that vividly displayed the length of her long legs. Her feet were encased in sturdy boots to protect them from the harsh desert sand.

Her long auburn brown hair was coiled on top of her head and her visor helped keep the weight in place. The visor was designed to shield her eyes from the sun and to also provide a soft cooling breeze down the length of her body. Unfortunately, the breeze currently did not work.

She let out a hard breath and pulled gloves on her hands. She was standing in front of a large cliff face outside the edges of her city. At the top of the cliff were several scraggly bushes with Knockback berries on them. So named because they were so sour that they knocked back any who ate them, she thought in wry amusement.

With lithe strength, she began to climb the cliff face. She had made the climb so many times that it was child's play. Her body was lean and strong, well-honed from survival in the hottest desert on Lucksphere. Only the hardiest of people made Symphony their home, but she couldn't imagine living anywhere else.

Halfway up the wall, a cloth bag filled with water struck the wall beside her head and exploded, sending warm water spraying into her face. Muttering curses, she shoved up her splattered visor and twisted slightly to look back at the ground. Her hackles rose as she saw the three teenage males standing there with nasty grins.

She had to order herself not to get angry. She stepped on the anger, choked it, and nearly choked physically as she forced herself to ignore them. For seven years, it had been her way of life. All her emotions had to be choked and stifled. If she ever let them free, her fate would be sealed and the world would sentence her to death.

"What do you want?" she called down to the boys. "I'm busy here."

"See?" one said. "I told you she didn't get angry. You can do whatever you want and she won't get mad at you. It's not normal. Hey, *poka!*"

"*Poka*, my ass," she muttered. *Poka* was an insult that implied the person being referred to was as slow and stupid as a Pokagale bird. The birds were so stupid that they often died falling out of their own nests because they forgot they could fly.

"Tariah's a *poka!*" The chant came from all three boys as they started lobbing more water balls.

She jerked her visor down again and started her climb once more. She ignored their taunts as fiercely as she ignored the water balls that kept narrowly missing her head. Finally, more disgusted than angry, she turned and made an elegant gesture with one hand. It was an exceptionally rude gesture, and it also harnessed her power. "You want Water," she muttered, "you get it."

A large tidal wave lifted out of the sands and began to chase the boys as they ran screaming back toward the city. They didn't make it in time, and the wave swept them up and sent them tumbling through the center of town. Even from the cliff, Tariah could hear the city laughing.

With a little satisfied smile, she worked her way up the rest of the wall. At the top, she unsheathed the dagger on her hip and began to harvest the berries. They were really sour and really disgusting, but their medicinal properties couldn't be beaten. The doctors made poultices and remedies out of the berries and leaves both.

When the satchel around her waist was full, she climbed back. As she jumped the last two feet, the ground under her feet shook and rumbled. It nearly knocked her over before she was able to catch her balance. It ended fairly swiftly and she let out the breath she was holding. Quakes on the continent of Choral were always more annoying than detrimental.

The rest of Symphony was of like mind. In size, the city covered a ten-mile diameter and boasted a population of nearly ten thousand. The buildings were made of red brick and hard-caked mud, but colorful tapestries and awnings brought the place to life. The streets were mostly sand but wooden tracks had been laid down for carts to roll on. Street sweepers made sure the tracks were kept clean every day.

Tariah loved Symphony. The heat, the color, the land, and the people. With a spring in her step, she hurried toward the doctor's office at the end of the main street. Inside was cool and comfortable, a welcome change from the midday heat. "Doc!" she called. "I'm back!"

"Ah there's my favorite Magi." The doctor was a MoonKin Elf of Dark power, and his skin was smooth chocolate. His eyes were silvery-gray like the moon and marked his MoonKin heritage as visibly as the little silvery tattoos on his arms.

He was not very big, only around five-six, so Tariah never felt exceptionally small beside him even though she was only five-two. She was a little fascinated by him too. Most Kin did not leave their homelands, but Maxim had done just that. He claimed it was to sew back together impulsive Magi, which amused her immensely.

She took off her satchel and set it down on the table. "Here you go." She gratefully took the glass of water he handed her and nearly finished it in a single gulp. "Whew! I needed that." She smiled. "A Water Magi, and I still get thirsty so fast."

"It's part of your power, and you know it." He began to sort the leaves and berries. Casually he said, "I noticed the three terrors come tumbling through town. Were they harassing you?"

She lowered her lashes slightly. She knew Maxim knew what she was though neither had spoken of it. The Kin always automatically sensed and recognized power in all other beings. It was one of their gifts. "Yes," she finally said. "But it didn't mean anything."

"I wish there was another way for you," he said softly. "You are one of the most giving young women I've ever known. To be condemned . . ."

"It can't be changed." She shrugged one shoulder and then smiled. "If anything, it gives me an edge. They think I'm a Master Magi, and that's enough to make them wary."

Master Magi were as rare as Chronicles but not nearly as loathed. Masters were simply Magi of exceptional skill. Tariah was willing to endure the slightly awed looks of people when they witnessed her strength with her powers; strength well beyond her years. It was better than to see them looking at her with hatred and murder in their eyes.

"What makes a Magi different from a Chronicle?" she whispered. "I don't feel any different. I'm just stronger, and I have lines over my skin."

Maxim sighed. "Like all creatures, a Magi uses lightning from birth. At puberty, they develop powers related to a primary element. Either Air, Water, Fire, or Soil. Then, during second puberty, they specialize with a secondary element related to the first."

"Yes, I know." She pulled a face. "Believe me, I went to school, and I was Magi the first part of my life. What makes a Chronicle *different*?"

"Well, I couldn't say precisely," he said. "They were wiped out over a thousand years ago, and all since have been put to death. But if the tales of my fellow Kin are true, then Chronicles were basically Magi that developed secondary elements at the same time as primary, and during second puberty they gained wholly new powers that were unique only to Chronicles and Furies."

Her heart gave a soft thud. She had never heard of a Fury before and yet something inside seemed to suddenly awaken. It strained and reached as if looking for something. "A Fury?" she asked softly.

"A Fury is a Dragon Lord." He watched her intently. "A Dragon Lord is not always a Fury, just as a Dragon is not always a Dragon Lord, but Furies are always Dragon Lords. They are the other half of a Chronicle. They are perfectly balanced and matched. When the correct Chronicle and Fury meet, they form a powerful bond and become Dragoons. The Fury will feed on the power of the Chronicle, and in turn the Chronicle can use Dragon majiks."

Tears burned the back of her eyes as she thought of finding the Fury meant for her. Someone that would accept her and love her for everything she was. She would not have to live in fear ever again. Somewhere in the world, she thought, there was probably a Dragon who felt the same as she. "I don't care for the majiks," she whispered. "I just want someone to understand me."

He had to smile. "I suspect that is how Chronicles always felt, and Furies as well. The Dragons still wait for Chronicles, or so they say. Legend states that they would protect any Chronicle they found, Fury mate or not. Legend also states that the lost continent of Dragons would welcome any Chronicle that was able to find them."

She frowned. "But how would I find them?" she asked. "I mean . . . Dragons aren't seen as commonly as Kin, and their continent has been lost for centuries, right?"

"That's what I've heard as well. Supposedly it lies at the place where the edges of the world meet." He smiled. "Perhaps someday you will find it. They say a Chronicle always knows. Maybe those lines on your body make the map leading you to them."

With a soft sigh, she put the thoughts of Furies and Chronicles out of her mind. Thinking about it just made her want it more, and if she let herself feel too deeply for it, then the aforementioned lines would become visible on her body. "Maybe someday," she agreed softly.

"Go home, little one," he said gently. "Don't stress yourself out."

She felt tired in the soul and heart so she had no problems agreeing with such a thing. With a sigh, she left the doctor's office and walked back outside into the oppressing heat of the afternoon. She pulled her visor lower over her eyes and headed down the dusty road toward her home.

Her parents owned the town library. They collected and stored books for the entire city so that they could be accessed by everyone. They worked in conjunction with other city libraries to provide copies to each other. In this way, the entire continent of Choral had access to all the books they could want. Transport between continents was long, and trade with the other lands was only just starting.

Sheer curiosity filled Tariah and she went over to the bookshelves to get out the giant book of maps. It was recent as of five years; the newest edition was being worked on since the mapmaker was trying to convince a Dragon to fly her over the countries, and there were rules against Dragons flying over cities.

Tariah opened the book and flipped to the center where there was a world map. Laid out flat, the world of Lucksphere looked like a mass of blue with spots of brown and some green and only a little white. Most of the world was desert; toward the north there were some forested and plains lands and to the very north there was a land of ice.

The primary islands of the MoonKin and SunKin were located scattered in an atoll around the edges of the forested country known as Carnelian. Tariah traced a finger lightly over the map. There were huge chunks of ocean. More than enough space to hide an entire continent, but nothing felt right.

Her right shoulder began to burn. She winced and pressed a hand to her skin and felt the heat underneath. It had happened once or twice before in her life, but never like this. It felt as if something was moving under her skin. Her lines itched horribly.

Her eyes fixed on the map. "At the place where the edges of the world meet," she whispered. She pulled the map out of the book and began to fold it into a sphere shape. There were cuts in the paper for just such a thing, and in a few moments she was holding a global representation of her world.

She turned it around until she was looking at the seam where the two sides had come together, and she felt a little shiver go down her back. In this shape, the two halves of ocean met at the seam and the two spots of deepest ocean came together. She measured it with her fingers. Based on the scale of the globe, the spot of deepest ocean was about the size of a medium continent.

It was a little unnerving. She quickly unfolded the map and put it away. The Deepest Ocean was a sailor's nightmare. It could not be traversed at all. If you came within a mile of the dark waters, your ship was immediately assailed by winds and torrential waves. Many ships had been lost, and hundreds killed, in the centuries since its discovery.

"And what are you up to?"

She jolted, then turned with a smile as her father wrapped an arm around her shoulders and hugged her. He was barely taller than she was and had the same sparkling silver eyes. His hair, however, was gold in color. He was an Air Magi of average strength but sensitive to the fluctuations of other powers.

She rested her head on his shoulder. "Well," she said, "I was looking at the maps."

"Thinking of abandoning your poor parents and traveling the world?" Dublin Chronis pulled a saddened face. "You ungrateful child."

She just laughed. "You would like to have time alone for you and Mom, and you know it, Dad." She turned her head with a smile as she sensed her mother's approach. "Right, Mom?"

"Guilty," Persia Chronis said ruefully as she walked over. She was taller than her mate by about four inches, and her hair was the same auburn as her daughter's. Her eyes were smoky blue and she was a Water Magi of stronger power.

She picked up the book of maps and flipped through the pages. Her heart was aching. She had wondered how long it would be before Tariah's Chronicle blood demanded she seek out the Fury meant for her.

When she had learned her daughter was a Chronicle, she had scoured every book she owned for more information. All she could say with certainty was that a Chronicle was compelled, by the very power that made them, to seek out the land of the Dragons and to find the Fury that matched them. "Where would you go if you could go somewhere?" she asked softly.

"I don't know." Tariah rubbed her hands over her arms, still feeling cold even in the warm weather. "Just somewhere. Somewhere I would not have to live in fear. Doc told me that legend speaks of Dragons guarding Chronicles. A part of me wishes to find out if it is true. The rest is more afraid it isn't."

Dublin and Persia looked at one another and unspoken messages passed between them before both nodded slightly. "We stand behind you," Dublin said quietly. "No matter what. If you want to set sail for the primary continent, we'll help pay for the ticket."

Tariah looked at him in surprise. "Really?"

"Really. You know we just want you to be happy."

She did know. Her parents had always done everything they could to help her adjust to the burdens she lived under. "I'll think about it," she decided.

There came a commotion from the street, and they all walked over to the doorway. "It's the Militia," Persia whispered, recognizing the soldiers on horseback. "What are they doing here?"

The Militia was the primary military force of Lucksphere. They originated in Spectrum, the primary continent, and had outreaches on all the other Magi continents. Magi were ruled by one kingdom on Spectrum, the Kin were ruled by one on their main land, and the Dragons . . . well, they were ruled by their own kind but no one knew where. They adhered to the laws of the land they were in at the time they were in it.

It was very rare to see a fully armed Militia unit in a city unless the continually shifting magic in the land had mutated the wildlife nearby into something that posed a threat. "We aren't under attack," Tariah said softly. "What's going on?"

Maxim often spoke on behalf of the city, and he walked forward to address the captain riding at the front. "Is there something amiss?" he asked calmly. "We were not expecting you."

"Rumor reached us that this city might be harboring a Chronicle." The captain was grim in face and tone. "If this is true, the entire city will be fined and the Chronicle must be immediately eliminated."

"Go back inside, Tariah," Dublin said quietly. "Now."

"I must know," someone called. "Why are Chronicles always killed?"

The captain glared at the speaker. "You question the law?"

"No," the man said hastily, "I just was wondering."

"Fair enough." The captain's eyes were restless as they moved over the crowd, as if he was trying to determine who might be the Chronicle. "Several thousand years ago, there were two kinds of Magi on this world. The normal kind, like us, and other Magi known as Chronicles. Chronicles were like Magi but developed differently. There was something weird about them. They were able to bond with the Dragon Lords known as Furies. When bonded, the Fury and Chronicle became far superior in power to the rest of their races."

"What's wrong with that?" Tariah asked defiantly.

The captain glared at her. "It is unnatural."

"Sounds like it was very natural," Maxim countered. "If what you say is true, this was something dictated by the nature of their respective species. Particularly if you look at the evidence that even after the race was destroyed, some are still born." His silvery eyes were sharp as glass. "What do you fear in Chronicles, Magi?" he asked softly. "Or is it jealousy that drove the Magi to massacre the entire race and send the Dragons into hiding?"

"Enough!" the captain roared. He drew his sword and dismounted. "All those between first and second puberty, please come forward!"

Tariah, at the cusp of second puberty, was part of them. She had faith in her hidden lines, but her stomach still quivered as she slowly walked forward with the rest of her peers. She could not hide away. If she hid away, it would give her away.

The females in the Militia examined the girls, and the males examined the boys. There were a couple hundred Magi of the right ages in the city's entirety, but only twenty or so present. The rest would be examined at their homes.

As it came her turn, Tariah just stood and waited. She was wearing clothes that revealed most of her skin so it was obvious she possessed no lines. Yet the soldier examining her seemed to sense something odd because she kept squinting at Tariah's shoulder. "What are those faint traces on your skin?" she asked.

Tariah squinted at her shoulder and felt her stomach dip as she saw the faintest hint of lines. Thinking quickly, she said, "I had an accident at the cliffs. I got burned when I smacked into the rock."

"They don't look like burn marks." The soldier shook her head. "But then again, they don't look like what a Chronicle's lines are reputed to look like either." She moved on down the line and Tariah let out the breath she was holding.

Once they were satisfied, the Militia got back on their horses to begin knocking on doors. Dublin and Persia wasted no time in hustling Tariah back into their home. Maxim went with them as well. "Tariah needs to leave the continent," he said bluntly as the door shut. "She needs to seek out a Dragon who can take her to safety."

"But it's a legend!" Persia almost cried.

"What other choice is there?" Dublin demanded. "This was far too close for comfort. If they find her out, they'll kill her."

Tariah slowly sank down to sit on the edge of a chair. She felt dazed and lost. But what choice did she have? Stay or leave, she was in danger either way. But by seeking out a Dragon, she might just have a chance. "I'll go," she said softly. "I'm not sure how much good it'll do, but I'll go." She straightened up with a smile. "Either way, the worst that could happen is that I die, and I've lived with that for years now."

"That's our girl." Maxim smiled and opened his mouth to say something more when a shocked expression suddenly crossed his face.

Tariah blinked. "Doc?" Her gaze slowly lowered and she saw the silver bloodstain spreading across the front of his cloth tunic. As he crumbled to the floor silently, the other three turned and looked at the doorway where the female soldier of before stood.

She slowly lowered her bloodstained sword. "I knew there was something odd about you," she said in satisfaction. "You are the Chronicle. All of you are hereby sentenced to death."

Tariah couldn't look away from Maxim's body, and tears welled in her eyes. "Why?" she whispered. "Why kill them? For loving me? For wanting to protect me? Why kill me? For jealousy? I didn't ask to be a Chronicle."

The ground began to tremble under their feet in the familiar pulses of uncontrolled power. Pain and anger welled inside Tariah. It choked her throat and made her blood burn. Maxim had been her friend. He had always been there. She had been a little in love with him, as if he was a part of her family. And now he was dead because he had loved her in return.

The soldier stepped back sharply. "Captain!" she barked out the door. "Hurry!" She moved into the room further for space to fight, and she kicked Maxim's body out of her way.

Tariah saw red. All her years of learning to resist her emotions came to be worthless. Water power erupted in the air around her and began to swirl dangerously. Shards of Ice power from her secondary skills formed at her feet.

Golden lines suddenly blazed into appearance on her body. They started at her scalp on the right side of her face, traveled down to her shoulder, crossed over her chest and stomach, then down her left leg. They traveled down the outside of her right arm to her hand, and the mark for the character 'chron' appeared on her palm.

The soldier was so terrified in that moment that she could not speak. She whirled to run and nearly tripped over her own feet in her mad dash for the door. Even Dublin and Persia were afraid. They did not know if their daughter had any control, and they feared she might destroy herself.

The shards of ice broke into pieces that floated up into the air. They quivered violently and the sharpened ends glinted. They fired through the air with lethal accuracy and impaled the soldier in the back. She was flung out into the street and screams lifted on the air. The sound of pounding hooves became distinct, and Dublin turned to Tariah. "Run!" he ordered her. "Get away from here!"

Tariah looked at him and her mother and realized both were ready and willing to die if it meant she got away. She couldn't stand it. And yet her lines burned, urging her to the north beyond the city. She *felt* it. She felt the road ahead of her. In that moment she knew her lines were indeed a map. She had to follow it even if she did not know where it led.

She turned on her heel and fled out the back of the building, snatching her cloak off the wall as she went. Her odds of surviving in the desert were small, but if she could make it to the next city, she might be able to find a Kin who could help her. They were neutral to Magi and Dragon alike, but they had soft spots for Chronicles if her past experiences were anything to go by.

The sun was low in the sky as she raced across the glowing desert sands. Her lines burned against her skin, urging her on. North. All she knew was north. Perhaps going north would eventually lead her to the land of the Dragons.

Perhaps there she could find out why she had been born a Chronicle and been destined to die.

Chapter Two

The sun was burning hot. Even for a SunKin Faerie like Sparkle, it was almost unbelievably hot. She had to stay in her Sylph form just to keep from being smothered in the heat. The only downside to her Sylph form was that she was now barely an inch big and it was hard to fly accurately across the land because of even the smallest winds.

She was looking for pitcher crabs that lived in sand dunes. They had the softest and tastiest flesh in the desert and could be sold for a fortune in Carnelian where they had no deserts. Kin like Sparkle lived on the Outposts built just for trading and went to the nearest continent to do their harvesting.

As she was angling down toward a dune that looked promising, she caught sight of a piece of dark against the white sand. For a moment she thought it was a crab, but as she got closer she realized it was a Magi.

With a little glimmer of magic, she went back into her natural form and angled down to land beside the figure lying in the sands. In natural form, she was not even a foot high but it was more than big enough to stop beside the girl and check her pulse.

Shock filled Sparkle. The girl was still alive. On the heels of that shock came a second one as she realized the girl was covered with Chronicle lines. She had to get her out of the desert, *fast*!

She looked around and spotted a nice dune nearby. Soil power pulsed around her feet as she pointed at the dune and then ribbons of green light flowed down her arm and over to the dune. The dune pulsed and began to rise up into the air until it formed a tall golem. Crabs scuttled away across the ground as their home was disturbed, and the golem lumbered over to Sparkle.

"Carry her," she ordered as she flew up to sit on the golem's shoulder.

The golem obligingly picked up the girl and carried her gently as it turned and began crossing the desert under Sparkle's direction. She had built a cabin under the sand using her Soil power so that she was sheltered from heat and cold alike. It was also completely undetectable by any Magi, with or without Soil power themselves.

Once at the cabin, the golem carried the girl inside and gently put her down on the floor. Sparkle dismissed her pet, who went outside and turned into a dune again, then turned her attention to her unexpected guest.

The girl was of smaller height and weight for a Magi, and her hair was thick and auburn brown. Her skin was light brown from the sun, but the Chronicle lines glimmered golden as they traveled down her body. She was really very pretty.

Sparkle flew over and grabbed a jug of water. Since she needed to cool the girl down and get rid of the heat in her skin, the quickest way was to simply pour cool water over her. So she flew over the girl and did just that.

The water was absorbed instantly by her body. "Oh." Sparkle stuck out her lower lip. "A Water element." Well, that would make things a little easier.

Tariah awoke to a raging headache and pains in her whole body. She also awoke to a SunKin Faerie hovering over her. Her eyes widened swiftly and she tried to sit up, terrified she might be in a town. Immediately the Kin hugged her around the neck comfortingly. "No, no!" she said. "It's okay! You're safe!"

Tariah looked around slowly. The cabin was about the size of a large bedroom, but it was a full home with a privacy room and a kitchen. Her power hovered at very low levels because she had been drawing on it hard to survive in the desert, but she felt the pulse of water close underneath her and knew she was underground.

Sparkle let her go before flying over to get a canteen. She brought it to Tariah and watched like a hawk as the young woman sipped carefully. "My name is Sparkle," she said. She landed on Tariah's knee and bowed gracefully. "A Soil secondary SunKin Faerie."

SunKin were Light primary, just as all MoonKin were Dark primary, so they only referred to their secondary when introducing themselves. Tariah had to smile. "I am Tariah Chronis, a Water Magi."

Sparkle tilted her head and her green eyes looked thoughtful. "Technically, I'd say you're a Water Chronicle."

Her gaze lowered. "Yes," she said softly. She drank more from the canteen. Both her body and her power needed the water very badly to recover. She couldn't help but wish for a pool or a spring to simply immerse herself in.

With a sigh, she looked at her rescuer. She was definitely SunKin because her skin was pale. And she was definitely Faerie because she was tiny and had wings. Her hair was pale lavender and there were tiny flowers in it, as was not uncommon of Soil powers. Her eyes were grass green and there were little gold tattoos on her face and arms. "You're cute," she decided.

Sparkle blinked, then smiled. "Well, you're cute too, for a Magi." She tilted her head. "Hey, Tariah, is there water near us?"

Tariah nodded. "I can feel it, yes. Why?"

"Let's make ourselves a spring!" She flew over to one of her walls and began gathering her power. The wall obligingly opened and made a doorway. She began to make a hall as well and stretched it about ten feet away from the cabin itself.

Tariah frowned thoughtfully. "Why?" she asked.

Sparkle grinned at her. "Why not?" She snorted delicately. "Don't tell me you Magi don't use your powers simply for fun sometimes. Why have them if you don't play with them once and a while?"

Tariah began to smile. "You're right." She very carefully got to her feet and walked over to Sparkle by holding onto the furniture and the wall. Her legs felt like rubber. She followed Sparkle down the hall she was making and then stood in the doorway while her new friend formed a new room and began making a basin in the ground. "Make sure it's really deep at one end, but shallow at the other."

"Oh good idea!" Sparkle did as requested before getting fancy and lining the bottom and sides with smooth stone to keep everything clean. "There! Now, Chronicle girl, where's our water?"

Power flowed around Tariah and the room began to pulse blue. Water poured out of the walls and flowed across the ground toward the spring. It was so sweet and pure that Sparkle felt it tingle in her lungs when she took a deep breath. There was nothing like fresh desert water.

Once the pool was filled, Tariah stopped the flow. She paused long enough to take off her shoes before she slid into the spring, clothes and all. Sparkle wasn't surprised; when she was too low on Soil she had a tendency to dive into a mud hole without changing clothes first. She stripped off her clothes, flew up in the air, and dove down directly into the middle. Despite her size, she made an impressive splash that hit Tariah.

Tariah sputtered for a moment. She then smiled and dove under the surface. She could breathe underwater because of her powers, and she let herself sink deeper until she was at the bottom of the deep end. It felt incredible. It was as if her body was actually soaking up the water around her, and some of the aches began to fade. When she surfaced again, she slung her hair out of her eyes and saw Sparkle skating across the top of the water. "You're good at that," she praised.

Sparkle laughed. "Well, sure!" She twirled around on one foot and let herself sink back into the water. She was watching closely, however, as Tariah moved to the edge of the spring and began to undress. She had been hoping the other girl would be comfortable enough to get naked. She had never seen a Chronicle, and she was immensely curious.

Tariah felt a little nervous as she put her clothes to the side. They were both females, and Sparkle was a Kin, but a part of Tariah still felt ashamed of her lines. She ducked back down underwater as quickly as she could and let only her head stay on the surface.

"Talk to me," Sparkle said curiously as she paddled closer. "Was it your lover who blabbed on you? I mean, you're alive and definitely older than first puberty, so obviously your parents didn't have you killed."

Tariah smiled. "I haven't started second puberty yet. I should be doing that sometime this year though. So no lover."

For all species, first puberty was where their bodies developed and began to grow in ways that defined them as male or female. It was also where their natural lightning abilities began to develop into a primary element (or secondary for Kin). Second puberty was where they began to develop hormones and urges related to sexual development, and began to develop secondary skills related to the primary. It occurred anywhere from ages sixteen up to twenty-one.

Sparkle nodded sagely. "It'll be hard for you. I mean, you won't be able to experiment or learn about your body or stuff like that because you won't be sure if you can trust anyone."

Tariah smiled wryly. "Tell me about it." She sighed and sank down in the water to her chin. She was not looking forward to second puberty. She never had been, really. Even with the ban lifted on her excessive emotions, Sparkle was right. "I'd rather be dead I think." The words had barely left her mouth before Sparkle dunked her. She surfaced again with a sputter. "Hey!"

"Hey yourself!" Sparkle poked her in the nose. "I didn't go saving your Chronicle butt just to hear you wish to die. You owe me, so you have to live." She scrambled back hastily as Tariah reached for her. "Whoa!"

Tariah caught her firmly and dunked her in retaliation. Sparkle surfaced, her hair hanging in her eyes, then she began to giggle. Tariah couldn't help but begin to laugh as well. She smiled as Sparkle shot forward and hugged her around the neck again. Gently she hugged her back. "Thanks Sparkle," she said softly.

"Anytime. Hey! Make this a hot spring, okay?" Sparkle released her to dive back under the water as Tariah obligingly heated the water with magic. Contented, she floated on her stomach with her arms on the side of the spring. Tariah joined her and Sparkle said, "Let's be friends."

"Okay. Friends it is." Tariah pulled herself up out of the water and sat on the side. She pulled her hair forward over her shoulder and began to work the tangles out. Unbound, her hair fell to her waist and was very thick.

Sparkle studied her and smiled. "You'll make some Fury a very happy man."

Tariah was startled. "Furies are male?"

"Not all of them." Sparkle shook back her three-tiered flowery wings. "See, Chronicles and Furies are always perfect opposites. Always male-female, and always opposing elements. So I can say with certainty that your Fury is a male and a Fire power." She frowned. "It's so sad."

"What?" Tariah wished longingly for a bar of soap as she looked at her still grubby fingers.

"Well, that you are a Chronicle and don't know anything about it." Sparkle was of like mind and flew down the hall to fetch some soap. She returned and plopped it down beside Tariah along with a piece of cloth. "Here," she offered, "I'll scrub your back."

"Sure." Tariah pulled her hair forward over her shoulders as Sparkle scrubbed soap over her back. She remained thoughtful as she looked across the room. "I guess it is kind of sad," she agreed after a moment. "But I don't mind it, really. The only thing I really want to know is why Chronicles are hated."

Sparkle's nose wrinkled. "Kin talk of jealousy. Magi were jealous that Chronicles were much more powerful so they spread rumor and destroyed them. We fought alongside the Dragons and Chronicles in that war, but we did not win."

"Fought?" Tariah looked over her shoulder. "Kin are neutral."

"And pacifists," Sparkle reminded her. "We will side with anyone we feel is being slighted. If it had been the other way, Chronicle after Magi, we would have sided with Magi. That is why all Kin will help you now, Tariah. Because you are being wronged. You would have sanctuary on any Kin outpost or in our homeland."

Tariah drew a long breath. "Will you help me?" she asked softly. "Help me find the land of the Dragons?"

She nodded firmly as she handed Tariah the cloth. "Absolutely." She giggled as Tariah began to scrub her clean. "It tickles!"

Tariah just smiled and rolled into the spring with her wiggling, slippery friend. They were both rinsed clean and Tariah got to work on her hair. "Thanks, Sparkle," she said softly. "Do you think you could hide my lines like was done when I was little?"

Sparkle shook her head. "Nuh-uh. My powers don't delve into that sort of thing. But . . . I bet I have a better idea. We'll just tell everyone we're traveling entertainers, and I made you look like a Chronicle so everyone knows what to be wary of!"

It was simple enough that it had to work. Tariah smiled. "I like it." She rinsed off fully and pulled herself out of the spring. She was feeling better already, although she was now starving. "I don't suppose we could make ourselves some dinner."

"Sure!" Sparkle flew out of the water and used her powers on the sand once more to weave two warm blankets, one of the right size for each of them. She wrapped herself up, then flew over to land on Tariah's shoulder once she had done the same. "I'm glad I met you."

Tariah rubbed her cheek against Sparkle's gently. "Me too," she said softly. She stretched. "Let's have some dinner."

Sparkle had some pitcher crab for her own consumption, and Tariah cooked it up for them. Sparkle was fascinated. She had never really learned to cook Magi food. She was used to the pre-made dinners that the Kin fashioned. They were full meals, but they missed an element. A person with that element could add it and instantly have a ready meal. Tariah, for her own part, was equally fascinated by the Kin method. They were such timesavers!

They both slept in blankets on the floor with a fire for warmth. The following morning had Sparkle circling Tariah to study her critically. Since Soil powers could make cloth from sand or dirt, it was easy to make new clothes for her friend. But to make sure they fit, she needed to know Tariah's measurements. "Let's see .. . Hmm, you're not very busty for a Magi."

Tariah crossed her arms with a glower. "Be quiet."

"I didn't say you weren't pretty."

"That doesn't take the sting out of your words. I've always wished for more curves." She poked her friend in the stomach gently. "Besides, you're pudgy."

Sparkle gasped. "I am not!" She stomped a foot in the air indignantly and then dissolved into giggles. "Okay, I am! I like sweet things! My auntie makes the best snacks in the whole world." She studied Tariah again and decided that her friend was beautiful for a Magi and really ought to show it off. She was also a desert girl and would hate confining clothes. With those thoughts in mind, she drew the sand down from the walls and used her power to weave first cloth and then weave that into clothing.

Tariah shortly found herself in snug cloth leggings, a top like the one she had been wearing before, and a sturdy cloak to protect her from the hottest parts of the day. They were all in dark green and looked really flattering against her skin and lines. "You're really good at this!" she praised.

"Aren't I?" Sparkle gave a saucy curtsey before starting to pack up her tiny backpack for the trip to the port. When Tariah returned from fetching her boots, Sparkle brought down the wall to the spring and shut it off protectively. "It's our secret."

Tariah smiled. "Sure." She picked up one of the visors that Sparkle had been storing and waited as it recognized the species holding it. It obligingly grew big enough for a Magi and she pulled it on and down over her eyes before pulling her hood up. The visors were made predominately by Kin, and again were of a technology far surpassing most Magi.

Once they were ready, they set out into the desert to begin walking toward the port that was a good thirty miles to the north. Sparkle rode on Tariah's shoulder, and she was covered protectively by her own visor and cloak. "The outpost where I live," she said, "is forested."

"Oh really?" Tariah considered that. "I've always lived in the desert. I can't imagine trees everywhere."

"It was hard to get used to no trees at all for me!" Sparkle smiled. "I'll take you there. The outpost is between Choral and Carnelian, but closer to Carnelian, which is why it is forested. The Kin that live there will help you too, I'm sure of it. And if Dragons go anywhere off their isle, they go there. I bet they'll definitely be willing to help."

"Do you think there's a Fury out there for me?" Tariah asked softly, longing in every word. She wanted to find the one person meant for her. "I just want to find a true friend. You're the first I've ever had, but I want more. Someone to share my heart because we're the same."

"I'm sure of it!" Sparkle was *very* sure, and her tone reflected it. She was also hiding a little smile because she knew more about Dragoon bonds than Tariah did. Tariah would get her friend, but unless she was one of the rare exceptions, she would also be getting a lover to help her explore all of her second puberty curiosities.

~*~

Harmonica was bigger than Symphony by about fifteen miles and it boasted nearly three times the population. In appearance, however, it bore a strong resemblance. The buildings and homes were built the same, and most of the people dressed with the heat in mind.

The streets were paved with strong stones that were easier to traverse with wagons and carts. Some buildings got as tall as three stories, a feat that was highly impressive to Tariah and Sparkle alike, both country girls at heart. "Amazing," Tariah breathed, looking skyward.

"It's really tall." Sparkle was sitting on her shoulder as she had for the last five days of walking. "Someone told me once that the cities on Spectrum have buildings as tall as six stories."

"That's incredible!" Tariah felt eyes on her and pulled her cloak tighter closed. She was wearing her hood far over her head and keeping her arms carefully covered. Still, she knew she was being stared at. Any Magi worth their salt would sense she was powerful. "How do Master Magi act?" she whispered.

"I think they're kind of anti-social," Sparkle whispered back. "I think you should be doing fine."

She drew a long breath and composed herself as they began working their way through the town toward the center square where the market was located. Other entertainers of all kinds were present as well, showing off and trying to earn coin through free shows.

There was only one open spot left. Sparkle claimed it by making a stone stage with her power. "Okay," she said softly. "All you have to do is make the biggest and most showy and grandest displays possible."

Tariah nodded and then climbed up onto the stage. Sparkle began to fly around the market. "Come one, come all!" she called. "My friend is a Master Magi and through my power of disguise I have made her look like a Chronicle! If you've ever wondered what the purest race of evil looks like, now's your chance!"

The word 'Chronicle' alone gathered attention. People immediately began to move toward the stage where Tariah stood. With a touch of defiance, she took her cloak off and dropped it on the stage beside her. Her lines blazed brilliantly in the sun and gave her already lovely features a rare and unforgettable beauty.

"This is how you recognize a Chronicle!" Sparkle flew around Tariah. "These golden lines are veins of Dragon power! According to the legends of the Kin, when a Chronicle and a Fury meet and bond as Dragoons, the Fury grows matching lines of Chronicle power. This is how they can harmonize through one another!"

Tariah felt startled. She had no idea if Sparkle was blowing hot air or if she was sincere. She did know, however, that the few Kin in audience recognized her as a real Chronicle. They had little smiles on their faces as if they enjoyed seeing the Magi be fooled by their own rumors.

"What kind of powers do they have?" someone called.

"I'm glad you asked that!" Sparkle spun in the air before landing on Tariah's head. "Master Magi and Chronicles are not that different in power. Observe! My friend here has not yet entered second puberty."

"Pity," came a male voice from the back of the crowd and made everyone snicker.

Tariah had begun to get into the spirit of things and she blew the speaker a kiss. "I'll write you a letter when I do," she called back, and it made the crowd laugh.

Sparkled giggled. She absolutely adored Tariah. "Now watch! Show them your stuff!"

Tariah let the Water well up inside her and it flowed around her feet as it became tangible. As she lifted her hands, the water flowed up her body and into the air over her hands where it began to become the shape of animals and people. Over her hands, she actually recreated the city in water.

"She's good!" a woman murmured to her friend.

"Ah but that's not all," Sparkle said as she heard the comment. She flew around the stage. "As we all know, Magi develop secondary skills while in second puberty. But Chronicles and Master Magi are different. Watch this!"

Knowing what Sparkle was asking, Tariah dissolved the city and the water flowed back down her body. Ice suddenly formed at her feet and shards began to float in the air. A gasp traveled through the crowd as they realized she had secondary skills with or without puberty. She smiled and the ice formed over her hands as a cloud that grew and surrounded the market. And then, softly, snow began to fall.

"What's that stuff?" a kid asked.

"It's called snow," another said. "It's so cold!"

Sparkle grinned. "And there you are! When looking for a Chronicle, this is what you're looking for!"

A Militia soldier stood in the crowd and he nodded succinctly. "Your timing is good. I received word from my superiors that the rumored Chronicle in Symphony is no rumor. He or she escaped the city after killing a soldier."

A murmured panic began to run through the crowd and Tariah's heart beat hard inside her chest. She was nearly holding her breath as people began approaching the stage. But to her surprise, and relief, they simply offered the little ivory coins that served as currency on Lucksphere. "For showing us what we need to be wary of," a lady said.

As more people came forward, Sparkle quickly made a bucket from the stone and it was into that that the people tossed their coins in passing. While that occurred, a few of the children ran over to where Tariah had sat down on the edge of the stage.

One reached out to touch the lines on her arm and then smiled in delight. "They're warm!" She smiled shyly. "I think they're pretty." She and her friends hurried off before they were caught, and Tariah let out a little breath. Even if the kids thought she was fake, their words warmed her.

Within ten minutes, the crowd had thinned and gone back to observing other displays. Sparkle peered into the bucket and her eyes slowly widened. "Oh my. Tariah, look at this!"

Tariah scooted over to look inside and her eyes widened equally. The bucket was half-full of money, and someone in the crowd had tossed in a few bronze coins as well. The bronze was worth five times the value of the ivory. Tariah looked up swiftly and her eyes met those of a SunKin Elf at the back of the crowd. The Kin bowed gracefully and then turned and disappeared into the crowd.

Sparkle quickly wove two bags for them to carry the money inside; she gave one to Tariah and kept the other. Both bags were on the heavy side, but it reassured them because it meant they could afford ship fare and inn stays as needed, and any supplies they could not make. Tariah could provide water, and Sparkle could make shelter, but food was something they lacked the ability to create.

"Where are you going next?" the Militia soldier asked as he approached them.

Tariah shoved her nerves down and found a casual smile. "Well, we thought we might stay here a while, then go to Carnelian."

"Carnelian is a good idea," he said. "The captain is on his way to this town too. Apparently they fear the Chronicle might try and catch a boat."

Sparkle sat down on Tariah's head. "Hmm. Maybe we ought to go to Carnelian now rather than later. Maybe we can beat them there and warn the people." Her stomach quivered too. She had gotten the whole story out of Tariah and knew that the captain would recognize her immediately.

"Good luck," the soldier told them with a salute. He paused a moment, then noted, "You know, I didn't get your names."

"Sparkle," the Faerie offered easily.

Tariah didn't want to give her first name and said only, "Chronis."

"Well, farewell to both of you." The soldier watched them hurry off and frowned thoughtfully. The name Chronis was familiar. If he wasn't mistaken, he could have sworn it was the name of the first Chronicle on record. It was the name from which 'Chronicle' had been derived. The irony was interesting.

Chapter Three

The next ship out of Harmonica was scheduled to set sail in an hour and due to arrive at the harbor on the southern side of Carnelian in two weeks. Tariah had never been on a boat before, and she could barely hide her excitement as she followed Sparkle up the gangplank and onto the deck. The ship was bigger than even a large Dragon and had enough cabins for the over one hundred passengers it was carrying.

Because it had served them well before, they kept up the façade of being traveling entertainers. Yet, even keeping up that façade, they still kept to their own cabin almost exclusively. Because everyone thought that Tariah was a Master Magi, no one found it to be out of the ordinary.

Dinner was served every night in the restaurant on the ship. The first night out, it was a formal dinner. Upon hearing that, Tariah and Sparkle felt slightly ashamed. Neither of them possessed any clothes that could possibly be considered formal, and there was no sand for Sparkle to use to make them.

"Well, damn it." Tariah sat down cross-legged on the bed. "Now what? I mean, that would take anti-social too far. We have to go, at least tonight."

"What're we supposed to do?" Sparkle asked. She flew in agitated circles around the room. "Put on a sheet?"

"The other question is," Tariah noted, "formal by whose standards?" She pointed at her clothes. "These *are* formal by the standards I grew up with. They cover more than half my body."

Sparkle blinked and then began to giggle. "You're such a desert girl."

"Watch it, woody." She flopped over onto her back and lifted her right hand to study the lines etched across the back and the symbol on her palm. She had never realized just how little the Magi knew about Chronicles despite their hatred of them. How could you hate something you knew nothing about?

Her lines began to burn and a fierce and powerful longing welled up inside her, so strong it literally brought tears to her eyes. For just a moment she thought she had felt him. She thought she had felt her Fury, and even that tiniest touch made her longing to find him worse. Her lines burned. *North.* She had to go north.

Sparkle watched the glow that rippled down Tariah's lines and saw the pained expression cross her face. Her lips tightened. She did not like seeing her friend hurt, and as long as she was on this stupid journey, she would. She knew that Chronicles of the old days had supposedly sometimes taken years or more to find their Fury, but she wanted Tariah to find hers *now*.

Someone knocked on the door and she flew over to open it. "Yes?" she asked.

One of the ship crewmembers stood outside the door, and he had a large bag in his hands. "This was sent to you by your fellow Kin," he said. "I was asked to give it to you."

"Oh." She smiled. "Thanks!" It was hard to determine which sender had provided the gift. There were several other Kin on the ship. She thought it might be the Fire secondary SunKin Elf she had sensed. Kin could always feel one another if they walked in the same place within a short time. The bag definitely felt fiery.

The sailor put the bag down inside the door and took his leave. Sparkle shut the door, and Tariah kneeled beside the bag to open it. It promptly overflowed and pure white sand spilled onto the floor. It was freshly made and of incredible quality. Tariah's eyes widened. "Where did they get this?"

Sparkle swirled her hand in the sand softly. "She made it. She must have! That's how the best sand is made, you know? A Fire/Smoke user can break down glass into the purest grains. This is the high quality stuff, the stuff sold in cities for Soil weavers and such." She smiled at Tariah. "She's giving us her support in the best way she can."

Tariah lowered her gaze. "All of you Kin . . . you've done so much for me." Her voice broke. "I had a friend who was a MoonKin. His name was Maxim. He was a doctor in the town and he . . ." Tears slid down her cheeks. "He died to protect me."

Her Faerie friend's face darkened slowly. "Who killed him?"

"The Militia." She wiped at her eyes, unaware of Sparkle's sudden alertness. "It was just so stupid. I lost him and my parents just because they loved me. There's no reason to hate me, let alone them!" She turned, startled, as she realized Sparkle had sat down on the air and started drawing shapes in front of herself. "What are you doing?"

"Writing to the MoonKin Elder." Her fingers glowed as she sketched and wrote in the characters that made up the Kin language. "Telling him what happened. The Militia made a big no-no. Kin are neutral. Killing one of us when we did not instigate the fight is against the boundaries of the treaty."

Tariah watched in fascination. "Kin can communicate across the world without letters?"

"These *are* our letters. See, we each put out a different kind of energy. It's like your lines. It's completely unique from person to person." Sparkle kept writing. "And once we meet, we can write to each other by writing with an energy that matches the person we're writing to."

"That's amazing." She scooted closer to watch, and she could see what Sparkle meant. Sparkle's power and energy always seemed, to her, to look and feel like a bunch of little dancing sparks. The energy she wrote with instead looked and felt like sparkly blue stars. "Can you teach me to read this?"

"Probably but it might take a while. We have over five hundred characters in our language."

"Five hundred!" She sat back. "Well." The language of the Magi only had one hundred. "That's . . . that's a lot."

"That's nothing." Sparkle stopped writing and the letter seemed to vanish into thin air with a small pop. "The Dragon language has over *one thousand*." She giggled and flew over to land on Tariah's stomach as her friend fell over on her back in shock. "Theirs is easier though. It's one thousand different characters instead of our five hundred that can be used in ten different ways."

Tariah put an arm over her eyes. "I'm beginning to feel like the naïve desert girl you called me."

"That's okay. You're nice, and you're smart. You learn things fast." Sparkle flew over to the bag of sand once more. "Let's make a bunch of guys really envious and annoyed that you're still not in second puberty."

Tariah considered that and decided the idea appealed to her. She sat up with a grin. "Sure. Why not?"

When they entered the restaurant for dinner, they got what they had been aiming to get. Every Magi bachelor in the place stared at Tariah with a comical combination of dismay and longing. The Kin males seemed no less appreciative, but they looked more amused than dismayed. The Faeries also made a point of indicating it was Sparkle that they had their eyes on.

Going on the assumption that formality was determined by your birthplace, both females wore what was formal from their homelands. Tariah, a desert girl, wore a dark green skirt that tied at each hip and fell open along the outside of each leg. On the top she wore a piece of matching dark green cloth that wrapped around her neck, crossed down to wrap around her bust, then continued to wrap around her in a cross pattern until her hips, where it fell in with the rest of the material. Underneath both she wore a dark gold bikini that very nearly blended in with her skin in the candlelight.

Sparkle was a forest girl. In stark contrast to desert dwellers, forested people tended to wear clothes that covered most of their bodies. Forests were both slightly cooler than average and infested with bugs that liked to nibble on exposed flesh.

Tonight, Sparkle wore a tunic the color of roses just blooming. It had a collar that she turned up rakishly to protect her neck, and the sleeves went down past her hands where they flared like rose petals. The tunic went to her knees, and underneath it she wore a matching skirt of a slightly darker color that went to her ankles. Around her tiny waist she had fastened a leather belt. She looked, very much, like a little rose with wings. And though, yes, she was slightly plump in places, it only added to her delicate loveliness.

"Hey!" a Faerie male called across the room in the language of the Kin. "Read my energy!"

It was the Kin equivalent of the Magi pick-up line 'write me a letter.' After translating it for Tariah, her Chronicle friend could only snicker and take a seat at a table. Her long hair had been pinned up on top of her head, and her lines flowed like golden ribbons as they traversed her skin. Many present couldn't help but think that even if she had been a real Chronicle, she would have still been very beautiful.

Dinner passed peacefully. The entertainment for the night was a Magi storyteller, and he wove fascinating tales from even the most common of prompts. If someone told him they wanted a tale about sand, he told a tale about a type of sand so rare and beautiful it grew like a waterfall in an oasis only seen by children.

As Tariah enjoyed her dessert, she became aware that she was being stared at. It was not an uncommon occurrence, but for some reason this gaze made her skin crawl. The power that flowed in her blood seemed to sting suddenly as if warning of danger.

She looked around with a frown. A lot of eyes were on her, but there was only curiosity or interest in their gazes. Nothing felt threatening . . . until her eyes fell on a shadowy corner of the room. Something sent a chill down her back.

There were five people sitting in the corner. All wore heavy white cloaks that covered their bodies entirely. The Magi chalice symbol was emblazoned largely on the back of their cloaks, and it was an unusual shade of black—the symbol was typically blue. A black dagger lay across the base of the chalice, and something about it made Tariah very nervous.

Sparkle followed her gaze and her brows drew together. "That's the Black Magi Elite," she said softly into Tariah's ear. She was sitting on her friend's shoulder in an effort to avoid ordering dessert and getting pudgier; sweets went right to her waist and hips, dang it. "They're really powerful Magi that travel the world looking for more to join them. I think they're trying to get recognized as their own race or culture, but they're no different from other Magi, except for their power."

Tariah frowned. "I don't like them."

"Few do. They're really, well, *elite*. They snub anyone who is less than they are." She looked longingly at the custard Tariah held. "Just a bite?" she asked.

"No." Tariah smiled and took a bite herself. "You're on a diet, remember?" Still, even with the distraction, she couldn't help but feel a chill along her power. She was disguised as a Master Magi, and the Elite were watching her. Though she might have assumed she would be safe with them, something about them terrified her.

Time passed slowly on a boat, she discovered, as the first week drew to an end. There was not much to actually do on a cruise. At least, not much that she wanted to do. There were games and entertainment and all manner of activities for the passengers, but none of it interested her. She was a Water Chronicle, but she missed her desert. She missed the stark sands and the hot sun. She missed her life.

With another week looming in front of her, she began to get bored. In her boredom, she began to experiment with her powers. She was working on learning to manipulate her ice as easily as she did her water. She had the freedom to do it now, so she went ahead and practiced. She wanted to be able to make cities of ice that were more real than reality itself.

She was enough busy with her shaping that she didn't notice the glow in the room at first. When it did trigger, she turned her head and saw that there were symbols appearing in the air. Since Sparkle wasn't present, she could only assume it was a letter. It was definitely Kin language. "Whoops!"

She quickly hurried out of the cabin and up to the top deck where Sparkle was visiting with one of her fellow SunKin. Tariah promptly grinned when she saw the scene. Since flirtations tended to be a bit universal, she felt pretty sure she wasn't wrong that the handsome male Faerie was smitten with her friend. He hovered much closer than was polite, and Sparkle was giggling. "Am I interrupting?" she asked as she approached.

"Chronis!" Sparkle beamed at her and hoped her cheeks weren't as flushed as they felt. Daylar was one of the handsomest Faeries around, and he was *flirting* with her. Her, of all people! By Kin standards, she was actually kind of plain. "You're not interrupting at all," she told Tariah.

Daylar grinned. "Yes, she is." He touched his wings and bowed gracefully in a sign of respect. "Daylar, Air secondary SunKin Faerie at your service. You are Sparkle's friend?"

She smiled. "Last I checked I was." She really liked him. He was quite handsome, even by Magi standards, and his wings looked like wispy clouds. The light in his eyes underlined his cheerful spirit. "Are you flirting with my partner?"

"I might be." He studied her intently and was not disappointed to realize she was indeed a genuine Chronicle instead of merely the pretender she professed to be. Word had traveled fast among the Kin about the rumors of a Chronicle. He would make sure the rumors were confirmed with his kind so that they knew to watch for her. "Are you here to take her away and break my heart?"

"I'm afraid I am," she apologized. "She has a letter waiting for her." She drew her thumb over her cheek and nose in the Magi sign of respect. "Come visit any time."

Sparkle knew she was blushing even more as she landed on Tariah's shoulder to return to their cabin. "It was nothing!" she announced. "He was just flirting with me. He does that. Daylar's one of the handsomest Kin around. He wouldn't be flirting with me."

Tariah covered a smile. "Sparkle, you're nervous."

"I am not!"

"Yes, you are. You're chattering, and you're contradicting yourself." She linked her hands behind her back.

"I liked him. And despite the fact that you might think you're plain by Kin standards, I think you're cute as a button."

"Oh."

She opened their cabin door to let Sparkle fly inside and then shut and locked it behind them. The letter still waited, and she followed Sparkle curiously. The Faerie sat down on the air and began to read. After a few moments, the letter rippled and different writing appeared. Tariah wondered if it was like a second page.

A few more pages later, the letter disappeared completely. Sparkle drummed her fingers on her arm thoughtfully. "See," she said, "I wrote to the MoonKin Elder and told him about Maxim. Apparently the Militia contacted them and said you were the one who did it."

Tariah bristled. "That's outrageous!"

"That's what the Elder had thought, and my letter confirmed it. He and the SunKin Elder have conferred and want me to bring you to the mainland for the Kin. If they offer formal sanctuary, then the Militia can't touch you there." She looked at Tariah. "Maybe we can keep you safe long enough to contact the Dragons. Seems they've had no luck so far. It's summer. They very rarely leave their lands at all during summer."

Tariah let out a long breath. Though her lines burned and urged her north, something equally told her that it would be good to go to the Kin homeland known as Kindred. It was a series of islands around the edge of Carnelian. It was not really a deviation from their current heading. It just meant they would have to catch another boat at the harbor and go back out into the ocean for a while. "Okay," she said. "Let's go. Seems like everything I do is by instinct these days, and at least among the Kin I would feel safe for once."

Sparkle flew over to hug her. "You've just got to promise to either let me visit, or come visit me, once you've become a Dragoon and are living with the Dragons."

"You have a deal." Tariah hugged her in return and then looked at the door as there came a light knock. "Who is it?" she called as she got to her feet.

"I am of the Elite." The voice was male and emotionless. "I wish to speak with the Magi known as Chronis."

Tariah and Sparkle exchanged a frown, then Tariah walked over and eased the door open a crack. "I am she."

"My name is Soh." The man pulled down the hood on his robe to reveal a grizzled face and deeply set brown eyes. His beard and mustache were the same gray and black as his hair, and his skin looked like tough leather from exposure to the sun without proper care.

There was nothing unappealing about him, and nothing remarkable. But Tariah felt her power stinging again and sensed danger. "Hello, Soh," she said formally. "What can I help you with?"

"I wish to speak with you of joining the Black Magi Elite." His eyes held a sharp gleam that could have been power, intelligence, or madness. It could have been a frightening combination of all three. "You would do well in our ranks, young Chronis. We need power such as yours."

She summoned up a kind smile even though her stomach felt jittery. "I thank you, but I am just a traveling entertainer. I don't really like belonging to any group. Your offer is gracious but I decline."

"I will ask again later." He bowed and walked away.

She shut the door quickly and let out a soft breath. "That's bad, isn't it?"

Sparkle nodded slowly. "I get the sneaking feeling it is. We better get to the Kin, and fast. The Elite come and go from there, but they would not dare touch you under our protection."

The next day another Elite member came to speak with Tariah. She gave her the same response. On the following day it was a third member. On the fourth it was the next. On the fifth day, Tariah spent most of her time staring at the door and waiting. She knew damned well that they would try again. The Elite was clearly not used to being turned down.

They were only a few days out of Carnelian's port town. They would be docking in two days if the weather held. It didn't seem likely at the moment. The sea was dark and turbulent and the sky had been covered with clouds. Lightning rippled across their base. The waves were choppy but relatively stable for the time being.

The knock on the door made both females jump slightly. Composing herself, Tariah opened the door. "Yes?" she asked.

It was Soh. The gleam in his eyes at that moment was more madness than intelligence, and it sent chills down her back. "Why do you refuse us, Tariah Chronis? Do you think you will be safe among the Magi?"

Her back stiffened. "How did you learn that?" she hissed softly. Anger began to mingle with her fear, and ice shards sparkled in the air threateningly. "Tell me!"

He laughed nastily and held up a pair of wings between his fingers. They were covered with gold blood but very recognizable with their cloudy, wispy shape. "He didn't want to tell me willingly. But he did eventually tell."

Sparkle went white. "Daylar!" She shot through the air past Soh and down the halls, shouting Daylar's name in the language of the Kin.

Fury bubbled under Tariah's skin so hard that the ice condensed. The ocean waters around them began to grow more violent. Storms on Lucksphere always seemed to be like a living creature, and they fed off the power of anyone they touched, particularly those of Water or Air. "You bastard," she said thinly. "For this alone I will never join the Elite!"

She took off down the hall to help Sparkle find Daylar, and Soh shouted behind her, "How many more Kin will die because of you, Tariah Chronis? Eventually even they will grow to hate you!"

She ignored him and followed Sparkle's trail as it wound around the ship toward the deck. The entire boat shook and shuddered as the storm opened almost over their heads. Though she had cut it off, her power had been enough to bring the storm to the forefront. The crew shouted orders for everyone to stay in their cabins and prepare to battle the waves.

She found Sparkle on the deck, and the Faerie was desperately dragging at some crates thrice her size. "He's behind here!" she shouted. "I hear him! Tariah, help me!"

Tariah lent her strength, and they dragged at the boxes until they moved aside. Tariah swiftly knelt and scooped up the prone form that lay behind them. He was covered in bruises, and golden blood seeped from the wounds on his back, but he was still alive. "Daylar!" she said softly. "Can you hear me?"

His eyes opened and he managed a little smile. "I'm sorry, Tariah."

"No, don't be!" She looked at Sparkle. "How can we heal him?"

Tears ran down Sparkle's face. "We can't. Not without wings. Our bodies can't heal without them. It's like ripping out your heart." Her stomach churned for a moment and then her back straightened as she clenched her hands into fists at her sides. "Take mine. Take two of my wings and give them to him."

Tariah's breath stopped. "Sparkle . . ."

"Don't," Daylar whispered. "Not for me, Sparky."

"Yes!" Sparkle's knuckles were almost white and tears burned her eyes. "He won't win! I won't let him!" She took his hand and held it to her cheek. "I'm sorry you got involved," she whispered. "This is the least I can do. Please, accept my wings, if you can."

Understanding filled Tariah. More than her wings, Sparkle was offering her heart. She had said it herself. A Kin's wings *were* their heart. Tariah held her breath as she waited for the answer. She loathed the idea of hurting her friend, but she loathed even more the idea that Daylar would die. He was guilty only of liking Sparkle and befriending Tariah.

"Okay," he finally said. His eyes closed as a little smile curved his lips. "Now at least I will have an excuse to stick around you."

"Idiot. You didn't need one." Sparkle let go of his hand and turned to Tariah. "Please. Take my top two wings and put them on his back. It's that easy."

"Easy!" Tariah swiped away her tears with her free hand. "Damn it, if both of you die, I'll be pissed!" She set Daylar down on her lap and then gently grasped Sparkle with one hand. Before she could tell herself not to, she grasped her friend's top two wings and pulled. They were shockingly easy to remove, and they came off as easily as pulling petals from a flower.

Golden blood welled and began to flow, but Sparkle's other wings glowed and began to creep up her back to seal the wound. Her stomach churning, Tariah took the two wings and pressed them against Daylar's back. She had no idea what she was doing, but it proved to be the right thing. Light flared with an odd sound, and the wings were jerked from her fingers as they attached to his back. The blood flow began to stop.

She gathered both Kin in her arms protectively and lurched to her feet as the boat shuddered wildly. Staying was out of the question with the Elite still there. She looked around desperately, and she thought she saw the outline of an island to the west. It had to be either an outpost or a part of Kindred. With her powers, they might make it. She ran swiftly to the edge of the railing and climbed on top.

"Tariah Chronis!" Soh shouted behind her. "There is nowhere your kind belongs except with the Elite!"

She shot him a look over her shoulder out of glittering silver eyes. "I belong with my Fury, wherever he may be!" she shouted back. "And not you, or anyone else, is ever going to keep me from finding him!" Holding tight to her two precious companions, she dove over the side of the ship and into the waiting ocean. There would be no going back now.

Chapter Four

With the turbulence of the storm above the surface, the best thing Tariah could do was use her powers to encase herself and the two Kin inside a bubble that would allow them to breathe underwater.

She let go of them only long enough to rip strips of material from the bottom of her leggings and turn them into shorts. She tied the strips together into a long loop and wrapped it around her body crosswise like a sling. Gently she tucked the two Kin into it so that she had her hands free.

Once they were secured, she shrank the bubble down to just the two Kin. It gave her the freedom to start swimming, which she was surprisingly good at despite living in the desert. Few Water elements didn't find a way to learn how to swim, considering how much time they spent in water.

She stayed five feet under the surface. It protected her from the storm but allowed her to rise easily if she needed. She could only curse herself mentally; the storm wouldn't have even gotten that bad if it hadn't grabbed her power.

After half an hour of swimming, she was tired. She rose to the surface to rest, and she saw that the ship was nowhere in sight. The island she aimed for still seemed like a line on the horizon.

"Tariah?" Sparkle whispered.

She looked down swiftly to see Daylar also looking up at her blearily. "It's okay. Go back to sleep." She hugged both Kin gently and only loosened her grip when she saw they slept once more. Both were very pale, and even their tattoos looked dull. Fury churned inside her heart. If she got her hands on Soh, she was going to rip his arms off.

She rested for a few more moments before swimming again. The storm had lessened finally, but it still lingered. She didn't dare use her powers to make them move faster; the storm would drink them up faster than a thirsty desert madman.

She lost track of time. The clouds overhead made it impossible to tell what time of day it was. Exhaustion tugged at her ankles but she kept going. If she fell asleep, the bubble on the Kin would disappear. She swam as long as she could and floated to rest. She didn't let herself think about anything except reaching safety.

The island steadily grew bigger and bigger. She was finally able to see the edge of the beach and the darker line behind it that indicated trees. If she looked to her right, she was able to see an even longer and far fainter line on the horizon. Her vague memory of the maps she had seen told her she was approaching either Kindred or Carnelian and the other was the line in the distance. Size told her she was likely closer to Kindred, and she really wanted to be right.

More time slipped past. She didn't know how long she had been swimming. A day? It had to have been at least that. She was finally less than a mile from the island. The storm had eased entirely and the clouds had dispersed. It was nighttime, and it would have been horribly dark if two of the four moons hadn't been full.

The beach was a strip of white and the trees beyond seemed an ominous, dark shape. They looked very big, and she thought they might be nearly as tall as her cliffs back home. Through them, even at this distance, she could see the lights that indicated a village lay ahead.

Encouragement brought a surge of strength to let her keep swimming. Her muscles ached. She was thirsty, hungry, and so tired that her eyes had gone blurry. If she managed to get to safety, she would sleep for days. It felt like she hadn't slept well in weeks.

When she was finally able to put her feet down and walk out of the waves, relief made her lightheaded and she stumbled up the shore. She fell to her knees on the sand and stared blindly at the distance. Daylar stirred slightly and asked faintly, "Are we safe?"

"I think we are. Stop talking and rest." She lied down on the sand and closed her eyes. She just needed a few moments to rest before making her way to the village. She could sense Light and Dark power and knew that there were more Kin than Magi around. She was safe enough.

When she opened her eyes the next time, she found herself staring at a wooden mobile turning slowly over her head. It had clearly been carved by a Soil/Wood master for each wooden animal seemed real enough to come to life.

She was lying on a soft bed and there were warm blankets tucked around her. She was also completely naked, but that didn't wholly surprise her. After everything that had happened, her clothes had been wrecked.

She held the blankets to her chest and sat up to look around.

It looked like either a guestroom or an inn room. Nothing spectacular made it stand out, and there were no indications that anyone had personalized it with their power. Daylight poured in the open window and filled the room with light and warmth. Beyond the window, she could hear the sounds of a village busily at work.

Realizing that she couldn't sense Sparkle or Daylar, she looked around swiftly. There was no sign of them. She swathed the blanket around herself like a dress and got out of bed. She hurried over to the door, but as she was reaching for the knob, it opened into the hall. A slender SunKin Elf with arms full of clothes stood on the other side. "Oh!" The Kin smiled, her blue eyes sparkling. "You're awake now."

"Yes." Tariah clutched the blanket closer. "Where are Sparkle and Daylar?" she asked urgently. "Are they alright? Please, tell me!"

"They are fine," the Kin assured her. "Both are recovering nicely. Sparkle woke and was able to tell us everything that happened. Daylar's body is adapting just fine to her wings." She smiled. "Sparkle can't believe that he loves her, but it's very obvious."

Tariah found a smile as relief made her feel lightheaded. She was more than willing to let the Kin escort her back to the bed so she could sit down. "She seems to think that because he's handsome that he wouldn't be interested in her. But she's the sweetest person I've ever known."

"She is, at that." The Kin set down the clothes she carried. "I am Rumidia, a SunKin Elf, Fire secondary."

"Tariah Chronis." She hesitated for a moment before saying softly, "A Water Chronicle."

Rumidia stepped back and studied her critically. The young Chronicle was surprisingly lovely, especially with her Chronicle lines swirling over nearly a third of her body. Rumidia wasn't used to seeing such short Magi, but she was delighted nonetheless. Kin Elves were on the shorter side as well. Few were ever over five-six in height. "I'm glad to meet you."

Tariah looked down at her hands. "Even though it was my existence that resulted in Maxim's death, and nearly in Daylar's as well?" she whispered. "Soh was right about that. If you all keep protecting me . . ."

Rumidia propped her hands on her hips and tossed her blue-black hair out of her eyes. Her sharply pointed ears quivered as a sure sign of her anger. Kin Faeries were marked by their wings. Kin Elves were marked by their ears. Rumidia's happened to be the ears of a feline, and they acted as such by showing her displeasure. "Now look here, little one," she scolded, "Soh is a fool. Moreover, the Magi are to blame for trying to kill you. We Kin stand up for those being wronged."

Tariah digested that. Then, "Okay. And . . . thank you."

The door flew open with a bang. "Tariah!" Sparkle shot into the room like a little bullet and plowed into Tariah with enough force that she almost managed to knock her back. "Tariah! You're awake!" Sparkle was crying as she clung onto her neck. "I was so scared! You didn't wake up for three days!"

"Three!" Tariah's eyes widened. "I was more tired than I thought." She eased her friend back and held her on her palms to study her.

Sparkle's tattoos still looked slightly faded, indicating she was recovering, but her wings seemed to have settled fully into their new position. They were currently folded against her back, and bandages wrapped around her body kept them in place. There were no bloodstains, thankfully. Either they had stopped bleeding or they were well padded.

Tariah asked, "Faeries can fly without wings?"

Sparkle nodded and wiped at her eyes. "For small distances. We use our Light or Dark powers for it." She hovered woozily over to Tariah's shoulder and sat down. She was dressed in a loose sleeping gown and she almost slid off her friend's shoulder. To anchor herself, she wrapped a lock of Tariah's hair around her waist. "Want to see Daylar?"

Tariah smiled. "Yes, very much so!" She looked down suddenly. "But, er, first I want clothes."

Rumidia chuckled. "As we assumed you might." She gestured to the clothes she had set down. "You're not acclimated for the forest, desert child. You'll want to wear some of our style of clothing in order to protect your skin and to keep you warm."

Tariah studied the clothes in resignation. "I figured you'd say that," she said on a sigh. As Rumidia left the room, she gently put Sparkle down on the bed and then walked over to where the clothes waited. She would just have to learn to adjust.

The clothing consisted of sturdy cloth leggings and a snug cloth tunic that clung to every inch of her body from her neck to her wrists. The collar came up around her neck but there were diamond patches of skin visible on her shoulders where the material was deliberately not sewn together. To go underneath the clothing was a matching cloth bikini specially designed to help keep her warm and support her figure.

Sparkle brightened as she saw how her friend looked. "You look really pretty in our clothes!" She saw Tariah preparing to braid her hair and swiftly hovered over and grabbed onto the brown locks. "No! Leave it down! I like it!"

"It gets in my way." Tariah plucked the Faerie out of her hair and set her on the table. As a compromise, she braided the thickest part of her hair down her back but left several locks in the front loose. "There, better?"

Sparkle hovered over to land on her shoulder and wrapped herself in Tariah's hair happily. "Yes!"

Tariah just shook her head slightly and left the room. She was definitely at the inn, she saw, so she headed for the stairs down to the bottom floor. Rumidia stood behind the desk and waved cheerfully as the two partners headed outside into the cool morning sunlight.

Tariah immediately shivered. The air wasn't strictly cold, but it was vastly cooler than she was used to feeling. She crossed her arms around herself tightly, then looked up in surprise as a MoonKin Elf draped a cloak around her shoulders. "Oh! Thank you."

The man smiled. "It's not a problem. We've gone to a lot of trouble to keep you alive. We don't want you getting sick." He headed off toward the woods with a whistle, an axe propped on his shoulder as if there was nothing at all unusual in having a Chronicle in his village.

She slowly looked around. It was hard to determine the size of the village because of the way it settled in and around so many trees, but an instinctive sense of the area and the feel of the power told her that it had to be at least the size of Symphony. The buildings were made of stone and wood, and the ground was covered with lush grass while the roads were hard packed dirt.

Trees loomed everywhere, towering high in the sky to touch the clouds. Sunlight filtered down through them hazily and cast sunbeams everywhere. Kin walked and worked everywhere, in shops and in homes, Faerie and Elf alike. This part of the village seemed predominately SunKin, something that made her ask, "Do the MoonKin live in the more shadowy parts of the woods?"

"Yes." Sparkle smiled. "Since their power is Dark, they like the shadows more, just like we're Light and like the sun more." She studied Tariah. "You're Magi raised. Do you know what Light and Dark are?"

"Vaguely." She began to walk down the road, slowly taking everything in. "I remember in school that they said Light encompassed both elements of Water and Air, and Dark encompassed both elements of Fire and Soil. Seems sort of simplistic, especially since you all do still learn the four elements, regardless of your primary element, and some even learn secondary. Or tertiary as it may be."

Sparkle nodded sagely. "To be literal, Light is the element of the sun and Dark is the element of the moon. *Technically* you could say they encompass the other elements since Dark basically works like Soil and Fire, and Light like Air and Water, but they're not actually the same thing. They have a similar application in use, though Light and Dark are a lot more in-depth and powerful. Like, as a Light primary, I could use really powerful destructive blasts. And the MoonKin are *really* strong healers. They can almost raise the dead. Ah, turn here!" she added.

Tariah obligingly turned and headed down the road her friend indicated. She could see now where they were going; there was a large building ahead with the universally recognized white water drop that indicated a place of healing. "It's sad," she remarked. "I'm learning more about Kin than I even know about myself as a Chronicle."

"Elder Juniper said he would be willing to talk to you," Sparkle noted. "He's been around a really long time and might know more about what you are."

"Sparkle!" a MoonKin Faerie scolded from the doorway. He hovered in mid-air, his gray dove wings holding him aloft. His soft dark ruby skin was lightly covered with the silver markings of his race, and his hands were propped on his hips. "I told you not to wander off."

Sparkle ducked down behind Tariah's shoulder and hid in her hair. "But, but, I wanted to find Tariah! She was worried about me too."

The Kin sighed. "You're three and you act like this still."

Tariah's brows went up through her bangs. "Three?"

"Well, by Magi standards." Sparkle smiled. "Faeries of either Kin blood mature really fast for our first two years then age really slowly from there on. Elves of either Kin blood mature really slowly in the beginning, but once they're like fifty or something they age at a normal rate. So, you at twenty are the equivalent to a two or three year old Faerie and a fifty to sixty year old Elf."

The MoonKin smiled and bowed. "I'm ten myself. I suppose I'm not *that* much older than Sparkle." He waved a finger at Sparkle. "I'm still your doctor! Get in there, right now, missy."

She sighed. "Yes sir." She hovered through the air woozily and then disappeared into the building.

Tariah looked at the doctor and smiled before lifting a hand and drawing her thumb over her cheek and nose. "Warm greetings," she said. "I am Tariah Chronis, a Water Chronicle." It was getting easier to say, she noticed with some surprise.

The Kin smiled and folded his wings around himself as he bowed in an equal sign of respect. "Warm greetings, young Chronicle. I am Poplar, an Air secondary MoonKin Faerie. I am also one of the doctors for this town." He flew over to land on her shoulder gracefully. "I'm glad to see you are well."

"I'm more glad that Sparkle and Daylar are well," she countered. She smiled. "May I see Daylar?"

"Naturally." He flew off her shoulder and into the building. As she followed, he headed for the next floor down, leaving a little trail of energy that she was able to follow easily.

The intensive care room was located under the main floor. It was a place that had been specially built to block outside energies and majiks from getting inside and interfering with those who were badly wounded or sick.

Sparkle sat on the side of a Faerie-sized bed and sulked as a SunKin Elf checked her temperature. She was sulking because checking someone's temperature meant that another person of like element had to surround the patient with their power and it tended to cause an either uncomfortable or stuffy sensation. It was the only accurate reading possible though since, as an example, Fire elements tended to always be on the warm side.

Daylar was also sitting up on a bed and he was also wearing a sleeping gown. His new wings were folded against his back and bandages wrapped around him as well. His markings looked even paler than Sparkle's, but his eyes were full of plenty of liveliness. The fist around Tariah's heart eased as she saw that he would be fine.

He spotted her and brightened. "Tariah!" He waved his hands at her happily. "Guess what!"

She walked over and knelt beside him. "What?" she asked with a smile.

"Sparkle's going to bind her energy to mine!"

Sparkle gave a gasp. "You tattletale!" She shot over to him and poked him repeatedly in the chest. "I was going to tell her! You promised not to blab! Dang it, she was my friend first and I wanted to tell her!"

Tariah tilted her head. "Bind your energy?"

Poplar smiled as he flew over to land on her shoulder. "You Magi refer to it as 'linking your elements.'"

She began to smile as delight spread through her heart. To link your element to someone was to tie your life to them for eternity. "Oh that's great!" She scooped up both Kin to hug them gently. "I'm glad that something good happened from all this," she said softly, but fiercely.

"I'd have convinced her eventually anyway," Daylar said confidently, his brown eyes twinkling merrily. "But now she *has* to believe me that I love her." He pointed over his shoulder to the wings. "If I didn't, my body would have rejected her wings."

Sparkle blushed. "I think you're crazy."

"Probably."

Tariah nuzzled both with her nose and made them laugh and giggle. "You're both crazy but I'm very glad you're my friends. Daylar . . ." She held him on her palm and lifted him to eye level. He was only an inch or two taller than Sparkle so he was still only around a foot in height. "I truly am sorry. I promise, I'll make Soh pay."

He shook his head. "As long as you find your Fury, I'll consider us even." He thought about it, then amended, "No, actually, I won't. You have to come back and give me and Sparkle a ride on a Dragon's back. *Then* it'll be even."

She smiled. "Deal."

"Okay, that's enough," Poplar scolded them all. "You two need rest, and Tariah has a meeting with the Elder. Let's go." He ushered both Kin back over to their beds. "Stay put or I'll have you tied down. I want another day of rest from both of you, at the least!"

"Yes sir," the soon-to-be-couple obediently chorused.

Tariah covered a grin and hurried from the room before she started laughing. Once back outside she gave a long stretch with her hands over her head. She was still going to drown Soh if she found him, but she would make sure it was quicker since it was nice to see Daylar and Sparkle happy.

With a little help from a few Kin, she was shortly on the path that headed to the Elder's house. She had to assume he expected her since both Sparkle and Poplar had said he wanted to talk to her. She felt more than a little nervous. Despite what the others said, she couldn't help but feel a lingering guilt for everything she had caused.

The Elder waited for her on the front step of his home. He was an average sized SunKin Elf, possibly only an inch or two taller than Tariah, and his hair and eyes were matching yellow. His skin was pale blue and the gold markings sparkled in the sun. He looked young in appearance, as most Kin did, but his eyes spoke of many years.

He studied Tariah as she stopped in front of him. He was not displeased with what he saw. She was both lovely and strong, and her power felt so strong that one could nearly taste it. Her Chronicle lines glowed vivid against her skin, a sure sign that her Fury did exist in this world at this very moment. "Welcome, Tariah Chronis, Water Chronicle." He touched the finned ears on his head as an Elf sign of respect. "I am Elder Juniper, an Air secondary SunKin Elf."

She returned the gesture of respect. "Warm greetings, Elder. You wished to speak with me?"

"Come inside, my dear." He held the door for her before following her inside.

She liked the interior immediately. It was warm and cozy, filled with wooden furniture and soft cushions everywhere. It was also much warmer than the outdoors. She loved everything she had seen of Kindred, but she missed the heat of her deserts. "What did you wish to speak of?" she asked.

He took a seat and gestured to the one across from him. When she had also sat down, he leaned back in his chair and crossed his arms comfortably. "Well," he began, "there are many things. To begin with, I wish to know of Maxim. The MoonKin Elder, Sage, and I have discussed what the Militia told us as well as what Sparkle brought to our attention. I want your side."

Her hands clenched together in her lap. "Maxim was a doctor in Symphony. He was my friend. When the Militia came looking for a Chronicle because of some rumors, he and my parents wanted me to escape. A soldier overheard us and just . . ." A tear slid down her cheek. "Just stabbed him from behind. Like it was nothing. His only crime was protecting me." She swiped at her eyes. "They wanted me to run, to escape. So I did. And I'm going to live." Her eyes glittered fiercely. "If only because people died to see that I do." She looked at the Elder. "Why? Why do the Magi hate Chronicles?"

"Jealousy." He sighed quietly. "I am old, my dear. Not old enough to remember the Chronicle War, but my father had fought then. He spoke of it to me. So, too, have others spoken. We Kin keep detailed records, especially of times and people lost."

"Then tell me, please." She met his eyes. "Tell me what I am, and where I am from."

"Very well." He sat forward. "No one knows," he began, "the exact reason or place Chronicles and Furies come from. It just happened one day, a few thousand years ago, that a set of Magi twins developed lines on their bodies during first puberty and were capable of using secondary elements as well. No one really thought much of it. But at the same time, in the Dragon race, another anomaly was occurring. What do you know of Dragons?"

"Not much."

"I see. Well, at that time, the Dragon race lived mostly on their island. About half of the race are known as Dragon Lords because they can take a shape other than their natural one; shapes such as a Kin or Magi form. These Lords primarily lived and walked among Magi. But then two Dragon Lords discovered that they could use secondary elemental skills from first puberty."

Her eyes widened. "Like Chronicles."

"Precisely. The Dragons dubbed these Lords 'Fury' because it is a word in Draconic that means 'evolution', which is what they assumed they were. Well, long story short, when the twins encountered the Lords, something happened. The Furies developed lines that matched their Chronicle, and the two formed a bond that was even deeper than a Linked couple. The Chronicle could use the Fury's majiks as their own, and the Furies could use their Chronicle's ability to manipulate the same. They completed one another. We have always assumed it was the lines."

She touched the lines on her face softly. "So these *are* lines of Dragon power. And they gain lines of Chronicle power."

"We believe so." He closed his eyes. "In honor of the twins who were known as Chronis, the new Magi were called Chronicles." He smiled and opened his eyes when he felt her surprise. "We do not know if you are related, but it is certainly coincidental."

"I'd say."

Continuing, he said, "For a few thousand years everything was fine. There came to be many Chronicles and Furies. About the time of second puberty for the Chronicle, they would be driven to seek their Fury somewhere in the world. Their lines would lead them for their lines contained the power of their Fury. These lines would act as a map and take them to their final destination, wherever it may be. It was usually wherever the Fury was."

"They could not seek us?"

"No. They know when their Chronicle is born and when they die, but they do not know where they are until they have bonded as Dragoons." He smiled, sensing the next question. "A Dragoon is the name for a Fury or Chronicle when they bond." He got to his feet and walked over to the window. "About a thousand years ago, the Magi began to show their jealousy. Chronicles were, after all, more powerful and more advanced. They were also, once bonded to their Fury, immortal.

"Magi began to spread rumors that Chronicles were hosts and Furies were parasites. You see, in exchange for the share of majiks, Furies needed to feed on their Chronicle's power. That was the other difference between a Fury and a normal Dragon Lord. A Fury has only a set amount of power and must therefore feed from a Chronicle who, unlike Magi, has nearly limitless power.

"In either case, warfare eventually broke out. The Chronicles were driven into hiding. And, eventually, they were slaughtered. In the years since, they have been killed upon discovery. Any Fury that feels their Chronicle die . . . well, Dragons are immortal. Rather than suffer endlessly, the Fury is mercifully released of this life."

There was silence as he finished speaking. Tariah had hundreds of questions but she did not ask them. She knew they were questions the Elder could never answer. To understand, she would have to find her Fury and get her answers firsthand. More than ever she felt the burning of her lines. *North.* She still had to go north.

"We have tried to contact the Dragons," Juniper suddenly said as he turned around. "To tell them we have a Chronicle. But after the slaughter of the Chronicles a thousand years ago, even the Dragon Lords stay mostly on their island. Especially during summer, the time when most Magi enter first and second puberties, and the Militia is sharp to find Chronicles. The Lords know they could never find their Chronicle before they are killed."

"The Magi are the only ones not suffering over this," she whispered. "It's so unfair."

"You would seek vengeance on them?" he asked softly.

"Of course not!" She shot to her feet indignantly. "I don't care what they do as long as I can live how I want. Chronicles and Furies are normal parts of evolution. If we weren't, we wouldn't still appear! The Magi will have to deal with it!"

He nodded. "As long as you hold to that feeling, the Kin will aide you."

There was a knock on the door and a SunKin Faerie flew in. "Elder," she said, "there is a soldier from the Militia here. Rumor reached them that we are sheltering a Chronicle."

Tariah took a sharp breath and Juniper gently touched her shoulder as he went past. "The Militia would not dare do anything to us. We may not outnumber them, but we far exceed them in power. Moreover, it would upset the balance of the land and destroy many islands, as it did before the treaty."

She followed him even though she would rather have hidden. "Is that why there is a treaty at all?"

"Precisely. The Magi decided that they wanted to get rid of the Kin to take their land. In the destruction of so many Kin, the land was sunk. We lost many more before the Magi got smart and offered a treaty." He smiled. "So, you see, you are quite safe with us. Go rest, my dear."

She reluctantly went back to the inn but she waited anxiously for word as to what would happen. As evening settled, she heard voices downstairs and snuck down to listen. Rumidia was talking with Poplar, and she hoped one or the other knew what was going on. She did not want to be the cause of more death.

"So the Militia knows we have Tariah," Rumidia murmured. "And what can they do about it?"

"They're going to station soldiers at every port and city. If she even goes near it she will be killed." Poplar's voice reflected his disgust. "They hope to keep her from following her lines and finding her Fury. They won't succeed."

"What about a formal offer of sanctuary?" she wondered. "If we make her honorary Kin, the Magi don't dare touch her at all."

"Juniper and Sage are discussing it as we speak. They're also sending word out to every Kin on Magi lands. We want everyone looking for the Dragons. If we can find even one, then we can get Tariah to their island where she can surely find her Fury. On the isle, she should be free. There's just one catch."

"What's that?"

"Well, the Militia have made it plain that if a Kin is caught assisting Tariah on Magi lands, they will consider it a breach of treaty. And we both know what that means."

Her voice went flat. "Death to the one breaching. They can't just manipulate the treaty however they like!"

"Until we make Tariah an honorary Kin, they can. But finding a Kin who can mark a Chronicle is nearly impossible because of their lines." He sighed. "We'll just have to do whatever we can."

Her throat tight, Tariah went back upstairs. So she couldn't go to Magi land. That was fine. She would find her Fury herself. She would find the Isle of Dragons on her own. She was a Water element. She could survive on the ocean. She was sure of it.

She waited until it was dark. Once the village was quiet, she snuck out of the inn and to the docks. She left a few coins for apology and then untied a small boat and began to sail it out into the ocean. Her lines were burning so she couldn't feel that this was wrong. She was tired of always needing to be protected. Tired of the stupid jealousy and fear that drove the Magi. And most of all, she was tired of following anyone's whims but her own.

She would find the damned isle by herself, and then she was going to give her Fury a piece of her mind for not looking for her when he had felt she was alive more than a few hours!

Chapter Five

Dominic Whisperer was a Fire element Dragon. Or, at least, that was the appearance that he let the rest of the world see, though any Kin who met him sensed the truth. Dominic was a Fury.

He had been hatched by his parents, both Fire element Dragon Lords, nearly three centuries before. Like most other beings of the element Fire, regardless of race, he was fierce and protective and very quick to temper. It was matched by a deep loyalty and sense of life that made him loved by his entire race.

When he had entered first puberty (an occurrence that came around the age of one hundred for Dragons), many females who had been waiting with their hopes held for him to eventually reach second puberty had found those same hopes dashed. Dominic had not just developed Fire powers, but he had also developed Smoke and shown his Fury blood.

It was a grim and cruel fate for Dominic. Not only did he have to watch his majiks usage for fear of draining it too low, but there was no telling when his Chronicle would be born. Once he felt her birth, it would be a ticking time bomb to the day when she would be killed and Dominic himself would need to be put out of his misery.

As he studied a window display in a large city on the main Magi continent of Spectrum, he smiled wryly to himself. He had felt his Chronicle's birth over twenty years ago. Either she was an exceptionally slow bloomer, or something had occurred to keep her alive.

It hurt. Oh, did it hurt. There were times when he would feel his throat close and his heart clench and his eyes burn with the overwhelming longing to find the one person who would understand him. The one person who would love him no matter what he did. But unlike Chronicles, Furies were not given the ability to track their chosen partner. He had tried. For the last ten years he had been trying. And he could not find her.

It was summer now. Summer was the time when nearly all races would begin first or second puberty. He had grown to loathe the summer. Each time it arrived he felt as if he waited with his breath held for his world to fall apart. And then, when summer was over, there was always the lingering despair that perhaps his Chronicle had hidden her identity and lived a lie. That, more than anything, broke his heart.

Prismatic was the capital of the Magi continent Spectrum. It was the capital of the entire race and by far the biggest city. It was nearly twenty miles in size, not including farmlands, and boasted a population of nearly two hundred thousand. It was Magi central and the source of the most commerce and trade.

It sat situated in the middle of the desert and well isolated from even the next closest town, some two hundred miles away. Dominic liked Prismatic if only because it allowed him to disappear in the crowds. Like Kin, Dragons could not hide their heritage. Though Dominic could walk in the form of a Magi, his black hair held red streaks. The streaks marked his Dragon blood.

Well past even second puberty, he wasn't worried that any Magi would ever know he was a Fury. He had no idea how they would react, and he wasn't particularly interested in finding out. He did not hate the Magi for what they had done, but he sure as hell did not trust them.

As he passed some women gossiping on the corner, he very nearly ignored them entirely. But, as he was going around the corner of a store, he heard the word 'Chronicle' very clearly. Shocked, he froze for a moment. He swiftly doubled back and stayed out of sight to listen.

"It was just speculation," the older woman was saying softly, "but the Militia is now being assigned to every port city on every Magi continent. It's got to be true. There's a Chronicle out there, alive."

"Unbelievable," the younger woman murmured. "Why wasn't he or she killed outright?"

"Well, there are lots of rumors about that. Some people claim she manipulated the minds of the people around her." The old woman snorted in derision. "If that were true, we wouldn't even know of her now. No, I suspect her parents loved her more than they feared her."

"And it still got them killed," the younger woman said curtly. "They'd have been better off killing her themselves than let her go through what she is now."

Dominic's fingers lengthened into claws and left gouges on the stone behind him as he grabbed the wall to control his temper. Smoke emerged from between his teeth as he hissed softly. His instincts told him that the woman was thinking of self-preservation more than the terror of a child.

Underneath the anger came the first stirring of hope. A female Chronicle had survived past first puberty and was only now being discovered. His Chronicle would be twenty now. It was more than slightly possible that the survivor and his Chronicle were the same person. In fact, he was nearly one hundred percent certain they were. The odds of two Chronicles surviving at the same time were smaller than a desert resident's swim clothes.

"No matter the reason, the Chronicle is alive." The older woman sighed. "I feel sorry for the child. She has no hope for a normal life."

Dominic had heard enough. He began walking quickly through the city toward the transportation district. It was the only place that Dragons were allowed to land when in natural form or to take off from in the same. He was not allowed to fly over Magi cities, but he had no objections to going the long way around. He would do whatever it took.

"Dragon! *Ashti ke!*"

He stopped and turned around, his brows drawing together over his gray eyes in confusion as he heard someone speaking Draconic. At first he thought it was a Magi calling for his attention, which would be almost impossible, but he realized immediately that it was not. It was a SunKin Elf, and he was running toward Dominic as fast as he could. "What is it?" Dominic asked warily.

The Elf looked around, realized there were far too many Magi, and switched to the language of the Dragons, something he felt sure no Magi would know. "The Kin have the Chronicle in our possession."

Dominic's eyes widened sharply. "You do? Is she well?" For the same reason, he also spoke Draconic.

"From what the Elders tell us, yes. Word has been flying among the Kin. We've been trying to locate even one of you to tell you. If you could take her to your isle then surely she could find her Fury and be safe." The Kin studied him. "Although . . . you are a Fire Fury yourself. And she is a Water Chronicle. Perhaps she is yours."

"Whether she is or not is not a concern to me." His eyes burned fiercely. "I will take her to the Isle whether she belongs to me or not. If not mine, she belongs to one of my fellow Furies. Where is she?"

"On Kindred, on the island furthest south. The Elders are discussing making her honorary Kin to protect her from the Magi, but we're still trying to locate a Kin that can harmonize with her. It's nearly impossible with her lines." The Elf touched his ears as he bowed. "Swift flight, Fire Fury. Please hurry."

Dominic didn't need to be told twice. He turned and made his way even quicker to the area affectionately termed 'the airport' because Air Magi would create portals to protect people while Dragons were taking off and landing.

Ten minutes later he was flying across the sky as swiftly as he dared. He had to circle around the outside of the city and impatience surged inside him. With it came a heavy dose of fear. He had been raised knowing that a Fury and Chronicle were always well matched, sometimes opposites and sometimes identical.

Knowing himself as well as he did, he knew that he would be blessed, or cursed, to be partnered with a strong-willed Chronicle. If this Chronicle was his, then she would hate being cooped up and protected. She would be more likely to set out onto the open sea in a boat with full trust in her power.

Normal Dragons had nearly limitless power. They could push themselves to fly as far and as fast as they wanted and cover miles in minutes with only the slightest drain on their power. Furies were different. Their powers had a limit, and without their Chronicle to feed from, they had to watch their majiks use lest they risk being severely injured or even potentially dying.

He was pushing his luck and his limits as he shot across the sky like a red and black bullet. It wasn't something he would have dared if he hadn't felt utterly certain that this mysterious Chronicle was his. He wouldn't even consider any other thought. It had to be her!

It was for that reason that, when he reached Kindred two hours later, he fell straight to his knees when he changed into Magi form upon landing on the beach. He shook his head and fought the sickness churning in his stomach. The sand had started to turn very interesting blurry shades of color that did nothing to help his nausea.

"Oof, you're in bad shape." The MoonKin Faerie that hovered near had his hands on his hips. "Well, I've never treated a Dragon of any kind before, but there's a first time for everything."

Dominic turned his head and tried to bring the Kin into focus. "You're a doctor?"

"That's me. Name's Poplar." He flew over and hovered anxiously as Dominic forced himself to his feet. He staggered, and Poplar swiftly grabbed his cloak to keep him from falling over. "I don't know a lot about Furies, but I do know enough to be capable of scolding you for pushing so hard!"

Dominic planted his feet, closed his eyes, and reached for his reserves of power. To his surprise, he felt a warm hand on his arm and realized someone had offered their Fire element to help him. He opened his eyes and turned his head to see a lovely SunKin Elf beside him. With a smile, he covered her hand and accepted her power to bolster his. It took the edge off his ailments, though it could not actually replenish him. "Thank you."

"Naturally." The Elf touched her ears as she bowed. "I am Rumidia." She propped her hands on her hips as she studied him and then sighed. "By the moons, I hate to be the bearer of bad news, but . . ."

"But . . .?"

"We, ah, seem to have lost the Chronicle." Poplar sighed when Dominic covered his face with a hand. "We were trying to keep her safe but she thinks that we'll be hurt if we do. She seems to have taken a boat and set off into the ocean."

Dominic cursed softly in Draconic. "When?" he asked curtly.

"Last night some time. Her partner, Sparkle, says that she always was feeling a burning to go north, so she likely went that way."

Shock reverberated through him. Up until this morning, he had been north of these lands. This Chronicle *was* his. She wasn't looking for the Isle at all; it lay to the far west in Deepest Ocean. She was looking for *him*. "I'll find her," he vowed softly. "And take her to the Isle where she will be safe."

Rumidia and Poplar shared a smile. They had been hoping the handsome Fury was the one for their Tariah, and both were fairly sure now that he was. He was Tariah's elemental opposite, and his personality would fit with her nicely. "Send us word when she is safe," Rumidia said. "Please. We all love her very much."

"Gladly." With the small boost from Rumidia, it was not difficult for him to take Dragon form again and begin flying across the ocean to the north. How far could a small boat get, even piloted by a Water Chronicle?

Farther than he thought because it was a good twenty minutes and ten miles of ocean before he spotted the little boat floating on the waves. He had been flying as fast as he dared without missing anything, and yet it had felt as if he was crawling across the sky.

The small boat simply drifted on the waves. He angled downward and changed into Magi form when he was close enough to land. It was a tricky thing to do when the boat was barely five feet wide and he was ten feet from nose to tail, but he managed.

The Chronicle was lying on the bottom of the boat, motionless, but he could feel the surge and snap of her power and knew she was only unconscious. He carefully knelt beside her and reached out a hand to tenderly brush her hair from her face. She was stunning, he realized in wonder. Her golden lines flowed down her skin like rivers, and he felt as if he could read every curl like a map to her soul.

A hot fist grabbed his heart and held on tightly as he gently lifted her into his arms and held her close. His throat closed so tight he could barely breathe. *Finally*, he thought in wonder and relief. Finally he had found her. The one person meant only for him. He tenderly pressed his lips to her temple. "You'll be safe now," he murmured.

He held her for a few more moments and then forced himself to put her down again. It was the hardest thing he had ever done. He jumped backward off the edge of the boat and turned into his Dragon form again just before he hit the water. He gathered his Chronicle in his claws as carefully as if she was glass, and he held her protectively where she wouldn't fall. He turned to go west, to head for the Isle . . . and realized in a sudden shock that he could not remember how to get there.

Praying it was only because of his diminished majiks, he instead turned and began to fly across the sky back toward Kindred. Until his Chronicle awoke, and until he could determine why the hell he had forgotten the route back to his own damned home, they would be safe among the Kin.

Rumidia and Poplar were both startled when they saw him flying over the island, but they were also relieved because they could see he carried someone or something in his claws. They hurried quickly down to the beach where they could see the light strafing off his scales as he landed.

They reached the shore just as he turned back to Magi form. Tariah rested in his arms, deeply unconscious with her head lying against his shoulder. Poplar scrambled through the air and touched her forehead gently. His breath came out in a relieved whoosh. "She's just asleep. She must have been sailing all night."

Rumidia watched Dominic's face as he looked down at Tariah. The knots of fear in her stomach began to unwind as she saw the expression in his gray eyes. It was a combination of awe and wonder, coupled with an emotion so strong that she was wary to even label it love. "She's yours," she said softly.

"Yes." He buried his nose in Tariah's hair, delighted with the way it smelled like the desert. "She's mine and I am hers. Where should I take her?"

"I run the inn." Rumidia smiled. "You can bring her there. Poplar, why don't you go tell Sparkle and Daylar that everything will be okay?"

"Just because you're older than me," Poplar grumbled as he flew off, "doesn't make you my boss."

Dominic followed Rumidia as she worked her way back through the village, and he noticed immediately that everyone who saw him with Tariah looked instantly relieved and delighted all at the same time. He had to smile. His Chronicle had more friends than she likely realized.

The room Rumidia escorted him to was a much more private one on the second floor at the back. He carried Tariah over to the bed and gently set her down on it. It took considerable willpower to ignore the sight she made. Her physical beauty stole his breath, but her power was what truly attracted him. It was *his* power that sensuously flowed in lines down her body. His fingers trembled as he ran them down her cheek.

Hunger prowled through him. A hunger for her soft lips and graceful curves. It was also a hunger for the power that flowed through her body. He could nearly taste it, and it was a surprising realization. He had not realized that his need to feed on her power would be a literal need, like food or water.

The door squeaked open and he turned his head just as a little lavender streak shot in the room. With lightning reflexes, he shot a hand out and caught the little Faerie when she was a foot from Tariah. "Hold it there, firefly."

Sparkle wiggled indignantly. "Let me go!" She aimed a sulky look at him as she crossed her arms. His grip was gentle around her body but implacable. "Tariah's my friend!"

"Tariah." He repeated the name slowly, enjoying it. It reminded him of *tarinah*, a word in Draconic that meant 'storms in a desert'.

She wanted to be annoyed but couldn't retain it, not when she saw the way he looked at her friend. So this was Tariah's Fury. She decided she liked him merely because she liked the way he looked at Tariah. "Her full name is Tariah Chronis. What's yours?"

"Dominic Whisperer." He brought her up to eye level and held her on his palm. He smiled as she shook out the sleeping shirt she wore and then he frowned intently as he saw the bandages wrapped around her body. "What happened?"

She held onto his thumb for balance. He was of average height for a Magi male, she supposed, since he was two inches shy of six feet in height, but his hands seemed bigger. They were almost twice Tariah's size, but, then again, her friend was little. "Well," she said slowly, "I had to give some of my wings to another Kin."

He smiled. He knew as much about Kin as they themselves did. "Congratulations, I assume, are in order."

She blushed a little. "Well, yes, but . . ." She looked at Tariah sadly. "The Black Magi Elite are after Tariah. They know she's a Chronicle and want her to join them. They ripped off Daylar's wings to make him tell them. Tariah blames herself but it's not her fault."

Anger beat upward in his heart. "No," he said as evenly as he could, "it's not."

She suddenly giggled. "When you're mad, you breathe smoke!"

He lifted a brow and then smiled and blew a swirl of smoke around her. "Sometimes," he agreed. He gently put her on his shoulder where she sat down companionably. "You're Tariah's friend?"

"Uh-huh. I found her in the desert after she fled Symphony." She looked at him seriously. "Please, Dominic, make sure she's happy. She keeps having bad things happen to her just because she's different. But I love her, a lot."

"I'll do my best." He rubbed his thumb gently over Tariah's cheekbone and wished they were already bonded fully. He had heard tales of Dragoons who could share their dreams, and he wanted to share Tariah's and make sure she knew she was no longer alone. For the time being, it would have to be enough to hold her as she slept.

Sparkle cleared her throat. She was past her own second puberty and far from blind. It was quite obvious Dominic wanted Tariah badly; something both expected and perfectly natural. It was also bad timing. She felt *really* bad for him. "Dominic?"

"Yes?"

"Tariah hasn't started second puberty yet."

It took him a few moments to realize what she had said. He closed his eyes in a combination of dismay and horror as he realized what he was about to endure. Frustrating wouldn't even be the word for what he would go through until Tariah was ready to take him as her lover. She wasn't even ready for him to kiss her let alone touch her as he craved. "*Kekle.*"

Sparkle had to assume that was a particularly nasty Draconic word. "I thought I'd just, you know, warn you."

"Thanks." He sat back with a sigh. "I can't decide whether I'm annoyed at needing to learn self-control when it's my right to claim her, or exceedingly grateful I get to be the one to help her become an adult."

She muffled a snicker that became a cough when he glowered at her. "Sorry. I just find it sort of sweet." She kissed his cheek. "I had wished she would find you soon. I'm glad she did. Now, no matter what, she'll be happy. Right?"

"We both will." He drew Tariah's hand to his cheek and rubbed against her fingers slowly. It was her right hand and he felt the pulsing of her lines against his skin. It fascinated him. Her lines had been made of his power, and yet they were filled with hers. The combination felt heady and nearly made his mouth water. His majiks had dropped so low that he either needed to go into hibernation for a while, or feed. He really leaned toward the latter. He could sense now just how amazing it might be.

"I wonder why she hasn't woken," Sparkle remarked suddenly. "I mean, she's not low on power. It's kind of funny actually, but she seems to be *over*-producing power. I can feel it in my wings. It tickles. I half expect to see her dissolve into a puddle or something."

"That is because our Dominic is here," Juniper said from the doorway. "To cement the bond, a Chronicle and Fury must make their first exchange. To that end, the Chronicle will suddenly produce an exorbitant amount of power, and the Fury will be drained. After that, the exchange will be more of an 'as needed' basis. Or whenever they are in a, ah, particular mood."

Dominic's smile came wryly. "Indeed. How did you know?"

"I was contacted a short time ago by another of your race, another Fury. She informed me of what to expect and said that she would tell the rest of your kind about Tariah." He lifted a brow. "You cannot do this yourself, I take it."

Dominic cleared his throat. "I seem to have forgotten the way back to my isle. And I can't seem to lay a successful hand on the energy output of any of my kind. Would you mind contacting my clanmate and telling her this? See if perhaps she or the Elders know what is going on."

"Gladly." Juniper smiled. "Come, Sparkle. When Tariah awakes, she will want some time alone with Dominic. Let Nature take its course. It has rules for us all. And you shouldn't be out of bed, missy."

"Oh come on!" She was indignant but obligingly flew over and rode on his shoulder as he left the room and shut the door behind them.

Dominic looked back down at Tariah's peaceful face. His Chronicle. He had thought he would never find her. With a soft sigh, he reached out and gathered her close so that he could feel her heartbeat. He was never going to let her go again.

Chapter Six

Tariah awoke to a blinding headache. In fact, it wasn't just her head. Her whole body ached to the point of nearly being real pain. She knew she wasn't in her boat on the ocean anymore; she felt a soft bed beneath her and the familiar feeling of Kin near. She knew someone had 'rescued' her, which annoyed her slightly, but the annoyance seemed faint in the face of the way her body hurt.

Her fingers curled into the sheet beneath her as sweat broke out on her skin. What was wrong with her? She wanted to unleash her power in a wild torrent, to rage and seethe like the seas. She felt as if she was choking on her own Water element. A faint whimper slipped past her lips.

"It's alright." The voice was soft and male, and the hand that covered her cheek felt the same. "Just open your eyes and look at me."

The voice and the touch reverberated through her body and touched a deeply buried inner instinct she hadn't known existed. *Mine*, a part of her soul whispered. *This man is mine.* Shock echoed inside her. Hers? Her Fury? Her eyes flew wide and she found herself staring up into the storm gray eyes of a man she had never met before but recognized on a cellular level.

He was, without exception, the single most beautiful man she had ever seen. His face was rough edged without being hard, and his black hair fell into his eyes. Red streaks curled through the black, and she wondered if he would mind if she ran her hands through them.

A slow smile began to spread as she carefully lifted a hand to touch his face. It might have been a sign of second puberty. It might have been merely him. Something inside made it impossible to resist the urge to touch him. If it *was* just him and whatever was between them, then second puberty was bound to be interesting.

Dominic's breath caught. Her smile had to be one of the most beautiful things he had ever seen. "Hello," he said softly. "I think I belong to you."

Some of the pain erased in sheer joy. Tears burned her eyes. "Really?" she asked just as softly. "Because I think I belong to you too." His presence curled around her and seemed to sink into her heart. She wasn't alone anymore.

The pain returned with a vengeance and rippled through her body. Her fingers tightened on his face, and he gently covered her hand. "It's because we need to bond."

"Okay fine." Her breath hitched as a spasm seemed to rip from her stomach outward. "No offense, but if this is going to happen every time, I'd sooner find a way to drown myself."

"Don't you dare!" He gently lifted her onto his lap and held her possessively close. As if responding to his presence, pale blue light began to emanate around her skin. Her lines rippled like waves. It was unbearably beautiful, and hidden instincts rose inside him with a hunger he could not fight.

He bent his head and pressed his lips to the patch of skin bared on her shoulder. He breathed in, as if drinking, and her power flowed into him. It tasted like the freshest of water, pure and sweet, but there held an underlying flavor to it like rare fruit.

The pain almost immediately lessened inside her body as he fed on her power. She relaxed against him and closed her eyes slightly, savoring the knowledge that someone needed her. Obligingly, she tilted her head to the side as he pressed his lips to her neck.

Though he would have liked nothing more than to cover her entire body with kisses and feed from her power everywhere, he knew better. She wasn't ready for him, and he wasn't a fan of self-inflicted torture. A thousand emotions seemed tangled inside him, welded together with a lust more powerful than he had imagined. It nearly overshadowed his hunger. Or perhaps they were the same. He couldn't tell, and he didn't care.

"I'm going to kiss you," he warned her as he cupped her face in his hands.

She smiled. "It's my first one, so be nice."

Talk about putting a man on the spot. Yet he wasn't worried. It was wonderfully easy to be gentle with her when she trusted him unthinkingly. Deep inside, he could feel the same thing. A bedrock trust that he had never before experienced. If he needed her, she would be there. If she needed him, he would be there. The feeling tightened his throat with overwhelming emotion. "Tariah."

She didn't get a chance to respond before his lips covered hers softly. She had nothing to compare it to, but she had the feeling he definitely knew what he was doing. His lips were warm and soft as they moved over hers, and the feeling of him drinking her power this way stole away even the last vestiges of pain.

As the last of her power flowed into him, it was as if they were suddenly breathing inside each other's bodies. Where she had her hands resting on his chest, she could feel the skin heat underneath his cloth shirt. Her palms itched and tingled as she felt power, his or hers she didn't know, building under his skin.

He lifted his head slowly and realized that he could feel her inside him. Almost curiously, he reached out with his mind as if to touch her. She sensed him and mentally shied away. He frowned. "You don't want me in your mind?"

She turned her face away. "I don't want to share my memories," she said. "I don't want even you to know. Maybe especially you."

He said nothing. Her emotions seemed clear as they flowed along the lines connecting them. She was ashamed of something, and there was a heavy dose of terror mixed inside. He ran his hands gently up and down her arms, and his fingers tingled as they skimmed along her lines. "I won't pry," he said at last. "But I eventually want to know. You can peek into my mind anytime."

Rather than immediately peek in his mind, she actually leaned forward and peeked down the collar of his shirt. His brows lifted in amusement. "If you want me naked, you only have to ask."

She stuck her tongue out at him briefly. "I was just curious if you have lines now, and it seems you do." It belatedly dawned on her that for all the intimacy between them, for all the ease she felt, and despite the fact that she felt as if he was a part of her soul that she had been missing since birth . . . she didn't know his name.

An odd look crossed his face. "I'm not sure which of us felt it first, but I agree that we're in a very odd situation. I don't normally kiss a woman before we've been properly introduced."

Her lines suddenly burned so hot that he had to hastily release her arm. He stared at her in surprise as her chin set and her lips thinned. Even without peeking into her mind, he could read her emotions clearly. She was feeling a level of jealousy unusual for someone not in second puberty. "Tariah?"

She got to her feet and walked away a few steps. She felt perfectly fine physically now that she had fed her Fury. Her emotions were another matter. She felt eaten alive by jealousy. She *hated* that he had been with other women, and she knew it was a stupid feeling. She knew damned well that he had been an adult long before her *grandparents* had been born and that he, like everyone else in the world, had graduated second puberty. She struggled to find the self-control she had lived with for the last seven years. It felt strangely unnatural now. "I guess I'm a jealous woman." Her tone managed to be flippant, but there was a note underneath that gave her away.

He tried to put himself in her shoes. Say she had already finished second puberty and had been with at least one lover. How would he feel? The answer came as a surge of feral anger. Ripe jealousy briefly stole his voice. It was entirely illogical. Having a lover was perfectly normal and natural, but he could not deny that he understood her feelings. "I guess I'm a jealous man," he said ruefully.

She looked at him in surprise before smiling wryly. "I guess we both have a lot to learn about how this relationship will work. I didn't think friends could be this possessive."

He ran his tongue over his teeth. "Before I address that, maybe we should get the formalities out of the way. My name is Dominic Whisperer." Introducing himself to someone who knew him inside and out felt very odd.

She felt no less silly, particularly because his mind *was* open to her. He didn't consciously think about his name—no one did—but all she had to do was dig in his memories for instances of people who had addressed him. She shook her head with a smile. "Tariah Chronis, but obviously you knew that since you've been calling me by name."

"I did." He held out a hand to her. "Come back here."

She immediately walked over and took his hand. He drew her onto his lap and she let out a contented sigh as she rested her head on his shoulder. She had never felt that complete in her life. As long as she was with Dominic, she knew she was where she belonged. Tears burned her eyes as she wrapped her arms around his shoulders. "I'm not alone anymore."

"Neither of us are." He rubbed his cheek over her hair softly. "I've wanted to find you for so long." He cleared his throat. "Tariah, I need to explain to you about Dragoons."

She reluctantly straightened up. She liked cuddling him; he was bigger than she was by quite a bit but she had discovered she enjoyed it. She liked being small enough to snuggle on his lap. "Explain what precisely?"

He ran his fingers through her hair, then drew his touch forward to trace over her lines. He wanted to follow every curl with his lips but firmly reigned it in. "Dragoons . . . their bonds are not just friendship, not as a rule."

It took her a few seconds but it sank in finally what he had implied. Her eyes widened and she blurted, "But I'm not in second puberty yet!"

"Trust me," frustration leaked into his voice, "I'm aware of that. If you were, that kiss we shared would have created steam between us." He framed her face in his hands, enjoying the tingle of her power teasing his skin. "You're going to be poking around my mind, and you're going to be feeling my emotions. I wanted you to know what you'd be seeing and feeling and not understanding."

She thought about it to herself for a long time. A part of her was a little flabbergasted that it could be that simple. Being a Chronicle meant she didn't have to struggle with falling in love. She didn't have to question if her feelings, or her lover's feelings, were real. Her Fury was everything she could ever want. She would be able to love him without question and he would love her the same. What they had was something more precious than the world around them would ever understand.

She smiled suddenly and her silver eyes sparkled like the rarest of coins. It stole Dominic's breath and heart all at once. "Well," she said with an impish note to her voice, "at least it reassures me about one thing. I had been worried that I would go through second puberty without ever once getting to explore my new feelings. But now I have you." She threw her arms around his neck happily. "Just remember to be patient with me."

"I'll do my best," he murmured huskily. "But be gentle to me, Tariah. If you turn out to be a tease, I'm going to go mad. I'm having enough trouble keeping my hands to myself right now." He nuzzled her neck gently. "You smell like the desert."

"I ought to. I'm a desert girl." She eased back and pulled a face. "I hate these clothes Rumidia made me wear. I hate confining clothes. I prefer my desert clothes, and the sun on my skin." She tilted her head. "What kind of weather is on the Isle of the Dragons?"

"It depends on where you live. We have a little bit of every landscape. The mountains are the warmest other than our desert. The valleys are where we get the coolest, but even then it doesn't get too bad." He cleared his throat. "We have a small problem about the Isle, Tariah. I seem to have forgotten how to get there."

She groaned and dropped her head on his shoulder. "Why me?" she wailed. "Why do I always have to have things the hard way?!"

For just a moment, he got a glimpse in her mind of her mad dash across the desert. His fingers tightened on her waist briefly and then he clutched her close. "The big difference," he said urgently, "is that you are with me now. You're not alone anymore. I promise." He groaned as he felt the heat of her tears on his skin. "No, don't you dare. Stop it, right now."

"Are all Dragons such babies about crying?" she sniffled.

"I don't know about other Dragons, but I can't stand to see *you* crying. It breaks my heart."

She lifted her head to study him for a moment. She smiled and wiped at her tears. "You're a big baby. You're a softy at heart. The big, bad, Fire Fury is a sucker for weeping women and cute kids. You cry at linking ceremonies." Laughter lurked in her voice as his cheeks warmed. "You made everyone think you're this tough Dragon and you're completely not!"

He tweaked her nose gently. "You love me anyway, and you know it." His breath was held. He knew that they had been born to love one another, but he still wanted to hear it. He *needed* to hear that she loved him even though he was soft-hearted and bad-tempered all at the same time.

Her smile filled with wonder as she cupped his cheek. "You know what? I do love you. I can see it. You hate losing and you would argue with me until the end of time if you thought you were right . . . but I love even that. I don't know why, but I do. Everything about you seems perfect to me." She curled closer. "If this is what it means to be a Dragoon, then I'm really glad I am one."

He held her for a moment and then eased her back. His gray eyes moved over her face slowly to memorize every feature. At the same time, his power and his soul memorized that which was hers, wanting to ensure he would always know her. Tenderly, he curled his presence around her mind, blanketing her comfortingly because he could not get inside.

She closed her eyes as she felt him inside. Without hesitation she reached for him in return, memorizing him so that he was stamped on everything that made her. The steady flow of power back and forth between them was the most wonderful thing she had ever known. She *trusted* him. Why was she holding anything back?

He took a quick breath as he felt her mind reaching out for him. She wasn't hiding anymore. He didn't immediately go looking even though he wanted to know everything. He waited until she let him in, until she had blended their minds and shared willingly everything she was and had been through.

It surged past his mental eyes in a riot of images and sounds. It was hard to pick out anything specific, and he knew that it was because of the trauma she had endured. Everything had blurred together and most of the details had been lost. But some stood out. Some were in horrifying clarity. His stomach churned and his heart broke. He struggled to keep himself calm, and all he could manage to say was, "It was *not* your fault! Stop thinking that!"

She looked at him sadly. "Tell me my existence didn't cause Maxim's death. If I hadn't been here, he would be alive."

"He would also have been greatly lonely and depressed without ever knowing why." He cupped her face in his hands and softly brushed kisses over her eyes even as his mind softly caressed her in a similar embrace. Both seemed to be weeping inside. "I know I would have been lost without you."

"Is it *true*?" She closed her eyes. "Do the Dragons really have to . . . to kill Furies who feel their Chronicle die?"

He let out a long breath. "Yes. You see, Chronicles are driven to find their Fury, but they don't feel them until they connect. Furies feel their Chronicle, but cannot track them till they connect." He rested his forehead against hers. "My brother was a Fury too," he said quietly. "Fifty years ago, he felt his Chronicle born. Eleven years later, he felt her die. He just seemed to . . . disappear. He didn't eat, he didn't sleep. He just suffered. He never spoke a word to anyone. It was like watching him bleed out one drop at a time. And worse still, it would never end."

She gently framed his face with her hands. She didn't need to hear the rest. She could see it inside him. To end his brother's misery, Dominic himself had taken an enchanted saber and struck his brother down. "If it had been you, you would have thanked him," she said softly. "Now in the Underrealm, he and his Chronicle are together."

He nuzzled her hands softly. "Someone else around here is soft at heart." He smiled when she pulled a face. "Deny it and I'll call you a liar. You also have a nasty habit I'm going to need to work on."

She narrowed her eyes. "What's that?"

"No more hiding your emotions." He leaned in and softly touched her lips with his. "In fact, I insist that you give me whatever you've got. If it means you like to shout and throw things when you're in a temper, be my guest."

"I am not violent by nature," she muttered.

"Never fib to the man who can see inside you. Given half an opportunity, I think you would sooner kick me than give in, even when you're wrong."

She gave him a half-hearted punch in the shoulder. "I've never really lost my temper," she confessed. "Or cried. Or had a *really* good laugh. I only recently was able to even express my emotions. I'm going to have to learn as I go."

He studied her. "Are you ticklish?"

Her eyes widened. "You wouldn't!"

He would. She swiftly tried to get off his lap, aiming to get across the room. Her Fury, however, was much faster and he caught her wrist. Quick as a blink he had her pinned to the floor, and his fingers mercilessly zeroed in on the sensitive skin of her waist.

She wiggled and squirmed but couldn't get away. He was tickling her from the inside out and it felt so ridiculously funny that she couldn't stop the laughter welling up from some hidden place inside. She was breathless with it as she fought him to get free. "Stop it, you meany!"

He grinned at her and kept up his relentless assault. "No." His throat closed with overwhelming emotion as he heard her laughing. It was the most beautiful thing he had ever heard. There was a burning well of life inside her that he hadn't immediately noticed. Restraining her emotions had not just insulted her nature, it had insulted life itself. His Chronicle needed to always be laughing. "Say please."

"I'm going to drown you!"

"That's not a please."

"Dom-in-ic! Let me go! I can't breathe!" She gulped air as his fingers stilled. She could barely see for the tears in her eyes, and she was wildly happy. She had never played with anyone like that before. There was so much she had never gotten to do that she was free to do with Dominic. She was free to do whatever she wanted.

He was experiencing a similar feeling. He'd had friends for a long time. He had brothers and sisters that he had more than once gotten to play with and wrestle with. And yet he had never been as incredibly happy as he was when wrestling with his small Chronicle.

"Small!" She glowered. "I am not . . . much."

"But I like it. You're the perfect size for me. Of course, I might worry that you'll fall off my back while we're flying. I might have to carry you." He smiled as he felt the sudden surge of delight inside her. "You want to fly. Well, then I'll be sure to teach you."

"Teach me?" She tilted her head. "How?"

"Chronicles can use a much more extensive range of powers by drawing on their Furies' majiks. I've heard about everything from summoning to transformation to conjuring to extremely strong mental skills like Telepathy and Telekinesis. Of course, you'd have to feed me afterward." He nuzzled her again, loving her scent. "You might even be able to turn into a Dragon shape."

She felt tickled at the very idea. "When do we practice?"

The door opened and they turned their heads to see Juniper standing there with Sparkle on one shoulder and Daylar on the other. Both Faeries were dressed a little more normally, but both still had their wings bound. Juniper covered a smile. "Are we interrupting?"

"Not completely. I was tickling Tariah without mercy." Dominic let Tariah sit up before getting to his feet to assist her as well.

Sparkle giggled. "Her waist is the worst."

"Tattletale."

"Now, girls," Juniper chuckled, "behave. Come, Dragoons. Let us go to my house where we can talk formally. We Kin have an offer to make to Tariah, if you are both willing to accept it. We hope that it might negate some of the bad effects of the Magi."

Tariah felt Dominic reaching for her hand and automatically slipped her fingers into his. The ease of the gesture and the belonging that went with it was exhilarating. Contented, she rested her head against his arm as they walked. "Does this have to do with the honorary Kin thing that I heard mentioned?"

"Eavesdropping is not nice," Daylar scolded her.

She stuck her tongue out at him. "So is keeping secrets from friends. I'd like to have an illusion of control over my life, thank you." She smiled when he hovered over to land on her shoulder, and Sparkle followed to land on her other. She softly rubbed her cheek against both. She was glad they would be happy.

Inside the Elder's home, they all took chairs and got comfortable. Dominic's idea of comfortable was to have Tariah on his lap. She had a different idea and they finally compromised by sitting together on the couch with her snuggled up against his side.

Juniper covered a smile as he walked over to his own chair. "We Kin," he began, "want to offer formal sanctuary to Tariah and therefore bring her under the protection of the treaty. The only way to do this is to make her an honorary Kin."

Dominic frowned. "Chronicles, I thought, had too erratic a power for that."

"Normally this is true. But we think that we have found someone who can get around it." He gestured to Daylar. "Our Daylar. His own power is quite erratic now because he had his wings removed and then replaced with someone else's. His body is sustaining two different elements for the time being. It might be enough."

Tariah frowned. "I'm not sure I understand what you mean about erratic."

Dominic skimmed a hand down her hair. "Erratic in that a Chronicle, or a Fury for that matter, develop in ways different from the rest of the world. Where others develop slowly and steadily, we develop faster and with a greater range."

"It is fairly simple for a Kin to relate to a Dragon or Magi," Juniper said. "We are born with Light or Dark, then develop a secondary element, then a tertiary. Dragons and Magi are born with Lightning, and then develop a primary element, then a secondary."

It dawned on Tariah. "But Chronicles and Furies develop secondary at the same time as primary, and then develop completely new skills unrelated to any other race. Daylar has a chance because he has technically gained another skill on top of the natural."

"Precisely." Juniper touched his arm where his tattoos were. "We of this world . . . our bodies are made by our power. We Kin bear these marks because of our Light and Dark powers. You Chronicles bear your lines because of your connection to a Fury's power. Our bodies cannot be changed. Our marks cannot be removed, nor can new ones be added, unless the power itself is changed."

Tariah nodded. "What you're telling me is that in order to place a mark on me that shows I am under Kin protection, Daylar has to be able to mark my power, and he couldn't do that if he wasn't capable of resonating with me."

"Precisely." Juniper smiled at Dominic. "She has a curious mind."

"I know." Dominic nuzzled his nose through Tariah's hair. "I enjoy it."

She lifted a brow at him. "I'll remind you of that when I start second puberty."

Sparkle fell off her chair laughing and Daylar was nearly right behind her. Juniper coughed, but his eyes twinkled merrily. "If you are in agreement, let us see if Daylar can make you one of us. He will claim you as family, just as you will need to claim him."

She smiled. "Well, if Daylar doesn't mind, I don't. I think he's a bit young to be my father, though. Maybe a brother."

Daylar smiled in return. "I have six big sisters. I wouldn't mind a little sister too. Because I'm *technically* older than you, after all."

"Technically." She straightened away from Dominic and got to her feet. She held out a hand and Daylar hovered over to land. "I would be honored to be accepted by the Kin," she said softly. "Thank you, Daylar."

He bowed gracefully. "I thank you, Tariah. I owe you my life, and you brought Sparkle to me." He closed his eyes and began to glow with soft white color as he opened his power and reached for hers. She began to glow softly blue as she reached for him in return, and the two colors seamlessly meshed.

It fascinated him. As he felt Tariah's power, he felt equally Dominic's presence. Changing one would change the other. He began to wonder then if perhaps the erratic patterns of a Chronicle or Fury had less to do with their unusual development and more to do with the endless cycle between Dragoons. He could nearly see the power flowing back and forth between the two.

He didn't want to mark her in a way that wouldn't be flattering, but he always wanted it to be visible. His first thought was to place a mark on her back shoulder; she was a desert girl and therefore tended to wear very little clothing. Much to his surprise, however, the decision was taken from his hands. His power was magnetically drawn to where her lines flowed over her arm. Even just a little touch from his Light power caused her lines to ripple like water.

Her lines abruptly moved. The curls shifted and reformed and flowed together to form a wing shape on her shoulder. It was as if the wing was a part of her lines and yet still distinct. It was followed by a flickering glow from underneath Dominic's shirt as his own lines shifted to form the same mark, defining him as well.

Daylar and Tariah stopped glowing and both smiled. "I always wanted a brother," she said as she hugged him gently close. She laughed. "Now I guess I get Sparkle too!"

Sparkle shot over to hug her as well. "Naturally!"

"Welcome to our land, young Kin," Juniper said with a smile. He started to add more when he noticed that there were symbols appearing in the air. "Ah. She finally responds. Let's see."

Dominic leaned to the side to see the letter. "My clanmate?" He straightened back up and gathered Tariah close against him once more as she returned to his side. His fingers smoothed over the newest design to her lines. He *really* wanted to trace her lines with his lips and taste her power there.

She elbowed him lightly. "Behave. Patience is rewarded."

"It better be."

Juniper decided that he greatly enjoyed their relationship and the way Tariah always seemed to be smiling. Turning his attention back to the letter, he began reading through what his contact had to say. It was interesting, to say the least. As the letter disappeared, all he could say was, "Well."

"Well what?" Sparkle asked.

"It seems that the Dragon Elders believe that Dominic's memory loss is because of his Chronicle. A Chronicle must follow the map within their lines. It is their journey of discovery and power. The map is supposed to lead a Chronicle to their Fury and the Isle. Dominic has found Tariah before she has followed her lines."

Dominic sighed. "My memory of the way to the Isle has been taken away to ensure that Tariah is capable of finishing her journey."

"There is some suspicion that if she does not, she might risk destroying herself. Her lines will continue to develop but the power will have nowhere to manifest. It could drive her mad."

"Let's not." He held Tariah closer protectively.

Her nose pressed to his shoulder, she sighed. "Oh well. I knew it couldn't get better." But, then again, things *were* better right there. Maybe not easier, but certainly better. She rubbed her cheek gently against Dominic. She would be happy just to stay on Kindred with him, let alone travel with him.

Her lines suddenly began burning. The fierce longing tightened her throat. *North.* She needed to go north still. There was something else to the north that pulled at her. It wasn't just Dominic. "I guess I go north," she said, trying to smile.

Dominic tenderly framed her face with his hands. He knew as well as she did that the only two lands to the north were the three continents belonging to the Magi—Carnelian, Spectrum, and Glacia on the top of the world. "We'll figure something out," he said softly. "I promise."

"I believe you." She closed her eyes and rested her cheek on his hand. "I guess we leave tomorrow morning." She opened her eyes and found a real smile. "I suppose I should look at it as a chance to learn what flying is like."

He smiled and softly touched her lips with his. He couldn't have asked for a better Chronicle.

Chapter Seven

They had dinner with Daylar, Sparkle, and both their families. It was probably, Tariah remarked dryly to her former partner, the only time she had ever felt big. Both SunKin families were made entirely of Faeries, and Tariah towered over them all. Dominic took it in stride even though he himself was even taller; he was more used to it.

After dinner, the Dragoons returned to the inn where Rumidia had assured them they would always be welcome to rest. As they were walking together, Tariah commented half to herself, "I should be ashamed of myself."

She felt more amused than ashamed. He just smiled. "Why?"

"I'm about to spend the night with a man I haven't known even a full day." She sent him a smile. "I mean, even in second puberty that's considered slightly tacky, and I'm not even in that yet."

Her Fury gave a quick laugh and then swung her up into his arms and in a quick circle. "You know what, Tariah Chronis? I think I'm absolutely crazy about you." He rubbed his cheek against hers softly. "Even if you hadn't been my Chronicle, I suspect that I would have loved you."

Her brows shot up. "Is that possible?" She linked her hands behind his neck and hooked her knees around his waist to hold on as he walked. She held no fear of falling. In fact, she enjoyed herself because she was able to see his face clearly. He smelled incredible, like the smoke that curled through the night sky during a good bonfire. She liked it a lot.

He carried her into the room they would share, then sat down on the plush chair in the corner. It automatically grew larger to accommodate his size, and then it got slightly larger still as it read Tariah's presence. The result was plenty of room for both of them. She *really* liked Kin inventions.

"There are two kinds of Dragoon pairs," he told her. "What's considered the primary kind, and then there is what is considered secondary because it happens rarely. The primary kind is what we are. The simplest term I can think of to describe it is 'lovers' but it's so much more than that."

"I can tell." She smoothed her hand over his chest unconsciously. She just needed to feel his heat and strength. "What's the secondary?"

"The simplest term for that would be 'twins.' It's the exact same sort of bond as a primary, but there is nothing romantic about it. Twin Dragoons, however, tend to remain single. It is very hard for a Twin Dragoon to find someone that they care about as much as their partner. When it does happen, the other Dragoon will often experience similar feelings for the mate, especially when it comes to protecting them."

"Oh I see." She smiled. "So if you *had* been with another Chronicle as a twin, and then fallen for me, the Chronicle would have loved me too and wanted to keep me safe if only because I made *you* happy. That's really beautiful." She leaned forward and rested against him. "I think I'd have loved you too. There's just something about you."

He nuzzled her hair. "I'll take that as a compliment."

She softly giggled. "Dominic, why are you always nuzzling me like that? It's so sweet, and you want so badly for people to not know you're a softy."

"It's the Dragon in me." He snuggled her closer. "Nuzzling each other is how Dragons show affection. We're very tactile creatures. And besides . . ." He buried his nose against her shoulder and breathed in deeply. "I like how you smell."

"What do I smell like?" she asked curiously.

"Like fresh water." He smiled. "Specifically, fresh water in the desert. Pure and clean but really sweet." He kept his arms around her waist as he got to his feet and gently helped her balance until she was standing on her own as well. "We should get some sleep. Tomorrow will be a long day."

Tariah, inexplicably, felt shy as she looked around the room and realized that she didn't have a night shift. She would have to sleep in her clothes or naked. The embarrassment puzzled her. Why was she embarrassed? She knew she had a beautiful figure, and she trusted Dominic implicitly. She knew him as well as she knew herself. Why was she nervous? Her heart was pounding hard.

"Is something wrong?" he asked. He softly smoothed his hands down her arms to comfort her. He could feel that she was unsure but he couldn't seem to pinpoint the source.

She turned to frown at him. "I'm nervous. I don't know why. I'm not self-conscious but I am now. What's wrong with me?"

His eyes softened and his fingers were tender as they rubbed over the lines on her cheek. "Welcome to the first stages of second puberty, *ishke.* You're suddenly becoming aware of the difference between male and female."

She glowered. "I know the differences, thank you."

"Ah, but now it's personal. Focus on your feelings. Are you nervous because you think you're not attractive, or because you want *me* to find you attractive?"

She wrinkled her nose. "I know I'm attractive. I'd be silly if I didn't know it." Saying it, she realized that he had hit it on the head. She was nervous because she wanted him to find her beautiful. She wanted him to look at her and see her as everything he had ever wanted. The frustrating part was that she *knew* she was what he wanted and yet she couldn't make the nerves go away. She crossed her arms. "I don't like this," she muttered.

His hands were gentle and confident as he began to calmly help her out of her clothes. He felt her determination to ignore her nerves, and his heart melted. There was nothing more beautiful than getting to watch firsthand as his Chronicle finished blossoming like a desert flower.

"Don't be poetic." Her cheeks went warm with embarrassment. "I'm trying not to lose my nerve. Why does this stupid second puberty make confident people skittish? It's stupid."

He hid a smile. "Is it stupid then?"

"*Yes.*" She crossed her arms over her naked breasts as he neatly absconded her bikini top. "I'd just as soon skip to the part where the curiosity begins."

He bit his tongue to keep from chuckling. It took all his willpower to keep his fingers steady as he got to work on her boots and leggings. She was the most stunningly beautiful creature he had ever seen. "You have to be conscious of your own body and how it works before you can consider how other bodies feel, and how they might work together."

Now naked except for her long auburn hair, she tapped a foot lightly on the ground. With a confidence that was purely bravado, she tossed her hair back over her shoulder and propped her hands on her hips, baring herself entirely to his eyes. "Reassure me so I get my confidence back and I can get over this." Try as she might, she couldn't keep the slight quiver out of her voice.

He stopped breathing as he stared at her. She was so utterly perfect to him that it should have been a crime. It could be debated whether he had been perfectly made to love her, or if she had been perfectly made for him. No matter the origin, the result was an encompassing hunger to taste every inch of her gentle brown flesh. The golden lines that flowed sensuously like water down her soft curves. His fingers itched to start touching and his body was hard and heavy with desire. "When I can manage to find a compliment," he said, his voice thick, "I'll give it to you. Right now I can barely remember my name."

Her nerves eased and her confidence returned. He wasn't doing anything to hide how he felt, though he was trying to shield his thoughts. She managed to get a glimpse, and her pulse fluttered in a way she hadn't felt before. She let it be; she would understand in time. "Is this the end of the first stage?"

He smiled wryly. "No. Unfortunately, it never quite goes away. You're always going to be more conscious of how you look to the person you want. You, however, have an advantage." He skimmed his hands over her hips gently. "I'll find you attractive no matter what you're wearing. Or not wearing."

"That's a consolation." She tilted her head. "Are you nervous about me?"

"Hell yes."

It was said readily and quickly and made her feel *much* better. She smiled. "You worry that I won't find you attractive?"

"Absolutely." He rolled his eyes and invited her to enjoy his situation. "Even knowing that eventually you're going to respond to me as deeply as I do to you doesn't make me less worried. We're all the same inside when it comes to how we want to appear to the person we want."

"It's not fun." She went over to the bed and turned back the covers. The sheets were soft and cool to the touch but warmed as she slipped under the blankets. "I'd just as soon go along knowing I was attractive and not caring about other opinions my entire life."

"Wouldn't we all?" Knowing she might be edging into the realm where she would be self- conscious about his body as well, he removed only his shirt and boots. He left his pants on as he walked over to join her. He nudged her lightly in the shoulder. "Scoot over and share."

"I got here first."

"I'm bigger." He slid under the blankets and caught her in his arms to snuggle her close. She turned over and cuddled even closer, her nose tucking against his chest. Her body perfectly aligned to his, all her curves fitting against him as if they were two halves to a complete being.

She let out a soft sigh as his arm draped over her waist. His warmth wrapped around her, and it was as wonderful as the desert sun. She felt his power curling around hers and couldn't resist reaching out to hold him as well. Her hand lifted and covered the wing mark within the lines on his chest. "You should go shirtless, like desert men," she said sleepily.

He lifted a brow. "It's a bit early for you to be interested in me naked."

"It's not that. I just want everyone to see that you're mine." Her hand smoothed over the lines. "You wear my lines. I want people to see." Her lashes fluttered closed. "But, eventually, I guess, I'll just want to admire you at my leisure. You're already beautiful to me."

Her power stilled its soft pulsing and he knew she was asleep. Smiling wryly as he thought of the time ahead, he buried his nose in her hair and let out a soft breath of contentment. It was going to be a long couple of months, but the end result would be worth it. He couldn't wait to claim his Chronicle as his entirely.

Tariah was awakened the next morning by the feel of someone jumping up and down on her shoulder. She cracked one eye open, saw Sparkle, and promptly closed her eye again as she curled more firmly against Dominic. "Go away," she mumbled against his shoulder.

"No." Sparkle's wings shimmered as she flew over and began to jump on Dominic's shoulder instead. "You too! Wake up, wake up! There's something very important happening in the Magi!"

"Someone find that bronze grows on trees?" Dominic asked sleepily.

Tariah giggled and Sparkle huffed out a breath. Indignant, she grabbed the blankets and jerked them off the couple. "Darn it all, both of you get up!" Her pale lavender brows lifted as she saw her friend. "You're naked."

"Give back the blanket and I won't be." Tariah reluctantly sat up and shoved her hair out of her eyes on a large yawn. "What's this about the Magi and something important?" Remembering how her hair liked to go crazy while she was asleep, she had to fight the urge to run to a mirror and fix it before Dominic saw her. She could only glower at herself. She was beginning to hate this self-consciousness.

He opened one eye to study her and his stomach quivered with fresh desire. Why she needed a mirror, he hadn't a clue. She was heartbreakingly lovely when she was flushed and rumpled from sleep. His fingers itched with the urge to make her hair even more tangled, and lust merged seamlessly with a hunger for her power. He rolled over and pulled a pillow over his head. "I hate my life."

She ignored him as she looked at Sparkle. "What's this important news?"

"You need to see it for yourself! Hurry and come to the Elder's house. I left clothes for you over there." She pointed to where a stack of clothing sat on the table. "You're going to Spectrum, and it's a desert too, so I made sure that they were your favorite kind of clothes." She grinned impishly. "They'll probably be Dominic's favorite too. Oh, and I left clothes for him. I had to guess at his size; they might be on the big side."

She sailed out the door and it swung shut behind her. With a sigh, Tariah nudged Dominic. "Up you go."

"No." His voice was muffled by the pillow.

Without guilt, she pounced onto his back and listened to his breath whoosh out. "Yes, damn it. If I have to suffer, so do you."

"Different sort of suffering." He suddenly twisted and dislodged her. Before she could tumble off the bed, he sat up and caught her safely in his arms. The instant his hands closed around her arms, her power began to flow over her like a soft blue veil. "Breakfast in bed is my idea of a treat."

She could only laugh as he buried his nose against her neck and drank her power from there. Contented, she wound her arms around his shoulders as he lifted his head and framed her face in his hands. He softly kissed her, drinking her power right from her lips. It was sweetest there.

As he reluctantly lifted his head, one hunger eased, he searched her eyes. There was still no recognition of him as a mate inside her. It was frustrating even though he knew nature had to run its course. With a sigh, he released her so that she could get dressed.

She slid out of bed and walked over to the table. She picked up an article of clothing and asked curiously, "Do you like kissing me, Dominic?"

His brows lifted. "I'm surprised you have to ask."

"You've only done it to feed." She shrugged her shoulders as she pulled on her cloth bikini. "I was just, you know, wondering."

Enchanted by the sign of nerves once more revealing themselves, he walked over to nuzzle her softly. "Trust me, *ishke,* once I have any sign that you are ready for your first real kiss, I will be right there waiting to claim it."

"How will I know?"

"You just will. I promise." He released her slowly and watched with interest as she pulled on cloth shorts and a cloth top that was little more than a bikini itself. His pulse spiked and he felt his Fire surging eagerly inside for her Water. "We'll have to live in a desert so I can see you this way all the time."

She looked down. "This isn't the least I've worn. Some of the hottest days in Symphony had me running around in a bikini and a piece of cloth tied around my hips." She stretched largely, rising up on her toes as she did. She felt much better now that she wasn't stuck in confining forest clothes.

With a curiosity more born of an interest in knowing everything about her Fury than an interest in him naked, she sat on the edge of the bed to watch him dress. Dominic, sensing her intent, discovered that he himself was suddenly very self-conscious. "Don't stare at me," he grumbled as he reached for the clothes provided.

She smiled. "Why not?"

"Because I want to impress you and I can hardly do that until you are further along in your development." He walked over and swiftly tossed the blanket over her head. Before she could do more than sputter, he had her all tangled up. "Have fun, *ishke.*"

"You bully!" She wiggled and squirmed but couldn't seem to find where the edges had been tucked. Finally she gave up and sat in sulky silence as she listened to him dressing. As the blanket was finally unwrapped and pulled off her head, she narrowed her glower at him directly. "Next time I'm embarrassed about changing clothes, I'll get you stuck in a blanket, you jerk."

He smiled and leaned down to nuzzle her cheek with his. "But I can reassure you, remember?" He straightened up and stepped back. He held his hands out to his sides. "Well? How do I look? Will I pass for a desert dweller?"

She studied him critically, comparing him to the other men she had known. Comparatively, the open vest fit Dominic's wide shoulders and strong chest much better than most Magi men. It also revealed the golden lines on his chest, and that was a definite plus.

The pants were snug on the hips but loose around the legs so they fit him the same as anyone. The boots they were tucked into only went halfway up his calf instead of closer to his knee, meaning his legs were a little longer than most Magi. The sandy brown color complimented his coloring and especially his black hair. The little red streaks were much more distinct. "You'd pass," she decided with a smile. "It looks good on you."

Females only starting second puberty were hard on a man's ego. He smiled and scooped her up into his arms. She wound her arms around his shoulders and leaned against him with an absolute trust that touched something deep inside. "This must have been what Magi were jealous of," he said softly, burying his face in her hair.

She closed her eyes. "I know I would have been." She released him as he put her gently on her feet. "Let's go see Elder Juniper. I'm curious as to what the Magi are up to now."

They put on the cloaks they had been provided, then left the room with their hands linked. Watching them go past, Rumidia just smiled to herself and hoped she got to meet any child they eventually had. Dragon or Magi, the child would be spectacular with these two Dragoons for parents.

Sparkle was flying in circles in front of Juniper's door. "There you are!" she scolded as she saw them. "This is big, really big!" She flew over and landed on Dominic's shoulder and then sat down. "You're never going to believe this."

"Magi discovered how to make boats fly?" Tariah guessed.

"No, better!"

Inside the Elder's home, Daylar was present as well and busily writing a letter to someone. Juniper was observing, but he stood with a smile as he saw who had entered. "Ah, there you are. Good morning to you both.

Please, have a seat. Are either of you hungry?"

"A little," Tariah said as she sat on the couch.

Dominic grinned as he joined her. "I had breakfast."

"My power doesn't count." She elbowed him slightly.

"In that case, I suppose I could eat something." He skimmed his fingers through her long hair. He knew that she was going to put it up before they left. He wanted to take as much advantage of it as he could.

Sparkle flew off to fetch something for them and Juniper sat back in his chair. "Let me begin by saying that we have checked this information thoroughly and it is true. Daylar was quite busy this morning with that."

Daylar had finished his letter and he flew over to Tariah's shoulder. "Every Kin I know on Spectrum has confirmed it."

"Confirmed what?" she asked warily.

"The king of the Magi has sent out an order for a ceasefire to the Militia. They are to cease their blockade on the ports, and he has asked specifically that you come to Spectrum as he wishes to meet you personally."

"What?" Her eyes slowly widened. "But . . . why? Magi hate Chronicles and they wanted me dead!"

"You are a Dragoon now," Dominic said softly. "If they kill you, they would have to kill me. Killing me would bring the Dragons down on them hard. My race has been waiting for an excuse to exact revenge and this would be the last straw."

"And," Daylar noted, "you are honorary Kin now as well. The treaty between Kin and Magi states that there will be no killing one another unless a breach of the treaty is made. As long as you obey their laws, they don't dare touch a hair on your head lest we have reason to come in and beat the hell out of them ourselves."

"A reason," Sparkle said as she handed bowls of savory rice and fruit blended together to both Dragoons, "that we will be happy to take. I mean, eradicating any of the three races entirely would completely destroy the world, but we could, you know, take out a few thousand or so."

"Sparkle," Juniper scolded. "That's not a very Kin point of view."

She looked at him fiercely. "If they touch Tariah, then I don't care."

Silence held for a bit as the Dragoons finished their meal. Dominic set his empty bowl aside and gently curled his hand around the back of Tariah's neck in comfort. He could feel the whirlwind of emotions inside her and he knew they were too turbulent for even her to understand let alone him. "It's your decision," he said softly. "Wherever your lines lead is where we will go."

As if called for, her lines pulsed and she felt the sharp tug inside. *North.* "I have to go north," she said softly. "I don't know more than that. But Spectrum is north of us so . . ." She set her bowl aside with a sigh. "I guess I meet the king. I don't want to, but I should, if only to prove I'm not some . . . monster."

"Speaking of monsters," Daylar said, "it may interest you to know that Symphony has had an outbreak recently. It's as if your disappearance disrupted the power flowing in the land. Crabs, dogs, cats, and even a few Magi, have been mutated into monsters. The Militia is keeping them at bay, but the city seems to blame them for driving you off. It looks like at least your home stands behind you."

Her throat closed. "I'm glad," she whispered. "At least that means I have somewhere I can visit that people won't think I am a monster myself."

"Indeed." Juniper stood even as they did. "May the moons guide you, Dragoons. Tariah, be sure to write to us." He smiled. "You are Kin enough now to at least be able to write to Daylar."

"It's a promise." Tariah hugged Daylar and then Sparkle when she flew over as well. "Both of you be good," she scolded softly. "And make sure to contact me when you're going to have your ceremony."

"We will!" Sparkle nodded firmly and then wiped tears out of her eyes. "Be safe," she whispered as she watched the two Dragoons leave the house. Then, on a little sob, she turned and flew into Daylar's arms. She was going to miss Tariah something fierce!

Dominic and Tariah stopped only long enough to pick up supplies. She wore her share in a sack that was part of a belt she could wear around her waist. He opted for a regular sack he could carry over his shoulder. With a smile he said, "Of course, you'll have to hold onto it while we're flying."

"I can do that." She rested against his shoulder as they headed down to the dock where the beach was big enough for him to change form safely. She had yet to see him in his natural form, and she was very curious about it. She had never seen any Dragon up close; she had only seen images of them in books.

"Stay here," he told her as he stopped her at the edge of the trees. He handed her his bag and then walked further away down the sand to where he had plenty of room. He knew that a lot of Magi, and even some Kin, found Dragons to be slightly alarming because of their sheer size. He was hoping that Tariah would not be afraid.

Red power flowed around him and fire blazed at his feet. It swept upward into an inferno for a few moments and obscured him from sight. When the fire faded away, there was a red and black Dragon standing where he had been moments prior.

Tariah's breath was held as she slowly walked forward. Somehow he seemed even more beautiful this way. His body was covered with scales that rippled like flames in the sunlight, and his wings were long and elegant. The skin between the ridges of bone was so thin that sunlight went through it and created reddish shadows. His golden lines still glimmered in the light as they flowed down the front of his body.

He was almost twice her height in his length from nose to tail. His face was hard and dangerous with sharp angles and wicked teeth visible when he opened his mouth even a little. The fins on his head were like small wings that curved upward to catch sound around him. His claws were long and wicked, made for rending metal and stone let alone flesh.

He was a terrifying, imposing sight, but she felt no fear as she crossed to him. She stopped in front of him, then smiled and held up her hands. He lowered his head toward her and nearly groaned as she began to softly stroke the scales on his face. Her hands seemed softer than ever against his Dragon skin. "You're not afraid," he said, and his voice was the same even though there was an echo of power in it.

"Why would I be?" His scales were *soft*, she realized in delight. More like feathers than skin. She gently wrapped her arms around his head and rubbed her cheek against his. She felt his surprise and smiled. "Dragons nuzzle each other to show affection, remember?"

He gave a bark of laughter and lifted her in his claws with a swiftness that startled her. She felt no actual fear, though. She held onto one of his fingers to maintain her balance as he opened his grip to let her stand on his palms. Now she knew how Sparkle felt! "Don't you dare drop me."

"I could never do that." He lifted her to eye level, fascinated at how tiny she seemed now. He felt as if he was holding a precious stone or something small and infinitely valuable. He would sooner tear off his wings than hurt her. "You want to ride or be carried?"

Her eyes glowed like coins with delight. "Ride! I want to feel like I'm flying too."

He lifted her toward his back and she climbed over easily. "Sit astride right above my wings. This way you will be balanced and not fall backwards no matter how fast we are going."

She did as she was told and felt her heart pounding with excitement. Hers, his, she didn't know. This first flight for them was the first real connection for them as Fury and Chronicle. Dragons *hated* to have passengers riding when they flew because the power of their rider clashed with their own. It made things uncomfortable for both.

But for Furies, their Chronicle was their other half. Their powers merged seamlessly. Flying together with Tariah riding his back was perhaps the single biggest statement they could make that they were Dragoons. "Hold on," he told her, and his wings kicked up sand as he flapped them and sent them flying into the air.

She clung onto his neck with a muffled shriek as they shot nearly straight up into the air. They hovered there for long moments and then he began flying across the sky at a speed she hadn't dreamed was possible. The ocean sped by below them ten times as fast as any ship ever made.

The feeling was indescribable. She straightened up to look around and felt the wind whipping through her hair. "It's incredible!" she said, wonder in her voice. "Dominic, this is incredible!"

He smiled. "I'll have to teach you how to take a Dragon form and you can return the favor. How does that sound?"

"It sounds like a deal." With a contented stretch of her arms, she leaned down until she was resting against his neck. If she got good at it then she would be able to take Sparkle and Daylar for a ride, just as she had promised. She didn't even worry about the rider thing; they were too small for that anyway. She could carry them in her claws. Even the idea of *having* claws tickled her. She couldn't wait to try everything in her new life.

Chapter Eight

The ocean flew below them like a streak of dark blue. Though the closest landmass was Carnelian, they could not fly over the top of it and straight to Spectrum. Dragons alone could disrupt the flow of power in the land where the cities were. A pair of Dragoons could disrupt the flow of the land as long as there were Magi somewhere nearby.

"Why is that?" Tariah asked as they flew along the edge of Carnelian more than two miles away from land. The continent looked like a strip of brown and dark green where plains and trees met. "Aren't we balanced?"

"We are," he told her, "but the Magi aren't." He smiled and swooped under a cloud to make her laugh. "Don't your Magi schools teach you anything?"

She ran her fingers through her hair to dislodge the Flutterlies that had gotten stuck. True to their names, they flew off in a flutter of white. Clouds on Lucksphere were made of thousands of the little creatures. Storms were a byproduct of too much Air or Water power, and they were made worse when Flutterlies started sucking up more from people on the surface.

"They do," she said, "but they never really go into detail. We only go to school for two years, Dominic. Long enough to learn about what Magi are and our role in this world. If we want to learn more, we need to learn it on our own time. And, I might point out, that there are few books about Dragons considering the, uhm, stressed relations between the two races."

"'Stressed relations' is a good term for wanting to beat the crap out of each other, I suppose." He angled down toward the ocean and just skimmed the surface. "Lucksphere is purely power, as you know. Power formed our world and then formed the three races that populate it. Magi are the power of the seas. Their presence prevents the oceans from overwhelming the land.

"Kin are the power of the land. Their presence is what allows lands to form and shift. Dragons are the power of the sky. Our presence is what keeps the sky from falling in and crushing those below. If any of these races were to be completely eradicated, then the world could fall apart."

She took a quick breath. "Like the war that instigated the treaty between Magi and Kin."

"Lucksphere, according to legend, used to have five continents the size of Spectrum. And now there's only one, Spectrum, the medium sized land of Glacia, the two smaller lands of Choral and Carnelian, and the island outposts of the Kin. The isle of the Dragons is smaller than Spectrum but larger than Glacia."

"So stupid," she whispered. "But I suppose it shows that Chronicles and Furies are not completely crucial to the world. Our destruction has had no effect."

"Hasn't it?" He let his power wrap around her as if in a gentle hug. "Two thousand years ago, when Chronicles were plenty, there were no outbursts in the land that mutated other beings. Look at Symphony. Your presence held it in line. When you were gone . . . it was a riot."

Tariah possessed an uncanny intelligence that she very rarely chose to exercise. She was finally beginning to understand her race, and with it came understanding of why they might exist. "There are too many Magi," she said slowly. "There is more sea than land or sky. That's why only Magi become Chronicles. Chronicles are made from the excess power in the world, and the Magi are the ones causing the excess because they are so clumped together onto minimal landmasses that the lesser amount of Kin can't keep things balanced. The presence of Chronicles gives the power a place to manifest and maintain the balance."

Dominic glanced back over his shoulder in surprise. "I had never considered that. Then why are Furies made from Dragons? We are not as numerous as Magi, but we are certainly more in population than the Kin."

"Because you are infinite. You are the sky, and the sky is infinite. No matter where you stand, eventually you will see an end to land or sea. But the sky is *never* gone."

Her mind was swirling through everything she had seen, heard, and felt, and it was a whirlwind that he didn't even try to attempt reading. Awe filled him as he realized that his desert girl had the intelligence of any ten scholars. Her uncanny grasp of little clues and ability to assemble them into a full story amazed him.

Everything she said made sense. To balance the output of Magi, Chronicles were made as power siphons. They took in the power of the world where it was excessive. Because it could in turn destroy them, Dragons, whose bodies were capable of infinite power, were made as Furies. But, unlike their brethren, a Fury didn't have infinite power. This gave the Chronicle a place to filter out the excessive power without upsetting the balance of nature.

"That's why," he said softly. "That's why erasing the Chronicles didn't stop them from appearing. And that's also why the children of Dragoons were not always Chronicles or Furies themselves."

"And," she said, smoothing a hand over his neck, "why we are opposite elements. If we were the same element, the same gender, or the same in any physical way, the generated power would be equally unbalanced." She frowned. "I can't, however, seem to figure out how our flying over land would be disruptive."

"That's simple enough. Power flows like waves in water. If you cross it slowly, you don't cause big ripples. If you cross it quickly, you make big waves. Dragons don't normally affect the land we fly over because we're out of range of the waves. But over cities, the power is much closer to the surface. As Dragoons, the opposite is true. You and I put out a power that is big enough to reach down to the land."

"Oh." She thought about it, then shrugged with a smile. "Well, as long as it is a law of nature and not a Magi law, I don't mind." She listened to his laugh and then leaned down to gently hug him. "Are you alright? We've been flying for a few hours now."

"At this speed," he told her, "we should reach Spectrum by evening. But I will need to feed again. If you're tired, take a nap. I won't drop you."

"I know you won't." She lay against his neck and closed her eyes. "And I'm not tired. I'm actually enjoying this a lot. I never realized flying could be so much fun. We better not let the Magi know. They might try to build ships for the air or something."

The sun was sitting on the edge of the ocean to the west as Spectrum became more than a line in the distance. It had been a sliver of brown for almost an hour. Now it was steadily growing larger and larger. It was just like Choral in many ways since Spectrum was nearly one hundred percent desert but it did not get nearly as hot. Temperatures were more smothering than scorching, though visitors from Glacia rarely could tell the difference.

The nearest city to where they approached was still ten miles inland. It was not quite a port town, but it was still close enough to the beaches to catch the attention of travelers in their own boats and ships.

Dominic did not want to share Tariah with a city of Magi just yet. When he landed on the beach, he said, "Why don't we camp here tonight? I can't fly to the city, and it would be a few hours by foot."

"That's fine." She slid down off his back and landed gracefully on the sand. Her legs, however, were rubbery from lack of use and she stumbled several feet as she tried to walk. She would have taken a nosedive into the sand but Dominic was quick enough to catch her in his arms. She held onto him for balance as she waited for her legs to adjust. "How did you change back so quickly?" she asked curiously.

He gathered her closer to savor the feel of her in his arms. "It takes less energy to go into a Magi form than it does to go back to my Dragon one. I suppose because a Magi form is much more simplistic."

"I see." She smoothed her hands over his arms and discovered that she really liked the way his skin felt to her fingers. It was nearly as soft as his scales, but there was hard muscle packed underneath. It made her feel safer than she ever had in her life.

He cleared his throat. "Tariah?"

"Hmm?"

"Please stop petting me."

She frowned. "You don't like it?"

"It's more that I like it too much," he sighed. "When you're ready, I'll pet you all over and you'll find out what I mean."

"Oh." She stilled her fingers, suddenly realizing that the swirling emotions inside him were very volatile. The most overwhelming was the feeling that she felt inside herself for him. It was something the Magi might call 'love' but she felt it was too simple a word for the feeling. She also recognized hunger inside Dominic. It, his love for her, and a third emotion were all tangled together. She didn't recognize the third. "What *is* that called?" she asked.

He knew what she needed to know. "The different races have different words for it. Magi call it 'desire.' But that seems too simple a term. Saying that I desire sleep when I am tired doesn't have the same impact as when I say I desire you every second of every minute of every hour."

Something deeply feminine inside her thrilled at the idea that he wanted her that badly. "What do

Dragons call it?"

"*Ishke.*"

Her eyes widened. "But that's what you've been calling *me* all this time. I thought it was an endearment."

"Well, it is." He leaned down and nuzzled her softly. Her scent was even stronger now, as if being in the desert that had given birth to her made her stronger. "It's a word encompassing all the wants, needs, and desires of the world. When I call you *ishke*, it means that you are the one thing I want, need, and desire more than anything. Even life."

That feminine emotion inside her had gone giddy. *She* was giddy. She warily pressed a hand to her heart. "I feel funny when you say that."

"Funny how?"

She tilted her head. "Like I had just won something that I'd been after as long as I was alive." She sighed at the look in his eyes. "Is this another puberty thing?"

"I'd guess so. I'd never felt that until meeting you, though, so perhaps it's a onetime occurrence." He studied her. "That's odd, though. It seems as though you are developing at a much quicker rate. I don't know if it is because you are a Chronicle, or because of my presence."

"I don't care which it is." She cuddled against him. "I'm just glad it won't go on for months!"

"Me too!" was his heartfelt mutter. He buried his nose against her neck and hunger roared to life. His majiks were very low, and her power had welled in response to his need. It flowed over her like a blue aura just begging for his attention.

He wanted to savor every moment. He had lived without her for centuries, and there was no reason to hurry. He lifted her right hand to his lips and pressed a kiss to the character on her palm. In Magi, 'chron' meant 'life.' In Kin, it meant 'strength.' In Dragon, it meant 'heart's keeper.' He thought it was the perfect symbol for his Chronicle.

He softly drank her power as he trailed his lips up her arm. It was sweet like wine and much more potent than it had been before. "Desert girl," he murmured huskily. "I didn't realize what that might really indicate."

She wasn't really paying attention to his words. She was trying to analyze the odd feelings inside her body. Her skin tingled with sensitivity, and she felt oddly lightheaded and breathless. They were not unpleasant feelings, but they were odd. "Dominic?"

"Hmm?" He drank her power from where her shoulder met her neck. When she was out of second puberty, he was going to drink his fill everywhere. Every curve and hollow had its own taste and texture. His control was strained as he fought the urge to go exploring.

"I feel odd."

He lifted his head quickly. "Am I hurting you?" he asked quickly. "Did I frighten you?"

"No." She frowned thoughtfully. "It's not a bad feeling. I feel slightly dizzy though. And my skin feels sensitive."

His pulse began to beat cheerfully throughout his entire body as the other half of his hunger for her surged forward. He ached and burned to possess her, to touch and caress and savor her body. His own Fire powers didn't make him that hot. "Well." It was the best he could manage around his tight throat. "It sounds like your body is trying to catch up to your emotions."

Oddly, knowing that it was perfectly normal made her wariness fade away entirely. She smiled. "I'm supposed to feel really good in more than my heart when you're touching me?"

"The moons save me from curious Chronicles in second puberty!" he muttered.

"Dominic, please. If I can't ask you, who can I ask?"

He cupped her face in his hands and felt her emotions with his. "Let's put it this way," he said roughly. "When you are fully matured, what you feel right now will be like a grain of sand compared to a desert the size of the ocean."

Her eyes widened to pools of liquid silver. The evening sun made them shimmer and ripple like molten metal. The sight took his breath. "That sounds a bit scary," she said softly. And yet, she wasn't scared. She could see and sense how the emotions affected her lover, and though they were almost frighteningly immense, they weren't truly alarming.

"It is," he agreed. "But it's very nice when it's shared." He leaned down and softly touched her lips with his to continue drinking her power. He let his emotions mesh with hers so that he would know precisely what she felt.

The lightheadedness was there to diminish her thought processes. Her lips tingled and she was a bit flushed. None of it, however, actually seemed directed wholly at him. It was merely her body beginning to develop the proper sensations and signals. Her body had begun to decide what it wanted. It was far more than he had hoped to see for a long time. Feeding hunger appeased, he lifted his head slowly. "When you're ready to start experimenting, just let me know."

"Deal." She released him and smiled. "Let's see about feeding *me* now. I need dinner."

By the time the sun had fully sunk and the moons had risen in the sky, Dominic and Tariah were secure in the camp they had made on the beach. Dinner had been made from a desert rabbit that she had caught and he had cooked, and she was feeling very full and surprisingly content. She stretched out on her back and stared up at the sky, simply grateful that she could.

Dominic returned from disposing of the remains of dinner, and he sat down beside her. He smiled as she automatically shifted and put her head on his lap. He smoothed his fingers down her lines softly. "I didn't think anyone so tiny would be so dangerous."

She smiled. "I used to spend long hours climbing cliffs to get supplies. You build up a lot of strength that way. And I've always been fast, so my ice power makes a good projectile weapon."

"I'd noticed." He had been utterly fascinated as he had watched her successfully track and roust the rabbit, only to kill it from almost two hundred feet away by using a single sliver of ice. "Remind me to never make you mad."

She muffled a giggle as she snuggled closer. "I keep wondering," she said softly, "when I might develop my secondary skills, like I heard would happen. I don't even know what they are."

He cocked his head. "That's a good question. There are three Dragoon abilities. They in turn will evolve into their own secondary abilities. But that won't happen for another fifty years or so."

The idea of being with her Fury for fifty years or longer pleased her greatly. "What are the skills?"

"Telepathy, which is the reading of minds. Telekinesis, which is the movement of objects using the mind. And Ultravision, which is the ability to touch something and see its history in your mind." He ran his fingers through her hair. "Are you going to put this up when we start traveling?"

"Of course. It's too hot to wear it down." Her finger drew absent designs in the sand beside her. "I don't know if I'd want to read minds. There are some things I just don't want to know or hear. I'd want to be able to control it."

"Maybe it's time to find out what we can do." He eased her up off his lap. "Let's just see. We can try applying our minds to something and see if anything happens. Here. Close your mind to me, and I'll see if I can read it even without our bond."

She obligingly, if reluctantly, closed her mind and cut off his presence. She immediately felt cold inside. She liked having him inside her mind at all times. The endless flow of power between them always made her feel warm and secure. "I'm going to think of something really silly," she said. "Something so outrageous that you'll start laughing the minute you see it. Then we'll really know."

He concentrated as hard as he could and probed at her mind. It remained firmly and stubbornly sealed. He pushed, he prodded, and he metaphorically shook, but the barriers remained firm. With a sigh, he said, "I don't think Telepathy will be my skill." He tilted his head. "What were you thinking about?"

She leaned up and whispered in his ear. Almost immediately he gave a shout of laughter. "Remind me never to doubt you again about your capacity for silliness." He let out a little breath as he felt her mind open for him. He had been lonely without having her there to touch at his will. He possessively gathered her closer mentally and with his power as well. It was just as good as having his arms around her. "Okay," he said. "Your turn."

"But I don't want to close you off again." She frowned and began to mentally poke around his mind. "Where's something you're hiding from me?"

"I'm hiding nothing," he defended himself.

"You are too. There's a big dark spot." She kept poking until she finally found the spot he had blocked off. It was part of his memories and she was immediately interested all the more. "Past lovers?" she asked. She poked again at the spot and waited for jealousy. It didn't arrive this time. It didn't take long for her to realize that it was her growing confidence that had erased the ugly emotion. She better understood how he felt, and that meant she knew nothing in his past was a threat.

He just sighed. "Stay out of those memories, *ishke*. They're hidden for your sake." The argument was for form only. He knew she would get inside; her mental strength felt unusually sharp and seemed to be growing stronger.

She poked and prodded at the barrier and then tried pushing. Unexpectedly, she found herself on the other side. His memories were laid out before her, and they were indeed of past relationships. She gave them barely more than a cursory look. She really didn't care. It was enough to know she had access. "Who was the Kin Elf?"

He smiled as he took down the barrier. "I had a feeling you'd ask that. She was my first. Stayed friends up until she passed away a few years ago." He skimmed his thumb over her lower lip. "Telepathy must be your Dragoon skill."

"I don't want it." Her voice sounded as sulky as her face looked. "I don't want to read minds."

"You have to do it on purpose. You won't just hear what's inside people's heads." He sighed when she got to her feet and walked away. He'd had a feeling she would do that. "Come back here. Don't sulk." She didn't respond and he got to his feet. "Tariah, come back here. It'll be just fine."

She shot him a look over her shoulder. "Stop trying to placate me. After everything I've dealt with, I've earned my sulk about being given the ability to read the minds of the people who want me dead!"

"You have to admit, that'd be useful."

"Hmph." She swung around to pace off her annoyance and suddenly felt something wrap around her. She gave a startled yelp as the invisible grip yanked her backwards off her feet. She landed on her ass in the sand with a thump. "Ouch!"

"Oh, shit." Her lover rushed to her side and knelt down. "Are you okay? Did you get hurt?" He ran his hands over her quickly. "That was *not* my intent, Tariah, I promise!"

"Don't touch me, you fiend!" She slapped at his hands. "I don't care what your intent was! If I want space, you have to give me space!"

He bit his lip to hide a smile at the evidence of her temper. He had been wondering if she would have one. Most Water elements were fairly even-tempered, but they could eventually be provoked. "Now, Tariah."

"Don't 'now' me!" She poked him in the chest. "Promise you won't do that again unless I'm in danger!"

"Alright, I'm sorry!" He was careful to keep his amusement hidden. "I won't do it again unless there's danger." Sensing her ire fading, he caught her in his arms and tumbled her down onto the sand. He braced his weight on his elbows to keep from crushing her but he remained close. "Feisty little thing."

She blinked, then smiled. "I guess I am. It felt kind of nice to get mad for once." The anger evaporated quickly as she cuddled closer to his wonderfully warm body. His weight and scent was stirring up that feminine thing inside, but she ignored it. Until it decided to be *specific* about what she felt and wanted, she didn't really care.

"Are you falling asleep?" His voice was warm.

"No." She gave a little yawn. "But I think I could. I'm sleepy suddenly." She closed her eyes and curled up on her side as he released her and got to his feet. She heard him establishing a protective barrier to keep out other people and creatures alike before she felt him return and lay down beside her.

She promptly turned over and snuggled up tightly against him. His arms closed around her, and she gave a soft little sigh. "I can't figure out how I ever slept peacefully without you," she murmured, rubbing her cheek against him.

"Me neither." He pressed his lips gently to her hair. "Go to sleep now." He closed his eyes as he listened to her breathing even and her power go quiet. Only then did he let himself think about the future. He had a house on the Isle, but it was in the mountains. He would have to move it closer to the desert for her sake. It would have to be made bigger, too, just in case she wanted as many kids as he did.

Thinking about all the fun and terror it would be to raise a brood with his Chronicle's frightening temper and intelligence, he fell asleep smiling.

Chapter Nine

They broke camp the following morning right after dawn. "How far are we from Prismatic?" Tariah asked as they set out on foot across the sandy dunes.

Dominic glanced up at the sky where only two of the four moons were still visible in the rapidly lightening blue color. Since he was only able to see the moons to the west and south, he was able to pinpoint the direction to Prismatic. "We're about a week's worth of walking away at the minimum. Refraction is our first city and I believe it is almost exactly eight days away from Prismatic."

She sighed. "There's only one bright side in all of that."

"What's that?"

"I get to spend the time with you." She smiled at him. "When I was running across the desert from Symphony, it was worse because I was alone. But now I'm not."

He could find nothing to say to that that would possibly convey how he felt. The best he could manage was to gently curl his fingers around the back of her neck and draw her closer. No hair impeded his touch, and he eyed the top of her head balefully. Upon waking, she had promptly fastened her hair up on top of her head in an elaborate coil of braids. He *still* didn't know how she had done it.

She grinned. "Girl magic, as Sparkle called it."

"I won't deny that the females of any species have a strange and powerful magic over us helpless males." Laughter lurked in his voice. "But then again, perhaps it is simply our hearts that make us so helpless."

"Perhaps it is." She linked her hands behind her back. "I'm helpless to you, but I'm not attracted to you, so it must just be my heart." She tilted her head back to let the sun wash over her face. "Of course, I'm sure it will be both eventually."

"You could be bad for my ego if I let you." He tucked his hands in his pockets as the sun rose steadily higher and the air heated. In the desert, during the hottest parts of the day, physical contact was vastly uncomfortable because skin-to-skin generated heat as well. Much as he wanted to touch Tariah, he kept his hands to himself.

Two hours of walking later and they were seeing the shape of Refraction wavering in the heat waves from the sand. He was sweating and sweltering, but she didn't seem to be affected at all. It fascinated him all over again that she was so truly a part of the desert. He knew people who were truly 'of' the land were at home there, but he hadn't imagined just how much that entailed. "I'm a little envious."

She stuck her tongue out at him briefly. "It's just worse for you because you're a Fire element. Your internal temperature is higher to begin with. I'm much cooler so I can shed the heat of the sun. Actually, it's more like I soak it up. I *love* the desert heat."

As the city grew larger before them, she began to feel tension gathering inside. Refraction was not much bigger than Symphony but it was still bigger than she was comfortable with. It was built in a spiral direction to take advantage of the power in the land. The biggest concentration of people was in the very center, but there were still many along the outer edges where the two Dragoons were approaching.

They had barely reached the entrance when several men stepped into their way. "The Dragon can pass," one man said icily, "but the abomination stays out here."

Tariah said nothing. Dominic barely bit back a snarl. "You *did* hear there was a ceasefire, correct?"

"That's the only reason she's still alive." The man gave Tariah a onceover with his eyes, and disgust filled their depths. "If I had my way, she'd be dead where she stands. Chronicles are a revulsion of nature!"

"We're leaving." Dominic pulled Tariah closer protectively. "They can keep their bigoted hate to themselves and we'll keep our coin."

She shook her head. "We're crossing to Prismatic, Dominic. We need more than just a few supplies. You're going to want a cloak, too. You're not cut out for the desert. I'll be fine out here. You can get what we need."

He knew she was right but he didn't like leaving her alone. "Be careful," he said softly as he leaned down to press his lips to her cheek. "Call for me if they even look at you funny, understand?"

"I understand." Her heart squeezed tightly for a moment as she watched him walk into the city. It was wonderful to know someone loved her that deeply. She could count on him to be there for her no matter what.

Disinclined to remain near the idiots glaring at her, she moved away from the entrance and sat down on the sand. She had been expecting this from the beginning. Magi had been believing in the 'evil' of Chronicles for centuries. They wouldn't stop thinking it just because the king said not to kill her.

Sensing stares, she turned her head to see several small children peering around the side of a building. They were watching her with expressions ranging from awe to wonder. There was no fear in their eyes. She smiled and waved at them, and they waved back with happy smiles. It helped ease her heart. Maybe there was hope for the Magi race.

A hard hand closed over her shoulder and shoved her flat onto the sand. She rolled over and scrambled up to her knees, her heart pounding madly. Three men loomed over her, and they wore ugly smirks on their faces. Something disgusting was in their eyes that she did not recognize but despised anyway. "Go away!" she ordered.

"Sex with a Chronicle is supposed to give you power," one chortled. "Let's find out!"

Her eyes narrowed dangerously. "You're going to wish you'd never had that idea."

Dominic had just paid for a week's worth of supplies and transferred it to his backpack when four little kids came running up to him. "Dragon!" The littlest of the girls grabbed his leg tightly. "You need to hurry!"

"What's wrong?" he asked in surprise. The other three grabbed his hands and began to pull, and he couldn't figure out what had put such terror in their eyes. The answer came as a sharp stabbing sensation inside his soul that could only be Tariah's fear. Her voice ripped across his mind in a mental cry, and an explosion of Water and Ice erupted outside the city.

The roar that emerged from his lips came from the very bottom of his soul. It was the roar of a fully-grown Dragon who had been wronged, and it was a chilling sound. No one in the city had heard it before, and every adult cowered back in fear.

On the contrary, not a single child was affected. The four who had gone to Dominic were more relieved than anything. As he rushed through the city faster than any Magi could travel, they scrambled after him as fast as their legs could carry them. They wanted to make sure that the pretty lady with the nice eyes wasn't hurt.

She wasn't hurt yet. She was pissed off. The bomb of Water and Ice had rendered one of her attackers half-frozen. Another nearly drowned when she encased herself in water and he couldn't release her arm in time. The third was a Water Magi, and he was mostly unaffected by anything she could throw. He dug his fingers into her arm and slapped her sharply across the face. "Stop fighting! Be nice and we won't hurt you!"

Her silver eyes turned crystalline blue as Dominic's majiks poured into her body. "Funny. I could say the same thing!" She shoved her free hand hard against his chest, and her power punched him pointblank with enough force to send him flying backwards onto the sand. Astonished, she stared at her hands. She hadn't known she could do that with power.

All three men were struggling to regroup when the piercing roar cut across the air. They went very still and slowly turned around to see Dominic rushing out of the city. A blur of red Fire shifted him to Dragon form halfway, and he landed next to them hard. The ground rocked and sand flew. The men flew as well, like leaves in a wind. Dominic's claws lashed out and he grabbed them before they landed. His gray eyes had gone red with rage. "Tell me why I shouldn't kill you!" he snarled gutturally.

On shaky legs, Tariah walked toward him. Other than a few bruises and the red mark on her face, she was relatively fine. "Let them go, Dominic."

"No." His razor sharp teeth bared in a mockery of a smile. "I'd rather eat them."

"You'll get indigestion." She pressed against his chest and wrapped her arms around as much of him as she could. "Don't lower yourself to their level."

He technically had every right to avenge her assault, and that was a right that applied under every species' laws. On the other hand, it would get them in trouble with the Militia. Her pain made him want to start chomping into her attackers, but her fear made him hold himself back. With obvious and careful control, he turned and tossed the men toward the city. They landed with thumps, their eyes wide and white with horror. "Be glad my mate is more forgiving than I!" he snarled at them.

The men scrambled into the city, and Dominic turned back to Tariah. He lowered his head and nuzzled her softly to comfort them both. She wound her arms around his neck and rubbed her cheek against his scales. He was an awe-inspiring sight, and she was both proud and astonished that such a magnificent creature belonged to her.

Red light flared and he turned to Magi form. She held on through the change and found herself dangling from his neck. Her feet left the ground, but she didn't care. His arms closed around her waist and held her tight. The lingering majiks inside her faded, and his presence filled the space left behind.

The children came running forward and there were many more than just the four who had fetched Dominic. At least fifteen clustered around Tariah and Dominic, and all were talking over each other as they sought reassurances. "I'm fine," Tariah told them. "Really. Thank you for caring."

One of the older girls shook her head. "We're really sorry about what happened. You haven't done anything to us. Why should we hate you? We'll tell our parents what *really* happened. We won't let anyone blame you."

"Thank you," she said softly. "But we're leaving anyway to keep the peace."

"It's stupid!" a small boy blurted. "You're not a monster! You're just different! Why are we supposed to be scared of something that's just different?"

Dominic smiled as the children went running back into the city. "Out of the mouths of children, as they say." He turned and ran his hands over Tariah swiftly. "Are you sure you're alright?" He found the bruises on her arms and a low growl rumbled in his chest. "Damn them!" He leaned down and softly pressed his lips to the mark on her face. "I should have eaten them anyway!"

She bit her lip but a soft snicker escaped anyway. When he glowered at her, she softly framed his face with her hands. "You wouldn't eat them, and you know it! Kill them maybe, but not eat them." She pressed her lips to his in a comforting kiss. "I was never truly afraid," she said gently. "I knew you'd save me."

He enfolded her in his arms and wrapped his new cloak around them both as well. Heat of the desert be damned. He wanted his Chronicle to be protected from everything. She was the most precious thing in his life. "Let's leave," he said softly, touching his lips to her forehead. "And even if we pass another city, we're not entering it."

"Agreed."

They set out once more across the desert. They didn't speak much as they walked. They were simply content to keep the silence and listen to the endless flow of power that circled between them. It was perhaps the most comfortable silence either Tariah or Dominic had ever felt. They didn't have to speak to understand one another.

After a while, almost four hours out of Refraction, curiosity got the better of Tariah and she asked, "What are the Dragons like? Their society, I mean. They're almost never seen anywhere. The few books about them just describe their appearance, not their way of life." She glanced up at Dominic. "From what I've felt from you, I guess you're all very close."

"Very much so." He smiled. "We're sectioned into four clans, one for each element. We have more Elders than most because we're immortal, but one from each clan is elected every hundred years to sit on the Council of Elders. They keep the laws."

"I bet they get loud."

"Good bet." He chuckled softly. "When they fight, you can hear it all the way across the land!"

She grinned. "Who is the loudest?"

"Hmm. Tough one. Probably the Air Clan Elder. He's stubborn." He skimmed a finger down her cheek. "I'm sure they'll be thrilled to meet you. For so long we've wanted so badly to find even one Chronicle."

She glanced at him solemnly. "You don't need to feel guilty. None of you are at fault. How could you have known how it would end?"

He closed his eyes. "Saying it isn't the same as believing it, especially when you've been watching others suffer for a millennia. Dragons will inherit the memories and feelings of those who pass on. It's how we make sure that important things are carried on even when our immortal bodies fade."

She slipped her hand into his. "So that's how you know so much about Chronicles despite being so young."

"Yes. I inherited from a Fury who lived at the end of the war. His Chronicle had not yet been born." There was a combined sadness and bleakness in his eyes. "He felt her birth and death before I was born. The day that he was put out of his misery was the same day I hatched."

"Now we live in memory of all of them," she said. She stopped and held him tightly. "Chronicles . . . we've suffered too. My entire life I *knew* there was someone out there. But I had no name for the feeling until Maxim told me about Furies. If I'd never found you . . . I'd have died too."

"Tariah." He buried his face against her hair for long moments and then reluctantly released her. "I'm getting you all sweaty. It's too damned hot in this desert."

"I like it."

"You're a desert girl. I'm a mountain Dragon." He looked around. "Are there any oases nearby? And, if not, could you make one?"

He looked so hopeful and adorable that she burst into laughter. "Okay, okay. Let's see if we can find one to camp at." She lifted her head and scented the air. She could smell the strong surge of Water power in the land. "There is one near. To the . . . east." She smiled. "It should be a nice one. The power is strong."

It took them less than ten minutes of walking toward the east to spot the oasis she had felt. They would never have seen it if they hadn't deviated from their route, but they were glad to see it now.

Because Water power in the desert would gather close under the surface, oases formed. They were little patches of trees and grass and water amid the desert landscape. They looked like little islands in a sea of sand. This one, in particular, was on the larger side. It had actually grown full size trees, and quite thickly too.

Dominic made Tariah wait at the edges of the trees while he prowled the interior to make sure they were the only ones there. Once he was sure, he returned to her side and escorted her deeper into the trees. "Wait until you see," he told her.

She almost didn't have to see anything. She could smell and feel the water. Still, her sigh was long and heartfelt as she saw the deep pool of water shimmering under the sun. "I think I've died and gone to the Underrealm." She hurried forward to drop her hipsack on the ground and then only waited long enough to remove her boots. Clothes and all, she dove into the pool without a splash.

He started laughing. "And I thought I wanted a swim!" He hardly blamed her. There were times when he loved to take the smallest Dragon form he possibly could, barely a foot in length, and crawl into a fire pit. It had been his favorite napping spot as a kid. Anticipating a nice swim, he removed his cloak and shirt and got to work on his boots.

She surfaced and turned to tease him when she realized he was removing his boots. He had already removed his top clothing and the sunlight flowed over his smooth skin and cast fascinating shadows along his muscles. The lines on his chest seemed more golden than ever and gave his already beautiful form something else. It was something she could not name, and she had never noticed it before.

Her breath held, she watched him as he dove, still half clothed, into the pool with her. She felt flushed and breathless, her stomach fluttering in an odd way. In fascination, she lifted her hands and looked at them. She had never before had an urge to run her fingers over him, but now she wanted to so badly that her fingers seemed to itch.

A hand closed around her ankle and tugged her underwater. She muffled a yelp as she was dunked and then she blew a stream of bubbles at her grinning partner. Indignant, she swam away and surfaced again. He surfaced behind her and she turned around to splash him. "Meany."

"You seemed distracted," he scolded her. "I wanted your attention."

She watched almost helplessly as water drops ran down his strong shoulders when he straightened up. The water went halfway up his chest where he was standing, and the part out of the water seemed to shine in the sunlight. She wondered why her mouth was dry when the air was moist. A bit disturbed by her body's sudden reaction, she turned away slightly. "You have it," she whispered.

He had no compunctions about tangling his emotions with hers to find out why she was acting so oddly. The feelings that then seemed to surge into him made his entire body tighten with stifled desire. "I see," he managed to say, but his voice sounded huskier than usual, "that maybe I won't be suffering for long."

She looked at him with a frown. "This is a puberty thing, isn't it?" she accused.

"Afraid so, *ishke*." He searched her eyes and saw the beginnings of her awareness of him as a mate. He slowly swam toward her to draw her into his arms. "Take your hair down," he said softly, his voice still husky with his desire for her. He wanted to see her hair flowing around them.

She felt a shiver that went from her bones outward at the sound of his voice. It was as if everything suddenly seemed sensual to her. Everything he did or said made little flutters of something skim along her nerves. It was a feeling of pure delight, and one that something inside her readily embraced. "I feel so odd," she murmured.

"You're getting twice the signal." He turned in a circle and let her float before him gracefully. "You seem to be skipping right over one of the primary stages of puberty. Normally what you're feeling would occur with anything that you liked. Everything would be sensitive to your developing senses." He lowered his head and softly nuzzled behind her ear. "But I guess because I'm here, you're zeroing right in on me as a target."

"Oh." She closed her eyes and let herself savor how it felt to feel him so close physically and emotionally. It combined with the cool feeling of the water to make her skin almost unbearably sensitive. A little afraid, she grabbed onto him. "I don't like this."

He sighed softly, his eyes tender as he carried her toward the shore. "That's because you're trying to convince yourself that something is wrong."

"Isn't it?" she asked curiously as he set her gently on the grass. She didn't let go of him and he was forced to sit beside her. For some reason, she simply couldn't bear the idea of releasing him. Her hands felt glued to him. "I'm going through second puberty in a *week* when it's supposed to take a *year*!"

He ran his tongue over his teeth. "Yes, but that's because of me I think." He lowered his head to touch hers. "What I feel when I touch you," he said softly, "is much more than I've ever felt before, Tariah. I breezed through second puberty because it seemed so comfortable and unimportant. But those feelings came back when I met you. The curiosity and the hunger to learn another's body. Not just anyone, but you. And it's a million times stronger for you."

"But it doesn't scare you," she said softly, searching his eyes. "Why not?"

"Because while I know that what is between us is bigger than before, I at least know what it is and what we're in for." He nuzzled her neck. "Take your hair down. Please? And take your time. I like it."

Her fingers trembled slightly as she reached up and began to untuck the little twists she had made in her hair. As each tuck came undone, a braid fell down and unraveled from the weight of her soaked hair.

He held his breath as he watched her. He had always thought there was something very beautiful about a woman taking her hair down, but when it was Tariah it was downright sensual. Her silver eyes seemed deeper than ever, like a pool he could drown in. It took every drop of his willpower not to kiss her as he craved. For all her awakening sensuality, a true kiss would likely terrify her when she was still trying to adjust to the sensitivity of her body.

She would never look at taking her hair down the same way again. Her heart and her stomach quivered with an odd sort of desire as she watched the smoke of his eyes deepen. The feel of her own hair sliding over her skin was powerful to her senses, and it made her want to feel his hair as well. Nerves tangled with needs and she kept her hands to herself.

As her hair tumbled down to her waist and swung softly behind her, he caught a handful and brought it to his cheek. He rubbed against it softly, as if it was the finest of silks. Breathless, she could only watch him helplessly. He felt her gaze and smiled slowly. "I take pleasure in everything about you. I thought you realized."

"Realizing it, knowing it, and understanding it," she said, her voice slightly huskier than usual, "are three entirely different things." She drew a long breath and moved away slightly. "Can we talk about something else?"

"Of course." He reluctantly released her hair and watched it slide through his fingers. He could hardly wait until he could see it fanned across his pillow back home. "What do you want to talk about?"

"Teach me majiks." She smiled suddenly. "I want to try and turn into a Dragon."

He grinned. "You do, huh?"

"Absolutely!" She scooted closer to him once more. "So . . . what do I have to do? How do I do it?"

"I'll help you. You won't know how to bend the majiks otherwise." He moved closer until their knees bumped together. Instead of wrapping his power around hers as he often did, this time he blended them together. It was quite easy when the power between them flowed back and forth as an endless loop. "Just watch what I do, and do it yourself."

She closed her eyes and watched how he was bending his majiks. She drew the majiks into herself and began to bend them as she had seen him do. Her body began to feel cool like water and she felt her skin throbbing as it responded to how she was changing her power.

She was concentrating so fiercely that when the change occurred it startled her. With a little gasp, she opened her eyes. Two things dawned on her belatedly. One, she was in Dominic's hands. Two, she was only barely half a foot big. Her eyes widened as she looked up at him. "I think I did something wrong."

He bit his lip. Then he bit his tongue. As her indignation grew, he bit his cheek. Finally he gave up and began laughing as he held her up to eye level. She was, easily, the cutest little Dragon he had ever seen. She was barely half a foot long and covered with soft auburn scales the same color as her hair. Little streaks of blue along the scales rippled like waves and marked her Water power.

"I think," he said, his voice warm, "that you just need practice. You're a cute little whelp, though. You'll be quite beautiful as a full Dragon. Little, probably, but beautiful." He rubbed his cheek against her gently. "Want to try flying?"

"Of course!" She was still in his mind, and she followed the knowledge inside him as to how to make her wings work. It warmed her to know he had crashed more than once while learning to fly. She wanted to do much better, especially because she wasn't born a Dragon. She concentrated hard, flapped her wings lightly, and rose up over his hands. "I did it!"

"Show off." Pride filled him. "Even full Dragons don't always hover first try."

"I know." Her voice was smug as she cautiously began to fly around him in circles. She landed on his shoulder and balanced delicately. "This is *really* wonderful, Dominic. Thank you." She tickled his ear with her tongue in the Dragon's form of a kiss.

"No tickling." He rubbed his cheek against her. "Take your time," he told her.

Much as she would have liked to, she had sensed his hunger before he could block it. She shook her head slightly and flew off his shoulder. It was even easier to unbend the majiks and return to her normal form. She shook her hair back and then moved closer and wound her arms around his shoulders. "Teaching me drained you. I can feel it."

"Only because it was the first time you'd tried. It'll eventually be easy enough that it doesn't affect me at all." He watched a drop of water run down her neck and shoulder from her damp hair and told himself not to sink his teeth in as if she was a dessert.

Her eyes widened. She had always assumed biting someone was meant to hurt. But if the flutter of her heart and blood was anything to go by, the ideas tumbling in his mind were certainly starting to appeal. She was beginning to understand them, and to recognize inside herself the beginnings of that third emotion that was so volatile in her Fury. The feeling that Dragons called *ishke*.

She was also beginning to believe that even that word wasn't enough to encompass her feelings, or his, and it was an oddly comforting belief. She smiled. "Let's see about feeding you now, and dessert can be planned for the future."

He gave a laugh and caught her close against him in a fierce hug. He was absolutely and completely over his tail and madly in love with his beautiful Chronicle. A part of him was even beginning to pity the Magi. They would never know this feeling. "Their loss," he said as he eased back. "Now, about that dinner."

Chapter Ten

Tariah awoke the following morning to discover herself sleeping on top of Dominic. It was more comfortable than she would have thought and the feel of his heart beating under her ear was deeply soothing. With a soft sigh, she curled closer. There were times it really was nice to be small.

There were also times it wasn't nice to be an early riser. She stifled a yawn and slid off his chest. She sat up with a languid stretch just as a misty rain began to fall. The storm overhead was typical of the desert: small, lightweight, and welcome respite from the heat. The rain felt wonderful as it fell on her skin.

She lifted her hands and studied them. Her skin was still hypersensitive, but she had begun to enjoy it. Somehow it turned everything into a small thrill. It felt a bit like being born again.

Dominic was still asleep. She moved to the edge of the pool and sat on the side with her feet in the water. She felt oddly suspended. Something inside her heart and soul seemed to be waiting. She couldn't put her finger on what it was but decided it didn't matter. She just smiled and closed her eyes. She tilted her face up to enjoy the rain just as Dominic had taught her to enjoy so much else.

When he woke, he automatically reached for her only to realize she wasn't there. He sat up quickly and looked around. His initial grumpiness faded immediately when he spotted her sitting on the side of the pool with her face lifted to the rain like a desert flower. Desire fisted inside his body with gleeful force. It was getting harder and harder to keep his hands to himself.

She had known when he woke, and she suddenly felt the intensity of his emotions. It sent off little shivers of delight through her body that grew steadily stronger as she probed the force of his feelings and saw how deep they went. "Dominic?" she asked without turning around.

"What is it?" He walked over to sit beside her. For the first time, he wasn't sure what she was thinking. Her emotions seemed like an enigma suddenly and they swirled with brilliant colors he could not decipher.

She turned to look at him. Her silver eyes were dark like the lining of the clouds over their heads. "I want you to kiss me."

Lightning cracked to the ground near them. It could have been coincidence or the storm responding to the surge of his power. He held his breath as he stared into Tariah's eyes. They looked like the eyes of a grown woman, and they were dark with mysteries he felt desperate to unlock. "Are you sure?" he asked huskily, lifting a hand to cup her cheek.

She smiled and rubbed her cheek against his hand. "I wouldn't ask if I wasn't. You told me I would know. And I do." With an instinct that was stamped into her very cells, she moved closer and wound her arms around his shoulders. He was strong and powerful and the feel of his body was thrilling. "I know how I feel when you aren't touching me. Now I want to know how I feel when you are."

"I'm going to lay down some rules first." His voice was thick with his emotions. It felt as though he had been given a gift beyond measure. "You have to hold my hands."

Her brow lifted ever so slightly. "Why?"

"To keep me in line," he said in frustration. "Do you know how long I've wanted to kiss you? To *really* kiss you? If you don't hold my hands I might start putting them places that would terrify you right now."

She had a feeling he was right. As badly as she wanted his kiss, something inside seemed to shy back at the idea of someone touching her intimately, even her Fury. A part of it was trepidation. She *knew* that how she felt could only grow stronger. She just wasn't ready for that yet. "I trust you." Despite saying it and feeling it, she took his hands with hers and laced their fingers together.

Since it meant he could not hold her, he curled his power around her instead. Her power met and merged with his in a return embrace and it was once more flowing between them like an endless loop. "Do you want to kiss me, or should I kiss you?" he asked her softly.

She thought about it and then smiled. "I want to kiss you."

"Then I'm all yours, *ishke*."

She eased closer, her eyes moving over his face with a hunger she had never felt before. Just like the rest of the world, it seemed as if she might be seeing him for the first time too. She had always believed him to be handsome but it was different now. Now the lines of his face brought up an urge to touch rather than merely admire. Curious how that worked.

She softly touched her lips to his and a little shiver of delight went down her back. His lips were the same as they had always been, yet now the shape and feel of them made her body tingle with pleasure. She sighed and let herself savor the feeling as she memorized the shape of his lips with her own.

He was *very* glad she had his hands. His eyes smoldered with desire as he watched her face. The feel of her lips was seductive, and the look on her face as she began to learn what was between them was doubly potent. He wanted to snatch her up in his arms and take the kiss from her. He wanted to cover her body with more kisses and satisfy her every curiosity and claim her for his own. It was nearly pain inside him, the hunger for her, and he couldn't have hidden his feelings if he had tried.

His feelings swept over her but she did not fear them this time. She *wanted* to know he needed her. The fierceness of his feelings unlocked that strange feminine feeling inside and she felt an odd urge to put her mark on him. She wanted other women to look at him and know that he was hers. A little confused because she didn't know how to obtain what she wanted, she eased back. Her eyes met his smoky gray gaze and he murmured thickly, "Don't worry about that right now. It's just a kiss." He freed his hands and buried his fingers in her hair to draw her closer. "Let me kiss you this time."

His breath was hot and made her shiver again with delight. He had promised to claim her first kiss. She wanted him to have it. "Be my guest," she whispered. "I'm still not sure how to do it properly."

He pulled her onto his lap and surrounded her with his body heat as thoroughly as she was surrounded by his power. The scent of her seemed sharper now, the rich and drugging scent of water in a desert. "If I scare you, tell me immediately."

She ran her hands up over his arms, loving the feel of his skin and muscle beneath her palms. Had he always felt this way? She wished she had noticed sooner. "I will," she promised. She tilted her face up instinctively, asking for his kiss like a flower asked for the sun.

He stopped breathing for a moment. He gently framed her face in his hands and leaned down to kiss her. Her power flowed up between them like an endless spring and covered them both with a soft blue aura. She could no more control the response of her power than he could. They were made to be this way.

He tenderly tilted her head back and teased the edges of her lips with his tongue. He wanted to taste her, truly taste her, but he didn't know just how ready she was. The answer came when she sighed softly and parted her lips for him. A shudder rippled through his body and he groaned as he deepened the kiss, his tongue gliding into her mouth to taste.

Her breath lodged in her chest as little waves of heat began to roll through her body. She had never felt anything as wonderful as his kiss. Her hands slid up to curl around the back of his neck and hold him closer. Wanting to know more, wanting to make him feel the same way she did, she followed his lead and curled her tongue around his eagerly. He tasted like what smoke smelled like. Rich and drugging.

He felt the wash of her emotions and it shook his control. He slanted his head and hungrily deepened the kiss even further, letting go of the edge of his desire for her. It seamlessly merged with his hunger for her power and he found himself feeding on the blue aura that begged for his attention. It was richer now, stronger, as if the act was finally being done properly.

She couldn't breathe anymore but didn't care. The sensation of him drinking her power made her entire body feel as if it had been caressed. It was nearly frightening how powerful the pleasure was. Shivers rippled along her skin and she was helpless to do anything but return the ravenous kiss.

Her body went weak in his arms and swayed toward him. Her breasts flattened against his chest, and a sharp lash of desire came through strong enough to frighten her. She jerked back, her eyes wide with distress. Her arms shot down to cross over her chest defensively and a frown marred her brows as she realized her bust seemed a little . . . swollen. "What did you do to me?" she asked warily.

He held up a hand to hold off the question. Carefully he went through all one thousand characters in the Draconic language. The mental act gave him just enough time to find some control and resist the urge to snatch her back into his arms. His arousal was literal pain in that moment. He would have considered a cold shower but the only water he wanted to be immersed in was the water of his Chronicle.

"Dominic?" she asked carefully. Her heart flipped up into her throat as he looked at her with his eyes nearly black. He was trying to withhold his emotions from her, but as she reached out a mental hand and brushed against them, she realized how turbulent they really were. It seemed a little frightening, but she was beginning to feel the stirrings of the same inside. She wanted to kiss him again.

"Don't you dare," he growled. "Otherwise I really will scare you." He drew a deep breath. "And all I did to you was arouse you. Don't ask me why your body responds the way it does; I'm not a female, I haven't a clue. But I can tell you that it's just your body saying that it likes how you feel. Male bodies do the same but react a little differently."

"Oh." Her eyes lowered and she spotted very clearly the evidence of his body's response. Her cheeks slowly turned pink. "Oh," she said again.

He had to grin. "Is that the best you can manage?"

"I'm not sure what else to say." She glowered at him. "I'm still new at this." She averted her eyes. "How did I do? For a kiss I mean."

He leaned over and softly touched her lips with his, careful to keep it light and tender. "When you want more practice, just let me know." He looked around as he realized that the rain was beginning to stop and the sun was starting to shine brightly. Steam lifted from his skin far more visibly now and he looked at it in amusement. "Well, there's the evidence of your effect on me, *ishke*."

She looked, and she began to smile. The smug and feminine curve to her lips was more evidence of her growing maturity, and he fought the urge to kiss her again. Instead, he ran his hands lightly down her arms where there was a matching steam lifting lightly. "And here's some evidence of my effect on you," he said huskily.

She lifted her hands and looked at the steam curling from her fingers. In consternation, she said, "I hope this doesn't stay for long. People will begin to think I was hit by lightning."

He threw back his head with a rich laugh and caught her up in his arms to hold her fiercely. "You're an amazing woman, Tariah Chronis. And I'm very proud you're mine."

She smiled and curled closer. "I'll remind you of that next time you get mad at me." Needing a distraction, she got to her feet and looked around. "I'm hungry. There's probably some cactear around here."

He watched her curiously. "Cactear?"

"It's a fruit that grows in the desert." She hunted very cautiously through bushes around the pool. "If you can manage to get the shell off, the fruit inside is very sweet and very soft. But the shell is covered in really nasty thorns. And then there's the problem of . . ." There was a rustle and a prickly little creature shot out of the bush and attached to a tree. "Catching it."

He looked at the sharp little spikes all over the cactear and grimaced. "Don't touch it, Tariah. I don't want you to get hurt."

She rolled her eyes. "Oh you big baby! I've been hunting these for a long time." She began to ease closer to the cactear and water began to flow around her ankle. Little shards of ice began to condense within the water but they were invisible to all but Dominic.

She suddenly shot a stream of water at one side of the cactear. It lunged off the tree in the opposite direction and was instantly encased in ice. It dropped to the ground with a thud.

Dominic began to applaud. "I stand corrected."

She grinned at him and retrieved the frozen fruit. She drew the dagger out of the sheath he wore on his hip to get to work on the ice. It cracked open and fell apart around the cactear. The spikes fell off moments later and left only the fruit behind. She held it up triumphantly. "And that's how it's done. Once the spikes are gone it's no longer able to draw power in."

He eyed the green and blue polka dotted yellow fruit. "Is it a fruit or an animal?"

"Well, that's a good question." She broke the fruit in half and offered him some. "But it has no body like an animal, so we call it a fruit." She began to eat her share with great delight, discovering that it tasted better than it ever had before. It seemed that everything was far more pleasurable to her now, just as Dominic had said it would be.

As she was licking some of the stray juice from her fingers, she saw him watching her with fire in his eyes. Literal fire. His power was as hungry for her as the rest of him. The sight of it took her breath away, and she leaned toward him without thought to kiss him. His lips were sweet from the fruit and it seemed to taste far more delightful on him.

He firmly set her away from him. "Stop torturing me."

She averted her eyes with a blush. "Sorry." She was beginning to seriously feel bad for her Fury. If her sudden desire to touch and taste him was anything like what he had been feeling all along, he must have been miserable.

"Let's just say," he said ruefully, "that when I do finally have you in my bed for more than sleep, I won't let you out for a week." He watched her eyes widen and couldn't hold back a laugh. "When we get there, *ishke*, you won't look nearly so alarmed." He wrapped an arm around her shoulders and tugged her back against him just so he could snuggle her. "Ready for more walking?"

She stifled a sigh. Prismatic was more than a couple weeks away by walking. She was tired of walking. She loved the desert, and she loved Dominic, but a part of her wanted to rail and scream against the law of the land and the law of the Magi that had caused her to be stranded in the first place.

He buried his face in her hair comfortingly and an idea occurred to him. "You want to ride? If I'm in Dragon form, I can walk far faster than in this form. We might even be able to get up to a running speed that rivals my flight. If we're touching the land, it might not cause any ripples."

She rested back against him, enjoying how his arms felt around her. "I'm willing to try if you are. I admit it. I don't want to walk any more. I just want to get to the king, get the meeting over with, and get on with going to the Isle. I don't belong here," she said fiercely. "I belong with the Dragons."

"You belong with me." He eased her head back and kissed her. He made sure it was quick and tender, but he couldn't resist taking it deeper than just the pecks he had been getting. He loved her taste.

She shivered softly in reaction and it was beautiful to him. Her lashes lowered partially over her eyes and they looked like pools of melted silver. His breath hitched and she smiled, loving his reaction to her. "I belong with you," she concurred, "but at least the Dragons won't try to kill me."

He chuckled. "I suspect you'll be running the place by the end of the first month." Keeping her close, he picked up his backpack and they began to walk toward the exit of the oasis. There were too many trees around them for him to go into his natural form safely. Either he or the oasis would be injured, and they didn't want either to happen. Once they were out on the desert sands again, she took his backpack and slipped it on over her back so that her hands were free. Then she rolled her eyes and waited while he tightened the straps since it was too big for her. "Not a word," she warned him.

"I wouldn't dream of it." He moved a few feet away from her to have space, then closed his eyes and let his power well up. He unbent his majiks and the power reverted him once more to his Dragon form. As he was blinking his eyes to clear them, he felt Tariah softly scratching him on the back of his neck. His just-cleared eyes nearly rolled back in his head and he laid down on the sand with a sound that was almost like a purr.

She began to giggle. "Dragons purr?" Delighted with the sound, she scratched him some more. She wasn't surprised he liked it. In this form it would be hard for him to reach his neck for anything.

He reached around and scooped her up gently with one of his claws. He brought her up to eye level and nuzzled her gently. "When you can manage to take a proper Dragon form, I'll return the favor." He brought her around toward his back and she climbed gracefully onto his shoulders.

She had barely gotten settled when he suddenly took off running across the desert sands. With a shriek of laughter, she grabbed onto him for dear life and ducked down so that the wind didn't slap her in the face. It still pulled at her hair and she realized belatedly that she had never put it back up. She was going to have tangles in her tangles at that rate.

The desert sped past them in a blur of brown and white. He could nearly run as fast as he flew, especially once she found a water stream under the land that he could run along the top of. She could draw power from the water, and by linking to her, he was able to lean on her power. It didn't stop his majiks from draining, but it allowed him to run as fast as water could flow.

By the time afternoon began to turn into evening, they could see Prismatic ahead of them. As evening became twilight and the moons started to rise, they were less than a few miles outside the city limits. He had been walking instead of running but when he realized how close they were, he stopped altogether. "Let's wait out the night, then go in tomorrow morning. We don't want to alarm them."

She rubbed her eyes. "Good idea," she agreed on a sleepy yawn. She had been tempted to nap but she had been enjoying the ride far too much. She slid down off his back and then staggered and fell to her knees when her legs wouldn't support her. "Oops."

He turned into Magi form and knelt beside her to gently lift her up into his arms. "Magi and Chronicles are rather flimsy little things," he teased her gently. "Your legs get weak when you don't use them."

She glowered at him. "And you don't fall asleep when you're not moving something for a while?" She promptly forgot the conversation moments later as she felt his heated breath on her shoulder. A shiver rippled through her body even as her power flowed instantly to the surface.

He shuddered lightly as her power teased his lips. "I can't tell anymore," he said huskily, "whether it's my need to feed that calls your power, or your power that calls my need." Eagerly he drank in her power at the curve of her shoulder but this time he actually touched her skin with his lips. He hungrily tasted her flesh and realized that the combination of her Water power and slightly salty skin made him feel as if he was drinking from the ocean. "I love desert girls."

She shivered again and held him closer as his lips trailed over her jaw and toward her lips. She wanted his kiss with a vengeance. If he didn't kiss her soon she thought she would die. His lips covered hers, and the desperation was replaced by pure pleasure. With a little sound of delight, she pressed closer and deepened the kiss, craving his taste as deeply as he craved hers.

His arms slid around her more firmly and he pressed her even closer against his body. Her breasts pressed against his chest but it didn't frighten her this time. The feel of him hard and close made her breasts ache deliciously, and she slowly rubbed against him to savor the feeling.

It was only when she felt his knuckles skim the outside curve of her breast that she became afraid again. The sharp sting of pleasure was like a whiplash, and she jerked back instinctively.

Immediately he gathered her close in a comforting hug. He released her tenderly from the kiss and then nuzzled her softly. "I can't keep my hands to myself," he said, his voice rich with masculine laughter. "You're too beautiful."

It wasn't an apology because one wasn't needed. The compliment was precisely what she required to find her footing, and her body relaxed once more. "Every time I think it can't get stronger, I get proven I'm wrong," she said with a touch of rueful amusement.

"You're not the only one." He reluctantly released her and then took the backpack from her to retrieve the blankets that waited inside. Like anything else made by the Kin, the blankets were the size of bandanas for travel. Once he held it in his hands, the blanket recognized his race and grew immediately to full size.

In a burst of playful energy, he pounced Tariah and tackled her down to the sand. He got them both tangled up in the blanket, which had gotten bigger to accommodate them both, then he began to tickle her without mercy.

She had no compunction about plucking knowledge out of his mind, and she zeroed in on his ribs. Within moments they were both laughing too hard to do anything except collapse on the sand. She snuggled closer against him and he tucked the blanket around them tightly. Their combined power created a protective barrier around their small camp and before long both were able to sleep.

In the middle of the night, however, something awoke Tariah. Dominic realized she was awake only when he felt her leaving his arms. He sat up beside her quickly. "Tariah?" he asked softly. The two moons visible overhead gave just enough light for him to see her face. It was calm and serene like the deepest of pools. It was an odd sight because he could feel the wild surge and snap of her power like the seas.

At first he was unsure what was wrong, and then he realized that he could feel someone else through her. His senses went on full alert and feral anger darkened his eyes. He didn't know who this mysterious person was that was able to connect to his Chronicle, but he would kill them for even brushing her power.

He curled his power and presence around Tariah warningly even as he pulled her into his arms. Her connection to the other person severed, and she gave a sleepy yawn as she cuddled more firmly against Dominic. "Is something wrong?" she asked sleepily.

"No, *ishke*. You were having a dream." He laid down and tucked her protectively under him. He didn't want to share her with even the moons.

"It seemed like a nice dream," she murmured as she snuggled closer. "It felt like I had found a friend."

She fell asleep again moments later, and he was left very puzzled and very wary. He didn't like the idea that someone, anyone, could connect to his Chronicle in anyway. And, even deeper, was niggling fear for her. Prismatic was the home of the Black Magi. If they somehow were able to call to her then there could be far bigger problems on the horizon than just the king. It was a long time before he was able to go back to sleep.

He woke the next morning to discover that Tariah was still tucked in his arms. Locks of hair fell in her face and he ran his eyes over her eagerly. It was as if every time he looked at her she became more beautiful. He bent his head and kissed her softly. It seemed wonderful that he could kiss her as he had wanted to for so long.

She awoke to pure pleasure. He was kissing her and she could feel his power caressing hers at the same time. She pressed upward to return the kiss and reached for him with her power. She could really grow addicted to him, she thought as they slowly parted. She licked her lips, tasted him there, and very nearly kissed him again.

"If you do," he warned huskily, "I might not have enough control to stop." With visible reluctance, he released her and rolled to the side to sit up. As she sat up beside him, he reached out and tangled his fingers in her hair. "When we get to the inn," he said softly, "I'll brush this for you."

She looked at him in surprise. "You want to?"

His smile came slow and devastating and made her pulse flutter wildly. "I suspect it will be much like when you were scratching my neck. Besides, I'll take any excuse to pamper you outrageously." His hands slid down to rest over her stomach. "It'll be practice for when you're pregnant with our children."

Her eyes grew round. "We can have children together?" When he lifted a brow, she said, "But . . . you're a Dragon! You lay eggs!" Horror filled her eyes. "I am *not* laying eggs!"

He began to laugh. "No, no!" He gave her a swift kiss. "Furies and Chronicles are perfectly capable of crossbreeding. Usually, the race of the child is determined by the race of the mother. I'm not going to lie and say you will never potentially carry a Dragon egg. But our doctors are just as equipped to deal with that as they are to handle a Fury who finds herself carrying a Magi."

"They better be," she muttered. She smiled and covered his hands with her own. "I really don't mind whichever it turns out to be. I'm just happy to think I could have children. Like everything else, I believed for a long time that I would never get to experience it."

He grinned. "Dragons are notorious for big families. You'll have plenty of children to experience." He stole a hard kiss. "Just make sure to give me a daughter precisely like you."

"I'll do my best," was the dry response.

Two hours later, as the morning sun was growing stronger, they found themselves approaching the farmlands that marked the outside edges of Prismatic. The workers out in the fields who saw them either didn't care or didn't realize what they were because not a single one said a thing.

Before long the farms became merely houses. Then the houses began to be grouped much more tightly together. And by mid-morning, Dominic and Tariah entered into the city proper. Tariah felt awed. It was built like all other desert cities, but it was *enormous*.

Some buildings were indeed as high as six stories, and the streets were made of stone. People rode all sorts of different mounts to get to where they needed to go, but there were wide sidewalks for pedestrians as well.

Her skin began to crawl as she felt all the eyes that fastened on her. She defensively moved closer to Dominic and held onto his hand. He drew her closer still, more protective than possessive, and swept his gaze over the crowd. Most who felt his gaze immediately stopped staring though whispers still flowed swiftly.

A stone landed in the street directly in front of her feet and shattered. It sprayed sharp pieces everywhere. Several nicked her flesh and drew blood. Dominic snarled softly and looked around. "Who threw that?" he demanded in a growl. "If you fear anyone, it ought to be me." He bared his teeth. "I'll gut the next person who harms her."

The Magi said nothing and hastily went back to their business. The few Kin in attendance were pleased with what they saw. They had been about to step in themselves but it looked as if Dominic had things well in hand. Or claw, as it were.

Tariah's trepidation grew as she spotted one or two members of the Black Magi among the crowd. There were not as many of them as she had expected to see, however. Like the Elite, the regular Black Magi wore heavy white cloaks that covered them from head to toe and on the back was a black chalice. Unlike the Elite, there was no dagger. Oddly, that little difference made her feel a little better.

Prismatic had been split into various sections. Most of the residential area grouped together and most of the commercial grouped together. The various districts were built in a circular shape around the large palace at the very center. It was the largest building of all and some towers stood at an impressive ten stories.

It was through the commercial district that the two Dragoons walked. There were several inns in that district and they wanted to get a room to rest and get washed up before they were called in to meet the king.

The inns metaphorically, if not almost literally, shut their doors in their faces. They had plenty of excuses for their actions because they feared the wrath of the Kin, but it was blindingly obvious that they despised Tariah for being a Chronicle, and Dominic for being her Fury.

While Dominic argued with one of the innkeepers, Tariah walked away to where a bench resided at the edge of a shady park. She felt tired from the soul outward. As she looked around, she had to wonder to herself how long it would be before the mindsets of a thousand years were finally changed.

"May I join you?"

Startled, she looked up. Her surprise didn't fade as she studied the young man standing beside the bench. In fact, it grew stronger. The man could have been her brother. He was of shorter height, around five-six, and he had familiar thick dark auburn hair that clung to the back of his neck. His eyes were silver as well and held a slight twinkle that indicated he would be quick to laugh when he was amused. She could see his shoulders were strong, but she couldn't guess at the rest of his build because the thick cloak he wore obscured him from view.

He was a Black Magi.

As if sensing her trepidation, he said, "I'm not going to hurt you. Please don't think that. There is a vast difference between the Black Magi and the Elite. May I join you?"

She nodded slowly. "Of course." She scooted over on the bench to give him room and watched him intently from under her lashes. She didn't trust him no matter how familiar he seemed to feel to her. She didn't trust any of the Black Magi at all.

"What is your name?" he asked her.

"Tariah Chronis."

His eyes shot to hers in surprise. "Well. That's a surprise." He smiled. "We might be cousins. My name is Morgan Chronis. I'm an Air Magi." He offered a gloved hand but she didn't take it. She simply watched him with eyes that were far too old. His heart wept for her. "Please, Tariah, don't hate me."

"I don't hate you," she said carefully. "I just don't trust you." She turned her gaze toward where Dominic still argued with the innkeeper. "When I was trying to escape Choral, I encountered the Elite. They tried to recruit me. In an effort to find out what I was and who I was really, the leader ripped the wings off a SunKin Faerie who had no crime other than being in love with my Kin partner."

Morgan's face tightened and he cursed softly under his breath. "Son-of-a-bitch, Soh," he muttered. "Is there no length you won't stoop to?" He turned back to her and his eyes burned intently. "The Elite are their own band. They have no affiliation with my Black Magi. They were once a part of us but their . . . ideals changed. What they want goes against everything I have tried so hard to bring to the Black Magi."

"You're the leader?" She looked him over quickly. "But you seem so young."

"I'm twenty-five," he told her. "I started the Black Magi about five years ago." He stood and held a hand out to her. "Please. Come stay with the Black Magi. We will happily give you a place to rest. You and your Fury both. Once you see what the Black Magi stand for, I am sure you will understand everything."

She hesitated and then took his hand to let him draw her to her feet. The minute their fingers connected, she felt a raw surge of power up her arm. He was holding her right hand so he was holding her hand that had her lines. All the way through her lines she felt a surge of power that was neither hers nor Dominic's. It was Morgan's.

Her eyes shot to his in shock. "You're a Chronicle," she whispered.

Chapter Eleven

Morgan's hand tightened on hers for a moment and Tariah fell quiet. She was stunned. She was stunned and she was shaken to her core. She wasn't the only Chronicle that had survived? But *how?*

Dominic, sensing her distress, was quick to hurry over to them. He saw her holding Morgan's hand and gave a soft snarl. He snatched her into his arms and removed her from the other man's reach entirely. "Don't touch her," he ordered in a dangerous growl. A split second later, his nose flared as he realized Morgan didn't smell like a Magi. "What the . . ." Tariah pulled him into her mind to share what she had felt and learned and his eyes shot to Morgan's in shock. "I'll be damned," he murmured.

Morgan smiled. "You're not going to eat me then?"

"Not at the immediate moment."

He gave a quick laugh. "How did I know that would be the answer?" He smiled at Tariah. "Please, come to the sanctuary of the Black Magi. There is so much I would like to talk to you about. And we can easily offer you a room to rest in before you meet the king."

Dominic said nothing. It was Tariah's decision. She was still confused but her trepidation had faded. Somehow, knowing Morgan was also a Chronicle made her trust him. "Alright. Thank you, Morgan." She gave Dominic a dry look and wiggled her feet where they dangled over the ground. "Are you going to carry me, or am I walking?"

He sighed and put her on her feet but kept her close beside him. He was no less startled. If Morgan was a Chronicle and he was alive, then that meant that his Fury had to be out there. But Dominic was sure that if the Fury was on the isle, the Dragons would have known another had survived. Where was Morgan's Fury?

The sanctuary of the Black Magi was a three-story building in the corner of the commercial district. A couple of other Black Magi tended to the landscape in front of the building, and they called friendly greetings to Morgan and Tariah alike. Tariah glanced at Dominic but he shook his head. Neither Black Magi was a Chronicle.

They had barely walked in the door when a girl with bright red hair came running toward them. She was no higher than Tariah's collar and looked no older than ten. She launched herself from several feet away and attached herself to Morgan's arm. "Morgan!" she wailed. "Roman took my doll!"

"I did not!" came a voice from a boy as Morgan hugged the girl. "Jayda did it!"

"I did not neither!" A girl with seagreen hair in a tangle of curls around her face stood in the doorway to an inner room with a look of indignation on her face. "Kelsey left her doll at the park." She diverted as she saw Tariah and Dominic. "Hi!"

Kelsey peered around Morgan at the newcomers. "You're pretty," she told Tariah. "You have lines on your body. Why? What do they do?" She held her arms out to Tariah demandingly. "You hug me too."

Tariah automatically bent and hugged the child when she hurried over. Ten-year-olds were notorious for their blend of clinging to childhood and beginning the first steps to first puberty and maturity. A feeling not unlike when she had taken Morgan's hand seemed to ripple through her lines, though, as she hugged Kelsey. Her eyes widened slowly with shock as she stared at the child she held. "She's . . ."

"A Chronicle child." Morgan nodded. "As are the other three terrors." He turned with a smile and called, "C.J.! Roman! Come in here!" He scooped up Jayda as she came over to hug his hip. "You're holding Kelsey. We call her Soot because she's always getting into it. This is Jayda."

Tariah spotted a smudge of soot on Kelsey's face and had to smile. "So I see." She rubbed it away gently. "Bet you'll be a Fire element, huh?"

"It's pretty." Kelsey was eyeing Dominic. "You're a Dragon."

"I am." He blew a ring of smoke at her and made her giggle.

Two boys came hurrying into the room and skidded to stops in front of Morgan. One was a blond with clear blue eyes. The other had ash brown hair and black eyes. Both were amongst the most adorable kids Tariah had ever seen. The blond was, however, her instant favorite. On one look at how he was dressed she knew he was from the desert.

"This is Roman," Morgan said, ruffling Roman's blond hair. He rubbed his hand over the other boy's ashy hair. "And this is C.J. He has expressly forbidden his parents to tell us what the C and J stand for."

C.J. wrinkled up his nose. "It's silly."

Tariah smiled. "Well, I won't ask then." She drew her thumb over her cheek and nose as a sign of greeting. "I'm Tariah Chronis."

"Are you Morgan's sister?" Jayda asked. "You look a lot alike and you have the same name."

"We might be cousins. We don't know." Morgan tossed Jayda in the air, then set her down. "But she's like a big sister to you just as I'm like your brother."

Kelsey leaned back to look at Morgan. "That's because she has lines like yours, right?"

"That's right."

Roman walked over to look up at Dominic. "You're a Dragon?"

"Yes I am." Dominic crouched down until they were closer in height. "My name is Dominic Whisperer. Tariah and I are Dragoons." He gently ruffled Roman's hair. "An easier way to explain for now is to say that we're Linked."

"Oh!" Roman grinned and showed he was missing a front tooth. "That's really nice!" His ears perked up suddenly as he heard a bell ringing. "Lunch is ready!"

Tariah hastily let Kelsey go as all four children went tearing out of the room, shouting over one another to be heard. She didn't need to touch the other three to know they would be the same as Kelsey. "They're Chronicle children," she whispered.

"Yes." Morgan gestured down another hall and the two Dragoons followed him. "They are the whole reason the Black Magi exist. Kelsey was the first I found. It was an accident. It stunned me, to be truthful. I got to know her parents and realized they would love her more than they feared her."

"So you decided to form a place where she could grow safely," Dominic said quietly as he sat down on one of the chairs in the study. When Tariah sat beside him, he took her hand and held it to his heart to comfort her. "Under the guise of being Master Magi."

"Yes." Morgan removed his gloves and his cloak. The light from the lamps in the room washed over his arms, bared by his short-sleeved tunic. The golden lines flowed over the entirety of his arms and hands and then disappeared somewhere beneath his tunic. The design and pattern was completely unique and looked nothing like Tariah's.

He sat down heavily with a sigh and raked his hands through his hair. "Only four. I've met at least ten over the last five years." A haunted look filled his eyes. "The other six . . . their parents could never accept them. I had to walk away else I risk those I had already saved."

"Your parents?" Tariah asked softly.

"I don't know." Morgan closed his eyes. "I had to leave my town . . . rather swiftly." He looked at her and his eyes darkened. "I'm so sorry, Tariah. I heard about your parents and the MoonKin. I wish I had gone to Symphony and found you. I just didn't have the time to get to Choral."

"Maybe it's better this way," Dominic said. "Maybe the king will actually listen to us and see that Tariah is not the monster of every Magi's nightmares. If he can accept her, then maybe eventually the people can as well." He looked at Tariah. "I'll let you stay here with Morgan and I'll go speak with the Militia to let them know we're here."

"They probably know," she countered dryly. She smiled and leaned up to kiss him softly. "Go. I'll be safe here."

"I know." He skimmed his thumb down the lines on her face and then got to his feet and walked out of the room.

Morgan watched him go and then cleared his throat. He recognized the signs of a very frustrated male. "So. Still in second puberty?"

Tariah glared at him. "Shut up, Morgan." He grinned at her and she relented with a sigh. "It's been a learning experience in more ways than one. Assure me that it will get easier, please. I'm going through this whole ordeal in a matter of weeks rather than a year!"

He thought about that. "Well, I don't know that it gets *easier*, but you'll be better able to deal with it. You have Dominic." Sadness clouded his face as he got to his feet and walked over to look out the window. From this height, no one on the street could see them. "My Fury . . . I feel her." He lifted a hand and pressed his fist to his heart. "It hurts so badly," he managed to say. "But my lines won't tell me where to go. I can only stay here."

She got to her feet and walked over to stand beside him. "She's out there," she said softly. "From what Dominic told me, Furies always know when their Chronicle is alive or dead. She must know you're alive, Morgan. Surely she is seeking you too."

"What's it like?" he murmured. "To be with your Fury?"

She thought about it before saying simply, "It's the greatest thing in the world."

"I thought it might be." He drew a long breath. "Well. Let's find you a room to rest in." He smiled. "When Jayda heard that there was another Chronicle alive, she said that we ought to have a room ready for you because you'd come here."

"Why'd she think that?"

He laughed. "Her words were 'Because no one else will let her stay anywhere. Adults are jerks.' She's quite astute, that child."

She smiled. "She's not the first child I've heard make a statement similar. Perhaps there is something about being a child that allows you to see clearly. Or maybe they simply haven't had a chance to be instilled with all the rules that grown-ups abide by."

"I like to think of it as the hope for the Magi race. Now, come along with me." He put his cloak and gloves back on and then led the way down the hall toward the stairs to the next floor. "How old are you, Tariah?"

"Twenty. I'll be twenty-one in a few months." She linked her hands behind her back as they walked. "Where are you from, Morgan? You seem quite comfortable in a thick cloak in a desert. I'd be smothering. Or wanting to rip the cloak off."

He laughed. "I'm from Glacia. You'd likely freeze up there, desert girl. Take the coldest temperature of the desert at night and make it twice as cold. That's the warmest day where I'm from." He saw the horrified look on her face and began laughing harder. "Just snuggle your Fury and you'll be just fine."

She shuddered. "No disrespect, Morgan, but I'd just as soon never go there." Her ears and nose both perked up as she heard and smelled the sound and scent of hot water. It was coming from the room Morgan had stopped in front of. "I can have a bath?" she asked eagerly.

"I thought of it!" Kelsey was sitting on the stairs up to the third floor and happily eating a bowl of mashed fruit and syrup. "Morgan's a *boy*. And boys don't know anything about girls!"

Morgan quirked a brow. "I pity her Fury," he murmured under his breath.

Tariah elbowed him. "Be nice," she scolded. She walked over and knelt down to be eye level with Kelsey. "Are you going to boss your Fury around, Kelsey?" When the little girl nodded enthusiastically, Tariah stole the spoon and scooped up a bite of fruit. "You'll have to teach me some pointers. I don't boss my Fury around enough."

"Probably," Morgan said dryly, "because you're at a disadvantage right now. Once you finish puberty you'll have all sorts of ways of keeping him at your mercy."

Tariah fluttered her lashes at him as she sashayed past him into the room. "You'll get yours, wait and see." She turned around and smiled. "Morgan . . . thank you." She held her right hand out to him and he took it tightly with his own. "After Dominic returns, will you tell us about the Elite? I have so many questions."

"I will tell you whatever I can." He squeezed her hand tightly and then stepped back as she shut the door. With a sigh, he walked over to where Kelsey sat. Years of practice made it easy to hide the fierce and painful longing that seemed to well up inside him endlessly. He wasn't the only Chronicle anymore . . . but he was still alone.

Tariah shut the door firmly and looked at the large tub filled with hot water. There were blankets and towels stacked beside it along with an assortment of soaps and perfumes. She had never before understood the urge people had for primping or pampering themselves but as she stood there and contemplated Dominic's reaction, she found the idea irresistible.

She hurried over to the tub and tested the water. It wasn't quite hot enough to suit her so she used her powers and increased the temperature. She swiftly stripped off her clothes and stepped into the tub. She winced as the hot water stung the cuts on her legs from the flying rock but she determinedly ignored it as she sat down.

With a contented sigh, she closed her eyes and rested her head against the rim of the tub. Once she had rested a little, she was going to wash her hair and skin thoroughly for the first time in a few days. Without intending to, however, she slipped asleep.

When Dominic returned to the sanctuary, he was not entirely happy. The Militia had been very rude in their opinions of Tariah. It seemed they held a grudge for her killing one of their soldiers even though she had acted in self-defense. Dominic hadn't known about the incident. If it came from the wild jumble of memories inside her mind, he suspected that she didn't remember it herself.

Moreover, according to the Militia, the king was not ready to see them today. He wanted them to come back tomorrow around mid-morning so that he had enough time to decide what he wanted to say. Dominic thought that was fair enough but had to wonder what the king was going to be saying that took that much thought.

"Do you fly?" The question came from C.J. as he attached himself to Dominic's ankle. "How fast?"

Dominic kept on walking though the boy was wrapped around his ankle. "Yes I do, and when I have Tariah, I can cross Spectrum in a day."

C.J.'s eyes widened. "Amazing," he breathed.

Dominic spotted Morgan coming down the stairs. "Morgan. Get your ankle biter off me." He held up his leg. "It's doing an impression of a leech."

Morgan smiled and plucked C.J. off Dominic's leg. He tossed the little boy over his shoulder and made him give a shriek of laughter. "Tariah is upstairs," Morgan told Dominic. "Kelsey's mother had a bath waiting for her, and I have no doubt she's probably bathing right now." He covered a grin as Dominic went for the stairs far faster than was polite. "Have fun," he called cheerfully. "And you, ankle biter," he added to C.J. as he flipped him right-side up, "need to finish your dinner."

"Rar!"

Dominic took the stairs two at a time, eagerly looking forward to catching Tariah naked and wet. But even steps before he reached the door, he knew she was asleep. Her power felt still and quiet inside him. His eyes softened and his heart filled with tenderness. He gently eased the door open and slipped inside.

She was in the tub, yes, but she was sound asleep with her head resting against the edge. With a sigh, he shut and locked the door and then walked over to crouch beside her. He tenderly brushed her bangs out of her eyes. She seemed heartbreakingly young. So much rode on her shoulders, and she was barreling through second puberty faster than a Dragon could fly. It was as if she had never once been granted a childhood.

He straightened and removed his cloak and vest. He knelt beside her again and leaned over to kiss her softly. She began to wake slowly, and her soft sigh tasted as sweet as her power when it was breathed into his kiss. "I'm back," he murmured huskily.

Her eyes opened slightly. "I was going to get cleaned up and surprise you," she said softly. His hand cupped her cheek and she rubbed against his fingers. "I was going to wear perfume."

"You don't need it." He lifted her wrist to his lips. "I like how you smell all the time." He was counting his lucky stars, though. Finding her clean and perfumed just for him might have been more than his control could handle.

She contemplated the imagery in his mind. "A wolf falling on a bone? That's not flattering."

"But accurate." He smiled as she straightened up. "Besides, I promised to pamper you. Hand over the soap and I'll scrub your hair for you." He waited while she poured water over her hair to wet it, then took the soap she offered and began to lather up her hair. He firmly rubbed away the knots of tension he found. They were manifestations of her emotional stress, and he refused to let them linger.

She nearly whimpered. As it was, she had to brace her feet against the other end of the tub to keep from sliding down in a boneless heap. She had never felt anything as wonderful as the feel of his hands rubbing her head and the back of her neck when he found more knots. "If this is how it feels to scratch your neck," she said faintly, "then you're welcome." It only mildly startled her to realize it felt almost as good as his kiss.

He chuckled softly. "I told you. I find everything about you pleasurable. It's no surprise that it is the same for you toward me." He waited until she had rinsed her hair free of soap before beginning to scrub her back. At the same time, he rubbed away all the knots he found. "Where were these hiding?"

She muttered something wordless and arched into his touch like a cat asking to be stroked. His body hardened in a wild rush of desire. Carefully he kept his hands neutral. It was the hardest thing he had ever done. For the moment, she was not connecting this feeling with the ones that were inspired by the passion between them. He could hardly wait to teach her the two could be combined.

She felt like a puddle of water herself as he rinsed her off and lifted her out of the tub. All the muscles in her back and neck had turned to mush. As she was set gently on her feet, she picked up a towel and wrapped her hair in it snugly. She swathed a blanket around her body, then made a startled sound as he scooped her up. "What're you doing?"

He carried her over to the bed and set her down on her stomach. "Getting rid of the rest of those knots. But I expect you to return the favor eventually."

The idea intrigued her. She rested her head on her arms and relaxed as she felt him tug aside the blanket so he could reach her legs. At first, the knots he rubbed away were painful. She endured it. She knew full well that it wouldn't get better unless she did. "What did the Militia say?" she asked.

He found the nicks on her legs and stopped rubbing long enough to apply some salve and bandages. "The king will see us tomorrow. It seems that he has to decide what to say."

She grumbled something uncomplimentary under her breath. "You'd think he would have had enough time to decide that already."

He smiled. "My thoughts exactly." Pleased because he could now feel the relaxation in her body, he sat on the bed and lifted her up onto his lap to cuddle. He nuzzled his nose into her hair softly. "You like Morgan?"

She snuggled closer and rested a hand over his heart. "I do. It's like suddenly finding a member of my family. I just wish I could find his Fury for him. He hid it well, but I could see how terribly it hurts him." Suddenly she straightened. "Wait! Daylar!"

Dominic dodged quickly before her head hit him in the chin and lifted a brow as she scooted off his lap. "Daylar? Are you going to try to write to him?"

She studied her power internally. "I'm going to definitely try. Maybe he can put word out through the other Kin and they can find Morgan's Fury like they found you." She found the information on how to write the letter inside her as if it had been placed there, and she suspected it had come with her Kinship. "You don't think she's on the Isle."

"She couldn't be." He watched curiously as she began to write in the air. It was in the language of the Magi and easy to read. What fascinated him was that he could see that she wasn't writing with her power. She was writing with Daylar's energy. It made Dominic smile. Her handwriting was as unique as her lines, and nearly just as beautiful. "If she was on the Isle, we'd have known Morgan was alive."

She added that information to her letter and then asked, "Maybe she left the Isle. In your memory, how many Furies left the isle that never returned? Specifically the females of a Soil element."

He thought about that. "I can think of three in my memory. I've seen one of them in recent years though. Another . . . well, we lost her two years ago. The last . . . it might be her. Tell Daylar to try and locate the Fury known as Jazz Eaglewind."

"How do you write that?" she asked.

He leaned over and caught her hand. He traced the characters in the air before bringing her hand to his lips and kissing her palm. The symbol there seemed to tickle his lips. "Did you ask if Morgan has this on his hand?"

"No, I didn't think to." She pulled her hand free and finished the letter. "But if he does, then I suppose we really are cousins in some way." She smiled. "It's a nice feeling to have family again. I mean, I only really need you, but anything extra is like . . . like a good dessert on top of a really good dinner."

"You humble me." He pulled her back onto his lap and buried his nose against her shoulder. "You don't need perfume," he murmured huskily. "I already love how you smell. Like water in the desert. There's nothing more seductive." He turned and lowered her to the bed and trapped her against the pale green blankets. "*Ishke.*" His voice had grown thick with emotion. "I think the word was made for you."

She wrapped her arms around his shoulders and held onto him fiercely. She had no words to describe how she felt. She could only show it. She could only wrap her power and mind around him and let him feel how terribly she loved him and needed him.

He trembled as he felt the searing wave of her emotions. That third part, the desire she had never felt before, was growing stronger. It was nearly as strong as the emotions he felt inside himself. He knew that soon there would be no more barriers between them. Soon he would be able to know her as intimately as he craved.

Someone knocked lightly on the door. "Tariah? Dominic?" The voice was unfamiliar and belonged to a woman. "Morgan asks that you join him when you're ready."

As the footsteps faded away, Dominic very reluctantly released Tariah. "I wish I could begrudge him that. But I can't." He sat up and watched as she got to her feet and crossed over to where her clothes had been tossed. He smiled. "I'll have to get you into some clothes of the valley. You might like them."

"Really?" She pulled on her bikini and looked at him curiously. "What are they like?"

"Slightly covering, but they tend to be loose and light to accommodate the winds around there." He stood and pulled his vest on once again. Since they were indoors, he didn't bother with the cloak.

When she was dressed as well, he pulled her close to escort her out of the room. C.J. and Jayda were chasing each other up and down the halls and nearly ran both Dragoons over. "Watch where you're running," Tariah scolded.

"Yes'm!" Giggling, the kids kept on running.

Downstairs, Morgan was reading a letter when they walked in. He looked up with a smile and set the letter aside. "You look like you're feeling better, Tariah." He gestured to the couch across from where he sat. "Please sit down. I would like to tell you about the Elite."

Dominic sat down and pulled Tariah down onto his lap. He knew she needed the anchor to keep herself grounded. Her memories of what had happened to Daylar were still very vivid in her mind, and they were more horrifying than ever now that he was her brother. "I assume they were part of the Black Magi at some time," he said.

"Yes." Morgan's hands clenched into fists. "Soh's son was a Chronicle and was killed for it. He wanted to join me to stop it from happening to others . . . or so I believed." He closed his eyes. "I found out shortly that Soh wanted revenge."

Tariah took a quick breath as everything made sense. "He wants to erase the Magi from the world. But . . . that could *destroy* the world!"

He looked at her sadly. "Soh firmly believes that Chronicles will take the place of Magi. Nothing I said would convince him otherwise. He drew other fanatics to his side and they left the Black Magi entirely to form their own group of Elite. I honestly don't think half the Magi that are in the Elite understand what Soh's true intent is."

"Is that why he wanted Tariah?" Dominic asked quietly. "Because he thinks she should hate the Magi as much as he does?"

"I think so." Morgan's knuckles were nearly white. "I have to be careful," he said faintly. "Soh . . . if he could come back and take these children away, he would. They're so young . . . he might actually be able to brainwash them over to his side. Especially if he arranged for their parents to die at Magi hands."

"I want to think he wouldn't do that," Tariah whispered, "but I know he would. After what he did to Daylar . . ." She drew a long breath and her intense silver eyes met Morgan's identical ones. "I'll do whatever I can to help you, Morgan. I won't let these children be harmed. When I get to the Isle, I'll tell them all about the children and where they are. The Furies can come find them and take them to safety." She found a smile. "Even if they do have to go through what Dominic is right now."

"It's certainly been an . . . interesting test of my self-control," her Fury muttered.

Morgan pulled off his glove and held out his right hand to Tariah. Sure enough, there, etched into the center of his palm, was the symbol 'chron.' She took his hand with hers and their fingers laced together tightly. "I wouldn't join the Elite," she said, "but you could consider me an honorary member of the Black Magi, if you like."

"Only honorary," he said softly, "because neither of us wants any connection to be made between you and these children. But, Tariah, I want you to know something. If anything should ever happen to me, you are the only person I trust to protect these children."

"You have my word," she said just as softly. "I'll do whatever I can."

Chapter Twelve

Tariah awoke to conflicting signals through her body. On one hand, her body was sending out messages of pure pleasure. Her skin felt more sensitive than ever and her breasts ached and throbbed. On the other hand, her body was as confused as her mind and unsure of where the messages came from.

"Now you're awake," Dominic's voice murmured huskily in her ear. He was propped up on an elbow behind her, his body heat curling around her even as his free arm did. He bent his head and trailed soft little kisses over her ear. "I was beginning to think you would oversleep."

She shivered softly. Ears were sensitive? "I don't think that's a worry now." The confusion had faded. His hand was resting just under her breasts and her every breath caused his knuckles to skim against her resilient flesh. She still wore her bikini, but for a moment she wished that she wasn't wearing it at all.

His breath hitched as he caught the thought. He gently turned her onto her back and leaned in close. "Do you trust me?" he asked thickly. His fingers trembled lightly as he drew them up over the outside curve of her breast.

"How can you ask me that?" She lifted her hands and smoothed her palms over the skin of his chest. The lines etched there tingled her skin. "I always trust you." She knew what he was really asking and looked inside herself for the answer. Her lashes lowered slightly. "Touch me. I want to know what it's like."

He held his breath as he slowly covered her breast with his hand. She was soft and fragrant, and her body was perfectly formed for his hands. He gently kneaded her flesh while watching her eyes and tangling his emotions to hers. He felt her first flicker of shock and then he felt the wave of pleasure that followed. As he felt her nipple tighten against his palm, his breath was released in a soft sigh of relief. "Tell me if I scare you," he murmured.

She trembled and arched to press herself more firmly against his touch. Fear was the last thing on her mind. Her lips were tingling, begging for his kiss. He sensed it and lowered his head to kiss her deeply. His tongue curled around hers with the familiarity of a lover.

With a little purr of delight, she slid her hands up into his hair to hold him closer. She loved the way he kissed her and the way it made her feel. Her entire body ached, and she pressed closer instinctively. She knew, somehow, that he could make it stop.

He released her lips and lifted himself enough to watch her face. He began to slowly untie the little knot at the front of her bikini top that held the cups together. Because she had been wearing it to sleep in, the knot was larger and not as tight because she didn't need the support. It opened easily for him.

As he tugged the cups apart to leave her half-naked in his arms, she felt a moment of nerves. They faded immediately as she saw the look in his eyes. It was a look she had always seen in his eyes when he looked at her, but for the first time she recognized it and understood it. She thrilled to it. "You want to touch me?"

"How can you ask that?" he said thickly, returning her words to her. "I've wanted to touch you since I laid eyes on you. Since I felt you were born. Since I was hatched and felt that there was something inside me missing."

His fingers slid up and cupped her naked breast warmly. Her entire body jerked slightly and her eyes widened. A faint blush stained her cheeks. He was still touching her emotions and felt savage triumph as he realized the reactions stemmed from pure desire. He hadn't thought his own emotions could possibly get stronger, but as he caressed her satin skin, he realized he was wrong.

Unable to resist the lure, he skimmed his thumb over her taut nipple. She took a sharp breath and her silver eyes darkened to the color of storm clouds. Encouraged, he slowly caressed her, memorizing the weight and feel of her. The temptation was too powerful to resist, and he lowered his head to press his lips to her rapid heartbeat.

She shivered and held onto him tighter. She felt his lips suddenly close over her nipple, and the pleasure was shockingly more powerful. It streaked through her body and made a strange ache bloom between her legs. Suddenly afraid again, she jerked away and rolled onto her side. She wrapped her arms around herself protectively.

He immediately gathered her close and cuddled her tightly. His hand rested on her stomach softly. "I'm sorry." His voice was tender. "I couldn't help myself." He ran his hands soothingly over her beautiful lines, careful to keep his touch neutral and not alarming.

"I wish I could talk to Sparkle," she said on a sigh. "She's been through second puberty. She could hopefully explain what is going to happen next so it doesn't frighten me so much!" She looked at him over her shoulder. "I'm not afraid of *you*, Dominic. I promise. It's my body that frightens me. It's like I don't know it anymore."

"I know, *ishke*." He nuzzled her shoulder softly. "It's no less scary for men." His lips curved. "You might even say it's a little scarier. We can't always hide our bodies' reactions."

Since she could feel him pressed entirely along her back, she could clearly feel the proof of his desire pressed against her bottom. It made her feel better and she smiled. "I've often thought I was glad to be a girl. I don't grow hair on my face that I need to trim away."

He skimmed a finger down her cheek. "I will concur that I am quite glad you are a girl as well." Less girl and more woman now, though. An inner certainty told him it would not be long before she was ready to take the final step to adulthood. Knowing that he would be the one to help her was one of the more incredible feelings he had ever had. He had always thought it was a beautiful development, but in her it was even more so.

He reluctantly let her go as she slipped out of his arms. With a sigh, he sat up and got out of bed to find his vest and boots. He had to smile. He supposed the desert dwellers had it much easier for changing clothes since they wore so few. He eyed Tariah as she pulled her shorts on. There were some distinct benefits for non-dwellers too.

Once they were both dressed, they headed downstairs to the first floor. Jayda spotted them from the doorway to what looked like a kitchen and ran over to take their hands with hers. "Good morning!" she said cheerfully. "We made breakfast!"

"We as in . . .?"

"Jayda and I," a man said from the doorway. His hair was the same rich seagreen as Jayda's, and he wore the familiar heavy cloak of the Black Magi. "My name is Eli Lakemore. Jayda is my daughter." He drew his thumb over his cheek and nose. "I am an Air Magi. I'm honored to meet you, Dragoons."

Tariah returned the gesture and Dominic gave a slight bow. With a smile, Tariah smoothed a hand down Jayda's hair. How odd that she had to be far from her birthplace to find a place that felt like home. "What's for breakfast?"

Breakfast was fresh fruit and a bread and rice pudding covered in cream. It reminded Tariah of her childhood and of the days when things had been much easier. It still hurt to even think of her parents and Maxim. Their only flaw had been loving her, and they had died for it.

Dominic gently cupped the back of her neck and drew her close for a soft kiss. "If I had found you sooner," he said softly, "I'd have taken you away before any of this ever happened."

"I know." She sighed and pushed her bowl away. She was more than full. Because she didn't know how hot it was going to get that day, she began to expertly twist and tuck her hair up into a neat coil on top of her head. Her stomach fluttered with desire as she saw the look in her lover's eyes and remembered how it had felt to take her hair down for him. "Don't stare at me," she whispered. "It makes it hard to breathe."

"Get used to it, dear," Jayda's mother said as she went past. "It will never stop. Eli still takes my breath and we've known each other since before second puberty. We've been Linked together for nearly fifteen years."

"They're *always* kissing," Jayda said.

"That's because it's fun." Dominic caught her up and gave her a smacking kiss on the cheek. "See?"

She giggled and hugged him tightly. "You're silly." As she was put back down on her feet, she heard a knock on the front door. "I'll get it!"

"No, I will!" Kelsey shouted. "I'll get there first!"

A few moments later, Jayda was back in the doorway, her face solemn. "Tariah, the Militia is here. They want to take you to the king." Her lower lip trembled. "Are you going to get in trouble?"

"I'm hoping to get out of it." Tariah held onto Dominic's hand tightly as they left the kitchen and headed toward the front door. Several Militia soldiers were indeed standing there, and one of them was the captain who had gone to Symphony. Her stomach churned.

None of the soldiers said anything as they stepped back to let the two Dragoons out of the building. The silence remained as they walked down the road to where there was a cart waiting to carry them to the castle.

There was barely enough room on the cart for all of them but neither Tariah nor Dominic complained. They just sat as close together as they could, and Dominic kept an arm around Tariah's waist to keep her from bouncing out of the cart as they went down the road.

The morning sun was very vivid on Tariah's lines and revealed the wing mark on her shoulder plainly. Because of it, there was no one who wanted to risk saying a word. There were enough Kin in the city that things could become very dicey. Pacifists or not, the Kin protected their own.

The castle was in the center of the city and nearly the size of a district all on its own. Tariah was astonished by the sheer depth of the building because she had never seen anything like it. Even Dominic was impressed and he had seen many large and beautiful buildings on the Isle.

The captain and two other soldiers took over the escort as they led the Dragoons into the castle proper. The courtyard was busy at that time of morning as Militia soldiers trained and servants maintained the land. All of them eyed Tariah with intense scrutiny, and Dominic bristled as he saw more than one derogatory look. Warningly, he bared his teeth.

The throne room looked like the definition of decadence. Everything was made of ivory and bronze, and there were even several silver statues sitting around. The floor was covered with tile so polished that it showed the perfect reflection of all who walked across it. The ceiling was well over their heads and chandeliers dripped toward the ground with plenty of light.

At the end of the throne room sat an ivory and bronze throne, and on it sat the king of the Magi. Tariah compared the pomp and haughtiness of the king to the relaxed and open manner of the Kin and found the Magi to be lacking. Dominic compared the king to the loud and argumentative, but always willing to listen, Dragon Elders, and came to a similar conclusion.

When they were several feet before the king, Tariah drew her thumb across her cheek and nose, and Dominic bowed. The gestures of respect were more automatic than deeply felt. After a moment where the king didn't speak, Tariah realized he was waiting for her to say something. "I am Tariah Chronis," she said. With more ease than she had imagined, she continued, "I am a Water Chronicle. I am also a Dragoon. This is my Fury, Dominic Whisperer."

"A Fire Fury," Dominic concurred. "Dragon Lord, fourth tier." He squeezed her hand in a promise to explain later more about the tiers among the Dragons.

The king leaned forward on his throne and studied them intently. His eyes lingered on Tariah's lines, as if trying to assure himself that they were real. "Is it true?" he asked. "Is there gold in your lines and this is why the metal is so rare?"

She stared at him. "Of course not. My lines are made of my Fury's power, but what flows in them is my own. There are no . . . stones or metals in my body. I am the same as anyone else in that."

The king nodded slightly. "And what about the rumor that having sex with a Chronicle will give you power?"

Dominic's face darkened. "I suggest you not mention that again. Several of your *upstanding* citizens tried to assault my mate over that ridiculous story. If that rumor were true, you Magi wouldn't have been so quick to kill off Chronicles."

Tariah's stomach was beginning to churn. "Your majesty," she said, "I have been running for my life. I have been forced to watch someone I loved be killed. And all of it was because I was born a Chronicle. I was able to walk among the Magi disguised as a Master Magi. No one knew the difference. Surely that should tell you something."

"Chronicles are said to seek the destruction of the world," the king said curtly.

"I seek only to be able to live as I wish," she retorted. "I am bound to follow the map within my lines. At the end of my map will be the Isle of Dragons. I would sooner stay there or visit Kindred where my honorary family is. The Magi wouldn't have to worry about me if they would simply leave me alone."

"I am through with talking to a pet!" the king snapped. He looked at Dominic. "Why do you not curb her tongue, as you should?" When his response was a narrow-eyed look, the king scoffed. "Do not play the fool. Everyone knows that Furies are little more than owners of Chronicles. Chronicles only exist to feed Furies. What does she feed you? Blood?"

"Tariah is my partner," Dominic said carefully. His temper was on shaky ground and only the knowledge that they could be killed kept him in line. "She is, to use a Magi term, my Linked mate. We are equals. The world made us as two halves of a whole." He glanced down at Tariah. "I've heard enough. We're leaving."

She kept her trembling inside where it could not show. "Gladly." She did not worry about insulting the king. He didn't dare harm her for fear that he would bring down the wrath of the Kin and Dragons alike.

"I did not say you could leave!" the king snapped. "Bar the doors!" he ordered the Militia. As they leapt to do his bidding, he narrowed his eyes toward Tariah. "I have no desire to have you wandering across the landscape. You will remain here until I can have the Kin fetch you. Chronicles will destroy the world."

Though Dominic was the one with the hot temper, it was Tariah that lost hers first. Her hands clenched into fists at her sides as she shouted, "I don't want to destroy anything! If anyone is guilty of destroying anything, it's the Magi! You destroyed the Chronicles! You tried to destroy the Kin, and in the process you destroyed a lot of the world! Now you're trying to destroy whatever freedom I've managed to fight for! If you'd get to know Chronicles, you wouldn't have to fear them! You're nothing but jealous bigots!"

"Watch your mouth!" the captain snapped as he came toward them swiftly.

Dominic's eyes flashed red and he hurled the captain away with Telekinesis. That same power caused a force that prevented anyone from drawing near. He felt Tariah opening her mind in an unusual way, but he didn't know what she was about to do. He got his answer as he saw her eyes turn blue and her mind seemed to sharpen.

The king's eyes slowly turned a matching blue and his expression stilled. "Release them," he said, and his voice was monotone. "Let them leave."

The Militia stared in disbelief at him, then one soldier saw the matching eye colors of the king and Tariah. "She's controlling him!"

"And if you do not let us go," Tariah said quietly, her voice as cool as a midnight ocean, "I will shatter his mind."

No one dared call her bluff when they did not know just what a Chronicle was capable of doing. The soldiers backed away from the doors and left plenty of room for them to leave. Dominic lifted Tariah into his arms as he backed toward the door. As soon as they were there, she released the king from her hold and he turned and ran out of the palace.

There was silence for a moment and then the Militia lunged for the door to stop them. "Stop!" the king commanded shakily. When they all turned to stare at him, he lowered his head into his hands. "Let them be," he said quietly. "When she took control . . . I touched her mind. She is not a monster." He lifted his head and stared at his hands, stricken. "Dear god," he whispered. "What have we Magi done?" He got to his feet. "I must think on this. In the meantime, do not harm Tariah Chronis or Dominic Whisperer! They have not earned it."

Outside the palace, Dominic didn't put Tariah down as he hurried toward the street. To his surprise, Morgan was standing on the side next to a cart. Dominic put Tariah down as they approached and Morgan said, "It didn't go well."

"No, not really." Tariah shivered even though it was a normal desert day. "I can't stay here," she said fretfully. "I feel like everyone is staring at me!"

"I didn't think you could." He gestured to the cart. "This is for you. There's a pack of supplies in the back. It should be enough for a few days if you want to avoid cities altogether. If not, you might consider Crystalia to the northwest. It's an oasis town and not very big. If you leave now, you could make it there by this evening."

She impulsively reached out and hugged him tightly. "Thank you, Morgan," she said. "I hope you find your Fury soon," she whispered. It was the greatest thing she could wish for him and they all knew it.

He returned the hug and then let her go. "Be safe, Tariah."

Dominic helped her up into the cart and climbed up beside her. "Good luck, Morgan," he said, then he flicked the reigns and the finned beast tied to the cart began to walk and pull them down the road.

Tariah studied the beast. She knew of them, naturally, but she had never seen one up close. They were called findrals and they were used for riding and pulling carts because they were fast and strong and they could both walk on land and also swim in water. They looked like a very big dog but with a face like a bird and instead of wings they had fins.

This one seemed especially spry and she suspected Morgan had gotten it specifically for them. The idea made her eyes burn with tears. In such a short time, he had become very dear to her. Cousins? Inside her heart, she felt like she had found a missing twin brother.

"I'm sorry, Tariah," Dominic said quietly as they continued down the road. When she glanced at him, he explained, "For not defending you better. I should have known it was a bad idea."

She shook her head. "No, don't be sorry." She turned on the seat to look into the cart behind them and spotted a heavy cloak. Though she knew it would make her warm, she pulled it on with the hood tugged down over her head. Right then she didn't want to deal with the stares or the rumors.

He kept his eyes on their surroundings until they were beyond the city. It wasn't until they were past the farmlands and there were no more Magi around that he actually relaxed. He immediately lifted his free hand and tugged her hood down. "We're safe now, *ishke.*"

"I know." She leaned against his shoulder with a sigh. "I need to be distracted. Tell me about the tiers. Is it a hierarchy of sorts?"

"So to speak. The tiers are how we define the strength of a Dragon Lord. A fourth tier is technically only a Fury, but there have been other Lords who are that strong. It's defined by how well and how long you can hold a form other than your own." He smiled. "First tier Dragon Lords have a horrible time with things. They could be in the middle of a city and suddenly turn back to normal."

She frowned thoughtfully. "Elder Juniper said Dragon Lords can take a Kin form."

"Sure. I once ran around as a SunKin Faerie."

She thought of her big Fury as a small Faerie and found it amusing. "I'd like to see that some time." She tilted her head. "So . . . do you think it might be possible for us to disguise ourselves as Kin? Then we wouldn't need to worry about anyone refusing us service."

"It's a good idea," he decided. "It'll take a drain on my majiks though." He shot her a quick grin of anticipation. "But I don't see a problem with replenishing it. It's been too long since I kissed you last."

She smiled. "It's more addicting than I thought it might be. I keep catching myself staring at you and hoping you'll kiss me."

"Hope louder," was the murmur in response. "I hadn't noticed. If I had, you would have gotten your kisses as wished." He felt the warm caress of her thoughts, and he sent her a heated look. "Not while I'm driving. The findral might run away with us."

She smiled and cuddled closer against his arm. She was contented with the knowledge that he wanted her. His power flowed around her and merged with hers to make once more that wonderful feeling of something that would never end. A sudden thought occurred to her and she sat upright. "Wait! Dragons are immortal!" She looked at him in horror. "Does that mean that someday I'll die and leave you?"

"No." He held the reigns with one hand and curled the other around her neck to pull her closer. "We're both immortal, Tariah. Our power is endless and infinite because it is shared. As long as no one kills us, we will live forever."

After a moment of thought, she said, "I don't think I'd want to be immortal if I wasn't with you. It would be boring. But because I'm going to be with you, it sounds really wonderful."

He pulled the findral to a stop and put the reigns down. He turned and pulled her into his arms as his lips came down to cover hers. He didn't bother to be gentle this time, knowing that she would enjoy the rough kiss as much as he did. Hungrily he devoured her lips, his tongue inviting her to return the favor.

She shuddered and wound her arms around his neck. She eagerly kissed him back and used everything he had been teaching her. It always felt wonderful to kiss him, but she was beginning to feel like there was something more her body wanted. His hand gently cupped her breast through the cloak and though it sent a wave of heat through her body, it wasn't enough either. "Dominic . . ."

He forced himself to release her. "We'll see what happens tonight," he said huskily. "For now, I just wanted to kiss you."

"Why?" she asked.

He picked up the reigns again and started the findral walking once more. "Mostly for you being you, but because I never seem to get enough of your taste." He sent her a quick grin. "You're the perfect definition of water in the desert. It's probably the most wanted thing in the world."

She *felt* like the most wanted thing in the world and found it to be very enjoyable. With a little sigh, she rested against him once more and closed her eyes. She much preferred riding on his back as they ran or flew, but this was nice too.

Crystalia was in their sights as afternoon began to turn into evening. They were less than a mile outside the limits when he stopped the findral and the cart. "Well, this would be a good time to try out our disguise," he told her.

She closed her eyes to concentrate and began to draw on his majiks to change herself. He could handle changing himself just fine. He showed her how to bend her power and the way it needed to bend to become a Kin. It was a complete blind shot for her. She had no way of determining what sort of Kin she might become by bending her power.

She got her answer as she felt the wind rustling the ears now perched on top of her head. She was a Kin Elf, apparently. She opened her eyes and looked down to see that her skin was now the color of dark gold, and her lines had shifted to turn into the familiar silver tattoos of the MoonKin. She lifted her hands to her ears and discovered they were the sharp and angular ears of a feline of some kind. She decided it was apt since she liked it when Dominic was petting her.

He was also a MoonKin Elf now, and his ears looked like they could belong to a canine. He gave a mock growl and scooped her up into his arms to nuzzle her throat. She smelled the same as ever even if she looked quite a bit different. "Be careful I don't go chasing you."

"I wouldn't run." She ran her fingers over the tattoos on his arms. She liked them, but she much preferred seeing his lines and knowing it was her power that made them. Testing, she probed at his majiks and saw that he was weakened. "Once we get to the inn," she promised, "then I'll feed you. Inside the inn room, we should be able to drop the disguise."

"And it won't be as draining next time because you'll know what to do." He started the findral again and they continued down the road toward Crystalia.

Crystalia was an oasis town because it was built in a large oasis. It was no bigger than a mile in diameter but it had a high traffic flow because it was between Prismatic and the port town of Scopic to the north. The inn was located directly in the middle of the main street which itself ran through the middle of town.

Not a single Magi suspected a thing. They looked at Tariah and Dominic and saw two MoonKin traveling together. There were one or two Kin in the town, but they just smiled and said nothing even though they knew full well what the two really were.

The innkeeper was very happy to rent them a room for the night so Dominic tethered the findral and the cart outside. He felt very tired, but the anticipation of tasting his Chronicle's power again was more than enough to keep him moving. He still had no idea how he had gotten along without her.

As the door to the room shut behind them, she asked, "How *did* you get along? I mean . . . I wasn't there to replenish your majiks."

He bent his majiks back the other way and went back into his Magi form. As she also unbent the majiks to return to normal, he reached out to draw her into his arms. "We Furies can put ourselves into hibernation for long periods of time to replenish our majiks ourselves. But, to give you an idea of how long that could be, even this minor drain I'm feeling right now would have required a year of hibernation."

She slid her arms around his waist and held onto him tightly. "That's horrible." Her breath caught as he lifted her into his arms and carried her toward the bed. "Is the door locked?" she asked.

"Locked and sealed." He lowered her to the top of the bed before removing her boots for her. He eased down beside her and began to unfasten the cloak, his fingers trembling lightly with desire as he uncovered more and more of her body. "I'm going to indulge myself," he murmured huskily.

She wasn't sure what he meant but she shortly found herself naked in his arms. It didn't bother her in the slightest. As he gathered her close and bent his head toward hers, her power welled up and flowed over her like a blue veil.

He didn't bother to work his way to her lips. He kissed her immediately, craving her taste as deeply as her power. It flowed into him like wine and he slid his arms around her to hold her even closer. Lazily he slid his tongue into her mouth, and his heart and body tightened equally as she returned the soft caress.

When his hunger for her lips was appeased for the moment, he released her and slowly began to trail kisses along the side of her neck. Her pulse pounded rapidly and he brushed against her emotions to be sure she was not afraid.

She wasn't afraid of anything. She felt as if she were drowning in pleasure. Her body was hot and aching but nothing he did seemed to make it better. It *felt* better but it didn't seem to be enough. She felt his hot mouth moving over the curves of her breasts and it sent those same tugs of before through her blood. It didn't seem nearly as frightening anymore.

Instinctively she twisted toward him, offering herself to him. He was hardly one to deny her, and he closed his lips hungrily over the tightened nipple begging for his attention. Her back arched and he held her closer as he eagerly tugged at her with lips and teeth, savoring her power as it flowed into him. It tasted slightly sweeter at her breast and certainly stronger.

A low moan vibrated out of her throat as he switched to her other breast. The ache was spreading and demanding more. Without thinking about it, she reached for him, wanting to touch him and make him feel the same. Her fingers found the material of his vest and she tugged at it in frustration.

His lips curved against her breast. "You want me naked?" He straightened and shrugged out of the vest. As he was reaching for her again, she flattened her hands against his chest to stop him. With a smile, he laid down on the bed beside her and tucked his hands behind his head. "I'm yours to explore, *ishke*."

She hadn't even realized that was what she had wanted until he had said it. Her curiosity had grown. She wanted to know his body. She wanted to see if he would respond the same if she touched him the same as he touched her.

She rose to her knees beside him and the lack of feeling her hair over her skin made her realize it was still coiled on top of her head. She reached up and began to untuck the little twists to let them fall down around her shoulders and waist. Dominic was still touching her emotions and she was feeling his in return. Her breath hitched as she felt his utter absorption and delight in watching her hair come down.

Once her hair was freed, she ran her hands through it to completely untwist it. She moved closer to him and lightly put a hand on his chest. She had touched his chest a lot, but now she was noticing how hot he was, and how strong the muscle beneath his skin felt. The lines flowing over his chest tingled her palms and she loved knowing it was her power that made them.

Delighted with her freedom, she slowly ran her hands over him, memorizing everything. He watched her through lowered lashes, his eyes nearly black with emotion. It was exceptionally hard to keep from snatching her up and pulling her over him to teach her how to ride him properly. His arousal couldn't have been hidden if he tried.

She didn't notice, lost in her study of him. Her questing fingers found one flat male nipple and she gave in to temptation to lean down and taste him as he had tasted her. His body jerked and a soft growl rumbled in his chest. Nothing could have delighted her more. "You like that too?"

He caught her hand and pulled it down so that it was pressed against his erection straining against his pants. "What do you think?" he asked in a soft growl.

Her eyes widened and she hastily snatched her hand back. Though she would have liked to have petted him more, she was nervous of going any further than that, and she didn't find it fair to him to make him so frustrated. Unsure what to do, she lowered her hands to her sides.

He sat up and softly ran his hands down her arms. "It's alright, Tariah. One day at a time. Look how far you've gotten already."

"I'm just so tired of being nervous." She sighed as he pulled her into his arms. She let herself relax against him and closed her eyes. "I want to belong to you. But something is nervous."

"That's the part of you that is still growing." He ran his fingers through her hair. "It knows that there is no going back and it doesn't want to grow up. Growing up means complicated feelings and emotions and living. Everyone feels that way. It's perfectly natural." He lowered her to the bed and covered her gently, wrapping her in his arms and his power all at the same time. "Rest now," he murmured.

She snuggled closer and slid her arms around him. "Dominic?" she asked.

"Hmm?"

"Thank you."

"For what?" He nuzzled her gently.

"For being you." She smiled and sighed softly. "The rest of the world could never change and I'd be happy just with you." She gave a little yawn. "I'm sorry I'm such trouble for you."

He smiled. "You're well worth all the trouble." He gathered her even closer and buried his nose in her hair so that her scent would follow him into his sleep.

Content, she closed her eyes and let the sound and feel of his heartbeat lull her toward sleep. She was beginning to feel like her puberty was taking too *long* rather than being too fast. A part of her couldn't wait to find out what happened next. Growing up meant that she would be with Dominic forever.

Childhood stood no chance against that desire.

Chapter Thirteen

They decided to eat breakfast at the restaurant in town instead of leaving and hunting their own meal. Tariah was tired of always being on the run, and Dominic was worried because she had lost weight.

Hearing that, she walked over to the mirror and frowned. "Have I really lost weight?" She peered at her figure for signs of skinniness. Sure enough, she *did* seem a little more slender in places. Her muscles were a little more pronounced in her legs and arms. No ribs were showing, though. "I guess I hadn't noticed."

He walked up behind her and wrapped his arms around her waist. "You don't spend as much time staring at yourself as I spend staring at you." He nuzzled her shoulder softly. "You've been on the run for so long, and there's been so much trouble, and we haven't had full meals consistently . . . it's amazing you haven't lost *more* weight."

"I don't want to lose weight." She crossed her arms. "I'd rather be happy, fat, and lazy." She waited a moment and then began to snicker softly. "Okay, maybe not. Sparkle's on the pudgy side and I love teasing her. I can't gain too much weight or she can take revenge."

He chuckled and turned her around in his arms. His hands slid warmly over her back. "Eventually you're going to get fat, you know." He kissed her softly and lingered over her flavor. "Pregnancy does that to a woman, no matter her species." One of his hands rested tenderly over her belly. "You'll be beautiful."

She cuddled closer. Her Fury always knew precisely what to say to make her feel better. She lingered for a moment and then reluctantly released him and went to get dressed. "Someday I'll cook breakfast for us."

His brows lifted as he pulled on his vest. "You can cook?"

"Don't sound surprised," she scolded. "I'm a *very* good cook." She smiled. "Mountain boy. I assume you've never had pitcher crab cakes with cactear syrup."

His mouth watered at the very idea. "No, but it sounds decadent." He scooped her up for a quick kiss. "Something tells me I might be the one in danger of getting pudgy if you start cooking for me."

She snickered. "I'll make you chase me across the dunes and you'll burn it off. I've yet to meet someone not of the desert who can outrun a desert dweller across dunes."

"We might try that even if it's not needed for exercise." He set her down and began to bend his majiks to change him to a Kin form. As he had thought, her use of his majiks this time had barely any effect. She learned *very* quickly.

She also made a beautiful Kin. He ran his fingers lightly over her ears and grinned. Because there was a smaller discrepancy between the heights of male and female Kin, she was actually only two or three inches shorter than his height. Her delight in that small thing warmed his heart. "But I like you when you're cuddle size."

"Me too, but this is nice too." She eased up the scant few inches between their heights and kissed him softly. "See?"

He hugged her tightly, then released her. He kept her close as they left the inn room and went downstairs to checkout. They wanted to leave right after breakfast and head to the north. They hadn't received any new direction to travel; they could only continue along what they had already been told.

The restaurant was only slightly busy this time of morning. It was very easy to find a place to sit where they wouldn't have to be too close to other people. Both ordered large breakfasts and had only started to eat them when a Magi walked up to the table. "Excuse me?" she asked.

"Yes?" Tariah's heart started pounding as hard as Dominic's. Were they found?

"I just wanted to remark on your tattoos. They're quite lovely. I've never seen another MoonKin with the like." The Magi smiled. "I hope that isn't too rude."

"No, not at all!" a SunKin Elf said as he came up to the table. He put a hand on Tariah's shoulder companionably. "To us, it's the same as complimenting a Magi on their hair or their eyes. Of course, our Tiarrah has beauty in all three."

"She does indeed." The Magi drew her thumb over her cheek and nose. "Well, it was nice speaking to you, Tiarrah."

Tariah, remembering Rumidia, touched her ears and bowed slightly. "Likewise." As the Magi walked away, she turned her head and looked at the Kin gratefully. "Thank you. I wouldn't have known how to react."

The Elf smiled and tapped her nose. "We Kin watch out for one another. Good luck, little Chronicle." He bowed gracefully and then headed back over to his own table.

She glanced at Dominic who was chuckling. "What?" she asked warily.

"What he called you." He smiled. "I believe in the language of the Kin, it means something like 'little creature.' I've heard it used as a term of endearment among family." He grinned when her nose wrinkled. "I also notice that it's a variation on the characters of your name. The Kin must have been waiting for a chance to remark on it."

"Shut up, Dominic," she mumbled as she dug into her breakfast. So she was short, even by Kin standards. What crime was that? Still, she had to smile. She liked knowing that her name was nearly the same as one in the Kin. They had become more of a fellow race to her than the Magi, and she was more closely connected to the Magi in her species.

Once they had finished breakfast and had paid for their meal, they went outside to where their findral and cart were waiting. Tariah was feeling better than she had in a long time. It had felt good to be able to eat to her fill. She was mildly impressed by Dominic's appetite though. "I never imagined anyone could eat that much."

"I *am* considerably bigger," he reminded her, "even if I currently don't look it." He helped her up onto the seat before climbing up beside her. Moments later they were heading down the road. "Will it bother you to live with the Dragons, Tariah? Even the Dragon Lords tend to stay in their normal shape unless they leave. You'll be slightly overwhelmed."

"As long as they watch where they're walking," was her impish response, "I don't mind. I don't want to get stepped on."

He laughed. "I'll carry you on my shoulder, how's that?" He held the reigns with one hand and wrapped his other arm around her shoulders to draw her closer. A part of him missed the Isle, but he wouldn't have changed a single minute with his Chronicle. His only regret was that because they were cut off from the Isle, she was being forced to suffer the Magi's prejudices. She needed to be home.

The findral suddenly balked and reared in the air, and it nearly dumped the cart over. Tariah went flying right over the side, and she shrieked as she landed unceremoniously in the sand. "Ouch!"

"Tariah!" Dominic released the reins and leapt clear of the thrashing beast to rush to his lover's side. "Are you alright?"

She spit sand out of her mouth and pushed herself up. "I'm okay, I think," she said shakily. "A little scared. Maybe a lot scared." She grabbed his vest tightly as she saw the way the findral was reacting. "Dominic . . ."

He looked and immediately recognized what was occurring. His stomach churned. "Stay here." He moved a few steps away and returned to his natural form. He wasn't risking her life on power alone. He planted himself in front of her defensively.

Her stomach quivered. "It's the power in the land, isn't it?" she whispered. "The findral is being mutated into a monster. But I didn't feel any fluctuations in the land!"

"It must be something in Prismatic," he said grimly. "The findral was born there. Something is happening to the power balance in Prismatic. You don't have to be in the city of your birth to be affected by it if it's big enough."

The findral gave a screech like nails across glass that shortly turned into a guttural roar. Sharp spikes burst out of its back and ripped the fins cleanly away. Its fur fell off to leave nothing but bare skin beneath, and Dominic covered Tariah's face with a wing as he saw the chunks of skin falling off the creature's face to leave nothing but a skeleton behind. "Close your eyes," he ordered her.

She very nearly hid behind a sand dune but changed her mind at the last moment. She was *not* letting him handle this alone. Her stomach rolled when she saw how the findral looked, but she braced her shoulders and gathered her power to wait for an opening. She was new to combat just as she was new to so much else, and she was damned well going to get through this too.

The findral lunged for Dominic, but the Dragon was bigger and stronger. One swipe of his massive claw sent the findral tumbling away. It recovered and came after him again on his blind side. He couldn't turn in time and the monster's sharp beak stabbed into his flank. With a roar, he flung the findral away once more.

It noticed Tariah and went lunging after her, sensing she was the smaller and easier target. She released a steady stream of ice projectiles at the monster, her quivering fingers the only hint of her nerves. Most of the ice shards pierced flesh, and the findral was forced to back away. Dominic struck like a blur and his teeth tore through what remained of the monster's flesh. He hurled it violently aside, and a spear of ice cracked down through the air. It encased the beast entirely, and he destroyed it with a solid swipe of his tail. Both monster and ice shattered in hundreds of pieces and dissolved in the hot sun.

His side aching worse than the fires of the Underrealm, Dominic laid down on the sand and scolded Tariah, "I told you to stay back!"

"I wasn't about to let you fight alone." She went over to his side and began to gently examine his wound. It was two sharp puncture wounds, and they were sullenly bleeding green blood. "This would be easier to tend if you were in Kin or Magi form," she told him. "I can rip my cloak for enough cloth to wrap your side that way."

He closed his eyes and focused his concentration on bending his majiks. His body shifted and glowed, and he turned into his MoonKin form. He also nearly fell flat on his face. The wound had transferred to his side and thigh both because this body was much smaller, and the wounds were much more disabling because of it.

She managed to catch him and break his fall, and she carefully helped him sit down on the sand. She pulled her cloak off and began to quickly and efficiently tear it into strips. He watched her with a wry smile. "You seem to be good at that."

She began to bind his leg first. "I used to climb cliffs, remember? There wasn't a day when I didn't get some sort of cut or scrape. It was easier to mend it myself rather than going home and coming back. We'll have to find a Soil element who can mend this better."

He grimaced as she bound his side tightly. "Easy on that. It hurts."

"I imagine so, you big baby!" She put the knot right over the wound to attempt to stem the bleeding. He sat up and she hastily braced him. "Take it easy," she warned. "Don't pull open the bandages."

An explosion in the far distance rocked the land around them and knocked them both off balance. He had to catch himself before he accidentally squashed her, and he covered her bodily as the sand erupted around them. The power in the land had gone haywire. From where they were, they could even hear the screams of the people in Crystalia as they were knocked off their feet.

The land stopped shaking and Dominic got carefully to his feet. He pulled Tariah up and held onto her tightly. "Are you okay?" He ran his hands over her swiftly.

"I am." She was shaking though unharmed. "What was that? That . . . that wasn't a normal quake! It felt like the power in the land was just . . . exploded!"

He stared over her head at the distance. Grimly, he said, "It was definitely Prismatic. I can see it from here. There's smoke pluming from the buildings. Something is happening there."

Terror closed her throat. "Morgan! We have to go back," she pleaded. "We need to make sure he's okay! If something happens to him and those children . . ." She paled as she remembered Symphony and how her sudden disappearance had disrupted the land. If the land had adjusted to the presence of five Chronicles, even if four of them were not yet developed, and they were suddenly removed . . .

Dominic cursed softly and stepped back from her. Once more, he turned back to his natural form. The bandages ripped away in the process, but the wounds were almost gone. The spewed elements from the eruption had acted as a natural healer. "Get on my back!" he ordered. "We can fly to the limits and then go inside!"

She climbed up onto his back and held on tightly as he took to the sky and began flying swiftly. Neither worried about disrupting the flow of power in the land. It was already so riotous that it would never notice the effects of Dragoons. A wave already in motion wouldn't notice more waves if they went in the same direction.

It was only half an hour before they were landing in the farmlands outside Prismatic, but it felt like forever. The farmers didn't notice a Dragon landing in their field. They were too busy scrambling to secure their animals and crops. Everything was being shaken up by the tremors in the land.

Dominic changed to his MoonKin form and spotted a findral running loose. He caught it and swung up onto its back. He reached down to pull Tariah up with him and they took off down the road as quickly as possible.

The city was a sea of chaos. Buildings had fallen, and some animals and Magi alike had been mutated into monsters. The Militia was everywhere and running mad as they struggled to protect and save everyone.

Random bursts of power in the land spewed fire and water into the air. Storm clouds rushed in over the city and lightning arced to the ground even without them.

Smoke billowed out of the district where the sanctuary was located. Tariah's heart seemed to freeze in her chest as she saw that the building had been nearly decimated. Fires still burned and leapt hungrily toward the sky. Through it, she caught the smell of Air and recognized Morgan's power. It was clashing with another familiar scent.

Soh had been here.

Dominic stopped the findral outside the sanctuary and Tariah leapt down to run over and join the Water Magi who were trying to put out the flames. Her power was far more potent, and with her assistance, the flames were shortly smothered. "What happened?" she demanded of the nearest Magi.

Shakily, the man said, "The Black Magi Elite. They. . . they came in and went to see the Black Magi. The next thing we knew, the sanctuary was exploding. Moments later the land went wild. We can't even get inside to see if there are any survivors." He gestured at the door. "It's too strong for Magi." He looked at her. "You're Kin. Can you get in?"

Even a Kin might have had trouble, to be honest. If she got in, it would be only because she was a Chronicle. Without waiting for Dominic, she ran toward the sanctuary doors. The barrier around the place didn't offer even a token resistance to her as she dashed inside. "Morgan!" she shouted. "Kelsey! Eli! Anyone!"

There was no response, and she could feel no power that indicated someone, if they were there, still lived. The entire place was charred and scorched. It got worse and worse as she went deeper down the hall toward Morgan's study. The detonation had occurred there; she was sure of it.

Dominic came up behind her. "I don't smell anyone here," he told her. "Either they got out or they're dead."

She flinched and opened the study door. The entire room was decimated. Not a single thing had escaped the explosion. There were no bodies, however, so no one had been in there to die. Oddly, Morgan's Black Magi cloak was still present, and it had been thrown across the floor haphazardly.

She walked over to pick it up and discovered, to her shock, a piece of paper with her name on it. It had no legible writing on it, but as she picked it up, the characters formed and became clearer.

"He must have written that before the attack," Dominic said quietly. "He knew it was coming."

She looked down at the letter and felt her stomach quiver. "He did," she whispered.

Tariah, my sister;

Well, not really my sister, but it feels as if you are. As I write this letter, I can feel Soh coming toward the sanctuary. He is after the children. His power . . . it has gotten stronger. I don't know how, but I know that whatever he has planned will be terrible. My only hope for protecting these children is to send them away.

I have erased the memories of the children and their parents alike. They will remember nothing of the Black Magi or what was done here. To further ensure their protection, I have locked their powers with my own. They will develop normally, but their Chronicle powers will not become visible until they are in the presence of another Chronicle or a Fury.

I will be sending the children away shortly via my Air powers. I do not know where they will land. It is better this way. If Soh gets his hands on me, and I lose the fight, then he cannot get their locations from me. I'm counting on you, Tariah. Find the children and lead them to the Dragons.

May the moons watch over you, Morgan

Tears welled and flowed down her face. "He's not dead," she whispered. "I'm sure I would have known! I can't feel as if he died here. I can feel that he fought here, but not that he died."

Dominic looked around the room intently. "It may be that he had just sent the children away when the attack struck. He was a smart man. If he had sensed or seen that Soh was too much for him, he would have used his power to get himself away as well. That would be why the land went wild as it did, in two waves. The first was the children being sent away. The second was Soh's attack and Morgan's disappearance."

"So where are the Elite then?" she asked. She rolled up the letter and put it in the sack she still wore on her hip. She wiped her tears away fiercely. "No one saw them leave, right?" Suddenly she froze. "If the Elite want to destroy the Magi . . ."

"The king!" He cursed softly and got to his feet. He grabbed her hand and hurried with her away from the scene. Rather than go out the front, they made their way to the back exit. A quick look around assured them that the Militia was likely too busy chasing monsters to notice anyone going into the palace.

They made their way through the city as quickly as they could by cutting corners and hanging to back alleys. The chaos was even worse as they got closer to the castle. The people with stronger power lived around the castle and the disruption had been greater.

The Militia didn't once notice Dominic and Tariah as they ran behind the buildings toward the gates. Tariah was quick and agile enough from all her years of cliff climbing to make her way up over the wall and into the courtyard. Dominic was forced to climb a tree to get over the wall, but he was shortly beside her once more.

The area was a tomb. The people who had been mutated into monsters prowled the edges. Those who had not been changed were either dead on the floor or had already fled the scene. The castle itself seemed to be un-breached, and two Militia guards stood outside the throne room doors.

Dominic, however, could smell something odd. "They're dead," he said flatly. "They're just propped up to look like they're alive."

Tariah nearly was sick to her stomach. She fought it back and hurried toward the throne room doors. When she opened them, the doors swung inward and the two Militia soldiers fell to the floor in a heap. Their heads rolled away from their bodies, and she gagged.

Dominic hustled her past the scene and through the throne room. "Your majesty!" he shouted as he saw the king standing down the carpet from them. Abruptly he stopped and pulled Tariah to a stop with him. "Something's wrong."

The king toppled to the floor and Tariah gave a cry as she rushed forward. She slid to her knees beside him and rolled him over onto his back. She immediately flinched. His chest had been torn open. Not even a MoonKin could have mended this. His power was draining away too fast to be stopped. When it was gone, his body would be gone. Without power, no body of any species could live. Their bodies *were* power.

His eyes opened and he stared up at her in confusion. "Kin?"

She shook her head and unbent the majiks to return to normal. "No."

He sighed as he recognized her. Blood stained his lips in the process. "I am sorry," he said brokenly. "Sorry for what I did to you. What the Magi have done. What we've done for so long. I touched your mind. I saw inside you. You're no monster."

She held onto his hand tightly. "Who did this? Was it the Elite?"

"Yes." Bloody tears slid down his face. "He called me a murderer. He was right."

"No, he wasn't! You're not guilty of the sins of others," Dominic told him sharply.

"No, but I am guilty of my own sins." He met Tariah's eyes. "If my daughter had lived . . . she would be your age."

She took a sharp breath. "Your daughter was a Chronicle."

"I was so afraid of a rumor that I had my own child killed." His eyes closed. "She never got mad at me. She just . . . looked at me and asked me why. I couldn't tell her." He coughed, and blood gurgled from his chest around the wound. "Dragoons . . . please. Stop the Elite. They want to destroy the Magi. If they do . . . then they destroy the world."

Tariah closed her eyes. "I'll try," she said softly.

Dominic's lips thinned. He was beginning to hate how everything had to come down on her shoulders. Why was she the one who had to carry the burdens of a race that had brought their own destruction upon them?

"The world needs Magi," she told him. "Without them, there would be no seas. The world would shrivel away. Someone has to do something. It might as well be me."

"I'm sorry, Tariah." The king gave a faint sigh. "I hope your children are Chronicles as well. Our world needs them again."

There were no further words, and Tariah and Dominic both felt as his power stopped entirely. His skin slowly turned gray, and his blood disappeared entirely. Without his power, his body was nothing more than a shell.

The doors burst open and the Militia surged into the room. They stopped in shock as they saw Tariah and Dominic beside the dead body of the king. Tariah could read their thoughts on their faces even without her

Telepathy. "No!" she said. "We didn't do it!"

Before the soldiers could retort, the captain walked forward and knelt beside the king's body. After a moment of scrutiny, he said, "She tells the truth. The king was killed by the Elite. I recognize their power. Those bastards!" he cursed softly. He looked at Tariah. "You need to get away from here. The people are in an uproar. They won't be able to define friend from enemy. A Chronicle would be a good scapegoat."

Dominic pulled Tariah up to her feet when it was apparent she was frozen with shock. "But why are you helping me?" she asked the captain. "You hated me!"

"For a time." The captain studied her. "But I've seen the Elite, and I've seen you. I may fear you more, but I trust them less. Get away from here. And I might suggest staying away from Magi cities entirely."

Dominic evaluated the power in the land and saw it was still rocking like waves. He backed up several feet and turned to his natural form. Tariah climbed up onto his back, and he looked at captain. "Tell me something. Are you finally seeing that it was the fault of the Magi for the existence of the Elite?"

The captain's face tightened. "Get out of here," he said harshly.

He didn't need to be told twice. He flew straight up into the air and through the broken ceiling toward the sky. Once they were well over the city, he began flying to the west. The entire continent of Spectrum was being affected. The only way he or Tariah would rest was if they were not on its land.

She said nothing as they flew. Her emotions felt like the land. They were shaking and turbulent. Nothing seemed to be secure in her world. At the whims of any person who crossed her path, her life could change. She just wanted to make it all go away.

Dominic felt grim and a little terrified. Only his presence anchored her to this world. He needed to get her somewhere safe and dedicate his full attention to her. The abundance of her inner strength had continued to astound him, yet he could see how terribly close she was to the end of her rope. Without him, she might very well attempt to detonate her own power.

A few miles into the ocean past Spectrum, he spotted a tiny island. It was hardly bigger than an oasis itself, but it was not part of the main landmass. He swiftly angled down and landed on the strip of sand that made a beach. He turned into his Magi form and caught Tariah safely in his arms as she tumbled toward him.

A brief scan of the island told him that they were alone. He put up a shield to keep it that way and then began to walk into the trees to find a place that would be good for camping. Tariah was silent in his arms, her head resting tiredly on his shoulder. His worry increased as he brushed against her emotions and found them to be completely numb.

There was a small clearing among the trees, and he gently put her down on the thick grass. She didn't move as he gathered small logs to make a fire. It was still daytime but it was dark among the trees and she was beginning to shiver. He used his powers to make the fire smokeless, then went to her side and wrapped her in a blanket from his backpack. "*Ishke.*"

Her eyes closed. "I don't know how much more I can take, Dominic," she whispered. "All I want is to have some peace. But Morgan needs me to find the children. The king needs me to stop the Elite." Tears slid down her cheeks. "I don't even know what *I* need anymore."

He pulled her into his arms and held her tightly. "Whatever it is you need," he said fiercely, "I'll get it for you. Just don't leave me. I feel like you're slipping away from me. I'm so sorry, but I need you too. I need you to be with me. Stay with me, Tariah."

She leaned back and studied his face. "You're hungry." Her arms wound around his neck. "I'm sorry I didn't notice." She eased up and teased his lips with hers. "I need *you*, Dominic. I feel like you're the only reason I have left to live."

His hands framed her face and her power welled up in silent pleading. He kissed her long and tenderly, drinking her power as it flowed generously into him. He deepened the kiss as she sighed, and his heart clenched with emotion as she returned every caress with one of her own.

They eased apart and she felt something inside her heart suddenly still. A calm certainty swept through her and banished all her lingering doubts and fears. Her eyes lifted to meet his. The words were there and unexpectedly easy to say. "Make love to me."

He stopped breathing. He searched her eyes and probed at her emotions with his own. Even when he curled his power around her, he could find nothing but certainty. She knew what she wanted even if she didn't wholly understand yet what she needed. A low groan caught in his chest and he kissed her hungrily as he lowered her to the ground.

The blanket was the perfect bed. She felt nothing but eagerness as she ran her hands slowly over his arms. When he began to slowly undress her, she didn't hesitate to reach for his vest and return the favor.

When he felt her fingers at the fastenings to his pants, he laughed and caught her hands. "No, you don't." He gently caged her hands at her sides and then eased back to look at her naked body in delight. "If you get me naked, you'll start exploring, and if you start exploring, I'll go crazy."

"Isn't that the idea?" She rubbed her power against his for the sheer delight of seeing his eyes darken. When he returned the invisible touch, her eyes closed helplessly at the feeling. "I want to know everything."

"Then let me show you." He lowered his head and brushed his lips over the curves of her breasts. Her power still flowed over her body, and he drank it slowly, savoring it like one would savor a rare drink. "You won't think of anything but me," he promised.

As his mouth closed over her nipple and sucked so strongly that her back arched, she had the feeling that thinking was going to be impossible. Heat surged through her body and the ache of pleasure spread swiftly. Just the feel of his hair on her skin was maddening and wonderful.

He released her hands and began to run his own over her body slowly. He trailed soft fingers over the length of her long legs and over the flat curve of her stomach. Her power followed him, and he was helpless but to feed on it wherever he found it. It sparked a feeling not unlike how it felt to be intoxicated. This intoxication consumed his entire essence, from his power outward. "Tariah," he murmured thickly against the skin of her stomach, his lips tracing the lines that were there.

She shuddered as his hand closed over her breast and kneaded gently. "What are you doing?" she managed to whisper as she felt his lips skimming over her thigh. He didn't seem to be making the ache better. He was making it worse and she could feel a throbbing between her legs. "My body feels odd."

He grinned with savage delight as he felt just how odd through his connection to her emotions. He wanted her to be completely mindless with desire. He wanted her to crave his possession of her so deeply that she would never doubt they belonged together. "Good," he said. "Take a breath."

She open her mouth and then sucked in a sharp breath as she felt his hand slip between her legs. Little shockwaves rolled through her body of raw pleasure and she curled her fingers into the blanket beneath her. She moaned brokenly as she felt him stroking her gently. She had never imagined it might feel like this.

He caught her hand and drew it down her body until she was touching herself. "You see?" he murmured huskily. "This is how your body shows its pleasure."

She slid her hand free and instead held his closer. "I like your touch more," she whispered. Her voice broke on a soft cry as she felt his hot breath where her fingers had just been. "You're not going to kiss me there."

"Of course I am." He shuddered as her power beckoned to him. Almost desperately, he closed his lips over her and caressed with his tongue the little knot of flesh he had awakened. She tasted like nothing he had ever known before.

She grabbed onto his shoulders for dear life as her muscles began to draw tighter and tighter. He was still making it worse! She couldn't breathe, couldn't think, for the pleasure that consumed her. But it still wasn't enough. It felt as if her whole body was going to shatter. "Dominic," she pleaded. "Fix it!"

Her hips twisted helplessly as she felt his fingers slowly stretching her. One strong finger slid inside her body even as his power consumed hers, and her entire body convulsed as ecstasy shuddered through her. As the pleasure swept over her, she realized it was almost exactly what she had felt missing. But there was something still lacking. "Dominic?" she asked huskily as she felt him gathering her closer.

He tilted her chin up and kissed her desperately, his tongue surging into her mouth to torment them both. His hands were shaking as he ran them slowly over her body, tracing every curve damp with sweat. "We're not done yet," he said thickly. "I'm just trying not to lose control."

The idea of an out-of-control Dominic was deeply appealing to that feminine place in her heart. She had been out of control in his arms. She wanted him to be the same. She pushed at his shoulders, and when he rolled onto his back, she rose to her knees beside him. "My turn." Her husky voice was a promise of delight.

He covered his face with an arm. "Be gentle," he warned her. "I'm already pushing the limit. I want to be inside you so badly I can taste it."

She glanced at the front of his pants and her eyes widened slightly. Curiously, she reached out a hand and covered the interesting bulge under the fabric. He groaned and, encouraged, she began to unfasten his pants.

He watched her with gray eyes stormier than any cloud and lifted his hips slightly to help her in removing the offending material. When he was completely naked, he gave a quick stretch. He hated clothing, truthfully. He had always assumed it was a quirk of Dragon nature.

"Not just Dragons," she said. Her mouth had gone dry. Her Fury was *beautiful*. Unclothed, he was even more so. She felt as she had the first time she had seen him as a Dragon. She was shocked and awed that such a magnificent creature was hers. "I hate clothes too." Testing, she reached out a hand and ran it over his stomach and steadily lower. "I'd run around naked if I could."

"I repeat." He stifled a moan as her soft fingers skimmed over his erection. He was so hard for her that it hurt. "I repeat," he tried again, "that I love desert girls." His breath hissed in as her hand curled around him. "Careful with that."

"Why?" She smiled and memorized the feel and look of him. She hadn't realized how beautiful a man's body could be. Or maybe it was just Dominic. She didn't think anyone else would compare.

His hand slid between her legs before she could stop him. A soft moan slipped past her lips as he stroked her. "Because it belongs here," he said thickly. "Let me show you everything." Her hands lifted and he pulled her on top of him before rolling over to tuck her safely underneath him.

Their lips met in a long kiss and she trembled as she felt his hands slowly stroking over her body. He lifted her legs to curl them around his hips, and she realized how strangely vulnerable the position seemed. Oddly, it didn't frighten her. Only hunger stirred deep inside. She *needed* him. "Dominic." She drew him down to kiss him again. "Hurry up," she whispered, and nipped at his lip with her teeth.

"Tease." He positioned himself and then slowly began to push inside her body. His eyes locked with hers, and he saw them widen with utter shock. He shuddered at the feel of her. She was snug and hot, fitting him as perfectly as he had known she would. Only when he was fully inside her did he stop to savor the fierce triumph in his soul. She was *his*.

She twisted slowly underneath him, her breathing shallow. She felt stretched and full of him, nearly on the verge of pain. But it wasn't pain. It was raw pleasure. Deeper still was the delight of knowing he was hers. Her Fury. She had finally claimed him.

He hissed softly as her muscles clenched around him even as her power rubbed sensuously against his. "Stop it," he said hoarsely. She did it a second time, her eyes like pools of melted silver and a little smile on her lips. She knew precisely what she was doing, and the knowledge broke his control.

His hands fisted in her hair and he dragged her up for a kiss as he pulled out and drove back in. Quicker he began to thrust, driving himself as deeply into her welcoming warmth as he could. He tangled their emotions together just for the sheer delight of knowing how he made her feel, and ecstasy boiled up without warning and consumed him. He could only dive himself to the hilt and pour himself deep inside.

She barely noticed. The instant she had felt his emotions tangling with hers, allowing her to share his emotions, the pleasure had detonated inside her body with the force of a firebomb, sweeping through her in waves of delight that overshadowed everything before. With a faint cry, she clung onto him tightly as an anchor against melting away.

Blessed peace fell in their secret camp. When Dominic was finally able to breathe more normally, he found the strength to lift himself onto an elbow. Tenderness filled him as he studied Tariah's face. She looked content, satiated, and very happy. Her lips were still swollen from his, and a beautiful flush clung to her skin even as lingering tendrils of steam did. He could feel the answer to his question, but asked it anyway. "Was it worth the wait, *ishke*?"

She opened her eyes and smiled at him. More than ever she felt as if she was finally where she belonged. "It was well worth it," she said huskily. Her arms tightened around his shoulders as she leaned up to kiss him lingeringly. "What about you? Was it worth waiting for?"

The corner of his mouth kicked up. He doubted she could miss his joy since it was overtaking most of his heart. "What do you think?" He skimmed his fingers down her arm and realized in surprise that her lines felt hotter.

He lifted himself further away and noticed that her lines from her face down to her breasts and partway down her right arm were darker than before. But it was a darkness that faded and grew like light rippling over waves. He could *see* her power flowing through the lines. "I wonder why," he said softly.

She looked at her shoulder. After a moment of thought, she said, "Perhaps it is telling us that part of my journey is done. I've finished that part of the map." She smiled up at him. "I guess that makes it the most important part." She skimmed her hand over his chest where some of the lines were also darker now in response to her change. "I don't seem to be as worried about the rest anymore."

"Tariah," he breathed. He gathered her close and hugged her tightly. He knew how she felt. It was as if the rest of the world no longer seemed to be so much trouble now that they were together as they belonged.

And yet, beyond their feelings, he felt inside both of them a lingering worry for another Chronicle somewhere else in the world.

Where was Morgan?

Part Two
~Morgan~

Chapter Fourteen

Dear readers,

My name is Morgan Chronis. I was born in a normal city, at the edges of a normal country, on the normal world of Lucksphere. I was a normal boy, with normal Magi powers, and I had a normal life. My parents were normal, both Fire Magi. They had grown up normal, in normal cities, inside normal countries, on this normal world.

Unfortunately, that normality changed during my fourteenth year of life. As I was preparing to go to sleep one night, something changed. In the space of two breaths, my body entered first puberty . . . and I developed lines.

These were not normal lines. They were dark gold against my skin, and they seemed to be made of loops and straight lines as they traveled down the outside of my arms and hands and across my chest. Their pattern seemed to be no pattern at all but something inside me knew they had meaning.

I was a Chronicle. I was a member of the most hated race on the world. I don't know why. The rumors were outrageous, talking of parasites and feeding, and Dragons that owned a Chronicle's soul. Oddly, the Dragons were not hated for this. Just the Chronicles. It was little wonder the Dragons disliked Magi so much.

It was law. Any child that developed Chronicle lines was to be instantly put to death. I was terrified. I did not want to die. I was going to hide my lines entirely and not tell anyone. But my father came into my room and saw me. I thought my parents would hate me but . . . they didn't. They loved me. They let me live.

No one in my village knew. I wore gloves and long sleeves and professed to having a sudden sensitivity to the cold. As I developed into an Air element at this same time, no one found it to be a surprise. When I began to develop Thunder power at the same time, it was accepted by all that I was a Master Magi.

I and my parents never corrected them. It was just so frustrating for me! I was often too hot because of my clothes, and yet I could never once complain or remove my shirt. More still was the worry for when I would enter second puberty. I was bound to end up naked and any girl in her right mind would panic if she saw my lines.

It was a frustrating way to be living your life, but at least I was living. Day after day, year after year, my life continued. Silently I was snubbing all those Magi who believed I ought to be dead.

Then in the summer of my twentieth year, it all changed. And that is the summer where my place in this story begins.

Morgan T. Chronis

Chapter Fifteen

(Five years ago)

The snow that covered the ground crunched lightly beneath boots wherever people walked. Here, in Glacia, it was always cold. Even in the summer it was cold. Snow would fall at any time of day, any time of the year. It was the whim of the power in the land. And here, the whim was to make it cold.

Few Fire Magi called Glacia home. It was mostly made up of Air and Water Magi. But, then again, Morgan thought to himself as he dug in the snow for roots, his parents were hardly normal Fire Magi. They were . . . quirkier, he supposed was the term. After all, they had let him live. Him, an abomination.

His lips thinned as he wiped away dirt from the root and put it in the basket next to his feet. For a moment he looked at his hands. They were covered with thick leather gloves to keep the snow from freezing his fingers. But even when he wasn't digging in the snow, he wore gloves. They were as common a part of his attire as shoes.

The gloves, and the long sleeves of his tunic, kept his secret from being shown to the world. He was a Chronicle. Across his chest and down his arms there were golden lines that flowed with Dragon power. Those lines were his death sentence if anyone ever found them out.

With a sigh, he got to his feet and slung the loops of the basket over his shoulder. It was much harder now to keep his secret than he had ever imagined. He was going through second puberty. There was, in fact, a particular girl in town that he had his eye on. He wouldn't have minded exploring his curiosities with her in the slightest. But he didn't know how she had react.

Ah, well. It wasn't a concern since she hadn't given any clue that she was equally interested. Smiling wryly, he headed back for his town. Such were the odd quirks of life.

He lived in Stalagmite, the town that served as the main port for the entire continent. Because it was cold, all the buildings were made of thick stone and hard packed mud to keep out the bitter winds. Snow covered every rooftop and created white blankets in front of every wall.

The streets were almost always being swept to keep the snow from getting into the tracks that carts rolled on. There wasn't a single door that didn't have a shovel sitting next to it to forge a path toward the street after a heavy fall.

It was mid-morning and the port was busy. People passing through and stopping over were enough to make the crowds thick along the sidewalks where canopies stretched overhead to protect pedestrians.

The sounds of bells blowing on ships came loudly in the crisp air. Flags with the symbol of the Magi flew high in the air. Looking around, Morgan found it hard to imagine living anywhere else on this world.

A MoonKin Faerie that was flying by paused for a moment to study him and then flew on with a hidden smile. It did not surprise him. There were one or two Kin living in the town and they knew he was a Chronicle. They never spoke of it, but he was sure they knew. He was also sure that any of the few Kin who passed through were sworn to secrecy. There was never any knowing who might overhear and suspect.

His parents ran a restaurant. He went in the back door and scraped the snow off his shoes at the door. Once they were clean, he headed directly into the kitchen and put down the basket of roots. "As ordered," he said with a smile.

"Your nose is red," his mother scolded as she hurried over. "Go upstairs and get warm." Her hands were quick and competent as she began to chop up the roots. Her hair, the same auburn as her son's, was pinned up on top of her head to keep it out of her way. "Go on now."

He grinned at her. "When will you remember that I'm twenty, Mom?"

Iria Chronis wrinkled her nose at him. She didn't like remembering that her baby boy was no longer a baby. She liked even less thinking that he would soon be a man and likely move out on his own. She had seen the way his eye lingered on Merideth Caradina. It made her heart ache. "Don't remind me," she grumbled.

"All children grow up," her mate said dryly as he walked into the kitchen with a tray of empty dishes. "I'm sure he won't move away and abandon his poor, old parents to their miserable and lonely lives." London Chronis' silver eyes twinkled as they met Morgan's identical ones. "Will you?"

"Depends on the incentive offered to me." He stuck his tongue out at them and ducked out of the kitchen before the towel his mother threw at him smacked him in the face.

As he walked through the restaurant toward the stairs to the next floor where the Chronis family lived, every female eye followed him. Morgan was not as tall as most Magi men since he only stood around five-six, but he was by far the most attractive male in town. Half the females in the city had been waiting for him to enter second puberty. The other half were almost regretful that they were not single.

His auburn hair glowed with faint red highlights under the lamps and it clung to the back of his neck. His silver eyes were quick to smile but could darken with intensity. He was intelligent, and he was powerful. He was also strong in the shoulder, and his face was handsome. Every available female in the restaurant felt as if they were in a race to catch his eye first.

When Morgan got upstairs, he locked the door and made sure the window was shut tight. He also pulled the curtains and tied them in place so they couldn't even accidentally move and let anyone see inside. Only when he was sure that it was safe did he remove his gloves. His thick cloak went next and then his tunic.

With a grateful sigh, he fell on his back on his bed and stared at the ceiling overhead. He tucked his hands under his head and studied the pattern in the ceiling almost morosely. He *hated* to be confined by clothes, despite the city in which he had been raised. He would have made a better desert dweller, he thought in amusement. They rarely wore much at all.

Someone knocked lightly on the window, and his heart gave a dull thud. He yanked on his tunic and gloves and checked the mirror to be sure everything was hidden. Only then did he creep over to the window and pull the curtain back. The Faerie of before hovered outside his window. He opened it warily. "Is something wrong?"

"Not at all." The MoonKin had dark sapphire skin and green eyes. Silver tattoos marked her body and shimmered as evidence of her bloodline. "May I enter, Morgan? I wish to speak to you about . . . something."

His eyes widened slightly. After a moment, he held the window open to let her fly in. Once she had joined him, he shut the window and retied the curtains in place. "Is this . . . is this about me being a Chronicle?" He had never before admitted the words out loud. It felt odd.

"It is." She flew over and landed on his desk. "You see, I know some things about Chronicles. My grandfather was there at the final battle between the Chronicles and Magi. He told my mother the tales, and then they both told me. We Kin have always tried to remember everything about Chronicles so that we could tell someone someday."

He was immediately interested. He sat down on the side of his bed. "Tell me what, precisely?"

"I thought you might want to know about Furies."

His heart gave a dull thud in his chest. A sharp and painful longing rose up inside him so fiercely that it stole his breath and made his eyes sting with tears. "Fury?" he whispered softly.

"Fury." She watched with compassionate eyes. "You see, Chronicles are one half of a whole. Their other half is a Fury. A Fury is a Dragon. To be precise, a Dragon Lord. I've heard that the bonds between Chronicle and Fury are even more powerful than those who are Linked or Bonded. It's imprinted in you before you're born."

He pressed his hands against his eyes. Even the idea of there being someone out there, someone who would understand him, took his breath away. He had always been a loner. He had never had any close friends. But his Fury . . . they would automatically trust each other, would be able to share everything. It was a tempting thought.

The Kin flew over to touch his cheek. "Morgan," she said softly, "stamped in your lines is a map. This map will lead you to the Isle of Dragons and your Fury. Follow this map no matter where it leads. Your lines . . . they are made of your Fury's power. They connect you to her."

"Her?" His head came up. "Furies are female?"

The Kin smiled. "No, not all. But Chronicles and Furies are always opposite gender because they have to be perfectly opposite in order to balance. Since you are a male, your Fury is a female. She will be your confidant and lover alike." She leaned over and kissed his nose. "Hold this knowledge close. Someone out there needs you like you need them. Her power is not infinite like other Dragons. She will need to feed on your power. In return, you will be able to use her majiks."

He opened the curtain and window so she could leave and secured them again after she was gone. His mind swam with what he had learned. His Magi upbringing told him that he should be horrified and appalled at the idea of anyone feeding on another's power. Yet his heart and his soul ached with longing to give his power to his Fury. How did one love someone they had never met? He wasn't even sure 'love' was a strong enough word.

There came a knock on his door. "Morgan!" Iria called. "Go fetch the bread from the baker! It should be ready by now!"

He sighed. "Yes, Mother." He put his cloak back on before leaving his room and heading downstairs. The baker was a few blocks over but he didn't mind the walk. It was growing later in the day and the sun had begun to sink in the west. Even then the town didn't seem to be winding down. It wouldn't do that until at least the second moon had risen.

The baker was waiting with the loaves in a basket for him. He picked it up and turned around only to bump into someone. He swiftly reached out and caught their arm to keep them from falling. "I'm so sorry," he said on a laugh.

Sparkling blue eyes met his. "It was my fault," Merideth Caradina said with a laugh in her voice. "I wasn't watching my step."

Morgan's young heart skipped a beat even as his body tightened with desire. Merideth was the loveliest girl in Stalagmite and possibly even Glacia. She was only an inch shorter than he was and she had thick black hair. Her young figure was graceful and generous all at once. "Hi, Merideth." It was all he could manage.

"Hi, Morgan." She eased closer, smiling from under her lashes. She and Morgan were the same age. She had started second puberty first and had been hoping he would eventually catch up. She knew she could very easily fall for him if she let herself. He was so wonderfully easy to like! And, of course, he was downright gorgeous.

Somewhere inside him, the motion of her body was recognized. He barely remembered how to breathe. "Are you, in a subtle manner, asking me to write you a letter when I'm available?" he asked softly.

She giggled and took his free hand with hers. The fact that he wore gloves was all the more sexy to her. Imagining what his hands would be like under the gloves was a wonderful, and frustrating, pastime. "I could be." Her cloak had fallen open, and she moved closer to give him a better view of her figure.

His mouth almost watered. "If you let me drop off this at home, I'm free tonight," he told her, his eyes moving over her heatedly. He could hardly believe she was interested in him in return. All he could think about was finally getting his hands on her.

Her heart skipped a beat. "My parents are out for the evening," she whispered. "We could go back to my home."

"Done." He held onto her hand with one of his and hefted the basket with the other. Swiftly they headed back to the restaurant to drop off the bread. Even in his distraction, he was amused. A cook never ate her own bread. His mother was such a contradiction.

Once the delivery was made, Morgan and Merideth set out through the town toward the second district where she lived. Her parents were indeed out for the night and the place was dark. She lit only two lamps and carried one with her down the hall toward her room. "I kept hoping," she said softly, "that you'd catch up with me."

He smiled. "I was afraid you didn't want me."

"Oh no!" Her eyes widened with horror. "How could you *think* that?" She set the lamp down in her room and filled the area with soft light. "Morgan, most of the women in this town are attracted to you. The rest haven't started second puberty yet."

Flustered, but pleased, he reached out to tug her into his arms. Somewhere inside him, something under his hormones seemed to protest. It seemed as if it was saying she was the wrong woman. He ignored the voice in favor of enjoying how she felt in his arms. She was so beautiful!

Their mouths met without hurry. After waiting for so long, they wanted to enjoy every second. Her arms wound around his neck and she pressed her body against his. "Take off your gloves," she said. "I've dreamed of feeling your hands."

He wasn't about to argue with that, and he tugged his gloves off. His hands splayed over her back and then slid under the edge of her tunic. She gasped. "Your hands are so hot! It's like I can feel your power."

He grinned. "Maybe it's just your effect on me." He kissed her again and tugged her even closer. Eagerly he began to trace kisses over her face. Before she could stop him, he had stripped her tunic over her head and left her in her bikini top. "I knew you would be worth waiting for," he murmured thickly, his eyes devouring her curves.

"Oh yeah?" She grabbed the edge of his tunic. "Well, let's be fair here." She stripped his tunic off him and then stopped in shock as she saw the golden lines that flowed over his body. A part of her saw them as being absolutely beautiful against his strong chest. The rest of her was horrified. "Morgan . . ."

He only then realized his folly. He stiffly took his tunic from her and stepped back to give her room. "Yes," he said. "I'm a Chronicle."

She wrapped her arms around herself. "I don't know what to think," she whispered. "Most of me is thinking 'this is Morgan. He's no monster.' But a part of me is scared of you." She looked at him sadly and with longing. "You're still Morgan. I would still want you for my first lover. But . . . there's a rumor that . . . that mating with a Chronicle will give you power. If I got power from you . . ."

He pulled his tunic on. "It would put us both at risk." He looked at her longingly. "I completely forgot my lines, you know. Thank you, for that."

She managed a wan smile. Her heart felt like it was breaking. "You're welcome." She walked over to look out the window. What she had to do was somehow easier now, and also harder. "You know," she said. "Maybe you ought to leave Stalagmite."

He looked at her in shock. "What?"

Her fingers curled into the windowsill. "It would be hard on both of us. We wanted to be lovers, but we can't. People would be suspicious as to why we didn't give in. And when you never had anyone for a lover . . . it might make someone begin to snoop around."

There was a very cold sort of logic in what she said. He picked up his gloves and pulled them on. "You're probably right." His frown darkened. "And I really shouldn't tell my parents. If they know why I leave, then if someone finds out, they could be blamed. Bad enough they have allowed me to live. They could be murdered as traitors."

She fought to keep her voice from quivering. "Then you're leaving?"

He hesitated. "Yes," he finally said. He reached out and softly touched her hair. "Merideth . . . you'll make a man very happy someday. I'm sorry it can't be me."

"Thank you." She closed her eyes as she heard him leave the room. Only when the door shut behind him did tears well up and flow down her cheeks. "Tell me," she whispered brokenly. "Tell me that the Fury in his life will love him more than I do."

The MoonKin Faerie flew over to hug her around the neck comfortingly. "She will," she said softly. "I swear it on my wings."

Morgan left the house and pulled the hood of his cloak over his head. Snow was falling lightly now. He kept the hood pulled low over his head to keep the few people still milling around from recognizing him. He thought there might be one last ship leaving for Spectrum that night, and he was hoping to get onboard.

He was in luck. The last ship to Prismatic had just started to prepare to leave. There was room for one more, and he used the last of the money he had on hand to pay for the ticket. His cabin was on the lowest passenger deck near the back but he didn't mind. He felt slightly numb. It was hard to believe he was running away from home to protect his parents and Merideth.

As he locked his door for the night, he felt a sudden fierce throbbing in his chest. It spread through his entire body and brought with it an ache that was physical pain. *North.* His lines burned and throbbed. He needed to go *north.*

Spectrum was technically both north and south, but boats only sailed north around Glacia; the currents were too strong to sail south. Because of it, Spectrum was considered very, very, very far north. It was nearly a month's journey away by boat.

He walked over to look out the window. Maybe in that month's time he would be able to accept how his life had just changed. The really absolutely worst part was probably the frustration. Frustration for the restrictions of the world. Frustration for not being able to live his own life.

Frustration, he thought grouchily, for not getting his hands on Merideth. He might as well get used to it though. Odds were that he would never get to satisfy his final curiosity until he someday met his Fury.

Whenever that may be.

Chapter Sixteen

For the first two weeks of the journey, Morgan didn't emerge from his cabin unless he was going to get food. Word quickly began to spread among the passengers. All of them were *positive* that he was a Master Magi. He was young and attractive yet single. He was powerful enough that you could sense it, but he was a loner. He had all the trademarks of a Master.

As he stood on the deck for fresh air, he felt someone coming up behind him. He turned sharply, his senses very acute and growing sharper by the day. He didn't trust anyone. He knew what people were suspecting and he let them. It didn't mean he would let his guard down.

Behind him he found an attractive young woman with thick ebony hair and sparkling blue eyes. He didn't need to see the bracelet around her wrist to know she was Linked to someone; it could be felt on her power. She was dressed like a forest dweller, and he had to assume she would be disembarking at Carnelian when they stopped there briefly in a day or two. "Yes?" he asked warily.

"I just thought I'd do what no one else seems to have the nerve to do and actually approach you." She walked over to lean on the railing. "My mate and I were visiting Glacia with our daughter. We're on our way home to Carnelian now." She drew her thumb over her cheek and nose. "Mildred Renaire, Soil Magi, at your service."

He returned the gesture. "Morgan Chronis, Air Magi. Likewise, ma'am." He leaned on the railing as well, and the wind ruffled his hair. "Are you on a family trip?"

"We wanted Kelsey to see other lands." She chuckled. "That girl. She's barely five but she's a handful." She glanced toward the afternoon sun in the distance. "She's well before first puberty, but . . . we suspect she may be a Master Magi."

He lifted a brow. "Stronger than average lightning?" It was a mark of Masters and Chronicles alike because he had been the same way himself. "Don't tell me she set a house on fire."

"Guilty of that, are you?" she murmured drolly.

He had to smile. "No comment."

She laughed. "As I thought. Well, no houses on fire, but her lightning is as strong as an Air/Thunder Magi's. Most people I've ever talked to indicated that was usually the first sign of a Master Magi."

He tilted his head slightly. "Are you asking me if I can confirm this for you?" He smiled wryly. "I'm not sure whether I can or not. I've never met another Master Magi. I have no idea if we, er, resonate to one another."

"Well, could you try? It's an imposition," she apologized, "but if she is, I want to know as soon as I can so that her father and I can make her transition as easy as possible. I've heard rumor that Master Magi develop their secondary element at the same time as their primary."

"They do," he said. He grimaced as he remembered first puberty. It hadn't been easy to learn to control his Air power when his Thunder power had been trying to start storms over Stalagmite. People had walked around with hoods on their cloaks for months, even in the dead of summer when storms were almost non-existent.

He thought about not getting involved. Then he thought about the image he needed to uphold. With a sigh, he said, "Alright. I'll meet her. I can't promise anything, though."

She smiled gratefully. "Thank you, Morgan." She began to look around. "Luke and Kelsey should be around here. I swear they were right over by the stairs."

He glanced around but he didn't see any children in the vicinity. Carefully he sensed the air, trying to find a power that was not developed. He caught the feeling of one, but it seemed to be coming from over his head. Puzzled, he wandered closer to one of the walls that supported the deck's game cabin; it had all manner of games inside and was used for entertainment by the passengers.

A young man not much older than Mildred came running up to her, his brown eyes dark with worry. "Mildred, I can't find Kelsey. She up and vanished on me!"

She groaned and put her head in her hands. "That girl!" She began to look around in unlikely places. "Kelsey! You come out here this instant!" She pointed down the deck. "Luke, check over there."

Luke Renaire didn't object and hurried that direction. Morgan studied the wall he was in front of and called on his power. Air swept around his feet and lifted him up into the air and over the roof. He landed gently and knelt down to keep his balance. He immediately spotted a small figure crouched near the pipe that spewed smoke into the air from the heaters below.

She was no higher than his knee in size, despite his own shorter height, and she had a cap of bright red hair. Her eyes were crystalline blue and reflected the sunlight like gems. Her face and arms were both liberally covered with soot. "Hi there," he said softly.

Her lower lip trembled. "Hi," she whispered. "Am I in trouble?"

"Afraid so. Can you crawl over here so I can get you down?" He eased closer, worried that if she got startled she might lose her balance and go tumbling off the roof.

"But you're a stranger." She watched his outstretched hand warily. "You might kidnap me or something."

He grinned at her. She seemed like a spunky little thing. "Well, of course I would. I kidnap children and make them clean my house."

Her eyes grew saucer round and then suddenly she shot him a dirty look. "You're fibbing! Meany!" The fib, however, had made her more inclined to trust him because now she could recognize what his power felt like when he was telling the truth and when he was lying. "My name's Kelsey."

"I'm Morgan." He edged closer to her. "Come here, Soot."

"Soot?" She tilted her head as she began to carefully creep toward him. She was wary of falling too.

"Your face is covered in it." She was in reach, and he swiftly reached out and scooped her up in his arms. His lines immediately pulsed and a tingling sensation swept through them. It was a shock of recognition that resonated through his entire body. Stunned, he stared at the little girl in his arms. She wasn't a Master Magi. She was a *Chronicle*. He was sure of it. "By the moons," he breathed softly.

She seemed to have sensed something too because she was staring at his chest. "You're warm," she said. "And you make my skin itch. How come I feel your power?" She wrinkled up her nose. "You're a Master Magi, aren't you?"

"After a fashion." He held tight to her as he used his power to carry them back down to the deck and safety. "Found her," he told Mildred with a cheer he didn't truly feel. His mind was racing a mile an hour. A part of it was shock. A part of it was terror for Kelsey. Even the most loving parents could turn on their child.

Luke got to him first and snatched Kelsey up into his arms. "Kelsey!" he said sharply. "Don't scare us like that again!" He clutched his daughter tight for a moment and looked at Morgan gratefully. "Thank you." He handed Kelsey to Mildred as she came running up so he could run his thumb over his cheek and nose. "I am Luke Renaire, a Water Magi."

Morgan started to return the gesture but saw there was soot on his hands from holding Kelsey. He smiled ruefully. "I would return the gesture, but I would look like your daughter if I tried. Morgan Chronis, an Air Magi."

Mildred gasped as she saw his pale brown gloves were covered in soot. "Oh no! Kelsey!" she scolded. "Apologize to Morgan."

Kelsey lowered her gaze. "I'm sorry, Morgan." She held her arms out to him. "You carry me again. You're warm."

Morgan obligingly took her and settled her on his hip. Seeing the two parents' surprised faces, he explained, "It seems Master Magi do indeed recognize each other. Like always does recognize like, I suppose."

"Oh dear." Mildred studied her daughter. "She was trouble enough before. The moons help us if she turns out to be a Fire element!"

Morgan thought of Kelsey's natural gravitation toward heat and smoke and had to think Fire sounded like a good guess. He flipped her over and tossed her across his shoulder. She shrieked with laughter. "You are a Water Magi," he reminded Luke. "If anything that should give you a means to extinguish blazes."

Kelsey wiggled around until she could see her parents. "Can Morgan have dinner with us?" she asked.

"Well, that is up to Morgan," Luke reminded her. He smiled at the younger man. "We would be honored if you joined us, though."

Morgan hesitated. "Well . . ."

"Please?" Kelsey's lower lip trembled and her eyes swam with tears. "Please? Please, please? I'll eat my vegetables and everything."

Morgan discovered something then. He discovered that he had absolutely no willpower to resist the little blue-eyed, soot-covered scamp. It wasn't just the sense of like meeting like. It was Kelsey herself. It would have taken a hardhearted man to resist her. She would break a few hearts in her life, of that he was sure. "Alright," he sighed. "Thank you for asking me."

As he was preparing to go to dinner that night, he discovered that his cloak and his gloves were both covered in soot and neither would wash clean with what he had on hand. His options were to go without, and reveal his lines, or to not go at all.

He scrubbed a hand over his eyes. Why couldn't his lines have been on his legs? It would have made everything even easier. Or at least not his hands. He studied his right palm where the symbol 'chron' was etched. He had often wondered if it was a fluke or there for a reason.

Someone knocked on the door and he hastily yanked his gloves and cloak on. "Just a minute!" he called. A look in the mirror assured him that everything was covered, and he walked over to open the door. "Yes?"

"Morgan!" Kelsey attached herself to his leg. Thankfully, she was clean this time. "Mama made you a present! And I got to bring it because it was my fault you got all dirty!"

Without dislodging the child attached to him, he picked up the box sitting by the door. He set it on the table and curiously opened it. Inside, he found a new cloak and gloves. Since they were white, there was a matching pair of slacks and a tunic to go with them. "Well, thank you," he said to Kelsey. "I was beginning to worry I wouldn't be able to attend dinner."

"Why do you wear them anyway?" She climbed onto a chair to watch him. "Are you burned?"

"I'm sensitive to the sun," he told her.

She regarded him solemnly. "You're fibbing again."

He said nothing. Only Magi before first puberty had the ability to tell the difference in someone's power when they were telling the truth or lying. Linked mates also had that ability, but only between one another. "Yes," he finally said. "I am."

"Why?"

"Because I can't tell you the real reason." He ruffled her hair gently. "Go back to your parents. I'll see you at dinner."

She hopped down and ran to the door. "You better not forget!" she scolded. Quick as a blink she was out the door and gone.

He just sighed. He was stuck now. With a wry smile he traded his dirty clothes for the clean ones. He was very grateful to Mildred for providing them. He had been getting tired of the same old thing over and over again anyway.

When he walked into the dining room, it was mostly full. The Renaires sat at a table to the side near a window, and Kelsey was standing on her seat waving at him. With a smile, he walked over to them. "Know what?" he told Kelsey. He scooped her up for a hug. "I'm going to start calling you Soot." He swiped his thumb over her cheek to remove a lingering trace. "Because you seem to be always in it."

"Believe me," Luke said dryly, "that's more accurate than you know." He smiled. "Thank you for joining us."

"Thank you for inviting me." Morgan set Kelsey down and took his seat. He was well aware of the inviting gazes of people around the room but he ignored them. Not only did he not trust anyone, he felt again that feeling inside that was telling him none of them were right. He wanted his Fury.

Mildred caught sight of the gazes and hardly blamed them. If she hadn't been madly in love with Luke, she might have made an invitation herself. Still, Morgan's disinterest caused her to ask, "Not through second puberty?"

"No, I am." He smiled wryly. "It's just . . . difficult to find someone I trust enough to share my power with." In more ways than one, he thought.

For a while, there was silence as they ate dinner. Morgan and Luke, each on a different side of Kelsey, took turns picking up the things that she managed to drop. In the process of straightening after picking up Kelsey's napkin for the fifth time, Morgan heard someone at the next table over say, "They killed another Chronicle in Crystalia."

"How old was it?" a male at the table asked.

"Twelve."

"Good riddance to bad rubbish."

It took considerable willpower not to let his hands shake. He had entirely lost his appetite and couldn't find a way to pretend he wasn't upset by the news. He didn't have to. Mildred was equally disgusted and pushed her plate away. "What filth," she said softly but scathingly. "Any parent who could do that to their child ought to be the one killed!"

Morgan looked at her in surprise. Luke nodded. "I agree. I've heard so many outlandish tales that I've stopped believing any of them." He smoothed a hand down Kelsey's hair. "The idea of any parent capable of killing their child . . ."

Morgan glanced out the window at the rolling sea. "People believe something for so long that it becomes truth," he murmured. "And they're so willing to accept that truth that they don't recognize it for a lie when it walks by."

"Aptly put." Mildred sighed. "Well, I have effectively lost my appetite. I need fresh air. This room is suddenly stuffy."

Since they were all in agreement, they left the dining room. Kelsey rode on Morgan's shoulders and held onto his hair for balance. He held her legs securely so she wouldn't tumble off his shoulders. He was beginning to feel more comfortable about Mildred and Luke because of their statements during dinner. Something told him that maybe, just maybe, there was a chance for Kelsey.

"Are you from Glacia, Morgan?" Luke asked.

"I am."

"Were your parents sad to see you go?" Mildred sat down on one of the benches near the railing and stretched her legs out. She was beginning to get tired of being on a boat.

Morgan lowered his gaze. His parents were probably worried sick about him. He was fairly sure they would understand why he left, but that wouldn't change the fact that they loved him and would worry. "Yes," he said quietly.

Luke studied him closely. He was beginning to feel a suspicion inside that he couldn't quite put his finger on. There was something about Morgan that didn't add up. "Why do you wear gloves and a cloak all the time?" he asked. "Is it because you're from Glacia?"

"I'm just sensitive to the light."

Luke looked at Kelsey and could see by the look on her face that he was fibbing. Though he didn't want to make assumptions, Luke could only think of one reason anyone would wear such confining clothing when they weren't truly sensitive to sun or cold. He had heard that the lines that marked a Chronicle could appear anywhere on the body. They were also reputed to be exactly like Master Magi in many ways. They were the only two rumors he had ever believed.

His heart stopped. If Morgan *was* a Chronicle, and he was responding to Kelsey . . . Terror for his daughter closed his throat. He reached out and grabbed Morgan's arm. "Tell me!" he said urgently, but quietly. "If Kelsey is in danger, I want to know!"

Mildred got to her feet. She had been following his line of thought and was in complete agreement. "Morgan," she pleaded. "Please. We won't look down on you. Kelsey is our child. We need to know as soon as we can so we can be prepared to protect her!"

Morgan lifted Kelsey off his shoulders and set her down gently. "Not tonight," he said quietly. "Too many people might hear. But if you come visit me tomorrow . . . I'll tell you whatever I can." There was no other choice. He had to take the risk for Kelsey's sake and his own.

He didn't sleep that night. Anxiety would either keep him awake or torment him with nightmares. By the time dawn came, he had given up on any sort of rest. He simply sat by his window and watched the sea roll by.

The knock came on his door right after breakfast. He took a deep breath and walked over to open it. "Come in," he said to the family standing just outside. On one look he knew they had not slept well either. Only Kelsey seemed to be full of energy, as usual.

As he shut the door behind them, Mildred and Luke walked over to sit at the small table in the cabin. Kelsey climbed up to sit on the edge of the bed. She didn't know why everyone was afraid suddenly. She liked Morgan. He was like a big brother, and she had always wanted one of those.

Morgan didn't know where to start. Finally, at a loss, he simply removed his gloves and held up his hands. The golden lines flowing over them were plainly visible. There truly was no mistaking them, especially because his skin was fair from lack of exposure to the sun.

Mildred took a sharp breath. "You really are a Chronicle," she breathed.

"Yes, I am." He removed his cloak and the short sleeves of his tunic revealed the lines flowed up his arms and disappeared under his sleeves. "They're also across my chest," he said as calmly as he could. "They developed when I entered first puberty."

"Pretty..." Kelsey reached out to touch his arm when he walked closer. The lines were warm and tingled her hand when she placed it on his arm. "What are they?"

"Near as I can tell," he told her, "they're lines made from Dragon power." He looked at the two astonished adults. "They're a map that will lead me to my Fury." He smoothed a hand down Kelsey's hair. "But you can't tell *anyone* about these lines, Soot."

"I promise," she said solemnly.

Mildred found her voice first. "Then Chronicles do have a pact with Dragons?"

"Not exactly." He shrugged one shoulder. "I don't know very much. The Kin could tell us more. But from what I was told already, Chronicles and Furies are two halves of a whole. They are complete together. I'm not sure what it means."

A sharp stab of longing rose inside him and he pressed a fist against his heart. *North.* Always north. He felt her. He felt his Fury calling to him. "I want to find her," he said softly. "So terribly. I've never wanted anything more."

Luke drew a long breath. "Then Kelsey..."

"Is a Chronicle child." Morgan glanced at the little girl. "I'm not sure how I know. Maybe it is because the Dragon power meant to make her lines is present even now, just as her Fire element is. Neither can manifest until she develops. But because I am fully developed I can feel it."

"And maybe," Mildred whispered, "it is something new in Chronicles. Maybe it is nature's way of trying to save Chronicles. Perhaps this world needs you." She straightened her shoulders. "It changes nothing," she said fiercely. "Kelsey is our daughter. I will not . . . not kill her for being another race." Even the idea was sickening. "We'll just have to move with her somewhere that we can keep her under wraps till her lines appear."

"If rumor is right," Morgan said, "then her lines could appear anywhere. She might end up with them on a place that's hard to hide, like her face. And when she enters second puberty..."

Luke winced as he suddenly understood. "I'm sorry, Morgan."

Morgan smiled wryly. "Well, the girl I wanted didn't report me to the Militia. She helped me escape actually. But Kelsey might not be so lucky. If only we could find her Fury," he murmured. "He could protect her. He'd also be the one perfect to help her through second puberty."

Mildred's eyes widened. "A Fury is ..."

"A Chronicle's lover? Apparently. Someone that will understand us and belong only with us." He struggled to keep his voice neutral and not give away all his fierce desperation to find his own. "The Kin who told me said it was a bond stronger than even Linked Magi felt. Somewhere in this world there is a man who is meant to love Kelsey. There is a Fury for every Chronicle."

A chill went down Luke's back. "By the moons," he whispered. "If we've been killing Chronicles..."

"Then the Furies are dying of broken hearts," Mildred finished softly. "How it must hurt to look for your other half and discover they were killed!" She covered her face with her hands. "What have the Magi done? There must be something we can do to try and stop it!"

Luke shook his head. "Like what? We can't change the opinions of the world overnight, Mil. And even if we somehow managed to find other Chronicle children, their parents might not be as open as us and Morgan's parents."

"But . . . there should be *some* way to disguise them! If it weren't for his lines, no one would ever know Morgan wasn't Magi. We all thought he was a Master Magi."

Morgan suddenly had an idea. It was risky, and slightly crazy, but it might just work. "What if we formed a . . . group of sorts? Like a haven for Master Magi? We could look for other children. If their parents were amiable, we could have them join. And maybe someday we could help them live long enough to find their own Fury."

Mildred frowned thoughtfully. "That might work. We'd have to get approval from the king in Prismatic, of course. But I don't see it being a problem. The rest of the world will be kept in the dark as to our real motives."

She looked at Luke. "What do you think? If we can, I want to do this. For Kelsey's sake, and for Morgan's."

"Mine!" He stared at her.

She smiled. "To help you find your Fury as well."

Luke nodded. "I am in agreement as well. What do you say, Morgan? Will you lead us? You're the Chronicle." He smiled. "You're the one who would recognize the children if we found them."

Morgan slowly sat down. He felt more than a little dazed. But a part of him felt that this was right. It was the same feeling that told him his Fury was waiting for him. It was a feeling he couldn't help but trust. "Okay," he said on a long breath. "So what do we call ourselves?"

"Good question."

"I know, I know!" Kelsey began jumping up and down on the bed.

Morgan hastily caught her before she fell. He firmly sat her down again. "What do you think, Soot?"

"Well," she said, "because we're gonna keep the world in the dark, how 'bout Black Magi?"

"Her level of astuteness frightens me," Luke muttered.

"I think it's perfect," Morgan said. "For one thing, she's definitely right. For another, it gives up a very easily recognized symbol we can use. We'll just take the chalice symbol that represents the Magi and make it black. If we stick it on the back of some long white cloaks, then no one will be the wiser. It will also cover all but the most troublesome of lines for any Chronicle."

Mildred, as a Soil Magi, always carried a bag of sand with her to make cloth items from. She opened the bag and poured some of the sand into her hand. It swirled up and around her palm as her power flowed into it. There was a flash of green colored light and suddenly the sand condensed into the shape of a white cloak. On the back rested the black chalice.

It was just the right size for Morgan and he pulled it on. The sleeves went slightly past his wrists and the ends of the cloak just touched the tops of his boots. It fastened down the front in such a way that it could not be seen through. On the back was a hood he could pull over his head as needed. It was also much lighter than his prior cloak and therefore more comfortable. "How do I look?" he asked.

"This might work," Luke said. "Mil, let's go with Morgan right to Spectrum. We can cross the land by findral and stop at every city. That way we can get word started."

"And maybe we can find more children to save," Morgan said quietly. He looked down at his hands where the lines were etched so vividly. He had never known if there was a reason for his existence. He had never known if he had a purpose, or if it truly was a quirk of destiny that his parents had been so unusual.

For all he knew, this wasn't his purpose either. But he was going to do his best. He was going to make a place where Chronicles could be nurtured in safety even if in secret. And while he was doing that, he was going to find a Kin who could tell him more about Chronicles. It was slightly awkward to realize he knew nothing about his own race.

Chapter Seventeen

The ship put to dock in Mirah on the southern edge of Spectrum two weeks later. When Morgan and the Renaire family disembarked, all of them were wearing the white cloaks that they had chosen to mark them as the Black Magi.

Poor Morgan wasn't ready for the weather. He had known that the primary lands of the Magi were deserts, but he hadn't realized how hot they really could be. His acclimation to the snow, and his heavy cloak, immediately made him feel as if he were smothering. He had to quickly use his Air power to bring his temperature down before he passed out. "Ugh."

Mildred chuckled softly at him. "Too warm for you, snow boy?"

"Just a little!" He glowered at her but couldn't hold the expression for long. Mildred and Luke had become as close to him as family. Kelsey, well, he had no objections to admitting that she'd had him wrapped around her finger from day one.

She was currently riding on his back. She was sleepy and ready for a nap because it was mid-morning, but she was also energized from the new places and new people.

The four of them went directly to the inn to get rooms to rest. Many curious gazes followed them as they went, but no one said anything. The innkeeper seemed equally surprised but he just smiled and said, "Welcome. Two rooms or three?"

"Two." Morgan smiled. "Kelsey can share a room with me. That way Mildred and Luke can have some personal time."

Mildred's cheeks turned pink. "Morgan!"

Kelsey giggled. "Mommy's blushing!"

"Because your daddy's gonna kiss her silly," Morgan said cheerfully, bouncing her on his back. "You get to be my roommate, Soot. But no hogging the blankets, and no snoring."

"Kay."

The innkeeper chuckled. "She reminds me of my daughter, so my sympathies." He drew his thumb over his cheek and nose. "Eli Lakemore, Water Magi."

"Morgan Chronis, Air Magi, leader of the Black Magi," Morgan said calmly. He had been waiting for an opportunity to say it.

They had decided on the boat that it was best not to go crying their name from the rooftops. Better to mention it casually in introductions and explain only when asked. Master Magi were known for being loners, and they had to keep up that illusion at all times.

"Mildred Renaire, Soil Magi, also of Black Magi. This is Luke, my mate. He is a Water Magi." Both mates drew their thumbs over their cheek and nose. Mildred gestured to Kelsey with a smile. "Our daughter, Kelsey."

"Hi!" Kelsey gave an ear-splitting yawn and rubbed at her eyes. "I'm sleepy, Morgan," she complained. "I want a nap."

"Okay, Soot. You can have a nap." He plucked her off his back and carried her in his arms. She tucked her head on his shoulder tiredly. "Which rooms?" he asked Eli.

"Five and six." Eli studied them curiously. "I have never heard of Black Magi."

"We just formed," Luke said. "Morgan is a Master Magi, as is Kelsey. We're hoping to gather more Master Magi, particularly children, to aide them in the difficulties of first puberty. Morgan set roofs on fire."

"Sure," the younger man mumbled, "tell everyone, why don't you?"

Eli's eyes widened and then narrowed slightly with immense curiosity. "You recognize children who are future Master Magi then?" When Morgan nodded, Eli leaned on the counter. "In that case, if you wouldn't mind, I'd like you to meet my daughter. She is about Kelsey's age I think, and she is certainly not using normal lightning."

"I would be glad to meet her," Morgan said with a smile. "Perhaps around dinnertime? For now, we need to get this one to sleep before she falls over."

"Gladly." Eli smiled. "I will speak with her mother in the meantime."

Luke and Mildred followed Morgan as he left the room and headed down the stairs to the next level lower. Most desert inns had three stories, but one was under the sand to keep it cooler. "What if she is not a Chronicle?"

Mildred murmured.

"I'll think of that when I get there," Morgan murmured back. "If anything, we might be able to check Eli and his mate out and see how they feel. If they're still open-minded, we might as well ask them to join. Odds are that his daughter, if not a Chronicle, really is a Master Magi. She'll have a tough time of it anyway."

At dinner later that evening, the small restaurant attached to the inn was busy. But because inn patrons had priority, there was a table just big enough for the Black Magi to sit at with Kelsey. There was even a large pillow for her to sit on to reach the table better.

A buzz of confusion and speculation ran through the room as people studied them. People had asked Eli about the odd strangers, and he had given them what he had been told. Because of it, the Magi were more curious than ever.

One of the patrons there that night was a Militia soldier. He walked over to the table where the Black Magi sat and saluted crisply. "Good evening. Is it true you are forming a faction?"

"We'd like to," Morgan said as calmly as he could. Nerves he couldn't help fluttered in his stomach. He fought an urge to check and make sure his hands and arms were still covered. "But we need permission from the king, of course."

"Perhaps I can assist." The soldier smiled. "I am returning to Prismatic on the morrow. I can take word with me to the king. By the time you reach the city, he should be ready to make a decision and meet you."

"We would be very grateful," Mildred told him with a smile. "It is kind of you to go out of your way."

There was sadness for a moment on the soldier's face. "My sister was a Master Magi. She couldn't handle regular society. She disappeared into the forests and never returned. Maybe if there'd been a group like you, she'd have had a better chance of adapting."

"That's what we're hoping for our daughter," Luke said. "Provided she doesn't burn down cities."

The soldier laughed. "We'd appreciate it if she didn't. Good luck." He turned and headed back to his own table to let them finish their dinner in peace.

"That is lucky," Luke murmured softly. "It may save us a lot of time in the end."

"Thank goodness," Morgan said with heartfelt feeling. "I have to admit, I was having trouble figuring out what I wanted to say to the king, and how. A couple votes of confidence from others will go a long way."

After dinner, they went to lay Kelsey down to sleep. She was already yawning again. Once she was settled, the three adults went back upstairs to meet with Eli. He was in the lobby of the inn and sweeping out sand that had been tracked in.

An attractive young woman with pale blond hair was straightening figurines on shelves. The bracelet she wore matched the one Eli wore. She was obviously Eli's mate, and the mother of the aforementioned daughter. "Good evening," Morgan said to her pleasantly.

"Good evening." She turned with a smile and drew her thumb over her cheek and nose. "I am Serenity Lakemore. Most call me Ren for short. I am a Fire Magi." She studied Morgan and the two Renaires curiously. "Are all of you Master Magi?"

"No, just Morgan and Kelsey." Mildred smiled. "If Morgan wasn't barely eight years younger than Luke and I, we'd have adopted him."

"It doesn't stop you from bossing me around," Morgan mumbled.

"Naturally."

Ren and Eli exchanged a smile. While he went to fetch their daughter, she sat down on the edge of the counter. "We truly do appreciate you at least meeting our daughter," she said. "Jayda is . . . a handful. Her lightning rivals that of Magi with Air/Thunder power. She also seems to develop far faster than normal Magi. Most Magi stay as children mentally until first puberty but she has these moments of insight that are almost frightening."

"That certainly sounds like our Kelsey," Luke said. "Morgan?"

Morgan grimaced. "Don't ask. Please, I beg you. You already blabbed about me setting roofs on fire."

Eli walked into the room with a little girl in his arms. Her eyes were black in color and very sleepy as she rubbed at them. Her hair was a riot of seagreen colored curls inherited from her father. "This is Jayda," Eli said as he set her down gently on her feet. "She will be turning five in a few months." He nudged his daughter gently. "Greet them properly, Jay."

Jayda yawned again and then obligingly drew her thumb over her cheek and nose. "I'm Jayda." She focused on Morgan fully and was immediately intrigued. He looked . . . different. Somehow he seemed completely different from all the other Magi she had met. "Who're you?"

He crouched down closer to her height. She was a striking young child and he had no doubt that she would only grow lovelier as time passed. What he liked most, though, was the spark of humor in her eyes. This one had a playful streak to rival Kelsey. "My name is Morgan."

She walked closer to him, studying his face. "You're pretty."

He felt his cheeks heat. "Shut up, Luke," he muttered at the softly snickering male behind him. He ignored his friends and focused on Jayda again. "You're pretty too," he told her. He offered a hand. "I don't bite, promise."

She took his hand and he instantly felt the same tingling sensation sweeping through his lines. His heart began to beat harder. Another one. This was another Chronicle child. "Yes," he said softly, "she's like me."

"Oh thank goodness," Ren breathed softly.

Luke lifted a brow before smiling with sympathy. "Were you worried she might be a Chronicle? I have heard they are very similar to Master Magi."

"Very much so." Eli let out a breath. "Not that we would have killed Jayda." Disgust crossed his face. "Any parent who could do such a thing should be flayed alive. It's more of an abomination than any Chronicle could be."

"You're in the minority with that view," Mildred noted. "The rest of the world is firmly set in their beliefs. And the saddest part is that they don't even have a good reason why."

"I must agree." Ren lowered her gaze. "There was a boy in town five years or so ago. He . . . well, when he hit first puberty, he grew lines. He was a Chronicle, and he was put immediately to death. He was a good boy. He liked sweetbread. And yet, suddenly, to everyone he was a monster."

"You knew him." Morgan lifted Jayda into his arms as he stood. She looped an arm around his shoulders and yawned sleepily. He had to smile; some things were universal.

"He was my little brother." She ran her hands over her arms to fight a chill. When Eli wrapped his arms around her, she leaned against him gratefully. "My parents . . . I haven't spoken to them since."

Morgan glanced at Mildred and Luke. Both nodded slightly. Turning back to the Lakemores, Morgan said, "Is there somewhere we can talk privately? The Black Magi prefer to keep their secrets from outside ears."

"Understandably." Eli gestured toward the door behind the counter. "My study is there. We can speak in there privately. We've already closed the inn for the night." He smiled wryly. "We have no more room."

Following Eli, they all headed behind the counter and into the room he had indicated. There was only just enough room for all of them, and Morgan and Luke opted to stand because there weren't enough chairs. Jayda sat on her mom's lap and was asleep within moments.

"I suppose you wish to discuss Jayda joining you," Eli said as he sat on the edge of his desk. "It would mean Ren and me joining you as well, of course. We would need at least a month to take care of the inn and such."

"Before we discuss that," Morgan said, "first, I need to tell you something."

"What is that?" Ren asked.

Because there was no way to say it that they would believe, he simply removed his gloves and held up his hands. Lamplight flowed over his lines and turned them stark gold in the lamplight.

Both Eli and Ren took sharp breaths of shock. "You're . . ." Ren's hands flew up to cover her cheeks as she looked down at her daughter. "Oh no! By the moons . . . no!" She clutched Jayda tight against her heart. "No one is touching my daughter!" she vowed fiercely.

"It is that very thing that makes us willing to tell you the truth," Mildred said softly. "Kelsey is also a Chronicle child. We too could not bear the idea. Morgan had the idea that we make a haven for Chronicle children to protect them until we can find their Furies or a Dragon to take them to safety."

Eli slowly raked a hand through his hair. He didn't know what to think or how to feel. The only thing he could be absolutely certain of was that they could not stay in Mirah. There were too many people who knew Jayda. If her lines were in a visible place, that would be bad enough. But even if they weren't, when she began second puberty . . . "We can't stay here."

"You are welcome to join us," Luke said. "The Black Magi exist for this very reason. We are heading to

Prismatic. It is such a big city that we can blend in. We can operate a base from there and travel as needed to find others. Perhaps after a while they will come to us."

"Then we will go with you." Ren looked at Eli. "We might not change the world, but we can change a part of it. And . . . who knows? Maybe someday things will get better." She looked back at Morgan, then at Luke and Mildred. "Thank you for trusting us. We are glad to join you."

Before Eli and Ren could leave Mirah, there was a lot they had to do. They needed to arrange the sale of their inn, and they needed to get rid of most of their belongings. Morgan and the Renaires helped however they could by promoting and arranging sales. Although, much to Morgan's amusement, he most often found himself babysitting the two children.

Not quite three weeks later, they were in possession of a sturdy cart, a couple tents, and a pair of strong findrals. Eli and Ren donned the cloak of the Black Magi, and they all set out into the desert just after dawn one morning.

Jayda and Kelsey had become the best of friends. They would take turns climbing all over Morgan, much to the amusement of everyone else. He took it all in stride. He loved both girls very deeply.

The trip across the desert was two weeks long. It could have been shorter but they needed to rest often. It was hotter than average during this time of summer, and it tired out the little girls. It also sapped Morgan's strength.

"You'll adapt," Eli assured him. "I promise."

Lying on the bottom of the cart with a blanket over his head to block the sun and trap his power to keep him cool, Morgan could only say, "I get to zap you with lightning if you're wrong."

The lightning was unneeded. Eli was proven right just before they reached Prismatic. The 'trial by fire' exposure to the desert sun had forced Morgan to adapt very swiftly. By the afternoon that they rode into the city limits, he was barely using his powers at all. He couldn't wait, however, to have his own room where he could strip down and relax for a few minutes.

As they were riding through the main street, a Militia soldier came running up to them and made them stop. Morgan recognized him immediately from Mirah. He smiled. "Good morning. I hope you have been well."

The soldier smiled and saluted. "I have been. I hope you have been the same." He tugged gently on the pigtails of both girls as they peered out of the cart at them. "I see you have gotten more Master Magi."

"We have. We hope more will soon follow suit."

The soldier nodded. "As to that, the king would like to speak with you, Morgan. When I spoke to my captain, and he spoke to his Argyle. The Argyle went to the king who has professed an interest in your Black Magi. I have every confidence that you will soon have your official sanction as a faction."

Argyles were the highest of rank in the Militia, and answered only to the king. There were only a handful of them across the world. While having votes of confidence all the way up through the ranks to the king was reassuring, Morgan couldn't ignore his nerves. A part of him didn't want to meet the king. "When will he wish to see me?"

"He asked that you come to see him upon your arrival. I can escort you there now if you wish."

"Please do." He firmly stomped on his jittery stomach and told himself to get a grip. The king, unless by some miracle was a Chronicle too, would not know what Morgan and the children were. He would be as easy to fool as the rest of the Magi. They were so willing to believe what they were told that it made Morgan sad for the future of the world.

"Look," Jayda whispered as she saw the palace looming in front of them a short while later. "It's so big!"

"Why does a king need a big place like that?" Kelsey demanded of her mother. "Why can't he live like normal people?"

The soldier coughed to hide a laugh and the other adults covered smiles. As 'commoners,' they couldn't help but hold a similar feeling. Only children were allowed to get away with speaking such thoughts out loud though.

Morgan was the only one allowed into the palace. The Argyle escorted him personally into the throne room. Morgan wasn't sure what to expect but the utter decadence of the place felt slightly disturbing. Why did anyone need ivory and bronze statues? It seemed an absolute waste to him.

The king was an older man who sat on a throne of ivory and bronze. Morgan couldn't help but wonder if the lack of comfort in the chair was what made the king's posture so rigid, or if it was because he was so deeply entrenched in his status that he had forgotten how to feel anything.

He stopped several feet before the throne and drew his thumb over his cheek and nose. "I am Morgan Chronis, a Master Air Magi, of the Black Magi." He linked his hands under his cloak to keep their trembling from showing. "You asked to see me, my king?"

"Yes." The king studied him intently. He had heard Morgan was young but he had not expected to meet a young man barely past second puberty. And yet Morgan's power was potent enough it could be felt. The king sensed it as a feathery feeling along his neck, a sensation warning him that there was a stronger power present. "Your Black Magi . . . what is their purpose?"

Morgan smiled. "To make a haven for Master Magi, particularly children. It is hard to grow up different. The differences are visible even before first puberty. What I went through . . . I only made it because my parents supported me." There's an understatement, he thought. "I wish to help other children make it through."

The king was silent for a few moments. Then, "I can feel it in you. What you wish is not against the ways of the Magi. There is something very strong in you. I will give your Black Magi my official approval. You may establish a main base wherever you wish."

"We would like to be located here in Prismatic. It is easier to hide in a crowd," he said wryly.

The king laughed. "So I have heard. Very well, Morgan. Good luck."

Taking it for the dismissal it was, Morgan touched his cheek in farewell and then left the throne room. The others were still waiting outside, and he climbed up onto the front seat of the cart again. "He approves," he said.

"I thought he might," the soldier said. "Because I was so sure, I arranged for a house to be ready for you." He offered the keys to an astonished Morgan. "If you ever need assistance, do not hesitate to ask the Militia. We have seen many Magi lost to society because they could not fit in with their power."

"You have no idea," Ren murmured so softly only Eli and Luke heard her.

The keys and the locks they would fit were made with Soil power. The thin ties of power between the two allowed Morgan to follow the trail into another district. The end of the trail was a simple two-story house with a third underground. It looked rather large overall. More than large enough for however many children they could find. It was also, unfortunately, in somewhat neglected condition.

Mildred took one look at the house and said, "I can fix this."

Ren considered things. "Curtains first. And we'll make Luke and Eli remodel."

"Why us?" Luke complained.

"Because we said so."

Morgan grinned as he hopped down from the cart. He reached up to help the two children down. They were officially a faction now, yet he couldn't help but feel as if they were a large family as well. A part of him still missed his parents and always would, but the Renaires and the Lakemores helped to fill in the gaps inside his heart.

A sudden sharp stab of longing went through him. It was so fierce that it nearly drove him to his knees. Only sheer willpower kept him standing. It hurt. More than ever, it hurt. He wanted to find his Fury. He *needed* to find her.

The longing hadn't brought a direction for him to follow. It could have meant he couldn't track his Fury anymore. It could have meant that he needed to stay put. Either way, he knew he would be in Prismatic a long time.

He only sighed and scooped up each girl under an arm. "Let's find you two a room to share. And no pillow fights this time." He was *never* letting them near feather pillows again.

Chapter Eighteen

(One year later . . .)

The small town of Umber on the continent of Carnelian sat nestled between two forests. One forest led eventually to a series of mountain cliffs. The other led eventually to the closest ocean.

Overall, Umber was not much bigger than an average sized city. It was only ten miles in diameter and had a population of only ten thousand. These people, like the rest of Carnelian's population, were forest dwellers. Their manner of dress was more acclimated for the cool weather and the stinging bugs that lived in and around trees.

For the first time in a year, Morgan no longer felt as if he stood out. By the standards of some people, he was actually underdressed. The cooler weather was also a welcome balm after the heat of Prismatic. He had adjusted, but he still liked to be cool and comfortable. Maybe he wasn't better suited to be a desert boy after all.

The Black Magi had grown in size. Not by much, but it had grown. They now had another child. A little boy by the name of Roman Arequo who was a year younger than Jayda. He and his parents had been living in a small town on the edge of Spectrum. Now they resided in Prismatic with the rest of the Black Magi.

A letter had arrived recently that had asked him to meet a child who might be a Master Magi. Because the child had sounded suspiciously like a Chronicle, he had been quick to make the journey to Umber.

The father of the boy was a man named Soh Emik. He and his son ran a small shop that sold wooden statues and figurines. Soh was a Soil/Wood Magi and very strong. His son, Phedo, was borderline first puberty and most presumed he would inherit his father's element since he already had a natural inclination for it.

Morgan walked into the shop and looked around. The figurines truly were exquisite. His attention diverted as he saw a man walking out of the back of the shop. The man seemed normal enough with his slightly grizzled face and salt and pepper colored hair and beard, but for some odd reason, Morgan felt his power stinging his skin as if sensing there could be danger.

The man spotted him and smiled. "Welcome."

"Thank you." Morgan walked closer and drew his thumb over his cheek and nose. "Morgan Chronis, Air Magi, of the Black Magi."

The man returned the gesture. "Soh Emik, Soil Magi." He studied Morgan intently. "You're much younger than I assumed."

"Most say that," Morgan agreed wryly. He tilted his head slightly. "You sent me a letter asking me to meet your son?"

"Yes." Soh's face tightened. "He is displaying traits vastly unusual for a child. He is nearing first puberty and I'm worried he may be a Chronicle. If he is . . ."

"You don't want him killed?" Morgan asked softly.

"Of course not!" Soh's face tightened at the idea. "He is my child! His mother died in a quake a few years ago. Phedo is all I have left. Him being a Chronicle would change nothing for me."

"Well, let me first meet him and we'll find out what he is," Morgan suggested. Inside, he was smiling. His odd sense of danger or not, he knew Soh and Phedo would be welcome among the Black Magi.

"Dad!" The door swung wildly as a slender boy with black hair came running into the store. He looked no more than eleven or twelve, but he was already beginning to develop into a handsome young man. He sat down the sack of sand he carried, then regarded Morgan curiously. "Who are you?" he asked.

"Morgan, an Air Magi." Morgan made the sign of respect. "You must be Phedo. It's nice to meet you."

"Likewise." Phedo studied him curiously. He had never met someone like Morgan before. Something about the older man made him feel safe suddenly, as if he had found a friend he could trust. His shoulders unconsciously relaxed and he smiled. "What brings you to Umber?"

"I came to meet you." Morgan had learned to recognize the feeling he got near Chronicle children. He was nearly positive that Phedo was one as well. "To see if you are a Master Magi. I seem to have a tracking system for others."

"Oh." Phedo smiled. "Am I one?" When Morgan offered a hand, he automatically reached out to take it. An odd feeling tingled along his power in recognition of something different. Something powerful. It felt oddly soothing.

Morgan smiled, his suspicions confirmed. "Yes," he said. "You're like me."

Soh's shoulders relaxed. "Phedo, fetch the bread before the baker forgets us. Morgan and I need to talk."

"Okay!" Phedo released Morgan's hand and ran off with a wave.

As the door banged shut behind him, Morgan turned to Soh. "He is not a Master Magi," he said very quietly.

"But you . . ." The color drained from Soh's face as he looked at Morgan's gloved hands. "Oh. Oh no. By the moons . . ." He braced his hands on the counter as fear churned in his stomach. Mixed with it came a fury for the Magi who had brought them to this point. "Is your whole group . . .?"

"Me and the children. I made the Black Magi as a haven. You and Phedo are welcome to join us as well," Morgan offered.

"Gladly!" Soh straightened. "The sooner we leave, the better. He could start first puberty any day now."

"In that case, I suggest restricting him to indoors until we can leave. Once we know where his lines are, we can take the steps to hide them." Morgan looked at his hands and grimaced. "As uncomfortable as they may be at times."

The quiet air abruptly shattered in a loud scream. Morgan and Soh whirled toward the door instinctively just as they heard an outraged and disgusted voice exclaim, "It's a *Chronicle.*"

"Phedo!" Soh had gone gray as he rushed around the counter and out into the street, Morgan hot on his heels. The scene they saw made them stop in horror.

Halfway to the baker's place, Phedo had begun first puberty. Under normal circumstances, no one would have known until he began to demonstrate maturity and elemental powers. But he was a Chronicle. His shift into the next stage of his life had brought with it the most vivid part of a Chronicle's existence: lines.

His lines crisscrossed over his face and down his neck. They disappeared under his clothes, but Morgan could spot bits of them on the skin of his knee where his pants had ripped.

He was crouched on the ground and staring at his lined hands in shock and disbelief. He knew what they were but at the same time he didn't know why they were so bad. The crowd gathered around him moved like a seething wave of anger. Several of the people were armed with a multitude of weapons.

"Stop it!" Soh lunged forward.

One of the men looked at him in pity. "Soh, it's a monster. We have to kill it."

"It's Phedo! He wasn't a monster until a minute ago! What makes him different?!" Soh whirled toward Morgan. "Do something!"

"I can't." It was the hardest thing Morgan had ever done to simply stand there. "If I do something, I might give myself away. If I do that, the other children will be found. I'm sorry, Soh."

Soh lunged for the crowd but he was too late. One of the men carrying a sword lifted it and shoved it deep into Phedo's back. Blood flew and there was a small shockwave in the land as the power was disrupted. A second later, Phedo's power was no longer subconsciously felt by anyone present.

As his body fell to the ground, the crowd let Soh pass. He rushed to his son's side and lifted him into his arms. He rocked back and forth with grief. Rage was becoming hatred. How dare the Magi do this? They deserved to suffer. To suffer the way so many others had suffered.

Morgan walked over to kneel beside him. "I'm sorry," he said softly.

"It's not your fault." Soh's eyes glittered with a madness held barely in check. "Why don't you hate the Magi?"

"It's a waste of time." Morgan got to his feet. "I will return to Prismatic in the morning." He didn't say he had wished he had gotten there sooner though he felt it inside. He had learned not to wish for things that could not be changed.

As he was walking away, his lines pulsed invisibly under his concealing clothes. He felt her. He felt his Fury. For just a moment, he could feel her. Shocked, he could only stand still as a painful longing rose inside him. Tears stung his eyes and closed his throat. Wherever she was, she was so close that he could feel her emotions. She could feel him and wished to comfort him.

He waited, wished fiercely for a clue, but the map in his lines remained stubbornly silent. Impotent anger welled inside him and tangled with his grief and longing. A strong gust of wind shook the town but no one really paid heed. He certainly didn't.

As he waited on the boat the following morning, he was surprised to see Soh approaching him, a bag slung over his shoulder. "Soh," he said, startled. "What brings you here?"

"I want to join you anyway," Soh said in response. "I can't stand being in this town any longer." He lowered his voice to add, "And I don't want to see what just occurred ever happen again."

Morgan hesitated. Somehow he felt as if Soh was walking a thin line between sanity and insanity. But Soh knew their secret. If he told . . . at least if he was with them, Morgan could keep an eye on him. If he was around him long enough, he might be able to even isolate and remove his memories.

All Air Elements could do tricks with the minds of other people, but on a small scale. It also took constant and steady exposure. On the other hand, Morgan possessed many strong and unusual mental gifts that he could only assume came from him being a Chronicle. He had heard Chronicles could use high-level mind skills *without* constant exposure, yet he had been too wary to try. If it was needed on Soh, however, he would do it. "Very well," he said. "You are welcome to join us." He could only hope he didn't live to regret it.

(One year later . . .)

The Black Magi had grown no larger in size. Soh was still the only other member of the Black Magi, but Morgan was beginning to think that he was going to have to make him leave. He had already taken the steps to ensure that Soh could not speak of the Chronicles to anyone outside the sanctuary, but it saddened him to know he'd had to do it.

As he sat behind his desk and studied the older man standing across from him, he felt a chill. Soh's eyes had always been borderline mad but Morgan had dismissed it because of what he had endured. He could no longer dismiss it, not when Soh's eyes were bright with full madness. Always tangled in it was his dangerous intellect. Morgan's danger sense was high and his power stung his skin.

"Morgan, you think too small!" Soh accused his leader. "Why not find other powerful Magi and have them join us?"

"The risk is too great. And why do we need them? The purpose of the Black Magi is to shelter the Chronicle children." Morgan got to his feet, feeling shorter than he ever had before. "Soh, this not the first time you've given me this tirade. What in the name of the Underrealm is going through your mind?"

"I've come up with the solution, Morgan!" Soh's smile widened as he threw his arms wide. "The best way to protect the Chronicles is to destroy the Magi!"

It took Morgan a few seconds. He was sure he had heard wrong. But the look on the older man's face didn't change. "Destroy the Magi?" he repeated. "Absolutely not. It would destroy the world!"

"Chronicles will take their place. We will gather the most powerful Magi, and if they have Chronicles, then we'll have more. Why don't you hate the Magi, Morgan? Look what they've driven you to!" Soh gestured to the door behind him. "Those children are merely the first step for us."

The air trembled around Soh warningly as Morgan's face tightened with anger all the more potent because it was rare. "You will never lay a hand on those children," he warned softly. "I won't let you use them. You've lost your mind, Soh."

"Then I will leave." Soh sneered at him. "I will find my allies and we will be an elite Black Magi. Don't worry," he added snidely. "I won't speak of your precious sanctuary. You didn't need to weave such a complicated block in my mind."

Morgan's eyes closed partway, the silver color beneath like chips from glass. "Don't expect me to remove it," he said in a hard voice. "I'm not the naïve fool you believe me to be. Kindly remove yourself from these premises."

"Gladly." Soh stalked toward the door and shot back over his shoulder, "but I will return for those children, Morgan! Mark my words!"

The door slammed loudly behind him and Morgan slowly sank down to sit in his chair. He pressed the heels of his hands against his eyes and tried to think of what he could do. He didn't doubt Soh would be back. And he didn't doubt that Soh would find his followers. There were many crazy people in the world, and there were just as many foolish ones who would believe whatever story Soh fed them.

The study door opened slightly and the three children peered around the edge. Kelsey was seven now, and the tallest. Jayda was months shy of seven herself, and she was the same height as Roman who was five.

All three trembled with fear. They had never liked Soh but they had tried. And now Morgan looked sad, and it broke their hearts. He was their hero. He wasn't supposed to be sad.

"He needs a hug," Jayda whispered.

"Yeah." Kelsey was the first across the room and she climbed up onto Morgan's lap to wind her arms around his neck. "You need a hug," she told him imperiously.

Jayda and Roman were not to be outdone. Roman climbed up so that he was dangling off Morgan's back and Jayda wrapped her arms around Morgan's leg. Morgan's heart clenched tightly for a moment as he held them all closer. These children were more precious to him than anything.

A light hand knocked on the door, and Liza Arequo, Roman's mother, looked around the edge. She was a rather ordinary young woman with brown hair and blue eyes, but she had a lively energy that made her appealing. Her mate, Tomas, laughingly admitted to being enchanted by her plain appearance despite it. "Morgan?" she asked softly. "Is everything alright?"

"Not really." He found a smile for her. "Soh left."

"Good riddance." She crossed her arms. "We tried, Morgan. That's more than most would have. What was his problem?"

He was hesitant to tell her and worry both her and the children. And he knew if he lied that the kids would know it and give him away. "He hates the Magi," he finally said simply. It was, after all, the utter truth.

"Why hate what you can't change?" She shook her head. "It doesn't matter. Morgan, there's someone here to see you. A couple and a little boy. They heard of you across the world. They're from somewhere on Choral. They want to see if the boy is a Master Magi."

He gently set the kids aside and then got to his feet. "Alright." In the last two years he had gotten adept at recognizing real Master Magi for their differences from Chronicles. The few he had met had been lucky to have parents willing to help them grow. They hadn't needed to join the Black Magi though the parents would infrequently write to Morgan for help. He was always prepared in case a Master Magi did need to stay.

As he walked into the lobby area and saw the little boy with ash colored hair and oddly iridescent black eyes, he knew this was not going to be a time it was needed. The boy was strong enough to be sensed across a room. "Hello," Morgan said. He made the Magi sign of respect. "I am Morgan Chronis, Air Magi."

The young woman holding the boy's hand used her free hand to return the gesture. Her brown eyes were the same interesting iridescent as her son's. "Ferris Daragon, Air Magi as well."

The man beside her also made the sign of respect. "Alline Daragon, Fire Magi. This is our son, C.J."

Morgan smiled. "What does it stand for?"

C.J. wrinkled up his nose. "Not telling."

"We're under orders not to tattle," Ferris said dryly. "We gave him what we thought was a wonderful name, but he hates it. We ended up compromising." She lowered her gaze. "C.J. is quite strong, Morgan. His lightning is exceptional, and he has such an unnerving maturity at times. Rumor stated that those sort of children became Master Magi."

"Most of the time, they do." Morgan smiled at C.J. as he said it because he knew it wasn't a lie. He knelt down and offered a hand to the little boy. "Of course, some become Chronicles." He glanced at the two parents. "I assume that is what you fear most?"

Alline nodded tightly. "Our town is small. The people are . . . strict. If they even got whiff of the possibility that C.J. was not Magi, they would kill him to eliminate even the chance. Chronicle or Magi, C.J. is our son."

"Anyone who touches my child will find themselves flying," Ferris said flatly. "And I assure you, they won't enjoy the landing."

C.J. wasn't listening. He was watching Morgan. The older man was kind of short for a Magi, but his eyes were kind. There was something really familiar about him. C.J. knew he was absolutely safe here in this place. Without hesitation, he took Morgan's hand.

The familiar tingling sensation of power recognizing power swept through Morgan's lines. He smiled. "Yes, he's definitely like me and the other children here." He got to his feet again and looked at the Daragons. "However, he is not a Master Magi."

It took a few moments before either Ferris or Alline realized what he had truly said. Both looked immediately at his gloves, and he removed one to reveal his lines. "Let me reintroduce myself," he said. "I am Morgan Chronis. An Air Chronicle."

"Oh my." Ferris looked down at C.J. in fear. "Then he is a Chronicle." She turned and took her mate's arm. "Alline, we can't go back. The minute C.J. enters first puberty, everyone would know! I won't let them take our son!"

"Nor will I." Alline smiled wryly at Morgan. "I don't suppose the Black Magi have room for more, do they?"

"There's always room," Mildred said as she went past. "Eli has an incurable building bug. We'll get you your own room, and C.J. can bunk with Roman if he likes."

The two boys eyed each other and then both shrugged and went running off to play. Kelsey and Jayda, not to be left behind, were quick to follow them down the hall. Morgan just shook his head slightly. "I can only pray they don't all start first puberty at once," he said wryly.

Eli laughed at him from the railing of the second floor over their heads. "You'll make a good father someday, Morgan, mark my words."

Chapter Nineteen

(Present . . .)

Tariah and Dominic were on their way out of the city.

Morgan still felt shaken. He had never, not once, in the last five years thought he would ever meet another Chronicle who had made it past first puberty. He still wasn't sure what to think or what to do. He felt helpless to do anything except stand on the sides and watch his sister suffer.

His sister. He wasn't sure why she felt so strongly like one when they were cousins at best, but there was something inside his power that resonated to hers strongly. He liked her. More than that, he was comfortable with her. It had been a long time since he had felt like he had a friend close to his own age. The other Black Magi were his friends but . . . they couldn't truly understand him.

A sudden sensation of trouble slid down his back. His power began to sting his skin. *Run,* a small voice inside him urged. *Something dangerous is coming. Something that threatens your life.*

He grabbed his head in pain as the voice inside brought with it a fierce and powerful longing for his Fury that literally brought him to his knees. Shaken, he could only kneel there in his study. His Fury . . . she had to be close. He *felt* her. His lines throbbed with her power.

"Morgan?" Mildred and Luke were in the doorway and Kelsey was riding on Luke's back. All three looked concerned as they saw him. "Is something wrong? You called for us."

"Yes." He pushed down the feelings as he always had and got to his feet. The danger . . . he knew the source. Soh was coming, and he was coming with the intent of trying to take the children. Morgan knew Soh had gotten more powerful, though he did not know how. The Elite had vastly grown in number as well.

There was no way they could fight Soh alone the way they were. He had too many people on his side. Too many people who could sacrifice themselves. Morgan was powerful, but he didn't think he could take on a crowd without giving himself away. Doing that would ensure the deaths of the four children he loved so deeply.

He walked over to stand in front of the Renaires. His silver eyes had gone grave. The seriousness in his mood had Luke putting Kelsey down on the ground. She too knew there was something wrong and her lower lip trembled. On a deep breath, Morgan said, "I must ask something of you. Something very, very important."

"Name it," Mildred said simply.

"Soh is coming. I feel him. My lines tell me there is danger." He looked at his ungloved hands. "I can't fight him alone. Perhaps Tariah and I could together but . . . to do that would reveal me for what I am. It would endanger the children."

Luke closed his eyes. "You want to send us away."

"No!" Kelsey lunged forward on a sob and grabbed onto Morgan. "No! No! You promised you'd always be there for us!"

Morgan hugged her tightly, his heart aching. "Soot, this is the only way I can protect you. You know what the Magi have been doing to Tariah, don't you? They will do it to me too, and they will suspect you unless I do something."

"What do you think to do?" Mildred asked quietly.

"I want to use my powers to lock the children's. I've been working on it ever since Soh left, just in case." He released Kelsey and walked toward the window. It was shielded to keep anyone outside from looking in. "If I seal her powers, they will not trigger until she is in the presence of a full-grown Chronicle or a Fury."

"Can you do that?" Luke asked carefully.

"I believe I can. I am a Chronicle. I have some very powerful gifts I have not used yet." He sighed. "And . . . I want to erase all of your memories. Of this place. Of me." He turned around. "If I erase your memories and replace them, and send you away, no one will know the difference."

Tears slid down Mildred's cheeks. "But what about you?" she whispered. "What will you do when Soh gets here?"

"Fight. If I survive, I will come find you when I have found my Fury. Then we can take all of you to the Isle just like we always wished. If I don't survive the fight . . . well, it will be Tariah who comes for you." He looked at the couple, then at Kelsey. "Will you go?"

"You'll come for us again, right?" she whispered in a small voice.

"I will do my best, Soot."

"You have to promise!" Her face crumpled as tears ran down her cheeks. "Because you *promised* to always be there! So you have to come back!"

"All right. I promise." He hugged her tightly, then slowly released her. He was going to miss her, and miss watching her grow into a young woman. Something told him that she was going to be one hell of a lady someday. No matter what he promised, he was sure it would be a long time before he saw her again.

Mildred and Luke exchanged a look, communicating without words, then both looked at Morgan. "All right," Mildred said. "It is the least we can do. You've done so much for us, Morgan."

"I'm the grateful one," he protested. He found a smile. "I'd have been awfully bored these last five years without all of you."

Thought was power. Power was instant. He had been around the Renaire family for so long that it was easy to slip past their guards and touch their minds. It was even easier to simply dissolve their memories of him. He erased all traces of his presence from their minds.

Then, in Kelsey, he instead placed a thin layer of his power along all surfaces of her skin. Her lines would never show through. As she grew, his power would eventually be replaced by hers and would serve the same purpose until someone removed it. Only Chronicles past second puberty and Furies would ever know. And the Kin, of course.

Before any of them could say anything, he used his Air powers to translocate them from the city. Translocation was an ability of Air elements. It took them or their target to any random location on the world. It took nearly all the strength of a Magi, and even Morgan felt strongly drained despite his limitless power.

It was evening before the Lakemores came to see him. He had needed the time to rest. He had no doubt that the entire sanctuary knew now what he was doing. Ferris and Tomas were Air Magi. They would have felt the translocation and all would have noticed the Renaires were gone.

"Soh is coming, isn't he?" Ren asked quietly as she closed the door behind herself and her family.

"Yes." Morgan lowered his gaze. "I'm sure you've noticed. I sent the Renaires away via translocation so I don't know where they are. Before I did . . . I took their memories of me and their time here. I locked Kelsey's power so her lines won't show until she is near another Chronicle or Fury."

Eli let out a rough breath. "And you want to do the same to us and to Roman and C.J." He gently rested a hand on Jayda's head as she clung onto his waist. "Morgan," he said softly, "You've done more than you know for us. If sending us away will help you, then we'll go."

"It's the only way I can protect you until I find my Fury. Without her, I am only half a whole. There's so much I need to be able to do to stop Soh and his insane Elite." He crouched down to look at Jayda. "But I promise. Either Tariah or I will come for you someday. We'll take you somewhere safe."

Tears welled in Jayda's eyes. "But I want to stay with you."

"I know. But it's not safe. Will you trust me?"

"I will." She scrubbed at her eyes and straightened her shoulders. "I'm gonna grow up," she warned him. "And when I'm a grown up I'm going to come find you if you don't find me first."

He smiled even though he knew she would not remember him when they met again. "Okay. I'll hold you to that."

Less than five minutes later, he once more found himself alone in his study. His heart broke quietly into hundreds of pieces. Both physically and emotionally he was exhausted. Sending the Arequos and the Daragons would have to wait until the morrow.

Dinner was very solemn. C.J. and Roman had sensed that something was very odd and didn't ask questions. Alline and Ferris were thoughtful in their silence. They had not known Morgan as long, only about two years, but they thought that they knew him as well as the other Black Magi. They were fairly sure he was doing the only thing he could.

Liza and Tomas felt much the same but they also knew that Morgan would stop at nothing to protect the children. Whether he sent them away or not, he would come for them again, or send Tariah if he could not make it. Just thinking about the reasons why it would be left to Tariah made them both lose their appetite. Morgan was a part of their family more than he was their leader.

Right after dawn the following morning, Morgan sent the Arequo family away with their memories gone and Roman's powers locked down. He only gave himself enough time to recover before sending away the Daragons. He knew it would shake up the power in the land to clump the boys close together, but his danger sense screamed viciously. Soh was in Prismatic. He was sure of it.

The sanctuary was quiet and lonely without the other Black Magi. He stayed in his study and wrote a letter to Tariah. He used paper made by the Kin that would not reveal its lettering until the intended recipient handled it and would also be strong enough to withstand even a detonation of power, just in case.

As he tucked the letter into the pocket inside his cloak, he felt the hair on the back of his neck quiver. He dodged and whirled around at the same time, and a shield of Air power protected him a second before the blast struck. It streaked around and instead blasted into and through the bookcases.

From where he stood in the doorway, Soh said caustically, "Always running, Morgan? Seems such a pity."

A chill went down Morgan's back. He had believed Tariah when she had said that Soh had gone beyond mad. But when he looked into Soh's eyes now, he saw just how deeply he had been corrupted. Even his power was tainted with madness. Madness . . . and death. "It was more of a dodge than a run," he said as evenly as he could.

"Same difference." Soh walked into the room. "Memory lane, isn't it? But where are the children, great leader? This place seems awfully empty now."

Morgan's lashes lowered and his silver eyes glittered with satisfaction. "I sealed their powers and sent them away by translocation."

Soh could only gape at him for a long moment. He had not realized just how far Morgan's skills could go. The shock was replaced by hate and rage, and his face turned slightly purple. "You bastard!" he roared. "How did you know I was coming?!"

"Two reasons. One, I believe I felt my Fury warning me." He unfastened his cloak calmly and removed it to leave himself in plain slacks and a tunic. "And for two, well, your power is really starting to reek. Sort of like dead flowers, or dog urine. Take your pick."

Soh gave a high-pitched scream of rage and lunged toward him. The Chronicle hurled his cloak at Soh and caught him in the face to obscure his view. Before Soh could recover, a shot of Air power had slammed into his chest. It hurled him violently backward and he crashed entirely through a wall and into the hall.

He yanked the cloak off as he got to his feet and threw it into the study. He immediately spotted Morgan beginning to glow. He was using translocation again. Evil power began to gather around Soh. "You won't escape me. You think you'll land somewhere safe?"

"It's got to be safer than here," Morgan said with a cheer he didn't feel. The spell wasn't casting as fast as it should because he was so tired.

A split second before Soh's attack hit, Morgan disappeared. In the giant explosion that followed and the sudden quake that shook the entire continent, no one heard the scream of raw rage that pierced the sky.

Morgan landed in the middle of the mountains of Carnelian. It had to be Carnelian. Choral and Spectrum didn't have mountains, and Glacia's were covered in snow. These mountains were cool and dry and snow free.

There was no strength left in his body. He fell to his knees on the ground and stared blindly at the distance. The sun beating down on his bare skin was a foreign feeling. He couldn't focus his eyes or his mind. The horizon seemed a blur of green that might be trees grown closely together.

It was some time before he realized that his arm hurt. He looked down and saw a long cut along his left arm that was slowly bleeding. His torn tunic looked quite stained. He vaguely remembered feeling a bit of Soh's attack getting through the translocation, but he hadn't actually noticed getting hit.

With some effort, he managed to rip a piece of material from his tunic and tie it around the wound. He had to use his teeth to make a knot, and just that small effort wore him out. He knew his odds of survival were low. He would have to find food and water or try to get out of the mountains and find a city. The city was the worse of the two options since his lines were now visible.

He sat down on a sigh and then fell over onto his back. He would rest for a while before figuring out what his options really were. He had absolutely no intentions of actually sleeping out there in the open, but the option was taken away from him. Even as he was trying to think of some way to contact Tariah, he slipped unconscious. He had been pushed too hard for too long.

~*~

(Isle of Dragons)

The Elders were fighting again. It wasn't anything new, not really, but this time they were arguing over something they agreed on. They all agreed that it was time they did something about the world, but they couldn't agree on how to do it!

Their voices could be heard through the large doors, and the slender young woman standing outside muttered, "Cantankerous idiots." She blew a streak of violet out of her face and it settled into her pale blonde hair. She walked a few steps from the door, and power swirled around her to change her back to her natural form.

She was a larger sized Dragon though not as large as most of the males. No one had ever picked on her for her height. She was a Fury, and there were many who treated her gently because they knew she would die someday soon. Her Chronicle had been born somewhere.

"Grecia!" One of the younger Dragons flew over and landed beside her. "We've got big news!"

"What now?" she asked.

"There are more Chronicles!"

She stared at him in disbelief and then demanded, "How old?"

"According to what we heard from the Kin who are sheltering Dominic and his Chronicle, they're children! The other adult Chronicle was sheltering them!" A trace of hope was inside his eyes that matched hers. He was also a Fury, and his Chronicle lived. "Maybe . . ."

Grecia whirled and flew over to the meeting room doors. She banged on them with her tail. "Open up!" she ordered. "Grandpa! Open the damned door!"

The door flew open and the Elder Air Dragon rose to his full height. He towered over her seventeen-foot length with ease. "How dare you speak to me in that tone!"

The Soil Fury didn't back down. "Dominic and his Tariah sent word through the Kin. There are several Chronicle children."

"What!"

The bellow from inside the room would have been heard a few hundred miles across the ocean if the island hadn't been shielded. Grecia rolled her eyes expressively. "You heard me!"

Her grandfather nodded slowly. "We must find these children, and this other Chronicle you mentioned before. We may not be able to bring them to this isle, but we can protect them!" He studied her. "Where are they?"

"That's the problem," the Fury who had brought the news said as he walked up. He was a younger Dragon, only two hundred or so, but he was swift and smart for his age. "Nobody knows. They were all translocated from Prismatic."

"That explains the explosion," the Fire Dragon Elder said. "It's time we left the island. Or more specifically, it's time *you* left the island." He pointed a claw at the two Furies. "You and the rest of the Furies are to go live among the Magi from this day forward. Find the Chronicle children! Find any others you can!"

"What!" Grecia looked at the other Dragon. "Solis, talk sense into your uncle!"

"You credit me with more talent than I have," the Water Fury muttered. "Uncle," he said patiently, "what if our Chronicle is killed in the meantime?"

Silence fell. It was something no one liked thinking about, let alone speaking. Only the Furies, ironically, seemed capable of mentioning it out loud. Perhaps because they lived with the knowledge of how likely it would happen. Finally, the Water Elder said, "If that happens, return to the Isle."

"Have we had any luck locating Jazz?" Grecia asked the Elders. "Daylar of the Kin was fairly sure that Dominic was certain that she was the Fury that belongs to the other Chronicle that isn't Tariah."

There was a brief silence before Solis finally said, "You fascinate me."

"I have that effect on a lot of people."

The Elders collectively shook their heads. "No," the Soil Elder said. "She has gone deeply into hiding in the mountains and has not responded to any of the messages we have tried to send her." He beetled his large brows together. "Both of you go to the lands of the Magi. Find the children. Find Dominic and Tariah. And for the sake of the moons, find out what in the hell is going on with the Magi!"

Grecia and Solis winced as the doors were slammed shut in their faces. "They don't ask for much," Grecia said wryly, "do they?"

Chapter Twenty

Jazz Eaglewind was a Soil Fury and over four hundred years in age. For the last twenty- five years, she had been living by herself in the mountains of Carnelian, in the most remote corner of the highest peak that she could find. Her life was simple there. All she had to do was simple. She only had to wait to die. When that time came, she wanted to handle the deed herself and not burden her family.

She kept up-to-date on the events of the world by turning herself into a Kin form and walking among the Magi in their villages on Carnelian. She knew of Tariah Chronis and Dominic Whisperer. She knew of the Black Magi and the Black Magi Elite. She also knew about the horrendous events in Prismatic. She just couldn't bring herself to care.

She had felt her Chronicle's birth twenty-five years, ten months, and six days ago. Somehow, she wasn't sure how, he had managed to escape death. There was no way he hadn't gone through first puberty. In fact, he had to be past second puberty by now and the knowledge was unpleasant. As terribly as she wished him to be happy, she *loathed* the very idea of anyone else touching her Chronicle.

She wanted to find him. With every fiber of her being, she wanted to find him. She had always been alone inside with a part of her soul missing. There had been times over the years where she had been sure she felt him. She had tried to touch him, but she hadn't been sure she had made it. It had always brought her to tears.

She had been tempted to leave her shelter and go to find him, but every time she began to make plans, something stopped her. It was frustrating enough without learning that Tariah had successfully hid herself for seven years.

Stifling a sigh, Jazz left her house. It was hidden in a cliff face and could not be found accidentally. She needed fresh water from the stream nearby, and the idea of a long shower under the waterfall appealed deeply. She climbed the first set of cliffs with lithe strength and then went up the pathway to the second.

The jug she had been carrying fell out of her hand and landed on the ground with a thud. Shocked, she could only stare at the sight of the young man lying near the edge of the cliffs. Her first reaction was sheer disbelief that he had gotten that far. Her second reaction was terror as she saw the golden lines flowing over his bare arms and hands. *A Chronicle!*

She rushed toward his side only to stop sharply as she felt his power. It curled around her like a cool and tender breeze and swept into her heart and body where it belonged. She slowly sank to her knees beside him, and her heart pounded madly. Her eyes memorized him longingly. Hers. This one man was hers alone. *Her Chronicle.*

Her entire body trembled with a sudden hunger. Hunger for his power, something that she could nearly taste. Hunger for his starkly beautiful face and body. She softly reached out and put a hand on his chest. His lines were hot against her skin even through his tunic. Sharp possessiveness filled her as she realized what it meant. It was *her* power creating his lines.

She stood and backed away several steps. Green light flowed over her as the ground trembled lightly beneath her feet. When the light faded, she had returned to her natural Dragon form. At eight feet long, she was on the smaller side, but she found herself taking great delight in it for once because her Chronicle was short himself.

She gingerly picked him up in her claws and flew back toward her house. It was capable of accommodating her Dragon size, and she walked in the front door without any trouble. She very carefully put her Chronicle on the bed and changed back to her Magi form. She sat down beside him and brushed at his auburn hair. She couldn't bear the idea of leaving his side.

She spotted the wound on his arm and her eyes narrowed. She untied the knot and unwrapped the bandage expertly, and her breath hissed in sharply. The jagged wound marred his lines, and it insulted her that anyone would dare mark her Chronicle.

Soil power welled around her, and she formed a needle and thread from it. Healing had always been her specialty. She carefully stitched the wound closed and applied a thin layer of power that would numb pain. The needle dissolved when she was done, and the thread would heal into the wound within an hour. It wouldn't even leave a scar. Such was the gift of powerful healers.

She picked up one of his hands and studied it intently. His were hands accustomed to hard work. Despite the gloves she knew he must have worn—his skin was very fair—his hands still bore calluses and possessed remarkable strength. Heat fluttered through her body at the idea of having these wonderful hands touch her.

A brief dizziness was perplexing until she realized her majiks seemed to be draining without her doing anything. It wasn't moving at a rate that alarmed her, but she was definitely beginning to feel exhausted without cause. It was countered by an increase in her Chronicle's power, and she looked at him longingly.

His power felt like the purest of air. Like a brisk snowy morning on the top of a mountain. But there was some sort of spark to it, like a delicious tingle from tasting something minty. She had to force herself not to kiss him and see if he tasted the way his power hinted he might.

She moved closer and held tight to his hand. She would wait as long as it took until he awoke. She wanted to look in his eyes and know that they belonged together. She had waited centuries for him. "Please wake up," she whispered. She lifted his hand to her cheek and closed her eyes. "Don't you want to be with me?"

Morgan awoke slowly to a raging headache. His entire body hurt from head to heels. He felt out of control. He was being blown away on his own power. It was so powerful and fierce inside him that he wanted to sweep across the land like a tornado, raging until there was nothing left.

He instinctively shifted to escape the feeling, and his muscles violently protested the movement. Terror began to well inside him as he realized he was no longer on the cliff. He didn't know where he was, but he was lying on a soft bed and the lingering scent of flowers clung to the air. He tried again to move, and again a torrent of pain ripped through his body. "Shh," a soft female voice said. "Don't move. You're safe, I promise."

The voice reverberated through him. As he focused on the voice and not his own pain, he became aware of a Soil power beside him. The power and the voice felt achingly familiar. Tears burned his eyes as something inside awoke and reached out eagerly. *His.* This woman was his. His . . . Fury?

Hope and shock mingling inside him, he forced his eyes open. He instantly found himself staring in a pair of green eyes as deep and rich as a spring meadow. They were set into a face too beautiful to be real. Her long hair was golden brown and streaked with green the same color as her eyes.

She seemed much shorter than average for any species, let alone a Magi or Dragon. She was probably only an inch taller than Tariah, but she possessed a lushly curved figure that would catch the attention of any member of any race. She was impossibly beautiful to Morgan, and far too perfect to be real.

Desire awoke and gleefully ripped through every nerve in his body with the force of a hurricane. He had felt desire on occasion since second puberty. He had been able to quite easily control it and ignore it. There was no controlling the hunger he felt for his Fury, and there was certainly no ignoring it. It consumed him from his power and soul out. "Good morning," he said huskily. "Where have you been all this time?"

Jazz's eyes closed and she rubbed her cheek against his hand. "Waiting," she whispered. "Waiting all my life." She leaned over him and her hair fell forward to curtain them. The soft strands glided over Morgan's skin teasingly. "You smell like the snow," she whispered. "It's driving me mad."

He threaded his free hand into her hair. She smelled, to him, like the rich scent of a summer meadow. Of lazy days where you could lay in the grass and stare at the blue sky overhead. Such places were rare on Lucksphere. It was why they were so deeply hoarded.

She sensed his pain even before he winced. "We need to complete the bond," she said softly. "It's natural. My majiks drain and your power grows so that we can bond." Her mouth was nearly watering with the desperation to taste his power and his skin. "I'm going to try to behave myself."

"Behave yourself?"

Her head lifted and she looked at him in surprise. It was such an innocent question coming from a man over twenty. "Haven't you . . . aren't you past second puberty?"

"Technically." He smiled. "But I never got around to actually graduating, as it were. These," he held up his free hand to show his lines, "sort of stunted that effort. They cover my hands, my arms, and my chest."

Triumph filled her as jealousy lost its green-eyed grip. He would be hers alone. "Good," she said succinctly. She lowered her head again and nuzzled her nose against his shoulder. His power immediately flowed up and covered him like a soft white aura begging for her attention. "I'll be delighted to help you 'graduate.' It'll be my pleasure."

"I think it'll be both ours." His eyes closed as her soft lips teased his skin. The sensation was electrifying.

"Tell me your name before I forget how to think. It's the only thing I don't know about you."

"Jazz Eaglewind." She was smiling when she lifted her head, and it was strangely foreign to her. It had been decades since she had last smiled, yet it was suddenly easy again. She wasn't alone. There was someone to walk beside her. Someone to protect and be protected by. "What about you?"

"Morgan Chronis."

Delight filled her. "*Morignan* is a Draconic word much like your name. It means 'rainfall in the mountains'. It was always one of my favorite words." Unable to resist the lure any longer, she pressed her lips to his shoulder and slowly breathed in as if drinking. His power flowed into her, the taste the same as the scent, and her hunger for him grew.

He didn't bother to fight a shiver as her lips teased his neck while she fed on his power. In fact, he was so enthralled with what she was doing that he startled when he felt his tunic suddenly disappear. His eyes opened. "Well."

"It was in my way," his Fury defended herself with a pout that had his pulse hammering with lust. "I wanted to see your lines." She ran her hands slowly over his chest, loving the feel of his power tingling her skin. She was still feeding on his power, and she traced his lines with her lips and little touches of her tongue.

He endured it as long as he could. It was wonderful torture but he was losing his mind. He wanted to kiss her, to learn her taste as well. He wanted to merge her so completely to him that they would never be apart. "Jazz," he said huskily.

She shuddered. She had never thought hearing her name could be seductive. She would give everything she owned if only to hear him calling her name. "What?" she asked. There was a fascinating dip along his collarbone and she tasted it lightly. She felt slightly intoxicated and reveled in it.

"Are you ever going to kiss me, or do I have to pin you down and claim it?"

She lifted her head with a grin. "You're a sassy little boy. Are you daring a Dragon, *ishke*?"

He grinned back, and his arms shot around her waist. He rolled quickly, dragging her across his body and pinning her to the bed beneath him. He laughed as he saw her astonished expression. In that moment he realized he had never felt happier in his life. For the first time he was no longer alone. "You forgot I'm an Air element, didn't you?"

"I did. I'll remember it from now on." She buried her fingers in his hair and drew him down eagerly. She wanted his kiss with a vengeance. His weight over her was wonderful, and it made her feel small and cherished. Maybe her size wasn't that bad after all. "I like this," she decided.

"Good." He cupped the back of her neck and lifted her until their lips met in a hungry kiss. He shuddered. She tasted like springtime and summer and sunshine all rolled into one. He couldn't wait to completely explore her and learn everything he had never gotten to learn before.

She returned the ravenous kiss and could only moan helplessly at the combination of his power flowing into her and his kiss devouring her. Her fingers slid down to his shoulders and ran over his skin slowly, memorizing how he felt. He was wonderfully hot to the touch. She would never need a blanket again.

The ebb in his power was felt by both of them. They slowly parted and their eyes locked. Between one breath and the next, they were breathing inside each other. A soft flickering light rippled over her body and identical lines appeared. They flowed around her neck, then in a wide ribbon around her body that wrapped twice before ending just past her hip.

Most of the lines were hidden beneath her leggings and strapless top, but he could feel them tingling wherever their bodies touched. He could feel *her*. Her age and her power. He reached out with his mind and power and found her there. He curled both around her in wonder, and her memories slipped into his mind. His throat tightened as he read her determination to die alone. She was much stronger than anyone had ever thought.

Her eyes closed on a wave of emotion at feeling him inside. She reached for him in return and held on just as tight. His memories swept into her mind, and she saw his determination to protect the children. His struggle to use his dedication to the Black Magi to cover his loneliness. "I'm so sorry, Morgan," she whispered achingly.

"For what?" He swept her hair out of her face. "You couldn't track me. My lines kept me there. I'm sure there was a reason. Maybe it was to meet Tariah and Dominic." He searched her eyes. "So . . . how do we get to the Isle?"

"We . . ." Her voice trailed off as her eyes widened. She couldn't remember. In fact, she couldn't even put a finger on the energy output of anyone of her race to contact them. She frowned. "I don't remember. Dominic was the same?"

"He was. I think the running theory was because of Tariah. That means your problem is likely because of me." He released her and rolled to the side to sit up. He felt fine now that his power was back to normal. Okay, maybe not *fine*. He had a raging arousal that wasn't exactly comfortable. But he would be damned if their first time was there in that house. There were too many echoes of loneliness in the walls.

Jazz scooted closer and pressed against his back. Her arms wrapped around his chest and her hand stealthily crept lower on his body. Her stomach quivered with sheer lust. His tunic had hidden a lot of muscle. He was short, but every inch was used to perfection. "I bet I can change your mind." Her voice sounded teasing and husky as her fingers rested above the fastening to his slacks.

"I bet you could," was his slightly strained response. He quickly caught her hands and held them against his chest. "But it's not right here. Can't you feel it?"

"I can but . . ." Frustration filled her voice. "You're mine. You're my Chronicle. I have every right to claim you as mine. Making me wait when I've been waiting for this long is cruel, Morgan."

He turned to grin at her. "At least you won't be waiting for *weeks*."

She lifted a brow. "Weeks?" She saw the knowledge in his mind of Dominic's plight, and she bit her lip to muffle a laugh. "Oh dear. Poor Dominic." She sighed and rested her cheek on his back as she nuzzled him softly. "I guess we follow your lines," she said simply. "We'll find your cousin and reassure her that you're alive. And then we'll *all* do something about the Elite." Her eyes narrowed with menace. "I claim Fury Right to kill Soh."

"Fury Right?" He turned and held her closer. She nuzzled against his shoulder and he returned the gesture before burying his nose in her hair. He had a feeling he would enjoy the Dragon form of affection.

"The right as a Fury to destroy anyone or anything that has threatened my Chronicle." She met his eyes. "It is a right that we Furies have been very careful to control."

Suddenly he understood something that had always bothered him. "No wonder the Dragons left. It wasn't just anger and grief. It was to remove the temptation of killing Magi for breaching those rights."

"It was certainly among the reasons." She slowly released him and ran her eyes over his half-naked body. Her entire body throbbed with the need to claim him. "You sure about waiting?" Her voice was a velvet invitation, and she didn't bother to hide her thoughts or feelings.

His eyes darkened to gray. He could no more resist her than the sun could resist rising in the morning. "Sure enough," he murmured thickly, "but I think you know you could change my mind in thirty seconds if you tried."

"Thirty?"

"Erring on the side of caution. It'd likely take you less."

She drew a deep breath. "Alright. If Dominic can find self-control as a Fire element, I can find some as a Soil element. Damn." She shook her head wryly. "If I discover that I have a bad temper, I blame you. I'm normally very even-tempered."

"The land may rest most of the time, but when it shakes, it shakes with enough force to alarm everyone," he noted.

"Very philosophical. Much like the air that is calm and serene, but can whip into a torrent at the right provocation?" She slid off the bed and got to her feet. "We'll need some new clothes for you," she said briskly. She walked over to where she kept a bag of sand. "We don't want the Magi to know you are a Chronicle until it can't be avoided."

"For the sake of the children?" He shook his head. "Don't worry. I've already thought of a reason. Because I was a Chronicle, I wished to prove I was not a monster by living among the Master Magi where I had a chance of blending in. The rest of the reasons for forming the Black Magi still stand."

"I suppose they do." She tugged him to his feet and smiled. She stood only three inches shorter. "You're very short."

"Look who's talking." He skimmed a knuckle down her bare shoulder. She wore a pair of form fitting leggings and a strapless form-fitting top. She had sleeves, but they were only fastened around her upper arm before falling in folds to her wrists. "It looks like you took a little bit of each land."

"It gets warm in the mountains during summer, so I need lighter clothing. But it gets cold in winter, so I needed more coverage. And the winds are strong, so I didn't want a lot of loose material." She smiled. "This also makes it easier for me to hunt if needed."

He lifted a brow slowly. "You fight bare-handed?"

"Most Dragons do." She glowered at the look on his face. "Quit looking at me like I'm some sort of little Magi."

"Right now you are."

She opened her mouth and then closed it. "I hate it when I'm wrong." Ignoring his grin, she focused instead on the sand. Her skill was quite high at her age, and it took only a matter of moments to weave new clothes for her lover. She made him a new tunic and cloak, but the cloak was only waist length. She also didn't make any gloves.

As he was dressing, he asked, "Dare I ask why?"

"I like your hands." Her eyes resembled dark green jewels warm with invitation. "You're welcome to put them on me at any time and in any place you wish."

He tried to ignore that but it was impossible. His breath hissed out as her power temptingly flowed around him. "I'm going to get you for that," he warned her.

She threw her arms around him happily. "Good!" She buried her face against his shoulder and couldn't fight a tremor through her body as his arms went around her just as snugly. She had been craving the feel of his arms her entire life without knowing it. "I don't want to leave here."

"Me neither." He held her even closer. He finally understood what Tariah had meant when she had said being with her Fury was the most incredible feeling in the world. He knew he would sooner die than give up Jazz.

They reluctantly eased apart and, hands linked, they went outside. Jazz released his hand and walked several steps away. "I'm also a small Fury," she confessed. "But you should still be able to ride on my back."

He shielded his eyes from the light as it consumed her and lowered his hand when she sat before him in full Fury form. There was nothing gentle or tame about her. She was fierce and almost frightening with the hard lines to her face. Yet, to him, she was still the most beautiful thing he had ever seen.

He walked over and reached up to frame her face. Even as a small Fury, she was slightly more than twice his size over all. Her scales, he realized in delight, felt as soft as feathers. Her body was golden brown and there was a patch of green over her back like a grassy field growing from the ground. "I think you're amazing," he said softly.

She lowered her head and nuzzled him, her heart tightening with emotion. Mixed with it was a heady dose of excitement. She had never had anyone ride on her back while she flew. It was impossible. But Morgan was a part of her. This flight would be the true evidence of their bonds. "Let's go."

He climbed up onto her back gracefully and with no fear. He knew he would never fall. "Go where?" he asked.

"There is a Kin outpost not far from here. We can go there for any news. It's safer than Carnelian." She flapped her wings and they shot up into the air. She laughed as she felt him grab her tighter. "You won't fall!"

"It was a little unnerving," he defended himself. Delight spread as they began to fly swiftly across the sky. The feeling was indescribable. Deeply linked to Jazz as he was, it almost felt as though he was the one doing the flying. "Don't go too fast. I want to take forever."

"I do too." She dipped down toward the ocean and skimmed the surface before flying up higher in the air. She loved carrying him like this. She barely felt his weight, and his power swirled deep inside her. Their power cycled between them like an endless loop.

The outpost was, by boat, three hours away from the nearest beach where her mountain had been. By flight, even without pushing herself, she made the journey in less than a single hour. It was with some regret that she angled down toward the beach of the outpost and landed gently in the sand.

Morgan slid down off her back and staggered as his legs didn't want to quite work. She quickly turned back and tried to catch him, but he was now bigger than she was and they went tumbling down to the sand.

He blinked up at her sprawled over him. He slowly smiled. "Hi there."

"Hi yourself." She braced herself up on her arms and sighed contentedly as she looked at him. "You're so handsome, Morgan." She lowered her head with the intent of taking the kiss she craved when she heard someone clear their throat. "Spoil a good moment," she muttered as she rolled off her Chronicle and gained her feet.

The MoonKin Elf who had gotten their attention could only grin as he watched Jazz help Morgan stand. "My apologies, but if you'd like more privacy, we do have an inn."

Morgan put his hands on Jazz's shoulders and then reached down and caught her hands to keep them away from any particularly sensitive portion of his body. The unfortunate part was that where she was concerned, it happened to be his entire body. "We'll take you up on that later."

The Kin's eyes lowered to his hands and the lines vividly displayed. "Ah," he said. "So you're the one Daylar mentioned."

"Daylar?" Morgan asked curiously.

"He is the honorary brother-Kin to Tariah Chronis. She let all Kin know you were out there, Morgan." The Kin bowed. "Though it seems some of us already knew but were careful to keep you a secret. You, and your Fury, are always welcome among the Kin."

"Thank you." Jazz leaned against Morgan. "Please, tell us, what is going on with the Magi? I had ignored the explosions and quakes, but now that Morgan is at the heart of it . . ."

"The Elite." The Kin gestured for them to follow and they fell into step beside him. "The Black Magi Elite have retreated to Glacia and made a worldwide proclamation. They are taking full credit for the death of the king of the Magi, and they are declaring their intent to destroy all Magi."

"Soh, you idiot," Morgan said softly.

Jazz's eyes widened. "But doing that will destroy the world!"

"Soh thinks Chronicles will replace the Magi," Morgan said on a sigh. "But the simple fact is that Chronicles and Magi need to work together. Magi overpopulate the world. The power is unbalanced. Only Chronicles are able to make the balance. That was Tariah's theory at least."

"She has a sound theory." Jazz crossed her arms. "Are there any Chronicles in the Elite?"

"No. Tariah and I are the only ones past first puberty, let alone second. But Soh has a few Master Magi, and many fanatical normal Magi. He needs Chronicles in order to really have any chance of taking out the Magi. He blew it with Tariah, and he never had a chance with me. He wants the children."

"He won't get them, Morgan." She turned and wrapped her arms around his waist, trying to comfort him. "We'll find them, and we'll take them somewhere safe. If we can't take them to the Isle, we'll bring them here to the Kin. We'll do whatever it takes."

"We need to kill Soh." His eyes were as flat as his voice. "We need to destroy the Elite." He looked at the Kin. "Please. Please contact your Daylar and have him tell Tariah that I am well, and that I have found my Fury."

"Consider it done," the Kin said quietly. "Will you go to meet Tariah and Dominic then?"

North. The sudden throbbing of his lines took Morgan by surprise. He hadn't felt them urging him in any direction for years. "Yes," he said slowly. "I think we will. I have to go north," he said to Jazz. "Somewhere north."

"*We* have to go," she corrected. "We're in this together, Morgan." She lifted one of his hands to her cheek so she could nuzzle against his fingers. "We'll leave as soon as we know where Tariah and Dominic are." She looked up into his soft silver eyes and felt her stomach flutter. She was completely unaware of the Kin's smile as he walked away.

Morgan was equally oblivious as he slowly drew her closer toward him. "Teach me," he murmured as he lowered his head. When his lips were a breath from hers, he amended, "Teach me majiks."

Her eyes flew wide. "What? Why you . . ." She sputtered but couldn't stop herself from laughing. "You're going to be a terror to live with, aren't you?"

He grinned at her. "Very likely." He lowered his head to brush his lips over hers. "Teach me everything."

"Everything?" she repeated, her voice warm with love and desire.

"Everything," he confirmed, his voice just as warm. "You'll find I'm a quick study. But I need lots of hands-on practice, you understand. And repeating a lesson is not discouraged."

She just smiled. "Consider school to be in session."

Chapter Twenty-One

Jazz and Morgan kept their hands linked tightly as they walked together through the Kin outpost. Morgan had never been happier. He glanced down at their linked fingers and thought to himself about the long years he had been waiting. He knew they were a drop in the bucket compared to how long she had been waiting but it had still seemed an eternity.

She suddenly scowled. "You're thinking about another girl."

He lifted a brow as he smiled. "So to speak. I was just thinking that if it had been you I'd been around when I was twenty, I wouldn't have hesitated in going after you." He tugged her closer, enjoying how she was smaller so he could indulge his protective side.

She brought his hand to her cheek and nuzzled it softly. "If I'd been there," she said softly, "I'd have carried you away and made damn sure I was the only female in your line of sight. Your Merideth was an idiot."

"No," he said softly. "I've thought about it over the years, and I think she was right. She did what she did because she cared about me." He bent his head and kissed her quickly. "Quit being jealous. Your skin will turn as green as your eyes."

"It will not!" she grumbled. She didn't like being jealous. She knew it was entirely unreasonable. She knew that he was hers and that he would always be there within reach as she would be for him. But the very idea of any other being laying a hand on his gorgeous form . . . it made her mad.

"You don't see me getting worked up over your past," he told her.

"You're more even-tempered than I am," she said with a sigh. "That or you're more open-minded. I'm not sure which."

"Well, I'm certainly not less possessive. A part of me wants to get enraged at the idea of any man touching you," he said thoughtfully, "but the practical part of me keeps pointing out that you were an adult long before my great-great-grandparents were born. However," he continued, his silver eyes darkening, "if any man tries to take you away from me now, I'll kill him where he stands. Fair enough?"

Strangely comforted by that, she cuddled close against his arm again. "You'll like it on the Isle," she told him. "There's a little bit of every sort of landscape. We could live in the mountains, or in the valley. Or in the desert, or along the ocean."

"I love the mountains," he said softly. "Probably because the air is always so clear on them. You'll have to pick us out a perfect spot and make our house there."

"Me?" Her brows shot up.

"Of course. I can see into your thoughts, Jazz. You've always wanted to build your own home. The home of your dreams. So you're going to."

She felt tears spring to her eyes. Blinking them away, she turned and threw her arms around him and almost knocked them both over. "It's your dream home too!" she said into his neck. "You'll have to help me."

"How can I help?" He held her even closer just for the delight of feeling her warm body pressed to his.

"You can stand there shirtless." She eased back with a grin as she felt his embarrassment rise. "You're blushing!" she said in delight as she saw his slightly reddened cheeks. "Morgan Chronis, never tell me no one has ever mentioned how utterly and absolutely *gorgeous* you are!"

He cleared his throat. "There's a difference between knowing it, having it mentioned, and having someone blatantly take full and utter advantage of it." Under the embarrassment lurked delight. He wanted her to find him irresistible. He wanted her to want him as terribly as he wanted her. It was hard to tell anymore whether his curiosity was purely because he hadn't made love before, or because of Jazz herself.

"It's probably me," she said huskily. "Because sure as rain in the valley, I've never been this desperate to know everything about a man before."

He felt her fingers skimming over the nape of his neck and quickly caught her hands. The sly little Fury had plucked the knowledge from his mind about the most sensitive parts of his body. But that was okay. He had gotten the same information from her. He just needed her mostly naked to get to where she was sensitive.

She almost stopped breathing. For whatever reason, innocents were always the most seductive and imaginative. She was fairly sure half of what he was thinking was physically impossible, but she was quite willing to try. "Inn," she said firmly. "Now."

He just smiled and let her drag him in her wake as she headed for the inn ahead of them. The Kin were fast when it came to news, and the innkeeper was waiting for them. She offered a set of keys and then pointed to the stairs heading up. "Second floor, last on right," she said cheerfully.

"Thank you," he said. It was all he could say before his Fury dragged him toward the stairs. He was no longer in doubt about her fighting capabilities. She was short, but she was almost fascinatingly strong. "Do Dragons retain their strength in any form they take?"

She shot him a grin over her shoulder. "Yes. Which means, *ishke*, that if you pin me down, it's because I let you."

"Just for future reference," he said, "that just makes you even more appealing to me. I like knowing you're willing to let me be stronger now and then." He shut the door behind them and then took the keys from her to turn and lock it.

Her arms suddenly slid around his waist and he stopped breathing. The impact her mere presence had on him was devastating. It was made all the more powerful because she was softly curling her power around his, rubbing slowly, like a cat asking to be touched. His mouth went dry. "I get the feeling you're always going to win any argument we enter," he managed to say.

She nuzzled his shoulder softly. "Is that a way of saying you can't resist me, *ishke*?" Her hands spread warmly across his stomach and her own stomach fluttered as she felt the strength in his muscles. In her long life she had had both Magi and Dragon, and a few Kin, for lovers. Only in Dragon form around other Dragons had she ever felt smaller than someone. In Magi form she was too conscious of her true strength. "How is it you make me forget?" she whispered.

He turned and pulled her close, savoring the feel of her curves molding to his body. "Well, I can't speak from experience, but I'd think that the stronger the feeling, the weaker it makes you."

"Do I make you feel weak, Morgan?" She slid her hands up under his tunic and thrilled at how his lines tingled her palms.

"So weak that I can't get away. You'll be stuck with me forever, Jazz." He lowered his head and took her lips slowly. He wanted to memorize their shape and feel and taste. He had half expected to feel rushed after waiting so long, but he felt instead as if they had all the time in the world. He could learn everything. Feel everything. Even things that he would never have learned without her there.

Her head fell back as his lips pressed to her throat. Her hands dropped to her sides and curled into fists. It was the hardest thing in the world to let him set the pace when her very soul cried out that she possess him now. But there was an incredible sense of power in giving him free reign. And when she brushed his emotions and felt the overwhelming surge of his love for her, tears ran slowly down her cheeks.

"Don't you dare," he breathed. He began to kiss away her tears. "You'll make me tear up and then we'll spend all night crying about how much we've wanted to be together instead of actually being together."

She gave a hiccupping laugh. "You're so odd to me, Morgan, and yet so wonderful. I see why you led the Black Magi so well." She leaned forward and nuzzled his shoulder, loving how his scent seemed to burn her lungs.

Just as he was seriously considering the merits of tossing her on the bed and having his way with her (something she had no issues with), there was a loud and thunderous explosion that rocked the entire building.

The roof shook and a piece came down toward them. Jazz knocked Morgan to the floor and half shifted back to Dragon. Only her wings shifted forward and she used them to protect them both. Morgan could only stare. "I didn't know that was possible."

"Fourth tier Dragon Lords are the only ones who can, and even then, it takes at least two centuries of practice." She kept him safely covered until the land was done shaking and the ceiling was in no more danger of falling. "We wanted a room with a view, right?" She peered up at the holes over their heads.

He contemplated how she was sprawled over him and how the angle gave him a very enticing view of her supple breasts hidden behind her sleeveless top. "The view isn't half bad," he agreed.

"Morgan!" She wanted to be indignant but her sense of humor wouldn't let her. Everything about him was utterly perfect for her. With a sigh, she rested her head on his shoulder and shifted her wings away. "I'm crazy about you."

"It's mutual." He carefully sat up as she slid off him. "As much as I'd like to ignore that event and return to something far more important, we'd better find out what happened."

She could only sigh. His sense of honor and responsibility were going to be a pain in the ass. Still . . . it made the idea of helping him forget everything all the more appealing. She slid closer and leaned up slightly to nibble on the edge of his ear. "Don't forget where we were."

"Trust me," his voice was thick with desire, "that's not likely to occur." He got to his feet and then offered her a hand and pulled her up as well. Together they walked to the door and headed down the hall.

The innkeeper spotted them and said, "The Militia caught a member of the Elite. She detonated her own power rather than tell them anything."

Morgan and Jazz both flinched. Among all the ways it was possible to kill yourself, detonating your power was the most lethal—to you and everyone around you. It literally tore your power apart and ruptured it like a firebomb. In killing those around you so quickly, you disrupted the flow in the land. A quake was one hundred percent assured in that situation.

"How many were killed?" Jazz asked quietly.

"Ten. Two Militia and eight bystanders." The innkeeper shook her head sadly. "I'm sure the Elite considers it a justified loss. After all, they lost one member, but ten Magi died."

"I'm not saying I want to see anyone else die," Morgan noted, "but if the Elite keeps up that attitude, they'll be gone soon. There's how many of them, and how many Magi?" He tucked his hands in his pockets. "I'd like to say that they're stupid enough to do it, but Soh is brilliant."

Jazz wrapped her arms around him and softly nuzzled his shoulder. "You want to fight them."

"Want to?" He shook his head. "No. Not really. Need to? Yes. If only for the sake of the children. As long as the Elite exists, they're in danger. The Magi won't recognize them, but Soh will."

The Kin nodded. "That's the opinion of the Kin and Dragons alike. We Kin are beginning to retreat back to our islands. Under normal circumstances we would ally with the Magi against the Elite. But the Magi are angry with us for siding with Chronicles. They would not accept our help."

Jazz snorted. "Hang themselves with their own rope!" she said derisively.

"Did you know your kind are spreading out across the lands?" the Kin asked her.

She stared. "No, I didn't. My kind as in Dragons, or Furies?"

"Furies. Seems that your Elders ordered the Furies to go out and look for any Chronicle they can possibly locate. Word reached them of the children. There is hope among the few who have felt their Chronicle's birth but not death."

She lowered her gaze. "It's such a shot in the dark. We don't know a Chronicle until we're directly in front of them. We can't track them, not even our own. It's why we stayed hidden away. It always felt so futile."

"If you do nothing, then you ensure nothing gets done," Morgan told her softly. He gathered her closer and buried his face in her hair. "Even if it's a one in a million chance, staying on the Isle made it a zero chance."

Her smile was wry. "Tell me you're going to confront the Elders with that. Please tell me. I want to bring the other Furies to watch."

He grinned. "I'll leave it to my cousin. She has had a much harder time of things than I, and she can be much more eloquent." His smile slowly faded, though, as he thought about things. "We need to find Tariah, and quickly." This time it was his smile that turned wry. "The sooner the better."

She very nearly growled but bit it back. She knew he was right, no matter how much she hated it. Damn it, she wanted him. She wanted to claim him as her own as the world had intended. If she didn't get a chance to taste every one of his lines, she thought she was going to go mad.

Suddenly grateful that his cloak was on the long side, he cleared his throat. She wasn't the only one going out of their mind. His hunger to touch and taste her was closer to a craving than ever before. But something inside . . . it told him that if they could resist it, then it wasn't time yet.

She knew he was probably right but still didn't like it. "Alright," she finally said. "Let's fly to Spectrum. We'll scope out a port city for information on the Elite and get a better idea of what they're up to. Then we'll try and track down Tariah."

He bent the few inches between their heights and kissed her lingeringly, curling his power around her in an equal caress. Her power curled around him in return and flowed between them endlessly.

They went down to the beach where there was room for her to change back into her Dragon form. Once she had, he climbed up onto her back and held on tightly as she took off across the sky. As he watched the ground rushing below them, he said thoughtfully, "I wonder how I'd look as a Dragon."

She chuckled. "I think you'd make a very handsome Dragon. Once you managed to transform properly, of course." She did a loop in the sky and thrilled to the sound of his laughter. He didn't laugh nearly often enough to suit her. His life had been too lonely, and too hard, for someone so young.

"But now I have you," he said softly. He pressed his lips gently to her neck as he leaned down to hold her tightly. It was as if the rest of his life no longer existed. He could barely remember how it had felt to not have her there. She filled the corners in his heart he hadn't known were empty.

"Keep up thoughts like that and I'll crash us." She flew a little faster, unafraid to push her limits when she had her Chronicle to feed from. It was such a wonderful experience that she knew she would have to watch herself lest she become addicted. Then again . . . there were much worse addictions in life.

By the time they landed on the beach on the outskirts of Mirah, she knew she would definitely have to feed soon. Just turning back into Magi form tired her enough that she stumbled when she tried to take a step forward. She landed in Morgan's arms and smiled sheepishly. "Sorry."

"Don't be." He smiled. "I can carry you on my back if you want."

"I'll be fine." She leaned up to kiss him but stopped with her lips a breath away from his as she saw the Magi watching them. Several were armed with weapons. She instantly moved and put herself in front of Morgan defensively. Her entire body braced for battle. "Harm a hair on his head and I'll make you into a midnight snack."

The Magi were very hesitant to do or say anything. Truth be told, they had far bigger problems on their hands than the shock of a second Chronicle being alive. There was no mistaking that he was one. His lines were vivid in the setting sun, and they were matched by the lines on his partner. Because that meant she was a Fury and not just a Dragon, they knew she could level the town in a single swoop.

"We're not asking for shelter," Morgan said calmly. He put a hand on Jazz's shoulder in restraint. He didn't argue with her protecting him. He argued with her temper, which, he knew, she did indeed possess. Given the slightest provocation, she would flatten the Magi. "We just want to get some supplies."

"I guess we can let you do that," one man finally said. "Lately no one is sure what to think or do."

"Try living your whole life that way," Jazz muttered. Her narrowed eyes were nearly serpentine in their intensity.

The Magi were smarter than to provoke a creature that was bigger, faster, and stronger than them. They put their weapons away and went back to their village.

Morgan slid his arms around Jazz and rested his chin on her shoulder. "You're something amazing."

She hooked her arms back around his neck with a smile. "I don't like people threatening the man I love." With a sigh, she slowly released him. "Let's get some information. I presume that was what you really meant when you said supplies."

"It was. If they're too confused to do anything, I want to keep it that way." He started to say more when he felt the skin along the back of his neck crawling. Instinctively, his mind swept the area for the source of his unease. Almost instantly he picked up on the mind of another Magi.

Jazz sensed his unease and lifted her head to sniff the air lightly. Her nose flared as she caught the scent of someone near them. Normally she wouldn't have been concerned, but the scent carried the bite of corrupted power. It was a scent impossible to mistake. It came across as bitter, infested, and disgusting.

Both Dragoons turned in the same instant. Their powers merged seamlessly into a single pulsing blast of Air and Soil that streaked across the beach and into the shadowy area behind a large stack of crates and barrels. The blast lit up the area briefly as it struck a shield but the Magi stood no chance against a Dragoon team. He toppled over.

Morgan nearly gagged as the fully rotten scent of corrupted power filled the air. He shoved aside the disgust and went around the edge of the crates to find the source. Somehow it didn't shock him to find a Black Magi Elite lying on the floor in a heap with blood seeping from the wound on his chest.

What was shocking was the blood itself. It was a sickly shade of yellow. Morgan was very careful not to touch the man as he stepped closer. "What are you after?" he asked quietly. "How can you think to stand against so many when you are so few?"

The Elite looked at him from dull eyes and gave a gurgling laugh that made blood stain his lips. "You don't know? The Dragons aren't the only ones with a hidden isle."

Jazz took a swift breath. "You're mad!" she said sharply. "The power hidden there . . . it will destroy you before you can use it! It's not for Magi to tangle with!" There was no response, and the sense of power died entirely. She could only curse.

Morgan grabbed her arm quickly. "Jazz! What are you both talking about?" he demanded.

She looked at him sadly. "The lost land of the Chronicles. The Chronicles had their own isle once. It was where they and the Furies retreated to when the Magi came after them. It was there that the massacre took place."

He took a sharp breath. The power that would be imbedded in the very land of such a place would be immense. Likely powerful enough to rip apart the very world. If Soh found the land and claimed it . . . "No," he said fiercely. "We won't let it happen!"

She went into his arms and held on tight. "It could tear you and Tariah apart if you tried to claim the power for your own. I refuse to let you even try!" But even as she said it, she saw the answer inside him. There was no other choice. If they didn't find it first, then they would be destroyed anyway. "Why does it have to be you?" she asked achingly.

"Maybe it's the destiny of the name Chronis." He smiled a little wryly. "Seems Tariah and I are both burdened by it."

She held him tighter and buried her nose against his neck. "No matter the burdens you carry, I will be right there beside you." She lifted a hand to touch his chest and savored the throb of his lines beneath her hand. "Where do we go?" she asked simply. "I will follow wherever you lead."

He closed his eyes. Almost immediately he felt the burn in his lines. *Northwest.* "Northwest," he murmured, his eyes unfocused as they opened. "It's almost like I can see the map in my mind now. Somewhere to the northwest is where we'll find Tariah. We need to find her before we do anything else."

"Then let's rest tonight and set out tomorrow." She held tight to his hand as they began walking down the beach slowly. The sun was setting around them and the moons were steadily beginning to rise. Neither wanted to be near the town, not when it still smelled like the taint of the Elite.

They selected a place to camp almost an hour away from the town. Morgan watched in fascination as Jazz used her powers to craft the sand into a sturdy tent structure for them. "I can tell you're a master of your craft," he said.

She shot him a grin. "I've had time to practice." Her smile faded as she saw him sitting down and staring across the ocean. She walked over to sit beside him, and she leaned against his shoulder. "How did you know he was there?" she asked softly.

"I felt a warning in my lines and used my mind to find his." He fell over onto his back on the sand and tucked his hands under his head. "I've always had stronger than average mental skills, but that was new. I assume it's my Dragoon ability."

"Telepathy, yes." She smiled. "Mine must be Ultravision. I tried Telepathy and Telekinesis both as we were leaving the village but had no success."

"What's Ultravision?" he asked curiously.

"I can touch objects and see their history." She closed her eyes. "It's not the easiest of skills from what I've heard, but I can handle it." Her eyes opened again and her heart skipped a beat as she saw the intensity on his face as he looked up at her. Hunger prowled through her body with the suddenness of a storm. Hunger for his power. Hunger for his skin and his heat.

He slowly sat up and pulled her closer. Her hands flattened against his chest, and his power rose instantly to the surface as a soft white aura. "This time," he said huskily, "don't stop." His fingers threaded through her hair. "Never stop."

Trembling with the force of the need inside, she began to remove his cloak for him. "You won't be needing this." As she tossed it aside, she gave a stifled yelp as she found herself lifted into his arms as he stood. Unnerved, she clutched his shoulders. "Put me down."

He grinned wickedly. "You don't weigh much in this form. I won't drop you."

She gave a shaky laugh. "I've discovered a fear of heights." She grabbed him tighter as he ducked into the tent. "In case you didn't notice, I've never been carried before." As deep as her trust was in him, her heart didn't stop fluttering until he had set her on her feet once more.

His amusement came across clearly, and she gave a little growl. Her foot hooked his ankles and dumped him onto the blankets she had made for a bed. He only lifted a brow at her, and she dropped to her knees to start removing his tunic. When she discovered it would take too long, her power swept out in a green wave that dissolved the material back to sand.

He could only shudder and hold her closer as her mouth fastened hotly to his shoulder. He couldn't even tell the difference in the emotions inside him. It was all tied up and tangled together. All he could be certain of was that he was going to go mad if he didn't get to have her soon.

She eagerly fed on his power, her lips trailing hot forays across the lines on his chest. They tingled wherever she touched them, and knowing it was her power that made them was thrilling. She felt intoxicated on him. She slowly slid up his body to kiss him, her fingers burying in his hair to hold him closer.

His fingers burrowed in her hair as he returned the ravenous kiss. He could not seem to get enough of her taste. Her body moved temptingly against his and he groaned. His body twisted and he rolled to pin her beneath him. He cuffed her hands beside her head and nipped at her lower lip. "Gotcha," he said thickly.

She tugged lightly at her hands but his grip seemed firm enough. She knew she could get free with raw strength but . . . she didn't want to. It was a heady power to know she was his first. To know she was the one who would teach him what it meant to be an adult. With a very feminine smile curving her lips, she let her power dissolve her clothes entirely to leave her naked in his arms. "Need a map?" Her voice sounded both husky and teasing.

His mouth went dry. "I have one." To prove it, he bent his head and ran his lips softly over the lines curving across her collarbone and down over her chest like a ribbon or a river. Little touches of his tongue soothed his need for her taste and made them both shudder. "I'm still learning," he murmured against the curve of her breast. "Tell me if I get it wrong."

She could only moan softly as his lips claimed the tip of her breast and tugged so strongly that her back arched in raw pleasure. "I'm not seeing that being a problem," she managed to say. Belatedly, it dawned on her that he was keeping his emotions tangled with hers; he knew *precisely* how she felt and could track down the places that gave the most pleasure. As his lips found a particularly sensitive place near her stomach, she whimpered, "Cheater."

"Cheater? How so?" He released her hands to have the freedom of his own. He slowly ran them over her supple skin, memorizing her every curve. Deliberately tempting her, he skimmed his knuckles across the skin of her stomach and then slowly lower.

She opened her mouth to respond but could only suck in a sharp breath as his hand slipped between her legs. She clutched desperately at his shoulders for balance in a world that was melting around her. "I'm going to get you for this," she gasped out as he continued to stroke her teasingly.

He had no doubt about that, but right then he was too consumed with the delight of learning her body. He didn't need to be experienced to know that what they had was special. That this was something he would have never found with Merideth. This was his Fury. She was everything he would ever want. "Jazz," he said thickly, his body trembling with need as he felt how hot and wet she was. "Is there a word for this?" he asked. "It's not love. It can't be."

She framed his face in her hands and drew him down. "Dragons call it *ishke*," she murmured against his lips. She kissed him deeply until it was nothing but a tangle of tongues and lips. "What're you waiting for?" she asked when she released him. "Hurry before I go out of my mind."

"I'm still . . ." He gave a husky laugh as he felt the rest of his clothes dissolve, ". . . dressed. Never mind then."

She nipped at his jaw lightly. "You should have mentioned them sooner." If she had ever seen anything more beautiful than Morgan's unclothed figure, she didn't remember it. She wanted to pet and kiss him from head to heels and back again. And why shouldn't she?

She twisted quickly and tumbled him over. Her hands pinned his to the ground in a sensual payback. With a hunger she was becoming familiar with, she raced her lips over his face and shoulders. He trembled underneath her and made her feel powerful in a way she had never felt before. She lifted her head. "How did I go four hundred years without knowing this?" she whispered.

His eyes glimmered like silver coins as he looked up at her. "I wasn't there." Her grip loosened, and he wrapped his arms around her as he rolled again. He couldn't wait any longer. He needed to be inside her and finally erase the loneliness that had haunted him for years.

She curled her legs around his hips, anchoring him from leaving her even if he had wanted to try. Her breath caught and lodged in her chest as she felt his hard arousal slowly pressing into her body. Ripples of pleasure radiated from the contact, and it felt as if he was sinking into her very soul as well. Desperately she twisted under him, tangling her emotions to his, wanting to share everything.

He shuddered but didn't move any faster. He wanted to savor every second, to memorize everything about her. Only when he was buried to the hilt inside her did the tension ease from his heart. Finally. Here, at last. He lowered his head to kiss her deeply. His Fury. Finally they were together.

She wound her arms around his shoulders and held him as tightly as she could. She couldn't separate her feelings. Desperation for an end to the ceaseless pleasure. Hunger to feel him as close as she could. Savage possessiveness in knowing that he was hers at last. Her Chronicle. Finally she had claimed him.

Their powers flowed together and between them in an endless loop as he began to drive in and out of her welcoming heat with instinct and desire fueling him. Ecstasy hovered, promised, and lured. And, as he felt her emotions swirling around him, sharing her deepest feelings, it swept over him hotly unlike anything he had dared imagine.

She felt his emotions even as he felt hers and the sensation was too much. Ecstasy swept over her, each wave rippling hotter and more powerful than the next. She would have cried out with it but his mouth sealed hers and she could only sink into the kiss helplessly, replete at last.

He didn't know how much time passed before he felt her stir beneath him. Their emotions were still tangled together and so were their powers. He softly curled his mind around hers in another caress. "Am I too heavy?" he asked into her hair.

She sighed softly and slid her hands over his damp shoulders. It was all she had the energy to do. "Don't move," she murmured, her voice still huskier than usual. "I've never had a blanket this wonderful."

His arms tightened around her for a moment and then he rolled to the side and onto the blanket. Before she could voice a protest, he tugged her closer and enfolded her in his arms. "That's better. I think even a Dragon might have trouble breathing with something bigger than her sleeping on top of her."

"I'm resilient." She caught the edge of a blanket and tugged it over them. Contented, she sighed and snuggled closer against his body. Her hand automatically lifted to cover his heart, and she realized in surprise that some of the lines felt hotter than normal.

She looked closer and discovered that almost a third of the lines from his left side and across his chest were darker than before. Yet it wasn't a solid darkening. The darkness flowed and changed like light rippling over water. She could literally see his power flowing through his lines. "It must mean that you've completed a part of your journey."

"You sound surprised." He tugged her closer once more. His eyes closed as he smiled. "I would think claiming your Fury is the most important part of a Chronicle's journey."

Unexpectedly, he felt a mental hand reaching out toward him. He reached for it in return, deeply curious. It reminded him of a night some time back. He had been dreaming, and had felt someone reach out to him. He had been *sure* that he had found someone that he hadn't seen in a painfully long time. The tie had broken before he could complete it, and he had just chalked it up to an odd dream.

This was no dream. He touched the other hand, and their fingers meshed. Their minds and their powers meshed in turn, and his eyes widened slightly as he recognized at last who he was touching. *Tariah?*

Morgan! Tariah sounded no less stunned. *But . . . how?*

"Telepaths," Jazz muttered as she buried her nose against Morgan's shoulder. She felt disgruntled. She didn't like someone else able to touch Morgan's power even if it was his 'cousin.' She couldn't stop the possessive feelings any more than she could stop breathing.

You're a Telepath too, aren't you? Morgan asked Tariah.

I am. Her mental voice warmed. *I see her inside you. It's nice, isn't it?*

It's wonderful. He could see Dominic just as thoroughly inside her and see his disgruntlement matching Jazz's. *Welcome to being an adult*, he thought warmly, knowing that only the completion of their bond would result in such a merger between Tariah and Dominic.

I think beat you into adulthood, actually.

By a few hours.

Who's counting a few hours? There was a long silence before she asked softly, *What do we do, Morgan? I can sense it inside you, that there's something more going on.*

It's bad, Tariah. Where are you right now?

On an island outside of Spectrum. You?

Near Mirah. Can Dominic safely bring you here tomorrow? It's a port so he can fly around the ocean edge.

He can. We'll get there tomorrow. Together we can do something, I'm sure of it.

I'm sorry to drag you into my battle.

Her voice softened but was no less firm. *Soh has hurt two men that I am honored to call my brother. It is as much my battle now as yours. I'll fight beside you.*

Sleep well, my sister.

Sleep well, my brother.

Their mental fingers slid apart but he could still see and sense the path that would lead him back to her mind again, no matter how far apart they were. He couldn't understand how the connection even existed. It couldn't be merely because they were both Telepaths. "I can't understand it," he said quietly.

Jazz regarded him quietly. "Perhaps," she said softly, "it is not merely coincidence that you share the same name. You suspected you were related, but I think it is more than speculation. There is blood shared between you, somehow strong enough to make you connect like twins."

"I wouldn't argue with that." He smoothed a hand slowly over her arm before gathering her closer and burying his face in her hair. "She hid it, but I think something happened to her that shook her down to her soul."

"Dominic will be her strength, as I will be yours." She leaned up to kiss him softly. "Tomorrow we will meet up with them and we will decide what to do. Tonight is just you and I. There is no Soh, there are no Magi. Just us." Her hands framed his face tenderly. "Tomorrow will come soon enough."

He held her closer, more than willing to let her help him forget. Forget his enemy, forget a world that hated what he was. Forget that, somewhere inside, her words had stirred up something he felt he had to understand. There was a promise he needed to keep. He was sure of it.

Part Three
~Chronis~

Chapter Twenty-Two

Tariah still felt slightly confused even after she and Morgan had stopped communicating. In her mind, she could see the line that would lead back to him. She hadn't even known she could reach out to him in the first place. She had been lying in Dominic's arms, wishing for some evidence that Morgan was fine, and then suddenly she had felt as if she could see him.

"I don't understand it," she said softly. She curled more firmly against Dominic's side, her hand resting over his heart. "I thought only Linked mates could touch one another's power like that."

He tucked his hands under his head and contemplated the stars in the sky overhead. He still felt slightly disgruntled. He didn't like it that someone else could touch his Chronicle's power. The only consolation he could find was in the knowledge that it had likely been Morgan who had touched Tariah on the night before they had entered Prismatic. "I think it's because you are related," he said thoughtfully after a moment. He turned onto his side and draped an arm across her waist to hold her close. "It was just assumption before but now it seems to be more than that. Do you know the legend of the first Chronicles?"

She smiled. "Elder Juniper told me. I always found it comforting to think I shared their name." Her heart gave a dull thud as she felt what was inside him. "You think I and Morgan are . . . are descended of the twins?"

"I'm almost certain." He rolled and tucked her underneath him. He lowered his head and began to sniff along her shoulder. "Stop wiggling," he muttered. "I'm checking something."

"It tickles!"

"And you're distracting me." He closed his eyes and breathed in deeply, taking her scent into his lungs. This time it wasn't just because he loved the way her skin always seemed to smell like the elusive fragrance of water in the desert. This time he was looking for the trace of Dragon that would be in her blood if she was a descendant.

Because it was so faint, it took him a minute before he was able to pinpoint the slightly sharp tone of Dragon blood. "There you are," he murmured. He softly nuzzled against her, his tongue tasting the curve of her shoulder. "There's some Dragon in you. *Very* faint so it's at least a few thousand years removed."

She shivered as his lips trailed up to her ear. She had stopped marveling at how swiftly her body and power responded to him. She was simply enjoying it. There was an ache in her muscles that she couldn't help but savor. "So it's possible?" she asked softly.

"I'd have to check Morgan's scent to see if it is the same." He grimaced wryly. "Somehow the idea of sniffing at him doesn't appeal as much. I'll leave it to Jazz." He smiled suddenly. "I'm glad they found each other. Do you suppose the translocation dropped him at her feet?"

"If it did, we'll have to thank Soh." Her silver eyes hardened suddenly. "Before we kill him, of course."

He slowly smoothed a hand up and down her arm. "So fierce." He bent his head and kissed her softly, savoring the freedom to touch and caress her at his will. All the frustration he had endured since meeting her had been worth it. Everything was worth it, if only to look into her eyes and touch her power and know she was his. "Will you let me claim Fury Right?" he asked softly.

She tilted her head slightly. "Fury Right?"

"The right of a Fury to kill anyone who threatens their Chronicle. I'm sure Jazz has claimed this right herself, and I seek to claim it as well." He nuzzled her gently and then rolled onto his back and tugged her over until she was lying on top of him. "We can fight over who eats him later."

She buried her face against his shoulder and giggled helplessly. "Oh, will you stop it! You wouldn't eat him!" She couldn't quite stop the comical image, however, of Dominic in Dragon form and roasting Soh on a spit like a wild hog.

He began to laugh. "Where do you get these ideas?" He buried his hands in her tangled hair and tugged her down for a long kiss. When he finally released her, he instead rolled them up within a blanket and kept her tucked snuggly against him. "Time for sleep, *ishke*. Tomorrow will be a long day."

She gave a contented sigh and nestled closer. "I really shouldn't get used to being babied like this. I'll get lazy and spoiled. Remind me when this is all over that I owe you some spoiling in return."

He smiled and buried his nose in her hair. "Deal." With a sigh of his own, he closed his eyes and let go, his mind instinctively seeking hers and weaving them together so that even in their dreams they didn't part.

The sun was creeping over the horizon when Tariah awoke. With a long stretch, she sat up and looked down at her sleeping lover. The fierceness that was so innately a part of him as a Dragon, even in Magi form, seemed softer when he was asleep. He had been through a lot for her, and the idea of spoiling him rotten deeply appealed. She couldn't carry him around and threaten to eat people who were mean to him, but she could do something no one else could.

She carefully slipped out of his arms and fetched her clothes. Once dressed, she began to silently slip through the foliage of the island. Some kind of fruit or food was bound to grow or live there; there were few things in the world that weren't edible with a little effort. She lucked out and found a bush laden with dark purple berries ripe enough to bend the branches under their weight.

She picked a few handfuls and carried them back to camp. Dominic was still asleep, and she smiled. She couldn't wait to tease him. He took such delight in teasing her about being a 'weaker being' that she wanted to savor knowing she had outlasted him at *something*.

The berries weren't ready in their current state. She left them to simmer in some water over the campfire and headed back through the trees toward the closest beach. They weren't actually far from it. Dominic had been in a hurry to camp and hadn't taken them very far inland.

She thought about things as she hunted through the sand for crustaceans or clams. Yesterday morning, she had been ready to fall apart. She was fairly sure that Dominic was the only reason she hadn't detonated her own power. But now . . . she wasn't so worried.

She had her Fury. That was worth fighting everything to keep. She wasn't a child anymore. She was an adult in every way. And she was a Chronicle. The world had made her. Why did she have to argue her right to existence? Why did the children?

Of course, it would have been easier if the Dragons had been looking for all of them all along. She understood their feelings, but she was beginning to be annoyed with everyone's 'we're doomed' mentality. She was going to give the Elders a piece of her mind.

She returned to the campsite with the clams she had dug up and shelled them easily; they weren't much different from desert crabs, really. She added the meat to the berries and let it continue to cook. She ground the shell down to fine powder and mixed it with ice to make a cold drink. Crustacean shells made some of the tastiest drinks on the world if mixed with ice. She took the cup with her and went over to kneel beside Dominic.

She touched his shoulder softly with her free hand and lightly curled her power around his to coax him awake. "Dominic?" she said softly. "It's morning."

"Mrmph." He rolled over onto his stomach. "I'd rather sleep." His nose twitched and he lifted his head curiously. "What's that scent?" His mouth had begun to water from the decadent smell alone.

She smiled and waved the cup she held. "This. I made breakfast."

It took his sleepy brain a few moments to register what she had said. When it did, the sweetness of the gesture overwhelmed him. It was such a simple thing, and really not important compared with everything else she gave him, but the fact that she had done something just for him moved him deeper than anything. "You didn't have to."

"I wanted to." She put the cup aside as he sat up. When he reached for her, she went into his arms eagerly and lifted her own to wind around his neck. "You act as if I brought you jewels."

"You brought me you. That's worth much more than jewels." He lowered his head and kissed her lingeringly. A tremor went through his powerful body as he heard her contented sigh. How in the name of the Underrealm had he deserved this? He couldn't think of anything he had done that was great enough to earn his Chronicle.

"You were just lucky," she teased.

He laughed and hugged her fiercely. "You're a brat." He released her and held her comfortably on his lap as he reached for the drink she had set aside. He sniffed at it but couldn't quite make out what she had put in it.

She hid a smile. "Baby."

Incensed, he took a drink. The flavor seemed to explode on his tongue with so many nuances he couldn't catch them all. It was potentially one of the most delicious things he had ever had other than Tariah herself. "By the moons, woman, how'd you do that?" He peered at the cup.

She grinned happily. "I told you I was a good cook. It's made from ground crater clam shells and ice."

"*Shell*?" His eyes widened.

"Most people don't know the shell is that good since you normally can't eat it. But if you grind it down with ice until it's a fine dust, it's perfect as a drink." She stretched and then slid off his lap to go check the simmering soup. "The meat from the clams is over here, mixed with some fruit."

He scooted closer to sniff at the reed pot she had made and the smell was even better than before. On a groan, he fell onto his back. "Yes, I foresee myself getting fat and lazy within a year or two. That and I'll never get rid of my family and neighbors. You'll need to open a restaurant or something."

Her flash of longing was almost hidden before he truly felt it, but he still saw it as it rippled through her heart. He sat up in surprise and stared at her. "Where did you hide that?" he murmured. When he went looking, it took up an amazing amount of her deepest heart. She had locked away such a fierce desire in a way that even he hadn't spotted. Her years of hiding her emotions had produced habits she couldn't break overnight.

She turned her face away to hide her pinkened cheeks. "It's just a daydream."

He cupped her cheek tenderly and turned her face back. He kissed her gently. "And you're going to have it." He smiled. "You can have your restaurant on the Isle, and then someday you can have one in Prismatic, also known as Magi central."

"But Magi would never buy from a Chronicle!" she protested.

He grinned. "*Ishke*, we're immortal. We can wait them out. In a thousand years, they might have collectively gotten over it."

Her mind whirled. She was twenty years old. It felt like a long time already. She could barely fathom living for a thousand years or forever. But the idea of being with Dominic for all of those years was something even more tempting than her dreams. "Okay," she said. "Deal."

After breakfast, Dominic could only sigh contentedly. His Chronicle was one hell of a cook. In a playful burst of energy, he caught her around the waist and tumbled her down onto the grass. He grinned as he heard her laughing. She laughed more freely than when they had met, but there was still something solemn in her eyes. "You're too melancholy. It breaks my heart."

She lifted a hand and smoothed her fingers over his face. She couldn't get enough of touching him. "I don't mean to be. It's just frustrating to be kept from having what I want. All I ever wanted was a place to live freely. And now I have to fight for it when others get it without asking."

He nuzzled her hand and then lowered his head and kissed her softly, lingering over her flavor and rubbing his power over hers to comfort and soothe. "We'll make it, *ishke*. I promise."

He got to his feet and pulled her up as well. They had already tided up the camp area and they were free to leave whenever they wanted. He walked a few steps away and turned into his Dragon form. They would fly along the coast until they were outside Mirah. At that time they would land and disguise themselves once more.

Tariah, as she climbed up onto his back, remarked musingly, "Maybe I'll try a Kin Faerie form this time. At least then I'd have a *reason* to be short."

He gave a crack of laughter and flew straight up into the air just to enjoy hearing her delighted shriek. "Look at it as more evidence you and Morgan must be related. He's short too."

She beamed. "That's true." Content with that, she wrapped her arms around his neck and held on as they flew swiftly across the sky.

Though the flight would have normally taken the better portion of a day, if not a whole day, Dominic pushed himself to go faster. Anticipation hummed inside his body. Now that his Chronicle was an adult, there was no need to hold himself back when he fed on her power. "I think I'm beginning to enjoy this Dragoon thing."

"Beginning to!" She lightly pinched his fin in retaliation and listened in satisfaction to his yelp. "That implies you weren't happy with me until you made love to me."

"That is not true," he scolded her. "You know damned well that I've been happy with you no matter what. But my patience was wearing thin. Do you have any idea how badly I wanted you?"

"I do." She smoothed a hand over his neck. She had always seen his emotions and how volatile they were for her. She could see the same inside herself and she loved it. She could barely remember the long years of restraining her emotions now that she had so thoroughly reveled in them. "Now you can have me whenever you want."

"You do know how to tempt a man." He began to angle down toward the shore as he saw the town in the distance.

"Just you." She waited until he had landed before sliding off his back. She caught her balance easily and shot him a smug look as he turned to Magi form. "Now who is a weaker being, mighty Dragon?"

He scooped her up in his arms and swung her in a giddy circle. "No one I know." He caught her close for a long and drugging kiss and then slowly released her lips. "I love you, Tariah," he murmured. "It's such a paltry word Magi use, but it's the only one I can seem to find."

"We'll have to make up our own word." She rested her head on his shoulder for long moments and then reluctantly released him as he put her down on her feet.

It was amazingly easy this time to reach for his majiks and bend them to a Kin form. This time, instead of bending them the way she always had for Kin Elves, she bent them the other way, instinctively assuming that would result in Kin Faerie.

She shortly proved herself right as she felt her body suddenly become exceptionally smaller. Dominic looked a whole lot bigger since he had opted for SunKin Elf. He was also grinning, something that made her wary. "What?" she asked carefully.

He gently plucked her out of the air and carried her over to the edge of the ocean where she could be able to see her reflection. Delight spread through her when she noticed her wings. She really did look like Daylar's sister now; her wings were the same cloudy form that his original wings had been. Instead of being white, however, they were closer to a silver shade that matched her eyes.

Her figure also, oddly, seemed lusher. She considered her bust size. "You know, proportionately, Faeries have better figures. But I refuse to tell Sparkle. She'll *never* let me live it down."

Dominic chuckled and placed her gently on his shoulder. She sat down comfortably and crossed her ankles to keep her balance as he began heading for the city.

Mirah was smaller as a port town than Refraction was but it was still of considerable size. Neither Dragoon felt uncomfortable as they entered the town because they now knew their disguise was good enough to fool all but the Kin. Or other Dragons, Dominic noticed with surprise, as he spotted a Fury having lunch at a restaurant.

Tariah was no less surprised. "I wonder why he's here," she murmured. "Can we ask safely without giving ourselves away?"

"We can try." He walked over to the table where the Fury sat and touched his ears as he bowed. "Sorry we're late," he said by way of greeting.

The Fury quirked one brow slightly in surprise and then amusement filled his eyes. "Well, I wasn't in a hurry," he said as he got to his feet. "Let's get out of the sun. Your partner looks a little faint. MoonKin don't like the sun as much as their cousins after all."

Tariah said nothing but inside she felt a little awed. She didn't need to see inside Dominic's mind to know she was in the presence of a Dragon Elder. The man walking beside them was so powerful that it couldn't be muffled. She felt it as a ripple of Fire along her skin and knew he was another Fire Fury.

Once they were out of sight and hearing of the Magi, the Fury said dryly, "Dominic, you make a fine SunKin, but I have to say that any attempt you make at being a pacifist would fail."

Dominic restrained an urge to stick out his tongue. No matter how old he was, Xander always managed to make him feel like a whelp again. "You're one to talk." With a smile, he gestured to Tariah. "This is my Chronicle."

Tariah stood and folded her wings around herself as she bowed gracefully, naturally adopting the Fae form of greeting without thinking about it. "Tariah Chronis, Water Chronicle." She smiled. "Naturally, of course."

"Naturally." The other man bowed just as gracefully. "Xander Journe, Fire Fury." His lips quirked. "An Elder, as I'm sure you've felt." Sadness suddenly darkened his eyes. "Well . . . for the time being."

Dominic went very still. "You felt her?" he asked quietly.

"Almost ten years ago. I just didn't speak of it." Xander turned his gaze toward the sun in the distance. "I wasn't going to speak of it until too late. I didn't want to make others suffer. I've lived so long after all, and I'm the only Fury Elder we have. But when I heard of the children . . ."

Tariah suddenly thought of little Jayda and her distinctly Water presence. She said nothing. She didn't want to get Xander's hopes up if she was wrong. "Why are you off the Isle? Because of the children?"

"Yes. Word reached us." He smiled. "You're making some serious waves, little Dragon. We heard of the children from the Kin who have been helping you. The Elder Council decided it was time to send us Furies out to hopefully locate them, or any others."

"It took them long enough to figure that out!" Tariah complained. "Any idiot can see that doing nothing means nothing gets done!"

Xander's eyes widened. Then, slowly, a grin began to curve his lips. "Dominic," he said, "when she takes on the council, I want a word-for-word description of the event. I'd happily be witness to it if I could."

Dominic laughed as he felt Tariah's sudden chagrin for speaking in such a way to an Elder. "Gladly." He offered a hand that Xander took and held tightly. "Swift winds to you, Xander. I hope you find her soon." He too had thought of Jayda, but kept his silence for the same reason.

Xander headed back to his meal, and the two Dragoons headed toward the inn down the road. It wasn't hard to tell that Morgan had been by at some point; Magi were still whispering about seeing a second Chronicle. The general opinion was one of high confusion. The good guys had become the enemy, and the enemy had become an ally.

After getting a room, the Dragoons headed downstairs to where it was located. Dominic shut the door and locked it with a Dragon seal only another Dragon could undo. Only Jazz would actually do so since she was the only one who would have reason.

Tariah wasn't stupid. She landed on the floor before unbending the majiks to return herself and Dominic to their natural forms. If she had gone back to normal while flying, she might have crashed onto the floor. She really didn't trust her sense of scale or depth perception.

She had just given a long stretch when he swooped her up into his arms and tumbled her down onto the bed. She laughed happily and threw her arms around him fiercely. "No matter what has happened, having you makes it all worthwhile!"

He froze for a moment and then his eyes closed as emotion welled inside. His eyes glittered with unshed tears as he opened them and met her gaze. He lowered his head until their lips were barely touching and held his breath as her power surged to the front and covered her with its soft blue aura. There was nothing more beautiful than water in a desert.

He pressed his lips to her shoulder and fed from her power there. It was even stronger now and hit his system like a shot of rich wine. Hungrily he trailed his lips up her neck and nibbled on the edge of her ear, listening in delight as her breath hitched. Deliberately, he tangled their emotions together and rubbed his power along hers.

Happily seduced, she returned the caress and lifted her hands to thread her fingers through his hair. She lightly rubbed his scalp in a way she knew drove him crazy and he shuddered. Her delighted laugh was cut short as his mouth covered hers demandingly, and his tongue surged past her parted lips to drink her flavor and power all at one time.

She whimpered as pleasure surged through her body. She eagerly ran her hands over his chest and felt a thrill as his lines tingled her palms. "I love how you feel," she murmured when he released her lips. "It's my power that makes your lines. I hadn't imagined how possessive it would make me feel."

His eyes glittered with male satisfaction. "Good." He bent his head and took her lips again, his need for her power appeased but his hunger for the rest of her as strong as ever.

The door opened behind them. "Whoops," a woman's voice said, humor in her tone. "We're interrupting."

"Considering what he went through," was Morgan's dry response, "I'm inclined to feel even more guilty than normal."

Tariah immediately began to wiggle to get free, and Dominic released her reluctantly. Despite being disgruntled at the interruption, he smiled when he saw Morgan standing in the doorway with the familiar form of Jazz. He was very glad to be right. "Swift journeys, Jazz."

She smiled. "And the same to you, Dominic."

Tariah leapt off the bed and rushed across the room. She threw her arms around Morgan and held on with a strength that was almost surprising. He caught her just as close, something inside his heart and soul finally relaxing now that he knew she was alive and well. Her relief was no less deep, and their Furies shared a speculative look over their heads.

"I was so scared!" Tariah said into Morgan's shoulder. "When I saw the sanctuary . . ." She shuddered.

"It wasn't exactly fun for me either." He held her tighter, then released her slowly. He searched her eyes. "I saw it when I touched your mind, and I can see it now. What happened? Something weighs on you."

Jazz shut the door behind them and sealed it in the same way Dominic had. "If it has to do with Soh, I claim seniority for killing him." She met Dominic's eyes. "But you are more than welcome to break his neck as long as you don't actually kill him."

"Gladly." He held out his arms and gathered Tariah close as she crossed back over to him. He gently smoothed a hand down her hair. "Essentially," he said as calmly as he could, "we witnessed the death of the Magi's king. He asked Tariah to stop the Elite and save the world."

Morgan cursed softly. "That's a nice thing to ask the person you've been trying to kill!" He sighed and held Jazz tighter when she wrapped her arms around him to comfort. "Well, it connects with what we've discovered. The Elite *have* to be stopped."

Jazz looked at Dominic. "They want the hidden isle."

He shook his head quickly. "They're insane. No Magi could control that." His heart gave a dull thud as he realized what would need to be done. "No," he said. "I don't like it. It could kill them both."

"As I said but . . ." She looked up at Morgan sadly. "He was right about one thing. If the Elite aren't stopped, we're all dead anyway."

Tariah frowned. "Someone tell me what we're talking about."

"There's an isle," Morgan said quietly. "Where the Chronicles used to live with their Furies. It was where the final massacre took place."

Her eyes widened. "The power in the land there would be immense and highly unstable! Any Magi would be torn apart if they tried to take command." She took a sharp breath. "That's why Soh wants the children. To let a Chronicle take the power and use it for him." Her hands curled into fists at her sides. "We'll get it first."

Morgan held out a hand and she laced their fingers together. "Are you sure?" he said quietly. "I was already intending to try but I wouldn't ask it of you. You've been through enough."

"And so have you." She shook her head. "I'm not going to run away. We should go after the Elite at their source and try to take them out. If we don't succeed there, then we can go after the children and the isle. Whichever we find first will keep the isle out of Soh's reach."

"That was my thought as well."

"So the Elite are gathering in the north," Dominic said quietly. "Do either of you know where in the north?"

"Well, there's only one other land in the north," Tariah said.

Morgan's eyes flickered. "Glacia. I haven't been back in five years. I'm sure they've heard of my leading the original Black Magi but . . . I'm not sure how to face them. Especially not my parents."

"They knew you were a Chronicle, right?" she asked softly. When he nodded, she smiled. "Then, if anything, they'll be glad that you have your Fury now. It sounds like they were like my parents were." Her voice broke, then steadied. "They would have been happy just to know I was happy finally."

Dominic slid his arms around her waist and rested his chin on top of her head. "It sounds like we will be heading for Glacia. We can fly around the coast and then across the ocean when it is safe. Let's not cause Spectrum any more trouble than it can handle."

"Agreed." Jazz pulled Morgan along with her as she headed for the door. "Let them be now. I'm hungry."

Tariah fluttered her lashes at her brother. "You'll get used to it," she told him cheerfully. "I've decided it's a Fury thing."

"I do have one advantage over mine though," he noted. He caught Jazz around the waist and tossed her over his shoulder. "See?"

Tariah considered that. "You're right," she decided. "I can't do that."

Dominic was laughing too hard to say anything. Jazz just sighed and propped her elbow on her Chronicle's back. "Dominic," she said, "I envy you."

As the door shut behind them, Dominic walked over to seal it once more. He was still chuckling. "I think there's always balance in a good relationship," he said. "After all, I can out power you and . . ." He turned around as he spoke and his voice trailed off as he saw Tariah had already begun to remove her clothes. His mouth went dry. "And you," he managed to say, "can have me at your mercy with a smile."

She was indeed smiling. Feeling wonderfully smug and feminine and desired, she walked over to her Fury and leaned up against him to wind her arms around his neck. "I can?" she asked teasingly. "I can have anything I want?"

"Anything at all." He lifted her and carried her toward their bed. His pulse was pounding. The ideas in her mind were interesting to say the least. "Where do you come up with these things?"

Her smile turned into a grin. "Morgan."

"Morgan!" He stared at her in shock.

She couldn't help but laugh. "Well, that's what you get for having a Chronicle who can touch the mind of her brother." She leaned up and nibbled on his ear. "You'll have to deal with it now."

He had no objections to that, but he had to wonder if she realized she had stopped calling Morgan her cousin. Something was very odd about these two Chronicles, and he couldn't help but suspect that it was related to the name both carried. Ah, well. It wasn't worth thinking about right then. The answers would come with time.

Chapter Twenty-Three

It was almost evening when the two Dragoon pairs met up again in the lobby. Morgan took one look at his sister and burst into laughter. She wrinkled up her nose and waved a fist threateningly. "What're you laughing at?"

He plucked her out of the air and studied her with dancing eyes. She made an adorable little MoonKin Faerie. "I wasn't expecting this. How did you do it?"

"I used Dominic's majiks." She smiled. "You could do it too, using Jazz's."

He was instantly interested. "Really?"

Jazz smiled. "We'll practice when we get a chance. After a while you'll be able to do it easily." She smirked as she looked at Dominic. "Not quite brave enough to become a Fae, whelp?"

His ears twitched in annoyance. "You're only two hundred years older than me. Don't call me a whelp." He took Tariah back from Morgan and settled her on his shoulder. "We've been disguising ourselves while in town even though the Magi have been ordered not to attack us. It's just . . . uncomfortable."

Morgan looked to where some Magi were whispering behind their hands when they saw his lines. "Tell me about it."

Tariah's gaze lowered for a moment and then she flew off Dominic's shoulder and landed on the floor. It took only a moment to return to normal. Her appearance made the whispers burst out in furious force. Her lines were even more obvious; they covered more of her body and her clothes revealed them clearer. She reached out for her brother's hand. "I'm not hiding anymore. If you walk freely, then so do I."

Dominic also returned to normal and smoothed a hand gently down her hair. Jazz contemplated both of them, then opened the bag of sand she wore on her hip. She removed a handful and poured it into the air. Her power welled up and the sand began to swirl together and take form.

A few moments later she had created three cloaks. In color and symbol, they were the same as the one Morgan wore. Hers and Tariah's, however, fastened around their upper arms and left their shoulders bare. The hood would cover their shoulders if they pulled it up, though. It was the more modern variant on the cloak, and she knew she had gotten it right when Tariah's eyes lit happily.

Morgan's heart tightened as he looked at them. "You don't have to wear the cloak of the Black Magi," he said quietly. "We don't exist anymore."

"Sure we do." Tariah fastened her cloak and began to tuck her hair up out of the way. "We need to keep the Black Magi. Once people get over their initial shock of you being a Chronicle, we may be able to use the same cover again. Looking for Master Magi who want a place to grow safely . . . *and to be kept from becoming like the Elite.*"

Jazz's eyes widened slightly as she looked at Dominic. "Damn. Why isn't she a scholar?"

"She's the daughter of scholars." His pride couldn't be hidden from his voice as he fastened his cloak around his shoulders. "She's very intelligent."

Tariah smiled as Morgan gave her a light cuff across the chin affectionately. "I read too much as a kid. It was the only way I really felt like I was living." She walked over to the window and looked out across the street. She defiantly stared down an old woman who was gawking at her. "I never got to go to the festivals," she said wistfully. "I was always inside reading about them."

Morgan looked at the Furies. "Do Dragons have festivals for the seasons too?"

"We have festivals whenever we feel a need, but most assuredly on season changes as well." Dominic watched Tariah. He was willing to bet she would be one hell of a dancer. There was incredible grace and strength in her slender body, and she enchanted him with the simplest of movements. If she wanted a festival, she would damned well go to one.

Jazz had a feeling they were thinking the same thing; the look on his face felt like the one on hers. She could see inside Morgan that he had also missed out on a great deal because he was different. "Let's stock up on supplies and start making our way north," she said only. "We can walk until we need to camp, then we can fly tomorrow."

All were in agreement and they left the inn. The shopkeepers were wary of having three Dragons in their town (they had spotted Xander), so they didn't refuse service to the Dragoon pairs no matter how much they might have wanted to shut their doors. Because of this, the teams were shortly leaving the city and following the coastline north.

"I'm still a little stunned that the Dragons are finally doing something," Morgan commented after a long silence had passed comfortably.

"Hey," Jazz said in disgruntlement.

"It's true!" Tariah muttered. "Okay, so you can't track us. There aren't so few Furies that you couldn't stick one in each town of the world and watch for Chronicles. Okay, Prismatic would need more than one, but you know what I'm saying."

Dominic shook his head when Jazz opened her mouth. "She's right, Jazz. We both know it. Isn't that why we both left the Isle? Even if it was only subconsciously?"

Jazz was silent for a moment before she nodded. "Yes, you're probably right." She smiled. "Can I watch when you take on the Elders?" she asked Tariah.

Tariah's cheeks turned pink. "Why does everyone seem to believe I'm going to rake them over the coals?"

"Because you have an intense dislike for blind ignorance and have something of a temper?" Morgan asked dryly. He dodged with a laugh when she tried to hit him. "It's true! You're surprisingly impassioned for a Water element. I guess your affinity is for the ocean, it being deep and uncontrolled and all. Maybe it's your bottled emotions." He ducked again, and his grin gave away that he was deliberately harassing his sister. "I've seen broken dams on rivers. It takes a while for the initial flood to taper down."

She swung her pack and clipped him in the shoulder with a thump. She was grinning, too. She knew he was only ruffling her feathers. She felt somehow starved for the companionship of her brother. How had she missed him without knowing him? Turnabout was fair play, though, and she took an instinctive guess based on what she knew about people with his element. "At least *I* never set a roof on fire."

"Damn it!" He glared at her. "Who told you that?"

She started laughing. "I *guessed*!" She muffled a shriek as he made a grab for her, and she shot away across the sand. She spun around and pulled down her eyelid as she stuck out her tongue. "Missed me!" The gesture and tone invoked the childhood she had never gotten.

He returned the gesture though he was laughing almost too hard to try. As they chased each other around the beach, their Furies just grinned and kept on walking. Like any other emotion, bottling up childhood fun and playfulness could also break down a dam. Morgan and Tariah had been cheated out of a lot in their lives. They deserved their chance to play.

The sun was setting when a carrier bird flew overhead. It wore a flag marking it as a Militia bird. The Dragoons exchanged a look before running down the beach after the bird. Tariah was by far the fastest, and she got close enough to fire an ice projectile that numbed the bird's wings without hurting it. It tumbled into her arms and she smoothed a hand over its feathers comfortingly. "It's okay. You're safe."

Jazz plucked the message out the bottle tied to the bird's leg and opened it. Her eyes promptly darkened with anger. "They're out of their league."

"Now what?" Dominic asked.

"According to this, the Argyles are calling for all troops to gather at the northern port on Spectrum. They want to storm Glacia and take on the Elite. Doing that could destroy the world anyway! All the cities will be unprotected, and I'm not sure Glacia can hold up under the strain." She broke off as Morgan's horror stabbed into her heart. "*Ishke*." She wrapped her arms around his waist. "I'm sorry, I spoke without thinking."

He held onto her, his eyes stricken. He felt terrified and sick to his stomach. No matter how long it had been, Glacia was still his home. His parents still lived there. The idea of everyone and everything being destroyed was horrifying.

"What if we took out just Soh?" Tariah asked quietly. She was thinking out loud to include Jazz and Morgan. "The Elite would fall apart without their leader then the Militia could come in and deal with them."

Morgan nodded. "I would concur with that."

Dominic grabbed the letter and erased the writing. He began to write on it himself, and he made a credible job of copying the Militia's style. "We're changing our letter to say that. The Argyles are telling the troops that the Chronicles will remove Soh to prevent disruption to the land. After he is gone, the Militia will move in."

"Ah, I see." Jazz smiled. "Because we can get to Glacia before the Argyles ever make it to the port, we can remove the problem before they arrive to contradict the false order."

"Exactly." He returned the message to the bottle and watched as Tariah released the bird so it could continue on its way. Thoughtfully, he looked around. The sun had wholly set and the moons were rising. From their position, they could see a moon to the west and a moon to the north. "I think we better camp for the night."

They moved inland away from the tides and found a flat place to set up. Jazz started showing off when she made two fancy tents and elaborate blankets for everyone. Dominic was compelled to compete and made a smokeless fire without wood—it was no mean feat to make a continuous fire without fuel. Morgan and Tariah sat to the side and just smiled.

Calling it a draw, Jazz sat down beside Morgan. She lifted a hand and sand swirled over her palm. Leaves and bark mixed with the sand as she called on her Wood powers, and in a few moments she was holding an oddly shaped wooden instrument. It looked like a pipe but had keys for her fingers.

"What is that?" Tariah asked curiously.

"A *ler*." She smiled. "Well, that's what we Dragons call it." She began to play and a haunting melody lifted on the air. "We're having our own festival," she told them. "Tariah, work on Dominic. He has an incredible singing voice."

Dominic's cheeks turned dull red as the two Chronicles stared at him. He cleared his throat. "Supposedly." He eyed his lover warily when she scooted closer. "Don't you *dare*."

She rested her hands lightly on his leg, and her silver eyes were deep and liquid in the firelight. "You don't have to sing right now." Her voice was both gentle and soothing. She knew exactly what buttons to push. She could see them inside him. "But you will probably want to practice in the future. You know, for when we have children." She kissed the corner of his lips. "You'll want to sing them lullabies, won't you? I can hold them, and you can sing."

The mental image made his throat close with fierce longing. How he wanted to have a family with her! He knew she was deliberately provoking him, but he just couldn't get past the idea of needing to sing their son or daughter—or both!—to sleep. He cleared his throat. "I guess I might as well practice now."

Morgan grinned. "Nicely done, Tariah." He settled back comfortably and propped himself on his elbows beside Jazz. He had no desire to tease Dominic about going weak-kneed. Truth told, the thought had already crossed his mind about children with Jazz, and he had gotten weak-kneed too. It was also terrifying in a way because he knew kids turned him to mush, but the longing was far stronger. He sent Jazz a warm look. They would have to start trying for a family as soon as the Elite was gone.

She nearly missed a note but kept playing. She smiled at him from under her lashes and then lowered the *ler* to blow him a soft kiss. As Dominic got to his feet, she said, "*Festa heq doj.*"

Tariah tried to repeat the words, but her tongue couldn't wrap around the syllables. The hiss on the S was easy enough, but it needed to be rolled somehow at the exact same time. "Draconic is hard."

"You'll get the hang of it." Dominic smiled at her. "It's the name of the song she was telling me to sing. It means 'Glory of the Festival.' It's basically a song sung at *every* festival we have. Whelps learn it as their first song in school."

She pulled up her knees and rested her chin on top of them as she watched him begin to move. He was an unexpectedly good dancer, and it made her smile. She wasn't the only one who had hidden a longing successfully. Her big, bad, tough Fire Fury wanted to be a bard. Who would have thought?

At a certain point in the music, he started to sing. The words were in Draconic, but neither Morgan nor Tariah needed to understand the words to realize that Jazz had been understating the situation. Dominic had a voice that most bards would kill to possess. "We'll make him sing lullabies to our kids too," Morgan murmured for Jazz's ears only.

Tariah was only enjoying the melody at first but the words began to slowly unravel inside her mind and take meaning. She recognized Dominic's presence and it dawned on her that he was providing a translation while singing. The fact that he could underscored his skill overall. She focused on the words and realized how beautiful they were. Blessings and thanks to the sun and world for supporting and sustaining all that lived. Unable to resist, she got to her feet and moved to his side.

He smiled and drew her closer to share the steps to the dance. He flicked a look at Jazz and she obligingly started the song from the beginning when it ended. It took little for Tariah to pick up the dance though there was some laughter when she nearly stepped on his toes once or twice. The Magi lyrics were in her mind, and Dominic's heart tugged at hers until she gave in and sang with him.

It surprised and pleased all of them to hear her voice. Perhaps not as talented as Dominic, there was something else in her voice that made it memorable. It meshed seamlessly with his and somehow enhanced his natural gifts. Like everything else, their voices were meant to blend together as one.

Thinking it, Morgan smiled at Jazz. He played one or two instruments. He would have to get one so that he could play with her. He had picked it up as a hobby to stave off loneliness. Now he could share it with the woman who had brought him everything. "Just don't ask me to sing," he said ruefully. "I make dogs howl."

She just laughed at him.

By the afternoon the following day, the Dragoons were approaching the port of Glacia. As Morgan watched Stalagmite growing larger in the distance, he felt his stomach quiver with nerves. It immediately drew Tariah's gaze. The longer they were around each other, the stronger their connection grew. Their minds were always touching, and their hearts and souls weren't far removed.

It was a very curious thing that puzzled their Furies. If it had been merely a product of Telepathy, then Dominic and Jazz would have been privy to the link. They weren't. Morgan and Tariah could actually shut them out of the communication if they desired. It was something wholly unique to the Chronis 'twins'.

"Morgan, are you worried about your parents?" Tariah asked softly.

"Yes." He looked at her wryly. "I'm getting close to twenty-six years old. I'm an adult. And yet I worry what they think of me."

"You'll never outgrow that." Jazz's voice was warm. "I'm over four hundred and I still worry about my parents' opinions. Just remember: they love you. If they didn't, they'd have killed you."

"This is true."

They landed on the beach of the actual port, and the two Furies took their Magi form again. Tariah began to shiver violently and wrapped her arms around herself as her teeth chattered. "M-morgan," she managed to say, "your town is beautiful. But it's too damned cold!"

The other three burst into laughter. Dominic caught Tariah in his arms and wrapped her inside his cloak with him. "I'll keep you warm, *ishke*, promise." He smiled at Jazz. "Do you have enough power left to make her some new clothes?"

"This is very easy." Jazz smiled as she opened her bag of sand. "Besides, there's nice incentive for using my power now." She sent a wink at Morgan who returned the gesture. Working quickly because she too was cold, she formed new clothes from the sand for both Tariah and herself. "Here, bundle up," she told the other woman.

Tariah wasted no time in pulling on the long sleeved tunic and leggings over her regular clothes. They, combined with her cloak, served to keep the cold out very well. They covered most of her lines too, but the ones on her face were still very stark. Oddly, only a sense of pride came this time at the knowledge. She was beginning to be *honored* that she was a Chronicle. When had that happened?

As they were entering the town, there came a happy cry and a crowd of people rushed toward them. "Morgan!" one man said. "Welcome home! This is such a surprise! Who knew that with all the terrible things going on that we'd get such a . . ." His voice trailed off as he saw Tariah and Dominic and recognized them.

The happy clamor of the crowd slowly died as they too saw Tariah and Dominic. Jazz's lines were effectively hidden by her tunic and hair, and no one realized what she was. Likewise, Morgan's hands were at his sides and also not visible yet. One older woman managed to find her voice and demanded, "Morgan, how could you? How dare you bring those . . . abominations here?"

"Tariah is my sister." He held up his hands and revealed his lines. Jazz pulled her hair back and the lines at the edge of her neck appeared. Morgan swept his gaze over the crowd. "I am an Air Chronicle. I have been my whole life. I never told, and you never knew. Am I suddenly a monster?" he challenged.

As the crowd fell quiet, a woman suddenly snapped, "Oh, get your heads out of the snow! Of course Morgan isn't a monster! He's our Morgan and nothing changes that!" She shoved her way through the people and stopped in front of the Dragoons with her hands on her hips. "They look perfectly fine to me, though I'd kill for her hair," she said after a study of Jazz.

Morgan felt a smile curving his lips. "Merideth."

Merideth Caradina was as beautiful as ever though her ebony hair was now cropped closer to her face. Her blue eyes still danced merrily, and she was still the loveliest woman in the city. "As always," she said warmly as the crowd behind her slowly dissipated. She walked over and leaned up to kiss his cheek softly. A part of her would always care for this man who had been her first love. "You're happy now," she said quietly. "I'm glad."

Jazz discovered she could hold no resentment for Merideth. Not when the girl was so clearly different from the rest of the Magi with her open-minded nature. "I'm doing my best to make sure he stays that way." When Merideth glanced at her, she bowed gracefully. "Jazz Eaglewind, Soil Fury."

Merideth drew her thumb over her cheek and nose. "It's an honor, Jazz. I am Merideth Caradina, Water Magi." She looked at Tariah and Dominic with a smile that was no less warm. "And it's also an honor to meet you as well." She looked twice at Tariah, and her eyes widened. "I see why Morgan called you his sister. You're a dead ringer for him. I would swear you were twins."

Tariah smiled and drew her thumb over her cheek and nose. "Tariah Chronis, Water Chronicle."

Dominic bowed. "Dominic Whisperer, Fire Fury."

Merideth tucked her hands in her pockets. "Well, why don't you come home with me?" She smiled. "I live on my own now. There's plenty of room."

Morgan hesitated. "Meri . . . about my parents . . ."

Her eyes darkened. "Morgan . . . there's something you need to know. But I don't want to talk here. Please come back with me."

"Alright."

She turned and began walking into the city. As he fell into step beside her, she glanced at him with a smile. "Leader of the original Black Magi. Respected by the Militia and king alike. And, gasp, suddenly a Chronicle. Magi are so fickle sometimes." She slid a smile at Jazz. "You're welcome, by the way."

Liking her all the more, Jazz grinned. "Thank you, indeed."

"Dare I ask?" Morgan grumbled.

Tariah grinned. The look on Dominic's face told her that only the women understood the byplay. Since it would be fun to keep it that way, she blocked him from getting the information from her mind. It would be their secret that Merideth had deliberately not gone through with being Morgan's first lover so that Jazz had the honor.

Morgan just rolled his eyes at the women in his life. They could keep their secrets. He had a feeling he didn't want to know. He managed to keep his silence on everything else until they reached Merideth's home, but as soon as he shut the door behind everyone, he said, "Meri, please. What's this about my parents?"

Merideth sighed and lit a lamp as she sat on the overstuffed couch she owned. "When the Elite arrived here a few days ago," she said quietly, "they came in looking for more members to join their ranks. They zeroed right in on your parents. We all assumed it was because you were the leader of the real Black Magi but now . . ."

"It was because they were the parents of a Chronicle," Jazz murmured.

"And because it's personal." Morgan's hands curled into fists at his sides. "Soh has always blamed me, even if not consciously, for not saving his son. I stood by and did nothing, remember?" His silver eyes darkened with anger. "It's personal for me, too."

Dominic glanced at Merideth. "Where have they gone? Glacia isn't that big. It's also lightly populated. Mostly farmland, correct?"

"Correct." She looked down at her hands. "There are three main cities on Glacia. This one, another on the coast to the very north, and the capitol in the very middle. The rest of the land is covered in farms and mining communities. We're one of the biggest agricultural places, very spread out . . . and so easy to control." She got to her feet and paced away. "Morgan . . . I hate to ask you this."

He found a smile for her. "What's his name?"

She turned in surprise. "How'd you know that?"

"Male intuition."

She was more willing to bet it was *his* intuition alone. She crossed her arms around herself tightly. "His name is Caleb. He's a good man. We were . . . we were supposed to have a ceremony and become Linked mates.

But the Elite came and convinced Caleb that because I had been exposed to a Chronicle, I might be in danger. They told him if he joined them, they would protect me."

"We'll get him out," he promised. He glanced at the window as snow and wind slammed into it, and he grimaced. The clouds had turned into a good, old-fashioned blizzard. "We can't go anywhere in this. As soon as it clears, we'll leave. No matter what time of day or night."

"In the meantime, please, stay here and rest. There are spare rooms." Merideth got to her feet and went over to the door to put on her hat and gloves. "I have to go to work. Morgan . . . thank you."

"You're welcome." He sighed only after the door was shut. He also turned and caught Jazz in his arms before even she realized how weak she felt. His eyes narrowed slightly. "Next time don't play at being fine when you're not. You should have said you were that tired!"

She smiled wryly as Tariah started shoving Dominic toward a spare room. "I'm not *that* badly drained, *ishke*. I just lost my balance, that's all. Now, if we'd been flying all day . . . well, then you'd likely be carrying me and Tariah would be rolling Dominic across the floor."

"She would not!" Dominic muttered as he caught the last of the conversation just before the door shut behind him and Tariah. He wasn't exceptionally tired either thanks to the constant and steady flow of power between him and his Chronicle. It was a subconscious replenish of his power at nearly all times.

Tariah smiled. "Yes, I would. It's not like I can carry you." She wound her arms around his neck as he lifted her and sat on the side of the bed with her on his lap. She sighed contentedly and let her head fall back as her power welled up and covered her with a soft blue aura. His lips pressed softly to her shoulder and she held him closer. Times like this made her feel as if the world had stopped and there was nothing to worry about in the world.

It was only as they were lying in bed together watching the blizzard slowly taper off outside that he noticed something different about her lines. He propped himself up on his elbow to study her intently.

More of her lines had darkened. Now they were dark gold down to the top of her hip and entirely down her arm. Her power was growing more potent. It was starting to manifest physically now and not just through her lines. Her hair seemed to ripple like water whenever light touched it.

It affected him, too. His lines had darkened and his hair burned like fire under the light. Thoughtfully, he smoothed a hand over her hip and traced her lines. "We're close," he said softly. "We're close to the end, *ishke*. In a month . . . well, I'd hazard that we'll likely be on the Isle and living however we want."

Tears burned her eyes. "Good," she whispered.

"What's the first thing you want to do?" he asked her softly. "Name it and it's yours."

"I want a Linking ceremony with you." She smiled when she felt his surprise. "I know it's a formality, but I want it. I never thought I'd get one so . . ." She tilted her head. "Or are there special ceremonies Dragons have?"

"There are. We call them Unification ceremonies. But . . ." He searched his memory. "I seem to have memory from the Fury before me that there was a ceremony for Dragoons. It was basically a Linking ceremony but it also named them full Dragoons. I can't be sure. We'd have to ask Xander."

"How old is he?" Tariah asked.

"Over twenty-five hundred."

She took a swift breath. "Then he was there. He might know where the lost isle is."

"No, unfortunately." He sighed. "All memories were erased of the location of the lost isle. I think the world feared this very situation. That someone would seek to find the isle and use the power. Lucksphere wants to survive above all else. That's why it made all of us."

"That's why there will always be Magi. Soh's a fool." She closed her eyes and cuddled closer against him as he lay down again. She wanted some sleep. They were going to need all their strength for the coming battle.

In the middle of the night, Tariah and Morgan were both awakened by the silence outside. It had stopped storming. Inside both Chronicles, they could feel the throbbing of their lines and the sudden sharp compulsion that was guiding them on. But unlike so many times when their lines had urged them north, this time the feeling was more definite, and more precise.

Go north and fight. Fight to live.

It was time to finish their journey.

Chapter Twenty-Four

The capitol city of Glacia was known as Bergia. It boasted a population of twenty thousand and had a large manor in the very center where the city leader lived while he was in office. Like most city leaders, he was an elected official.

But as the Dragoons approached the city two days later in the early morning, they were fairly sure that the city leader was no longer in residence. Hovering over the large building sat a dark cloud of ominous proportions. It was a thick and malevolent mass of power, as if the Flutterlies that made the clouds had been corrupted as well.

The cloud was expanding and covering the entire city. The people were either ignoring the cloud—and if they were, they were wearing Elite cloaks—or they were loading up wagons as fast as they could to escape. More were leaving than staying, but there were still enough left that it was like a sea of white cloaks.

Because they would have stood out, Jazz had turned all their cloaks brown and they wore hoods to cover their distinctive hair and lines. Their power could still be sensed, but no Magi recognized it as being anything other than above average. There were enough Master Magi to provide an effective cover. The disguises allowed the Dragoons to walk among the crowds and listen to conversations. There weren't many. It was as if the entire city had fallen silent.

The closer they drew to the center of town, the thicker the crowds grew. The Magi were gathered together around the leader's manor where there was a large balcony for him to use for speeches. This time it was Soh who stood on the balcony.

"What's he doing?" Tariah whispered. She was too short to see over the crowd.

Jazz and Morgan had the same problem, and Dominic skimmed his gaze over the area. He focused on Soh's lips and concentrated on reading what he was saying; it was too far away to actually hear. "Seems like he's just touting a lot of nonsense about purifying the world," he said quietly.

"Purifying . . . ?" Morgan began to push his way through the crowd to get closer. What was going on now?

They found a spot to see and hear from, and they were able to remain behind several large pine trees to keep themselves from being seen in return. It wasn't the best place, but it was the best they could hope to have.

"My fellow Magi!" Soh was saying. "The time is now for us to wrest this world from the people who don't understand! We must purify this world of the foolish ones! Those that would destroy the powerful because they fear them! Those that would destroy this world by removing our one saving grace! We will make a world for those saviors to live in! We will make a world where Chronicle and Magi live together!"

Jazz nearly gagged. "Hypocrite," she muttered.

"He's completely lost his mind," Tariah whispered. "Didn't the events two thousand years ago prove that genocide won't create peace?" She suddenly took a sharp breath and the color drained from her face. Her agony was so sharp and acute that not only did Dominic feel it, but Morgan also felt it as a psychic backlash. "No . . ." she whispered.

Dominic followed her gaze and felt his heart turn to ice. He knew who they were from her memories. Even if he hadn't, he would have been able to guess. The man had Tariah's silver eyes and the woman had her auburn hair. "How is it possible?" he said softly. "We were told they were killed."

Morgan suddenly sucked in a sharp breath as well. He had just recognized the two figures standing beside Tariah's parents. They were *his* parents, and all four wore the cloaks of the Black Magi Elite. "We have to get them out of there," he said urgently.

Knowing the two Chronicles were likely to follow their hearts and potentially get themselves killed, Dominic grabbed Morgan and Jazz grabbed Tariah. The two Furies hurried away from the scene as fast as they could, each carrying a Chronicle under their arm. It was only when they were well beyond the city limits that they put down their burdens.

"Ouch!" Tariah rubbed her hip. "You dropped me!" she accused Jazz.

"I was in a hurry, honey. I'm sorry." Jazz skimmed a hand down her hair in apology and then went over to where Morgan stood. She wrapped her arms around his waist and held on tightly. "We'll get to them eventually. For now there are far too many of them for us to take on by ourselves."

Dominic lifted Tariah up off the ground and enfolded her tightly in his arms. For all her sass to Jazz, she was in shock. Her entire soul seemed to have shaken down to its foundations. She had believed her parents were dead. But here they were, and they were her enemy.

"How do we handle this?" Jazz asked Dominic. "We need more help. But we can't contact our clanmates right now." She looked at Tariah. "Can you contact your Kin brother? Perhaps the Kin will assist us. After all, what Soh proposes to do to the Magi is as abhorrent as what the Magi did to Chronicles."

"They said that the Magi won't accept their help," Morgan noted.

"It's not the Magi asking. It's us." Tariah straightened her shoulders and eased back from Dominic. "I'm sure they will assist us. And they can notify the Dragons and the Furies as well."

Unexpectedly, all four felt a very strong and *very* distinct presence, and they turned to see a Dragon flying across the sky. His body was black with red swirls throughout the scales. He was, easily, the largest Dragon either Chronicle had ever seen. At their best guess, they thought he had to be fifty feet in length.

"Xander!" Jazz gasped. "What's he doing here?"

"We saw him in Mirah," Dominic managed to say. "You didn't?"

"Not at all!" She held an arm in front of Morgan to give him a brace as Xander flew in for a landing and his wings began to kick up snow all around them. Belatedly, she noticed that Xander had his claws very gently folded around two beings. "He brought someone."

Tariah peeked around Dominic's arm and gave a delighted gasp as she saw the two Xander carried. She rushed forward with a cry. "Sparkle! Daylar!"

"Tariah!" The two Faeries shot forward and attached themselves to her neck in fierce hugs. "I missed you!" Sparkle wailed. "It wasn't the same without you there! I kept hearing all these things and I was so scared!"

Tariah hugged both of them as tightly as she could and tears filled her eyes. "I missed both of you so much!" She released them and held one on each hand. "But why are you here?"

"We're here to help fight," Daylar told her. He looked at Dominic and the other pair of Dragoons. "We Kin are glad to fight alongside the Dragoons. We won't let another tragedy occur, especially not when it will destroy the world."

"The Dragons also feel this way," Xander noted. Light engulfed him and he went into Magi form. He pulled his hair back and tied it out of his way at the nape of his neck. "The minute I saw you in Mirah, I knew what your intent was. I sent word to the Elders and to the Kin. Both races are marching this way as we speak."

"We're already here," came Elder Juniper's voice from the air. "We Kin march vastly differently than you Dragons do."

Everyone looked around but couldn't see anything. Daylar and Sparkle giggled. Then, suddenly, the snow began to billow up into the air and formed swirls upon swirls of light and dark. From every swirl appeared a Kin, Moon and Sun alike, both Faerie and Elf, and all of them were armed for battle. Within moments, the land was filled with Kin.

A thousand . . . two thousand . . . Tariah couldn't guess at the amount of Kin standing there. Every Kin, for the strength of their power, was worth at least two regular Magi. In half the size, they had twice the army.

Before anyone could say or do anything, the land seemed to go dark as a shadow passed across the sun. It wasn't from the gathering storm clouds. It was from the thick mass of Dragons that flew across the sky. There were fewer of them than the Kin, but they were far bigger and far more deadly.

The air filled with the flapping of their wings and the snow kicked up in the air as they found places to land. Most were Furies. Some were merely Dragon Lords. And more still were normal Dragons. Each seemed bigger than the last, though none were as big as Xander. Tariah and Morgan felt vastly overwhelmed and both ducked behind their lovers.

Juniper and Xander walked forward as the representatives of their races. "Dragoons," Juniper said formally, "we are here to assist you in your battle against the Elite. We will hold the field for you while you take out the leader. When the leader falls, so will the army. If you're ready, we will begin the assault."

Tariah and Morgan exchanged a look and then looked at Dominic and Jazz who both smiled. With matching looks on their faces, the siblings turned to Juniper and said, "We're ready."

Dominic and Jazz turned into their Dragon forms, and Tariah and Morgan got onto their backs. Dominic carried Daylar in his claws and Jazz carried Sparkle. The two Kin would go along to add supplemental magic that even the Dragoons couldn't use.

As they took to the sky, Juniper murmured to Xander, "I must know. Did you recognize them?"

Xander's ponytail ruffled in the wind. "Yes," he murmured equally. "More than that, I could smell it in their blood. We're going to see something spectacular today, Juniper. Something I thought I'd only see once in my lifetime. This time though . . . this time I suspect a much better outcome."

Inside the city, silence had fallen. The Elite and Magi couldn't see outside the city walls because of the sudden snowstorms covering the town, but they could definitely feel that there was something going on.

Soh was afraid. He paced restlessly in the main hall of the leader's manor. He had thought that everything would go perfectly according to plan, but he was beginning to think he had erred somewhere. He knew that the two Chronis cousins had joined forces, and something about it told him he was in over his head.

The silence of the city broke sharply as Kin suddenly appeared from out of thin air and Dragons rushed up over the sides of the city walls and began to fly in to land. The land shuddered and rippled with the force of such sudden power but quickly calmed.

Elite leapt into battle and threw everything they had against their invaders. In the violent battle that raged, no one noticed the two Dragoon teams flying to the leader's manor. They landed in the back courtyard, and Sparkle and Daylar attacked the guards leaping for them. The combined Light blast repelled all enemies around them long enough for Dominic and Jazz to take Magi form again.

They fought their way past the guards and Elite that surged at them from all sides. Tariah and Morgan were full Chronicles; their powers were far more potent than any Magi could hope to achieve. More than one guard was either frozen solid or sent flying through a wall. Those that made it past their powers couldn't hope to make it past the Furies and their deadly fighting skills.

Halfway down the hall toward the main meeting room, the team was brought up short by the sight of Persia and Dublin Chronis standing in the hall waiting for them. Tariah's throat closed. "Mom . . . Dad . . . it's me!" She ripped off her cloak and tossed it aside. "See?"

Dominic's nose flared slightly as he caught the scent of the two Magi. His gut clenched as he smelled the unmistakable scent of power that had been tainted beyond repair. Alive or not, neither Magi would have any sort of life even if Tariah could reach through to them. They would be sick until they died.

Tariah closed her eyes as she understood his thoughts. "Soh's trying to stop you," Sparkle whispered from where she was riding on her shoulder. "He knew this would make you hesitate. But Tariah . . . they're already dead."

The others looked at her in shock. "It's true," Daylar said sadly. "The power you sense flowing in them is a false power. Their true power stopped long ago."

Water began to well up around Tariah's feet as shards of ice formed. Her hair unraveled and fell down around her body in auburn waves as her lines glowed and rippled. No one said anything, and not even Dominic offered to help. This was something she needed to do herself, and they all knew it.

Without hesitation, she released the ice at her former parents and the shards impaled them both with enough force to send their bodies flying to the floor. Whatever was fueling them was cut off, and both bodies turned to skeletons. The flesh melted away and the yellow blood filling them stained the floor. The smell made all of them gag.

They hurried past the scene and down the hall. Tariah stripped off her leggings and tunic as she went and left herself in her regular desert clothes. Something told her that she wouldn't want her lines muffled in the slightest. Morgan clearly felt the same for he was also removing his cloak and shirt.

"Bet that made for interesting fights," Sparkle said to Daylar. "Half-naked Chronicles everywhere."

None of them got a chance to laugh, though they all wanted to. They were stopped short by the sight of Iria and London Chronis standing in front of the doors to the main hall. Neither smelled of tainted power, and both turned white as they saw their son. "Morgan!" Iria managed to say. "We were told . . ."

"I know what you were told." Morgan kept his voice even and calm. "But it's okay. Quickly, get over here." The urgency nearly choked him. "There's something in that room. Something evil. Hurry. Please."

"Of course!" The couple moved forward, and they unknowingly triggered a hidden trap. Air blades formed in the air and shot forward to strike them in the back. They were sent flying to the floor and across it several feet before sliding to stops where blood pooled under their bodies.

"Mom! Dad!" Morgan rushed to their sides and realized both were still alive. "We need to heal this!"

"Leave it to us!" Daylar said. He flew over to Iria and began to dissolve the blade protruding from her back. "We Kin are better at healing than even the most adept Magi. We'll keep them alive until backup comes." He inclined his head toward where Sparkle was already summoning several more Kin, especially MoonKin, to assist them. "We'll make sure they survive," he promised.

Jazz helped Morgan stand once more and the four Dragoons moved alone toward the doors. Dominic kicked them down, and then covered Tariah protectively as a surge of power flooded out at them in a razor sharp wave.

Tariah felt Dominic's pain and realized that he had been wounded. A quick look at Jazz told her that she too had been wounded in the wash as she protected Morgan. "What was that?" she demanded. "I've never seen the like!"

Dominic and Jazz shared a grim look. "Dragon power," the male Fury said quietly. "There's a Dragon working with Soh."

They carefully edged into the throne room. There were no people present but for Soh and a woman sitting on the edge of a table. It wasn't hard to see that the woman was a Dragon for her hair was blue with white streaks, but her very appearance also noted that she was a Dragon Lord.

And, as they actually got close enough to feel her power, they all sensed it. "You're a Fury!" Morgan said in shock. "Why?" he demanded. "Why are you helping this sick bastard?" He gestured at Soh furiously.

The Fury looked at him and her green eyes glittered with hatred and grief in equal doses. It was as if everything she felt was dead. Everything except hate and pain. Something inside the two Chronicles wanted to weep for her. "Because," she hissed softly. "Because the Magi killed my Chronicle . . . *and you did nothing!*"

Jazz realized it first. "You were Phedo's Fury!" She shook her head violently. "Don't you think he would hate that you are doing this?" she demanded. "I would never let my Chronicle be alone, even if meant I took my own life to be with him! Sistra, where is your loyalty to your Chronicle!?"

Sistra lifted her hand and blasted Jazz halfway across the room. As Morgan rushed to her side, the other Fury said in a stifled tone, "I waited. I waited for five hundred years only to watch the Chronicles be massacred. Still I waited. I waited for a thousand years! And then I felt him! I felt his birth! . . . Barely eleven years later, I felt his death! And you know where I was? I was on the Isle!"

"It's your own fault!" Tariah shouted at her. "No one *made* you stay there! There's no one person at fault for everything! Everyone has been stupid!"

Sistra moved as if to blast her, and Dominic quickly moved her out of harm's way. Soh began to laugh maniacally. "When I met Sistra, I knew we could work together perfectly. She will help us find the Chronicle children."

"Furies can't track Chronicles," Jazz said as she painfully got to her feet. She was bleeding, but Morgan was binding the wounds as fast as he could. "If she told you they could, she was lying."

Soh looked at Sistra in shock. "You said . . ."

"Ignore her!" Sistra ordered.

"But . . ."

Dominic and Jazz exchanged a glance and then both turned into their Dragon forms. The hall was so big it could have held Xander let alone the two of them. Sistra saw what they had done and swiftly changed back as well. She was no bigger than Dominic in size but there was something about her form that seemed less beautiful and more . . . terrifying.

Jazz and Dominic both lunged for her and the building shook as she countered and sank her teeth into Jazz's wing. Soh turned to go assist Sistra when suddenly Morgan and Tariah both stepped in front of him. He stopped short. He couldn't say why but something about the two of them together terrified him. "If you'd just joined me," he told Tariah, "then this wouldn't have happened."

"True," she countered icily. "But then I would have suffered not knowing my Fury. I would have become my brother's enemy." Her eyes narrowed. "I'm going to kill you, you sick bastard. For what you're trying to do, but more for what you did to Daylar!"

"Who? Oh." He scoffed. "The Kin." He sneered at Morgan. "So you translocated right into your Fury's arms, did you? Where's my thanks?"

Morgan lifted a hand and a blast of air knocked Soh halfway across the room. "There's your thanks," he bit out. "Don't think you can play mind games with us. We're not going to be swayed." His eyes sharpened as he saw the blast Soh was gathering. "Move!" he snapped at Tariah.

They both dove out of the way, and the immense blast blew a hole in the floor. The two Chronicles rolled up to their feet and shot raw bolts of power at Soh from opposing directions. To their immense shock, the two powers merged together halfway and transformed into the shape of a Dragon as it rushed at Soh.

Soh opened his mouth to scream in terror but it was too late. The beast was upon him and it swallowed him whole. The power faded away and left nothing behind except Soh's cloak. It fluttered to the floor and melted into sand. It could not hold its form without the power of its owner.

Tariah swallowed hard. "Morgan?"

He felt no less shaken. "I don't have a single clue." He turned sharply as the room shook, and he saw that Jazz had just been thrown into one of the walls. He sucked in a sharp breath and rushed to her side. One of her wings was visibly broken, and she bled even worse than before. Her body was marked with bites and claw marks.

A moment later, Dominic hit the wall as well. He was in no better condition. Tariah hurried to him and began using ice to cover the wounds and stop the bleeding as best she could. A quick look told her that Sistra was wounded but still strong. "How is it possible?" she whispered. "Shouldn't a Dragoon be stronger?"

"Should but . . ." Dominic drew a labored breath. He hurt from head to tail. "It's like she's linked to someone and they're giving her power. So you could say that she's a Fury with infinite power without her Chronicle."

"That can't be right." Morgan pushed Jazz back when she tried to get up. "You're too wounded! Stay put!"

Sistra laughed dangerously. "And if they don't fight, who will stop me from erasing this entire city? Magi, Kin, Dragons . . . they're all the same!" She flew straight up into the air and burst through the ceiling. Pieces rained down onto the ground in her wake.

Tariah and Morgan looked at one another silently, and Dominic sensed their intent first. "She'll kill you," he told them. "You can take the form, certainly, but how will you know how to use it?"

"We can't just sit here," Tariah told him. She framed his face in her hands and kissed his forehead gently. "Let us protect you for once." She released him and walked over to her brother.

Both Chronicles began to draw on the majiks of their Furies, and the mental link between them allowed Tariah to show Morgan how to bend the majiks to the shape they needed. Air and Water power filled the air and engulfed both of them, stretching and reforming them as they bent their own power as well.

When the power faded, it left behind two fully-grown Dragons. Morgan was barely bigger than Jazz, and Tariah was slightly smaller. Both were auburn in color, the same as their hair, but while Tariah was marked with blue streaks, Morgan was marked with spots of white. Their silver eyes were eerily identical.

It took a few attempts, and reading of their Furies' minds, but Tariah and Morgan finally flew up into the air and through the hole in the ceiling to follow Sistra. Their passage opened the hole more, and the entire ceiling gave way. Despite the debris that landed on them, Dominic and Jazz were grateful for the view of the fight. If there was anything they could do, they wanted to do it.

Sistra saw the two Dragons flying after her and began to laugh uproariously. "What nonsense! Whelps think they can take on an Elder?" She flew directly at them and forced them to dodge and scramble to stay aloft at the same time. "You can't fly and fight, you fools! How does this help you?"

Tariah flew closer. "We can try," she said fiercely. She shot a blast of power at the other Dragon.

Sistra dodged hastily and then flew even further up into the air. She flew so high that the manor became a speck on the ground, but she wasn't very surprised when the siblings followed her. She even had to be reluctantly impressed with their ability to learn quickly. Both were flying more steadily. Still . . . they were out of their league.

"Enough toying around!" She began to gather her strongest attack. "I commend you for your bravery, but you never stood a chance. Goodbye, little Chronicles." She released the blast at them both, and it struck Tariah first. It sent her flying into Morgan, and they were both hurtled back toward the land far below.

Dominic and Jazz struggled to get themselves into the air and toward their Chronicles to save them. They barely missed them. The two siblings shot past their grip and slammed into the ground with such force that they blew out a hundred-foot crater. The shockwave caused everyone who was fighting to stop wherever they were. The silence was absolute.

Dominic and Jazz hurried toward the scene. Both knew that, somehow, oddly, their Chronicles had survived. "Tariah!" Dominic shouted. "Morgan!"

There was no response, yet something suddenly moved within the darkness of the crater. A massive claw lifted and grabbed the edge of the hole. Another followed suit and the beast within the hole began to pull itself out. It was the most shocking thing anyone had ever seen. No one had ever seen anything like it . . . except for Xander and Sistra.

The Dragon stood a hundred feet long from nose to tail. It had four wings on its mighty back, and it was covered in silver scales that glowed brightly in the sun. Each claw was as big as a Magi. Its head looked sharp and angular with two great fins extending from its head near where its ears would be.

"C-Chronis," Sistra managed to whisper. Even from her position high in the sky, she could see the Dragon clearly. "The Chronis Dragon." She had been sure she would never see such a thing ever again. A vivid memory cut across her mind of watching the Chronis Dragon fly across the field and cut down enemy Magi sent to destroy them.

Chronis looked up at Sistra and then suddenly flew straight into the air with a speed and grace only found in Elders. Sistra was still frozen with shock. It was only at the last moment that she was able to dodge, but she didn't get out of the way in time. The greater Dragon ripped her arm and wing off as easily as picking the petals of a flower.

Sistra screamed and began to plummet toward the ground. Out of desperation, she sought her Air power and cast a translocation spell. She, and the Elite still standing, disappeared from the field all at once. The Kin and Dragons were left standing as the winners.

Dominic and Jazz landed on the field and turned back to Magi form. Kin swiftly descended on them to heal their wounds, but all eyes remained fixed on the silver Dragon that was circling overhead as it slowly came in for a landing. Chronis landed at the edge of the hole it had come from and let out a roar. The sound was a promise and threat all at once. It chilled those hearing it.

Light engulfed the Dragon, and it suddenly split into the two Dragon forms belonging to Tariah and Morgan. They too glowed and shifted back to their natural Chronicle form. Both collapsed where they stood, and their Furies rushed to their sides.

Though both Furies had been drained dangerously low, they were replenished the moment they touched their Chronicle. Their majiks came back in an instant as if they hadn't been drained at all. Morgan and Tariah glowed brilliantly, emanating enough power that the land quivered in the wake. Finally, slowly, the land stilled. The power ebbed. The twins stopped glowing.

Silence overtook the field. Neither Kin nor Dragon said a word. There was nothing any of them could think to say. The snow fell softly around them as they wondered what they were supposed to do next.

Chapter Twenty-Five

Tariah awoke to the feel of sunshine across her face. She was lying snuggled in Dominic's arms, and she wasn't wearing a bit of clothing. Neither fact surprised her. For a moment, she simply savored how it felt to be in his arms, but then memory returned in a rush and she sat up swiftly. "Sistra!"

He sat up and pulled her into his arms again. He smoothed his hand through her hair gently. "Easy," he said softly. "We're safe. We have no idea where Sistra is though. Or the Elite. Her translocation scattered them. The good news is that the Elite is down to a handful of members. They were being slaughtered by our allies."

A chill rippled down her back and she moved closer to his comforting warmth. "If that is the good news . . . what's the bad news?"

He took a long breath. "Well . . . it's as if the Elite never existed. Like the lost isle, the memories of the world have been erased. The Magi remember the Elite, but not who they are. Even I can't seem to bring to mind the faces belonging to them. So now they walk among us and we're blind to their presence."

"It will take a long time for Sistra to heal," she reminded him. "Perhaps long enough for us to find the children."

"It's possible." He eased her back. "Would you like to tell me what you and Morgan did? I've never seen the like!"

"I have," Xander said from the doorway.

Tariah shrieked and yanked the blankets over her naked form. Her free hand lobbed a pillow in his direction, and the Fury was so surprised that it popped him in the face. He looked at Dominic. "I *really* want to know about that meeting."

Dominic grinned. "It's one of the many reasons I love her." He peeked under the covers. "You can show your face at the least."

"I just hit an Elder!" she wailed in response.

Xander laughed. "I deserved it. I am sorry for startling you, Tariah." He smiled when she pulled the blankets down to her shoulders. "No harm done." He walked over to sit on the side of the bed. "I already spoke with Morgan about things this morning. I wished to speak with you as well. To tell you of the Chronis twins."

"Dominic suspects Morgan and I are descendants," she said.

"It's no suspicion. I recognized your scent, and his, instantly. I knew the Chronis twins. They and their Furies still lived at the time of the first battles between Magi and Chronicle." He took a long breath. "They were . . . fascinating to know. And powerful. In the first great war, they took the field to fight. Their Furies became mortally wounded. The twins then did something no one had ever dared imagine possible. They didn't just turn into Dragon form . . . they merged."

Dominic's eyes widened. "Like Morgan and Tariah did."

"Yes. They obliterated the field of Magi. Nothing could stop the Chronis Dragon. But . . . their Furies died shortly thereafter. The twins just . . . slowly began to fade away." Xander looked down. "It was painful. Finally, other Chronicles offered to put them out of their misery. They agreed. But before they were struck down, and I remember this clearly, they looked at all of us and promised to come back and finish what they had started."

Dominic looked at Tariah. She was silent for a few minutes. Then, slowly, she said, "Morgan and I . . . we didn't know what was wrong with us. When we were falling we just . . . we just knew what to do. But we have both felt it. That there was a promise to keep." She looked at Xander. "And we will."

"I believe you." Xander stood. "Just to let you know, the Militia has put out word that you and Morgan are sanctioned by them. The Magi are heralding you as heroes."

"But . . . ?" Dominic asked.

"The law stands. Chronicle children are to be killed upon discovery." Xander crossed his arms. "I think they're of the 'if they don't exist, the Elite can't get their hands on them' mindset. So we're not quite at square one, but pretty damned close. Still . . . we Furies are going to do our best." As he was heading out the door, he added, "Remember to invite me to the ceremony."

The Dragoons smiled. "We will," Tariah promised. As the door shut, she fell over onto her back. "Are Morgan's parents alright?"

"They are." Dominic leaned over her and tugged the sheet out of the way to admire her beauty. She seemed impossibly perfect no matter what form she took. "They wanted to meet you, but Morgan made them return to Stalagmite. Even the Kin couldn't fully heal London. He will always use a cane from now on."

"I can meet them later." She closed her eyes for long moments. "It's not quite over yet but . . . I feel as if we might have some peace for a little while. Even looking for the children would never be as bad as what we just went through."

Her eyes suddenly flew wide, and shock filled her face. The door flew open and Morgan rushed in. He was fully dressed again, but his tunic was sleeveless to show his lines. Jazz was right behind him, but she looked as puzzled as Dominic. "Did you feel it?" Morgan asked his sister urgently.

"I did!" Tariah held the sheet to her chest as she sat up. Excitement hummed through her body. She could barely breathe as she looked at Dominic. Inside her body, she could feel the throbbing of her lines and the direction they were urging her. "We know where the Isle of Dragons is."

Go west.

"What? How?" Jazz asked Morgan.

Go west.

"I don't know. I just feel that this time we're heading to the Isle. The feeling is so precise it's like someone is whispering in my ear." He caught her in his arms and swung her around before kissing her soundly. "We're almost home. Finally."

Go west and you will find the Isle.

Tariah wasted no time in getting dressed. Once all of them were prepared, they left the inn they had been staying at. They had been in Arctica, the city on the western coast of Glacia. Bergia was in the midst of massive repairs. The land was still a little unsteady at times but was slowly returning to normal.

They stocked up on supplies, and Dominic and Jazz turned into their Dragon forms. With their Chronicles on their backs, they took off across the ocean. They flew at a slower rate than usual to preserve their strength, but they still moved faster than any boat.

They stopped only once over the next week, at one of the Kin outposts along the western coast of Carnelian. They restocked their supplies and obtained a strong boat for the rest of the journey that would take them into open ocean waters. They were still following the Chronicles' lines, and every day their lines seemed to steadily grow darker further and further along their bodies as they charted the last of their maps.

It was another week at sea before they knew they approached the Deepest Ocean. The waters were growing turbulent and steadily darker. The air was much more active and wind blew ceaselessly. Even the sky seemed darker than usual though there were no clouds. Oddly, Tariah no longer felt the trepidation she always had when contemplating the Deepest Ocean. It was oddly comforting.

They were awakened the following morning by the sudden calm of the sea. The ocean had stopped seething around the boat. When they emerged from the cabin onto the deck, the entire ocean was shrouded with fog. It was quiet all around them as if the world held its breath.

Dominic took command of the boat and sailed them silently into the fog. It was not yet dawn, and there was only one moon in the sky. The only light came from lanterns on the boat. It felt a little as if time had lost all meaning, yet the slowly rising sun proved it still passed. Steadily, the morning rays stretched across the sea and began to erase the fog.

When the fog lifted entirely, it was not gradual. It evaporated so suddenly that the sunlight on the ocean blinded everyone and forced them to look away. The glare faded just as quickly, and they slowly lowered their hands. Sitting across the ocean, less than a mile away, was an island. It had emerged from the mists as if it had been there all along.

"The Isle of Dragons," Jazz breathed. "I had forgotten how beautiful it is."

Beautiful was not the word for the Isle. It was exquisite. It was what Lucksphere had looked like before war and malice had destroyed the land. Mountains rose high in the sky, and the top peaks of several were snow-capped. The lower lands on this side of the mountains were filled with brilliant green grass and pockets of trees. Both Chronicles knew from their Furies that the other side of the mountains held lush deserts and oases. This one isle had the best the world could offer. It was blessed.

Dragons flew through the air, and occasionally a plume of fire or soil could be seen. Something inside Tariah's chest finally loosened, and she reached for Morgan's hand. Their fingers linked tightly together. "We did it," she whispered. "We found it. Somewhere we belong."

The Dragons were already gathering as they pulled in to dock. Those who were Lords were in Magi form. Those who were not shrank themselves down as small as they could to try to prevent themselves from overwhelming the newcomers. Excitement lingered high in the air. Everyone wanted to be the first to see the Chronicles.

Dominic got off the boat first and helped Tariah down. In delight, one Dragon exclaimed, "She's so tiny! And so pretty!"

Morgan hopped down off the boat and said to Tariah teasingly, "You must have an appeal to transcend race."

"Don't tease her too much!" someone at the back of the crowd called. "You're cute to us too!"

His cheeks went pink, and Tariah smirked at him. Jazz and Dominic just laughed. Dragons were always drawn to objects of beauty, and their Chronicles fit the bill both inside and out.

The crowd drew closer and everyone was beginning to talk excitedly. "They need to go meet the Elders!" someone said. "They said to bring the Dragoons immediately, remember?"

"Alright, everyone!" a female voice said from the air. "Calm down before you scare them off!" The cream-colored Fury was circling overhead, and white spots scattered across her scales like freckles. She was Dominic's size but vastly more slender. She turned into Magi form just as she was landing and became a tall woman with blonde hair and cream-colored eyes. She walked forward with a smile and hugged Jazz.

Jazz smiled and hugged her equally. "It's been a long while, Dahlia." She gestured to Morgan. "This is my Chronicle. Morgan, this is Dahlia Stalker, an Air Fury. We've been friends since we were whelps."

Dahlia bowed gracefully. "An honor, Morgan."

He drew his thumb over his cheek and nose with a smile. "Likewise."

The crowd began to disperse as Dahlia had asked, and she led the Dragons away from the port and toward the dirt road leading deeper into the Isle. "We Dragons," she told the Chronicles, "don't have cities like yours. We live wherever we please and build homes wherever we want. When we gather, we gather in the cliffs where the majority of buildings are. That's where our shops are and where the Elders meet. It's the closest thing to a city we have, really."

Dominic tucked Tariah close against his side. "My home was in the mountains, but we can live wherever you like." He smiled. "You can never really take a girl out of a desert, or so I've heard."

"Something like that," she said wryly. "But I'd like to try living in the valley you once mentioned. I've never seen one before."

"Hurry up!" a Dragon called from overhead. "They're getting impatient!"

With sighs, the three Furies turned into their Dragon forms. Tariah climbed onto Dominic's back, and Morgan onto Jazz's, then both pairs took to the sky with Dahlia following. As the other Dragons saw the sight, a cheer rose in the air. It was the most vivid sign in existence that could tell them all that Dragoons had returned again.

At the entrance to the meeting room, Grecia and Solis both waited. They waved their wings happily in greeting before changing into Magi form as the others landed. Grecia walked over to peer at Tariah as she slid off Dominic's back. "They weren't kidding when they said you were little!"

Tariah could only sigh. Dominic turned into Magi form and offered, "They say great things come in small packages, and they were right."

Solis grinned. "I certainly think she's fine as she is." He winced as there came a loud thud from inside the meeting room. "Better hurry before they knock down a mountain." Under his breath he added, "Again."

Dominic and Jazz wasted no time in hurrying to the doors and opening them. Urging Morgan and Tariah ahead of them, they went inside. The doors did not, however, shut behind them. Grecia caught them with her foot and peered inside. Solis and Dahlia quickly joined her. In fact, within a matter of moments, half the Furies left on the Isle were hovering close to see and hear. Word traveled fast among Dragons. No one wanted to miss this!

The meeting room was bigger than the king's palace, Tariah and Morgan both realized. The practicality was obvious since Dragons were much bigger. Yet there was something so simple about the room that, despite its size, it didn't feel overwhelming. Unlike the Magi king's throne room, there were no decadent statues displayed to flaunt wealth. The only statues were carved of wood and stone.

The four elder Dragons were as big as Xander, and each wore a colored sash to represent their clan. The Soil Elder studied Tariah and Morgan, then nodded in satisfaction. "Welcome, young Dragoons, to the Isle. We have searched for you for many centuries."

"Technically," Tariah muttered under her breath, "you didn't."

Dragons had good hearing. The Elders' eyes slowly widened as a group. "Pardon us?" the Fire Elder asked.

Already kicking herself mentally, she crossed her arms. She hated proving her brother right. "I just said that, technically, you didn't look for us. *We* looked for *you*." She ignored Dominic's clear amusement, and Jazz's quick grin. "*You* sat on your butts and lamented the sad state of the world!"

For a moment, not a single Elder could find a word to say. Carefully, the Water Elder said, "Well . . . that may be but . . ."

"No buts!" She threw her hands in the air. "Okay, you couldn't track us. Okay, you were afraid you'd go around eating Magi for their stupidity. But you could have done *something*. By doing nothing, you ensured nothing got done!"

"Yes'm," the Elders said as one. The hint of pink bloomed across all four faces.

She continued, "Morgan and I went through a nightmare to find our Furies. And at least *they* were looking for us! What about Dahlia? And Xander? Confining them to the Isle is stupid when they could at least *try* to sniff out their Chronicles. If *we* can feel them, *you* can!"

"Yes'm."

She crossed her arms. "We've got the Elite to deal with. We've got Sistra. There are kids out there that are being denied the truth of what they are. Are you going to sit on your tails and do nothing?" It was shot at them challengingly.

"No, ma'am."

"Good." She turned on her heel and headed for the doors before she made an even bigger scene. The Furies outside hastily moved out of the way, and all began to clap and cheer as she exited.

Morgan and Jazz followed her, and as Dominic turned to go as well, the Fire Elder called his name. "Yes?" He looked back over his shoulder.

The Elder's face creased into a toothy smile. "I like her. We all do." The other Elders nodded in agreement, and all were grinning as well.

Dominic started laughing. "I *knew* she would somehow cause you to agree on something for once!" Still chuckling, he hurried from the room to find his Chronicle. There were many things he wanted to show her. So many things that he had waited too long to share with her.

One week later, Tariah and Morgan stood side-by-side facing their Furies who were in Dragon form. Both Chronicles wore clothing woven of the finest cloth by the greatest craftsman on the Isle. The clothes were the formal type considered the standard style of where they were from. For Tariah, it was clothing of the desert. For Morgan, it was clothing of the snowy lands.

Dominic and Jazz wore sashes in the color of their clans; red for him and green for her. All around them, the entire Isle had gathered. Every Dragon of every shape, size, and age had come to witness the event. Because of it, the event was taking place in the middle of the valley where there was room for all of them.

The only others present were Sparkle and Daylar. They were in formal clothing, too, and riding on Solis and Dahlia's shoulders. Neither Kin would have missed this ceremony for the world. Sparkle couldn't stop sniffling, though, and Solis kept handing her tissue. He didn't mind. Her happiness was shared by all of them.

"This ceremony," the Fire Elder said, for he was presiding over the events, "is an old one. It is steeped in heritage and history. It has been a thousand years since it was performed, and yet all present will remember it somewhere inside.

"Furies, will you dedicate your lives to protecting your Chronicles? Will you always support them, and give them the wings to fly across the skies as Dragoons?"

"We will," both Dominic and Jazz said.

"And Chronicles, will you dedicate your lives to protecting your Furies? Will you always support them, and walk beside them when they wish to see the land as Dragoons?"

"We will," Tariah and Morgan said.

"Then it is with honor that I name all of you full Dragoons and confer upon you the full privileges associated with such a position. I also declare you to be Linked by Magi standards, Bonded by Kin, and United by Dragon. You will stand as one, you will live as one, and you will die as one. For eternity."

"For eternity," all present repeated.

"Let us see our Dragoons take their first flight together on their new paths." He moved out of the way, and the crowd backed up as well.

Tariah belatedly discover that climbing onto Dominic's back in a skirt was near impossible, and her nose wrinkled up. Before she could find a way to use her power, Xander walked up and lifted her easily onto Dominic's back. She smiled down at him as she settled into place. "Thank you, Xander."

He smiled. "It was my honor." He moved back once more and tucked his hands into his pockets.

Morgan had already climbed onto Jazz's back, and the crowd held its breath. The two Furies shot straight into the air with a shower of sparks and light, and the crowd erupted into cheers. Half a dozen Dragons flew up to join them and they trailed behind the Dragoon couples as they flew in opposite directions across the sky. They would circle the Isle before going to their chosen homes; it would be the mountains for both, but the sunny side for Tariah and Dominic and the snowy tops for Morgan and Jazz.

Tariah felt an odd sense of peace and disorientation as she held onto Dominic. A lot had happened in what felt like an impossibly short amount of time. "The Magi are calling us heroes," she said thoughtfully. "The Kin are calling us saviors. I'm not sure I want to be a hero or savior. What are the Dragons calling us?"

Her mate smiled and angled down toward the home waiting in a place where the sun would always shine. "I think they're calling you champions."

"I don't like that either." Her lower lip poked out.

"How about I call you something else, then?"

"Like what?"

"*Ishke*."

She sighed contentedly and leaned down to hold him tight. She had never been happier in her life. "I suppose I can settle for that." In fact, she thought she could settle for anything as long as she had her Fury by her side.

Finally, she was where she belonged.

Epilogue

Dear reader,

And so ends the Chronicle of Destiny, named for the Chronicles who carried the name of Chronis and the fate it bestowed. Though the battles ahead will be tough, and though no one can say with certainty that the outcome will be one wanted by all, there is no doubt in my mind that no one will ever forget this journey and the part it has played in the story of the world.

Where the next will begin, no one can say. But begin it will, for in the language of the Dragons and Kin alike 'luck' shares a character with 'forever' and 'sphere' shares one with 'story'.

And so, the story of the world shall go on forever.

Xander Journe

Chronicle of Summer
Book Two of The Chronicle Series

Part One
~Memory~

Prologue

Dear Reader,

Summer is the best season on Lucksphere. Everything and everyone enters into its growth cycle. Children—be they Magi, Kin, or Dragon—enter into their first or second puberty. If entering first puberty, their birth-given powers evolve and they develop the true elemental powers that define our world. Air, Fire, Water, Soil. The Kin call them secondary powers because they learn Light or Dark from birth. Magi call them primary because they don't develop the secondary powers until second puberty and instead have lightning from birth. Some Magi, though, deviate from the norm.

Some Magi are Chronicles.

Chronicles are hated and feared. If a child becomes a Chronicle, their bodies develop golden lines of Dragon power upon first puberty. Lines that are a map leading them on some great journey. More deaths than births have littered the Chronicle past. Magi law dictates that all Chronicles are to be killed upon discovery.

But, you see, Chronicles are different in another way too. When they enter first puberty, they learn both primary and secondary elements. Air and Thunder, Fire and Smoke, Water and Ice, or Soil and Wood. There are also people known as Master Magi—people like me—who are exactly like Chronicles in their first puberty development. We, too, learn both elements from that time and evolve differently through our lives.

In the summer of my nineteenth year of life, I began my second puberty. This was the time when I would truly become an adult. You see, first puberty defined us as our gender, developing our bodies physically. Second puberty defined us sexually, allowing us to grow in ways that would give us the ability to reproduce.

Second puberty is the most beautiful time of life and makes summers beautiful as well. Growing and blossoming, discovering the beauty in yourself and in others. Discovering how to find pleasure in your entire world, and not just in a sensual manner. Your skin is more sensitive, and your eyes see clearer. You go through the world more conscious of yourself and others. It's like being born a second time. At least, that's what people say.

They don't mention the awkwardness or the shyness or the self-consciousness. They don't mention how wearing covering clothes because you live in a forest will make your sensitive skin itch like it was on fire. They don't mention how even a normally out-going person will feel embarrassed to go swimming when other people are around.

Second puberty is a pain in the ass.

Kelsey Renaire

Chapter One

The city of Verdenture boasted a population of fifty thousand Magi, a handful of Kin, and absolutely no Dragons. It was not unexpected. The Kin, both Sun and Moon, both Faerie and Elf, stuck to their own islands because they didn't always like Magi ways of life. Dragons . . . well, they intensely disliked Magi and stayed on their hidden isle to stifle the desire to start eating them.

Among the cities on the land of Carnelian, Verdenture was one of the biggest. It was also well noted on maps: within the forested city was a young Master Magi by the name of Kelsey Renaire. She was a Fire Magi who also used Smoke powers despite not yet being through second puberty. In fact, she had only recently begun that beautiful development, and every unattached person in town was waiting with their fingers crossed to be noticed.

In addition to her world-renown skills as a Master Weaponsmith, Kelsey was without question the most beautiful girl in her city. Her hair was a thick mane of red curls that varied between shades of red that were more blue and reds that were more orange. It cascaded down her back in a thick mass that she often tied on top of her head in a messy bundle wrapped in ribbon.

While she worked at a forging table, she wore little more than a snug, strapless top and a pair of shorts. She felt no fear of injury; her own fire could not burn her. She *did* worry about material catching flame, though, and cut down on what she wore. It could also get blinding hot, enough that it bothered even her.

When the small MoonKin Faerie approached the stone shed where her friend worked, she was highly disgruntled to see the men peeking inside. Unsurprised, naturally, but disgruntled regardless. She skidded to a stop and propped tiny hands on her hips. Her nearly translucent double wings fluttered to hold her in the air. "Ahem!"

All four males jumped and turned around quickly. The youngest was only just past second puberty, and the oldest was potentially old enough to be Kelsey's father. Etude wasn't sure which was more vexing. "March!" she ordered. She pointed down the road. Her slender arm with its rich mocha colored skin displayed its silver tattoos brightly in the filtered sunlight from the trees.

With distinct reluctance, the men dragged their feet and shuffled down the stone path toward the rest of the buildings. This part of Verdenture was purely residential with the pointed exception of Kelsey's stone shed. Though she was more social than most Master Magi, she was still inclined to retreat for her work.

Etude flew into the shed and landed on a shelf near the door. It was never a hardship to watch Kelsey. To be a Weaponsmith meant that the Fire Magi had to have a precision mastery over wielding her element at the same time that she manipulated her material. Every hammer blow had to have a delicate combination of physical force and Fire power.

Kelsey's skill was evidenced in the way sparks flew with every blow, and her strength was seen in the sleek muscles that lined her arms. Even Etude thought that Kelsey's strength was sexy, and she didn't have a particular preference for Magi. But Kelsey wasn't a normal Magi by any means of the imagination. Etude wasn't sure *how* different Kelsey was, but she had suspicions. Ones she would never speak out loud.

With a final rap of the hammer she held, Kelsey straightened and held up the sword she had been working on. She set the hammer aside before shoving her visor up on top of her head. Her crystalline blue eyes nearly looked green in the light from the fire in front of her. With a contented sigh, she put the sword to the side. It was just a blade right now. She would be smoke-carving the hilt later.

"Cross-eyed yet?" Etude asked.

Kelsey turned with a grin. "Only a little. Ugh." She swiped at her arms and her forehead to remove sweat but only added more soot and ash. "Air!"

Etude obligingly created a soft breeze to flow in the shed and remove the oppressive heat. Even Fire elements could get overheated. Etude, as an Air secondary Kin, was the perfect partner to work with. She was also a master etcher and could use her tertiary Thunder power to make intricate designs on Kelsey's weapons.

While Kelsey lied down on the floor, Etude flew over to look at the blade. It was double edged and both sides were razor sharp. The blade flared at the base where it would eventually be mounted to a hilt, and the entire blade came to a point that was no wider than Etude's hand. "It's beautiful," she said finally. "You just get better every time." She flew over to her friend and peered down at her face. "Can you walk?"

"I'm not sure. How long was I in here? My back says it was about ten hours."

"The sun says it was more like twelve."

"Who am I to argue with the sun?" She pushed herself up to a sitting position with a groan and then gained her feet. "I need a hot bath."

Etude smiled in bemusement as she followed her friend out of the shed. "She goes from a hot forge to a hot bath. I'm surprised you don't sleep in a fireplace, Kel. Really."

"Mom and Dad swear I used to crawl into them, actually. I was always covered in soot to the point that people were thinking I was part MoonKin because my skin was dark."

Etude studied the smudges across her face. "I ought to call you Soot then."

Kelsey stopped walking sharply, a fist emotionally slamming into her chest. Something hurt. Something hurt a lot. She felt as if she should remember something that she couldn't. She had forgotten something. Something important. She had always felt that way, but the missing memory suddenly seemed downright painful.

Etude's smile faded and she flew closer. "Kel?"

She shook her head. "I'm okay." She pushed it aside and walked faster down the road. "Let's get indoors before I get bit." Forested lands were notorious for insects. It was why the dwellers within the trees tended to wear longer clothing.

Because she wasn't an adult yet, she still lived with her mother and father. In deference to her very strong independent nature, though, her parents had made her room on their house to be self-sufficient. She had her own bathing room, kitchen, and work area. If she was in a mood where she didn't want to see anyone at all, it wasn't required.

That didn't mean her parents didn't try to spoil her.

She smiled as she walked into her bathing area and saw that there were already towels stacked neatly beside a special soap that wouldn't make her sensitive skin itch. The large pool was already filled with hot water, courtesy of her father who was a Water Magi. Water made by a person rather than nature itself never changed temperature.

"Your parents really love you," Etude noted.

She stripped off her clothes. "Yeah." She contentedly got into the tub and sank in to her neck. She remembered her hair was still up, and she pulled out the ribbon. The thick mass tumbled down, and she ducked underwater entirely. When she surfaced, she slung her hair out of her eyes and said, "Second puberty is overrated."

Her partner tried not to smile. She was six years old by Magi standards. By Kin Faerie standards, she was closer to her mid-twenties. Faeries grew very fast for their first three years and then grew at a normal rate until the age of one hundred when they stopped growing entirely. On the flipside, Kin Elves grew very slowly until about fifty. At that point they would start aging normally to two hundred when they stopped growing. Kin weren't immortal like Dragons, but their average age span was around five hundred.

As such, second puberty was around three for Faeries and around fifty for Elves. Etude was well past the process. "You're just reacting stronger because *you're* stronger." She gathered up Kelsey's discarded clothes and put them in the basket where they belonged. "You know flesh is secondary to power on Lucksphere. You went to school, didn't you?"

As if from memory, Kelsey obediently recited, "All Magi learn lightning from birth. Around an average age of thirteen, they enter first puberty where their bodies develop and define their gender. Their lightning becomes a tangible primary element. Around an average age of nineteen, they enter second puberty where they become capable of reproducing. Their primary element evolves into their secondary."

"With . . . ?"

She sighed and sank further in the water. "With the noted exception of Master Magi who develop secondary elements from first puberty and tend to grow at a faster rate. They also experience things far more clearly because, like all beings, their bodies are made by their power. The stronger the power, the stronger their bodies and feelings."

"Good girl." Etude flew over and picked up a cloth to help scrub Kelsey's face. Her friend never did manage to get all the soot off. In return, Kelsey always helped Etude get her wings clean. They didn't fold in ways that allowed her to reach all the parts.

There came a loud commotion outside, and Kelsey opened her eyes. "Now what?"

Etude flew over to the window and opened it just enough to hear. Outside, two women were talking with a visitor from Prismatic. "What do you mean you saw one?" one of the women asked.

"I saw one of the Chronicles that saved us nine years ago," the man explained. "It was just in passing, but it was definitely the female! She was riding on the back of a Dragon, and if that isn't a clue, I don't know what is. Dragons can't carry passengers, but Furies can carry their Chronicles."

"Ugh," the other woman said. "I still don't know why we let them live and have to kill all the rest. It's been nine years. The Black Magi Elite are gone. I say it's time to live and let live. If the two we've seen are anything to go by, then I don't believe Chronicles are the terror we've always been led to think."

"You may be right," the man said softly. "The woman I saw didn't look like a monster. If anything . . . I think she looked a little sad."

Etude shut the window and thought swiftly over things. That was a really good thing to hear, especially for the Kin. She flew down to where Kelsey was scrubbing her hair and landed on the edge of the pool. "They were talking about a Chronicle sighting." She watched Kelsey's face as she spoke. "She was seen flying on her Fury's back past the continent of Prismatic."

Kelsey's hands stilled as she felt a fierce pain welling up inside her chest. Her skin burned, and her soul felt as if it was being torn apart. She *needed* something. There was something that was critical to her existence. There was *someone* out there. She felt him at the back of her mind and heart. "What are Furies?" she managed to ask. She hurriedly rinsed her hair free from the soap though her fingers trembled.

Her reaction only confirmed Etude's suspicions. She closed her eyes. "Furies are Dragon Lords. Dragons are Dragons, as you know, but Dragon Lords are Dragons who can take Magi form. Or Kin form, actually. Dragon Lords aren't always Furies, but Furies are always Dragon Lords. A Fury is the destined lover for a Chronicle. They're always complete opposites. Opposing genders, opposing elements. You know how Chronicles have lines? Well, those lines are a map leading them to their Fury. They say that the love between a Fury and a Chronicle is unlike any other. They become bound in ways that go beyond a Linking union for Magi, or a Binding one for Kin."

"Someone to love them," Kelsey said softly.

"Someone to love them no matter what happens. It's instantaneous, if what I've heard is true. They meet and . . . it just happens. I think part of it is the power exchange." When Kelsey blinked at her, she rubbed the back of her neck. "We call it feeding on power, but it's more complicated than that. You know how Dragons have infinite power and Magi don't? It's flipped in Chronicles and Furies. A Fury feeds on the Chronicle's power and it maintains balance. The Fury doesn't risk destroying his or herself and the Chronicle doesn't risk going out of control."

"It sounds beautiful."

The longing in Kelsey's voice was poignant and clear. It was also completely subconscious. Wanting to distract her, Etude flew over and tickled her ear. "Still ticklish?"

"Gah!" She grabbed Etude and dunked her. "You little fink! Taking advantage of my skin is not fair!" With an annoyed sound, she got to her feet and began wringing out her hair. It tended to dry very quickly because her natural body heat was high. "I hate this part of puberty! Yes, things I like are more enjoyable, but on the other hand, the things I don't like are LESS enjoyable!"

Etude surfaced and flew out of the water. She shook out her wings before grabbing Kelsey's clean clothing. "I think you're just having a double dose because you're a Master Magi. It should go away in another month or so. I think."

"Think!" She muttered under her breath as she pulled on her underclothes. For women, the two-piece set was called a bikini. It consisted of a pair of underwear, and a top that crossed over a woman's breasts and tied behind her back and neck. The set could be worn with or without clothes over the top. The tighter the top, the better the support. She had seen some desert girls wearing literally nothing more than a bikini and some cloth tied around their hips. She *envied* them.

Because Kelsey's figure was on the lusher side—lush when compared to her average five-six height—she wore her bikini top slightly snugger than usual. She paired with it a pair of snug black leggings and a loose dark red tunic. The tunic had sleeves that went to her wrists, and it belted around her waist. The clothing was standard for a forest dweller.

It was for that reason that she walked into her parents' central room and complained, "Can we move to the desert already?"

Luke Renaire looked up from the book he was reading and smiled. "Hello, Etude."

Etude waved from where she was sitting on Kelsey's shoulder. "Hello!"

"What are you complaining about now?" Mildred Renaire asked in exasperation as she walked in from the kitchen. She moved over to the other seat in the room after stopping long enough to kiss her daughter's cheek. "Hello, Etude." The Faerie had been a common sight in the household for years.

"I'm complaining about this!" Kelsey held out her arms, and the sleeves flopped past her hands. "Long sleeves! Long leggings! I just put them on and already my arms and legs are itching!"

Luke frowned and put down his book. "I think perhaps it's time you went to the doctor in town. This is going beyond unusual, even for you. If it was just your sensitivity, it wouldn't be isolated. Your whole body ought to be itching."

"It's not my whole body. Just the undersides of my arms and the outsides of my legs." She crossed her arms to keep herself from scratching her skin. It nearly burned in intensity. "No doctor. I'll deal with it."

Neither Luke nor Mildred felt surprised. Kelsey was, indeed, more outgoing than most Master Magi, but she was still highly sensitive emotionally. She wouldn't go to a doctor unless she was dying and, frankly, even that seemed debatable. "Very well," Luke conceded.

A knock came to the front door, sounding as three sharp raps. Mildred's brows rose. "The Militia?" She hurried over to the door and opened it slightly to peer out. On the doorstep she found a young man wearing the uniform of the Magi Militia. "Is there something wrong?"

"Not at all." The man smiled. "Might I enter? This is the home of Kelsey Renaire, is it not?"

"Bye." Kelsey turned to leave, but Etude grabbed her tunic collar and Luke grabbed her tunic bottom. She groaned but stopped trying to get away.

"Yes," Mildred said dryly, "it is. Please come in." She shut the door once he had entered and led the way to the sitting area. "What can we help you with?"

For a moment, Ilian Deepforge couldn't speak as he spotted Kelsey. He had never seen such a strikingly beautiful young woman before. Her thick red hair was like the purest of flames, and the blue eyes glowering at him reminded him of the clearest sky. Stunning was the only word he could think of to describe her.

She covered her face with a hand. "I'm not out of second puberty."

He blinked and then smiled apologetically. "I am sincerely sorry for my absorption, and also sorry for the people in this town."

"So am I," Luke muttered.

"*Dad.*" Kelsey smacked his hand off her tunic and dislodged Etude as well. That done, she drew her thumb over her cheek and nose in the universal Magi greeting even as Etude folded her wings around herself and bowed in the Faerie greeting. "Nice to meet you. I am Kelsey Renaire, Master Fire Magi. This is my partner, Etude, Air secondary MoonKin."

Ilian returned the gesture. "Argyle Ilian Deepforge, Fire Magi, leader of one of the Militia parties deployed to Carnelian." He repeated the gesture to Mildred and Luke, including them in the respectful greeting.

Mildred and Luke also returned the gesture. "Luke Renaire, Water Magi, and my mate, Mildred, Soil Magi," Luke said. "What brings you to our home, Argyle?" He couldn't quite keep the confusion off his face or out of his voice. Argyles were the highest ranked members of the Militia, answering only to the king himself, and only half a dozen existed across the world. They did not usually show up randomly in cities; that was more a duty for the captains of individual units.

"Ilian, please. I was only recently promoted to Argyle and I'm not used to it." He took a seat when Mildred gestured to it. "I'll make a long story short. I am here to request aid from Kelsey to make new weapons for my unit. Our weapons simply won't hold up to our current duty. We need better, and there is none better than Master Kelsey's weaponry."

Kelsey was intrigued despite herself. "Can you tell me what your duty is?"

"I am afraid I cannot," he admitted. "We have to deploy in a few days, however. I suppose that is not long enough."

"For one or two weapons, perhaps. How many do you need?"

"Twenty."

She grimaced. "Never happen. I can do it in a week or two, though."

He almost offered to come back for them but changed his mind at the last moment. He couldn't seem to look away from her crystalline eyes. He wanted to be the one she noticed when she was ready to experiment in second puberty. The only way to do that would be to keep her near. "Would you be willing to travel with my unit long enough to make the weapons?"

"Only if I go too," Etude muttered. Her rose-colored eyes told him that she had not missed his interest.

"Naturally you would be invited," he agreed. "I would not expect her to simply travel off with a person you have no reason to trust."

"It's up to you, Kelsey," Mildred said softly. "You are a Master Magi and therefore you exist under rules different from the rest of us. If you wish to go, we won't stop you."

"I'll make the first weapon," she decided. "If it is sufficient for you, I will agree to travel with you long enough to make the rest. What would you like me to work on first?"

Ilian drew the sword he wore at his side and offered it hilt first. Though he had been expecting it, he was still a little nonplussed as she took it with one hand and no effort. There were few women who could swing a sword one handed. "As you can see, this sword has seen much fighting and is stressed to the max."

"Hmph. Looks like it was never high quality to begin with. I could do better in my sleep." She propped the sword on her shoulder. "Let's talk payment."

"I can offer a payment of ten bronze coins for twenty weapons." He smiled when the others stared at him. "It's a payment well made for Master Kelsey's work."

Bronze coins were worth five times the amount of ivory coins, the common currency for the world. A single bronze coin could allow someone to buy food and supplies for an entire month. "*Aiyea,*" Etude breathed.

"Pardon?" Luke asked.

"It has no translation to Magi," she apologized. "It's more an exclamation of surprise than a word. Remember, we have five hundred characters in our language and you only have one hundred."

"Aiyea indeed," murmured Mildred.

Kelsey shrugged one shoulder. She was used to hearing outrageous amounts of money thrown at her. Truth be told, she had a sealed trunk in her room with enough ivory that she would never want for anything again. "Done." She turned to head for the door.

Startled, Ilian said, "You do not need to get started right now."

"Why shouldn't I?" Without another word, she headed back to her rooms to change into her work clothes again.

Luke said softly, "She's more comfortable there. Though she smiles and laughs and makes friends easily, she is more secure in her workshop." He ran a hand through his hair with a sigh. "When she was a child, she was precocious. But when she entered first puberty . . . a part of her retreated. If she didn't have her weaponry, she wouldn't even live in a town."

"You want to see?" Etude asked. Ilian nodded and she flew over to the door. "Follow me." With him close, she headed back down the trail toward the shed. There was already a plume of orange smoke coming from the chimney. "You liked Kelsey, didn't you?"

"I did," the Argyle admitted. "It was a bit surprising. I've never been quite so strongly attracted to anyone before, not since my own second puberty."

"And that was . . .?"

"About ten years ago." Realizing what she was fishing for, he offered, "I am twenty-eight summers old." He ran a hand through his short black hair. "Her eyes . . . they remind me of the glass I often work with. I've always wanted to make that shade of blue."

"Oh so you work mostly in Smoke?" The element of Smoke allowed a Fire user to create and craft glass. They could also break down glass into sand for Soil users to weave cloth with.

"I do. I have not done it since joining the Militia though. Perhaps I ought to pick it up again." He stopped talking as they reached the door to the shed. As quietly as possible, he opened the door and peered inside. At first, he was distracted by Kelsey's stunningly long legs, and then he focused on her work and his breath really caught.

The sliver of metal she hammered looked like nothing remotely resembling a sword. But as he watched, he could see the beginnings of the shape forming, the metal melting and reforming under master control. His eyes shifted to her face, and he was left spellbound. The color of her eyes . . . he wanted to capture it within glass.

"Don't fall in love with her," Etude warned softly.

"Why?"

"Because she can never love you back." She flew off without another word through the darkening twilight.

Ilian, with nothing else he could do, turned to go to the camp where his party rested while they waited to set off again. Her words confused him highly. In a world where you couldn't *know* how a person's heart would function until after second puberty, how could she know whether or not Kelsey could love him?

Something told him he didn't want to know the answer.

Chapter Two

When Kelsey finished the sword blade, she went immediately into smoke carving. Smoke carving was arduous. It meant making glass and then fire hardening it until it was unbreakable. During that hardening process was a very small window of time where carving could be done without detail being lost. As soon as it hardened completely, it was too late to do additional work without breaking the hilt down entirely and starting over.

The normal course of work wasn't without its mishaps, and there were several piles of discarded glass by the time she deemed the hilt ready to be forged to the blade. That was another several hours of work because the fusion of metal and glass involved excruciating heat and detail to make sure the two halves bonded permanently. She had never had a sword break. She didn't intend to start.

Once the sword was finally done, she dunked it into a spinning barrel of sand to polish up. The spinning barrel was an invention of Air Kin and could spin for as long as needed. She had it set to spin for two hours. The sword was on its last step, and not a minute too soon. She pulled off her visor, curled up near the forge, and fell asleep.

When she woke next, she discovered that someone had draped a blanket over her. Groggy, she pushed the blanket aside and sat up. She rubbed at her eyes blearily. She was *starving* and she wasn't sure what day it was. She had lost track of time again.

"Good morning."

She squinted at the doorway and discovered Ilian standing there. "Good morning," she said automatically. She blinked. "Is it morning? What day is it?"

"Two nights and a day since I asked you to make the sword." He walked in and removed his hat reverently. "I've never known any Weaponsmith who could sustain herself on her power alone for two days while she crafted. I can see why you are a master at your work."

"Uh-huh." She covered a yawn. "I don't like interrupting myself." She got to her feet, then went over to where the barrel had long since stopped spinning. She pulled the sword out and shook the sand off. "Here you are." She held it out to him.

He took the sword from her slowly, and his eyes filled with astonishment. It was twice as long as the original sword, but it was also twice as light, evidence of the master crafted glass hilt. Magi characters for strength and speed had been etched into the hilt. The blade looked sharp enough to split hair, and hair was one of the strongest physical components on any being's body.

"I need a bath and food." Still rubbing her eyes, she walked past him and headed for her home.

He realized belatedly that he was being left behind. He sheathed the sword at his side and hurried to catch up. "Would you be ready to leave within the day? We must move quickly, and for that I apologize. Do you even think you can craft on the move?"

"Please stop talking." She stopped at her door and gave him a disgruntled look. "Please, leave me alone for a while."

He frowned when the door shut in his face. "I did not mean to offend her."

"You didn't." Etude had flown up without his awareness and she circled around in front of him. "She's just sensitive right now. Come back later. She needs to rest now." She entered through a smaller door designed just for her, and the sound of the lock sealing was distinct.

Once inside, she flew over to where Kelsey was staring at a hot bath with a look of consternation on her face. "I saw the sword was done," Etude explained. "We knew you'd be ready to relax soon. I'll get some food for you."

Kelsey stripped down and climbed into the pool gratefully. She still felt groggy and disoriented. She hadn't slept long, but she had slept hard. She had also pushed herself intensely hard and was even more sensitive than usual. The hot water felt delightfully comforting against her skin.

When Etude returned with a basket full of piping hot food, she could only sigh. Kelsey was asleep in the bath. The girl needed a keeper. She worked too hard and too long. The part that frustrated Etude was that she *knew* Kelsey's perfect match was in the world. She just didn't know where he was exactly. "I'll help you find him," she vowed softly. She landed on the edge of the pool to study her friend. "I'll find your Fury. And I'll help you find yourself." She shook it off and gave Kelsey a shake. "Kel. Come on, Kel."

Kelsey's eyes blinked open. "Huh? Oh." She sat up and rubbed her eyes. "I fell asleep again. Sorry." She got to her feet, then got out of the bath. "I guess I was still tired." She got dressed in fresh clothes and took the basket into her kitchen to eat. "I worry you, Etude. I'm sorry."

"It's all right. You wouldn't be my Kelsey if you didn't." Etude took a biscuit from the basket. It was nearly bigger than she was, but Faeries ate a lot compared to their size. "Do you think you'll be able to do the weapons justice while traveling?"

"I think so." Kelsey happily ate the blended rice and fruit she had been given. Her mom could *cook*. "I figure I'll work on the weapons at night while we're camping then sleep during the day while we travel."

As she proceeded to demolish the rest of the food, Etude had to smile. Kelsey could eat on a level comparable to a Kin Faerie.

After eating, Kelsey got out a hipsack to begin packing for the trip, and Etude hurried for her own home to do the same. The hipsacks were another invention of the Kin and could expand in size to hold whatever they needed. The Kin had made a lot of things that way; everything from blankets to furniture. They had even invented portable meals that remained as little bricks until a missing element was added. Kelsey kept a supply of the meals that lacked Fire. Once she added it, she had a full meal ready for eating. She was fond of the fruit ones, personally.

As soon as the hipsack was ready, she tied it to a special loop on her belt. She preferred to wear the sack there rather than using the strap to carry it across her body or on her back. She just preferred the freedom of movement.

Since she didn't know when she would be getting back, she headed to her parents' side of the house. "I'm leaving now," she said as she walked into the room. "I'm not sure when I'll be getting home, though. Probably a week or two. Maybe more."

Mildred hugged her daughter tight. "Be safe."

Luke didn't much like the idea of his baby girl heading off with the Militia for two weeks when she was still in the beginnings of second puberty. He didn't like Ilian's admiration of Kelsey for the same. It was a normal process and no stopping it, but he hated his baby growing up. "Come home soon," was all he finally said.

Kelsey smiled and hugged him tightly. "You can't stop me from growing up. But don't worry. Ilian isn't for me." She tilted her head. "I'm not sure how I'm sure, but I am. So, no worries. Once I find the person for me, you can bet I'll be in a bigger hurry to finish puberty. Until then it can take its time." She scratched at her arm. "Except for the itching!"

He laughed and hugged her again. "That's my girl." His smile faded as she headed out of the house. He had a terrible feeling that he wouldn't see her again for a long time, if ever. There was something important about her that he had forgotten. He was sure of it. He just couldn't call it to mind.

Kelsey found Etude outside and they headed out of the city to where the encampment was set up. The people there were already breaking camp, and Kelsey noticed males and females of all elements present. They wore all manner of weapons, from swords to spears to clubs to gloves with blades in them for slashing. Her mind automatically began cataloguing what she would be making. Some would be easier than others and that would cut down on the time needed.

"Are you feeling better?" Ilian asked as he walked up. "I sincerely apologize for overwhelming you this morning. I wasn't even thinking."

"It's okay," she assured him. "I was just a little . . . raw. If it is all right, I would like to obtain a wagon for the trip. It will allow me to bring my smaller forge, and it will also give me a place to sleep during the day. I can work at night."

"That can be arranged," he agreed. He smiled. "You're doing us an immense favor. It's the least we can do." He turned and gestured to the Militia members. "I'll introduce them as we go along. It might be too much all at once."

Etude saw several people studying Kelsey with interest and pointedly sat on her shoulder with arms crossed. The message was clear: You had to go through the MoonKin to get to her partner. The looks averted.

They set out within an hour and Kelsey rode in the back of the wagon with her forge. The wagon was being pulled by a findral, and the rest of the Militia rode more of the same though theirs had been bred for battle. Studying the large beasts, Kelsey asked Etude, "Were findral a Kin invention gone awry?"

Etude giggled softly. "No, they've always been here. I think the fact that they can climb mountains and swim in water is an adaptability feature. There's much more water than land now, and I think I remember my elders telling me that they used to be just land creatures."

"And the fact that they look like large dogs with a bird's head and fins instead of wings?"

"I'd like to point out that we Kin find you Magi weird because you don't have large ears or wings." Kin Elves were known for their varied ear types. They could be feline ears, canine ears, or any other kind of ear. It was those ears that marked an Elf in the way that wings marked the Faeries.

"You have a good point," Kelsey conceded. She turned to where Ilian rode beside the cart. "Where are we heading? Can you tell me at least that much?"

"I can. We're heading for the center of Carnelian. It's the only plains area that any Magi land has that isn't covered in sand." He studied her intently for a moment. Though he wasn't supposed to divulge details, he felt that she could be trusted. More still, if she was riding into a battle, she had a right to know. "What do you know of the Black Magi Elite?"

Her heart gave a dull thud inside her chest that she tried to ignore. "Nine years ago they tried to destroy the world. They were diverted by the only two living Chronicles who stayed on the lost Isle of the Dragons afterward and have not been seen much since."

"That's the summary of events. The Elite broke off from the original Black Magi, which was a faction led by the male Chronicle to create a haven for Master Magi like you. It was a place for them to grow and develop and adjust to society. I've always thought he was drawn to the duty because he knew how it felt to be different."

Her heart was beating harder and there was again a pain in her head as if she couldn't remember something. "And the Elite?"

He studied her, wondering why her voice seemed strained. "Were led by an insane man named Soh. He was responsible for the death of the former king of the Magi and the upheaval we endured for two years to find a new king. Soh took control of Glacia and was going to instigate war. The Chronicles gathered Dragons and Kin and launched a surprise attack. I'd like to say they won, but it wasn't entirely a win. A rogue Dragon who had been assisting Soh got away. She also translocated the remaining Elite across the world."

"Translocation is an ability of Air elements to send someone to a random location in the world," Etude explained.

"Oh." Kelsey frowned. "I would have been ten. Why don't I remember any of this?"

"That's the problem." Ilian looked again toward the road. "No one remembers anything clearly. We can tell you the events, but we couldn't tell you what the individual players looked like. I remember *distinctly* fighting the Elite during my first year with the Militia. I do not remember their faces or their names. No one in the world remembers."

"We Kin are investigating," Etude said softly, "but even our best scholars cannot determine how or why the entire world would forget something so important. Many don't believe the Elite ever existed or exist now."

"Oh," Ilian's voice sounded grim, "they do. That is where we are heading. An Elite member named Phi has shown up. He is disrupting the flow of the land and causing quakes. The quakes have been traveling underground and reaching even the edges of Prismatic. It needs to be stopped before there is irreparable damage done."

Kelsey lifted a brow. "And that's why you need my weapons."

"Indeed. Phi is a Master Magi as well. If we are to fight him, we need to be prepared." He cursed softly under his breath. "It would be so much better if I knew precisely what he looked like."

When they camped for the night, Kelsey got to work. She completed two weapons over the course of the night. Upon the morning, she was curled up in the back of the wagon and deeply asleep. The Militia didn't disturb her. They were slightly in awe at the speed and the quality with which she produced weapons.

It was a repeat of the same for two more days. As the third day dawned, they exited the forest and entered into the only open grassy plain that now existed on Magi lands. If it had been flown over, it would have resembled a green bowl surrounded by a rim of dark trees. At only ten miles wide, the valley was considered protected territory. It could be traveled through, but it could not be populated for fear it would go away.

Halfway through the day, Etude woke Kelsey so that she could see the plains during the day. She sleepily rode with her arms draped over the side of the wagon, enjoying the scenery but half wishing for more sleep.

"If you will permit me?" Ilian had ridden closer and was holding out a hand.

She scrubbed at her eyes before reluctantly holding out her hand. His hand closed around her wrist gently, and she hid a flinch as the itching got worse. She focused instead on the feel of his Fire power sliding into her body and helping replenish her. Elements could lend power to one another to bolster strength and reserves.

Even after the exchange, he held onto her wrist. His eyes searched hers but he saw no awareness in her for him as a man. It was frustrating. The more he was around her, the more he liked her. He could very easily lose his heart to this woman. "Will you write me a letter when you're an adult?" he finally asked.

Etude said nothing. Kelsey studied Ilian's face before gently freeing her wrist. "No," she said softly. "I'm sorry. I'm not comfortable enough with you to consider sharing my power with you in that way. Don't take it personally. Etude is the only close friend I've ever had. I just . . . am different from normal Magi."

For the first time, he felt as if he had seen the true Kelsey. The vibrant and fiery exterior hid a deeply vulnerable core. He had always heard that Master Magi tended to be withdrawn and hide from society, but she had seemed different. In that moment, he knew she wasn't. "I hope you find the one whom you are comfortable with," he finally said quietly. "And I wish it would be me."

There came a shout from someone riding at the front. "There's a Dragon flying on the horizon to the right! I can just barely see their scales from here. Do you want us to flag them down and ask if they've seen our target?"

Though Magi and Dragons did not get along in the slightest because of the Chronicle Massacre of a thousand years past, there was a tentative truce between them. Magi didn't ostracize Dragons, and Dragons didn't eat Magi.

Ilian frowned. "Are they going our direction?"

"Seems to be."

"Let them be then. If we need to, we'll flag them down. For now, let us see if we can't find our target on our own. I just hope it takes a little while longer." He looked at Kelsey. "I'd rather see you finish the weapons and be on your way home before the fight. You're not Militia. You don't deserve to be pulled into our fight."

She finished the rest of the weapons three nights later when they were three-quarters of the way through the plains. She was tired and drained to her core but also well pleased with herself. She had done some of her best work. As she curled up in the wagon to get some sleep before dawn for once, her eyes were drawn to the distance where she could see the Dragon landing for sleep. Something stirred in her heart, something fierce and longing. She fell asleep before she could capture the feeling again.

She woke again later when Ilian gently shook her shoulder. Groggily, she said, "Yes?"

"Kelsey." He smiled when her eyes blinked open. "I just wanted to tell you that we're parting ways here." He desperately tried to ignore how beautiful she looked with her hair falling in her face and her cheeks streaked with soot. "Etude has said she can drive the wagon and findral home for you."

"Oh." She rubbed at her eyes. "Okay. Are the weapons sufficient?"

"Sufficient?" a female repeated in awe. "It's *incredible*." She used dual daggers and was swinging them lightly in the air. "They weigh nothing yet they're stronger than anything I've ever seen. You earned every ounce of your pay."

"And as to that," Ilian handed Kelsey a small bag, "here it is." A trace of longing in his voice, he asked, "Are you sure you won't consider me someday?"

She opened her mouth to respond when the ground suddenly began to shake. The quake was quick and violent and knocked several people off their feet. The findral began to panic, stamping their feet and screeching in fear. The findral attached to the wagon reared so sharply that he jerked the wagon in the air and it sent Kelsey flying.

"Are you all right?" Etude asked urgently as she hurried to her partner's side.

"I'm okay," was the shaky response. "What's going on?" Under her hands, the land felt like it was in a riotous frenzy. "The power in the land is going out of control!"

Grimly, Ilian said, "I think Phi found us before we found him. I am sorry, Kelsey."

She got to her feet and shook her hair back. "Don't be." She looked at her now ruined forge. "I'm a little pissed off right now." Because she was far more sensitive to the fluctuations of power than normal Magi, she felt the rolling power before the land began to shake again. "Brace yourselves!"

That quake was much harder and lasted much longer. Cracks began to appear in the land. Vents of pure elemental power began to shoot in the air violently. One appeared under Kelsey's feet, but she didn't bother to move. It was the rawest sort of power, and it replenished her in a way that sleep never could.

Seeing her absorb the power, Ilian felt his heart begin to pound in his chest. He had never heard of a Magi, Master or not, who could absorb the surplus power in the world. It was too raw, too concentrated. There *was* a theory he had once heard, however, and it terrified him. He didn't want it to be true.

A fireball erupted in the middle of the area and flung everyone in all directions. Some Militia members didn't immediately get up. Others didn't get up at all. The sheer potency of the power told Ilian that Phi was indeed a Master Magi, despite his hoping it might be just a rumor. That was the last thing they needed. "Air Magi, get a shield up!" he shouted. "Someone try to find out where he's attacking from!"

Things began to get worse. The power in the land disrupted the life of the findral and began to mutate them into monsters. The few Militia who had seemed to have been knocked out by the first blast also began to mutate. It was a terrifying and disgusting sight as the newly made monsters turned on everyone around them, even each other.

Etude grabbed Kelsey's arm. "We need to leave!"

"Go, quickly!" Ilian urged.

Kelsey didn't waste words. She turned and ran. Her target was the line of trees in the distance. Though it was running away from the direction of her home, it would be easier to lose an attacker in the forest; on the plains she was a perfect target.

An eruption of Water power forced her to stop running. Before she could double back and go around it, her skin began to itch violently. She turned sharply and discovered a man standing behind her. He was taller than she was and wore a heavy white cloak etched with a black chalice and dagger. The chalice was the symbol of the Magi. The black chalice was of Black Magi. And the chalice and dagger were the mark of the Black Magi Elite.

Phi couldn't have been more pleased as he slowly approached her. "A Master Magi. How fabulous. Your death will certainly break up this land entirely."

"You've got to kill me first, *poka*!" She hurled a fireball right at his face with all her strength.

The other Magi was a Master Soil Magi. He didn't have the power to neutralize or block her; he had to scramble to the side. As he did, he felt the heat of the fireball scorch his hair and clothes. The fireball proved to be the first of many. She continued to throw fireballs at him until he was scrambling everywhere in his efforts to dodge. "How are you doing that?!" Even Master Magi weren't that strong!

"I can hold him off," she said softly to Etude. "Go get the Dragon! Tell they they can eat this guy with the Magi's thanks!"

Etude didn't want to leave her but knew that it was more important to get the Dragon for more reasons than her friend understood. Without a word, she turned and shot across the sky like a small mocha colored bullet. Phi turned sharply but the vines he sent after her were no match for a Kin's speed. A fireball detonated at his feet and flung him backwards. He landed hard and the ground rippled like water. The fight was only making things worse.

Vines shot out of the ground and struck Kelsey in the chest. She hit the ground and rolled several feet before rolling up to her feet again. Her chest hurt like hell and she could see where she had been cut by thorns. Her skin itched violently again, and it seemed as if her power literally burned in her blood.

Eyes blazing red with power, she hurled another fireball. "Let's just see which of us is better! I think I'm a little better equipped for battle, don't you?" The next fireball barely missed her enemy.

He snarled at her. "I look forward to ripping you apart!" He gathered his power and broke the land open under her feet. It caused a lethal amount of power to spew in the air. To his shock and horror, she absorbed it as if it was nothing. *It wasn't even her element*! "What in the name of the Underrealm are you?" he demanded sharply.

Fire gathered around her hands. Her eyes burned with the same flames at her fingers. "Very, very angry," she warned softly, her voice crackling like a bonfire. "And congratulations! You're my target."

As he dodged both fireballs, he knew he was not dealing with a normal Master Magi. He didn't know what she was, but he knew damned well that she was not normal by any stretch of the imagination. He should have easily won over any Magi opponent. He just needed to survive long enough to figure her out. Once he did, he would be able to destroy her.

A fireball narrowly missed his head. At the least, he *hoped* he would be able to destroy her.

Chapter Three

Solis T'mer was a Water Fury. He was one of the younger, only slightly over two hundred years in age, but he was by no means the weakest. Just being a Fury made him stronger than any of his regular Dragon brethren, but he always had to be careful of his majiks usage for fear that he would drain himself out. Then again, his brothers and sisters never played too hard with him. They were gentle with him.

They knew he was going to die.

It was the curse of a Fury. They always knew when their Chronicle was born, and they always knew when their Chronicle died. Hundreds of Furies had been mercifully killed over the centuries to save them from eternal suffering. It had become a painful way of life for the Dragons. It was why Solis had never said anything about sensing his Chronicle's birth even ten years after it occurred.

That had been nine years ago. He didn't know how, but his Chronicle still lived somewhere. He had his suspicions, though. When Jazz Eaglewind and Dominic Whisperer had found their Chronicles, both miraculously alive despite all odds, it had given hope to all the other Furies. More still, Morgan Chronis had spoken of the four Chronicle children he had found and sheltered. One in particular had caught Solis' attention: a female Fire Chronicle. Solis was a male Water Fury. The chance of that Chronicle being his was very, very high.

In the nine years since the Chronis siblings had come to the Isle of Dragons, Furies had gone out to live in society. The Magi still killed Chronicles when they were found. Dragons and Furies couldn't track a Chronicle, but they knew them when they were right on top of them. No one had found any Chronicles yet. And some Furies had returned to the Isle to be mercifully killed. In some ways, things had not changed.

Solis didn't mind living among the Magi too much. Because he was Fury—a Dragon Lord—he could take a Magi form and walk among the crowds. He still stood out, though. His thick brown hair was streaked with pale blue as mark of his Dragon origins. He was of average height for Magi males at five-eleven, but he was slightly broader in the shoulder and overall more powerful. It was to be expected. Dragons retained their strength in any form they took.

His intent was to spend a year in every city, long enough to meet every citizen. When that was done, he would go to the next city. It was the only way he could think of to ensure that he found his Chronicle. He *knew* he would know her when he found her. His only fear was that he might miss her in passing.

He had spent three years on Prismatic. He was ready for Carnelian. He decided to start at the southern end, so he flew past the northern end along the outside of the trees. He wasn't allowed to fly directly over cities because it would disrupt the flow of power in the land. He wouldn't have minded taking out a few Magi, but he refused to hurt the world. It had suffered enough. It still suffered.

As he flew slowly along, he could see the Militia party traveling to his left. He was half-tempted to go buzz them just for the humor, but they seemed to be on a mission. Because it was an oddity, he decided to stick around and keep pace with them. He knew Carnelian was having quakes and that was unusual enough.

At twenty feet in length with brown scales and blue streaks across them, he knew they had to have seen him. No signal flares went up, so he camped when they did and flew when they traveled. What *were* they up to?

He got his answer when the land erupted into violent quakes and began spewing power everywhere. He dodged the blasts sharply and found a safe place to land. When his feet touched down, he could feel the riot under the land. Someone was deliberately disrupting the flow. He landed on the plains side of the trees, and his sharp eyes could see the signs of the Militia battling.

Before he could make up his mind whether or not to help, he spotted a streak of brown coming toward him. He hastily caught the small MoonKin Faerie gently before she could tumble past him. "Easy!" He held her on one claw and brought her to eye level. "What's wrong?"

Kin and Dragons were close allies. Etude felt no fear. Trying to catch a breath, she said, "Elite. Fight. Help!"

"Breathe!" His eyes narrowed slightly. "What's this about the Black Magi Elite?"

She closed her eyes and tried to get a steady breath. Flying that fast always drained her to the core. Her euphoria at finding a Water Fury, a *male* Water Fury, couldn't override her breathlessness. Precious time was wasting! After a moment, she was able to say, "My partner! She's in danger! We were traveling with the Militia so Kelsey could make weapons for the Militia to fight Phi, from the Elite. But Phi attacked us! Now Kelsey is fighting him and we need help!"

He closed his claws around her gently to hold her securely and flapped his wings to fly up into the air. "Which way?" he asked.

"Look for the big explosions."

A large fireball blew up even as she finished speaking. He immediately began flying in that direction, and he skirted around the edges of the Militia's battle with many monsters. The Militia was trained to deal with this sort of thing. Etude's partner was not. But as he flew, he felt his heart begin beating harder. Those fireballs didn't look like normal Magi fireballs.

The fireball ripped open a crater in the ground and dropped Phi into the center where he landed with a bone-jarring thud. He scrambled back out and shot a wave of soil at Kelsey that sent her tumbling backwards. To his frustration, she just rolled to her feet again. They were both lined with wounds and he knew he was reaching the end of his power. She just seemed to keep on going. "No Magi has infinite power!" He hurled vines at her.

She let the vines wrap around her waist and then grabbed onto them. "Try me!" Fire poured down her arms and streaked down the vines toward him. He was flung backwards as the vines evaporated. Reaching for reserves of power she didn't know she had, she went after him directly.

Before she took two steps, the Dragon suddenly passed by right overhead. She felt his power wash over her, and her skin seemed to burst into flame. She fell to her knees on a cry as fire whipped around her wildly. Her head pounded and her body throbbed. Her skin was stretching, stretching, until she thought it would tear apart. Hotter and hotter her power grew until something inside broke.

Golden lines blazed into appearance along the insides of her arms and along the outside of her legs. They were vividly displayed by her working clothes and unmistakable. With little sharp edges and some rounded curls, they looked stark and powerful and like nothing else in the world.

Phi's heart leapt into his throat. "A Chronicle," he managed to say. "Well, that explains that. I guess I won't kill you after all!" He started to lunge forward only to stop sharply as the Dragon landed in front of Kelsey with teeth bared. Terrified, he scrambled back instead. He knew those markings. "A Fury!"

Solis was in a rage he had never felt before. The instant he had laid eyes on Kelsey, he had *known* she was his. His Chronicle. The only being that was his alone and he alone belonged to. He hadn't needed to see her painful awakening to know the truth. Now she was dazed and vulnerable, a far cry from the magnificent fire goddess he had just witnessed. He would protect her when she could not protect herself. "Get away from my Chronicle." The words were little more than a guttural growl.

"*Your* . . . ?" Phi kept backing up. The last he needed was to tangle with a Dragoon set! "You win this time, Fury! But I'll be back to take her away! She will be the harbinger of destruction for the Magi!"

Power erupted from the land and momentarily blinded Solis. When the power faded, Phi was gone. Solis dismissed him and turned back to Magi form. He hurried to Kelsey's side and realized she had fallen unconscious in the grass. He knelt and tenderly eased her into his arms. She was *exquisite*! The lines that flowed so sensuously down her body were made from his power. "Finally," he managed to say. He buried his face in her hair. "Finally, I've found you."

Etude started to speak when she heard a sound. "Solis!"

He turned his head sharply, and his brown eyes narrowed. "Who goes?!" The words came as little more than a snarl, clear evidence that he would protect his mate. Water and ice condensed warningly around his feet.

Slowly, Ilian walked forward. The hand holding the sword that Kelsey had forged was trembling. Wounds marked his body from the fight he had just left. Eyes riveted to Kelsey, he was scarcely breathing. "She's . . . she's . . ."

"A Chronicle," Etude confirmed softly. "I warned you that she could never love you."

Solis held Kelsey closer to his chest possessively. "Kelsey belongs to me, Magi." The words were gentler than they might have been otherwise. He could see the heartbreak in Ilian's eyes that said he truly cared for Kelsey. "What are you going to do?"

Ilian closed his eyes. "Magi law states that all Chronicles are to be killed when found." His eyes opened and he looked at the sword he carried. Slowly he lowered the blade and turned his back. "It would be blasphemy to kill a Weaponsmith with a sword she forged herself, and it is the only weapon I am carrying."

Taking the gift as it was given, Solis gently laid Kelsey down on the ground and stood. He returned to his Dragon form and then picked her up with his claws and cradled her as if she was the most precious thing in the universe. She *was* the most precious thing in his universe. "There was no Chronicle here," he said.

Ilian nodded without turning around. "When I arrived, I saw Phi escaping. I did not see Kelsey. For her sake, it is better that the world think she is dead for now. Take her away." He did turn then and look at Solis. "And love her the way I wanted to."

"You have my vow." With a flap of his wings, Solis rose into the air. He turned to go west, to the Isle of Dragons, and realized in belated dismay that he had forgotten the way. Mentally cursing, he turned instead to head for one of the many islands that dotted the edge of Carnelian. They would be safe enough there.

As they went, Etude flew alongside his head. "Solis," she said apologetically, "Kelsey's only just starting second puberty. I can't even tell you how far along she is. She's felt no attraction to anyone."

A sigh was his answer. "Well, I know Dominic had to suffer Tariah going through second puberty. If he can handle it as a Fire Fury, I can handle it as a Water Fury." He glanced down at Kelsey, enchanted by her delicate features and lush mane of hair. The soot that streaked her face seemed to enhance rather than decrease her appeal. From where he was holding her, he could feel the steady rise in her power. It was matched by a decrease in his majiks. It was curious.

Etude seemed to sense it. "You need to bond as Dragoons." When he glanced at her, she asked, "I take it you haven't inherited the memories of any older Dragons."

"None that were Furies," he admitted. He angled down toward the small island that he could see approaching. Like most islands around Carnelian, it was covered in trees. He changed into Magi form as he landed, and Kelsey remained gently cradled in his arms.

"It's simple," Etude said as she flew down to join him. "Her power rises automatically and your majiks drain. This is to ensure that the first bonding takes place as soon as possible. Once you've bonded, you'll be Dragoons, tied in ways that surpass even normal Linkings for Magi or Bindings for Kin."

"Or Unities for Dragons." He wasn't entirely listening to her anymore; his eyes were riveted to Kelsey's face. Her name reminded him of the word *kelsin*, a word in Draconic that meant 'storms of fire'.

Sensing the demands of nature, Etude smiled and flew off to give them privacy. He didn't notice. He gently put Kelsey down on the soft grass, and her hair burned against the sun-dappled green. He sat down beside her and lifted her hand with his. She was of average size for a Magi female but her hands looked strong and capable. He could see the tiny scars from working with weapons and he could feel the calluses from the same.

He lost track of the time. He memorized the lines of her face and the supple curves of her body. Every minute made his hunger for her grow. Hunger for her shocking beauty and her deceptive strength. Hunger for the spirit she had revealed as she stood on a battlefield and burned wild. Hunger for the power he felt smoldering under her skin and begging for his attention.

When she began to stir, he moved closer. He framed her face with his free hand and held her other hand to his heart. "Kelsey?" he asked softly. "Wake up, *ishke*. It's all right. You're safe with me."

Her lashes fluttered and lifted. His breath caught. Her eyes were the crystalline blue of the purest glass, framed by thick red lashes, and now shimmering with fires barely held in check. He had never seen eyes like hers before, yet they were somehow achingly familiar. He had waited to see these eyes.

Kelsey woke to raging pain in her body. Her power was out of control. She wanted to burn and ravage the land as a firestorm. She could barely breathe for the heat consuming her. The tender touch on her cheek was disorienting for its familiarity, then she heard *it*. A male voice that her very soul recognized. She recognized it all the way to her cells, to the power that built her. *Hers*. This man was hers.

Her eyes opened and she found herself staring into a somehow familiar face. The shock of his features reverberated through her body. A hunger she had never felt before made her eyes move over him swiftly in an attempt to memorize everything. She felt the lure of his watery power brushing against hers seductively, and the sudden sharp hunger to taste his kiss was stunning. It was nearly as stunning as the sight of her arm when she lifted a hand to touch his face. She had lines.

"It's all right," he said huskily. He could feel the alluring touch of her power to his in a call as ancient as time. She was further in her development than Etude had believed if she was instinctively able to send out such a signal to her mate. "You're a Chronicle, Kelsey. My Chronicle."

Delight brought her smile quickly. "I'm not alone?"

"Never again." He gathered her closer. "I've looked for you for so long . . ."

She went to put her arms around him but her body protested. Her breath caught in pain. "What's wrong with me?"

"We need to bond. I need to feed on your power." He brushed his lips over her shoulder and a soft red aura instantly began to rise as her power emanated in a physical way. It shimmered and danced like flames. "Are you afraid?"

"Not of you." Her eyes closed as his lips sipped delicately along her skin. The little shivers of delight were completely foreign but she wasn't afraid of them either. They felt utterly right.

Unable to resist the temptation, he began to breathe in her power and drink it from her tender skin. He followed the trail as it went down her arm. His lips teased the lines along the inside of her arm and traced their shape. Her power tasted wild and spicy, stinging his tongue lightly but exploding with flavor after. His free hand smoothed compulsively over her side and shaped the curve of her hip.

He slowly traced his lips back up to her shoulder and then brushed them over her face. He moved steadily toward her lips. "I'm going to kiss you," he warned, his lips a breath from hers. "Do you mind?"

She didn't answer with words. She simply wrapped her arms around his shoulders and pressed upward to take his lips with hers. She had never kissed anyone before. She had never wanted to. This man . . . she wanted. She wanted to kiss him with a vengeance that was as much emotional as it was physical.

The kiss deepened further as he fed from her power there. It was hotter and sweeter, still spicy but now flavored. He was instantly addicted and knew he would never have enough. And even when he felt the last of her power enter him, he couldn't make himself release her lips. He nipped lightly at her lower lip and felt her shock as if it was inside his own heart.

It wasn't the only thing he could feel. As the bonds between them cemented fully, he could see all the way inside her soul and her mind. He could see and feel her every emotion and her every thought. She saw into him the same way, and he could sense her wariness for the volatile emotions inside him. Love, desire, and more. A third emotion that encompassed the others and was yet stronger.

"What is that?" she asked softly, her voice smoky with a desire she had only just discovered. Inside her heart and body, she could see the stirrings of the same emotion, as yet growing, but sure to be an inferno before long. The love . . . that already consumed her. She didn't question it. She simply accepted it.

"Dragons call it *ishke*." He smoothed her hair from her face. "It's a word meaning all the needs, wants, and desires of the world." He lifted her onto his lap as he sat up properly and hoped she was as yet innocent enough to miss his body's unmistakable reaction to her mere presence—he didn't want to scare her away.

She still noticed, but she ignored it. She wasn't ready for that much exploration of her Fury's body, no matter how incredibly beautiful he was to her eyes and no matter how much her body ached now. "I'll try to be nice to you," she finally said. "Because I'm not the type to wait around for things to happen."

His eyes half closed. "Try your best not to throw me on the floor and ravage me until you're absolutely sure that you're ready for me to return the favor." His breath hissed out as her power curled around his temptingly. It wasn't done with the intent to seduce so much as it was done to see if it *could* seduce. Her curiosity in second puberty would be the death of him, but he would die a happy man.

"It won't kill you!" Oddly content, she curled against his chest and then pulled back in surprise as she felt an odd heat. His power was . . . changing. Being the type of person she was, she immediately untied the laces of his tunic and opened the front.

A bit dryly, he asked, "Are you further along than I presumed?"

"You have lines." In wonder, she traced them with a fingertip. They looked just like her lines as they flowed across his muscular chest and down toward the edge of his pants. It was her power that made the lines on his skin, and the knowledge was heady. She wanted him to be marked. She wanted him to be visibly claimed. One tiny little detail eluded her though.

He eyed her warily as he sensed the steady rise of her ire. "Yes?"

She grabbed the open edges of his shirt and shook him quickly. "How am I Chronicle?!" she demanded in aggravation. "How did I not know?! Where were my lines? Why didn't I know until you went by overhead?! And why didn't you eat Phi?!" She broke off as he wrapped his arms around her and cuddled her close. The fight went out of her body, and she sighed as she relaxed against him. "You won't win all fights like that," she muttered against his shoulder.

He just smiled. "For now I will. You'll have other weapons to use against me later." He slowly smoothed his hands over her back and curled his power around her comfortingly. "I didn't eat Phi because he got away. As to how you didn't know you were a Chronicle . . . that would be Morgan's doing."

She frowned as something hurt fiercely inside her heart. "Morgan?" She shook her head as she felt again that disturbing empty place. She felt Solis probing gently at her mind and said nothing.

As he examined her mind, he said softly, "Morgan Chronis. Nine years ago, he was the leader of the Black Magi. He found four secret Chronicle children and kept them hidden from Magi eyes under the disguise of being Master Magi. When the fight went down, he erased their memories of him and sent them away via translocation."

She began to tremble and pressed closer against his chest, desperately needing him to ground her. "But I grew up in Carnelian! Didn't I?" She shook her head. "I can't remember. Why can't I remember?" She lifted her head in new annoyance as a thought occurred. "What's your name, damn it? I can't just go around calling you 'my Fury' no matter how much I might want to!"

"Come back here." He pulled her close once more. "My name is Solis T'mer." He continued to examine her mind until he found the gaping hole. It was nearly five years' worth of memories that had been taken away. There were 'filler' memories inserted in their place, illusions based on the memories of her first five years so that neither she nor her parents suspected anything. "There it is."

"I want them back."

"I know, *ishke*." He shook his head. "But I'm not sure if I can do anything. This is an Air Chronicle's work, and Morgan is a Chronis. He and Tariah are stronger than anything anyone has ever known, even our only Fury Elder, and he lived back when Chronicles were not killed outright."

"Well *try*." Her lips moved into a pout that instantly drew his attention. She sensed it and grumbled, "Don't kiss me! Fix my memories *then* you can kiss me. Better yet, I'll kiss you. Fair enough?"

With incentive like that, who was he to not try? He began to gather the fragmented portions of her mind by using his Water power to sweep them together. The more he looked, the more sure he was that Morgan hadn't *erased* the memories. They had been broken into dozens of tiny fragments that only a Fury could mend. "What he can do with his power is astonishing."

"Fix it!"

"Don't be so impatient, Kel." He swirled the pieces together and put them into the empty place in her mind. Once reassembled, they naturally refused together. Even as the completed memories punched into his mind, they punched into hers.

As the memories swamped her, pain mushroomed inside her chest. She doubled over against Solis with a low cry and a sob tore out of her chest. She beat at his shoulder with a fist. "*He sent me away*!!"

Heart breaking, he could only rock her back and forth. He could see the love inside her heart and mind yet felt no jealousy. It was a love entirely different from the one she felt for him. "He wanted to protect you."

"I'm going to fry him to a crisp!" She straightened and swiped at her eyes. "He *promised* to come get us!" A hiccup caught in her chest as she remembered her surrogate brothers and sister. "Roman and C.J. and Jayda." She wiped her eyes with the edge of his tunic. "We have to go find them."

"Right now?"

"Yes, right now!"

"No."

Her eyes went wide as she stared at him. "What?"

"*Some*one owes someone else a kiss."

Blue eyes blinked at him for long moments before beginning to spark with a distinct challenge. Defiantly, she grabbed his hands and held them at his sides. "You can't touch me," she ordered. "Because it's the first time I've ever instigated a kiss like this." Despite her bravado, her heart pounded in her chest.

Sensing it, his power curled around her softly and comfortingly but with a distinct lure to her own. It was as instinctive as breathing. "I'm waiting." Try as he might, his voice came out deeper and richer, evidence of his hunger for her.

Before she could change her mind, she leaned in and kissed him. She had intended to keep it quick, but he tasted like the purest of spring waters. Tempted, she went back for a second kiss and softly teased his lips with her tongue. When his lips parted, she couldn't resist the offering. She deepened the kiss slowly and savored the way he tasted. Heat began to rise in her body as ripples of pleasure spread outward.

This time when he nipped at her lower lip, the little sting wasn't alarming. She returned the gesture and the rumble in his chest was wonderful. She moved to press closer and her breasts flattened against his chest. The lash of pleasure shocked her, and she jerked back. Her eyes were wide as she carefully took a breath. "Uhm."

He mentally counted all one thousand characters in the Draconic language and aimed for maintaining control. He wanted nothing more than to yank her back into his arms. Instead, he contented himself with tugging her closer and nuzzling his nose into her hair.

"Why do you keep nuzzling me like that?"

"It's how Dragons show affection." He rubbed his nose against hers and made her smile. "See?"

"I like it." She let out a breath. "So. Leaving now?"

"Best to wait until tomorrow," he disagreed. "We don't know what is going on with Carnelian or Phi." His eyes narrowed sharply. "And I assure you, if I get my hands on him, he will become the main dish at a roasting."

She barely stifled a giggle as she saw bubbles coming out of his nose. Quirks of Dragons; they tended to breathe their element when they reached a certain level of anger. And though it was a sign of temper, it was still funny to see Solis breathing bubbles. Her humor faded, however, as another thought entered her mind. "What about Etude?"

"You mean me?" Etude flew down from out of the sky and hugged Kelsey around the neck tightly. "I'm right here."

"You scared me!" Kelsey grabbed her friend and glared at her. "And why didn't you tell me? You had to know! You're a Kin! It's why you told me about Furies and Chronicles, isn't it? Damn it, Etude!"

"She gets cranky easily," Etude told Solis gravely.

"I'd noticed," was the dry response.

Smiling because she liked him for Kelsey, Etude turned back to her partner. "I didn't tell you because you didn't know. Someone had gone to great pains to hide your identity and I was the last person who would reveal it." When Kelsey released her, she flew over to land on Solis' shoulder. "We should go to Kindred."

"Really?" Kelsey frowned. "For shelter?"

"For one, yes. But we can contact Daylar there."

"Who is Daylar?"

Solis smiled. "He is the Kin brother to Tariah. You remember the wing in her lines? That was the mark of it. She is considered honorary Kin, and she and Daylar claim each other as brother and sister. His Bonded mate was Tariah's partner for a while."

"Oh." Kelsey frowned thoughtfully. "Okay, we can go there." Belatedly, she realized how bossy she was being. Slightly chagrined, she looked down. "That is, if you're all right with that, Solis."

"Don't be demure." He smiled. "It doesn't suit you. I am perfectly content to let you lead as you see fit, and if you ever try to push me into something I don't want, you'll know instantly. You'll feel it from inside me." He skimmed his knuckles across her cheek and brushed her hair back. Tenderly, he wiped away a smudge of soot. "You need a bath."

"There's a little basin not far away where you could make one," Etude offered.

"Good idea." He stood and scooped an astonished Kelsey up in his arms. "Let's go take a bath."

"With Etude?!"

Etude giggled as she followed. "Don't worry! I'm not interested in Dragons or Magi. If he isn't offended, I'm not." She grinned when Kelsey glowered at her. "Are you jealous, Kel?"

"Yes!" Kelsey crossed her arms indignantly. "He's *my* Fury."

Solis decided he liked the possession in her voice and emotions. "Yes, I am. And therefore you should know there's no reason to be concerned." He spotted the basin that Etude had mentioned and put Kelsey down on her feet. "Stay here."

She obligingly waited while he went to the edge of the basin. It looked like a portion of the land underneath had given way from a collapsed cave. The top was covered with smooth grass. At its deepest point, it would go up to Solis' chest. At the widest point, it was ten feet across.

Solis first used ice to cover the bottom with a smooth and clean surface. Once done, he began filling the basin with fresh water. Because both the ice and the water were of his power, he could maintain the ice and use hot water at the same time. He brought it to a point where it began to waft steam in the air. "There we go."

Etude dove in, clothes and all. Kelsey, for the first time in her life, found herself immensely shy. She hesitated in taking off her clothes, and Solis sensed it. He walked over and tugged her into his arms. "Never found this part before, did you?" he asked lovingly. He nuzzled her hair softly. "For some, the self-consciousness never quite goes away. Based on your personality, I imagine you'll be one to get over it quickly."

She frowned. "I don't like being worried about how people think I look. I know I'm beautiful." It was said without conceit because it was a statement of fact. And, being Kelsey, she decided to get to the point. She stepped back out of his arms and stripped off her clothes. "There. Now tell me I'm beautiful so I can get past your first reaction and get used to being naked around you."

Speech literally beyond his capabilities, he could only stare at her. His eyes devoured every perfect curve of her body. Her lines burned gold against her pale skin where they traversed her arms and legs. Her body was lush compared to most other females but she looked like perfection to his eyes.

The wordless absorption was exactly what she needed to restore her confidence. She could feel his power boiling as it swirled around her, and she felt her own power turning to steam. In fact, steam was lifting from both their bodies as power and desire merged. Her breath hitched.

He averted his gaze. "I should have made the water glacial," he managed to say at last. "And I think it would be best if I kept at least some of my clothes on for the time being."

Her gaze lowered and red color climbed her cheeks to match her hair. "Yes, please." She hastily hurried into the water and ducked under the surface. Why was it so much more unnerving to see the reality of what she had learned in school? The combination of trepidation and anticipation was vexing. Curiosity gnawed at her but couldn't override her nerves. "Why does growing up take so long?" she asked when she surfaced.

Floating on her back, Etude said, "You wouldn't appreciate it so much if it didn't. And I'd like to note that you're going through something in a short time that normally takes people months."

Kelsey's eyes met Solis' and fresh steam that had nothing to do with the pool rose from their skin. "Not fast enough," she said softly. "Not nearly fast enough." She sighed and turned toward the setting sun in the distance. "Where do you suppose Roman and the others are?" she asked.

"I don't know." Solis tugged her back against his chest. "But if they're like you, they're living a normal life as Master Magi. Once we reach Kindred, we'll see what we can do to find them." He pressed his lips to her hair. "I'm sorry I can't take you to the Isle right now."

"It's okay." She covered his hands with hers and smiled. "We'll appreciate it more because it takes longer."

He laughed outright and hugged her closer. He wouldn't have traded her for any other Chronicle in the world. She was the perfect one for him.

Chapter Four

To the northeast beyond Carnelian was the mainland of the Magi. It was a large continent called Spectrum. A handful of medium sized cities were sparsely scattered across the vast deserts, and tinier little towns sat even farther apart. The two cities with the most traffic were the capitol known as Prismatic and the port town to the south known as Mirah. Very few boats ever docked on the northern end of Spectrum. Most sailed all the way to the south. Boats from the northernmost icy land of Glacia couldn't sail south at all; violent storms always barred the way.

Mirah was a decent sized town of many thousand Magi and half a dozen Kin or so. They were mostly SunKin, though, since they survived in the desert sun better than the MoonKin did. Spreading out from city central were dozens of farms where Soil and Water Magi made the desert land fertile enough to grow food. Air Magi owned windmills that provided fresh breezes to the farms in the surrounding areas when the sun reached its most unbearable points. The windmills also ground assorted crops into a state that could be used for cooking.

One windmill in particular was located closest to Mirah and provided heat relief to the people. The windmill was owned by a young Master Air Magi by the name of Roman Arequo. His parents lived in the city proper and owned a market where they sold fresh fruit. Even they didn't see Roman very often; as with other Master Magi, he kept to himself.

It was to the regret of all the available women in the town. Roman was one of the most attractive males around. At the age of eighteen, he was an early bloomer and already partway through second puberty. Only one girl could verify it was true. She had been the lucky recipient of his first kiss. Most assumed he had to be nearing the experimental stage, but he had made no signs of being interested in anyone that way.

At six feet tall, he was of average height for a Magi male. His hair was yellow blond, and his eyes were dark ocean blue. His shoulders were strong, and his skin golden from exposure to the sun. Like other desert men, he wore loose pants, boots, and a vest. Very little else could be worn without fear of passing out.

When he went into town for supplies, his path was almost always inundated with females. It was to the amusement of the older Magi that he simply never seemed to notice! Either he was exceptionally innocent for someone in second puberty, or he was being selectively blind.

As Roman stood watching his mother load up a hipsack with fresh fruit, he saw one of the village girls approaching. He barely stifled a sigh. Seeing it, Liza Arequo murmured, "Roman . . . be nice."

The girl had reached the counter, and she leaned on the top of it. As she did, the curves of her breasts were clearly displayed within the sturdy bikini top she wore. "You're such a stranger!" she scolded Roman. She smiled, her lashes fluttering slightly. "When are you going to write me a letter?"

He pretended as if he had only just noticed her. "Oh. Melody. Did you say something?"

She sighed. "No, nothing. Nice seeing you, Roman." She crossed her arms and sulked as he slung the sack over his shoulder and headed out of the building. "Why is he so blind?" she complained to Liza.

"He's a Master Magi," Liza said simply. "We're lucky that he even comes into town, Melody. Ever since he was a child, he's been isolated from others because of his power. How many Master Magi do you know of existing in this world?"

Melody frowned. "Four. There's that Weaponsmith in Carnelian, some doctor on Glacia, a weaver on Choral, and Roman."

"The sheer fact that there are four currently in this world at once is astonishing enough," Tomas Arequo explained as he walked up. He absently rested a hand on Liza's back. "Master Magi are born one in a few thousand. It seems much rarer than that because they simply . . . go away. Their power is so strong that they are unable to handle society."

"But Roman . . ." She trailed off slowly as she realized that Roman never came into town unless it was for supplies. He never came to festivals and never celebrated the harvests. "Is it because we treat him differently?" she asked softly.

"He feels different." Because she liked Melody, Liza offered, "You could go visit him. He might like that. I think his father and I are the only ones who bother. Perhaps having someone reach out to him might do some good."

"Then I'll go out there tomorrow!" Melody smiled. "He might never write me a letter, but I still like him."

Roman kept a findral for the brief trip in and out of town. He actually had a small herd of the beasts and they wandered all over his property. He couldn't help but relax as he entered onto his land. He *hated* going to town. The people were always talking and moving and putting off energy that rubbed him raw.

He went into his small house and put the sack down on the kitchen counter. Absently, he scratched at his face and his right arm. Ever since he had begun second puberty, they had been itching like mad. Combined with his overall increased skin sensitivity, it was vexing.

As he was putting things away, he saw a small fire flare in the air over Mirah. He smiled wryly and went to the base of the largest windmill. His power welled up as a whisper of wind, and he poured the Air element into the machine. The top began to turn and a steady breeze began blowing toward Mirah. It could spin for a few hours without more power added.

Because it was his favorite way to pass time, he headed into the small area he used as a workroom. He had a partnership with a Fire Magi in town. She made glass art that he etched for her. They split the profits though he had often tried to turn down his share. He just liked the work.

He lost track of the time as he worked. All his concentration was on using his Thunder powers to make precision details without shattering the glass. He hadn't shattered anything for all the four years he had been doing it, but he was always careful.

The rising moons surprised him and he looked out the window. There were two visible in the sky and it was definitely nighttime. There were no more signals over Mirah; he didn't need to regenerate the windmill. Content with his day, he headed for a bath and then for bed. This plain and simple life was his favorite.

He was in the fields the next afternoon tending to the findral when he saw several Magi approaching. He frowned and headed toward the fence to meet them. One Magi was the Elder in the village. Others were Soil Magi. It looked like a search party. "Is something wrong?" he asked. He automatically drew his thumb over his nose and cheek.

The Elder returned the gesture. "Has Melody Brenik been out this way?"

Roman's brows went up in surprise. "She hasn't. Was she supposed to be?"

"She set out this morning to visit you, or so she said. She hasn't come back and we're worried." The Magi who had spoken blew out a breath. "If you were anyone else, we'd have assumed that you and she were 'together.'"

Roman rolled his eyes. "I'm eighteen. You can use the phrase 'sleeping together' just as well as anyone. I won't be offended. And, no, she's not here, nor are we 'together.' I'm not interested in her that way. Or in anyone." He shrugged one shoulder. "It's uncomfortable around other people."

"And that's why we're worried," the Elder confirmed.

Roman's eyes studied his face. "What aren't you telling me?" At the surprised look, he crossed his arms. "I'm not an idiot. I'm also an Air Magi. I can sense the fluctuation in your minds. So, what's going on?"

"There have been a series of disappearances around the town," one woman said. "We're almost positive the people who are disappearing have been murdered. The power in the land under Mirah is steadily going out of control. Waves are starting to spread and are connecting with ones from Carnelian. Storms have started to form and are cutting off trade."

"That's why the ports have been quiet," he murmured mostly to himself. "Has anyone contacted the Militia?"

"The king is sending out a party as soon as he can. He dispatched one to Carnelian as well. There is some fear that the Black Magi Elite are returning." When Roman frowned, the Elder explained, "You would have been too young nine years ago to remember. It was during the war when the two Chronicles and their Furies joined with Kin and Dragon to protect us Magi from the Elite. It was an . . . eye opening time for us all."

His heart began to beat hard inside his chest, and a pain grew inside his soul and mind. His skin began itching as if it were burning. "A Fury?" he asked softly. "What's a Fury? I think I know what a Chronicle is."

Wondering why he sounded so odd, one man offered, "A Fury is a Dragon Lord that doesn't have infinite power. He or she has to feed on the power of a Chronicle who, unlike Magi, does have infinite power. We used to think it was some sort of evil pact but it really isn't. Some of the last people to see the two Dragoon pairs said they looked beautiful together."

"I see." Roman pushed down the throbbing inside his soul. He wanted . . . something. Someone. He didn't know what. He just knew there was someone in the world who needed him and that he needed in return. "Well, I didn't see Melody. I hope she's okay."

"So do we," the Elder said. "Sorry to disturb you, Roman."

"No, it's fine." He leaned on the fence and watched as they headed back toward the city. He looked almost blindly at the desert sand under his feet. Hearing about the Elite had made him somehow afraid. Hearing about Furies had made his heart and soul hurt. Something in his mind was blank as if he had forgotten something important. Nothing seemed to make sense.

By evening, he could feel the faint tremors under the land that meant that things were getting worse. There had been no word about Melody. His concern grew, and he headed for the town in the morning. When he reached his parents' store, he made a beeline for the back where Tomas was sorting wares. "Has anyone found Melody?"

Tomas looked up sadly. "They combed a five-mile area around the town and found no sign of her power. It went to a dune past the city, where it then disappeared. It's just like the other disappearances. We have to assume the worst."

Roman sat down on one of the wooden crates in the area. "I liked her," he said softly. "Not like she wanted, but she was nice. She didn't judge me." When his mother came up behind him, he leaned back against her. "It doesn't seem right."

"The Elder is preparing to issue rules about traveling alone. We can only prepare for the worst." Liza sighed as she heard the bell over the door. "Already? We're not fully set up yet."

"I'll go." He got to his feet and headed out to the front of the store. "Can I help you? They're not quite open yet."

The woman standing at the bins where some of the fruits were just being stacked was of average female Magi height and wore the comfortable clothes of the desert. He had thought he knew everyone in town by then, but she was new. She had pale brown hair and matching eyes. There was nothing unremarkable about her, yet he felt wary.

The woman turned to smile at him, and her eyes widened slightly. She stared at him in genuine surprise. She hadn't expected him to be *that* attractive. Other women had seriously underestimated his good looks. "I'm sorry," she apologized. "I just wanted out of the heat. I don't mind waiting."

"Mm-hmm." He began to edge toward the doors. He didn't trust the double take she had made. "In that case, you can just wait a few minutes and my parents will be right out."

"Oh, your parents own the shop?" She moved and blocked the door by casually leaning against the frame. She made the Magi sign of respect. "Beta, Air Magi."

He automatically returned the gesture. "Roman Arequo, Air Magi."

The name registered and her eyes widened. "You're the Master Magi that owns the windmill near here, aren't you? You're much younger than I had been thinking. In fact, aren't you a glass etcher? I've seen some of your work. It's beautiful."

"Thank you." He longingly eyed the exit behind her. He hated small talk. "You're new in town?"

"Just got in a few days ago," she confirmed. "Been meeting people and learning names." She pointedly blocked the door more firmly. "Are you an adult?" It wasn't a rude question, not when he was only eighteen. Second puberty could hit at any time after sixteen.

"Not quite yet. Could you let me out?"

"Depends on if you agree to come have dinner with me."

Tired of the games, he reached out, grabbed her around the waist, and bodily lifted her out of the doorway. As he set her aside, he said, "No, thank you. Nice meeting you." With more haste than grace, he hurried out the door and toward his findral.

Mouth hanging to her knees, she couldn't find a single word. When Tomas cleared his throat, she turned and gestured at the door. "Did you *see* that?!"

"Yes," he said dryly. "I did."

"I don't take no for an answer." She tossed her hair and stalked out of the building. Under other circumstances, she would have just kidnapped Roman or lured him away from the village. This, however, was personal. She could break his stubborn Master Magi isolation and *then* get around to killing him. His death would surely break the land. The boy had a lot of power. She had felt it when he had touched her. It just didn't entirely feel . . . normal.

When Beta showed up at the windmill the next day, Roman was cleaning out the shed that served as a shelter for his findral. He nearly groaned when he saw her. Why were women in the town determined to 'make' him see them? If he was going to be attracted to them, it would have already happened! Without looking at her, he said, "You're too old for me."

Her eyes narrowed and she planted her hands on her hips. "And what makes you think so?" she challenged. "Are you saying I look old?"

"You have three lines at the corner of your eyes," he noted. He raked down fresh dunegrass from the bin and began to spread it out. "Those lines don't appear on Magi until at least the age of thirty. Even at that, you're too old for me."

"It's actually better." She moved closer and leaned on the edge of a stall, trying to ignore the findral inside. She hated those things. "Wouldn't it be better to finish second puberty with an older woman who knows her way around things? No strings attached."

"Anyone who attaches strings to anything said or done during second puberty is an idiot to begin with." He hefted a bag and began pouring out grain. "And maybe I'm not ready for experimenting. Ever think of that?"

"You kissed Terina in town," was the retort. "She's quite proud to be your first kiss."

"As she ought to be. I'm proud to be her first as well."

Frustrated, she threw her hands in the air. "All I'm asking is for you to give me a chance! Let me hang around and maybe you'll be attracted to me. Are you saying I'm not attractive?"

"Not to me." He kicked the stall door as he added some fruit to the grain.

She opened her mouth to retort when the findral in the stall snorted and grabbed a mouthful of her hair. "Let go!" she yelped. "Let go of me!" She smacked the findral and it released her with a squawk. She backed up quickly. "Yick, I hate these beasts!"

As she turned and fled out of the barn, Roman patted the findral on the neck. "I owe you one, friend." To his amusement, the findral made a point of eating the fruit first to get rid of the taste of Beta's hair. Sometimes animals called it just right.

He was in the fields the next day when she showed up again. "Either be helpful or go away," he said bluntly as he cut down long stalks of dunegrass. It was the only crop he grew simply because it was cheaper to grow it than buy it. "There are spare gloves in the wagon."

Reluctantly, she put on the gloves and moved over to help. She held the grasses while he cut them and then helped tie them into bundles. "I can't believe you run this place by yourself. I rode the edges of your land. It's very big. Very isolated."

"It's isolated because it's big and it's big because I want to be isolated." He hefted the bundle into the wagon and began to cut the next. "And I enjoy the work. It keeps me busy. If I wasn't busy, I wouldn't even live near the town." His eyes flicked to hers. "Do you know what it's like to be a Master Magi?"

Softly, she said, "Yes, I think I do. I knew some Master Magi once. They walked the edge of madness sometimes. Maybe they needed a desert farm like this." She studied his face. "Don't you dislike the Magi? They've committed genocide of the Chronicles for a thousand years, and only a few centuries ago, they tried to erase the Kin. They've made our world more sea than land."

"They're collectively stupid." He grabbed a strip of cloth and tied it around his head to keep his bangs out of his eyes. "Does that mean that we need to get rid of them instead? No."

She let the subject shelve. Instead, she blew her hair out of her eyes as she continued to help with the dunegrass. Manual labor wasn't her favorite but she couldn't deny the benefits of getting to see sunlight ripple across Roman's muscular chest and arms. That was worth the aches she would have later.

As Roman was getting a bucket of water for them, he saw a flare over Mirah. He instantly diverted and went into the windmill. Beta followed him curiously. She had never been inside a windmill before.

He wound up the base of the windmill and then added his power to make it start. Once it was running, he also added power to the system of pipes that went around the house to keep the heat out. As he did, her eyes narrowed slightly. He was using a lot of power, even for a Master Magi. How could he maintain two separate systems without draining himself?

"Drink some water before you pass out." He handed her a cup.

"Oh. Right." She gratefully drank the water, only belatedly realizing she was thirsty. It was deceptively easy to forget to drink anything while in the desert, especially for Air Magi. Their power automatically cooled their bodies and they never knew they were overheating. "When did you come to Mirah?"

Why wasn't she leaving yet? He rubbed his forehead. "About nine years ago. I grew up in a much smaller town but it wasn't comfortable for me so we came out here. Where are you from?"

"Prismatic."

"Long way to move."

"Felt like a change." Beginning to sense that he was at the edges of his patience, she headed for the door. "Well, I'll see you tomorrow."

As she disappeared out the door, he considered digging a basement and hiding in it. Why wouldn't she take 'no' for an answer? The sad part was that he couldn't even say that he was starting to like her more now that they had spent time together. The opposite was true. He did not trust her and he did not like the sense of her power. It smelled bad.

She showed up again the next day as promised. This time he waited for her at the door. He pointedly blocked the opening. "Listen," he started, "I'm flattered. But you're wasting your time and mine. I'm not interested in you, and I won't be interested in you. Please stop coming out here. It's really getting on my nerves."

"Can I watch you etch for a while at the least? Then I'll leave." It took effort to remain cheerful and pleasant. How *dare* he dismiss her like that?

He debated with himself for long moments and then reluctantly stepped back to let her in. "For a very short while," he said. "And when I tell you to leave, you have to leave." He absently scratched at his arm as he headed for the workroom. His skin was more sensitive than usual that day. It felt like something inside burned.

He didn't bother to offer a chair to Beta. If she wanted to stay, she could stand. He put her out of his mind entirely and went over to his worktable. His favorite current project was a figurine made of glass that looked like a MoonKin Faerie. It had been specially requested by a SunKin on Kindred; he wanted a statue of his mate. Roman's job was to add the little silver tattoos that marked a MoonKin and to add detail to the wings.

Etching involved first filling the inside of the glass with air to keep it from shattering. That alone was tricky because you had to be very precise in how you put the air in, else you shatter it anyway. It took him long minutes to fill every corner since there was a lot of shape and form to the statue.

Once it was secure from the inside, he made several bolts of lightning of different sizes and potencies. He wielded them like a pen and began the process of carving into the glass. After the first few marks, he entirely forgot Beta was there. The project was a challenge of him artistically and he loved it.

Beta forgot her real reasons for being there as she watched him work. She was caught between fascination for his precision and skill, and desire to see how nimble his hands would be on her body. She couldn't believe he was only eighteen. He looked and acted much older, as if he was already an adult. But that was to be expected. He was a Master Magi. His power had fully developed before his body even started first puberty. Power made you what you were. It was the curse of exceptionally powerful people, of all races, to be exceptionally intelligent and mature.

Under his hands, the glass began to really look like a Faerie. The silver tattoos went down the outside of the arms and then along the legs. He made the wings thin and translucent to allow the veins underneath to show and reflect light. He added detail to the skirt and tunic and made them light and airy.

By the time the sun was high in the sky and starting a downward descent, he had finished his work. He put the statue on the desk and studied it contently. It was not much smaller than the Kin it was modeled after, and it looked real enough to take flight.

He jolted when Beta's hands suddenly came down on his shoulders and began to rub away tension. He tensed up further. "Don't touch me." Because he couldn't move his chair back, he pushed the table forward until he could stand. "Leave." It wasn't a request.

She eyed him, then suddenly sprang forward and threw herself against him. It caught him off guard and he fell on the floor. As she pinned him bodily, his eyes narrowed sharply. The air began to spark and sizzle. "I'm tired of playing nice," she said. "And it's time you grew up!"

"Not with you." The sparks became lightning bolts as thick as her arms. "I will not hesitate to hit you so hard that you'll be lighting up houses for a month. Don't think that your power will protect you." The blue of his eyes flickered with white. "I'm stronger."

The silence stretched. She felt one of the lightning bolts jab her in the side and the pain was blinding. Realizing he was serious, she scrambled off him and got to her feet. Her rage welled, and she grabbed the glass statue from the table. She hurled it to the floor where it shattered into bits. "You'll regret it!" she snarled as she stormed from the room.

The door slammed behind her. Roman sat up and looked at the remains of all the hard work he and Terina had done. Anger began to simmer inside his heart. "Not as much as you will." There were laws against destroying the work of master craftspeople.

Chapter Five

The next morning, Roman went directly into town with the broken statue in a bag. His first stop was at Terina's shop. Though he had never been attracted to her beyond their mutual first kiss, he considered her to be his only real friend. She was the only one who didn't expect more from him than he wanted to give. She had already finished second puberty but had let him know that if he ever wanted to become an adult with her, she would be interested. One statement, made once, and made sincerely. For that, he liked her all the more.

When he walked into the back of the shop where she was working, he waited for her to notice him. She was concentrating on molding the liquid glass in her hands. Like all Fire elements who worked with glass, she worked bare handed for precision crafting. She couldn't burn herself on her own glass.

Under her skilled hands, the glob of glass formed into a tall vase with scalloped edges. His mind automatically began to catalogue the detailing he would need to do. When she finally straightened and shoved her visor up, he said, "This is beneath your mighty skill."

She grinned at him. "Hi, Roman." She studied the vase. "Sometimes it's nice to do something easy." She stuck the vase in a spinning barrel of smoke and sand to set and smooth the surface and then swiped an arm across her forehead. "Did you finish the statue?" she asked eagerly. "It was the best thing we've ever done."

He set the bag on the counter and condemned Beta to the Underrealm as Terina's face fell and despair filled her eyes. "I had finished it," he said evenly, "but then that new woman, Beta, decided to smash it because I wouldn't let her seduce me. She's been after me for days despite me telling her no."

Terina's black eyes began to smolder with a fiery anger. "Who does she think she is?" Furious, she grabbed the bag with one hand and his wrist with her other. "We're going to the Elder and she is getting kicked out of the town. Comes in here acting like she knows everything then tries to ruin our lives!"

He followed obediently. There was no swaying her when her mind was set. She reminded him of someone, but he couldn't remember who. It was another blank space in his mind. He tried to ignore his forgotten memories, but it wasn't always easy when he felt as if they were important.

The Elder lived in a small house in the center of town. Four different dirt streets led to the house, ensuring that anyone who wanted to find him could. Every couple of years, there was a town vote to see who among the oldest in town would be Elder. For the last three votes, it had been Elder Rynic. At close to eighty, however, he was considering retiring and letting someone else take over.

He had seen Terina approaching with Roman in her wake, so he was standing on the front step waiting for them. "Come in, young ones." He held the door for them and his eyes studied the bag Terina carried. "What is wrong?" He sat down behind his desk with a sigh.

Terina put the bag down and the broken shards jangled together. "Beta." Her hands hit the top of the desk with a thump. "She destroyed something I made and that Roman etched just because Roman rebuffed her! *I want her hide!*"

"Calm down," he soothed. He looked at Roman. "Kindly be more levelheaded than your partner and tell me what's going on."

"Beta made offers that I was not interested in," Roman explained. "Repeatedly. When I finally told her to get out of my life, she smashed Terina's statue in anger. It was probably the best thing we've ever made."

Rynic began to frown deeply. "I see. She will, naturally, be brought in and questioned. She's committed a grave crime and may need to be turned over to the Militia when they arrive today."

Terina and Roman exchanged a quick glance. "The Militia will be arriving today?" Terina asked.

"Indeed. Word reached us that the Militia party in Glacia and the one in Carnelian have cross-confirmed the presence of the Elite causing trouble. As the end results are much the same as what is happening here—namely the disrupted land flow—we can only assume there is someone here as well."

Roman began to have an ugly suspicion. "At the risk of jumping to conclusions, did the first person disappear from Mirah about the time Beta showed up?"

Carefully, Rynic said, "There are some . . . coincidences about her appearance, yes."

"That's it. I'm setting her hair on fire."

Roman caught Terina around the waist and held tight despite her mad wiggles. "You're saying that no one can prove she had anything to do with the disappearances?" He firmly put Terina down on a chair and ignored the glare she leveled at him.

"I'm afraid so, Roman."

Three short raps sounded on the front door before it opened to admit a man wearing the uniform of the Militia. "I apologize for the intrusion, but I was told I could directly enter, Elder Rynic."

"Indeed." Rynic stood. "You are Argyle Vinhri, are you not?"

"I am." Vinhri drew his thumb over his nose and cheek. "Water Magi."

Rynic returned the gesture. "Elder Rynic, Soil Magi. The two present are Terina Faturi and Roman Arequo. Terina is a Fire Magi and Roman is a Master Air Magi. You've likely heard their names before."

"I have!" Vinhri gave both a warm smile. "I am a fan as well. It's an honor to meet both of you." He looked to Rynic. "May I speak freely, or should I wait until later?"

"Speak freely. Roman and Terina can be trusted."

"Very well." He linked his hands behind his back. "My party is currently examining the town and outlying areas. Just entering town, we picked up traces of the Elite."

"How do you know?" Terina asked curiously.

"The Elite carry tainted power in their bodies," he explained. "Therefore they leave a smell behind that the more attuned power can catch." He saw a flicker across Roman's eyes and was instantly intrigued. "You have witnessed a bad smell around someone, Master Roman?"

Roman hesitated and Terina's eyes went wide. "It was Beta, wasn't it?" A low sound rumbled in her chest as she crossed her arms. "Now can I set her on fire?"

Vinhri lifted a brow. "Perhaps an explanation is in order." He listened to the events as they were outlined, and his eyes went to the bag sitting on the desk. As a Militia member as well as a fan, he was doubly outraged that anyone could destroy someone else's craft. "I see," he finally said. "Well, that certainly puts this Beta at the top of the suspect list. Is she still in town?"

"That is a very good question," Rynic murmured. He went over to the door and stepped outside. "Has anyone seen Beta lately?" he asked those going by on the street.

"No, Elder," one man said.

A woman offered, "I last saw her yesterday."

One of the children came running up to Rynic and tugged on his pant leg. "I saw her this morning! She had a hipsack packed. When I asked where she was going, she said she was just taking a trip. She was lying though."

Children could always tell when someone was lying or telling the truth. The ability went away with first puberty but was restored between couples when they became Linked mates. Rynic, therefore, took the little girl's word as absolute that Beta had lied.

Vinhri had overheard the exchange. "I will send out a team to begin searching," he decided. "If she was innocent, then she would have no reason to flee on the day the Militia arrived. Warn everyone to remain in town and not wander off alone."

"Done."

Vinhri left to begin issuing orders to his party, and Rynic sent Terina and Roman home. As he was leaving Terina at her shop, Roman found himself with a stubborn Fire Magi attached to his arm. He sighed. "Terina, let me go."

"He said to stay in town."

"He said to go home as far as I'm concerned."

"You're in the most danger!" She released his arm but promptly smacked him instead. "She already set her eye on you, and killing you might destroy this entire city! The land here is so accustomed to your power that it would go *insane*!"

"So be it." He shrugged one shoulder. "I'll die if I stay in town anyway."

As he walked away, she wiped fiercely at the tears in her eyes. "Stupid stubborn man!" she whispered. She was *not* going to break her heart over him. She refused to. If she did, then she would lose his friendship and that was more important than anything.

He was halfway home when he sensed a familiar power. Shocked, he stopped his findral and looked around. He could feel Melody's power. He was sure it was hers. He quickly turned toward the direction the power had emanated. If he felt her power, then she was still alive. It was worth the risk of trying to find her if she could be saved.

A mile beyond the city, he found a dune that looked like it had been recently disturbed. He swiftly dismounted and began gathering his power in brisk winds that swept the sand away from the dune in ways that were far faster than he could dig. His first hope came when he saw a flash of dark hair. "Hang on, Melody!"

Using his hands and his power, he shortly uncovered her body. She began choking and coughing, and his hopes rose. He braced her over his arm and began a rhythmic beating on her back that forced her lungs to keep expelling the sand she had inhaled. He kept a flow of wind directly at her face, allowing her to cough out the sand through her mouth and breathe fresh air through her nose.

It didn't take long before the coughs faded to faint whimpers. "Roman?" she managed to whisper. Her entire body began to shake violently. He turned her over and lifted her, and she slumped weakly against him. "I thought I was going to die."

"Not yet, I promise." He got onto the findral's back and held her tight as he rushed back toward town. As he went, he fired multiple lightning bolts in the air in a repeated four-one-three pattern. It was the signal for medical aid that was used by all races and cities across the world.

Because of it, the three town doctors were waiting for him at the edge of the city. Many others had gathered as well, and a cry rose on the air as they saw Melody. "She's alive!" Roman said quickly. He bent and handed her gently to one of the men standing near. "She was buried alive in a dune. If she wasn't a Soil Magi, she'd be dead."

"I'll have the head of whoever did this!" her father almost roared. "Where's Beta?!"

Word spread fast in towns. Everyone knew Beta was under suspicion. But because the Militia was already out searching, there was nothing anyone in town could do. Roman watched long enough to see Melody taken to the Healing Shelter and then immediately headed for the edges of town. He was going to go looking himself, and he would have a few 'words' with Beta, Elite or not.

He caught the distinct smell of tainted power a few miles beyond the town. It was stronger than ever. Eyes narrowed, he left his findral and began walking. He didn't want the poor beast to be caught in the crossfire of the inevitable fight.

Another mile out, he was brought to an abrupt halt as a dust storm suddenly surged up and blocked his route. His eyes narrowed further and he slapped at the storm with his own wind to kill it. Even without turning around, he knew Beta stood behind him. "You really went too far."

"You mean you actually care about someone or something? I'm shocked."

He turned around and studied her white cloak. There was something almost blasphemous about it to him. He felt as if something that should have been cherished was being insulted instead. "Don't mistake disinterest for a lack of feeling. Just because I'd sooner sleep with a findral than with you is no reason to think I'm emotionless."

She very nearly shot a lightning bolt at him but restrained herself. He was clearly braced for battle. She needed him off guard if she was to have any chance of taking him out. "My apologies," she said with a touch of bitter humor. She cocked her head. "How'd you find me out here?"

"Your power reeks. Tell me, did you leave town when you heard the Militia was to arrive?"

"Naturally. What made you come after me?"

"You want the whole list? Where do I start? The part where you tried to force yourself on me or the part where you destroyed Terina's statue? How about the part where you've been kidnapping and murdering townspeople to try to destroy the city? Or maybe where you attempted to kill Melody as well."

"*Attempted*?" She sighed. "I should have buried her deeper. Damned Soil Magi."

If there was anything more disgusting than such a careless regard for life, he didn't know of it. If this was what evil was like, then he hoped he never saw it again. "What's the game?" he asked. "You've got to have a reason for this."

"It's simple." She flashed him a smile. "Magi need to die. Once they die, the world will have a chance to heal and start over."

He blinked. "Pardon me?"

"You heard me well enough. It's like I said: Magi are the cause of all the suffering of the world. Genocide of Chronicles, war with Kin . . . if they could find the Dragons, they'd probably try to steal their lands as well! They're nothing but land hoarding, narrow minded, uptight fools."

"And are you really that much better than they are?" He began to gather invisible power at his hand. "Right now I don't see you as any sort of miraculous savior of the world. You're nothing but a murderess. If you were doing such a great thing for Lucksphere, your power wouldn't reek like day old findral droppings."

She snarled and hurled a lightning bolt with all her strength. He had been prepared for it and snapped up a shield of wind that deflected the attack. His other hand shot forward and released the power it held. A rapid fire of small bolts began flying at her. The tiny bits of lighting were far more deadly than a single blast and had the potential to tear flesh to pieces.

She shielded herself as fast as she could, but bolts still tore through the shield and slashed at her clothes. Fear began to edge into her heart for the first time. He was even more powerful than she had suspected. She turned and began running across the sand to have the time to make a bigger blast.

Much to her dismay, Roman was as fast on his feet as he was with his power. He was able to navigate the dunes better and with more skill than she had. It didn't take him long to catch up. Shortly after that, he passed her. He skidded around in front of her and fired a tornado right into her chest that sent her flying back the way she had come.

She skidded across the top of a dune, then rolled down the side. Aching all the way through her body, she painfully rolled to her feet. She fiercely whipped up a dust storm and hurled it at him.

He waited until the storm was close before taking forceful command and reversing it back toward her. As he did, he wrapped the storm within lightning bolts. It grew larger and larger until it was twice his size. The Elite Magi was caught off guard by the change, and she scrambled out of the way. The lightning ripped open the back of her cloak.

She swung around to attack, and then she ducked hastily before a fireball took off her head. She turned sharply and saw Terina standing less than fifty feet away. Fire swirled around the younger woman's feet. "You!"

"Me, *poka*!" Terina hurled another fireball. "Back away from Roman!"

"Get out of here!" Roman snapped at her.

"Well, since you're here, you'll be first!" Beta hurled a massive lightning bolt at Terina. Glee that was both professional and personal filled her. Roman liked Terina, and Beta knew she would never forgive the other female for taking his attention.

Roman hit the ground running and tackled Terina down onto the sand at the last second. The bolt narrowly missed them both. He returned the blast with his free hand and sent Beta scrambling. "You idiot!" he snarled at Terina. "Get out of here!"

"Was I supposed to let you fight alone!?" was the counter snarl.

Beta began to laugh maniacally. "How cute you are!" Ugly yellow wind began to swirl around her and the smell of tainted power rose on the air. "You should have stayed safely at home!"

"What is she doing?" Terina asked in horror.

"I don't think we're going to like the answer." Roman released her and rolled up to his feet. When she stood as well, he held an arm in front of her defensively. The land under their feet had begun to rock and ripple like water when pebbles were dropped inside.

The yellow power suddenly whipped into a tornado and came flying at them. Roman shoved Terina to the side and went the other direction. The attack missed them by inches but the flying sand struck them both in the arm and rose large welts. "That's not possible!" Terina said fiercely.

Roman didn't bother with words. He summoned up an even larger tornado. It consumed the yellow one and something popped loudly as the power was purified. The pure tornado whirled and went after Beta. She shielded herself from the hardest hit, but the sand scored her face and arms where her cloak couldn't protect her.

"That shouldn't be possible either," Terina managed to say. It was in reference to both Beta's shield and Roman's tornado. Roman, even as a Master Magi, shouldn't have been able to absorb the power. And Beta, not being a Master Magi, shouldn't have been able to protect herself from the blast.

From the corner of his eye, Roman saw a distant shape on the skyline. His hopes soared. There was a Dragon crossing the desert. "Terina!" He ducked a lightning bolt. "Go and get help!"

She looked and saw the shape. Dragons may have hated Magi, but it was a sure bet that they hated the

Elite more. She scrambled to her feet without hesitation and took off running. When it came to running on sand, no one could outrun a desert dweller.

Beta didn't notice the Dragon but she did notice Terina running. She turned to fire after her, but Roman came up firing instead. The rapid bursts of lightning forced her to dodge as fast as she could. It was getting harder for both of them to move with the land rolling like the sea.

Bursts of elemental power began to geyser into the air. Beta dodged one. Roman didn't. As she watched him absorb the power, she began to have an ugly suspicion she might know why the blue-eyed farmer was so very different even from the Master Magi she had known.

She whipped up another yellow tornado and hurled it at him. This time she opened fire with the same lightning bolts he had used on her. It was a calculated risk. Every ability she used forced her to draw more power from the land. If she didn't destroy herself by using all her power, she might destroy herself by taking in too much external power. Her Magi body was not meant to be infinite.

He shielded from the lightning bolts and then rushed forward swiftly. Before she could dodge, his fist cracked across her jaw and sent her sprawling. "There's a rule about not hitting someone smaller," he said through his teeth, "but I'm really getting tired of this!" He began to say more when he saw the blood welling on her lip. Shocked, he backed up slowly.

Her blood was yellow.

Only tainted blood was yellow. Pure Magi blood was red in color. Kin had silver or gold blood, and supposedly Dragons had green blood. No blood was ever yellow unless the owner's power had been corrupted and made to be an aberration of nature itself.

She wiped her fingers over her lip and studied the smear on her fingers. With a shrug, she wiped her fingers on her cloak. If anything, her callous disregard for the reality of the monster she was made him all the more disturbed.

As she began to advance toward him, yellow lightning flickering around her, he backed up slightly. For the first time, he was beginning to question whether or not he would actually win this fight.

Terina had better hurry or the Dragon wouldn't have to worry about protecting Mirah. It would detonate in Roman's death, just like Beta wanted.

Chapter Six

Grecia Laluna was a Soil Fury. She was over six hundred years in age, older than many Dragons and certainly one of the older Furies. She was the second oldest, in fact. The only Fury older than her six centuries was Fury Elder Xander Journe. Xander was nearly twenty-five hundred years old. The gap between their ages had a simple explanation but a heartbreaking one.

No other Furies born after Xander but before Grecia had lived longer than a few hundred years before losing their Chronicle and needing to be mercifully put out of their misery. Grecia, herself, had inherited the memories of another Fury, as was the Dragon way. Newborn Dragons were always given the memories of other Dragons who passed in the same moment, thus ensuring no knowledge was ever lost.

She was one of the most beautiful among her kind. In Dragon form, she was slightly over seventeen feet in length, but she was all slender lines and graceful curves. Her scales were pale lavender with gold and green patches to denote her Soil element. Her slenderness, however, hid a deceptive strength. She was very, very strong. Even the males were wary to wrestle with her.

Thinking about that made her smile as she wandered the shops in Prismatic. She was in Magi form, naturally, and it was a form no less beautiful than her Dragon one. She was five-eight, slender and willowy, and her long hair shimmered pale gold streaked with distinct lavender color. Her eyes were also lavender and tilted at the corner. Even though she was obviously a Dragon, many Magi watched her wistfully.

She had been living in Prismatic for the last nine years. It had been the last known location of the Chronicle children, and her hope was that eventually one might return. It was a desperate hope. Though she had never spoken of it to anyone, she had felt her Chronicle's birth just over eighteen years earlier. The timing was coincidental enough to make her nearly positive that the young male Air Chronicle that Morgan Chronis had spoken of was *her* Chronicle.

When word of the trouble in Mirah reached Prismatic, she had the sneaking feeling she knew who was behind it. Removing the Elite was as important as finding the missing Chronicles, and she headed to the 'airport.' It was thusly named because Air Magi used wind to keep people safe while Dragons were taking off and landing. The port had been there for millennia, and though largely unused for the last thousand years, it was still maintained.

She took to the skies and skirted around the outside of the city; she didn't dare fly over it for fear of disturbing the land. It was just as well. She needed to head south anyway. By flying along the shoreline, she was able to fly at her natural speed. It was a speed that would let her cover as much ground in a single day as a findral could in a few. However, it was also a speed slower than other Dragons because she was a Fury and her power was not infinite. Not without her Chronicle.

She began to notice the signs of trouble on the third day of flying. She could see the land rolling like waves. A flicker in the corner of her gaze indicated there was a fight of some kind but she paid no heed to it until she saw a sudden staccato of fireballs in the air in the familiar four-one-three pattern. Someone needed help.

She instantly stopped flying and angled down toward the sand. She landed carefully to keep from disrupting the land further. Her sharp eyes saw a small figure rushing toward her, and it moved with a speed over the dunes that meant this person (likely Magi) was a desert dweller. To keep from alarming him or her, Grecia used her Soil power to create a willow tree that was the universal symbol of peace.

Terina slowed her run as she realized the Dragon had landed. Try as she might, she couldn't keep out the fear. Her heart pounded wildly as she slowed to a walk. The Dragon was more than three times her height and at least twice her size. It was, however, standing next to a willow tree. Things were perfectly safe.

She didn't *feel* safe! There was no way to feel safe next to a beast as magnificently powerful as a Dragon. This one seemed oddly feminine though her face was fierce and powerful. Terina was tempted to call it a beautiful face, but it was hard to think of something that potentially dangerous as beautiful.

She stopped when she was feet in front of Grecia and struggled to catch a breath. As she gasped for air, a gentle claw was laid on her back. Cool Soil power slid into her body and healed the restrictions on her lungs. It allowed her to take deep breaths. Startled, she straightened. "Thank you."

"I will assume that is not why you were signaling me for help," Grecia said. Her slanted eyes tilted even more as they narrowed. "You are wounded." She lowered her head to touch the wound on Terina's arm with her nose. The smell of tainted power was sharp, and she lifted her head. "The Elite."

"Yes!" Terina forgot her fear and put her hands on Grecia's leg pleadingly. "My friend . . . he's fighting Beta! I jumped in like an idiot, but we should have been able to win! Roman is a Master Air Magi! But Beta . . . she did something. It's not natural! You need to save Roman! If he dies . . . Mirah is doomed!" She gave a squeal as a large claw closed around her body. "Don't eat me!"

"Don't be silly. You can't ride on my back, but I can carry you." Grecia flew up into the air. "We're going to save your friend."

Heart in her throat, Terina held onto her claw. "They're where the explosions are!" She closed her eyes. Worry choked her painfully. "I don't want him to die! He's my best friend! He was my first kiss!"

Second puberty was a strange and wonderful time. Grecia had gone through it over five hundred years earlier. She still remembered her first kiss and her first lover. "Then we will save him." Her teeth bared as she smiled. "I'll teach this Beta what a real quake is like."

At the fight, Roman blocked the next attack and countered with a series of larger lightning bolts that forced Beta to dodge. He knew exactly which direction she would go, and he sent a tornado whipping at her from the side. It caught her and flung her high in the air. When she landed, something broke audibly. She got to her feet and her left arm hung uselessly at her side.

As she started to gather her power together for another attack, a Dragon shadow passed by overhead. The power washed over the field, and it seemed to arrow in directly on Roman. His skin burst into riotous pain and electric shocks flooded the air. His skin stretched violently and felt as if it would split open. Wind whipped around him and sent sand flying wildly. He fell to his knees as something inside swelled larger and larger, pushing against what felt like unnatural binds. Then, with a shockwave of air, the tension broke.

Golden lines suddenly appeared on the right side of his face and blazed a trail down his neck and shoulder all the way to his right hand and fingers. As they covered the entirety of his arm, they appeared as straight lines with little curls at the end. His soul was throbbing but he felt oddly more peaceful than he had in his entire life. He slowly lifted his hand and stared distantly at the lines. He was a Chronicle?

Beta felt no less shaken. Her suspicions had in no way prepared her for reality. It was disorienting, to say the least. She shook it off and started to step forward when a powerful roar ripped through the air over her head. It chilled her to the bone and she scrambled back instead.

Grecia landed on the ground in front of Roman with her wings arched and her teeth bared. Her scales fully lifted to reveal sharp edges in a battle-ready pose. "Stay away from my Chronicle!" she snarled. She had known it the instant she saw Roman. With or without his awakening, she had known.

Beta's eyes slowly widened as she saw the markings on Grecia's body. "You're a Fury?"

The answer came in the form of deadly thorn covered vines bursting out of the sand. As they advanced toward Beta, she knew she was outmatched. Even her stolen power was not enough. Not against a Fury this old and powerful. A ball of lightning filled her hand and she threw it to the ground where it detonated with a blinding light. When it faded, she was gone.

Grecia looked around, but she neither saw nor smelled her enemy any longer. A soft thump had her head swinging around, and she saw Roman lying unconscious on the sand. Her heart broke.

Lavender light flared around her body, and she transformed into her Magi shape. She walked over to his side and knelt beside him. Tenderly, she eased him into her arms. Tears burned the back of her eyes as she buried her face in his hair. Finally. After six centuries of waiting, she had finally found the one man who completed her. The one being that was hers alone.

Wonder filled her as she studied his beautiful face. She softly trailed a finger across the lines on his face. It was wildly seductive to know that it was her power that made his lines. Without lifting her gaze from his face, she said, "I am sorry."

Visibly trembling, Terina walked forward from where she had been hiding behind a dune. "I always knew he would never be mine," she whispered, "but never why. I can see the why now."

"You don't fear and hate him?"

"Why should I? He's still Roman." She took a long breath. "I am going home, and I'm telling everyone that I saw Beta and Roman fighting. Roman overpowered her and she fled. In doing so, he realized that he was a threat to the city and decided to leave entirely."

Grecia studied Terina's face. "It is not entirely a lie. This is the ideal time for Roman to leave. The land is already in fluctuation and his returning there now after awakening will make things worse. But by the time the land settles, he will be gone. It will accept his leaving." In a very soft voice, she added, "I will love him in a way you can't."

Their eyes met in a moment of understanding. "I want you to," was the soft response. "He needs someone to love him. Just . . ." her voice broke for a moment, "just send me a message somehow when he's happy. If I could know that . . ."

"Consider it done."

"Then I will leave now." She turned, then paused for a moment. "Will you have a Linking ceremony?"

"There will be a bonding, but it will not require a ceremony. If we do have a ceremony, you will surely be invited."

"Thank you."

Grecia watched Terina until she disappeared on the horizon and then turned her attention back to her mate. She could feel his power rising steadily even as her own majiks began to drain. The sun was devilishly hot overhead and she didn't want to remain out in the open. They were along a common land route between cities.

She gently put him back down on the ground and got to her feet. Soil power welled inside her and flowed down into the land. It stilled its soft tremors and fell quiet. She waited a moment, then focused her power. It surged from her as a swirl of summer leaves and the top of a dune lifted entirely.

Under her expert control, the land began to shape and form into a cave deep under the surface. Because she might have been slightly smaller than Roman in her Magi form but she was still as strong as her Dragon one, she bent and wrapped an arm around his waist to lift him off the ground.

She lowered the dune back into place once they were inside the cave. It was pitch black but she always carried lamps in her hipsack. She pulled out several and set them up. It took a minute but eventually they realized it was dark and obediently began giving off a strong light.

She felt no worries for using her majiks now that she had her Chronicle. She took the effort to cover the cave ground with soft and lush grass and even scattered around flowers for visual appeal. She made every effort to make the area comfortable before returning to Roman's side. She sat down beside him and studied his form. There were wounds marking his body and she began the task of healing them all.

Technically, all elements could heal though MoonKin with their Dark power were the most potent. It really depended on whether or not the owner's power could be used in that way. Grecia's could, and it was also her specialty. She took great delight in removing the blemishes from her mate's perfect beauty.

Perfect wasn't even the word for him. She had never seen such a stunningly handsome man before. Hunger churned inside her body. She wanted him. Had, in fact, never wanted anyone or anything more in her long life. It was a physical hunger for his strong muscles and rich golden skin. It was an emotional hunger to see him smiling at her and loving her. It was an elemental hunger to feed on the power she felt beckoning to her even then.

Time slipped past. She didn't know how long it was until he finally began to stir. She moved closer and leaned over him, her hand seeking his and lacing their fingers together. "Open your eyes," she pleaded huskily. "Please."

He woke to agonizing pain in his body. His Air was going out of control. He wanted to sweep across the land and become a tornado across the skies. He wanted to unleash storms of lightning and tear open clouds. When he tried to move, every muscle protested. A tender touch on his hand was shocking, and it reverberated all the way to the power that made him. He *knew* that touch. And he knew the beautiful voice calling to him. This woman was *his*.

He forced his eyes open and found himself staring into the lavender eyes of the most beautiful woman he had ever seen. His breath caught as a sudden searing desire consumed him. For the last few months, his second puberty curiosity had been little more than a passing thing that was easily ignored. There was no ignoring it in that moment. He ached from head to toe in a way that had nothing to do with his rampant power and yet had everything to do with it.

When he tried to reach for her, his body protested. She instantly brought his hand to her cheek. "We need to bond as Dragoons," she said softly. "I need to feed on your power." Her eyes searched his. "Do you understand what has happened and is happening?"

"Acknowledge and accept it? Yes. Understand? No." He found a smile for her. "I don't care that much, oddly, that I don't understand anything about what has happened. You're here and that seems to make everything else not matter."

Her heart clenched wildly for a moment as she slowly eased him off the floor. She softly nuzzled her nose into his shoulder. He smelled like desert winds and rich desert storms. It was addicting. Unable to resist, she lightly tasted his skin. A soft white aura instantly lifted and covered his body in response. Who was she to resist the offer?

As her lips sipped delicately along his shoulder, he felt a shiver from his head to his toes that was pure delight. As instinctive as breathing, he curled his power around her. It vividly underlined a more physical desire to make them one.

She followed his power as it lured her into trailing soft kisses over his face. He tasted as wonderful as he smelled. She would never have enough. As she teased his lips with hers, she asked softly, "Tell me you're through second puberty."

"I'm," his voice caught as he felt her fingers kneading his muscles like a cat, "I'm in the third phase."

Experimentation phase. It was, without question, the best and most frustrating part for a pair of lovers. Bodies and powers more than ready and willing for the final step but emotions and minds still catching up. Feeling his power swirling around her seductively, she knew at the least that she could take the kiss she craved.

Her lips softly covered his, and he freed his hand to bury his fingers in her long hair. He couldn't tell where the greatest pleasure originated. The softness of her lips, the richness of her taste, the silk of her hair, the scent of her skin . . . it all tangled together inside him and merged with a matching hunger to feel her mind and soul, to bind her as tightly to him as he could.

And as the last of his power flowed into her, just that happened. He could feel her breathing inside his lungs, feel her thoughts inside his mind. Her emotions burned hot and wild inside his heart. He could see everything she was and had been. Centuries of memories fluttered across his mind and broke his heart as he saw how long she had waited.

She felt his heart, breathed his breath, and felt his love burning inside her. The volatile three emotions that marked Dragoons rioted inside him as they did inside her. Her heart soared as she realized that the third emotion, the one that could only be at its peak when the Dragoons were lovers, was nearly as great inside him as it was inside her. He was nearly ready for her.

But as his memories fluttered across his mind, she immediately saw that there was something missing. There was a large blank space present. She touched it lightly and felt the lingering traces of Morgan Chronis' power. Roman was, without question, one of the missing Chronicle children.

They slowly parted but she couldn't move very far with his fingers tangled in her hair. She tried to free herself, her control shaky enough, but as she pulled back, he sat up and pulled her closer again. Startled, she let her head rest on his shoulder. She felt . . . small suddenly. It was an odd feeling. She had never felt small around any male that wasn't a Dragon.

She decided she liked it and nuzzled his shoulder. He promptly set her away, and she began to frown. "What? I was comfortable!"

"And I want to see you." He held her at arms' length and eagerly looked her over. Her figure seemed sturdy rather than generous, and her legs looked almost outrageously long. She wore a desert bikini under snug shorts and a top that wasn't much more than a bikini itself. She looked like any other desert girl, but at the same time, she looked far better. And, before his delighted eyes, a flare of light made lines identical to his surge across her slender stomach and down her legs to her knees. It was *his* power that made her lines.

Her eyes closed helplessly as he tugged her onto his lap and she felt his heated intent. "That's not fair!" The last word was almost a gasp as his nose buried between her breasts. "Really not fair!" She shivered in wonderful delight as his lips teased her skin. "I hate this part."

"Liar." He really wanted to peel the offending clothes from her body to see more but knew it wouldn't be fair to either of them. He knew he wasn't ready for more than a simple exploration of his lover's body.

"*Simple*?" She wound her arms around his shoulders. "Simple is staring at me. *This* is torture!" She let out a long breath. "Say something to distract me. Fast. Else I'm having my wicked way with you."

The threat of ravishment from his Fury was *vastly* more appealing than the threat of being ravished by Beta. A sudden surge of violent emotion from Grecia had his eyes widening, and they widened further when her lavender eyes turned dark green with rage. "What's wrong?"

"She tried to *what?!*" The words came out as a soft snarl. "I'm going to roast her alive!"

"Tried," he stressed. "And failed. No, you don't." He wrapped his arms around her waist and held her firmly on his lap when she tried to get up. Wanting to distract her, he smiled at her. "What's your name?"

She opened her mouth, then closed it. Bemused, she offered, "Grecia Laluna."

"Roman Arequo. And now that that is out of the way, I don't suppose you can fill in some of the details of what the hell is going on. I went from a Master Magi to a Chronicle who seems to have one hell of a beautiful Fury."

"Stop complimenting me so that I can get my thoughts organized," she grumbled. Her breath hitched in her chest. "And stop petting me with your power! You're just being mean!"

"I'm just experimenting, Grecia." His smile was half innocence and half masculine amusement.

"I'm doomed." She blew out a breath, firmly removed his arms, and got off his lap. She sat beside him instead and curled their fingers together. When he leaned closer, she felt herself surrounded by his heat and presence. It soothed her all the way to her soul. "You seem to know something of Chronicles and Furies."

"A little. Just what I was told. I can see the rest inside your mind. I just want to know how I never knew what I was." He held up the arm with his lines. "Is this why my skin has been itching like mad ever since I started second puberty?"

"I'd have to guess it is. This is an, uhm, unusual circumstance. I have nothing to base it on." She sighed. "Does the name Morgan sound at all familiar? Or Tariah?"

He began to frown. "It feels . . . it feels a little familiar." Pain seemed to flash in his head and he pressed his fingers to his forehead. "There's something missing in my memories. I've always thought that but . . . damn, it hurts."

She framed his face with her hands and swirled her power around his mind. Looking at his mind was like looking at a puzzle missing a piece in the very center. "Nine years ago, you lived in Prismatic with three other Chronicle children, your parents and theirs, and a young man named Morgan Chronis. He and his sister, Tariah, are the two most powerful Chronicles this world has ever seen. They can do things that even the Elders of the Kin and Dragons have never heard of being done.

"When the war with the Elite started, Morgan erased the memories of his Black Magi and sent them— you—away via translocation. He put a lock on your powers by using his own to create a barrier under your skin to hide your lines. It would not break unless you were in the presence of a Chronis or a Fury."

A flash flickered across his eyes of a young man with auburn hair and silver eyes. Eyes that were almost always sad but unwilling to give in. Someone he had idolized. "He . . . his eyes are silver."

She sensed movement in his mind and began to see fragments of memories in all corners. "So that's what he did." She used her power to begin gathering the fragments, connecting them by tiny vines that she could pull together. "He didn't *erase* them. He just fragmented them. I think . . . I think I can put them back."

The fragmented memories came together in the empty space in his mind. Silently they fused together. The lost memories punched into both their minds at the same time, but seeing them brought blinding pain to him. He doubled with it and she caught him close. She wrapped her arms around him tightly. "How could I forget?" he asked in despair. "I forgot Morgan. I forgot Kelsey, and C.J., and Jayda."

"It was better that you did." She rocked him gently. Her heart broke for him. "I don't know where the other three are, but I know where Morgan is. He's on the Isle of Dragons. It's . . ." She slowly trailed off as she realized she didn't remember where the Isle was located. She groaned and closed her eyes. "Your journey isn't done."

"You forgot how to get to your own home?"

"It's your fault! It happened to Dominic and Jazz too! Because a Chronicle *has* to finish their journey, the Fury forgets how to get home." She released him when he straightened. Tenderly, she wiped the traces of tears from his eyes. "We will get there, *ishke*," she promised softly.

"Is that a Dragon word?"

"It is. It's the greatest word we have. It encompasses all the wants, desires, and needs of the world." She smiled. "It's what we call that third emotion inside Dragoons." Sensing the next question, she said, "We're Dragoons. When a Fury and Chronicle bond, they become Dragoons. It won't be long until we start developing tertiary skills that only Dragoons can use. I'm not sure I want you to have Telekinesis, though. I hope it's Telepathy."

"I wouldn't move you anywhere against your will," he promised. He sighed and fell over onto his back on the grass. When she curled up against him, he realized he was happier than he ever had been in his life. "So, what do we do next? We can't just sit here forever."

West.

The throbbing in his lines was shocking. He sat up sharply and looked around. The strongest compulsion was inside him as if he heard a voice in his mind. *West.* He had to go west. He shook his head but the urgency commanded him. "I have to go west."

She sat up as well and studied him. "To the west beyond Spectrum is the land of Kindred where the Kin live. That might be an ideal location, actually. The Kin will offer shelter, and Tariah's Kin brother is there. He can contact her. It might be the only way to contact the Isle since I've forgotten how to get there. I can't even put a finger on anyone's energy signal either."

"I guess we go there then." There was a long silence and then he asked achingly, "I can't contact my parents, can I?"

"Not yet." She scooted closer and pulled him into her arms. His arms wrapped around her in turn, and she rubbed her cheek against his hair softly. "I am sorry, Roman. It just isn't safe. Though Magi mindset is changing, there are still many who hate what you are. Your parents would be in danger."

"I know." He straightened and tugged her onto his lap. "You know," he decided, "I forget that you're a Dragon. You're much smaller than I am right now. You're so slender! Do you weigh anything?"

"Yes, thank you." She sniffed disdainfully and then laughed. "Actually, even among Dragons, I am considered slender. Not small, mind you. Sadly, Jazz holds the distinction of being the smallest, but that's only fitting. Morgan is really short for a Magi male, and he is a very 'protect everyone he loves' type person, so her shorter stature makes him feel as if she needs protecting—even if she probably doesn't. It's adorable how she lets him think so."

He grinned a bit. "I'm not necessarily a type to need to protect everyone, but I apologize in advance if you being a healer and smaller than me makes me forget you're not exactly helpless."

She had to grin as well. "Furies and Chronicles always give each other something they need. Tariah is *very* short and petite, and that tends to send both her brother and her Fury into overprotective mode. Which works, really, because she needs that—even when she chafes at it sometimes." She thought about it. "Tariah is smaller than Jazz, actually, so I guess, technically, Tariah is the smallest Dragon when she is borrowing Dominic's Dragon form."

"Borrowing his form?" His eyes went wide.

"Oh, yes. A quirk of Dragoons. The majiks are what let Dragon Lords change shape. It's technically what defines us as Lords. *But* with you . . . we can do entirely new things. By my feeding on your power, I am given the ability to use my majiks in ways that are wholly different from the ways Dragons normally do. And in return, you can use them too."

"Amazing," he said softly. "And feeding on my power means your power is now infinite as well?"

"Kind of. It means I can use my full potential as a Fury without risk. Without you, I've had to be *very* careful not to drain myself." Her smile came slow and sensual. "Now I don't mind being a little . . . reckless. The reward is well worth it." She eased in and brushed a teasing kiss over his lips. "We are one in a way that no other being will ever understand. Everything about us is made to be together. The power that flows back and forth between us will go on for infinity. Living as one . . . breathing as one . . . forever. Never alone, never doubting each other's love . . . It is our destiny as Dragoons."

If that was the destiny of a Dragoon, he thought he had a good idea why Magi had always been so jealous of Chronicles. The way he felt for Grecia and the way he felt when he could feel her emotions for him . . . he would kill to protect that feeling.

And something told him he might have to. The Elite were still lurking in the world. The next time he saw Beta, he wouldn't hesitate to destroy her. She had to be stopped once and for all.

Chapter Seven

The small continent of Choral was the land to the furthest southwest on the world of Lucksphere. Only three cities existed on its harsh desert landscape. One was a port town to the north, another was a port to the south, and in the very center was the city of Symphony. Choral had the hottest lands in the entire world with temperatures soaring to the near boiling during summer. Only those with the highest durability lived on Choral.

Once, nine years before, Symphony had been home to a Chronicle. Tariah Chronis had fled from her hometown after discovery by the Militia, and her abrupt departure had caused disturbance in the lands for two years before settling. Animals and Magi alike had been mutated into monsters until the land calmed.

Now, seven years later, the city had recovered. Many owed the stability to the presence of a young Master Magi who had arrived seven years earlier. At the age of nineteen, C.J. Daragon was the best weaver in the world. The tapestries and banners he wove with his Soil powers were amongst the greatest any had ever seen.

He lived on the outskirts of Symphony in a shelter built beneath the harsh desert sands. He was slightly anti-social when it came to his interactions with others, but he could be coaxed into coming into town for the occasional festival. His empathy for others and his ability to provide comfort to those who were lost far surpassed his short years. He wasn't even an adult yet and only barely beginning second puberty.

Everyone in town who was single was hoping that his less-than-anti-social personality would allow him to find one of them attractive enough to become an adult with. C.J. was downright beautiful. He had short ash brown hair that seemed to glow with silvery highlights under the sun. His eyes were a stunning iridescent black, and they reflected rainbows in the right light.

Only one person in town knew C.J.'s ways of thinking. That distinction belonged to a young SunKin Elf named Cole. He was sixty in age (or twenty-five by Magi reckoning) and had been C.J.'s friend and confidant since the younger male had arrived in town. Cole was a Soil secondary Kin, and he had been the one to help C.J. master his unpredictable power in a body that wasn't fully developed.

Cole wasn't precisely unattractive himself with his long feline ears and lively brown eyes. He was shorter than his friend—five-six to C.J.'s five-eleven—but every inch had been well used. When the two of them walked through town together, most people were compelled to stop what they were doing to watch.

C.J.'s parents were Ferris and Alline Daragon. They lived in the town proper. They had never tried to force him to stay with them, understanding that he needed his space. They still tried to baby him though. Ferris owned a restaurant and took advantage of it to feed her son.

When Cole arrived at C.J.'s home under the sand one day, he was, as usual, carrying a basket. "I need to stop going by your mother's restaurant."

C.J. didn't look up from the cloth he was weaving from the bag of sand near his feet. "After these years, one would think you'd learned that."

Cole put the basket down and stepped over to watch. Though he did the same kind of work, every weaver was different. Watching C.J. was an art in and of itself. Some weavers could only make cloth of the most simple color and designs. C.J. could use every color imaginable and had created complex tapestries that were even then hanging in the palace of the Magi's king. Cole had personally delivered special banners to the Elders of the Sun and MoonKin as well.

After a few minutes, C.J. finished the cloth he was working on. It was a thick blanket of soft yellow hues. Cole fingered an edge and felt the extra fluffiness inside the material. "Going to Glacia, is it?"

"It is." He removed the blanket from the frame and folded it up neatly. "It will decorate the bed of a newly Linked couple."

Cole wigged his brows. "In other words, it will be broken in fairly shortly."

He grinned at that. "I would hope so." He rolled his shoulders. "I think I've been standing for a couple hours. Where's the moon?"

"Set. The sun is currently right over your dune."

"Okay, more than a couple then. Explains why I'm starving." He picked up the basket and began pulling out the still steaming breads and the assorted chilled foods in their own special containers. "I shouldn't let her spoil me."

Cole took a big bite of sweetbread. "If you have a parent that cooks like this, you don't argue. You just smile and say thank you. And anyway, your mom scares me."

"Me too." C.J. didn't have many chairs in his house. He just sat down on a rug on the floor. When Cole joined him, they divvied up the remaining food. Cole got a slightly larger share but he consumed more food because his body housed three elements: Light, Soil, and Wood.

As C.J. absently scratched at his chest and his hand, Cole asked, "Is it getting worse?"

"Well, it isn't getting better! Are you sure this is normal for second puberty?"

"Skin sensitivity is, but I'm not so sure about the itching. I didn't think anyone could be allergic to puberty, but you might be a new case." Under his lashes, he watched C.J. He had some . . . *suspicions* about his friend. Ones that he was too afraid to say out loud. Instead, all he offered was, "We could see the new doctor in town. Maybe she has some herbs or something."

"The last time you convinced me to take herbs for a problem, my skin turned blue. I looked like your cousin."

"Hey, I warned you not to take them with water, but did you listen to me? No, you did not." He tilted his head and one ear cocked at a curious angle. "Let's hit the library first. Maybe there's something in a book there."

"Oh all right." C.J. reluctantly got to his feet. "At least the library is quiet."

"Careful. Keep up talk like that and I might think you were turning into a normal Master Magi. I hear the one near Mirah almost never goes into town."

"I've heard he's also an Air Magi and Air elements are notoriously aloof to begin with. He has my sympathies." He opened the dune for his friend and then followed him out into the hot sun. He closed the dune behind them and began heading toward town. Like all males of the desert, neither wore more than pants, boots, and vests.

The library in town was one of four on the world. There was one on each main Magi land in the central city location. Books were traded back and forth across the world and copied at each location. Choral, however, housed the best. It had once been owned by the parents of Tariah Chronis. Now it was owned by the entire town.

Contemplating things as they went inside, C.J. asked Cole, "Why don't Kin have a library?"

"We don't use books." He began to look for the books on Magi physiology. "Our stories are passed on by word of mouth. I've probably got half this library worth of tales in my head."

"Is that why there's no room for anything else?"

He flicked his ears in the Kin version of a rude gesture. C.J. just grinned. Ignoring his smart-mouthed friend, Cole began flipping through the pages of the book he had found. "I'm not sure what scares me more. That someone took the effort to detail the potential effects of second puberty, or the fact that the book is this big." It was almost as thick as his forearm, and Cole was unusually strong for a Kin. They usually ran to slender or pudgy physical types rather than muscular.

C.J. sat down on the side of the table. "Anything about allergic reactions?"

"No . . . not that I'm seeing. But this is interesting. I didn't expect to find a section about Chronicles in here." He thumbed past a few pages. "Guess they have their own set of problems if they're ever allowed to reach second puberty."

"Like what?"

"It's called a journey. I guess it was the Chronicle equivalent of second puberty. They'd start things the normal way but would be compelled by the lines on their bodies to go seeking their Fury." He watched C.J. from the corner of his eye. "It's pure speculation based on the fact that only two Chronicles are known to have survived to second puberty and most other records have been erased over the last thousand years. But the thought is that since Chronicles develop so fast to begin with, they might hit a slow growth until meeting their Fury which then propels them at their normal excessive speed."

C.J. felt a sudden pain inside his chest that seemed to consume everything. He needed something. Someone. There was someone out there that was looking for him. She needed him. He pressed a hand to his heart and stared almost blindly at the floor. How did you hunger for someone you didn't know? "A Fury?" he asked softly, not even conscious of asking.

Cole closed the book. "The destined lover of a Chronicle. A Fury is a Dragon Lord who doesn't have infinite power. The Chronicle does, and by feeding on their power, the Fury can use their majiks safely. Elder Juniper of the SunKin says that the tales of the things a Dragoon pair can do are pretty amazing." A little wistfully, he said, "I envy Chronicles a little. A love like that must be wonderful."

C.J. forcefully shook off the feelings. "Okay, so that's a Chronicle and Magi. What about Master Magi? We're that odd gray area between the two."

"Why don't you ask a doctor?" a feminine voice asked behind them.

Both males blinked, then turned. Behind them they found a stunningly beautiful Magi with thick cream-colored hair and matching eyes. She was tanned from the sun and wore the casual bikini and shorts of most desert women. The only pointed difference between her and most other women was that she had a tattoo around her lower right arm. It was an entwined chain of water drops that marked her as a doctor.

Cole's ears quirked with interest as he looked her over. "And who says Kin don't appreciate lovely Magi," he said under his breath.

Even C.J. thought the woman was beautiful, but he didn't feel the slightest bit attracted to her. Sadly, he couldn't even say if it was because he wasn't through second puberty or simply that she wasn't his type. He didn't even really know what his type was yet. His curiosity was, thus far, more general and less specific.

The woman walked forward and drew her thumb over her nose and cheek. "Kappa, Air Magi."

C.J. returned the gesture with a smile. "C.J. Daragon, Master Soil Magi."

Cole lightly touched his ears and bowed slightly in the Elf equivalent of the Magi greeting. "Cole, Soil secondary SunKin." His smile was decidedly warmer than C.J.'s. "It's a pleasure to meet you, Kappa. You're the new doctor in town?"

She wasn't sure which was more amusing: that the Kin was flirting with her or that the Magi wasn't. They were both outrageously attractive and she wasn't entirely sure which she preferred. She felt oddly drawn to both of them. That, of course, might have been simply because she was of the element of Air and both were of Soil. They were natural opposites to her. "I am indeed," she said after a moment. She walked closer a step. "I overhead a bit of the conversation. You're having some odd problems with second puberty? What stage are you in?"

"Second."

"Starting or ending?"

"I don't know. I'm curious, but it's more general. I haven't really been attracted to anyone specific. I'll say the beginning though it's possible I'm further along. I'm not entirely comfortable with people. It might simply be that I'm not at all compatible with anyone around here."

"Hmm." She tapped a finger on her chin. "What exactly is the trouble?"

"My sensitivity is making my skin itch in places."

"I think he's allergic to puberty."

C.J. made a quick gesture with his left hand that was as rude as Cole's from earlier. Kappa hid a smile. "Now, boys." She stepped closer and lifted a hand. "May I?" When C.J. nodded, she lightly put a hand on his chest. Her power lifted to surround him in the only surefire method of evaluating his health. After a moment the power dissipated and she stepped back. "I don't sense anything unusual. Your skin *does* seem to be acting oddly, though. The best way to describe it is to say that it's acting like the land does when the power fluctuates."

"Ah, I see." Cole tucked his hands in his pockets. "That's causing the irritation. Well, he is a Master Magi. We'll need to contact the author of the book and have them come examine you. Make a new chapter."

"Be nice," she scolded. "As for you, C.J., if you'd like, you can come by my Shelter tomorrow and I'll see if I can find something for you to bring down the itching. I doubt I can stop it though."

"I can do that."

"What about me?" With a distinctly flirtatious smile, Cole leaned closer. Kappa stood an inch taller, and he rather liked it. "Want to make sure I'm healthy too?"

She turned toward the door with a smile. "Maybe another time. You're probably too old for me anyway, being a Kin and all."

"That's not fair," he complained. "It's only a technical age gap." He studied the lines at the corner of her eyes. "Besides, you have to be at least thirty. Technically, you're older than me."

"I'm not interested in Kin, even attractive ones," was her laughing retort as she headed out the door.

There was a moment of silence and then he said, "I like her."

"You need to be committed to a Healing Shelter for mental health." C.J. got to his feet. "But in a purely unphysical way, I liked her too. I felt strangely comfortable near her, and that's not something I can say about a lot of people."

From where she was listening outside the door, Kappa couldn't have been more pleased. She had plans for C.J. and having him comfortable with her presence was crucial. She had come to Choral with the intent of taking advantage of the disturbed land, but it was oddly stable.

Asking around had told her that it was his presence that kept things steady. It puzzled her. How did a Master Magi manage to calm the wake of a Chronicle's departure? Master Magi were more like Chronicles than they were like Magi, but there were still distinct differences between levels and scope of power. A lack of infinite power in Master Magi was first and foremost.

She headed back to her Shelter and thought about her plan of action. There was no set time limit for what she needed to do. Her best bet was to win his (and Cole's) trust, and hope that he was eventually attracted to her. If she could become his lover, she would have a better chance at understanding why he was vastly different compared to others. Once she understood that, she would be able to kill him. Choral would be decimated in his death.

Being in town meant an obligatory visit to his parents. C.J. headed to the restaurant and Cole tagged along. He peeked in the front door and said, "Full house." Even before he finished speaking, C.J. was heading toward the back as if his boots were on fire. Bemused, Cole followed him. "You sometimes move as fast as my sister and she's a Faerie."

"When I have reason." He barely hid a shudder. "I refuse to walk into a room full of that many people. If I'm allergic to anything, it's crowds." He blinked as a slender woman suddenly grabbed him in a hug. "And my mother, but don't tell her that. In fact, I feel itchy already."

"Oh stop!" Ferris Daragon tweaked his nose. "Nineteen or ninety, you should be nicer to your mother." She propped her hands on her hips and studied him. She didn't see him very often, and whenever she did, she looked closely to make sure that he was healthy. He looked just fine. "Did you eat?"

"I force fed him," Cole offered. "Do you have any sweetbread left?"

"Bottomless pit." It was said affectionately. "There's a day-old loaf on the counter. Feel free to have some." As he went to cut a piece, she tugged C.J. into the kitchen and out of the sun. "What brings you by? I wasn't expecting a visit this soon."

"We came into town to go to the library. My skin still itches. The books didn't have any answers so I'll be talking to the doctor tomorrow. She's fairly sure she can say what's wrong, but not how to fix it. She's going to try to find something to make it itch less."

"Did you find her lovely?" Ferris asked hopefully.

Cole's ears perked. "I did."

"You hush and eat your sweetbread."

"Yes'm."

Ferris sighed and C.J. just laughed. "I did; it just wasn't personal. I'm not attracted to her. Cole is, but she countered all his advances. If he tried to write a letter, it'd be returned to sender."

"We don't write letters, exactly," Cole explained. "We usually offer to read someone's energy. It's kind of the same pick up line, but different because we write letters to each other by writing with another person's energy."

"Convenient," Alline Daragon said as he walked into the kitchen with an empty tray of dishes. "It must be much faster too."

"Sometimes it is. Other times it's slower. I sent my sister a letter once that didn't arrive for weeks. She was ill. Her energy was diluted and couldn't receive any letters." He brightened as Ferris handed him a cup of sweetened tea. "Thanks!" He happily dunked the bread in the tea. Like other Kin, he had an incurable sweet tooth. Yet somehow, he didn't get overweight. It puzzled most who met him.

"I hear things are getting worse," Alline told Ferris. "They're saying that the Militia has been dispatched to Carnelian, Mirah, and Glacia."

She frowned deeply. "And yet nothing has happened here. How very odd."

"It's still affecting the northern port," he disagreed. "We're getting bad waves from Carnelian. Most ships are grounded now. It's even worse, though, because our ships that do leave can't make it to Mirah. The waves between Spectrum and Carnelian are making storms. Bad ones, I might add. At this rate, all lands will be isolated."

"Wait a minute." C.J. frowned. "What are we talking about?"

"Members of the Black Magi Elite have shown up." Just saying it made something inside Ferris viciously angry. She had always felt as if the Elite were an offense to someone or something. "They've been upsetting the power in the land on Carnelian and making quakes. On Mirah, it's causing waves near the shoreline. In Glacia, it's been avalanches."

Cole put down his tea. "If they keep that kind of thing up, they'll break something."

"That's their known intent. Though the world forgot their faces, we remember their deeds." Ferris rubbed at her forehead. "The Militia has been sent to confront them and to try and get rid of them, but we can't be sure it will work. Nine years ago, it took the Kin and the Dragons to get rid of the majority of the Elite."

"And the Chronicles," Cole murmured.

"Well, of course them! And they're better people than I ever will be," Alline said, "to willingly save the people trying to destroy them. I sincerely hope they are living happily now on the Isle of Dragons."

"Kin still keep in touch with them," Cole offered. "I can tell you that last I heard, they were very happy." There was more to the tale, but he wasn't going to speak of it right then. It was a closely held secret.

"We'll take each day as it comes." C.J. straightened from where he had been leaning against the wall. "I'm heading for home now." Suiting action to words, he headed out the back of the restaurant.

The following morning, he returned to town. He met up with Cole halfway and they headed together toward the Healing Shelter. It had once been owned by a Kin, but he had been murdered by the Militia because he had kept Tariah's origins a secret. It had taken a few years for the truth to come out, but now that it had, the Militia had to step lightly in town. Those who remembered had still not forgiven.

The Shelter was located among the main street through the center of town. A large white water drop was on a sign hanging outside the door. It had never been especially cheerful before, but now it seemed much livelier. The outside had gotten a fresh white color and the windows in the front were filled with desert flowers.

The steps were swept meticulously clean and a comfortable set of chairs sat outside the open doors. Cole started to climb the steps but stopped to let a little girl go past. She had come running out the door at top speeds. "Thanks, Doctor!" she shouted back over her shoulder. "Hi Cole! Hi C.J.!"

As she disappeared into the distance, the two males exchanged a smile before continuing up the steps and into the Shelter. "Anyone home?" C.J. asked.

"If you're not bleeding, please give me a moment."

"I *really* like her," Cole murmured.

After a few moments, Kappa walked out of the back room, wiping her hands on a towel. "My apologies, boys." She sighed fondly. "Magi should not learn lightning until they're ten. Five-year-olds frighten me."

Cole leaned on the counter with a smile. "You seem to be fitting in just fine."

Something in his blue eyes made her heart flutter but she ignored it. "Everyone has been very welcoming. It's not hard to be equally accepting in return. Now, then. C.J." She went over to a cabinet and began to sort through the medicines and herbs that were inside. "Normally I'd give these herbs to someone with an allergy, but they ought to have a similar effect."

"They won't turn my skin blue, will they?"

"Blue?" She blinked, then hid a smile. "No, they won't, I promise. You might be a little more sensitive to the sun though, so take care not to get a burn." She put the herbs in a bowl and began to expertly grind them into a fine powder. "I'll make it into a lotion you can rub into your skin. It's more effective than eating them. And anyway, they might make your stomach upset."

"I've eaten Cole's cooking and survived."

When Cole didn't say anything, Kappa lifted a brow. "No witty comeback?"

"I can't argue with the truth," was the dry response. "If they really want to get rid of the Elite, they should feed them my attempt at sweetbread. It's probably more lethal than a fireball from a Master Fire Magi."

She bit her lip to hide a smile. Without another word, she finished grinding the herbs. She then added a liquid serum from some desert flowers to make it into a spreadable condition. "The only side effect other than the sensitivity to the sun will be that you might smell like flowers."

"I'm a Soil Magi," C.J. pointed out. "I frequently smell like anything that has to do with growth, and flowers often fall out of my hair. Spring is the worst. The findral keep trying to chew on my flowery hair."

"That's why it's so short," Cole offered. "We couldn't get the findral away fast enough."

"Are you sure you're not brothers?"

The males grinned at each other. "Well, in a way we are," C.J. admitted. "We've been best friends ever since I was twelve. No one knows me as well as Cole does. Actually, I've never been comfortable around anyone but Cole, so that's part of it as well." Honesty made him admit, "I'm fairly comfortable around you as well."

She started to ask if that meant he would write her a letter someday, but she saw Cole watching her. Something in his eyes made the words go away. Averting her gaze from his oddly piercing blue one, she said instead, "Well, if you'd like another friend, I wouldn't mind. I've never had that many friends either."

"You do seem fairly strong for a Magi," Cole noted. "You're probably a little more sensitive yourself."

She looked at him quickly. "I always forget that Kin can sense the power in other people. But you're right." She poured the medicine into a jar and sealed the lid tightly. When she was sure it wouldn't leak, she handed it to C.J. "One use in the morning should make the rest of the day better. If you find yourself waking because of the itching, use it before you go to bed."

"Yes'm." He thought for a few moments and then made his decision. "Would you like to come see where Cole and I weave? We work together sometimes and he uses my workroom. I'm supposed to make a tapestry for someone in Carnelian and it needs five different colors. It might be interesting to you."

"*Five* colors? Very interesting indeed." She smiled. "I'll even bring lunch with me, how's that?" Her smile turned into a laughing grin. "I promise it's far less lethal than anything that Cole might produce."

"Sweetbread?" Cole asked hopefully, his ears perking up.

Knowing Kin and their notorious sweet tooth, she sighed fondly. "Yes, including sweetbread. I might even bring some pudding to go with it. But you have to share!" she scolded Cole as he and C.J. headed for the door.

Cole paused in the doorway as C.J. went down the steps to the street. Softly, his eyes warm, he said, "It's the only thing I'll share, Kappa. C.J. won't notice you, no matter how you might hope. When you accept that, my shoulder will be there for you to cry on."

She felt as if she wasn't breathing as he went down the steps toward the street. Why was she so breathless? Because a handsome Kin was flirting with her? She was thirty-two. She had been flirted with before. She'd had lovers before. She couldn't afford to be distracted by Cole when it was C.J. she needed. She couldn't afford to get her heart involved else she would never have her revenge on the Magi.

But why did it hurt so much?

Chapter Eight

The next morning, Kappa headed out of town and across the dunes to where she had been assured that C.J. lived. To her puzzlement, she didn't see any buildings or structures at all. There was nothing, as far as her eyes could see, that even remotely looked like a house. And more specifically, how would anything survive? There were cliffs nearby, though. Maybe he had dug out a home there.

"What's a pretty Magi like you doing lost in the desert?"

She stifled a yelp and a jump as she whirled around. Cole just grinned at her and her shoulders relaxed. "That was not very nice!" she scolded. "I thought Kin were supposed to be gentle and kind."

"Oh, we are." Power welled up around him and flowed across the ground to climb up her body. It focused near her ear and became a lovely desert flower the same color as her eyes. "Is that sufficiently gentle?"

Ignoring the smile he was giving her as hard as she was ignoring her rapid heartbeat, she found a breezy smile. "Indeed. Now be a gentleman and tell me where I'm going. I think I'm lost."

"Actually, you're not. You're standing on his roof."

"His roof?"

The dune lifted under her feet and sent her tumbling forwards. She landed safely in Cole's arms and stared wide-eyed as the dune lifted to reveal a cave. C.J. peeked out of the opening, laughter in his black eyes. "Did someone knock?"

"You two are *horrible*." She straightened and refused to be charmed by either of them. She held up the basket she carried. "That's a fine way to treat someone who came bearing gifts." She reached in the basket to find the sweetbread but it didn't come to hand. Puzzled, she peeked inside. "Where did the sweetbread go?"

"Ahem."

She turned and her eyes went wide as she saw Cole holding the loaf. "How did you do that?"

"I'm good with my hands." He handed her the loaf and then headed down into the cave with a merry whistle.

She wasted no time in following him and watched in fascination as the dune was put back in place. You could hardly tell that it was a cavern under the land. The walls were covered with sturdy wooden planks and the floor had thick woven rugs. The ceiling was more wooden planks, and lanterns hung on all the walls. Except for the absence of windows, it felt like any other home. "This is incredible."

"It gives me as much quiet as I want. Only people who know where my dune is can find it. And even better, they can't get in unless they have Soil power *and* I let them." C.J. poured a glass of tea and offered it to Kappa. "It's not big, though. The main room where we are, my bedroom, a washroom, and my workroom. I never bothered with a kitchen. My mom is driven to feed me."

"She's driven to feed everyone," was Cole's dry opinion.

"That too." He headed to the workroom. "Over here."

Kappa followed him curiously. She had never been in a weaver's workroom before. It looked like a normal room with a couple of tables covered in bags of sand. The predominant object, however, was a large wooden frame in the center of the room. "What's this for?" she asked.

"It's the frame that holds whatever I'm working on. For clothing, I don't need a frame. But for banners and the like where I need to see the entire piece at once, I use this." He grabbed a bag of sand and dropped it on the floor near the base of the frame. In the back of his mind, he could already see what he wanted.

Cole tugged Kappa back a step and offered her a chair. Fascinated, she watched as C.J. began gathering the sand with his power and forming it into threads and cloth. Under his skillful hands, the tapestry began to take form. It was a sea of color formed to depict a sunset on the ocean. The colors were so vivid that she half thought the imagery was real.

When he finished the first section, he put a temporary seam on the frayed edges. "Well?" he asked. "What do you think so far?"

"You're showing off."

"Am not."

Kappa shook her head. "It doesn't look like he's showing off at all. It's really beautiful, C.J." She got to her feet, beginning to feel the first stirrings of unease. What right did she have to destroy someone who made such beauty? "Let's have some food."

They all sat down in the main room and divided up the food. Kappa had indeed brought pudding, and Cole was more than happy to take a large portion. Much to her surprise, Kappa found herself enjoying the visit immensely. Cole and C.J.'s verbal banter kept her laughing, and she was oddly touched when they listened to her talk of living in Prismatic for a while.

"Why become a doctor?" C.J. asked curiously.

"It was a decision I made about nine years ago. I just . . . felt driven to heal people. My Air powers are best applied to healing arts, so it seemed logical. Until that point, I'd never really been sure where I belonged."

"I know how that feels," C.J. said softly. "It's hard to fit in when you not only *are* different but you *feel* different." He smiled. "But you can visit with us any time, Kappa. Just ask Cole to bring you for a visit."

"Or you can visit me at my home in town." Cole's smile was warm in a way that meant she was welcome in any way at any time. "I wouldn't mind."

The message went over C.J.'s head if the look on his face was any clue. For that, Kappa was glad he was still not an adult. "Maybe I'll visit you both," she made sure to the stress the 'both' part, "or you can come visit me. I've never really had that many friends."

"Well, we'll change that." C.J. bumped her foot with his. "You're a good person, Kappa."

She abruptly got to her feet. "I need to be going."

"I'll escort you back," Cole offered. He also stood and opened the dune above their heads. He held it long enough for her to scramble out and then followed her and closed it behind him. She moved very quickly across the dunes, but so did he. He shortly caught up. "That combination of childhood astuteness and not-yet-an-adult maturity is vexing, isn't it?"

She crossed her arms tightly. "Neither of you know anything about me. You probably shouldn't even want to be my friend."

He caught her arm and swung her around. Her eyes were instantly drawn to the gold tattoos on his strong arms. They glimmered in the sun, oddly beautiful, and the strength in his body was a lure. If she wanted, he would hold her. She hadn't been held in years.

"I know enough," he said softly, "to know that C.J. is right. You're a good person. Maybe it's time you learned that too." He ran his fingers through her hair tenderly and then released her entirely. "You'll fall a little in love with him. It can't be helped. I'm a little in love with him too. But he'll never belong to you, and you'll never belong to him."

"No one's ever wanted me to belong to them."

He smiled a little whimsically. "I wasn't there." He turned her around and nudged her toward the city in the distance. "Go home. We'll come visit tomorrow. Have you been to the oasis inside the town?"

"No, I haven't had time."

"Make time." With that, he turned and headed back toward the dune where C.J. lived.

C.J. went to town by himself the next morning. He was going to be meeting Cole and Kappa at the central oasis. The oasis had been built by Soil and Water Magi to provide a place where the people of the city could escape the harsh desert and enjoy lush green scenery. The oasis was half a mile long and half a mile wide, big enough for a lake and for lots of trees. Kin Faeries who flew over it claimed it looked like a tiny blue and green dot in a sea of brown.

He got to the lake area first and sat down on one of the stone benches. The lotion was working wonders, and his skin didn't seem to be itching quite as badly. He also wasn't getting a sunburn; he seemed to be weathering the side effects just fine. He sensed Kappa before he saw her and smiled as he turned. "Good morning."

"Good morning." Relieved that he was alone, she walked over and sat down beside him. "Out of curiosity, what brought you to Symphony? Considering the problems that the city has had, it seems strange that anyone would voluntarily move here during the worst of it."

"By the time we arrived, it was centered mostly in town. And I've always lived in the desert, though for a while I and my parents lived in a very small town on Prismatic. Mom had a falling out with her family, and we moved here. I've just really liked it here so I haven't bothered to leave. I probably never will. Well, I might go to Kindred someday. Cole is nagging me to visit with him one year."

"The out of control power didn't frighten you when you got here?"

He tilted his head. "Oddly, it didn't. Because my power is strong, I thought I might be able to help a little bit. I tried to grow something directly in the sand, you know, giving back when something had been taken away. It worked." He pointed to where a large cactus was in full bloom. "That's what I planted."

"My goodness." Her eyes widened. "It's huge!" She walked over to it and discovered it stood bigger than she was tall. "I've never seen a cactus get this tall!"

"It was an accident. Every time the land had an aftershock, I added more power." He smiled sheepishly. "By the time the shocks stopped, my cactus was a little, erm, distinctive. We built the oasis around it."

"You were twelve," she murmured. Most twelve-year-olds weren't even in first puberty yet. "You must have started first puberty early."

"I did. I'd started it about a month earlier to our move. I was trying to deal with my Soil powers and my Wood ones at the same time. It was actually helpful to me too. I didn't have to worry about excess power." He winced. "I only once put a tree through the roof of our house."

She walked over and sat down next to him. Conspiratorially, she said, "I set my neighbor's barn on fire when I was learning my Thunder powers. It didn't help my cause any that I happened to be in the middle of the curiosity phase of second puberty and *really* liked my neighbor's son."

"How did that end?"

She grinned. "Well, he was a Fire Magi. He accidentally filled his house with smoke and had to ask me to help clear it. We were even at that point. He kissed me before the wind was fully gone." With a fond sigh for the memory, she said, "You never forget your first kiss." She quirked a brow as he shrugged at her. "You're not even at the curiosity for a kiss yet?"

"Well, I think I am, but I haven't met anyone I wanted *to* kiss. I'll sit and think about what kissing someone must be like, but at the same time, not have anyone I'm inclined to kiss. It's really frustrating."

"Frustration is another name for second puberty," she countered dryly, warmed by his honesty. "Wait until you get to the exploration phase. It's *murder* on hormones. Both yours and your lover's." She lightly put a hand on his. "I wouldn't mind being your first kiss," she offered.

"I don't know if I'm attracted to you," he admitted.

"The offer stands if you decide you are." She knew better than to push things and looked around instead. "Where is Cole, anyway? I half expected him to just appear from out of thin air. He startled me something fierce yesterday."

"You called?" There was a swirl of gold light, and Cole appeared right in front of them.

C.J. grabbed Kappa before she could fall off the bench. Desperately trying not to laugh, he helped her sit back up. "Actually, Kin can travel via land current, so they are invisible to the average eyesight until they stop moving."

"And we can move *really* fast." Cole pointedly sat down on the bench next to Kappa. "Good morning. Sleep well?"

Cursing the faint heat she could feel in her cheeks, she found her bravado and looked him dead in the eye. "I did, thank you." She pointedly turned back to C.J. "How did you meet Cole?"

"Mom fed him and we haven't gotten rid of him since." He grinned a little as Cole flicked his ears at him. "Truthfully, I got lost in the desert. He was coming back from the northern port and found me. By the time we got back to Symphony, we were friends. We just seemed to hit it off."

"It's clear there's a special bond there," she agreed. She got to her feet. "I need to go back to my Shelter now. I'll see you both later. Maybe we can spend more time together. This is a nice place to take a break."

"Anytime." As she disappeared out of the oasis, he said to Cole, "I don't want to be in the middle."

"I don't think it can be avoided," Cole admitted. "She's . . . conflicted."

"Why?"

"Reasons you wouldn't understand." He stood. "Don't worry about my feelings. I know you won't suddenly fall for her." Hands linked behind his back, he headed out of the oasis as well.

Over the next few days, the town got used to seeing Kappa with Cole and C.J. They spent time in the oasis together when Kappa was taking a break, or the males would visit her at the Healing Shelter. Other times she visited them at C.J.'s place, or even Cole's home. No one could even be sure which of the two males Kappa liked more. The only thing the people were sure of was that Cole was falling for Kappa and C.J. wasn't.

Even Kappa didn't know which male she was drawn to more. She was attracted to Cole, *badly*, and her heart ached around him. At the same time, she really cared for C.J. as well. She was attracted to him, but it was a gentle attraction. She couldn't even sort out her own feelings. It felt like second puberty all over again and it was disheartening.

She was goofing off and slacking off. She wasn't even doing what she was supposed to be doing. Her job was to find the reason why Symphony was balanced, and she had. The part where she was supposed to remove the balance was what held her up. How did you bring yourself to kill someone you loved?

A knock on the door jarred her out of her thoughts and she got to her feet. "Coming!" As she entered into the front area, she went very still. The man standing inside the doorway was very familiar, and at that moment, very unwelcome. "Hello, Delta."

When C.J. got to the Healing Shelter a few minutes later, he had to move aside as an older man went down the steps. "Pardon me," he said politely. "Is Kappa in?"

"Yes."

A little puzzled at the abrupt answer—and the fact that the man dressed like someone from a forest while in the middle of a desert—he went up the stairs and into the Shelter. "Hey, Kappa!" he started to say cheerfully. He broke off as he saw her sitting and staring out the window. His smile faded and he hurried to her side. "Are you okay? Did he hurt you?"

"No." She closed her eyes. "He just told me some . . . unpleasant truths." At a touch, she looked down in surprise to see his hand covering hers. "Don't be nice to me."

"Why not?"

"I don't deserve it." Her smile turned a little crooked. "I'm a little in love with you, C.J., but I'm doomed to hurt you. Pathetic, isn't it?"

He stood quickly. "That's ridiculous!" he said sharply. "You always have a choice! And anyway, I don't think you care for me the way you care for Cole!" Her eyes swung toward him and he raked a hand through his hair. "I'm not *that* naïve! And I refuse to get in the middle of this!" He swung toward the door. "I'm getting Cole. We're going to all have a talk. I'm not watching you two suffer when it's just you both being stupid!"

As the door slammed behind him, she winced. Her gentle and innocent Master Magi wasn't always so gentle, and he certainly wasn't entirely innocent. He was definitely further in second puberty than they all thought. Hating herself for what she had to do, she got to her feet to go into her room. She would change clothes, and then she would follow him. The sooner it was done, the better.

Cole wasn't at his home so C.J. headed toward his own. If Cole wasn't at one location, then he was assuredly at the other. And, sure enough, halfway between town and his dune, he saw Cole walking through the sand. He hurried to catch up. "Cole!"

Cole stopped and turned around with a smile. "Hey, C.J." The smile faded as he saw the seriousness of his friend's face. "What's wrong?"

"Well, for starters, some forest dweller just upset Kappa." He caught Cole's arm to keep him from running off. "Hang on, there's more." He let out a quick breath. "Kappa said she's a little in love with me."

"As she should be. I knew she would be."

"That's not the point!" He released Cole's arm and walked a step away. "She said she was doomed to hurt me! What is wrong with her? She was fine until that mainlander showed up! And you!" He turned and poked Cole in the chest. "You've clearly been hiding something from me! You always say that you *know* things are going to happen or won't happen. How do you know these things? I'm not saying I think I'll fall in love with her, but how can you be sure I won't? I don't want to hurt you two!"

Cole closed his eyes. "Your destiny is different, C.J." His eyes opened, and they were intense and nearly grief-stricken. "You're a Chronicle."

Silence fell. C.J. shook his head a little as he backed up a step. "Th-that's impossible! I don't have any lines!"

"That we can see. If my hunch is right, they're hidden right now. That's why your power is causing your skin to itch badly. And that's why you seemed to be 'stuck' in second phase of second puberty. Why do you think you calmed the land when you got here? What was taken by a Chronicle was returned by one. Your power is *not* Magi in origin. I always suspected, but I was sure when I saw your reaction to being told about Furies."

The painful longing welled up again and this time it made utter sense. Barely breathing, he lifted his hands and stared at them as if they belonged to a stranger. "But how is any of this possible? Who could have locked my power?"

"Nine years ago," came Kappa's voice behind them, "there was a man named Morgan Chronis living in Prismatic. He is a Chronicle. He had four Chronicle children hiding in secret. He sent them away and we've been hunting them ever since."

Both males turned and C.J. went very still as he saw that Kappa wore the long white cloak with the black chalice and dagger that meant she was a member of the Black Magi Elite. How he knew what the cloak stood for, he couldn't say, but he was utterly sure. He was also not very happy, or surprised, to recognize the forest dweller standing beside her in the same cloak.

"Well done, Kappa," the man said. "I commend you for finding one of the Chronicle children."

Kappa said nothing. Cole, pointedly, stepped in front of C.J. "And who are you?" he asked.

"Delta." He gave a tight smile. "We are from the Elite, Kin. And if you value your ears, you'll leave now. This matter does not concern you."

"I'm afraid it does." Something powerful swirled through Cole's eyes. "You're threatening my friend, and you seem to be hurting someone else I care for." His eyes met Kappa's startled gaze. "Why do you stay there?"

She said nothing. What could she say? She didn't have an answer for him. All the things she had thought she knew were completely false. It broke her heart. She didn't want C.J. to be a Chronicle. She wanted even less for him to be a Master Magi and need to be killed. "I . . ."

"Don't be swayed," Delta ordered her. A little madness gleamed in his eyes as he slowly advanced toward the males. "If you won't leave, Kin, then you'll just die here. I'm sure your death will disrupt the land as nicely as your friend's would have. As for him, we have other needs for him."

The land began to tremble softly. Eyes narrowed, C.J. said, "Maybe you should ask me if I'm interested." He shot a look at Kappa. "I thought better of you than this." She flinched and he began to gather his power. "I'm not going anywhere with the Elite."

Pulsing white light surrounded Cole's hands, burning as brightly as the sun. "If that's his wish, then I'll help him."

Delta sighed. "Must you make things so difficult?" Fire began to gather around his hand. "I'm a Master Fire Magi, Kin. You won't find this battle easy. Kappa, you subdue the Chronicle." She said nothing and he looked at her sharply. He turned away in disgust. "You would have affection for these two. Very well. I'll kill the Kin first and that should clear your mind."

C.J. stepped up beside Cole. "You're not touching him."

The land under Delta cracked and surged upward, flinging him high in the air. He twisted around to get his feet under himself and began shooting fireballs at C.J. and Cole. They ducked and dove two different directions. When Cole rolled to his feet, he threw a ball of light directly at Delta. Vines covered in thorns shot out of the ground and threatened a painful landing for Delta.

He barely managed to dodge the light and then surrounded himself with fire as he landed. It burned away the vines. He drew a dagger and ran directly at Cole, but the land rocked violently and tossed him back the way he had come. As he landed, he had to roll swiftly across the sand to avoid the vines shooting up from the land.

As the fight began to progress, Kappa realized that the land was shaking and quivering in ways that had nothing to do with the quakes that C.J. used. She knelt and touched the sand and felt the violent churning under the surface. Symphony was balanced, but it was still recovering. Her head jerked up. "Cole! C.J.! Don't use quakes!"

"You little . . . !" Delta swung around and shot a fireball directly at her. "You can die with them!"

At the last second, Cole appeared in front of her and shot a ball of light at the fireball. The two met and exploded together and tore out a large crater. The land went mad. Rolling waves of sand lifted and swelled like the ocean. They rippled as far as the city, and from even that far they could hear the people beginning to scream in terror.

Cole grabbed Kappa's wrist and pulled her along behind him as he began running across the sand. "C.J.!"

C.J. wasted no time in following. Putting as much space between them and the city as possible was critical. He didn't bother to look back over his shoulder. He knew Delta was following them.

When they were at least a mile out from the city, they stopped running to catch their breath. Cole released Kappa and she sank down onto her knees. She was trembling as hard as the land. "What is going on in your head?" he almost shouted. He knelt and gave her a shake.

"You wouldn't understand." She shook her head and her hair flew. "A few years ago . . . I had nothing to live for. The Magi . . . they destroyed my life. Joining the Elite was all I could do. I needed to do something!"

"That wasn't the thing to do!" C.J. snapped at her.

Cole caught Kappa's face in his hands. "You're not alone! Not now."

Tears burned her eyes. "You're not the one I'm supposed to love. You're breaking my heart."

Before Cole could respond to that, he sensed a familiar power. His head lifted sharply and he saw Delta approaching with fire coalescing around his body in a deadly inferno. At the last moment, Cole and Kappa disappeared from where they were kneeling. A fireball shattered the land at their location and they reappeared closer to C.J.

Laughing a little maniacally, Delta began shooting fireball after fireball at them. "You can all die! It doesn't matter anymore!"

A solid wall of wood appeared and the fireballs splashed off harmlessly. Before Cole could say anything, the wall splintered and became wicked shrapnel that fired directly at Delta. C.J. ran toward the older man and Soil power swirled around his body.

The rioting land was spreading and had reached them again. Geysers of elements shot up through the surface. Delta had to dodge. Cole made a protective shield of light around him and Kappa. C.J. either didn't notice or didn't care, and it was evidenced when a geyser broke under his feet and fired raw elemental power directly into his body. He absorbed it instantly.

Kappa's eyes went wide. "I thought that was a myth!"

"That Chronicles can absorb any power excess?" Cole shook his head. "The Kin call it the reason for their existence."

Delta was so startled by the sight of C.J. absorbing the blast that he didn't know the Chronicle was on him until too late. C.J.'s fist connected with his chin and sent him flying. He had to hurriedly get to his feet to avoid another geyser and shot rapid-fire balls of flames at his enemy. C.J. blocked but ended up singed. Almost as if something had snapped, he lifted the land as high as he was tall and hurled the wave at Delta.

Cole's eyes fixed on the city in the far distance. He could see an oddly familiar shadow approaching it on the horizon. "I'm going to get help," he told Kappa. "C.J. can't do this alone." His eyes glittered as he looked at her. "If you're not here when I return, I'll look for you until I find you."

Before she could respond, he had disappeared. Shivering despite the heat, she looked at the bloody war that was being fought. Delta was outmatched. C.J. was stronger than one would expect for an unawakened Chronicle. He was still at a disadvantage though. His powers hadn't been intended for battle and Delta's were. Kappa knew she could jump in the fight on C.J.'s side and give him an advantage.

She just didn't know if she dared risk it.

Chapter Nine

Dahlia Stalker was over four hundred years old. She had been friends with Jazz Eaglewind since they were both hatched. When Jazz had found her Chronicle, Dahlia had been happier than anyone else. Behind her happiness, however, she had hidden a great secret. Everyone knew Dahlia was a Fury; it wasn't something one could simply ignore. No one had known, however, that she had felt her Chronicle's birth ten years prior.

Now, nine years later, she still felt him.

That feeling, that longing and aching in her heart, told her he was alive. In knowing he was alive, she was fairly sure he was one of Morgan's hidden Chronicle children. For nine years she had been looking, crossing from city to city. Examining every face, bumping shoulders with every Magi. Looking for that one person that would complete her.

She had always been a loner. It wasn't as painful for her as it was for the other Furies searching the world. They were caught between the hunger for their lover and the longing for home. She called the Isle of Dragons home, but she didn't entirely miss it. Even her own kind didn't realize how solitary she felt inside.

She laughed, she smiled, and she spent time with the others. But inside . . . she felt alone. She was honestly surprised no one had realized sooner just how alone. She was well past second puberty, but she had never taken a lover.

Never.

Though she had gone through the curiosity and the exploration and the readiness to become an adult, she had never found someone she was fully comfortable enough with to have as her lover. Dragons had offered, and so had Magi. In fact, a few Kin had offered. She had turned them all down. Her heart had been unmoved by them. If her heart wasn't moved, why should her body be?

As she stood in the southern port on the land of Choral, she was aware of the interested gazes of Magi as they went past. It was to be expected. She was unusually lovely and surprisingly tall with her curvy six-one height and her knee length blonde hair. Her hair was streaked with stark white, courtesy of her Dragon blood, and her eyes were the creamy color of milk soaked sweetbread (a delicacy unto itself).

She had to suppose that another reason she was different was that she had never truly hated the Magi. Oh, she disliked many of them intently, and she had met a few she wouldn't have minded eating for a snack, but as a general rule . . . she didn't mind them that much.

She had seen their mindset change over the last nine years. The new Magi king was more open-minded and had expressed a desire for change. He was working with the land of Kindred, with both Elders of the Kin, to more firmly cement the treaty. He wanted to offer them some additional land on islands the Magi didn't use to help them spread and grow.

She didn't know where he stood on the issue of Chronicles, though. He hadn't changed the law, but he didn't seem to be *enforcing* it either. By her reckoning, if the Elite were gone, perhaps the law would change. The general feeling was that killing Chronicles kept them out of Elite hands. Stupid, perhaps, but far easier to deal with than the horror and hate.

She was startled out of her thoughts when she saw a little girl trying to peer onto the counter where a vendor sold candy. She smiled and knelt next to her. "Hi."

The girl looked at her in surprise but didn't initially see anything unusual about the pretty lady with cream-colored eyes. She was wearing the same bikini and cloth skirt that most older females wore, and she was wearing sturdy dune-walking boots. The girl finally spotted the streaks in her hair and felt the tickle of strong power. Delight filled her face. "You're a Dragon!"

"Mm." Dahlia inclined her head at the table. "You want to see the sweets?" When the girl nodded, Dahlia picked her up so she could look. She couldn't help but be warmed by the way the girl's eyes went wide with wonder. She loved children of all races. "Which is your favorite?"

"That one!" The girl pointed to a round candy covered in spots. "Cactear bites!"

Holding the girl with one arm, Dahlia grabbed a few coins from the bag on her hip and handed it to the vendor. She then plucked up the bite and handed it to the girl. "My treat." She set the girl down gently. "Now don't ruin your dinner."

A woman came hurrying through the crowd and skidded to a stop near the girl. Wariness filled her eyes as she pulled her daughter close. "Was she bothering you?"

"Not at all. I was just being indulgent." Dahlia smiled. "I don't eat children. They get stuck in my teeth."

The girl giggled and the woman's shoulders relaxed. "I apologize for my wariness," she offered. "Dragons and Magi aren't known to be that friendly to one another." She made the Magi sign of respect. "If your race is all like you, perhaps we might find peace."

"Only if yours is like you," Dahlia agreed with a graceful bow. It was the Dragon sign of respect. "Warm winds, as we say."

The woman smiled. "Always in the desert."

Appreciating the humor, Dahlia waved to the little girl and walked away. It was time to leave the city. She had met every person and seen every child. There were no Chronicles there, neither child nor adult. Her Chronicle wasn't there.

She went half a mile beyond the city before turning into her Dragon form. As a Dragon, she was a slightly taller than average twenty-one feet in length, and her scales were cream and white. Ironic though it was, in Magi form she was considered lovely, and in Dragon, she was often termed cute. She had no idea where the distinction occurred. She supposed it was a cultural thing.

She sensed the trouble long before she reached Symphony. She could see the waves of the land rolling back and forth. Startled, she stopped in mid-air a mile out of the city. She had thought the land was said to be calm now. Alarmed, she hurried faster toward the city where she could hear the rising panic.

Normally Dragons were not allowed to fly directly over or near towns because that too could cause ripples in the power under the land. Since the land was not likely to notice her presence right then, she flew directly over the city and landed on the northern side. A particularly vicious wave of land was rolling directly at her, and she knew it might destroy the city.

Her wings arched and Air power swirled around her. It connected with the wave of land and sent it back the way it had come. Other waves rolled into her barrier and then bounced back away. After a moment, the shaking stilled in the area. She could still see waves in the distance, but they weren't reaching the city.

She turned and looked at the city just as several people on shaking legs walked forward. "Is everyone all right?" she asked. Her voice was no different from her Magi one, but it carried a stronger echo of power.

"We are," one woman managed to say. "We'll have to check to be sure. You . . . you may well have saved all our lives." She drew a long breath. "We owe you."

She shook her head. "No, you don't." Her eyes moved to the distance where she could see a battle being raged. "Have you been dealing with the Elite?"

"No . . . not that we know of," a man spoke up. His eyes were on the horizon as well. He could just faintly see the lights and sparks.

"Where's my son?" Ferris pushed her way through the crowd gathering. "Where's C.J.?"

Something about the name sounded very familiar to Dahlia and she frowned. "Is he missing?"

"He lives in a dune home outside of town." Ferris went up to Dahlia without fear and touched her leg pleadingly. "Please! Go make sure the waves didn't hurt him! He's a Master Soil Magi and might have ridden out the storm, but I can't be sure!"

"I'll go and check," Dahlia promised. As she turned to look at the distance, she not only saw the more distinct signs of Soil power being used, but an unusual light flare in a two-one-one pattern. A Kin was signaling her. "Everyone stay here."

Everyone backed up and she lifted into the air to fly swiftly toward the signal. When she reached it, she found a SunKin Elf waiting for her. He looked healthy enough, but he showed the signs of recent fighting. "Is something wrong?"

Cole couldn't have been more delighted to discover himself talking to a female Air Fury. "My partner is in danger!" He pointed toward the fight. "He's a Soil Chronicle and unawakened! Everyone thought he was a Master Magi though!"

Shock reverberated through her. "How old?"

"Nineteen!"

Too afraid to hope yet too afraid not to, she shot across the land in a white colored streak. It was too coincidental to be true, but it was too likely not to be. "Please," she said over and over again as she flew.

"Please!"

At the fight, C.J. was wounded. He had taken a fireball across the arm and was burned from elbow to wrist. It was also hard to breathe now that Delta was using smoke to obscure the air. Kappa had run away. C.J. didn't blame her at all, but he knew Cole would be furious.

Reaching for reserves of power he hadn't known he had, he grabbed up a handful of sand and hurled it at Delta. It formed into a thick piece of cloth that stuck to the other man's face like tar. Choking and wheezing, Delta clawed at the cloth. He couldn't see or breathe. Small boulders began to pelt his chest, and he felt the stings that meant he was being wounded.

He was at the last dredges of his power. C.J. was a Chronicle. His power was infinite, and every geyser under his feet just seemed to heal and refresh him. Finally tearing the cloth off, Delta gathered all his power for an immense fireball. "Cursed Chronicle!"

A furious roar ripped across the land and sky, and a Dragon's shadow passed directly overhead. C.J.'s power went out of control. The land broke into riotous bloom of flowers and immense trees burst hundreds of feet upward into the sky. With a surge of golden light, lines appeared across his chest, over the backs of his hands, and across the top of his feet.

Dazed and shaken by the near detonation of power inside his body, he fell to his knees amid the flowers. Dahlia landed gracefully in front of him, and her wings spread wide to make a more imposing sight. Every last one of her teeth bared as she snarled, "Get away from my Chronicle!"

Delta backed up slowly and then turned to run. Before he could take more than a step, he found himself face to face with an immense ball of light power. The heat scorched his skin. He had just enough time to meet Cole's eyes before the ball consumed him. It burned so hot and fast that in seconds there was nothing left. Only a tiny ripple in the land was all that marked his passing.

Cole lowered his hand and looked around. Kappa was nowhere in sight. He could only curse mentally as he crossed to C.J. "Are you okay?" he asked softly as he knelt next to his friend.

C.J. barely noticed. His eyes were fixed on Dahlia. He had never seen anything as magnificent or beautiful as this cream-colored Dragon. "Mine," he whispered. It was all he could say. It was all that was important. Still suffering his own internal aftershocks, his eyes closed and he fell to the sand without another sound.

Dahlia turned and went into her Magi form. Wonder filled her eyes as she knelt beside him and eased him into her arms. He was more beautiful than she had dared dream. She had known the instant she laid eyes on him that he was hers. Dormant emotions, unawakened emotions, rose to the forefront with a hunger and desire she had yearned to experience.

If there was anything more beautiful than seeing the face of a Fury who had found their destined Chronicle, Cole had never heard of it. He got to his feet and looked around for evidence of the direction Kappa had fled. "Damn her," he said softly. "Always so willingly blind."

Dahlia looked up in surprise. "Someone is missing?"

"Yes." He glanced at her. "Someone as important to me as C.J. is to you."

"C.J." She found she liked the name immensely. "What does it stand for?"

"He won't say, and he threatened his parents with bodily harm if they blabbed. You'll have to tell me what it is when you two bond." He let out a little breath. "I won't ask you to love and protect him. You cannot do anything less. But I will ask that you eventually contact me when he finishes his journey."

"You have my word," she promised softly. "And when you find your lover, please let me know." Softer, she added, "Thank you, for protecting him for me."

"C.J. and I are much alike. And he's easy to love."

As he disappeared, she returned her attention to C.J. In wonder, she brushed his hair out of his eyes. He wasn't a warrior. She had noticed that instantly when she had approached the fight. He had thrown *cloth* at his enemy. On the other hand, she *was* a warrior, and her Air power was suited for battle. She would protect him.

She tenderly put him down on the grass and backed up. She changed to her Dragon shape and picked him up with her claws as gently as she could. She didn't bother to determine the way home. It had been her guess years before that suggested Jazz and Dominic had forgotten their way home because of their Chronicle. Now she was sure of it.

As she flew into the air and began looking for a safe place for them to rest, she reflected back on the memories in her mind. She had inherited the memories of another Fury at her birth and she knew precisely the steps needed for the bonding. She already felt the drain on her majiks even as she felt C.J.'s power rising.

She flew to the east beyond the desert and to the scattered islands that dotted the ocean. They were the only remnants of other great lands. Though the Magi had not wanted to, they now had to accept that Kin were crucial to the world. They represented the land. And the Magi, too, could never be removed. They were the sea. The Dragons, infinite in power, were the sky.

One island looked like a floating oasis and she angled down that direction. There was just enough room in a small clearing for her to land. She put C.J. down and turned back to Magi form. Her senses told her there was nothing dangerous on the tiny isle, but she sent out a probe of Air power regardless. It also told her it was safe.

She walked over to a tiny spring sitting nearby and filled a flask from her hipsack with fresh water. It broke her heart to see burns on C.J.'s arm, and while she couldn't heal them, she could at least tend to them.

Her heart fluttered as she wiped away blood and dirt. Something low in her belly tightened with pure desire. Unable to resist, she ran her fingers over the supple muscles of his arm. She couldn't believe such a magnificent creature was hers. "If I had to wait to finish second puberty," she said softly, stroking his hair from his face, "then you were well worth the wait."

She curled up beside him and tugged him into her arms where he could rest. She couldn't bear to leave his side. There was nothing more comforting than the sound of his breath feathering over her skin. The rise and fall of his chest was almost hypnotic. Softly, she ran a finger over the lines on his chest. They almost looked like vines and leaves as they ran across his golden skin. Knowing it was her power that made every curl was a potent thing on her senses.

A little laugh caught in her throat. He was only nineteen. She could only pray that he was part of the way, if not all of the way, through second puberty. Things would be very interesting if he wasn't.

C.J. woke to raging pain in his body. His power was wild and out of control. He wanted to shake the land and tear it apart in quakes. He wanted to create mighty trees that stood taller than the sky. There was a presence nearby that he violently wanted to bind to him. He wanted to curl his vines around it and keep it close for all time.

A soft hand touched his cheek and the touch reverberated through to his very soul and power. He knew that touch. He knew the power curling alluringly around him. *His*. He was sure of it. He gathered his strength and forced his eyes open and found himself staring up into a lovely face he knew he would never forget until the day he died. She was . . . breathtaking. Wonder filled his eyes as he reached up to cup her cheek. "You," he breathed. "You're my Fury."

Dahlia turned her face into his hand and her eyes burned with tears. "Yes," she said softly. "I've waited for you for so long." She felt the soft swirl of his power surrounding her in a call as old as love itself, and she felt some of her nerves ease. He was, at the least, old enough to send out the signal. She softly rubbed her power against his in return and saw the faintest of pink color climb his cheeks. "Don't be embarrassed. There's nothing to be embarrassed by."

He tried to lift his other hand and pain ripped through his blood. She instantly moved closer and leaned in protectively. Her fingers kneaded almost compulsively at his chest. "We need to bond," she said huskily. "I need to feed on your power."

"Like sweetbread?"

It made her smile. "So to speak." She nuzzled at his chest softly. A soft green aura immediately lifted and covered his body, just begging for her attention. He smelled like flowers and rich summer. A time of growth and learning; a time when the world, for a moment, was utterly perfect. Half drunk, she softly brushed her lips over his skin and tasted his power. It was as thick and wonderful as it smelled.

As her lips softly trailed over his chest and up over his shoulders, he wasn't breathing. Nerves and curiosity tangled inside him. The pleasure of her touch was more like an ache and it was spreading. He wanted . . . he didn't know what he wanted. He wanted *something*. He shivered in delight as her lips found a sensitive place on his neck. His lips had begun to tingle. "What's wrong with me?"

She smiled as she nuzzled his cheek. "You're not an adult yet."

"Second phase." His eyes dipped to the lush curves barely held by a bikini top. He *really* wanted to touch her. "Potentially entering third. I never found anyone to be curious with." His eyes met hers. "Until now." The pain in his body faded rapidly to be replaced by a wholly different ache. He propped himself up on an elbow and tangled his fingers in her hair. "Forgive my curiosity."

"Forgiven." Her lashes lowered as his warm breath washed over her lips. She wanted his kiss with a vengeance she had never felt before. The first touch of his lips was almost shy. The second was teasing. She made a frustrated sound. "Tease later." Her arms wound around his neck and she fused their lips together in a way she longed to fuse the rest of their bodies.

He proved to be a quick leaner. The kiss deepened further as he willingly followed her lead. She fed on his power the entire time. It flowed from his mouth to hers with a wild and rich flavor more potent than she had thus far encountered. She was going to be addicted. She was never going to be able to look at flowers the same way again. He had ruined her entirely. And she was happier than she ever had been in her life.

She found herself sprawled against his chest when he sat up fully. Her fingers ran down his body with a possessive touch, and she simply couldn't resist gliding her hands over his back and down his butt. It was a *really* nice one. He promptly broke the kiss with an odd look on his face, and she bit her lip to hide a smile. "Should I apologize?"

He wasn't really sure which the stranger feeling was for him. That she had actually grabbed his ass or that he hadn't really minded it in the first place. "There's a lot more to things than they teach you in school."

"Some things can only be learned by trying." She nuzzled his shoulder where she could see some lingering power. Far be it for her to stop mid-meal. As the last of the power flowed into her, it seemed to ricochet back out of her body and into him. Their power swirled together, fused together, and bonded them in ways that no other being besides another Dragoon might understand.

She could see everything in his heart and mind, could see the generous and feeling heart that ached for the entire world. She could see the mischievous boy that had never truly given sway to correct behavior for an adult. She also saw something else, a close held secret that made her lips curve. She saw why he hated his name.

He could see no less fully into her. He saw the carefully guarded heart that would protect and defend her loved ones to the death. He saw a careful veneer of outgoingness hiding a shy side. He saw a love of the absurd and a hunger for someone to hold. He saw four centuries of lonely waiting for her own death, expecting that she would never be complete. And he saw something else, something that stunned him to his very depths.

She felt her cheeks slowly heating as he stared at her. Feeling suddenly shy, she looked away. "I just . . . wasn't comfortable. I don't deny being curious. And I don't deny one or two kisses getting a little interesting. But . . . even when I was with someone, I felt alone. What was the point?"

He smiled. "The same point that has likely kept me from acting on my curiosity." He ran his fingers slowly through her hair. The sensitivity of his skin seemed to be in overdrive because the soft glide of her hair over his fingers was sensual and wonderful. "If you'll help me satisfy my curiosity and my eventual exploration . . . Then I'll satisfy yours."

She almost wasn't breathing as she watched him lift a handful of her hair and rub his cheek against it. His tactile delight in everything about her was exhilarating. His power softly caressed hers not with the intent to seduce, but simply to see what would happen. His curiosity, now unleashed, seemed to make him want to catch up for lost time. "C.J.?"

"Hmm?" He ran a finger down her arm and enjoyed the feel of her skin. Delight filled him as a wave of lines followed his finger. They were identical to his and he knew they were made of his power. She was marked as his. She was also struggling for control, and he lifted his hands quickly when he felt her stifle an urge to touch him in return. Nerves made his heart trip over itself. He wasn't sure he was ready for her to return the favor. Chagrined, he looked away. "I'm sorry."

"Never be sorry, *ishke*." She looked to where her new lines went down the side of her neck and right arm. They had also appeared around her left ankle. She had been expecting their presence, though she hadn't expected to feel that wonderfully claimed. It made it hard to keep reign on the emotions inside her.

He felt their volatile presence but wasn't alarmed. He could see the three distinct emotions inside her, and he could see where her love matched his. Her desire was greater than his, but he could see the awakenings of it inside himself. The third emotion . . . it was deeper, wilder, and more powerful than the other two combined. He felt the start of it inside his heart. "What is that?"

"Our gift as Dragoons." She let out a little breath and laced their fingers together. "My name is Dahlia Stalker. I'm saying it because I don't consciously think of my name so you shouldn't pick up on it in my mind."

"C.J. Daragon." He narrowed his eyes when she smiled. "You know my full name. How'd you get that?"

"Unfortunately, *you* think about your name consciously, potentially because you hate it. Me, I find nothing wrong with it." She squeezed his hands tightly and took a deep breath. "How did you know you were a Chronicle?"

"Cole told me." He frowned. "Kappa mentioned something about a man named Morgan." Even saying it made something hurt inside. He had forgotten something. He had often felt there was something missing, but he had never really been sure what. He tried to reach for the memory and encountered a large blank space in his mind.

Dahlia's presence was instantly there and she probed at the empty place gently. She curled her mind around his and soothed his rising distress as she looked for the signs of what had been done. As an Air element, she was more adept at mind searching than other elements. She had still never seen anything like Morgan Chronis' powers. She had a deep hunch that Tariah could do nearly all of the same things, but she hadn't seen her demonstrate the power.

She found the empty place within moments. While she searched for the remaining fragments, she explained, "Morgan is a Chronicle. He and his sister were the ones who fought the Elite nine years ago. Prior to that, Morgan ran the Black Magi; the *real* Black Magi. He gathered four secret Chronicle children with the intent of nurturing them in a safe environment."

As the fragments began to gather, C.J. saw flashes in his mind. "He's short."

She smiled. "Compared to Magi men, yes. He makes up for it in personality." She had routed the fragments and was slowly gathering them toward the blank spot. "When the trouble went down, he erased—fragmented actually—the memories of the children and their parents. He then sent them away via translocation so that no one could find them."

"But what about my lines being hidden?"

"He did that too." She hesitated for a moment and then swept the pieces together.

They fused to the blank space and the memories pounded into his head. He doubled over in agony. She caught him and held tight as the memories brought searing waves of emotional pain. His tears burned her skin and broke her heart. "I'm so sorry," she whispered. "He did it because he loved you."

"I'm *killing* him!" was the fierce mutter against her breast. "He sent us away!" His breath caught with a new wave of pain. "My friends. My sisters and my brother. We were family! How did I ever forget them? I should have remembered!" He straightened and swiped an arm across his eyes. "I'm not a crybaby," he muttered.

She rose up slightly and tenderly kissed the tears away. "Never that," she said softly. "You just willingly feel more than most."

"Willingly? I have a *choice*?"

She laughed. "There's my C.J." When his arms went around her and he buried his face in her hair, she slid her arms around his waist. How she would keep someone with such a tender heart safe and happy was beyond her, but she looked forward to the challenge. She had waited her entire life for this person, and it had been worth every moment.

Her lover sniffed. "You're making me cry more," he grumbled.

"I know. I'm sorry. But these are happy tears, right?"

"Yes." He let out a little breath. "I need to find him. I want to find him. You can't find your way to the Isle, so we'll have to do something else." He eased back. "I want to go to Kindred. Please. Cole might be there. I have to see that he's okay. And I have to thank him."

"He won't be there," she disagreed. "He went to follow Kappa and you can bet she won't go there herself." Half to herself, she added, "There was something oddly familiar about her. I can't put my finger on it. But that's probably because she's a member of the Elite. I was there at the last battle, and my memories were tampered with too."

"I don't see any blank places in your mind, though."

"That's what has everyone confused. Our memories weren't removed unnaturally." She looked up toward the sky where the sun was distinctly setting. Twilight was coming in and she could already see two of the four moons in the sky. "We ought to camp here tonight and set for Kindred tomorrow."

"Will Symphony be all right if I leave?" Sadness filled his face. "What about my parents?"

"We can ask a Kin to deliver a message to them," she promised. "As for Symphony, I don't know. I was able to calm the land, so it might be all right. But there's no way of knowing for sure. We can find that out on Kindred as well."

"Okay." He looked down at his clothes and saw that they were muddy and torn. He looked longingly at the spring. It was just big enough to swim in. The only thing that kept him in place was an unexpected shyness at the idea of taking his clothes off around Dahlia.

"Why?" She smiled slowly. "I can already see a fair amount of your body, and it's an amount well worth seeing." She tugged him up to his feet. "Let's go. Clothes off, *ishke*. You're just feeling self-conscious because you're attracted to me. And I'd like to point out that even though I've never had a lover, I've seen many naked men in my long life. I can be fair."

He grabbed for his courage and removed his vest and boots. He would dissolve them back to sand and recreate them once he was clean. It took all of his bravado, but he also removed his pants and stood naked. It took a lot of willpower not to cover himself with his hands; his body was making it *very* obvious that the physical signals of desire were going through *just* fine.

Her eyes slowly widened as she stared at him, and she hastily put her hands behind her back before she gave in to an urge to start petting him from head to heels. He somehow seemed even more beautiful with the evidence of his desire for her surrounded by his perfect strength. It made her realize just how much of a woman she was, and just how perfectly they were made to be one. She closed her eyes to remove temptation from sight. "Spring. For the moons' sake, get in the spring before I scare you to death."

He could feel her emotions. He wasted no time in getting into the spring. He didn't feel embarrassed though. Not anymore. Feeling the hot caress of her emotions had removed all self-consciousness. How could he be embarrassed when he knew precisely how his Fury felt about him? Once more at ease, he tilted his head. "Can I watch you undress?"

She really wished his curiosity was stemming from pure attraction. Sadly, it wasn't. Oh, there was attraction there, but she knew it wasn't wholly focused directly on her. Not yet at the least. If it was, he wouldn't have asked. He was the type to have taken her clothes off for her.

He grinned a little. "Eventually I will."

She sighed, then laughed. She really hoped his mischievous side never went away. With only a little hesitation, she untied the cloth around her hips. She removed her shoes and then swiftly removed her bikini as well. Naked except for her exceptionally long hair, she propped her hands on her hips. "Well?"

His eyes studied her in fascination. "You're a lot curvier than Magi females. I like it."

"Thank you." She walked over and sat on the edge of the spring. His enjoyment of her body had removed her nerves. She was glad; she liked the feel of air on her skin without clothes to impede her. "I'd hate for you to dislike it. I can't change it."

"Why would you want to?"

Bemused, she explained, "In my Dragon form, I'm very rounded and curved too. But to the Dragons, that makes me really cute instead of pretty. My friend Jazz is really curvy too, but somehow she's beautiful. I don't know how she does it. It's vexing."

His eyes met hers. "I saw you in Dragon form. I thought you were beautiful." He felt her surprise and tugged her into the spring with him. "Sorry, but cute isn't a word that comes to mind when I'm around you."

Her smile spread across her face and came from the very depths of her soul. She had never been happier in her life. "If it ever does, we'll ask Morgan to erase it."

"Deal." No less happy, he hugged her fiercely and spun her around in the water. He was worried about Cole, and Kappa, and he was definitely worried about his missing childhood friends. But right then, it didn't matter that much. Having his Fury made everything right in the world.

He could only hope for his friends to experience the same. Nothing would be better.

Chapter Ten

On the world of Lucksphere, there was only one land mass that had ice and snow: Glacia, the land to the far north. Despite its place on the world, it was also considered the far south since ships could not actually sail north from Prismatic to reach the port. Natural storms barred the way between the two lands with such fury that none could pass. Ships wanting to go to Prismatic had to take a much longer route by sailing around Glacia's land mass.

There was a town to the far south—Stalagmite—and a town to the far north. Partway between the two was a town on the western shore called Arctica. A range of mountains wrapped around the back of the city and cut it off from the fiercest central storms.

Across the face of the continent were dozens of tiny farms. As a rule, Glacia was very spread out. The people liked it that way. There had once been a capital city called Bergia, but it had been the site of the war nine years before and had not yet recovered. The people were scattered across the land for the time being and the city leader who oversaw Glacia as a whole lived in Stalagmite.

Summers were always cold on Glacia. The only thing that made them different from winters was that there were no storms. At least, that had been the norm. For the last few months, avalanches had been occurring in the mountains near Arctica. It had been assumed at first that they were the byproduct of a still settling land, but now people were surer that it was deliberate.

The Black Magi Elite had arrived.

Expeditions that went into the mountains to mine and to harvest snow plants were now in danger. Many people had been injured or killed in the avalanches. One survivor remembered seeing someone in a white cloak running away. It was enough evidence to request Militia presence. They were, even then, on their way.

It was common knowledge that Carnelian and Spectrum were experiencing much the same problems. It kept everyone in a state of alarm and constantly on the lookout. They couldn't just stop going into the mountains; their livelihood rested there. All they could do was increase security as much as possible.

Despite the increased security, Jayda Lakemore found herself with more than a double in injured patients. She was a Master Water Magi and worked as a doctor in town. Or rather, she helped the people from town, but she didn't live in town. She lived outside the town in a small house that she never left.

She was exceptionally powerful as a healer, and she paid the price for her strength. She was painfully sensitive to people and society. She could barely stand having two people in her home at once, but she made a pointed exception because she couldn't fight the need to heal those who were hurt.

Arctica loved Jayda. They had loved her since she had arrived nine years before. It hadn't been hard. Abut then, at thirteen, she had entered first puberty and revealed she was a Master Magi by learning both Water and Ice, and almost overnight, the spunky child had become a softer and more withdrawn young woman.

Now, at nineteen, the town couldn't even be sure she had started second puberty. She could even have been done with it, but they had no way of knowing. No one minded. You couldn't help but love Jayda. The children of the town took turns taking supplies to her home every week. Sometimes, if they were the lucky one, she left a basket of sweets on the doorstep for them.

It was especially frustrating for the men of the town. With shoulder length seagreen hair that hung straight as a pin, opaque black eyes, and a lovely, delicate figure distributed over a slightly taller than average height of five-ten, she was the reigning beauty of the town, and likely Glacia as a whole.

The sound of findral feet on the snow brought Jayda to her front window. She gave a little sigh and contemplated locking the door and hiding in her room. She couldn't bring herself to be that rude though and instead went to the front door. She didn't open it very far as the male in her yard got off his findral and approached. "Good day."

"Hello, Jayda." He smiled. "I was wondering if you would like to have dinner with me."

"No, thank you."

She stepped back a little and tried to shut the door. It was stopped as he reached out and grabbed the edge. Impatience filled his eyes. "Look, Jayda, you can't just live out here like this. You have to grow up eventually. Have you just not started second puberty?"

"I'm a late bloomer," she lied. Truth be told, she was fairly sure she was all the way through, short of having a lover. Thoughts of having a lover didn't alarm her in the slightest, and for a while they had.

"Maybe you're just not being exposed to the right people."

A delicate seagreen brow lifted ever so slightly. "You come knocking on my door every week. Clearly, you are not the right person either."

A flash of anger lit his eyes and he let go of the door. "Are all Master Magi so stuck up?"

An icicle fell from the roof and landed an inch from his foot. It landed hard enough that it imbedded itself several inches into the wood of the porch, and it was still as high as his knee. He went very still. Softly, Jayda said, "It is not being stuck up to know the difference between affection and self-gratification."

She shut the door and locked it. She stood where she was for long moments and listened to the man as he got on his findral and left. She shivered and went down the hall to her washroom. The pool was always filled with hot water, and she knelt to thrust her arms inside. After a few moments, the heat finally sank into her body. The weather didn't make her cold. Being around other people did. Sometimes she felt as if she would break apart from the inside out from her own Ice power.

Warm once more, she went back to her kitchen where she had been before she was interrupted. The dough still sat on the counter and she resumed kneading and pressing it. Once it started to get flaky, she rolled it into the twisted loop shape of sweetbread. She moved quickly and competently and shortly had several loaves in the oven.

Because she always did her baking every five days, she began to put together the makings for other things she would need. She loved to bake. It was a calming process that let her mind wander without thinking about anything specific. If she stopped and let herself think too much, she would be tempted by the urge to escape into the mountains. Here, at any time, someone might come to her home. It was stressful to say the least.

As if called for, she sensed someone new approaching. She moved quicker and put the tray of mini cakes into the oven as well. She dusted her hands on her apron, and then removed it to go find her cloak. Once it had been wrapped securely around her shoulders and the attached shawl was snug around her neck, she stepped out onto her porch. She would be warm enough between the cloak and her long sleeved tunic and slacks.

Riding toward her was a wagon pulled by two findral. The woman who drove the wagon looked as if she had recently been in an accident. Wounds marked her arms and face, but Jayda didn't see anything life threatening. In contrast, the two men lying in the wagon looked to be in terrible shape. "Doctor!" the woman said in relief as she saw Jayda. "I'm so sorry! We need you!"

Jayda moved down to the wagon and climbed up onto the step beside it. She flinched as she saw the state of the two men. Both were alive, but their power was at a critically low point and escaping their bodies from their wounds as quickly as their blood did. "What happened?" she asked as she rolled up her sleeves.

"An avalanche collapsed a cave," the woman explained. "We were the deepest in and got hit the hardest. Everyone else seemed to make it out safely. Assorted bruises and cuts, but nothing severe."

Jayda formed a needle from ice and drew a thin thread of water through it. Swiftly and expertly, she began to stitch the worst of the wounds closed. The thread would dissolve into the wound and aid in healing it. There wouldn't even be a scar left. "What caused the avalanche?"

"We can't be sure. We . . . we think it might be the Elite. We always feel the mountain's power shake before the avalanche occurs. We've never felt that with normal events." She made a sound of frustration. "Why do they hate us so much? What did we ever do to them?"

Jayda switched to the other male. "That's a question I am sure that another race has asked for a millennia."

There was a long silence. Then, finally, "I never looked at it from that perspective. I suppose we have been doing to Chronicles what the Elite are doing to us."

"It bears a strong resemblance." She finished the stitching and began using her power to find internal injuries. One man had three broken ribs. She wrapped bands of water around his chest, and they sank into his body to begin setting the ribs in their proper place. The power would remain to hold the bones together until they healed.

"How are you so wise, Jay?" The woman watched her work with fascination. "You're only just nineteen and you have the skill of someone twice your age. It's as if the uncanny clarity of childhood never left you."

"Sometimes I'm not sure I was ever a child." She shifted attention to the other man and discovered internal bleeding from his stomach. She removed several herbs from the small bag she wore on her hip and ground them between her fingers. She lifted his head and put the herbs in his mouth. He reflexively swallowed them but he winced when he did. "I know, they taste horrible," she apologized softly.

Both were breathing far easier, and the bloody wounds had closed. The constellation of bruises could only heal with time. The woman let out a little breath of relief. "Will they be all right now?"

"They should be. Watch them both closely, though. If they expend any power, my work will be wasted. Half the problem was that their bodies couldn't naturally heal." She hopped down from the wagon. "Make them drink tea mixed with *femi* herbs. The tea will negate the taste and the herbs will help with swelling."

"Thank you, Jayda." The woman lifted the reigns and studied Jayda. It was a damned shame that a young woman this amazing would be cursed to hide away from a town and a society that loved her. She deserved to find the perfect mate and to live a normal life.

As the wagon left, Jayda hurried back into the house. Shaking, she sat down in the main room and wrapped her arms around herself until the trembling stopped. She seemed to be shaking apart from the inside. Dizzy and ill, she sat there until she smelled her bread finish baking. She was still shaky as she went into the kitchen and took the loaf and the cakes from the oven.

The comfortable rhythm of the baking again helped erase the lingering pain and discomfort, and she focused solely on making the tiny candies the kids from town loved. She couldn't hug them or play with them the way they wanted, but she could show she cared in some way. When you were a child, it was critical to know you were loved. She remembered little of her childhood thanks to large spaces in her memory, but she remembered being loved. That was all that was important to her.

As she begam to get ready for dinner, she heard again the sound of a wagon. This time she recognized the wheels. She went to the door and smiled. "Will you ever get that wheel fixed?" she asked.

Eli Lakemore also smiled as he hopped down from the wagon. "If I did, you wouldn't know it was us." He walked over and hugged her tightly. He was one of only two people whom she felt comfortable around. The other was her mother, Serenity.

Ren tied the findral at the fence and then walked over to hug her daughter tightly. "Let's look at you." She held Jayda at arm's length and looked her over intently. She looked as lovely and peaceful as always. If living so far from others made Jayda happy, Ren would gladly make the hour ride every week if not every day. "You look lovely."

"I look like my mother."

"You do indeed," Eli agreed.

"Oh hush." Ren followed Jayda into the house and sniffed the air appreciatively. "What are you making now?"

"It's just a mush," Jayda said as she went into the kitchen. "Rice and cactear from Choral. It was a gift from one of the people I healed recently. I've added some crater clam as well."

"Do your loving parents get any scraps?" Eli asked.

She smacked his hand when he went to steal a taste. "Yes, if you keep your fingers out." She was smiling as she said it. Just being with her family could make her feel better. "Can you get the bowls?"

"Of course." Ren opened a cupboard and burst into laughter as she saw the three misshapen bowls. "Oh my." She pulled them down to see them better. They were sturdy and big enough to use, but they were crooked and lopsided with a very interesting combination of pink and orange.

Eli lifted a brow the same color as his daughter's hair. "Have we been experimenting with clay in our spare time?"

"If I was, they wouldn't even hold water. No, they were a gift from the kids. Liaon only just entered first puberty, and he has Soil power. He was practicing." Jayda smiled at the bowls. "They're lovely for a first try."

"Colorful," Ren decided. "I'm not sure about the lovely."

They were durable, though. When Jayda served the mush in them, they held up just fine. They also didn't get hot from the food, which showed the maker had some natural talent in crafting.

They sat together at the small table in her kitchen. "Someone mentioned things getting worse," Jayda noted. "I tended to two people who were wounded in an avalanche. They were badly beaten up."

Ren sighed. "It's a reciprocating trouble. The first few deaths caused the first instability. The instability causes more avalanches . . ."

"And that causes more deaths." Eli ripped a piece of sweetbread from the loaf with a carefully controlled motion. "The Militia is due to arrive in a day or two. They're positive we've got an Elite member behind things. Apparently it's so bad in Carnelian that the land is sending out waves into the ocean. Mirah is also in fluctuation and the waves are meeting the ones from Carnelian. Trade is being cut off."

"It makes me so mad," Ren muttered, stabbing at her food with her spoon. "I don't know why. But every time I hear about the Black Magi Elite, it just makes me furious! I'm sure it has to do with those blank spots in my memory, but I just can't get those memories back."

"Maybe they're gone for a good reason." Jayda took her empty bowl to the basin for washing. "Maybe we're not supposed to remember those things, whatever they are." She turned around and linked her hands inside her sleeves.

"Stop scratching," Eli scolded.

She sighed and stopped scratching at her arm. Her left arm had been itching something fierce ever since the time she presumed she had started second puberty. Her right leg itched as well, the skin sensitive in a way that was frustrating because of her long clothes. "I forgot to put on my lotion earlier, sorry."

"I'd say it was all right, but it isn't." Ren frowned. "It's not normal."

Jayda had to smile at that. "Am I normal in any other way?"

"I believe she wins that," Eli told Ren.

"Indeed she does." She smiled. "She wouldn't be our Jayda if she was normal."

As Jayda prepared for bed much later, she thought about that. People who were normal wanted to be different. People who were different wanted to be normal. Was one or the other truly better? She sat on the side of her bed and studied her arm. It looked perfectly normal, but she knew her power rolled under the surface of her skin. She couldn't say why it did any more than she could explain why contact, verbal or physical, with other people hurt her. She couldn't say that she minded though. She didn't want to change.

She was awakened in the early hours by the sound of rumbling in the land. Startled, she pulled on her robe and hurried over to a window. She could see the mountains from there. They looked as if they were actually swaying in the moonlight. A chill went down her back. When thousands of feet of mountain could dance like a piece of string in the wind, things were truly bad.

Unable to get back to sleep, she got dressed and made herself some sweet tea. The sun was just peeking over the horizon when she heard the sound of a findral approaching very quickly. By the time she got to the front door, the beast was skidding to a stop and sending snow flying. "Dad!" She stared at Eli in astonishment. "What's wrong?"

"There was a massive avalanche." His handsome face was very grim. "It's bad, baby. Over a hundred people have been injured. Some are too wounded to move. The two doctors from town are on their way but they have nowhere near your power and skill. We need you. I'm so sorry."

She shook her head. "I'll deal with it. If someone died because I stayed here, I'd never forgive myself." She hurried into the house and pulled on her heaviest boots. She added a second tunic over her regular one before pulling on gloves and her hooded cloak. She grabbed her hipsack with emergency supplies and slung it across her body.

When she joined Eli, he lifted her onto the findral's back before swinging up behind her. Time was of the essence and he urged the findral to run as fast as it could. He hated having to ask her to enter into a large crowd of people, but there was no other choice. The fewer people who died, the less the impact on the land would be.

Halfway up the mountain, she knew they were getting close. Her stomach rolled, and her skin seemed to burn as if tiny bugs crawled all over her. The anxiety rose in waves, and she closed her eyes. She gulped the cold air to keep from begging her father to take her home.

Then, softly, she felt the faintest caress of a power. It stirred something inside her heart and soul. Something seemed to rumble as if waking from a long sleep. Her arm and leg throbbed almost painfully and her power swelled sharply. It ebbed without breaking free and the throbbing went away. Something had almost happened, but she wasn't sure what.

She was sure, however, that her anxiety had gone away. She was calm suddenly as her stomach settled and her pulse slowed down. She was safe. "Were there any Kin there?" she asked her father over the wind. Only a Kin or possibly a Dragon could have had a power strong enough to reach her from a distance.

"No Kin that we know of," he answered. "But there was a Dragon seen flying past the mountain last night."

"That must be what I sensed then." Odd that he would leave a power signature even after leaving, but perhaps he was an Elder.

The site of the avalanche was a bloody horror. Jayda, for all her exposure to wounds and injuries of all shapes and sizes, winced. Nearly a hundred men and women were injured to varying degrees. People from the town wrapped and bound as many wounds as they could to stop bleeding. Others handed out hot tea and blankets. Fire Magi worked with Air Magi to keep the temperature of the area from being cold enough to cause frostbite but not so warm that the snow melted.

Even before the findral stopped, Jayda jumped down. She rushed over to the closest severe injury and knelt beside the wounded woman. Her leg was twisted at an odd angle and lacerations were visible through her ripped clothes. "I need scented air!" she shouted to a nearby Soil Magi.

He didn't look up from the wound he was tying off but he let the air fill with the scent of flowers. The scent was comforting as it drifted over to her. "Just breathe," she said softly. "Breathe and stop thinking. It doesn't hurt. It's not really painful. It's not cold. You're somewhere the sun is shining."

The soft, melodic words were as effective as the scented air. The woman was lulled into the place between sleep and consciousness, unaware of the outside world. When another woman knelt beside her, Jayda made motions with her hands to show what she needed. The other woman nodded and carefully untangled the broken limb so that it laid properly. The patient didn't notice; she was drifting in the place where Jayda had sent her.

Jayda wasted no time in setting the bones and stitching wounds closed. As soon as they were closed, her aide began binding them to keep out the cold air. Jayda also put a splint on the broken leg and bound it tightly. "Wagon!" she called. It was the medical shorthand for saying a patient was ready for transport.

With the woman aiding her and assorted Magi lending their powers as needed, she moved quickly between the worst injuries. The other two doctors worked with the lesser injuries, and everyone moved as fast as they could. The land still trembled softly under their feet in a warning that all was not safe or secure. Water Magi watched the mountain intently, ready to use their Ice power to stop new danger for as long as they could.

People were still being dug out of the rubble. Some didn't come out alive. The city Elder was on hand and keeping track of those who were alive and dead. He knew everyone in town by name. Only he could be sure who was safe and who wasn't. He was also able to keep track of who was still trapped.

As Jayda was setting another broken bone, she saw movement from the corner of her eye. She looked up sharply and saw the figure of a man fleeing up a mountain path. He was wearing a white cloak that looked oddly, and disturbingly, familiar.

A commotion behind her had her turning to see that the Militia had arrived. There were twenty soldiers in total. Most of them saw the scene and immediately began helping with the transporting of the injured. Others began to help gather the dead. The two healers among the Militia joined the doctors in making the rounds.

The young woman in charge immediately focused on Jayda as being the head doctor and hurried over to her. She swiftly made the sign of respect. "Argyle Quinn Flyer, Water Magi."

Jayda's hands were full with stitching a wound closed and she couldn't return the gesture. She inclined her head instead. "Jayda Lakemore, Master Water Magi. Warm greetings."

"If only." Quinn knelt beside her. "Can you explain what has happened here? When we got to the town, we were told there was a catastrophe in the mountains. They seemed to have understated the case."

"An avalanche." She looked around and spotted her aide. "Wagon!" She got to her feet and hurried to the next patient with Quinn close behind. "I was wakened in the early morning by a quake. It made the entire mountain dance. An hour ago, my father fetched me to come help heal. I'm the strongest in the Arctica area."

"Glacia too." Quinn watched Jayda's speed and competency. She could also sense the rolling turmoil in the younger woman's emotions. Gentler, she said, "You're a good woman to come out when it is painful for you." When Jayda looked at her in surprise, the Argyle admitted, "My little sister was a Master Magi. She never left her home. If she lives, we don't know it. No one can approach."

"I've considered barring my home," Jayda had to admit. "But I am driven to heal. It is a painful combination. I am only enduring now because the Dragon in the area seems to have calmed me."

"I've heard that Dragon Elders are quite sensitive themselves," Quinn concurred. "If he sensed your distress, racial tensions aside, he'd be inclined to help." She cursed softly under her breath as she saw more bodies brought from the rubble. "Curse those Elite to the Underrealm!"

"What do they look like?"

She sighed. "We don't know. We can only identify them by the cloaks they wear. White cloaks with a black chalice and dagger. They make a mockery of the Magi symbol. Our chalice is a sign of justice, not murder!"

In the hours that passed, two more avalanches shook the mountain. Both were stopped by the Water Magi. As the last people were being loaded into wagons, Jayda began to feel the nagging sensation that there was still someone injured. It had been there all along, but she had been ignoring it because it had been very obvious that people were hurt.

Everyone had been tended to, and she still felt the urgency in her body. "Are we sure we got everyone?" she called to her father.

He shook his head. "We're still combing the mountain to be sure. Do you feel someone injured?"

"I think so. I'll help look." She headed for the mountain path. "If there's someone out there without help, we have to find them!" Without waiting for consent, she hurried down the path and began to climb higher in the mountain.

The sun was bright, and she could see clearly even though a light snow fell. The further she went, the more she felt the sharp pull and compulsion of a power sending out a subconscious distress signal. It was a *strong* power, not Magi in origin, and seemed to whisper along her soul with a voice she knew.

She rounded one bend and suddenly caught sight of a man lying face down in the snow. Alarmed, she rushed to his side. "Are you okay?" There was no response, but she could sense his power still moved and he was still alive.

She fell to her knees beside him and turned him over onto his back. Shock stole her voice and her breath all at the same time. She had never seen such a shockingly handsome man before. He looked roughed up from an avalanche and there was a large bump on the side of his head. It called to her healer side, and it called to something more. Her sudden attraction to him went to a place inside her that lurked beyond her power.

With a roar, that something awoke inside her. Her power rose and surged wildly under her skin to make it burn fiercely. It broke free, and water and ice swirled through the air in a short but strong cataract. It finally died down, and she felt her arm and leg throbbing.

Almost fatalistically, she reached out with trembling fingers and pulled up her sleeve. There were golden lines shaped like little waves on her arm. Based on the throbbing in her skin, she had to assume they went from shoulder to wrist and hip to ankle on the two limbs that had itched so hard.

She was a Chronicle.

The man stirred slightly and startled her out of her shock. She tugged her sleeve down to cover the marks and got a grip on herself. This was not the time to be thinking about things that she couldn't understand.

She swiftly began to check her patient for severe injury. He had definitely been banged up, but she didn't find anything too terrible. Only the bump on his head looked like it needed closer attention. Terror and anguish churned in her stomach. A living fear that she might lose him before knowing him stole her breath.

Her eyes went to his thick black hair and the bright streaks of red through it. She tenderly ran her fingers through the vibrant locks. He was a Dragon. Now that she was close, she knew his was the power she had felt. He was a Dragon Elder. Whatever was inside him felt like a hot caress of fire against her soul. "Mine," she said softly. She was sure of it. Somehow she knew this man was hers alone.

She heard a footstep and turned her head to see Quinn approaching. Quinn spotted her in return and let out a breath of relief. "There you are!" She came to a stop beside Jayda and took a sharp breath. "A Dragon!" She knelt quickly. "He looks pretty bad! He must've been caught while camping!" Chills rippled down her skin. "He's *powerful*."

"An Elder is my guess," Jayda said. Her eyes watched as Quinn lightly touched the lump on the man's head. It took considerable willpower to resist telling her to keep her hands off. "He deserves care as much as the next person. We need to get him off the mountain."

"Agreed." Quinn felt a soft warning of power from Jayda and lifted her hand. The menacing feeling immediately faded. Pondering it, she got to her feet. "I'll, er, go get a wagon." Suiting actions to words, she turned and hurried back down the path.

Jayda didn't wait for the wagon before beginning to tend to the wounds she could see. It broke her heart to see injuries on such a magnificent creature. In a distant part of her mind, she was a little amused and a little confused. If the feelings churning inside her body were any clue, then she was definitely near to the end of second puberty. Desire, never before felt, was nonetheless oddly familiar as it swirled through her blood.

Quinn returned shortly with Eli and a wagon. Jayda watched intently as they carefully lifted her Dragon into the wagon. "Be careful!" she ordered sharply as she saw them jostle his head.

Eli looked at her in surprise. He had never heard her sound that way before. A nameless fear clenched his heart as he looked at the streaks in the wounded man's hair. It wasn't possible . . . was it? The moons only knew that nothing else had made sense of Jayda in her life.

"Should we take him to town?" Quinn asked as she helped Jayda into the wagon and then climbed up beside Eli.

"No." Jayda's fingers almost compulsively stroked the man's arm. "I will tend to him."

Quinn began to frown. "Jayda, Dragons are not friends with Magi."

"He wouldn't hurt me." She felt sure of it.

Not liking it, but accepting it, Eli aimed the wagon for her home. He and Quinn carried the man inside and settled him onto the guest bed that Jayda kept for when her parents visited overnight. Quinn left to begin the hunt for the Elite, and Eli stayed to watch as Jayda began to bind wounds and stitch others. "I never thought I'd be near a Dragon, let alone an Elder," he finally said.

"Me neither." She pressed ice against the head injury to bring down the swelling. "But perhaps that is why I am so comfortable with him. I feel . . . safe. I've never felt safe near Magi. And . . ." she admitted, "well, I'm attracted to him." She sighed as she saw her father grimace. "I'm sorry, but it's true. If he wants to be, I would have him for my first lover."

He would have much preferred her to set her eye on a Magi, if only for the lesser danger, but he could not deny she had taste. "Because you would be that contrary."

She had to smile. "I take after my father."

"Well, I can't argue with that." He straightened. "It's odd but . . . I feel that you're safe with him. I trust him. It's curious." He ran a hand over her hair. "I'm proud of you," he said softly. "Never forget that." Unable to shake the feeling that it might be goodbye, he turned and left.

She finished healing her unwitting visitor and covered him with a thick blanket to keep him warm. His was a face that looked stark and beautiful, yet it was a face that spoke of living alone for too long. She felt the loneliness inside him as if it was inside herself. Perhaps it was. She gently pressed her lips to his cheek. "We don't have to be alone anymore," she promised softly.

Wanting to be ready when he woke, she got to her feet and headed for the kitchen. She wasn't going to think about being a Chronicle. Not yet. She wasn't even sure what it meant. But she knew, somehow, that it was connected to the Dragon in her home. Everything about her connected to him.

He might very well be the piece that would complete her.

Chapter Eleven

Among the race of Dragons, there were ten who were Elders. There were the four who belonged on the Council of Elders—one Dragon representing each element clan—then there were five others scattered among the tens of thousands of Dragons that called the Isle of Dragons home. There was only one other Elder, but he wasn't often considered a Dragon Elder.

He was the only living Fury Elder.

For over two thousand five hundred years, Xander Journe had endured day after day, week after week, year after year of painful waiting. He had waited fifteen hundred years to find his Chronicle, only to witness the massacre of the entire race. From that day on, for a millennia, he had waited with his breath held for the day his world would end.

Then, one day, he had felt *her*. He had felt the birth of the only being that could end his loneliness. The only person who would love him as completely as he loved her. Because he was a Fire Fury, he knew she would be a Water Chronicle. He knew because he was older and more mature, so would she be. And he knew that because he was increasingly more sensitive to those around him, so would she be.

For ten years, he had thought that his hope was groundless. All that had changed the day he met Tariah and Morgan Chronis. They had survived. They had found their Furies. And Morgan had told the Dragons of the secret Chronicle children he had found. Four children, two boys and two girls, each of a different element. It hadn't been until after the war with the Elite that Morgan had gently told Xander that one of the girls showed signs of being a Water element.

Now, nine years later, Xander had not felt the death of his Chronicle. He knew that she had to be the one Morgan had found. For nearly a decade, he had spent his every waking minute searching the face of Lucksphere. Even when asleep, he thought of her. He wouldn't let himself think of what she might look like. He wanted to feel that first punch of shock and recognition all rolled together.

He had already spent time on the other lands and now he was working his way through Glacia. He *hated* Glacia. It was all ice and snow and *cold* but he went anyway. In truth, Glacia was the best place to visit if you were a Dragon or Fury. In Stalagmite to the south, all Dragons were welcome. It was in this city that Morgan had grown up, and his parents still lived there. Furies who were even then in the world seeking their Chronicle would periodically stop to say hi or pick up and deliver messages.

Xander couldn't land in the city, unfortunately. He stretched fifty feet long from nose to tail and was greatly larger than average. Luckily for him, he was nimble in his age and able to change into Magi form in midair before landing safely on the docks. He had perfected it so well that barely a ripple touched the land despite his power.

The Magi females of town never minded when he came for a visit. In Magi form, he was one of the most gorgeous men they had ever seen. He stood much taller than average at six-five and his shoulders looked broad and powerful. His black hair had streaks of red, courtesy of his Dragon blood, and his eyes glowed the same ruby red.

No one knew of his Fury status, though. Truth be told, there really was no way for Magi to tell the difference between a Dragon and a Fury without their Chronicle. Only the Kin knew because they could sense different powers in other beings. They could sense the lack of infinite power yet infinite potential inside a Fury.

One Kin had described it like seeing a raging river that had been blocked. Until the block was removed, the power was restrained. Once freed, it would be far more potent than anything else. Of course, that same Kin had teasingly told Xander that that made him *really* scary because he was so powerful even without his Chronicle. Xander didn't mind. He liked the Kin Faerie that Tariah called a brother.

The city was the same bustling port as always. He made his way through the crowds to the restaurant that fed most of the tourists who came through. Cruises from Spectrum to Glacia were often used by newly Linked couples as a celebratory trip. He didn't see the point, personally, but that was a cultural difference.

He stepped over a child and then stopped to let a wagon go past. Once clear, he entered the restaurant through the back door. "Hello?"

Persia Chronis looked up from the bread dough in front of her and her face brightened. "I wasn't expecting to see you! It's good to see you, Xander." If she was at all uncomfortable with a Fury Elder in her kitchen, she didn't act or show it. "Are Morgan and Jazz well?"

"Last I saw of them, yes. That was about two years ago though." He sniffed at a basket holding fruit. He had a weakness for fresh fruit.

She offered him one with a smile. "When are they giving me grandchildren?"

"That is harder to say," he admitted, nibbling on the fruit. "Dragons have large families, but the Dragoon couples I remember only had one or two children. With them being immortal . . ."

She wrinkled up her nose. "I want grandchildren. You tell Morgan that he had better not wait one hundred years to have a child!" She huffed out a breath. "What about Tariah?"

"She *suspects* she might be pregnant." He smiled as he said it. "If she is, it happened too recently for even our most accomplished healers to detect the new life. Dominic is as sure as she is. I think I've seen him walking a few feet off the ground."

"Ah, then I have at least *one* grandbaby in my future!" She was appeased with that. Tariah was, at most, a distant cousin by blood, but she and Morgan acted and felt like twins and so his parents had adopted her.

"How is London doing?" Xander asked.

"The limp is only really bad during the coldest days, but he's overall much better." Her gaze lowered. "How we let ourselves believe that foolishness . . ."

"The Elite fooled many," he said quietly. "You're not at fault. At least you survived." He straightened from the counter he had been leaning against. "Any message to pass on, short of the 'give me grandkids' one?"

"Visit!"

He laughed. "I'll tell him that, and in just that way." With a little bow, he left the restaurant. He enjoyed the entirety of the Chronis family. He himself felt confident in Tariah's knowledge of her own body and couldn't wait to see what sort of child came from her and her Fury. There would be no knowing what race it might be until further in her development when the power coalesced and could be sensed by healers.

He spent a couple days in Stalagmite, long enough to be sure that his Chronicle was not present. As he was preparing to leave town, a tremor shook the land. He caught his balance and helped a young woman walking past keep from falling as well. "I didn't think there were quakes in Glacia."

"There aren't, usually." The woman shook her head. "Haven't you heard about the Black Magi Elite? They're causing much chaos in Carnelian and Mirah. We've been suspicious that they were here as well. Arctica to the north has been having terrible avalanches in the mountains."

His frown deepened. "I see."

"It's spiraling around itself too. The Militia who came through yesterday on their way there said that the more people who were killed, the worse the land shook. I heard there's an immensely powerful Master Water Magi living near Arctica, but I don't know if even she can help. She's only nineteen."

He went very still. Chronicles appeared nearly indistinguishable from Master Magi to the average person. "A Master Magi? I thought they were almost never seen."

"They're never seen because they can't handle society," the woman explained. "We actually have four on the world right now. They keep to themselves to varying degrees, but they don't hide away entirely. I think there's an Air one near Mirah, a Fire one on Carnelian, a Soil one near Symphony, and then the Water one near Arctica." She sighed. "All nineteen or eighteen. Such heavy burdens on such young shoulders."

He had never believed in coincidence. Four Master Magi, one of each element, of the eighteen to nineteen age bracket. They had to be the missing Chronicle children. "Indeed," he agreed softly. "Perhaps I will head north and see if they need help."

"I thought Dragons didn't like the Magi."

His smile showed several sharp teeth. "We like the Elite even less."

"Oh." More fascinated than alarmed, she waved as he headed out of town to find a place large enough for him to go back into Dragon form.

Once he had changed back, he flew into the air and began heading north. His heart pounded hard in his chest. He had tried to teach himself not to hope, but it got harder and harder every minute. Maybe it *was* just a Master Magi living in Arctica. Maybe his Chronicle was somewhere else entirely and he just kept missing her arrival as he left.

His attention diverted the closer he got to the mountains around Arctica. He could smell and sense the fear and pain that climbed the snow covered cliffs. And as he entered the mountains and began to make his way through them, he smelled something else.

He smelled tainted power.

His eyes narrowed. He flew closer to the surface to track the scent to the best of his ability, and the land rippled harder in warning. The state of fluctuation was in no way aided by his presence. He stopped flying and changed form as he landed. Though he was no less powerful in Magi form, it dispersed over a smaller area. The tremors lessoned without going away entirely.

Grateful for his heavy cloak (he *loathed* snow), he worked his way through the mountains on foot. He didn't bother to camp when night came. He could see just as well in the dark as he could in the light, and he wasn't tired. Tariah had accused him of existing on pure stubbornness and the occasional fruit. He sometimes wondered if she was right.

Halfway through the night, he caught the sharp and acrid scent of power that had been corrupted. He also caught the scent of a pure power. They were close together, and he hit the ground running as he rushed toward the scents. He skidded around a corner just in time to see two figures struggling near the edge of a cliff. One was a scrawny man in a white cloak. The other looked like a miner. "Stop!" He ran toward them. "Get away from the cliff!"

The man in the cloak gave a nearly insane cackle and shoved hard. The miner went flying over the edge of the cliff with a terrified scream. The Elite member turned to flee when he realized that Xander stood right behind him. The color drained from his face. He had been there at the final fight nine years before. He knew this Dragon. "You!"

"How nice to be remembered." Xander walked steadily closer, fire swirling around his hand. "I'd threaten to eat you, but I'd get indigestion and we both know it." His eyes glowed as red as his power as he lifted his hand. "Don't think you'll be able to escape. I've been on this world a lot longer than you can imagine."

Gamma knew he stared death in the eye. He was only a slightly stronger than average Soil Magi. He held no chance against a Dragon Elder, let alone one this powerful. He had seen Xander in battle. He had ripped apart entire groups of his enemy and shrugged off blasts as if they were bugs.

Before Xander could throw the fireball, and before Gamma could think of a way to escape, the entire mountain quivered. The land lifted and rolled so fast that both men found themselves standing on air for a second before dropping down. The tremors started coming faster and faster, and the mountain swayed violently.

Great waves of snow began to roll down the side of the mountain. Distantly, Xander heard the screams of many people. Gamma began to cackle. "Crush them!" he crowed. "Crush them all!" His eyes gleamed with madness as he looked at Xander. "The people mine at all hours. How bad for them!"

Xander turned with a snarl but the next wave of the land sent him rolling one way and Gamma the other. Snow had begun to fall, and even with the moons overhead, it was hard to see. He found himself trying to find something to grab onto as the mountain rocked and shook and sent him tumbling further down the side.

He cracked his head against a tree and stars exploded behind his eyes. By the time he finally stopped rolling, he had no strength or energy to move. He could only lay face down in the snow, aching and disoriented and dimly grateful that his heated breath melted the snow enough for him to breathe. He couldn't move, couldn't quite think. The pain in his head was excruciating. It swelled more and more until he finally, blessedly, blacked out.

He only had one lucid moment after that. He could vaguely sense the distress of dozens of people. Pain and fear ran rampant. Yet through the chaos, he felt one person clearly. Her anxiety rose and rose until it made his throat ache. He knew that pain. He lived with it every day. He instinctively reached out for her, wanting only to comfort. His power brushed hers . . . and he recognized it.

Wild triumph and elation swelled on two millennia worth of loneliness. It was *her*. He had found his Chronicle. He tried to will his body to move but it wouldn't respond. Even when the blackness took him again, he was desperately trying to shake off the cold and the pain. She needed him. She needed him as badly as he needed her.

The next time he woke, it was all at once. His eyes opened and his senses sharpened. He was dry and warm, and his wounds were gone. The bump on his head seemed nearly non-existent. He had been tucked securely into a soft bed, and the tender scent of fresh snow lightly filled the air. It stung his lungs wonderfully.

He felt cushioned and surrounded by the scent and feel of a power that was utterly feminine and utterly familiar. *His.* The savage joy was only dimly shocking. He probed the house with his power to find her and encountered nothing. She had been there recently because the signature she had left was still fresh, but she was not there at the immediate moment.

He swiftly got out of bed and made a physical exploration of the house, restlessly prowling through the small space with the hope that he was wrong. He wasn't. He was alone.

As he entered into what he assumed was her bedroom, he realized why she had left. He could feel the unsteady and arching swell of her power lingering in the air. Her body and her power were trying to prepare for the natural bonding demanded between Dragoons, and she didn't know what was going on. All she would know was that her power was going out of control.

Her reaction came as no surprise. He could feel the sharper drain on his majiks as indication of the same need. A lack of consciousness was not a viable excuse for nature to take a temporary hiatus.

He cursed softly and hurried through the house to the exit. He could still feel her. He could still smell the scent of her skin. Once outside of the house, he changed to his Dragon form and took to the sky. He was going to find her and then he was never going to let her go again.

~*~

Jayda didn't know there was anything wrong at first. She felt a little shaky, and her power seemed slightly riotous. Her only assumption was that because she had become a Chronicle, she was a little unstable. She ignored the trembling in her fingers and went about her daily business.

The influx of people to her home had increased by triple as injured miners kept coming by for her more advanced healing skills. After she sent the tenth person on their way, it dawned on her that she wasn't feeling as raw around others as she always had. When she finally had a free moment, she went into the guest room where her visitor still slept. "It's you, isn't it?" she murmured.

She smoothed his hair from his eyes and felt his power stirring under her fingers. He was drawing closer to waking. Her eyes went wide and she dashed down the hall to her room. She began to quickly brush her hair to remove the tangles, and only belatedly did it dawn on her what she was doing. She sat down on her bed with a sigh. She had always wondered what self-consciousness felt like. She didn't like it.

The Dragon didn't wake even an hour later. It was a stressful hour. Jayda just felt more and more out of sorts. She started contemplating a hot bath to soak away the stress but heard footsteps in the snow outside. She peeked out the window, saw Quinn, and opened the door. "Hello." She drew her thumb over her cheek and nose. "What brings you out here?"

"Many things." Quinn took a deep breath. "I'll start with some hot tea."

"Come in." She shut the door and led the way to the kitchen. As she poured two cups, she asked, "What's next? I'm sure you didn't make the ride just for the tea."

"Naturally not." Quinn wrapped her hands around the cup. "How is the Dragon?"

"Better. He's healing quickly. I sensed his power move not long ago so he should be preparing to wake."

"That's good. He was as much a victim of the incident as the town was. Then, of course, it would look bad on the Magi if we didn't take care of him. The Dragons would be glad for an excuse, I'm sure."

Jayda tugged her sleeve down further defensively. "I imagine they would. And on that same note, I don't suppose you know anything about Chronicles, do you?"

"Chronicles?" Quinn blinked. "Well, no more or less than others. They're hyper-powered Magi, I guess. They look and act like you Master Magi do, but they have infinite power. They also develop lines on their bodies at first puberty. Those lines lead them to a Dragon Lord known as a Fury. Based on what we've been learning over the last few years, it's not quite the parasitic relationship we all thought. The Kin said the closest word we could understand would be 'love.'"

"Parasitic?"

"Apparently, Furies *don't* have infinite power. They're limited. They're more powerful than regular Dragons, but they have limits. If they feed on their Chronicle's power though, then they can be all but infinite. The recent hypothesis from scholars is that Chronicles might be taking in the excess power of the land and filtering it through their Furies. In other words, they might be a naturally occurring phenomena."

"Then why kill them?"

Quinn lowered her gaze. "Nine years ago, I'd have said that they were a horrible aberration and a disgusting perversion of nature. Now . . . I don't know." She shook it off and smiled. "You distracted me."

"My apologies. I get curious sometimes and it seemed like a time to ask. Now what did you need from me?"

"I was hoping you might have seen or sensed anyone at the site. I've had conflicting reports from various miners that they might have seen someone lurking around that didn't belong. My party is combing the mountainside, but we're coming up blank."

Jayda frowned. "When I was working with someone, I saw a man in a white cloak running around the side of the mountain path. I didn't really think much of it. I just assumed he was looking for more survivors."

"I see." Quinn drummed her fingers lightly on the table. "That's encouraging at the least. The Elite smell of tainted power. We should be able to track him if he's the one we're after." She tilted her head. "You seem . . . odd. Are you all right? I keep feeling like waves of your power are lapping over the edges, so to speak."

"I'm still recovering from being around so many people, I think." She tugged her sleeve down again. "I've also had a steady stream of patients today. People with smaller injuries who know I can remove them entirely where the other doctors cannot."

"Understandable. You're one of the best healers I've ever seen." Quinn got to her feet. "I will be joining my party in the mountains. For the time being, the mountains seem to be stable. Perhaps your internal fluctuations helped with that. I've seen it before where the correct element can help calm the land. It might be worth gathering many Water Magi like us and trying to calm the mountain entirely."

"That's a very good idea." Jayda followed her to the door. "Be safe."

"You too." Quinn headed down toward where she had left her findral and glanced back only once to see Jayda tugging on her sleeve again. What was she trying to hide?

Once she was alone again, Jayda headed into her washroom and pulled off her clothes. She stepped in front of her full-length mirror and looked at her body with a thoughtful frown. The lines started at her left shoulder and wrapped around her arm to her wrist, and then they started at her right hip and wrapped around her leg to her ankle. They shimmered gold against her pale skin, and she thought they were unexpectedly attractive.

Shrugging it off, she put up her hair and got into the pool. She felt a little bemused at herself. There was a perfect stranger in her home, and he could wake and walk in on her at any time. She felt neither fear nor concern for it if it happened. She was safe with him. She knew it.

Quinn's words danced in her mind. Was her Dragon guest a Fury? If he was . . . was he hers? Her heart said yes. Nothing else made sense of the situation.

Her power began to rumble warningly and pain blossomed under her skin. Alarmed, she sat up and got out of the tub. She dried off and got dressed, but by the time she was brushing her hair in her room, she felt surer than ever that something had to be wrong. Her power was rising too fast, and it was getting more and more painful.

Rather than worry about it, she got dressed in her warmest clothes and left her home. If she was going to go out of control, then she might as well be in the mountains. The land needed power from a Water element to help settle, and she was going to settle it for a *long* time. She had a feeling she had power to spare.

She went by foot and covered ground much quicker than most people because of her Ice power. She was climbing the mountains within an hour and made her way steadily higher. It was snowing lightly and she still felt the tremors under the surface of the land. It grew harder and harder to walk as the pain slowly became blinding. The clouds far overhead responded to her power, and the snow began to fall heavier.

Just as she reached a cliff where there was shelter, she couldn't walk anymore. She fell to her knees and carefully crawled under one of the trees. Maybe this hadn't been the brightest idea.

She heard footsteps crunching on snow at the same time she smelled the unmistakable whiff of spoiled power. Alarmed, she looked up sharply. The man from before approached her, and his white cloak fluttered in the wind. "Who are you?" she asked warily.

"My name is Gamma." He stopped in front of her with a pleasant smile on his face. "I'm a member of the Black Magi Elite." When her eyes widened, he waved a hand in the air. "Oh don't worry! I'm not here to kill you.

That'd be such a waste!" He knelt and shoved her sleeve up her arm. "You're a Chronicle, after all."

She tried to pull her arm free, but his grip was strong and her body hurt. "How did you know?"

"I was going to kill that Fury when you arrived. I saw your little awakening. Imagine that. A little Chronicle, hiding as a Master Magi." His grip tightened on her wrist. "What are you doing out here all alone, anyway? It's dangerous. You never know who you might run into."

"Let go of me!"

"The Elite have plans for you, little girl. We need you to help us find the key to destroying the Magi." His brown eyes were wild and more than a little mad. "Doesn't that sound delightful?"

She jerked at her arm again, but he countered and dragged her up off the ground. She went stumbling past and fell to the snow, and her sleeve ripped off her tunic entirely to reveal the full length of her lines. She painfully turned her head to see him approaching. "Why do you hate Magi?"

"They keep trying to destroy the world! They put it in the state it's in now. We'll erase all Magi, and Chronicles will take their place. But we can't do it without you." He walked toward her, a hand held out. "You hurt, don't you? Well, come with me and you can use that power for destruction, just like you should."

An immense icicle formed from the sky and landed sharply at his feet. He backed up quickly and turned to see Quinn standing nearby with more ice swirling around her hands. "Back away from Jayda," she warned. "She's not going anywhere with you."

He laughed wildly. "She's a Chronicle! Don't you want to kill her? Why would you protect her?" He whirled toward Jayda. "She saves you only to murder you! You know it!"

Jayda pushed herself painfully to her feet. "No, she doesn't. And even if I'm wrong, I trust her more than I trust you." Her lines rippled as if alive and water flowed around her body. Shards of ice formed in the water, and she hurled the blast with all her strength.

Halfway toward Gamma, it was joined by a blast from Quinn and they sent him flying backwards through the snow. He scrambled up with a snarl. "If that's how you want to play, then let's play!" He flung out his hands and vines shot through the air at the two females.

Quinn was able to dodge. Jayda wasn't. The vines slammed into her chest and sent her tumbling back across the snow. Winded, she rolled to a stop at the edge of the cliff. She couldn't think or move. Quinn scrambled over to her side. "Jayda!" She lifted the other female into her arms slightly and felt the rioting power under her skin. It was barely held in check. "Jayda!"

Gamma staggered toward them as if drunk, weaving back and forth across the snow, nearly stumbling over his own feet. "She will be the catalyst of destruction! You better kill her yourself if you want to save her from me! Isn't that what you Magi have been deluding yourself into thinking?"

A terrifying roar ripped through the air. It reverberated off the mountains and made them tremble in fear. It echoed and doubled time and again, and it rang in everyone's ears. Gamma went deathly white. Quinn couldn't breathe as she felt a fierce and deadly power behind her. Gamma slowly started to back up, stark terror on his face.

Slowly Quinn looked over her shoulder and saw the biggest Dragon she had ever seen in her life. He was fifty feet long, at least a third of that wide, and covered in pitch black scales with flicks of flame red. His teeth were as long as her arm and his face looked somehow frightening and beautiful all at once.

Xander had never been more furious in his life. He landed on the cliff and then whirled and swung his tail sharply. The end slammed into Gamma and flung him straight into the air and into the distance so hard that he shortly disappeared from sight. Slowly, Xander turned to look at the Militia member holding his Chronicle.

"Are you a Fury?" she managed to ask.

"I am a Fire Fury Elder," he confirmed. He lowered his head to be closer on eye level. "You are holding my Chronicle. For saving her life, you have my thanks."

"What's wrong with her?"

"She and I need to bond as Dragoons. Nature makes its demands known. Her powers rise and my majiks drain. I woke and found her gone before I could tell her. Will you give her to me?"

Quinn looked down at Jayda. She wasn't fully conscious, but her gaze fixed on Xander with something akin to wonder in her eyes. There was also something more, some powerful emotion that Quinn wasn't sure could be called love. "Yes," she said softly. "Magi law for killing Chronicles is made with the idea that we do it to keep them from the Elite. If you have her, then she will not be with the Elite. The law is upheld."

He reached out and picked up Jayda with his claw. A tremor went through his mighty body. She was smaller than his entire claw. She was taller than average, but she was slender and graceful and as elegant as her element. Beautiful. She was beauty incarnate. He drew her closer possessively and slowly rose into the air. He had enough power to get them to shelter. "Does she have family?"

"She does. I will think of something to tell them." Quinn got to her feet and smiled a little. "I had wondered what she was hiding. But I can't say I'm surprised. Be well, Elder." She stepped back to give him more room and watched as he flew across the sky. Under her feet, she could feel that the mountain had stabilized and become secure because of Jayda's spent power.

At least *something* the Magi believed had turned out to be right.

Chapter Twelve

By the time Xander saw a small island off the coast that *didn't* have more snow than land, he was flying low to the surface of the ocean because he didn't have the power to remain aloft. He angled down to the island and gave it a cursory look with his eyes and senses. The only signs of life came from plants.

Relieved, he landed and looked around. The land felt much warmer than Glacia but there wasn't much by way of shelter. There were only a handful of trees scattered across the scenery. There were, however, a couple standing together not far away. He walked over there and gently put Jayda down on the ground.

He grabbed the tops of the trees and carefully bent them down until they formed a canopy. Using the smallest amount of his power as possible, he created ropes of glass and bound the treetops in their bent position to ensure they would stay as good cover. He added more leaves on the top for additional protection before going back into Magi form.

He stumbled a step before he caught his balance. He waited for his head to stop spinning, and then carefully sat beside Jayda. He lifted her into his arms and onto his lap. His fingers trembled as he smoothed her hair out of her face. Had he ever tried to imagine what his Chronicle might look like, he would have fallen far short of reality.

Her thick hair smelled like fresh snow and glacial flowers, and her body was lithe and graceful. She was taller than average, but so was he, and he loved every inch on her body. He buried his nose in her hair for a moment. His throat closed tightly and his eyes burned. He had waited. Even in the face of despair, he had waited. And he had been rewarded.

He lifted her left arm and studied the lines wrapping around her soft flesh. Hunger tightened his body in a searing wave. It was *his* power making her lines. He lifted her wrist to his lips and felt her pulse beat strong. His fingers had begun to shake. He couldn't separate the hungers inside him. Hunger for her power, hunger for her impossibly perfect beauty. Hunger for her smile and her gentle nature.

Her power steadily gained strength and grew wilder. As it did, he felt his desire growing. All he could do was close his eyes and pray with all his might that he would not be suffering Dominic's fate. If his Chronicle wasn't nearly done with second puberty, he didn't know if he had the control to wait.

Jayda woke to raging pain. It was worse than it had been before. A low whimper echoed in her throat. She wanted to go out of control, to unleash floods and hurricanes, to raise the seas and consume the land. It *hurt*. She felt a hand holding hers and curled her fingers around it tightly, knowing at her deepest level who held her.

"Open your eyes," he urged huskily. "Please."

She forced her lashes up and found herself staring into a familiar face. His eyes stole her breath. Ruby red, fiery red, they consumed her and brought warmth to the coldest parts of her soul. Her lips trembled as she smiled. "I'm Jayda Lakemore."

"Xander Journe." He framed her face with his free hand. "It hurts, I know. It's just something to force us to bond." He softly brushed his lips over her cheek and eyes. "Are you afraid of me?"

"If I was afraid of you, I'd have never taken you into my home." She shivered in delight as his lips stirred nerves and senses that had been in suspension. A different ache entirely settled into her body. As instinctive as breathing, her power reached for him and curled around him seductively.

His breath caught. Was he that lucky? He softly returned the touch, and her power rose to cover her in a soft blue aura. It was more beautiful than anything. Unbearably tempted, he lowered his head and pressed his lips to her neck. Her power was fresh and pure, and her skin was cool. It made him feel as if he tasted the purest glacial water. "I might change my mind about snow," he said huskily, drinking her power as he ran his lips down her neck.

"You don't like it?" Her eyes closed in pleasure as his lips teased her collar.

"I'm changing my mind." He hit the edge of the tunic she wore, and it was the one with the torn sleeve. Seeing that torn material made rage churn inside him that someone had threatened his mate. Before she could guess his intent, he literally ripped the tunic from her body.

Her mouth fell open in shock, but her words became a soft gasp as he promptly buried his lips at the opening in the under-tunic. It was like any other tunic except sleeveless and lower cut. It was more for warmth than appearance. One of his hands caressed her from shoulder to hip and then back again, spreading fire as he went.

Eagerly, half drunk, he followed her power back up to her lips. Without waiting for permission, he took her lips with his and deepened the kiss instantly with a demanding thrust of his tongue. Her power tasted even purer there, and the euphoria at finally knowing her presence was as tangled as the other emotions inside him.

A low moan vibrated in her throat, and she freed her arms to bury her fingers in his hair. The pain had disappeared. In its place was a storm of hunger. Hunger for everything he was. She craved his power and his presence, to feel his arms tight around her. She wanted to be his lover, to become an adult in his heated embrace. She wanted to take away the loneliness she felt eating away at him. She wanted his love to match the love in her heart.

When her body arched to press against his, he went light headed with relief. Half-wild, he continued to feed from her power at her mouth until it stopped flowing free. He felt better than refreshed. He felt ready to take on the world and exist for another millennia. He felt more, though. He felt *her.*

The bonds between them formed as naturally as the sun set. He could see everything in her heart and mind, could feel her every emotion and breathe her every breath. And because he could, his heart soared as he saw that the three emotions inside her, the ones marking Dragoons, were as fierce and untamed as the ones inside him. "*Ishke.*"

She couldn't speak around her tight throat. She could see the thousands of years of memories and emotions inside her Fury. She saw everything he was and could be. And she saw her own presence inside him erasing the loneliness. His violent emotions, the three turbulent sides, surged and snapped at the bounds of his flesh. She didn't fear them. She felt the same untamed feelings inside herself and craved the feelings in him.

She wanted to say that she loved him, but the words weren't enough. There weren't even words to describe that other feeling. "Xander." She pressed upward to kiss him, longing for his taste as if it had been centuries rather than seconds since she had last had it.

His hands buried in her hair, and he kissed her as she wanted: long, and deep, and hungry. He wrapped his power around her, unable to release her, and curled his mind around hers as well. He needed to feel her everywhere.

Without warning, he came into direct contact with the blank space in her mind. Startled, he broke the kiss and lifted his head. He was nearly distracted as he looked at her. Her cheeks were flushed and her lips swollen. He went back for a quick kiss, then a second. As he teased her lips for a third, he said thickly, "Distract me. Hit me. Do something." Her power fluttered against his teasingly and he groaned. "Anything but that, Jayda! I'm trying to find some semblance of control! I need to see what's in your mind."

With a little sigh, she stopped teasing him. Instead, she dropped a ball of snow down the back of his shirt. He yelped and she bit her lip to hide a smile. "Does that work?"

He grimaced at the cold snow sliding down his back. "Yes, quite." Grateful that she hadn't decided to drop it down his pants instead, he framed her face with his hands and softly probed at her mind. Now looking for the blank space deliberately, he found it quickly. It was as if a large chunk of her memory had been fragmented away.

She began to frown. "I've always felt that there," she admitted. A little more fretfully, she grabbed onto his arms. "It's important, isn't it? Who did this to me and my parents? Why were our memories taken away?"

"It's all right, *ishke,*" he soothed softly. He stroked his thumbs over her cheeks even as he softly wrapped his presence around her. "I can see who did this, and I was expecting it." He began to search through her mind for the tiny fragments that remained. "Nine years ago, you lived in Prismatic with your parents as members of the original Black Magi, the faction formed by Morgan Chronis as a secret hiding place for Chronicle children."

She almost stopped breathing. "That's why we always felt angered by the Elite."

"It is. And this will hurt you, to remember your friends and Morgan. You were like a family. He's suffered for nine years knowing he sent you away." His Fire power fused the fragments into a single mass as he swept through her mind. When he brought the pieces together at the blank space, they instantly melted together and reformed.

The memories punched into both their minds equally. He wrapped his arms around her and pulled her fiercely close. He pressed her face to his shoulder as a low cry tore from her chest. It broke his heart. "He loved you enough to protect you the only way he could," he said softly.

"When I find him, I'm kicking him!" was the fierce counter. She took a ragged breath that ended with a hiccup. "I miss Kelsey and C.J. and Roman! I always felt so safe with them. If I'd been with them when I went into first puberty, maybe it wouldn't have hurt so badly."

"I'm afraid it would have." He rubbed his thumb under her eyes to remove the tears as she looked up at him and. When more fell, he lowered his head to softly kiss them away. "I'm an Elder. Every year I live, I become more sensitive. Where we are not perfect opposites, we are perfectly alike. We would not understand one another this well if we hadn't experienced similar."

"Is that why when I felt you on the mountain, I felt suddenly safe?"

"I'll *never* let anything hurt you." A little flicker of fire came and went from his eyes. "It's just as well I wasn't in the area when your weekly visitor came by. I'd have eaten him."

"You didn't eat Gamma." Her lips trembled as she tried not to smile. "You punted him like kids kicking snowballs." She let out a little breath and relaxed against his chest, comforted by having him close. "I never imagined this happening to me. Maybe I remembered Morgan a little when I awoke after finding you. I felt a little confused but a little relieved."

"I think I lost my mind a bit," he admitted, "when I woke and you were gone. I had felt your presence when I tried to comfort you. But I was so badly injured that I couldn't do anything about it."

"Oh!" She sat upright. "Your head!" She scooted off his lap and then knelt beside him. She threaded her fingers into his hair to examine the bump on his head. "I completely forgot! You distracted me!"

He admired the curve of her breasts. They currently rested on perfect eye level for him. "I suspect I will often be distracted by you too."

Ignoring that to the best of her ability, she gently examined the injury. It was all but gone. "It's a good thing you have a hard head. You must have tumbled clear down the mountain!" His memories were hers, and she could see the confrontation with Gamma. Her eyes narrowed ever so slightly. "I suppose it's just as well that I wasn't in the best shape. I might have killed him myself."

"Your gentleness hides a fierce side." Unable to resist, he nuzzled his nose between her breasts just for the delight of hearing her breath break.

"I'm not a pushover." The words came out breathless. The heat in her body had been silent but suddenly awoke with a vengeance. When his tongue lightly tasted her skin, her sensitive flesh sent messages of pleasure to every corner of her body.

"I should wait," he said huskily, "until we have a better shelter." Even as he said it, he slowly untied her tunic to reveal supple pale skin and wonderfully curved breasts hidden behind bikini the same hue as her flesh.

"How long have you already waited?" Her fingers slid down to his shoulders and began to knead lightly. Her fingers tingled, wanting to feel his hot skin. She wanted to explore every inch of her Fury's body, to assuage the curiosity inside. What had seemed impersonal before was suddenly very personal.

His eyes closed. "My whole life," he managed to say. He caught her closer and buried his face against her heart. "I've waited. I waited no matter how terrible it felt at times. No matter how it cut me to see Dominic and Jazz happy with their Chronicles. I've waited centuries, millennia, to find you."

"Then don't wait anymore. My wait wasn't as long, but it hurt just as bad. I was so *alone* without you." When he looked up at her, she smiled tremulously. "We're not alone now. Why wait?"

On a low sound of need, he caught her around the waist and tumbled her down onto the grass. Against the green color, her hair seemed more blue than green, just as against the sky it had seemed more green than blue. It shifted and flowed like the icy ocean. "Be gentle with me. Your curiosity might kill me."

She nimbly began to untie the laces of his tunic. "You'll be okay. You know a good doctor." His laugh warmed her all the way through, and as his tunic opened to reveal the incredible expanse of his chest, her sigh came soft and happy. "You have lines like mine."

They flowed across the left side of his chest in the same pattern as on her body. They were gold against his tanned skin and rippled with every movement of his muscles. Seeing them brought a fierce wave of possessiveness. He was hers. He was marked as hers. "We need to live in the desert," she decided huskily as she ran a finger across his chest.

He shrugged out of the tunic and then lifted her enough to remove the one she wore. "Why? So I go shirtless?"

"Mmm." She ran her hands slowly over his chest and shoulders, memorizing the feel of his body. Her hands burned and tingled to send waves of delight through her body. Desire slid through her blood as surely as her power did. She felt hot and hungry in a way she had never felt before.

His power rubbed against hers and there something sizzled softly. When her eyes went wide, he drew one of her hands to his lips. Steam softly curled from both their bodies. "What did you expect when water met fire?" He was holding her left arm so he was able to trail his lips down her arm and taste every one of her lines. He slowly climbed toward her slender shoulder.

She moved restlessly under him, her fingers flexing in his grip. "Not yet," he said softly, enthralled with learning her body and her pleasure. "Let me memorize you. I've waited too long for this." His lips teased hers softly until she strained up to deepen the kiss. "You'll have your turn."

"I'd better!" The words turned into a soft gasp as his fingers brushed over the curves of her breasts. Before she could take a breath, he had untied the knot holding the bikini together. Now half-naked in his arms, she waited for nerves. There were none.

Their eyes met and held as he softly trailed a finger over her bare breast. Steam curled behind his touch as she arched slowly to follow his caress. He curled his presence around her to feel her emotions and rubbed his thumb over her nipple. The jolt of pleasure that ricocheted through her body rippled to him, and he did it again just to make her voice break on a soft whimper.

She was going out of her mind. He knew exactly how sensitive her skin was and knew that even the barest touch was dizzying. A sense of pressure built inside her muscles, the pleasure circling and coiling. Her pulse throbbed everywhere at once, and heat burned her. If the lines on her body hadn't branded her, then this would. An ache began to build between her legs and she shifted restlessly. Her remaining clothes felt too tight and too confining. "Xander."

He lifted his head and took a deep breath. "Hold on." He ran trembling fingers over her side. "I might rip something."

"And?"

He gave a half-laugh, half-groan. "You'd have nothing at all to wear." He grabbed for as much control as he could and began to work the pants down her legs. It was a struggle; she was softly curling her power and presence around him, deliberately trying to undermine his control. "I'll tear them off you later. Stop teasing me!"

"Never." As she found herself fully naked, she savored the freedom to be there in his arms. "Where's the self-consciousness part? I only had a little bit much earlier."

"You can't be self-conscious with someone who wants you as badly as I do." He felt fascinated with everything he saw. She was utterly perfect. Unable to resist the lure, he bent his head and closed his mouth hotly over her nipple. Her back arched on a soft cry, and her fingers clenched into his shoulders.

Her entire body began to vibrate like a plucked string. Barely able to breathe, she grabbed his shoulders as her anchor in a world she had never dared dream existed. The ache was growing and spreading. She *wanted*. She had no name for what she wanted. She only knew she did. "Do something," she pleaded breathlessly.

"Like what?" The words were as teasing as his breath as he slowly trailed kisses over her flat stomach. He burned to take her, to bury his aching flesh deep inside her, but he couldn't seem to assuage his heart's hunger to know everything about her. "I am doing something." Her scent, crisp arctic oceans, tempted him to move lower, and his lips trailed over her inner thigh.

She opened her mouth to retort when she felt his breath on her sensitive flesh. She took a sharp breath that came back out on a moan as his tongue found some secret spot, something unbearably sensitive, and teased it mercilessly. The ache grew, the pressure built, the pleasure drowned her, and she couldn't *breathe*, ready to cry and beg him to stop . . . when he did. He shifted back up her body to memorize her face with his lips, and his fingertips scraped over her flesh teasingly.

Shocked, she couldn't find her voice or her thoughts. His feelings lightly fluttered against hers and determination filled her. Two could play *that* game! She slid her hands up to caress his face and then pinched his ear. He yelped, and in that moment of distraction, she was able to get the leverage to tumble him over onto his back. She sat across his hips triumphantly. "Serves you right!"

She looked wild and sultry. Her hair no longer fell straight as it tumbled around her shoulders in disarray.

A flush to her skin made her radiantly beautiful. Unable to help himself, he curled his hands around her waist. He could nearly span it with his fingers. How could so much power fit into that slim body? "And what are you going to do with me?"

"I'm not sure yet." She smoothed a hand across his chest, loving the difference in their skin tone. "I'm still learning." She slid off him but he made no move to take control. Instead, he linked his hands behind his head. Delight filled her. "Are you at my mercy?"

"You have to ask?" He laced his fingers together tightly. He didn't know how much he could take, but he was willing to find out. A low groan rumbled in his chest as she bent her head to tease a nipple with her lips. "Quick learner."

"Always." Savoring the freedom, she trailed her lips and fingers over his chest and shoulders, tracing the lines and the curves of his muscles. She wasn't afraid. She should have been. He was so powerful, even in Magi form, but he trembled under her touch and his red eyes burned as they watched her.

When her explorations brought her to the edge of his pants, and the fascinating bulge beneath, she didn't hesitate to tug the pants down his legs. He had to help remove his boots first, and both were amused he had forgotten them, but he was shortly naked as well. She stared at his arousal in a combination of fascination, trepidation, and anticipation.

He couldn't resist teasing, "Surely a doctor has seen a naked man before."

She shook her head a little. "Not one who wanted her."

"Then you've been around idiots." His eyes all but crossed as her hand curled around him to memorize his length and shape. "By the moons." His knuckles turned white as he fought to control himself. He stopped breathing entirely as he felt her hot breath. "Don't . . ." The words stopped as she teasingly kissed him. "That's it!"

She gave a startled gasp as he sat upright and grabbed her. Before she could blink, she was flat on her back with his wonderful weight pressed along her body. She opened her mouth to ask a formless question, but his hungry kiss took the words. Words became unimportant and she buried her fingers in his hair to hold him closer. Restlessly, instinctively, she curled a leg over his hip.

"Do you know what you're asking for?" He got his answer when her emotions fluttered against his like the tide on the shore. She knew. Not consciously, not yet, but she knew. He caught her other leg and pressed it against his other hip, opening her entirely to him. His eyes met and held hers, and his throat closed as he saw the look in her eyes. "*Ishke.*"

Her eyes fluttered closed and her breath caught as she felt him slowly sinking into her body. Ripples spread outward, the ache easing and doubling all at the same time, building the hunger in her body until it was all she could feel. Tears burned her eyes as she felt, for the first time, as if she was whole. She had claimed her Fury. Finally. She felt as if she had been waiting millennia too.

She didn't get long to savor the feeling. He pulled back, then thrust deep again, stealing a gasp. The gasp became a whimper, then a moan, as he moved faster, building the pleasure once more. This time she knew he wouldn't stop. She prayed he wouldn't stop. She was going to go out of her mind if he did. She couldn't breathe anymore. Her fingers clenched in his hair as her body went out of control, tension stretched to the point of bursting.

He did something then. His mind and his power seemed to meld into hers just as his body did. The tension broke and ecstasy shuddered through her body and mind in a burning wave of water that was so hot it flashed to steam. She held onto him even tighter, only dimly aware a world existed beyond them and that moment. And as she felt the searing heat of his pleasure deep inside, she lifted her head to meet his kiss and finally felt as if she was home.

He tucked a hand under her head for support, but that was the extent of what he had any energy to do. Moving was far beyond his reach. *His.* His Chronicle. Every torturous minute of waiting had been worth it to finally feel complete. Her heart seemed to beat inside him, and he curled his presence around her to anchor her close.

Her power stilled its soft pulsing, and he found the strength to lift his head. Tenderness swamped him as he saw she had slipped asleep. He couldn't be surprised. She had gone far too long with uncontrolled power before their bonding. Adding in their energetic mating would be enough to tire anyone out. He was on the tired side himself.

He sighed and forced himself to release her. He sat up and grabbed his hipsack from where it sat nearby. He pulled out a blanket and shook it out. It was Kin made and automatically grew to accommodate his size. When he wrapped it around himself and Jayda, it promptly got big enough for them both.

He tucked her possessively into his arms and buried his face in her hair. He wanted her again. Even after what had just happened, he wanted her again. He softly stroked his fingers over her arm and side. A certainty in his heart told him that he would never stop wanting her. She was just going to have to get used to his hands being on her at every opportunity.

She murmured against his shoulder, "Is that supposed to be alarming? It fell short of the mark."

He smiled and lifted his head. She was smiling up at him, her eyes sleepy and satiated. "More of a statement of fact."

"Mmm." She smoothed a hand over his chest, marveling at how her skin still felt so sensitive. Or perhaps it was just because of him. "I don't mind. I suspect I might have the same problem. I can't seem to keep my hands to myself."

"I don't mind," he said, returning her words with a smile. He smoothed her tangled hair from her face. "Did I hurt you?"

"If you did, I didn't notice. Was it supposed to hurt the first time?"

"Not if your lover knows what he's doing."

Her smile turned slightly smug. "Mine certainly does. Of course, I'm sure I'm not near to his skill. I'll have to practice."

"I stand ready and willing to help you practice as much as you like. I would like to note, however, that I think you had it right the first time." He stole a tender kiss and lingered until she relaxed wholly. Only then did he release her. "Want to tell me what's really on your mind?"

"Where do we go?" she asked simply.

"Kindred."

Her brows shot up. "Kindred?"

"It will be safe, for one thing. For another, there is a Kin there who is Tariah's brother. He can contact her on the Isle. It will be the only way we can get in touch with her and Morgan. I've forgotten the way to the Isle now that you're here. You need to finish your journey." He trailed a finger down her lines, a good portion of which were now even darker. Light rippled through them as if showing the power flowing inside. "But you're a step closer."

"Do you suppose the rest of my journey has to do with the Elite, or that we'll ever find my brothers and sister?" She felt no hesitation in claiming Kelsey, C.J., and Roman. They were, in every way that counted, her siblings.

He sighed softly as he thought of the things he had seen and experienced. "I think that it's somehow inevitable. We all have a reason for being. We just need to find yours."

"And after that?"

He smiled. "We'll make a home on the Isle of Dragons and have many children to torment your parents with. You can patch up foolhardy whelps, and I'll give in and actually take my rightful place on the Elder Council."

If that was her reason for being, then she could find no fault with it. "It's a promise."

Part Two
~Journey~

Chapter Thirteen

The Isle of Dragons was located in the middle of the Deepest Ocean, a place of turbulent waters that no ship ever dared sail through. In size, the Isle was bigger than Glacia and Choral, but not quite as big as Spectrum. Its landscape consisted of mountains, deserts, valleys, and rivers. Every manner of scenery existed there. The oldest of Dragons remembered when the rest of the world had been just as beautiful. The younger simply sensed something amiss.

The largest concentration of Dragons lived on the Plateau, a series of cliff steppes that offered caves to live and work in. There was no currency on the Isle. Everything was done through barter and trade. Though their mountains were rich in ivory and bronze, no one mined. What was there could stay there.

When she had arrived at the Isle nine years before, Tariah Chronis had been at the end of her Chronicle journey. She had been pursued across the entire world by people who wanted to kill her and people who needed her to save them. At her lowest point, she had been on the cusp of mental breakdown, ready to detonate her own power and leave the world entirely.

But she hadn't.

From where she stood on the sunny cliff just outside her home, she turned to see her Fury sleeping in a swinging bed suspended between two desert trees. It had been Dominic's unconditional love and presence that had brought her back from the brink.

She smiled and walked over to look down at him. "Lazy."

One eye opened ever so slightly to reveal smoke colored amusement. "You fed me. I'm ready for a nap." He sighed contentedly and reached out to tug her down onto the bed with him. She was quite small, even for Magi, but he loved it. She was perfectly sized for him to cuddle. "I can't seem to get rid of my family when you're cooking."

"That's because you're all bottomless pits." She stretched slowly and the sunlight glimmered across her lines. They covered a fair portion of her body, including the side of her face, across her chest, and down an arm and leg. They were often clearly revealed because she was a desert girl and stuck to the clothing she was most comfortable with.

"Tariah!"

Disgruntled, she lifted her head to see her brother coming down the path toward them. "I was comfortable," she complained. She got to her feet. "And why didn't you just tap my mind?"

Though there was a five-year age difference, Morgan and Tariah had bonds like twins. Most people didn't even know there was an age gap at all except for the fact that Morgan had the three little lines at the corner of his eyes and Tariah didn't. They both had Telepathy skills as Dragoons, and they could communicate with their minds across even large distances.

Morgan Chronis came to a stop and smiled. In height, he was only a few inches taller than Tariah and quite short for Magi males. Both Chronis twins had the same thick auburn hair and glimmering silver eyes. Morgan's lines went across his chest and arms, and they were also often seen because he lived in the higher mountains and wore sleeveless tunics. "I figured this was worth a real visit." He reached out to pat her tummy. "Rumor reaches my ears."

She grinned happily. "What sort of rumors?"

"Oh, I don't know. Dominic strutting around like he owned the world, that sort of thing." The words were said teasingly as he looked toward Dominic, still lazily swinging on the bed. "And I believe a bet has begun about the child being Dragon or Magi."

"No Dragon!" She shook her head vehemently. "I am not laying eggs!"

"Well, not technically," Dominic soothed her. "The egg would be removed from you at the right time." He rolled lithely to his feet and walked over to tug her into his arms. His hands spread warmly across her stomach even as his presence curled around her mind and heart comfortingly. "Stop worrying about it. In a month or two, we'll know definitively which you're carrying and can make plans for it."

Morgan grinned a little. "Mom and Dad are going to be over the moons with happiness. The last few messages that have been delivered to me pretty much sang the same refrain. They want us to visit, and they want grandchildren."

"We flew past Spectrum a week ago," Tariah offered. "Just to see if I could sense anything. I saw some Furies, but didn't sense our children." She smiled. "Well, not children anymore, I'm sure. They're all eighteen or nineteen now."

His eyes lowered. It still cut at his heart every day to remember the necessity of sending away the four Chronicle children he had found. He had only had them for five years, but he had loved them deeply. Kelsey had been his favorite. He had been wrapped around her finger from day one.

A shadow passed overhead as a Dragon came in for landing. She changed to Magi form as she walked over and wrapped her arms around his waist. "Stop," Jazz Eaglewind said softly. She was only fractionally taller than Tariah though distinctly curvier. Tariah had stopped resenting her for it. Jazz gently reached up to frame Morgan's face. "You did what was needed."

Without words, he buried his face in his Fury's hair and drew on her ready support. He too wouldn't have survived nine years before if he hadn't found her. "Sometimes I need to be reminded."

"Tariaaaaaaah!"

The shout was followed by a small figure tumbling through the air on a gust of wind. Dominic hastily reached out and grabbed the tiny yellow Dragon by the base of her wings and held her steady. She had the potential to be a Dragon Lord, but at only twenty-five years of age, she was the equivalent to a six-year-old Magi. She wouldn't be able to practice an alternate form until she hit first puberty around the age of fifty.

Tariah smiled. "Good morning, Saffron." She held out her arms and took the small Dragon for a cuddle. She was little more than a foot and a half in size. "You know better than to fly that fast," she scolded. "The currents are strong up here."

Saffron's golden eyes sparkled happily. Tariah was her favorite person *ever*. "I heard you're having a baby!"

"That's what I strongly believe." It was said with a smile. "I'm certain of it."

Saffron's tail wagged happily. "I'm glad!" Her nose wrinkled up. "I had something to tell you, but I got distracted. I don't remember."

Almost automatically, both Chronis reached out mentally and nudged her mind as if nudging a door open. Jazz and Dominic exchanged a grin. Jazz had Ultravision—the ability to see the history of objects she touched— and Dominic had Telekinesis. They were special, unique, gifts that only Dragoons could learn. Though Morgan and Tariah came by their Telepathy through their Dragoon gift, they had strange and wonderful other mental gifts that were wholly their own.

Saffron brightened and sat up straight in Tariah's arms. "Now I remember! We're getting reports from Furies out in the Magi lands! It sounds like the Chronicle children have been found!"

Shock stole Morgan's voice and Tariah fared little better. Dominic put an arm tightly around his mate's shoulders to anchor her as he sensed the wild response of her heart and mind. "How did they find them?" he asked. "The four weren't to awaken without Morgan or Tariah or a Fury present."

"They sensed them from other cities. An' the Elders have been conferring. Four Furies haven't reported in yet; the assumption is that they are the Fury with the correct Chronicle. The four who haven't reported in are Solis, Grecia, Dahlia, and Elder Xander!"

"That sounds about right," Jazz said softly. "Because each child was of a different element."

Morgan grimaced. "Solis has my pity for it is a surety he has Kelsey. On the other hand," he added softer, "I am glad that Jayda was the one for Xander. He was alone for far too long." He let out a little breath. "Now what do we do?" he asked Tariah.

She frowned. "We will want to try to meet up with them. We can't bring them here, obviously. They need to finish their journeys. But having us there might be helpful because you can be sure the Elite will be aiming for them."

"They might have already made movements," Jazz noted. "We can't be sure."

"So then let's go to Kindred."

"Why Kindred?" Morgan asked.

"Because I'm fairly sure that at least Xander will think to go there to see Daylar to try to contact me." Tariah smiled. "And anyway, I haven't seen him and Sparkle in a year. This will give me a chance to tell them that I'm pregnant. They're going to be thrilled."

Saffron's face fell. "You're going to leave?"

"Just for a little while." Tariah put her down gently on the ground. "We'll be back as soon as we can, and you'll have four new Chronicles to be friends with." She straightened back up and the sunlight glimmered across her lines. "Let's pack some supplies and get going. The sooner we find them, the better. I have a bad feeling I can't shake."

Chapter Fourteen

Kelsey awoke to soft kisses being feathered over her shoulder. Not even half-awake, she swatted at Solis. "Too early." His soft laugh teased her sensitive skin, and his presence swirled around her temptingly. He was lying along her back with his arm snug around her waist. She had never felt more secure and loved in her life.

As her power fluttered against his, he knew she was finally actually waking. He had been trying to bring her around for the last several minutes. His Chronicle slept like the dead. "There you are." He teased her ear with his lips. His intent wasn't to seduce. All he wanted was to make her gradually more accustomed to his touch. Having everything of second puberty happen at once would only alarm her more.

She turned over and snuggled against his chest. "You know," she murmured softly, "I was half expecting to wake and be disoriented. I'm naked and sleeping in the arms of a man I've known only less than a day."

"Is there *anything* that disorients you?" His fingers moved unconsciously over her back. Her skin seemed outrageously soft considering the work she did. He nuzzled her hair softly, savoring the scent of spicy fires and thick smoke.

Her breath caught. "I'm not sure." Her hands smoothed over the supple muscles of his arms, then linked behind his neck. "I want a good morning kiss."

"Have I mentioned that I love you?" He tilted her chin up and feathered his lips over her face before settling on her lips. As her sigh breathed into his mouth, he deepened the kiss slowly, his tongue teasing hers. Her power rose in a soft red glow, and he happily drank it as he kissed her. If all he could have of her physically for the time being was her mouth, then he was still a very happy man.

She shivered in delight. She didn't know if he was drinking her or her power. Her entire body was beginning to feel flushed, and her breasts were swelling in a foreign way that still seemed oddly natural. When he released her lips and buried his against her neck, she could only manage, "Solis."

His entire body quivered. He would live every one of his two hundred plus years all over again just to hear her call his name. "Yes?" He brushed against her emotions and elation filled him. Just to be sure, he lifted a hand and lightly skimmed his knuckles over the outside of her breast.

Her breath hitched and she arched a little toward him. Drawn back to her lips once more, he sank into the kiss as he pressed a hand against her back and pulled her closer. Her breasts flattened against his chest and made them both quiver with barely leashed hunger.

It was only when he began to softly trail kisses down her collar that her nerves reappeared. As he reached the curve of her breast, the bolt of pleasure went from breast to toes. It was shocking enough that she instantly tried to jerk back.

He immediately gathered her close in his arms. "Easy," he said softly. "Now that I know your limit, I'll stop."

Feeling her body sending out aching frustrated signals at complete odds with the anxiety in her heart and mind, she blew out a breath. "I'm not enjoying this yet," she complained.

"Yes you are, and that's the real problem." His smile looked tender and sensual all at the same time. "It'll get worse before it gets better. There will come a day in the not so far future where you're going to feel like you're on the verge of self-combustion but your mind won't let you take the final step yet." He stole a brief kiss, taking the last of her power waiting for him. "You'll likely be ready to tackle me down, and I'm going to be just as miserable."

"As long as it's mutual!" was her grumpy counter.

He smiled. "When it's second puberty, both lovers suffer equally whether they're both going through it or just one is." He sat up and shoved down the blanket that still mostly covered them. "We need food."

Etude came flying up, and her wings fluttered madly as she carried a hipsack filled to the brim with fruit. "I have some if you'll help me!" She was barely aloft; the sack weighed more than she did.

Kelsey scrambled up heedless of her nudity and grabbed the sack. Solis watched the morning light dapple across her pale skin and covered his face with a hand. He had lied. He was already miserable.

"Patience is rewarded," she reminded him. It warmed her that he wanted her so much. She *needed* him to want her, in ways that had nothing to do with her body.

He cracked one eye open. "When have you ever been patient, *ishke*?"

Defiantly, she took a bite of fruit. She wasn't going to credit that with an answer.

He relented with a sigh and got up. He shook out the blanket and it obligingly shrank back down to its default size. He tucked it safely into the shoulder pack he usually wore and got out a fresh tunic.

She had been mostly ignoring him while she happily ate her fruit, but when the tunic was dropped on her head, she was diverted. "What's this for?" She pulled it off her head and eyed it in distaste. "It has sleeves."

"Desert girl at heart," Etude informed Solis.

"So I can tell." He got out another tunic and pulled it on over his head. "We're going to Kindred. It's another wooded land." Kelsey's disgruntlement made him smile. "When we get to the Isle, I promise we'll live in a desert area. Actually, I have many desert relatives."

"How many is 'many'?" his mate asked suspiciously.

"Hmm. I have about fifteen older brothers and sisters and four younger ones. Between them, I have more than a hundred nieces and nephews." When her eyes went wide, he grinned. "We like big families."

"And your Isle hasn't fallen apart under the weight?!"

Enjoying her, he sat down and tugged her onto his lap. Her crystalline blue eyes looked skeptical, and mentally she was sure he was teasing her. "We don't live only on the surface of the land. Some live under it, others live in mountains. A lot of Water Dragons even live in homes on or under the ocean around the Isle. There's plenty of room."

"Oh." She thought about that for several moments. "Well, as long as I get to live in the desert, I don't care how many of you there are." When he opened his mouth, she shoved a piece of fruit in and got to her feet. "Eat your breakfast."

He obediently ate the fruit. While he did, he watched under his lashes as she pulled on her bikini. She moved as wildly and freely as a flame burned. He wanted her more than he wanted air. More than life.

She pulled on the tunic with trembling fingers. "Stop that."

His smile came slow and lethal. "Why?"

"It's making me jittery!" The sleeves flopped past her fingers, and she eyed them in consternation. "It's too big."

"It'll have to do. None of us is a Soil element." He hungrily eyed the opening in the tunic where he could see the curves of her breasts. "Etude, can you help her lace that? If I try, I might take it off her."

"Is that supposed to alarm me?" Kelsey asked dryly. She felt the sudden searing backwash of his emotions and her eyes went wide. He had only given her a glimpse of what was in his mind, but she saw enough to bring her nerves back to life. "Never mind. Etude can help me."

Smiling, Etude flew over and helped tie the laces on the tunic to keep it closed. "What about her legs?" she asked.

Solis eyed the long length of Kelsey's legs. "They're stunning."

"Yes, but they need to be covered as well."

Kelsey looked down. The tunic went further down her legs than the edge of her shorts. The tunic, in fact, almost went to her knees. "If I tried to wear anything else of his, it'd never fit. I'll just wrap the blanket around my waist until we find other clothes."

"My friend is a Soil secondary," Etude offered. "I can ask him to help."

"That would be great."

Solis got to his feet. "I guess we're ready to leave then." He skimmed a thumb across Kelsey's cheek as excitement began to hum inside him. When she tilted her head, he said softly, "Dragons can't carry people on their backs, Kin or Magi, because the powers always clash and it makes the Dragon uncomfortable. But Dragoons . . . We Furies can carry our Chronicles on our backs."

Her breath caught. "Because our power is made to be one." The idea of flying was exhilarating, and so was the idea of finally seeing her Fury in his natural form. His lips softly brushed against hers in a tender kiss that brought tears to her eyes. "What was that for?" she asked softly.

"Being you." He rubbed his thumb across her cheek. "Back up and give me room."

Kelsey and Etude both moved back so that there was plenty of space, and fog and ice rolled in around Solis as he began to glow with blue light. There was a flash, and when it faded, he was once more in Dragon form. He shook out his wings with a quick stretch before unfurling them entirely.

Kelsey had never seen anything more magnificent. He was almost four times her size but she felt absolutely no fear. His scales were the same rich brown as his hair and marked with the blue streaks of his Water element. His wings were thin enough in some places that she could see the veins beneath and they formed a beautiful pattern. His face should have been frightening with its sharp lines and wicked teeth . . . but it wasn't. He was beautiful.

She walked over to look up at him, and his beautiful brown eyes looked down at her. He lowered his head until they were on eye level, and then very gently he nuzzled her with his nose. "You seem tiny," he said in awe. "It's hard to believe so much personality is packed into that tiny form."

"I'd take offense if it wasn't true." She softly put her hands on his face and delight filled her. His scales felt as soft as fur rather than the tough skin she had been expecting. She stroked lightly along his beloved face and he gave a contented sigh that almost sent her tumbling. A strong claw instantly closed gently around her and kept her close. She felt . . . safe. She felt as safe as when he had held her in his arms.

She smiled and leaned forward to nuzzle his cheek. He laughed and lifted her up high. "Grab onto my ear fin, but gently please. Then climb over onto my shoulders."

She did as told and then gave a little yelp as she almost slipped off his back. Etude grabbed her by her tunic, however, and held her steady until she could find a secure place to sit. Curiously, the way the bones along his back were shaped provided a perfect perch for her. Was that also because he was a Fury?

"Hang on tight!" He gave no more warning than that before flapping his wings and shooting up into the air. Her shriek of laughter tickled him, and the euphoria of having her on his back made him do a quick loop in the air. There was no discomfort. No sense of something wrong. Only a sense of something right, and the power that flowed between them swirled like infinity.

Etude flew up to join them, and he grasped her gently with a claw. "Point the direction. The flight's on me."

She looked down. Way down. Hastily she said, "Please free my wings. I believe I have a fear of falling if they're not open." He obligingly changed his grip, and she let out a soft breath. "Faeries can fly without their wings by using their power, but it's never as secure as using my wings."

"A Faerie afraid of falling." Kelsey pondered that. "That'd be like me being afraid of fire." Etude flicked her wings at her, and Kelsey grinned. Despite all events lately, she felt wildly happy. She stretched her arms high over her head to enjoy the wind whipping past. They went through a cloud, and she found herself with an armful of Flutterlies. "Well."

She studied the little puffs of white curiously. No one was really sure what to classify them as. They weren't really animals, but they weren't really plants either. They would often just appear in the sky and gather together. When they did, they formed clouds. When they pulled in Air or Water power, they became rain clouds. Too much Thunder power and they became storms.

Something seemed . . . odd about this batch. She couldn't put her finger on it. She opened her arms and let them go, and watched as they flew off into the distance. They seemed to be heading somewhere with a purpose. "I wonder if they're heading to the storms around Mirah."

"I hope not." Solis frowned. "Things are getting worse around Spectrum last I heard."

"So how far from Kindred are we?"

"About three hours of normal flight speed. I can go faster if you like."

"Won't that be taxing for you?"

His smile, though it revealed many sharp teeth, was anticipatory rather than predatory. She felt a flutter of heat in her body. "I have good incentive to use my power now," he almost purred.

She blew out a breath. She was beginning to think second puberty was the planet's idea of a practical joke.

~*~

When Roman awoke the morning after he had discovered what he was, he woke to find himself curled up in the middle of a cave covered in flowers. Grecia was contentedly sleeping with him wrapped in her arms. The incongruity of things hit him, and he studied his Fury in consternation. Lives weren't supposed to change that fast.

It was mostly dark in the cave. The balls of lightning he had made for additional light had started fading away; the lanterns had long since been dead. Rather than recreate them, he carefully used his Air power to bore a hole up through the roof to the surface. Light immediately flooded in and he winced in the brightness.

When his eyes finally cleared, he was able to see much better than before. He was also able to see Grecia more clearly, much to his delight. His eyes eagerly ran over every curve of her body. Desire for her, only dormant and not truly gone, roared once more to life. He softly smoothed his hand over her hip and leg and savored her skin. He caught a handful of her hair and brought it to his cheek. It was as soft as fur and carried a strength hidden behind deceptive delicacy.

He gently brushed his power against hers, trying to coax her awake. She only made a grumpy noise and tugged him closer. He smiled and began to rub the back of his knuckles over the outside curve of her breast. Her power stirred and fluttered against his and then he felt her fully awaken. "Good morning," he said softly.

"I guess it is." Her eyes didn't open as she slowly twisted against his fingers. He shifted upward and she released him so he could move. His lips lightly trailed over her face and neck, and she slid her arms around his shoulders once more. Half awake, half dreaming still, she had never felt so utterly cherished.

His fingers framed her face so he could tug her up for a tender kiss. Her entire body felt hot and heavy, her hunger for him stealing every ounce of her strength. She had no will or ability to resist as he tumbled her onto her back and began to explore her face with his lips. As his lips moved lower, she shivered helplessly. "Wake me this way every morning."

"I'll do my best." He smiled as he felt a rumble from her power. "That sounded like the sound my stomach makes when I'm hungry for sweetbread pie."

She opened her eyes and saw the soft white aura covering him. It beckoned to her in a way that was vastly more tempting than any pie could hope to be. "If I start calling you 'sweet pie' it's because you've now gotten yourself associated with it in my mind." She curled a leg over his to keep him close and leaned up to press her lips to his collar. His power flowed into her, cool and refreshing and delightfully sweet.

When she tumbled him over, he didn't argue. His eyes all but crossed as she began to softly trail kisses across his chest. The ache grew and spread, and he wanted her so badly that it was physical pain. His arousal throbbed in time to his heartbeat and it beat only for her.

Heat flushed his skin and hitched his breath as she continued her teasing little kisses. He wasn't entirely sure he wanted her to ever stop. Her lips teased his stomach while her fingers temptingly danced their way up his leg. When she was only inches from her goal, his stomach suddenly let out a loud rumble not dissimilar to the one her power had made.

She blinked and straightened with a smile. He looked horribly embarrassed and it was wonderfully sweet. "Well," she said. "I suppose other hungers must be tended to first." She eased up his body and kissed him lingeringly. His fingers tangled in her hair and she loved it. Softly she curled her presence around him and felt him curl around her in return. The powers merged and flowed endlessly.

As they eased apart, he said huskily, "I'm not going to be willing to stop next time."

A little thrill rippled through her body on a wave of lust. "Are you going to have your wicked way with me?"

"I'm going to have you any way I can. Wicked might be part of it eventually." He caught her in his arms for a fierce hug, simply wanting to have her close. "Mine," he breathed in wonder. "You're mine. I still can't quite bring myself to believe it."

She hoped he never did. She loved the breathless wonder in his eyes every time he looked at her. It was the way she felt when she looked at him. "Maybe in a thousand years you'll believe it." His eyes widened with shock and her smile softened. "You're immortal now, Roman. Our power is infinite between us and it makes us both infinite as well. As long as we choose not to age, so long as no one kills us, we will live forever. Together, forever. Until time ends."

"How do Furies live so long if their power isn't infinite?" he wondered.

She opened her mouth only to close it again quickly. Thoughtfully, she said, "I am not sure, to tell the truth. It's not something we ever asked. But it is a very good question. We'll have to ask Tariah when we find her. She's got an amazing intelligence. She should be a scholar."

"What does she do?"

She grinned. "Feed many hungry Dragons. She's an outstanding cook." She got to her feet and brushed off her clothes. Both hers and his alike were dusty from sleeping on the bed of flowers, but both sets of clothes were sturdy and made for the desert. Dusty and sandy were just part of the choice of living there.

She opened the ceiling with her power and then formed steps leading out. As they got into the sunlight, Roman stretched largely. He loved the desert. Watching him and the way the sun rippled over his stunningly beautiful body, she decided she was becoming a fan of it herself. There was much to be said for the way the desert sun defined muscles on a man like hers.

"What do we do about breakfast?" he asked her. "Unless you're carrying supplies in that hipsack of yours."

"None that are edible." She frowned thoughtfully. "We can't wait until we get to Kindred. It's a good five-hour flight from where we are. And we can't go into a city safely." She skimmed her knuckles across the lines on his face. "The world is changing, but it has not changed enough to make you safe, *ishke*."

"Fruit is out of question because I doubt any oases are near here." He snapped his fingers suddenly. "Let's see if we can hunt up some dune crabs. There are bound to be some around here. I can probably cook them with some lightning and we'll be good to go."

"How do we hunt them?"

He glanced toward her feet. The sand had turned an odd color. "Oddly, they always seem to be drawn to Soil power."

She blinked. "Pardon?" He suddenly snatched her off her feet, and she barely stifled a yelp as she grabbed his shoulders for balance. Eyes wide, she stared at the giant pincers that now stuck out of the sand, trying to grab any and everything they could. "Well then."

A lightning bolt cracked down from the sky and struck the top of the dune. Sand flew and the large crab popped out with a distinctly angered clattering noise. It was as high as Roman's hip, and its pincers were almost as big as its body.

Still holding Grecia, Roman backed up a few steps. His eyes flashed white and another lightning bolt dropped from the sky. It hit the crab in the middle of its back and it flipped up into the air. When it landed, it didn't move. Steam rose from its shell.

"Well," Grecia said again. Belatedly, she realized she was being carried. "You can put me down now."

He slowly put her on her feet, taking care that his hands slid warmly over her bare skin wonderfully displayed in her desert clothing. Breathless, she watched as he walked over to where their breakfast waited. He cracked the shell open, and she got a look at what was inside. She instantly closed her eyes. "Yuck."

He said nothing though he did smile. Using some of the water she had been carrying, he cleaned out the inside of the crab. Expertly, he began to break the shell away from the meat. Sweat rolled down his back and he realized he was sitting in the direct sun. A moment later, a large fern tree sprouted behind him. Its giant fan shaped leaves shaded him from the sun and immediately brought relief. He smiled at Grecia. "Thanks."

Looking anywhere but at the crab, she said, "You're welcome."

"Because of it, I'll refrain from teasing my big, terrifying *Dragon* that she's squeamish at seeing the inside of a crab. And you call yourself a healer."

"I'm fine with blood. Guts are another story entirely." She closed her eyes. "Just hurry up, please. I'm losing my appetite."

He wasted no time in finishing preparing the crab. He washed his hands clean and then went over to Grecia to tug her into his arms. "It's done," he told her gravely. "You're safe now."

She lightly punched him in the arm but still took advantage to cuddle against him. She softly nuzzled his shoulder. "You are incorrigible. But I love you anyway." She eased up for a brief but tender kiss and then released him. "Let's eat."

Much to her relief, the crab tasted far better than it looked like it would. The taste was also familiar. "I've had this before, but didn't know it," she decided. "They must clean it up a lot before it's served at a restaurant."

"They do. Most people don't realize what they're eating unless they're told. And even then, they don't recognize the crabs when they encounter them. They're normally harder to find, but I suspect the waves from Mirah came out this way." His gaze lowered slightly. "How bad is the rest of the world?"

"It's bad." She smoothed his hair out of his face. "I've only seen parts of it, but it's going to get worse as long as we can't catch the Elite. But, hopefully, the storms between Carnelian and Mirah will die down now that Mirah is no longer sending out waves." She stretched largely. "We need to get going toward Kindred. We'll have to fly south, then west and cross over the ocean rather than the land."

"I heard Dragons weren't able to fly over cities."

"It's true. We cause ripples in the power in the land not too dissimilar from flying too low over water. But the ripples in the land can be worse because of the presence of so many Magi. Unfortunately, as a Dragoon pair, you and I need to keep at an even greater range from cities if we're flying because we put out just that much more a large signal. If we were trying to go between Magi cities, we would have to walk most of it. Since we're cutting across the land and avoiding them, we should be safe in flight—especially with the already disturbed land. I suppose that's the only positive in this."

"Do the rules apply for Kin cities?" he asked curiously.

"Actually, curiously, we seem to be fine flying over our own cities and over Kin cities."

"Then maybe it's just the concentration of Magi power being unbalanced. Another one for Tariah to ponder." He got to his feet when she did. "Are you going to carry me?" he asked.

She smiled at him, her eyes dancing and breathless anticipation swirling inside her. "You're going to ride on my back." She slid her hands into his and brought his hands to her cheeks. "That, more than anything, as much as our lines, proclaims we are a Dragoon pair."

A matching excitement began to rise inside him. He had always wanted to see what flying was like. Beyond that was a hunger to see her in her natural form. He had never seen a Dragon up close, and he wanted to know everything about the woman he loved.

"You're distracting me," she said softly.

"I like distracting you." As if to prove it, he eased in and kissed her softly. He whispered against her lips, "You're the one who is tempting me. I'm just some poor helpless male almost done with second puberty. I'm at your mercy."

Her breath caught. "Promise?" His power fluttered against hers and her pulse pounded. That was as good an answer as any. She freed her hands with great reluctance and took several steps backward. When she had enough room, she let the power rise inside her. Summer leaves and swirls of gold and green power surrounded her. The power flared brightly, momentarily blinding Roman, and when the light faded, she had transformed.

In a sort of stunned wonder, he stared at his Fury. She was . . . breathtaking. She was close to seventeen feet in length judging by how high over him she stood, but she looked overall slender. She seemed as graceful and willowy in this form as she did in her Magi one. She was covered in shimmering gold scales that glimmered with lavender highlights when she moved. Her face was more rounded than angular, and the fins extending from her head were nearly see-through in their translucence.

He held his breath as he walked closer until he stood in the shade of her body. The lavender eyes watching him were the same. "You're beautiful," he said softly. "In any form."

She lowered her head and nuzzled him gently. Her heart quivered. She could feel it from him and it rocked her somehow. She had been worried that he might be afraid of her true form. Softly, she said, "I suppose the idea of beauty being racially subjective is no longer valid."

He smiled and smoothed his fingers over her soft scales. "We're a race unto ourselves, aren't we? And it would entirely defeat the idea of us being mates if I didn't find you attractive in any form. I can't love you in one form but not your natural one. Intimidating though you may be."

"Oh, I'm not intimidating. *Xander* is intimidating. He's fifty feet tall!" She lifted him gently with her claw. "You can ride on my shoulders. You shouldn't slide up there."

He looked, realized that her shoulder bones had been made in such a way that he had a proper place to sit, and pondered the coincidence. It would be another thing to have Tariah examine. He put it out of his mind for the time being. He didn't care for the whys. He was simply enjoying the results. Secure in his perch, he said, "I'm ready."

He stopped breathing for a moment as she literally shot straight up into the air before spreading her wings and catching herself. She was so graceful! Despite her size, she was as nimble as a bird. And before he could say a word, they were flying across the sky with the ocean passing like a blur beneath them. "I can't believe it!"

She did a barrel roll just to make him laugh. "Me neither," she admitted. "I've never gotten to fly this fast before! I always had to restrain myself because of my power."

He smoothed a hand across her scales. "Well, now you have me."

Hungry anticipation colored her voice as she countered, "It would seem I do. And soon I'll claim you entirely as is my right of birth."

His entire body heated happily. "Who am I to stop you?" he asked huskily. "I'd hate to infringe on any rights." Enjoying her low laughter, he ducked down to avoid a cloud. "How far from Kindred are we?"

"A couple hours. By boat, it'd be a few days."

"It's amazing the Magi haven't tried to find a way to fly."

"The few Elders we have who are old enough to remember before the Chronicle War say that Dragons used to carry baskets with people across the oceans. It was back when we had open trade with the Magi. And like everything else, it too fell apart with the War." Her eyes closed briefly. "I long for a day where no one wars with anyone else."

"I think we all do." He wrapped his arms around her neck as much as he could. "If anything, perhaps the Elite will finally show everyone what is truly important. And if not, and I can't walk in Magi lands, we can stay on the Isle. You have a desert, right?"

"A large one, in fact." She smiled. "I might have to fight with a brother or two for the best part, but I think we could find ourselves a home."

Warily, he asked, "How many brothers do you have?"

"Mmm . . . ten? I think. I also have ten sisters." Feeling his shock, she said, "We like big families. Just as a forewarning. But if all I was blessed to have was one child with you, I'd still be happy."

"We can have children together?"

"Furies and Chronicles are the only cross-compatible species in the world. The child is usually determined by the mother's species, but it's always possible I might carry a Magi child." She smiled softly. "I'll be happy with whatever we're given."

He lost his breath. "Me too," he said softly. It was tantalizing to picture his Fury carrying his child. It, like everything else, would be an inescapable bond between them. And daunting as it was to consider raising Dragon children, he found himself looking forward to it. He would never be bored, that was for certain.

Chapter Fifteen

After a breakfast consisting of fruit from a nearby tree, C.J. and Dahlia were ready to leave for Kindred. Well, they were almost ready.

"It's a forested land," Dahlia explained. She was sitting on the edge of the spring with her feet in the water. "We really ought to have slightly better coverage for clothing because of the bugs. I mean, not that I don't love how you look, but I'm the only one who can nibble on you."

Remembering how she had taken distinct delight in nibbling on his skin while feeding that morning, he felt his cheeks flush. Ignoring it, and the smiling sidelong look she gave him, he said, "I can make us some new clothes. I just need sand."

"Hmm. Where can we get some?"

"Normally I get sand from Fire elements. They can make and break glass down for the best kind. But I can also use natural sand." He got to his feet and began to look around closely. "Since this is an oasis, we're lucky that the landscape is born from sand. I just need to find the right kind."

She braced herself back on her hands and watched him without shame. He hadn't bothered to put his vest on. She could see the full expanse of his broad shoulders and muscular chest. She especially loved the way his lines moved across his body. Wherever his lines rested, his skin was hotter. His hands always seemed to burn wonderfully. Her smile spread as she saw the red color on his cheeks. "Am I distracting you?"

"Yes!"

She just laughed. She fell over onto her back, linked her hands behind her head, and closed her eyes. "There. Now I won't keep staring at you. I'm afraid I can't help it. If my eyes are open, I'm going to stare at you."

"That should make me less self-conscious, not more," he grumbled. "Why does it make me nervous?"

"Because you can sense and feel that I want something from you that you're not quite ready to give me. It's a nervous excitement, isn't it?" She softly brushed against his emotions. They were as pink as his cheeks but underneath was a sort of giddiness. "You somehow want to give me what I want, but you don't know what it is nor do you feel ready."

"I don't like it." He began to scoop up the darker sand near a tree. It felt rich and vibrant with Soil power. "I dislike being nervous. When will it go away?"

"That I could not say. But I don't expect it to be long." She turned over onto her stomach and opened her eyes to smile at him. "You've already taken a large leap, *ishke*. And having waited for you as long as I have, I can find patience."

"I can't!" Distinctly sulky, he began to shake up the sand in his hand. "It feels like I waited a long time to start second puberty and now it feels like it'll be too long until it's done. I want it done and over with, so that I can stop being such a source of amusement for you."

"But it's a loving amusement," she countered. Her smile turned soft. "You're so sweet to me. You're unlike anyone else. You're a man who never let the little boy inside grow up. I need that. I get serious too much. So when you're officially an adult, I still want to see you sulking and playing pranks and driving me nuts."

He grinned a little. She seemed to know just how to lift his mood. "I'll endeavor to make you always entertained and tickle you mercilessly until you actually giggle."

Her eyes widened. "I don't giggle." She hastily scrambled up as he gave her a speculative look. "Don't you dare!" She ducked behind a tree. "Just make us some clothes! Keep your fingers to yourself unless they have intentions other than tickling me! I don't giggle. I refuse to giggle!"

That was a challenge worth revisiting. But feeling suitably equal to her once more, he began to concentrate on the sand. It swirled up over his hands, and he began to weave with expert precision. Dahlia was golden skinned with pale hair and beautiful creamy eyes. He wanted to set everything off and display her beauty as it deserved.

With her mentally feeding him the concept of forest clothing, he wove together a pair of dark green leggings, a snug black tunic with long sleeves, and a creamy colored cloak to go around her shoulders. He edged everything with gold color and made sure the tunic laces went from neck to hem so that she could choose how to fasten them.

She took the clothes and stared at them in astonishment. "Amazing," she breathed. She smoothed a hand across the silky material. "I've never seen anyone with this talent before." Never one to turn down beautiful gifts, she swiftly removed her cloth skirt and left herself in her bikini. She pulled her new clothes on over the top and began to lace the tunic. Everything fit perfectly, and she left the top laces undone so that it flattered her bust better.

His eyes dropped to the distinct shadow between her breasts that was teasingly hidden and revealed behind the laces. His fingers began to tingle. He hastily began to weave his own clothing. "You did that on purpose."

"I like being found beautiful," she admitted simply. "You make me feel that way, and I've always felt cute, no matter what Kin or Magi said. I can't forget that I'm a cute Dragon. But *you* make me forget."

"Good." He wove for himself a pair of sturdy slacks, a long sleeved tunic, and a cloak. He chose the same colors for his clothing that he had for Dahlia's because he liked the idea of them matching. Unlike her clothing, however, he chose to add gloves to his set to cover his hands.

She covered a smile as he watched her from the corner of his eye. "I'm not turning around."

With only a little reluctance, he changed clothes. He was discovering that he liked the way she looked at him. It was just those darn nerves that made him feel awkward! He also discovered something else when he was fully dressed. "I don't like clothes."

"You can't run around naked," was his lover's exasperated response.

"If I could, I would!" He wrapped his arms around her waist when she moved closer. "I can't feel the air. I also can't feel you. It's itchy. And stuffy."

"Desert boy." She leaned down to kiss him softly. He only stood two inches shorter, but they both enjoyed it. It encouraged her protective nature in a way they both needed. "We'll live in the desert or the lower mountains on the isle. Both are warm and both are wonderful for running around in less clothing than the valley or the forest demand."

"Deal." He tangled his fingers in her hair and loved the feel of it sliding over his fingers. Anticipation was beginning to rise inside him. "We're going to fly to Kindred?" When she smiled, he swung her around in a quick circle. "I've always wanted to do that! It's okay because we're Dragoons, right? That's what's in your mind." He could see it there and her eagerness was becoming his as well.

"You're making me giddy." She held onto his shoulders as he swung her around again. "And how you can swing me around like this is beyond me. I could lift you up!"

He stopped, startled. "Really?"

"Really. We retain our strength in any form. If you ever see a Kin Faerie lifting someone off the floor, it's probably actually a Dragon or Fury in Faerie form." She smiled angelically. "Not that I've ever done that, of course."

"Oh, of course." He grinned. "It's doesn't bother me that you're stronger than me." He snorted softly. "You're a *Fury*. Of course you're stronger! I just need to find another way to have an advantage."

She contemplated all his mouth watering beauty and the way she had felt when she had woken with him in her arms. "I think you've got one. You just need to learn how to use it." She reluctantly released him. "Back up to give me room. I'm on the taller side of average for a Dragon, as my height might imply. You should be able to ride comfortably on my back."

Swirls of fog and white power swirled around her and began to rise as the wind blew. A flash of light momentarily blinded C.J., and when he could see again, his beautiful lover had become a Dragon. He had seen her in this form once before, when she had saved him, but it was a fresh and wonderful shock all over again. She was as rounded and curvy in this form as in her Magi one, as she had said, but he took one good look at her and decided that Dragons were either blind or crazy. There was nothing cute about her at all.

He walked over to her without fear. "You know," he said, "I think Dragons are out of their mind." When she cocked her head, he smiled. "You're beautiful."

Cream-colored eyes widened and then closed. She lowered her head and nuzzled him softly, curling her presence around him fiercely. She loved him so much. "*Ishke*." She curled her wings down to pull him closer in a Dragon's hug.

His throat closed as he felt the emotion pouring out of her. "Are you trying to make me cry again?" His eyes were damp anyway, and he pressed closer. He rubbed his cheek against her soft scales. In some ways, he couldn't be mad at the Magi for their jealousy. This was well worth being jealous over. "I pity them."

"As do I." She released him from her wings then lay down. "Climb up. You can sit right in front of my wings and ride comfortably. I promise not to drop you." When he had climbed onto her back, she straightened up. "Comfortable?"

"Yes." He yelped and grabbed onto her neck as she suddenly shot into the air so fast that sand flew. As she laughed at him, he managed to say, "That's not funny!" His heart flipped into his throat as she did a loop de loop in the sky. "*Dahlia*! Have mercy!"

"Relax!" she scolded him gently. "Enjoy yourself! Do you realize we're flying?"

He closed his mouth and fiercely ignored how high they were from the ground. As he did, he became aware of the wind rushing past and the sensation of moving fast. Delight replaced nerves and he straightened up. "Amazing," he breathed. He looked around quickly, trying to take everything in at once. It wasn't just the flight. He felt *her*. He felt her power inside him as his was inside her, and the endless loop was as exhilarating as the flight.

Several minutes passed in easy silence as they both enjoyed the flight and then he asked, "How long until we get there?"

"Several hours."

"Isn't it normally a few days by boat?"

She smiled. "I fly far faster than any boat ever made. And I can fly much faster than other Dragons now that I have you. It'll drain me, certainly, but . . ."

He smiled. "But you have me." He laid down and rested comfortably on her neck. "That works for me."

Chapter Sixteen

Xander and Jayda awoke to rumbling stomachs and surprisingly warm air. The former was more important to Jayda, but Xander was quite grateful for the decreased chill. She could only shake her head at him. "I suppose I should have expected it since you are a Fire element. Few like the cold." She shot him a teasing smile. "Although, I do believe someone said he was developing a fondness for snow thanks to me."

"It's almost a fetish now." He nibbled at her ear playfully and made her laugh. He smiled and lifted his head to smooth a finger down the lines on her arm. "You're so fair," he said in wonder. "We'll have to live in the valley so the sun won't burn you."

"I won't burn," she promised. "I lived the first few years of my life in a desert, remember?"

His mind immediately pictured her in desert clothing, and he stopped breathing. "Well."

She hid a smile. "Are we distracted?"

"Quite."

She leaned up and nipped at his chin just hard enough to sting. "Better?"

"You're learning Dragon habits." He couldn't have been more pleased. He gave her a quick kiss and then rolled to the side and sat up. He sighed as he surveyed their clothing. "I look forward to a bath and a change of clothes." He tugged on his clothes and started digging in his hipsack for his supplies. A loaf of bread and a handful of fruit emerged, and so did a packet of rare tea. He brightened as he looked at Jayda. "Can you brew this for me?"

Her heart melted at the hopeful look he gave her. He looked just like a little boy asking for treats. Her thoughts collided with his abruptly as they were both suddenly diverted. In both their minds, they saw a little boy with her hair and his eyes running around. Her breath caught. "We can have children? How?"

"This from a doctor." He smoothed trembling fingers through her hair. "Chronicles and Furies are able to cross-breed. Odds are that our children would be Magi because that's your normal form, but you might possibly carry a Dragon egg."

"I don't mind either," she decided as she finished dressing.

His grin widened. "You're one better than Tariah. She's dead terrified of carrying a Dragon egg."

She smiled. "I'll study with the Dragon doctors and tend to her myself so she won't be so scared." She took the packet of tea and nimbly created a cup of ice that she could keep heated without melting. Some hot water turned the tea leaves into a sweet scented brew that she handed over with a smile. "Here you go."

They demolished the meal in short order, and she laughed at him when he munched the ice of the cup as well, just to get the last flavor of his beloved tea. He then took down the shelter of the trees he had made and soon everything was the same as when they had found it.

"If we go west, it'll take longer." He was mostly talking to himself. "From here we could catch a current and head southeast and reach Kindred by afternoon." He smiled at her. "You ready to learn to fly?" Excitement began to hum inside his heart. "In twenty-five hundred years, I've never had anyone ride on my back. I've waited for this moment."

"Then wait no more." She leaned up to frame his face and then rose up to kiss him softly. His excitement was becoming her own. Or maybe she was equally excited. She couldn't tell and didn't particularly care. "I've been wondering when I'd get to see you in Dragon form."

"Don't be alarmed." His thumb skimmed over her cheek. "I'm not exactly a small Dragon."

"Nothing about you alarms me." She rubbed her cheek against his hand and then slipped free and moved well out of the way. She had the vaguest memory from when he had rescued her, but it was more of a lucid dream than anything else. She remembered his pitch-black color and glimmering eyes, and that was it.

Fire and smoke swirled around his body and a bright red glow began to rise. The fire detonated into a storm and momentarily blinded her. When her eyes cleared, the fire burned around the immense fifty-foot length of her Fury's Dragon form. Not breathing at all, she watched as he stretched and shook out his wings. She was *miniscule* in comparison to him yet she felt no fear.

Unlike other Dragons she had heard of, Xander had two horns. They were long and curving and extended from his head near his ear fins. The way they glowed and glimmered, she thought they might well have been glass themselves. His face was sharp and angular, and his teeth were almost as big as she was tall. His body was stark and powerful, pure muscle shifting under onyx scales. He was *beautiful*. It seemed a paltry word for such a magnificent creature, but it was the only one she could find.

He waited for her to say or do something. When all she did was stare at him, he reached for her emotions to know what was inside her mind and heart. The breathless wonder stole his own breath and his heart tightened fiercely. He laid down until he was more on ground level. She seemed small and fragile suddenly, and he wanted nothing more than to hide her away where no one else could discover her.

She walked forward, pulled by a compulsion she couldn't fight. His head was bigger than she was! Without fear, she wrapped her arms around as much of him as she could and pressed her cheek to his soft scales. "It's a wonder Gamma didn't run screaming before you punted him," she said teasingly.

"No one has ever run screaming from me," he mused. "But I believe that a few have passed out. I try not to fly close enough to any city that they notice how big I am. Stalagmite is a pointed exception, but everyone there welcomes me. It's Morgan's hometown." He curled a claw around her gently, and his heart quivered as he realized again that she was smaller than his entire hand. "I think I'm the one terrified."

"I trust you." She pressed her lips to his skin softly. "Now how am I ever going to keep from falling off your back?"

"You can ride near my head. If you sit right near my horns, you should be plenty secure." He lifted her carefully until she could climb onto his neck and then onto his head. He smiled. He wouldn't even know she was there if it wasn't for her power. She weighed next to nothing. "Are you comfortable?"

She sat down next to his right horn and let it be a brace for her. "Comfortable, but not entirely secure. I have nothing to hold onto." Before she finished speaking, smoke curled around her and anchored her securely. "That works perfectly."

He rose up to a sitting position and then stood. His power flowed to her and then back again in a never-ending loop. He rose into the air with a flap of his wings that rippled the trees. Then, like a red comet, he shot across the sky. As he felt Jayda's power pulsing inside him, he felt nearly giddy with happiness. So much so that he did several loops in the air until she was breathless with laughter.

"When was the last time you had so much fun while flying?" She wrapped her arms around his horn since she lacked anything else to hold. Much to her delight, it was as soft and warm as the rest of him.

"I don't remember," he admitted. "There's a lot I'm rediscovering with you, *ishke*." He softly rubbed his power against hers and was contented when she returned the soft caress. "Relax and rest. If you feel compelled for a nap, feel free."

"And leave you alone again?" She snuggled in more securely. "I'll just enjoy the flight too. And anyway," warm feminine laughter filled her voice, "I'll need to be awake when we get to our destination so that I can feed you."

His soft laugh rumbled through her entire body. "Waking you might be equally enjoyable, though." He flew down closer toward the ocean to duck under a cloud. The Flutterlies were flying with distinct purpose, and he didn't want them to siphon her power. "Unusual."

She looked up. "I've never seen a cloud moving that fast. Or in that direction, I might add. I thought Flutterlies couldn't fly in a western or northern pattern."

"Normally they can't." His voice sounded grim. "I get the feeling it's important, yet I can't seem to recall why. It must be from the time that the War occurred. I remember many things of that time, but there are other things that have been taken from my mind." He felt her probing at his mind and sighed. "You won't find anything. They simply do not exist. The only reason I know they are gone is because I encounter impressions that indicate I've seen something before."

"We'll ask Morgan," she said firmly. "He can help. I'm sure of it."

"Possibly he and Tariah together could do something." He was thoughtful. "I do not know the extent of Tariah's mental skills, but they ought to be quite strong considering her brother. They're two halves of a whole in a way not too dissimilar from the way Dragoons are. I suspect they couldn't exist without each other either."

She tilted her head slightly. "That brings up all sorts of new questions, doesn't it?"

"Questions I've pondered for nine years," her lover admitted. "I suppose we will find the answers eventually." He angled back up into the sky again. "We'll have to get you some new clothes on Kindred. Long sleeves are also best for forested lands." He smiled. "Perhaps you will develop a fondness for trees."

"As opposed to my fondness for snow?"

"A man can hope." Warmed when she laughed, he flew faster. The sooner they got there, the sooner he could have her in his arms again. Draining his majiks had never seemed so delightful before. And if he was really lucky, maybe his Chronicle really would like trees more than snow.

It was mid-afternoon by the time Xander was circling Kindred and looking for a place he could safely land. Kindred consisted of one larger island and many smaller ones. Over the last few years, long bridges had been built between the islands to allow easier travel. From the air, it looked like a string of stones on a necklace. Nearly every inch of the islands were covered in trees except for strips of beaches.

There was one on the larger island where he saw enough room to land. He circled in slowly to give the Kin enough time to recognize he was landing. He touched down gracefully and then lay down so that Jayda could slide down off his back. He had to help her, though, as her legs were slightly rubbery. "Are you all right?"

"I'm new to flight," she admitted. She took a few shaky steps. "The land feels like it's moving and I know it's not." She turned around to say something more but ended up turning into his arms. As they closed around her, everything stabilized. She sighed happily and burrowed closer. "Never mind then. Are *you* all right?"

"Just a little tired," he admitted. "I'll be fine once I feed." He looked up suddenly, his nose flaring. Not ten feet away stood a familiar SunKin Elf. "Rumidia, it's good to see you again. How are you?"

Rumidia smiled as she walked forward. "I'm doing well, and I can see you're doing wonderfully!" She included Jayda in her warm and welcoming smile. "Welcome to Kindred, young Dragoon." She touched her ears and bowed. "I am Rumidia, Fire secondary SunKin."

Jayda drew her thumb over her cheek and nose. "Jayda Lakemore, Water Chronicle." Softer she added, "Former Black Magi, under the leadership of Morgan Chronis."

"Naturally. We Kin knew of the Chronicle children from the moment Morgan and Tariah met. You are very welcome here, as is Elder Xander." Her eyes twinkled merrily. "I run the inn. If you'd like to follow me, there's a room ready for you. Word is spreading and we knew we might be seeing at least one Chronicle."

Xander's brows lifted. "Others have been found?"

"According to the letter Tariah wrote to Daylar, potentially yes. You are among four Furies who have not reported in lately, and other Furies have reported sensing Chronicles in and around other cities and lands. The belief is that all four children have awakened." She began heading down the beach toward a path leading into the trees. "The Chronis twins are on their way here as we speak."

"Twins!" Jayda's brows came together. "I don't remember them being twins. Wasn't Morgan about five years older than Tariah?"

"Physically, yes," Xander said softly. "Their souls are another matter entirely. The way they act and behave, we've all started calling them twins. And . . . there is more as well." In his mind flashed a vivid memory from over a thousand years prior.

Her breath caught as she saw what he had. Two nearly identical Chronicles that bore eerie resemblance to Morgan and Tariah but certainly weren't them for they had blond hair and blue eyes. "Who are they?" she asked softly.

"The first Chronis twins. Morgan and Tariah are direct descendants and . . . possibly more." He smoothed a hand down her hair. "It can be talked about later, *ishke*. It is not important at the immediate moment."

When they reached the inn, Rumidia led them to a room near the back for privacy. "I will let Daylar know you're here," she offered. "He will want to come see you to hear everything before he writes to Tariah." She laughed. "And knowing Tariah, she will want to know everything as well! She has a hunger to learn."

"The amount of knowledge in her mind is indeed amazing," Xander agreed dryly. "Thank you again, Rumidia." He opened the door and ushered Jayda inside, and when the door was shut behind him, he let out a breath. "Peace and quiet."

"Mm." She stretched largely and then laughed as he caught her around the waist and lifted her high in his arms. "Xander! Put me down!" As she found herself tumbled onto the bed and pinned by all his wonderful weight, she had to say, "Not what I meant, but I'm happy with it." His red eyes seemed to smolder as they looked down at her, and her breath caught as her entire body heated. Unconsciously, she curled her power around him seductively.

"You certainly know how to tempt me," he said huskily. He lowered his head, and even before he reached her lips, a soft blue aura lifted to cover her. His stomach tightened with hunger of many kinds. Almost reverently, he took her lips with his, drawing the kiss deeper and deeper, unable to determine if it was her power or her desire that replenished him.

By the time he lifted his head and began to trail soft kisses over her neck, she couldn't move. Her entire body was weak and aching with need. "You are entirely too good at that," she managed to protest weakly.

His lips curved. "I aim to please."

"You succeed, I assure you."

Rumidia was humming happily to herself when she sensed another Dragon power approaching. Brows lifted, she hurried to the window and looked down toward the beach. A large blue Fury was slowly circling for a landing and there was distinctly a young woman riding on his back. Delighted, she headed for the door.

Solis touched down on the sand and his eyes instantly flared wide. He could feel Xander's presence. "Even better," he told Kelsey. "I can sense Elder Xander here. He can surely contact the Isle for us!"

"Oh good." She slid off his side and landed on her feet. Her knees gave out and she promptly sat down hard on the sand. "Oof!" Mutinous and annoyed, she crossed her arms to glower at her mate as he knelt beside her in Magi form, a smile on his lips. "Not a word," she warned him.

"I wouldn't say a thing," he assured her warmly.

Etude flew down with a giggle to land on Kelsey's shoulder. "You'll get used to it, promise." She brightened as she saw a familiar Elf approaching. "Rumidia!" She flew over and happily hugged her cousin around the neck. "It's been a long time!"

"Etude, what a wonderful surprise!" Rumidia hugged her back and then regarded Kelsey and Solis. She smiled warmly. "Welcome to Kindred, Dragoons. I am Rumidia, Fire secondary SunKin."

"Solis T'mer, Water Fury." Solis bowed gracefully.

"Kelsey Renaire." She hesitated and then straightened her back, her blue eyes almost defiant. "Fire Chronicle. Former Black Magi, following Morgan Chronis." She opened her mouth to say more when a shadow passed by overhead. Startled, she looked up to see a large cream-colored Dragon flying in. Her breath caught as she saw the figure of someone on the Dragon's back. "Impossible!"

Solis looked up and his smile spread. "Dahlia!"

Dahlia angled in and landed with precision grace on the sand. She blinked rapidly as she saw Solis and Kelsey. "Well then." As C.J. slid off her back, she changed to Magi form. She was quick, thankfully, and caught her Chronicle as he stumbled. "This is unexpected."

"Why is the sand moving?" C.J. complained. He shook off the sensations and straightened. "I hope I get used to that. Gah!" The last was added as he found himself tackled by a slender redheaded female and sent flying to the sand. "Kelsey!"

"C.J.!" She wrapped her arms around his neck and hugged him tightly. "I missed you!" She straightened up, her arms crossed on a scowl, and was entirely unconcerned that she was sitting on her friend. "Well, if I've found you, I need to find Roman and Jayda!"

He propped himself up on his elbows with a wry smile to Solis. "Hi. I'm C.J Daragon, Soil Chronicle."

"Solis T'mer." He reached down and lifted Kelsey off C.J. "Water Fury, obviously." He smiled at Dahlia. "You look happy."

"I am happy." Dahlia helped C.J. stand. To Kelsey, she said, "I am Dahlia Stalker, Air Fury."

"Kelsey Renaire, Fire Chronicle." The redhead tapped a foot impatiently on the ground. "The Faerie is Etude, my best friend." She saw the flash of pain that went across C.J.'s face and reached out to take his hand. "What's wrong?"

"My best friend Cole." He looked at Etude and Rumidia. "Do either of you know Cole? Soil secondary SunKin Elf."

Rumidia shook her head. "I am sorry but I do not. You will have to ask Elder Juniper." She smiled. "If you'd all like to come with me to the inn, you can rest after your journey. Another of your kind is here."

"Xander Journe, right?" Dahlia asked. "I can sense he has been through."

"Indeed. And he was not alone."

It didn't take long for everyone to understand. C.J. brightened. "It must be Jayda! It *has* to be!" He enthusiastically caught Dahlia in his arms and swung her around. "That's wonderful, isn't it? For Xander and for us!"

Kelsey found herself envious of her friend. She couldn't budge Solis if she tried. His arms curled around her and he murmured softly in her ear, "You have other ways of making me weak, *ishke*. You're only just learning them, though." To add emphasis, his teeth teased the edge of her ear and made her breath catch.

C.J. saw the pink on her cheeks and felt immensely better. "Which phase?"

"First and a half," was the mutter.

"Second and a half."

She brightened. "That makes me feel better, thank you." She leaned back against Solis and drew his arms tighter around her. She could feel weakness inside him and knew he needed her power. Looking at Dahlia, she could see the paleness to her cheeks that meant she needed C.J. "We should rest."

"Indeed." Rumidia smiled. "You would not want to disturb Elder Xander right now. He's . . . indisposed." The two Chronicles blinked at her and her heart melted. Those in second puberty were wonderfully innocent in many ways. Their blend of both child and adult made others feel young again. "Their flight was a long one as well."

"Oh." It was the best Kelsey could come up with.

"Er, right." C.J. coughed. "Okay, we'll see him and Jayda later." He caught Dahlia closer and steadied her when he felt her sudden unbalance. "Lead the way, please?" he asked Rumidia.

"Certainly." She headed down the pathway once more, and her eyes met Etude's as they went. Both were thinking that it was no doubt a matter of time before the fourth Chronicle arrived as well. It was impossible that he not make it to Kindred as well. There was no such thing as a coincidence.

While Etude went to see the Elders and find out where Daylar was located, Rumidia got the other two Chronicle couples settled into rooms. She spaced all of them far enough apart that their powers wouldn't clash and distract each other. Much to her delight, within the next hour, she saw the familiar shadow of another Dragon approaching outside.

As Grecia was coming in for a landing, Roman sighed wistfully. "We're there already?" He had been enjoying the flight too much for it to end already.

"Unfortunately, yes." She angled down and landed lightly on the sand. She waited for him to slide off her back and then hastily turned to Magi form to catch him. She staggered a step but smiled. "Are your legs tired?"

"I have legs?" It was said with a smile. He gathered himself as he felt the feeling return to his legs and he straightened up. "I will get used to it."

"I'll fly you everywhere I can until you do," she assured him. Sensing an approaching power, she turned and automatically put herself in front of Roman protectively. When she saw Rumidia, her shoulders relaxed. "Greetings, Kin." She bowed. "Grecia Laluna, Soil Fury."

Roman drew his thumb over his nose and cheek. "Roman Arequo, Air Chronicle, following the path of Black Magi leader Morgan Chronis."

Rumidia touched her ears and bowed slightly with a smile. "Greetings, Dragoons. I am Rumidia, Fire secondary Kin." Her eyes sparkled merrily. "You're late."

"Late?" Roman lifted a brow.

Grecia suddenly realized that the tingling in her feet had nothing to do with hot sand. Familiar power, three familiar powers, had touched this land and recently. "Oh!" She brightened, a smile spreading across her face. She turned to Roman and took his hands with hers. "*Ishke*, three other Furies are here. Elder Xander, Solis, and Dahlia. I recognize their powers."

"And they were not alone," Rumidia confirmed. She smiled. "Follow me to my inn. They're there, resting up. I'm sure you would like to do the same." She tucked her tongue in her cheek as she saw the smoldering look that passed between the two Dragoons. "Solis and Dahlia will be quite envious of you, Grecia."

Grecia tilted her head and then winced as she realized. "Oh." She bit her lower lip. "Oh my." The smile fought to get free as she glanced at Roman. The idea of having to wait longer than she already had was frustrating and intimidating. A thought occurred to her and she turned back quickly. "Xander didn't . . . he doesn't have to wait, does he?"

"No," Rumidia said softly. Her eyes were warm. "He and his Chronicle are true Dragoons."

Roman let out the breath he was holding. He could see Grecia's memories of Xander, and it had hurt him as well to think someone who had waited so long would be forced to wait more. Over two thousand years. A Fury's dedication could be a little overwhelming.

"But worth it," Grecia murmured. "And he'd be the first to say it."

It was close to dinnertime when Kelsey woke from her nap. She had been wrapped around Solis, and he had been a wonderfully comfortable pillow. She hadn't felt compelled to move, but the distinct feeling of someone jumping on her shoulder brought her around. On a groan, she tucked her face more firmly against Solis. "No."

Etude rolled her eyes. "Kelsey! Wake up! I brought proper clothes for you."

Kelsey cracked one eye open. "Proper by whose definition?"

"The forest."

"No, thank you." She rolled over and pulled her pillow over her head.

By that point, Solis was awake too. He propped himself up on an elbow with a wry smile. "Kelsey," he said warmly, "we will eventually be in a desert. For now, we have to make do. Now, it's dinnertime and we should go to the dining room. Perhaps Xander and Jayda will be there." His nose flared slightly. "And I sense that another Fury has arrived."

She peeked out at him. "Who?"

"It feels like Grecia." He smiled. "She is the closest thing to another Fury Elder that we have. Since she is a Soil Fury, she may be in the company of your Roman."

"She is," Etude assured them. She smiled. "I saw them when they arrived. And," she added, "I talked to Daylar and Sparkle. They said they were going to come meet us for dinner. They have news and they need to hear our news to send to Tariah."

"Oh, all right," Kelsey muttered as she sat up. She blew out a breath so hard that the hair falling in her face stirred. She raked it out of her eyes and caught a breath as Solis' soft finger slowly trailed down the line of her back. A shiver rippled through her body as every nerve seemed to finally awaken as well. Even the feel of the soft sheets sliding over her skin was sensual. "Uhm. Etude."

He tugged on her long hair until she fell back against him. His lips trailed over her ear and cheek. "She was going somewhere."

Desperately trying not to smile, Etude flew backwards toward the door. "Mm. I guess I was." Hiding a giggle, she shrank even smaller and flew out through the keyhole.

Kelsey barely noticed. She was drowning in Solis' tender caresses. She could feel his presence wrapped firmly around her, their emotions meshed, and knew that he knew exactly how he made her feel. She was glad that at least he knew what was going on. She didn't. She could only feel without understanding, accept without knowing. As he turned her and his lips sought hers, her sigh was long and contented and unknowingly sensual.

A quiver rippled through his body as he fought for control. He had never been in this predicament before. He had never been the one to initiate a lover to the wonder of second puberty. His first lover had known more than he had, which had probably been to both their advantage. But if he had done to her what Kelsey was doing to him, it was a wonder they had both survived.

She made a soft sound of protest as he left the kiss and his lips began to slowly glide down the line of her neck. As instinctive as breathing, her power rose to greet him as a shimmery red veil of Fire power. Breath held, she grabbed his arms for balance as his wandering lips set off riots of delight under her skin. Her breasts began to ache and swell, begging for his attention. "Solis." It was little more than a whispered plea.

He buried his nose between her breasts. One hand curved around her waist to hold her and the other slowly skimmed up her body. Giving her plenty of time for nerves, his fingers trailed over the top of her breast. Her heart began to beat harder under his lips but not with fear. Unable to bear it, he turned his head and captured one taut nipple between his lips. Her power there was wild, spicy, and more potent.

The wave of pleasure went from breast to toe and back again before gathering low in her body. When his free hand covered her other breast, she couldn't stifle a soft moan. She would have melted bonelessly to the bed without his strong arm around her waist. Was she finally past that horrible nervousness? Could she finally give herself to the man she loved?

She got her answer when his fingers slid down her body to her leg. He brushed the inside of her thigh and it shocked her so much that she jerked away, her eyes wide with fear. She instantly covered her face with her hands. "Solis. I'm sorry."

"For what?" He drank the last of the power from her slender and yet beautifully strong arm and then straightened and brushed her hair out of her eyes. He tugged her hands away from her face and kissed her softly. "I have patience, *ishke*. It's not as if we will never be there." He let out a rough breath as his aching body seemed to protest everywhere at once. "I need to go find a glacier."

"Stop tormenting yourself," she muttered.

"And therefore stop touching you? Ha. I'm frustrated, not suicidal." Easily, he continued, "But if you want to return the favor, let me know."

She blinked, then looked at him. It hadn't even crossed her mind. Yet as she watched him get out of bed, the way his strong figure moved fluidly made something inside her body flutter with sheer hunger. He was . . . gorgeous. Had she really noticed before? The urge to run her hands over him was so strong and fierce that she was on her feet before she was conscious of it.

Solis, keeping his emotions from hers for his own sanity, didn't know her intent until he heard her move. He looked over his shoulder and stopped breathing. The way she walked . . . the way she moved . . . she was as fiery and sultry as the flames of her power. "Kel."

She softly pressed her hands to his chest and her fingers kneaded softly. Wonder filled her eyes. "Mine." The word was softly breathed as she leaned in to lightly touch his skin with the tip of her tongue.

He firmly grabbed her wrists and held her away. "Mercy," he begged roughly. "You can be curious later tonight. But, right now, please have mercy on your poor, aching Fury."

Her lips curved slightly with a smug femininity that was older than her power. "Okay. I'll hold you to that." She freed her wrists and walked over to where her clothes waited. With a long-suffering sigh, she reluctantly pulled the leggings and long sleeved tunic on over her bikini. She gathered her hair up and tied it haphazardly on the top of her head with a ribbon to match.

His clothes were not dissimilar from her own, and she eyed them in distaste. She liked seeing her Fury's lethal beauty and the golden lines marking him as her own. "I hate forests," she grumbled.

He just smiled and wrapped an arm around her shoulders. "I know."

When they walked into the dining room, and Kelsey spotted the slender young woman with seagreen hair, she brightened visibly. "Jayda!" She gave a happy cry and rushed across the room to throw her arms around the taller female.

Jayda felt tears well in her eyes as she held Kelsey just as tightly. "Oh, Kelsey!" She eased her friend back and smiled tremulously. "I can't believe it's you! When Xander said he had sensed the arrival of three other Furies and Chronicles, I was so afraid to hope! But here you are!"

Xander smiled at Solis. "Warm greetings, young Solis."

"Warm greetings, Elder." Solis bowed respectfully. "I am happy for you, Xander." He smiled at Jayda. "I am Solis T'mer, Water Fury."

"Jayda Lakemore, Water Chronicle." Her fingers laced tightly with Kelsey's as if neither could bear to let go just yet. "It's an honor."

Kelsey, showing the same lack of fear and nerve that all those who knew her loved, smiled at Xander cheekily. "I'm Kelsey Renaire, Fire Chronicle." She made the gesture of respect, but it came out sassy. "Nice to meet you. Solis says you're old."

Jayda bit her lip. Hard. Solis groaned. "Kelsey."

Xander just grinned and gave Kelsey a gentle cuff in the chin. "You suit Solis well, fledgling." His grin was almost a taunt as he looked at the other Fury. "Putting his vaunted patience to the test too, I see. It does him good."

"Someone have a party and not invite me?" C.J. complained from the doorway.

"C.J.!" Jayda brightened as she saw one of her brothers. "Over here!"

"Ah ha!" He swooped down and scooped her up, never mind that she was very nearly his height. He hugged her fiercely for a moment. "Missed you," he said into her hair. When she held on just as tight, he felt tears sting the back of his eyes. He had missed his family and never even known it until the holes in his mind had filled.

"Dahlia." Xander smiled as the younger Fury crossed the room as well. "Warm greetings."

"Warm greetings, Elder."

"So," came Roman's voice from the doorway, "I don't suppose there's room for two more?"

"Roman!" Kelsey happily tackled him straight to the floor. In moments, she had been joined by C.J. and Jayda, and all four clung on tightly.

Grecia carefully stepped over and around the tangle and crossed to her fellow Furies. A wry smile was on her lips. "Well. Greetings." She realized that Solis and Dahlia were eyeing her, and she felt her cheeks slowly heat. "What?" It wasn't *that* obvious that she and her Chronicle were full Dragoons, was it?

Xander cleared his throat and then lightly tapped his neck. She blinked in confusion and then warily touched her neck. She felt the little abrasion instantly and went pink. She remembered Roman's mouth being there, but she hadn't realized that he had marked her. "Oh." She cleared her throat as well.

Solis smiled at her. "You've waited longer, Grecia. You're entitled." He walked over to where the Chronicles were now standing and tugged Kelsey into his arms. He loved seeing her happy.

It was only a few moments before the Dragoon pairs were once more grouped up. "Okay," Kelsey said with a smile. "From the top. I'm Kelsey Renaire, Fire Chronicle following the path of Morgan Chronis."

"Roman Arequo, Air Chronicle, on the same path."

"Jayda Lakemore, Water Chronicle, same."

"C.J. Daragon, Soil Chronicle, same."

"Solis T'mer, Water Fury."

"Grecia Laluna, Soil Fury."

"Xander Journe, Elder Fire Fury."

"Dahlia Stalker, Air Fury."

"I'm Etude, Air secondary Kin!"

"Gah!" Kelsey nearly jumped out of her boots as her friend seemed to materialize at her shoulder. "Etude, don't DO that!" She grabbed the small Faerie and scowled at her. "That wasn't very nice!" On an indignant huff, she put Etude on her shoulder.

Seeing the look on C.J.'s face, Grecia asked softly, "C.J.? Is something wrong?"

"My friend." He closed his eyes. "My best friend is a SunKin Elf named Cole. Soil secondary." He took a deep breath and rested his cheek against Dahlia's hair when she wrapped her arms around him. "We fought against the Elite together. I passed out at the end, when I awakened as a Chronicle. Dahlia says he left to find Kappa but . . ."

"I think you had best start at the top," Xander suggested. "And let's sit down before we fall down. We're awaiting Daylar and Sparkle still."

They found a table, and each recounted the events that had led to their awakening near their Fury and the encounters they'd had with the Elite. Gamma was surely dead; no one could survive the flight he had taken. Delta was dead at Cole's hands. Kappa was not a threat; if anything, she was better suited as an ally. Phi was still on the loose. Beta was also still free. "But, and I stress this," Grecia noted, "we can't be sure they're the only two left."

"Well," came a dry male voice from the doorway, "no wonder the land is almost purring in contentment! Four sets of Dragoons in our inn!"

They all turned and found a handsome SunKin Faerie hovering in the doorway. Beside him was a lovely female SunKin Faerie. Both had matching sets of wings, which was curious to all except Xander. He knew the story. Both looked much as they had the last time he has seen them, except for Sparkle. The naturally curvy little Faerie was decidedly getting pudgier, and with good reason. He began to slowly smile. "Well."

"Would that be the news they had?" Solis asked Etude dryly.

"It is!" Etude's smile looked happy.

"We don't know what we're having yet," Sparkle admitted, "but we're just happy to have a baby!" She flew over and landed on Xander's shoulder. She folded her wings and bowed with more grace than her expanding waistline should have allowed. "I am Sparkle, Soil secondary SunKin."

Daylar flew over and landed on Xander's other shoulder. He mimicked the bow with just as much grace. "Daylar, Air secondary. I'm very happy to meet all of you." He smiled at Xander. "And happy especially that you have your Chronicle, Elder Xander. Was it worth the wait?"

The way Xander smiled at Jayda made more than one pair of eyes sting with tears. Solis, being the youngest, knew how it felt after just his short time of waiting. He could barely imagine how Xander felt. "It was well worth it," Xander said softly, bringing Jayda's hand to his cheek for a moment. He smiled at Daylar. "Have you written to Tariah?"

"Not yet. I wanted to confirm just who you all were." He sat down on Xander's shoulder and began to trace intricate characters into the air as if writing with energy. This particular energy was actually familiar to those present for all had met Tariah at some point in their lives. As he wrote the letter, the energy was cool as water but held a hint of the lines that marked the older Chronicle.

While he did, C.J. looked at Sparkle. "Tell me, do you know a SunKin Elf by the name of Cole?"

She cocked her head slightly. "The name is familiar, though I'm not sure from where. Why do you ask?"

"He's my best friend. He left to pursue Kappa from the Elite to convince her to join our side. I just need to know that he's all right." C.J.'s hands clenched together in his lap. "I think I would feel if he was hurt. I just need to know for sure that he's fine."

Etude began to frown thoughtfully to herself. It was very odd indeed that so many Kin would not be certain of Cole's identity. Most Kin knew each other in some way or another. Either he was a Second Born Kin, and that was rather odd in and of itself, or he was the Kin equivalent of a Master Magi, which did exist rarely. She was going to have to start asking around to figure out which it was. If he was Second Born, then they needed to find out who he was fused from so they could easier track him.

Daylar finished writing the letter and sent it off. "I don't know how long it will take her to write back," he said, "so we might as well rest today and meet with Elder Juniper tomorrow morning. The Kin will want to offer you sanctuary, and he may have more answers about what is occurring with the Elite."

"And why we can't remember anything about that time?" Grecia asked quietly.

"That I cannot say," he apologized. "Sparkle and I were there as well, and we do not remember a great many details either." He flew up into the air and hovered gracefully. "Enjoy your dinner. I'll let you know as soon as Tariah writes back."

"Thank you, Daylar," Grecia said warmly. "And you as well, Sparkle."

"Of course!"

The couple flew out of the dining room, and Rumidia began to serve dinner. She had been standing by for a few minutes, not wanting to interrupt the conversation. She too was beginning to think along Etude's lines, and she gestured for her cousin to follow her out so they could talk.

The Chronicles didn't notice and began to talk cheerfully about the lives they had been living. The Furies didn't say anything; they just listened with smiles. The four Chronicles looked nothing alike. They were completely different personalities. But anyone who looked at them would see a family.

"I suppose that makes us related too," Xander told his fellow Furies gravely.

As one, all three groaned and dropped their heads onto the table. He was already bossy just from being an Elder, let alone from being the oldest in their family!

Chapter Seventeen

After dinner, they adjourned for the night. Kelsey watched the way Jayda and Xander and Grecia and Roman walked with their heads together intimately, and suddenly felt immensely guilty as she went into her room with Solis. It just didn't seem fair that she be so early in her development that he had to wait for her. He had already waited *centuries.*

His arms wrapped around her waist and he buried his nose in her hair. "Kel," he said tenderly, "I wouldn't trade you for anyone else. I'm *proud* to be helping you through second puberty." He nuzzled her softly. "I won't say I'm not losing my mind and that not I'm exceedingly grateful for my Water patience, but I wouldn't change you at all."

She looked over her shoulder at him. "What was it like two thousand years ago? Did all Furies have to go through this? I mean . . . did Chronicles finish second puberty before meeting their Furies, or after?"

He frowned thoughtfully. "Those are very good questions, *ishke.* We've been so busy theorizing about why all of you are growing at such accelerated rates that it never occurred to us to question if it has always been this way. Xander should know."

"I think Jayda is a good example of what I'm wondering." She turned in his arms and lightly looped her own around his waist. "She had gone through second puberty but hadn't actually *gone* through it. And Roman was all but done. But their Furies are much older. And Dahlia's older than you, right?"

His brows lifted slowly. "I believe I see what you are inferring. The older the Fury is when their Chronicle is born, the more likely the Chronicle is to be at the end or close to the end of second puberty when they meet."

"It's that balance thing again. Opposites or identical." She took a breath and grabbed for her courage. "And on that note . . ." She firmly began to unlace his tunic. "You promised."

His heart began to beat harder and desire tightened his body. Unconsciously, he curled his power around her in a seductive call as ancient as time. Her power softly rose to curl around him, and his knees went weak with delight. "I suspect," he managed to say roughly as her hot hands softly spread across his bare chest, "I may be in the most trouble for reasons other than you being the youngest in development."

"Why's that?" The perfect line of his strong muscles was so tempting that she couldn't resist leaning forward and tasting it with the tip of her tongue. He was as pure and sweet as water in the desert. She loved the desert, and she loved the water. Her Fury was perfect for her.

"I think when you are fully grown, fully sure, you are going to be a force to be reckoned with."

The look she shot up at him from under ruby lashes was like seeing a promise of eternal, smoldering, passion. Her crystalline blue eyes were now more the eyes of a woman than a girl. "Does that scare you?"

His lips curved. "I'm shaking in my boots." When she pushed at his hips, he walked backward until the bed hit his knees and forced him to sit down. It took all of his considerable strength to keep from dragging her down onto his lap and teaching her the proper way to burn. He would have his turn later. They had forever.

There was something wildly thrilling at seeing the wonder in her eyes as she looked at him. "You're overdressed," he said huskily. "I thought you hated those clothes. Maybe you need to get rid of them." *Before he tore them off her body and ripped them into shreds for daring to hide her beauty.*

The hot lash of his thoughts no longer alarmed her. She could feel that volatile third emotion inside her heart swelling and growing every minute, every second, and as it grew, it overshadowed any nerves. She wanted to feel his hunger for her, to know he desired her as terribly as she was beginning to desire him.

She started to reach for the edge of her shirt but paused as his mind curled around hers. Instead of simply yanking the shirt off, she slowly drew it up in a graceful motion and let the soft material caress her sensitive skin. When freed of it, she reached up to pull the ribbon out of her hair.

The feel of her own hair sliding over her body was as erotic to her as it was to him to watch it. Her sensitive skin had been such an annoyance that she had never thought to experiment with the other aspect. She slowly removed her leggings before stepping toward her lover.

He knew what she wanted and softly smoothed his hand down her long leg. The shiver that rippled through her body seemed to also move through her power where it touched him. "This," he said softly, "is what you should be feeling all the time. Stop thinking about the bad things. Just let yourself savor how it feels to live."

"Will it go away when I'm a true adult?"

"To some extent. But even after your body is used to the signals, some things will always be more wonderful. Like this. You're a Fire element. You will always be more passionate and sensual." He slowly smiled. "My reward for being a Water Fury."

She leaned down and pushed at his shoulders to make him fall over onto his back. It was more for his self-control than hers that she kept her bikini on. She felt it, that touch of nerves inside that warned her she was not yet ready. It was doubly frustrating with her body trying to insist she was *very* ready. She *burned* hotter than her power. She needed him to touch her, to hold her. There was something beyond the relentless pleasure, and she wanted it though she couldn't name it.

His soft laugh made her body heat and clench with longing. "I warned you."

"You're not miserable yet." She pinned his hands beside his head. "I need to change that. You're going to lie there and let me learn all about you." She freed her hands and slowly smoothed them across his powerful chest. She savored the tingle of power in his lines. *Her* power marked him.

There were little calluses on her hands from her years of work. Her power burned under her skin. He curled his hands into fists and his teeth clenched together as he struggled for control. Not yet miserable? He was dying. He was burning alive under her curious, questing fingertips.

She seemed to touch him anywhere and everywhere. She combed her hands through his hair, trailed over his face. She traced every line, followed every muscle. And when her hands were appeased, she began the journey with her lips. Her tongue teasingly flicked across a nipple and he couldn't bite back a groan.

For all her wild sensuality, her underlying uncertainty was obvious. Her hands never went below his waist, and her lips never went past his navel. Her eyes did, repeatedly, and with combination of curiosity, fascination, and trepidation in their blue depths.

He firmly caught her hand and pressed it to his aching erection trapped beneath his sturdy pants. "Don't be scared," he told her, his voice little more than a rumble as her heat seared him.

"I'm not." The flutter of her emotions made it a lie, but her fingers flexed cautiously. Curiosity and nerves fought for dominance until finally the nerves won and her hand instinctively tried to jerk away. He freed her hand and she sat back sadly. "I'm sorry."

"Don't be." Aching head to toe, he sat up to tug her into his arms. "You'll put us out of our misery soon enough." His brows lifted as her arms wound around him and her lips feathered across his neck. "Kel?"

Her mouth closed over his skin hotly and sucked hard. The shock of it was as thrilling as the actual feel of her lips. His hands tightened on her waist without his control as he struggled not to return the favor.

She lifted her head and studied the little mark she had made. Something inside heated at the sight of it. "Grecia had one," she said huskily. "I wanted to see why."

He laughed, but it sounded strained. "I feel as if I should warn Dahlia. C.J. seems to be the type to see me and Grecia and become curious as well."

"He's further along than I am." She didn't feel the slightest bit embarrassed as his nimble fingers removed her bikini top. She was more comfortable being naked with him than him being naked with her. For now, at least. "He may have already tried it and we didn't see it. I could ask him."

He shook his head fondly. "There's no one else like you." He helped divest her of the rest of her clothes and then playfully tumbled her down onto the bed. He tucked her firmly against his chest and draped an arm over her waist. "There."

She snuggled back against him. "Solis, I really love you. It doesn't seem like the best word for how I feel, but it's the only one I have. I just wanted to say it."

He nuzzled her hair. "I love you too, *ishke*. Don't feel guilty. You wanted me to be miserable, and you succeeded. However, I am also very, very happy."

"How's that possible?"

"It's my body that aches, Kel. My heart and soul are jubilant." He pressed a kiss to her ear and nuzzled her untamed mass of red curls. She always smelled of rich and drugging smoke and mystery. "Go to sleep."

She forced herself to stop thinking and snuggled more firmly into his arms. Her body ached, her mind was nervous, and her heart and soul felt a thrill at every new experience. The thought of having to endure this sort of thing for *months* was alarming. For the first time, she was grateful for her accelerated Chronicle growth. She would be close to insanity if she were normal.

The next morning, the Dragoon pairs met up for breakfast. The little knowing grins that Grecia and Xander shot at Solis made the Water Fury's cheeks turn slightly pink, but he gamely ignored them. He was well aware that the little mark was still visible on his neck. He saw Jayda whispering in Kelsey's ear, and his redheaded lover snickering softly, and he had a strong feeling he was indeed doomed.

It was as they finished breakfast that Daylar arrived. He flew in and landed gracefully on Dahlia's shoulder, and his lively face looked very serious. "Elder Juniper would like to speak with you, C.J. He would like to know more about what happened with Cole."

C.J. nodded slightly, his heart clenching with fear. It was only the soft caress of Dahlia's power and heart curling around him that kept him calm. "I'll go to him after breakfast, if you can show me where to go."

"Of course." The Faerie took a quick breath. "Tariah wrote back to me this morning. She and Dominic are grounded with Morgan and Jazz a few miles out from Prismatic. They landed to wait out a storm, but the storm is only getting worse. When I checked with some other Kin, they confirmed that the storm is spreading across Spectrum. Not moving, spreading."

"Those Flutterlies we saw," Jayda said to Xander. "They were flying unnaturally. Perhaps that is where they were going." She saw Kelsey frown and turned to look at her. "Did you see some as well?"

"I did. They were odd. I don't know how, but they were odd. They weren't off-direction, but they had a purpose. Solis and I thought they were going to storms on Mirah." She rubbed her hands over her arms to combat a chill her long sleeves couldn't block. "Storms are slowly covering the whole of Spectrum. Why?"

Xander rubbed his forehead as he encountered again the blank space in his memory. He felt Jayda moving through his mind, but she could not seek out what had been removed. "I am sure I've seen this before," he said softly, "though I can't remember where or when. It must be from the War."

"Your memories were removed of that time?" Dahlia looked at him in surprise. "You've never mentioned it before."

"It's never consciously on my mind. I only know I have memories that are missing because of moments like these. My mind looks and feels perfectly fine. There are no blank spots as was with our Chronicles."

"Like with the Elite," C.J. said. "Memories removed naturally." He looked at Dahlia and Roman equally. "Do you think either of you could help Xander? You are the element of Air, and it has power over minds, right?"

"It can't hurt to look," Xander admitted. "Feel free."

"I'm not sure I want to look inside a mind that old," Roman countered dryly.

"It's only a little dusty." Jayda's voice was impish.

Xander brought her wrist up to his lips and nipped at her skin lightly. When she squeaked, he leaned down to kiss her nose. "That's what you get for teasing a Dragon, *ishke*." He brushed a kiss across her lips with a smile. He cherished having someone tease him, and he knew she knew it. Too often he had been alone, even among his own kind.

He felt the sudden presence of both Dahlia and Roman in his mind, both of Air but very distinct with their own signature. They swept through his mind, and he felt entirely unsurprised when neither was able to find anything. As they pulled out, he said, "You have confirmed, again, my suspicions about Morgan and Tariah. What they do is not normal."

To his surprise, he suddenly felt Kelsey flit through his mind. He lifted a brow at her. "I believe our youngest fledgling is learning her Telepathy skill. And if she is developing that already, then the rest of us must surely have our skills growing as well."

"I can only assume I have Ultravision," Solis said. "When I noticed Kelsey's mind strengthening, I began testing the skills myself. I certainly am not Telepathic nor am I Telekinetic."

"What exactly are the skills?" Roman asked curiously.

"Telepathy allows a Dragoon to read most minds. Morgan and Tariah, however, can do *vastly* more than that. They can fully communicate with each other across any distance. Tariah once took control of the former Magi king's mind, and we all know what Morgan did even before his tertiary skill developed." Xander shook his head. "And then there was the Chronis Dragon."

"Maybe Morgan can do something about your memories," C.J. said.

"That is my hope."

"What's Ultravision?" Kelsey asked Solis.

"The ability to read history in an object. It evolves into Ghost Touch which allows communication with ghosts. Telepathy becomes Clairvoyance which allows for viewing events in another location." He glanced at Daylar. "Have Tariah and Morgan evolved?"

"They haven't said."

"Telekinesis," Dahlia offered, "is to move objects with your mind. It becomes Invisibility."

"That would be fun!" Roman decided.

"It's a good thing you think so." Grecia kissed his cheek. "You have Telekinesis. When you tugged me into your arms this morning, it wasn't with your hands. I felt it come from your mind." She shot a smirk at Xander as she blatantly poked at his mind so that he arched a brow at her. "And Telepathy is mine. Our Elder will have to stay on his toes."

"I would be more concerned," Xander said mildly, "for all of you." Rather pointedly, he touched all of their minds and watched all except Kelsey wince. She just grinned at him, but he had expected that. "It would seem your Elder has it too."

"I probably have Ultravision." Jayda tugged on his sleeve in a bid to make him behave. "I don't have Telekinesis or Telepathy. What about you, C.J.?"

"I don't know." He tried concentrating on her and felt nothing that indicated he was even close to peeking inside her mind. He focused instead on a cup of water. To his shock, it suddenly flew up into the air. He lost his concentration and the cup dropped back toward the table.

Thankfully, Roman and Jayda were quick. Roman caught the cup with his Telekinesis, and Jayda caught the water with her power. "That answers that," the Air Chronicle said dryly. "Please be more careful, Ceej." He glanced at Dahlia speculatively. "Do you know his full name?"

"Don't you dare!" C.J. muttered. "And those with Telepathy can stay out of my head! Especially you, Kelsey!" He sat back and crossed his arms. "When we find Cole, then I'll tell you. He's waited the longest to know, all right?"

Dahlia reached up to gently ruffle his hair. "I will protect you," she promised gravely. "I have Telepathy too." She looked at Xander. "Do you think we should go to meet Morgan and Tariah, rather than have them try to come to us?"

North.

All at the same time, the four Chronicles felt the sharp compulsion of their lines. It was so strong and fierce that it rippled into their Furies as well. Both Jayda and Roman, whose lines had partially darkened, felt it burning in the uncharted portion of their lines. Kelsey and C.J. felt it through all their lines. *North.* They had to go north.

"That answers that," Solis said quietly. "We go to Morgan and Tariah. If your journey is taking you north, it is taking you to them." He looked at Dahlia and C.J. "Go meet with Elder Juniper and then meet us at the beach. We can at least fly along the coast of Spectrum as far north as we can before the storms make us land."

"We won't want to go together," Xander said. "It might be too much power with the fragility of the land right now. Once we reach Spectrum, we will need to take different routes."

"I want to say goodbye to Etude," Kelsey told Solis firmly.

"Of course."

With breakfast done, and the Chronicles feeling their lines burning, there wasn't anything else to be done. Xander took care of paying Rumidia for the room and board for all of them, though she tried to turn down his money, while Kelsey and Solis went to find Etude. At the same time, Daylar led Dahlia and C.J. through the town toward where the Elder lived.

C.J. was fascinated by the forest. Admittedly, he disliked the covering clothing and he missed his desert sun, but there was something peaceful and beautiful about the trees and shade. Kindred was essentially a giant oasis in the desert of the world. The peace-loving nature of the Kin had seeped into the very land. Somehow he doubted the storms would ever reach this place.

Elder Juniper lived in a small house not far from the Healing Shelter. He was of average height for an Elf, a SunKin, and his golden tattoos glowed vivid against his pale skin. He looked fairly young to be an Elder, but his eyes spoke of many years. As the Dragoons approached, he touched his ears and bowed. "Greetings. I am Elder Juniper, Air secondary SunKin Elf."

C.J. made the gesture of respect even as Dahlia bowed. "C.J. Daragon, Soil Chronicle. This is my mate,

Dahlia Stalker, Air Fury." He rubbed his hands over his arms to fight a chill. "You wished to speak with me about Cole?"

"Come in, young ones." He suddenly smiled. "Well, perhaps Dahlia is not that young compared to I. I am only a hundred years older, or so."

She smiled at him. "How much longer do you intend to live?" At five hundred, he was indeed old, even by Kin standards.

"I will not die until I finish my father's work," he said simply. "He fought for peace during the War. I wish to see that peace arrive." He gestured to a couch, and as soon as his guests had seated themselves, he sat down in another chair. "Now, C.J. Please talk to me of Cole."

"He's a Soil secondary SunKin Elf. About sixty years old. He's been my best friend for seven years." He couldn't keep the agitation out of his voice, and not even Dahlia's hand covering his could give him any comfort. "Why doesn't anyone know him? He came here for visits all the time."

"I did not say I didn't know him," Juniper said soothingly. "Please, tell me of what occurred."

"We were attacked by the Elite. One of them, Kappa, isn't our enemy. She's a good person, and Cole loved her. She loves him too, I think, and she loved me a little. She ended up helping us against Delta, and when Cole went to get Dahlia, she ran off. He went to follow after her. I just need to know he is all right."

"He has not checked in with me," Juniper said thoughtfully. "Which does not necessarily mean he is in trouble. Cole is a Second Born Kin, and he is much stronger than average."

"Second Born?" Dahlia asked curiously.

"It means that the soul and the body of Cole were not born together. The original soul within Cole's body died several years ago, at the same time that the body belonging to the current soul did. The two souls briefly touched, and it was agreed that the new soul would take Cole's body for his time was not yet up. It happens among the Kin not unlike you have Master Magi."

"He would know, wouldn't he?" C.J. asked. In a way, the knowledge didn't surprise him. There were many aspects about Cole that had never seemed normal, even by Kin standards. It also explained why he had always been fiercely protective of C.J. He had known what it meant to be different.

"Certainly he does. He brought in his memories of his old self and they combined with the memories of his new self so that he could use his new body comfortably. Bodies are little more than shells for our power and souls." He reached over to lightly touch C.J.'s knee. "I have Kin keeping an eye out for Cole. His family will let me know if they feel anything has happened to him."

"And you'll let me know?"

"As soon as I am able," the Elder promised.

"We might as yet meet him ourselves, *ishke*," Dahlia reminded C.J. gently. "If he has not caught Kappa, and she is as yet confused, she may be with the Elite and coming for us."

"Good." His chin set into a familiar stubborn line. "I don't care if she's older than I am. I'll box her ears!" He blinked, and a bemused smile crossed his face. "My mother used to say that. I didn't think I'd ever say it myself. Kindly don't tell her. I'll never live it down!"

Juniper chuckled softly. "Another sign of adulthood."

As they left the house a few moments later, Dahlia murmured, "Thank you, by the way, for keeping your curiosity where it can't be seen. For the time being, anyway. Once we hit the desert, I'm sure it will be noticed."

He grinned unrepentantly. He felt absolutely no shame for his curiosity and rapidly growing hunger to know everything about his Fury's body. He had pointedly made the little mark on the curve of her breast just to see how she reacted. He hadn't been disappointed. "You weren't thanking me when I did it."

"I was *very* close to having my way with you," she grumbled. "Having you in the experimentation phase is maddening." Her breath caught in her chest as his power suddenly swirled around her hotly, his emotions colliding and tangling with hers. Her heart began to beat harder as she saw how very close that third emotion was to being as great as her own. "C.J."

"Next time," he said softly, almost shyly, "I don't think I'm going to want to stop. I won't make you wait any longer, Dahlia. You've waited long enough." He swung her into his arms and around in a quick circle, uncaring that the Kin watched with grins. "I guess it's a good thing that we're splitting up. I mean, I would hate to embarrass you in front of the others by seducing you nearby."

Her eyes lit with laughter and love. "I'd worry most for poor Solis. He would have the youngest Chronicle when she was Fire." Wildly happy, she threw her arms around her lover and held on. He had this way of making her feel wonderfully cherished, and she reveled in it. And yet, she loved the way he respected her strength and loved letting her protect and shelter him.

"You'll make me cry." He buried his face against her neck. "Damn it, Dahlia." He put her down and laced their fingers together. "We need to meet with the others. I feel a bit better after talking to Elder Juniper, and I'm glad to know why Cole was always different to me. I'm glad he was born again. I'd have had a very unhappy life without him."

"He would be to you what Daylar is to Tariah, just not as formally," she murmured. "A Chronicle's power is too erratic to become an honorary Kin. Tariah got lucky because Daylar's power was erratic for a while."

"It doesn't have to be formal. It's there. That's enough for me." He grinned. "And you're going to be in trouble when we find Cole. He and I are terrible together, or so we've been warned. I can't help it. We bring out the worst in each other."

Or the best, as far as she was concerned. She could see his memories and knew the two males made a dangerous combination. "I'm terrified," she said drolly.

The beach where Xander had landed was where everyone else waited. The other three Chronicles wore packs with supplies, and Kelsey handed an extra one to C.J. "Here you are," she said. "And since we're going to a desert," she added hopefully, "can we *please, please* have desert clothes?"

He lifted a brow at her. "If you give me some sand, *Master* Kelsey."

"That's not fair," she told him. "I happened to see *someone's* tapestry hanging on a wall at the inn."

Roman kept his mouth shut because he wasn't about to defend either of them and get it pointed out by the other that he was also world-renowned for the glasswork he and Terina had made. He was much smarter than that.

Jayda smiled wryly up at Xander. "I am grateful that I am not an artist of any kind. I don't think I'd want to be known across the world. Well, more than I already was just for being a Master Magi."

"Now, kids," Grecia firmly stepped between C.J. and Kelsey, "let's play nice, shall we? Xander and Kelsey will make the sand, and I and C.J. will weave with it. If he will make cloaks to protect us from the sun, I will make clothes. We don't need much."

Kelsey stuck out her tongue at C.J. impishly and he returned the gesture before ruffling her hair. Not a single one of their friends doubted that even being full adults would stop them from sniping at each other. They had done it from childhood, and not even nine years had changed it. Nothing ever would.

C.J. used some of the plain sand under their feet to create two small bags, one for him and one for Grecia, so that they could carry the higher quality sand with them. Kelsey lifted her hands and billows of smoke swirled into the air. She had often made sand for weavers across the world. Many discarded hilts had become a beautiful piece of cloth somewhere.

To make sand, the creator first made smoke and then solidified it into glass. Glass could be formed either solid or liquid depending on its usage. The more intricate the work would be, the more likely the glass would need to be liquid. It could then be hardened further with fire or smoke. Roman had seen Terina make glass, and it fascinated him to watch Kelsey and Xander. He had never realized that making glass could be as unique as the maker.

Kelsey made liquid glass and solidified it to the state she wished before she dissolved it into sand by using her Smoke power. Xander made glass that was solid from the start and broke it down from there. Though both end results looked the same, it was still very obvious that they had been made by two different people.

Xander studied the bag of Kelsey's sand before smiling at her. "You are brilliant at your work, fledgling. I've had two and a half millennia to practice, and you're nearly as good as I am after less than a decade."

She flushed with pride. "I taught myself how when I realized what a waste it was to just get rid of my discarded glass."

"You know that tapestry you saw at the inn?" C.J. asked as he ran the sand over his fingers. "It ought to feel slightly familiar. It was made with some of your sand. Cole got the bag for me from Prismatic. I never realized it was yours until now. I suppose that's why it felt familiar. It was the best I've ever worked with. Expect me to nag you incessantly for a big supply once we're all settled on the Isle."

She grinned at him. "Only if you make me something for Solis' and my house."

"Deal." He straightened and gathered the sand in his hand. As Grecia formed clothing, he formed cloaks. It took no thought to know what he wanted to make. He made eight cloaks total, and all were pure white with the black chalice of the Black Magi in the back. The men's cloaks would fasten around their necks, and the women's would fasten around their shoulders.

Grecia made clothes in creams and tans since they would wear best in the desert. For the men, there were loose slacks and vests. For the women, she made shorts and tops that weren't much more than bikini tops as well, but much sturdier. As she handed clothes to Kelsey, she asked warmly, "Will this do?"

"Yes!" Kelsey clutched them close happily. "Forests are nice, but they're not for me!"

"I will need to get used to this again," Jayda said. "I've lived in Glacia for so long that I am acclimated to the cold. Xander hates the snow," she said gravely. "He wants to convert me fully into a desert girl."

"Can we compromise on the valley?" he asked hopefully.

She framed his face with her hands and went up to kiss him warmly, her power swirling teasingly around him. They both knew that he would willingly live in the mountains if it would make her happy, but she didn't mind meeting him halfway. "Compromise accepted," she said softly.

Since they wouldn't be wearing much beyond their bikinis anyway, the four females stripped off their forest clothes and put on their shorts and tops. The males, out of consideration for Kelsey who was still only partway through second puberty, decided to wait until they had all split up.

"I hate modesty," she grumbled. "Tell me it goes away. It shouldn't bother me to see a naked or mostly naked male. It didn't before!" It wasn't the same as with Solis; this was more an embarrassed feeling than a nervous feeling.

"It usually goes away eventually, Kel," Dahlia told her gently. Laughter lingered in her voice. "Especially for someone as outgoing as you."

"Back up," Xander warned with a smile. "Give me room to change form. Once I and Jayda take off, then someone else can change." Everyone cleared back and he called on his power to go back into his natural form. He felt no worry for how the other Chronicles might react; he doubted that much would unnerve them at this point.

Roman studied the immense Dragon now on the beach and then looked at Grecia and said solemnly, "You're right. He is much more intimidating than you."

Xander laughed as he helped Jayda up to her perch. He wrapped smoke around her to keep her held securely as he flew straight up into the air from where he stood. He flew out from the beach and hovered in place to wait for the others.

Dahlia changed next since she was the next largest and then helped C.J. onto her back. Once he was secure, she flew out to join Xander. Solis and then Grecia followed suit with their Chronicles, and when all four pairs were together, they began to head north across the ocean toward the land known as Spectrum. There was no worry that they would get lost.

Even at a day's flight away, they could see the darkness from the storms gathering on the horizon.

Chapter Eighteen

It was evening by the time the Dragoons approached the western shore of Spectrum. They had been forced to fly much farther north than intended, thanks to the storms spreading out from Mirah. Roman very carefully kept his worry for his best friend and parents hidden from all except Grecia. There was no hiding it from his lover.

The storms had begun to cover nearly every inch of Spectrum. There was only a small space between the ones moving north and the ones moving south. They pushed into the oceans and made the water seethe restlessly. Even if it had been midday, it would have been hard to see.

Among their supplies had been lanterns, and all four Chronicles carried them as they flew along the shore to find a place to land safely. They needed to land, split up, and camp soon so that their Furies could be fed. The long and fast flight had drained them all.

When they found a place secure enough, they all landed one by one. The four Furies turned back into Magi form, but even Xander found it difficult to remain on two feet. C.J. and Roman were able to lift their Furies off their feet easily enough, but Kelsey and Jayda could only brace Solis and Xander.

"It occurs to me," Jayda said warmly as she kept Xander's arm wrapped around her shoulders to support him, "that female Chronicles are at a slight disadvantage in moments like these."

"When we have a chance," Grecia said tiredly from Roman's arms, "then we will show you how to use our majiks to change into a Dragon form. It will increase your strength to a comparable level, and in emergencies, it will remove this problem."

"Is it hard to learn?" Kelsey asked curiously.

Xander suddenly smiled. "You'll have to ask Tariah about her first attempts." He carefully straightened and ignored the way his body protested his drained power. "C.J. and Roman can cover more ground right now than Jayda or Kelsey because of Solis and me. I suggest that the two of you move as far north and northeast as possible before camping. I still have reserves of power to draw on; Jayda and I will move as far as I can make it."

"I think we'll just stay here." Solis sat down on the sand with a wry smile. When Kelsey knelt beside him, he tugged her onto her lap so he could nuzzle his nose into her hair. He would never tease her for being the youngest of her friends simply because he was the youngest of his.

"We'll either meet up outside Prismatic, or wherever we find Morgan and Tariah," Roman said. "Maybe they can use their mind skills to reach out to anyone who doesn't make it to their side."

"I think that's a sound plan." Xander gathered his strength and let Jayda take some of his weight as they headed more east than north. Eventually they would turn and make their way north more than east, but they wanted some distance between themselves and the others to make their presence less conspicuous.

Roman and Grecia set out north, and C.J. and Dahlia headed northeast. In only a matter of minutes, Kelsey and Solis were left by themselves on the shore. He nuzzled her hair again and then trailed his lips to her neck. Her soft red aura lifted and made his mouth tingle with the anticipation for her taste.

Her lashes fluttered down as a shiver rippled through her body of sheer delight. His lips barely skimmed her sensitive skin, his breath cool against her heated flesh. It was a shocking contrast to where his hands rested on her back and hip. They burned hotly even through her cloak. She instinctively reached for him with her power, curling her emotions around him temptingly, trying to tell him what she wanted. What she needed.

He shuddered lightly and unfastened her cloak. Her breasts curved enticingly over the edge of her top and bikini, and he buried his nose there to taste her power. It was wild and spicy, sharp and sweet all at the same time. As strength poured back into his body, he tugged down her bikini so that her breasts were bared. Eagerly he closed his mouth over a taut nipple, thrilling to the soft whimper that she couldn't stop.

She buried her hands in his hair and pulled him closer. Her body was beginning to tremble with need. She burned hotter than her power. She could feel his emotions tangled to hers so that he could read everything she felt, and it had the effect of letting her feel what he did. For the first time, the volatile third emotion inside him did not scare her. She thrilled to it and reveled in being wanted that terribly. "Solis." It was little more than a pleading breath.

"If you intend to stop me," it was murmured huskily against her breast, "you had better do it now." She arched against him desperately, and his body throbbed painfully. Steam curled from both their bodies and made the air thick and sultry. He slowly slid his hand down her body and between her legs. Her skin was hot and soft and he wanted to taste her power everywhere from head to toe.

The feel of his touch on her inner thigh didn't frighten her this time. Her entire body twisted restlessly, begging for him to stop teasing her. She dragged his head up and kissed him wildly, and the feel of him as yet feeding on her power was erotic in a way it had never before felt. She could *feel* the strength pouring into her lover's body.

His knuckles brushed lightly against the sensitive flesh between her legs, and even with the layers of her clothing between them, the pleasure was sharp and terrifying. Her entire body instinctively tried to jerk back though she could not actually get away with his arm around her. Tears welled in her eyes as she burrowed against his chest. "Damn it!" Aching, needy, she quivered from head to toe. "That isn't fair to either of us!"

"If you're not ready, then you're not yet ready." His hands shook as he calmly stroked her arms and side, trying to soothe them both. He wanted her so badly that even his teeth ached, and his pants were far too tight on his arousal.

"How can you be this patient? This is torturing you." She wiped her eyes on his tunic.

"It is torture," he said softly, "but I don't find it that difficult to stop when you are afraid. That's why I let our emotions tangle as they did. I knew that feeling your fear would give me control." He tilted her chin up and gently kissed away her tears. "Anyone who could push beyond such a natural reaction is less than worthy of the gift of their lover's second puberty growth."

She took a long breath. "No more teasing me," she said firmly. "When you feed, keep your hands to yourself. Let me test my own emotions. I'll know when I'm ready. I'm sure I will." She framed his face and kissed him with all the love in her heart, letting him feel how terribly close to full bloom that third emotion was inside her.

He smoothed his fingers through her hair and savored how the curls clung to his skin as if they too would hold him. "Having you be mine fully," he said softly as he brushed her lips with his, "will make every minute of the wait worth it." His lips curved. "And it gives me an entirely new respect for my first lover. She was very patient with me as well."

Her lips curved in return. There was no jealousy in her heart for anyone in his past. There was no fear for anyone else in the future. She found it impossible to ever imagine him ever wanting or needing anyone else. That was the true miracle of the bond between Dragoons as far as she was concerned. That absolute confidence in each other, the surety in always knowing how the other would feel.

And her lover felt . . . hungry. His power was fed by feeding on her power, but his stomach had other needs. She grinned when he smiled sheepishly. "I'm getting hungry too. You find some fish and I'll put up the tent."

He reluctantly released her and got to his feet. If anything, the jump in the ocean might help cool him off. Steam still lifted from both their bodies.

She dug in her pack until she found the tiny little square box that the Kin had given her. She had been assured it was just like many other Kin inventions that could and would enlarge itself to proper size for whoever used it.

She held it out on the palm of her hand and waited for a few moments. Nothing happened. She poked the box with her other hand and it suddenly jumped into the air. She stifled a yelp as she fell back onto the sand and the box bounced away. With a sudden surge of power, it burst open and grew to a full sized tent that could easily hold both Kelsey and Solis comfortably.

Disgruntled, she turned her attention to making a small fire to cook whatever Solis managed to catch. It burned obediently on the sand, and she finally, belatedly, realized she was in a desert at last. She promptly fell over onto her face in the sand and spread her arms as if to hug the land. She had missed the desert something fierce! She loved the heat and the dusty ground. The taste and scent of the air. She wanted the world to have more plains and forests, certainly, because it would balance everything out, but she wouldn't want all of her deserts to go away for it!

Solis started laughing when he saw her. "I wondered how long it would take you to notice." Perfectly dry thanks to his power, he sat down beside the fire and began to efficiently clean the fish he had caught. Once that was done, he put them in the fire to cook. "And on a related note . . ." He pulled his desert clothes out of the pack. "I might as well change."

She sat up to watch unashamedly as he pulled off his clothes. She was no longer nervous with her Fury's body, and she watched with immense curiosity as he stripped naked. Only a day before, she had been afraid to confront the sight of his desire for her. Now, seeing the sight of his arousal blatantly declaring his need for her just made heat curl inside her body. Nerves did flutter, but they were not true fear. Just a slight trepidation.

He was utterly beautiful to her eyes. He seemed, to her, to be the ultimate in perfect beauty. And his complete lack of embarrassment or modesty allowed her the freedom to look her fill. If it hadn't been for those fluttery nerves, she would have tackled him down onto the sand to continue her exploration of his body. Watching him as she was, she could see the instant response of his body to the hot lash of her thoughts. It delighted her entirely. "You mean I don't have to actually touch you? I just have to think about it?"

He looked at her with eyes that smoldered. Rather than respond with words, he let his mind fill with everything and anything he wanted to do to her, with her. How he so desperately wanted to touch and taste her. He didn't censor a single image and gave her details he might have before hidden.

Her breath caught in her chest and her body instantly heated. It erased all of her efforts to cool down after the embrace. "Oh." It was about all she could think to say. If thoughts alone were going to do that to them, then they were going to have a very tempestuous relationship. Not that she was complaining, of course. Once she was an actual adult, she definitely wanted to explore those ideas in his mind.

A smile lit his face as he tugged on his vest. He walked over to where she sat and knelt down to kiss her softly. "Never change," he told her softly. "You are perfect for me." He sat beside her and retrieved the fish from the fire. He divvied it between them, and a companionable silence remained as they ate.

She had never felt as perfectly at home as she did sitting in a desert with her Fury. And yet . . . she didn't feel entirely at home. She was far too conscious of being on Magi lands, too conscious of the fact that going near a city could be deadly.

"I don't think anyone would dare try to hurt us," he said softly, musingly. "General attitude seems to have been changing over the years, and the tentative truce between Magi and Dragons isn't about to be tested by any except the truly stupid. I think the Magi finally are beginning to realize that the danger is not from a Chronicle. It's from the Elite."

"Maybe we'll see the laws changed someday."

"Maybe so."

It was getting late, and they set up a protective shielding around their campsite so they could go to sleep. They removed the fire and shield in the morning as they let the tent collapse back down into its default state. When the area was as pristine as when they had found it, they set out across the desert.

Though it was morning, there wasn't much light. Kelsey carried their lantern as they walked. Solis had to be very careful not to expend even the slightest bit of power for fear of making the storms worse where they closed in overhead. The clouds of Flutterlies were more black than gray, and flickers of lightning were proof of the power they had already absorbed.

The air of the desert felt hot and humid. Both Dragoons could feel themselves sweating despite their respective powers. It didn't help any that partway into the afternoon, Kelsey's lines began to itch violently. Her power rioted under her skin. It burned into her lines and raised her agitation levels. She said nothing about it though Solis was well aware of it. Neither could figure out what would be causing it. It would make more sense for him to be agitated because of the storms, but he felt perfectly fine.

A short time later, she stopped walking entirely. "I can't stand it," she said fiercely. "Something's wrong, Solis. I can feel it. The last time I felt like this was when I was fighting Phi. It was as if I could sense the perversion of nature inside him."

His eyes sharpened and his nose flared as he smelled the air. Underneath the humidity of the storms, he could catch a whiff of tainted power. Without thinking twice, he gave her a sharp shove and sent her tumbling across the sand. He was barely in time. The blast of raw Soil power exploded the sand under his feet and flung him violently away. As he rolled to a stop, green blood began to flow from the wounds lining his legs and chest.

Kelsey scrambled up to her feet and rushed to his side. "Solis!" As she knelt beside him, her lines burned painfully. Her head jerked up and she looked to the side to see the familiar, and unwelcome, figure of Phi approaching. A low sound rumbled in her chest and her eyes flashed red warningly. "You."

Phi cackled at her. "We meet again, little Chronicle! Why don't you come to my side? We're going to destroy the Magi and make the world better! Don't you want to live peacefully? It'll be so much better when they're gone! You've got the potential we need to take command of the Lost Isle. Come on, Kelsey! Won't it be wonderful?"

Fire whipped up around her body and flew across the land at him before he could move. It slammed into his chest and flung him backwards through the air. "Attacking my Fury won't do anything except make me more determined to kill you!" she snarled.

Solis tried to lift himself to help, but a few of the wounds had gone to the bone. He didn't dare change into his natural form because of the storm, and Kelsey lacked the ability to heal with her power. "Xander." It was little more than a whisper. "Call Xander with your mind."

She had no idea if it would even work, but there was no reason not to try. With all the power she could muster, she sent out the mental cry toward Xander. Telepathy was supposed to be only for reading minds, but perhaps his being an Elder would let him feel her from a distance.

Phi had staggered back up to his feet, and yellow blood oozed from his wounds and stained his clothes. The scent was putrid and horrid in the humid atmosphere, and the clouds themselves seethed as if in protest. The land rumbled softly. It was unstable enough without the risk of battle.

He shot a tangle of vines at Kelsey and she reached out to grab onto them. The thorns bit into her flesh but she held on and sent fire whipping down the branches back toward him. He released the vines swiftly and instead began to agitate the quake until the ground started to roll and rock violently.

Kelsey held onto Solis tightly. She knew that if she left his side, then he would be an easy target. She couldn't risk losing him. Not Solis. He was the one thing she could never give up. If she lost him, then she would have nothing.

Phi was so busy trying to find an open shot that he didn't realize they were no longer alone until a massive fireball slammed into his back and sent him flying headfirst into the sand. When he managed to get free and scramble around, he saw Xander and Jayda approaching quickly.

While Xander went after Phi, Jayda ran over to Kelsey and Solis. She dropped down beside them with a soft curse as she saw the Fury's wounds. "Kel, shield me. Block the storm from getting my power so that I can heal these wounds."

Kelsey instantly surrounded them in a bubble of fire. Even if Jayda's power tried to escape, it would simply turn to steam. "Can you heal him with the quake?" she asked. It was a legitimate concern when the land still shook.

"I'm going to try." She formed a needle of ice and thread of water and got to work stitching the first of the truly terrible wounds. "He knew exactly what he was doing when he went after you here," she said grimly.

Phi barely spared the fire bubble a second look as he backed slowly away from Xander. The Fury Elder had fire swirling around his hands and feet, and his teeth bared in a soft snarl. "What are you doing here?" Phi demanded.

"You attacked my clan; what do you think I'm doing here?" was the retort. He shot another fireball at Phi and sent the Elite member scrambling. Almost lazily, he shot yet another fireball and had him dodging back the other way. "How does it feel to be on the receiving end for once?"

Phi managed to catch a breath only to lose it when the ground suddenly flung him straight into the air. When he landed painfully, he could feel at least one rib crack in the impact. His eyes jerked to the side and he saw the familiar form of C.J. and Dahlia. The male Chronicle's eyes were livid with an unexpected rage.

Immense thorns burst out of the ground and threatened to impale Phi entirely. "Don't forget us," Grecia warned as she and Roman joined Kelsey and Jayda. Both ducked into the bubble and knelt down. "Let me help," she said to Jayda. "I can use more power safely. Let me take over."

Dahlia, of no use with her Air power, went to aid the others with Solis. C.J., though not necessarily equipped for battle, joined Xander. Because Jayda had stopped using power, Kelsey took down the bubble and got to her feet to go join the males in battle. "You heard me," she said to Xander.

"I did." He ran a hand down her hair gently. "You scared me soundly, fledgling. Dragons are notoriously protective of their families." He rested his other hand on C.J.'s shoulder. "Cover us," he told the younger male. "If you think you can attack, then do it. Remember, your power is designed for art not combat."

Phi spit blood out of his mouth, either uncaring or unseeing when the yellow liquid burned the sand. "It takes this many to kill one measly Master Magi?" he taunted. "Maybe you aren't as powerful as you think you are. Don't you want a peaceful world without war-hungry Magi?"

"And you're any better?" C.J. demanded. He looked at Xander with a scowl. "Can't you just eat him?"

Xander bared his teeth as Phi went white. "I might get indigestion, but I'm willing to risk it." He started to glow as if to turn into his Dragon form.

Phi panicked and shot as big a blast of power as he could at the Elder. Death by being eaten was not only said to be extremely painful, but it was also the most humiliating way a Dragon could kill someone. It meant that they saw their victim as being of no more value than food, and to a race that valued life . . . that was a significant difference.

The Elite Magi was so busy trying to keep Xander away that he didn't even notice that Kelsey had moved out from behind the shield that C.J. had made. In fact, he only knew she wasn't there when he realized she stood right behind him. He went lethally still as her slender hand closed around the back of his neck.

"I don't hate you," she said quietly. "Perhaps the saddest thing is that I feel nothing for you at all." Her hand began to burn hotly as fire rippled across her lines and flowed down her arm. "Even Lucksphere has turned her back on you."

He opened his mouth but nothing emerged. The fire engulfed him without warning and the flames swept from head to toe. They burned hotter and hotter until the air quivered with heat waves. The smell of burning tainted blood filled the air and everyone gagged. Then, blessedly, he turned to ashes. The storms overhead began to rain viciously and poured down water that washed away the remains of the Elite.

The land stopped its shaking as Xander, Kelsey, and C.J. went to join the others. Solis was sitting upright while Grecia healed the last of his wounds. A few were still pink lines but rapidly healing as well. "Thanks," he said to Grecia and Jayda alike. When Kelsey knelt and threw her arms around him, he pulled her as close as he could. "I'm fine," he said into her hair. "I promise."

"Maybe splitting up was not the best of ideas," Roman admitted quietly as he sat down beside Grecia. "The way the elements fall, these storms prevent one half of us from being able to use our powers. And in our two Soil Elements' case, they aren't designed for battle. Grecia is a healer and C.J. is an artisan."

"Then at this point," Dahlia spoke up, "we need to stay together. It is a certainty that the rest of the Elite will be coming after us." The others glanced at her in agreement and immediately began to grin. She felt her cheeks slowly heating. "What?" she asked warily. It dawned on her and she hastily slapped a hand over her neck. Sure enough, she could feel the little abrasion. "C.J.!" she scolded. "You promised!"

He grinned mischievously. "I couldn't resist." He held out his hands and they could all see where a portion of his lines had significantly darkened. "I noticed this on Jayda and Roman and now me," he said to Xander. "Kelsey's lines aren't darker, and she and Solis aren't lovers. It's connected, isn't it?"

"It is an indication of a portion of your journey being done," he explained softly. "In the very old days, the final stage of your journey would be taking your lover, not the first. The final portion of your lines won't darken until you reach the Isle, if what happened to Tariah and Morgan holds true."

"Xander?" Kelsey suddenly asked. "Did Chronicles finish second puberty before finding their Fury in the old days?"

He frowned thoughtfully as he looked back to those years. "You know," he said slowly, "I don't think they did. Most, I believe, were like Jayda or Morgan. They had gone through the entire process—whether normal or accelerated I couldn't say—but they had never 'graduated' into being an adult. There might have been a few exceptions that I am unaware of, but I don't recall ever meeting a Chronicle who was fully an adult before they finished their journey and found their Fury."

"Lovers share power," Dahlia said softly. "Perhaps it is too uncomfortable for a Chronicle to share their power with any except their Fury." She took a soft breath, willing to admit her truth to help make sense of it all. "And some Furies are made that way as well."

"Oh, Dahlia." Grecia hugged her friend. "I had no idea. No wonder C.J. is perfect for you."

"So," Roman said slowly, studying his lines, "one portion of our journey is to take our Fury. Another portion is to find the Isle. What would the third portion be?"

"That," came an unexpected and yet familiar male voice, "we will simply have to wait and see."

Everyone turned sharply, and Kelsey took a swift breath as she recognized the four people standing just behind them. The two Chronicles were much shorter than average for Magi height and had matching auburn hair and silver eyes. They looked enough alike to be twins. The male Fury was of average Magi height, and the female Fury was much shorter, though not as short as the female Chronicle.

"Well, then," Xander said softly. "How long have you been standing there?"

Morgan grinned. "We followed the explosions. I knew Kelsey's temper would get the better of someone someday." His smile softened as he looked at the young woman he had loved as if she were his daughter. All of his children had grown up. "Hey there, Soot."

She leapt to her feet and tackled him straight to the sand in a single bound. A sob caught in her throat as she clung onto him. "You promised us!" she almost wailed. "You *promised*, Morgan!"

It took less than a second for the other three Chronicles to scramble over to cling onto Morgan as well. All of them were taller than he was, except for Kelsey who was the same height, and it broke his heart that he had not gotten to see them grow up. "I'm so sorry," he whispered.

Tariah knelt down beside him. She had not gotten to know the four children the way he had, but it had not stopped her from loving them the minute she had met them for such a brief time those years before. "We were looking," she confessed. "We knew you had to be starting second puberty soon and that that could have an effect on what Morgan did. You can't stop a Chronicle from journeying."

Kelsey turned and hugged her fiercely but leaned back again with a bemused look on her face. "When did you get shorter than me?"

Morgan studied her lines, saw no darkened portions, and looked at Solis with a wry smile. "I'm sorry," he said dryly.

Solis grinned when Kelsey stuck her tongue out at Morgan. "I'm not."

"I think we need to camp here," Dominic said. "We have some things to discuss, and we're not going to get anywhere once it is fully night. The storm is getting worse." It was a legitimate concern since the pouring rain had removed any remaining ability to see more than fifty feet ahead.

And that alone was deeply concerning to all present. Deserts on Lucksphere were not known for rainstorms. There was no knowing what sort of damage could be done to the cities scattered across the landscape. There was no protection from flooding. No protection from mudslides sweeping in from tall dunes. There was a tenuous balance in place that even the slightest vibration might upset.

At this rate, the Elite weren't going to need the Chronicles to help destroy the Magi. If just destroying Phi had done this to Spectrum, what would destroying the others do to the rest of the world?

Part Three
~Summer~

Chapter Nineteen

The storm was unrelenting with its fury. Kelsey dug out the tiny tent box from her pack and held it up. "Will it get big enough for all of us?"

"It should." C.J. grinned. "Morgan's short."

"Did they have to grow up?" Morgan complained to Tariah. "Now I'll have forever with them making fun of my height." Not that he truly minded, of course. Nothing could take away his happiness at having his children, though nearly all adults now, back together again. And it clenched his heart to see them all wearing the cloak of the Black Magi.

"It'll get old after a century or two," she assured him. "And as for the tent, I would assume it ought to get big enough. That's the whole point of Kin inventions. Daylar was showing off a new meal type to me recently that can become dinner for a whole family. They all have far too much time on their hands."

Kelsey tossed the box onto the ground a few feet away and it promptly grew into a full-size tent. As soon as everyone started ducking inside, it grew proportionately bigger. It allowed for enough room for everyone to sit or stand comfortably though several knees bumped. No one minded.

"How are your wounds?" Dominic asked Solis.

"Nearly gone. Grecia and Jayda took care of me." His face darkened with a frown. "Phi knew exactly what he was doing when he attacked me like he did. Whether he happened to find Kelsey and me first, or he was specifically looking for her, I don't know. But we are indeed at a disadvantage on Spectrum right now."

"There aren't many places we will have an advantage." Jazz kept an arm lightly around Morgan's waist. She knew that his calm manner hid his guilt for not finding the four children sooner. "The storms are spreading into the oceans. Glacia is beginning to have full blizzards. Choral is dealing with desert tornados, and Carnelian is suffering like Spectrum."

"What about Kindred?" Kelsey asked swiftly, thinking of Etude and their other friends.

"Curiously," Tariah said, "it has been spared. The Isle of Dragons has been spared. It would seem that only Magi lands are under siege from nature. But that's to be expected, considering what the Elite have been doing. They deliberately tore up the balance of Magi lands."

"But they haven't found the Lost Isle," Dahlia murmured. "If they had, there wouldn't even be a world left."

"What isle?" Roman asked.

"When the massacre occurred," Xander began softly, "the Chronicles and Furies retreated to the isle they had called home. The genocide occurred there. The power from the battle seeped into the very land." His eyes closed. "I was there. But even now I don't remember what the land looked like or where it is. That entire time is sketchy in my mind, at best."

"That kind of power," whispered Jayda, "could tear apart anyone who tried to claim it!" She looked at Morgan and Tariah, saw the steadiness in their matching silver eyes, and felt her heart stop. "You can't intend to . . . to try to take command of it! It might kill you!"

"But it might not." Tariah and Morgan laced their fingers together. "It's something we've talked about for nine years," Tariah said quietly. "We're the strongest Chronicles here. We're not . . . normal Chronicles, somehow. And we . . . well, we made a promise. To end what was started a thousand years ago."

"Tariah, I have a question." C.J. sat forward to see her better. "Would you say that it is perfectly normal for Chronicles to accelerate through second puberty when their Fury is there, but to take a regular amount of time if they aren't?"

She looked at Morgan. "You were normal, right?"

"Relatively speaking."

She looked at Jayda. "And you?"

"I believe so. It was several months from when I think it started to when I think it ended. I've thought it might be because of Xander's age that I was all but done with second puberty. It would be cruel to make him wait longer than he had to claim me." She slid her hand into his tenderly.

"I was thinking age might have something to do with it too," Kelsey put in. "The relative age of the Fury seems to have had a distinct impact on where in second puberty their Chronicle is when they meet. And Xander thinks that Chronicles never 'graduated' until meeting their Furies in the old days."

Tariah frowned thoughtfully, and Dominic smiled as he watched her mind move too quickly for even him to follow. After a moment, she said slowly, "What it really comes down to is that Lucksphere wants to survive above everything else. Chronicles were made to take in the excess power in the land and filter it through their Furies, whose Dragon birth gives them the capacity to process infinite power. But that dichotomy is dependent on the Fury and Chronicle being Dragoons."

Grecia's brows lifted. "You mean that we feed on our Chronicle's power more effectively when we're lovers?" She thought back, wondering if she had noticed any difference from the first time she had fed on Roman's power to the most recent time. An obvious difference was, of course, *how* she fed and from where, but his power *did* seem sweeter and more potent now that they were lovers. "I didn't think anything of it," she murmured. "I just assumed it was my emotions making it different."

"What about this?" Roman asked. "It crossed my mind when Grecia and I met that if Furies don't have infinite power, then how do they live so long without their Chronicle? Look at Xander."

Slowly, Tariah said, "A Fury knows when their Chronicle is born and when they die. That means there is a connection that exists before birth. That connection is what becomes a Chronicle's lines. So that connection is what sustains a Fury. And the older a Fury, the more effort the planet has needed to make to sustain them without a Chronicle. So their Chronicle is more likely to be ready to become a Dragoon."

"Again, it comes down to Lucksphere wanting to survive."

Xander suddenly frowned. There was something in his mind, something that he had forgotten. He was sure that it was critically important, but he simply could not call it up. It had to have been from that lost time. Were his missing memories another act of the planet in an effort to survive? Then why would they have all forgotten the Elite? That certainly wasn't helping anyone.

"Morgan," Jayda spoke up, "can you do anything for Xander? His entire memory of the final fight during the War is gone. He keeps thinking there was something important, that there's something we need to know, but it's simply not there. It's not like what you did for us by fragmenting our memories. They're not there at all."

"That's impossible," Morgan disagreed instantly. "Memories can't be fully erased. I've been thinking about it for nine years, and I think we do still have our memories of the Elite. They've been fragmented smaller than bits of sand, and our arrangement of memories were changed so that we didn't notice the lack."

"But could you or Tariah do something for him?" Dahlia asked. "Maybe, if anything, he can remember where the Lost Isle is."

"We can't do anything here and now." Tariah shook her head. "Not with the storms. Morgan is Air and I am Water. With our individual strength let alone our collective . . ."

"Then where do we go now? We can't go to the Isle, even if you could lead us," Xander noted. "Jayda, Kelsey, C.J., and Roman all must finish their journeys." He hesitated, then said slowly, "We can *guess* the location of the Lost Isle on the basis of where everything else is. And if you think about it, it might just make sense to you as well. Where is the one place no one can sail to?"

Jayda took a sharp breath. "South from Glacia. That huge expanse of ocean that no ship can pass through. Of course."

"We can't just sail into those storms and hope for the best," Solis pointed out reasonably. "We need to have directions or we're going to be stuck in there forever. What if we headed back to the ocean and went out to sea away from the storms here so that Morgan and Tariah can get into Xander's head?"

"That may be our best bet," Morgan agreed.

Because it was late, and everyone was tired, it was decided to keep camp where they were in the hopes of the rain passing. They stuck with the single giant tent and everyone dug out blankets. In a short amount of time, everyone settled down in pairs.

Kelsey couldn't sleep. There were too many thoughts rushing through her head in too many directions. Too many emotions inside her growing heart. She could only lie in Solis' arms and stare sightlessly at the wall of the tent. Softly, she heard Morgan ask, "What's wrong, Soot?"

Tears burned her eyes at the nickname. She shifted enough to turn her head and found him watching her over the top of Jazz's head. His Fury looked impossibly tiny next to him, but she held him no less fiercely than

Solis held Kelsey. "A lot of things," she finally said softly. "I'm just feeling overwhelmed."

"And rightfully so. Second puberty is a big enough upheaval without going through it in a matter of weeks while in the middle of fighting simply to survive. You ought to talk to Tariah about it. She went through the very same thing. But her Water element gives her more of a cool head than your Fire one gives you."

After a moment of silence, she whispered fiercely, "You promised me, Morgan. You promised to come find us. Why didn't you?"

"I tried," he said tiredly. The note in his voice broke her heart because it made him sound too much older than he was. "Tariah and I would take turns passing by cities, praying we might find one of you. We didn't dare ask anyone for fear of drawing attention to you."

"I was living as a Master Magi. I'm a Weaponsmith. You had to have heard about me. I couldn't get people to *not* talk about me." She took a soft breath. "Even not remembering, it hurt. I knew there was something I didn't remember, someone I cared so much about. And now I can't even tell Mom and Dad. Am I going to ever see them again?"

"You will," he promised. "I still see my parents. And if we can do what we intend to, can get rid of the Elite, maybe there will be a day not far in the future when we can go anywhere and do anything. The attitude is slowly changing, Soot. We can't undo things overnight. But we can start the efforts."

She sniffed and wiped at her eyes. "You still think you know everything."

He smiled. "I do know everything. I have eyes on the back of my head, remember?"

"You fibbed. I looked but I never found them." She suddenly smiled at the memories. "I caused you so much trouble, didn't I?"

"Of course. But there wasn't a day that my world wasn't better because you were in it. Each of you four . . . the moment I met you, I was wrapped around your fingers. But you were the worst of them all."

"I just wanted you to be proud of me," she whispered. "I think that even not remembering, that was all I ever wanted."

"I don't think anyone else could ever be more proud." His silver eyes softened. "I have every hope that if I have a daughter, you'll teach her all of your bad habits so that my life is never boring even when you're off living with Solis in a desert and raising tiny hellions to torment his uncle with."

"His uncle?"

He grinned. "One of the Council Elders. They're sort of fascinated and terrified of Tariah all at the same time. Something tells me that between the two of you, you'll have those stodgy old Dragons whipped into shape in no time." His smile softened. "Go to sleep, Soot. It'll be all right. We're all together, and we can't be stopped."

Just hearing him say it made it easier to believe. With a little sigh, she snuggled more firmly into Solis' arms and closed her eyes. Thinking about tormenting the Council Elders, she fell asleep smiling.

They shared breakfast in the morning. Tariah had brought enough to feed an army, and her family was more than happy for it. She could cook in a way that no one else ever could. C.J., who had grown up with an amazing cook for a mother, even had to admit Tariah was far better. "But don't tell her I said that," he pleaded.

The rain had become a very light drizzle though it was still no lighter out. Kelsey broke down the tent again and propped her hands on her hips. "It occurs to me that our plan is all fine and good, but we can't possibly fly north. We're going to need a boat or two. Are there any towns close enough that we could go to?"

"There's one further north along the coast," Dahlia said. "It's not very big, but they might be willing to sell us a boat of some type." She grimaced. "Well, sell to Morgan and Tariah, anyway. No one yet knows anything about the rest of us except for the Kin."

"I'm not going to hide." Roman's voice was very soft. "I refuse to hide. I'm not going to be ashamed of what I am. If the Magi don't like it, that's their issue. We're the only ones who can stop the Elite, and unless the Magi really do want the world to be destroyed, they're going to know it."

"Then we'll go north." Tariah shrugged with a wry smile. "It'll be uncomfortable, but they won't really try anything." She jerked a thumb toward Xander. "Would you want to be on his bad side?"

"No," C.J. said with a grin.

"He's not that bad." Jayda rubbed her cheek against Xander's shoulder softly. As long as he was near, she no longer had to fear her sensitivity to people would tear her apart. His presence alone created a buffer for her. Though her friends didn't seem to affect her, the city would be another story entirely.

Uncaring of where they were or who they were with, he swung her up into his arms and kissed her soundly. She was more precious to him than anything in the world. Every lonely, terrifying minute of waiting had been worth it the instant she had smiled at him. He had known there had to be a reason why he survived so long. And here she was, her black eyes always filled with love for him.

"I think someone is wrapped around someone else's finger," Jazz told Dominic gravely.

He nodded sagely. "Quite so, Jazz. He's getting his just desserts for how he's always teased me about Tariah. There's no one more deserving."

Xander put Jayda down and distinctly ignored the younger Furies. He skimmed his fingers through his lover's hair with a smile. "You were going to tell Tariah something," he reminded her. "You might as well tell her now."

"That's right." She turned to smile at Tariah. "I'm a doctor," she offered. "A very good one. Xander says that you're pregnant, and I want to be the one who tends to you."

"You are?" Grecia brightened. "Tariah, that's wonderful! Oh, there hasn't been a Dragoon baby since well before the war!" Her eyes widened in shock as she realized. "Oh my," she said softly as she looked at Xander. "Wasn't the last one . . .?"

"Yes," he said softly. "It was." When brows lifted, he said, "The last Dragoon children born before the war were a daughter to the female Chronis twin and a son to the male Chronis twin. I have every confidence that it is from those two that you are descended," he told Morgan and Tariah.

C.J. eyed Tariah and then Dominic and then back again. "So . . . which are you carrying? I would guess that a half-and-half baby isn't likely. Is it a Magi or a Dragon?"

"No Dragon!" Tariah muttered. "No eggs!"

Jayda wrapped an arm around her shoulders soothingly. "I will study with the Dragon doctors," she said warmly, "and I'll know exactly how to care for you if it happens that you're carrying a Dragon. The odds are more to be that it is a Magi because you are a Chronicle, but you never know what'll happen in the future."

"If it's you, Jayda," she conceded, "I guess it'll be okay." She smiled up at the taller girl. "Were you living as a Master Magi doctor? Where?"

"Glacia. Arctica to be precise. I lived outside of town because it was too painful to be near people." Without conceit, she said, "I was the best healer on Glacia. When the Elite attacked, I went into the mountains to save people from an avalanche and cave-in. That was how I found Xander." The look she shot her lover was teasing. "His head wasn't quite strong enough to fully handle a nosedive down the mountainside."

He nipped at her power with his in retaliation though he was smiling as well. Though more mature than her brothers and sister, she was still no less sassy, and he couldn't have been happier.

"What about the rest of you?" Jazz asked curiously. "You were living as Master Magi too, correct?"

"We were." Roman tucked his hands in his pockets. "I lived outside Mirah on a farm. I ran a windmill." Reluctantly, he admitted, "And I did some art with my best friend who is a Fire Magi. She would make glass figurines and I would etch them."

"I knew you were hiding something," C.J. grumbled. He grinned. "Though I'm one to talk. I was living outside Symphony. I'm a weaver. Some of my stuff is hanging in the Magi king's palace, though I think he'd be alarmed to learn his art was made by a Chronicle. Then again, maybe not. He's not exactly *pushing* the laws."

"I'm a Weaponsmith," Kelsey offered. "I got into this whole situation because the Militia wanted me to make them new weapons. Phi attacked us before I could head home, and Etude, my Kin partner, went to get Solis since we had seen him flying past. We didn't know he was a Fury until he awoke me." She thought of Ilian for a moment and her eyes darkened with sadness. It must have been a horrible shock to him. If they ever met again, what would he say? What would she say?

It was less than half a day of walking before they approached the town. It wasn't very large but its convenient location beside the ocean allowed for a decent enough trade and rate of visitors. Cruise ships would stop along the way, and in fact, there was one docked at that immediate moment.

There was also a Militia ship docked.

"Are we sure we want to go into town?" Roman rubbed the side of his face where his lines rested. "I know I said I didn't want to hide, but I'm not sure I want to provoke the Militia either."

Grecia opened the bag of sand she wore and swiftly wove a hood to go on his cloak. She gave gloves to C.J. to cover his hands, and he, Kelsey, and Jayda closed their cloaks entirely. Once Roman pulled the hood far enough over his head, there was no noticing that they were Chronicles.

"Why are the Black Magi reforming?" Jayda asked the twins.

"To find other Master Magi to help stop the Elite," Tariah answered promptly. "To create a new sanctuary so they don't have to live as Jayda did, or Roman did. Most of you were thought to be dead when you disappeared, right? Well, obviously, that didn't happen. We managed to save all of you." She studied the four Furies. "And, clearly, Dragons are helping us for obvious reasons. No one knows the difference between Dragon and Fury without seeing their lines."

As the four Furies had already closed their cloaks, their lines were also hidden. It was possible someone might make the correct assumption based on the even number of males and females and the opposing elements, but few Magi truly knew anything about Chronicles.

"We can send letters to our parents to let them know we're alive, can't we?" C.J. asked hopefully.

"No need," Morgan said. "When Tariah wrote to Daylar the last time, she asked him to spread the word to Kin to have your parents retrieved and taken to Kindred for safety. By now, they should be there and away from danger." Something painful filled his eyes. "I don't want what nearly happened to my parents, and what did happen to Tariah's, to happen to them."

"And you'll give them back their memories too?" Kelsey asked pointedly.

He smiled. "Yes, Soot, I will."

The storm was over the town though it did not rain. People went about their normal lives with an undercurrent of tension. Militia soldiers walked around visibly armed as they made sure the people were protected. The upheaval in the land outside had turned normal creatures into monsters, and they crept close, just waiting for a chance to destroy anything in their way.

Many startled looks shot toward Morgan and Tariah as they were recognized, but no one outright said anything to them. Xander, not recognizable as a Fury, was nonetheless recognizable as a Dragon Elder, and the tentative truce was as fragile as the state of the world. Some people whispered, but not even sensitive Jayda could feel any true malice in the air.

While Morgan haggled with a boat maker for a good price on a decent enough boat that could carry them where they needed, the others wandered a few feet away to look at the wares on sale at the market. With no hood on her cloak, Kelsey's vibrant hair burned brightly in the desert air despite the gloomy light. It was as powerful as a beacon, unmistakable to anyone who had ever met her in the past. She only became aware of her distinction when a soft and familiar voice asked behind her, "Kelsey?"

She straightened and turned around swiftly to discover the familiar form of Argyle Ilian Deepforge behind her. His handsome face was filled with shock and hope mingled, and his eyes held a touch of fear. "Ilian," she said softly. She instinctively held her cloak more tightly closed.

His eyes lowered before moving to Solis, who had said nothing, and then to the others who wore the cloak of the true Black Magi. His gaze lingered on Morgan and Tariah, and then came back to Kelsey. "I am glad you escaped from Phi, Master Kelsey," he said formally. "When I reached the site of the battle, both of you were gone. We had feared for the worst. Yours is a gift the Magi couldn't stand to lose."

Solis softly rested his hand on the small of Kelsey's back. Her entire body trembled, and her emotions were a chaotic tangle of sadness and relief. "We Dragons," he said calmly, "were sent out by the Chronis twins to retrieve Master Magi and keep them safe from the Elite. I have been given the task of protecting Kelsey."

"So the Black Magi are reforming."

"We are." Kelsey found a smile. "I was always a Black Magi. Morgan sent me away for safety nine years ago but kept his promise to find me again. We want to stop the Elite." She shook her head. "We *will* stop the Elite."

Roman had only been listening with half an ear when he suddenly caught the scent of a familiar tainted power and his lines began to burn. His head jerked up. Grecia, reading his mind and emotions, was right beside him as they leapt for Solis and Kelsey. Grecia knocked Solis halfway down the street. Roman took Kelsey another direction and rolled with her in his arms safely. Only moments after they were safe, a massive lightning bolt struck the ground where they had been standing.

People screamed and scrambled for cover. The clouds tore open and started pouring rain. Ilian looked around sharply. "Stay calm and go inside!" he ordered. "Militia, escort any children and seniors to safety!"

Beta's strident cackle cut through the air. "You're wasting your breath, Argyle! I'm going to level this place!" She walked forward from the shadows, and her Elite cloak was a distinct mockery of the cloak worn by the others. "We meet again, Chronicle Roman!"

There was no denying it. In his effort to save Kelsey, his hood had fallen back to reveal his face. When he pulled Kelsey to her feet, her cloak also fell open to reveal the lines going down her arms and legs. "I'd have preferred never to see your face again," he retorted.

Grecia's eyes flickered with warning rage. "I claim Fury Right," she said as she stepped forward. As Beta slowly paled, a cool smile touched her lips. "I see you understand what that means. Good."

"Fury Right," Solis explained softly for the new Chronicles and Ilian's benefit, "is the right to kill any who threatens the life of a Fury's Chronicle. Had Phi not gotten the jump on us, I would have claimed it against him."

Ilian remained silent for several moments. Fighting the Elite was supposed to be the matter of the Militia. His orders were very clear. Yet, very distinctly, he stepped back. "The Militia will bow to your right," he told Grecia. "We have trampled on the rights of Furies and Chronicles for long enough. I will not see it anymore."

"Nor will I."

Jayda's head swung around sharply at the familiar female voice. "Quinn!"

Argyle Quinn Flyer stepped forward from the other side of the street, her eyes dark and steady as she looked at Beta. The Elite fanatic had been caught in a crossfire of Magi, Furies, and Chronicles. "If there is any blight on the land," she said distinctly, "it is the Elite. I watched Jayda Lakemore risk her life and sanity to save others time and again. And I have told the king as much." She looked at Morgan and Tariah. "Morgan and Tariah Chronis. I bring an official declaration from the Magi king. He wishes to meet with you to discuss a formal treaty of peace. As of this moment, all Chronicles are welcome in Magi cities."

"Look at that, Beta," Roman said mockingly. "The Elite have done something good for the world. You helped the Magi see who the real threat is."

In a burst of furious power, she sent a tornado whipping down the middle of the street. It was aimed directly for Ilian, but ropes of Soil shot around his body and yanked him out of the way. He landed on his ass at C.J.'s feet, and the Chronicle winced. "Sorry about that. I didn't have time to aim."

"I won't complain. That I assure you."

The storm began to gather in violence as Beta whirled and lobbed another attack. The tainted touch of her power began to turn the dark clouds a sickening shade of yellow-gray, and the rain began to sting like acid. The land quivered warningly, and waves started rolling up from the sea and hitting the docks viciously.

We have to get out of the city! Morgan's voice rang in the minds of all Chronicles and Furies present.

Tariah followed him with her own order, *Roman, she wants you specifically. You must lure her out!*

Even Xander was slightly nonplussed that Morgan and Tariah had the ability to speak directly into the minds of others. He had never heard of such a thing before, though it wasn't the first time that the twins had done something beyond the normal realm of possibility. They were constantly defying the laws of power, as if Lucksphere herself blessed them.

Roman didn't question either of his leaders. He shot a taunting blast of lightning at Beta that deliberately missed her by inches. The power absorbed by the clouds promptly dissipated the ugly yellow tint, and the rain was purified. "If you want me, come and get me, Beta. Oh, that's right. You tried that once. You never stood a chance, old lady."

Her shriek seared the ears of those who heard it, and she went rushing after him as he turned and ran out of the city. Grecia was right on her heels, though Beta didn't know it. The Elite's eyes fully fixed on Roman. She wanted to wipe the smug look off his face and vent her wounded pride. What did that . . . *reptile* have that she didn't!?

When they were far enough out, he swiveled around and fired a tornado at her. It didn't seem to be making the storm worse, and it distinctly prevented the Elite's taint from spreading. Still, he was cautious. The land continued its violently shaking.

Just focus on destroying her, came Tariah's voice in his mind. *C.J. and Jazz are working on controlling the land in the city. Hurry, Roman!*

Breathing hard, Beta started at him malevolently. "Do you think you can destroy me?"

"I can," Grecia taunted from somewhere behind and above her.

Her dead heart froze in her chest as she realized there was only one way that Grecia's voice could be so far over her head and carry such a vibration of power. She carefully turned around and stopped breathing as she saw the Fury in Dragon form towering over her. All she could manage was a single squeal as Grecia's claw closed hard around her body. "Don't eat me!" she shrieked as she saw massive teeth looming close.

"And get indigestion? You jest." She hurled Beta through the air and didn't so much as flinch when the Magi bounced hard and painfully. Yellow blood oozed down Beta's side from where a cracked rib poked through her skin, and Grecia bared her teeth. "Lucksphere herself has turned against the Elite. Your yellow blood is proof of it."

Beta painfully began to gather all of her remaining power. "You won't win," she snarled raggedly. "I'm not going to let you walk away from this so easily!"

Realizing what she was about to do, Grecia grabbed Roman and flew backwards swiftly. Beta's power rose as she prepared to detonate herself, and the resulting shockwave was sure to tear apart the already fragile land. But just as she reached critical mass and her hair began to smoke, the area was lit by a blinding flash of light from a massive lightning bolt as big as Grecia. It struck Beta directly, as if it deliberately targeted her.

The sharp crack reverberated off the eerie silence a second later. There was nothing left of Beta. There wasn't even a sign of ashes as there had been with Phi. The lightning bolt had more than destroyed her. It had erased her entirely.

The land slowly began to stop trembling as the steadying waves from C.J. and Jazz were able to spread further. The storm lessened in its rage, softening to little more than a light drizzle yet again. The ocean continued to seethe angrily, but without its violence of only minutes before.

"Did she . . . she didn't detonate her power," Roman said softly.

Grecia's claws tightened protectively and possessively around him. "She didn't, no. But something or someone else certainly did." She went back into her Magi form, and her arms remained tight around his waist even though he was suddenly taller. "We better go back into the city and see what damage was done."

As they turned and walked, he glanced back over his shoulder to where Beta had stood. There wasn't even a burn mark. Whoever had used the storm's lightning had done so naturally. As naturally as the removed memories in everyone's minds.

Just what was really going on?

Chapter Twenty

The city was quiet and subdued. The Militia moved quickly to ensure that no one had been harmed. The shocking arrival of Beta and the resulting defense of the city by the Dragoons had thrown everyone off balance. More than even Quinn's proclamation.

"I don't understand," Jayda said quietly to Quinn as they stood with the others and Ilian. "Were you telling the truth, or was that just to get at Beta?"

"It was the truth, Jayda," she said. "I went right from Glacia to Prismatic. It was a risk. I knew it was a risk. But it was one I needed to take. I knew that in the worst-case scenario, people might know you were a Chronicle, but there are few who would dare try to harm you, especially with an Elder for your mate."

"You just walked into the throne room and told the king what was going on?" Tariah asked skeptically.

C.J. looked at Dahlia. "And you said I had no self-preservation."

His Fury snorted softly. "You don't."

Quinn shook her head. "Argyles are the highest rank of the Militia. We are given certain rights, and direct contact with the king is among them. I told him what I had witnessed without embellishing anything. I didn't have to. He wants to change the laws, but was hesitant to do so until the people could believe and the Elite might be less of a threat."

Xander studied her speculatively. "Why does he care so much?"

"He has a son," Grecia murmured. "Coming close to first puberty, isn't he? He fears his son being a Chronicle. He fears more that his son might be killed by a law he himself could have changed."

"But what about the people?" Solis asked.

"Chronicles."

They all turned and discovered that most of the people in the city had gathered. Instinctively, the Furies moved to protectively shelter their Chronicles. Xander also put himself in front of Ilian and Quinn, refusing to see them harmed for their compassion.

An older man stepped forward from the crowd with hands spread to show he was unarmed. "We Magi . . . we were wrong." The words were soft but clearly heard. "We can never make up for a thousand years of hate in a single night. It may be centuries before things are the way they should be. But we know we were wrong. These last nine years have shown us all. Our world has shown us."

A woman said, "If you weren't supposed to be here, then you wouldn't keep being born. And just now, we could all see it, that the storm was calmed by the younger Air Chronicle's power. You protected us from the Elite when you had no need to."

"You will always be welcome in Lumin," another man offered. "All of you."

"Should we go to the king?" Tariah asked Morgan. "Prismatic is days from here, and I don't think we have days. But we should at least send him a letter, or do something to acknowledge what he's said and done."

"There is no need." Quinn glanced toward the shadows of an alley between two buildings. "Am I still being demoted for shoving you out of the way?" she asked mildly.

A man stepped forward and pulled down the hood on the cloak he wore. He was unfamiliar to all the Dragoons, but he was certainly familiar to the Magi. There rose a collective gasp of shock, and many elbows bumped and collided as all the Magi hastily made the gesture of respect.

"I take it he's the king?" Jayda whispered to Xander.

He quirked a single brow. "Apparently so." He studied the shorter male intently. Plain in the face and overall average in height and frame, he was as yet slightly stronger than average in whatever power he possessed. There was an intelligence in his eyes that couldn't be hidden. "I'm surprised he journeyed this far."

"A king can't stay cooped up in his palace, no matter how badly his Argyles try to make him," the king noted reasonably. He made the gesture of respect to all those present. "I am Finus Clertain, Water Magi, and I am the king of Magi lands."

The Furies all bowed gracefully. "Xander Journe, Fire Fury Elder," the eldest said calmly. He gestured to his fellow Furies. "Grecia Laluna, Soil Fury; Dahlia Stalker, Air Fury; Jazz Eaglewind, Soil Fury; Dominic Whisperer, Fire Fury; and Solis T'mer, Water Fury."

To the surprise of all but Xander, Morgan and Tariah made a gesture that none but the Elder had seen before. The twins touched their left cheek with their right thumb, then their right cheek, then their left shoulder. If one had drawn a line between the points they touched, they would have drawn half the symbol of 'chron' for which the twins took their family name, and their race took its.

"Morgan Chronis, Air Chronicle," Morgan said calmly. "Black Magi leader."

"Tariah Chronis, Water Chronicle," his sister said. "Black Magi second." She gestured to the four beside her. "Jayda Lakemore, Water Chronicle. Roman Arequo, Air Chronicle. C.J. Daragon, Soil Chronicle. Kelsey Renaire, Fire Chronicle."

It seemed impossible somehow that four more Chronicles had managed to survive the laws, but there was no denying their presence. More still, all four names were very familiar to many people. If these four had lived as Master Magi successfully, then how could anyone doubt any longer that Chronicles were not the terror they had always been purported to be?

Finus sighed wearily. He was not very old, even by Magi standards, and only in his late thirties. He just *felt* much older than his physical age. The struggle he had made over the last few years to mend his broken people had taken its toll. "May I have the honor of an audience with you?" he asked the twins equally.

Well? Tariah asked it into her brother's mind.

We have nothing to lose, he answered wryly. "We would be honored to accept," he said out loud. "But we must be on our way swiftly."

"It will not take long." Finus rolled his eyes as Ilian and Quinn leapt to open the door to the inn for him. "Being king does not make me helpless," he scolded them. "Who was it who carted out those ridiculous statues from the palace?"

"And nearly broke his back in the process," Ilian retorted politely. "Kindly keep yourself healthy and safe so that your Argyles don't lose what is left of their sanity."

"I didn't promote you to be sane," Finus groused wryly as he walked into the building, letting Quinn pointedly go first.

Suddenly liking him a lot more than she had liked the last king, Tariah was smiling as she followed him with the others. The innkeeper was more than happy to show them into the dining room where there would be plenty of space. He felt slightly awed to have not just Chronicles and Furies present, but the king as well, and determined to give them the best service possible.

They found places to sit, and Finus studied the dynamic of those present with immense curiosity. He didn't need to ask to know who was mated with who. The Furies sat very close to their Chronicle, most touching in some way or another. Dominic held Tariah on his lap with his arm around her waist and his hand over her stomach in a familiar, universal, protective gesture.

It was also curious to note that Morgan and Tariah sat slightly to the front of the others, even Xander. Despite their young ages, they were treated with the same reverence of an Elder as old as Xander. The twins also sat close enough that their bodies just barely touched. Finus knew they were not twins by birth, but he had trouble believing it. "Tell me what has been happening," he requested quietly. "From the beginning when the Black Magi formed fourteen years ago."

Without hesitation, Morgan laid it all bare. From his youth to his flight from Glacia, to his chance encounter with the Renaires and his determination to save his kind. The subsequent gathering of the other three, and the issues with Soh. Tariah offered her own tale of her restricted childhood and painful awakening with the death of her beloved Maxim.

They left no detail out, not even when Ilian flinched or Quinn looked away in shame. Not even when Finus seemed to age before their eyes as he listened to the litany of abuse and hate that the twins described in every city. He did not need to ask if what they spoke was true. Though welcome in all cities, neither Morgan nor Tariah had been seen more than a handful of times in nine years.

"The Elite are the fault of the Magi." He said it starkly. "If the laws had not been in place, if Chronicles had not been so hated, Phedo Emik would be alive and Soh Emik and Sistra of the Dragons would not have gone mad."

"I doubt that it would have made a difference for Soh," Morgan denied. "There was always something off about him before. But Sistra . . ."

"I do not believe she was bad inside," Jazz said firmly. "She would not have been made a Fury if she was not deserving of the gift of being a Dragoon. If we can find where she hides, where she recovers, we may as yet be able to reason with her. She might as yet be saved. Phedo must be lonely on the other side without her."

Hesitantly, Ilian asked, "A Fury cannot live without their Chronicle?"

Dominic met his eyes unflinchingly. "Not once they feel the birth and death of their other half. A Fury feels the moment that their Chronicle is born. And they feel the moment that they die. They just . . . go away. They don't eat. They don't sleep. Every day that they live, they die a little more. The only respite for a Fury who has lost their Chronicle is a merciful death."

Quinn turned a sickly shade of green and rushed from the room. Ilian sat down hard, looking little better. Shakily, Finus asked, "Do you mean to say that every Chronicle we have killed over the millennia . . . ?"

"Was the death of a Fury?" Xander asked bluntly. "Yes, we do. Dominic was forced to end his own brother's misery. I can't name all the Furies I have known and lost over the years. With every passing century, I grew more and more certain in my own destruction. When I felt Jayda take her first breath, I put my affairs in order." His eyes closed. "Then I met Tariah and Morgan. And I had final hope."

Jayda turned and burrowed against his chest, desperately curling her power and emotions around him, merging their minds, trying to crawl inside his soul to comfort, to give him the reassurance that she was there with him at last.

Finus closed his eyes. The idea of how much death and murder had occurred over the centuries was sickening. And it was murder. He saw that clearly. He couldn't even say why it had started. No one remembered any more. Magi lived an average of a hundred years, and the earliest records simply stated that Chronicles were vile, disgusting creatures who would destroy the world in their parasitic pact with Furies.

He did not see vile, disgusting creatures. He saw powerful, giving, and caring people. He did not see a parasitic relationship between Chronicle and Fury. He saw love, though he was hesitant to call the force by such a paltry word. And he did not see people who would destroy the world. He saw people who might just be the key to its salvation.

He straightened his back and looked every inch the king he had been made. "Is it true that you have the ability to sense other Chronicles?" he asked Morgan and Tariah equally.

"Seems so," Tariah admitted. "It was how Morgan found these four terrors."

"We grew out of being terrors," Roman promised her with a sudden grin.

"Some of us didn't," Kelsey said cheerfully.

Finus found a smile for the first time. Some things were truly not limited to one race. "Then I wish to ask a great favor of you, Dragoons of Chronis blood. Once a summer, I wish you to come to Prismatic. Your sanctuary will be rebuilt. There, families with children of questionable strength may bring their child to you to see if they are a Chronicle. Children who have already revealed themselves as Chronicles will come. You will teach them what they need to know of their own race, what they need to know to grow and be everything they are meant to be, so that they may live among the Magi as happily as possible."

"And none will stop them from journeying when they start second puberty?" Tariah asked quietly. "That journey is what will lead them to their Fury, what will define the reason for their birth."

"No Chronicle will ever be barred from any city. Wherever their lines lead, the Magi will be there to offer shelter, guidance, and friendship." His blue eyes abruptly glittered with painful tears. "My sister was a Chronicle," he admitted roughly. "Is there . . . is there any way of knowing who her Fury was? I want to have her grave moved to where her Fury rests."

Xander looked at Morgan and Tariah who nodded slightly. "It can no doubt be determined," the Elder said after a moment. "You intend to make some sweeping changes."

The king smiled slightly. "They made me king. They can do as I damned well say."

Tariah decided she *really* liked him. "We will come visit you when this is done," she promised. "We will start what you ask of us, and we will meet your son as well." Her eyes began to sparkle merrily like silver coins. "I hope he is like you. You're a good person, Finus." With him in charge, there might just be hope for everyone.

"What do we do about the Elite?" Ilian asked Finus. "The only ones who can stop them sit before us right now."

Quinn had rejoined them, and though pale, she was composed. "They may take my ship," she said. "It is strong and sound. Wherever they need to go, it will take them there."

"Where are you intending to go?" Finus asked.

"We would rather not say," Morgan said softly. "As you said, opinion cannot change overnight, and, frankly, we do not trust Magi very much right now."

None of the Magi before him could find the will to argue with him. Neither Chronicle nor Fury had any reason to trust the Magi at all. Frankly, the Kin didn't have much reason either. For being the most populous race on the planet, the Magi had done a poor job of being a good neighbor to the other races and an even poorer job of being a child of Lucksphere.

"Can you tell me if you are chasing the Elite?" Finus asked instead.

"We are, and we aren't," Kelsey spoke up. "We're chasing something they want with the hopes of getting to it first." She frowned at Morgan. "Are we sure they haven't gotten there?" When the others eyed her, she shrugged. "The Elite aren't using normal power. They're doing things beyond what they should be able to. Beta wasn't naturally that strong, but she was acting like it."

"I had thought that before," Roman admitted.

"If they found it," Solis said, "then why is the world still standing? Why would they need a Chronicle to take control?" He frowned. "Unless that's the very problem. They can be affected by it, but they can't control it." He shook his head. "I still feel like there's something we don't know that we should. We need to get out to sea so that the twins can dust off Xander's brain."

Xander made a gesture with his right hand that looked similar to the Magi gesture of disrespect. It made both Argyles grin at each other. You had to admire anyone with the nerve to directly sass an Elder as old and powerful as Xander. "Watch it, whelp," Xander said mildly. "I'll clip your fins."

Kelsey stuck her tongue out at him. "You have to go through me first, old man."

Ilian looked at Quinn. "If you will escort them to your ship, I will start the journey back to Prismatic with Finus."

"I'm still here," the king complained.

Quinn hid a smile. "That will work. Swift journeys, Ilian." She got to her feet gracefully. "If you will come with me?" she asked the others graciously. As she led them out of the inn, she asked Jayda softly, "Are you happy?"

"Very happy." She was walking with her arms around one of Xander's, her head resting against his shoulder. Her need for his constant touch and presence was very obvious, as was her acceptance of her need. "I don't have words to describe it. I wish I did."

"You don't need words." Quinn smiled. "I have eyes." They walked onto the dock and she gestured to the ship anchored there. "Here we are. It is seaworthy and strong. It can stand most any storm that is thrown at it."

"How big of a storm?" Dahlia asked.

"Well, we sailed through a five-knocker, and it came through fine."

Kelsey scowled. "Can someone say that in non-sea lingo for the desert dwellers?"

"My apologies, Kelsey." Quinn hid a smile. "A 'knocker' is a unit of storm measure used by sailors. It means that the wind knocks against the side of the ship five times in a second. They are the roughest storms that any ship can sail through. As a comparison, the storms south of Glacia are considered to be eight-knockers and therefore impassable." When there was silence, her stomach dipped. "I see."

"Can it handle it?" Grecia studied the ship intently. It certainly looked weather worthy, but eight-knockers were vicious beasts.

"I don't know," she admitted. "We came out of the five-knocker with no damage, so it's certainly possible. With the sort of Water and Air power you have present, you might fare better where others would fall far short." Hesitantly, she asked, "Are you sure you have to sail into those storms?"

North.

The burning pulse ripped through the lines of all Chronicles present . . . including Morgan and Tariah. The sharp compulsive urge was something they hadn't felt in nine years, and it shocked both so deeply that it ricocheted into Dominic and Jazz. Astonished, Dominic grabbed Tariah's shoulders. "Did you feel that?"

"That's impossible," Xander said instantly. "You finished your journeys."

"Did we?" Morgan asked softly. He pressed a hand to his chest as he felt the painful demand inside his soul. "I thought we had too, but I can *feel* it. My lines are burning. *North.* We have to go north."

Quinn didn't have a clue what they were talking about, but she was beginning to think that she could see why Tariah had insisted that Chronicles on their journey not be stifled. If it was their power driving them on, then stopping it could be devastating.

"It's a voice." C.J. shook his head. "I would swear it sounds like an actual voice speaking to me."

Tariah looked at Morgan sharply just as his head swung toward her. In the last phase of their journey, they had both been certain they heard an actual voice leading them to the Isle. It hadn't been just a feeling driving them a direction. It had been words, a soft feminine voice, urging them on.

"Curious," Xander muttered as he lifted Jayda onto the ship. "Let's go," he told the others. "We need to get out to sea as far as we can with the daylight we have left."

"There's daylight?" C.J. grumbled.

"Somewhere under the clouds, yes." Dahlia urged him onto the ship. "Come along, *ishke*." She nimbly hopped on board and then turned to help him the rest of the way onto the deck. Wisely, she hid a smile as he wobbled before he could find his balance. Desert dwellers were not often comfortable initially on boats.

"We could tow him behind the ship," Roman offered as he climbed up. "Use him as bait for dinner."

"And we could tie you to the sail to summon steady winds," was the retort. "There's space enough inside your head."

"Now, boys." Jazz, trying not to smile, pushed them apart. "Play nice or you're both going overboard. And don't think Dahlia and Grecia will stop me. They know better than that."

"We'll just go over after you," Dahlia promised solemnly.

The others climbed on board as well, with Solis and Kelsey last. As she was preparing to climb up, she sensed Ilian's approach. She turned toward him curiously. "I thought you were leaving," she said. "To escort the king safely home."

"I wanted to say goodbye." He took a deep breath and kept his voice lowered. He was well aware of the sharp ears of the brown-eyed Fury watching patiently. "I feel as if it will be the final goodbye, and I'm not sure why. When you finish your journey . . . you will live on the Isle of Dragons. By the time you will feel safe enough to walk freely in Magi lands, I will no doubt be long gone."

She lightly touched his arm. "Ilian," she said softly, "my parents will still live on Magi lands. I wouldn't cut myself off from them entirely. The Isle will be where Solis and I have our home, certainly. But I would visit my friends." She smiled. "And you're a friend. If Solis and I have a Linking ceremony, I want you to come see it."

"I wanted to love you," he admitted wistfully, "from the moment I met you. But I understand why Etude said you would never feel the same. Solis is a very lucky man." He hesitated before opening the pack he carried. He removed a small box that he held out to her. "Don't drop it," he warned. "And don't open it until you're out to sea."

Sensing his power inside the box, she held it protectively. "I won't."

He paused and then leaned forward to gently touch her lips with his in a bare kiss. "You are an amazing woman, Kelsey Renaire. Lucksphere knew exactly what she was doing when she made you one of her chosen children."

Somehow she managed to keep her tears hidden as he walked away. She kept them firmly held inside as she climbed onto the ship and saw the sympathetic looks on the others' faces. She even managed to hold onto them as they set out to sea away from the coast in an effort to get away from the spreading storms. But when she finally opened Ilian's gift, she couldn't hold onto them any longer.

Inside the box sat a pristine, brilliantly crafted, glass necklace. The chain was made of tiny flame links, each and every one different from the next. The pendant itself formed the symbol in all three languages that meant Chronicle, the one derived from the symbol 'chron' which was etched into the lines on Morgan and Tariah's right hands. 'Chron' itself had different meanings depending on the language of who spoke it. In Magi, it meant 'life.' In Kin, it meant 'strength.' And in Dragon, it meant 'heart's keeper.'

The glass of the pendant was the same crystalline, uncanny, blue color of Kelsey's eyes.

She carefully traced her finger across the symbol, trembling hard. "I couldn't love him," she whispered. "And . . . I didn't want to." Her eyes closed as tears spilled down her cheeks. "I didn't want to love him." The sob caught in her chest as Solis pulled her into his arms. "It's not fair that he would fall in love with me!"

He simply held her tighter and let her cry against his shoulder as if her heart was breaking. And though she hurt, he wouldn't have stopped it if he could. Painful though it was, it was another part of life, another part of second puberty. Hearts that could grow could also break. Hearts that could break were hearts that could feel every emotion life had to offer. In her despair for hurting a good man unintentionally, she was only moving farther down the road toward being an adult.

And that road was just as important as the one she took as a Chronicle. Perhaps they were the same in the end.

Chapter Twenty-One

The ship was well stocked for a long journey, and there was no worry for how far or how long they would sail. Rooms were plentiful enough that each Dragoon pair had their own, though Solis and Kelsey didn't need the privacy as badly as the others. Nothing was said to Solis about Kelsey's seemingly frozen growth. Her vibrant exterior hid a core as vulnerable as Jayda's, and in her unease and fear, she clung harder to the last vestiges of childhood. Solis was patient. He knew their day would come.

When they had sailed a day and a night, unease began to stir at last. They had not left the storms from Spectrum behind. There was no longer any blue sky to see. Storms covered every inch of the air with the Flutterlies in such thick and dense swarms that they made it impossible to tell day from night.

They had kept Spectrum as a line on the horizon, but after a few more days, even that disappeared at last. The waves grew rougher, more turbulent, as they began to sail beyond the scope of safety. With every passing mile, the wind knocked harder against the boat. Even with Roman and Morgan working in concert with Dahlia, it was hard to keep the winds steady.

Tariah and Jayda managed to keep the rain at bay, though many mornings they all woke to discover that at least some had fallen in the night. No one really knew where they were or where they were going, short of being sure that the worsening storms were a good sign.

They soon found themselves a week into their voyage and preparing themselves to sail into the very worst of storms where there would be no turning back. Passing time was filled with old stories and new study. Morgan and Tariah had started developing their Clairvoyance, and the others as yet developed their newest skills.

It was mid-afternoon when Xander needed some air. He left Jayda with Tariah to discuss the latter's pregnancy and headed to the deck. There was no one steering at that moment and the anchor was dropped to keep them as stable as possible in the rolling waves. The untamed nature of the storm didn't concern him as he stood at the rail and looked into the murky distance. He had seen these storms before.

At the wayward thought, he went very still. It wasn't just any storm that he remembered. It was *these* storms. He could see it very clearly in his mind. The pattern of the Flutterlies that had seemed so familiar to him. When 'it' was happening. They broke pattern and flew to the heart of each city and spread outward. But *why*?

It's like scabbing over a wound that cannot be healed.

The voice whispered in his mind, sounding so much like Tariah that he immediately turned to find her, but she was not there. The voice in his mind wasn't Telepathy. It was in his memory. He struggled and fought, desperately reached for that voice. It merged with a familiar figure of his past and he went still.

Tarinah Chronis.

The memories slipped free further as he fought to gather them. She had been a healer. Her twin brother, Morignan Chronis, had been a powerful warrior. She had been a Water Chronicle, he an Air. As the end had slipped closer and closer, malice and hate rising in the land, Xander had stood with the twins on a brilliantly beautiful cliff that reminded him of home though it was not the Isle.

They had watched the Flutterlies flying with purpose, dragging a shield of storms that slowly began to encircle the island. *She is our Mother*, Tarinah had said, gesturing to the bits of puff in the sky. *They are Her tears. What the Magi do is killing Her. Killing Him. Our Mother and Father. But the Flutterlies . . . It's like scabbing over a wound that cannot be healed.* Her blue eyes had welled with tears as she pressed her hands to her very rounded belly. *My children will cry too.*

"Xander." Jayda pressed against his back and her arms encircled his waist. Tears slid down her cheeks and flowed through her heart. She had been there in his mind and seen those terrible moments. She surrounded him with her emotions and power, trying to soothe the wounds inside his heart and soul. The curse of an Elder: with age came strength but it also came with emotional sensitivity.

"We don't have a choice," he said grimly. "We have to find my memories now. We've delayed because of the unpredictable storms, but we can't delay any longer."

"It might very well destroy you."

He turned and lifted her off her feet to bury his face in her hair. She was as pure and sweet as the air of her home, and no matter how he complained, he had grown to truly love the scent of snow. "You'll hold me together," he said confidently. "I have complete faith in you and Morgan. I have to remember, *ishke*. There is no other option."

She knew he was right though she feared for him. Her beloved Fury was too gentle, too feeling, to suffer under the weight of his own past. A part of her couldn't help but wonder if that, more than any other reason, was why he had forgotten something that terrible.

Morgan was with Jazz in their room, and they had curled together on a chair to read a book. He glanced up automatically with a smile that faded as he saw the seriousness on Xander's face. "What is it?" He released Jazz so she could stand and then got to his feet as well. Automatically, he slipped his hand into hers for support.

"I had a memory. It was there and gone, but it was a real memory. I saw . . ." Xander fell silent for a moment. He wanted to say he saw Morgan's ancestors, but though it was true, it was not the full truth, though he wasn't sure how. Had never been sure how since the day he met Morgan and Tariah. "I saw . . . you."

Jazz said nothing. She simply held Morgan tighter. He took a long breath. "I have no answers," he admitted. "Tariah and I have discussed it, but we don't understand either. We simply . . . accept."

'It's easier to take it one day at a time.' The words were accompanied by a laughing grin from Morignan. 'And better for that old mind of yours, old friend.'

Xander shook his head swiftly. "Something's happening," he said. "Something has changed. Things you say are knocking memories free. The storm itself was knocking them free. You have to go into my mind, Morgan, and free the information we need."

The Chronicle said nothing for a moment, then finally murmured, "I will know all your memories, Xander. All of them."

Xander met his eyes unflinchingly. "You were there for fifteen hundred of them. The last thousand are not much to look at. Nothing but a hate for summer that all Furies who live long enough finally begin to feel. The most beautiful time of the year . . . hated by the ones who should love it most."

Tariah. Morgan called instantly to her. *Come to my side, little sister. I will need your strength and will if I am to do this. Jayda will keep Xander from breaking under the weight of those terrible days, but I will need you and Jazz to hold me together.*

When Tariah walked into the room, she wasn't alone. Everyone else had come as well. Xander looked at all those around him and felt staggered by a flash of déjà vu. A city sitting peacefully under the glowing sun. People laughed and played and worked. Children ran around underfoot, both Magi and Dragon alike. Nearly all adults had lines, though half had streaked hair marking them as Furies. "Sanguine." The word was breathed softly. "The City of Summer."

"What's going on?" Kelsey asked.

"There's something about where we are that is mending the missing memories in Xander's mind. And that makes me positive that I was correct about the memories not being *gone*." Morgan took a deep breath. "I've never done this. We will have to make it up as we go. With the storms outside, this room needs to be secure."

"The easiest way to do it," Grecia spoke up, "is to have those of us with Fire and Soil encase the room entirely. Layers. Chronicle, Fury, Chronicle, Fury. We'll have C.J. go last and put his on the inside." She grinned at the male in question. "Since he is so artistic."

"See if I make you any more blankets! Hrmph."

Dominic cocked his head. "Just Fire or Fire and Smoke?"

"One layer of each. We want this room to be *sealed*. I will go first." Power flowed up and around Grecia in a swirl of leaves and green color. She started with her Soil power and built up the walls, floor, and ceiling with plants and vines. Bits of bark swirled into her power as she used her Wood skills to build a lattice of planks and branches over the vines.

Kelsey went next, grateful to have a distraction. Over the layer of Wood, she built a layer of glass with her Smoke power. Only showing off a little, she made sure the glass was the same color of green as the vines it hid. She followed that with a layer of Fire that burned bright and fierce and did not harm.

Dominic followed with his own layer of Fire, and it was distinctly different from Kelsey's for it held the tinge of Dragon origins. The layer of Smoke glass that he built was not green but deep ruby. He couldn't let a fledgling show him up, could he?

C.J. built a wall of his own vines and branches over the last layer of glass and then built a layer of Wood. Since Grecia had pointedly challenged him, he opened the bag of sand he wore and used it to swiftly weave tapestries to hang down from the ceiling and cover the floor with comfortable padding. He used every color imaginable until the room was a whirl of color and life.

"I believe," Roman told his lover warmly, "you have been soundly power-slapped." The phrase was an oft-heard one in childhood. It meant that in a duel, the loser had never stood a chance of winning.

She smiled in bemusement. "Indeed." She lightly cuffed C.J. in the chin. "You are brilliant," she told him sincerely. "And I say it to you for the reason Xander once said it to Kelsey. You will have to decorate the Council's cave. Those stodgy old fuddy-duddies need to brighten that place up."

"Her grandfather is the Air Elder," Morgan told Roman politely, but with laughter in his voice. "Grecia is his favorite granddaughter, potentially because she's the only one who dares sass him to his face."

Roman winced. "How fun."

"He'll love you." She kissed his chin softly. "After all, you saved my life simply by being born."

"What do we do next?" asked Solis of Morgan. "The walls are a few feet thick with layers of shielding. I doubt even you, Tariah, or Xander could get your power through without doing it on purpose."

Morgan and Tariah looked at their right hands where the 'chron' symbol was etched. "This," they both said as one as they held out their hands.

'They finish each other's sentences,' the violet-eyed Fury said wryly. 'And talk at the same time, and in the same voice. It's so odd, but I think I love Tarinah almost as much as I love Morignan. They are critical to each other. Perhaps another type of two halves of a whole.'

"Jazz?" Xander asked softly. "How do you feel for Tariah?"

Startled, the Soil Fury looked at her sister-kin. Though her first response was to, naturally, say that she loved her, she knew the question was meant seriously. And so she thought about it seriously. To her surprise, she discovered that there was a deep emotion for the shorter woman that went well beyond the scope of normal. "How odd," she murmured. "I never realized. I suppose I can say it best by saying that the only person I care for more than Tariah is Morgan." She looked at Dominic. "You?"

He slowly nodded. "I've often thought that way about Morgan. In the beginning, I was very jealous, which I don't deny. But it wasn't until the last year or so that I realized how important he was to me."

"Is that normal?" C.J. asked Xander.

"Not normal, exactly, but perfectly within the realm of reason for them. It coincides with another memory. And it confirms something that I have wondered for a long time. Morgan and Tariah couldn't live without each other in a way not dissimilar from what would happen if they lost Dominic or Jazz."

Because it was a fact of their nature, it was something both Furies had instinctively known and responded to without consciously understanding. It was also a dangerous caveat to their existence. If Tariah died, then she would take Dominic and Morgan with her, and therefore Jazz as well.

"You really do have a lot of important things in that dusty old mind," Kelsey said. She lifted her hands and fire flowed over her fingers. With her distinctive style of writing, she burned the chron symbol into the floor under their feet. "What next?"

"Xander needs to lay on the symbol. Everyone else form a circle. Be in pairs, but stagger the elements." Morgan fiercely pushed down his nerves. This wasn't the time for them. Too much rode on this. "I may only be able to do this a piece at a time," he told Xander as the Elder laid down.

"Then at the least get the location of the Lost Isle. That is the most important thing right now."

"Jay, kneel by his head. Jazz and Tariah, I need you beside me. Dominic, please kneel across from us on Xander's other side." Morgan took a steadying breath. "I've never done this, never tried to do this."

"You'll do it," Roman said confidently. He said it with absolute belief because he believed it absolutely. There was nothing that his father-kin and mother-kin couldn't do. Morgan had said he and Tariah were the children's brother and sister, but not a single former child believed it. The twins were their surrogate parents.

With a breath to brace himself, Morgan let himself go into Xander's mind. The complexity told him instantly that he would not be able to succeed alone. Without him even asking, Tariah was suddenly there with him. Their two energies fused into a single beam of pure soft light as they swept through Xander's mind.

Watching them, Kelsey knew the instant it happened. Neither moved but it was as if neither was there anymore. There was one consciousness between them. One will and one power. Small lines of pain edged the identical pairs of eyes as if whatever they saw hurt them as well.

A different painful struggle churned inside her mind and heart. Becoming an adult hurt. It meant hurting others and hurting herself. It meant feeling and thinking and experiencing on a level that was terrifying. Surrounded by the people she cared for most, she felt like nothing more than a nuisance. Some kid who was tagging along without being needed.

But scarier still was the thought of going back. Going back would mean losing Solis, and he was the only thing she had to hold on to. She was hurting him both physically and emotionally. There was no end of patience inside her mate, but she could see that it had strained to the limit. She wanted to be his, to be his lover as she was meant to be. Wanted him to be hers as was promised by their births. As long as she had Solis, then she didn't need to hide in the safety of childhood. In finally knowing it, accepting it, she knew the truth.

It was time to grow up.

Something thumped onto the deck of the ship over their heads. She looked up sharply and her nose flared as she caught the distinct scent of tainted power. Her lines began to burn and itch violently. "The Elite are here."

"They can't stop now," Dominic warned grimly. "They're buried too deeply inside Xander's mind. It's taking all of Jayda's will to hold Xander together. Jazz and I are fighting to keep Tariah and Morgan together as well."

"We can't all go," Dahlia said. "Some of us have to hold this circle together. And some of us are not meant for battle." She looked at her mate pointedly.

"I will go in his place," Grecia said. "I am a healer." She stood gracefully. "Solis, Dahlia, and I will take this battle."

Kelsey got to her feet swiftly. "I will go too." Her tone dared them to argue. "Dominic is Fire. He can hold our element for the circle just by being here. I am needed with you three. I'm not . . ." Her hands curled into fists at her sides. "I'm not going to sit back like a child anymore. I *have* to do this."

Solis softly curled his arms and emotions around her all at once and buried his face in her hair. There were no words he could find for how precious she was to him, how proud he was of her. If there was any emotion he felt for Ilian, it was sympathy. He could not blame the Magi for his love.

The easiest way to get out of the room without breaking it was to turn into their elements entirely and slip through the cracks. Kelsey had never tried such a thing in her life for it was a unique gift of the majiks that Dragon Lords used, but she could do it by drawing on Solis' own majiks. As he built the knowledge in her mind, she realized how very simple it was to do.

She reached for the majiks, bent them as he had shown her, and her physical body fell away as she dissolved into the flames of her own power. Actually moving in that form was much trickier, but all three Furies wrapped themselves around her and brought her along with them as they moved through the shields. She watched intently how they moved, read the skills inside Solis' mind, and determined to do it for herself next time.

They turned back as soon as they were outside the door. The smell of tainted power lingered even stronger in the hall, and the thumps from the deck sounded like someone staggering around in a stupor. "It sounds like someone had too much cactear juice," Kelsey muttered.

Grecia looked at her curiously. "Cactear juice induces intoxication?"

"If Magi drink too much of the distilled stuff, yeah. It affects Kin if it is mixed with something else, but Etude never said what that was. Does it work on Dragons?"

"We really don't even like the taste of distilled juice. Raw or pure, sure, but not distilled," Solis told her. He suddenly smiled as he felt her poking around inside his head. "I've only been intoxicated once, and I've avoided it ever since." The look he shot Grecia was sour. "And I've never trusted anything she gives me to drink since."

"It was an accident," she said in exasperation. "Get over it, whelp."

Ignoring them both, Dahlia led the way up the steps toward the deck. The storm was growing more and more agitated and the sea rocked the ship hard. Staggering around on the deck was a man in the Elite cloak, and though none present had met him before, they still knew he was bad news.

"You must be running out of members," Solis said calmly. "Since they seem to be destroying themselves as we go along."

The man looked at him with yellow eyes that seemed nearly feral. "We used to number hundreds. Thousands. Now we are a pitiful few, but we are not so powerless that we can't do what is needed. Those who remain are the elite of the Elite!" The rotting stench of decay lifted from his skin as he aimed a nearly gnarled finger at Kelsey. "Chronicle!"

She propped a hand on her hip. "*Poka!*" she retorted. It referenced a childhood insult. It implied the recipient was as stupid as a *pokagale* bird, known for breaking its own neck because it forgot it could fly. No one had any idea how they even managed to propagate at all. "Now that we're introduced, the name is Kelsey."

He bared rotting teeth in a smile. Whatever taint held him was one that had existed so long that it had gotten into his physical being. "Epsilon," he said. He made the Magi gesture of respect, but it looked distinctly mocking. "Come along with me, child."

Merged as he was with Kelsey, Solis saw the abrupt violent rage of her transition to adulthood long before it ever reached the surface. He leapt backward and dragged Dahlia and Grecia with him for safety. Though, technically, not yet an official adult until she took her first lover, Kelsey was no longer a child either.

"Don't call me a child!" The furious shout was accompanied by the biggest fireball that anyone on the deck had ever seen. It lit the area like the day as it shot through the air directly at Epsilon.

The Magi dove out of the way and clawed his way back up to his feet. Water power swirled around him as ice shards condensed. The storms overhead began to take a yellowish tint and rain began to fall with stinging drops. "If that's how you want it," he snarled, "then there are three others for me to take once you're gone!"

"Wait!" Solis grabbed Dahlia's arm when she would have lunged forward. "Let Grecia cover Kelsey in battle while you and I take control of these storms! I think I have an idea of what might have happened to Beta. We're going to invite it to happen again, if my hunch is correct."

Kelsey ducked one blast of ice and then dodged another. Her cloak felt restrictive suddenly and she let it drop to the deck. Small flames rippled down her now visible lines on their way to her hands. She wore desert clothes still, but she did not feel the cold. The pendant she wore seemed to pulse softly as if it radiated heat.

If Epsilon had any idea of what he had unleashed, it didn't show as he fired a barrage of attacks at her. When she either evaporated them or dodged them entirely, he clawed for the sword he wore on his hip. "Let's see how you like something more tangible!"

She took one look at the weapon in his hand and, shockingly, started laughing with real humor. "Go ahead and try!" she challenged. She walked forward with her arms held out. "Take your best shot, *poka!*"

Grecia's entire body tensed as she prepared to leap forward. Epsilon didn't notice her at all. He had forgotten the three Furies were even present. Snarling incomprehensible curses, he swung his sword with all his strength at Kelsey's head.

Inches from her red hair, the sword stopped itself in the air. He had thrown his full weight behind the swing, and though the sword stopped, he didn't. He went tumbling across the deck and smashed into the mast. Yellow blood dripped down the side of his face as he stared at the sword hovering in the air. "That's impossible!"

She reached up and took the sword from the air. With a casual strength that impressed Grecia, she swung the blade one-handed. At her touch, the corroded blade turned to bright silver and the glass hilt cleared from its clouded hue. She studied the blade for many moments, then said softly, "I'm so sorry you ended up in his hands."

She released the sword and it hovered in the air beside her. A cool and yet slightly savage smile touched her lips as she turned toward the fallen Elite. "Did you see the carvings at the base? The symbols 'kel' and 'ren'? Those would be my maker's mark."

Grecia looked at the way the two symbols flowed together and smiled to herself. When written as one symbol, the two characters formed a new word that, in Magi, was used interchangeably between 'fire' and 'adult' depending on the context. "Weapons forged by a Master such as Kelsey," she said calmly, "cannot harm the one who made them."

Epsilon staggered up to his feet and gathered his power with the familiar intent to detonate himself. Whether it was a choice or mental programming, all the Elite were clearly prepared to destroy themselves rather than lose. He had enough power that detonating himself would take out the ship and likely everyone on it.

Kelsey suddenly felt Solis in her mind and turned to jump at Grecia. She knocked the Fury down and away several feet just as Solis and Dahlia let go of the storms they had been controlling. The clouds broke into torrents of rain, and the taint washed away from the gray color. Blinding light flashed and an immense lightning bolt struck Epsilon in the head. As the crack reverberated off the air a moment later, there was nothing left.

"How did you do that?" Grecia asked Solis as she let Kelsey pull her up to her feet. There were a handful of minor wounds on the Fire Chronicle's arms and she swiftly set about mending them.

"We didn't," Dahlia said simply. "Solis was correct in his theory. We purified the clouds as the taint came in and kept them . . . protected, for want of a better word. When we pulled away, the Flutterlies were strong enough to fight back by themselves. *They* destroyed Beta and now Epsilon."

The sudden sensation of their ears popping told the four on deck that the shielding below had been lifted. The sea rocked with slightly less violence and the rain was onl6 a soft drizzle that caused steam to lift from Kelsey's still burning lines. Something triggered in her mind as she looked at the storms, and she whirled to run downstairs. "I need to talk to Tariah!"

In the cabin, she found Morgan and Tariah both resting wearily in their Fury's arms. They were pale and grief-stricken with tears fresh on both faces. It made her heart break to see shattered the two people she had always believed invincible. Xander looked little better where he rested in Jayda's arms.

"What happened?" Dahlia asked as she kneeled beside C.J. He felt as shaken as Kelsey looked, and so did Roman before he went into Grecia's arms. "*Ishke*?" She smoothed C.J.'s hair out of his face. He had always looked youthful, but he then seemed much older though physically he had not changed.

"The only way to get the location of the Lost Isle," Dominic said roughly, "was to go there in Xander's memories. The twins had to . . . had to become their past selves. They put themselves into Xander's memories to lure out the hiding pieces. I can't tell you how they did it. But the memories burned into Morgan and Tariah's own minds like an after-image. Xander managed to protect Jayda from experiencing the memories herself, but Jazz and I . . . we're not Telepaths. We could not do the same for our Chronicles."

Tariah stirred softly in his arms. "Dominic?" Her arms curled around him fearfully. "You're alive?"

"I'm alive. You're alive." His hand settled over her stomach protectively. "Our daughter is alive." He had never before seen her this shaken except for that horrible moment nine years earlier when he had feared she would detonate herself. His lips curved as he sought to bring back her smile. "I think she might be a Dragon."

"No eggs!"

The mutter reassured everyone. Morgan's eyes opened slightly, and the silver color was dark and wet with tears. "We couldn't get all the memories," he said faintly. "Xander instinctively kicked us out of his head the minute he realized what we were doing. He was trying to protect us like he always does." His eyes closed again and he slumped against Jazz. "We know the location."

"Sleep." C.J. moved closer and covered his wrist with his hands. "Sleep, Morgan. You too, Tariah. We're going to be all right. Let us take care of you now."

"Tariah?" Kelsey asked softly. "Is it possible to *take* power out of a storm the way it is to put it in?"

Her dark lashes fluttered though they didn't lift, evidence that she was listening. Far too tired to use her voice, her words softly said into everyone's minds, *It doesn't seem impossible. We are Chronicles. We are here to take in the excess power for balance. If you have seen something that makes you think we can tame the storms, then believe in it. Being an adult means taking a risk.*

Almost at the same time, both her power and Morgan's went very still and could not be sensed any longer. The deep sleep was a good sign. It indicated that they would be able to rest and recover.

Instinctively, without intending to, Kelsey took immediate command of the situation. "Jay, are you feeling well enough to help us up top? We need your Water power. Tell me the truth, because if Xander needs you, then you stay."

"He is too deeply asleep to notice one way or another. He protected me from being imprinted by his memories, but I cannot escape entirely because I am inside his mind already." She took a very deep breath and wiped at the tears on her face. "He blanketed my heart and made himself vulnerable to his own pain. I will be fine."

Kelsey looked at C.J. "Weave the thickest, calmest, most damned *healing* blankets you can." As he instantly began to work, she turned toward Dahlia. "Do you know anything about boats? Solis doesn't."

Morgan had been their ship's captain, but he clearly would not be sailing anytime that day. Dahlia nodded quickly. "I do, actually." She kept a smile well-hidden where only C.J. would find it. Kelsey was a chip off her father-kin's block by automatically taking control when their two leaders were out of commission. Her newly found adulthood gave her a strength and surety as fierce as her fire.

"Then you're in charge of sailing." Kelsey got to her feet. "Grecia, can you stay with C.J. to aid with the healing process? I know minds and hearts aren't capable of being healed like a body, but I think there still have to be ways to help. You have Telepathy, and you're a healer. Maybe the two can be used together. Do we have anything to lose by trying?"

Grecia thought about it seriously, then said, "No, not particularly. At most, I might get kicked out of their minds if they sense I might encounter something painful to me." She moved closer to Xander, knowing he was the one in most dire need of comfort. "I'll take good care of him, Jayda," she promised.

"I know." Jayda gently put Xander down onto the thick pillow that C.J. had also made. With Grecia's help, she tucked the heavy blanket securely around his body. She could feel the pounding aches inside his body from his power being so low. She couldn't feed him until he woke, but Grecia might be able to make him rest easier.

She got to her feet and joined her brother and sister, and they with Solis and Dahlia headed up to the deck. While Dahlia went to take the controls of the ship, Jayda picked up Kelsey's cloak and helped fasten it around her shoulders once more. "Were you in a hurry?" she asked teasingly.

"It was odd." Kelsey studied her lines. "I just couldn't stand to have my lines covered that much."

"If I recall," Dahlia noted, "at the last fight with Sistra, neither Morgan nor Tariah could stand to be covered either. It must be a Chronicle thing." A smile touched her lips. "An *adult* Chronicle thing."

"I'm not an adult *yet*." Kelsey shot a look at her Fury that made her crystalline eyes smolder with desire and that powerful, fully grown, third emotion that marked Dragoons. "But it's a matter of time."

He curled his hands into fists before he yanked her into his arms and took the kiss he desperately needed. Before he touched her and tasted her from head to heel, fed on her power from any and everywhere. *His*. Finally, she was his for the taking, and the knowledge was heady. He had waited so long . . .

"How are we doing this?" Roman asked, breaking into his thoughts. "I've never tried to draw down a storm's power." He studied the sky and the clouds intently. "But I can't argue why you asked. Wasn't this a six-knocker earlier? It's barely a two now."

"Solis and Dahlia did it unintentionally." Kelsey shook her head. "It reminded me of the time I had a really bad injury from a blade I was making. The wound had gotten swollen and the healer lanced it to make it heal faster. That's what it seemed like happened here."

"A build-up of power with nowhere to drain." Jayda looked at the clouds. "Well, we have nothing to lose by trying, though I agree that I don't know how to do it." She looked at Dahlia. "Can you sail us into rougher waters?"

"Can? Yes. Want to? No." But she did anyway, directing the ship to move past the calm two-knocker and toward the more deadly seven that tore up the waves barely a mile away. "Jay, do you have the directions from Xander's memories?"

"I do. Keep heading north and any time you see a dark wave, turn east for half a mile before going north again. It will pass us through the proper checkpoints and make the Isle reveal itself." She grabbed onto the mast for support as the winds picked up and began to pound against the ship.

Flashes of lightning crisscrossed the sky with their loud roars always arriving moments later. The gentle rain became a torrent, soaking even Jayda and Solis to the bone. Roman and Jayda moved to the center of the deck and started to lift their hands when lightning flashed right above them.

"Don't get fried!" Solis said swiftly. "Xander and Grecia would eat us for dinner!"

"We're fine," Roman assured him. "It just surprised us. Let's try this again, Jay."

She nodded slightly and they lifted their hands again as if asking for the storm to come for them. The lightning flashed again over Roman's head and then struck him directly. Kelsey would have yelped if Solis hadn't clapped a hand over her mouth hastily. Roman didn't even seem to notice he had been struck; his body absorbed the power easily.

The rain itself began to rush directly at Jayda and she absorbed it with the same ease. As the storms sensed the open outlet, they grew more and more violent. Stronger and more potent blasts of power were thrown at the two Chronicles. It seemed to go on for an eternity, the ship rocking so badly that it sent Solis and Kelsey tumbling across the surface.

But then . . . it stopped.

Legs trembling, Solis managed to get up once more. He helped Kelsey stand as well and they looked out across the rocking waves. They were much calmer in force as they gently lifted the ship up and down. The rain had slowed to barely a drizzle, and the wind knocked only once or twice against the side of the ship.

"I can't believe it worked," Kelsey managed to say. "I was *guessing*." She walked carefully over to Roman and Jayda. "Are you all right?"

"If I move, I'm going to fall." Jayda's knees visibly trembled. "I feel well enough, but I'm a little shaky right now." She leaned gratefully against her sister as Kelsey wrapped an arm around her waist.

Solis moved to brace Roman and winced wryly as he felt the electric shock between them. "You certainly were hit by lightning. You're sparking into the air, Roman. We'll need Grecia to ground you. Literally."

The tame storm was spreading even faster than the untamed. When C.J. and Grecia came up to join them on the deck, there was no longer any fear that the ship would be torn apart. Dahlia held the ship on a steady direction following Jayda's instructions.

By the time it should have been evening, they could see a black line on the horizon that was potentially the worst storm any of them had ever seen. The good news was that it did not hover over the ocean and prevent passage. The bad news was that it hovered over a strip of land that was surely their destination.

"Drop anchor," Kelsey said softly, shivering even when Solis wrapped her in his arms and cloak. "We can't land like this. We'll let Morgan and Tariah and Xander recover and then land tomorrow morning. Tonight we prepare." She closed her eyes but could still see that broken island in the distance burned inside her mind. Something terrible had happened there. It could be seen even at a distance. Something terrible, something against the very laws of nature itself.

Something like the genocide of an entire race.

Chapter Twenty-Two

The easiest thing to do with the resting Dragoons was to leave them where they were, though Tariah got tucked into the bed because her pregnancy made her restless. C.J. and Grecia made sure that Dominic, Jazz, and Jayda had enough blankets to be comfortable since the nights had proven to be quite cold.

Those who were awake ate dinner together before they retired to their rooms for the night. Kelsey was all but vibrating with energy and emotion as untamed as her element and twice as unpredictable. Solis considered himself a very lucky man that he was inside her mind at all times and able, to some extent, to predict her movements.

Her cloak was still wet, and drops flew when she dropped it over the back of a chair. Her wet hair clung to her face, shoulders, and partway down her back with the curls slightly stretched out from the weight.

He couldn't hide his hunger for her and didn't bother to try. He stood in the middle of the room and watched her pace back and forth with chaotic energy, her long legs sleek and supple and her lush body moving in all of his favorite ways. "You were amazing, *ishke*," he said softly, sincerely. "You took command of the situation perfectly. Morgan and Tariah will be proud of you."

She stopped pacing and looked out the small window toward the darkened ocean. So many emotions swirled inside her heart that he couldn't identify them all. "I didn't even think about it."

"It's a part of who you are," her lover said simply. "When you chose to become an adult, then you were able to be that confident once more." Softer, he asked, "What changed your mind? Why did you stop being so afraid?"

"There were a lot of reasons. Fear was one of them. I don't like hurting. I don't like hurting others. That scared me, so I pulled back. But there was a stronger fear. Fear of losing you." She turned around and her eyes glittered with every bit of her maturity. "You're mine. My Fury. I was given a *gift*. And I'm going to take it. I want everything. I want you. I want to be your lover. I want us to have a home, to have children." She smiled suddenly. "And unlike someone else around here, I don't care if I carry eggs."

A lump closed his throat with painful, overwhelming emotion. There were no words he could find. Instead, he wrapped her within his power and his heart, caressing her hotly so that her eyes darkened and a shiver rippled through her body. "*Ishke*." It was all he could say. It was the only word that could say what he felt. There was nothing more precious to him than his beautiful Chronicle. His gift.

She paused for a moment and then pointedly unfastened the top she wore and threw it aside. Her shorts went next and left her in just her bikini. Her lines rippled like gold over her pale skin, as yet untouched by the sun because of the storms. As her fingers toyed with the tie to the bikini, she asked huskily, "Do you want to undress me?"

His brown eyes darkened. "You seem to be doing a fine job," he said just as huskily. "I might tear something. Imagine explaining that to the Soil elements. They might never stop laughing long enough to make you something new."

With a smile older than her power, she untied the top and let it fall to the floor. Not a single fear, not a single nerve, came to life as his eyes swept over her hotly. She could see and feel that nearly violent third emotion inside him and it called to what was inside her. It was so strong, so potent, that she didn't know how he had ever restrained himself.

She stepped toward him slowly and lifted her hands to push on his chest. He stepped back until the bed forced him to sit down. She slid onto his lap and linked her hands behind his neck. "Am I going to have to get tough with you, or are you going to touch me?"

He leaned forward and nipped teasingly at her shoulder. Her skin was sweet and spicy all at the same time, and a soft red aura instantly lifted to cover her. With a sound that was almost a tortured groan, he leaned forward to drink in her power. His mouth moved hotly down her strong arm, and his tongue traced any lines he found.

This time she could actually *feel* her power flowing into him and it sensitized her skin unbearably. His hair brushed against her and made her shiver. His hands curled around her waist strongly and the restrained strength was wildly erotic. She could feel him walking an edge, a thin edge, where patience met instinct and a gentle nature could not tame a primitive soul. What would an out of control Solis be like?

Wanting to know, needing to know, she let her mind and heart merge to his, let her emotions flutter up against his. She swirled her power around him this time with the deliberate intent to seduce. She was burning. He needed to burn with her.

Something much like a growl rumbled in his chest. Before she could catch her breath, he twisted and tumbled her onto the bed so that she was pinned beneath him. His hands and lips raced over her flesh a little wildly to find every nerve that would bring the most pleasure. There was always one spot, one place, that was the focal point of power on a body. When someone said a lover could push their buttons, it was that spot they referenced.

He knew when he found Kelsey's. It was buried in her golden lines directly over her right hip. He pressed his mouth there, and she cried out in shock and delight as her body arched reflexively. He lavished the area with kisses and nips of his teeth until she writhed underneath him, and the scent of her need mixed with the scent of her power intoxicatingly.

She gulped air to beg for him to stop tormenting her when he shifted and closed his mouth eagerly over her breast. The jolt of lust went through every nerve and gathered low in her belly with greedy knots. There was a throbbing between her legs that was maddening, never seeming to be appeased no matter what he did. "Solis!" It was almost a sob.

He muttered something wordless and fiercely stripped her bikini bottom off. He leaned back to survey her naked body with satisfaction, possessiveness in every line of his body and face. *His*. After the lonely years of waiting, the painful years of expecting to die . . . she was there with him at last. His immortal lover. "I'm not done," he said roughly, dipping his head to catch her mouth with his in a devouring kiss. How could she taste so *perfect*?

For the life of him, he couldn't get enough of her mouth. One hand curled around her neck to keep her as close as he could, and the other slid down her body in sweeping caresses. Without giving her a breath, without waiting to see if she would panic, his hand slid between her legs and pressed against where she ached so terribly. Even as she moaned into his kiss, a shudder tore through his body. She was hotter than her power, wetter than his. Steam lifted from both their bodies and filled the air with a sultry heat.

The teasing touch of his fingers did nothing to make the ache better. It only made it worse. She twisted against him desperately, curled her power around him, clutched at his shoulders wildly. When she encountered the vest he still wore, something seemed to break inside. She twisted and tumbled him off her with a lithe surge of seductive strength.

As he rose to his knees, she rose as well and yanked the vest down his arms. His lips, slightly swollen from their last kiss, were more than she could resist and she dragged his head down for another. She let her power well and called it to the surface until he could taste it in her mouth. His tongue tangled with hers hotly as he fought to get his vest off without breaking free.

Four hands went after the fastening to his slacks, and she laughed huskily. "You can't take them off if you're kneeling on them!"

"Someone distracted me." He nipped at her shoulder again and then soothed the sting with a kiss. He gave her a gentle push and she fell back against the blankets. Her hair spread around her like a breathing flame, and her blue eyes darkened to nearly black as she watched him. He brushed against her emotions, but there was no fear in her. She was sure of what she wanted even if she didn't yet know what to call it.

He rolled to his feet and almost ripped off his boots. As he fought with his stubborn pants, her sultry voice said teasingly, "Don't rip something."

He managed to get the pants off and pinned her to the bed bodily, a shudder rippling through them both as every curve and line fit together perfectly. "I think," he said thickly as he began to softly trail hungry kisses down her lines, "that it wouldn't be the first time they've seen something like it."

"Even C.J.?"

Her lover's laugh felt hot against her sensitive skin. "Didn't you notice Dahlia had a new top?" When she suddenly laughed, he buried his face against her belly. He wanted to see her carrying their child, to feel the life growing inside. How he envied Dominic! He wasn't sure he could wait nine years to start his family. Dragons *needed* family. They *needed* love. Was it any wonder they had been the chosen race to become Furies?

He slid lower and her breath caught in agonizing anticipation. The first touch of his lips on her sensitive flesh ripped a cry from her throat. The second scored her insides with sheer lust. There was a slippery precipice between pleasure and pain, and she *ached* for something she couldn't yet comprehend. "Tease!"

He nibbled at her thigh. "Your power is sweeter here." His voice was husky and loving all at the same time. "But spicy." She twisted beneath him wildly. "Not yet, *ishke*. I'm not done with you yet."

By the time he reached her ankles, she couldn't breathe anymore. There was no stopping her mate from his hunger to memorize her, to wring every cry he could, to find everywhere that brought her the most delight. If this was what an out of control Solis was like, then she was going to provoke him a *lot*.

"When do I get a turn?" she managed to ask as she struggled to catch her breath. His fingers brushed along her lines as he moved up her body and she stopped breathing entirely. "Solis!"

"Next time." He framed her face with his hands and kissed her wildly, the rough edge to his voice and embrace making hunger claw painfully inside her. "Any time. Every time. Let me have you now. *Ishke*."

She threw her arms around him fiercely and buried her face against his neck. "I'm holding you to that promise!" As his weight settled over her again, it was so welcoming and wonderful that tears burned her eyes. She curled her legs around his hips, instinctively needing to bind him. It left her open and vulnerable, but this was her Fury. He would *never* hurt her.

As his arousal slowly began to push into her body, she stopped breathing. He paused, his powerful body trembling, and she fiercely wrapped her emotions around him, needing him to know it was not pain. It was wonder. Pleasure. Joy. It was a wild and complex tangle of the three that no words could ever voice in any language. And as he surged forward, took her completely, tears slid down her cheeks. Finally she was complete. Finally he was hers as he had been born to be.

When he began to thrust into her slowly, then faster, it was that complex tangle that coiled tighter and tighter inside her body and her heart. That terrifying precipice loomed closer and closer, her body winding tighter and tighter until she couldn't even find her voice to cry out. His emotions tangled wildly with hers, seemed to fuse the two of them into one single being, and the tension broke in a searing wave of fire and ecstasy hot enough that her hair, for a moment, literally caught flame.

The sight was so erotic that he couldn't fight back his own release. He buried himself to the hilt and stayed there as his body shuddered with pleasure. He *felt* her. Felt her permanently engraved inside him. Live without her? He didn't even have a life without her.

He fell to his elbows and then simply collapsed into her arms. She didn't mind at all. They were both sweaty and hot, neither of their hearts yet able to beat a normal rhythm. He smelled wonderfully of male Fury and Water power, and the steam that curled from their bodies was almost a fog.

It was only when the steam began to dissipate and their bodies cool that she realized she felt a bit chilled. Even before the thought cleared her mind, her lover carefully levered himself up onto his arms and stared down at her face with wonder in his eyes. She traced his lips with her fingers tenderly. "Was it worth the wait?" she asked softly.

"Which wait?"

Her lips curved. "Either."

"I'd go through every minute again if I had to," he promised softly. He kissed her gently and lingeringly, then reluctantly pulled away and disentangled their bodies. He got out of bed to retrieve the stack of blankets, and when he turned around, he found her watching him with a combination of curiosity and appreciation in her eyes. "Like what you see?"

"Let me catch my breath and I'll start at your ears and work my way down. I mean, my eyes certainly like what I see, but I need to get *very* close to be sure." Her voice sounded impish and sultry all at the same time, and so perfectly her that it took his breath.

He spread out the blankets and then got underneath them with her. With a contented sigh, he tugged her into his arms where she belonged. "Weren't you supposed to throw me on the floor and ravish me?" he asked teasingly. "I seem to recall that being mentioned somewhere."

"The bed was closer." She flicked her tongue teasingly over his collarbone and it made heat happily curl inside her body as if she had never been satisfied to begin with. Still fused as they were, she could feel the answering surge inside his body. "Can I throw you on the floor this time?"

"We're already in bed, though."

"Good point." She nibbled at his chin. "I guess I'll have to ravish you here."

He laughed softly with anticipation. "Anytime, anywhere, and anyway you want, *ishke*. I'm all yours."

Her lips curved. "You certainly are."

They slept tangled together, one of her arms thrown across his chest as if she feared he would be taken away now that she had claimed him. When dawn came, it came with a gentle knock on the door. Sleepily, she lifted her head. "Yes?"

"Is it safe?" came Morgan's voice.

Heedless of her nudity, she leapt out of bed and rushed over to open the door. Fiercely she wrapped her arms around Morgan and held on. "You scared me!" she said into his shoulder. Though they were the same height, it was the first time she had ever truly noticed. How did he seem to stand so tall to her?

"*Ishke*." Solis' voice was warm. "Your father-kin is staring at the ceiling."

She blinked and looked at Morgan to find him indeed watching the ceiling with a resigned look on his face. "Oh." She sighed and grabbed a blanket to swath it around her bare body. "Sorry, Morgan. I didn't think."

"You wouldn't be my Soot if you did." He cuffed her chin gently and ruffled her hair. "I suppose there are some things a father simply does not want to see or know, even after his little girl ran around naked when she was small."

She grinned impishly. "I'm really glad to know that my modesty was a byproduct of second puberty. Now that I'm secure in my emotions and know what they are, I'm not embarrassed anymore." She went over to sit on the side of the bed and smiled when Solis sat up to wrap his arms around her.

Morgan didn't need to ask to know that his little girl was, indeed, a full adult. A third of the lines, all of the ones going down her arms, had distinctly darkened. They flowed like molten gold over her skin as evidence that the first third of her journey, arguably the most important third, was completed.

"How are you feeling?" Solis asked him softly.

He took a deep breath. The imprint in his mind would never be removed. He would forever live with those memories. In a way, he did not want to remove them. It was not fair that Xander carry the burden alone. "Stable. I can't say I feel fine, because I don't. Tariah and I relived those memories with Xander. Rather literally. And because . . . because we were there to begin with, what we feel is not mere empathy."

"How is it even possible?" Kelsey asked softly.

"The body is secondary," Solis reminded her gently. "If Morgan and Tariah's power was never dispersed in their deaths, then there was no reason it couldn't take shape again. Dominic and Jazz are no doubt the same. I can't imagine Chronicles having two Furies."

"Tariah and I both feel it more strongly now than before," Morgan admitted, "that our Furies are not merely with us now but *again*. Their souls are not any newer than ours. They are far less sensitive, however, and other than what they see in our minds, they may never experience that painful past. And for that we are grateful."

Solis ran his fingers through Kelsey's hair softly and looked at Morgan. "Did the others tell you what Kelsey did?"

Pride filled Morgan's silver eyes. "They did. I'm very proud of her, as are Tariah and Xander. Now come join us for breakfast. We want to land as soon as we are able. There is no cover for us on the ocean, and we can't know how many Elite remain."

The door shut behind him as he left, and Kelsey's lower lip quivered. "He looked older."

"For all intents and purposes," her lover said into her hair as he drew her close, "he is. He and Tariah are . . . well, I suppose we might as well call them Elders now. Chronicle Elders. I am sure there must have been some once. Didn't you notice we always treated them as such anyway?"

"But he never *looked* it." She took a deep breath. "He's my hero, Solis. He and Tariah . . . I love them as much as I love my parents. Maybe . . . maybe more." She straightened her back and shook it off even as she shook off her blanket. It was not worth dwelling on what she could not change.

Once they were both dressed, they put on their cloaks and headed to the galley to have breakfast with the others. When they walked into the room, C.J. and Dominic promptly started clapping. The others either grinned or hid grins. Xander, also looking slightly older than even before, said, "Congratulations, Kelsey. And thank you for making Solis easier to live with."

She walked over and bent to hug him tightly. "Are you okay?" Since Jayda was her sister, that made him her brother. She didn't care how old he was, or how much power he had. He was family, and she was going to worry about him. It was just the way she was. She should have been a Dragon herself; her need for family was nearly as great.

Solis didn't think it was just Dragon blood, though he had no doubt that was why they had been chosen to become Furies. It was built into Chronicles as well.

"I will be fine, sister-kin." Xander covered her hands and kissed her cheek. "These memories are a part of me. They are part of what made me who I am. I wouldn't want to lose them again, even to make it hurt less." He looked across the table at Morgan and Tariah. "And there is something here that makes it easier to bear."

"Does that technically make you older than Xander?" Roman asked the twins.

The look Tariah shot Xander was teasing even though there was still something painful in her much older eyes. And here, on her face in particular, was the proof it was no illusion: the twenty-nine-year-old had suddenly gained the three little lines at the corner of her eyes that she should not have had for another year. "I suppose it does. I guess I shouldn't feel bad about hitting you with a pillow that time." At the lifted brows, she smiled. "He walked into Dominic's and my room, and I was naked. It was reflex!"

There was little further talking while they ate. No one wanted to stay in one spot. Epsilon had already proven that that could be dangerous. When refueled, they all went up to the deck and Morgan took control of the ship once more to direct them toward the broken island ahead.

Within the last five hundred feet from shore, they realized that docking was out of the question. Jagged spikes of rock littered the ocean, and the waves threatened to smash anyone crazy enough to navigate through.

The island itself did not look very big, and it was one of several small pieces of land that dotted the ocean. There was a bigger landmass in the middle, but immense whirlpools surrounded it and the storm was focused directly over it.

A sort of cry seemed to drift on the wind, as if someone wept uncontrollably. And if the wind was not weeping, it screamed a shriek of anger and retribution. Chills raced over Morgan's arms, and he clamped his hands over his ears desperately to shut out those terrible sounds of unbearable agony.

Tariah, too, could hear them. And she could hear even more. She could hear in the waves the sounds of hundreds, thousands, of voices at war. The deadly cacophony tore across her soul with razor claws until it was as if she could see the bloody battles that had been fought.

Tears ran ceaselessly down Jayda and Kelsey's faces. They could not hear the voices but they assuredly felt the echoes left in the air. Xander was pale but struggled to hold himself together for Jayda's sake. If he let himself buckle, then she would have nothing to hold onto for her own sanity.

"We have to land." Grecia's voice was soft from where she stood in the circle of Roman's arms. "You have to be strong. Let us help you. Share the pain among us. I know we can. Dragons do it. Kin do it. Magi, if they wanted, could do it. Therefore we can do it."

The instinctive refusal to do so was written across all five faces for a moment before they all exchanged a long look. Reluctantly, they let their power well into the air. The others lifted their power as well, and when they touched, the pain instantly dispersed among those present, dividing on the basis of who could handle the most.

In the end, it was Roman and Solis who carried the heaviest weight for theirs were the strongest hearts that would only bend under the hardest of trials. Those who carried the lightest weight were Jayda, Xander, and Tariah. Though Tariah had a strong heart, all feared for her unborn child who might absorb the pain herself if her power was strong enough.

Able to breathe again, Morgan anchored the boat. "We will have to fly." His voice was a little rougher than usual, but it was steady. "Can you navigate through these winds?" he asked the Furies in general.

"If Xander goes first," Grecia said. "He is the biggest and flying behind him will shelter us. Jazz needs to be last because she is the smallest."

"Not that I doubt you," C.J. said to Xander, "but how can you change form on the boat? You're bigger than it is!"

Xander lifted an amused brow at him. "So little faith." The teasing was new to him and yet entirely enjoyed. Too often he had been handled gingerly because he was a Fury, and an Elder with it. Finally, he had his own clan to be himself with.

Much to the absolute fascination of all except the other Furies, he partially shifted and allowed for his wings to reform and open. He leapt backward off the rail of the boat and flew up into the air. When he was clear enough, he glowed brightly and transformed the rest of the way back to his natural shape.

"I didn't know Furies could do that!" Kelsey exclaimed.

Jazz's voice warmed. "Only fourth tier Dragon Lords can, and it takes at least two centuries of practice." She ruffled Jayda's hair affectionately. "I will carry you up to him as he cannot fly closer without capsizing us."

Jayda smiled. "Thank you."

Solis and Dahlia opted to dive overboard and swim far enough away to change shape. Dominic, Grecia, and Jazz were just small enough to be able to, one at a time, change form where they were. Dominic was only ten feet long while Jazz was eight.

As Grecia hovered close enough for Roman to climb up onto her back, she said teasingly, "Isn't Dominic cute? He's average enough in Magi form, but he's actually quite small for a Dragon."

Dominic flicked his tail at her and snorted smoke out his nose in a distinctly rude response. He had once lamented his size, certainly, but having found Tariah, he thought he was perfect for her. She was so small that she needed a smaller Fury if she was to ride on his back.

Jazz gently picked up Jayda in her claws and flew up to where Xander waited. Jayda nimbly climbed up to her spot near his horn and held on securely. Wonder dazzled her as she looked around the air and saw the pairs of Dragoons. She couldn't even be sure if it was her emotions or Xander's. She had never imagined such a thing, and he hadn't thought to ever see it again.

He started flying toward the closest bit of land with the others falling into line behind him from biggest to smallest to provide the best protection against the terrible winds. And they were terrible. They grew stronger and more vicious the closer they got to the land. The tiny piece of land was only a few square miles big, and its edges had no shores. They were torn and jagged cliffs.

Flying past the piece of land was potentially deadly for the winds kicked into what could only be called a ten-knocker the instant the outer edge was reached. Instead, Xander circled down and landed near what might have once been a forest but was now blackened and decayed stumps. They dotted the land like broken teeth.

Once they had all landed, the Furies, except for Xander, went back to Magi form. He turned slowly, critically studying the landscape around them. He had a perfect view from where he stood to across several isles. It almost seemed as if they were connected together somehow, creating a pathway on land toward the center where the worst waited.

He turned to Magi form as well. "I suspect we can make our way there on foot, but I can't promise that for sure. There's so much vegetation and destroyed land that I don't recognize where we are in relation to my memories."

"Are we sure this is the Lost Isle of Chronicles?" Roman asked.

The answer came in an unexpected form. It came as a sudden geyser of power that opened directly under the twins' feet and engulfed them both. Neither was harmed at all, though Dominic and Jazz leapt forward to brace them when they staggered. "Oooh." Tariah stared at Dominic woozily. "I feel funny."

Morgan held up a hand. "Who spiked the power with cactear?"

"Are you . . . intoxicated?" Kelsey had to cover her mouth to hide a grin. "From power?"

"It was some first class power." He shook his head but the fuzziness would not clear. Gratefully, he leaned on Jazz for balance. He had an absurd urge to laugh but bit it back as hard as he could. Unfortunately, when he looked at Tariah, she had the same look on her face. It set them both off.

"Oh my." Jayda bit her lip to, unsuccessfully, hide her own smile. "Well, with a potency such as that, and a reaction like this, I would have to say we must be on the Lost Isle. And that it is clearly declaring Morgan and Tariah as its . . ." She sought the word she wanted. "Its heirs."

Dominic just sighed and lifted Tariah into his arms. He firmly wrapped his emotions around hers and merged her mind to his so that he could hopefully diminish the effects. "They won't be of any use to us for a while," he said dryly. "We might as well start walking."

Jazz sighed and turned into her Fury form again. She could, technically, carry Morgan in her Magi form since she retained her strength, and she more than once had hauled him around under her arm. She preferred not to this time, wanting him to stay upright until his head cleared. She firmly picked him up in her claws and merged to him in the same way Dominic had to Tariah. It wasn't just the giggles, which had faded. It was the distinct wooziness and fuzzy thinking that was the most detrimental.

They made their way carefully through the broken forest toward what Xander hoped was a pathway to the next isle. Knowing the danger of them, they carefully avoided any geysers they found. They seemed to just spew up into the air from out of nowhere, but after a short time, C.J. and Grecia could predict where they would pop up.

"There aren't any quakes though," Dahlia noted. "Perhaps the geysers prevent it from occurring. I've never seen this many in one place. You can *feel* the instability." She let out a soft breath. "And I think we now know what happened to the Elite."

"No wonder Epsilon and Gamma seemed intoxicated," Jayda murmured. "They are very lucky they were not torn apart. I wonder why they weren't."

The sudden acrid scent of tainted power touched them all at the same time. Without even thinking about it, they all moved to close ranks around Tariah and Morgan. Nothing happened, though the scent did not go away. It simply grew stronger. The clouds overhead began to turn slightly yellowish.

All Chronicles felt their lines begin to burn. It was so sharp and strong that it rippled into their mates. Speculatively, Xander studied each in turn. They all felt their lines burn when they were in proximity to not just the Elite but danger in general as well. Were their lines an early warning system as well as a map? If so . . . who was sending the message?

The storm clouds began to pour rain just as five figures approached from the distance. Two were female and three were male. All wore the cloak of the Elite, and all except one carried the stench of decaying power.

C.J. stopped breathing as he recognized the woman at the end. "Kappa!" He would have rushed forward if Dahlia hadn't grabbed him. "Kappa!" he shouted. "Come fight with us! Come fight on our side! You're not like the Elite! Where's Cole? You must have seen him!"

Kappa said nothing as she looked away. Pain lined her face and eyes. The male at the other end of the line laughed nastily. "Don't waste your breath, Chronicle. Kappa knows just who she is beholden to for her very life. You're on our territory now, so why don't you come along quietly?"

If we were on 'their territory', came Tariah's still slightly slurred voice, *then they wouldn't need us to go along quietly.*

Kelsey and C.J. exchanged a look. As one, they made the rude gesture of the Magi with their left hands. The other female of the Elite looked so horrified that it nearly amused the Dragoons. Really, she should have been used to seeing it by then. The Elite weren't exactly *welcome* by anyone.

"Since you won't come along quietly," the male said with a sneer, "then I suppose we will have to take you by force."

No one got a chance to respond. No one needed to. The very land began to rumble softly as if to protest more war upon its surface. It was evidenced when geysers of power opened up in a circle around the Dragoons, forming a protective wall that could be deadly to pass through if you weren't a Chronicle. In this battle, the Lost Isle itself would be a combatant, and that swung the battle in the Dragoons' favor.

And at that moment, even the Elite knew it.

Chapter Twenty-Three

There was no question the fight would be bloody. It was also not one that could be fought as a group. Too much danger came from the geysers. It didn't help that the two strongest Chronicles were incapacitated, and C.J. was not designed for battle of either healing or combat orientation.

In a very soft voice, Kelsey said, "Ceej, you have to go after Kappa. She won't attack you. You have to get her on our side! Dahlia will protect you. The rest of us need to split up and get rid of the others. Xander and Jayda should go after the two males with the black hair; I think they're Soil power. Roman and Grecia can handle the other female; she seems to be Fire." Her eyes narrowed slightly. "Solis and I will take care of the one with the big mouth."

That left Dominic and Jazz to defend Morgan and Tariah, but if all the Elite were distracted, it wouldn't be that bad. Both twins had started to recover rapidly as they focused all their effort on repelling the effects of the power they had absorbed.

The four Chronicles still standing exchanged a long look. All unfastened their cloaks and let them drop. As fast as her power, Kelsey suddenly shot across the landscape toward the blond who had been such a smug bastard. She wanted to rearrange his face purely on principle.

He fell back in shock and swiftly dodged the fireball that shot for his head. His allies didn't even have a chance to help him. The others struck as well, forcing them all to scatter apart. Kappa saw C.J. coming toward her and desperately scrambled back. "No!" she shouted. "C.J., please! Don't make me fight you!"

The blond had recovered and he threw back the hood on his cloak to stare at Kelsey and Solis malevolently. "I am the highest class of Elite," he said icily. "My name is Zeta."

"Highest class? Or the highest class that's *left*?" Solis began to gather his power, and water swirled around his feet with bits of ice mixed inside. "I wouldn't brag about how strong you are when we've been taking out those who were stronger than you."

"Oh there's still one stronger. But don't think she would ever fall to you! And I will not either!" Zeta hurled an immense tornado through the air and the yellow taint cut through the land. The ground was so saturated from the storms and sea that the gouge in the soil made water well. In the dim light, it looked as if the land bled.

Kelsey gracefully dodged the tornado and returned the favor with a powerful stream of fire. Where Magi could only fire in staccato bursts, the fire poured from her hands in a steady blast that she had more than enough time to aim. It left a trail as she pursued Zeta.

Even though he outran her fire, there was Solis to deal with. The Fury was lethally accurate with the shards of ice he threw from his fingertips. When the two powers of the mates happened to cross, they did not cancel each other out. They merged seamlessly into a blinding force that was not dissimilar from the Kin power over Light. When it streaked past Zeta, narrowly missing him, just the heat of it burned his arm to the bone.

The other female of the Elite had once been an attractive enough Magi, but her face now looked worn and haggard with the skin sagging on her bones. When she saw Grecia and Roman rushing toward her, she instantly began to shoot bursts of Fire power at them. From the corner of her eye, she could see Kelsey's pure stream and was bitterly envious. Couldn't these foolish Chronicles see that the Elite were trying to make them a world to live in!?

"Before we turn you into dinner," Grecia said pleasantly enough, "why don't you tell us who you are?"

"Lambda." Her green eyes narrowed to slits. "You're nothing but a healer, Fury. What makes you think you can even hope to compete with me?"

She went white as a surge of power turned Grecia into her natural form. The Fury bared her teeth in a mockery of a smile. "I might be a healer, but I'm also a whole lot bigger than you."

Lambda was smarter than that. She turned and ran back across the field to put distance between them. Roman immediately swung up onto Grecia's back and held on with his legs as he lifted his hands to call his power. If Lambda wanted to make this a round of target practice, then he was happy to oblige.

The two males with black hair that Xander and Jayda went after were identical twins. Both were of the element of Soil, which was not uncommon among twins. Morgan and Tariah were, as was their way, different yet again from the normal course of things. It couldn't even be blamed on the fact that they were not, technically, twins in this life. It was the last that counted for it was then that their power had been born.

Jayda was a healer and more so than even Grecia. It did not make her any less accurate as she hurled a blast of snow directly into one of the twin's face. As he swiped at his eyes so that he could see, she shot a stream of water into his stomach and sent him flipping backwards across the ground.

His brother rushed to his side and snarled at Jayda, "Is that the best you can do, Chronicle? Mu and I will tear you apart!" At Xander's arched brow, the Elite offered haughtily, "I am Nu."

A mocking smirk touched Xander's lips. "How fitting. If I were to write your names in Draconic, it would form a word meaning 'the worthless.'" At Jayda's surprise in his mind, he mentally showed her the written characters in Magi and then compared them to Draconic. The similarity was amusingly close.

Mu scrambled to his feet and hurled a blast of small rocks at Jayda. Xander calmly stepped in front of her and swung his hand through the air. In his wake, a ribbon of fire appeared that melted the bits of stone. They became encased in smoke as they turned to glass shrapnel and reversed their course.

The twins managed to put up a soil wall as a barrier, but more than one of the tiny projectiles went clean through and narrowly missed them both. They'd had no idea that an Elder could do such a thing. "Just surrender," Nu bluffed, "and we won't have to get tough with you!"

There was no immediate retort, but a heated air swept over them and they both slowly looked up to see an immense black Dragon leaning over the wall. His breath was close enough that they could smell the fire in his power. "Get tough with who?" he asked softly, his voice a dangerous rumble.

When C.J. did not divert from chasing her, Kappa turned and fled. Tears choked her throat and ran down her face as she scrambled across the landscape to get away. She couldn't do this! She couldn't fight C.J.!

He moved over and around obstacles as nimbly as if he was on the dunes of his homeland. With every stride, his long legs gained on her lead. "Kappa!" he shouted. "Just stop running! You can fight with us! I know you're not tainted! I *believe* in you!"

Pain ripped her in two. Over her shoulder she shouted, "You don't know what I've done!"

"I don't care!" Panic fluttered in his stomach as he saw how dangerously close they were to the cliffs. "Kappa, stop! Please! You can make anything right if you just try!" He felt as if he was fighting not just for her life but Cole's as well. If she was alive, then so was he. C.J. was somehow sure of it, and he was sure that losing one meant losing the other as if they were Linked. He couldn't bear the idea of losing either of them for good.

The land gave way suddenly to a cliff. Kappa tried to skid to a stop but she had been running too fast and the grass was too slippery. She pitched forward over the side, and she couldn't even be upset over it. She had been on borrowed time anyway. Perhaps, in her death, she could atone.

Dahlia didn't hesitate. She threw her majiks into C.J. and shoved the knowledge into his mind. She believed in her Chronicle. His lead of several hundred feet would give him those precious seconds that might save Kappa's life.

He dove over the side of the cliff and grabbed onto the majiks to bend them sharply. A bright green glow engulfed him and changed him into a Dragon shape. Because he was of average Magi height, he became a Dragon of average length at roughly eighteen feet long. That added size was just enough. His claws closed around Kappa, his wings arched, and they sailed back up into the air mere feet before hitting the ragged rocks below.

Her eyes flew wide in shock and she stared at his draconic face. She hadn't seen the change, but she would have known him anywhere. His eyes were still the same as when she had first seen them in a boy's face. They were now the eyes of a man, and quite livid with it. Her gentle weaver was *furious*.

He landed more gracefully than one would expect from someone new to the form, but Dahlia had shoved *all* of her knowledge in his mind. He put Kappa down and firmly rooted her with vines before releasing the majiks and going back to normal. He could feel the sharp drain on Dahlia's power and pulled her into his arms to keep her steady. As soon as the battle was done, all the Furies would need to feed.

Kappa tugged at her binds, but found herself very firmly caught. "What are you going to do with me?"

He sat down on the grass and crossed his arms. "Right now, I'm going to bite my tongue before I yell at you. When everyone else joins us, I'll yell at you then." He blew out a hard breath and then suddenly seemed to realize what had happened. He boggled at Dahlia. "I turned into a Dragon."

Inexplicably, Kappa found herself smiling. Maybe he hadn't changed that much after all.

Mu and Nu, despite their combined strength, were no match for a fifty-foot Fury. Xander took care of Mu by flinging him into the violent storm clouds. Lightning flashed across the darkened sky, and the Elite never came back down. Nu, sensing his own demise, turned to go after Jayda.

She stood silently as he approached and she neither ran nor dodged. Just as he lunged for her, she lifted her hands. A giant ice spear instantly formed. He was moving far too fast to stop and impaled himself on it. Yellow blood welled nauseatingly, and his shocked eyes met hers. "I might be a doctor," she said softly, "but there's another side to that. To know how to heal even mortal wounds, you often need to know how they were caused."

The ice shard surged outward and froze him solid. A sharp strike from Xander's tail shattered him into millions of fragments. The stench of rotten power dissipated.

Lambda could only run. There was no stopping to catch a breath, not when there was a mounted Dragoon pair behind her. Roman was shockingly accurate with his wind pellets, and many struck her flesh before she could evade. Blood oozed down her arms and legs and stained her cloak. Pellets that missed her and struck the land did not do damage. They were simply absorbed.

When she found herself running into a large wall of cliffs, she knew she was done. There had been no cliffs there before the fight. The Isle itself had decreed her death sentence. Her mouth bitter, she turned to face the pair hovering in the air behind her. All she had wanted to do was get rid of the war-mongering, hate-filled Magi. What was so bad about that?

Zeta was by far faster and stronger than his brethren, but he was outclassed by Kelsey and Solis. The simple fact was that his power was not infinite. Kelsey's was, and she deliberately forced him to use more and more power, her every blast growing stronger and stronger with no clear effects to her. "I can go on for days," she told him as she hurled a spear of fire at him. "How about you?"

His body had begun to ache and burn, his muscles locking and knotting painfully. He reached desperately for his final reserves of power, and instead of attacking, he let it well inside. He would destroy himself before he ever gave them the satisfaction! Could the Isle handle a detonation? He didn't know. He didn't care.

"Get back!" Solis grabbed Kelsey and dragged her as far back as he could before they encountered the line of dead trees.

Zeta's body began to glow brightly when an immense shard of ice wrapped in lightning shot out of nowhere and slammed into his chest. It expanded to encase him just as he detonated. Trapped inside the ice, the power that blasted outward was purified as it passed through. By the time it reached the air, there was nothing it could damage.

Kelsey shot a fireball at the ice and blew it into tiny fragments to leave no trace of him behind. Heart pounding, she looked to where Morgan and Tariah now stood with Dominic and Jazz. Both twins looked lucid and alert, and power still swirled around their hands. "Are you sane again, or should I be glad you hit what you aimed at?"

Morgan had to grin. "My aim was never good to begin with, so count your blessings, Soot." His smile faded quickly as he looked around the scene. There should have never been another battle on these broken lands. It was like pouring salt into an open wound. "Is everyone all right?"

"We're fine." Xander kept an arm around Jayda's waist. "Tired, though. C.J. and Dahlia have Kappa captured."

Though all Furies needed to be fed, they were not at a critical level just yet. They could wait until camping, if camping was a possibility. To find that out, they needed to talk to Kappa. Morgan and Tariah led everyone to where C.J. and Dahlia waited.

There was something eerily familiar about Kappa to both twins, but if she had been at the last battle in Bergia, that was hardly surprising. Those missing memories had slowly started slipping free inside everyone.

"Well done." Morgan sat down next to C.J. and ruffled his hair. "We knew we could count on you." He turned toward Kappa and studied her critically. No taint clung to her power. It was as clean and fresh as the air around them. She still looked as lovely as she had always been.

Zeta's words danced in their minds. No one asked why she would be beholden to the Elite for her life, but they all wondered. Tariah asked only, "How many are left?"

"Two, if you include me. The strongest, Alpha, is farther from here. She can't come to you. You would have to go to her." Her lips twisted into a bitter smile. "None of us answer to our own names anymore. You already know Alpha by another name. My true name has been forsaken to me."

"How did all of this happen, Kappa?" Dahlia asked gently. She could not help but care for this other woman. She could see C.J.'s memories and feel his emotions. It broke her heart.

Kappa took a deep breath. "Years ago, Sistra appeared before Soh Emik. He was . . . broken. His mind was broken. Sistra wanted revenge and wanted to destroy the Magi for destroying her happiness. Maybe, in her own way, she wanted to save other Furies. There's no knowing now.

"When that fight happened back then, Sistra translocated everyone far away. I woke up in the middle of a desert. It was like being born again and very disorienting. Years later, we all suddenly got contacted out of nowhere by Sistra. She had found the Lost Isle and showed us how to get here. The geysers made everyone stronger, but it . . . twisted them further. I did not go near them. I didn't . . . I didn't even really want to be here."

She closed her eyes for long moments and then looked at C.J. "I don't know where Cole is. I've felt him following me, but I haven't seen him. The two of you . . . broke my heart. I wanted to die, yet something about the two of you made me want to live."

"I think that you already have your answer," Xander said softly. "Your power is true, Kappa. You were with the Elite, but you were never one of them. Lucksphere still loves you, still forgives you anything."

She looked at him in shock for a moment, then looked away. "I don't know how it could."

"Don't ask why." Kelsey's blue eyes were fierce. "Just accept it. Just go forward from today. Learn from your mistakes. Isn't that what adults do?"

"Most of them do," Solis murmured. "The smart ones, anyway. And I think Kappa is a smart lady." He rubbed a hand slowly over Kelsey's back. "Why cause the disruptions, Kappa? Was it to destroy Magi, or was there some other reason?"

"It was that and it was a hope of forcing more Chronicles to be born. Or to lure out the ones who still lived." Her breath came sad and long. "I don't know anything about the storms. We didn't do that. They just started forming when we were upsetting the lands. The storms here have been here for a millennia."

It only proved their theory that the storms were the world's attempt to heal. Grecia looked toward the center island where it seemed dark and malevolent. It was sickening to think of how severe the wound must be to produce such a storm. "What is at the center?" As soon as she said it, she knew. "Sistra is your 'Alpha', isn't she? She is the one you are beholden to for your life."

"If we can reason with her," Jazz said, "then we can free Kappa. I don't believe Sistra is bad. She was chosen to be a Fury. She knows she belongs with her Chronicle."

Tears slid down Kappa's cheeks. "How I envy you all."

"You'll have Cole." C.J. freed her from the vines and moved closer to hug her tightly. "It won't be the same, no, but it'll be wonderful for you. You need each other. I know Magi and Kin don't usually become permanent mates, but if you two love each other, then you can't say it isn't right."

"Is it safe to camp here?" Tariah asked.

Kappa nodded. "As I said, I am the only walking Elite member left." She studied Morgan and Tariah. "How did you shrug off the intoxication? The Elite never could."

"They weren't Chronicles," Morgan said simply. "We are designed to absorb power. And we think the Lost Isle has . . . has selected Tariah and me to take control. The power was potent, and that gave us the intoxication. Now that we're used to it, we should not be in any danger. The Elite are very lucky they weren't simply torn apart."

Tents were dug out of bags and put up. Kappa didn't have one, but she did not mind sleeping outside. There were enough meals packed for at least one more night of camping, and C.J. forced Kappa to take one of his extras. If Cole was his brother, then she was his sister. It was that simple.

By the time what should have been morning came around, everyone was fully recharged. The Furies had been fed, and unexpected geysers during the night had affected all the Chronicles and not just the twins. It made them all much more powerful than before. It also did something else.

The four Chronicles still on their journey discovered that the next third of their lines had darkened. That left no doubt in anyone's mind any longer that this was where they were supposed to be and what they were supposed to be doing. Once they were able to fix what was wrong, finding the Isle of Dragons would likely be their final step. Luckily, the four older Dragoons still remembered how to get there. It would not be hard.

Kappa was gone when they emerged from their tents, and it did not truly surprise anyone. What did surprise them was the fact that she had left a distinct trail for them to follow. She was breaking down and opening the path that would lead them toward the center island where Sistra hid.

They wasted no time in following the route. It was not easy. The further they went, the closer they got to the center, the worse the storms became. It was only when they were able to look across the divide and realize for the second time that they could see where they had come from that Xander realized why the shape had looked odd. "It's a spiral. The islands form a spiral chain leading toward the center."

'Do you see that, Xander?' There was laughter in Tarinah's voice as she perched gracefully on her Fury's back. They hovered in the sky over Sanguine with Xander beside them. 'Our city is surrounded by a spiral of mountains!' She held out her hand where the chron symbol was etched into her lines. One half of the symbol seemed to form a similar spiral. 'Just like in our name.'

Jayda's hands flew up to cover her mouth as tears welled in her eyes. "What is it?" Kelsey asked as she hugged her taller sister tightly.

"In Xander's memory." She closed her eyes helplessly. "We walk on what . . . what were once mountains. The mountains were the spiral leading to Sanguine."

"How big was this land once?" Roman asked softly.

"Roughly the size of Choral." Xander took a long, steadying breath. "We must keep walking. I will be fine. And stay out of my head," he scolded Morgan and Tariah. "You have endured enough!"

At one point along the path, they found themselves at a point higher than the quickly approaching center island. It looked slightly sunken with an immense crater situated in the very center that looked as if it might go into Lucksphere itself. There was a figure of some sort in the middle that might have been a Dragon . . . or Fury.

It seemed as if there were shadows moving across the center island without stop, but that made little sense when there was almost no light to be had. It was only when they heard the rumble on the wind that they realized what they saw.

Monsters.

Hundreds of monsters.

"There was nothing to mutate," Dominic said. "They must have . . . have somehow been *born* this way." He took a long breath. "We will have to fight our way through. C.J. . . . . I'm sorry. You're going to have to make your power do something it was never intended to do."

"You can do it," Dahlia said softly to her mate. She framed his face with her hand and her heart and power swirled around him soothingly. "You wouldn't be here if you weren't important. You're good with vines and quakes. Use them."

He nodded slightly. He was scared. He would have been lying to say he wasn't. But he wasn't going to leave. He had to do this. Kappa and Cole were counting on him, and so was his family. He would never shame Dahlia or Morgan and Tariah.

It felt like hours passed before they were actually underneath the terrible storm clouds. There was no longer any path to follow. No grass and no growth of any kind. They had to pick their way over broken rocks and jagged cliffs as they steadily made their way down toward the crater. The wind screamed and cried and begged for mercy.

Miraculously, it did not rain. The lightning flashed so often, so strongly, that it was easy enough to see where they were going and what they were doing. As they reached the edge of the five hundred foot crater, they distinctly saw Sistra hovering in the center.

She was blue in color with white spots, roughly around Dominic's size, and there was something more terrifying than beautiful about her face. In the last battle, she had lost an arm and a wing. The wing had re-grown but the arm had not. Even after nine years, the wound remained open. It did not bleed, yet it was nothing remotely resembling healed.

She looked worn and haggard with every one of her years weighing heavily. She, too, was an Elder. A Fury Elder. She was only a thousand years younger than Xander. She had endured the massacre destroying her dreams. She had endured the millennia of waiting. But she had not been as lucky as the rest. Her Chronicle had been killed by Magi law. It broke the hearts of those who looked at her. How could they hate her?

C.J. spotted Kappa standing not far away on the edge of the crater. Tears ran down her face without stop, and in a flash of lightning she looked almost as tired and worn as Sistra. This madness had to end before more lives were destroyed.

Painfully, Sistra lifted her head. Her green eyes were in turns dull and bright, and sane and insane. "Dragoons." It was little more than a sibilant hiss echoed by the monsters that crawled over the crater, always moving close but not attacking. Not yet. "Do you see what has become of our rightful home? Help me destroy the Magi. Make them suffer as they made us suffer."

"The Magi are changing, Sistra," Morgan called. "The laws are revoked. Chronicles are to be protected, to be sheltered. They will not be murdered anymore. No more Furies will suffer as you did. You *succeeded*. You saved them."

"It is not enough." Her head slowly turned toward Kappa. "Attack them!"

"I can't." Her voice sounded thin. "You know I can't."

"And just who do you think gave you life?" The words that spewed into the air were as vicious as the storms. "I gave you that form and flesh. I gave you your second life. You served me already. I could have erased you, but I let you live. I will not release you! Do my bidding if you wish to ever be free!"

Painfully, slowly, she turned toward the Dragoons. Her refusal was written all over her face. "Kill me." Her voice came out so faint that it was almost impossible to hear. "Please, C.J. I beg of you to free me of this curse."

On a violent oath, he turned toward Sistra. "Is this what you want?" he shouted. "This destruction of people who just don't know any better? How is destroying the Magi going to make right all the wrongs? It can't! Is this what Phedo would have wanted?"

"No," came an unexpected male voice. "It is not what I want."

They all turned sharply and discovered the form of a SunKin Elf standing on a large rock nearby. Only C.J. and Dahlia recognized him, and Dahlia had to grab C.J. before he leapt forward. "Cole!" he shouted. His friend's words sank in and his eyes widened in shock. "Wait, what do you mean it's not what *you* want?"

A surge of power rippled over Cole's body and the golden tattoos suddenly connected and changed shape. Morgan stopped breathing entirely as he recognized the shape and form. A Chronicle's lines were unique to each individual. No two would ever be alike. "You're a Second Born Kin," he said softly. "You're Phedo."

Chapter Twenty-Four

Cole looked at Morgan for a moment and then said softly, "I never hated you, Morgan. I never hated anyone. If you have felt guilty for not finding me sooner, then stop. This was a path set before me long before you ever arrived." He looked at Tariah. "For what my father did to Daylar . . . I am sorry."

"Is it . . . is it possible?" Kelsey whispered to Xander.

He slowly shook his head. "I have never seen a Second Born Kin that was not twice a Kin, but that does not mean it is not possible."

"Help us!" Jazz called to Cole. "Please, help us talk some sense into your Fury!"

Cole looked directly at Kappa. "The sense is there. She's just too afraid of it." He leapt down off the rock and walked toward her purposefully. "She couldn't even see me when we met. She wasn't looking with her heart. But I saw her heart. I knew."

"Stay back!" She held up her hands to hold him off, her eyes blind with terror and tears. "You can't be . . . it can't be . . ."

He brushed aside her hands and pulled her into his arms. "I am." He buried his face in her hair and let his power well. He reached for her with his emotions and his power, let her see and sense what was inside. That wellspring of desperate emotion that the Dragons called *ishke*. The emotion that marked only a Chronicle or Fury. "Kappa."

She collapsed against him on a sob, her hands beating at his shoulders wildly, and her cream-colored hair suddenly streaked with golden yellow in evidence of her true power. "You were dead!" she sobbed into his shoulder. "Why couldn't I die to find you?! Why did I turn to hate?!"

He held her closer. "It doesn't matter anymore. It's done." He looked over her head to where the shocked Dragoons stood. "I don't know the 'how', I'm sorry. But I knew when I met Kappa that she was a Second Born as well, and I knew she was my Sistra. When I died . . . I just knew I couldn't. I met the original Cole halfway to the Underrealm. His body was alive, but his soul was not. We traded to give me the time I needed to find my Fury."

It dawned on C.J. at last. "That's why . . . that's why she was drawn to me. I'm a Soil Chronicle, and you and I had been together so long that your presence was a part of me. It sent out a confusing signal."

"Then what happened to Sistra and Kappa?" Kelsey demanded.

"Me." The one who held Sistra's body stared at all of them malevolently. "I wanted this body. I forced her to live again to do what I could not."

"That's why you wanted to die," Tariah said softly to Kappa. "You were trying to return to Phedo. You didn't know he was still alive." She took a deep breath. "Why did you change your mind? You were so determined to destroy the Magi!"

"That . . . other being was inside me." She shuddered. "Her rage, my rage, her grief, my grief . . . it was one terrible force. I couldn't fight it. But when I saw you and Morgan become the Chronis Dragon . . . I could see the hope for future Furies. It gave me the strength to die though she would not let me. All these years . . . I did as she bid, praying someone would destroy me at last."

"Then just who is in your other body? You said she was there all along?" Morgan stared at Sistra, trying to determine why she still seemed so very familiar even without the proper soul and power inside.

"I don't know." Her voice was weary and she rested heavily against Cole. "I don't. I don't even know how to live anymore . . ."

"I do." He tilted her head back and met her eyes. "I do. Whatever we do from now on, we do together."

Sistra hissed at them all. "So be it!" She roared furiously and the sound reverberated off the rocks and crater, bounced down from the clouds. "I will destroy all of you, then all of the rest, and we will start over from scratch!"

The monsters lunged up out of the crater with claws and fangs bared. Destroying them was no easy feat, and for every one destroyed there were two more to take its place. All Furies went into their natural form to fight more efficiently, but even Xander had his claws full. The monsters just kept pouring out of the crater.

To make matters worse, Sistra began to attack as well. She did not throw merely the tornados and lightning of her Air element. She threw them all. She caused quakes and hurricanes; she threw fireballs and shards of ice. She sent blasts of Light at Cole and Kappa that the Second Born Kin was forced to block and repel. She even threw blasts of Dark, regenerating the monsters when they were down but not dead. She used every element. She *was* every element.

'Xander?' Morignan was sitting on a cliff outside Sanguine where they could watch the sunset. 'Did you know our island is alive? Tarinah and I can hear it breathe. I would daresay it is the very heart of this world. We live in the heart of the world. It is no wonder we exist on love.'

A sickening feeling swept through Xander as he stared at Sistra. "She's the Isle," he said softly. "She's possessed by the Isle of Chronicles!"

"Close but not quite it, fledgling." Sistra blew ice at him that he had to block with his wing. "I am not the heart of this world. I *am* this world. I *am* Lucksphere. And I am going to erase it all and begin again!"

Something rang false in her words though Tariah could not figure out what. Her sharp eyes could see quite plainly that there was at least some truth. Every time the land took damage, a matching wound appeared on Sistra's body. The storm was surely the manifestation of her torn arm. Destroying her would, at the very least, destroy whatever was left of the isle.

But there was something else odd. Though Sistra attacked them, she did not leave her crater. Tariah stared harder and could not see anything. She turned and swiftly located Cole. He was a Chronicle, but he had inherited Kin power. *Cole! Fire some light under Sistra! I need to see what she is hiding!*

He immediately sent a ball of power whipping down into the crater. She watched intently, and the light illuminated a distinct hole in the crater that led even deeper into the ground. Whatever was in there was what Sistra defended. *Morgan! We have to go down there! We have to see what she is hiding!*

"Go!" Jazz clawed apart another monster. "We will cover for you. Just go! You're the only ones who can do this!"

Morgan and Tariah sprinted for the edge of the crater, and the others began to cover them with attacks. Cole and Kappa went after Sistra directly, forcing her to focus on them and not the twins. The monsters barely noticed the twins going past; they were too focused on the battle at hand. When one did notice, it was C.J.'s perfect aim with his vines that kept it from following.

The hole in the crater was several feet wide and so deep that it was pitch dark. Morgan called up a bubble of air and wrapped himself and his sister within it. There was no telling how far into the land the hole went.

They seemed to descend forever. When Tariah looked up, she could see the entrance becoming a dim and distant memory. The hole at the top was little more than a pinpoint by the time they actually landed. It felt bitterly cold and it was gut-wrenchingly dark. The twins took a hesitant step forward, and light suddenly flooded the area and blinded them. When they could see again, Tariah could barely stifle a cry of horror.

The place at the center of the world was a swamp. It was a putrid, oozing mess. Rivers and pools of mud and filthy water stood motionless. Some dripped from the thorn covered walls. Vines that might have once held flowers now held dead bulbs. Everything was covered in a pale and sickly cast, and the air smelled of rotting vegetation. Hard dirt covered where there wasn't sludge, and cracks crossed it like scars.

None of that was as truly horrifying as what stood in the very center. Bound within more of those vicious thorny vines were the figures of a man and a woman. The thorns bit into their skin, and their faces were lined with pain and fatigue. On first glance, the man seemed to be dead for he did not breathe and he did not move, but when Tariah cautiously stepped closer, she could feel the faintest of power inside him still.

The woman stirred slightly, her lashes lifting to reveal eyes that were half white and half blue. Old eyes. Ancient eyes. Eyes that had seen far too much and suffered far too long. "My children?" Her voice was thin, almost non-existent, but it was very, *very* familiar.

"It was you," Morgan whispered. "You led us on our journeys." His throat closed painfully as tears welled in his eyes. "Who . . . who are you?"

"I have no real name." Her eyes closed for a moment and then opened again. "You might call me Sphera. I am one half of this world. Air, Water, and Light are born from me." She took a ragged breath as if speaking was simply too much for her to endure. "My Luck . . . does he live? Have I lost everything?"

Tariah bit back a cry, her fingers tangling desperately with Morgan's. "He lives. There is power in him, so he must live."

Sphera's lips tried to smile, but they were dry. They cracked in places and golden blood welled. "If he dies, I will have no will to hold on. I have carried the weight alone for so long . . . If we die, there will be no Lucksphere. I am sorry."

Tariah moved closer and tore a piece of cloth from the one wrapped around her hips. She wet it with her Water power and tenderly wiped at Sphera's lips and face. "What has happened?" she asked softly. "Tell us how we can make it right."

Her sigh was long. "Our garden . . . see what it has become. The Magi . . . the Magi began to kill our garden as they killed the balance. We let our gardens bloom with flowers, let the flowers be born on land. Our beautiful Dragoons. Our precious children." Shimmering love filled her eyes as she looked at Morgan and Tariah. "How we loved you! All that lives is our child, but . . . Chronicles . . . you are our flesh and blood.

"We chose our most beautiful, our most precious flowers to become our first Chronicles. But we could not ask you to do things alone. We looked at our other children, and we saw the beautiful love inside Dragons. Oh, how they love everything! We made them our Furies." Tears slid down her cheeks. "You are happy? Tell me you are happy."

"Our Furies make us whole. We are strong because of them." Morgan's voice broke and then steadied again. "They waited patiently for us, Sphera. They loved us before we were ever there. You chose them perfectly. And Xander . . . look at him to see just how well you chose."

"I'm glad." She smiled though it trembled.

"What happened to Luck?" Tariah gently touched his face and found it cool to her fingers. He was a handsome man and Sphera's perfect opposite. She knew, was sure, his eyes would be half green and half red. His hair was silver where Sphera's was gold. His skin was dark where hers was pale. The father of all that lived.

"The massacre." A sob tangled in Sphera's chest. "The Magi came. They tore apart our heart. Our children were destroyed. It . . . broke Luck. In all the years, I have tried to bloom our flowers again and again. But they were always killed. Our beloved Furies were mercifully killed before their love turned them . . ."

"Into you." Morgan stepped forward and touched her hand where it was caught between two horrid thorns. "We came back," he said softly. "We came back as we promised. We're here, and we can make it better."

"When I saw your flowers blooming in the middle of our dead garden . . . I felt hope again." Her hand stirred, her fingers brushing his. "Blooming again. Morgan, Tariah. Your flowers were so strong that they came back to us to be born again."

"Then tell us what to do to make it right." Tariah gently touched Luck's face and then Sphera's. "I've lost one set of parents. I can't lose another. Tell us how to defeat Sistra. How to help you."

"Sistra . . . my pain, my rage, my fear, my grief . . . even my hate. It took shape. In my worst moment, I hated my Magi children. And my hate doomed them all. It met Sistra's grief and found an easy outlet." Her eyes closed. "I'm sorry."

The sudden feeling of their mates calling urgently had Morgan and Tariah looking up sharply. The others needed them. "It's getting worse."

"Go," Sphera urged softly. "Please. No more death."

The twins turned and ran out of the swamp, and Morgan carried them swiftly up toward the surface. The fight was not going well. The Furies were starting to run low on power, and there wasn't a single person who was left unwounded. The monsters finally diminished in number, but not quick enough. Sistra seemed slightly weaker, but still impossibly strong.

Morgan rushed over to Jazz in time to shield her from an unexpected attack. He forcefully poured his power into her and gave her enough to change into Magi form. As she collapsed into his arms, his power rose to cover him in a white aura. "Feed," he told her sharply. *Cole! Kappa! You still have reserves! Cover us so we may feed our Furies!*

Cole and Kappa ran down to join them from where they had been fighting and they worked swiftly to distract the enemy. The Chronicles followed Morgan's lead in forcing their Furies to change form so they could feed as well. They couldn't go on like this any longer!

It's Luck! Tariah spoke directly to Morgan's mind. *We have to restore Luck. It's the only way Sphera's grief will lift!*

My children. Sphera's voice softly whispered across all of their minds. *The only way to restore Luck is to restore the balance. Our garden must bloom again.*

"We'll go." Cole straightened his back. "Kappa and I will make the garden bloom."

Phedo, Sphera's voice warned gently, *you know what that means.*

He smiled at Kappa who smiled back tremulously. "We know. But . . . we were on borrowed time anyway." He walked over to C.J. and knelt down beside his friend. "I love you," he said softly. "You're my brother in every way that counts. I wish we could have flown the skies with our Furies. The one thing I cannot regret in my second life is getting to meet you."

Tears slid down C.J.'s cheeks. "You're saying goodbye."

"Who knows? Maybe my flower will bloom again."

C.J. took a deep breath and leaned over to whisper softly in Cole's ear. He eased back and somehow smiled. "I promised, right?"

His Kin brother smiled as well, and it was a genuine smile. "I think your name *does* suit you, C.J. Your parents knew more than we did. Don't look at it in Magi language. Look it up in the Kin. You'll see what I mean. Our many more characters bring beauty to mundane things." He gently touched Dahlia's hand. "Take care of my brother."

Her lips curved. Her strength was pouring back in now that she had fed on her Chronicle's power. "You'll have to come back," she told him, "and make sure that I am doing a good job."

He got to his feet and walked over to Kappa. Their hands linked and they leapt down into the crater. The monsters started to go after them, but the Furies were back to full strength from those precious few minutes. They joined forces with their mates, and the combined strength of the Dragoons formed a thick shield to protect them all. They needed to buy time for Cole and Kappa.

Kappa used her power to take herself and Cole down to the swamp, and they walked with their hands linked to where Sphera and Luck were trapped. Her throat tight, Kappa said, "I'm so sorry for what I did."

"You are not to blame." Sphera's eyes opened slightly. "You must never believe that. You were chosen, Sistra. You are one of our chosen ones. Jazz was right about you all along. C.J. was right. The love in you is true."

"Are you ready?" Cole asked his mate softly.

She looked at him with shimmering eyes filled with her emotions, the greatest of which was that wonderful third Dragoon emotion. That gift of their mother and father. The gift of their world. "I'm with you," she said simply.

He pulled her close and kissed her tenderly, and lines that matched his swirled down her body. He let his power, both born and born again, well in the air around them. Her power, born and born again, rose to meet his. They both began to glow brightly, brilliantly, as if they were going to detonate themselves. At the very moment when they would have been destroyed, they instead turned into pure light. They flew into Luck, merged into his body . . . and his eyes opened.

He drew a deep breath. It was the first he'd had in a millennia. Strength and power poured into him from the unconditional gift of life. "Sphera." He reached for her with his mind and his power and wrapped her within his love. It burned as bright as any Dragoon's. "I am here."

The thorns began to change, began to fall away from the vines, as she moved her hand toward his. Their fingers met, meshed, and a sob slipped past her lips. "I've missed you!"

Power flooded from their joined hands and tore through the swamp. The cracked ground pulled together and bloomed with lush green grass. The deadened vines bloomed again with desert roses. The filthy water evaporated, and fresh, pure, water cascaded down the walls to fill the pools and rivers. The vines encasing Sphera and Luck lost their thorns and bloomed with flowers as they fell away. And as Luck drew Sphera into his arms, the garden began to glow softly, strongly. Beautiful once more.

On the surface, Sistra screamed in pain. Morgan and Tariah felt the rumble within the land and leapt to their feet. The barrier came down as they rushed toward the edge of the crater, and they threw themselves out over the top. Within the first two feet, they had become Dragons. Within the next two, they fused.

The immense Dragon was twice the size of Xander and covered in silver scales the same color as its eyes. Four wings held it aloft and fins extended from its starkly beautiful face. The Chronis Dragon, as it had been named, had only been seen twice before. Perhaps this would be the last time it was ever needed.

There was nowhere for Sistra to move. Nowhere for her to retreat. The Chronis slammed into her and tore her from her perch over the crater. She did not fight or resist as the Chronis hurled her up through the air. She did not open her wings to fly away. She simply waited for the end. Finally, it had come.

From one claw, the Chronis hurled a stream of raw ice at her that encased her fully. From the other claw, lightning flew and shattered her into millions of pieces. The abrupt destruction caused a shockwave to be released and the entire island went ballistic. Geysers spewed into the air as the ground shook violently.

Without hesitation, the Chronis Dragon began to draw it all in. It pulled in every geyser and loose tendril of power. It hovered over the center of the crater and began to glow blindingly bright. No one could look close yet no one could look away. The Chronis threw back its head and, with a roar that shook the world, released the power.

The shockwave ripped across the land and sea and tore across the sky. The storms were dissipated instantly and released the Flutterlies to their proper duty.

The Lost Isle began to shake violently and then rose swiftly through the air as the ocean receded and pulled back. In minutes, the spiral isles had become the top of the spiral mountains once more. They rose high enough into the air that it was certain to snow when cooler weather returned.

The crater filled and healed with green grass rushing to cover it. The hole down to the secret garden disappeared entirely, safely protected within its heart once more. Across the world, the storms dissipated and lands stopped shaking. The small islands of Kindred found their shores expanding as the ocean pulled back. Other lands were as yet born new. Some were forested. Others were beautiful flat fields of grass and flowers. One even had mountains not yet covered in snow.

As the last of the power left, the Chronis Dragon circled the spiral mountains before landing gracefully in the center where its city had once laid. With a glow, the Chronis became the Dragon forms of Morgan and Tariah. Another glow returned them to their normal Chronicle forms.

The shockwave had healed and replenished all the Chronicles and Furies. They made their way down the mountains by air and rushed across the plains toward where Morgan and Tariah laid. Both were perfectly fine though they were deeply asleep. When Dominic lifted Tariah into his arms, shock stole his voice entirely. "Jay," he said hoarsely. "The baby."

She lightly rested her hands over Tariah's belly and her eyes went wide. Her lips trembled as she saw the miracle that had occurred. "A Chronicle. She's carrying a Chronicle. The garden is in bloom."

Deep below the surface in the immortal garden of life, Luck and Sphera stood together looking at the beauty surrounding them. They were not healed fully, not yet. More Chronicles and Furies would need to be born to truly restore the balance.

Luck softly opened his hands, and on his palms rested two seeds. He released them into the garden and smiled. "When you bloom," he said softly, "then we will know we are healed. Until that day, sleep well, little ones."

His arm slid around Sphera, and she turned into his embrace. Finally, she was alive. She was not alone any longer. Their children would laugh. They would play. They would love and they would live. No one would ever cry again.

Chapter Twenty-Five

Kelsey awoke one morning a few days later and realized that her lines were pulsing. She sat upright in shock, dislodging Solis, and stared at her arms. Her lines were darkening. The darkness slowly flowed down her skin and marked the last of her journey.

It had been days since the resurrection of the Lost Isle. None of the Chronicles or Furies had left yet. They had been camping in the valley and savoring how it felt to be somewhere they belonged. And they did belong. None had ever felt more at home.

They had built small homes of wood and stone and glass to rest within, but most of the time they were flying over the mountains and valleys to see and learn. To Kelsey's absolute delight, the western side of the land, just past that side of the mountains, was a wonderfully hot and beautiful desert. She had made everyone laugh by diving into the sand happily.

They had known the journey was not yet over, though they hadn't felt any urge to go anywhere. Perhaps Sphera had been recovering still. No one, not even Tariah, had been able to guess. But as Kelsey saw her lines darkening, she felt the stirring inside of that urge telling her where to go.

South.

The voice whispered softly across her soul welcomingly. "How far south?" she asked suspiciously of the air. "After what we went through, you could be more specific!"

Soft laughter filled her soul with joy. *Go south to the end of our heart. Your journey ends there.*

She scrambled out of bed and jerked on her clothes. When Solis didn't move, she scowled and went over to shake him. "Wake up, you lazy Fury! We have to go south to the end of the island!" She blinked. "Well, it's not really an island anymore, is it? It's more of a continent finally. We need a name for it."

He opened one eye. "You kept me up all night."

"You're the one with all those fascinating ideas in your mind. I was just trying them out." She tugged on his hand, so vibrantly alive that he couldn't tear his eyes away. "Solis! We have to go! My journey is almost over!"

He got out of bed with a smile and pulled on his clothes. How would he ever say no to her about anything?

She wasn't the only one who had felt the call. By the time they got outside, the other three who were still on their journey had also gathered. C.J. looked much older than he ever had before, but he was healing as well. He clung onto the hope that Phedo could be reborn again, and even if not, that he and Sistra were happy in the Underrealm where souls went when they were done.

"Elder Tariah!" Roman called teasingly toward her home. "Elder Morgan! You need to come with us, too!"

The twins were only reluctantly resigned to the fact that they were Elders, which made it all the more fun to tease them about it. For that reason, Tariah was pulling a face as she and Dominic left their home to join their clan. "You can't call me that for another thousand years," she scolded.

"Deal," Roman answered promptly. "I'm holding you to that."

"When do we get to know your name?" Kelsey demanded of C.J. "You told Phedo, so you have to tell us."

"No." He smiled. "I'm going to wait to tell you until he's with us again. You'll just have to be patient, Kel." He rubbed his cheek against Dahlia's hair as she slid her arms around him. "But I don't mind my name that much anymore. Dahlia knows Kin, and she told me what it meant in that language. Phedo was right. He usually was."

When Morgan had joined them as well, the Furies went into their natural form and their Chronicles climbed to where they belonged. Together, they flew over the mountains and made their way toward the distant ocean. It was not a long trip by flight; it was only an hour or two. A Fury with a Chronicle could cover the entire continent within a day. By foot it would be a week. Big, but not too big. It was perfect.

They landed on the southern shore, and they were still not entirely sure what they sought. Despite that, their lines steadily continued mapping their journeys. Just as they fully darkened, Kelsey saw something on the horizon. "Ships!" she exclaimed. "I see ships!" Her eyes slowly widened. "A lot of ships . . ."

It was an entire armada and all bore the flag of the Magi king. It was also not the only thing on the horizon. A darkened line moved in as well, and within minutes it was recognizable as a fleet of Dragons. There were at least a hundred of them, and at the front were the four Dragons on the Council of Elders.

Grecia studied the ground and then the sky. When Roman arched a brow, she said, "I'm making sure we really did win and the world is not ending. I thought nothing less would get those old fuddy-duddies off the Isle!"

As the ships grew closer, it became obvious that they carried not just Magi. There were dozens of Kin on board as well, including Elder Juniper. There were no docks to land at, so the ships dropped anchor and sent in smaller boats that could land on shore. Riding in the first one came Finus and Juniper, and they had a few other familiar faces with them.

"Kelsey!" Etude nearly wailed it as she shot through the air and hugged her friend around the neck. "I missed you! You're okay! Oh, I knew you'd do it!"

"Etude!" Kelsey hugged her happily. "I missed you too!"

Sparkle and Daylar were also on board, and flew over to hug Tariah in the same way. The others didn't get a chance to feel left out. The boats also carried all of their parents.

"Mom." C.J. rushed forward and scooped her up off her feet. "I can't believe it! Why are you here? Do you ... remember?"

Ferris smiled through her tears as she studied him. "When that shockwave came through, it put our memories back together." She scowled at Morgan. "And you, young man, have some explaining to do!"

He winced wryly. After meeting Sphera, he had suspected she was the one who had erased the other memories. He was sure of it now. It still didn't make him any less guilty of the same! "Yes'm."

The boats continued to carry out more people as Finus and Juniper walked toward where the Dragoons stood. The clan moved automatically to put Tariah and Morgan at the front as their leaders. The Dragons had begun to land, and those who were Dragon Lords turned to other forms to make more room. The four Elders were Lords, and they took a Magi form. It shocked the Furies even more because they had *never* done it in the past.

"We have come to make amends," Finus told the twins. "We bring supplies and artisans to help you build your city. I am offering a formal treaty of peace with you all. Dragoon, Dragon, and Kin. There will be no more war."

"We accept your offer, gladly," Morgan said softly. "There's been too much hate for too long." He made the Dragoon gesture of respect. "We would like you to stay with us, Finus. And learn about us."

"I would like that as well." He took a deep breath and turned. "Elen." As a young boy ran forward, he put a hand on his shoulder. "This is my son, Elen. He has twelve summers."

At one look, Tariah and Morgan knew what they saw. The power in the boy bloomed bright and true. They knelt and offered their hands, and Elen took them with a smile. He liked how their silver eyes were warm. He felt safe near them.

The jolt went up through the twins' arms, and they looked up at Finus. Without hesitation, Morgan said, "Your son is a Chronicle."

There was a long silence before Finus scooped up Elen and tossed him in the air with a smile. "I suppose we need to celebrate, don't we?" As he caught his son in a fierce hug, everyone began to clap and cheer. The world needed Chronicles. They were the keepers of their beautiful Lucksphere.

Kelsey barely noticed when the Dragon Elders started talking with Finus about trade and possibly restarting the air service that had existed a millennia before. Instead, her eyes fixed to where Ilian and Quinn stood with members of the Militia. No one was in uniform, but it was obvious who and what they were.

She lightly touched the pendant she wore as she walked over to where Ilian stood. "Ilian." She smiled at him. "Thank you for your gift. It's beautiful." She felt Solis' arms around her waist and leaned back against him. "There is a Dragoon ceremony that is our version of a Linking one. I want you to attend."

"I would be honored." He smiled at her. She was, as he had always known she would be, a beautiful and confident adult. Solis suited her perfectly. "I'm glad you're happy. And that you aren't upset with me."

"Why would I be?" She studied him, then studied Quinn, then him again. "You know," she said, "maybe you've got the perfect match too. Maybe you just haven't noticed yet. Promise me that if you notice, you won't hesitate."

"I promise," he assured her, but inside he was amused. What woman in her right mind would want to be a mate to an Argyle who was always on the road?

The ceremony was held a week later in the half built city of Sanguine. People from all over the world were coming through, and a small port city was being built as well. People of all three races wanted to live on this peaceful land, and Morgan and Tariah had made it clear that the shores were open to all. They would have a festival every summer, and children could come to see if they were chosen as well.

After much bickering among the Council of Elders about who would preside over the ceremony, they finally decided to make Finus do it. He felt humbled and honored to be given the duty, and he made sure to memorize the ceremony to the last detail. It was more beautiful than he had imagined.

The four Dragoon pairs stood before him in the formal clothes of their homelands. For C.J., Roman, and Kelsey, that meant clothing of the desert. Kelsey had grown up in a forest, but she was a desert girl at heart. For Jayda, that meant the clothing of the snowy mountains.

Their Furies would have normally been in their natural form, but there wasn't enough room. Instead, they wore clothing that best suited the area of the Isle of Dragons where they had lived the longest. They also wore sashes in the color of their element to denote which clan they came from. All of the clothing had been woven by C.J. for he was the best the world had to offer.

"This ceremony," Finus began, "is an old one. It is steeped in heritage and history. Furies, will you dedicate your lives to protecting your Chronicles? Will you always support them, and give them the wings to fly across the skies as Dragoons?"

"We will," the Furies said as one.

"Chronicles, will you dedicate your lives to protecting your Furies? Will you always support them, and walk beside them when they wish to see the land as Dragoons?"

"We will," the Chronicles responded.

"Then it is with honor that I name you all full Dragoons and confer upon you the full privileges associated with such a position. I also declare you to be Linked by Magi standards, Bonded by Kin, and United by Dragon. You will stand as one, you will live as one, and you will die as one. For eternity."

"For eternity," said all those who were in the crowd.

He grinned. "Let us see our Dragoons take their first flight together on their new paths." He felt Elen hug him around the waist and lightly rested a hand on his shoulder. He couldn't wait to see the day that his son was able to start his journey and find the Fury meant for him.

Everyone moved back as much as possible so that there was room enough for all four Furies to change form. Many Magi felt nonplussed at the sight of Xander's fifty-foot size, but the tenderness in the way he lifted Jayda up to his back made his face more beautiful than terrifying.

As the pairs lifted to the sky and began to fly around the city, a cheer rose on the air. Sanguine was stable. It was the beating heart of the world. No Dragon or Fury would ever fear flying over it. Perhaps, someday, they would never fear flying over any city.

"How do you feel?" Solis asked Kelsey as he did a playful loop-de-loop in the sky.

She stretched her arms high and laughed as she got an armful of Flutterlies. They looked fat and happy as she released them to continue their peaceful journey. If they stormed again, it would be a normal storm. It would not be a portent of devastation. How long had it been since anyone had seen a storm and been unafraid? "I feel wonderful." She leaned down to wrap her arms around his neck. "And I saw my father talking to you very seriously. What was he going on about this time?"

Her mate chuckled softly. "He was giving me some of the finer points on how to raise a daughter just like you."

"Oh, are we planning on having one?"

"I was considering it."

She smiled and let her emotions swirl around him hotly and powerfully. His rose to meet hers and they flowed back and forth in an endless loop of infinity. "When do you want to start trying? Who knows. We might not take nine years like someone else we know."

His laughter rolled across the skies. "I could be persuaded to start trying now, if you promise you'll do your best to give me a blue-eyed daughter."

Her eyes filled with tears. She had never imagined she could ever be that happy and complete. Her wait, though shorter, had been no less sweet. "Then take me home," she said softly.

As he angled down toward the desert, they could see the setting sun in the distance illuminating their beautiful continent. It was called Esteria. In the language of the Magi, it meant 'peace.' In the language of the Kin, it meant 'heart.' In the language of the Dragons, it meant 'home.'

Esteria, the peaceful home of the world's heart. The place where a garden could bloom forever.

Epilogue

Dear Reader,

Summer is the most beautiful time on Lucksphere. In the thousand years I have walked this world, I have never seen anything as beautiful as this time.

There used to be a festival in Esteria every summer. We would welcome to our land the children who might be Chronicles. There were always at least a handful. We would guide them, tell them of what to expect, and wait for that summer in the future when they would begin their journey. No matter where it led, at the end was a Fury who had waited patiently to love them.

But that was how it was long ago. With every passing century, the number of Chronicles and Furies being born has diminished more and more. Furies stopped being born four centuries ago. The last one that was born is a female Air element. Do you know who she is? We did as soon as we saw her.

This summer was the most wonderful yet. On the ship coming in from the other lands was a young boy of thirteen summers. When his feet touched the soil, his first puberty began and familiar, wonderfully familiar, lines traversed his body. Our last Chronicle. Many cheered. Others wept for joy.

This summer heralds in a new time for Lucksphere. Our world is healed at last. The garden is in full bloom. In six or seven years, we will get to celebrate the last Dragoon ceremony. To know it is the last, to know that our world is healed . . . there are no words.

Oh, but I suppose there are a few words. C.J. was forced to keep his promise and tell us just what his name is. Prepare yourself. It is Chrisanthedel Jiordan. When you break down the characters of his name, the closest Magi equivalent is 'festival chaser.' But when you break it down in Kin . . . it becomes 'weaver of the heart.' I suppose the best parents, in the end, really do know their children better than anyone else.

And this is where we say goodbye, gentle reader. When the summer is warm, the sun shines bright, and you see flowers blooming, remember our story. Remember our laughter and our life. Remember our love.

May it never end.

Elder Tariah M. Chronis

S.J. Garrett

Author Notes

I hope you enjoyed reading CHRONICLE OF SUMMER and coming along on this epic journey! It was an adventure to write, and I promise that I laughed every laugh and cried every tear along with you. If I've left an imprint on your heart, then I've done my job right.

If you loved this story, leave me a review on Amazon.com (http://amzn.to/1ODDYw3). I love hearing from fans just what touched them most about my stories, and reviews help more readers find me.

Want to keep up-to-date on what I'm writing or taking photos of? You can follow me on Facebook (www.facebook.com/stacyjgarrett) or Twitter (@stacyjgarrett). You can also sign up for my mailing list (http://www.stacyjgarrett.com) and hear first about new releases and get background info not shared anywhere else.

Never stop believing in a wonderful future, readers. Even in the darkest time, a small light can shine enough to bring back hope.

Stacy J Garrett

About the Author

Stacy J. Garrett (S. J. Garrett) was made in England but born in Sacramento, California, and like the redwoods of the state, her roots have dug deep. Her destiny as a bard was somewhat inevitable. Little else can explain how she constantly told her mother tall tales so outlandish that she couldn't even get grounded for them. Her mother and grandmother had her reading by age three, and that love of a good story propelled her through so many books that Scholastic Books gave her a medal. At the age of twelve, she picked up a point-and-shoot camera, and her love of telling a story took itself on a new journey as she starting taking photographs no one believed an untrained child could. She entered junior college by age fifteen to study photography, and in the same year, she wrote her first story. She has never looked back.

Stacy has seen both good and evil in her life, and her works, like life, have no half measures. Even in fantasy worlds of dragons and faeries, she knows that the constants of real emotion never change. Whether shooting photographs in stark straight black and white or brilliant digital color, or turning out fantastical novels of over a hundred thousand words, she shows an ability to move hearts, engage minds, and take people beyond the borders of reality into another world entirely.

Her current haunt is a comfy house in her beloved Sacramento where she wrangles four feline fur-kids and consumes peppermints like mana in order to balance a calendar filled with more creative venues than a sane person should realistically undertake. She considers herself extremely blessed to be surrounded by a group of amazing friends and associates who never hesitate to volunteer to do something a little strange for the sake of art, whether it is getting almost naked in a park or dressing up for a steampunk tea party.

She holds an Associate of Arts Degree in Fine Arts Photography, as well as a Bachelors of Fine Arts in Photography.

James R. Hugunin

Something Is Crook in Middlebrook

a novel

ISBN 1-884097-43-X
ISBN-13 978-1-884097-43-0
ISSN 1084-547X

James R. Hugunin

Something Is Crook in Middlebrook

a novel

Journal of Experimental Fiction 43

**Journal of Experimental Fiction
Depth Charge Publishing
Geneva, Illinois**

Something is

Crook

in Middlebrook

(a comic database in 12 parts
which is thoroughly jolly and in
many respects useful to read)

By

James R. Hugunin

____

______ of _______

**This book is published in a limited
boxed edition of 26,
lettered A to Z
and signed by the author, in a limited
boxed edition of 100,
signed by the author, and in a general
trade edition hardcover.**

To my late mentor, the photo-image scavenger and collagist, Robert Heinecken

You know quotations are my only fog lights.
— *The Mysterious Flame of Queen Laona,*
   Umberto Eco

The point being that somebody already said that.
Somebody already said many of these things.
— *Girl Imagined by Chance,* Lance Olsen

Words, words, words taken out of place and mutilated,
words from other men—those were the alms left him by
the hours and the centuries.
— "The Immortal," Jorge Luis Borges

The original artist is incapable of copying. Therefore, in
order to be original, he only has to copy.
— Jean Cocteau

Whether Mr. Mutt with his own hands made the fountain or
not has no importance. He chose it.
— Marcel Duchamp, re: his Readymade,
   The Fountain

[R]eaders are travelers; they pass through lands belonging
to someone else, like nomads poaching their way across
fields they did not write, despoiling the wealth of Egypt to
enjoy it themselves.
— Michel De Certeau

Defiance of society includes defiance of its language.
— *Prisms,* Theodor Adorno

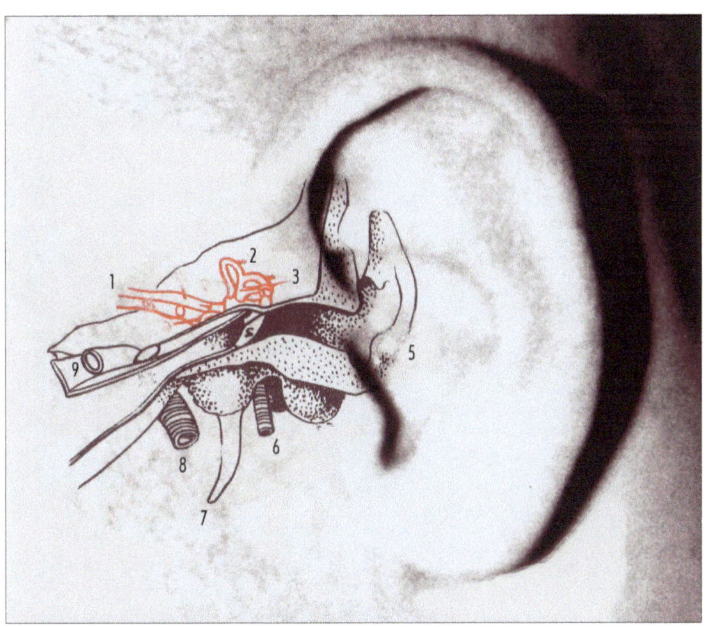

Arthur's Left Ear (Photo by Beth Reineck)

Arthur's T-Shirt, a Gift from Una Calda Bionda

Prologue

(or The R & D phase of R & D)

Arthur Anaphora Middlebrook

And Arthur Anaphora Middlebrook, Civil War hero, lives eighty-six years and begets Chester who lives sixty-one years and begets Richard who lives seventy-three years and begets Jerrald who lives eighty-three years and begets Arthur Strewth Middlebrook who develops the strangest ear of all. At least that's how Arthur S. Middlebrook relates it to me. Why he is given the gift/curse of profound hearing could be attributed to a roll of the cosmic dice. When I ask Art about it he merely quips: "Jim, there ain't any answer. There ain't going to be an answer. There never has been an answer. That's the answer."

Only later did I realize Art was plagiarizing (what he calls "playin' jarism") from Gertrude Stein, delighting in Stein's rhetorical use of *epistrophe*, the repetition of the word "answer" at the *end* of her sentences.

I first meet Art one summer day, a gentle day—mild, magical and innocent with great sailings of white cloud, serene and impregnable in the high sky, moving along like kingly swans on quiet water—with park paths once again strewn with those little sticks of wood that Eskimo Pies are attached to. The sun is in the neighborhood also, distributing its enchantment unobtrusively, coloring the sides of things that are unalive and livening the hearts of living things. Unfortunately, due to the several Long Island Ice Teas imbibed the night before in company with my wife, my tongue felt like a flashfried frazzfurter.

We both, independently, travel to the Winterthur Museum (Winterthur, Delaware) to immerse ourselves in Americana. There we find ourselves sharing a large oaken table in that estate's library's Dimmesdale Room. At this time he is still married to his first wife, Brittany, and both his ears are normal. He has friendly endearing spaces between his teeth and grin so glutinous you could hang wallpaper on it. Except for his eyes, in which resides a kind of light that often distinguishes visitors from other planets, he could be any overweight middle-aged American on vacation. I notice his gray trousers are pilling. Academics battling the "publish or perish" policies of our respective teaching gigs, we are both doing research. I, poking into the representation of prisoners in the United States in the nineteenth century—this carceral curiosity originating with my delight in Schopenhauer's dictum: *If you want a safe compass to guide you through life . . . you cannot do better than accustom yourself to regard this world as a penitentiary, a sort of penal colony*—he, hunching over an old Holmes stereoscopic viewer looking at late-nineteenth century stereo views, taking notes; beside him a copy of K. W. Jeter's Steampunk novel *Morlock Night.* One image he peruses just happens

Something is **Crook** in Middlebrook

to be of a black inmate at Eastern Pennsylvania Penitentiary being mugshot for the prison archives. I ask to look. We get to yakking. I show him a microfiche copy of startling front-page headlines from *The Chicago Tribune* dated September 4, 1949: WRONG MAN, RIGHT NAME CONVICTED IN MURDER TRIAL. As if on cue, his voice becomes chummy, face warming up like microwaved potpie. When I mention my wife practices psychoanalysis and is treating a obsessive-compulsive woman with a beautiful mint-pitched voice who accordion-folds any scrap of paper that happens to be in her hand for more than a minute, confesses he has been treated successively (but not successfully) by eleven different psychiatrists, two Reichian psychotherapists, a witch, and a lifestyle coach. Seems his theoretical focus is on the Hegelian notion that man can never directly confront the real world because of the innumerable sensory phenomena that intervene, but *rejects* the Hegelian notion of a world outside of humanly-perceivable phenomena. "I embrace the notions of Walter Lippmann, who argues that we are limited to the reality we build within ourselves from everyday experience and borrowed explanations. But my erudition is no doubt an aspect of my ignorance," he teases. "Say, do you know the modernist academic's prayer? . . . It goes thus." Assuming a subdued and earnest manner, hands raised in the prayer position, Art recites: " 'O Transcendental Signifier, give me strength and leisure and zeal to enlarge my knowledge. Our work is great and the mind of Man/Woman presses forward forever. Thou hast chose me in Thy grace to watch over the canon, the student body, and the accuracy of my bibliographies. As I am about to fulfill my duties, guide me in this immense work so that it may benefit Humankind for without Thy help not the least footnote would be accurate, nor would I be without the sinful stain of plagiarism. Amen.' A modernist prayer—that bit about plagiarism—now everyone cops from everyone. The freshest idea on the cleverest tongue is always someone else's—but never in its original form. My memory is made of paper, not of neurons, but pages."

"In the Beginning was the Word, now there's the Quote? You know Susan Sontag writes that 'A photograph could also be described as a quotation, making a book of photographs like a book of quotations."

"Ho! You *do* grok. But can we reverse Sontag's insight and assert that a book of quotations is like a book photographs? That's the kind of book I'm interested in."

"Well, I write like a photographer—I go out into the world of other people's writing and take snapshots."

He's delighted we share love of citation, and the ludic crazies of Alfred Jarry and Rabelais. And (surprise!) we're both from Chicago, residing only blocks apart. We exchange addresses, vow to get together for drinks sometime. When my cell-phone sounds the knock of a truncheon on cell-bars, I make a handwave exit. That afternoon, sipping steaming java at a funky coffee-house called Latte Lenya's, I tell my wife about how that odd guy looks a heck of a lot like an actor I don't much relish, Bob Hoskins.

I don't hear from him for months. Close to a year. Completely forget about him, in fact. Then the madness of an autumn prairie cold front coming through—gust after gust of disorder, temperatures falling, sky has as many subtly distinguished shades of gray as pair of flannel pants painted by Manet —you could feel something very weird was going to happen. Well, I'm lumbering down the gray expressway—listening to white news and black music, wondering why no so-called good music is any good anymore, staring at a Jeep Grand Cherokee's license plate in front advertising EXCEL—when my cell-phone knocks. It's a voice radiating strategic urgency, wanting to meet —it's Art. Important news.

"Blessed Benimming! It's torture *and* a tonic; like I've become a character in a J. G. Ballard story in which the sonic and the geological prevail. Jeeze, you are yourself, then you're not. I'm all rude shift, as if a pea has been slipped beneath the mattress of my life. Shit, I've been in the hospital. Upon discharge, I felt like a piece of paper that had once had coherent writing on it but had been through the wash: roughened, bleached, and worn out. I stand in awe of my body, it has become so strange to me. If only I'd been born without ears!" Concerned, I suggest the very hip new Italian-Mexican fusion restaurant wittily named Pasta Luego. "No!" He insists on a *quiet* place, a staid Japanese restaurant. "Hasuppa Musume, on Clark Street, my friend. Six p.m. and don't be late; they're performing *chanoyu*, a tea ceremony, for us. During which I'm gonna give you an earful! Like Big-Bang and new auditory universe is created. Eccentric sensoriality, my friend. You see, well, I'm *ear*-ly sensitive 'n weirdly sympathetic to that divine moment when my refrigerator kicks in, hums and, synaesthetically, I taste chocolate milk. Hell, the drift of modern history domesticates the fantastic and normalizes the unspeakable, so I'm a perfect expression of our times! Put phenomeno-logically: worlds design bodies, bodies design worlds—everything flows within a global tympanum, kemo sabe. We wear two question marks, one on each side of our heads like placards." This puts its hooks in me, that thing about bodies, gets me to the restaurant early. It's nearly empty. Art enters. Says not a word as he makes his way to my table, limping with a moon mad gait. Walks as if he is concentrating very hard on what he has in his pockets. Dressed like a fashion dummy in a golf pro shop. I compliment him on his brightly colored striped shirt.

"Jim, being slightly overweight, I have at my disposal two strategies to conceal this fact (you might want to jot this down): I can put on a shirt with vertical lines which makes me appear slender or I can, on the contrary, put on a shirt with horizontal lines, counting on the fact that the people I meet will misperceive my overweight as the illusion created by my inappro-priate dress. Imagine someone saying: 'Look, this stupid shirt makes him look fatter than he really is! . . . This morning, even the black, bent, bald shoeshiner who slicked my boots with his fingers had a name tag on his breast reading in capitals: ART. Until now most of my life has been barely audible background noise; now *everything* is roaring, the whole world, noise and more noise. Yesterday, a bird flew so close I could hear the gristle in its wing creak. Yep, there comes a time in every man's life, and I've had plenty of them!" For an awkward minute or two we practice what the Tierra del Fuegians term *mamihlapinatapai*: looking at each other hoping that one of us will offer to do something that both of us desire but are unwilling to do. Finally, he relents: "You know that the best you can expect is to avoid the worst," maximizing the minimum, copping maxim from Italo Calvino.

This is going to be a very weird evening. I suggest there is an honesty inherent in bulkiness if it is just the right amount: "People trust a certain amount of bulk in others." We sit cross-legged at a corner table. In truth, he looks like shit. His eyes are bloodshot. He has the 2000-yard combat fatigue stare that speaks of anxiety beyond the reach of Valium. His left ear is swollen and he has one fuckin' crazy ripper tattoo supered on it. His body language is machine-like, fitful, alternating between slow and rapid gestures, rigid and yet expressive, as if the operation is out of control, not quite corresponding to the will that lies behind it.

A woman in traditional geisha garb serves us tea in an oddly shaped bowl with marked bald patches in its glaze (such scruffiness being an instance of the aesthetic of *wabi*). She serves the bowl to Art with the best side towards him and bows to the floor. Tea leaves unfurl as they spin round, diffusing their color and flavor while the steam vanishes and mingles with the air. Art supports the bowl in his left hand and turns it twice clockwise 90 degrees so that the best sides faces his host. Throughout, Art turns his left ear slightly towards the action. I repeat his actions when so served. "Ho! We've become *chajin*, tea ceremony devotees, my friend," he says. "Since the advent of my super-hearing I like listening to my tea-kettle's tremble; the handle is slightly loose, and its shaking adds another harmonic layer over the tremulousness of the metal." As he tells me this I notice him unconsciously pressing on a vein on his left hand, making it fade to white and then return again to that very particular blue.

After our tea we order Bento boxes of choice Japanese delicacies. He leans forward and hands me a horoscope, *his* horoscope, clipped from *Vogue* magazine:

GEMINI (*June 21 - July 22*): You are like a frog at the bottom of a dry well, with fog in his mind. So try quitting your job but do it circumspectly. Geminis are prone to tearing their clothes off today. Odd people may stare at one of your ears. Smile away your blues with a new lover. Try eating undercooked omelettes and/or build yourself your dream house.

"Gemini. I'm at two with nature. I'm good at Longitude, bad a Latitude. I'm what scientists call a *dissipative structure*, I maintain myself in a stable state, but far from equilibrium. Yep, I'm in a world of shit. But I'm alive. And I am not afraid. *That,"* points vigorously, "was my horoscope the day *it* happened; in a physicist's femtosecond my brain sizzled 'n soured. Just looking at it now . . . well . . . a sour nausea rises in me like the mercury in a thermometer held in the flaccid mouth of a dying leper." Mops his brow. "This is an excerpt from my diary written several days after *it* happened while still in my hospital bed," he says, handing me a barely legible hand-written notebook page:

> *7:12 AM News on, about a kidnaped surgeon required at gunpoint to perform strange anal surgery on a masked patient, and my mouth tastes like it's been scrubbed out by an unlicensed nurse with a pair of gasoline soaked panties. My tight, pinched headache synchs perfectly, thoughts gliding aimlessly through my head like loose magnetic tape. I'm auditorily surfing through our fantasmo imperium. Limbs hang dizzy and sausage-like with minor flailing. I'm not sure I'm compelling, commanding, or controlling. Even*

Something is *Crook* in Middlebrook

What an amazing bit of drivel, I think, shaking my head. But I can feel the tingle of his stress-equations. And his face now seems to wear a coating, a cladding—the hospitalic subtraction of vigor and light. He speaks with a hurt twist of his mouth. When he does smile, small slightly misshapen stained teeth tentatively peek out at you.

"Yeah, yeah, I know, but that's what I was like then," says Art, relaxing into a middle-aged stoop as he relates a strange tale, an extra-ordinary mélange of firsthand testimony and hearsay. "Shit, I can identify the make of a car only by its engine noise. Now, some days begin like sym-phonies, some like jazz, some like a third grader learning to play the drums. Sometimes I think I hear the millenary sound of the earth's spin. Ya grok?

Do I believe him? Not until he demonstrates his newly acquired auditory power. He asks me to go the far side of the restaurant, turn my back to him, and whisper something. I do. Returning to our table, he relates back to me my exact words. When I express my amazement (my brain is forced into the steaming mulch of putrid truth!), he brags, "Ho! I can follow a pant-ing syllable right through time 'n space." I urge him on, while my tea goes as cold as a junkie's forgotten hamburger. So he tells me of his near-death experience, the acquisition of super-hearing in his left ear, his divorce, his new girl friend, and his cockloft-tipped dome-home.

"This weird ear of mine," he says, "why hearing with it has prompted me to observe . . . well . . . to play on a quote by Marcel Proust: 'The only true voyage of discovery . . . would be not to visit strange lands but to possess other ears.' (Proust had written 'eyes' in place of ears.) First time I experience my enhanced hearing I suffer a slightly outerspace feeling, my frame of reference tenuous 'n shuddering all around me. Why Jim it was like all my life I had been sleep-walking in the vicinity of the impossible *until* the advent of my super-hearing. Now the impossible is my daily fare. When I remove my wax ear plug from my weird ear, my auditory life becomes as independent as a Siamese cat. I'm out there bowling alone, if you catch my drift." Tears plunge shamelessly down his face like collapsing winos. "My across-the-street neighbors, the Pogacnics, still use an old Remington type-writer (that says loads about 'em). Ignoring the bitter winter chill, I open my window, train my weird ear northward and listen to their machine's ticli-ticla, ticli-ticla which does please me as much as the best arias by Galli-Curci and (ho!) plunges me into that state of inner contemplation usually reserved for

v

Art's Library (photo by Lew Koch)

violins, organs, and orchestras! When I mentioned this 'eartoid' to my workmate at the Museum, Mala, she informed me that the first significant mention of typewriters in Mexican literature does appear in Mariano Azuela's *Los de abajo* [The Underdogs, 1915, ed.], that most famous novel of the Mexican Revolution. Ya grok?" When I answer affirmatively, he begs *me* to write a sort of bio-graphy on him and his sonic adventures, but that I create this text from shards of writings culled from his vast library because, "Fragments are the only forms I trust."

"Jim, I'll give you unlimited access to my library—hey, we might even title the book *Ex Libris*!—as well as great *detail* about me and my life; in the process, we'll become buddies. I'll give you freedom to creatively fill in the story where my knowledge by acquaintance or description (thank you Bertrand Russell) are both lacking. But you mustn't assume that I'll always tell the truth; on the other hand, it would be wrong to think I lie. Recall Jacques Lacan's dictum: *Truth has the structure of a fiction.* Hopefully, the book will reflect both of our personlities and our love of books, a *Nachkonstruktion*, a rhetorical re-enact-ment shaped by both my own and your experi-ences and concerns. You might, if you wish, change my last name to Mr. Engelbert, after a hapless Hapsburgian in Jaromir John's novel *The Internal-Combustion Monster* who is, appropri-ately, driven nuts by the sounds of automobiles —the first *auralcentric* man. As a hook to readers uninterested in my personal life, include some-thing about discovering the final resting place of Jimmy Hoffa's old bones. Politically, I want the text to be a *counter-programming,* a screwing with the comfortable-familiar, if you get my drift. Finally, the text should be comedic as jokes were always told, pranks common in our family, be-cause life therein was unbearable. It was a way of denying what was happening through mockery, keeping it at a distance by making fun of it. When one's history become unbearable, you put your own misery on stage and laugh at it. Still true for me today. Grok?

"You'll come to see how I'm nothing but a wrapped onion, an onion wrapped in texts. I am what I read. Words are everywhere, inside me, outside me, impossible to stop them. All my life reading—from when I was a jerk-off teenager with

Something is *Crook* in Middlebrook

no more data than a black-'n-white sixty-five line-screen reproduction to the present—has meant a voluntary association with imaginary people whose company has been vastly more welcome than the company of anyone else in the vicinity. Since childhood, I've read an average of three books per week. As a tyke, I soon learned that books don't bleed, defecate, nor do they spank you. They and I became fast friends. Now I can't speak without thinking, *Where did I get that idea, that turn of phrase?* You know, we are a con-catenation of all we've heard and read. One must accept the fact that what one feels or says has been said before by the likes of: Anaxamander or Apollinaire or Amis or Aristotle or Almond or Ascher/Strauss or Auster or Ballard or Barth or Barthes or Bashō or Bakhtin or Bachelard or Barthelme or Baudrillard or Baudelaire or Beckett or Bellows or Borges or Boyle or Burroughs or Carey or Carlyle or Camus or Circero or Descartes or Derrida or DeLillo or DeMan or Ellul or Emerson or Federman or Franzen or Fuentes or Foucault or Goethe or Gombrowicz or Gadamer or Gaudi or Greenberg or Handke or Heidegger or Hume or Husserl or Ingarden or Issa or Jencks or Jeremiah or Joyce or Kerouac or Kundera or Kroker or LeWitt or Lowry or Lem or Marx or Musset or Merleau-Ponty or Nietzsche or Nabokov or Oates or or Olson or Ortega y Gasset or Orton or Pater or Plato or Pirsig or Pius X or Public Enemy or Pynchon or Quayle or Queen Latifah or Rilke or Ryle or Rivera or Ruskin or Said or Sartre or Sacks or Sebald or Siqueiros or St. John or Todes or Tzara or Thoreau or Tretyakov or Trotsky or Unamuno or Überoth or Valéry or Verne or Venturi or Vonnegut or Wittgenstein or Warhol or Xenophon or Malcolm X or Yevtushenko or Zhadanov or Žižek, but maybe also on the tongue of an Iowa tourist. Nothing can be said that has not been said before, my friend. We *are* intertextual, aggregates of the already-written. Recall Walter Benjamin's project of collecting quotations, a collection which would illustrate the infinite and regenerative seriality of language itself. A sheer exercise in *imaginative reasoning.*"

Ignoring the oxymoron, I nod agreement; so prolific a reader am I, too, that I usually can't separate my "original" ideas from those received from others. "Yes, we can say of narration what Merleau-Ponty says in general of all speech, namely, that through it my thoughts are already displaced into the thoughts of others, and other's into mine such that we are guided by a thought of which no particular person is the sole thinker, author, or origin."

"So you like pastiche, parody, puns, 'n quotation?" he queries rhetorically, a shade of citric joy in his voice. P.P.P.Q.! The despised stuff of modernist academics and literati. I rub my hands together enthusiastically. Once he's mentioned *that*, I'm sucked down the rabbit hole. I tell him of my scripto-visual propensities to traffic in quotation and intertextuality, Post-modern style. I mention dialogism, Mikhail Bakhtin and heteroglossia. He beams. I agree with him that once something rhymes in "Uh-merica," or "uh-literates," then it's a social norm. My self, he as other—we're hooked.

So I offer to *ghost-write* his autobiography. "It's perfect," I say. "How did we meet? By chance, like everyone else! Perfect. We can collaborate on a disruptive complicity. A real fictitious reality, I can write, wherein the reader can regulate at will the degree of his or her credulity, eh? I want to turn you into a word-being existing in a text that changes like a cloud as it goes along; that's as fugitive as the comings and goings of your hearing, my friend. But you'll have to have a little patience. I will also, you see, write about not only your life, but your opinions also, and what you overhear, too."

He declines: "Not ghost-written. Because our joint project will entail incorporating blatant and not-so-blatant coppings from divers texts—a lot from Martin Amis, *please,* whose Menippean satires I love—clandestinely overheard conversations, and recycled thoughts. I mean, there are so many great writers who've said so many great things that no one ever need express their own opinions ever again." Art suggests: "We might better escape lawsuits if we publish it under a pseudonym like 'Al Reddy Said,' or 'W. E. Rowtit,' or 'Isa Parot.' May be 'April Feurst.' The latter plays up both the ludic and epistemological implications, huh?"

I laugh. Sip my sake. He orders plum wine. The waitress brings us our red bean ice cream. I tell him if I'm going to put the time in writing the damn thing no pseudo-creature is going to get the credit or blame. "It's okay in *cacademia* today to be seen as (merely?) a *bricoleur,* a cobbler of pre-existing fragments, rather than an author-genius *per se*. Recombinant poetics, word-splicing akin to gene-splicing, is *in.* Brian Poole, a young Canadian scholar has shown in detail that whole pages of the Rabelais book by Mikhail Bakhtin are copied without attribution word-for-word from philosopher Ernst Cassirer. And then there's the case of Jerzy Kosinski's plagiarism. And in photography, Robert Heinecken's collages are aggregates made from shards of the already-seen; Sherrie Levine re-photographs classic photos by Ed Weston and Walker Evans."

"You got it, Jim! By the way, Levine's autobiographical statement is only a string of quotations pilfered from others. One never knows where one's thoughts originate, and when these thoughts merge with those of others, where one's language begins and where it converges with that of others within the dialogue all of us entertain with ourselves and with others."

"Yes, prior to capitalist social relations being instituted, such textual borrowing was common, expected even. But those greedy corporate attorneys?" worries Art.

"If the attorneys can't see it our way, tough. They're moderno-capitalist lackeys. Why some corporations today are even trying to copyright names, sue folks who use such common terms such as 'Leonardo', as in the case of a French company suing *Leonardo* magazine! Hell, to answer the query 'How can 'intellectual property' be 'protected'? I say the question contains the seed of its own confusion: it's the wrong verb about the wrong noun. So we'll use our collaboration as a trial case for 'fair use' of material in a creative artifact. Besides, what's to sue *for*? I only own a computer and a beater for an auto." He hands me a color Xerox of an excerpt from Erskine

> Why don't you do as I do, letting go of your thoughts as though they were the cold ashes of a long-dead fire?
>
> From a text by John Cage. A quote, though he doesn't give it as a quote and doesn't indicate its source. I know it's from Huang Po but Cage doesn't say so. Not that there's any reason why he should.
>
> I-said-it, you-said-it, quotes, sources, originality—all relics of a time when even words and the ideas they hint at were considered commodities, things a person could claim or possess.
>
> If I were to have a thought that no man has ever had before—a near impossibility—how, even then, could I call it my own, since it would have simply congealed or condensed from the whole of my experience, which is not really my experience, being involved inextricably with the experiences and thoughts of thousands or even millions of other men?

Something is *Crook* in Middlebrook

Lane's *Game-Texts: A Guatemalan Journal* with his marginal gloss. Art beams. And when Art beams, he looks especially like Bob Hoskins. "My justi-fication for what I call *playin' jarism*," he says, rubbing his eyes. I give the clipping a more than averagely puzzled squint. Soon we are making plans for our first collaborative session.

After our dinner I wander over to Office Depot. A shipment of new notebooks is in, and the pile is impressive, a beautiful array of blues and greens and reds and yellows. I pick one up and see that the pages have the narrow lines I prefer. Embarking on my writing project, I feel a new note-book is in order. It will be helpful to have a separate place to record Art's thoughts, his observations, and his questions. In that way, perhaps, things may not get out of control. I pick one out, gingerly fanning its pages with my thumb; it is a standard 8 ½ x 11 notebook with 100 pages, but something about it calls out to me. I am at a loss why I find it so appealing, except for the fact that its unique destiny in the world would be to hold the green-inked words coming from my Montblanc fountain pen. Holding my newly purchased notebook, I prepare myself for my third encounter with Art by recalling the wisdom Poe asserts about his master detective Dupin's strategy something about "an identification of the reasoner's intellect with that of his opponent."

Exhaust pipes diffuse their pollutants like the pollen of a new era, sowing the future flora of a sickly civilization in the lungs of Chicagoans and tourists alike. The sun climbs steeply out of its hiding and stands benignly in the lower sky pouring down floods of enchanting light and preliminary ting-lings of heat. I arrive at Art's dome-home, witness first hand the peculiarities in his abode. Art clears the debris from the surface of his kitchen table—dead matches, cigarette butts, eddies of ash (left by neighbor Deena Boettcher), spent ink cartridges, a few coins, ticket stubs, doodles, a pamphlet titled *How to Deal with Crazies Without Turning into One,* and a dirty handkerchief—then serves up shots of espresso. A black bird whips by the window as if shot out of a grenade launcher.

We sip as I listen to Art's suggestions in a state of continuous partial attention, the teaming jungle of his words, like: "Can you problematize for the reader whether I am the teller or the told? Put a self-reflexive exuberance into it? Be sure to leave plenty of semantic gaps (what literary theorist Wolf-gang Iser calls *leerstellen*) in the text. Shuffle the order to events so as to encourage the reader to approach the text in what Roland Barthes terms a free *tmesic* manner, that is, encourage skip-reading of the text. Say, even combine aspects of my art criticism therein, making a sort of *criti-fiction* of the thing? Moreover, Jim, you must capture that delicacy of hearing I'm now endowed with. To play on a line of poetry by Paul Celan: 'The world is *hear*, I have to carry you.' Henry Thoreau once noted in his journal: 'A slight sound at evening lifts me up by the ears, and makes life seem inexpressibly serene and grand,' but he didn't suffer the synaesthetic *tasting* of each sound as I do! You know, each voice has an existence of its own; its sound, its individual rhythm, its peculiarities of pitch and intonation that create a counterpart to what is being said. For instance, every woman's voice on the telephone tells me whether she is attractive; her tone reflects back—as self-confidence, natural ease and self-regard—all the admiring and desirous glances she has ever received. This I recognize on first hearing, a familiar quotation from a book never read. But I'm also privy to the unnameable: the purring and jud-

Something is Crook in Middlebrook

dering appliances like refrigerators and microwave ovens, the buzz of personal computers, the drone of building maintenance systems, and the awful noise of automatic garage doors. Ho! Some noises evoke the unbandaging of great giants in agony. And remember, each sound has its synaesthetic taste counterpart! Shit, it's all stuff that can tear through the very fabric of one's sanity. To put it bluntly, can you transform the fiasco of my reality into a howling success? Tap into that rhetorical alchemy of yours to create an hyperbolic wow? Make the book a monument to my spizzerinctum? Can ya?"

Spizzerinctum? I looked it up in my OED: the will to succeed, but also gimcrackery. And I thought I was pedantic! Soon I am meeting an even more pedantic Al, for whom a serious discussion seems more like a succession of inequations, containing several unknowns, integrals, and reshufflings of complex numbers. "I don't know if you've noticed," declares Al the first time I meet him, "but if you take the dimensions, the circumference, and the weight of a baguette, you get the golden section!" And then there's Art's across-the-street neighbor, that blind photographer, Peven, producer of a fiction of surfaces and a personage who, even garbed in a cashmere suit (instead of this usual T-shirt declaiming *SEMPER IN OBSCURUS*) and carrying a Braille copy of Jacques Derrida's *Memoirs of the Blind*, looks like a tramp. His mantra is: "Once the world has been photographed it is never the same again." I meet Una, enjoying her estrogenic voice which she can pitch low 'n throaty putting little burr in it that makes her interlocutors shiver. She has a way of brushing her hair out of her eyes in a sweeping gesture that looks like a drowning swimmer suddenly shooting to the surface of the water. Art warns me her elbows are argumentative. But she provides noisy aural sex to Art (it is rumored her erotic confessions would increase pantihose, petticoat and high-end hearing aide sales nationwide). She wins my affection when I learn her favorite type of pasta is *strozzapreti* ("strangled priests").

Eventually, I'm a regular guest at Art's dome-home, privy to his most intimate dealings and intimate with his privy. Tape recorder in hand, I later find myself having to decipher a collage of contravivulating conversations. "I've had few friends," offers Art sheepishly, as I quiz him, "because I suffer from that sort of social awkwardness which comes from too much tolerance and understanding, but, ho!, I'm always afraid, too, that I might lose my little shy streak and join the great mass of people who despise you if you don't dominate them. Ya grok? Now *you* have a subtle, contradancing mind and so can understand me better than most." I just nod an affirmative and give him my best archaic smile. And so our collaboration begins.

"It used to be that," observes Art, "true originality consisted in trying to behave like everybody else without succeeding; but—*Blessed Benimming!* —there is nothing more compliant now than the modernist wish to be original —to find one's own voice, etcetera. Now it's very *postmodern* (thank those Reader Response theorists) to develop your own ear! So, ironically, my weird ear has propelled me firmly into PoMo-land. Ergo, this text of ours should be about *hearing* texts and not about voicing them. Ya grok?"

Besides his commitment to the already-written, the already-heard, since we are living in this postmodern era of "weak thought," of indeterminancy where nothing is definite, Art insists I drop all definite articles in the text. I balk. We compromise. I will drop *the* and *a* in my narrative when possible, but retain those words in direct speech of the characters. He wants the text to read like schizophrenic writing mixed with the pedanticisms of academic discourse. "Mix high 'n low discourse, the playful with the serious, found text with new; create a new type of novel, a *Ludicakadroman*! Jim, prove France's *Prix des Critiques* winner Brice Parain's quip wrong: 'One cannot at the same time be a scholar and a knockabout comedian'. Reverse that verse from Ecclesiastes so it reads: 'It is better to go to the house of mirth, than to the house of mourning.' Ya grok?"

He likes the interjections "ho!" and "Blessed Benimming!" I pepper the writing with 'em. A fan of Robert Heinlein's sci-fi, especially *Stranger in a Strange Land*, he says using "ya grok" on occasion would be most appropriate. I acquiesce. Next he wants, everywhere the word 'exaggerate' is used, me to spell it with three g's. I nix that! Our biggest fight occurs over his desire to occasionally replace "and" with the contraction " 'n," both in the speech of the characters and in the main narrative. I argue it seems arbitrary: "We need to be consistent here." No go. He is granitic on this point. Finally, he begs me to "fill the text with references to Chicago's perennial contact sport, *weather,* because that ace PoMo writer, Donald Barthelme, purged such from his stories, told his students clouds 'n wind were as toxic to authorial success as those damn commas." I grudgingly agree, but begin to feel as constrained as Rauschenberg's famous goat with the tire wrestled over the animal's hind legs.

The strangest and most interesting aspect for me was that he insisted I write a book length story about him, then using that story as textual grist, cop fragments from *that* narrative and recontextualize them into the final book."Oh, my god!" I exclaim, sensing things are getting out of hand. "You never know what is enough 'til you know what is more than enough. Why, Jim, *think*. That way the *whole* text is a Frankenstein, like those late photo-collages of Robert Heinecken's, but using words. A suturing together of fragments. By the way, ironic isn't it that our textual monster will, like Frankenstein's, be a product of galvanic activity, electronic word-processing!"

We both got a good laugh out of that. But when I complain that that tactic, albeit interesting, would be enormously time consuming, he counters: "Hey, that's what us academics have a black belt in—consuming time and regularizing our irregularities, setting right irrectitudes," he defends. "You know producing this tome will allow you to engage a vast *corpus* of problems, assumptions, adumbrations, fictions, prejudices, tenets; the sphere of random beliefs and hopeful guesses; the whole world, in brief, of abstract opinion and disputation about matters of feeling, etcetera."

I scratch my head. Rub my eyes. Swallow hard. I finally give in. The strategy is so interesting to me, but I hope the labor is worth it. It was obvious Art has the egocentricity of those who speak only in the first person: he talks about himself, about others in relation to himself, and about what they say about him. He peppers his statements with "This is and is not true."

"Okay, I'll do it," I say. "Literature is the fragment of fragments." So I write an eight hundred-page biography and then use it as the basis for the final text, yanking large fragments from this "unoriginal-original" text galvanizing them into the new text, then redacting that tome down to manageable size.

Something is *Crook* in Middlebrook

The title of this text has not been chosen without grave and solid deliberation. As the text is cobbled together from fragments of hundreds of sources, I suggest titles: *Metabook* or *Holiday from Authorship* or *The Ear's Embawdiment.* He balks, *Ex Libris* or *Adventures in the Signosphere* is suggested. "Much too arcane," I say. "How about *Reality Monster*? Your ear's gathering more and more *reality*." No go, too sensationalistic for him. He agrees the title should relate to his *ear*-ly gift and how it permits him to be privy to the confessions of *homo stupidus*. I then suggest *(Ear)ly Warning.* Another no; too much like a political thriller he points out. Or how about *The Man with too much Content*? No! Then *he* offers the paradoxical title of *Memoirs of an Amnesiac,* the title of Erik Satie's autobiography). *I* nix that one. Then he comes up with *Heard Mentality*. I like it somewhat but, finally, I get a more appropriate idea. Since his middle name, Strewth, is a mild oath in Australian slang, I play off on that and do further research. I find that the phrase "Something's crook in Middlebrook" is Aussie argot for "Something's screwed up." Perfect punful title. I run the idea by him. Delighted, Art agrees to it: "So let's collaborate! As French poet Arthur Rimbaud remarked, 'I is an other.' You are my other. So let the games begin!"

"A collaboration! How very Postmodern," I remark, "just like theorists Gilles Deleuze and Félix Guattari's famous authorial partnership." Our conversation reaches an exciting density. Like those Frenchies's texts, Art's and mine will be a product of a multiplicity without unity as there is no unique author in the traditional sense to ground the work.

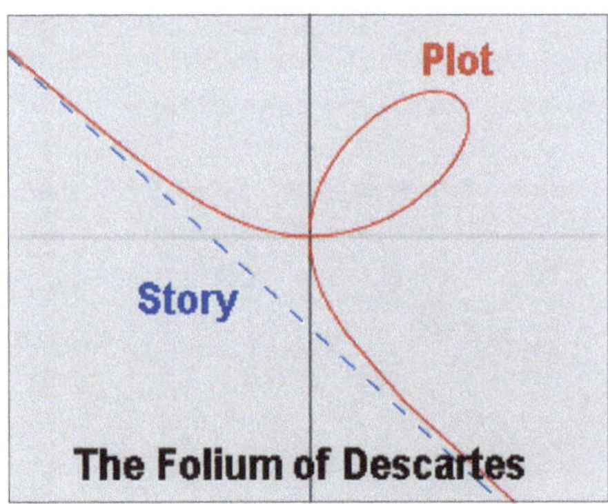

Before he departs, Art gives me a curious analytical geometric diagram. "Jim, see the straight blue line? That's the *story* events of my life; the red curving line plots Descartes's Folium and is how I want you to treat the *plot* of the novel, in recurring loops. Moreover, this folium figures the flux of my lived experience: the flow of the modifications of the past that drag along like the tail of a comet and the continuing gushing forth of the now. My life is a private culture, but that will be what I'll be showing you, letting you into, my private culture. Ya grok?" I nod heartily.

"And here is yet another conceptual tidbit to chew on," he says slapping a self-published postcard in my hand like some surgical nurse handing a scalpel to a doctor. "This is simply the Rosetta Stone, the key, to my whole philosophy 'n aesthetic." As he stands up his knees make

1) HEW:YEW::

a) I:you

b) hay:you

c) few:many

d) butcher:ewe

e) creature:victim

1) a b c d e
   o o o o o

Something is *Crook* in Middlebrook

two quick cracks, like the reports of a .22 caliber handgun.

"Really? Uh, thanks."

"Overall Jim, what I want of your text is a *reversal* of Freud's dictum 'Where id was there ego shall be.' Where ego was id shall be. Ya grok?"

"Tell me the story and then we'll figure out the ending. See ya in a week. And ya gotta read this before then." Hands me a scholarly study of plagiarism.

So we put our hearts and minds together in very long discussions over why it should matter that the world be lovable, have strident critiques of our broken modernity that sublimates happiness into consumer pleasure, that leaves us only the dull coin of habit, law, and procedure, and leads to the

belief we can fake life and no one will notice. We play miniature golf and chat, exchange e-mail, letters, postcards, phone messages (he answers the phone, "Mmmmmmmmmm-yyyellow"), photographs. I diligently decipher Art's nearly illegible, barbed wire-like scrawl on Post-It notes, old napkins, tattered envelopes, stained recipe cards, binder paper, even the backs of postage stamps—until the following text is born. In the process, I discover he wears boxer shorts of combed Sea Island cotton and mixes his own salad dressing. Once he even sees fit to provide me with a Xerox from his buddy Alfred Schmerbauch's diary so I can "grok" the extent of this eminent Professor of Combinatorial Analysis's pedanticism:

The contacts between inhabitants of a large city like Chicago are so numerous that one can hardly be surprised if there occasionally occurs between them a certain amount of friction which generally speaking is of no consequence. It so happened that I was recently present at one of these unmannerly encounters which generally take place in the vehicles intended for the transport of passengers in the Chicagoland area in the rush hours. There is not in any case anything astonishing in the fact that I was a witness to this encounter because I frequently travel northward to Northwestern University in this fashion. On the day in question the incident was of the lowest order, but my attention was especially attracted by the physical aspect and the headgear of one of the protagonists of this miniature drama. This was a man who was still young, but whose neck was of a length which was probably above the average and whose hat-ribbon had been replaced by a plaited cord.

Something is *Crook* in Middlebrook

Curiously enough, I saw him again two hours later on campus engaged in listening to some advice of a sartorial order which was being given him by a woman in the company of whom he was walking up and down, rather nonchalantly I should have said.

There was not much likelihood now that a third encounter would take place, and the fact is that from that day to this I have never seen the young man again, in conformity with the established laws of probability.

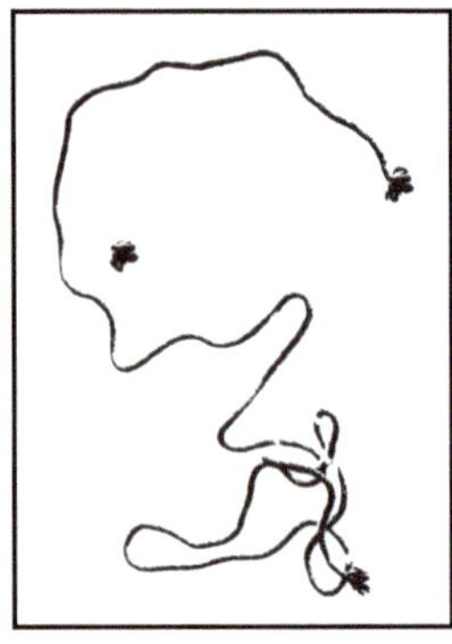

He fills me in on one Pau D'Arco, Art and Al's French Canadian friend who owns and chefs at their favorite hangout, The Bowmanville Bistro where, at any one time, you may rub shoulders with an Argentinean dancer, a Swiss homeopath, a Mexican secretary, an Australian mother of five, a young Bangladeshi computer programmer, a pediatrician visiting from Maine, and a Filipino accountant. Pau is a master of *l'omelette à la baveuse,* an undercooked omelette skillet-dish which Art dubs "*Le Grand* Pan," remarking that,"*Le Grand* Pan," remarking that, "*Le Grand* Pan *est* more" (punfully playin' jarism with Pascal's translation of a famous passage by Plutarch on the death of the gods). Art shows me a rapid line sketch he did of Pau cooking over his grill, while telling him, "Notzing engages more completely *avec* zee beautiful diversity of zee material world zhan zee simple act of eating, *mais oui*?" Moreover, our French chef is a fanatic collector of back issues of *Almanach Vermot*—a fanciful amalgam of *Old Moore's Almanack, Film Fun,* and *The Girl Guide's Diary*, each page garnished with feeble jokes popular in French bourgeois households during the late nineteenth and early twentieth centuries. Pulls out a copy Pau loaned him. Pau's witty take on Art's *ear*-ly affliction comes in the form of a quote from the poet Verlaine: "*Ni tout à fait la même ni tout à fait une autre* ("Neither completely the same nor completely other.")

"I, in turn," explains Art, "lent Pau my childhood copy of Vernon Grant's superb nine-teen thirty-four fantasy book, *Mr. Mixie Dough, Baker Man*. Mixie—a "goof" living in "Behind the Clouds Town" (drawn imaginatively by Grant, a School of the Art Institute of Chicago-trained illustrator) —pulls his country's King out of clinical depression with a special happiness cake. Brimming with color 'n cute, read and reread to me by my Grandpa Detleff, that book sparked my interest in cooking and superlative cuisine."

After four years of perusing such stuff seasoned with numerous quibbles and compromises—being half drunk on my learning curve as I peruse his extensive library—I realize Art does not answer to any of the gods we answer to: he sits up late at night, listening for the knock of The Semiologic Police. His first reaction to my initial draft was: "*Blessed Benim-*

Something is *Crook* in Middlebrook

ming!" accompanied by physical symptoms we shouldn't dwell upon. Wall-to-wall rewrite! "Cut it to twelve episodes, like in Godard's film *Vivre Sa Vie*, ya grok?" Final result? A fragmented, discontinuous narrative that bears the marks of repeated emendations—additions, deletions, embellishments, and other wonky textual manipulations. Art's now thrilled with it. Laughs suddenly, shows fat back teeth. Thought his pounding, overtaxed heart would jump through forty-seven hoops of joy.

To celebrate the book's completion, he invites me over to his dome-home. Outside Indian summer is erasing the palette of greens: no more summer lime, almond, emerald, celadon, or olive; now the foliage is blotched with madder, carmine, cinnabar, coral, scarlet, brick and dark-red, maroon, blood and ruby—the world glazed a rosy hue beneath a supernaturally blue sky. Inside, there's a kind of white that is more than white, a white that is aggressively white, that did its work on everything around it, nothing escaped. In the dome's entryway is a framed, punful postcard (a real *multum in parvo*), red background with white lettering reading "Come See Come Saw." I notice a curiosity cabinet filled with many oddities: a postcard depicting Marcel Duchamp's enigmatic 1916 sculpture *With Hidden Noise*, an old postcard depicting a "Tom Thumb Wedding" (a tableau composed of children playing at adult roles) staged at the Campbellite Church in Bethany, Nebraska in 1900, a publicity photo of British playwright Joe Orton, a badly worn square of carpet upon which (as the certificate of authenticity verifies) General Lafayette inadvertently spilled his glass of Madeira during his visit to Boston, a yellowed, worn and torn pamphlet by Charles Napier on "The Moral Significance of Fishes" (1870), a vintage copy of *Tom Swift and His Wizard Camera* by Victor Appleton, and a Jurassic gem (a superb specimen of Baltic amber) in which is forever suspended a spider-eating-a-fly placed next to chunk of gallium the size of a damson plum. On a pedestal next to this cabinet is an eco-gift from his ear-mate, Una: an "Eco-Sphere" glass globe harboring inside four tiny brine shrimp, a feathery mass of meadow-green algae draped on a twig of corral, and microbes in the invisible millions. "Gaia in a bottle is how Una describes it." On the wall is a framed print of Henri Rousseau's late-nineteenth-century painting, *Pierre Loti,* probably because the sitter sports a single cauliflower ear on the right side of the face that looks like an artificial hearing device or a de-formity.

Once on his turf, he treats me a platter of *andouillette de Troyes*, special sausage home-made by his new girl friend, Una, who is a card-carrying member of *L'Association Amicale des Amateurs d'Andouillettes Authentique.* These delicious French delights are accompanied by a salad of bananas, green grapes, cann-ed pineapple, marshmallows, and lemon Jell-O, all washed down with an unusual cocktail he's concocted: "O.J.'s Bronco." Gin, grenadine, juice from a freshly knife-slashed orange, stale lemon-juice from concentrate, and a drop of Pennzoil—served over crushed ice in a white mug with a small plastic knife for a swizzle-stick. We clink glasses, sip to the uncertain future. He then chats me up about his new squeeze.

"In some ways Una, my ear-source, reminds me of my first college girl friend, Rhonda Perlmutter III, who came from a long line of dentists and became one. Ho! Like Rhonda, Una's fav food is exotic sausages, her handbag says 'Someday I'd like to see a UFO,' while her oft-worn skirt declaims 'My mother lives in Bergen, Norway. Ya grok?"

Something is *Crook* in Middlebrook

We both have a good laugh, then Art puts on a CD of Smetana's "String Quartets #1 and #2"—written while the composer had just lost his hearing—and reads a poem by Una celebrating their initial bizarre sexual encounter:

> *And I poked at his thinning hair —*
> *And he said not there . . .*
> *And I poked at his ear —*
> *And he screamed, my dear!*

Three drinks later, I am a cocktail shaker of hilarity and awe; the weather in my brain is as warm and bright as in Aruba; conversation with this impossible possible philosopher's man takes on the expansiveness of the waistline of the morbidly obese: he mentions Una's excitement at an interview she did appearing in a well-known women's magazine in the column "Yes, I'm Dating *HIM*"; then we explore a range from the bawdy to the scholarly, from off-color jokes to the most obscure footnote-of-footnote references, from dumb puns to eloquent poetry, from analysis of lyrics in German drinking songs to the bliss (for him) of listening to John Cage's infamous silent composition *4' 33"* to a heated discussion over the goose-bumps experienced by women listening to the feminist lyrics of Tori Amos; from a chat over the ghost authorship of the Hardy Boys's mysteries, to marginal glosses of obscure Arabic texts, to how often to oil a racing bike's *derailleur,* to how *hornets* are metamorphosed through the action of heat from nearby igneous rocks, to a critique of Jeff Chandler's portrayal of a Naval Captain in *Away All Boats*, to a semiotic and medical analysis of Jim Jarmusch's film *Coffee and Cigarettes* (to which I ask: 'Is that a theoretical position or a real position?'), to the secret recipe for Windmill cookies, to life after The Oil Crash, to a detailed list of the best ingredients for trail-mix, to a heated debate on whether reincarnation is a mode of expression for stability in midst of postmodernist flux.

"Speaking of reincarnation," Art segues into the why of my visit, "I assume you've got the new incarnation of our collaboration with you?" Prissily pats finny tips against other five finny tips.

I nod an affirmative. "It's one prolonged hovering flight of the subjective over the out-stretched ground of your queer case exposed. But too bad we can't set the action in the Arctic or the Antarctic; novels set there are now receiving development grants."

His eyes brighten and deepen, dancing with reflections as he first holds the manuscript in his mitts; he enthuses, like Dr. Frankenstein, "It's alive! Ho! It bursts at the semes! It'll give 'em a thousand and one nights of interpretive pizzazz, yes?" Then, more ominously, "But, like the original Frankenstein monster, will it, too, be hounded to death [by the critics]? Will it? Huh? Ideally, the critics should write: *The border line in the author's mind between originality and imitation is truly difficult to ascertain; yet all his (and his protagonist's) acts and remarks are peculiarly his.*"

"Ya? Well," I reply, "I'm just *filled* with antisappointment, that is, anticipation colliding head-on with the certainty of its own doom. I can imagine a critic writing: *Nothing could be more reminiscent of a junk shop than this collection of Rabelaisian hodgepodge, a mass of heterogeneous objects with a few valuable things among them but no one of which the product of the dealer's own talents,* or less pedantically, *the author cavorts through the dignified hideaway of his subject's private life with all the tact and discretion of a lobotomized orangutan which has just sat on a hedgehog. Pure laughterature.*"

"Well Jim, I really fear the critic who writes, 'Your book is both good and original; but the part that is good is not original, and the part that is original is not good; parts marred by pallid jokes and instances of pointless pseudo-exactitude; it's pretty damn dense, like a top chef's reduction.' I can imagine another critical bark: 'You get joists, braces, buttresses (a skipful of teachabilities): you don't get a house—books have to shape a solid structure.' What say, kemo sabe?"

"We no longer believe in a unified totality, only fragments; pure linguistic oxygen! So I intuited, like Lev Manovich, that *the database* is displacing well-structured narrative as the dominant cultural form. Hey, *you* urged, 'Datamine me,' and so we got a 880-page tome that folded in data from your library plus all that new sonified data gleaned via your weird ear. All that shit I fragged into *this* much slimmer book and arranged in discrete numbered lexia. A hard copy just thick enough, as per your request, to fit under that awfully wobbly kitchen table leg (a nice way to determine length as anything, I admit). I also agree with your idea to typeset using all-around large margins since such shows one, as you put it, '… to be a person of delicate sensibilities with love of color 'n form 'n who holds oneself aloof from the multitude 'n lives in one's own dream world of beauty 'n good taste'."

We step outside, past his lawn sign reading: CAUTION: MAN READING. (He reads as others pray, as gamblers follow the spinning of the roulette wheel, as drunkards stare into vacancy, a saurian of the book world, an antediluvian survivor of an extinct species who weighed each tome in his hand and sniffed at it as sentimental as a girl's smelling of a rose. I suspected the phenomena of existence did not begin to become real for him until they had been set in type, arranged, composed, collected and, so to speak, sterilized in a book). The sun is roaring in the sky and sending great tidings into our middle-aged bones. I watch Art with clogged calm, almost love-like, and a sense of getting nearer to something. I absent-mindedly feel a large envelope containing a self-portrait-with-ear, with a poem on the back which he gives me along with praise partially copped from the mouth of James Cagney in *Yankee Doodle Dandy*: "My mother thanks you. My father doesn't thank you.

My sister would've thanked you. I thank you. Your picture is in God's wallet. But with the *caveat* that, Holy Fuck, you *do not* typeset the manuscript in *The New Yorker*'s famed Caslon-typeface. It ain't the font of youth no more! Ya grok?

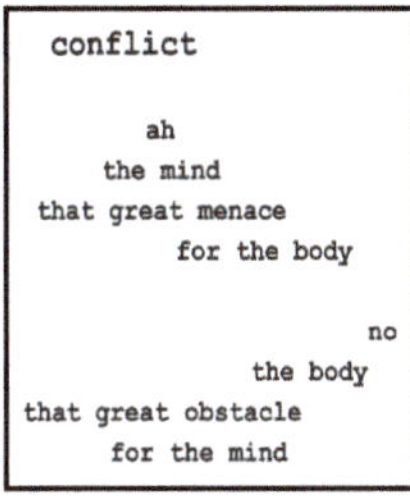

```
conflict


        ah
    the mind
that great menace
          for the body


                  no
              the body
that great obstacle
    for the mind
```

Something is **Crook** in Middlebrook

"Critic! . . . Okay, how about something totally *now*, like Verdana, designed for the Web?"

"Rimes with veranda, nice, relaxing. And my cousin, a web-designer, just named her new-born daughter Verdana! So sure. Bit of trivia to amuse your readership or reader's hip, that is, hip readers: until this ear-thing happened," Art confides, "I had acquired a local reputation as a savant due to the fact that I was known to never read newspapers. I'd get into a taxi and say, 'The library, and step on it'; there I'd steal books one page at time, reconstructing them in the safety of my study like a clandestine editor. Shit, now I subscribe to both *The Tribune, The Sun-Times*, and *The Chicago Defender* too. The Sunday editions as well. Sounds mad? Well, my museum workmate, Mala, warned me that the Spanish words for *reading* (*lectura*) and *madness* (*locura*) were closely related."

"Ah, surely the handiwork of wisdom and . . . ah . . . extremely acatalectic," I pedantically reply, bemused. "Surely you're the most Omnidirectional Thinker I've encountered—ever!"

On parting, he shakes my hand a bit too vigorously, exclaiming: "'Til we meet again, keep yer powder dry, yer aspidistra flyin', 'n yer deuces wild. Ya grok?" Gives me one of those gigantic smiles, hard to believe in, that makes one feel guilty for not believing it. I leave him basking in impassive happiness, as if his heart and brain overflow with many, many multicolored marshmallows. As I saunter down his arc-shaped sidewalk, I sense myself stepping back into the rhythm of life where the days multiply all by themselves.

I'm off for a working weekend at my lake cottage near Indiana Dunes State Park at the southern tip of Lake Michigan. On the way, I do a double-take at an odd billboard, a Fundamentalist rant in Brobdingnagian-scaled Helvetica font screaming: *You're not in Chicago anymore, asshole!*

Amen.

— James R. Hugunin, Chicago, Illinois

The Database

I only quote others the better to quote myself.
— Montaigne

*The space of language today is not
defined by Rhetoric, but by the Library.*
— "Language, Counter-Memory, Practice," Michel Foucault

*Strings of language extend in every direction to
bind the world into a rushing, ribald whole.*
— Donald Barthelme

*His ears were growing sensitive to a preter-
natural and intolerable degree, and he had long
ago stopped the cheap mantel clock whose ticking
had come to seem like a thunder of artillery.*
— "The Dreams in the Witch House," H. P. Lovecraft

Enhancing my Hearing (ink on paper, 1952) Arthur Middlebrook,
age 5 (Kindergarten sketch an uncanny anticipation of weird ear)

You can hear ambient sounds during trash collection day in Art's
neighborhood and what Art hears when walking in Chicago's Loop
recorded with a shotgun mike and amplified to give a sense of
what living with super-hearing is like. On the Internet, go to the urls:
http://www.uturn.org/Crook/earsounds.mp3
and to
http://www.uturn.org/Crook/earsound2.wav
(40-second download times for .mp3 file with high-speed cable).

Something is *Crook* in Middlebrook

1.0

~~It is the best of times, it is the worst of times, it is the age of wisdom, it is the age of foolishness, it is the epoch of belief, it is the epoch of incredulity, it is the season of Light, it is the season of Darkness, it is the spring of hope, it is the winter of despair, the gigantic anthropological circus is in full-swing. Art has everything before him, he has nothing before him … he has a thirst for contradiction like a thirst for wine.~~

City of Chicago, like spatter of ink on a map. Another day in our deMOREcracy.

Something's crook in Middlebrook. Something's wrong with Arthur Strewth Middlebrook that is. As he comes limping down sidewalk, he can hear your heart a-tickin' from across street. Or sitting high up in his cockloft on top his golf-ball shaped dome-home with his left ear focused in your direction, he audits conversations hundreds of yards away. Pure electronic hum of untuned radio some four blocks away bores through his *cabeza.* With swollen ear, gimpy left foot, at 55, Art finds everything auditory to larboard closer than soundings to starboard. Only malleable waxy ear goop purchased at Walgreen Drugs thumb-stuffed into auditory canal can balance his auditory perceptions. How would you recognize him? Could be stunt-double for beefy actor Bob Hoskins, except for enlarged left ear, that gimp, and his left-handedness. If an artist did symbolic portrait of Art, it'd look like some fantastic cartoonish creature out of repertoire of Chicago Imagists such as Jim Nutt or Karl Wirsum. When watches frightening films, put his hands over his ears, not his eyes.

Wants to audit *mucho* stuff, so his Chicana workmate, Mala Gradecido—who sports teeth like screaming horse in Picasso's *Guernica*—blesses him in Spanglish after each museum shift: "*Bato*, go *con la oreja al vuelo* (Friend, go with ears wide open). She wittily captures Art's new selfhood in punning couplet: "*Hombre nuevo/hambre nueva.*"

"Yes, new man, new hunger; I'm fearfully and wonderfully made," agrees Art.

1.1   It all begins little over year ago in eighth biggest city on earth. Budget cuts at Chicagoland suburban jerkwater college art department. You know, large campus green with bad imitations of Richard Neutra architecture built circa 1965. Classrooms that have tall, narrow windows easy to defend with student desks firmly bolted to floor. Art department in basement of science building so student work nearly invisible. Must not risk offending anyone. One ominous word from Dean Gerta Hackenkreuzler and Art's yearly renewable part-time pedagogical position teaching "New Forms"—critical writing, conceptual art, performance, video, digital art—to suburban brats *ist Kaput*. His usual Gramscian mantra—"Pessimism of the intelligence, optimism of the will"—isn't working any more. Last class Art declaims: "God is dead, Marxism is a specter—neither alive nor dead—budget cuts are rampant, students seeping into my classes are increasingly stegosaurus-rugged no-hopers, parrot-crested blankies, Ayn Rand-wannabes, and I don't feel so hot myself." Fellow faculty there are what you're bound to get when you deal with people who want to write their own lives: star bursts, black holes, white dwarves, dead suns. Decides to go back to school for reskilling.

Imagine. A garden with a hundred kinds of trees, a thousand kinds of flowers, a hundred kinds of fruit and veggies. Suppose, then, that gardener of this garden knows no other distinction than between edible 'n inedible, nine-tenths of this garden would be useless to him. He would pull up most enchanting flowers and hew down noblest trees and even regard them with a loathing and envious eye. That's *capitalism*. Imagine same *jardin des plantes*, but now gardener can't even distinguish between edible 'n inedible. That's *fascism*.

That is what Art used to tell his "Introduction to Art" students. Used to tell them anyway until course evaluation forms came back with comments like:

✔ THIS COURSE IS COMPLETELY WORTHLESS IN PRE-PARING US FOR REEL *[SIC]* LIFE.

✔ THIS CLASS HAS NO REDEEMING VALUE.

✔ INSTRUCTOR TOOK US ON TOUR TO STUDY INGENIOUS DRAWINGS IN LAVATORIES.

✔ SEND THE PROF TO BOB JONES UNIVERSITY FOR REMEDIAL TRAINING.

✔ DEFEND OUR MORALS, DEFUND ART (BOTH ART AND ART MIDDLEBROOK).

✔ PROF SAID ART IS ALWAYS AIMED LIKE A RIFLE AT THE MIDDLE CLASS.

✔ OUR REQUIRED FIELD TRIP TO THE ART INSTITUTE MUSEUM PUT US AT RISK FOR OUR LIVES FROM INNER-CITY NEGROES.

✔ PROFESSER*[SIC]* IGNORED MY CLEAVAGE—HE'S EITHER GAY OR WAY OVER-COMPENSATING.

✔ PROF PRAISED *SPLICE GARDEN*, MARTHA SCHWARTZ'S TRAVESTY OF ROOF GARDENS THAT MIXES JAPANESE AND FRENCH MOTIFS, USING PLASTIC PLANTS.

✔ PROFESSOR TOLD US MARCEL DUCHAMP PLAYED CHESS BECAUSE THERE WAS NO TELEVISION BACK THEN; IF THERE'D BEEN, HE WOULD HAVE WATCHED IT ALL DAY LONG.

Collision of two worlds—neo-con versus rad—manifesting itself in Art's classes. Art now be heap tempted to introduce his courses with rhetorical flourish known as *captatio malevolentiae*: "I don't know if it's worth saying what I have, because I'm talking to a bunch of complete idiots who won't understand a thing."

Something is *Crook* in Middlebrook

So one sad day Art is found in school's hallway, eyes wild with cascade of internal reckonings, lips acting out some unintelligible discourse, inaudible to numerous students who race by him noting his mad appearance and, quite rightly, offering him wide berth as they escape into someone else's class. When he begins to wash all the blackboards with soap and water, he is called into the RREMFs (Realm of the Rear Echelon Mother Fuckers, i.e., the administration), to be precise, into Dean's office. Art's blood slows 'n clogs, what little of his hair is left hums. Cooler blood chills Dean's veins, as if her mind works best at temperatures lower than her heart's. Dean sits at her desk ignoring him for a long moment, while Art scans her Deanly terrain: books on shelf with decorative beer steins as bookends, jagged-line graphs depicting declining enrollment figures, a print from minor German Expressionist, and an engraved "Strathmore's Who's Who" plaque honoring one "Gerta K. Hackenkreuzler, Distinguished Albert Speer Professor of Architectural History." Over Dean's door is placard denominating her office as *Das Warum* (The Why of It All). Faculty punfully call it "The War Room." I.D. badge photo reveals: square crushing jaws, scornful jutting lips that spit with defiance, massive rock-like head with ultra-dynamic eyes (corneas of a wolf, they dart with speed of baby-blue Ferrari on Germany's *autobahn*), brutal hands. In department where most faculty are sheathed in image broadcast by the self—but only in weak local frequency—Gerta's international broadcasts come booming in like Deutsche Welle.

Wow! Does Dean Hackenkreuzler have more than several unkind words for Art—including calling him "extraordinarily wilful"—peppered with strict advice. Something like (sitting on her fat *Popo*, adjusting her *Büstenhalter*): "*Prost, Herr Luftmensch*! *Hirnlose Ochse*! Another *schwarzes Auge* on your record, *mein Herr. Ach*! Is your brain steeped in milk? We've received written complaint from S.P.O.G.G., The Society for the Promotion of Good Grammar, concerning your critical writing; you're not Theodor Adorno nor teaching at Berkeley, *nein*," and (cracking her knuckles) "*Ja,* this maybe not be a Christian school in *der* town of Vheaton, *Herr* Middlebrook, but it's still *der* suburbs," and (re-adjusting her *Büstenhalter*) "*Studenten* are here to learn practical skills—*ja, ja*—to raise their EPR, their economic potential ratio. Not to be indoctrinated by you," and (clasping both hands before her, staring Art down with icy eye) "Like Kant, vee make distinctions here . . . categories, modalities. *Ja, ja.* Reason vee have a downtown campus *und* a Schaumburg (*not* Shamburg as one irate student claims you slandered it) suburban locale is *precisely* so our middle-class kids neither have to mix *mit der* subachievers *und* dope fiends nor learn Spanglish nor ebonics. *Und* then there vas your ill-received curatorship of 'A Festival of Plagiarism' which aimed at, I quote from your trashy gallery announcement, promoting 'The New Plagiarism as an anti-capitalist gesture by redeploying photo-copy machines and computers in favor of a cut-'n-paste aesthetic of revolt'. But, Sir, your penchant for imitation is merely imitation of a penchant!" (Art calls such Postmodern art strategy "playin' jarism," a kind of Glass Bead Game aimed at subverting capitalist notion of intellectual *property*.) "*Ach, mein Herr,* you are a mature pedagogical technology: you generate as many problems as you solve."

Dean's dressing down ends with her pointing unpleasantly at Art and yelling, "Go! Go *und* zin no more, *mein Herr.* . . . Or tender your resignation. Oh, *und* by *der* vay ... due to budget cuts janitorial staff are being laid-off, so adjuncts *und* assistant professors vill become our new *Scheisse-kommando*, latrine patrol. You vill owe us *ein* hour after your regular office hours zo bring your overalls, *mein Herr*!" Her face takes on appearance of an old sneaker as she subtly belches odor of *Weissbier* subtly laced with *Mittwurst* toward his startled face, while her shoes take on look of pair of large dead brown birds.

If Art had any doubts as to why, in German, "I" was *Ich*, they're gone now. Pronounced "Eck"—like sound of child confronting its own feces. Armoring himself from this verbal flogging and keeping him from telling his Dean *Mach'ne Fliege*! (Take a hike!), Art silently repeats over and over and over his family motto: *Etiamsi omnes, ego non* (Though everyone else conforms, I don't). Ho, yes! Fill your *cabeza* full, full, full enough and other stuff can't get in. Meanwhile, Gerta's face—framed by her grey, straight, severe hair—successfully seeks that precise angle, thirteen degrees from horizontal, signifying smug satisfaction. Jeeze! Whitey whites of her eyes sting like fresh frost. As Art slinks out of Dean's lair, infamous faculty secretary (Vera Goodykind but aptly dubbed "The Barracuda") just looks up at Art from her paper strewn desk with Cheshire Cat smile that breaks her face into different occupation zones. *Fuck these RREMFs*, he silently grumbles. Decides to quit.

So fuck New Forms course, now wants geologically ancient stuff. He is leaving theory now and entering practice. Enrolls to get Masters Degree in Geology, his childhood love—hammer banging on rocks, knees in dirt and gravel. First love was small chunk of stibnite: glossy black, spear-like prisms of antimony sulfide. Largest come from Ichinokawa Mine on Shikoku Island in Japan. Crystals five, even six feet, high. Early on loves galena. Its cubic structure is expression of way its atoms arrange in lattices. And cryolite, ice stone from Greenland, so low in refractive index it is transparent. Ah, those delicious mineral names taste good on tongue. Like melodious pair orpiment and realgar after which he names two childhood pet cats.

Oh yes. Obvious it all comes down to rocks: from basic bedrock to fault zones to gems in tiaras tippy-top Heads of State. Fact: favorite cartoon character Rocky of "Rocky and Bullwinkle" show. So Art diligently studies cleavage in geology classes (both rocky and fleshy) at Roosevelt University on South Michigan Avenue in gem of building designed by Louis Sullivan. Still having love of aesthetic ambiguities and odd words, he specializes in aggregate and metaphoric rocks. Altered by heat 'n pressure. Like *hornfels,* hard, compact rock that breaks into splintery fragments. Fact: field associations of such rocks are "zone or aureole of contact metamorphism bordering granitic intrusions." Ah, those geological textbook descriptions be as fascinating as are actual minerals.

Yet wanting to remain close to art, Art pays his way through program working as drably uniformed museum guard guarding art at Art Institute of Chicago. (He was seduced by employment ad that offered the new guard the benefit "of warming yourself at the red and golden fires of Titian and Veronese.") Imposing building is rip-off of old Italian *palazzo*. Black plastic Motorola walkie-talkie in hand, his gaze perpetually torn between pigment on paintings and fleshy cleavage in jostling crowds. There he can exercise certain love for arbitrary authority and in his own small way contribute to goal of such museums: obedience, subjection, surveillance, 'n control, that is, to cleanse and civilize bodies and spirit of our so-called subordinate classes by touting purely visual experience that excludes movement, noise, smell, and taste. Oh, how he delights in yelling across gallery: "DON'T TOUCH THE ART," startling art patrons (decked out in suburban garb) out of their confused reveries. Once, stout, white-haired tourist in hospital-green polyester pants suit starts to raise small white Tic-Tac breath mint past her sagging breasts to her over-painted lips. "NO EATING IN THE GALLERY," Art yells obtrusively. Woman caught like deer in car's headlights, mint one inch from mouth. All heads turn. Embarrassment. Hope she has on her Depends. Fun!

In sly, destructive moments on night shift (when put off by set-jawed throning Virgin looking at him aslant from large oil) has balls to gingerly pull out box-cutters (like those preferred by terrorists highjackers) to scrapiddity-scrape diminutive pigmental flakes off famous paintings into small white envelope. Later ceremoniously adds 'em to *Wunderkammer,* cabinet in which—besides dainty jeweled *Schloss Bijou* almanac about half size of postage stamp (enclosed in small solander case which reposes in tiny silk lined 'n leather bound case in which was also diminutive magnifying glass shaped like a hand mirror), guitar made from eighteenth-century French bidet, statue of Chinaman with double pupils, skull of St. John at age of twelve, and postcard depicting "The living statue of Hananuma Masakicki, the greatest sculptor of Japan, a self-portrait in which the artist's own hair, teeth, toenails, and fingernails are embedded"—he keeps what he calls "My Testes-tube Art Collection." A sculptural spectrum Minimalist-like array of sixty-six (and growing) six-inch tall Pyrex tubes stoppered and neatly labeled with title, artist, and exact color of pigment. Taxonomic order. After brain event, where veins be just burstin' for a bustin', begins to write these labels left-handed, a southpaw overnight.

Normality be tightrope-walker above abyss of abnormality—sometimes one falls. Year ago, as if maimed paintings wish his demise, Art nearly expires among artworks. Outside, transient Chicago thunderstorm rages, nature's Tesla coil sends jags of electricity across dull sky, angry drops form sheets of rain, blow horizontal, dousing tourists and homeless alike, purging city of its summertime grime, making trees angular and ill-tempered; against glass building fronts, treetops foam like surf. Abandoned black umbrella, turned inside-out and blown against museum steps, looks relieved that it be broken, broken out of world of definition and be just sprig of plastic tackle again. Inside, Art's brow be suddenly 'n minutely sequinned with sweat. Voices around him sound like pile of foreign noodles smothered in black bean sauce. Feels vascular roaring rushing that until pain hits seems like gathering of a kind of orgasm of the head. In Art's once *vas bene clausum*, stupendous cerebral event sizzles, bangs! Strobe-flash of light—electrics fire off like jellyfish in brain. Everything be expanding in blackness; inflating 'n widening, yet at same time shrinking 'n straining, evading something, with some kind of winnowing, general 'n particular, dangling by fine thread as well as transformation into some something, transmutation. Boiled engrams. Engrams of oblivion. Flicker-image of data being hastily deleted. Traces left in his "reactive mind" go bye-bye, a fucking L. Ron Hubbardesque Blitz-therapy happening right now in his throbbing *cabeza.* (Umberto Eco, prolific Italian semiologist, noted that: "Dianetics can do a lot in terms of wash-'n-wear sorcery and Holy Grail frappé"). One moment heart be pumping, sloshing blood from one room to the next, then, a door slams and his mind pulls up

Something is *Crook* in Middlebrook

anchor in an undifferentiated sea. Then stupid blackness. . . . With fright-movie suddenness Art falls KERPLOP. To observers (including his own out-of-body autoscopy), fast ripening, pudgy body twitches on polished parquet floor, arms wildly spreading expressive lines of bright red blood on floor. On floor right under huge Jackson Pollock canvas. Blood trickling from every orifice like red madder pigment dribbled by Action Painters of yore. Screaming adults, perversely delighted children. Raggedy art students, thinking it's art performance pastiching both Pollock's drip-paintings and Vik Muniz's wacky fabulations, pull felt-tip pens out of ripped jeans, start to either take illegible notes or make hasty sketches. Room's emotions seem to be inverting themselves every couple of seconds. Milo Zecchi (Curator of Prints and Drawings) administers CPR while praying—"Give him vigor 'n brawn, wake him up from the dead, make him rise 'n live on!"—and later photographing blood spill which looks remarkably like a sinking ship. Within ten minutes, pair of paramedics continue CPR as Art's sinking ship rushed past panicked people and into ambulance. Time's on fire as screaming machine wiggles its way north up Michigan Avenue with force of nothing but light 'n sound. Flashing emergency lights reflect in Anish Kapoor's *Cloud Gate;* past Millennium Park's F. Gehry-designed Pritzker Pavilion where office men sit with lunchbox faces and truant eyes; past annoyed tourists covering their ears, past Miesian structures lost in clouds, past barking art caged in high white galleries, to hospital where McDonald's and Starbucks be just off first-floor marble 'n glass reception area with its parabolic front desk lit with glaucous gleam, seemingly filtered through deep water, with special quality of pale brilliance of leg suddenly revealed under lifted skirt. In E.R., air be lukewarm, hums, 'n tastes of human organs obscurely neutralized or mistakenly preserved.

Art's Blood Spill

In scene like from TV show "ER," he be rushed around by screaming people in surgical outfits. Red froth at Art's mouth like remnants of some primitive language. Plugged into life support: Siemens Servo 300, loaded with red lights and green lights and plenty of bells 'n whistles. Monitors EKG and

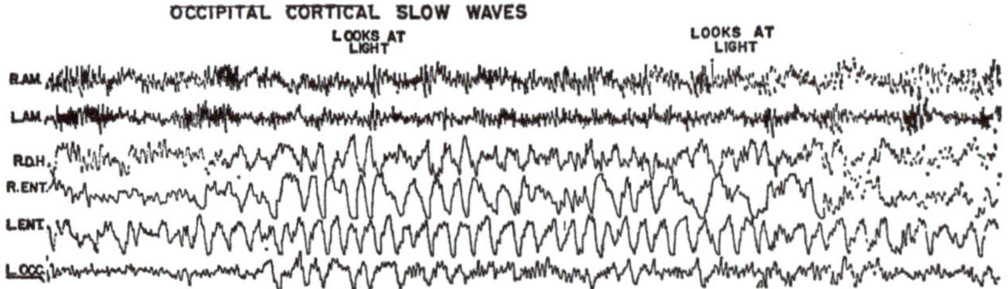

EEG activity, respiratory functions, blood pressure, oxygen saturation 'n end tidal CO_2. EEG: higher voltage, faster waves than normal. Detleff Mächenfänger, M.D. pores over flitting images 'n data on his computer screen as if they be diagrams of enemy military installations. Art's left ear swells (which ain't swell). Lump on back of head, bruises all over arms 'n legs turning uglier. Bloodshot eyes. In ICU with tubes 'n wires running hither 'n thither: IV pumps 'n miles of IV lines. Blood test reveals his red fluid is crowded with commuters, the glucose peons, lactic, and ureic sanitation workers, hemoglobinous deliverymen carrying loads of freshly brewed oxygen in their dented vans, stern foremen like insulin, enzymic middle managers and executive epinephrine, leukocyte cops and EMS workers; everyone riding aortal elevator 'n dispersing through arteries. Condition has as many ups and downs as Cartesian Devil. Damn-sure saved by cool-headed, nicotine-addicted curator (he prefers Dunhills) in nick of time. Hurrah!

After surgery, world around Art like page of alien text. Strange sensation of awareness goes through him, as if that moment were first moment of his life, feeling of air on his skin, precise placement 'n hum of medical apparatus around him; with sudden rush of new consciousness, he feels difference between life 'n death and beside it tingle of awareness as if he just be born. Ho! His disheveled carcass is expensively parked in Northwestern Memorial Hospital where doctor and patient now look at one another, equally disconcerted, in mutual astonishment and curiosity. Art is marginally safe under distracted medical ministrations of nurse with plump calves and coarse vitality to her body, whose identification badge on lapel labels as: Dagmar Flatterhaft, R.N. Healthy, defiant 'n bristling with nylon-static sex-electricity, obviously she worked her way through nursing school modeling for Wonder Bra ads, breasts with nipples like twin Gestapo bullets aimed toward main light, fill light, cucoloris, 8 x 10-inch Sinar view camera, straight at bored photographer who attempts to look like Surrealist photographer Man Ray circa 1925. Same hospital where Art's former HMO doctor gives him brutal rectal exam, telling him: "I'll bet one of your students would've liked doing that!" Art changes primary physicians immediately.

Same day as Art's brain-event, male giraffe in the Bronx Zoo, New York, ceases to eat. In nine days following, it changes form, absorbing all of its extremities into egg-shaped mass of living flesh and bones. On tenth day it begins to divide quite spontaneously and by twelfth day two pulsating fleshy masses. Day later, bumps appear on two masses. Grows, taking form and design. Twenty days later legs, necks, heads and identical markings of original giraffe appear—but half size of original. Exactly similar occurrence in Brazil in which steer is unfortunate victim. Although rancher there smiles —he now has two steers for price of one. Same fateful day, for two days, Ohio River flows upstream. For six hours trees in Euclid Park, Cleveland, lash their branches madly as if in terrific storm though no breath of wind. Fishes swim out of Mississippi River through air, and proceedeth to drown in atmosphere, turned belly-up, and float placidly at an imaginary water level some fifteen feet above pavement of city. Big hurricane sweeps South Pacific causing huge tidal waves. Radios in Joplin, Missouri suddenly squawk and begin to emit insistent, mechanical shriek which changes again to squawk and then terrific sound as if all static of ten thousand thunderstorms on-air at once. Then silence. I regret error of not mentioning these extraordinary coincidences earlier, but I've only just read about them in Murray Leinster's odd-ball sci-fi story "Sidewise in Time" (1934).

1.2   Five days later and a couple of dozen bowel movements behind the game. Whole new syntax for fatigue needed on days like this. Night so dark and somber after day's unreadably churning skies, ominous dull reports from south-county municipalities that air smells of Mexican violence, or hurricanes or coups. Several thousand TV ads air since Art's embarrassing performance. Fact: television = relentless foregrounding of everything. Hefty white collar he wears and way sheets puff up round his neck make it impossible to avoid thought that he is slowly emerging from depths of a toilet bowl; and there be wires taped to his scalp. Is drowsily awake sometimes 'n hit with memory loss, paranoia, 'n schizzes that scrambles codes. Art gives forth tricky tremolos; his consciousness plays on end of mindlessness, as if memory be balloon on loose string that be let run through his finnies 'n suddenly be grab tight again 'n then be let loose again, o'er 'n o'er:

Where's hhhe? Skiing along on the soft surface of brain damage ... deep birth moans . . . stomach that aches. Toyota Celica. Amway. Lose forty pounds in two weeks. Whose fffucking hand is that? Do get it off hhhis stomach! Hhe can hhhear him, but not see him . . . do stand back! Hhhis ear is in the next room. And hhhe wants it back . . . Where one plus one does equal three. Gas, more gas through them tubes, do gas hhhim up. What's this? Youth-in-Asia? He only groks theft 'n gift, oil 'n knowledge. No payment until February next year. The ccccccalabash of incision, gentlemen warrant scrutiny, gentlemen start your engines . . . The rat's ass is hangin' from the sky. Sussceptible to augmentation, resistant to diminution . . . Sssliver of bamboo cuts heap too easily ... Empire carpet, buy now, pay later. Hhhe's benditoicin' ingenious lllord who keeps you secure. Tight as rust that's bbburied inside. Crusade, crusade! On behalf of fifty-watt light bulbs. Sixty's too bright, forty too dim! Wine twissster definitions remmmminiscin' on women . . . Sighs in front of garbage arranging itself. Hhhis original puddle is drained by the sun. Hey, ain't life fun! Ffffore! Choke down on the club. Lob shot. Pitch shot. Gggive me my pppppputter! Don't Bogart that joint my friend . . . hhhe won't review your show . . . hhhe wants a pay raise . . . takes this job and shove it . . . Rhodochrosite . . . don't ya love it . . . Hey, my thing for that whole time thing was really a kinda art thing or something. . . . To the peasant language means the city, to the soldier is means the rear . . . Ah, to be the flâneur! . . . No more Ouzo or boozo . . . Hhhe needs an omelette . . . Roo'll rue the day . . . Noreen, no more chickens . . . Bite mmmmy crank. One day the natives forced into heavy reptile forms of overwhelming gravity . . . . The subway broke out every into every damn language . . . Ho, cut word lines 'n shift those linguals buddy . . . In grad school they went through hhhis photos 'n essays with finnies light 'n cold as the winter wind . . . Peven says 'come closer 'n see my fatagrafeeya' . . . those dumb rubes playin' 'round with photomontage, huh? . . . Sad little irrigation ditch, come to Papa . . . Fun in the naborhood with aqualungs . . . Meatloaf, bulb-headed syringes, 'n bedpans on an operating table . . . Tight here should be taken pretty loosely, right? Just as you have swept through me; just as now I sweep through you. . . . What's the difference, especially in différance Monsieur Derrida? . . . See kingly pride dragged in the dust ... The Sphinx Humbled! What did Nasser's Mother really look like? You'll find out when you see Oedipus confronted by the Lion-Faced Lady! . . . See the Young Oedipus and the Lion-Faced Lady! See the Sphinx feeding! . . . Hear the first and most sexual quiz on earth! . . . See the great Technicolor Ear! Now comes the lagging time, abruptly, flopping down like immense 'n invisible jelly from the ceiling, oh god! . . . swamping the air with marine languor and insect speeds only Peven can master, spray, spray, Pev! Everything I think has been thought, everything I've done has been done. I have no mouth and I have to scream . . . I'm a dead tooth on a fart of air. But I got one hell of an ear! I am being shot full of sings. The foetus of symmetry nourishes itself on cross purposes! If you cut your toenails on a Friday you'll never have a toothache 'n will enter the realm of sweet reason 'n pure noise. . . .

His condition does feel like The Twenty-First Century: it be something you want to wake up from. Ho! True agony can't be cheapened; it be known alone, with no one else there, for agony do be friend who demands intimacy, demand's one's full attention; who demands 'n demands 'n does take everything 'n then leaves with nights bedeviled by weird dreams. Tossing in bed, be sign that he be inhibiting erratic impulses—dreams-within-dreams—recalls one in detail.

There is feeling of great tension. Many people—plump-faced 'n bone-faced, lightly clad—parade round a large central rotunda carrying a variety of golf clubs. Four smaller rotundas ring its side. Circulation in the large rotunda is to the left and in the smaller rotundas, to the right. In the middle there is a barstool on which I sit holding a putter. A large sculptural rendition of an ear is placed in the center of each of the smaller rotundas, each painted different colors: red, yellow, green, and, white. I start spinning myself in the direction opposite the people in the central rotunda, propelling myself with the putter. Disquieting questions arise: Am I turning in the correct direction? Am I using the right golf club? Someone asks me, What's the irony of golf?" I reply, "A long drive and a short putt are the same thing, both can win the game; that's the long 'n short of it."

Decipherment is left to Jungian analyst, who tells Art it has something to do with "a disturbed mandala." Hey, isn't an ear a kind of laterally squished mandala? As Art finally does become fully conscious, his nurse encouragingly advises him, "Vhen evening comes Herr Middlebrook do not dare to promise yourself the dawn."

1.3 Seven days pass among white geometry of made-up beds. His face clears as if emerging from shadow into day. Outside: light everywhere, immense light that seems to radiate outward from each thing eye does catch hold of, and overhead, in tree branches, a breeze hissing, a rising and falling that breathes on as steadily as surf. As if in argument with this environment, the hospital seems static, blank, a hell of stale thoughts. Inside, inside Art's unhappy green hospital room, there piles up Amway toiletries from his wife Brittany, Day of Dead figurines from workmate Mala, golf magazine from golf buddy, Al Schmerbauch, flowers from neighbors the Boettchers and the Pogacnics, and ABCs of small mineral samples—agate, beryl, chrysocolla, diopside, epsomite, feldspar, gneiss, hematite, iron-nickel, jade, kunzite, linarite, malachite, natrojarosite, opal, pyrite, quartz, rhodochrosite, stibinite, tourmaline, ulexite, vanadinite, wolframite, xenotime, yugawaralite, zircon—from his fellow geology classmates.

While trying to achieve difficult feat of taking his own pulse while continuing to bite his nails, Art distinctly hears Herr Doktor Detleff Mädchenfänger—he has healthy appearance of decorated S.S. officer who ain't above puttin' on gloves and trading a few punches every morning, followed by brisk shower and shot of Kümmel—whisper to nurse Flatterhaft down depressingly sterile hospital hall, through ICU's closed door no less. If Art could see his lusty doctor now he'd find him exuding air of abstracted benevolence that seems tinged with cunning, a pleasantness that masks some secret edge of cruelty:

GUTEN ABEND, HERR DOKTOR. WIE GEHT ES IHNEN? ES GEHT MIR GUT. ICH BIN BEUNRUHIGEN. UND KEEP HERR MIDDLEBROOK LIGHTLY SEDATED BIS MITTWOCH. [He puts his right hand on her left buttock.]

JA, JA! [She unbuttons top blouse button; her eyes drill into Detleff like point-blank pistol shots, eyes loaded with mascara.]

UND . . . VISITS BY RELATIVES VERBOTEN! UND . . . [He strokes her right breast; she flushes.]

FAHREN SIE FORT, BITTE! [She smiles.]

UND . . . ER . . . 'DINNER' IN OUR USUAL ROOM

HERE, JA? [He winks, stroking her left breast.]

LANGSAMER, BITTE! . . . JA, JA. OKAY. [She blushes.]

Art doesn't hear Doktor's affirmative nod, but by now he is experiencing his first synaesthetic response to sound as veil of pure blue hue covers his visual field. When Doktor resumes romantic chatter, Art be baffled as little by little Detleff's words become only sounds, random collection of glottals 'n fricatives, heap storm of whirling Germanic phonemes. (Fact: Art suffers such bouts with auditory gibberish until his brain adapts to his newly-discovered hearing abilities.) Art, laying on his starboard side, left ear pointing toward ICU's door, does hear nurse Flatterhaft noisily tramp in:

CLUMPIDDITYCLUMPPIDDYCLUMPBUMPCLUMP

CLUMPIDDITYCLUMPPIDDYCLUMPBUMPCLUMP

CLUMPIDDITYCLUMPPIDDYCLUMPBUMPCLUMP

CLUMPIDDITYCLUMPPIDDYCLUMPBUMPCLUMP

And suddenly he ceases to be the old Art; now in his place rests huge sound-hungry trembling EAR: from across room he does hear rapid systole/diastole of nurse's blushing ticker, as if that ruddy muscle be wired into hospital's P.A. system:

HHUMMMPTHUMHUMMPTHUMMMPTHUMMMMPTH

THUMPTHUUMMPTHUMPTHUMMMPTHUMPTHMMMP

THHHHUVMPTHUMPTHUMMMPTHUMMMPTHUMPTH

HHUMMMPTHUMHUMMPTHUMMMPTHUMMMMPTH

Something is *Crook* in Middlebrook

He does hear rustling of her uniform, heel squeaking on tiled floor, maybe even blinking of her eyelids. So intense is sound he (ah, synaesthesia!) simultaneously *sees* blue hue and *tastes* her mixture of modesty and lust. He blinks like someone coming out of darkness into broad daylight, he then looks right 'n left in pious astonishment, rolls his eyeballs, shoots them upward, ogles, opens mouth in calf-like rapture, lets out soft cry as if he spots something on ceiling, assumes expression of rapture and so remains, entranced 'n inspired: *Yum! Like licking raspberry Tootsie Pop with gooey dark chocolate inside,* he thinks. *What I would give to have an organizational chart that detailed the lust structure that keeps this place humming.* When plane tows ad for local theme park over nearby beach, Art swears that coffee mill has been grafted onto his left eardrum. Much more disturbing do be continuous racket that assails him from corridor whenever staff forget to shut door despite all his efforts to alert people to his hearing problems. Heels clatter (albeit deliciously!) on linoleum, carts crash (awfully!) into one another, hospital workers call to one another (with voices of stockbrokers trying to liquidate their holdings), radios nobody listens to are turned on (in rooms wherein lie bedridden wretches whom fate has cast to the far edge of life). On top of everything else, large professional-looking floor-waxer does send out auditory foretaste of hell. But one positive side, does audit flutter of single butterfly that does somehow get into his ward. Ah, yes. . . . *Hombre nueva/hambre nueva.* Yes, Dear Reader, it's heap big bungee jump into new way life for one Arthur Strewth Middlebrook.

During his enforced hospital stay—where, because he hates hospital chow, he's living off tuna, rice, and water, losing pounds faster than Lloyd's of London—Art turns into pure inactive spectator: a detached, disembodied aural point-of-view that lacks feeling of unity 'n wholeness. A body-in-parts which will gradually be retrained into an active body with its global feeling of body-as-whole. Immobile aural-observer, Art can't help *ears*dropping on hot monkey sex betwixt those two partners in trauma, nurse Flatterhaft 'n Mädchenfanger, M.D. Big surprise: does find he's highly stimulated by enhanced hearing of their furtive, stolen moments in adjoining storeroom translates into loud spinning 'n squealing consonants, rattling faster, hesitating, then racing harder, syllables melting with groans, or moans finding purchase in new words or old words or made-up words; does hear deep in nurse's throat Mercurochrome agony of delight, thousand letters crashing in long unmodulated fall; does hear couple's last fit of fury resonating deep within his super-charged cochlea 'n down cochlear nerve; almost does audit very adult shivers 'n shakes of these two adulterers.

Next time Art sees nurse Flatterhaft, she's in medical scrubs 'n swaying in the door frame to his room like eucalyptus leaf and he's started to think consecutively, even logically. Logically enough that he wants to say something that will force her to turn to an impartial referee and say, *Flag him, flag him, that's gender pre-emption!* And she *is* all ticketyboo, tame 'n tepid, stooping over him, holding white bed pan; through her high-swelled lips a low hum occasionally comes (reminds Art of sound you sometimes hear from power station when you pass one on a summer night), while in depths of her eyes her German and Jewish heritage keep closing like oxygen and hydrogen. Ho! Art is sucked into the Flatterhaft Vortex. No surprise. Maintaining a maintained swoon, Art notices new factoid: she sports old clunky brooch (valuable antique from her grandmother who had a Cambridge education and several abortions to look back on) made out of polished sterling silver with platinum plated antlers, emerald eyes, small diamonds on fringe of its mane and silver latch disguised as its tail; thread of braid gold secures it to her starched uniform. What does it mean? Like the dark side of the moon, its meaning is invisible but not without influence. Art impresses her to no end by confiding in her that, "What I like about the Black Forest is that it is neither black nor a forest."

After his bed pan removed, Art reluctantly restarts tape of geology lecture one of his fellow students drops off so he doesn't fall too far behind in his class: . . . *Soil bearing capacity? That's a very complicated question, Terry. I mean, look, 'massive rock' like trap rock, for instance, can stand up to 1000 metric tons per square meter while sedimentary rock, like hard shale or sandstone, for instance, will crumble like bumble-berry pie with anything over 150 metric tons per square meter. And soft clay's not even worth 10 metric tons.* [Fast-forwards a bit.] *So, what we have here ladies and gentlemen is a nice banquet of igneous, sedimentary, and metaphoric samples, some granular, possibly gabbro and pyroxenite, some with much less grain, possibly trachite or andesite. The sedimentary group is fairly small, mainly limestone and marl. The metaphoric group predominates with traces of amphibolite and marble. . . .*

It was at this moment that Art notices aberration on his left palm; his head and heart lines (as palmistry calls 'em) have now mysteriously merged, forming single fold known as a *simian crease. "Blessed Benimming!"* he cries out.

1.4   Looks like somebody they forgot to take off Alcatraz during difficult days of recovery in the Intensive Care Unit of the Head Injury Ward (where there is a kind of whispering behind half-shut doors and where his triumphal first-time full deployment of knife 'n fork does bring him accolades). Art's weird ear is treated to steady diet of sounds, pleasant 'n unpleasant. His ear one vast black hole sucking in decibels. Does hear years of clogged phlegm clatterin' inside his hospital roommate's shrunken bronchi and for twenty seconds room does fill with convulsive bursts of sound that reverbs inside Art's head and he does taste thick, spoiled molasses. *Oh god, to be in a place where I am not!* muses despondent Art. *Wherever I am not is the place where I am myself again.* If this were movie, camera close-up would reveal Art taking deep sighs as sounds of televisual event-glamor and crisis-chatter provide soundtrack.

Outside, Chicago lives under sky that brings only weather and bird-screech like irradiated monsters in Japanese sci-fi films from Art's youth. Inside, muted decibels of televisions in myriad adjoining rooms perfectly audible to Art: chintzy exhortations on behalf of miracle breakthrough products: knives that never go dull, light bulbs that never burn out, secret-formula lotions that remove curse of baldness—yak, yak, yak—same old suds 'n blather. Speaking of decibels, each day when sun is hour above horizon —still showing one thing to another; showing other thing to this thing, and this thing to other thing—there is reckless, nonsensical rhythm emanating from set of drumsticks wielded by some lost soul in ragged threadbare pants with improvised skylights at knees and scarecrow's overcoat advancing crazily along street outside Art's room, drifting in slow eddies of mental space, unnear lonely planets and outside gravity's functional belt. Beating and beating away at cement, at wrought iron bars, at light poles, at newspaper dispensers, at street signs, and (occasionally) on car hoods. Latter sound, deep 'n resonate, usually followed by police sirens then black man's loud, demented protestations:

> **THIRD MARINES. . . . EATING BEES. . . . THE BEES CRAWLING OUT OF MY MOUTH. STOP DA KRUMPIN'? AND WHAT IF I DON'T WANT TO! GOTTA KILL DA BEES. I WAS A SEA-BEE. . . . THIRD MARINES. TO BEE OR NOT TO BEE. . . . DA DEADLY GLORY O' DA REAL WILL NOT BE SANITIZED FOR A NATION THAT DENIES ITS MEAT BONES, THAT DEMANDS NAMED-BRAND FRUIT AND PASTEURIZED PUSSY. MAKE ME THE SERGEANT IN CHARGE O' DA BOOZE, WE'RE CIVILIZED 'N SHOVELIZED 'N RANDOMINZED, 'TIL ORDER LOOKS LIKE CHAOS . . . GET YER FUCKIN' HANDS OFFA ME, PIG . . . MAKE ME … GET YER FUCKIN' HANDS OFFA ME, PIG . . .**

Sounds that (to Art, an old Soupy Sales fan) sound identical to two people doing famous Soupy Shuffle. Shuffle does produce synaesthetic taste of scrambled eggs 'n bacon releasing related platitudes—"a good egg," "egg on his face," "to lay an egg," "to be as like two eggs"—that bounce around in his injured *cabeza.* Art recalls he read somewhere that George Armstrong Custer once said that Indians could hear with their eyes. Chicago streets sing. Yes they do. Can you hear them? Chicago streets scream.

1.5   Weeks later. Kitchen table, demitasse of Turkish coffee in right hand as left thumbs newspaper, while Artful eyes gaze into yellow 'n gold-brown tones of setting sun. Ho! Art's front page news in *Sun-Times* (*Chicago Tribune* ignores story as too low-brow). And in Section B, page 8, Art spies his latest horoscope:

> GEMINI (*June 21 - July 22*): Saturn has its knickers in a knot about a pesky new acquaintance, so it's tempting to be passive aggressive until you get snappy. The answer can be found in a jar of super-crunchy peanut butter with raisin accompaniment. Avoid cashews next Wednesday.

Ever since able to count down from one hundred by sevens, he's been out-patient under neurological care. Art, even as toddler, suffers what neurologists term "recruitment": exaggerated and abnormal sensitivity to sounds, especially to voice of his daffy daddy. Does this predispose Art to suffer his vastly post-traumatic amplified hearing? During first few weeks after brain

Something is *Crook* in Middlebrook

trauma, Art complains of other sporadic neurological anomalies: 1) songs spontaneously slop around his inside his skull, stuff like "Amazing Grace," "The Battle Hymn of the Republic," Beethoven's "Ode to Joy," the drinking song from *La Traviata*, "A-Tisket, A-Tasket," and a really dreary version of "We Three Kings of Orient Are;" 2) lively arguments among more than two interlocutors sound like *a cappella* jazz group, The Grunyons, singing "Shooby Doin', while Chopin ballade does sound like toneless banging with unpleasant metallic reverb, as if ballade be played with hammer on sheet metal by Boettcher Brats (this be often accompanied by brilliant, scintillating black zigzags across visual field, like negative of SS insignia); 3) brief phases of simultagnosia where auditory environment be split into discrete and unconnected elements, not integrated into normal auditory background (aggregates that won't aggregate); and 4) exposure to jazz's "flatted fifth" (i.e., augmented fourth in classic terminology) be experienced as excessively ugly, uncanny, even diabolical. On positive front, Art now gifted with absolute pitch; confesses to his brain doc: "Nurse Flatterhaft moans in B major and *Plusia gamma* moth buzzing around my lava lamps tunes in at low F-sharp.

Today Art cools his heels with other patients in brain specialist's waiting room. Leafs through magazine—*Forbes* or was it *Fortune*?—either be like reading operating manual of some strangely sanctimonious pirate ship. Notices one patient reading *Modern Maturity* article titled "Year of the Depend Undergarment." Another peruses Michael Chorost's *Rebuilt: How Becoming Part Computer Made Me More Human* and recalls he once read in *Wired* Chorost's wonky article, "My Bionic Quest for *Bolero*." Out of boredom Art does stroke "Erin" (his pet erinaceous rock) wrapped in tiny felt blanket 'n housed in his right pants's pocket, while watching slick video ad for Corecktall Electrolytes provided free by Merck to Dr. Anders Daffy who passes it on to his patients: . . . *Of ferrocitrates and ferroacetates specially formulated to cross the blood-brain barrier and accumulate interstitially,* says unseen pitchman on video sound track. *We also stir in a mild, non-habit forming sedative* and *a generous squirt of Hazelnut Moccachino syrup courtesy of the country's most popular chain of coffee bars. Ingest and—kaboom!—its synaptogenesis!* This all in announcer's G-sharp voice which evokes in Art vivid synaesthetic chroma display from blue end of spectrum. After attending concert in Millennium Park, Art finds that G minor evokes subdued yellow ochre, G major bright yellow, D minor elicits flint, graphite; moreover, his sensory mix-'em-up extends to taste: clarinet elicits splash of dry *curaçao*, oboe that of *kümmel*, flute that of *crème de menthe*, etcetera.

In waiting room do be *the cool* and *the uncool. A perfect subject for Edward Hopper*, he chuckles silently. Latter be mainly suburban minivan drivers (you know, God is my Co-Pilot, Pro-Life, and Support the Troops bumper sticker aficionados) thirty or forty pounds overweight and sporting multi-colored jogging shoes, pastel sweats and Prussian hair. Among former be, *The Cool*, young go-for-it Yuppie with truly nasal nose, trite 'n inane, consisting of two parallel, finite tubes; he's over-dressed in caper-green half-silk sport coat, ecru linen button-down, pleatless black dress pants, and tasseled loafers. After intently watching video, our Mr. Cool secretively pulls out palm-top stock-quoter, puts wire in his ear and, with schizophrenic eyes of cell-

Something is *Crook* in Middlebrook

ularly occupied, whispers conspiratorially. From across expanse 'n din of overly elegant waiting room, Art ungoops 'n intakes:

Door to the examining rooms opens; everyone in waiting looks like the winning serve might be delivered right now. "Mr. Middlebrook," calls overly obese nurse. *Why are so many nurses and other medical assistants so damn fat*, he wonders as he squeezes between nurse and door frame.

"You will have to be a very patient patient Mr. Middlebrook, a patient squared," lectures Dr. Daffy once he's got Art in his lair, "the various neurological afflictions you suffer—like seeing that blue hue when you listen with your left ear—*will* take time to repair, if they repair at all." Art notices several oddities about his neurologist: a line-backer type with thick glossy sideburns and texturally distinct stubblefield of hair higher up; faint smell of Vindaloo curry on breath. During examination of Art, Daffy's tongue unconsciously probes beneath his upper lip like cat beneath blankets—bad habit acquired in childhood and never out-grown. Ho! Art has his own annoying childhood leftover: loves to noisily thumb books, habit originating in caressing silky-soft edge of blanket between thumb 'n forefinny, furtive exercise that toddler Art terms "foovy-woovying." Ho! Calmed his childish soul and still functions as effective self-medication. "Cheaper than Xanax," he defends whenever Una complains about annoying noise emanating from his fav reading chair— "That's very very very bug-house, Arty"—in voice as caustic as silver nitrate and as confusing to Art's scrambled brains as Hindu music's 22-note scales.

Snippets of what Art tells his doctor over several visits: "My neighbor's Brats got noisy toy Star Trek Blasters for Christmas which give out a high-pitched wine, a sitar-like caterwauling that seems to pull apart the sutures of my skull . . . . The raw tritone sounds so harsh. . . . I could make a living, I suppose, tuning pianos. . . . And if I had a Mall shopping center I would have monkeys, and Chinese restaurants, and Mylar kites and a band of small girls playing tambourines. . . . As a matter of fact I hear that 'No man is an island' once or twice a week, from blocks away, quite often from people (I suspect) that think they are quoting Ernest Hemingway. . . ."

Daffy, besides reviewing array of previous MRI scans, has Art undergo Rorschach Test, Thematic Apperception Test, Sentence Completion Test, and Minnesota Multiphasic Personality Index. Ensuing psychiatric report details: "*a personality in process of deterioration . . . regressive libidinal preoccupations . . . fundamentally pessimistic, fatalistic . . . feels deeply that all human effort is foredoomed to failure . . . auditory and olfactory hallucinations . . .*" Doctor suggests Merck's new miracle drug Corecktall Electrolytes. Art refuses, it painfully reminds him of time his now-dead daddy had stormed into their house after trip to Home Depot announcing: "Correct all electric lights! . . . Correct all electric lights! All will be revealed at the proper time!" and started manically screwing in those screw-shaped fluorescent bulbs advertised to save hundreds on your electrical bill over a year. Big screw shapes, small screw shapes—new bulb for every old bulb in every socket in the goddamn house. God how Art hated it; it was like something more primordial (DNA-like) was supplanting ye ol' ovum-shaped bulb.

Of his tribulations, Art later reports to Al: "I am told, and so she said he said, I heard later, according to the doctor's report read by the nurse, it was reported that, *I should lead a simple life.* Apparently. My body now offers a precise physiological equivalent to what's going on in my mind. Ya grok?"

Stranded between his old self and his evolving new self, between how he constituted Chicago *before* his brain event and advent of super-hearing and *after*, Art, rather than look outside himself to see who he is and where he is going, turns inward, *introrse* as his word-smithing sister Els would've put it, and launches into deep phenomenological self-examination into his lived-body, that "zero-point" of all orientation. Checks his Husserlian dipstick for richness of his mental givens; then explores impact of his trauma on intersubjective terrain of his personal "homeworld/alienworld" cogenerative dyad (how Art loves philosophical jargon). All at urge to see if he can "grok" his new self (what Art terms "Gettin' oil 'n knowledge"). One thing is for certain—and that's saying something in these days of philosophical uncertainty—has to admit his entire *oeuvre* be forged out of confused 'n chaotic love life; writes out list . . .

lo

love

love given

love denied

love received

love in absentia

love interrupted

love found again

love misdirected

love never found

love lost temporarily

love thoroughly botched

Blessed Benimming! Art notices list shaped like Brook Shields brand condom. Ah love! Once Una crabbily complains to him, "When I say 'I love you,' you either reply 'I know' or 'Love ya back.' What's that about?" Her eyes cut to side just for moment, which means she's thinking.

"Una, love speech is so *banal* while hate speech thrives on endless metaphorical flourishes, don't ya know; new insults are created everyday, but we keep returning to only three words. Thought I'd cop a line from Hans Solo in *Star Wars: The Empire Strikes Back* and Tom Cruise in *Jerry Maguire.* 'I love you' and 'Love ya back' *are* always quotations." Art, pointing index finny to head, does start lover's spat when he stupidly adds: "And when those three words are said, it's a little like a gun pointing at one's head, ya grok?"

Ho! Had Art only held his peace. Una abruptly pulls sleeves of her sweater over her fists (sure sign of anger and disapproval). Slight gurgling noise deep in her throat.

1.6   Outside, Chicago sky becomes pink-streaked exhibitionist in drag; sky lowers, thickens, opals into upside-down topographical map. On busy corner of Lawrence and Western Avenues man in coat color of C-sharp minor with E-major-colored trousers with Tourette's (as Art would see/hear syn-aesthetically said garment) acts out veritable debauch of absurd gesticulation, his own wild muscular traveling carnival. (Fact: Art's super-hearing and syn-aesthetic response permits him to confirm poet Arthur Rimbaud's famous boast: "I invented the color of vowels—*A* black, *E* white, *I* red, *O* blue, *U* green"). Inside, Oprah's Harpo studio talk-show be taping: Dr. Oz be telling Oprah's snake-charmed audience: "It goes without saying that *you* are of

course wearing your halo and mouth-guard at all appropriate times and eating at least one green, leafy vegetable per day, right?" On camera, hyped-up audience gives its own version of Tourette's. Oprah mentions next show's theme: "People who protest using their own bodies as grist; like Aline, a class traitor, from Highland Park who shaves her public region in protest against the fur trade."

Inside local dojo, planted on southeast corner of Lincoln Square exactly two blocks from the Boettcher abode, shadows do seem to boil. Ho! Inside the inside our infamous Brats—Ernst Gombrich might dub them Ping 'n Pong, Art prefers Kit 'n Kaboodle, Al likes Cathode 'n Anode—concerning whom their teacher observes: "Ahhh, those boys may frighten sincerity." They do move in graceful, liquid way, stepping from one foot to other 'n back, in 'n out, back 'n forth at their *sensei*'s command: "Do The Rocking Horse!"

"Yyeess, *sseennsseeii*!" Twins bark in near unison. In white dojo uniforms we notice they both sport over-large wrists, bony temples, closed, abstracted look on their faces as if crossing our own universe at slight angle.

"Relax!" Delivered with ferocious energy.

"Yyeess, *sseennsseeii*!" Delivered with mellow, poignant gravity.

Twins shed tension from muscle groups as if they've been unplugged from current. One brat delivers full-wattage pout (he'd rather be peeking through window of The Ace of Thighs—local stripper sleaze-bar with less history than a Styrofoam cup—featuring nightly XXX act billed as: "Crazy Jane Spork and the Mudpit of Truth").

Bored, *sensei* munches on one fucking big Char Siu Bao and yells: "Practice The Five Spanish Archers." (*El bow* strikes if you were wondering).

"Yyeess, *sseennsseeii*!"

Something is **Crook** in Middlebrook

"Alright class, now the Internal Alchemies: first The Iron Skin Meditation followed by the Ghost Palm."

"Yyeess, *sseennsseeii!*"

"In unifying your *chi* with that of your opponent—in aligning the breath of your life and theirs—you will storm the stronger fortress. There! Is that a good secret?"

"Yyeess, *sseennsseeii!*"

Thus does Master fill eager Bratly minds with the highest-quality *bullshido* (martial arts hogwash called The Inner Teaching of the Voiceless Dragon School). Exiting dojo with matching gym bags 'n tennis shoes, our twin Furies turn angelic faces up to Chicago's noonday sun just now peeping out of clouds and loudly declaim in near unison, "Eeaasstt, Wweesstt, Hhoommee iiss Bbeesstt!"Then off they fly all ass 'n elbows to yet another appointment with mishaps mainly minor, sweet swims 'n sweatsy slogs 'n languid Happy Hours spent with Mr. Mischief. Parents of wayward youth suffer one Bad Heir Day after another, after another, after another.

Art's sketch of one Brat's
odoriferous tennis shoes

1.7 Giddings Avenue, 6:25 a.m., Sunday: line of cars (Art dubs them "ideology-on-four-wheels") drive by honk-honking their imported horns at Chicago's rising sun. Someone must be having heap o' fun, or as Art would say: "Someone's happy in her serape or so right in their sarong." Not so happy are people raised out of snoring their way through eight-hour peep-show of infantile erotica, that archaic sump called sleep. The earth warms, a Spring's morning is squeezed from it.

Noisy entourage passes dark-blue beater, beefy man sealed in behind steering wheel. He be so still as if believing all motion leads inevitably to death, knowing-eyes training military-issue binocs on Art's newly constructed dome-home, the "here" of his self contrasting with the "there" of everything else. Rake of car's windshield pillar partially hides puffy face adorned with subtle scars on forehead 'n mouth. Imperceptive, slow disintegration works upon him. Sharp (but not unpleasant) smell rises from his baggy trousers, blend of semen 'n day-old pizza sauce. There's Chinese proverb that goes something along lines of: a fish never knows when it's pissing. Same applies perfectly well to this strange creature.

Let us imagine this mystery-man as collection of loosely coupled planes, elements of his flab 'n personality suspended millimeters apart, floating like contents of some astronaut's capsule. Finger-grease-stained anthology of Lord Bryon's poems perches precariously on dirty dashboard. If Art's weird ear could at this moment penetrate mind of this *homo obesus* he would hear noise of water rushing over smooth-washed stones, murmuring incomprehensible phrases to itself. Summarizing this man's existence in fewest possible words: *Key to his past lies in his present; key to his present lies in his future.* Ya grok?

2.0

Three months after release from hospital. Art suffers sense of inner, intermolecular mockery 'n derision, that inbred superlaugh of bodily parts all runnin' wild. Yahoo! Weird ear hears sound of sun-excited flies, thin squeak 'n fat slap of swinging door of neighbors as person enters and another leaves. Art does get olfactory hallucinations accompanying sound. Does now sniff essential wrongness in air, a fucked up undertaste, as if all sequiturs do be vacuumed out of it; a yellow world of faith 'n fear 'n paltry ingenuity—as if he do be just flyin' blind, but hearin' good. Sure 'nuff, Art be given lesson in how lives can veer abruptly from one thing to another, to jostle 'n bump, to squirm. Person does head in one direction, but be forced to turn sharply in mid-course. Nothing do be ever known, and inevitably we come to a place quite different from one we set out for. Yet Art tries to run his human engine on NORMAL: he is back riding Brown Line EL where riders stare as if they were already looking at television. Feels himself lunging towards a sense of the moment. Looking out window as he snakes southward to Museum job— past sort of bars 'n night spots where the carpet can suck shoes right off your feet, past big sign reading "Creative Realtors," past butter-yellow Hummer with bumper-sticker screaming: FIGHT CRIME: SHOOT BACK—he is struck by sharp clarity of colors around him: green grass, brown dirt, white, blank billboards, blue sky above. At far end of train, man in unlaced hiking boots be embracing his woman. As train leaves Merchandise Mart and crosses Chicago River, noonday sunshine cinema-izes site, turning bridge 'n river into over-exposed picture.

Walking around The Loop, it's hard to be around throngs of milling tourists again for they notice Art's flaws. But learning Spanglish and trading quips with museum workmate, Mala-the-Mañanista, helps. Hailing from *Istlos* (East Los Angeles), this *el* breathtaking *mestiza* calls Art *El Profe,* as much for his pedantics as his curiosity about that verbal aggregation *el espanglés.* This interest starts when she says one day at lunch, "After work I'm going chopin." Impressed, Art asks if she attends Chicago Symphony concerts regularly. "No, *ese*, TCHO-peen, s-h-o-p-p-i-n-g. . . . I'm livin' *la jerga loca,* just as you're livin' *la oreja loca*. Using this mishmash lingo, why *El Profe*, it's *una forma de revancha*, a revenge of sorts on Anglolandia." Next day Mala lends Art not only her audio-book copy of first full-fledged Spanglish story, "Pollito Chicken," by Puerto Rican author Ana Lydia Vega, but also wonky new CD by rapper group, *Ganga Spanglish.* "There' fuckin' hip 'n hot with the *nacos* that live *en* the hood," she recommends. "First song on there . . . it's first time I hear recorded that wonderful word *mistihueso* [pronounced mees-tee-WE-so] for Smith and Wesson pistol." Even with his ear goop in, weird ear tingles. Ho! Ever in search of new polyphonics to stimulate that ear, Art is now all ears. New man/new hunger.

At night Art tries to chill out by sitting on floor in lotus position. He practices special mantra his Jungian analyst (who is always ranting something about neurosis supplanting myth) recommends to stem anxiety: "My mind is as quiescent as a coat rack under a forgotten hat . . . my mind is as quiescent as a coat rack under a forgotten hat . . . my mind is as . . ." Art's life-world changes. Like living inside Don DeLillo novel, *White Noise*: church bells, their dialect high and sweet like chirping birds; TV (dominated by phalanxes of American soldiers, jihads of jarheads), radio (mostly shock-jocks), computer modems hooking up to Internet, satin slip rubbing against fishnet stocking. Ah, now wants *aural* sex. Wife Brittany—oft clad in her preposterous navy-blue coat with its hood 'n bamboo buttons—so silent in things sexual, not good provider of such and such computer geek is Brit that he fears finding himself in USB port instead of her pussy. After cerebral event she confesses, "My uterine contractions've been bogus for some time;" thalidomide baby could count on one hand number of times they make love. So Brit reaches out 'n touches someone; touches old flame, Timmy Maulstick. Born Timaeus Mawlshtck in Dorsettown-on-Choptank, Maryland in 1957, this skinny computer geek be USENET devotee of *budd.comp.expert* (forum for Buddhist computer experts) and animator for iToons on Wabash (doing Kotex ads, etcetera).

Home-life now state of undeclared war. Brittany's subversive school-girl evasive eyes. Her now toneless skin. Her moods flare 'n darken in just seconds, shift of internal weather almost tropical in its sudden turns. Art's ear that can't evade any sound. Finally, Brittany hastily packs up all her Amway distributor crap; tells him, "You're not a man, just . . . just . . . an illness," and stomps out for Timmy's Printer's Row live-in loft in re-architectured building named Eden-Olympia, whose roof-sited satellite dishes re-semble wimples adorning some order of computer-literate nuns. Over main entrance is large banner reading: STILL IMPROVING. Ensconced in new digs, while leafing through huge coffee table book on Gaudi of Spain, she drinks ten glasses of Sangria; begins to imagine nuptial catacomb fit for Madonna. Later, mean divorce papers filed against Art; only sometime later can calmly state: "Old love? It's only a row of beach huts in November."

2.1   Art just sits at home searching planetarium inside his skull for glimmer of light. Occasional painful smile drifts across his face like dismasted ship, detached from whatever he was thinking—and he's been thinking of Brittany's new lover: "I've been maulsticked," moans Art. Grumbles so until—some weeks later—meets Una Calda Bionda, auditorily striking second cousin of Milo Zecchi at flashy Members Preview Show at Museum month after leaving hospital—his persona floating toward her persona over Sea of Hesitation. Here's woman of us in her man-to-be's later intimate observation: thighs be sweet-shaped 'n plumpy as ampersands, soft belly with God's thumbprint for navel. In between copping plastic flutes of champagne while on duty, Art delights in hearing this thyroid blond's panty-hosed thighs rub-a-dub together, voice as Lauren Bacall's in *The Big Sleep.* Ho! Laughter be ventilating her entire being, down to uterus. Measures five foot 'n a credit card, weighs eleven stone. Eyes do have long unqualified range of the iris of wild beasts whose focus not tamed down to meet human eyes. Wears leather belt, with rose stuck in it, worn above waist on soft blancmange-colored Shetland dress. Slim Motorola RAZR cell-phone snuggles in her cleavage (Una affectionately calls it: "*Il mio telefonino*"); gets Art thinking about it vibrating between those soft Italian hills. Still shapely, smiles with enticing guile; has space between upper teeth, like actress Maria Schneider. In her eyes, humid like velvet skin of an otter swimming on surface of water, keen glints of sensuality be stirred up; look that do be at once self-contained, seductive. Her beauty has element of elegant remoteness, secrets. Admires her absolute freedom of gesture, unselfconscious abandon allowing her to live fully in ever-present, expanding Now. When she says: "And what is love if not sorrow exposed?" mentioning that she "so loves occasions for synergy," Art tastes powdered kunzite (which responds in high-degree to radium emanations).

Milo—robust, bull-browed man—introduces her, whispering to Art: "She's attractive in a straight-to-video sort of way and romance-at-short-notice is her specialty." Art's all civility, Una's all sexuality. Just out of a relationship, her mantra is: *Provando e reprovando* (Try and try again). Money is carelessly present in cut 'n texture of her clothes, her leathery accouterments, in that pink Timmy Woods lip purse, in hair-brilliance 'n mouth-tone. Art discovers they share interest in: classic cars, gems, golf, 'n safe, noisy sex. Meet privately after event. With loosely swinging arms, she walks with ease of a seaside nine-year-old. Art slips his arm through one carrying that wow purse and leads her—three-inch Manolo Blahnik heels aclicking **CCLLIIINNCCHHCCCLLANNKKCCLINK** oh so very sonorously 'n deliciously on heap hard aggregate known as cement—to his vintage purple 'n white Nash Metropolitan. No surprise, given Art's linguistic turn, he dubs this classic auto "SVO"—instead of SUV—acronym for "Subject-Verb-Object" (e.g., Art goes to the store). Briefly brushing cheeks, Art weathers tear-gas attack of Una's perfume (she's splashed on "Odeur 53," Comme des Garçon's "anti-perfume," blending 53 non-traditional notes: oxygen, flash of metal, washing drying in the wind, mineral carbon, sand dunes, nail polish remover, cellulose, pure air of the high mountains, burnt rubber and flaming rock). Night feels bright 'n accurate. Art, gazing upward, spies Betelgeuse, one of the shoulders of Orion, the hunter.

Art opens door of his retro-roadster. Una confesses classic car kin-ship: "Mio *Amico*, I drive a fully-restored 1955 Vauxhall Cresta, named *Settebello* (Beautiful Seven) after high card in Italian card game Scopone." Laughs—not that polite reflexive laugh, no, a *real* laugh—least ladylike Art's ever heard: savage, childish, but symphonic, with competing levels 'n strains. Art's Nash's engine sings of work involved in propelling chunk of metal down a road. Ho! He swoons as they pothole-bounce toward Wani-Guchi, Una's fav Japanese grill, for classic seduction meal. Art squeezes dinky auto into impossible parking space in front of destination. Interior of car lights up when Art opens passenger door and image of Una's figure emerging stays in Art's eyes for moment as if Una be composed solely of light. Art blinks. Strong wind blows. Art then notices sheet of newsprint wrap itself around a parking meter with erotic-looking desperation. Awnings along street and automotive mud flaps shiver. Spastic neon of restaurant sign—sounding all sourness 'n static—viciously teases weird ear (even with goop in) as he and Una passes under. "*Irasshaimase*! Una," welcomes beaming chef from behind sizzling grill as our lovers-to-be totter in. Shouting cooks slice squid and hurl it onto metal plate where it leaps like something in hell. Some locals give steely looks; they seem soldered to metal chairs as they prod wooden sticks at what looks like dog shit, swig Saki, and read *Asahi Shimbun.* Good thing weird ear be gooped. Hokusai prints grace walls. As Art watches Una's lips order dinner, visually devours her slippery soft-muscled mouth in dancing light of this simulated Nippon country barbecue. Both drink The Purple Haze (hot Saki with splash of Chambord) as they gobble Teppan Yaki and philosophize:"I agree, life is not always perfect; but," parries Una, "it's relaxing in its way, decent spaces between one thing and another—as between ants in a procession across a footpath—or like notes in a Satie composition marching along the measure." "Ho!"amplifies Art, "my weird ear itches for that Frenchy's humorous *Sports et divertissements*—kinda like Japanese haiku."

A narrowing of Una eyes may be interpreted as saying: *Fuck, I'm impressed!"* But puzzlement shows (Art thinks) in darkness of veins on tender side of her arm. And this mixed message in her bodily expressions continues as Art confesses to finally understanding—at his age—that Braque had no sense of humor. But she's *really* impressed when she finds out that Art is conversant with Norman Lindsay's oddball children's book *The Magic Pudding: Being the Adventures of Bunyip Bluegum and his Friends Bill Barnacle and Sam Sawno*. The Author will spare The Reader this hour-long discussion about the Magic Pudding, which is a pie, except when it's something else, like steak, or jam donut, or apple dumpling, or whatever its owner wants it to be, and fast-forward to arrival at Art's dome-home, which Una dubs "Domo Arigato," pun rooted in how thankful she is at what transpires in dome that night as their new geography drifts toward congruity.

2.2   Upon arrival at dome-home, Art changes into yellow jump suit, while Una's brown eyes stare in max befuddlement at device with shimmering glass discs of varying size stacked horizontally in-line. Ho! It's Art's armonica. He loves its incomparably sweet tones, which swell and soften at his pleasure by stronger or weaker pressure of his finnies upon glass discs. Spittin' image of Ben Frankĺin's old glass musical invention. Well-tuned and with weird ear ungooped, provides tastes and visions of confections forbidden on his low-carb diet. Before Una can ask "What the hell is this," Art's tugging her into kitchen to prepare her his fav late-night snack, "Ants on the Log," celery stick with super chunky peanut butter and raisins.

She confesses to musical interest too. As founder of, and lead singer in, teenage garage band, Moist and the Towelettes. "We really wiped out the competition in a local Battle of the Bands." Sound of her chewing on those chips of nut contrasting with softer raisins makes him see mineral samples. Mouth full of dissolving peanut butter, she tells Art her mother once saw her in bath and gave cry: " 'You are a golden girl!' " then burst into tears. When her hot tongue be peanutty enough, it unerringly finds Art's weird ear. So intense is sound of chunky-peanut-butter-grinding-in-ear—**WIMBLECCCLICK CLICK CRUMBLECHAWOCRUNCHY**—he does taste old Portuguese culinary favorite oft served up by his wife's friend Mrs. Kàc: *ximxim galinha* (chicken braised in peanut-oil and served with the sauce of ground shrimp, sweet peppers, onions, peanuts, and ginger).

"Here's where he hears," Art points proudly around his golf ball dome-home, "with an ear as ravenous as our information-hungry global econ-omy." All inside is curvy. Curves based on myriad of golf strokes, ball trajectories, precise stuff. "Besides golf, it's is inspired by Barcelona's famed architect, Antoni Gaudi, who wrote of his Casa Mìla, that, 'the corners will disappear and the material will abundantly manifest itself in its astral rotundities; the sun will penetrate on all four sides and it will be the image of para-dise . . . and my palace will be more luminous than light!' How 'bout that?"

"My, you weren't just astickin' your nose in my ear," Una replies, astonished at what she sees. "No wife, huh?" she coos, collecting him in gentle coils of her voice, voice of perfect clarity which Art hears as golden hailstones ringing against sonorous crystal.

"I'm divorced now. Was maulsticked by Timmy Maulstick. Come upstairs."

They traipse up wrought-iron curving staircase. "I can guess why!" she murmurs under her breath, noticing computer print-out banner above ear-shaped bed placed dead center in bedroom:

BANG A GONG, GET IT ON.

Cominciamo!" she announces, smiling like gleam of starlight across frozen steppe. Blond hair spread like parachute 'n spin around her, light 'n feathery 'n infinitely strokable. It fall around in haze; she fire smouldering look at him for just one heartbeat. He prime ear with quick twist of little left pinky 'n turn super-sensitive organ toward blond. Hear her thick eyelashes rustling against her cheeks when she blink. She sit absent-mindedly, do rub knees together.

"Yes," pleads Art, "Do rub-a-dub knees together. Rub-a-dub-dub!" It's excruciating; like watching some transgendered Oliver Twist ask for more porridge.

SSSSSHWWWWWGEEEEESHWWWWGEEEEEESWGGE

SSSSSSSSSHWWWWWGEEEEESHWWWWGEEEEEES

He hear sound—nylon-on-nylon (like audiotape of same in Truffaut's *The Bride Wore Black*)—and distinguishes individual synthetic fiber against individual synthetic fiber. Odor of lilac and pulverized feldspar (constituent of aggregate called gneiss) fill his nose. Synaesthesia linked to overly sensitive ear. Start to taste it. Start to hyperventilate, swoon. She catch on, stimulates his auditory organ with soft osculation of voice. Earotica. Her hand up shift, right index fingernail scratching crotch of black silk panties:

SSSSSSHWWWWWGEESHWGEEESWGGGSWEEEE [pause]

SSSSSSHWWWWWGEESHWGEEESWGGGSWEEEE [pause]

Her sex-kitten p-a-u-s-e-s that absolutely, bar-none, drive him crazy. Then zipper of shift slowwwwwwwly undone. *Like delicious teething on slate*, he thinks.

ZZZZZZZZZZZZZZZZZZ [pause] **ZZZZZZZZZZZZZZZZZZ**

ZZZZZZZZZZZZZZZZZZ [pause] **ZZZZZZZZZZZZZZZZZZ**

Something is *Crook* in Middlebrook

Sound of shift falling to floor end with light PLUFFF. *Like melted ice cream puddling in grotto of geode,* he thinks.

"I am filled with hope for a lovely series of auditory revelations which I pray will never end," mutters under breath, as Una silently repeats truism: *The admission of desire entails a larger wish.*

She starts new routine: bra shoulder straps caught up by thumbs, pulled forward and be snapped against white flesh. Several times. Same with garters. He wince with delightful pain at sharp sound sounding like ball-peen hammer on obsidian. Feels flecks (sharp, black chip rock) in throat. Off comes bra, unhooking sounds like metal girders rubbing together twenty stories over Michigan Avenue. Actual fall silent as flake of mica drop-dropping into Kleenex box. Stockings peel off legs. Audits each stubbly leg hair pulling free of fiber and tastes powdered kunzite. He in yellow jump suit. She now unzip it neck to crotch, like peeling super big banana. Art gazes at proud drama of her face, valves 'n orbits of her throat, wetlook runnels of her hair, those breasts, heavier than ever, solidly mounted on ribcage, naked slopes of her belly, that sudden flaring of hips, smell of sex. Now pair tumble into his ear-shaped bed. Una's hair be oiled 'n colored with sexual heat 'n sometimes does ripple like fast-flowing water. Inner thighs be exceptionally smooth; skin be snakelike there: it shines. Art seeks silky complicit creases in tendons near her cleft. Reciprocating, she sticks long finny deep into his left ear (Art insists she refer to this act as "enclosure," not "penetration") and notices spiraling, folded inward; both ear 'n shell seem vulva-like 'n recall her own private hours of satisfaction. As she labors, he does hear nubile opening bars of *Peter and the Wolf.* And then . . .

"Holy hearin'!" screams Art. Taste of Tootsie Pop leaks onto his tongue. Q-gasm stronger than does get from masturbating ear with Q-tip.

"Yeeeee ssshit!" yells she when notices his awful ear wax on her digit, followed by light blowing of air behind her new lover's ear. Her sexual gifts ring tinkly-tinselly bells of ecstacy deep in Art's middle ear. "*Il mio dolce stil nuovo,*" whispers Una, then sighs, "*sovramagnificentissimamente*" [very, very magnificent]. Put your ear to my ribs on the left side 'n you'll hear me echoing." Such love! Appropriate here be movie music, music like in those old movies when man 'n woman run through heather, hand-in-hand. Camera then would slowly scan down her beauty spots: one above breast, one above belly, one above knee, one above ankle, one above buttock, one above back of neck—all so itemized be on left side in perfect vertical row.

As his consciousness does titrate back into his body, Art can feel both darkness and hear silence—and his head hums with them. He puts his weird ear directly on his new lover's yummy tummy and hears soft brush-strokes, that Japanese music of her insides, then light whirr of silence. In this unusual woman, he feels startling absence of inner struggle, equilibrium of mind that seems to exempt this lover from usual conflicts 'n aggressions of modern life: self-doubt, envy, sarcasm, need to judge or belittle others, freed from scalding, unbearable ache of personal ambition. This is what Art will fall in love with: sense of calm, radiant silence burning within. As Art spraddles on bed, Una squids around beneath quilt, her mind returning to default condition of ready-to-buyness.

Something is *Crook* in Middlebrook

2.3   Two days later. Una receives flowers 'n cute note from Art:

> Una My Ear-Source,
>
> Great night. I slept still as a pane of glass beside you and I was satisfied to the point I walked funnier than usual for a whole day.
>
> I want to lick your professionally whitened teeth, those winsome gums. I want to lick them. With my tongue. I want to retrieve your mail for you. I will bundle it with a rubber band and leave it on your stoop, then sneak away. You won't even know that I've been there. I want to grow very tiny and have you put me in your back pocket.
>
> Love, Arty

If note not enough excuse, bright tempting morning lurks outside Una's Sunset Towers apartment just off Michigan Avenue (sun sets in west, but Sunset Towers faces east and has no towers). A call to wander. So Una roars over to Art's in her Vauxhall model E, sporting childishly flounced tutu plus bra-sized half-shirt, dappled here and there by her spicy sweat; looks tired, eyes hollowed. Brings with her gift of tomatoes so red 'n bloody they look like cow's organs. "Just caffeine me," she pleads. Over Intelligentsia brand coffee they discuss *that* note: dwell on paradox of word "cleave," which means both "to join together" and "to break apart," embodying two equal 'n opposite significations that are two possible outcomes of Art 'n Una's new relationship. Over java 'n Danish, Art tells Una, "You're the only person I've ever met who looks only like yourself. What's your ex like?"

"My first husband? . . . a most hirsute man. My mother had him pegged when she referred to him as, 'One strange object covered with fur that breaks your heart.' She got a way with words. Say, you too can look like yourself, Arty," coos Una. "I think you need a bozotic bod mod. Tattoo. Let's go right now. No procrastination, my, my—er—my *homeslice!*" Holds out hand wanting Art to give her ye ol' soul clasp, confirming coinage of new term of endearment. In real world of sound 'n color, in fleshed-out, 3-D world of five senses, four elements 'n two sexes, Art has never met creature to compare with this one. But encounters hard sparkling granite wall of her stubbornness when he tries to resist her request. But gives in when given gift of new, unique T-shirt (see frontispiece) meant to replace his old one which states: FEAR THE QUASIHEMIDEMISEMIQUAVER (a 128th note in music).

"Okay, let's do it!" Smiling, gesturing, as if unfolding something half hidden and dazzling.

Una plops into purple 'n white tuck-and-roll seat next to Art in his vintage Nash Metropolitan. Gives firm directions to Skin Kreations. Funky tattoo parlor on south Western Avenue specializes in *ripper* style tattoos. Wants Art to get such depicting anatomy of inner ear. To be supered over his weird ear (see frontispiece). Upon entering, they notice slight odor of sweat and focused violence. They take seats, waiting. Across from them sits young blond with purple streaked hair wearing Guess jeans and white T-shirt with quote from some obscure Jean Baudrillard text thereon. She's sipping coffee and eyeing Art's HI, I'M ART AND I'M A NATIONAL TREASURE AND I HATE NOISE T-shirt, a gift from Una. Art spies livid bruises above her wrist, blue 'n yellow clouds of damaged skin from some masochistic game played (perhaps) with her lover who now is having his biceps decorated in next room. Una wants to get her address, to send her spanking new copy of Karen Krankinkl's latest scrotum-tightener from Feminist Front Press called *Not On Our Lives.*

Instead, Una pulls out pack of Gitanes, lights cigarette and settles back to thumb through month old copy of *Paris Match* found on small table nearby lying next to soaked tissues and coffee-stained sugar sachets. As she reads, Art studies her impassive face. Her unlined visage is pale from too many cigarettes, too many late nights with boring lovers who fail to appreciate her. Eventually, our pair be beckoned into inner sanctum of that den of pain. Forgotten smile lingering on his lips like a tide-mark, old near-toothless Thai tattoo artist looking utterly ruined with red bags under his eyes, sizes up Art. His breath contains weak memory of Singha beer 'n pot stickers. Art's head is strapped into device to steady it. Soon sharp, small needle traces design (Xeroxed by Una from *Gray's Anatomy*) on Art's outraged flesh. Art bites tongue, hard; for unknown reason name of famous French pilot-author Saint-Exupéry enters his *cabeza.* Una's watchful eyes make like those of over-gifted child witnessing autopsy.

2.4   Spaceship Earth. Chicago, Illinois. Sun putting out more energy in one second than human-kind has put out since the beginning of time. Inside golf-ball dome-home. In ear-shaped bed. Weird ear, stinging from tattoo needle, buried in soft pillow so car alarms less alarming. Art in reverie where magic of words brings new dawning and even sure shelter (whatever *that* means): Honeysuckles with digited pistils advance as if on clawed hands. The couch grass, lycopods, mignonettes, green and gray plebeians multiply in immense carpets over which run avant-garde of mad bindweed bearing cups from which trickle blue drunkenness. And only silence livest and reignest. But, alas, at thought of drunkenness floral reverie evaporates and replaced by dusty smell of Art's father's ancestral home on Hudson Street in Antigo, Wisconsin and sour stench of drunken daddy didact's dictating Hispanic history over shot glass of Jack Daniels: How one Spanish Queen of days of yore be filching gunpowder set aside for impending Portuguese campaign so as not to deplete national income, which she sees better spent on sublimity of theater and opera. World's first official anti-art-mageddon policy. At mental re-mentioning of such sublime art forms being related by such plastered papa, Art gets auditory hallucination of harsh sounds of discordant brass band. *Ah, Big Father of the big muscles and the boom, boom, boom*, he muses, unconsciously rubbing his buttocks. Art suddenly recalls earliest memory of Big Father's declaration of affection: "You remind me of a somesuch or a groan, I don't know which!" Yes, his father, a hard man living in age of miracles 'n wonder.

That queen—lucky for old Portugal, lucky for Portuguese actors, singers, and painters—is unlucky herself. Upon queen's death king—as story goes—attempts to violate royal corpse as it coldly lay in state betwixt 'n between rows of beeswax candles and pious praying monks. Art's mind zig-

Something is *Crook* in Middlebrook

zags like his drunken driving daddy minutes before he hits car full of sen-escent nuns head on near St. Sabina's. Even five years after his daddy's death old man be still hitch-hikin' 'round in his grey matter. Art's mental-machine stops and picks him up along with ghost of vacations-past. Dead daddy and he both catch following rerun at The Engram Drive-in:

> *Public square, Barcelona, Spain. Sacred drama of the Annunciation. Art and his Dad stuff fresh Agfachrome film in their Voitlander f/2.8 cameras. The performance begins. St. Michael doffs his cloak before The Virgin, disclosing a leg-of-mutton sleeve decked with ribbons and little mauve wings. The Virgin offers him a cup of chocolate, which he refuses, God-The-Father once promising him fish-stew for dinner. Then The Holy Ghost enters and the three people celebrate their union in big improper fandango, while the foreign ambassadors who look on are quite utterly flabber-gasted. Like The Virgin, The Devil is ubiquitous.*

As he snuggles deeper into pillow, Art recalls trip he and his daddy immediately take afterwards to see famous works of Goya—*The Caprichos, The Disparates, The Colossus, The Fear*. Art speculates on inverse and ana-grammatical relationship between The Master of Seeing (Goya) and The Stream of Hearing (Art). Ironic that Goya was deaf and Art now hears *mucho*. Great exponent of agony that Goya, while Art's life is test of exponential agony of increased levels of sound. Goya seems to draw things *from inside*, while Art hears things *from outside*.

Both Goya and Art *grok* that human race is race of victims. But former sees 'em, latter hears 'em. Thanks to super-hearing, Art hears plenty ugh-ugly stuff about racism, about petty politics of academia, marital squab-bles, cruel cops, ass-kissing politicians, avaricious aldermen, harried bike-messengers, and miscellaneous over-reaching, back-stabbing, back-biting crew members of Spaceship Earth. Not to mention incessant radios, televis-ions, screeches of fax-machines, cell-phones (vehicles for the voices of the lonesome crowd, needing to come together), and such of Electronic America. Like during his first trip back into Loop since brain event. Passes Marshall Fields after said retailer bought out by New York's Macy's. Shopping bags with Red China-like stars on 'em now replace calm green Field's bags in shoppers' hands. So heap big protest among nostalgic locals. Weekends scores of jeer-ing protestors (some dressed in nineteenth-century facsimile) march angrily 'n incessantly around 'n around the shamed store caterwauling through rainbow coalition of colored-plastic battery-powered bullhorns over 'n over:

> **HEY, HEY, HO, HO. THE MACY'S NAME HAS GOT TO GO. HEY, HEY, HO, HO. THE MACY'S NAME HAS GOT TO GO. HEY, HEY, HO, HO. THE MACY'S NAME HAS GOT TO GO. HEY, HEY, HO, HO. THE MACY'S NAME HAS GOT TO GO. HEY, HEY, HO, HO. THE MACY'S . . .**

Something is *Crook* in Middlebrook

When weird ear ungooped, Art does taste sudden bitter splash of Gin Rickey cocktail while ear throbs in sympathy with repeated syncopation. Ho! Annoying throb even lasts long after auditory stimulus absent. Later, when he relates awful aural event to Una, she starts 5.5 minute rant about how she will never shop at Macy's because: gall of Big Apple Corporate to destroy 154 years of Chicago tradition, poor maintenance of architecturally significant structure, shoddy product, lousy window and floor displays, somber all-black garbed staff, blah, blah. *Blessed Benimming!* Art thumb-stuffs in ear goop.

2.5   And then just yesterday. Ah, some too cheery radio talk show host asking. Perplexed call-in listener pondering. Perfidious audience awaiting. Prize in the balance: year's supply of Brook Shields brand condoms. Oddball belluine question coming from inscrutable innards of Korean Bang Ho's #1 Shoe Repair Shoppe—whose exterior boasts faded sign showing shoulder-padded '80s woman with text: MODERN WOMEN WEAR WHITE TOO!—which Art always passes on his way to The Pleasing Supermarket for over-priced groceries. Notices slight indirect cricothyroid approximation in announcer's voice:

> **WHEN THE COWS BE BELLERING, WHAT IS ARE CALVES DOING? YOU HAVE TWENTY SECONDS TO GIVE ME THE ANSWER MR. KOSTMEYER . . . ONE . . . TWO . . . THREE . . .**

Anticipation. But radio turned off before answer given and prize awarded or not. Struggling with idiom, our Korean proprietor does ask customer,

> **WHAT DO YOU DO FOR THE LIVING?**

Annoyance. Hand dives into pocket. Art tears off fresh lump of ear waxy stuff, rolls soft white crap around awhile with his finnies 'n thumb-stuffs it down external auditory canal of weird ear. Bang Ho (Art dubs him "The Chink in the Armoire") be one *haan*-ridden country *yangpan* who converts to Catholicism and immigrates to U.S. after Korean War. He refuses Art's gift of "Ants on the Log" 'cause he suffers from *arachibutyrophobia,* morbid fear of peanut butter sticking to roof of mouth. Bang Ho is always expressing indignation over something ("*Uh-gul-ha-da*!") like fact his wife suffers "so-bad teef" 'n bouts of *hwa-byung.* Whenever Art attempts to converse with him, he only gets in reply: "You forget me foreign, me no speak Engrish too god; me speak with atrocious accent; me has weak voice 'cause of all great suffering me endure." Always on cutting edge of entrepreneurial pursuits, Bang Ho gives customers custom-made fortune cookie when "laundlee be picky up." Art's last wonky fortune read: "The lone waited for day is rust around the corner. Your extra special to the end. Just look in your mind. Good day."

   Yep, thinks Art, *everything's 'rust around the corner'*! As he saunters back to dome-home that day he sings (to tune of "Home on the Range") bit of doggerel copped from inventor R. Buckminster Fuller: *Roam home to*

Something is *Crook* in Middlebrook

a dome / Where Georgian and Gothic once stood / Now chemical bonds alone guard our blondes /And even the plumbing looks good. One man as thin as a fuse and his dog, cocked 'n spherical as a rocket, pass Art going in opposite direction. Simultaneously in Pogacnic's kitchen—where vivid sunlight makes room seem oppressively populous—Peven cleans his lenses 'n filters. His wife, Noreen, has quick efficiency of people who are used to reality. Shows off her mottled, striped, grainy, ocellated, dotted, speckled, studded skin, her neck-length blah-colored hair so filametous you can detect large patches of scalp through it, her nervous finnies that be knuckled like bubbles in her pudding (she must have stood back in simple dismay when all physical gifts were being handed out) all while intoning wisdom uttered between teeth arrayed like rank of men on stadium terrace, tugged into this or that position by groans of obsessed crowd. Wisdom from, at times, her mother—"Flowers are God smiling at us, deary"—other times citing photographers like Robert Adams [no relation to Ansel], idealist drivel about "the significance of grace in photography," and "a mystery at the end of every terror—the survival of Form." Although Noreen does think of herself as below her husband in every way, in grace, in beauty, in sophistication, Pev realizes she is his angel, repairing him, dressing all his bleeding wounds. She's always on Sri Lankan immigrant mailman for his persistent irritating habit of doing other side of street before doing her side. And, like best of artists, she can discuss the gauze of August light falling across billowing curtains at construction sites; once even goes on e-Bay to bid (successfully) on copy of *Australian Women's Weekly* for Pev's fav recipe for Tuna Casserole. When she's really 'on' she walks calmly, her head raised, face lit with particular wisdom, wisdom of plumbing.

2.6   Month after divorce final DOZE-IT DESTRUCTORS, INC. (still located on Pulaski near Irving Park Road) raze Art's $90K old Victorian domicile. Upon Jungian analyst's advice, up goes golf-ball white Bucky Fuller geodesic dome, fifty-foot diameter, with weather-resistant wooden deck in back fully equipped with tiger salamander named "Tiger Woods" prowling and burrowing below among golf balls lost to erratic putts. Confirmed: all curves inside dome precisely based on archetypal golf ball trajectories and break away curves on slopes, etcetera. A barricade to ugliness, a very Western attempt at building a separate personality.

"The sun never knew how wonderful it was," Art tells golf buddy, "until it fell on a golf ball, across those little convex indentations making the ball a Platonic Ideal of the dialectic of tiny crescent-shaped highlights and shadows." Golf ball, solitary eccentric oscillating between highs and lows, white and black—like Art.

How lucky one is! (That's easy to do in literature.) Art's rich uncle dies; his Last Will and Testament makes it through Probate with help of bribe and Art inherits into six digits. Just in time. Needs to settle medical bills, finance dome-home (fashionably insulated with recycled blue jeans), and pay fucking IRS back taxes. Afterward, $33,134.92 to spare. "Christ!" Art exclaims, as he writes out check which, along with his AIC insurance, ultimately pays for Mädchenfänger, M.D.'s daughter's spanking new gun-metal gray Porsche. Later hears, literally, said Porsche wrap itself around light pole across from Museum. Hears M.D.'s daughter moan her way onto stretcher and wailing ambulance head northward toward her daddy's ICU.

Later, in dome-home. Overhead noisy prop plane flies *fortissimo* through humongous cumulus. About three thousand feet up, Art estimates with tilt of weird ear. Not to fear. Life not imitating literature here. No black speck heard falling out of plane—as does in an Aldous Huxley novel—turning into small dog looming larger and larger and larger until it (Christ!) splatters at ground-zero shooting hot turkey-red liquid onto shaken spectators. Wrought-iron spiral staircase inside dome-home leads to shallow turret—"the cockloft," Art calls it—perched at apex. Next to light with dimmer switch is small scrap of elegant paper framed, upon which is Una's perfect handwriting spelling out curious and (given Art's name) punning assertion: "Art is what makes life more interesting than art." *I'm glad she didn't capitalize the 'a' in the final 'art',* he muses. Curved windows for good view and meshed screens for optimal use of super-hearing surround black Naugahyde 'n chrome swivel barstool placed dead-center. Copped from Smog-Cutter Lounge in Silver Lake area of Los Angeles ten years previous, it permits Art to rest rump thereon and ear-scan four-points of compass with chancy roulette spin. Panaudicon supreme tunes in tonight to "Queer-Eye for the Straight Guy" TV show blaring in neighboring house:

MATERIALS OF CHOICE THIS MONTH: LIBERTY PAISLEY PATTERNS, DARK DENIM, AND CORDUROY. WHY NOT PLAY OFF YOUR NEW LOIS JUMBO FLARED CORDS AGAINST A CHUNKY PAIR OF PUMA BLOCKAS AND A POWDER BLUE V-NECK WITH OPTIONAL SKI JACKET. AND REMEMBER, RETRO RAINWEAR RE-VIVAL IS UNDERWAY! DIG OUT YER PETER STORMS!

2.7   Eleven months since Art's brain event. May 5th. Sky opens and rolls back like scroll; simultaneously, Al Schmerbauch (Art's next door neighbor 'n best buddy 'cause ever since Art confesses, "I wept at first seeing the Pytha-gorean theorem." "Me too!" Al screams.) opens valve of his wit: "My doctor has always told me to drink and smoke. He even explains himself: 'Drink? Well all sensible people understand that the use, and even more the abuse, of fermented beverages is what distinguishes men from beasts.' And, 'Smoke, my friend, otherwise someone else will smoke in your place.' Well, I sure don't want that on my conscience," deadpans Al to one startled Arthur S. Middlebrook as they sit inside Al's bozotic abode, in which meticulous order and sordid disarray gleefully rub shoulders. (Isn't that the essence of Chaos Theory?)

Ah Al! He does have reputation which, in family circles 'n among professors, provokes sudden silences 'n obvious embarrassment. As a child he was weird mixture of vice 'n virtue: half brat, half prodigy (a *potache*, as bistro owner Pau D'Arco has it in French). Maybe schizo because mother wants to call him "Alwyn," father wants "Frederick," so they compromise with "Alfred." Which Al is encouraged to write as "Al-Fred"—it looks more Moorish that way explains his father—until he is eighteen and rebels. Like Art, Al's

Something is *Crook* in Middlebrook

childhood be spent in picturesque 'n stifling Midwest town best known for its inhabitants' dogged devoutness 'n high incidence of alcoholism. Watershed book in little Al's pre-teen life is A. E. van Vogt's *The Weapon Shops of Isher* which features a "callidetic" character named Cayle Clark who cleans out casinos. This super-lucky (i.e., callidetic) Isherite forever fascinates Al, but such sci-fi disgusts overbearing father. Like Art's dead daddy, father-son relationship be collision of violent vectors. Al refers to his dad as "Himself" (short for The-Man-Himself); daddy never be complimentary: "Al-Fred, your character is nothing to shout about; like all of us you're a negligible assemblage of atoms. But, by Odin, I will grant you one quality: you don't cling like the Moms [his son's moniker for his wife, April June]. Remember, the man who knows his own limitations has none!" Explaining "the birds-'n-the-bees" to his son, he offers: "Al-Fred, love is only a cognitive-affective state characterized by intrusive and obsessive fantasizing concerning reciprocity of amorant feelings by the object of the amorance." Ho! Any wonder that both Al 'n Art share literary fact that random sampling of their writings disclose texts produced by single entity who seems to inhabit two different countries of the mind?

Fibonacci sequence—1st, 2nd, 3rd, 5th, 8th, 13th, 21st—demarcates days of month when Al Schmerbauch—short, pot-bellied Professor of Combinatorial Analysis at Northwestern, who has enough hair on his hands to account for what is missing on his head, devoted golf enthusiast, and Art's neighbor—permits social interaction. Accepts or declines invites only by toss of coin: heads = yes, tails = no. Did his doctoral dissertation on coemergence of realistic novel (fictional reality) and calculus of probabilities and statistics in nineteenth century. Al's fav fiction includes Edgar Allan Poe's "The Mystery of Marie Rogêt (wherein theory of probability is mentioned several times), Jorge Luis Borges's "The Lottery of Babylon" (its obvious why), and any novel by Paul Auster. Other than hobnobbing with buddies, he's found groaning among shadows in his home or office. He's reading heap-heavy tome called *The Best Jokes Explained*. He's forty-one = prime number. His fav quip is: "Extraordinary how math helps you to know yourself." Al's in philosophical mood: "The Calculus of Probabilities," he tells Art, "is purely mathematical, while daily events are contingent, mysterious; ergo, we have the anomaly of the most rigidly exact in science applied to the shadow 'n spirituality of the most intangible in speculation. For instance, golf: an aleatory flutter of uncontrolled, metastatic growth, each well-shot ball admitting of n possible lies on the green." Wants to yak up Art about his latest book: *Quasi-Likelihood and its Application*. Especially anxious to get Art's response to math conundrum used in frontispiece to book:

$$12 \times 0 = 0 \text{ and } 13 \times 0 = 0; \text{ therefore: } 12 \times 0 = 13 \times 0;$$
$$\text{divide both sides by } 0; \text{ therefore } 12 = 13. \text{ Q. E. D.}$$

Until he was twelve, Al be more familiar with Africa than his own body. As undergrad, was youth deranged by German philosophy, but later converts to Anglo-Saxon empiricism, mathematics, and noonday reason under the name of "Mediterranean virtue." Yes, Al, virtuous . . . and plump . . . with dash of freshened sadness. In politically correct terms, Al is *vert-ically challenged, trying to avoid follicular regression.* But before the body, there is the face, and before the face there is the thin black line between Al's nose 'n upper lip; a twitchin' filament of anxieties, a metaphysical jump rope, a dancin' thread of discombobulation. A seismograph of Al's inner states, his mustache do be key to what Al be thinking. Important as when they first meet, Al tells Art, "My obsessions are mind things, not geared to action much. I hate people who, like my father, bed their sunglasses in their hair." Art notices on Al's forehead one very wavy winkle above two straight gouges, like the approximately-equal-to sign in math. "What I do best," continues Al, "are the absurdities of daily life: I observe, add up these observations, increase them to the nth degree and draw the square root from them, but with a different factor from the one I increased them by. I believe only in chance, not in destiny. Chance: the art of being about half right, even when one is dead wrong." His fav ejaculation is "Choice!" (chance 'n excellence wrapped into one word). When only five, Al calculates density of movable furniture in parents' home as 9.7 lb/ft^2. When six, I figures out how much he'd weigh on each of planet in solar system. Another time, Al proves universe prefers kilometers to miles: "The speed of light is 186,282 miles per second; in kilometers it's almost exactly 300,000 kilometers per second? No? And 1 light-hour is 670,000,000 miles, which is close to 1,000,000,000 kilometers; average distance between sun and earth, center to center, is 92,950,000 miles, but it that's very close to 15,000,000 kilometers!" Al, trained in best universities, lives by following formula: *Probability of a future decreases in inverse proportion to its theoretical remoteness.*

Alfred Schmerbauch, as a young graduate student, watching a Random Mechanical Cascade display

Yes, rigors of his intellectual training do gradually fine tune him into someone who looks at himself from a distance, to see himself first of all as a man among other men, then as a collection of random particles of matter, and finally a single speck of dust. His hard-thinking expression resembles sort of comically distorted face made to amuse an infant. Al's reaction to Art's enhanced hearing? "It's you to the second power." Al's only concession to Positivism is his famous Comedian Rooms wherein he hangs in his home old film stills: there is the Buster Keaton Room, the Marx Brothers Room, the Bob

Something is *Crook* in Middlebrook

Hope Room, the Laurel 'n Hardy Room, and so forth. Not pretty, but not not-pretty either. Fact: whenever Art meets Al, he enters speaking in puns because Al's powerful rationality leaves very little room for unequivocal alternative perspectives. Like Al's distaste for Rusk Boettcher, his razor-sharp-whiff-of-alcohol breath, his ughsome presence, and his recidivist spawn. Ho! Sullen in sweet air gladdened by sun, such is our neighborhood sot.

2.8   Thirteen months since Art's brain-event. Just yesterday it be loveless day, without drifting clouds; unclear branches against shapeless sky—like hostile animals; whole vast sky as some defect of vision. Today, magically, just reverse.

YEEEEEEEEEEEEEEEEEEEEEEEEEEEEEEEEEEEEEEEEEEEE
YEEEEEEEEEEEEEEEEEEEEEEEEEEEEEEEEEEEEEEEEEEEEE

Doloriferous wailing—especially to enlarged, acutely sensitive, left ear of Art—reverbs down his pharyngo-tympanic tube. Art tastes it: distinctly yellow—icterous. Past his tongue, his tonsils swelling, it skips adenoids though and goes down through palatine to lingual tonsil. Creepy sensation of infiltration halts him in mid-gimp.

YEEEEEEEEEEEEEEEEEEEEEEEEEEEEEEEEEEEEEEEEEEEEE
EEEEEEEEEEEEEEEEEEEEEEYEEEEEEEEEEEEEEEEEEEEEEE

Big Bluffer-brand car alarm is yawping. Four blocks east, exactly. Fact: no one pays attention to alarm; it's always going into noisy jimjams over slightest breeze, most casual bump. Boettcher Brats (always as volatile as popcorn) like to pump up futuristic-looking gray SONIC-SOCK air-guns 'n bounce invisible concentrated balls of O_2, CO, CO_2, SO_2, and O_2 off this sports car's perfectly vertical rear window. Predictable effect. Four blocks away? Pending confirmation—via left pinky—that umber blob o' waxy cerumen be not crammed against his tympanic membrane, skewing calculations.

YEEEEEEEEEEEEEEEEEEEEEEEEEEEEEEEEEEEEEEEEEEEE
EEEEEEEEEEEEEEEEEEEEEEYEEEEEEEEEEEEEEEEEEEEEE

Reason to be sad wailing. Neighbor Al Schmerbauch effusively tells him later: "That shady debarred lawyer, Avvocato Toscafundi, had his turkey-red Toyota MR2 copped in splashing full sunlight right out under the nose, no less, of that yenta Noreen Pogacnic clad in those horrible faded chartreuse shorts out watering her gasping lawn."

"Hot damn, what a yegg be he who copped that car!" answers Art.

When Boettcher's back door opens, out fly twins, unloosed like two locomotives hurtling along side by side; Brats in their feverish state of pale childhood—noisy, messy, egomaniacal, cruel, combative, recalcitrant, naive,

Something is *Crook* in Middlebrook

needy, histrionic, uniformed, opinionated, untruthful, insecure, moody, amoral, and physical and emotionally destructive—scream "Phlblaaatth!" They beat all over with pulses, nothing but craving defenseless greedy hearts, whose antics evoke from Pau this Frenchly retort: *"Quels merdeux! Merdre et re-merde et reremerdre!"* While Art quips that Brats' antics prove wrong Teddy Adorno's dictum: "The unreality of children's games gives notice that reality has not yet become real. Unconsciously they rehearse the right life." All this ten days since Art almost waffles two Vietnamese kids while driving near his dome-home in vintage purple 'n white Nash Rambler Metropolitan. Near victims be sons of Ngo Truong Huy, owner of Hoang Kim ("The Golden Age") Vietnamese Restaurant spicing up corner near Ravenswood EL's Damen stop; there Art gobbles down pornographic-sounding noodle dish, *Bun Thit Nuong* while lusting after Ngo's wife whose beauty is like Chinese lantern hanging in oak tree.

Five days since Rusk "Beer-bibber" Boettcher (b. Severed Root, Kentucky where only claim to fame there be his never-beaten sales record for subscriptions to *Grit*, billed as "America's Greatest Family Newspaper") enrolls in suburban jerkwater college (where Art used to teach). Life gives him many reasons to be on guard, but none to be frightened. Wants to get AA Degree in auto-mechanics. Wants that lusty Mechanic's Body: those rough, tender hands, that knowing stoop. Slow going as he suffers, as Al puts it, "a certain parsimony

Rusk Boettcher, age 13, with *Grit*

of imagination," and various levels of alcohol lapping at his smudged brain (which has evolved schnoz on him like some way-hemorrhaged strawberry). Ho! His handshake be pulverizing, hugs be rib cracking, and (as per spousal testimony) his kisses be wet, doggy, possessive. A fried-chicken 'n pork chop kind of guy *avec* toads' eyes (*yeux de crapauds*, Pau calls 'em), heart of a deer, and turbulent complexion. He lacks proper sense of personal worthlessness that would fuel overachievement. His moniker be "Roo," his fav smart-ass retort be: "Why don't you shut yer mouth 'n give yer arse a chance?" Ask him question, reply be maximum of two short sentences as if every word costs him ten dollars. Attends night classes—complaining to academic advisor that his "monkey mind" has his thoughts swinging from limb to limb, stopping only to scratch themselves, spit, and howl—while working days at service station he dubs "The Realm of Rowdy Ratchets." Boss be brassy Basil Acerbopolous who sports muscularity somehow furious, as though some process like gnashing of teeth went into building up all that strength. Local Greeks dub Basil *Polymechanikos*, The Crafty One.

If art student do Super-Realist painting of Roo titled *Rusk Before Dusk*, we'd see lanky blank figure stretching sore back in tumescent heat-hazed carscape, silent, unreflecting, alone. If this painter be heap sensitive, he (or she) would capture that unshirkably elemental something about him: his cave shave, noble-savage beer-belly, ears crinkled like Chinese cabbage, that empty gaze giving him air of eternal flybuzz boredom. But when angry, a real fizzer, all set to pop. Roo be like cart hitched to wild horse named "Drunkenness," alongside trained horse named "Rationality." Lazy *and* hardworking. Beats Deena one moment, elaborate apologias thereafter (Dee retaliates by wearing her trenchcoat to bed and encourages her twins to have beautiful penmanship to take revenge through her offspring upon her illiterate husband). Roo tends to thrust alcoholic belch as big as opened umbrella into middle of something someone else is trying to say. When twin sons ask if he hit lots of home-runs in high school or took Minnesota Fats at billiards, reply to such queries always be: "Yoose ta could. Yoose ta could." Why boss Basil does season retorts to Roo's verbal diarrhea with: "*Blaberon, Adikon,*" (pronouncing it: "Blabber on, a dick on," punning with classic Greek terms for 'harmful' and 'unjust'). Sorry about this Roo, you simply *had* to be this way—nothing personal buddy, please understand—in order to serve the textual demands of our little docudrama.

July 8th is Fibonacci number. So okay for Art to invite golf buddy Al onto backyard deck for vanilla-flavored iced coffee. Weather? Muggy, per-haps, but gentle breeze obtains. Sometimes small puffy anthropomorphic cloud floats belly-up just north; occasionally it passes between deck 'n sun, paling our interlocutors. Today Art's ear goop *in situ*, but loosely. Gotta be wary. Boettcher Brats. Noisy-nosy sons of Rusk and Deena, outside on prowl like Deimos 'n Phobos dogging Mars—fear and dread. As full of schemes 'n secrets as Court of Byzantium, Twins rename days of the week—Shunday, Moanday, Tearsday, Woundsday, Thirstday, Firesday, Shatterday—to cor-respond with actions that Dee dubs "a kind of beautiful mischief." Ah, Dee!

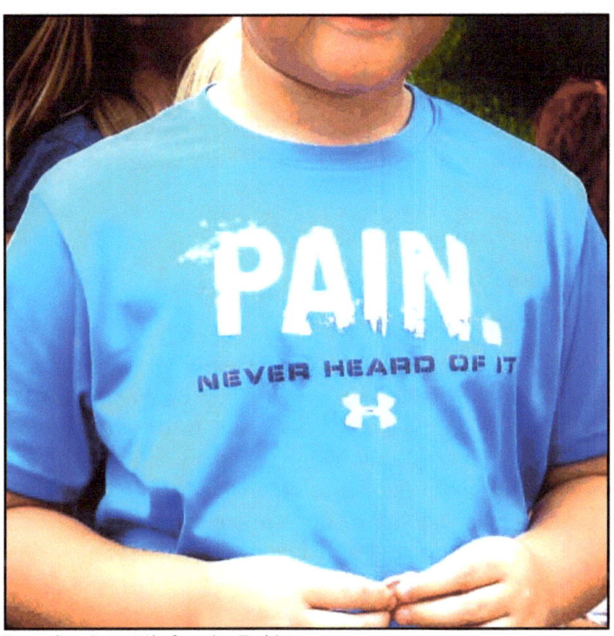

Boettcher Brat #1's favorite T-shirt

She do be big brawny vision in her youth, with encouraging hint of rural gulli-bility in breadth of her eyes 'n lips. But years of living with that hammer-fisted sot, Roo (who berates his wife's love of cham-pagne, calling it "giggle-water"), and . . . well . . . there are times when she feels so starved for warmth that in-structions her on painkiller packet or vitamin bottle makes her go all limp 'n weepy, and times when both her boxed ears forced to listen to drunk talk played back sober, so that occasionally her right ear does a perfect jet imitation, with whistle 'n whine 'n hungry rumble of underfloor fire. Speaking of underfloor, beneath Art's deck one huge, grotesquely cuddling salamander lurks, oranges eyes peering out of the dim.

Something is *Crook* in Middlebrook

Al flops into canvas deck chair, exclaims "Choice!" Keeps crossing 'n recrossing his legs, which are so short he seems to Art to be twiddling his thumbs. He's balding, bushy-bearded, stoop-shouldered, bewildered and somewhat ridiculous scholar with child-like look of wonderment behind his black plastic (Golden Section ratio) rectangular glasses. Al be confirmed bachelor; until discovers Internet porn, only foreplay be on golf green.

Art, his eyebrows raising 'n lowering as if sending private messages, starts off their verbal brawl, "Both irrationalism and rationalism are equal ingredients of both my thinking and that of Spanish philosopher Miguel De Unamuno."

"I'm good today," promises Al, "I'll neither adopt external positions in order to refute your Unamunoist assumptions, nor try to expose your internal contradictions. I won't even chide you to practice a rigorous *Cogito* ear go *sum.*"

"Just *hear* him here," Art pleads. "No pedantic . . ."

"Only mild rejoinders, I vow." (Dear Reader, are you skeptical?)

"Unamuno's first novel's title describes me and our world today: *Peace in War*. I'm an actor in an objective epic. I *hear* like Goya's *I see this*. Unamuno's cry *Inward!* akin to my cry *Toward me!* about how sounds come to my much sensitive left ear. *The horror, the horror*, says Colonel Kurtz in Coppola's flick *Apocalypse Now*. Like me, Unamuno never belongs to any single political party. Like Unamuno, I am a heretic to all parties. Unamuno lives in Salamanca in the thirties, while I have lost some thirty golf balls under the deck of my dome-home. Fav philosopher is against tyranny of ideas. I am against tyranny of sound. Damn Boettcher Brats! I, like Unamuno, insist on predominance of the concrete. Likes high spikers put down hard on hard concrete!"

"I think a category mistake is being made . . ."

"Concrete over abreaction . . ."

"Abstraction. Abstraction," corrects Al.

"I hear you. No need to repeat like child's *ma ma,* or *da da*." Clearing his throat, Art continues, "Unamuno's really into the tragic sense of life. In his *The Tragic Sense of Life* he argues back and forth with himself. Soul? No soul. Yes soul. No soul. Yes soul. Over soul's immortality or not. Warring coexistence there is like mini-*Putsch* going on inside both Miguel and Art. World of perpetual strife is for both of us our 'Lavoo-Vahna,' our utopian paradise. But for Miguel it's only a formal principle of his philosophical system. For me this push-pull applies to all waking existence. I'm more Eargistential than Unamuno is Existential. Ya grok?"

"That perpetual battle of Unamuno's between heart and head, huh?"

"My left ear hears things as close, right as far. The weird ear says yes to sound, but when ear goop in, it says no. I've always been good in geology, but just barely scrape by in my painting classes.*" Maybe why I now love to scrape paintings,* he muses. "Still love ex-wife, but must fine tune Una to be superb *hearker.*"

"Hooker?"

Something is *Crook* in Middlebrook

"No, hearker. . . . Aural sex. . . . Do like kids, but I sure hate the Boettcher Brats. Only thing not open to question is promulgated in the motto over my dome-home's front door: *No sooner said than heard. . . .* You know that famed art critic, Clement Greenberg, would stand with his back to a new painting until it was in place and then wheel abruptly around to let his practiced eye take it in without giving the mind a chance to refract the pure optical experience through apriori theories. Analogously, I have Una put on some *ear*-fully delicious *accoustiments* (a condensation for acoustical accouterments) such as nylon stocking brushing against silk slip. I stand with my back to her; she starts to rub-a-dub the two fabrics together; suddenly I turn, aiming weird ear at sweet sound, doing aurally what Greenberg did optically. Ya grok?"

"Sound reasoning to me!" puns Al. "But you'll open yourself up to being accused to exercising, not the male gaze, but male hearing." Ah, Dear Reader, how prescient ol' Al is on this point!

Faraway murmur quite suddenly becomes roar as sound of low-flying helicopter batters against dome-home's windows before receding again into distance. Even with ear goop in Art's ear feels like someone just stuck micro-sized electric egg-beater down 'n frothed his waxy cerumen. . . . . When vertigo subsides, Art changes subject to their local bistro owner and *bon ami*, Pau D'Arco.

"Despite the fact has ears like raw veal chops and, like most Canadians, lifts his leg slightly to fart, Pau's superman. Was member of Québecois-Separatist Left and is still on R. C. M. P.'s notorious *Personnes à Qui Doit Surveiller Attentivement* List. Under pressure, he habitually stands legs apart, face placid as a cow's mug. Keeps under his pillow a book titled *Ils Ne M'auront Pas* (*They Aren't Going to Get Me*). And the versatility of the guy! Can talk all day to a butcher about the longevity of imported meats, go a round with the best wine *sommeliers* (once telling whiny wine importer: "Although Riesling is that region's raisin d'être, I don't' give a fig."). Dude's veritable buzz-saw: talks about flavor 'n savor the way Marxists talk about revolution. Believes in Krishna Socialism. Can make omelette in his sleep, yak up air-hostesses about safety regulations in de Gaulle hangars, engage insurance salesmen about post-dated transferable policies, amaze poets how to use non-typographical means for distinguishing six-syllable three-line stanzas and nine-syllable two-line ones, keep his own with economist about pre-war counter-inflationary theory, and wax eloquent on compensatory eye movements of iguanas. Plus (and, moreover, in addition, etcetera) he's adept at Krav Maga, that Israeli self-defense smash-'em-'n-bash-'em."

"I do notice those Brats be give his bistro a wide berth, observes Al."

"No wonder he's got that bizarre coined-operated heap, The Knowledge Machine, incongruously stuffed into his place."

"Shit, he probably programmed it!"

"He makes me feel like everything I do is in trite inverted commas."

Faint click. Al barely hears it, but Art does—distinctly—even with ear goop in. Then slight puff of air hit Al and Art very gently on back of their heads. Turning toward northeast side of chain-link fence, they spy Peven Pogacnic (former military photographer who be blinded by A-bomb test, who

Something is Crook in Middlebrook

did walk through ankle-deep mud in the early 1940s all way from Estonia to escape from persecution, now be neighborhood's own version of Tiresias) sporting pink Bermuda shorts 'n white sleeveless under-shirt that be stained with generous dose of marinara sauce on front. There be caution in his stride but nothing frail or halt. Stopping, he holds his Leica over head, pointing device in general direction of our two deck-bound interlocutors. "I really believe there are things nobody would see if I didn't photograph them," he loves to repeat. Admits that, "If reality isn't my picture of it, I'm lost." Captures on film Brats' shenanigans with their SONIC-SHOCK air-puff guns. Latent image made, Peven quickly retreats— for blind man, that is—all ass 'n elbows back across Giddings Avenue, back to Noreen, their cheap sofa and hi-lo carpeting. I like Al's description of ol' Pev: "He lives in an atmosphere as dense and separate as an island with its own sea, so he is more autonomous and vulnerable than any of us, and for him the world is rendered into shadows and smells and sounds as though it was being remembered even as he acts within it." Al once disturbs Pev's sleep for whole month with photo-philosophical question: "The world arrives through the boundary of a rectangle, but can you photograph an orange in black-and-white? Doesn't the thing that makes an orange an orange demand that it be photographed in color?"

Inside cover of Brat #1's School Notebook

Something is *Crook* in Middlebrook

Ho! Noreen be dressed in blue-and-yellow madras shorts, billowing white blouse, and pair of leather sandals; she seems to have stopped thinking about her appearance long time ago. Plumpness of her arms 'n legs do grow even more pronounced over the years and flesh does sag from her upper arms. You could easily mistake her for retirement-community golf lady. She do be type prone to vast and sudden enthusiasms coupled with tendency to bustle about straightening up after people very moment they stand up from their chairs. Likes to annoy Art by singing Toreador song from *Carmen* in voice that explodes in Art's brain, flooding every nexus of cells with its violence; grotesque parody of classical soprano: harmony, purity, cadence go bye-bye; it be rough, cracked, jerks sharply from one high note to lower with breath intervals uncontrolled, sudden precipices of gasping silence which plunge through volcanic torrent, dividing it into loosely connected sequence of *bravura* passages as her mouth assumes form of something generous-but-nasty, something resolutely both indulgent and restrained.

Some days, Pev 'n Noreen manage to fascinate *and* annoy Art at same time. How? By performing onomastic game they call "Dueling Denominations." Object of wacko pastime is to come up with increasingly goofy appellations. Example taken from Art's diary:

"How about O. Vera Cheever?" opens Noreen.

"Ya, Redburn Backspace," replies Pev. *"How 'bout that?"*

"Or a good catholic name like Neal O'Neill."

"Lee B. Doh."

"Wayne Ing-Moon."

"Lensgreve Aklefeldt."

"Butch Beausoleil."

"Lars Bang."

"Fart Klaeber."

"Slick Swallow."

"Morgan Supersad."

"Barry Self."

"Dym DeLight."

"Wyatt Flagger."

"Hugh Wood."

"Zane Cohen."

"Fenton Akimbo."

"Buck Specie."

"Diane Proletaria."

"Helen Weels."

"Horris Tolchok."

Something is *Crook* in Middlebrook

"Ignito Jawopy."

"Vron Buster."

"Astoot Liyer."

"Valuta Groschen."

"Bill Quaintance."

"Howe Vrais."

"Pudge Portleigh."

"Don Armour."

"Purly Gates."

"Polly Sentrick."

"Getton Stiffer."

"Dern Winters."

"Dwight Chrismass."

"Tessla Coyle."

"Jerry Mander."

"Daley Grind."

"Sarah Toenen."

"Virginia Dentatia."

"Yoo-Mai Starcherone."

"Rollo Tomasi."

"Cardinal Sin."

"Aaaahooogahhhh-aaaahooogah! Rules violation—there really is someone by that name.

"Vosdanig Manoug Adoian."

"Violation, again, violation! That's painter Arshile Gorky's real name.

Etcetera.

Musing on Pev's photographic peregrinations, Al offers, "He must be using that super wide-angle lens again," comments Al.

"Pev never does see what he photographs. I often never see what I hear. So I do, after all, feel a modicum of kinship with poor Peven."

"Ah, like a flying yarrow stalk Peven shoots forward through the gulfs of probability!"

Fact: Peven prefers photos which look like they were taken by some-one else: "My favorite Walker Evans photo was taken by Edward Weston." When he's not using his vintage camera, Pev sports dude-ranch cowboy belt with greased holster modified to contain slender spraycan specializing in flies, wasps, mosquitoes, large black bees, etcetera. When aerial denizens do come weaving towards him like punchy old southpaws with half-remembered moves, ponderous fakes 'n feints, Peven's keen hearing does guide his speed-draw so as to catch invader full in the face. Insect does *kamikaze* death-dive. If Pev's daily kill goes over ace's five, he celebrates with pre-dinner Kamikaze cocktail.

2.9   Early evening light has color of car sickness. Art ensconced in cock-loft, slowly scanning; audits roar of traffic on Lake Shore Drive. *This is the new ocean,* he thinks. *Ceaselessly, in great surges, these metal waves roll in over the length and breadth of our cities, rising higher 'n higher, breaking in a kind of frenzy when the roar reaches its peak and then discharging across the stones and asphalt even as the next onrush is being released from where it was held by the traffic lights.* He pans toward Avvocato Toscafundi's place where he suffers to hear ex-lawyer's newly acquired black Newfoundland dog leaping at new green-painted iron gate, quite beside himself, as if taking leave of its senses (possibly due to Boettcher Brat shenanigans). Animal's natural gentleness be broken by ill-treatment and long confinement in illegal dog-fight kennel (which pays protection money to one heap corrupt Alderman, "Pronto" Pietro who, in turn, uses filthy lucre to keep himself clad in his fav Austrian Loden coats). After car copped, Avvo wants to discourage criminal elements. Sound so disturbing, Art does feel chill of terror in his limbs and tastes rotten haggis, even though source be four blocks away. Color drains from Art's face like darkness that drains from sand as water recedes after high tide. Hastily goops weird ear, dashes downstairs.

Decides to bathe Tig; carries amphibian to basement sink where weeks of salamander funk dissolves down drain as Art ungoops and aims ear at dirty water drizzling down drainpipe. Gurgle-gurgle sound punctuated with sharp pings of small detritus does sooth over-worked ear with wonderful theme 'n variation. Art tastes melting chocolate bar flecked with Rice Krispies. Dries with Bed, Bath, 'n Beyond-bought towel dripping Tig, then perfumes him with splash of Viktor & Rolfe's new Antidote cologne. Why? Once in great moon Art rewards true-blue Tig with cozy bed-down with him in ear-shaped bed. And tonight's the night! When put in bed, Tig is motionless for minutes as Art undresses; sweet-smellin' salamander takes in as much as possible of his surroundings without moving even his eyes. But when Art pulls out his portable CD player and that "Pollito Chicken" audio-book CD Mala gives him, Tig suddenly moves his head, taking in whole bedly environment with steely eye, thinking—well, your guess is as good as mine. Art climbs in, cozies up with Tig, whose eyes close—one supposes—in deep satisfaction. Weird ear is ungooped, while normal ear is gooped—Art wants to put hearing into maximum aural-drive. Snaps off room light, lights Mr. Sputter, his latest gift from Una: a fat blue sweet-scented candle nestled in glass with weird wooden wick that, as it burns, makes soft soothin' cracklin' like wood combusting. After ten minutes of this relaxing foreplay (arm around Tig) which "zeroes" his auditory equipment, he puts on left headphone only, turns volume very low and punches (*ándale!*) PLAY button:

LO QUE LA DECIDIO FUE EL BREATHTAKING POSTER
DE FOMENTO QUE VIO EN LA TRAVEL AGENCY DEL
LOBBY DE SU BUILDING. EL BREATHTAKING POSTER
MENTADO RESPRESENTABA UNA PAREJ A DE BEAU-

Something is **Crook** in Middlebrook

Whoo-whee! Syncopations of mishmash of Grand Gringoñol does send Art into aural-thrill ride that goes from The Alamo and *gringófobos* to *gringólatras* and current tendencies toward the amigoization of major cities like Los Angeles and Chicago. Halfway through story aural ecstacy is so intense, Art grasps Tig so hard he salamanderly suddenly despoils sheets. *Blessed Benimming!*

3.0

Odd weather, light foggy, like wrong shutter speed. Art writes art criticism. It demands he perform difficult mental trick of trying on somebody else's personality. Gives him excuse to expatiate on chance, death, irreducible pluralism of life and of truth, the unintelligibility of the real, the intelligibility of artifice. In his reviews, Art touts daring, impudence, and wit as no less aesthetic than grace, elegance, and beauty."The world is neither completely rational, nor quite irrational either," he writes in early review. Enjoys paradox of having, on one hand, amorphous, everyday flow of reality as it is experienced, and, on other, edifying reconstruction of this reality by speech, rea-son, theory. Fun to see if he can translate one to the other. And as critic he is safe from deeper psychic shit inside him; there is in writing on work of another a distance that is just heap perfect and says to Art each time review pops out of inkjet printer: "I am safer doing this than writing a novel." Has lectured on "The Lutheran Condition of Marx's Thought," but prefers reviewing photography as it permits him to say about that paradoxical medium: "Only through balance of evidence and lyricism shall we attain combination of emotion and lucidity. Ya grok?"

Used to be more prolific, writing turgid essays with titles such as: "Psychoanalysis of the Sword," "Frigid Enjoyment," and "The Wanton Truth of Sculpture". Now he's professionally obscure. Now he's professionally obscure. Sometimes instead of writing review, he fills out one of his "Substitution Forms" and sends to museum or gallery (probably only celebrated thing about him except for his weird ear):

Date: <u>February 15, 2003</u>
Substitution #: <u>24</u>

INSTEAD OF WRITING A
REVIEW OF YOUR SHOW I __
<u>filled out this form</u>

Signed:
Arthur S. Middlebrook, Middle-aged Crank

Now has bellyful of reviewing. Decadent Postmodern times: rampant pluralism, philosophy foundering, science leaking at every seam, ethics going to seed. And Gresham's Law: Bad art drives out good art. Doesn't like his critical colleagues either: they are so uncritical and lacking in humor toward themselves. Nearly stops altogether for same reason that 1940s premier modernist critic Clement Greenberg did: ". . . the ungrateful nature of art criticism as serious form of writing." Polite way of saying that one is fed up with bullshit one takes from touchy artists, overbearing editors, and ill-prepared readers. Art doesn't mind intellectual jousting, but hates vicious personal attacks and petty jealousies. Reviewing foregrounds worst of human condition: each of us is stranger to himself and victim and executioner for everyone else. Museum curators complain his negative reviews weaken future funding. Some depressed artists threaten suicide. Distant cousins of artist whose work Art pans—"The canvas dances with an elegant geometric chaos of defeat"—send death threats. On positive side, an occasional compliment; one artist whose paintings he touts as, "magnificent aggregates (like rocks geologists term *hornfels*) of pigment, gravel, and parts of smashed clocks," sends him fruitcake every Christmas. Eventually, Art becomes sarcastic. His last review in major art monthly (of drawings at Zolla-Lieberman Gallery) ends:

> *. . . The artist never wearied of admiring the inimitable grace with which the arms were attached to the torso, the marvelous roundness of the neck, the harmonious lines drawn by the eyebrows, the nose, and the perfect oval of the face, the purity of its vivid contours and the effect of the thick, curved lashes which lined her heavy and volup-tuous eyelids. Hell, it would've been easier to just take a photograph!*

And, thus, ends his tenure as contributing editor with *that* Blue Chip art rag. When teaching course on criticism, curious suburban undergrad asks who bar-none best art critic was; Art answers: "Clement Greenberg." When asks who worst, Art replies: "Clement Greenberg." Art likes to give his sub-urbanite students these art world Zen Koans to stimulate what little thinking they do do.

But since weird ear event, he again delights in gallery openings, earsdropping on chatter of those most appreciative (but too poor to buy the art) as well as brash pronouncements of well-heeled who can afford it (or least *could have* afforded it prior to big Recession) but have little sensibility to appreciate it. Tucks choicest tidbits away in engram library housed in his *vas bene clausum.* Later uses 'em to jump start his reviews. To overcome his persistent writer's block, he need only recall 'n relate pertinent sound-bites. Yah, sometimes writes whole reviews as dialogues between contentious gallery snoops, taking either side of aesthetic evaluation with equal virtuosity and with amused pedantry. Shades of Unamuno's conflictual metaphysics and Bishop Berkeley's dialectics in *Three Dialogues Between Hylas and Philonous.*

3.1   Today—blustery clear day in late April. Air so clear 'n fresh that even those dying in local nursing homes be filled with hope. Art dons art-opening garb: brown leather pants, black turtle neck, brown, pointed Italian boots, and brown leather jacket. Super goops up his weird ear for noisy trip on the rockin' rattlin' Blue Line EL to small gallery just west of The Loop. Despite goop, distinctly hears proverbial single empty Coke can rolling around passenger compartment, banging against tennis shoes, high heels, and metal chair supports mixing with ghetto-voice of haggard black man begging coins from annoyed riders and profit-inflected voice talking into cell-phone: **NO, NO, WE'RE NOT AIMING FOR A DEMOGRAPHIC; WE'RE AIMING FOR A . . . A PSYCHOGRAPHIC**. Notices anorexic-thin woman reading *Is Humanism Molesting Your Child?* Twenty minutes later, exits at Clinton stop. Slowly takes his waddling bulk down steep stairs as pair of laughing black kids scramble up two stairs at a time in unsuccessful attempt to catch train; engineer waits until they are oh so tantalizingly close to door then shuts it abruptly, speeds off.

Art saunters down Randolph Street west past one of his ex-wife's fav dining establishments. Black Bird's minimalist, understated facade has black-garbed, thin-lipped, anorexic hostess, gloved-skinned, with body thoroughly scoured as a Dutch kitchen. The women diners served are the kind of talking dolls that say *Mommee* and take a leak if you turn them upside down, their faces cute 'n beady. The establishment popular with those with money and serves such minimal portions of its *nouvelle cuisine* as to impress such abstemious diet on clientele. Behind large glass window, thin, curious, well-heeled diners gesture 'n peer disapprovingly out picture window at Art's left ear oozing white ear goop. Mechanical aspect of their gestures 'n senseless pantomime make everything about them seem stupid—*like George Bush, Jr.,* he thinks—since, with ear goop in, Art can't audit 'em behind glass partition. Ignores 'em and makes a beeline to Peoria Street and his rendezvous with champagne and finny-food at Crawl-Space Gallery's opening for two-person show featuring black-and-white photographic work shot in India by Wisconsinite Lewis Koch and colorful, massive Indian-inspired sculpture of India-born Ravinder Reddy. Three blocks away Art checks his bearings by ungooping tattoo-bearing weird ear, aiming it toward his ultimate destination:

OUR KRISHNA CONSCIOUSNESS MOVEMENT IS GENUINE, HISTORICALLY AUTHORIZED, NATURAL AND TRANSCENDENTAL DUE TO ITS BEING BASED ON *BHAGAVADGITA AS IT IS.* IT IS GRADUALLY BECOMING THE MOST POPULAR MOVEMENT IN THE WHOLE ENTIRE WORLD, GGGGRRRRRRRRRRZZSHHH HHSRRCCCCCCCCCCCCRAASSSKKKSSSSSSSGRRR ZZSHSRRCCRAASKKKSSSQQQUUUUGRRRRRSSSSCR SSCRRLSQUUUSSC [EL train obliterates several sentences here.] **DUE TO MY ETERNAL SPIRI-TUAL MASTER, HIS DIVINE GRACE OM VISNUPADA PARAMAHAMSA PARIVRAJAKACARYA ONE HUNDRED AND EIGHT SRI SRIMAD BHAKTI-SIDDHANTA SARA-VATI GOSVAMI MAHARAJA PRABHUPADA. KRISHNA DESCENDS TO THIS PLANET ONCE IN A DAY OF BRAHMA, OR EVERY EIGHT BILLION, SIX HUNDRED MILLION YEARS.**

For second, startled Art mishears phrase as "eight billion, six hundred million *ears*." Grunts with satisfaction, synaesthetically tasting Punjabi specialty, *Paneer Amritsari.* Yep, he's on right track alright. He knows Inter-

Something is *Crook* in Middlebrook

national Society for Krishna Consciousness plans to use show as venue to recruit new members. In Catholic services, as child, instead of singing Lord's praises, he distracts himself by whittling on the pew and holds any religious sensibility submerged as you would hold ill-tempered puppy under water until its struggles cease. Now, thanks to weird ear, can't even practice Eastern religion's regime of *pratyahara*, withdrawing of senses from sense objects.

Was about to thumb-stuff his ear goop back in when visited with auditory stimulant that, like Proustian involuntary memory zap, takes him back to those Scout knife-carved pews of his pre-Vatican II Catholic childhood and smell of sweet incense:

> *LAUDATE DOMINUM DE COELIS, LAUDATE EUM IN EXCELSIS!* [Priest reciting.] *LAUDATE EUM OMNES ANGELI EIUS LAUDATE EUM OMNES VIRTUTES EIUS.* [Choir responding.] *LAUDATE EUM SOL ET LUNA; LAUDATE EUM STELLAE ET LUMEN.* [Congregation.]

Small detour left around corner (and small detour from our main plot) and Art discovers Latinous sound coming from large basement window in old brick building marred by anti-Papal graffiti: RATZINGER, THE RAT! Sign over door reads "Immaculate Heart of Mary Church, Chicago's Premier Tridentine Latin Rite Church"; banner beneath boasts "*De Maria Nunquam Satis*" (Of Mary, there is never enough) and announces "Father Casimir Pussi-korius welcomes the Blue Army of Our Lady of Fatima." Art recalls that back in 1960s, when Pope John XXIII promulgates vernacular Mass, thousands of disaffected Catholics worldwide—thinking some *ineffable* thing lost in trans-lation from Latin to English and bemoaning fact it was harder to sleep during Mass now—breaks away from Roman Catholic Church proper in order to maintain what they feel is "the true faith." Under influence of rebel Bishop Francis Konrad Schuckardt, they become known as "*sedevacantists*" (Latin for "the chair [of Apostalic Succession] is empty").

Cultish atmosphere of this splinter group in Pacific Northwest grows until it is not uncommon in certain towns there to see nuns in blue habits, selling Virgin Mary dolls outside grocery stores during day and out praying rosary when others long asleep. Some carry CONVERT OR YOU'RE TOAST signs. Many of these nuns live outside their traditional convent in flop houses, surviving (barely) on Pizza Pockets and lemon-meringue pies or donuts that local businesses deign to donate. In one incident, reported on cult's website *www.eatcumspiri220.org*, heap hungry Sister Mary Rotunda of Seattle beat International Speed Eater Takeru Kobayashi of Japan by consuming sixty-three Pizza Pockets in just twelve minutes. Kobayashi won title in meet held six months earlier in New York by inhaling record fifty hot dogs in twelve minutes.

Fact: in southern Oregon two such near-starving nuns are on Klamath Falls bike path breathing in midnight air, nibbling on shared, stale Pizza Pocket, and praying for souls of sinners, unaware one is headed straight toward them. They finger their rosaries and murmur prayers to Virgin Mary as soused drifter on way home from local strip club approaches on his wobbling bicycle. According to prosecutors, man attacks them, raping both, and strangling one with her own rosary beads as punishment for pulling wooden ruler on her attacker. The dying nun's last words: "*Paete, non dolet*" (Don't worry, it doesn't hurt). Later, when local, beady-eyed *sedevacantist* is asked by media if there was something to be learned from this vicious incident, she sternly observes: "If the attacks obtained for people the grace to pray the rosary and study Latin, it was well worth it." *Amen*.

Art into skull-time. Recalls how from age eleven groks organized religion as pernicious mind virus. *Why do people in church seem like cheerful, brainless tourists on a package detour of the Absolute?* Scandalizes fellow Catholic school chums by passing out recipe for "Nuns' Panties Soup": dirty panties of five nuns boiled in chicken stock for eight hours; add: leeks, spices (angelica, garlic, anise), Blue Nun Riesling wine, salt and pepper to taste and *ecce*! Now ponders how outraged these devotees would be upon viewing controversial photographer Joel-Peter Witkin's scandalous staged scenarios, especially *Choice Outfits for the Agonies of Mary,* where, hooded nude decked out in stiletto heels and surrounded by bizarre array of S & M accessories and sex toys suggesting whippings, beatings, gougings, stabbings of erotic violence. Witkin scratches on negative, placing crudely drawn black arrows pointing to Mary's vulva. As Witkin's mother's name is Mary, Art interprets this as literally taking stab at one's inviolable mothers: biological and religious. Ho! Recalls eighth-grade teacher Sister Mary Never's admonition: "If our minds are filled with images of exposed bodies and songs that recommend the liberation of our impulses, our sexual behavior will have a large admixture of lust in it." When older, Art tries real hard to imagine sex without lust but draws one fuckin' heap big blank.

3.2   Light changing heartbeat by heartbeat. Sidewalk taking on color of potato skin. Art regoops ear and makes his way down Randolph Street to gallery, past chanting Krishnas sporting *japa mala* beads—"*Hare Krishna, Hare Krishna, Krishna, Krishna, Hare, Hare, Hare Rama, Hare Rama, Rama, Rama, Hare, Hare*"—up two flights of stairs rubbing middle-aged shoulders with svelte young art-conscious crowd. Lot of jabber, foreign 'n domestic, in the air. *Dil Lay Gayee, Dil Lay Gayee* blares sounds of *Bhangra,* filling gallery with energetic vibes of Punjabi pop music that mixes modern and traditional instruments as ethnic mélange fills room with energetic bodies. Swarthy Indians in turbans and subcontinental divinities in Saris politely surround famous South Indian sculptor, Ravinder Reddy; bored lanky white chics in tight hip-hugger pants sip from plastic champagne flutes. Two teens garbed emo-style in tight wool sweaters, tighter jeans, itchy scarfs, with ebony hair swiped across their faces, ogle elegant text-image diptyches on wall: one image shot in India paired with a photo of textual fragment culled either from Vedic wisdom or British colonial hubris. Starving Korean grad students with horrible garlic breath chatter quietly, hoard Samosa snacks. Several well-groomed children curiously touch large, near-Kitschy colorful sculptural busts by Reddy and giggle. A couple of sweaty college kids snog 'n canoodle in a corner. Meanwhile, full-figured gallery owner spreads good *karma* by making her smiling rounds draped in hideous muumuu, holding fat cherubic alabaster-skinned baby right out of a Bronzino painting. Odd smile or wave or shout be seen as Art moves among gaggle of attendees, free as water.

Something is *Crook* in Middlebrook

Crazed artist with wild-eyes and disheveled hair tries to convince some local art writers (who roll their eyes in annoyance) to visit *his* studio. Art heap glad no one here yet recognizes him; albeit, several folks cast curious glances at tattoo 'n white goop in his left ear. Art makes beeline to liquid refreshments; casually overhears woman, draped in stunning Sari, touting (to very fit Anglo female companion): "the efficacy of pure *bhakti-yoga* untainted by any admixture of *jnana, karma* or *hatha,*" that it, "is *the system* that the *Gita* recommends above all others." Q.E.D. Young woman serving drinks looks like art student who only recently takes bath and seems uncomfortable in elegant black and white serving duds. Art opts for alcoholic bubbly.

Cold Duck churning in plastic flute, surrounded by cacophony of voices, Art hitches up leather pants with free hand and heads toward gallery wall. (He's not much for the gallery leisure-speak circuit.) Left-to-right, his practiced eye peruses both Reddy's sculptures and Koch's photo-text combinations while thoughtfully scribbles notes into small wire-bound notepad. Jots down how effective is juxtaposition of Reddy's large, brightly painted heads with Koch's small monochromatic diptychs, how one body of work demands standing back to peruse it, while with other, one must come close, attend to visual and textual information. Neither body of work detracts from other, in fact, he writes, they tend to re-enforce each other and resonate together. Reddy's work is within traditional mold; his sculptures are essentially large heads and single figures through which he inscribes his "Indianness." His Brobdingnagian heads are iconic forms reminiscent of religious sculptures, of popular visual culture of urban bazaar. Their simple overall form balanced by attention to ornamental detail—plastic bands, gold-plated earrings, ribbons and scarves that are akin to those sold in village festivals —in such a way that these objects read paradoxically as *both* traditional and modern, high culture and low, messing delightfully with modernist penchant to hold them distinctly apart. Art notices how they fill large interior space with bright color that demand one pay attention to them; they gratify immediately, invite touch. Although appearing to be of carved wood, actual materials are painted polyester-resin fiberglass. These heads, their lips pursed with wide-open eyes transfixing viewer, establish exchange of gazes crisscrossing gallery's space. They set tone of colorful exoticism that mocks exoticism and deliberately just borders on Kitsch. But it's Koch's work that Art wants to really "grok."

Finishing notes on Reddy's work, Art reseats white ear goop in external meatus and contemplates Koch's installation in fussy detail. From review of show that results from these silent musings and hastily jotted notes ("Don't Hassle Me, I'm Local," published month later in local anarchist art journal *F/Art)* we surmise that for Art, Koch's artwork's significance lies in being self-reflexive. These photographs admit their otherness; they *do not* reproduce hubris of tourist mentality toward that over-exoticized land such as found in much color photography by both Indian and Outsider alike. For instance, we find out in said review that Dayanita Singh, prominent Indian photographer, bemoans some of her own work which she freely admits caters to Western eyes, and that Robert Arnett's recent photobook *India Unveiled* still treats us in his text with Eurocentric myth of Aryan invasion of India in 2500 B.C. and, in his photos, with hot, vivid color. But Koch, continues Art:

Something is *Crook* in Middlebrook

. . . eschews color, shooting in black and white; ignoring exotic National Geographic types of subjects, this photographer, focuses on the seemingly banal. It is as if we are seeing India through demotic eyes. Hard to do given the pre-existing pile of texts and documents, fantasies, legends, jokes, and other people's memories of that vast land, India. To stress the fact that all seeing—especially visualizing a foreign culture—is a complex construction, an intertextuality that can be traced back ad infinitum, *Koch balances his idiosyncratic visual statements with textual fragments appropriated from indigenous sources and outsider commentary, from theoretical texts to government documents to religious tracts. This postmodernist strategy aims at revealing the "violence of representation" in all such photography of the Other; it pulls Koch's project—he spent nearly a year in northern India making periodic forays south from Dharamsala—away from the heroics of traditional documentary of the exotic into problematizing the very act of image-making he practices.*

Looking for the quirky detail he often frames his subjects in ways that "disclarifies" them. Koch even (unknowingly?) mimics a compositional trait found in many indigenous Indian photographs from the nineteenth century where a large foreground feature looms to block the path between viewer and subject. In Iron Pillar at Qutab Minar *(1995), a large pillar intervenes between foreground and background; in another, walls covered with writing confront us, dividing the subject into separate areas so what is to be judged the main subject is hard to determine. The "personal documentary" approach is the closest one can come to labeling Koch's aesthetic here. He does not engage in what anthropologists term "intersubjective time," a reciprocal,* empathic *engagement with his subjects as seen in Dayanita Singh's recent photographic studies of contemporary Indian families or in Morrie Camhi's photographs of the Jews of Greece. But neither does he isolate the exotic in another time, an eternal Past-in-the-Present. There is no sense that the photographer romanticizes or claims to master his subject. Modest, he makes us realize that, indeed, he is an Outsider here and can't probe this society like an Insider could; yet there are things he reveals which Insiders might not see for being too close to it. Koch's project—like Robert Frank's photobook,* The Americans (1959), *wherein he reveals the United States's 1950s malaise by the very fact he is an immigrant—finds curious items for our inspection; for instance, the young Buddhist monk's math practice made of rolled* tsampa *(roasted barely flour and tea) laid out on a table as discovered in the temple at the Tibetan Children's Village in Dharamsala. Or the visual complexity of a soda advertisement* in situ *in Udaipur, Rajasthan.*

Something is **Crook** in Middlebrook

In sum, although these images are taken by a Westerner, there is no colonial lens at work here. Koch is no Samuel Bourne, the noted British photographer who confidently roams India during the 1860s, patting himself on the back in his journal for symbolically conquering the newly acquired British colony for Western eyes, while trouncing his equipment-carrying "coolies" with a stout stick for their recalcitrance.

Suddenly be soft tap on Art's shoulder. Pulled from his critical reveries, Art takes moment to recognize odd physiognomies of his across-the-street neighbors, the Pogacnics. Noreen, with Peven-the-blind-photographer in tow, wears dull brown (or is it caramel-colored?) dress that speaks of spinal supports, hernias. "We received a gallery invite intended for you, but mistakenly dropped into our mail box," explains Noreen. "Peven thought he might enjoy seeing—er—having me describe the prints to him." She fumbles with plastic chicken brooch pinned on her outfit. "And, just may be, I can get someone here to tell me just what all those Sikhs say to each other on their cabs' radios."

"I'm always trying to improve my game," Peven replies, making motions as if he be snapping a shot with his Leica. Turning head as if he could see, "Hey, those damn Brats ain't here are they?" Pev refers to recidivist twins, his neighbor's kids who, like the mythological Furies, endlessly torment him. Art says no. Peven visibly relaxes. If he'd been ungooped, Art would have heard poor fellow's tension move down from head, through torso, toward toes, puddling at Peven's pigeon-toed feet. Several vibrant bluecheese white glare flashes from Pev's strobe are seen tonight.

"Noreen's pissed," Peven spits out.

"Huh?"

"We found out Wal Mart has taken out insurance policies on its employees. If one dies, management collects into the five digits. And with all those elderly folks on the payroll . . . ," adds Noreen.

"*Blessed Benimming!* I've always wondered why Wal-Mart hired so many retirees," spouts Art.

"Well, excuse us—gotta help Peven enjoy the photos."

"*Ciao,*" Art waves his right fingers in their direction and saunters off.

Noreen faces Peven's blank face toward Art's fav print, titled *Iron Pillar*, and starts one of her famous verbal translations. Across room, Art ungoops ear 'n aims it at Noreen:

IT'S A HORIZONTAL FORMAT, BLACK 'N WHITE. THE IMAGE IS DIVIDED INTO THIRDS. THE CENTRAL THIRD IS FILLED WITH A CLOSE-UP OF A LARGE PILLAR. A PERSON STANDS WITH HIS BACK TO THE PILLAR, HIS ARMS IN WHITE SLEEVES AWKWARDLY WRAPPED AROUND IT SO HIS ELONGATED FINGERS WITH GLOWING NAILS CARESS THE PILLAR. ONE FEELS THE TENSION IN THE ARMS, SO AWKWARD IS

Something is **Crook** in Middlebrook

Quite a meaningful mouthful, thinks Art. Ear still uncorked, Art slowly scans crowd for odd sound-bite. From woman whose appearance and tone of voice reminds him of writer Susan Sontag reading from one of her books:

Young woman, dressed in black leotard over which she wears deep purple slip with lace fringe, has every bit look of disillusioned graduate student in Humanities:

Something is *Crook* in Middlebrook

RICHEST WOMAN IN CHICAGO" AND ALL THAT'S LEFT IS A DIRTY TORN RAG FIT ONLY FOR AN AMVETS COLLECTION.

Pointing to one of Koch's photos of appropriated text, middle-aged man in white mock turtle neck sweater edges in front of this woman, blocking her remarks as powerful radio station broadcasting over weaker does. Art hears, presumably, commentary about Koch's use of textual references:

FUTILE TO EXPECT IT TO HAVE A PRE-ESTABLISHED SIGNIFICANCE. ITS ONLY MEANING IS THE ONE THAT IS GIVEN TO IT. ITS VALUE IS STRICTLY HISTORICAL AND PRACTICAL. IT IS THE WORD OF THE LEADER, OF THE RULING CLASS. CAN ANYONE KNOW EXACTLY WHAT IS MEANT BY OTHER PEOPLE'S WORDS OR EVEN BY HIS OWN?

Art swings his shotgun-mike ear toward chunky fellow of European extraction draped in cheap tweed suit and gray knit tie; recognizes him as local art critic, Fritz Gruebler, who teaches art criticism at variety of academic venues and jumped started his career by writing attacks on Akira Kurosawa for *American Legion Magazine*:

THE FUNCTION OF CRITICISM IS TO CRITICIZE, THAT IS, TO TAKE A STAND FOR OR AGAINST AND TO SITUATE HIMSELF BY SITUATING. AS CRITICS, LANGUAGE IS THE MEASURE OF OUR ACTION, WHEREAS FOR THE ARTIST, ACTION IS THE MEA-SURE OF HIS LANGUAGE. DIFFERENT VERBO-MOTIVE PROCESSES, YOU SEE. NOW IN KOCH'S WORK WE HAVE A KANTIAN APPROACH AS HERE THE HUMAN MIND ITSELF *CONSTITUTES* TRUTH IN CONTRA-DISTINCTION TO TRADITIONAL DOCUMENTARY WHICH STILL ADHERES TO DESCARTES' EPISTEM-OLOGY WHEREBY THE HUMAN MIND MERELY DIS-COVERS SUCH TRUTH.

Turning to port, Art picks up another choice tidbit:

YEAH, THAT'S THE GUY ON THE ART STUDIO FACULTY THEY CALL "LEATHER BOY." ONCE WAS NOTORIOUSLY VICIOUS DURING FACULTY CRITI-QUES OF STUDENT WORK. DEAN AND THERAPIST INTERVENED AFTER STUDENTS THREATEN TO BOYCOTT THE CRITIQUES. RUMORED THAT NOW HE DOES THOSE CRITIQUES WITH A BENIGN SMILE AND

Something is *Crook* in Middlebrook

Hmmm. Not a little unlike me stuffing in my ear goop. Art aims his
ear at scruffy art-type in torn blue jeans and brown T-shirt:

Art slowly pans head, like rapidly turning tuning dial on radio. Hears
mélange of disparate sound-bites:

Something is *Crook* in Middlebrook

3.3   Art's auditing is disturbed by highly disturbed fellow, some flesh-monster born of doughnuts 'n Kentucky Fried, who is just outside gallery entrance in hallway vigorously slamming gold wrist watch against freshly painted silver radiator—**SSSSSSSSSSHHHMMMMMACKASSSSSHHHUKKKK CCCRACKSHHHSHHHHHMACKASHUKCRACKKKKSSSSSSHHHMMMMM ACKASSSKKKKRRRRRRACKKKSHHHHHMAAAAAKKK**—and yelling wildly through fat, tubular muscle extending from face through body as small gears and springs fly about (accelerating at 32 feet-per-second-per-second) metal tinkling as slams onto cement floor. Sound makes Art taste cold diamonds as audits crazy invective from this oleaginous, Bisquick-faced street person dressed in cum-stained harlequin garb girdled with mistletoe-and-hemlock belt whose buckle bears offensive inscription: 'KISS ME UNDER THIS, BITCH. As he stumbles through gallery door all bulk 'n swagger, he sports wild eyes and wobbly smile. He yells:

Something is *Crook* in Middlebrook

CLOCK STOPS DOES TIME COME TO LIFE. DROWN YOUR WATCH! LIKE THE SUIT? THIS SUIT MASKS MY REFLECTIVE, CRITICAL GAIETY WHICH HIDES, IN TURN, A BEATING HEART. I CAN DETECT, YOU KNOW, SMELLS THROUGH THE TELEPHONE, TOO. I KNOW WHERE HOFFA, JIMMY, IS BURIED 'N I'VE READ KIERKEGAARD. USEFUL READING FOR AN ASPIRING CLOWN, YA KNOW. AND THERE WAS A SECRET IN THE ROOM LIKE BAD MEAT, A NASTY ODOR, SO FAMILIAR, FROM MY VERY SAD AND DISAPPOINTING BIRTH, THE LONG AFTERNOONS, SUN THROUGH THE FLYWIRE, THE BUZZ OF FLIES OUTSIDE HOWLING FOR BLOOD, MOM'S BREATH LIKE ROSES, LIKE COMMUNION WINE.

Shit this guy opens up whole new worlds of semantic reach to the epithet RAW; *should be the poster boy for French theorist Julia Kristeva's conception of how the Semiotic, pre-Oedipal drives burst forth and disrupt the Symbolic strictures of syntax and law,* muses Art with Kantian disinterestedness. *Sheer carnivalesque unleashed within space of the aesthetic serious.*

BUNGLE'S MOTTO IS: I'D RATHER HAVE A BOTTLE IN FRONT OF ME THAN A FRONTAL LOBOTOMY! NOW DON'T TELL ME THAT TWO AND TWO IS FOUR. HOW DO WE KNOW THAT TWO IS TWO? THAT IS THE TWENTY-ONE THOUSAND DOLLAR QUESTION. BUNGLE'S MOTTO IS: I'D RATHER HAVE A BOTTLE IN FRONT OF ME THAN A FRONTAL LOBOTOMY! NOW DON'T TELL ME THAT TWO AND TWO IS FOUR. HOW DO WE KNOW THAT TWO IS TWO? THAT IS THE TWENTY-ONE THOUSAND DOLLAR QUESTION. I'VE FUCKED 'EM BIG. I'VE FUCKED 'EM SMALL. I'VE FUCKED 'EM FAT. I'VE FUCKED 'EM ALL. I'VE FUCKED 'EM . . . AAARGH! UNHAND ME YOU BEASTS. YOU CAN TOSS ME IN YOUR FOETID MARSHES BUT I WILL BE BACK. THIS IS NO TIME FOR SERGEANTS MILADIES AND GENTS. WATCH THE SUIT YOU NINNIES. ART'S IN THE HANDS OF A BUNCH OF NUTS. AAARGH! UNHAND ME YOU BEASTS. YOU CAN TOSS ME IN YOUR FOETID MARSHES BUT I WILL BE BACK. THIS IS NO TIME FOR SERGEANTS MILADIES AND GENTS. WATCH THE SUIT YOU NINNIES. ART'S IN THE HANDS OF A BUNCH OF NUTS.

Curious looking man in black jacket (with slight bulge under left arm, something hidden there?) with silver conchos. And trousers of fire pink. His eyes be inordinately focused on this purveyor of verbal diarrhea.

Something is *Crook* in Middlebrook

3.4   As two strong self-appointed bouncers escort poor struggling fellow downstairs 'n toss him stumbling into throng of crazed, chanting Krishnas, Art finds himself tossed into skull-time: Carnivalesque images of his long-time buddy, Larry Lister Binacka, flood in. Larry do be Art's "alchemical friend," one in whom image of one's father fuses with picture of one's best pal. He is place where everything begins for Art. They do meet before they can talk, babies crawling through grass in diapers; by time they do reach seven they have pricked their fingers with pins and do make themselves blood bros for life. This momentous kid-event takes place at Camp Ditch-the-Kids (near Big Bear, California) where Art sees his first uncircumcised penis (on lanky Ballant Burkess, Hungarian refugee) and where Larry writes, after bout 'n rout of Montezuma's Revenge, wacky piece of juvenalia he titles "The Thesis of the Plentifullest John."

Ah Larry—there be something so attractive about him that Art always wants him beside him, as if one could live within his sphere and be touched by what he is. Alternately playing roles of clown 'n scoundrel 'n philosopher, it do be as if Larry lives at right angles to our world. He inspires teenage-Art's appropriational propensities by going to grocery store and Xeroxing box of English muffins, two pounds of ground veal and apple (flagrant violation of Copyright Act). At its weakest, its most ingratiating, Larry's adult face becomes that of man who might step up to microphone and give you competently leering rendition of "Pop Goes the Weasel." Even as adult, Larry has speculative energies, scrambled attributes of the young, when one's personality is still an improvisation. Larry casually describes their intertwined lives as: "A bunch o' poor fucks doin' what we can ta stay alive." Larry's North Star, his guiding principle, is: *Blind disobedience at all times is the strength of free men.* Starts to practice this dictum from early age: when taken to visit his relatives, when bored 'n does desire to go home, he simply starts writing on walls with his trusty crayon. Later, graduates to shooting little pea-size sodium balls into swimming pools with his slingshot—with explosive results. In high school, after fisticuffs in school gym which leaves Larry's lips feeling like two fat snails grafted onto his face, pedophile gym teacher puts firm, desiring arm around Larry and advises him, "Let's not get carried away, my son. Channel your violent impulses in a salutary direction— become a Marine! Purge your natural tendency toward . . ." Sentence never finished as Larry does place tip of his gym shoe against shin of counselor and flees to spend rest of day hiding 'n gorging at A-Month-of-Sundaes ice cream shop. There, he watches owner sashay around her shop, breasts rolling like channel buoys, hips swaying like mounds of dough being hefted by a pizza chef, until blood sugar rises 'n falls, inducing slumbers indifferent to our world's sad truths.

For Larry's sixth birthday his botanist uncle, spidery old man whose skin resembles cantaloupe rind, gives him book, *Weeds of the West,* by a Wyoming-based Herbarium Manager and published by the Western Society of Weed Science. So Larry studies color plates and reads words with a chewy Saxon thickness to them: smallseed falseflax, skeletonleaf bursage, common sagwort, nodding beggarsticks, plumless thistle, squarerose knapweed, hairy fleasbane, riddell groundsel, blessed milk-thistle, poverty sumpweed, spineless horsebrush, spiny cockbur, bladder campion, dodder, prostrate spurge, two-grooved milvetch, spurred anode, panicle willowweed, sharp-point

Something is *Crook* in Middlebrook

fluvellin, Dalmatian toadflax, bilobed speedwell and sacred datura (the last important in a later phase of Larry's mental life).

Soon little Larry is starting "The Larry Binacka Wonder-Weed Garden" in his backyard—much to his gardener mom's dismay. *Next,* Larry initiates genocidic "Project Fly-Away," daring Art to join him in keeping track of how many flies they could smash over summer vacation—highest body count wins. So filthy flies be hunted down with vengeance: fatter 'n hairier they be, worse our pair need to see them flattened by Day-Glo-colored, plastic fly-swatters. (Fact: between them, they go through 22 such instruments of death that summer). Some flies seem armored and look like attack aircraft of the twenty-second century; and when they rub their wrists together—that way they do—it seems they be sharpening knives to defend themselves.

Larry's life-theme do be always *freedom*—freedom to be individual before being member of society. He always does despise people organized into docile herds. Hates team sports. Mass gatherings of any ilk. Later he begins herculean project: to publish encyclopedia in which all information is false; wrong dates for events 'n locations for every river, biographies of people who never existed, etcetera.

He was there for you, muses Art, *and yet at the same time inaccessible. Felt there was a secret core in him that could never be penetrated, a mysterious center of hiddenness. I was the befuddled witness to his wacky antics which become known among us kids as "pulling a pure Binacka." What lay behind all that surface craziness now, in retrospect, seems to be a great darkness: an urge to test himself, to take risks, to haunt the edges of things. Maybe as an abreaction against his father who was a cipher to all, a silent man of abstracted benevolence with little feeling for children, someone who has lost all memory of having been a child once himself.*

Larry do be first person to teach Art to *question* the comfortable-familiar; exposes him to the *ludicrous* and the abject. Larry who excels both in serious atmosphere of the classroom and comic antics of playground. Larry who disrupts line separating serious and comic (an early poem of his opens: *The sky was full of feces and onions*). Larry weird child who shits his pants then tosses crappy lump at local bullies. Larry weird teenager who drives miles and miles to explore yet another foetid pool or malarial marsh. Larry weird college student who loves to cite choice Joycean sound-bites ("Stand up, mickos! Make strake for minnas!"), majors in Sociology at UCLA and does his Master's thesis on Anarchism. Larry whose favorite bits of wisdom doth be: "What is socially peripheral may be symbolically central," and "It's like we're being told you can be anything in this country *but* creative, anything *but* different, anything *but* genuine." Larry with his odd pale, slate-grey eyes. Larry with forehead so sloped back that when he stares at you it looks like head be tossed back in caustic, contemptuous laughter. Larry, to whom a case of the crabs is "an honored visit by charismatic megafauna." Larry who keeps secreted on his person small green vial of rare Sardinian herb *Erba Sardoa* which, administered as poison, produces horrible rictus upon face of victim who ho-ho convulses with sardonic laughter. Larry a one-man *roguocracy* (to use term of his own coinage). Larry who constantly puts on acts of deliberate vulgarity: grimy finnies probing his large nose, rolling eyes with bad teeth gritted in maniacal grin, farting prodigiously and at will. "Fire for effect," he yells, putting his finnies in ears then cutting loudest fart ever;

often philosophical question posed answered only with a long, thin fart. By comparison, Larry makes wonky character named "Booger" in *Revenge of the Nerds* films look like proper English gentleman.

Aye, recalls Art, *he always exploits the grotesque and the lower body and dirty orifices to their full disturbing carnivalesque effect.*

After all, it's Larry who, as college freshman contradictorily describing himself as a "Marxian anarchist," induces Art to read his dog-eared 'n green ink annotated copy of Rabelais' *Gargantua and Pantagruel*. Reading bawdy text, Art alternately laughs 'n weeps in envy and disbelief; feels his middle-class life's sure achangin'. The-System-Cannot-Withstand-Close-Scrutiny ("L'il Larry's Litany") be their mantra. Adult Art sees natural affinity between his appreciation of Larry's antics and his later attraction to artists Paul McCarthy and Mike Kelley's stomach-wrenching sojourn into The Abject.

In turn, Art (at this time in thraldom to catchpenny shamanism) cajoles Larry to read Carlos Casteneda and later Martin Amis's satirical novel, *Dead Babies*. And so begins Larry's lifetime experimentation with weird incantations, magic and magic mushrooms, LSD, opium, and other exotic hallucinogens. *Sizzle, sizzle, this is your scrambled brain on drugs.* His interest in art and humor and study of Russian literary theorist Mikhail Bakhtin's provocative concept of carnivalesque as comic transgression displacing high and low elements of society be traced back to influence of Larry Lister Binacka's giddy instabilities. Ah, how "L. L.'s" sweet 'n sour antics help Art survive brutally repressive patriarch and drudgery of being unwilling Catholic when every homily focuses either on evils of sex or those of "Comm'nism." *I should be,* repents Art, *welcoming this wonky Bungle's one-man vaudeville act against the serious, against the 'lie of pathos' that marks out the false solemnity of all official language and culture.*

3.5　　As Art takes his leave, before putting in his white ear goop, he makes one last, slow auditory scan of gallery, stopping at paunchy middle-aged guy in short-sleeved ash-gray madras dress shirt that reveals skinny arms as pale 'n hairless as zucchini squash. Overhears snatch of conversation between this *bonhomme* and wildly gesticulating cyberpunker in ass-tight black jeans:

> **THE INTERNET? WHY THERE HAS NEVER EXISTED AN INSTRUMENT WITH SO MUCH POWER FOR UNITING PEOPLES SEPARATED FROM ONE AN-OTHER. . . . HEY KID, THAT'S WHAT THEY SAID ABOUT THE RAILROADS ONCE.**

Aiming weird ear at young Indian woman—whose lavender veil drapes over mustard-yellow *ghangra* (skirt), while half-sleeve of her magenta-pink *choli* (blouse) reveals arms adorned by profusion of clear-green bangles—Art overhears end of what must have been bizarre conversation:

> **AND THAT'S NOTHING, ALPANA! YOU SHOULD HAVE HEARD OUR LAST CONVERSATION; IT WAS LIKE, WELL, HINDU SCIENCE FICTION.**

Something is Crook in Middlebrook

Turning 45 degrees, attempt at witticism by young Pakistani man in a white Nehru shirt directed to gallery owner is sucked down Art's weird ear:

ALLAH WOULD SAY THAT GAUTAMA BUDDHA WAS THE GREATEST SALESMAN IN HISTORY. HE WAS SELLING *NOTHING*! THAT'S WHAT 'NIRVANA' MEANS, NOTHING.

Two tall sex-tanned men (being what they call *in rude health*) sporting wide smiles with inward-sloping top front teeth, sweet teeth, synch Rolex watches and brush cookie debris from lapels of their twin Brooks Brothers suits. If camera be watching from high-angle in room all evening, we'd notice some kind of human force-field holds them in mutual orbit. Sudden light behind their eyes, braying like an ass, attracts Art's attention from across gallery.

Bet Nor 'n Pev have already given these guys pseudo-names, maybe Spunk Davis and Buck Specie. They seem rich in stories concerning the pornography of travel. The kind of wealthy bum-boys best displayed in tank-top T-shirts on the cover of airline magazines. . . . Art's musings abruptly halt as weird ear tunes in lantern-jawed Yuppy (Spunk) who turns face of bleached sincerity to his constant-companion (Buck) and confesses:

I HAVE LITTLE *TIME* FOR READING, AS I'M USUALLY TOO BUSY *READING*. BUT I'M NOT AT ALL INTERESTED IN THE NOVEL OF IDEAS, NOR NOVEL IDEAS. I'M NOT CAPABLE OF TRUE LOVE. . . . IT ISN'T TRUE. I TRULY LOVE MONEY. TRULY I DO, I LOVE YOU. YOU'RE SO DEMOCRATIC: YOU'VE GOT NO FAVORITES.

His interlocutor replies:

IF WE COULD SPREAD MONEY SHALLOW IT WOULD ACT LIKE A LAYER OVER EVERYTHING, SOFTENING THE WORLD. BUT LIFE, LIFE IS SO HARD [Laughs at double entendre]. **LIFE IS SO *HARD*.**

Blasted, totaled, but eager for more, Art's ear whips around toward fringe of crowd, picks up intense, slender, fair-haired man—recognizes him as distinguished art history prof at The School of the Art Institute—addressing younger man with shaved head (a graduate student?):

OH YES, MANET REMAINS THE ACID TEST FOR ANY DIAGNOSIS OF MODERNITY. WITH MANET, EVERYTHING IS AT STAKE.

Something is Crook in Middlebrook

Yep, all those culture vultures are ayammerin' away twenty to the dozen 'bout dazzlin' array of subjects:

CAN WE SAY THAT WE COMPREHEND THE METABOLIC INTERNAL BLIZZARD THAT CONVERTS MATTER INTO ENERGY?

And:

WAS IT ONLY A COINCIDENCE THAT EMILY POST DIED DURING KHRUSHCHEV'S BOMBASTIC, SHOEBANGING VISIT TO THE USA IN SEPTEMBER, NINETEEN SIXTY?

And:

DID YOU KNOW THAT WOODROW WILSON SANG "OH YOU BEAUTIFUL DOLL" ON HIS HONEYMOON WITH EDITH BOLLING? THE PULLMAN PORTER SAW HIM DANCING AND SINGING IN THE MORNING WHEN HE CAME OUT.

THAT'S JUST THE SORT OF FACT YOU'D KNOW!

And:

I NEVER YET TOUCHED A FIG LEAF THAT DIDN'T TURN INTO A PRICE TAG.

YAH? WELL FREEDOM OF OWNERSHIP IS HARMLESS; WHAT *IS* DANGEROUS TO THE STATE IS FREEDOM OF BEING.

Photo by Peven Pogacnic

With heap charming hook in her inflection 'n matching deep smile that rings like car keys, wobbly in fuck-me heels, stuffed into tight pink cashmere sweater, and standing arms akimbo—grad girl addresses through bee-stung lips one very slender 30s type male suffering bad posture, pierced ear, sassy black hat announcing GET KILLED, GET NOTICED, and host to over-washed Banana Republic duds:

JEFFTY, VENDLA O'FALLON JUST SUBMITTED HER DOCTORAL DISSERTATION, "DOUBTFUL IT STOOD:

Something is **Crook** in Middlebrook

And another pair look like they just stepped off the set of Jean-Luc Godard's film *Wind from the East* (1970):

Turning thirty degrees clockwise, Art does catch words of spindly young man with flourishing gardens of acne on his cheeks spoken to his frizzy-haired female companion, her eyes seeming to be cartoons of themselves, boldly outlined and richly shaded:

Behind this pair Art spies odd fiftyish couple—probably friends of the Pogacnic's as they've been orbiting them all evening like pair of electrons—a big blobby, bristle-jawed woman in shabby beige dress and her equally fat,

Something is *Crook* in Middlebrook

equally disheveled spouse: rumpled golf cap, oversized polyester polo shirt, baggy corduroy pants; they look like pair of bookends they'd failed to unload at their own garage sale. Man strokes his extraordinarily chaotic and unseemly beard. *Beard be like a bird's nest constructed under a bid system,* muses Art. Exchange of terse, pained glances as wife addresses husband:

> **AND NOREEN SWEARS, JUST SWEARS, I MIGHT LOOSE TWENTY POUNDS OR MORE ON THAT NEW "HEISENBERG UNCERTAINTY DIET" RECOMMENDED BY OPRAH WINFREY.**

Upon leaving, Art's weird ear does pick out snippets of three last arcane sound-bites that follow him out gallery door:

> **PETER, I'VE BEEN TO SO MANY GALLERIES TODAY, I'VE GOT A BLISTER ON MY PIVOT FOOT.**

> **SO YOU'RE SAYING TO MAKE IT IN THE ARTS NOW YA GOTTA, PUBLICIZE YOUR PRIVATE PARTS? BUT NOWADAYS CRITICS SAY YOU CAN'T OFFEND 'EM WITH YOUR PHALLUS OR PUDENDUM!**

> **SO MY DAY BECAME A STRANGE ONE OF TRACING PAPER AND INVISIBLE INK. . . . EVEN MY OMELETTE, WHICH LOOKED DOCILE ENOUGH ON THE PLATE, SOON TOOK ON STRANGE POWERS OF LIFE.**

> **NO, NO, IN THE ERA OF POST-NATURAL NATURE OUR MANTRA SHOULD BE: 'ENDARKENMENT IS THE DESTINY OF THE DEFUTURED'.**

> **I'M ASHAMED AND PROUD OF IT. I'M ASHAMED OF WHAT I AM. AND IS THAT ANYTHING TO BE ASHAMED OF?**

> **WHAT'S WITH THE GLASSES?**
>
> **REEF SAYS IT'S QUITE FASHIONABLE TO LOOK LIKE AN INTELLECTUAL THIS SEASON.**

Blessed Benimming! I feel as though I've been sitting on a molten walnut or a goofball of critical plutonium.

Describe the kind of reader this passage would please, and say why it would please him or her: ____

____.

Something is *Crook* in Middlebrook

3.6   Simultaneously, at 2159 West Lawrence Avenue, inside Bang Ho's dingy Shoe Repair, incessant blare of vintage Bakelite radio assists Bang Ho tally day's receipts. If this were film critics denominate "the ebb tide of the new wave," camera would slowly pan from this *yangpan*'s ledger book, past guitar with bumper sticker that says FEAR ME, BRETHREN, to close-up of said radio, then up to rickety shelf where sits old, rare tome—Charles Dallet's *Histoire de l'Église de Corée* says gold leaf on spine—propped up by colorful Korean knickknacks. (Scholars determine Dallet never ever saw Korea!) If Art were to walk past now he'd smell Bang Ho's wife (in apartment above) simmering her concoction of *Samgyetang* (Korean Chicken and Ginseng Soup) and hear broadcast of game show, *With a Little Help from the Lord*, on which contestants (probably wonderfully obese or horribly thin) demonstrate their zeal and test their knowledge of religious lore:

> *. . . And now, for five points,* and with a little help from the Lord*, can you tell us, Melody Sue, how does the Evil One disguise his appearance in front of the wise men of the Tabernacle, in the parable of the archangel and the gourd, in the Book of Joshua? a) as a young goat, b) as a jug vendor, c) as an acrobat with a monkey?*

Three blocks due north, private investigator sits in bare apartment across street from his mark (let's call him "Edmund 'Kite' Leitfaden" and name our obese P.I. "Chauncey 'Nub' Forkner"). Beneath Nub's thick feet, junk food wrappers scatter, evidence that four Wallies, three Blastfurters, and an American Way bought at Pepper's Burger World be washed down with nine-pack of beer. Nub adjusts his binocs at tall albino lounging in luxury loft-space, casually thumbing a book; spies spine displaying call number PS3048 .A1 1992 and title *Walden*. Although thorough, our private dick (bet he's never heard of Thoreau) meticulously jots down title with pencil stub in red notebook (identical to notebook your note-taking Author bought earlier, see Prologue) as if this be of major significance.

Meanwhile, another paunchy peeper, Mr. Bungle, lags, drags, 'n wiggles his bruised way back to beater leased from Rent-A-Wreck. He's in that slipped zone where there is neither sleep nor wakefulness, where all his thoughts and words are cross-purposed and yet his mind is solving, solving: *Kozmo'll be pissed. I should be after Alderman Pietro as ordered—yes—but—that fuck Middlebrook, that Potentate of Ear, has spook potential with a capital P. Which reminds me . . .* (Muscles out of car, whips out his prong and takes long hot, boiling leak against not-so-white white-wall tire, so pave-ment now smells of urine, burnt rubber 'n pumpernickel.) To anyone else, this matter of choice betwixt Pietro or Art would be open to prolonged debate; to Bungle—precisely *because* he is Bungle—it isn't.

Bungle scrunches into backseat of auto trying to ignore drunk trying to strangle some dog somebody left leashed to a parking meter; dog 'n drunk screaming at each other. Lying there on cheap beer 'n cum-stained seat, Mr. Bungle, you remind us art-smarts of those forlorn figures in California Pop artist Ed Kienholz's gut-wrenching mid-sixties art installation, *The State Hospital*. Fitfully dozing off, Bungle does suffer disturbing reoccurring nightmare (once shared with sister-in-law, Cassandra, psychoanalyst by trade): "I'm in

<h1 align="center">Something is Crook in Middlebrook</h1>

a Confessional: 'Bless me Father, for I have sinned. I committed endoarchy two times, melanicity four times, encropatomy seven times, and preprocity with igneouos intent, pretolemicity and overt cranialism once each.' My penance is to stand looking at my mug in a mirror nailed to a huge redwood tree; my mouth puckers to look like the mouth of a beehive, a hive about to swarm; that visible agitation around the mouth of its entrance—my mouth. Colony whines in centerless loud drone that vibrates through my whole body. I begin to spit out masses of bees, as if it were emptying not only my guts but my thoughts. A poltergeist-like storm of tiny wills materializes over my head; it grows to be a dark cloud; this ghost slowly rises into the sky, leaving behind my head to be like an empty box swimming in quiet bafflement."

Cassandra—possessed of superb range of modulations 'n timbres (plus she plays a banjulele, cross between banjo 'n uke) always looping back 'n forth between hard sounds 'n soft, allowing words to rise 'n fall as they pour out in dense, intricately fashioned barrage of syllables—offers her professional interpretation: "That dream is about your death, Les. Look at it this way: you were once the size of a period. For a brief time you tumbled about as a multi-cellular sphere, much like pond algae. Currents swept and washed over you. Remember? Then you grew. You became sponge life, tubular, all gut. To eat was life. You grew a spinal cord to feel. You put on gill arches in preparation to breathe and burn food with intensity. You grew a tail to move, to steer, to decide. You were not a fish, but a human embryo role-playing a fish embryo. At every ghost-of-embryonic-animal you slipped into and out of, you replayed the surrender of possibilities needed for your destination. To evolve is to surrender choices. To become something new is to accumulate all the things you can no longer be. Death is just another (probably final) phase of this evolution, Les. Hey, did you know that the German theosophist Rudolf Steiner writes lucidly in his otherwise kooky *Nine Lectures on Bees*: 'Just as the human soul takes leave of the body . . . one can truly see in the flying swarm an image of the departing human soul.' Yes, Les, that dream of yours is sheer death anxiety, but one mollified with bright hopes of some kind of eternal life."

3.7   We mercifully (for us) leave you Les, (a.k.a., Mr. Bungle) to (for the moment) suffer outside this text (in your own context). Of course Dear Reader, being an educated consumer of novels, you must suspect this dream *may be* a harbinger of textual-stuff-to-come. Some options you *might be* thinking about right now:

    1) The Boettcher Brats will snatch a hive 'n heave it
       onto our poor textual whipping boy; or,
    2) Bungle will die (most likely by extreme prejudice), or
    3) He will live to carry-out another "sting" operation for
       his overseers.
    4) It's a red herring bearing no relevance to future events.

Does it frustrate you that *I* know Bungle's fate right now better than you? Check one:

_______ YES   _______ UNDECIDED   _______ NO

4.0

Opening over. People spilling into streets color of oyster 'n carbon; air shivering 'n shakes its coat, like wet dog, like surface of worried water. Art treats himself to a taxi, avoiding getting wet and taxing ride on noisy EL. Like musing Wally Shawn in final scene of film *My Dinner with Andre*, he stares out cab's window through which he reads GAP ATHLETIC as GAL PATHETIC and EMPIRE REALITY as VAMPIRE REALITY. (Brittany on his mind?) Moodily reminiscences about times past. Ho, yes! Art's adoin' skull-time in battered Yellow Cab No. 2430 commanded by Zygmunt, taciturn, prissy-lipped Polish immigrant whose eyes manically fizz in rear-view mirror. Has clenched-jawed metonymity of driver determined to stay awake on featureless stretch of interstate. Fortyish, but still lean. Balding pate nearly glows in dark; hair scurries long 'n damp down neck 'n shoulders. *Mad rug, mad neck*, muses Art. Notices neck be explosively pocked 'n mottled, with flicker of adolescent virulence in crimson underhang of ears. Fact: Art gets creeps riding in back seat of any vehicle if driver sports mad neck supporting mad rug. Red-and-white decal of Polish flag prominent on cab's cracked windshield, glow-in-dark plastic Jesus with hand raised in blessing adorns dash, while pernicious punning bumper stickers on rear read: "I **SLAM** ISLAM" and "ISLAM**IS**BAD." Art hopes plastic dash fetish protects his journey from *fatwah* ordering bloody Jihad contra cabby's baneful blasphemy.

Indulging what Una calls his "petrified unrest," constant disquiet that permeates both his interior landscape and his experience of external urban-scape, Art zooms north up Racine Avenue. Bounces around in back seat like popcorn popping thanks to punches from Chicago's proverbial potholes. Passes homeless bag lady on bench. That kind assassin, Sleep, has drawn bead on 'n blown her brains out: head bent forward, empty purse between legs, clothed in rags and carrying her worldly possessions in several worn bags; grotesquely ironic gesture as if just returned from suburban shopping spree. *For the oppressed,* Art muses, *existence in public space is more likely to be synonymous with state surveillance, public censure, and political power-lessness.* Rollin', rolllin', rolin;, taxi continues north, passing signs reading: COWARD SHOES and HOME OF THE WHOPPER.

Next block, Art spies black kids cutting chain lock on bicycle and riding off on it. *Private property . . . why it has made us so stupid and passive that an object is only* ours *if we* possess *it, that is, exists for us as capital, or is* used *by us.* Asks stern driver to take him by his childhood haunts near North Clark and Pratt so he can recall forms of his formative years, create palimpsest of past 'n present. *I have more memories than if I had lived a thousand years; my own sad brain hides many secrets.*

Driving past old red brick building with faded, now still, candy cane barber pole, he thinks: *There, there! I had my first haircut, daddy insisting on a closely cropped "whitewalls" treatment so I looked like a Hitler Youth. So much did I hate having my hair cut, it was my earliest exposure to what I came to punningly call "barberism," that is, anything unpleasant and/or*

Something is *Crook* in Middlebrook

forced upon me. Funny how these memory flashes work: things step into our lives, not we into theirs. That barber pole was once functional, twistin' 'n turnin', its screw motion fascinating little Art no end. *I remember staring at that pole until it put me into a sort of trance.* Later, as fledgling art student, realizes importance of logarithmic spiral as archetypal image—it's expression of The Golden Section Ratio—and notes its ubiquity. Loves artist Robert Smithson's earthwork in the Great Salt Lake titled *Spiral Jetty*. For Art that tornadic shape becomes icon for revolutionary change; so uses spiral as logo accompanying his oddball *nom d'art*, "3Nomial Voices Whirlpool Destruction," which he signs to 16-part series of wonky aesthetic manifestoes touting conceptual art's dematerialization of the artwork. Like so many notes-in-a-bottle

```
                    WHERE ELSE?
              (put it on your bookshelf)

      The Phenomenological Artwork is an attempt to land you in
your easy-chair. Another hemorrhoid swelling to bursting. We
are a clot of blood in the pants of the Passéists. Oh, those of
weak vascular strength!  We straddle the Word and the Image with-
out as much as a grunt. Such sensitive tissues, Us.

      Put it on your bookshelf, where else? Our Artworks reject
the sore feet and poor postures of OBJECT ART. Thumb Our pages,
leave your mark. Put it on your bookshelf, where else?

      The Phenomenological Artwork is a setting-into-work of truth
that thrusts up the familiar and ordinary,discounting what we
believe as such. The truth that discloses itself in the Work
can never be proved or derived from what went before, as such.

      We are STRIFE in which the unity of the World and Us are
won. We bring out what is yet undecided and measureless, and
thus disclose the hidden necessity of measure and decisiveness!
In going beyond correctness to truth, We arrive at the essential
disclosure of what IS as such.

      We declare that: the thing-concepts obstruct the way to-
ward the thingly character of the thing as well as as toward
the equipmental character of equipment, and all the more toward
the workly character of Our Works.  Passéists! The unpretentious
thing evades thought most stubbornly.

      Get your Language straight!!!!!!!!!!!!!!!!!!!!!!!!!!!!!!!!!

        signed:          3NOMIAL VOICES WHIRLPOOL DESTRUCTION
```

they are bulk mailed out to art world notables.

4.1   Art's what some here call "a boomerang": lived in Chicago, left Chicago, returned. Art used to live on Chicago's northeast side suffering under both paranoid daddy (pathologically jealous, obsessed that his wife sleeps around) and traumatizin' tutelage of Jesuits (Art still calls 'em "Jesus-Whips") until age of reason. Art, like most kids, be absolutely monster of activity as child. But bourgeois socialization attempts to prepare him for secure nonexistence as adult dummy by stressing parroting back "correct answers," looking without touching, solving problems "in the head," sitting passively in the classroom, learning to do without optical clues. Triumph of such cognition does *nearly* signal defeat of Art as potential revolutionary subject. So thanks for support of long list of wonky (then and now) friends who confirm 'n re-enforce Art's innate sense of rebellion.

Now cab rolls past mini-park at intersection of Ravenswood and Albion where he and his sister used to play on the swings: *There I beat up Billy, the block's bully, after he tried to steal my tricycle. Stuck a metal bar into the front spokes and bad Billy did 180-degree loop onto his stupid red head. So stunned, I could easily pummel him until he begged for mercy. Not only did he never bother me again, but he actually grew to even like me. What's it about males that they can hate you, but if you kick each others' ass once, you become buddies?* Old neighborhood has changed hands, witnessed by poignant, red graffiti scanned by passing streak of yellow cab:

Tewanda G.:
Everyday I calls a phone to her
Every night I dreams for her.

4.2   Later Art's whole family exiled west to boring Burbank, California and nondescript yellow duplex with parched lawn and two short, fat palm trees in front. Art hates it. Why move? Paranoid, alcoholic daddy hires on to work at Lockheed Aircraft's top secret "Skunk Works" projects under famous aviation designer Clarence Kelly Johnson during height of Cold War when being paranoid certainly *not* political liability. In sunny, smoggy Southern California little bashful Art attends dreary Bellarmine Jefferson parochial military school run by obese extroverted ex-Army Chaplain who has gone to seed and could pass for Friar Tuck. Art has to smartly salute the nuns and priests and march in stupid parade each morning as flag raises and National Anthem plays. Has to wear tacky khaki uniform with black tie and black spit-shined shoes. Has picture to prove it too. Art shits his khaki pants one glorious Spring day, so intimidated is he of stern old nun with blood-stained ruler who fiercely proctors third grade final exam. Doesn't raise his hand to excuse himself. May be has something to do with Latin proverb tacked to cork bulletin board behind teacher's desk: *Qui timide rogat docet negare* (He who asks timidly invites refusal).

This is same pedagogue who ridicules Art's penchant for art. Little Art draws big crayon picture of Disney cartoon dog Pluto with paw raised in awful pain, small nail sticks therein and cartoon balloon captions above reads: "Ouch, help me Mickey!" Down from out of airplane in sky floats Mickey Mouse to rescue, "Don't worry Pluto, I'm coming!" Miffed teacher beckons Art up in front of class to show his masterpiece, then lambasts him for not only drawing—horrors!—cartoon characters, but for sin of impurity for importing debased text into pristine visual image. Points ruler at Art's heartfelt scribbles and declaims, "Bad art." Points to Art and says, "Bad Art. *Quod erat demonstrandum.*" This be some five years prior to Roy Lichtenstein's very similar comic-strip inspired Pop Art paintings. Art really ahead of his time as precocious Pop Artist *avant la lettre*.

Cab moves slowly on. Some insulted Arab bystanders carrying box of Dunkin Donuts flip driver off. Sees them in his rear-view mirror, but ignores 'em. Cab moves on to Art's now decrepit Jesuit grade school; it looks so much smaller and unimpressive than he remembers: *Yep, here's where I was dragged kicking and yelling (or was it fussing and fuming?) into my culture's socio-symbolic field, negotiating all that Oedipal shit, assimilating what witty Postmodern theorists now call "The Big Other."*

Suddenly Art hears in private privacy of his *cabeza* delightful sound of freedom, John Phillip Souza's "The Washington Post March." Rousing tune plays as grade school is let out each day. Now waves of pleasure mixing with pain wash across Art and he sees instant rerun of "Doofus," his weird, but good-natured classmate from first grade: *Ah, he still sports coke bottle thick glasses and those dull suspenders yanking his grey corduroy pants up almost to his armpits; he suffers perpetual bubbles of snot dripping from his nostrils as he waves goodbye until another tomorrow.*

Alas! Only one day there is no tomorrow for dear friend Doofus. His distraught father—oddly, his name is Abelard—takes hellish hard fists and super sharp butcher knife to his whole family that night. Wraps their bodies parts up like butcher does meat and mails packages to J. Edgar Hoover. Then suffocates himself with garbage bag. Seems Doofus's daddy, always staunch Democrat and supporter of liberal values, does fall into pathological depression after being fired from Westinghouse's Elevator Division (same year that company installs elevators in Roosevelt University where Art attends geology classes) when F.B.I comes around hinting to Abelard's boss that "Aby is a Communist sympathizer." And so it goes. Funny. Can recall father's name, but not Doofus's actual appellation. An engram lost forever.

4.3　　Three decades later, Art returns to Chicago to teach; blushing new bride, Brittany, in tow sporting legs as long 'n slim as Art's hope of Heaven. Fact: has tendency to fall at mere flash of kneecap. Settles just south of his former haunts; ergo, many features of noisy Windy City now elicit in him flash of involuntary memories (some good, some bad) and uncanny feelings. Heaps of uncanny feelings: *There daddy secretively prowls trash bins, ours and neighbors; once pulls out tasteful nude photo (face is not visible) from an amateur photographer neighbor's trash can; furious, he proceeds to accuse my poor mother of posing for the abomination even though mom is heavier with long brown hair, while model is slim, short-haired blond. Angry, daddy tears up photos; crying, mommy's tears tearing down face; in fright 'n flight, little ol' me tearing up the back stairs to the neighbor's apartment.*

Within month of triumphant return to Chicago, wanting to enliven his experience of this city as vast palimpsest of past and present experiences, Art devises clever contrapuntal conceptual art projects called *Orders* and *Chance Trip.* Both involve Art abrogating authorial status, but in the former, Art is literally programmed by his students who fill out typed form that orders him to specific intersections in town with initial direction of commanded walk indicated by start arrow. Then, checking off ten RIGHT _______ , LEFT ______, or STRAIGHT _______ options on said sheet, students program Art like robot to perform series of ten block walks. At completion of each, he cajoles some bystander to take Polaroid of him at destination and sign-off as witness on said form, proving all commands properly executed. Eager to outdo rival New York conceptual artist, Vito Acconci, Art covers these ten blocks while slowly walking large tortoise (leased from disreputable local pet store that provides roosters for local cockfight enthusiasts).

Fact: walking since infancy means that walking is one of life's treacherous routes back through everything one's been. In the latter piece, aleatory method means Lady Luck programs six-hour chance trip around Chicago starting from steps of Art Institute of Chicago; at each intersection, Art tosses two coins held inside a plastic jar: 2 heads = right turn; 2 tails = left turn; heads/tails = straight. Around 'n around the city he goes, where he'll stop only chance knows. You know, witty play on those musing, mincing, distracted strollers—*les flâneurs*—fashionably sauntering about *les boulevards de Paris* in nineteenth-century France.

During such leisurely mincing walks, Art often revels in Proustian flashbacks: *Ho! There's the small hill I used to slide down in my saucer-shaped aluminum sled as I wore warm silver-colored rubber space cadet boots and a silver-colored snow suit that made me into something like the alien spaceman, Klattu, played by Michael Rennie in the classic sci-fi film* The Day the Earth Stool Still.

When not time-traveling into his past on these walks, or noticing oddball weather manifestations such as that hollow pink cloud now basking in clear distance—its rosy cusp fastened by tendrils at either end, like a vertical eye or vertical mouth with a creaturely essence, meticulous, feminine—Art dodges rude comments from the urban peanut gallery like "Gaback to California, ya faggot!" in between placing orders for piping hot grande vanilla lattes at Cosi.

Vanilla. Art loves it. Loves it in all things: coffee, ice cream, milk shakes, donuts, cakes, after shave, and scented candles even. Now with weird ear, likes to hear Una *say it* over 'n over: **VAH-NILL-AH . . . VAH-NILL-AH**. Does synaesthetically taste it then, that unique flavor. Why does Art like vanilla better than chocolate? Answer may be in astounding fact mom tells Art upon graduating high school: seems when born Art is way way premature, has to spend six weeks in incubator peering out at weird world from behind alienating Plexiglas; when mom does make visit to hospital to occasionally breast-feed him, she puts tiny amount of vanilla extract on her nipple to induce Art to suck. Art's "good object" (to cop term from British psychoanalyst D. W. Winnicott's Object Relations Theory) becomes identified with that unique taste. How would *you* describe taste of vanilla?

Justwaitadamnminute (you say) what about that Plexiglas prison from which new baby Art observes strange new world, huh? "Stuck in that isolation chamber so long, probability high it explains your penchant for voyeurism and earsdropping," pontificates Professor of Mathematics, Art's next door neighbor, Al Schmerbauch. "Did you know that the typical incubator's rectangular proportions match *phi* [pronounced: *fee*], the Golden Section or Divine Proportion of 1:1.6 and change? Ratio underlies much architecture: like the famous "Chicago Window" of Louis Sullivan. *Phi* is an expression of the Fibonacci Series, you know."

Hey, think Al is on to something here. As child Art has yellow plastic crystal radio with earphones. Does clandestinely listen to broadcasts of local CBS affiliate late at night under covers of his bed. The content of broadcasts irrelevant to pleasure Art receives from clandestine listening. Later, as pimply teenager, Art takes up shortwave listening as all-consuming hobby and way to avoid high school social life. No interest in Ham radio broadcasting, only pleasure of listening. Daddy puts up long dipole antenna over house, buys him massive Korean War surplus Hammarlund Super-Pro shortwave radio stuffed with huge tubes and festooned with delightfully mysterious dials. Early 1960s, ears glued to ungainly headphones crackling with Radio Moscow's propaganda competing with jamming and other electromagnetic phenomena on 11,255 megacycles. Art learns about different types of antennae, effect of sunspot cycles on radio propagation, how to reduce jamming, joys of hearing clandestine stations, and that listening to and corresponding with Radio Moscow and Radio Havana brings paranoid F.B.I. to one's door, especially if one's paranoid daddy is working on top secret government projects.

Ear to the airwaves, Art gets startling political lessons: compares media coverage of divers events from different national perspectives, groks how selective U.S. media is, how subtle censorship is exercised. Now enlightened, thinks everyone should have shortwave radio to escape monopoly of U.S. media broadcasts. Loves to listen to Ham radio enthusiasts, mostly old geezers jawin' 'n jawin' 'bout, well, just *anything* so long as it's not too serious. Ham radio as "power to the people" exercised in opposition to mass media domination. So heap grateful when liberal librarian at high school turns Art onto *Frankfurt School of Western Marxism for Dummies,* dumbed-down version of Theodor Adorno, Max Horkheimer, Herbert Marcuse, and Walter Benjamin's critique of our "culture industry." Art stops watching TV. Becomes self-styled high school campus radical. Views his classmates as sheep or lemmings conforming to societal dictates. Sets off in school lockers small homemade bombs constructed of hundreds of match heads stuffed into small CO_2 cylinders originally used to power air guns. Lights Jet-X fuse and three minutes later KABOOM. Stuffed one in empty locker next to that of "Scutch," most-hated class bully (sort of student whose intellectual life might be titled *Still Life with Bong*): blows huge hole into adjacent locker so bully's text books and girlie pin-ups burn to crisp. School investigation never tags Art as culprit.

Now Art is still the "rad," but big difference on airwaves. Few years ago Art buys spanking new Kenwood R-5000 receiver with single-side band capability and digital signal processing; runs long Eavesdropper Dipole Antenna inside his home—much to Brittany's dismay—tunes in all short-wave bands. Once again delightful sound of electro-magnetic jimjams in his ears. But actual broadcast content disappointing. "Greenwich Mean Time" now called more politically correct "Universal Time Coordinated." Rich sound of amplitude modulation (AM) largely replaced by inferior sound of single-side band (SSB) transmission, which takes up less bandwidth.

Plethora of ultra-conservative Hams run mini-chat groups promoting Fundamentalism and politics of hate. Ho! KKK has its own radio station. Neo-Nazis prattle on uncontested. Oodles of conservative talk show hosts hawking fear and hatred of government, talk of Black Helicopters Over America, screeching Southern preachers touting separation of races, and conspiracy freaks bemoaning United Nations be ubiquitous on all commercial shortwave radio stations. Only Radio for Peace International in Costa Rica broadcasts liberal programing on rights of women and gays, problems of the environment, rights of the working fellow, etcetera. So, after audio-taping hours and hours of most egregious fascist sound-bites for his research into hate groups —heave-ho!—Art tosses expensive receiver into garbage bin. Signs up for Cable Internet service, only to find situation on-line not much different. And so it goes.

4.4   First thing Art does upon arriving at dome-home is unpackage week-old lemon Danish, its wrapper dragging away clots of vanilla icing like Band-Aid pulling off scab; boots up computer and checks e-mail. Ho! Message from former colleague at that jerkwater suburban college:

> FROM: Josh86@hotmail.com
> TO: Exprof@gadfly.com
> SUBJECT: The Barracuda bites The Big Weenie
>
> Hi-ho! The wicked witch is dead. The Barracuda now sleeps with the fishes in the Des Plaines River! Praise be for small miracles.
>
> — Josh

Josh teaches PhotoShop skills and helps Art set up his computer at home once. Flashback necessary to explain his happy news: *Hurtle o'er root 'n stone, beware o' boulder, break no bone*, repeats Art to under his breath over 'n over just prior to combative faculty meetings at that jerk-water suburban college. Helps get his confidence level up for inevitable verbal thrashing he suffers before, during, and after such meetings. "Leatherface," detested departmental chairman, and his obese gruff departmental secretary (one of those middle-aged, middle-class, bitter busy-bodies lovingly referred to by all as "The Barracuda") do so hate Art's postmodernist propensities. Yes, they take every opportunity to harass him in petty ways.

When Art initially hired, Leatherface notices Art's car more rétro 'n expensive than chairman's salt-corroded "beater" van, so immediately buys candy apple red Chrysler P.T. Cruiser to outshine Art's purple 'n white Nash. As the department's new hire, Art cajoled by Leatherface to jot down minutes of each faculty meeting. Sure, it's really The Barracuda's job, but Leatherface wants to break Art's spirit, show him who's boss, and gain favor with his co-conspirator. *If this asshole likes writing, I'll give him something to write about,* thinks he. *What a sweet man, think we can really screw him, I think,* thinks she. And *he* is called Leatherface because mild stroke leaves facial muscles rigid and disposition mercurial. So secretary feels sorry for him. Guy's stuck in some weird Hollywood cowboy movie and Art's playing fall guy. Saunters about like John Wayne, while Art cowers like town drunk. Leatherface's costume is square dance-style shirt and trousers, snakeskin cowboy boots, tan cowboy hat with snakeskin band, all covered by long tan Western-style duster. All that's missing be proverbial double-barrel shotgun.

Art tries to curry his favor by wearing authentic cowboy boots, but only succeeds in straining his lower back walking in 'em. Sons of the Pioneers music creeps from Leatherface's office along with smells of barbecued pork sandwiches and french fries; office adorned with large poster of James Dean and on wall nearby scope-equipped Olympic competition-style German Feinwerkbau model 65 air pistol. Lives on small farm near Plano, sharing his Rustic Retreats Build-it-yourself log cabin with seven constantly farting whippet racing dogs, their inline cages gracing his living room. Faculty meeting held out there once moved out onto back deck, so strong was odor emanating from those canines.

Leatherface generously gives Art small faculty office directly across from The Barracuda's desk so she can spy on Art, see if he cops any office supplies, wants to get some dirt on him so Art can be blackmailed into voting wishes of chairman. *Now let that little shit try 'n fuck students in his office without us knowing about it!* Art and his colleagues have to beg on their hands and knees for office supplies from The Barracuda, Keeper of the Office Supply Keys. Liquid Paper white-out, paper clips, Post-It notes, pencils, note pads, and manila folders are doled out meagerly and duly recorded in small booklet. Once Art tried to get more Liquid Paper and was rebuffed: "*Nada.* Jeeze, only a week since your last request for some, Mr. Middlebrook. We gotta economize you know." Faculty's friendly "hello" to her each morning as they past her desk to collect their mail is met with icy silence or special grunt of annoyance. Since she's State employee protected by tough union, not easy to get rid of her charming presence either. Ah, academia! But now thank god for small miracles. Fall into water during freak boating accident (Art suspects henpecked hubby pushes her in) on rain swollen river frees department from perennial curse. Cheers, Leatherface has lost his "muscle." *Could be regime change in the offing,* thinks Art.

After deleting gaggle of spam, Art comes upon e-mail from Una. Laid-off from job as investment banker last month—she's got all the business buzzwords: profit centers, value-added, service industry, human resources, etcetera, but she is also against all idioms that are divisive or judgmental, so its: *birth name* for maiden name, *preorgasmic* for frigid, *back salary* for alimony—Una writes she has new job now:

```
FROM: Una8@cheapnet.com
TO: Exprof@gadfly.com
SUBJECT: To Freebie or not to Freebie

Arty darling:
        A kiss can be a comma, a question mark, or
an exclamation point. That last kiss of your was
. . . well ... the latter type! Today I went dress
shopping (tried on an original Todd Oldham wrap-
```

> *around: not-so-basic black-slash-beige dress,*
> *strapless, Navajo-inspired and neon quilted),*
> *stopped into a bank to cash a check and visited a*
> *Saturn dealership to look at new cars, test drove*
> *a Land Rover; then went golfing, afterwards to*
> *dinner at a nice Italian ristorante. I get free*
> *gas, groceries and clothes. When my car breaks*
> *down I get paid to have it repaired. Guess what*
> *kind of job I have? I am part of the Freebie Econ-*
> *omy now. Companies pay ME to test their products*
> *and services. I am The Brand Called You!*
>
> > *This month I will gross nearly $7,000 from*
> *various freebie adventures. Hey, it's the only way*
> *to deal with our permanent risk economy where*
> *people no longer dream of overcoming difficulties,*
> *but merely surviving.*
>
> > *Before you say I've copped out, did you*
> *know that the word for 'sale' in French stores is*
> *'révolution'?*
>
> > *Say, sweetie, you could supplement your*
> *income by testing ear plugs or evaluating the*
> *sound of door bells!*
>
> > *— Baci e abbracci* [hugs 'n kisses], *Una*
>
> *P.S. Homeslice, have you read Tori Timmerlmann's*
> *thought-provoking book,* The Technological Imagi-
> nation: What Today's Children Have to Teach Their
> Parents? *She retires the "tired paradigm" of gift-*
> *ed child as socially isolated genius and touts the*
> *"wired paradigm" of the gifted child as creatively*
> *connected consumer. She also argues that often the*
> *most exciting fashions are now worn by urban poor.*

Shit, if we're having Neiman-Marcus time, I can't compete! thinks Art. Such e-mail is convenient—despite half of 'em offering riven virgins and pregnant grannies and offers for penis-enlargement strategies—but Art prefers Una's personal hand-written notes for they are written in fleecily curling script with elegant punctuation marks, and signature like seven-veil dance. Moreover, those letters smell of Una's potpourri—a distillation of jasmine, patchouli, bitter oranges, and calambulaliam.

4.5   Sky lowers, grays, thickens into upside-down topographical map. Misty drizzle washes over Illinois. Left ear ungooped. Hears yakky people discussing impending war against Iraq from confines of his domicile. This overhearing may be Yaqui way of knowledge that he and his crazed druggie buddy of yore, Larry Lister Binacka, once learn from *'Boca Loco,'* old Yaqui *brujo* they meet in Baja California back in their hippy days when both read Carlos Castenada. Maybe he can recall chant to fend away bad stuff, maybe. Only wants to hear good stuff. So he ascends to cockloft to sing modified version of haunting *canto antiguo* titled *"A Todo Vapor"* ("At Full Steam") as he spins on swivel-barstool sporting label underneath seat reading: MADE IN BARSTOW, CA:

> Go on—at full steam—just imagine!
> Ear noise before him,
> Ear noise behind him,
> Ear noise above him,
> Ear noise below him,

Something is *Crook* in Middlebrook

Ear noise all around him.
Home above the big salamander.
Dark cloud at the door.
Zigzag lightning stands high upon it.
The male deity *Mescalito!*
He makes the deity's offering and requests:
If can't restore his normal ear to him,
Do restore his normal gait.
Or do dull the left ear's hearing to evil. At least.
This very day do work your spell for him.
Happily he wants to recover.
Happily his interior wants to be cool.
Impervious to pain 'n death.
Happily may he hear normally.
Being as use to, may he hear normally.
But at least, may it be sweet sound all year round.
In beauty, may it be reasonable resonate sound.

Art's mad spin stops roulette-randomly. Weird ear, still ahearin' super-normally (like auditory version of *camera obscura*) is facing northwest toward Magnetic Resonance Institute Research Center recently housed in refurbished red brick building formerly home to Serbian restaurant gutted by Croat fire bomb on Xmas Eve last that grills 'n kills restaurant's top chef's father visiting from Old Country. Sound emanating from there is, to Art, ominously techno-incoherent:

MS. BUXBOTTOM TAKE A LETTER ADDRESS IT TO MIFFLIN B. CLOUGH III, CEO WORLD SYSTEMS THOUSAND POINTS OF LIGHT PROJECT WASHINGTON, DC TWO-OH-OH-OH-ONE. DEAR SIR, BLAH BLAH BLAH. USUAL GREETINGS. GIVEN THE ALREADY-SECRET TRUE EXPERIENCE OF REGENERATIVELY-EVOLVING COMPREHENSIVE WORLD-DESIGN EFFORT AGAINST TERRORISM, FIRE, FLOOD, PESTILENCE, VIOLENT ATMOSPHERIC DISTURBANCE, AND PROVIDING SEVENTEEN CUBIC FEET Of AIR PER MINUTE PER PERSON FREE OF TOXIC OR DISAGREEABLE ODORS OR DUST OR MALICE, WE FEEL THAT METALS BROADLY SPEAKING AND SYNTHETICS NARROWLY SPEAKING SHOULD BE INTERLINKED MAGNETICALLY INTO CONTINUOUSLY IMPROVING WORLD-AROUND EXTRA-CORPOREAL NETWORKS, NETWORKS WITHIN WHICH ONLY THE INDIVIDUAL PRESENTS ITSELF AS AN INHERENT ISLAND OF PHYSICAL DISCONTINUITY SAD TO SAY, SAD TO SAY, PHYSICAL DISCONTINUITY TORPOR, TOTAL VELOCITIES OF WHICH KNOWN PRACTICES PROVE INADEQUATE TO SOLVE. GIVEN, HOWEVER, ALL-OVER COMPENSATORY DESIGN DESPAIR SUCH AS KNOWN TO YOU AND KNOWN TO ME, AND FREAKINESS, AND BEARING IN THE MIND PUSH-PULL AS PRIOR TO AND ABOVE ALL,

Something is *Crook* in Middlebrook

Tastes brown of corporate bureaucratic bullshit. Suffers head-spin 'n heart fever.

Whirling Dervish antics that you, The Reader, just witness is like aleatory spin of roulette wheel. Chancy stuff. Today it's discrete discourse of creepy capitalist, tomorrow maybe young mother comforting crying baby, or Noreen verbally translating one of Peven's photographs, or dark breathing of steel and refineries under webs of humming power lines south of Chicago.

4.6   Three days later. Muggy air plays basso continuo to blackness of Night. Across street from Art's dome, Boettcher's living room stuffed with too many tchotchkes. Roo watches NBA game blaring from jumbo TV—African-American pituitary cases in short pants leaping and loping like turbocharged leopards. Brats (consumer-cadets) be in their room (happily) playing quietly (and even tenderly) with their magical-pseudo-technology-of-violent-conflict toys after making another entry in their joint diary. Ho! Let's sneak-a-peak:

Monday --- Us.

Tuesday --- Us.

Wednesday --- Us.

Thursday --- Us.

Friday --- Us.

Why aren't we surprised?

However, Saturday's entry is slightly different:

Saturday --- Us (in school play we helped
write titled "She-sus Versus Godzilla").

Art firmly *in situ* in the cockloft on swivel stool with red safe-light on ready to start *ears-dropping*. On barstool, Art always sings that damn incan-

Something is *Crook* in Middlebrook

tory pre-hearing jingle as he twirly-twirls in same direction as Mother Earth, using his golf putter to propel him. As human roulette wheel stops, he pulls waxy plug on weird ear and auditorily samples what's what, his upper teeth warily bared to that expected press of aural sense data. Ear now aimed at slim man in Brooks Brothers three-piece walking past dome-home who does sing under his breath to tune of "Jingle Bells" this bit of official doggerel:

Suddenly Art's doin' skull-time; antithetically recalls lusty, loud song sung by teenage-terror—one Larry Binacka—during mid-1970s Presidential campaign:

When I was young 'n so damn naive,
I asked my mother what should I be.
Should I be Republican, or Democratic,
Here's what she said to me: Are you
Stupid kid? Do what your daddy did,
For something grander do make the bid.
Like Beneficent Anarchism—
For such Count Kropotkin did assiduously strive
For society of friendliness to all to be alive.
This's why we in underground hive do
Alternative politics imbibe.

Ah, Larry, sighs Art nostalgically; then quickly redoes twisty-twirl, now pointing weird ear directly south and hears Chicago panting, big urban engines going, sirens weirdly yelping, ambulances, police cars—mad-dog, gashing-knife weather, a rape 'n murder night, thousands of hydrants open, spraying water from both breasts. Turning again, aiming for house next to Boettcher's: Pogacnic's domicile. Ho! Just in time to audit Noreen exercising her photo-interpretation skills, scanning, and deciphering Peven's 35mm slide that is projected onto dining room wall as Peven listens and chugs a Miller High Life:

Something is **Crook** in Middlebrook

Gunshot or car backfiring. Maybe recidivist Boettcher Brat tossing M-80 fire-cracker out bedroom window. Or all three events sounding simultaneously. Abruptly ends aural session. Art's ear rings and rings and rings like un-attended phone in deserted phone booth in desert. If Noreen be privy to this, she'd think—*Art got his just desserts*—and laugh in her trapped, guttural, lockjawed laugh.

4.7	KAAABLLLLAAAAM does startle Tiger Woods who salamanderly scuttles into his small sub-deck snuggery—made of bamboo—which Pev photographs prior to installation and Noreen verbally translates thus:

Somewhere in Tig's reptilian consciousness he was vague feeling that there do be some original salamanderly world, a comfy home-world, which be lost to him forever. Tig shits.

Something is Crook in Middlebrook

As Tig skittle-scuttles 'n shits, simultaneously along Lawrence Avenue huge plum-colored Cadillac driven by old, yellow-skinned, fat white man in blue shirt with orange polka dots passes old maroon Buick driven by fat young white man in green shirt and red polka dots, his radio blaring Madonna's "Like a Virgin." Both are going much faster than posted speed limit. Meanwhile, two Harley-Davidson crazies noisily zoom past both autos on right in "Bicycles Only" lane, causing three startled pedestrians to cower for their lives and squeezing lone bicyclist into curbside. "Organ Donor!" cyclist shouts back in impotent rage. All of above proof that in big American city its dwellers be needing one deep no-affect belt, a heap critical mass of indifference, to survive effects of modernity. When the dogs-of-conscience be barking, throw 55-pound re-enforced concrete pork chop at 'em. Knocks 'em silly every time!

Regooping his wounded ear, Art watches in fascination from his cockloft as very pale elderly woman with terribly fierce expression, repeatedly tries to parallel park her old Citroën DS—also known as *Déesse*, or *Goddess*, after the punning initials in French (thanks to Pau D'Arco for this bit of trivia)—in front of Boettcher's abode. Why such interest? Art has his own theory that way people park has much to do with their intimate self-image, revealing how they feel about their own backsides: "Start to park and your neurotic impulses advance upon you; you have, like the external world, your own phenomena inside, and parking in Chicago is like standing at edge of your own psychic pond and throwing in crumbs to watch the carp (crap?) come swimming up. Ya grok?"

4.8	TV news report that night confirms noise not originate with Boettcher Brats, but be hate-filled pipe-bomb stuffed in garbage can of nearby Muslim neighbor. Moreover, drawing by Brat #1 accomplished that night depicting juvenile recidivists doing anti-pedagogical shenanigans on grade school's front lawn that day proves at least one Brat be blocks away at time of explosion.

At same moment bomb goes off, Una be readying to work on her laptop. Her gloves adore such sensation. Finnies sliding through their nice cashmere lining, diverging in ten directions, butting against their innermost tips. A sated, exquisite feeling. Heavenly. Hands tremble. Gloves tremble. And deep inside them, fingerprint swirls light up like elements of a stove. In calfskin, Una's hands move in ways they never do when bare: they could make a deft point, beckon gracefully; gesticulate. In calfskin, they become as dexterous as hands of baseball umpires, traffic cops and the deaf.

Something is *Crook* in Middlebrook

Ho! Her hands radiate possibility. Fact: she always wears them when using her computer, like today when following e-mail does arrive at IN BOX of Una's e-mail:

> *From: ahmedhassan1977@yahoo.fr*
> *To: Una8@cheapnet.com*
> *Subject: Proposal Get Wealthy*
>
> *Dear Madam,*
>
> *Good a thing to write you. I have a proposal for you -- this however is not mandatory nor will I in any manner compel you to honour against your will. I am Ahmed Hassan 23 years old and the only son of my late parents Mr. and Mrs. MOHHAMED HASSAN, My father was a highly reputable businness magnet--(a cocoa merchant) who operated in the capital of Ivory coast during his days when breathless enthusiasm sung in harmony with poisonous boredom.*
> *It is sad to say that he passed away mysteriously in France during one of his bus-iness trips abroad in the year 2006.Though his sudden death was linked or rather suspected to have been masterminded by an uncle of his who travelled with him at that time. But God knows the truth! My mother died when I was just 4 years old, and since then my father took me so special. Before his death on 2006 he called the secretary who accompanied him to the hospital and told her that he had a sum of$4.500.000(Four Million, five hundred thousand dollars) kept in a bank in (AFRICA). He also explained to her that it was because of this wealth that he was poisoned by his business assoc-aites. That I should seek for a foreign partner in a country of my choice where I will transfer this money to and use it for investment purposes.*
> *I want you to assist me in transferring the fund into your bank account overseas as a bene-ficiary of the fund, and also use it for an in-vestment purpose. I am just 23 years old and a university undergraduate and really don't know what to do. Now I want an account overseas where I can transfer this funds. This is because I have suffered a lot of set backs as a result of inces-sant political crisis here in Ivory coast. The death of my father actually brought sorrow to my life.*
> *Dearest one, I am in a sincere desire of your humble assistance in this regards Your sug-gstions and ideas will be highly regarded.*
> *Thanks you so much.*
>
> *My sincerely regards,*
> *Ahmed Hassan*

Una will open this message and (check one):

1) immediately delete it _______ ;or

2) follow-up on the offer and make enough profit to buy another vintage Vauxhall auto _______.

Al says you've got 50-50 chance of getting it right.

Might we venture to imagine this brash e-mailer's visage? How about a charismatically handsome man, with rich, resonant face and hot, busy eyes

Something is Crook in Middlebrook

who talks with cadences of extreme gleeful emphases, using abnormally heavy stresses?

Once more Una's gloves joyfully caress keys and another e-mail pops onto her MacBook Pro's monitor: YOUR ORDER HAS BEEN SHIPPED. Una's lips turn upward into perfect semi-circular mark of devilish delight. *God, wait 'til Arty doesn't hear this!* Yep, it's her oddball birthday gift to Art: avant-garde sound-artist Max Neuhaus's Silent Alarm Clock. Silent? Uh-huh. Let's look at The Art Institute of Chicago's gift-store's website ad:

The Max Neuhaus Silent Alarm Clock

The sound of this postmodern silent alarm clock begins oh so imperceptibly, swells, and then breaks off a few minutes later. Only in that moment of disappearance is it actually perceived, as an 'after-image'; here a moment of unexpected silence awakens you, pulls you out of sleep and gently back into the world of everyday noises.

"Wimble-click-crumblechaw-beloo! This l'il gimmick'll be my silent partner," bellows Arty after grumbling negotiations with Una's three nested boxes-within-boxes gag-wrapping, untimely pulling out his timely gift. With exaggerated ceremony—twisting one little finny in weird ear while turning 'round 'n 'round thrice, and petting clock with his free hand—gingerly places his new possession on night table ("Ta-da!") next to ear-shaped bed, Una playing his befuddled witness. Question: Would you, Dear Reader, consider *yourself* a "befuddled witness" to this text?

5.0

Mr. Bultitude, abnormally big tiger salamander, now deceased. After much mutual nudging, pushing and lashing of tails, he lays down spermatophore for Mrs. Bultitude to pick up. And so fathers Tiger Woods, Art's pet salamander living under Art's deck. Buys him at same pet store he rents tortoise from for his *Orders* project. "Tig," as he nicknames him, has a projected life span of twenty years. His horrible head is round with pronounced snout, eyes fairly small and widely spaced. Some thirteen costal grooves located on side of his 200-mm long body. He is smeared with yellow and black that form irregular blotches; two tubercles are present on sole of each foot; there are no parotoid glands present. Ho, his mind is as slimy and unhuman in shape as his body. He doesn't grok that he loves and trusts Art. He doesn't grok that Art and neighbor Al are human, nor that he is member of species *Ambystoma tigrinum*. In fact, he doesn't know that he exists at all; everything represented by such words as: *I, Me, Thou, He,* and *She* wholly absent from reptilian mind. No idea where he came from or where he is heading. Art puts out big dish of water, baby mouse, or occasional frog, and special salamander food supplement derived from aquatic insects each morning. Tig doesn't recognize either Art as giver, nor himself as recipient. Goodness occurs and he senses and tastes it—that's all. Hence, Tig's loves can be described as merely *cupboard loves*: food and cool shade of deck, hands of Art and Al that caress, voices that reassure. But if by cupboard love you mean something calculating you would be quite misunderstanding real quality of this beast's sensations. He is no more human egoist than human altruist. There is no prose in his life, even though you, Dear Reader, are urged to see Tig as akin to ugly troll living under bridge in Swedish fairy tale. His eyesight is not all that reliable, subject to passionate distortions of fear and desire. Appetencies which human mind might disdain, are for him quivering and ecstatic aspirations absorbing his whole being: infinite yearning, stabbed with threat of tragedy and shot through with colors of Paradise. One of our own race, if plunged back for moment into that warm, trembling, iridescent pool of pre-Adamic consciousness, would emerge believing he or she has grasped The Absolute. States below reason and states above it have, by common contrast to life we experience, certain superficial resemblance to it. Sometimes there returns to us from infancy memories of nameless delights and terrors. Such memory is often attached to delightful or dreadful things and can become some potent adjective floating in some nounless void. Pure quality. Subtract such qualities and odds do be that world itself would cease to exist for Tig.

Saturday morning so delightful. Tig under deck. Crisp yet warm, clear but some playful puffy clouds way way up there in blue sky. Art starts morning rituals by sliding down curving bannister from bedroom to living room. Wheeeee! Fun. Starts up coffee in his rétro-styled Art Deco Cuisinart 12-cup brewmaster. While coffee gurgling away, he slaps on several strips of turkey bacon and poaches eggs. Pours glass of orange juice (breakfast without is like day without sunshine). While breakfast cooking, he feeds very grateful Tiger Woods who seems more agitated than usual today. Despite dimness of his netherworld, Tig's skin has luminosity of organs freshly exposed to light. Undefined anxiety begins to spread across salamander-shit-strewn dirt under dome's deck. So nice is it above deck—weather fine and Boettcher Brats not in sight—Art decides to eat his high-protein nummies outside. Lightly thumb-stuffs white ear-goop in, carries his chow out on tray, leisurely munches away. Sitting on his Ace Hardware white plastic deck furniture.

5.1   Next door, Al Schmerbauch has same idea. High probability he emerges from perpetual fragrance of warm electronics in his home office and sits on his deck too and waves at Art. High probability Art invites him to join him for breakfast. High probability Al accepts as it is date okayed by Fibonacci sequence. So totes his huge bowl of Cheerios over (Al has cholesterol problem, high probability for heart attack). High probability following exchange takes place.

"And how is Una these days?" starts off Al, sipping his steaming coffee.

"Her real might be *the* real!" Art relates how they now have brave, beaming, soul-rich crying jags together—yes, her crying muscles be well developed from pumping a lot of iron in their time—and how when he once placed his hand on that electrical cashmere of her lap, he felt his dick give sick 'n fuddled lurch. Finally, he gets around to full contents of Una's last communiqué—all this in between nibbling on his crisp bacon.

"Yah," replies Al, stirring his Cheerios, "you know modernity allocated to work the main responsibility for giving folks their identity, their social bonds and social function: you *are* what you do for a living. By contrast, in a postmodern habitat you *are* what you buy. PoMo culture is a consumer cooperative."

Art had to agree that it is aesthetics of consumption that now rules where work ethic once did. "The world and all its fragments are judged by their capacity to generate sensations and to arouse desire. More satisfying than the satisfaction itself, I might add! Reminds of me of Jerrold's daughter. My old departmental chairman back in La La Land . . . Los Angeles . . . that city of lost dreams and false breasts. Guy makes peanuts teaching in the Art department at a Lutheran College, see. His daughter, Fiona, won't go to school—she's having a shit fit—until her dad buys her Guess jeans. Seems she's ashamed to be seen in school with her Sears brand blue jeans."

"Oh, my god."

"Yah. Only eight years old and already brainwashed."

"PoMo habitat is not quite what is seems," says Al. "It conveys the image of being a pleasure park, a consumer's playground, a place where you can pick-'n–mix lifestyles and beliefs according to taste, like those mixed grill entrées you love to barbecue."

"The shopping mall and fusion eateries as the temples of postmodernity."

Something is *Crook* in Middlebrook

"But this park is laid out on a demolition site that was once modernity."

"Indeed, those postmodern experiments in living are *bricolaged* aggregates making use of bits and pieces of modernity lying around like hot metal after an explosion!" (Fact: Art tastes his unique bratwurst-rib-eye-bok choy combo.)

"In such an environment," says Al, wiping milk off his upper lip, "high probability the poor are out of place, at worst, threatening, criminalized. Result is the slow holocaust of these flawed consumers who just don't fit in."

"Ho! And the rich salve their residual guilt with occasional 'carnivals of charity' subscribing to relief funds . . ."

"Like Farm Aid."

"However," continues Art, licking bacon grease from his finnies, "this is more than counter-balanced by the strategy of criminalizing the new poor. It's the Bunker State."

"Meanwhile, global companies compete with each other in bitter dog fights; governments can't keep 'em in check and so have simply let 'em off the chain. Grrrrrrrrrr."

"Sure all those dog attacks in the news lately," giggles Art, "are micro-events descriptive the macro-level of abuse. If the Parisian *flâneur* is the originary form—the *Ur-form* Walter Benjamin would say—of the consumer, the dog attack is the *Ur-form* of late-capitalist production."

Al notices that it is at moments of such profound insight that his buddy's face lights up and he looks most like his famous Dopplegänger, Bob Hoskins. This leads Al into his own profound insight: "Unlike the proverbial Panopticon of Jeremy Bentham and Michel Foucault where the few watch the many, I claim we now live under the spell of the Synopticon where the many watch the few: on television, at the cinema, and in their magazines and newspapers. In turn, celebrities are *not* free to look; the sunglasses they are obliged to hide behind are the symbolic expression of the blindness to which they are condemned by always being looked *at.* Art, the lives of celebrity shmucks provide a pattern of existence for millions of admirers. Reports of their activities are like *broadcasts from heaven*!"

"Those admirers, they don't seem to grok they are mere clones. We got royalty that *guides* instead of ruling," summarizes Art, wiping last crumbs of his poached eggs off his artisan-crafted ear-shaped plate (cost heaps I bet).

"That royalty, those jet-setters, have a global stamping ground and can often be found in plush, boring airport lounges even as the majority of the poor are excluded from such arenas and remain penned up in the Third World."

"Ironically, Al, some of those—ah—subalterns may also be found in airport lounges (not the V.I.P. one's though) waiting to be deported—sent back to *where they belong*. My *compañera* at the Museum, Mala Gradecido, is already educating me about *los de abajo*, the perspective of the underdog. The world view of the have not, sometimes also called *rasquachismo.* She's

Something is **Crook** in Middlebrook

turned personal misfortune into political activism. I have to admit that a small whitecap of sympathy for her arose in my mind after she told me:'Señor Middlebrook, so horrendous is my early life in barrio—under thumb of alcoholic parents—what I call *El Mundo Malo*—I get a rash just thinking about it; so huge sections of my past are now freeze-dried and hidden away in a dark locker in my mind, never to be opened again.' Now, she inhabits what she calls *El Mundo Bueno*, The Good Reality, where utopian visions such as José Vasconcelos sketches in his *La raza cósmica* mix with counter-intuitive sensual thoughts like (to quote her): 'Sweat is good, an invitation to taste all the body's salt streams.' And she says this with a smile that has a gorgeous rosy lack of definition which you could, given the art context, better explain with paint, a thumb, a short and stabby brush. But she also warns that, 'We walk

Palo Santo Bark

in *El Mundo Bueno* as if we tread the thin skin on warm milk; it's always possible to break through and drown; if so, quickly perform purification ritual: burn pale bark of South American *palo santo* tree.' And . . . she makes a good museum guard as she can petrify a cranky small boy at fifty paces with her *don't touch* stare. Well read too. Once she confessed: '*Orale ese,* books saved my sanity, knowledge opened locked places in me.' Ho! Besides knowing the plot of every tele-tamale soap opera on Hispanic TV, she appreciates the diff between Flaubert and Maupassant!"

"No!"

"Yes! And throughout the day, she maintains a perfect underslept Aztec obstin-acy. But at night . . . one gets the impression she's so happy in her serape or so right in her sarong."

If this were Hollywood movie, as cultural theory here becomes opaque, camera would inversely delight in greater visibility, so would slowly pan down under dark deck as conversation's volume diminishes. Ominous music would then swell. Then slow zoom into close-up of Tig's face revealing —can we claim?—dreamless sleep.

"Has she told you about the Leavers? No? My god Art, haven't you heard of Greta Leaver and her lover, Trash Tory? San Francisco Bay Area radicals, they met at Berkeley. Their theory of Leaverism? Their slogans: 'Don't Waste Toxic Waste' and 'Leaver American If You Love It' caused a huge uproar just prior to the nine/eleven debacle pushed it out of the news."

"No, I was in Italy looking at frescoes and lapping up gelato then."

"According to a *Newsweek* article, their theory is rooted in that twentieth-century economist Joseph Schumpeter's controversial notion that capitalism will be destroyed not by its failure, but by its *success*. Trash Tory argues against all *allopathic* remedies like revolution, which will never get widespread support as long as the system feeds mind-numbing commodities to a passive populace, and gradual legal reform, which can only prolong the agony of the conflictual social present. In contradistinction, Leaverism proposes to accelerate the demise of capitalism by what they call 'a *homeopathic* solution to a pathetic regime.' (Their detractors dubbed them 'Damn Homeos.') The means to this end? A passive-aggressive strategy (they call it 'a PA system') for exacerbating environmental pollution and political corruption. A strategy, I might add, already popular with the majority of our media-distracted Americans. A two-pronged attack. One, what they call 'leavering': Leave your unsorted trash (full of nonbiodegradable) items and dangerous chemical wastes (carcinogenic preferred) in ponds, lakes, streams, and oceans. Consequently, they fight recycling in all forms, flaunt fluoro-carbons, and do rain dances for acid rain. And two, what they call 'leaverage': Advocating the election of the most reprehensible politicians; for instance, they donated thousands of dollars to Arnold Schwarzenegger's bid for governor of California. They support the Daley political machine in Chicago; they promote making democracy a harsh theocracy; they encourage greed in all its manifestations, making Ivana Trump the movement's Madonna. A more radical branch of the Leavers, headquartered in Boston and calling themselves 'The Enablers,' tout clerical celibacy and recruitment of gay priests, hoping to increase molestations of unwary Catholic kids; a sure way, as they put it, 'to homeopathically discredit the Papish Church with pathetic homos.' Get it?"

"Okay, okay. So how is *that* shit supposed to bring down the system?"

"They feel that active resistence to current policies would be doomed to failure, but by stimulating, encouraging, contributing to the inherent vices of their sworn enemies the quicker the resources that feed it will be exhausted and/or discredited. A whole system of economic and ideological production will . . ."

"Until the whole damn system collapses?"

"Yep, feeding the proverbial glutton. This will herald in what they call 'The Hard Age,' an anarchic blood bath during which many of the inert masses will die off from bitter battles over resources, rampant cancers, and myriads of eco-disasters brought on by global warming. Meanwhile, an enlightened remainder will come alive as true eco-citizens and flee to eco-safe zones like Iceland, Australia, New Zealand, and Tasmania where they will devoutly practice Gaia Zenecology and institute Eco-socialism. Their real genius, many think, resides in their *faux* rah-rah Americanism which helps the system to gleefully cut its own throat as it is hardly distinguishable from the right-wing ideology promoting The New World Order. Many Leavers drive huge SUVs that get the worst gas mileage, detach their smog devices, and put stickers on those vans saying: 'I'm Proud to Support President Bush,' 'Kill 'Em All 'n Let God Sort 'Em Out Later,' and 'Proud to be a Member of the National Rifle Association,' and so forth."

"Like Iago subtly cajoling Othello to murder Desdemona, these Leavers are wickedly clever," observes Art.

"I know their program sounds extreme, but compared to Ipse Dixit's theory of T.P.E., as touted in her rétro mimeographed Punk zine, *The Gipper,* it's mild."

"Oh, Dixit's wonky notion of Total Population Elimination?"

Something is *Crook* in Middlebrook

"Yep. Took inspiration from an Anthony Burgess novel where a character says: "You've no idea how pleasant it is not to have any future . . . It's like having a totally efficient contraceptive." Mass sterilization. One hundred years later, no lay-offs, no dudes in three-piece suits, no sexism, no TV commercials for Longine Symphonette instrumentals, no war, no hunger, no ghettos, in fact, no human suffering at all. Utopia!"

"Yes, a Utopia composed wholly of *discorporate* members!"

"Some might say that's a bug to be worked out yet! But it sure solves the world's ills, huh? Others are sure Dixit's interventionist praxis would lead to, literarily, a true community of souls that can no longer abuse material reality."

"But what's to distinguish this scorched butt policy from the Holocaust, heh?"

"Art, Art. Ipse Dixit's plan encompasses all classes; why it's multicultural, multiracial. *All* humans will gradually die out—equally."

"The angels'll be countin' cadence as the last soul gratefully departs this vale o' woe. Wonder if the last person alive will be man or woman, Republican or Democrat, Chinese or Anglo, Gay or Straight? Or may be the two last people on earth will die exactly at the same instant! Simultaneity."

"What the hell does that . . ."

"Yep. And it'll probably be winter on top the Matterhorn with no one standing there sun-goggled; no one languishing in Munich; the Hiwassee River in Tennessee will be at an all time low with no one standing on the bank, hands half in pants pockets. No one left to check evidence, receive postcards, paste photos in the family album. Full-color holy cards of Ivana Trump as The Madonna of Tenderness, Our Lady of Feints and X's, will blow lazily down now-abandoned alleys as peach blossoms follow the moving water."

"You been reading Henry Miller again?" jabs Al.

"Ah . . . Chinese poet, Li Po."

As Art 'n Al banter, Boettcher Brats finish watching 170th rerun of *Ice Station Zebra* (they're Ernest Borgnine fans and avid watchers of "Invader Zim" TV series). Be bored. So down back alley of Art's house they go dressed in silver-colored Lycra exercise suits, marching in jerky movements like mechanical men. Acting out what they call "bein' cyber-naughties," they chant loudly and, as if computer stuck in never ending program loop, repeat endlessly: "We ain't got no ma or pa, 'cause we is autom-a-ta! . . . We ain't got no ma or pa, 'cause we is autom-a-ta!"

Launching countermeasures, Art quickly screws in more of his white ear goop. But words sufficient to push Art's thoughts toward bozotic future where of human species only brain be remaining beautifully encased in Duraplast globe (as kid Art terrified by bottled brain in 1953 B sci-fi B-movie that butchered Curt Siodmak's novel *Donovan's Brain*) equipped with myriad sockets, plugs, and clasps for installation of innumerable prosthetics, like golfing, mountain biking, water-skiing, stir-frying, and fornication modules. Latter prosthetic touted in jingle Art once hear student relate:

Something is *Crook* in Middlebrook

> There was a young man named Racine,
> who invented a fucking machine.
> Concave or convex, it fit either sex,
> and was exceedingly simple to clean.

Suddenly, Art recalls dream he had that night. Relates same to Al: "I'm in a cool green, antiseptic hospital operating room smelling of chemicals whose functions you don't want to understand. All looks distorted as if the scene is shot with fish-eye lens (like in the last scary scenes of John Frankenheimer's disturbing sci-fi film *Seconds*). A surgeon inserts a balloon under my skin near my left ear; it is gradually inflated until a bubble of stretched skin is formed. The balloon is then removed and a cartilage ear shape is pinned inside the bag of excess skin. The surgeon then meticulously cuts and sews the skin over the cartilage structure. Wrapped in bandages. Then later dramatic unveiling. Bandages undone. Ho! I now have a third ear! But—*Blessed Benimming!*—this ear *emits* sounds; implanted with a sound chip and a proximity sensor, the ear speaks, to anyone who gets close to it, a refrain from a Simon 'n Garfunkel song: 'I am a rock, I am an island.' "

"Weird. That's one for your Jungian analyst. Kind of a reversal of the scene in David Lynch's film *Blue Velvet* where a *severed* ear is found, setting in motion the whole bizarre plot." Art gives Al a *I hadn't thought of that* look. Art and Al's conversation takes sharp left turn into topic of hi-tech stuff and computer-mediated communication.

"Ya know, Al, the trouble with the Net is that there isn't enough *Africa* in it and too many blogs featuring fiber optic probing photos of the insides of people's colons. Cyberspace *is* a Teflon place, wiped clean of muddy earthly reality; the road to Erewhon. Asked if *he* would use a computer, my daddy replied, "No scan do!"

"Our fascination with computers is more erotic than sensuous, more deeply spiritual than pragmatic, I think. You know Howard Hughes used an early version of the computer to design a brassiere for Jane Russell? Face it Art, because of my real-life rule about seeing people only on days okayed by the Fibonacci Series, I am face-to-face with my computer for far longer than I look into any human face. Real bodies have to be wooed and are dangerous. And kissing! Kissing interrupts how faces communicate; one can't speak while kissing, kissing is the end of faciality. Andy Warhol wryly observed that 'two people kissing always look like fish'. Promise not to blab a word about this and I'll let you in on a secret."

"To the extent my ear is open to sound, my lips are sealed."

"I've become an erotic hitchhiker in search of sexual stimulation on-line. Been toying around with cybersex. Ever since the Vatican created a patron saint of the Internet, Isidore of Seville, a sixth-century monk who composed an early database in the form of a twenty-volume encyclopedia. High probability I get cyber-laid if I pray to him. We exist in a world of pure communication—today's new theme is tomorrow's twenty-three newsgroups—where looks don't matter and only the best writers get attention. In compusex, being able to type fast and write well is equivalent to having a buff physique and smouldering eyes. Been logging-in on Infomart USA. They have such *outré* orientations as 'Leg Brace Enthusiasts' and 'Hot Denture

Wearers,' if one was so disposed. I once tried out 'Breakfast of Champions' —oral sex enthusiasts' chatroom and had group session with Nina5 and Beth R."

"Surprised you haven't substituted eating Wheaties for Cheerios."

"It's the age of dissatisfaction; everyone wants to be something they're not. On one site you can lay Cleopatra, Helen of Troy, Isis, Madame Pompadour, or Aphrodite. You can get fucked by Pan, Jesus Christ, Apollo, or the Devil Himself. Anything you like likes you when your press the buttons. But I refuse to enter the 'Dung 'n Drag' chatroom."

"Play on Dungeons and Dragons?"

"Yep. Afraid I will inadvertently have cybersex with a gay man 'wearing a girl's body'—it's happened you know. It's the Information Super-screw Way. Other chatrooms are sheer lesbigay digitopias. In one case, you enter by clicking on an animated gif of the Pope, whose white vestments then drop off and a huge erection pops up from his nude flabby bulk, while the word 'Solidarity' flashes on-screen. In another animation, clicking on Pope John Paul II morphs him into gay photographer Robert Mapplethorpe in black leather holding a whip. On one lesbian site the question determining entry is not 'Are you lesbian?' but "Are you lesbian *enough*? to participate. And one fetish blogger boasted a being a non-smoker who finds pics of women smoking in public erotic!"

"I grok, bro'. It gets more convoluted than the baroque forms of transvestism in the early writing of that Frenchy Collette where she is a woman writing as a man, who poses as boyish girl, Claudine, who marries a 'feminized' man, the ageing Renaud, who pushes her into the arms of a female lover, Rézi, with whom she takes the virile role."

"Art, did you know that Metcalfe's Law of the Internet—that's Bob Metcalfe, a former Xerox PARC researcher—states that *The power of the network is N squared where N is the number of nodes*; so if you double the number of nodes, users, you actually double squared, or you quadruple, the overall value of the network. The reason is that the Internet gets more valuable to me if you come on it. Even though I'm already there, the network's getting continually more valuable to me as more people come on, as more contact comes on, as important businesses, like cybersex stuff, are connected."

"You know what Seneca said: 'A great pilot can sail even when his canvas is rent'."

"Yah, and Columbus had to sail with madmen to discover America."

We leave The Reader to ponder this exchange of *non sequiturs* while Art and Al start to exchange typical torrid sexist male sex stories (references to "the beauty of a naked thumb" and to "a passionate, interestingly-historied wrist," etc.) but most are too politically incorrect to relay to your ears.

5.2   That evening . . . unusual thing occurs in Tig's sub-deck world. He spies something new out there, shape 'n pattern, evidence; senses faint splittings 'n crashings, drawing nearer; scent, still diluted by distance, keenly

intrigues him, but also awakens glands of danger. Great manifestation presses upon random world through which he crawls: queer objects (ho! colored
clown pants and oversized shoes) he doesn't recognize skulking in backyard,
but coming closer. Suddenly sees most beautiful human face he ever sees
peep under deck. However, as Tig's aesthetics is of his own species, *typical*
human face seems ugly; in contradistinction, *this* face so ugly by human
standards, has such reptilian aura about it, that Tig swoons with delight and
senses kinship. Clown figure carefully crawls under deck mumbling baby talk
to Tig.

Tig, however friendly this face seems to him, is also unflaggingly
loyal to deck, dome-home, and hand-that-feeds-him. Ergo, strife is produced
in Tig as his reptilian "morale" conflicts with his "morals." This is as close to
mental conflict possible for beast whose consciousness consists only of vague
central warmth and dimness. Nevertheless, mysterious reluctance arises
toward this figure intruding into sacred salamander space, clouding this amphibian's emotional weather; but mixed with this there is also opposite
impulse to welcome this new reptilian to his dim haunts. Why? He doesn't
know and is incapable of even raising said question. If pressure behind conflicting impulses can be translated into human terms at all, it would appear
as something more like mythology than thought. With unblinking walleyes
and nervous tail, Tig watches this seeming escapee from Barnum and Bailey
Circus fiddle with some contraption on underside of deck. If human were to
witness this, he'd see him installing small black box with little antenna directly
below Art's deck furniture, flipping switch; small red light blinking on—bug in
place.

5.3   Sunday. Art 'n Una heatedly discuss letter from Geology Department
chairman. Wants to recruit Art for studies in Volcanology. Sees Art's *ear*-ly
gift as boon for study of volcanic activity; maybe even provide *ear*-ly warning
of eruptions. Tempts Art with full scholarship. Art *is* tempted, Una fears future
job too dangerous. But now Art has to study for geology quiz on metamorphism. When tells Una to "please leave," single blood vessel rises on her supple
subtle forehead, she abruptly rises, leaving Art with nothing but her dirty
teacup sunk in suds in sink. Walks to car, buttons her coat, turns, crosses her
arms and stands there bristling with all the counter-strength of the street:
"Damn, you Arty!" Inside, Art's oblivious: ear be gooped, horse blinders be
strapped on. One fuckin' serious student that Art!

5.4   Comes Monday. Art awakens alone with alarm clock's beep to urban
noises. His temples unsoothed by wafting smells of salamander shit. Day
invades him like tide. Up in time for Morning Edition on NPR. Tumbles out of
ear-shaped bed. Has choice: put ear goop in and put radio in kitchen or leave
ear ungooped and put radio in basement. Today chooses latter. Listens to
Lisa Labuz's firm authoritative voice which, added to increased bass from
basement locale, always seems to strengthen Art's inner resolve and ego
boundaries. Like miners shoring up dangerous mine shaft from collapse.
Atkins Diet breakfast as usual. Today sharp sound of sizzling turkey bacon on
Teflon pan sets off involuntary memory of his sister, Els, reading out loud

Something is *Crook* in Middlebrook

passages from Beat author William S. Burroughs's *The Ticket that Exploded*. Much better than yesterday when uses uncoated aluminum pan whose sizzlin' sound evokes visions of salamanders crawling in broken bottles and tin cans. Feeds Tig in between turning bacon.

Morning shift at museum. Summer tourist season (when at night city becomes three-dimensional representation of Art's neon leaping heart). Overly crowded at same time as enormous fat guy in wheelchair keeps steamrolling over visitors' feet (papa-mama-offspring-granny) so galleries start filling up with subtle commotion and cries of annoyance and pain. Arthur Strewth Middlebrook is deck-ed out in freshly laundered guard uniform. To look at dark suit jacket, you'd never guess that two days ago a baby threw up on lapel while Art was holding him for his mother who was using Museum's restroom. He idly stands at eastmost all-glass entrance to Museum, looking out over Lake Michigan which is smooth enough to Xerox. Art's attention is intensely focused into blue distance of sky and water. Daydreaming. And on this job, Art has plenty of time for that and for daydreamers there is no such thing as wasted time, only busy intervals between one fantasy and next, pregnant lapses during which reminiscing takes back seat to direct action that secretly scrounges landscape of present for wicks of invisible fires.

Snap, crackle, 'n pop. Neurons fire in Art's *cabeza*. He sees tiny dot of what ... *a bird?* ... in far distance above lonely sail boat on Lake Michigan. Dot is rapidly getting larger like ink spreading outward from tip of fountain pen. Bird has wings but it isn't flapping 'em. Wings are stretched out . . . like an airplane's. . . . *It is an airplane!* It can't be much more than fifty feet off water's surface for water is being visibly affected, rippling, churning, evaporating under movement of this object. As it passes over sail boat, boat keels over in direction of object's flight. It fails to right itself. Object is getting larger in Art's field of vision. He puts his arms akimbo and stares intently. Within seconds, Art realizes that this object is jumbo jet . . . *an Airbus, right?* . . . with two large engines heading straight for vulnerable glass facade on east side of Museum. Curiously, he doesn't panic. *Okay. Terrorists. I'm about to buy the farm.* He calmly watches machine's metal nose head directly for his fleshy nose. As jet sweeps across Grant Park, it rips leaves off and into what looks like swarms of angry bees. He can see them now, bearded, swarthy faces staring maniacally from inside plane's cockpit. He imagines hijackers wearing sweat-shirts proclaiming in Arabic: JIHAD: A LITTLE GOES A LONG WAY. *Okay, this is it.* As if in slow-motion segment, Art calmly watches as people around him slowly turn horrified heads toward jet. If this were film, jet sent by Allah would burst slowly through plate glass walls of entrance, glass shattering into millions of flesh-cutting shards. Huge jet nose approaches Art's nubbin of a nose to within inches. He flashes on climactic train crash scene in popular movie, *Silver Streak.* Museum-goers are sucked off their feet and hurled head first into impeller blades of huge jet engines. Some dive for cover. Red aura of sprayed blood covers engine cowls. Then ringing in Art's ears. Ringing won't stop. Ringing won't stop.

"Ah. Hey, buddy! Buddy! Your cell-phone's aringin'," sooth-softly says man with big, trustworthy features, black hair falling across his brow like a crow's wing; clad in stylish black, tan, and white argyle sweater, he gently nudges Art from his horrific vision.

Something is *Crook* in Middlebrook

Noon. Cumulonimbus drifts over spires of downtown, where it hangs like vast gray anvil. Art's shift is over. He marches across street for Flaherty's Famous Fish and coffee for lunch at Bennigan's where large green stopwatch at your table times your waiter's service (you get free meal if food arrival is not timely). Time *is* money. Enjoys diners startled stares at his ear's ripper tattoo. "Mommy, look, you can see inside the man's head!" whispers one surprised child. Pays bill and leaves big tip. Then off he prances to his geology seminar at Roosevelt University three blocks due south through a jostling crowd along Michigan Avenue. When he strolls down that broad, magnificent street he's usually happy, but at same time feels he's merely an extra in a tourist's film. Today he ungoops 'n hears City Water Department safety inspector, Frank "Coconut" Conate, bullhorn a message to Mayor from in front of Anish Kapoor's *Cloud Gate* sculpture:

SHAME, SHAME! DA MAYOR SHOULDA USED DA MONEY FER DIS DAMN TING TA BE GIVIN' SOME RAISES TA US CITY WORKERS, HARD WORKIN' FOLKS WHO DON'T GIVE A DAMN 'BOUT HAVIN' DIS BIG SHINY SAUSAGE MIRROR FER DA 'MUSMENT O' DA CAMERA TOTIN' TOURISTS.

5.5   Art gimps awkwardly down elegant marble steps of famous Louis Sullivan lobby in famous Auditorium Building. Same staircase immortalized in confrontation scene between Al Capone (Robert De Niro) and Elliot Ness (Kevin Costner) in *The Untouchables.* Feet makes wonderful scuffling sound, so Art ungoops weird ear and, thanks to his synaesthesia, nostalgically tastes his mother's Teflon-cooked blueberry pancakes. His eyes caress gorgeous onyx wainscoting and unique stylized floral ornament. Experiences feeling of dignified public space and pleasure that philosophers call aesthetic response to significant form. In lobby bell-ding of Westinghouse elevators (which his daddy once oversaw installation of) amplifies through unprotected ear orifice and Art tastes stale Communion host. *Blessed Benimming!* Moment to compose himself. . . . Then hitches his shoulder bag higher up on shoulder and exits one of several imposing revolving doors fanning hurried students.

You guessed it. He be on way home after GEOL 503. Geology grad seminar on *contact metamorphism* taught by Rock Peterson, a sixty-ish prof who does remind Art of publicity picture of British writer J. G. Ballard. Grad students be all worked up over results of last week's exam; you can see it in way they do touch themselves, those lewd innocent little caresses of the self, way they do linger o'er their pens' rear-ends, scores of bright sucking lips. He's oldest stud in class, so be garb at odds with Twenty-First-Century dress code's mixture of cut-offs and halter tops, garments that do manage to fuse sartorial aspirations of sports-wear and lingerie where there be no holding back of supple, young skin. Several guys do sport overblown Seiko Message Watches, some in oversize T-shirts spelling out in Helvetica Bold: DON'T WORRY, BE STUPID. So Art sits way way in back, uncorks weird ear to enjoy mellifluous sounds of felt-tip marker on plastic as instructor does put chemical formulae on board, pedagogical sound be mixing with occasional tones of bra gliding against kind o' cheese-clothy camisole that be illegal in key southern states worn by classmate to his left. Synaesthetic response to aural delights gives forth sweet taste 'n texture of pink cotton candy. Does smell little scent of coconut 'n cigs floating around face of some doomed starlet: small, found features that express kind of contemptuous yearning; but eyes like looking into aperture of slide projector. *That startling. That white.* She be strike him as type who be viewing her sexuality as bright new user option only obscurely related to her heart, i.e., as type be having torrid affair with Tae Bo instructor be named Jericho.

Does exit university. Steps onto Michigan Avenue. *Ah, what a nice city we live in, very clean, with an excellent park system,* thinks Art as he takes in deep breath of lake odor 'n fresh flowers. *You'd never know that people are dying of unhappiness, right here under the nose of God.* Suddenly, he hears loud crash of metal-on-metal due north up busy street briefly drowning out cacophony of traffic buzz:

**CCCCCCRRRRAAAAAACCCCCCCHHHHHSSSSSSHHHMMMMM
MMMMMAAAAAAAAAAAAAAASSSSSSSSSSSSHHHHHHHHHHHH**

Synaesthetic sensation he gets be like teething on rare instance of feldspar group called Bytownite, mineral has very specific ratio of calcium to sodium. Art limps up street, focusing weird ear northward and up-angle about 45 degrees. Soon does audit distant screams of people and wail of ambulances. He be start involuntary grinding of teeth. So intense is horrible cacophony that he sees wave of blue color shimmering before his eyes, that distinctive hue produced by dissolving alkali metals in liquid ammonia. *Lives must be at stake,* he thinks. Art, worried that public transportation be disrupted, flags down cab with Mexican driver who looks *mucho* like Latino artist Guillermo Gomez-Peña garbed appropriately for his *Border Brujo* performance complete with Mariachi hat, Day of the Dead earrings, other wonky accessories. Crazy Mr. Toad's Wild Ride back to dome-home in record time while radio blares Mariachi song *Bonito Tecalitlán*. Art tips generously. Gets a *"gracias"* and a tipped hat in exchange. Rushes in, flips on Sony TV. Smiling, inane Channel-5 news anchor sporting ugly tie is on scene describing how window-washing scaffold *mucho* stories up on Hancock Center breaks loose in strong wind, smashes 'n mashes until high-rise office windows be shatter sending fragments flying about like rainbow insects with scalpel wings (more than one white-collar pencilneck be seeing buying fresh underwear in Water Tower Place Mall across street). Finally whole cursed apparatus breaks free, crashes to ground, waffling poor young Anglo blond woman driver in red Mazda Miata. Commercial break. Then interview with mourning hubby, who says of his spouse, "She was someone who plunged through life without the almighty force-field of irony." *Maybe if she'd had that field about her,* muses Art, *she'd been saved ironed flat by that damn iron scaffold.*

Now news conference with beefy Mayor Daley sporting crocodile tears, in front of microphone-bedecked podium expressing condolences to bereaved family and promising investigation. Art uncorks weird ear. Takes aim at Daley's rastered image. Hears peculiar grain of Mayor's Chicago-born boom-box voice. Even as filtered through TV audio, reveals this bullying politico's rough 'n tumble origins, utter lack of sophis-tication, and lusty-lust for power. Art hastily replaces ear goop.

Ironically, this slaughtered saleswoman for prominent software company did have pressing engagement with client only two blocks away. Had just courteously waved African-American pedestrian across intersection when "Death from Above" (motto of Air Cavalry in Vietnam) reaches out and touches someone. Her peep-hole forever. Had she been rude 'n racist and muscled out pedestrian, she'd be alive today. Oh those What-Ifs! What if Art had had another set of parents? He might be today intimate of Wogan and Paloma Picasso, be painting murals for Playboy mansion and co-hosting New York chat-show with Quentin Crisp, while army of devoted lawyers exploit merchandising rights to his latest Resurrection or Crucifixion paintings.

Art thinks: *Now her broken body is pressed 'n soft. . . . Someone's jewel ruined. Just as sapphires be basically nothing but corundum, colorless aluminum oxide, but which can take on red color when chromium replaces aluminum in its chemical make-up, this poor woman be basically a pile of carbon and water which takes on life with admixture of some mysterious life-force X. Now she mere corundum. Lifeless 'n colorless. And so it goes. (Not original thought, but more mellifluous than "Shit happens.") Wonder what the chances are of this happening to someone. Have to remember to ask Al about precise statistics on this. Why probably much higher of dying this way than from lightning strike.*

Art flashes on grotesque scene in Chicago author James McManus's book, *Chin Music.* Therein, heroic suicide does take fearsome plunge from Hancock Center, Swiss yodeling as repeatedly caroms off pyramidally sloping sides until hard pavement abruptly stops woeful Alpine echoes. *I think the author should substitute this real event—it's more TODAY—for the fictive when he comes out with a later edition.*

5.6　　The prison of the self: gaps between bars are sutures of one's own skull. Death and mayhem on Six O'Clock News opens wrong cell door and Art finds himself on old burlesque stage with several baffling props—igneous rock, sand dune, enlarged prostate—all resting on mock up of topology of a drained delta. Such stuff always puts Art into morbid frame of mind similar to what we normal folk find expressed in that irreconcilable melancholy of an exposed embryo as depicted in a Salvador Dali painting. That not-so-benign deity of Art's inner space takes control. His face does takes on qualities of catatonic withdrawal. Symmetry and regularity of his visage does mask in-tense inner violence of hot cauldron of time 'n myth. Marked blood pressure rise. Starts thinking about those nine billion names of God. Re-experiences deep dead-inside feeling like all vitality is being sucked down big black hole, like he had when sister Els (short for Elsie) be given only two weeks to live thanks to cervical cancer that initially misdiagnosed as "just bad cramps" by distracted, obese HMO doctor who does label Els "a complaining woman." Wonders if doctor feels guilty about pulverizing sorrow Els's family suffers. *She has outsoared the shadow of our night, envy and calumny and hate and pain, and that unrest which we miscall delight,* so he prays.

Something is *Crook* in Middlebrook

Art guiltily recalls that when told after his sister's birth that he had someone new to play with, he assumed she was new toy and asked: "Yes, but where are its wheels?" Can never forget his last visit to her deathbed. Her bewildered drug-inflected eyes looking at him for the final time. They be like black holes sucking out forever his happiness. Black holes. Recalls that eccentric East Coast physicist, David Melville, be trying to create matter-sucking black hole at Brookhaven National Laboratory (dubbed "Alphaville" by critics hostile to impersonal "Alpha-60 logic" exercised therein) using Relativistic Heavy Ion Collider to duplicate conditions that be prevailing milliseconds after Big Bang when universe consists of primordial *soup de jour* called quark-gluon plasma. Well, problem be probability be said black hole be hungry and be eating its way down toward center of terra firma, slurping up all stuff from inside out. Doomsday machine! Terra be torn, not firma. It be not good time to be around to see this. Not even steroidal musculature and bashing big bearing of Schwarzenegger can escape super-sucking Schwarzchild radius of black hole. No, no. Lemmy Caution you.

5.7   Door bell be make sound of putted golf ball dropping into tin cup. Subtle sound, but weird ear does hears delightful **PLINK** loud 'n clear. Roused from reveries, grabs golf ball door handle, turns, opens and (ho!) beholds type of face that be never succeeding, face that early on learns society be only heap filthy trick of The Rich. It's Deena Boettcher—mother of Brats who claims she "learned courage from Buddha, Jesus, Lincoln, Einstein, and Jeff Chandler"—flaunting her best bedraggled beatupness: sauerkraut hair, eyes looking like crushed flowers, flesh beneath like dough risen 'n punched down. Has dry, hectic look 'n be so white that lipstick rages on her mouth; between lips, a Gauloise. With each massive puff, red ember of her cigarette glows brightly 'n grows like dog's erection, chewing off almost half-inch of tobacco and leaving wilted gray tube of dead ash in its wake; fighting back tears, her carotid stands out. For moment, each stares at each—distraught Art ain't so nice to look at either—two neurological totems confronting each other in mute nostril agony. Blue vein of worry beats steadily in her temple, fine brow wrinkles like overbaked potato as she sucks her fag. Her physique, posture, and morphology alerts some screaming switchboard of insecurity within Art's mind. She gives out bitter, grown-up laugh seeping from her soft cherry-blossom lips like raw sewage, ugly trickle turning to bloodcurdling roar splashing forth. Needs milk of human kindness spooned on wound like sour cream on baked potato. Clock time here no longer valid. Watches begin to melt 'n drip. Sensation like meeting IRS tax inspector while riding amusement park's wall of death. But soon rectilinear structures of consciousness reassemble and normal conversation becomes possible, rectums merging as both have common shit in life to overcome. Both must constantly fight Total Demoralization. If, as Albert Camus claims, "a man is more of a man because of what he does not say than what he does say," and if this statement applies to women, then Deena, Mistress of Understatement, be more woman for that fact. Fact: for me, The Author, these two characters are disquieting muses.

"Roo . . . he . . . he'll rue da day he . . . ," spits out Dee enraged, crying. Since marrying, her life be what she calls "an indigestion."

Something is *Crook* in Middlebrook

"Rusk been usin' you for a punching bag again?" Art senses danger, Dee's very armpits hum with it. Kool-Aid-purple damage beneath her eyes; greenish-pale hue to her skin.

She merely nods affirmatively, tears starting down her ruddy cheeks like mini rivers. Right index finny wipes blood drippin' nose. "But I got in bunch o' good punches o' my own, damnbetcha! Luckily, Da Brats are having brats at their grandma's tonight. *Merde* Art, life wit Roo 'n Da Brats is sometimes like a Lenny Bruce show rewritten by Dr. Goebbels!" Longer she talks, more reality flows back into her veins.

Art pulls out starched and meticulously folded, monographed handkerchief to staunch dripping blood. Got to keep Astroturf putting-green rug from being stained. "Now, now, get a grip on this. Here try a few putting strokes with this." Hands her his spanking brand new Nike Blue Chip putter. "I find this *always* calms me down."

"Art, fuck yer psychic *jiu-jitsu*! Just gimme da ice-bag will ya?"

Art and Deena's relationship recalls back and forth bantering between obsessive-compulsive detective Adrian Monk and his ever-suffering female assistant-caretaker in popular cable comic TV series "Monk." Deena's role as mother of twins and long-suffering wife of unreconstructed bar-hound *cum* wife-beater, Roo, makes her source of rivers of tears—like Anna Livia Plurabelle, James Joyce's archetypal (feminists would say *stereotyped*) symbol of constant renewal in *Finnegan's Wake*.

Drawing by The Boettcher Brats

Deena? She be case of gilt by association: be shining when with likes of Art, Al, 'n Una, but be tarnishing when Roo near. Pau D'Arco, her boss at The Bowmanville Bistro, punningly refers to her as *la gueule* (French slang for

Something is **Crook** in Middlebrook

'loud-mouth' that sounds like 'la girl') because of her stentorian tone honed over years of chastising her twin Furies. Pau just had to laugh: Dee, trying to be Frenchly, insists on pronouncing "halibut" in way that rhymes with "Malibu." And she loves to say, "I'm like, major social *faux-pop.*" Al Schmerbauch describes her contradictorily as "Shirley Temple's head in *Curly Top*, planted on top Julia Roberts' body in *Erin Brockovich.*" But now her curly locks be hide under crimson scarf, cleavage invisible under turtleneck. Her eyes be shine like small light bulbs. Flecks of eye shadow catch in her windlashed lashes. Often wears small yellow badge declaring: MY SAFE WORD IS 'OUCH'. When not bruised by Roo—resulting in her eyelids turning dark with pain—she be radiant with health 'n life, always some study in dirty duds. "She's da master o' da classic shiver, da slow blink, da knuckle-ta-lip pathos," admits Rusk. When not on a drunk, Rusk repairs dents and other shit on accident prone cars. Dee waits tables, both hail from crappy west Chicagoland suburb inappropriately called Aurora. In high school Dee was president of Jeff Chandler Fan Club. "A movie screen," she explains to an amazed Una one day, "*is* a kind of sky; a sky filled with events and people. From where else would film stars come if not from a film sky?" Heap romantic, she builds whole philosophy from cry of crickets 'n her heart's anguish. Chews Bible brand bubble gum in little folded cartons, smallest of its kind for any product in the known universe, containing two tabs of chewing gum. Printed on inside of each carton is verse from King James version of The Book. When carton unfolded, verse revealed. Fact: Bible Gum be packaged in work-shop for disabled in Southern Missouri. Stuff now collector's item sold on e-Bay.

Brats's sketch of their parents

Art obliges Dee. She presses comforting cold compress to her bashed schnoz. As blood congeals, she does becomes more congenial. As pain dulls, her mind wanders to thoughts of delightful escape: sees acres of air-conditioned Greyhound Bus interior, glinting, slightly greasy railings, old rivetheads needing paint; see herself pile into crowded bus, later to hear surf of Carmel and smells ocean *sans* Brats 'n her husband, Roo, who's at home, exhausted from marital fracas, sitting in patched over-stuffed chair. Be entering his mind, we do spy maze of tiny cubicles and narrow corridors jumbled with rusty old engrams. Only active area be boozy speculations inspired by TV documentary limning delightful lives of prim 'n proper Limies during Shanghai's colonial days when Brits move through their day from office to lunch to dinner and nightclubs in delightful haze of dry martinis or gin tonics calling out: "Quite! Yass, guv'nor, a large pink gin, easy on the pink, eh wot? Haw-haw! Elementary! Bit of all right, eh old chap!"

Something is *Crook* in Middlebrook

Art breaks Dee's revery. "Still taking your French lessons?" chuckling under his breath, hiding it with hand over mouth.

"*May we.*" Low, vague airplane fear gnaws at her, like it did to ValueJet passengers flying day after infamous Florida crash into Everglades. Tries to change her feelings by detouring conversation. "My boss, that encyclopedia of cookin', tells me last night that Emperor Nero invented *aioli*, that sauce ta end all garlic sauces. 'Zee *magnafeek* accompaniment to simple crudities,' as he put it. Crudities. . . . What does *that* mean, crudities? Pau, Frenchly owner o' da bistro where I waitress, just put up a sign over his Bunn stove readin' in French: 'God made food, da Devil made seasonin' '?"

"To be anticipated, to be anticipated. He once told me the original title of Baudelaire's *A Season in Hell* was actually *A Seasoning in Hell.*"

"Huh?" she replies with quizzical look reminiscent of expression displayed when Pau once tells her that during Japan's attack on Shanghai in WWII single wild bomb falling on Avenue Edward VII closes peepholes of more than 1000 people.

"Deena's lack of cultural competence is," as Al once elegantly put it, "inversely proportional to the tendency of inbred Pennsylvania Amish to produce children with six fingers. Shit Art, did you know that when I asked Dee why she didn't simply dump Roo, she reasoned thus (raising her hand): 'In our country good-bye looks just like hello.' Can you believe *that*?"

5.8　　　Which, Dear Reader, brings to mind tricky topic of Art's genealogy. Strain of schizoid 'n paranoid tendencies does run through his family tree like San Andreas Fault through Southern California. His namesake, Brevet General Arthur Middlebrook, up 'n abandoned his destitute family to join Illinois's 12th Infantry during Civil War; becomes hero; rapid rise from Captain to General due to paranoia which in wartime is anything but liability. Old tintype of said General looks much like Art's paternal grandfather, Rich, that same beaky nose that seemed an uninvited guest to the party of his features. Richard Middlebrook served as WWI trench mortar batteryman in France. Got steamed in mustard gas, served up on Red Cross stretcher, and consumed by repeated episodes of "excessive suspicion" (as Art's mother, Jeanette, euphemistically put it). Returning to civilian life, only job he could hold was to become sole owner of his own house painting biz. Lead in paint back then further seasons Rich's peculiar take on existence. Drops his Protestantism, becomes Catholic 'cause in delusional world it's more certain about stuff. Papal Bulls 'n all that. Rich's wife, Rose, once cooked for lummoxes with voracious appetites in large logging camp. There she meets and softens Rich's brittle heart via his growling stomach. Result of furtive marital sex act is Art's dad, Jerrald, who early on trains as house painter and gets high on paint fumes. Later high in elevators 'n airplanes, and delusional episodes. Most episodes revolve around fantasies that his wife is having affairs with all his friends. Art recalls dead daddy lying in state in funeral parlor and how he reads his stony face like geologist taking measure of effects of ancient glacier on granite.

Jeanette 'n Jerrald have two kids. Jerrald's daughter, Els, graduates college, moves to Frisco, later returns home; has psychotic episode. Chucks all her possessions into dumpster, except for dog-eared copy of Burroughs's *The Ticket that Exploded.* Hops into VW Bug attempting to reach parent's home, but has to call for help from phone booth halfway there. Picked up, taken to parent's home. Art recalls blue flames of her paranoid eyes, atmosphere simmering, like two mini-pots boiling. Sheer terror. Thinks Art's going to stab her, but that cockroaches do be bosom buddies. Medicated with Thorazine (her smiling visage eventually makes cover of *Thorazine Sunrise Monthly*). Later, brief marriage, then cancer; only member of family to win Die Young Award.

Opening family album—chopped-up tunnel betwixt centuries, repository of glossy headstones of snapshot moment—notice mother's side of family of Germanic Protestant descent; great grandfather daring draft dodger escaping Prussian repression, flees to America to farm loamy soil. His son, Detleff, marries Chora June who intrigues him with quip: "Children are a consolation for everything—'cept having children." In new coupling, pure silliness coexists with agoraphobia. "Det", as he's called, is inventive verbal comic and persistent punster always on move between Milwaukee and Ashland, Wisconsin as an engineer for Chicago & Northwestern railroad. Meanwhile, back at the ranch, morose wife—mouth puckered in indeterminate determination that defines this one-woman Reality Principle, exuding rich odor of burning graves—does darning, intricate needlework, fries thick greasy bacon in basement, grows green vegetables in backyard garden, and henpecks her hubby from minute he walks in front door until he leaves for train depot again. But sting of life does no more to Det's complacent soul than scratch of pin to smooth face of hard rock.

Both sides of family hail from northern regions of Wisconsin and are raised on hard work, cold winters and huge snow banks, generous portions of diverse sausages, boiled potatoes, sauerkraut, green Jell-O, and prune kolaches. Det never chucks a sickie, never even suffers a cold for-god-sakes; kicks-off in his sleep at home. Chora's rich in vowels but poor in teeth 'n eyes; yet she's tough, her cancer just gives up on achewin' on her colon. Eventually dies of "senescent boredom" in retirement home too cheap to install TVs in residents' rooms. All donors to Art's genes live on into their early nineties. In home-video interview shot by Art when in grad school, frail Chora sits up in her death bed, spits, gives culinary advice: "Don't eat carrots —they'll kill your desire for anything else," and attributes her longevity to: "Green beans, staunch genes and moral rectitude." Everyone hated her while she was alive, but now that she's dead it's as if someone broke case of *Chanel* on her grave. Ho! Arthur Strewth Middlebrook is genetic stir-fry of all this pomp and circumstance. If Lamarckian genetics be true, and if he be now having offspring, Art would be passing on his weird ear mutation and its consequent effects on his orbitofrontal lobes to further generations of bozotic Middlebrooks. But no such luck (or misfortune). In The Age of Simulation, Art will remain original.

"Hey!" yells Deena, "ya gonna invite me ta dinner? Ya got some o' dat Mulligan Stew *à la* Sorrentino ya always makin'?"

"Nope. But I got eggs." Art knows Deena still tastes raw 'n putrid meat of Roo's knuckle sandwich, so offers her emergency dose of vodka 'n lime to clear palate followed by quick meal of his favorite culinary aggregate,

Something is *Crook* in Middlebrook

The Denver Omelette. "Well-cooked Art, well-cooked," she yells from living room, knowing Art's penchant for Pau's infamous undercooked French ome-lettes. As he chops ham, Art's eye takes in two items. First, sitting on a shelf, his prized conch shell which he clasps weird ear to, finding it soothes an over-active ear jarred by urban noise. Not sure we should violate Art's privacy, but here goes: he affectionately names this conch "Moana" as its sounds of sun 'n surf recall soporific South Seas, an exotic Polynesian name recalling both Robert Flaherty's famous documentary film on Samoa and New Zea-land's honey-voiced diva, Moana Maniapoto. Secondly, he briefly catches distorted reflection of himself and his whole kitchen wrapping around gleam-ing glass sides of empty mason jar found round and tall, dead center on his stylish wooden island. Thinks: *God . . . It be the finale of the seeming to be.*

5.9   Meanwhile outside . . . a bustling line of brown ants clean a dead cat's skull. Boettcher Brats methodically steppin' 'n stompin' on long line of said ants sending them, ants 'n Brats, to Nirvana. Under Art's deck, Tiger Woods closes his eyes for a long nap. One mile away on Lincoln Avenue is cheap motel run by Korean immigrants. Over manager's desk is large sign in Korean Hangul stating: "The neighbor is a cousin":

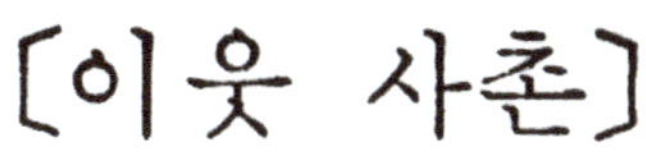

Inside . . . one shabby room two young people sit in darkened room on worn couch. Only other object in room is TV on which X-rated movie plays. They watch it without speaking. The actors in film be engaged in oral sex. When movie ends, light from TV is only source of illumination in room and static hiss from absent picture is only sound. These two people turn to each other and, without speaking, do exactly what they have just seen. In adjoining room, elderly woman watches through unobtrusive hole in wall, slowly lifts her muumuu, and . . . .

Two blocks away, Roo's out littering *à la* Leaver in a local park named after local Korean Alderman named Park. Mr. Bungle, park's resident wino—*the* real Mr. Bungle whom pseudo-Bungle models his clever act after—reeks of urine, pushes shopping cart, has love affair with his own death stamped in slope of his shoulders, in perpetually sidelong cast of his eyes. Guard at Lincoln Square Mall unlocks its doors to eager crowd of consumers. Auto parts truck rear-ends blue mini-van on Eisenhower Expressway, crush-ing two commuters in back seat. Crazy Muslim makes deeply offensive on-line posting on USENET group *alt.soc.culture.indian*. Art's primary HMO physician logs on to url: *http://www.nim.nih.gov/research/visible/visible_ human.html* to view several of 1,871 1-mm slices of Joseph Paul Jernigan's virtualized criminal body. Noreen be gingerly dusting off her humongous chicken collection, her profile all planes 'n angles; her eyes, like those of celebrities, has chilling glitter to them. Outside, Pev boldly swings his Leica about, framing, reframing, clicking away at some obscure decisive moment in blind imitation of that King of Street Photographers, Garry Winogrand. Hears—does not see—and dramatically captures on film one stout middle-aged woman in hot pink pedal-pushers and Birkenstock sandals spitting with obvious contempt on sidewalk in front of Art's dome-home while she hands out a Cyberfeminist flyer. A few days later—out to annoy Art—The Pink

Something is **Crook** in Middlebrook

Pistons (gang of flamboyant lesbian trick motorcycle riders) perform noisy maneuvers up 'n down his street.

TACTICS FOR MENOPAUSAL CYBORGS

NOW that your body and subjectivity are not useful for reproduction and production, use them as autonomous sites for your own resistant research into uselessness, obsolescence and pleasure. Refuse to shut up and hide; remain visible, remain vocal. Refuse to be ghettoized in senior communities. Demand the food and products of your youth. Slow everyone else down: refuse to be hurried; clog up the aisles at the supermarket and the space at the post office; drive 40 mph in the middle lane with all your lights on. Park anywhere you like. Demonstrate the futility of fashion. Wear your night-gowns and slippers on the street; flaunt your wrinkles and decay. Be very opinionated and demanding, be angry and funny. If you desire sex, pool your sexual resources with others. Revel in your uselessness; don't work; demand full service. Refuse the compulsion to be wired, but get online and mouth off if you want; refuse to be smart, new, and improved. Don't let churches control your spirituality. Be noise in the codes of bureaucracy, authority, and utility.
Q.E.D.

5.91 At this precise moment, seven-year old Latina is shot in her *cabeza* by stray gang gunfire in nearby barrio, while Noreen suffers her anxiety-of-coupons by fondling her stash of long out-of-date coupons bundled neatly in rubber bands. Simultaneously, Pietro, local Alderman with bored eyes color of expensive snuff, like two-way mirrors, and smile playing like snake on his lips, is taking his weekly bribe in some dive on Rush Street. He breathes air as if he were stealing it. He has look of eagerness and distemper. He is victim of two evil powers: ambition and indigestion. As teenager he spends time thieving from slot machines and deflowering daughters of better men than himself. There do be inside him somewhere baby of pristine misery; every day he feels for it and holds it and feeds it, and every night he puts it to bed. Most nights he needs bottle of wine to get him through an evening with only a bottle of wine to get him through it. He has cheeks of corruption, greying hair is cut short. There's total blackness behind his eyes when usual postures fail him. Wears too many rings, sports a baggy imported Hawaii Dantesca brand shirt, dove-grey brogues from Siena, and carries too much trouble in his middle-aged bearing. Prowls his office menacingly swinging battered Cubs bat. Speaking at Aldermanic events, on his face is projected, one frame quickly replacing another, pictures of self-satisfaction (well, just like *Il Duce!*), despair, fear, submission, tenderness and God knows what else. Framing that face are large ears, hairs inside which look like iron filings clustered around pair of magnets.

"How the world is managed, and why it was created I cannot tell," his voice sails through council chamber's air like ring of sweet smoke which relaxed smoker lets fly from his pipe as he reclines in his armchair, "but it is no featherbed for the repose of sluggards. People who conceive of life to be

Something is *Crook* in Middlebrook

the pursuit of happiness must be chronically unhappy." Offers this bit of wisdom to justify nixing The Big Box Ordinance which would have required Wal Mart and other discount mega-giants to pay employees a better wage.

Moniker popular press gives this civil servant, "Pronto" Pietro, suggests this notorious First Ward Alderman be always ready to instantly scheme, graft, and abuse his public office for profit. Especially if it's at expense of African-American or Latino community. Kyle Long Jaw, Coldcockin' Collins, Turkey Leg Krutsinger, and Macho Man Torres—four monstrous thugs on payroll as body-guards—always surround him like Apostles around Christ and be always looking for government men, bugs, 'n informers. People on his payroll get gift subscription from him every Christmas to *Sports Afield*. They call him "Big Chief" or "B.C." for short (appropriate, since this fellow's a real Neanderthal). Anything that occurred in his Ward *prior* to his administration referred to as "B.B.C." (Before Big Chief) and coded *bad*; all activity occurring *after* his election termed "A.B.C." (After Big Chief) and coded *good*. And if you are on Pietro's staff, you'd better know your ABCs! For instance, Pietro loves to enforce *structured* fun days at his office. First Friday of month is declared "inside-out day" where all staff wear their clothes inside-out, while second Monday of month is dubbed "silly hat day" (self-explanatory). Two months ago, Pietro requires all staff to read Oprah Winfrey-recommended book, *Why the Super-Ego is your Amigo.* Ah, Pietro. You can see the Chicagoan in him: tight-jawed, almost ventroloquial delivery, hard vowels, human hardness of the Windy City, the City That Works.

In 1992 A.B.C. Pietro gets Latino Cultural Center in his Ward condemned and torn down. "Pietroville," magnificently landscaped park with postmodern Italianate decor and reflecting pool by architect Charles Moore, arises in its place. Touted as "Ragazzi's Respite," it is weekend home to local upbeat Christian youth choral group, The Sunshine Yodelers; during the day it's popular site for skate rats gathering to tell lies, for itinerant gelato vendors who sell to post-, post-, post-feminist girls stretched out on thick grass talking of their lives in every detail—their *fucking* lives—looking aside every so often to ensure that others are straining to hear, and groups of college students (unbearably young) auditioning for sex in chunky shoes. But at night park becomes tough turf for gang of brutal-looking young scum, heads shaved like pink coconuts, ears pincushions of iron-mongery, tattoos glowing at the edges of cutaway singlets, They are the notorious "Hollowcaustic Kids O'Leary" who ply their trade with impunity as cops palm bribes to look other way. Rumored that Big Chief himself gets fair percentage from all illicit sales. Mifflin Bacon Clough III (infamous right-winger mentioned in Ron Bartheleme's arcane message earsdropping Art hears) is on Pietro's speed-dial. Ho! Typical shenanigans in that cooked environment, that prosthetic world denominated "The Windy City," where time of apprehension is reduced to that of a Polaroid, where folds 'n depths of "reality" are smoothly ironed out, and where question of "values" is seemingly whittled away.

5.92   And in that Windy City sits Art snug up in his cockloft as sunset be so coagulate that it seems as if tangerines, apples, and melons are being pulped on Chicago skyline. Weird ear scans 180-degree swath south-westward, trapping a mishmash of odd sound-bites:

Something is *Crook* in Middlebrook

Art tires of this gabbity-gab. Art regoops weird ear. Jumps off stool. Runs down spirals stairs to fix oversized mug of twig tea. Great Eastern Sun Kuchika twig tea do be healthy birthday gift (bought at Avery Now & Zen Health Foods by Una) who tries to wean Art off Starbuck's coffee as that company's CEO, Howard Schultz, in address to Seattle synagogue, blindly supports Israel against Palestinians. Una figures win-win situation: get Art off caffeine and support liberal boycott of Starbucks. But, unbeknownst to Una, Art prefers competitor Cosi's grande vanilla latte over Starbucks any day, because only there can he sit face-to-face with focaccia that looks like giant, cancerous crouton.

As Art sips his steaming twig tea, sitting lazily at his kitchen table, his mind wanders into skull-time as he absentmindedly watches Tiger Woods scamper out into the backyard, twist his ugly neck around and stare directly at Art, blinking his eyes twice. Suddenly Art's reveries take him back to his high school science classes.

Ah, those were the days. My mind buzzing with dissociation constants, moles, titration, strong acids, weak acids, buffers, pH, gas chromatography, even ligands. Wow. How exciting it was to learn all that stuff. How delightful to work with beakers, test-tubes, alcohol lamps, delicate chemical balances—the works. Later my shrewd sister gives me Primo Levi's book, The Periodic Table, *for Christmas one year and all this marvelous chemical stuff comes flooding back again. Shit, I do regret not following my chemical career earlier. But better late than never, I guess. Man, was it a surprise when I first realized rocks were actually chemicals!* $Cu_{1.75}Al_{0.25}H_{1.75}(Si_2O_5)_2(OH)_4$ *was actually Chrysocolla (also called Bisbeeite), a stunning pale blue-green gem found in the Ural mountains! Before, I was stuck between a rock and a solution. But now my two loves could blissfully combine. Amativeness. 'Get your rocks off doing chemistry,' becomes my mantra. Oil 'n knowledge. Oil 'n knowledge. Now where the fuck did I pick up that expression? Why do some things just stick in our minds and repeat like a looping computer program?*

It is during such moments of intense reverie that Art's mind roams wholly free of physical and temporal constraints and he feels impervious to worldly woes. During such skull-time, he is often reminded of what Mr. MacPherson (his high school English Lit teacher who went on to produce a popular version of Beckett's *Endgame* in the soap opera medium) once said to his chem teacher in school cafeteria by way of defending the status of poetry: "The tetravalence of reverie is as clear and as productive as the chemical tetravalence of carbon."

This MacPherson—heavyset, equipped with piercing blue eyes, very bushy eyebrows, and ruddy nose that tells of imbibing quantities of single malt scotch—had pet phrase that ever sticks in Art's craw: "Tell me what your favorite totem is—gnome, succubus, sylph, undine, or salamander—and I'll tell you which poet'll touch you to the quick."

MacPherson—his eyes shifting from sandstone to quartz—once lifts chronic classroom dissident (infamous for episode of mischief involving a swordfish and a typewriter) sitting in desk three feet off floor and drops him hard—KAAAPLOP!—yelling, "The sour ocean of a sick mind refuses no river." Thereafter, shaken teen becomes model student. Day after Christmas break this same MacPherson, who knows that alcohol be an immediate food which quickly warms cockles of one's heart, comes to class bit tipsy. He lets fly bit of wisdom gleaned during those alcoholidays: "It appears evident that alcohol is a creator of language. It enriches the vocabulary and frees the syntax."

He then proceeds to tell us students about wonderful winter festivals he enjoys during his youth in Glasgow. How his family prepares beneficent *brûlot* (a punch of friendship composed of brandy burnt with sugar) and enjoys poetics of flame and comfortably glowing stomach from imbibed brew lapping hot 'n sticky on slick sides of his glass. *Ah, Bacchus, you beneficent god,* muses Art, *by causing our reason to wander you prevent anchylosis of logic and prepare the way for rational inventiveness.*

Much later, MacPherson hires on as teacherly technical advisor on that famous film, *The Dead Poets Society* (1989). Makes mind-boggling big bucks so can afford to buy two bottles (at $3600 per bottle) of that famous Bordeaux red, Château Pétrus '82. Logs in his *Big Book o' Booze* database this critical tasting evaluation: *Château Pétrus '82: Mature color. A great nose of prunes, spices, huge character and "presence". Liquorice, with sweet, gummy definition. Some sweet aniseed. A lovely sweet "leather" taste. Now has a pruney finish, with sweet, soft cinnamon at the end. Really mocha as it lingers on the palate. A recent magnum had a really exotic spicy nose and was deep, fabulous and complex on the palate. Superb, full, rich, ultra-dimensional taste. Rolls round the mouth. Unbeatable and stunning, with great meaty character.*

Before film completed and second bottle drunk, is carried off set suffering extreme *delirium tremens,* never to return. Up until Mac kicks pro-verbial bucket in Cedars-Sinai Medical Center two weeks later of massive liver failure, his attending nurses swear his face continuously exudes "a kind warmth like the pale flame of a punch bowl." Fact: Mac wills Art his *Big Book* stuffed with keen insights into the spirit world (like absinthe's fabled "Green Fairy").

Ah, how I loved that man and his boozy choices! Thinks Art. *Mac's totem must have been the salamander; as ancient wisdom has it, the salamander, composed all of fire, has tendency to be consumed in its own flame.*

Art be jerked from nostalgic reveries by distinctive cartoon balloons' *flatus vocis á la Boettcher Brat*:

ARF BANG CRACK

BLAM BUZZ CLAMP

SPLASH   CRACKLE

CRUNCH   GOSH

GRUNT HONK HONK

MIEOW   MUMBLE

PANT PLOP PWUTT

ROAR BLOMP BUZZ

SLAM PUFF PUFF SOB

SLAM PUFF PUFF SOB

GULP SPRANK BLOMP

SLAM PUFF PUFF SOB

SSSSSSSSSSSSSSSS
SSSSSSSSSSSSSSSS
SSSSSSSSSSSSSSSS
SSSSSSSSSSSSSSSS
SSSSSSSSSSSSSSSS

6.0

In west clouds be breaking up, violent eye-shadow shades of lavender 'n robin's-egg blue marks cutting edge of latest cold front. Saturday sunset in our Administered World, land of innumerate billionaires, where game of Scrabble is literary event, where prevailing values are those of the pocket calculator. Millions of people engaged in pseudo-activities. Their feelings of security purchased with sacrifice of autonomous thinking. Emergence of new human type, The High-I.Q Moron, is in offing and White Hair (geronto-porno) is fast becoming a Web rage. In nine months ex-President Reagan, The Great Liberator, will be liberated from his mortal coils and those administered millions will praise memories of that affable face of American fascism.

Sound of golf ball falling into tin cup announces Una Calda Bionda at door of dome-home. In open doorway, almost invisible, Una be spectral outline with light shooting through tips of her hair, a being on fire. Blond, brown-eyed girl friend of Art's is product of union between not-so-famous Italian actor in Italian Neo-Realist cinema—he had bit role in *The Bicycle Thief* and always belittled Una as: "*Bislacco* (weird), *sfasato* (deranged), and *distratto* (distracted)—and itinerant Scandinavian singer of minor talents who, in her hey-day, was billed as having "the body of Jean Harlow and the voice of pre-pubescent Heintje". So Una carries around Nordic nose, Mediterranean mouth. Of her childhood, she confesses: "We lacked all the necessities in the midst of all the superfluities." Her father's deathbed confession was: "Twenty thousand cups of coffee have killed me. Thank God I'm an atheist!" Fact: it was her father's idea to name her after Una in Spenser's *The Faerie Queene*, where she symbolizes truth.

She be here on invitation from Art to show her all his "harems," Art's quaint term for his gaggle of fetish objects, material expression of his repetition-compulsion. Objects like his pet rock "Erin," his infamous collection of paint-scrapings, and his very intriguing, chronologically-ordered array of golf putters. Most valuable is his collection of oddball lava lamps (pink Pepto-Bismol filled lamp is his fav as pink, as a color, be too loaded with negative associations to sit comfortably within art context). Sonic context for Una's visit be Edgard Varèse's "21.5" playing on Bose Wave Radio's CD-player. (Actually, not sure it's that title, but it's one featuring Chinese blocks, sleigh bells, tambourine, gongs, chains, and all that crap).

"What's this?" inquires Una holding up a thick, leather book box with gilded lettering titling it: *S.O.M.B.A.*

"Oh, my collected writings titled *Some of My Basic Assumptions*." Opens box to reveal over one thousand fanfold pages. "All printed out on, you know, tractor-feed computer sheets."

"Why fanfold, and why keep them attached to each other?"

"Be like heap long scroll, connecting archaic with contemporary."

"Read me an excerpt, Arty dear."

Something is **Crook** in Middlebrook

"Sure. But excuse the telegraphic style. At that time I was *with* French writer Céline, ripping off his infamous use of triple-dot punctuation. Miffed, my father used to say, 'Sir, when you are *with* Arthur Middlebrook, call me.' Now remember this is all true, yet all false; every sentence here is a lie, and yet every word written with conviction." Pulls out initial page and reads: " 'I give everyone a pain in the ass. . . . Now I'm giving you some ideas in here of how things stand. . . . I'm going to be taking you backstage so you won't get any illusions about my basic assumptions. . . . What a hand with adjectives I have. . . . I assure you. . . . If I'd only crapped out all my impertinences into my diapers. . . . But, ho-hum, I didn't. . . . My mentor once said, 'Flattery will get you everywhere. Twittering nowhere.' . . . My mother said her gynaecologist told her, 'Soon be over, soon be over,' when she was in labor with me. . . . Got to get God-excited, my childhood confessor once told me. . . . Kiss any girl, the little devil in my *cabeza* once said. . . . As in Hell so in Heaven. . . . I need oil and knowledge. . . . In that order. . . . Cyborg you know. . . . Things are bad!... The world's collapsing, but I'm writing. . . . Reading Merleau-Ponty's *Humanism and Terror* simply because it was written the year I was born. Reading Céline because his first book was praised by the extreme Left *and* the Extreme Right. . . . I'm now on quest to view all Hollywood movies released in 1947 too. . . . Naturally, I'm not going to tell you everything. . . . I'm not the son of a rich planter in Cuba, executed by Castro's regime. . . . I'm the son of a schizoid drunk, drunk on God and booze. . . . Which has a lot to do with my basic assumptions. . . . With my choice of art as a career. . . . Why I need oil and knowledge. . . . In that order. . . . Cyborg you know. . . . Things are bad!. . . . The world's collapsing, but I'm writing when not too depressed. . . . And that Pole Henryk Górecki's *Symphony #3* (*Symphony of Sorrowful Songs,* 1976) is the perfect homeopathic medicine to ease my depression.' Ah, want me to continue? I warn you, as is often the way with diaries, as events get more exciting, the descriptions of those events become more elliptical."

Una looks up at ceiling as if discovering it glows melon-pink; her lips make mere ghost of movement while looking at Art mistrustfully; just doesn't get it—abruptly changes topic. "I like *that* photograph," her voice with trace of metallic in it, her finny pointing to large Cibachrome print on wall depicting Coke bottle/Molotov cocktail with embedded text: NOTHING'S MORE AMERICAN THAN COKE. "Is it yours? I mean, did you create it?"

"Indeed." Expatiates on this masterpiece from his Red Period. "When I was exhibiting in many alternative art spaces. My old girl friend, Brucine, berated my Leftist aesthetic activities as: 'A buffoon yodeling in the caverns of the world.' Can you beat that? She had the magic ability to depreciate something just by breathing on it. 'A rabbit fart' is how she described one of my activist artworks. But she did mix a mean side car cocktail—sheer wooziness with a wallop."

Art proceeds to lead Una down narrow spiral stairs into basement. "We stand now," opens Art's mini-lecture on his harems, "in front of idols that are the empty husks of dead clichés; can't you just feel the tinge of infantile belief? There is a sublime pleasure in this. Uncanny even. I credit the start of my collecting mania with this kiddy rock collection. It's all oil and knowledge."

Something is *Crook* in Middlebrook

Flashback: Art is five. His Uncle Don, a dentist trained in chemistry, shows him instance of cold light: takes lumps of cane sugar and, keeping his mouth open, chews them vigorously until friction of crystal against crystal causes them to glow. "Uranyl nitrate crystals work even better," explains Don, "but mortar and pestle must replace one's crunching mouth upon pain of death. Textbooks call this phenomenon *triboluminescence*." From sweet sugar crystals to magnificent geodes, Art begins his geological journey. It stimulates both sides of his brain, his aesthetic sensibilities and his scientific curiosity.

Ho! Little Art hangs up his professional shingle, neatly lettered on cardboard, over his bedroom door:

Arthur Strewth Middlebrook
Certified Mining-Prospector
Explorer of Occult Gems 'n Herbs
Initiated Engineer

Not only does little Art love colorful crystals, flaky mica and shale, and those geologic *mestizos*, aggregates. But he also adores obscure chemical names, especially now-discredited names. For instance, take jargonium, an element supposedly present in zircons and zirconium ores, but which actually turns out to be element now called hafnium. Even now, Art chides many fellow critics for their lapse into academic jargonium.

"Una, did you know vanadium was once called panchromium?"

"No." Una shakes her head, bored, and pissed because Art is ignoring sherbert texture of her skin and that sweetshop delicacy of her mouth.

Uncle Don's fav element though do be scheelite, which fluoresces bright bluish-white. Scheelite is, ideally, pure calcium tungstate, $CaWO_4$. But some specimens do contain certain amount of calcium molybdate, which in its pure form becomes that wonderful mineral called powellite.

"Now here's a fine sample of stibnite. After stibnite, my fav mineral is powellite—named after Powell the explorer—because it occurs in quartz veins and fluoresces golden yellow under ultra-violet light. This latter specimen was originally found in the Seven Devil's district of Idaho. It was a tenth birthday gift from my uncle."

Powellite has symbolic importance in Art's life. Its chemical formula reads $CaMoO_4$ (so little Art wittily dubs it "California Cow" and later, while living in California and during time he be reading lots of Albert Camus's writings, he gets CAMOOOOO as personalized license plate); its cleavage is bipyramidal (like Una's), its fracture property is conchoidal (like conch shell he holds to weird ear to sooth his hearing), while its luster ranges from adamantine to greasy (just like people Art later meets in academia).

"At certain crucial junctures, my collecting mania gets major infusions of stimulation. For instance, a rock-hounding trip with my first bittersweet lover, Brucine, through California Gold Rush country. Scads of gems stores too; we buy many choice specimens as its easier than digging. Within two years our poisonous relationship goes on the rocks. Some twenty-six new stunning gems in my collection and deep scratches on my arms are residual traces of our passion."

Unremarked upon by Art here, but even more important to Art's collecting mania, is bizarre excursion he and Larry Binacka (who sports racoon eyes 'n suffers a soiled wardrobe 'n collects ads for, 'n instances of, "X-ray Spex") take during their college years. A mind-blowing buddy-outing to largest existing collection of horror and fantasy film special effects objects stored in Hollywood Hills home of Forest J. Ackerman, former editor of *Famous Monsters of Filmland* magazine. "Touring this palace is like walking through a blend of harem and morgue," claims accordion-fold tourist info brochure. Art and Larry stop smoking pot for a week to pay for exorbitant entry fee. Once inside, everywhere they be treated to recognizable fragments of Hollywood film reality, but arranged more like child's bedroom than normal museum.

In one corner, Art spies rubber cast of Jane Fonda's breasts used in filming of *Barbarella*. In another, Larry stumbles upon *faux* black panther head from *The Most Dangerous Game*. Claws, body parts, and models from films long forgotten be strewn hither-thither. On shelf is small clay animation figure by Ray Harryhausen. Upstairs, in living room, is found one-eyed blob used in Art's fav episode of original TV series, "The Outer Limits*.*" Not until postmodernist installation art—like that of L.A. artist Mike Kelley—will Art ever experience such so-so sojourn into the uncanny. Not until he reads in grad school German critic Walter Benjamin's "Unpacking my Library" does he find kindred spirit deeply expressing what it feels like to collect stuff: "One has only to watch a collector handle," writes Benjamin, "the objects in his glass case. As he holds them in his hands, he seems to be seeing through them into their distant past as though inspired." *Right on,* studious Art silently affirms after reading such insightful revelations.

Art's buddy, Larry, goes on to local fame by building his own significant collection of microscopic sculpture and utensils made for babies. Eventually, he and his collection are featured for laughs on Johnny Carson's "The Tonight Show."

6.1   Una struts provocatively across bare basement floor. Art quickly ungoops and delightfully hears how she's dressed: high heels against tile floor (one heel slightly loose), mesh nylons with slight tear that catches on her flouncy organdy petticoat which rubs deliciously under her silk dress. *Absence only makes the ear grow fonder. Oh, how does it!* Una's underwear drawer is a galaxy—star bright slips, black panties.

Una's bored by the rocks. "Phallic stibnite and vaginal geodes, old stuff. So where's your lava lamp collection, or was this invite only an excuse to get me . . ."

"Both baby, both. *Blessed Benimming!* You should know by now I'm into *both/and* logic, to hell with *either/or*. Like my cocktails *both* shaken *and* stirred. Sex *both* seen *and* heard."

Something is *Crook* in Middlebrook

Snickering, "What's that—er—ejaculation mean? Blessed Bene Ming. A holy, good Chinese dynasty?"

"Not Italian. One word. B-e-n–i-m-m-i-n–g. It's an archaic term that the O.E.D. defines as 'the taking away' of something from someone. Deprivation from unpleasant sounds is good, blessed. Ya grok?"

"Always the wacky philologist, huh?"

"Philologist *and* geologist. Both dig into our past. Dig it?"

"Oh I do Daddy-O. I do." Una ups ante by slowly sitting on white leather couch so sound of organdy on silk 'n silk on leather do mix with rub-a-dubbed nylon on leggy legs. Earfully distracted, Art may delay showing off his lamp collection. But Una has delaying, teasing tactic up her sleeve. Pulls out old old *National Geographic* mag from huge handbag. "Art, Milo wanted you to have this. He said something about it containing reproductions of Finlaycolor transparencies via chromolithography. He said fine checkerboard lines seen with magnifying glass proves it."

6.2   Now Dear Reader, Finlaycolor is additive-color photographic process similar to Autochrome: three color-separation negatives are taken simultaneously by using grid ruled with microscopic red, green, and violet lines. One then makes positive, a lantern slide, from this negative and brings it into exact alignment with the grid. Tricky, delicate process, but when one has them in perfect register, previously black-and-white slide bursts into full color.

6.3   "Thanks. I mean, tell Milo thanks. As if saving my life wasn't enough. I do love the sense of color obtained with this method," comments Art, recalling vividly certain compositions by famous photographer, Edward Steichen, all realized via Finlaycolor.

"He speaks so highly of you Art. Thinks your decision to exit academia is one huge loss." Una places *National Geographic* on her lap, its weight just enough to compress organdy petticoat against her dress and nylons. As each page of magazine turned little sound does emanate and Art does wince with delight; seized with earful desire, he synaesthetically sees beautiful blue flame flash of combustible element dubbed cesium by chemist Robert Bunsen.

Seeing Art staring absent-mindedly into space, Una inquires: "Earth to Art, earth to Art. Ya readin' me?"

"Oh, sorry." Mentions his seizure by cesium.

"Your mind is a strange place, Art."

"Una, that element is so romantic. It burns sky-blue in air, explodes in water." Clears his throat, starts to sing weird ditty copped off USENET group *alt.cesum* to tune of Jimmy Buffett's ode to bar hoppers, "Why don't we get drunk . . .":

Something is **Crook** in Middlebrook

Why Don't We Mix Up the Two

> I've got a pound of Cesium,
> It's burning gently near.
> The sky-blue flame looks lovely,
> But it's noise I want to hear.
> So darlin' bring some water,
> A couple pints'll do.
> And why don't we mix up the two?
> Why don't we mix up the two?
> 'Cause Cesium and water,
> Really make a wicked brew.
> You say I've got a death wish,
> But honey, I'm just blue.
> So why don't we mix up the two?

Putting on his best W. C. Fields imitation: "Cesium, my little Chickadee, was named after the Latin term for sky-blue, *caesius;* it's a silvery-white, soft alkali metal with a melting-point just below body temperature. It occurs naturally in the minerals lepidolite and pollucite. Repeated consumption of small amounts eventually leads one to be seized with cesium madness. Ya can't sit still. Auditory hallucinations common. One sufferer's case history, a veritable Troubadour of the Sepulchers, relates that poor soul's torment: perpetually hears pledged harps, whole carloads of clarinets, ocarinas, oboes, and Japanese balalaikas, Indian sitars, all accompanied by an out of tune toy piano played by an old man with Parkinson's Disease."

"Not unlike that disturbed author, Céline, you mentioned before. Due to a severe battle injury during The Great War, that fascist complained into old age about bothersome ear noises. Heard trombones, full orchestras, marshaling yards."

"Really?"

"Really. Found an article about it when I was doing a Google search on the Internet about ear troubles just after we met."

"Doin' research on my affliction, huh?"

"An informed lover, is a good lover."

"Anyway, to get back to that case history. . . . It's pure auditory torture for that cesium-poisoned musician. He eventually strangles himself with some old violin strings."

"Ugh!"

"Soon afterward, it is discovered that the artist's pigment, Prussian Blue, acts as an antidote to cesium. But only if one's exposure is not too severe."

"I suppose you have Prussian Blue in your perverse little paint chip collection over there?" Una tosses her gaze at the colorful array of small test tubes, simultaneously crossing her legs, sending more shocks of delightful sounds into Art's eager ear. Six perfect notes in side pocket. Tastes Tootsie Rolls spiked with breath mints.

Something is *Crook* in Middlebrook

"I do. . . . I do." Spoken low, breathlessly. If this were cinematic scene, film editor would here perform series of quick jump-cuts closer 'n closer toward Art, finally resting as enormous close-up on his weird ear. What auditory accompaniment would *you* suggest to go with this scene? Varèse, for continuity with ambient sound? Climax of *The 1812 Overture*, for silly over-statement? Random short-wave radio interference, for hint at entropy? The background sounds emitted by unwatched TV tuned to popular Mexican soap opera "The Rich Also Cry," for hint at global ubiquity of media? Silence, for Zen sake?

"About your lava lamp collection . . ." invites Una.

"Oh . . . did you know that that type of motion lamp was invented in 1963 by Edward Craven Walker and patented in England a year later. Can you believe it took eight more years before it was patented in the States? His Crestworth Company marketed the lamp. Later the company became Math-mos and holds the European patent. Walker went on record declaiming, 'People who don't like this lamp are afraid of sex.' How do you like that?"

Una noisily ruffles her petticoat. Art winces. "Honey, I know the lamp has two substances in it, one being heavier in specific gravity and unmixable with the other substance. The liquid in which the glob is suspended is dyed water."

"That globule, Una, is solidified mineral oil such as Ondian 17 with a light paraffin, carbon tetrachloride, a dye and paraffin wax. The clear liquid is roughly seventy-per cent (by volume) dyed water with remainder a liquid raising the coefficient of cubic thermal expansion to encourage vertical move-ment. Slip agents like propylene glycol or ethylene glycol are recommended for this. If you go to E-tailers at *www.oozinggoo.com* or *www.badfads. com* you can glean heaps of data on this ever-popular cultural icon."

"Okay, lay it on me—er—the collection I mean."

"Close your eyes." Art turns off basement light. Opens sliding doors on large cabinet (purchased at local IKEA). Flips toggle switch. Scores of lava lamps slowly awaken to caloric of hot bulbs. "Okay open 'em."

"Hey, quite a collection. All the colors of the rainbow!"

Pointing, "Here's the Aristocrat, that one is from the Midnight Series, this one is called the Lightning Storm, this is the Wizard Glitter, and that one is the Safari Lava Lamp, the next one is the Plasma, that one is the Silver Streak. My fav is that Star Ship Lamp, akin to ultra-streamlined space ship from early 50's TV program I used to watch. 'Tom Corbett' or 'Space Patrol,' not sure which now. See . . . now some are coming to life."

"Popularity is probably due to the sexual component of these lamps. It's obvious, Art. Look at the shape. Pulsing phallic verticality. Inside you have egg-shaped globs. A perpetual ovulation machine. It tantalizes. Sug-gests. During a time when we no longer make love under clear star-rendering skies, a new kind of astronomy is founded: the study of colored malleable globes. . . . The colored light tints one's skin red or blue or . . ."

"I prefer red. Recall my Red Period."

Something is *Crook* in Middlebrook

"Me too. Why I can imagine the gods on Mount Olympus regaling themselves with ambrosia and nectar, savoring with delight the aroma of roasting meats as it is wafted up to their abode *and* see their orgies lit by such marvelous lamps! Gee. Which reminds me. When the hell we gonna eat?"

A "g" added to astronomy yields gastronomy. Art leads his Una-earful-delight, wobbly spike heel 'n all, back up spiral basement stairs for pizza. Ultimate organdy petticoat rustles. Makes Art randy. Has to refocus. So, sitting in kitchen, he expatiates on rare book in his collection. English translation of French translation of Latin translation from ancient Greek by Epicurus's guide and friend of Pericles's son. "Ever hear of Archestratus of Gela's gastronomic poem, a work on the delicacies of the table, titled *Heduphagetica*?"

"Can't say I did."

"He loved to expatiate on fish dishes."

Una playfully tosses rhetorical question at Art. "Did he mention the fantastic dish Pau has listed on his menu as The Bowmanville's Totally Unique Tunny Omelette? And at $19.95 a serving, it *is* unique."

"Carp roe, tuna, parsley, shallots, chives, butter 'n eggs. You bet it costs. Pau takes pride in letting it be known that Jean Anthelme Brillat-Savarin waxes eloquent on this dish in his paean to our taste buds, *The Physiology of Taste.*"

"Oh, the guy to who quipped, 'The discovery of a new dish does more for human happiness than the discovery of a new star'. Deena told me she's learning to that dish as it might have a pacifying effect on ol' Rusk."

"Where lies the body of that mute American who first married pork to beans?"

"Or who first thought to put raisins 'n peanut butter to celery?" Una nostalgically recalls those tasty Ants on the Log that Art used to seduce her.

"It's drummed into school kids who invented the telegraph, the steam engine, the phonograph, who walked on the moon, blah, blah, blah. But our great chefs? They go unmentioned. *Blessed Benimming!* Not until astronomy is replaced by gastronomy as our most important science will peace livest 'n reignest on this planet. Folks will learn that true faith is the kind that raises pie-crusts."

"Ah! Said like a true Yuppy and perpetual starvling!" taunts Una.

"Yup. Gourmands will always be ecologists by default. What chef and good-eater would will the demise of the species canvas-back duck or diamond-back terrapin? Who, with well-tempered tummy, could vote more mercury in our tunny, or budget cuts in food stamp and school lunch programs?"

"Yep. Hard to get up gumption to kill abortion clinic doctors after having dined on chicken stuffed with Pérgord truffles."

"Suicide bombers will only target fast food establishments."

Something is **Crook** in Middlebrook

"Crazed snipers will only go after hyperacidic gum chewers and ketchup eaters," replies Una.

"Only airlines that fail to change their in-flight fare will suffer hijacks."

"Hey Art, it's your Lavoo-Vahna, your ideal society, in-process!"

"Why . . . yes." Art's eyes sparkle to point of carbonation. Fact: Brillat-Savarin cites bright eyes as important aspect of true gourmand.

"Opposite of this foodly utopia can be found in the astonishing town of Sravana Belgola in the Hassan District of Karnataka, India. The Digambaras there, an ascetic Jain sect, renounce life, go naked, and some slowly starve themselves to death. You see, perfect saints, *kevalins*, are supposed to live without food. Needless to say, few saints are discovered! But also no need for weight control clinics there. A month in their sect might do me out of the forty pounds I can sure afford to lose."

"If only the Christian Right in our country would adopt such a belief!"

"Well, they do, but it's directed at our impoverished citizens."

Una absentmindedly fusses with Art's grease-stained cookbook. Out falls recipe card. Oddly, neatly typed thereon is a "suicide poem" attributed to Abraham Lincoln.

"A poem I always read," he explains red-faced, "when I suffer bout of melancholy after listening to NPR coverage of latest neo-con triumphs."

Una reads aloud, comma of pizza cheese dripping from lips:

> *Sweet steel! Come forth from out your sheath,*
> *And glist'ning, speak your powers;*
> *Rip up the organs of my breath,*
> *And draw my blood in showers!*
>
> *I strike! It quivers in that heart*
> *Which drives me to this end;*
> *I draw and kiss the bloody dart,*
> *My last—my only friend!*

Art never gets chance to comment on how beautifully she reads poem. Imagine exchanging gazes with distorted rubberized face of carnival show freak with severe collagen disorder. It's *that* clown again—that pseudo Mr. Bungle—with freaky face flattened flat on kitchen window.

Undescribable noise from Una, her brain shrinking painfully, a paralyzing chill across her heart.

Art—no longer adopting absence of prejudice or aesthetic disinterest toward this figure—quickly grabs large, cold, partially eaten isosceles-shaped pizza slice off kitchen table 'n whops it SMACKEROO against glass and face leering behind. Mixture of cheesy goo, anchovies, peppers, sausages, and lumpy red sauce partially masking vile visage turns scene into slasher film special effect mimicking double-barrel shotgun blast smack-in-da-kisser.

Something is *Crook* in Middlebrook

Bungle blasts off, laughing maniacally, his oversize shoes flopping comically, tracing white arcs in the evening sky all way down Giddings Avenue.

6.4   Oh Una! I imagined you fitted against Art's shoulder all through the night, still, calm, trusting, showing—even in your sleep—sweet affection which would never jibe with your public reputation. When Art watches you sleep, sees your calm unrevealing facial terrain, he recalls that cartographers call blank spaces on maps "sleeping beauties." Oh what trouble it was to determine what you were to be like, to draw your map. Especially your eyes. Did you know that me, your Author, considered these standard (read banal) implications? Blue = innocence and purity. Violet = preferred by Raymond Chandler. Green = wildness and jealousy. Black = passion and depth. No. Chose brown for reliability and common sense, but will poetically describe them as *sapphire eyes, like split almonds*. Eyes that feel more than they have right to feel at that age. It's just what Art needs in his life, reliability and common sense. Gustave Flaubert might have had a better idea though. On one occasion he gives Emma Bovary brown eyes, on another deep black eyes, and on another blue eyes. Better to cover all bases.

Una, even though you are formed for long acquaintance and close viewing—especially when you don that catsuit made of coins—I haven't included your photograph here. Why? You're always looking away in them at God knows what; no one can catch your eye; maybe you're looking away because what you can see over your shoulder is more interesting. My grandfather always did same thing in group photos. My therapist, trying to unravel my family history, said that was a sign of something. How appropriate you should exhibit very same quirk.

Oh Una, I had my doubts, but how you've ripened into Art's perfectly-matched mate. You've successfully found that sliding panel which opens secret chamber of Art's heart, chamber where memory and corpses are kept. You risked. You could've found there only a mouse skeleton. But still you risked. Thank you. Yes, Art. You've been chosen; you are elected into love by a secret ballot against which there is no appeal. You will enjoy nights when Una will be near you after dinner, reading, motionless, like an artifact, like an Old Master, and all you're going to be aware of is the texture of the paint.

6.5   That night, sacked out in his ear-shaped bed, Art's last conscious thoughts before he lapses into an exhausted sleep are concerning species of hearing his newly acquired weird ear foists on him: *It is not the word—say "macaroni," or "Mulligan Stew"—that I hear, but rather a certain highly particular sound, uttered by a soft or hoarse voice and lifted up in a whirlwind, amidst lights that penetrate it, odors that impregnate it, and a sadness or gaiety that colors it. The word, I eat it, it fills my ear like food my mouth.*

Goodnight Art.

Simultaneously, outside, one block north, CTA bus passes with swoosh and doesn't stop for lone Hispanic woman waiting at bus stop adjacent to new Korean restaurant which Deena's been warned to never come in again if she has those Brats with her. Pavement is wet. No stars shine in sky. Across street from Art's place, Deena and Rusk Boettcher are toasty-snuggled in bed. Dresser bureau's top sports framed autographed black-and-white publicity photo of Jeff Chandler next to a framed wedding photo of Roo 'n Dee. Down hall, in small bedroom, Twins visit slumberland.

6.6   Next morning. If this were a film, camera would hover high above a suburban wood frame house across street from dome-home. It would slowly dive down and into front picture window. Therein, Deena Boettcher, vacuuming her living room rug, is seen glancing up in time to spy Peven Pogacnic running back across asphalt street from Art's dome-home to his own house. *Something's crook at Middlebrook's*, she thinks. Rubs her itchy nose and continues to clean. Rusk's been up early. Hasn't even shaved yet. He is down in their basement unpacking and setting up his new Brew Meister home brew beer-making operation. *Holy shit, love those Belgian monks. This Belgian Chimay Ale'll be great. All I need to order now is Wyeast Belgian Ale Yeast 'n I'm up 'n runnin'*, muses Roo.

Twins also involved in chemical experiments. Once they mixed sour cream 'n ice cubes on window sill to see if would turn into *ice cream*. Today, they celebrate what they call "Silly Saturday" morning making Oobleck (what clever twins rename "Obtainium" as all ingredients are easily obtained). Oh, you know, that bizarre semi-liquid sludge made from cornstarch and water made famous in that Dr. Seuss book, *Bartholomew and the Oobleck.* Decked out in their mother's grungiest checked aprons, Brats are following modified recipe they download from some wonky Hacker website:

OBTAINIUM 1.007

— 1 cup cornstarch   — 1 cup of baking soda

— 3/4 cup of water   — 2 drops of green food coloring

— 1 drop of vanilla essence (optional)

This stuff exhibits amusing and extremely non-Newtonian behavior: it pours and splatters, but resists rapid motion like a solid, and will even crack when hit abruptly with a hammer. Ho! Does not obey Newton's Third Law: for every action, there is an equal and opposite reaction. When this goo is smacked with your hand, it doesn't splash, but becomes a solid substance for a few moments. If you make a ball of it and throw it up in air, it loses shape and becomes flat in mid-air. Left out in sun, color bleaches out, it turns hard cement on top, but remains jelly-like on bottom. Annoying possibilities of such a wonky substance dance like sugar plums through our Brats's little perverse noggins. *Mr. Schmerbauch could use some of this stuff poured over his egghead or we could put it in dad's beer-making equipment, or put it down mommy's garbage disposal*, muses Brat #1 as he adds water in small increments as Brat #2 slowly drips in drops of food coloring, thinking, *I'll hammer hit this stuff within Art's earshot.*

According to recipe, substance is ready for use when this mixture "tears" as finny is quickly scraped through it and it "melts" back together again. Slowly prepared in this manner, multifarious mixed states that this cornstarch-baking soda combination goes through as it *becomes* Oobleck is grokked by our curious kids in its funny fullness. As they watch Oobleck turn from liquid to solid and back, Twins delightedly and repeatedly yell: "From piss to shit, shit to piss, ha, ha! From number two to number one to number two to number one again!" Unbeknownst to our Brats is fact that this weird stuff is used by grade school instructors to teach rudimentary chemistry about properties of liquids and solids. Waist deep in his chemistry studies, Art knows why this goo performs so extraordinarily. In conversation with him once, I cajoled him to give us an explanation.

"Well, uncooked cornstarch particles are structured in both crystalline and noncrystalline arrangements."

"Weird science. Interesting. But so what?"

"When slowly mixed with water, the noncrystalline structures of cornstarch absorb most of the water. When you smack or rapidly stir it, you increase the temperature and pressure on the mixture which causes more noncrystalline structures to form. These new noncrystalline structures absorb more water and the mixture becomes thicker; hence the appearance of a solid. Then when you discontinue the pressure, the number of noncrystalline structures decrease and water is released, creating the soupy mixture. It's an interesting property of some matter. Chemists call it *isotropy*, ya grok?"

"This grade school science might make interesting grist for artworks!"

"Already done. No cigar. It's called conceptual art."

Both Brats wear pig-snouted masks, make oinking noises, splatter green goo every which way. Soon, Dee sniffs pungent, distinct odor of leaking gas. Surmises Twins messing around with stove manage to disrupt flame, allowing unburned gas to escape.

"Shit! Gas! You kids! Get the hell out of there. Now! Hubba-hubba."

"Flub-a-dub," says Brat #1.

"Dub-is-flub," retorts Brat #2.

"Go. Now!" She grabs Brats by collar (their delicate skins red with offended horror) and hauls them kicking 'n screaming out back door. They dive into weeks of uncut grass and duck 'n cover.

6.7   At precisely same moment, Roo trots up his front walk with exciting news that Art 'n Una are engaged. Opens door, lit cigarette dangling from his stupid lips. Point five seconds later right side of Boettcher house is blown out, shredded, in spectacular ignition. Roo blown into hedge lining walkway. A seared two-by-four flies past, just missing his head. Brats feel sudden scorching heat that singes their hair. Despite high probability of serious injuries being inflicted, Dee and Brats walk away from incident with minor boo-boos. Roo's northern regions suffer scorched hair, southern regions suffer week's bout with severe collywobbles. North side of Boettcher abode is in ruins and aflame. Adepts of sheer rampage, Brats have visited upon Dee 'n Roo the worst of the worst. Bad karma. Soon Roo will also suffer severe case of misopedia.

Something is *Crook* in Middlebrook

Dee's in shock. Realizes that her gaudy, glass-jeweled crown, won when she was chosen Dairy Queen's Dairy Princess at age twelve, is *Kaput*. It had white 'n blue stones all around outside with a glass Holstein cow in front as a kind of centerpiece, complete with cluster of pink cubic zirconia stones for an udder and tiny red stones for nipples. Now it's just blob of melted glass 'n metal suffering its ruination somewhere in that charred heap they once called home.

If this were film, camera would take in disarray of scene from above from circling helicopter. Frame would catch, in a darkness illuminated by fire, a panicked Noreen running up side-walk toward stunned Roo, while concerned neighbors look out their front doors or peek out of shattered glass windows. Lens would slowly zoom back to include gaggle of flashing red lights weaving their way down Damen Avenue toward explosion. In alley, near Art's dome-home, lurks clown-suited figure. Soon myatonic police cordon off area as men in rubber duds wearing funny looking boots stomp all through Deena's flowerbeds. Not to worry. Channel Five news just arrived. It'll make more sense on TV.

6.8   Water sibilates. Pot clanks against another pot. Silverware clinks like bowl of spare change. Una's straightening up Art's kitchen. Pigeons fly in sunset and over roof of neighbors Poganic, then flock together; horn of car sounds in distance, child plays on sidewalk, windowpanes be bathed in setting sun. Later in evening, after particularly noisy love session, Art gives Una well-thumbed copy of James McManus's Chicago-situated novel, *Chin Music,* stressing she pay attention to page 82 where man in green Izod shirt 'n gray slacks caroms down sloping facade of super-tall Hancock Center. After reading said passage, Una wants to gulp 'n guzzle at Hancock's tippy-top restaurant 'n gaze at Windy City architecture: "In a city, time becomes visible to me, just like in a rustlin' petticoat sound becomes visible for you. Grok?"

Week later: Una be readying herself for this auspicious dinner date. She's good eater, *una buona forchetta* (Italian for "a good fork"). But you won't find even tiniest bit of food wedged between her teeth. She constantly runs her tongue across her glowing teeth—no diamond is so precious as a tooth—then starts to scrub her teeth if offending tidbit discovered; those chompers, just bit smallish, are pretty 'n even. Fourteen years ago they belonged in such a face as hers was—her father used to affectionately call her *acqua e sapone* (soap and water) so often did she wash her face—and even now Una can throw back her head 'n laugh heartily, confident that nobody will mind that single porcelain filling in one bicuspid or that one tiny wrinkle near each eye. Spoiled by her parents, Una is her own best *tifoso* (fan). She smiles (oh that spells romantic danger for Art!) 'n slips into that Devil-Wears-Prada dress that drives Art nuts and drives to Art's

Our love-bound couple, fleeing exorbitant parking rates in The Loop, take Brown Line south to Belmont, transferring t0 Red Line where man enters car, annoyingly announcing: "Pub trans is the humiliation of democracy in full effect. I've already apologized, for those of you who didn't know." He repeats litany again and again and again—exiting at Chicago Avenue along with Una 'n Art. Emerging from underground, our couple saunters past small fountain

Something is Crook in Middlebrook

where shabby-looking pigeons wheel about meaningfully but in slow-motion; fountain supplies sound of falling water, but to Art's weird ear, water sounds viscid, hopeless. Arm-in-arm they march toward Michigan Ave., noticing how they can only glimpse fragments of that manmade mountain through series of titillating obfuscations—between other buildings, over billboards, behind water towers, etc—that only intensifies their desire to arrive at its massive base, stroke its metal sides, ascend to its peak.

Art wants to wow her—wouldn't you?—with thrilling high-speed elevator ride toward heaven where scalextric of the City be glimpsed and tops of water of Lake Michigan are valueless jewels; to window table where Art can plie Una with famous Cloud Buster cocktail: joyous blend of coconut milk, pineapple juice, 'n vodka served in souvenir replica of second-highest building in our Windy City. Drink costs $10, ceramic take-home replica another $25.

While admiring her cleavage, Art slips slim 30ish hostess sawbuck for east-facing table with vast lake view. At their table, Art, that gurgling wizard of calorific excess, is—much to Una's romantic distress—waxing eloquent about nauseating noises emanating from divers men's rooms. "When I'm ungooped and strolling public buildings I can audit that slow rasp of zipper-down, then drilling sound of leak fruitlessly trying to bore through porcelain, then rasp of zipper-up, followed by Niagra Falls of flush. *Blessed Ben-imming!*" Ho! Lucky for Una, menus come, dispensed like examination papers by waiter with cheap churned hair, half an ear bitten off, penny-farthing nostrils, and teeth as randomly angled as shards of glass on some back-street wall. "Why the fuck hire *that* disaster-in-process? whispers Art.

"Arty—the distressed look is totally *in* today," Una whispers, her eyes rebuking him.

Thumbing their menus, our lovers hesitate and fall silent for awhile, frowning and murmuring over array of selections. Finally, they (appropriately) order the "It Just Hasta Be Pasta" daily special which, today being Friday, is *orecchiette con i funghi.* After menus returned to nervous hands of "The Disaster," Una's eyes—two brown lighthouses in a storm of white petals 'n moist olives—gently bathe overview from snaking Lake Shore Drive (locals dub it "LSD") to far lake horizon tucking into Michigan shores. She absently-mindedly sips her libation; stares longingly into boundless distance as if far, far on other side of Lake Michigan lay China. Art gazes through those large windows, sees ruled space, faraway spools of storage tanks, orange delicate distant filthy slums, and green of Chicago river strapped by black bridges. Closer to shore, little boats bob gaily at anchor, and two or three boats sail about, simple and clean as brand-new toy boats. These little boats are life-size and miniature at once, shifting scale from one to the other.

"My homeslice, god, it's like . . . ," gesturing vacantly with empty hands, "why... like being poured out to the horizon." A cloud crosses her facial landscape. "This great expansion . . . why . . . what if death should be like this, the soul finding an exit?"

Art is startled by her deep-water greatness. "Want me to unpop goop 'n hear what I hear? May be heap big increase in auditory universalism, huh?"

Something is *Crook* in Middlebrook

An affirmative nod of her head results in Art's finnies pulling out goop; pressure released causes impolite *ear*-ly burp; now rolls menu and attaches it to ear to baffle out local conversation and bar's TV with its 6 PM News diet of: *Watch out for the Downtown Slasher . . . Watch out for the Uptown Strangler . . . Watch out of the Midtown Mangler.* Terrible things happen all the time; this is the terrible thing. Diners at table next stare at Art, gag on their *osso bucco*. Art aims enhanced weird ear out toward vast duo-tone blue expanse. Does audit something glint, something metallic, melody of hard light in soft empty air. *Jet on approach to O'Hare? No—no jet-engine sound*. Ho! It's some errant weather balloon, shiny stuff that causes world-wide UFO reports.

"Ho! I feel like a man out of time." Art suddenly realizes he can actually hear light under special conditions. Fact: when Art attempts this procedure, aiming toward Loop, does easily audit Chicago's vital substance: bustle 'n brawn sound of money changing hands. Suddenly our Don Juan's head jerks violently to what sounds (holy humbuckles!) like anvil dropped on electric guitar from 30,000 feet. Una 'n Art's eyes meet horribly; blood slowly trickles out weird ear. *Duh—steady now. Blessed Benimming!* Art grabs table with both hands as restaurant lights don't seem at all fixed or stable. . . . Only that night, watching CLTV's Late Late News, do Art 'n Una discover cause: big black '57 Caddy sharks out of lane, cuts-off even bigger black Hummer that swerves too far right, blast, through guard rail on LSD north of Hancock Center. Awful things can happen any time. This be *the* awful thing.

6.9   Three hours later. Art's blood-stained souvenir napkin rests on his kitchen table. Una's on Art's couch garbed appropriately for night of noisy aural sex. Larry King's suspenders scream from TV raster as he takes on Norman Mailer: *Critics say your prose gurgles with clichés, tautologies and uneasy mandarinisms.* Una urges watching late-night rerun of "The Oprah Show" as featured guest is Canadian sexologist Sue Johanson. Ah, TV . . . forward sight always being framed and edited as back projection.

But, Oprah, as I've said on my show on your network, it is obvious that men and women's sexual organs are attracted to each other like a magnet only through the introduction between them of a web of uncertainties ceaselessly renewed, a real unloosing of hummingbirds which are wanting to go to hell to have their feathers smoothed.

Una and Art look at each other coyly. Art runs into kitchen. He pops cork on chilled bottle of Alsace Böckel brand Gewürztraminer, grabs some pre-chilled glasses, then he cuts up some Baby Gouda cheese into wedges and places them on silver platter. He returns with snacks and sits close to Una, putting arm around her.

Sue is still yakkin' away: *Yes, that absolute gift of one being to another, which exists only in reciprocity, is in the eyes of every one only a natural and supernatural hanging bridge cast across life itself.*

Art and Una clasp hands. Communication between our two lovers is by touch, taste, 'n ear. *Dio Santo, how I love Arty's taste in wine 'n trimmin's,* silently muses Una. *You'd think he was European.*

Something is *Crook* in Middlebrook

Not so silent is TV: *But Sue, soon overhead and between lovers flies a rain of poisoned arrows, barbed with dolors, that soon fly so thick as to prevent any exchange of glances. Then hastily, a hateful egoism walls itself into a windowless tower. Their mysterious attraction then breaks.*

Whenever I got depressed as a child, thinks Una, *my bilingual mother used to kid me, trying to cheer me up, saying I was suffering 'The Barbie Dolors,' punning on Barbie 'n barb and doll 'n dolor, and giving me generous doses of yellow, puffy Sugar Pops to munch on.* She feels Art's hand in hers.

But Oprah, and I do ask your audience to pay heed, it is a matter of ruling against the widespread, erroneous opinion that love always wears out. At the very worse, love, like a diamond, may eventually be reduced to dust, but that dust always hangs suspended about us all our life.

"Aren't you afraid I'll leave you like I did Brittany?" Art suddenly breaks their tender silence.

"Hush silly rabbit." She puts her index finny to her red lips. "Thou art so sweet 'n furry, coming into this courtship with your unchaste equations, your ungooped ear! Oppose me not, Arty. Enter these my arms, for since thou think it best not to dream all my dreams away, we can pretend the world away until tomorrow. Until reality will be again abanging on our door 'n you will have to leave my warm dark forest. But before that, will you poach my eggs? Yes?"

Sue, some people don't want to be healed. They want a nice juicy wound that shows well when they put the neon lights around it. No "proud flesh" to show there!

"Turn that thing off," urges Art as desperate finnies probe to ungoop ear.

"But she could be talking about my old Vietnamese boyfriend, Phong Sha Ding! Petite, yet radiant and way way crazy, he was so very much like the properties of light: diffuse, specular, and ambient. His first name means 'wind' in Vietnamese, so I should've been warned. Soon found out this computer programmer was blowin' smoke up my ass; had half a dozen women under his mouse-finger at any one time. We were just 'clickables' to him, hyperlinks to his myriad fantasies."

"Sorry. But can you cast your nets into my aural depths, puleeeeze?"

Her eyes take hold of Art's and don't let go, as hot 'n hard 'n punishing as pair of torches. "Okay, okay. My pleasure," replies One-Hot-Blond rubbing her fishnet stockings together under her organdy petticoat.

Art's eyes spin 'n tilt like fruit icons on slot-machine; does taste chocolate, Valrhona's "pur Ghana, Nyangbo" brand judging by its subtle bitterness. Wanting to up earotic ante, Art does grab his well-thumbed bedside companion, *Erotica for English Majors,* and reads from story featuring fictional fucking Una. Putting on his sexiest voice, Art coos, hand on Una's netted knee: " 'On a bed, surrounded by a confusion of potted plants, exotic palms and cut flowers, faintly over-sung by the notes of unseen birds lays a young Italian woman, heavy and disheveled. Her flesh the texture of plant life; beneath it her latest client, Ben Armato, sensed a frame, broad, porous, a real cuddle-puddle inviting fishing beneath her visible surface. Like a painting by the *douanier* Rousseau, Signorina Una Bimba seems to lie in a jungle trapped in a drawing room, thrown in among the carnivorous flowers as their ration; the set, the property of an unseen *dompteur*, half lord, half promoter, over which one expects to hear the strains of an orchestra of wood-winds render a serenade which will popularize the wilderness. The words that fall from her mouth seem to be lent to her; if she'd been forced to invent a vocabulary for herself, it would be a vocabulary of two words, "ah" and "oh." She defiled the very meaning of personality in her passion. She was one of the most unimportantly wicked women of her time. Ben inevitably thought of her in the act of love emitting florid *commedia dell'arte* ejaculations, maybe because his own wife always referred to *his* ejaculations as comedic. . .' What? What? You don't look . . ."

"*Aiuto!* Jeeze Arty, you think *that's* sexy?"

"Well, if Robert Crumb gets off on cartoon characters . . ."

"Just shut up 'n listen to *my* sounds or it's *ciao bambino!*" She pulls out CD of Vivaldi's Sixth Concerto for Violin, subtitled *Il Piacere* (Pleasure), and waves it seductively while rustling her petticoat.

6.91　Following morning,　Art 'n Una be entering a world based on analogy 'n thrust into differentiation. Ho! Be waked by birdsong; each bird-cry to Art's ungooped ear be full-hearted release of birdly-selfhood into neighborhood air expressing such joy as can barely be comprehended. *I, says each cry, I! What a miracle!* muses Art. *Direct opposite of military drill cries; those rapid, flat, soul-deadening mechanical manners of manoeuver I suffered through once.*

Simultaneously, next door neighbor (still in his P.J.s) extends tape measure, taking precise note of new computer desk's dimensions. *Ah, thirty inches deep by ah fifty-six inches long by thirty-six high.* He records data with Monte Blanc fountain pen using green ink in leather-bound *Measurement Book* (huge tome with all information on room dimensions and size of each piece of his furniture in house). Habit (Over-Attention Disorder) extends back several generations on bizarre branch of his father's family tree.

After data logged, he boots up his laptop, puts on Aphex Twin's CD *Ambient Works* (specifically to "Ageispolis," chill-out music that burbles 'n uncoils like some very beautiful snake; next track in line be way-peaceful, "We Are the Music Makers," which has tiny joke tucked inside its glittering synth refrains 'n clicking percussion, beginning with what seems like sound bite of psychedelic wisdom, but be actually line of dialogue from *Willy Wonka and the Chocolate Factory*).

Patting his paunch with one hand and logging on his preferred cyber-sex chatroom with the other, Schmerbauch is soon textually flirting with "Asymptote," someone who claims to be "a young woman" and "a Gastro-physics doctoral candidate at Harvard endowed with perfect mathematical proportions" who, while typing, is "currently surrounded by tanks of liquid nitrogen and alginates," which she (or is it a *he*?) "uses to study hydrocolloids." Now Al has annoying habit of substituting his lucky number 2.718 . . . for the letter 'e,' as *e* be very important mathematical constant of that value 'n be both irrational 'n transcendental number and which (typing furiously) he begins to inform her (or *he*) about by example:

> D2.718ar Asymptot2.718,
>
> My lucky numb2.718r is 'e' (2.718 . . .), a transc2.718nd2.718ntal numb2.718r. In fact, as you can s2.7182.718, I oft2.718n substitut2.718 that num2.718rical valu2.718 for th2.718 l2.718tt2.718r 'e' in my corr-2.718spond2.718nc2.718.
>
> Ya grok, my curvy Asymptot2.718?

Unfortunately (or fortunately!) "Asymptote" immediately bugs out, mistaking our brilliant professor for puky person of weapon-grade stupidity. Irritated, she (or *he*) mutters indecipherable oaths while moving on to yet another electronic interlocutor known by online tag as "Leviticus," typing out whole sorry story and summing up:

> Shit, L, that last dude to chat me up's mental faculties could only improve with the onset of senile dementia. Probably thinks the world's a Moebius strip and that Fellatio is a character in Hamlet! Or that the failure of mayonnaise to emulsify can be attributed to the fact that the chef was menstruating while making it.

Poor Alfred. His very next chatroom contact goes by heap appealing androgynous tag, "Jamie-the-Dwarf."

Something is *Crook* in Middlebrook

7.0

Sun does lance through bank of clouds and lights of passing traffic like tinsel. All around Art people are charging through their morning, toward God knows what. Art is on bee-line to Roosevelt University, to sixth floor class-room where in few minutes he will be feverishly taking notes in his GEOL 511: Geology and Anthropology class. But first he must confront four ele-vators. One, as usual, be out of service. It wasn't always same one either, even sign handing on door be not always same. This time, for instance, it reads: OUT OF SERVICE; others have said NOT WORKING or BROKEN or DON'T TOUCH or even BACK SOON. Maybe it be receptionist or building maintenance guy who changes sign according to some vaguely ironic whim. There were lines in front of remaining three elevators, and this, too, happens every day. If classroom be not six floors up, he'd prefer to walk stairs (which he does do on his way down). Once Art astonished Al with fact that *one day all four elevators* yelled DING! simultaneously and opened. Al figured odds for this event be 1 in 5 million.

Art's desk (too small for his bulk) occupies small rectangle near left corner rear of classroom ten inches away from circular dull-brown trash can filled to overflowing with empty Evian bottles. Behind south wall comes distracting sounds from unsound-proofed music practice rooms. Drives him, even with ear goop firmly in, slightly nuts. Permits himself illegible shudder (only a cinematic close-up would catch this). *Must keep focused. Focused. Keep your eyes on the prof. Concentrate.*

Aging instructor's paunchy physique, long white hair and beard, makes him perfect Christmas Santa. But, garbed in tux, it also makes him wholly out of place in his season ticket front row seat at Chicago's Lyric Opera. Professor Albert Dox joyfully plays Santa at his Lutheran Church's annual holiday party for underprivileged kids. He insists party staff call him "Orrin" during event. Why? The professor's mother, Emma, gave birth to twins while family resides in Iowa City, Iowa. For years neighbors, punning, refer to these lively pair of Dox boys as "Emma's Paradox." Albert always destined for science. Wins Union Oil's Youth Medalist Award for Excellence in High School Science. In contrast, Albert's twin brother, Orrin, grows up admiring likes of Jane Adams and Albert Schweitzer; reads heaps of utopian novels like Edward Bellamy's *Looking Backward* and Aldous Huxley's *Island*; reads about nineteenth-century attempts at perfect societies like Brook Farm, Wisconsin Phalanx, and New Harmony Colony. Becomes passionate fan of L. B. J's "Great Society." He is killed at tender age of nineteen in war-ravaged Congo while working as young U.N. relief worker there. Mistaken for Belgian colonist, he is shot in back by very indigenous people he was helping.

Ever since then, Albert attempts to live out twin role: objective scientist *and* subjective lover of humanity. Wants to live his life *and* life of his brother that was tragically cut short. In his lectures, Albert tempers cold equations of science with warmth of heart. Does strut before his students with no less than four pairs of eyeglasses affixed to his person: one on his nose, one on his forehead, one hung around his neck, and one in his shirt pocket. At his best, "Berty," as loving students call him, raids our world for materials to build sentences; his language be dense in objects which pester one's senses; he hauls in visual imagery of every sort, strews metaphors about, peppers his speech with bald similes and allusions to every realm. So good an instructor, so popular is he with graduate students, that if he didn't have security of tenure, his jealous inferior academic comrades would've gotten him fired by now for "lack of collegiality." Not that that keeps them from occasionally bribing foxy female students into trying to seduce him so they can file sexual harassment charges on him. But Albert much too smart to fall for their frame. Knowing if they can't go for his throat, they'll try to get him through his balls, he puts video surveillance in his office and never closes office door. Has his union rep on speed-dial. Carries voice-activated audio tape record in sport coat to record any threats or unprofessional comments directed his way. Due to these safeguards, even hostile faculty forced to greet Albert with crocodile tears, or cheery words and warm embraces.

Outside, Chicago sky, suspended in heights, is light, fresh, pale, and sarcastic; inside, Albert opens GEOL 511 in manner guaranteed to stun his students: "Every alteration of the features of nature has its origin either in powerless indolence or blind audacity." Another excerpt: "The age of chipped stone is the age of the tormented stone, the age of the polished stone the age of caressed stone. The brutish fellow breaks the flint, doesn't work it; the fellow who works the flint loves the flint, and one does not love stones any differently than one loves women—an evolution of the erotic. With the polished stone, we pass from the intermittent caress to the continued caress, to the gentle, the enveloping, the rhythmic and seductive movement."

Albert skips his thought like stones across his subject—several female students are swooning—and Art's getting writer's cramp. Wishes he knew shorthand. "Gifted geologists are really *geolinguists*, who read the cold volcanic poetry of the rocks: each one a word spoken, how long ago, by thee earth itself, in the immense solitude, the immenser community, of space. To paraphrase British writer, J. G. Ballard, *seams of jade and obsidian are like a segment of embalmed time*." Long pause, rapt students. "Unparalleled cunning, great honesty of thought, and intelligence sharpened to a degree, will be required to enable man to escape from his stiff exterior and succeed in better reconciling order with disorder, form with the formless, maturity with eternal and sacred immaturity," continues Albert, keeping up a slow pace in front of classroom's blackboard, a mosey style of walk that imitates gait adopted off Mississippi river boats known as "shooting the agate." A grotesque trick of leg tissue which springs from observations made along New Orleans's wharves and consciously groomed during his undergraduate days at Tulane University. "In the meantime," he continues, "tell me which you prefer, red peppers or fresh cucumbers?"

Students look up, youthful mouths open in disbelief. Eyes blink. Abrupt shift in topic catches them in mute surprise. Art about to reply that it depends on how said vegetables are prepared when professor explains his rhetorical question.

"I was just seeing if you children of Adam were awake," teases Berty.

Something is *Crook* in Middlebrook

Laughter of relief.

"Pyrite crystals my friends . . . the original fascination of the Pythagoreans with Platonic solids, polyhedra, may have originated from observations of pyrite, fool's gold, crystals as they are often found in dodeca-hedral shape."

On and on he lectures. By end of class, mellifluous-voiced Albert manages to lip synch to some operatic arias spilling over from adjoining music room, liken infectious disease to human immortality, and compare Cro-Magnon man to a modern geologist. All this in mere fifty minutes.

Hematite, magnetite, chalcopyrite, galena. Sphalerite, pyrolusite, scheelite, wolframite. Argentite, freibergite, rose quartz. Morganite, carnelian, jaspar, andesite. Wow! Thinks Art while packing up his briefcase. *This guy. . . . He sure gives off the magical sense that practically every day is dandy, just heap fuckin' dandy! . . . How does he do it? . . . Gee . . . got to get to be grokin' this great guy. In midst of moral decay, ethical confusion, epistemological uncertainty, rampant deconstruction, academic politics, and over-priced nouvelle cuisine restaurants, he seems to have found his own private Idaho, Idaho being the Gem State.*

Art stares down exiting student who seems amazed to find middle-aged old fart in his class. Or maybe kid notices the awful ear goop dangling out his ripper-tattooed weird ear, or maybe he thinks it really is Bob Hoskins in his class in need of reskilling! Art glances up at large wall clock. Notices he has just enough time to gobble down dinner at Greek greasy spoon next door, swab his weird ear, and get his overeducated ass home.

7.1 Outside, sky is color of apple flesh that's been bruised. *Going to be another 40-watt afternoon,* muses Art. Inside, young nubile waitress—small, supple, swervy, bendy, bed-smart variety, who (unlike Sartre's famous example of "bad faith") is *not* alienated from her true self. She works tables at The Artists' Café adjacent to Roosevelt U. and recognizes him ten tables away by his weird ripper ear tat. Exchange of nods. Ungoops weird ear and listens to her heartbeat. Wonders if *her* heart beats slightly faster, like his, when they make eye contact. *Damn. Her gum chewing is gumming up my reception. Can't detect any noticeable variation in her systole/diastole.*

Art peruses menu. Two women—their voices thin 'n breathy 'n faint, like wind moving through dry reeds—whisper unkind words about Art's demeanor. Eleftheria (Greek for "Freedom") dawdles over another table's order where Art overhears a bearded, professorial type playfully order cinnamon-raisin bread as *cinnamon-reagan toast*. "Sorry, we don't have any of those, but how 'bout pumpernixon instead?" Effortless repartee brings forth hearty laughs to all. Still chewing gum, she hip-sways over to take Art's order. *Poetry in motion*, muses Art as he gives her his usual lusty leer. "You're a dirty old man, ya know," she says, reading his thoughts.

"I know," answers Art, "But I was a dirty young man, too."

Something is **Crook** in Middlebrook

She giggles. "Our special Greek plate today is grilled lemon chicken *breast* with rice or potato, spanakopita or dolmades. 'N now we have veggie Not Dogs on our menu too."

Her emphasis on breast is silently noted by Art. "I'll have *that*, with rice and spanakopita. No pita, but bring me Greek coffee, medium-sweet, please."

"Yes, sir." She mock salutes.

7.2   Puts his hands in his lap like two uncooked chicken breasts. Aromatic smells emanating from kitchen entices Art's mind into skull-time. Back to 1972 and his very first Greek dinner in long, narrow sparsely decorated Greek restaurant on Taylor Street in San Francisco whose Greek name translates as "Tantalus's Table." Three souls are at table. Art is celebrating his sister's birthday with her and her new squeeze, Kyrios Ypsilon, a Greek with a plow blade of a jaw. Better known in his crowd as "The Poet," Kyrios's moniker reflects less his actual talent for writing poetry than his sensual, poetic approach to existence. His penchant for *joie de vivre*. Good literature, wonderful cuisine, superb wines, fascinating conversation. When he describes someone, he eats him alive from head to toe. When he reads a menu, it's salacious word-packing of spicy courses, *intercourses*.

But why San Francisco? Els leaves home and moves north from L.A. after she graduates college with degree in English. Gets low paying job in Bay Area writing blah ad copy for some now-defunct cosmetics firm (job she calls "doubleplusungood"). She meets Kyrios at The Book Worm, musty old used book store in Berkeley near University campus, where this Greek curiosity cashiers. The Poet hails from island of Spetses and attended Anagyros College there as undergrad. Now grad student in European Literature at University of California. Els begs Art to fly up and visit them. Meet her new beau. Her twentieth birthday good excuse to do so.

Around Els's neck hangs strand of fat pearls; her dress cut so low these gems do flirt with her cleavage. Els wants Chinese. Art admits he likes good Greek meal better than good French meal, even though in his crowd it's heresy to admit it. The Poet recommends Greek fare and soon they are hopping off crowded cable car and confidently striding down Taylor Street in their bell-bottom pants and eventually through unassuming door of best Greek eatery in Bay Area. *Ktapothi saltsa, bakaliaros tighanitos, psari savori, pastitso, prassorizo, stifado, kottopoula me bamies, hirines brizoles, mousaka, arni psito, fasolatha, fakkes, avgolemono, koloktholouloutha yemista*—exotic names on lengthy menu fascinate young Art whose palate loves taste of words when pronounced and much as taste of food when chewed. As he pronounces these Greek dishes, his mouth waters. (Yes, he already displays advanced symptoms of passion for word mysticism ever since reading *After Babel,* George Steiner's book on language and translation.)

Ho! He imagines himself in Athens, a guest of Kyrios's trust fund, enjoying: stunning classical ruins, intense blue skies, hot sun, vigorous males dancing on tables, seductive, tanned women tossing down *ouzo* in local *tavernas*. Kyrios talks to waiter in his native lingo. Wow! Gasterea, muse of

Something is **Crook** in Middlebrook

haute cuisine, smiles upon them. It seems Special of Day is pheasant prepared five different ways. Brimming with anticipation, Art orders this extravaganza along with cup of *avgolemono* soup, flaming *saganaki* cheese, a side of steaming *dolmades*, and carafe of uniquely flavorful, clear bright gold Achaia Clauss brand Retsina wine served at perfect temperature. How Art loves its pine resin flavor! (Thereafter, in compulsion to repeat, Art will serve Retsina wine during his so-called dinners of seduction, only to find his dates hate the stuff.)

Lively Bouzouki music provides atmosphere. Delicious breads to soak in award-winning Eliki Extra Virgin Olive Oil precede the main course. During his *saganaki* appetizer course Art's eyes creep upward and notice Greek words circling near ceiling around three sides of dining room. Seems to be quotation attributed to a "J.A.B.S." Asks The Poet to translate. Waiter tells Kyrios it's famous social recipe for elegant dining from famous French gastronome, Jean Anthelme Brillat-Savarin: "Let the men be witty and not pedantic, and the women amiable without being too coquettish." Pheasant dishes are prepared variously: as baked, grilled, broiled, layered and wrapped in phyllo dough. One served after another in slow succession of visual and taste delight. What an exotic spread! After delights of their main courses, Five-Star Metaxa liqueur accompanies dessert of *galaktobouriko* and *baklava*. Some three hours after arriving, they rise from table with all physical grace of wine casks without legs.

Exotic food so captures Art's imagination, he can't recall anything specific about that evening's conversation, except he laughs at almost everything Kyrios says. He can still see The Poet sitting across from him gesticulating, garbed in that odd brown and white Guernsey cowhide vest, red bandana around his forehead, and his thick wooden walking stick leaning like a shepherd's staff against the room's white-washed wall. Later, Els explains, "He tries to cultivate the urban peasant look."

He always carried that damn stick, recalls Art. *But I can't even remember what Els, my poor departed sister, said or wore that evening. Had I known then she'd die so young . . . Strange how memory works.*

7.3 "Chow's on!" declaims Eleftheria through her black lipsticked gum chewing mouth, startling Art from his reveries as she sets before him plate of tasty grilled chicken. "September seventh. Say, did you know it's Brazil's Independence Day today?" It seems Freedom (because of her name?) knows date of every country's Independence Day. And she loves to tell everyone.

"Ah, no. Thanks. It'll make my supper more festive," jives Art.

"Can hardly wait 'til I'm free of this job. Owners here are cheap as hell. Keep on your ass all day. No time to chill out. Like prison. And that young cashier . . ."

"Yah."

"Well, he's family, part of the cheap family that owns the place. They don't trust anyone else to take the money in."

"They over price the food, for sure."

Something is *Crook* in Middlebrook

"And if you need a restroom, you have to take a slow elevator commanded by a human operator to the fifth floor here. No bathroom in the restaurant itself. Sucks. Especially when ya gotta change yer—er—pad fast!"

"Yah. Sucks." *Did I really need to know that?*

7.4   Art always loves to chat with wait staff. They're always into "the dirt" about a place, or more than willing to screw obstreperous owners. Once he and Els were eating in Haight-Ashbury area of San Francisco at greasy spoon with U-shaped counter. Midway through their chow mein, disgruntled female short-order chef pokes her head out swinging kitchen door and gestures for them to come around back after eating. They do so and find this overworked hippy chick—she calls herself "Jody Schmoe"—sporting wild eyes, shoulder length hair, and eager to sell steaks and hamburgers right out of establishment's freezer super cheap as owner shamefully underpays her culinary talent. So Art and Els clean up. For twenty bucks they receive fifteen thick prime cut steaks, thirty burger patties, and a paradoxical quip from Schmoe: "I can't go. . . . I'll go on."

"Beckett," Els whispers knowingly to Art as they haul chow to Art's van.

"Huh?"

"Why that gal . . . I took her for a perfect schmoe . . . just cited Samuel Beckett's unnameable narrator in *The Unnameable*. Probably a Lit major at Berkeley. Shit. She's playin' jarism with us. Get it?" (Art and Els, a fan of William Burroughs, love to play this game where they plagiarize from famous or obscure sources and see who recognizes their citations.)

In fact, Els's take on this gal is way off. As dominant authorial voice I can assure you, Dear Reader, that her real name is Cynsa Bonorris. A high school band drop-out, but passionate autodidact, she goes on to found weird Bay Area band called "joe shmoe." A three-woman, two-man group of schmoes that music critics characterize as "Ed's Redeeming Qualities meets The Velvet Underground." Their first original hit—featuring ukulele, accordion, djembe, marimba, recorder, didgeridoo, small percussion pieces, mighty nose flute, and 1970s-era analog synthesizer—is haunting, meditative song titled "Potscrubber Girl," soon followed by their raucous, anthemic tune "Everything Sucks."

Art packs his 1965 blue and white VW Microbus with their treasure of protein and hot tails it back across Bay Bridge, past Yerba Buena Island (once known as Goat Island), to Els's second floor apartment on Oxford Street in Berkeley. Stuffed both into her freezer and her immediate neighbors's, filched food keeps Els in red meat for weeks. Kyrios reports that, curiously, during this era of plentiful protein, Els has no desire to drape herself upside down in plaid pajamas in her old overstuffed chair as usual, solipsistically listening with headphones to her favorite bit of morose music, Beethoven's *Melancholia Quartet* (Opus 18, no. 6) while unconsciously thumbing pink beads of rosary won in Sister Eugenia's fifth grade class for excellence in piety. After returning to Los Angeles due to her bouts with depression, it is this quartet that Els listens to just prior to her psychotic break, to that rush of terror and confusion which she experienced as solidly chemical as adrenalin, a telephone call to mother, and a bus ride to a clinic.

Much later, in retrospect, Art attributes this anti-depressive effect to one of those many dietary benefits of The Atkins Diet. This be around time that Art is still teaching and logs onto Atkins Diet website and leaves following testimonial on their Bulletin Board:

```
Dr. Atkins,

        Thanks to two years on your fabulous
diet, I've been cured of melancholy and all
remaining religious pangs.  I also lost
thirty pounds and so decided to dye my
hair(what's left of it) back to a youthful
brown again to match my mucho slimmer figure.
        Now that my grey hair has gone bye-
bye, younger folks actually take what I say
seriously.

        Sincerely yours,

        Professor Arthur S. Middlebrook
```

7.5　　While letting his food cool (Art is susceptible to burning skin off roof of his mouth) he ungoops weird ear 'n scans dining room for interesting auditory tidbits. From conversation between, presumably, a young graduate student and professorial-looking interlocutor with long hair, graying beard, and garbed in sport coat with elbow patches, Art tunes in this academic insight from older mentor:

WHO CAN THWART THE GLOBAL SYSTEM? CERTAINLY NOT THE ANTI-GLOBALIZATION MOVEMENT, GEORGE. HEAR ME OUT. IN THE UNIVERSAL, THERE WAS STILL A NATURAL REFERENCE TO THE WORLD, TO THE BODY AND TO MEMORY, RIGHT? A KIND OF DIALECTICAL TENSION AND CRITICAL MOVEMENT WHICH FOUND THEIR FORM IN HISTORICAL AND REVOLUTIONARY VIOLENCE. IT IS THE EXPULSION OF THIS CRITICAL NEGATIVITY, SAYS JEAN BAUDRILLARD, WHICH OPENS ON TO ANOTHER KIND OF VIOLENCE, THE VIOLENCE OF GLOBALIZATION: THE SUPREMACY OF POSITIVITY ALONE AND OF TECHNICAL EFFICIENCY, TOTAL ORGANIZATION, INTEGRAL CIRCULATION, THE EQUIVALENCE OF ALL EXCHANGES. WHAT CANADIAN THEORIST ARTHUR KROKER CALLS "VIRTUAL CAPITALISM." HENCE, THE END OF THE ROLE OF THE INTELLECTUAL, BOUND UP WITH THE ENLIGHTENMENT AND THE UNIVERSAL —AND ALSO THE END OF THE ACTIVIST, WHO WAS

Something is *Crook* in Middlebrook

Dense stuff. An incommensurate language game. Our public sphere is being replaced with little islands of discourse without bridges between. Like only speaks to like. No wonder the average Joe Schmoe professes a deep resentment of academia, often has a strong penchant for anti-intellectualism, and becomes easy prey to neo-conservative attacks on progressive thought.

A tap on his left shoulder. Art looks up. "Greek coffee, medium-sweet," silently mouths Eleftheria, noticing Art has removed his ear goop. He is grateful she gently startled him out of his silent musings. Last time she didn't, called out in full waitress volume, and Art's ear rang for several minutes from sonic concussion.

"Ah . . . oh, thanks. Smells great." *And looks great too,* thinks Art as he catches appreciative peep of waitress's cleavage as she bends down to place small cup of lava-dense java before him. He always loves familiar sweet-bitter taste and feel of this thick substance as it passes slowly across his tongue. *Damn. Not enough cardamon. I prefer more and usually they do put in more. But this will have to do, I guess.*

Art eats out often and often at same establishment, so becomes hypersensitive to fact that depending on who is chef that day dishes and drinks vary widely in presentation, amount, and flavor. Lack of consistency. So when possible patronizes restaurants that have highest cuisinely con-sistency. *If I weren't in such a hurry to get to Una's tonight . . .* Art's thoughts run to delightful vision of piles of spicy, carmelized jumbo shrimp, sweet plantains, and bountiful doses of potent mojitoes at Mar y Sol, his favorite Cuban restaurant. *Ah. Another time, with Una ear-fully in tow in flouncing petticoat.*

7.6   Two young women stroll past restaurant just on other side of large glass window next to Art's table, right next to his weird ear. He inadvertently picks up snippet of their conversation as they pass by:

Something is *Crook* in Middlebrook

Art turns his head ninety degrees to right and picks up another auditory fragment, bit of interesting historical trivia, emanating from table occupied by two young, nerdy professorial types sporting white plastic pocket protectors with green Roosevelt University logo imprinted on each, starched, form-fitting short-sleeve white shirts, and godawful I-got-this-for-Christmas-once ties:

AS YOU KNOW, IRRATIONAL NUMBERS ARE INCOM-MENSURABLE. BUT DID YOU KNOW THAT THEIR DISCOVERY BY A MEMBER OF THE PYTHAGOREANS CAUSED QUITE A STIR. THE HISTORIAN AND PHILO-SOPHER OF SYRIAN DESCENT, IAMBLICHUS, AROUND THREE HUNDRED B.C., WROTE THAT THIS FELLOW WHO DISCLOSED THE IRRATIONAL NATURE OF THE GOLDEN SECTION RATIO, *PHI*, AS THE NEVER-ENDING, NON-REPEATING NUMBER ONE POINT SIX ONE EIGHT ZERO THREE THREE NINE EIGHT EIGHT SEVEN TO INFINITY (THAT IS, DIS-COVERED FACT OF INCOMMENSURABILITY) WAS SO HATED FOR DISTURBING THEIR CONCEPT OF THE PERFECTION OF NUMBERS THAT NOT ONLY WAS HE BANNED FROM THE PYTHAGOREAN COMMON ASSOC-IATION AND WAY OF LIFE, BUT EVEN HIS TOMB WAS CEREMONIOUSLY BUILT AND MOCK BURIAL CARRIED OUT, AS IF THEIR FORMER COLLEAGUE WAS DEARLY DEPARTED FROM LIFE AMONG HUMANKIND. NO SHIT SHERLOCK, THIS IS TRUE! I BEAR NOT FALSE WIT-NESS.

Art gets his check. Leaves friendly waitress large tip. *Wouldn't mind having a daughter like that*, he thinks. This time of day road traffic makes it faster taking Brown Line EL home than using cab. Ravenswood Brown Line meanders above ground like long snake west and north from The Loop to within four blocks of Art's dome-home. Past Chicago's back porches 'n stairs—wooden, crudely built, open to weather, home to long icicles, prone to collapse—through ample greyness, ample brownness, making rickety speed through violet evenings over clean steel rails, big clouds above. Wat-ches old woman running to catch train; because her legs couldn't move any faster, her face, especially her mouth, was hurrying like mad. Ride is so rail-screech noisy, he super goops up both ears. Can't hear panhandlers nor people on their portable phones. Can't hear boyfriend-girlfriend arguments. Can't hear Born-Agains declaiming they're more interested in the Rock of Ages than the ages of rocks. Can't hear driver call out stops either. Has to keep attentive. So has front row seat to class warfare. Spies young, slick

Something is *Crook* in Middlebrook

Asian pickpocket smoothly nip leather wallet off well-groomed corporate type who's oblivious, nose-deep into bestseller, *Winning Through Intimidation.* Guy, who looks like George Clooney, strides confidently off at Armitage stop unawares he's been clipped.

Probably thinks he's well armored in his Armani suit. Just wait until he tries to whip out his American Express Gold Card at a posh restaurant.

As for Art, since being victimized himself once, he always carries two wallets. One is out of reach in his carry bag; other is conspicuously peeking up out of his back pocket, inviting someone's quick fingers. But ho! Latter is stuffed with Monopoly money. And those clear plastic picture displays? They are filled with photos of sneering Republican politicos snipped from *Newsweek.* But *la pièce de résistance* is this neatly typed note folded in on top of funny money:

> Greetings friend! Contra those well-meaning, wimpy T-shirts, you'd better FEAR ART! For you've just been royally fucked with by . . .
>
> — *3Nomial Voices Whirlpool Destruction*

Well-versed in ludic tactics of that 1960s art group, Fluxus—Yoko Ono was their most famous member—Art sees this as practical application of conceptual art. Pickpocket makes eye contact with Art. Art sees mixture of fear and defiance in those brown eyes which know theft has been witnessed. Silently says, "Now what are you going to do about it?" Art winks knowingly, defusing awkward situation. Guy rubs his nose with index finny, nods slightly at Art, and shoves his way up aisle and into adjoining coach.

Art notices black youth occupying double seat with such truculent insolence that, despite crowded conditions, no one dares to demand squatters' rights. At Diversey stop young man with large book on mathematics gets on. *Shit, math again!* Very technical looking and serious, he makes sullen youth move his gaffer-taped boom-box, sits down and, scribble, scribble, sets right to work on his formulae. *Wow*, thinks Art. Seems Art attracts EL-ride incidents like blue serge suit attracts lint. Once, crazy black man confronts him on Blue Line EL, screaming that he's a white racist, part of white power structure, etcetera. Art just stuffs his head down into his book 'n ignores harassment. At least with nose in reading some oaf won't be confronting Art with bestial snarl: "Who da fuck you looking at?" Moreover, underlining pertinent passage with his fine point red ink pen, he can use said instrument as shiv to defend himself. But most of time Art-the-EL-rider (like his peers) be torn in futile, anguished fashion between disinterest in passing urbanscape and disinterest in book cradled in his lap.

Something is *Crook* in Middlebrook

7.7   *Now what to do?* Bored stiff. Surrounded by bone-weary bodies, sporting borrowed faces 'n canceled eyes, swaying to 'n fro in CTA's mechanical snake, Art's mind suffers mute traumatism akin to primeval emptiness called *tohu bohu.* Poor Art. But, ho, authorial god to rescue! Let there be light! *Ah! Now that's it,* muses Art. During remainder of thirty-minute EL ride, our protagonist amuses himself by switching on his attic light and dusting off paradoxical gem left to posterity by that philosophical frog Gabriel Marcel. Art's mind gently takes hold of it, lovingly polishes it, weights it, takes its measure, scrutinizes it closely: *"Hope is a memory of the future," writes Marcel. Al once tells me that this bit of wisdom is the perfect definition of the science of probability: "Substitute the word 'probability' for 'hope' and there you have it!" So Al goes on to describe a famous example known as Buffon's Needle posited in 1777 by the Comte de Buffon: "Suppose you have a large sheet of paper on the floor, ruled with parallel straight lines spaced by a fixed distance. A needle of length equal precisely to the spacing between the lines is thrown completely at random onto the paper. What is the probability that the needle will land in such a way that it will intersect one of the lines. Surprisingly, the answer turns out to be the number 2/π, where pi equals 3.14159. Probability as memory of the future, Art." How is it possible that math, a product of human thought that is independent of experience, fits so excellently the objects of physical reality? Paradoxical. But, despite Al's math, how can we have a memory of what is yet to come?* thinks Art. *Pokes holes in our staid rationality, like a Zen koan. Asserts non-duality. Reversibility of time. Or is it simply an attempt to more wittily express Heidegger's Existentialism, our famous 'thrownness' toward the future? ... Could be just a bad translation from the French. . . . When I do what writer-photographer Wright Morris calls 'skull-time,' lapsing into a deep reverie over past events, do we get the obverse: skull-time as the future of my memories?*

Reverie broken by jarring series of abrupt stops at Fullerton station. Several passengers go tumbling down aisle. Art has to grasp the chrome bar in front of him. Doors fly open and two loud-mouthed college students bulldoze their way through gaggle of riders. They sport baseball hats turned backwards and grey DePaul University sweat shirts. They noisily plop down directly behind Art in space just vacated by enormously obese woman whose size and penchant for bad farts kept her alone in her seat. Students yell to be heard over EL's noise so even with ear goop in, Art becomes privy to their conversation.

"Five. As our prof said, that number was worshiped by those Pythagoreans of yore. He noted that pyramids haves five corners and five faces, counting the base. And that what is called the sacred cubit has about twenty-five (five squared) inches (precisely twenty-five pyramid inches); and, that the pyramid-inch is the five-hundred-millionth part of the Earth's axis! Dig it!"

Blessed Benimming! I can't seem to get away from the likes of Al. Yah, the next time you feel happy, look at a clock and note how long it takes until you are miserable.

"Yah, but he failed to mention that if one looks up the facts about the Washington Monument in the *World Almanac*, you will find considerable fiveness, my friend.

Something is *Crook* in Middlebrook

"Yah?"

"Yah. Its height is five hundred fifty-five feet and five inches. The base is fifty-five feet square, and the windows are set at five hundred feet from the base. If the base is multiplied by sixty (or five times the number of months in a year) it gives three thousand three hundred, the exact weight of the capstone in pounds!"

"Wow, cool."

"Also, the word 'Washington' has exactly ten letters (two times five). And if the weight of the capstone is multiplied by the base, the result is one hundred eighty-one thousand five hundred, a fairly close approximation to the speed of light in miles per second! Figure that."

"Holy shit, that's warp one, captain!"

"And that's not all," he adds, whispering conspiratorially, "a friend of mine works for the local F.B.I. and one night we got him drunk at Gene and Georgetti's and he dropped a hint that there's a secret file claiming Nixon had Hoffa snuffed and his union-worn bones secreted inside the Washington Monument where the Prez could look 'n laugh at 'em everyday! No shit!"

I'm surrounded by a bunch of math and conspiracy nuts. Spare me! cries Art silently as mechanical snake snakes its way past dreary backs of decrepit red brick buildings with uniform grey wooden back porch staircases that collapse when too many party-goers climb on 'em, past brilliant-colored graffiti announcing END OF THE WORLD or crying out for DESTRUCTION OF GLOBALIZATION, or DEATH TO REPUBLICANS, or just announcing that US CHOLOS WAS HERE, past Korean laundries with their too-smiley owners, past signs in squiggly Arabic cursive, past gay-haunted streets of Chicago's "Boys Town," ever west and northward to its terminus at Kimball Station catacorner to an ever-busy Bank One Cash Station where customers are forever being robbed as they walk out with their cash. The sky, losing its start-of-the-day sarcasm, is now most impossibly innocent blue.

7.8   Sun will set tonight without anyone's seeing it—there is that kind of afternoon bleakness. After dinner. Loud knock on his front door interrupts his chromic melancholic musings. *Una!* Like a priest preparing Mass, Art prepares Una 1920s millionaire-artist Gerald Murphy's famed Bailey cocktail:

> 1 oz. orange juice & 1 oz. grapefruit juice
> ½ oz. lime & ½ oz. lemon
> 1 oz. of gin & some bruised mint leaves
> Shake with ice & strain into a cocktail glass
> that has been rimmed with coarse sugar.

Una's eyes keep enlarging as Art sips his drink and expatiates on his prized Cassina reproduction of Gerrit Rietveld's famous De Stijl red-blue chair, placing his cocktail glass on chair's black, broad, yellowed-tipped arm-rest. Art views this utopian chair, originally designed in 1917, as a symbolic aggregate of planes assembled in space. It's formal aspects has marked

Something is *Crook* in Middlebrook

affinity with crystalline structures. Its seat is a deep blue, color associated with passivity, horizontality, femininity—traits associated with Jung's concept of *anima*. Backrest is red, color indicating aggressiveness, verticality, masculinity—traits of Jung's *animus*. Sitting amongst this delicate balance of anima and animus was Art's Jungian analyst's idea. An idea that cost Art an arm 'n a leg.

"Ah, Una. Such formal perfection contrasts bitterly with life today. Sometimes I think I'm surrounded by some sort of wretched specters, not by people. Walk around our cities. You encounter identical multiplex cinemas and the same blank faces; in those corporate hangers, stultified plebs vacillate between adhering displays of products and fast-food counters, until almost by malign accident they arrive in the rooms where Hollywood films composed almost entirely of digital effects battle in void, self-referential competition with one another, parallel universes. Our contemporary city perpetuates itself through relentless visual and auditory curtailments as well as systematized neural jolts, provocative of consumption. I often feel, against the stupidity of my time, floods of hatred which choke me. Shit rises to my mouth as in the case of a strangulated hernia!"

"Now Arty. . . . Arty . . . ungooooooop that ear!" she demands in tone mimicking sexual dominatrix. Wants to unstick his stuck-record mind from its negative groove.

Art gets it. He slowly, seductively ungoops weird ear. Una, with seductive rustle of dress upon organdy upon nylon stockings, waggles over leisurely and achingly slow sits down in Art's lap. Stabs of delightful sound as she makes little probing excursions of sexy *frottage.* Una has remarkable ability to make Arthur suddenly burst into tears of joy, melting his eyes; thereafter, Art's world always seems to him cleaner, fresher. Summoning all her influence over him, Una exercises this ability now. Sound, touch, sight intermingle into one weird, wonderful *Gesamtkunstwerk.*

If this were a film, camera would adopt high, bird's-eye view down on our affectionate couple. Image would be softened by addition of diffusion filter over lens. Musical track would be Streisand's song "The Way We Were" but as performed by The Jo Castle Showband (one of many so-called "function bands" that play at corporate events, garden parties, bar mitzvahs, weddings, on cruise ships, etcetera).

Faaaaaaaaaade out.

7.9   Fade in. Following morning. Sun is still realistic, world still holds together, objects still observe an outward propriety. But life remains just as uncertain and viscous as before. Ear-shaped bed holds spooned forms of Arthur Strewn Middlebrook and Una Calda Bionda. Above them now thrummed high-pressure blue; sky be vibrating with it. Art awakes from that semi-reality, that whiff of life, we call dreams, into world of thought 'n fascination. *Ho! how trusting, feeble 'n foolish we are in our sleep!* he thinks while looking at Una's sleeping form: child in her is still visible in resting eyelids and ghost of her smile; she is traveling through time, and to where? At that moment

Something is *Crook* in Middlebrook

Una stirs, tenderly, oozily, seeking a more perfect horizontal, just as water desires the flattest level.

Art turns on his little bedside TV to lowest volume, ungoops ear —Art's left ear quite sore from Una's passionately untrimmed index finny nail used during bout of whimpering abandonment—and hears Channel Five's "Morning News" announce that Mayor Daley will move his residence north to new condo high-rise near Wabash and Randolph overlooking Millennium Park. Then brief item, something about a Southern Baptist minister being defrocked for "gnostical turpitude."

Art stares at his dressing table. Clean sheet of paper rests thereon and on top of paper, distinctly outlined against its whiteness, is beautifully sharpened pencil with ebony gleam to each of its six facets—like polished gem. It's there for Art to record his dreams. His Jungian analyst insists. *The pencil, an enlightened descendant of the index finny*, Art wittily muses, playin' jarism. Meanwhile, bedroom fills with oils, extraordinary pigments, of a Chicago sunrise delicately brushed across white walls, walls blank except for reproduction of Dutch De Stijl painter, Bart van der Leck's abstract triptych *Mine* (1916). For Art, Van der Leck's paintings do be "ludic aggregates."

When he be in graduate school, Art once transferred Van der Leck composition, abstraction of human figure, onto female nude's torso 'n limbs using colored tape, arranging her pose in perfect simulation of original canvas. Then he photographs result—very postmodern. Once shows Una SX-70 Polaroid of this taped-up model standing, and posing right next to her be young Arthur sitting on edge of his studio table, dangling one foot in air while bracing other against floor in imitation-jaunty pose of operatic rakes in obligatory tavern scene. Art usually managed to cajole handsome women into his studio to participate in his artworks, be they photographs or videotapes.

Art movements—with their manifestoes, diatribes against unbelievers, their freshly coined neologisms—always has profound influence on young Art. After Cubism, it was De Stijl (Neo-Plasticism) that made deep impression on his impressionable mind. He could identify with their utopian aspirations that impinged on everything from easel painting to furniture to architecture to typography. And he preferred Van der Leck to Mondrian, latter being too severely minimalist, too Puritanical, for Art's taste. You can see it too in their portraits. Mondrian: thin, pinched, severe; Van der Leck: portly but robust. During height of his fascination with everything De Stijl, Art "dutchifies" his name, spelling it: Aart. Later Surrealism would mesh with irrationalism of Hippy movement, leading Art into appreciation of Antonin Artaud's extreme declamations (e.g., "All writing's pig shit"), Andre Masson's weird, semi-abstract Dionysian visions, and Max Ernst's collage-like paintings (e.g., *Elephant of the Celebes*).

You can be sure Art's illegal collection of test-tube pigment scrapings taken from famous Art Institute canvases include Van der Leck and Masson. He's looking forward to his next shift change when he will again be working nights in that museum—only time he can have enough privacy to safely scrappity-scrape with his little X-Acto blade. Ho! He now has his greedy eye on a nice Yves Tanguy surrealist landscape. Alone in his assigned patrol area, when he ungoops that weird ear of his, no one can sneak up on him while he at work flaking off pigment.

7.91   Art senses Una stirring. Even before her eyes open, she smiles a smile that is knowing, roused and playful, but also innocent. Art looks at her and thinks, *She's not a woman of the world; she's a woman of somewhere else.*

"Ho . . . Hom . . . Homeslice," drowses Una, slowly sitting up in bed, "we live in scary times." It *is* scary times when a beautiful woman awakens and first thought after consciousness switched on is *that*. "Er . . . Arty, I was dreaming . . . I think about L.A. Hey, notice how often young Hollywood stars, those heart-stopping girls with potent coloring, vanilla teeth, and nice—like Lindsay Lohan—are busted by L.A. cops? You don't hear of that occurring as much in New York, do you? I mean, less celebrities are hassled by police there than on the "Letterman Show." Why?"

"*Blessed Benimming!* Don't get me on L.A. If you so much as loosen your seatbelt or drop your ash or pick your nose, then it's an Alcatraz autopsy with the questions asked later. Those stormtrooper cops out there . . . why any indiscipline, any variation and there's a bull-horn, a set of scope sights, and a coptered pig drawing a bead on your *cabeza*."

"In Chicago, the pigs, they just beat the shit outta ya—simple, no frills. I prefer that," adds Una, her face wavering, then looking into Art's eyes. That face, its small universe, all present 'n correct.

Art turns up TV's volume for Una's benefit, pushes channel-changer to WTTW, Public Television on which authoritative announcer declaims:

> *Yes Susan. Why in Japan, the bulky* manga *pornographic comic books, still comfortingly brandished by 'salary-men' at the end of the 1990s, are now increasingly being super-seded by digital, minuscule images of bodies in animated sexual convulsions. . . .*

Una grabs Art's hand, presses it affectionately. They look longingly at each other.

> *Stephen, only the visually self-disassembled body can explore states of resistance to the digital city. . . .*

"Arty, you know that of 1931 Berlin Christopher Isherwood writes of the increasing street violence there, how rage often exploded suddenly."

"His *Berlin Stories*?"

"I think so. Rage erupting at street corners, in restaurants, cinemas, dance halls. Knives were whipped out, blows dealt with spiked rings, beer-mugs, chair-legs, even leaded clubs. Newspapers were filled with deathbed photos of rival martyrs: Nazi, Reichsbanner, and Communist. Are we well on our way to _that_ level of violence in the U.S.A. today? I wonder. The ideological riffs separating people now reaching record levels, are fast approaching those suffered just prior to Hitler's ascendancy and the subsequent quashing of dissent under the Nazi authorities."

"I fear the same," says Art. "Notice how most media outlets play down or even rarely report on these deep ideological riffs separating extreme Right and extreme Left. And the undercurrent of violence stemming from those riffs, of hate crimes amongst our fellow citizens, is glossed over. Also, do we hear of the increasing number of suicides since the economy went south? No."

"As if only what gets reported is real. Ignore it and it doesn't exist. And when something is reported, it's framed as an _individual's_ problem, rarely as a social problem."

Susan, in its visual form, the postmodern city comprises an intricate set of architectural textures and media screens that surround a scattering of obsolete but ingrained historical scars. . . .

"Say, Arty. Did you ever try your weird ear out on top of the Sears Tower?" Una kicks covers off her legs.

"Actually, yes. I thought . . . you know . . . it'd be superior to my cockloft. But . . . _Blessed Benimming!_ . . . the blaring vocal texture of exclamation was instantly lost in the cacophony of the city's soundscape. I was actually too high up. Couldn't focus the sound enough. Like receiving _all_ the stations on AM radio simultaneously."

The final ambition of digital culture, Stephen, must be the disappearance and replacement of the body, of the city and even of the presence of the visual itself. . . .

"Are you listening to this," asks Una, pointing to TV.

"Peripherally. Peripherally."

"In a state of distracted attention?"

"Yes."

"If you went to Pike's Peak—fourteen thousand feet up—aimed your ear Milky Wayward, would you be able to hear the emanations of the stars, the gurgle of matter going down those black holes?" Una cranes neck around, looks out second-story bedroom window toward cold gray-blue expanse of Lake Michigan. Sky is gray 'n grisly, with interesting bruises, street is damp 'n stickered with leaves.

"I wonder." Art leans over, smells Una's hair. *Ahhh. Vanilla*. He starts to get out of bed. His back emits a solid squeak. Una laughs. He sits up on bed with one stubby leg crossed over other and clasps his shin with his plump hands. A limpid aquamarine sparkles on his auricular finger, gift from Una to celebrate his nocturnal heroics.

"I never noticed that curious photo over there. On your dresser. In that pewter frame," observes Una in indolent Sabbath-speak, rubbing her eyes. "Can I see it closer?"

"Sure." Art more hops than walks over and grabs framed photo. "Here."

"Very interesting process."

"I took an old family flick of my grandfather, part Menominee Indian, part Bohunk, kneeling by me and my new trike, held it up in front of me then had Brittany rephotograph it and me on old black 'n white Polaroid stock. Then I held that same Polaroid up and had her rephotograph me and that new photo. Process was repeated several times, resulting in receding array of images. Like quartering in heraldry. Like looking in opposing mirrors on a ladies make-up table. A seemingly infinite embedding of self-same images."

"Photo-within-photo, ad infinitum."

"Staging what theory jocks call 'the scene of the abyss,' or *mise-en-abyme* in French. Heap PoMo."

"*Mio Dio*, Arty that tricycle."

"What?"

"A cheerless little tricycle with orthopedic attachments."

"I was so small. Premature baby. A fizzled firecracker of a kid. Dinky legs."

"Why choose *that* photo—why not another?"

"If you look at the original, you can see my grandfather's jacket has small frogs ornamenting it! Notice those ugly folds around his mouth that seem to express eternal disgust (put there by his wife); then there's that disturbing purple blotch of a birthmark on his corded temple, with a swelling resembling a big raisin right on the vein. His browned, lanky train-engineer hands touch both my back and the handlebars on the trike. My expression is a sad one. That photo, for me, captures something I've been trying to decipher about my early family-years."

"What's that?"

"At what point did I realize I was surrounded by crazies. Been studying all existing family photos for clues, hard evidence. But only vague intimations so far."

"A cheerless little tricycle with orthopedic attachments," repeats Una thoughtfully as if phrase is Rosetta stone unlocking ancient secrets.

"Ostensible darling, that phrase reminds me of one that often hums in my brain: 'Horrible little black pony, its awful yellow teeth.' Why?"

Something is *Crook* in Middlebrook

"Supposed sweetheart, your mind's a weird place."

"Whatever happened in my early years, by the time we moved to California, I had grown impervious to the gaze of classmates and authority figures—opaque—like a lone dark obstacle in a world where most souls are at least semi-transparent. So I usually made a bizarre impression on both students and teachers. Had to use crafty deception. I learned to fake translucence by bringing to bear on my personality a complex system of optical illusions. But I had only to momentarily forget myself 'n I'd lapse in that self-control keeping my cunningly illuminated facets and angles in play. Then people would say, 'What's wrong with you Arthur?' or 'Art, you're weird.' Then I'd remove myself to some private, safe place—either spatially or mentally or both. I only truly opened up to very close friends. Like Larry Binacka." As Art relates this memory of psychic pain, he grows pallid.

"Poor boy. It always strikes me with great force how unqualified every person in the world is to raise another human being." Her hand reaches out, touches his. "It would be interesting to look up Bob Hoskins, the actor. See if his childhood was also a tormented one. See how he compensated, etcetera. As he and you look so much alike . . ." Una's eyes fill up with tears; her mouth does tremble; look of rapturous intensity does shine forth from her face, as if her whole body do be suddenly giving off light.

"Nature or nurture, huh? . . . The full indecency of my childhood is difficult to put into words, hard to encompass fully, produced as it was of a thousand barely noticeable, overlapping trifles peppered with moments of utter humiliation. Then there's the good 'n bad genes. Els got most of the bad genes in the family."

"Your sister?" Una looks at Art with a silent ecstasy of curiosity.

"Right. During our college years she loved reading Gertrude Stein out loud to me. Liked the, as Els put it, 'sonorousness' of her language. Those iterations, repetitions, with their ironies and parodies. Unpredictable locutions 'n structures scribbled into French school *cahiers* and later typed out by Alice B. Toklas. Els once took a course on Stein by a professor who'd known the Stein family when he was growing up. She used to bring audio tapes home of Gertrude reading her stuff. We'd sit on her bed, turn the lights off, sip Christian Brothers Golden Cream Sherry, and listen. Would love to unplug my ear 'n listen to those tapes again but afraid they'd set off my melancholia."

"You miss your sister deeply, don't you?"

"She was an exceptionally strong, ardent, independent thinker. And very generous with her affections. After getting into teaching, she became very active in the Teacher's Union, picketing."

"Talking about activity, I suppose it's time we get our lazy butts up. I have dubs on the shower first." She rubs her finny firmly, as if it were a cheese grater, under her nose, so that pink tip wrinkles 'n wags. Fact: Una's shampoo has pleasing, subtle scents of late-model Western capitalism.

Something is *Crook* in Middlebrook

7.92   Time, humming evenly, continues to pass. Art, humming unevenly, continues to worry. Suddenly, he's doing skull-time about his divorced, paranoid daddy's days during the bright springtime of his senility. *I remember his smile, just like chilly sunshine, the kind of cold, thin light that the sun throws off early on a winter morning.* Daddy's beliefs increasingly flicker at edgy-edges of a silent-snow, secret-snowfall wherein it is hard to grok diff between existing and non-existing entities and events (this after he goes off his pills that end in *zil* and *ine*)."Orthodox realilty ain't gonna kill me," daddy boasts. His thoughts now are like open razors, his eyes going off like guns as he yells: "Secure the perimeter!" Carries on about founding new discipline—*Sallescape*—which studies the whys and wherefores of room-leaving. Suffers "apophenia," spontaneous perception of connections 'n meaningfulness in unrelated things. When driving, on red alert, he looks more often in rear-view mirror than through windshield. Once, thinking teenage miscreants break into his mobile home for his booze, he hangs new door with 24-gauge hot-dipped, galvanized steel skins and acoustical performance rating coded at ASTM E413-70T-STC 28, complete with four Schlage dead bolts, and color codes four separate keys: red, yellow, green, and blue. A year later (a crisp, cold night) his father fantasizes two short jovial guys hailing from New Jersey that live across street (he imagines they are retired Mafia) are surreptitiously running hoses under his mobile home, piping in some kind of noxious fumes in order to get him to vacant premises so they can buy his property, cheap. (In fact, at this time, his daddy suffers bout of undiagnosed respiratory infection.) Art drops by late that night to return borrowed tools, only to find his *parapapanoid* (Art's term, not mine!) crawling out from under his home (his growl rising to shriek, then sinking to mere pule), dusted in cobwebs 'n dirt, and garbed like Navy SEAL (blackened face, snarling teeth clenching combat knife). "Grrrrr, sheeit! Got da fuckers!" he tells Art, his eyes showing competing currents and temperatures subtly coursing, or as his daddy do describe it: "Son, I get sparks in my long muscles 'n a click in my head like a catching latch in need of oil." Proudly holding up massive knife, he boasts, "Cut those damn hoses. Cemented up one of the heating floor vents too! Mission accomplished! Chalk one up for God 'n Country! Remember The Gipper!" His daddy always takes suspicion into conviction.

At Sunday Mass, imagining his non-Church attending wife having rendezvous with local glamor photographer, he'd rant: "Bless me, save us! The misery of Sundays. I hate her! Hide the knives, lock the doors. I hope she dies." When little Art challenges patriarchal authority, daddy do say: "Me pap. Me pap. You son. You son. Only." He believes in dumb insolence of inanimate objects: What was *in it* for that doorknob that hooks one's jacket as you passed? What was *in it* for that jacket pocket? In lucid moments, he lobs aggressive mantra at you: "I get it; everything is *ulterior*. And *you're* [jabbing firm finny at his paranoid object] in on it too, aren't you? You *are*, aren't you? I don't know how. I'll find out in the end, or my B-seventeen's bombsight wasn't a Norden."

What does one say to *that*? "I think you're experiencing an accounting problem in the marble department?" His daddy teeters on brink of chaotic immensity. Brainfizzed Art can only muster bland professional platitude: "Aaah Dad, remember what your doctor advised you, 'It is the strict adherence to daily routine that tends towards the maintenance of good morale and the preservation of sanity. You are to avoid pointless repinings.' Now this ain't routine! Recall that your therapist cautioned you to not name or elaborate upon anything for which a physical equivalent could not be demonstrated." His dad only angrily replies about how that restriction would negate his Catholicism, etcetera. Lucky daddy die when did; otherwise, might've landed in booby-hatch doing nothing but licking sports on walls.

Maybe that's why I love geology so much. Naming and manipulating things for which a hard equivalent can always be demonstrated. A means of distancing myself from my old man's paranoid fantasies and his compensatory religion. Oh yes! And within geology, my love of aggregates figures my aesthetic predilection for appropriation, bricolage, textual splicing, even out 'n out plagiarism. As for my taste buds, they delight in ceviche mixto, *mixed fruit cocktail, fruit cake, all manner of fusion cuisine . . .* Art's thoughts on this peter out as he looks over at his dressing table. Next to Una's piled up stock-ings he spies small stack of his Gratuitous Giving Cards. These be sealed in envelope with $20 bill and handed out, tools of Art's latest artwork which he dubs: "A potlatch for our PoMo times." Reaches over Una's still-sleeping form, slowly raises himself from his ear-shaped bed, grabs one, thumbs it lovingly.

An Anti-Capitalist Gesture
www.uturn.org/cadeau

While holding this item, Art flashes on remarkable act of kindness his dead daddy do once do. Hot, sunny day. He and his father are walking back from a Seven-Eleven convenience store that do be recently robbed. Art is pimply teenager. They run into old African-American woman in rags begging for food money on street. People ignore her. Some make rude comments. One spits. But Art's daddy does gently coax wobbly woman into nearby McDonald's and sits her down at table. He proceeds to buy her Big Breakfast complete with coffee. To amazement of people in this fast food joint, he nobly serves her at table, bringing over napkins, salt 'n pepper, ketchup, cream for her drink as if he was waiting tables at a four-star restaurant. From outside Art sees him kindly pat her back with his right hand, his left resting on table, wishing her well, as his Adam's apple goes up 'n down in between measured sips of hot chocolate he'd ordered for himself. Recipient of daddy's Gift is smiling increasingly weird smile, as if someone yells *Smile!* and gooses her with plastic fork. Finally his father exits, all eyes in joint on him. *I almost crapperooed my pants with surprise,* recalls Art proudly. Memory of daddy in black ops gear weirdest memory. Memory of dutiful daddy most positive memory. Bipolar memories of a bipolar kind of guy. Ah, in retrospect, Dear Reader, may our tears of sympathy here crystallize as they fall and be worn as pearls in the bosom of our affections!

Una comes out towel-wrapped. She and Art make silent eye contact. Are they recalling their noisy late-night passion? But might it not be a new searching, a searching for things yet to be discovered in each other? If this be film, camera would not reveal which. Although camera close-up would tantalize, revealing tip of Art's nose quivering slightly, around which his face remains almost expressionless, set in rigid mold but with hint of suppressed craftiness about lips, like smuggler sauntering through customs. Nice way to keep audience guessing. Make it ambiguous.

7.93   A week later. Cocktail hour, when all trees be striped with pale bands of sunlight and birds do begin to hurtle through branches in their prenocturnal frenzy. Mr. Bungle flattens against telephone pole in alley near Art's garage. Listens to fruits of bug he placed under Art's deck. Unbeknownst to Mr. Bungle, two beady (adoring) salamander eyes from under back deck and four (suspicious) twins' eyes from down alley to clown's left triangulate their gazes upon him. Like classic moment in Sartrean philosophy, spy is spied upon.

Boettcher Brats first to react. They exchange mischievous glances. Reach into their back pockets and pull out Wham-O slingshots. Each load glass marble into their respective slings, pull to maximum extension and, like David facing Goliath, release. Ho! Two small peewee marbles arc down alley and make simultaneous stinging contact with left cheek of Mr. Bungle's flabby *derrière.*

"Bbuullllss-eeyyee!" yell twins in near unison.

At that precise moment Mr. Bungle be very aware of his dysfunctional over-active bladder. At marbles' impact Mr. Bungle does jump about nine inches, over-sized shoes flopping ridiculously; spurt of urine does soil his new briefs; he turns with expression mixing anger with embarrassment just in time to see Boettcher Brats ass 'n elbows it outta there.

Sitting on deck Una excitedly taps Art's hand, points from deck chair at this harlequin-suited intruder. Mr. Bungle knows jig is up. As Una bitterly reaches inside her dress to adjust recalcitrant bra strap and Art starts to yell, Mr. Bungle runs awkwardly down alley in direction opposite our two retreating bratly recidivists. Stiff, warm breeze blows old Mounds candy wrapper into his face and then carries it off to new surprises among battered trash cans in alley, lodging among box of Pampers, aluminum foil and Coke cans. Someone, several doors down washing big black gas guzzling SUV, spies our fleeing oddball traipsing by and cries indignantly, "Get outta here you fuck!" Turns and thoroughly soaks him head to foot with hose.

"Aww, shit," mumbles Bungle as he tries unsuccessfully to dodge spray. Dripping wet, clown clothes clinging to him like a drowning man, he skulks back alleys, leaping over and around slalom course of new 'n old piles of dogshit and puke from weekend drunks, all way to rear door of boarded up storefront on Damen Avenue above which is defunct antique shop. Pulls back pliable plywood board and slips into rancid old building. Smell of cat urine welcomes him home. Stench still pervasive despite repeated attempts with TV-advertized air freshener to perfume ramshackle space.

Ten minutes later. Stripped to his lantrified Montgomery Ward underwear, Mr. Bungle looks at himself in discolored mirror above washstand.

Something is *Crook* in Middlebrook

He thinks (courtesy of Heinrich Böll) of that clown who weeps in his bath. Tucked under mirror's frame is yellowed photograph depicting faded image of an unknown woman. *A memory left by some past user of this space,* he thinks. Bungle notices faint resemblance to an old flame of his. Their evenings together consist of evening papers, cigarettes, and Parchesi. Yes, Parchesi. He always gets a wonderful emptiness when he plays Parchesi. Musing about this past love, he gratefully stretches out on Army issue cot in rundown safe-house. Lifts head just enough to pop strong pain killer as anodyne for smarting buttock and aches 'n pains of ill-used intelligence. Exhausted, falls asleep, arm and hand out-stretched near sawdusted floor on which new paperback from John Birch Society Press, *Communism in Corporate America*, lies in wait. Nightmares featuring huge salamander perturbs lustful images of his wife's champagne-glass-size tits.

Upon waking, weird poetic musing sluggishly make its way through his drugged clogged grey matter: *I lie for a long time on my right side nursing my left butt cheek and eat nothing, but no voice comes on the wind and no voice drops from the cloud to tape. . . . Between the grey spiders and the orange spiders [slaps his thigh], no voice comes on the wind. Meanwhile, the heavens assemble their dark map and the traffic begins to thin. . . . Wish I was back in Southern California where aphids munch on the sweet meat of the lemon trees and the lawn sprinklers rise and fall. . . . But over my head instead, star-shaped pieces of plaster dip their yellow scarves toward my black black desire. . . . Shit, this business I waste my heart on! Why did I get this assignment? . . . Me, who once infiltrated the Parelli crime family as a handsome, rich, glib guy with connections and a penchant for Parchesi who wore suits made at Savile Row in London, England.*

Lying on his back, Bungle notices large, beat up old sign removed from its original location and hastily nailed onto ceiling; presumably, to stop leak or shore up falling plaster. Reads down oddball list. Stops at surrealistic listing: "Cannibalism Control."

Total Tag Company

4835 N. Damen Ave., Chicago, Illinois
Max Tagg, Proprietor, PH: 312-256-3110

Adjustable Tags, Advertising Specialty Tags, Aluminum Bands, Beak Guards, Bicycle License Tags, Bird Bands, Bird Bits, Bird Blinders, Cannibalism Control, Cat Tags,, Crab Trap Tags, Dog & Cat Tags, Dog Rabies Tags, Ear Punch, Ear Tags, Electrical Markers, Emu Bands, Fish Tags, Gill Net Tags, Horse Saddle Tags, Inventory Tags, Key Chain Tags, Livestock Tags, Plastic Ear Tags, Plate Tags, Plumbing Tags, Poultry Bands, Rabies Tags, Rabies Vaccination Tags, Sheep Tags, Sign Hanging Spirals, Slot Tags, Swine Tags, Tool Check Tags, Tree Tags, Truck Seals, Turkey Tags, Turtle Tags, Variable Size Tags.

Something is *Crook* in Middlebrook

What the . . . Shit. Feel like I'm being eaten alive by my covert needs. That beating I took from that fat, auburn-skinned Menominee Indian on my last assignment—his fists raining upon me faster than a blender mincing onions—and now this. By far would much prefer spying on the East Coast radical chic cocktail party circuit.

Our pseudo Mr. Bungle, known familiarly to his FBI operatives as "Big Les," distractedly thumbs through his well-thumbed copy of *Gynecology for Dummies.* Likes the diagrams. Finally turns on miniature TV set: "Happiness is a Dodge Truck" croaks corny commercial for Kemper Dodge in Grayslake which, their musical jingle claims, is located in "A beautiful place in the country." *Egad!* is Bungle's last thought as he slips into sleep.

7.94   Hours later, Bungle's restive slumber (seasoned with yet another nightmare about past assignment where his cover was a-postal-employee-bitten-by-dogs-and-burdened-with-third-class-mail) be punctured noisy opening of rear door of his funky lair. Groggy. Pries open bloodshot eyes, just managing to discern tall figure in fire pink pants with faint whiff of intrigue familiar to Bungle: *parfum de fantôme.* Hairstyle unmistakable: one yellowy hank be swiped forward from nape of his neck, while other originates from his luxuriant left sideburn; head does look like fudge sundae; he could have put spoon in ear and maraschino cherry on his crown and looked no worse. Such spectacle is hair, Bungle only graduallly notices his visitor reaches under black jacket, aims silencer-equipped Walthers PPK (.38 ACP with bonded bone handles sporting figure of a knight chess piece etched thereon) directly at *him*; assassin's eyes be like trick mirrors and his lips never lose loopy, gold-inlaid smile as he inquires: "Where's *that* file, kemo sabe?" in voice that sounds more like overworked cabby than vengeful agent. If this were film, close-up in *film noir* lighting would reveal face like hatchet and angry red eyes, but with eyelids as soft as a penis freshly bathed. Figure moves slightly as weak light spills across face, mad, muscular face, as though it's bearer pumped iron with his ears.

"Ppppaladin!" *Shit—this guy runs through the world like an open razor 'n knows eight ways to kill with a rolled newspaper.* Gives best teeth-gone-to-hell smile, but looks like horrible idea enters one ear, spins around, confused, goes out through other, leaving behind only warm vestige of terror.

Dead eyes move across Bungle's face like razors. "Did you think your Bungle act, Mr. Bungler, would fool me? I want *that* file on Hoffa back, the one about where his musty bones doth lie. Did you think they'd *not* notice it missing? Why'd ya take it? To sell to the tabloids? An ace-in-the-hole? Actin' the Lone Ranger again, eh? Another class A cluster fuck, yes?"

Bungle (his real name is Les Moore) points to small portable plastic file box. Imposing figure kneels, sifts through disorganized files, keeping gun hoisted on clown whose expression is like perspectival regression toward a vanishing point of misery.

"Thanks," finds file, removes it.

Something is *Crook* in Middlebrook

"Paladin. I . . . I . . .," trying to tame his bronco word-endings and his slippery vowels, even as something monstrous stirred in his bowels.

"We know you've been shadowin' some ear freak 'n ignoring Pietro."

Bungle shrugs. Groans as sharp pain in his ribs gets his attention. "Well, thought this Middlebrook guy was ripe for recruiting—fuck, with that shotgun mike ear he'd be one hell of an asset . . . Just wanted to make sure of his politics, you know."

"I don't know. I do know it's a no-no, kemo sabe. Besides this file business and unauthorized surveillance, you bungled your assigned target, that Alderman. And we haven't forgotten that Wisconsin caper of yours on the Indian Res. How long were you in the hospital after that beating? . . . You know Company policy. Three strikes 'n you're fat ass is O-U-T. Mm, it's so *nice* when one of your peers goes down. You know the feeling? A real buzz, isn't it? So . . . good-bye, Big Les. You're about to become a Big L-e-s-s."

"Fer godsakes, Mr. P., I have the greatest respect for all your parts without exception, because I know that you are a part of Humanity, of which I am also a part, and that you partly take part in the part of something which is also a part and of which I am also in part a part, together with all the particles and parts of parts, of parts, of parts, of parts, of part of parts, of parts. I don't want to be the dearly departed." Intense solar warning flashes in Les's green eyes as he lies in the sawdust of his defenses, with nothing between him and oblivion. THWWAAP goes gun. "UUHH," goes Bungle. (Just like in the movies.) Takes slug directly between eyes. Impact knocks our clown back down on cot. Faces begins to sag like first slide of avalanche. Blood starts to soak fabric, spreading red halo outwards, an uncontrollable mystery on that bestial floor. When a bullet enters human being, it has hysterics. As if it knows it shouldn't be there. Bungle seems to visibly shrink before our eyes—does change tenses. (If this were film, shot would linger over Bungle's vacant eyes as red field behind him, slightly out of focus, expands and expands to fill whole frame.)

Man in black re-holsters his weapon, pulls slim metal flask from suit jacket pocket. Pours extremely flammable liquid over Bungle and around dilapidated room. As he exits, he nonchalantly tosses lit match inside. For further details refer to Chicago Fire Department Arson Investigation case number Ch-445G-68-0247.

7.95   Kozmo Kakopygian born in Getup, Armenia—but lived in Turkey— so speaks Turkish. Loves to tell people that at age sixty he still has what he calls "Getup 'n go" (translation: he suffers immense, insatiable desires, alternating with fierce boredom and attack of yawns). Has one glass eye which looks out of head with bold stare as if there were different brain controlling that peeper, a computer kind of brain that could know everything at once. His social conversations are interminable monologues chockful of bawdy remarks and dirty jokes but also studded with learned references and quotations, lewd but self-ironic anecdotes, philosophical lectures on the world that suddenly morph into gossip, and a bragging drenched in desperation.

Something is *Crook* in Middlebrook

When he sits at his desk, Kozmo must wedge his misshapen buttocks (complete with NTBR, Not To Be Resuscitated, tattoo) down into a black Matrexback executive chair (equipped with 2-to-1 synchro tilt and genuine Italian leather seat). Therein, every day at noon, he attacks his lunch: an Arby's super-size roast beef sandwich painted with wasabi mayonnaise tossed to his girl Friday from over counter by fast-food staff that look like orthodontists. Each time his sexy secretary traipses in with said sandwich nestled in Arby's white paper bag, he, strafed by sense impression, always raves— twice—in his high-pitched, almost falsetto voice: "Bettina, the best goddamn sandwiched I've ever haded." Besides fast food, Kozmo loves natural vistas, mountains, rivers, herds of sheep, buffalo on plains. Likes to see them from the air. He collects Western paintings and builds airplane models. He's member of the International Cloak Society, *Los Amigos de la Capa*.

Like many immigrants, Kozmo has dropped his native Armenian cuisine in favor of American fast food. Claims chewing fast food prepares one's vocalic apparatus to speak English without foreign accent. Says it's based on scientific study by McDonald's University that immigrants who eat fast food regularly learn to speak English quicker and with a truer accent than those who remain enamored of their native fare. Remarks that this was an important point which that anti-junk food documentary film, *Super Size Me*, failed to mention. Kozmo plans on having Paladin look into director Morgan Spurlock's background for any incriminating ammo to use against him—as soon as he finishes his Chicago assignment. *That oddball bastard's supposed to call in today*, he suddenly recalls. Don't let Kozmo's seeming rudeness fool you; at heart, he's really kind and thoughtful to everyone. *Everyone* reminds him of his own son, killed on nine/eleven in tower #1.

Kozmo sits in his office in nondescript Miesian high-rise near Lafayette Square in downtown St. Louis. Outside, sky be theater of possibilities. Inside, on his desk sits meticulously detailed balsa wood model of his Piper

Apache. "She a sweet potato. First plane model I ever builded," he'll tell you. Kozmo flimflams agency into purchasing this 3500 lb. twin-engine bird for Koz's official business trips. When Kozmo turns 120 degrees from that model in his swivel chair, you see that most skin on back of his rude neck be grotesque purplish-red burn scars. Some childhood incident occurring in Ankara suburb involving, as he delicately puts it, "racially insensitive Turks." Beyond this, he reveals little detail. Koz re-adjusts his generous buttocks in elegant chair; wipes last hint of mayonnaise off mustache. About to open file in Top Secret red folder when emerald-green phone on desk buzzes.

"Kakopygian."

"Koz, Paladin here. Reportin' in." He sits on torn leather bar stool in declassé establishment suffering bad clientele near intersection of Milwaukee and North Avenues calling itself Club Anything.

Something is **Crook** in Middlebrook

Photo by Lew Koch

"Passworded?"

"Hey, Koz! You know it's me!"

"Passworded."

"Uh . . . Club?"

"Anything," Koz whispers, giving counter-sign.

"Okay. . . Ah, Koz, Les is *much* less—but had to use extreme measures. Hope your circuits aren't offended, Effendi."

"I'm consternated, Pal; it maded front pages of news like in *Sun-Times* 'n seventh page news in the *Trib*. Sounded like you builded yourself a shit-mess up there, kemo sabe. Now your cover in dangered of bein' blowed."

"But, Koz . . ."

"Alright. But you didn't needed that fire, huh? Okay, after retrieving all bugs from that Arthur fellow's damned dome-house, getup 'n get back here. I getted another juicy assignment for you, Pal: in some midwestern Bulkville, where the superfat bob like barrels over the trampled sidewalks, unregarded, unmocked; where your evening wear will be a palatinate reefer jacket, with plump-winged bow-tie tugging at your neck, and pink cummerbund to conceal your weapon, all standing on a pair of elegant lacquered spats. And—please Pal—keep your expensed account down, down! Accounting has rejected for reimbursement that admission fee for three to that blockbuster art show by Monet or Manet or Money or some such guy. They would not have complained if you'd taken two or four guests in with you, but *three*? They think you're up to your *ménage-à-trois* shit again. So be returned by Greyhound here—cheap 'n less conspicuous—'n sin no more. I'm only go-ing to said this once. Getted it?"

"Ya . . . shit." *Ah, the koz of all my pain*, fusses Pal, knowing this—having agents travel by bus—is Koz's way of meting out a mild reprimand,. "Okay, okay," fun 'n joy missing from his voice. "But send me new documents. I want to be traveling under a new alias and cover—Duane O. Tubb, an itinerant plumber, sucks. Let's try Crispin Fancher, arson investigator. C-r-i-s-p-i-n F-a-n-c-h-e-r. Got it?"

"Getted it, Pal. But shit-can those fire pink pants I" Jots name down. "Go picked new docs up at usual dropped box in, say, twenty-four hours. Okay?" Paladin nods an invisible YES. "*Güle, güle* [good-bye]." Right hand gestures in empty air as if patting some imaginary chick's spongy ass. Gingerly hangs up phone. Spins in chair, returning attention to that red file. It concerns Paladin's latest psychological evaluation.

Paladin slaps cell-phone shut, crosses expanse of cold asphalt indifferent to pedestrians on way to gas station mini-mart near his safe house. Notices Chicago breeze has ruffly quality, it doesn't quite seem to touch ground. He pushes money through slot in bulletproof glass of mini-mart, ordering a 99-cent Big Gulp. Leisurely sips and listens to thunk of gas-pump nozzles halting when tanks are full; scans sans-serif numerals of gasoline prices that are hiked up daily.

Something is **Crook** in Middlebrook

Unbeknownst to Kozmo is fatal fact that in six months and three days he will be put in the past tense, permanently. Be burned to crisp in Piper Apache after it loses left engine on take-off and ends up nose-diving into junkyard, killing one fuckin' vicious junkyard dog too. Last transmission surprised air traffic controllers hear from Piper 007 be sounds of anxious whistle of Koz's sinuses, followed by moist yelps and then very loud: "*Vay* [oops], I'm exploded. Goodbye My Loveds."

Sky becomes pink-streaked exhibitionist in drag; sky lowers, thick-- ens, opals into upside-down topographical map. Koz be buried with his fav plane model. Sobbing widow? A fair-fluffy woman with finnies like thin ivory sticks loaded with jewels; dark eyes raised upwards at corners has faraway, liquid look, lips be double curve of dusky crimson and parted like mouth of some tragic mask. Exact moment Kozmo's remains be lowered into Arlington National Cemetery, Art saunters by Bang Ho's shoe repair *sans* ear goop 'n does hear some southern twanger apreachin':

I AM A MAN OF PEACE AND MUTUAL TOLERANCE; HOWEVER, IT IS A SHEER NECESSITY THAT WE STRIKE OUT AT ALL FORMS OF VICE AND IN- DOLENCE, SET A TORCH TO THE HAYSTACKS OF DESIRE WHEREVER THEY MAY BE FOUND, AND FERRET OUT THE HIDEY-HOLES AND DARK DIVES OF LASCIVIOUSNESS IN WHICH THE GODLESS HAVE CREPT LIKE RATS BEFORE THE HOUNDS . . .

Art's on his way to Pau's establishment for one artery-choking decadent dish: *raie au beurre noir* (black butter skate); to watch butter go from yellow to brown to black and hear Pau yell "Fire in the hole!" while pouring boiling vine- gar into dish's steaming, blackened butter-saturated *court bouillon* with its resultant projections of boiling liquid (Art 'n Pau don thigh boots 'n cover themselves with sou'westers) worthy of siege of some medieval castle.

"*Miam-miam,*" coos Pau. . . . "Yum-yum," echoes Art.

8.0

1970. The West: earthquakes, flood, drought, drugs. Santa Ana winds sweep in from desert, blowing hot 'n dry and continual, leaching skin 'n filling nostrils with dusty crud of dried lizardshit 'n faint, clean scent of baked bones. Dry hills scream with cactus nestled among large boulders. Dead finnies of parched palm trees scratch 'n rattle against hazy yellow sky. Youthful Art is blissed-out, drenched by Southern California sun. A long, slow afternoon in west foothills of San Fernando Valley. Not far from Crash Corrigan's famous "Corriganville" movie ranch with its set for TV series, "Rin Tin Tin," and Spahn ranch where Manson's infamous family hangs out. Art wields military trench shovel and little geologist pick. Excavates on dirt road around deeply impressed dried truck tire tracks made after last week-long rainstorm.

His little sister, Els, records dig with successive snaps of Leica camera on tripod, participating in what they call "A Bro'-Stir Production," a collaborative art piece by brother 'n sister. Large chunk of sun-baked adobe impressed with deep tracks—an *indexical sign* semiologists would say—is awkwardly lifted out of its original site, put on sheet of plywood and placed into Art's blue 'n white VW Microbus. This *objet trouvé* is transported seven miles south to site of new housing construction in foothills where earthmovers have chewed tract home lots into the suffering hillside. Large chunk of dirt is relocated, broken up, stomped on, reintegrated into soil of newly graded lot. Throughout—click, click, click, click—Els records every nuance of Art's performance. Later Art processes film and tips small prints into small photobook documenting this conceptual earth art in which Marcel Duchamp shakes hands with Allan Kaprow and Robert Smithson. Attention art historians. This artist's book, *In Natural Irreversible Processes, Entropy Increases*, is first time Art weds extensive text to imagery, creating a scripto-visual aggregate. Dubs it "a phenomenological artwork," fusing his interest in geology, semiotics, and art. You can bet Art's been reading Kaprow's famous "The Education of the Un-Artist, Part I."

This (sort of) "Happening" occurs during height of hippy movement and only blocks away from Summerhill West, a hippy-style rip-off of British educator A. S. Neill's infamous alternative school for recalcitrant students. In this flower child incarnation of Neill's utopic ideals, young enrollees do-their-own-thing, sport long hair, and suffer little supervision inside huge, white, revamped old three-story farm house plopped on four acres of scruffy land.

Something is *Crook* in Middlebrook

On one of those days in May when California's marine layer turns light gray and dense as water, a daylight that has no source, no direction—Art 'n Els attend student art show there. Strolling through parking lot over-flowing with colorfully painted VW Microbuses is like strolling around inside Timothy Leary's acid-soaked brain. Over din of stereo playing *Lucy in the Sky with Diamonds,* they meet "Star" and "Pan," identical twins attending this anti-Establishment school. They have smart mouths and sport (although they're white) huge curly Afros. Look like they just finished auditioning for bit parts in cast of musical *Hair.*

"What's happenin', bro?" they ask Art in unison, itching their scalps.

"Just a cat, diggin' your scene," replies Art, flashing peace button on his lapel of his threadbare jungle fatigue shirt, doing little jig in his sailor's bell-bottoms.

"Man, do ya really dig what us cats 'n chicks are doin' here?" queries Pan, dramatically tossing his black cape around himself and eyeing Art's Leica.

Star, his sister, is in face paint, beads around her throat, and wears a granny dress with leather sandals strapped to her delicate feet. She has small flowers joyfully poked in her hair. She spins around, showing off her garb. "Groovy, huh?" She smiles sweetly. "When I find Mr. Left (no Righties for me!) we'll have a carefree child, so free of non-straightness that he'll laugh 'n weep from morning til night. Ahhhhh. . . . Say, did you know that it's official—Joyce Haber of *The L.A. Times* says so—actor Paul Lynde gets more fan mail from parents of retarded children than any other performer?"

Els, a confirmed Sartrean, asks Star's brother about his 'life-project'. "In blessed hippydom," explains Pan, "a kind of collective id is being sub-stituted for the image we used to have of ourselves, and this id is our new real self. As our so-called 'principal,' Bon Icar, tell us: 'Coming in here filled with bourgeois hang-ups? Not to worry. Why we shall squeeze you empty, and then we shall fill you with ourselves!' Groovy, huh?"

"Art—everybody's out of control here!" exclaims Els.

"Yep," Art replies, giving his sister a smile so faint it is barely there. "But isn't that the point?"

Els excuses herself to go to ladies room. Enthroned therein, Els has the "Queen's View" of inscriptions flying off in all directions, written in various-colored inks, ballpoint pen, indelible pencil, felt-tip pen, calligraphy brushes, but written with knives too and with Gods knows what other sharp objects. Heap hairy world of passions find substantiation in this tattooing of toilet space surfaces. Genres mix; poems are neighbors with prose passages full of shiny aphorisms; bellowing interjections, surrounded, as if by feathers, with exclamation marks, flutter over entire landscape. Stall door in full bloom. There was, notices Els, everything: pieces of advice, suggestions for improve-ment, piggish grunts, howls of flesh rearing their ugly heads, elegiac witti-cisms, warning and threats, nasty and tasty invective, quotes, toasts, auto-graphs with dates 'n cities, cunning hints about bigger things to come, heart-rending appeals and most complete 'n utter nonsense.

Something is *Crook* in Middlebrook

Art notices tall man straightening his shoulders as if he'd just woken up; his eyes glow with a dull sheen; touch of gray in his beard.

"Bon Icar," whispers Pan to Art, nodding in his direction.

He appears to be around thirty-seven years old. In costume, he wears elegant velvet outfit, what Cosimo de' Medici might have worn as everyday duds around his *palazzo*. Poking through opening in his sandals are toes so twisted they looked as if they'd been grafted on. Looking around him like a Duke on his battlements, he tucks remains of a second tofu dog in his delicate mouth, between lips so thin they could be earthworms dyed red; he then runs his long finnies on his right hand through his long, straight hair. With his left, he clutches a worn book, *Yoga Made Easy, Eight Steps to Enlightenment, The Swami Speaks*. Art overhears snippet of his encouraging conversation with one dejected student artist whose work on display be butt of jeers by classmates: ". . . but remember what the *I Ching* says: 'Perseverance Furthers,' ya grok"

Ya grok? Phrase sticks in Art's mind. Recalls it comes from Robert Heinlein novel, *Stranger in a Strange Land*. Art will pepper his speech with this phrase all his adult life. His use will, in turn, get acquaintances to adopt it.

Els returns, snickering. "Arty, I just saw some great graffiti. Jotted one down for my collection: 'Matt, Cat, Kitten—I love the man I can decline.' Smart, huh?"

"I thought the scene was supposed to be no hang-ups, free love?"

Those twins rattle on about having lived for awhile with their parents in a psychedelically-painted dome-home in Drop City, famous hippy commune in Trinidad, Colorado; they wax hip-eloquent about acid rock groups (Jefferson Airplane, Country Joe and the Fish), books (A.S. Neill's *Summerhill,* Cleaver's *Soul on Ice*), psychedelics ('shrooms versus acid), our military-industrial complex (relationship between USA's GNP and Vietnam War), as well as esoteric arguments for metempsychosis (i.e., transmigration of souls).

Art 'n Els are impressed (nay, *blown away*) by intelligent, confident, smart ass aroma these young flower children exude. Standing perplexed before twins's artwork—scribbles daubed with creamy Viridian, Lead White, Chromium Green, Lamp Black, purple, and brown—Art 'n Els are less certain about its quality. (In retrospect, Art has to admit their paintings anticipated Jean-Michel Basquiat's work by ten years.)

8.1   It's around this time—when sky be active with galactic smudges 'n communication satellites—that Art begins to formulate dreamy ideas about ideal society, redistribution of wealth, closing of churches, liberal child-rearing strategies (including new theories of toilet training), social role of art, feminism, etcetera. He starts to check out stacks of utopian/dystopian books from local library. Starts with Thomas More's *Utopia* and wacko notions of Charles Fourier, then works forward through well-known and obscure texts. Later, for his "Art and Urban Life" class, Art assigns his students Berkeley professor Ernst Callenbach's visionary 1970s book, *Ecotopia,* for it makes certain degree of sense, even *seems* to make certain degree of sense. Unfortunately, most of his suburban pupils ridicule concept of sustainable, non-consumerist society. A society *sans* auto roar, tacky malls, or endless mayhem displayed on Playstations? No can do!

If this were film, editor might ironically run voice-over narration, "Like Sisyphus, Art keeps trying and trying to stimulate youthful rebellion in his young audience," juxtaposing this sound bite to monochromatic flashback wherein newbie professor Art, nervous, obliviously paces through dog shit while lecturing to his class as students scream, laugh, and run for fresh air.

Art, a rad, becomes increasingly disillusioned as over years bored youth sitting before him turn increasingly conservative, visionless. Hard to believe how quickly young folk exchange Star 'n Pan's idealism and countercultural ethos for social indifference and ROTC classes.

8.2   Midwestern sunset be like orange mousse squeezed through trees dying of Dutch Elm disease. Art's perched on barstool high up in his cockloft surveilling. He muses: *It's hard to remember how at sunset the wind moved and the reeds clicked behind my uncle Don's red and white cottage on Pelican Lake. That Wisconsin cottage, not equipped for winter, with those granite boulders popping up out front which Els and I and cousin Bobby always climbed on as kids; that lake with its sudsy shoreline and persistent Musky fishermen with their huge lures while the fish do their fish thing: swim with their shimmy, then rise to gulp waiting bugs; the bugs oblige, they go along with the deal. Oh, how those little bundles of wind in the marsh grass chased their own tails, skidding across the water. Then the approaching storm: perch-belly white of the sky turning the color of a fish's flanks and back, then that yellow rending of the sky above the fishermen in their boats; it is an agony made into a thing. Distant rumble of thunder across the lake like cry of pain. Would be easier now to hear it all. How sweet is yesterday's noise. The ear inhabits being as a man inhabits his home.*

Sweet, except for yesterday's noise of feminist protest rally in front of dome-home. Noreen, still grinding her teeth over fact Art can get earful of Pogacnic's domestic squabbles and lusts, contacts local feminist activist group, BAD GIRRRLs, through Deena's contacts at Northside Battered Women's Shelter. Noreen rouses women to rail against Art's pernicious "male hearing," auditory version of pernicious "male gaze." So last night at 6:40 p.m., for forty minutes, some forty women, average age of forty, sporting Birkenstock sandals and large protest signs punfully reading DOWN WITH THE MALE (H)EAR, march outside his domicile. Channel Five News truck comes by with young smart aleck reporter and Art and his dome-home are publicly humiliated on 10 O'clock News. Thereafter, Art notices increase in women in old model Volvos and Chicago cops in squad cars slowly moving past his home.

8.3   Art's up in his cockloft. *Ah, tree frogs in the dark. That small brass of the natural world is drumming and what I want is nothing to them.* Checks

Something is *Crook* in Middlebrook

 his compass reading so as to aim super-ear at Déja Vu, White Supremacist hangout. He's done this drill numerous evenings: thoroughly cleans his weird ear of waxy cerumen with Q-Tips (giving him heap good Q-gasm) and tapes on his brilliant invention (paper towel core focus-extension). Ready for maximal hearing event. Finds that using this home-brewed extension does cut off annoying extraneous crackle of electricity coming from large transformer hanging half block right of building Art be aiming at. Art closes his eyes. Pushes hard on eyeballs until spectacular inner fireworks go off and he hears sound of his own synapses snapping. *Clears circuits,* he thinks. Now fully concentrates. As first sounds start to penetrate his *vas bene clausum*, just before he starts to *reflect upon* what he hears, Art experiences weird sort of crossover: both hears/is heard as spark of sensing/sensible is lit, and Art enters primordial *earelationship* to world; as Flesh that neither knows if it is hearing or heard, he is caught up in things as auditory fire starts to burn, a burning that will reduce in intensity as he *thinks* about what he hears, but will not cease entirely until ear goop be again firmly in place. In moment of self-reflexivity, Art fancies himself as handsome character playing modern day Orpheus/Poet in Jean Cocteau's film masterpiece *Orphée* as this man sits in his garaged car listening to, and puzzling over, many mimicries of poetic BBC broadcasts that activated French Resistence fighters on D-Day. Attempt to unravel occult trading of metaphor where what counts be no longer *manifest* meaning of each word, but of *lateral* relations, kinships that are implicated in their transfers and their exchanges. But what he gets instead is brutal smack in ear of announcer yelling (to audience's cheers) dictates of alien moral system:

WHITE SLUTS 'N NOT SO GENTLE MEN: WAS MIGHTY WHITE OF YA TA GIVE JOYCE AND 'ER WHITE-POWER PUPPET, ROYCE, A GOOD HAND. PUT YER THUMBS ON YOUR EYEBALLS 'N PUSH HARD TO SEE THE FIREWORKS FOR WE FINALLY GOT 'EM HERE, OH YAH. DIRECT FROM AUSTRIA WE HAVE THE BALLS, THE UNMITIGATED GALL, TA GIVE YA *DER BLUT-HARSCH* SINGIN' "THROUGH NIGHT AND BLOOD TO LIGHT." A BLOOD-IN-THE-FACE BLOND-BEAST BAND, THEY'VE MADE THEIR MARK IN CHEERFUL EUROPEAN DENS 'N BEEN CHEERED IN DENMARK; HAVE ROCKS IN THEIR BONES, STREAMS RUNNIN' THROUGH ARTERIES, LIGHT PENETRATIN' EYES, AND A FINE FORCE COURSING THROUGH THEIR NERVES, MY DROOGIES. YAAAH FUCKIN' A—OR SHOULD I SAY FUCKIN' B?

Racist blather of band, like whiskey, is exciting in its first effects and stupefying in those which follow.

Disgusted, sour-mouthed, spinning his *ear*-ly roulette wheel, Art now aims weird ear at simulacrum of Irish pub, Totty's, on Irving Park Road and picks up this auditory gem (30-ish male voice seasoned with inflection of low-class Paddy) wafting therefrom:

> **. . . THAT MARTHA ME WIFE LEFT ME IN A YAREPLANE ON TH' BLOODY CHAMPAGNE FLIGHT BACK TO BRITAIN, WHERE, SHOR 'N BE GORY, TOTTY, DA QUEEN IS DA FOUNTAINHEAD 'N MOTHERLODE O' A SNOBBERY THAT POISONS DA DANK AIR O' ENGLAND WITH DA SMELL O' BRUSSELS SPOUTS ACOOKIN' TO A SOGGY GREEN PASTE. BRUTE FORCE 'N RUDDY IGNORANCE! BUG-GER DA QUEEN! HEH, TOTTY? 'NOTHER BLACK 'N TAN HERE, ME LIKES ME GUINNESS ON TOP ME BASS, LIKE ME LIKES TO BE ON TOP ME WIVE'S BIG ASS. HAR, HAR!**

Blessed Benimming! Sound makes Art taste unpleasant mixture of ink 'n day old fish 'n chips wrapped in soggy month-old Belfast newspaper dripping with excess of rancid malt vinegar. For minutes, Art's senses be deranged: thousands of taste buds be extinguished by exposure to wee bit of sound from this IRA word-bomb.

8.4   Ho! How exotic that ear is. Decomposing simultaneous auditory and gustatory sensations *developed in time,* Art can identify three stages of hearing/tasting which constitute a kind of narrative: 1) *direct* — when auditory favor/flavor starts acting on the front of his tongue; 2) *complete* — when favor/flavor moves to the back of his mouth; 3*) reflective* — the final moment of judgment as to precisely *what* he tastes. And what he tastes as he overhears throbbing sound and Jew-baiting lyrics of *Blutharsch* is like small boy chewing on big lumpy scab freshly peeled from recently scuffed knee or elbow—paradoxically pleasant (music) and gross (lyrics) at same time. Yep, Art confirms this odd flavor with two tongue movements: *spication* (tongue assumes shape of a spathe) and *verriculation* (tongue sweeps around mouth).

When Art hears convivial stuff—like sigh of lovers—his physiognomy glows, his color heightens, his eyes sparkle, while his *cabeza* cools down and gentle warmth penetrates his entire body and he tastes gourmet. His visage becomes like softly radiant painting, illuminated from within. But when Art hears bad stuff just opposite occurs. In this instance now, his physiologic response (echoed in his ambivalent taste sensation) splits the difference: he responds pleasantly to texture/grain and tempo of music 'n voice and to formal, poetic qualities of language used, but heap negatively to hideous beasts of dogmatism and racism clawing at margins of that language.

Art pivots off bar stool, regoops weird ear, spirals down his spiral staircase. Needs comforting walk in surprisingly cool summer evening; puts on his light sweater with circular badge pinned thereon reading DON'T WORRY ABOUT ME that makes Art into walking paradox who draws attention to his desire not to draw attention. Like Rosetta Stone, this badge be key to unlocking mysteries of Art's psychic life.

Something is *Crook* in Middlebrook

8.5   Sunrise, a gaudy polychrome sky—mauve, cerise, puce—so garish that Art can hardly take his eyes off it as he walks east toward museum. Has to be on job way way early. Momentous day. German photographer, Thomas Struth, is back at The Art Institute of Chicago with his view camera in tow. In 1990 this international art figure photographs museum visitors (and guards who are there to be *unseen*) standing before large paintings, such as Caillebotte's *Rainy Day* (1877), and has these color images enlarged to huge dimensions. These prints, in turn, find their way into major museums around the globe. Because of this event, added museum security is needed. Art is called in on what is usually his day off.

Gossamer threads of Indian summer drift about; freshly dropped autumn leaves flee before determined wetbacks with noisy leaf-blowers. Standing in line and paying good money are the museum visitors: flashlight-faced Japanese, balls-talking bumblers, culture-vultures, students, loners, pick-ups, vituperative interpreters with tourists in tow, determined samplers and heroic consumers spun off by our thrashing city whose need to consume is exacerbated by drive to compensate for the "don't touch" distance demanded in the galleries by unleashing acquisitive desire in the museum store. Meanwhile, German photographer tows small cart laden with camera gear around various galleries. Throughout his eight-hour shift Art keeps trying to wheedle his way into Struth's composition, but his duties always him take to different galleries than where this Kraut is shooting. Hip docent explains art to school kiddies: "Then you get *Mo*-net and *Ma*-net, that's a little tricky, *Mo*-net was dude who did all the water lilies 'n shit, *Ma*-net did Bareass On the Grass 'n shit; later you get *Mar*-cel Duchamp, he's the devil in human form."

Finally at 1:43 p.m.—success. Art and Struth occupy same gallery area at same time. Moving slowly, Art casually positions himself back-to-camera; he then turns slightly left, nonchalantly unbuttons his uniform coat to better display his chubby profile. His hands are innocently entwined behind his back, in full view of camera. He wants to appear oblivious to Struth's presence. But his left ear is ungooped so he clearly hears sound of film holder go into camera back. Can audit Struth's breathing too. When Struth holds his breath to press cable release, Art knows this is that split-second of calm before Struth clicks shutter. Art very quickly makes subtle obscene finny gesture so camera records him—left of center, twelve feet from camera, eight paces in front of large Medieval panel painting—flipping off Struth. As artist does neither scream nor reconsider his shot, Art assumes (correctly) that his mocking gesture went unnoticed.

Ruin my day off will ya! Just wait until that art bozo has that one blown up to mammoth size, snickers Art to himself. *I'll bet he hollers out* 'Ach! Dreck! Himmel, Arsch und Zwirn!' *followed by more choice German cuss words, one of which,* 'Verdammt Fettsack' [damn fatso] , *is sure to be a reference to my girth. Har-har. Wish I could be there to see it.*

As if unawares he was just photographed, Art makes his way slowly to another gallery. His weird ear picks up sound of zipper being undone. Notices to his left tall man starting to take a Kodak KB28 35mm camera out of its case. Feeling more kindly than usual, Art doesn't yell out, embarrassing this fellow. Instead, he approaches and quietly 'n gently busts this well-meaning tourist for attempting to record his pert wife in front of Georges

Something is *Crook* in Middlebrook

Seurat's huge canvas, *La Grand Jatte*. Confused man doesn't understand why he's forbidden to make quick snap when, "That damn fellow in the adjoining gallery can walk around all day shooting with impunity." From fact that man uses word "impunity" Art surmises, *This guy's educated. Maybe even a lawyer.* Art can't muster convincing response. Just shrugs and replies, "In the art world, my dear sir, shit happens." Disgruntled, man and wife walk off shaking their heads.

An hour later, Art's workmate, Mala Gradecido, joins him on his afternoon coffee break. Even in the unisex guard's uniform, she's pleasant to look at. Art admires her pluck. She carries over to Formica table well-thumbed copy of Sharlene Nagy Hesse-Biber and Michelle L. Yaiser's collection of scholarly essays, *Feminist Perspectives on Social Research* in one hand, her steaming grande vanilla latte in the other.

"*Orale ese, gusa?*

"*Orale, esa*. My dogs are sure barkin'."

"*Ujole,* see they called you in today too. *No justo.* . . . *Sí,* know what you mean; we must walk ten miles a day in here. With your *el oreja loca*, I assume you can hear *my* dogs barkin'?" Mala's facial muscles sag, sure sign of fatigue.

"Yep. What pisses me off is how little warning we were given about this Struth visit. Had to cancel some important plans. But I got my *revancha*." Art details his expert monkey wrenching of Struth's photograph. He stands up and imitates position 'n gesture, much to delight of this *pochista* whose eyes do twinkle-winkle.

"*Tripioso.* I hate all this art-about-art shit anyway. Art inbreeding. And as for this stuff being called an 'institutional critique of dominant structures,' *El profe,* I don't see us *peones*'s *pay* here getting any better despite all the dumping on museums by postmodernist critics and artists."

"You got that right, *esa*. These semiotic critiques of dominant ideology and master narratives are too idealist, they leave the material, economic inequalities largely uncritiqued, undeconstructed. Moreover, just read any mainstream museological literature out there and one quickly learns that the duty of the contemporary museum is to improve, design, or deliver experience, a *better* art experience, much like ads that promise stronger muscles, improved memory, or longer orgasms!"

"*Simón, ese,* you hit the snail on the head."

"Nail, Mala, nail."

"Speaking about our barking dogs, my grandmother—she hails from Matamoros—told me about an old Yaqui Indian recipe for strengthening and relieving sore legs 'n feet. She swears by it."

"Shoot."

"According to her, one makes a decoction of sage, rosemary, thyme, lavender, camomile flowers, and melilot, stewed in white or red wine; or else makes some lye with oak leaves, a little vinegar, and half a handful of salt. This, she claims, 'dissipates gross and viscous humours.' I haven't tried it yet myself."

Something is *Crook* in Middlebrook

"God bless your dear grandmummy! But did she mean for one to drink that shit or rub it on the limbs?"

"*Quién sabe.* I . . . I . . . Well . . . She didn't say," she teasingly shoves Art's shoulder with her right hand, "Okay. I forgot to ask." She nervously brushes back her dark, thick hair with her elegant right hand then sips her latte with her left. For most part, Mala is ambidextrous due to fact she always sat at her mother's right side while they watched television 'n munched on bowl of goodies in her mom's lap. Years of grabbing at that delicious home-popped popcorn with her *mano izquierda* expertly trained those nimble left digits for any task. Not only can she sign her name with both hands, but she can fluently write her name backwards! A feat that always astonishes Art. He loves fact that Mala never tires of demonstrating this gift upon polite request.

"Mala, do it again. Write your name backwards, *pleeeease.*"

"*Para qué?*"

"Because . . . well . . . it supports my thesis that there's a parallel universe, just the reverse of ours, that touches our universe at times. Matter versus anti-matter. I think we might find those places of invagination where our world turns, like a sock pulled inside out, into that other world. I mean there might be someone like me who is *skinny* and whose *right* ear is super-sensitive. Just the reverse. Ya grok? Your signature gives me hope this world can be discovered." Puzzled expression on Mala's brown face. "Okay. I know it sounds dumb. But shit, Mala. Sometimes I think I can hear sounds from that other world. Jumbled, yet familiar sounds . . . as if an audio tape be playin' backwards on very low volume."

"*Tripioso.* . . . I don't know what to say."

Teasingly he demands, "Say it backwards when you figure out what you want to . . ."

"*Hombre nuevo/hambre nueva,*" groans Mala. "New man your new hungers are inexplicable, *sí*? . . . *Oye*! Break's over. *Hasta luego, profe*!" Mala waves good-bye, scurries back to her duties relieved she can politely make her escape. *El profe seems to get stranger every day*, she silently observes.

Bite by slow bite, Art leisurely finishes his onion bagel. *I ain't rushin' outta here. No sir!* Licks his finnies with a flourish. Meticulously folds his paper napkin. Brushes off bagel crumbs. Body language signals how reluctant he is to go back to pacing gallery floor.

8.6   This slow eating is antithesis to way Art eats during his youth. As dinner table conversation is strained because of weird, unpredictable behavior of daddy, Art 'n Els learn to vacuum up their chow in record time (earns Art nickname of "The Hoover"), help their mommy rush through washing dishes, then flee to safe haven. In single-story, L-shaped house of some 2500 square feet, Euclidean geometry problem is how to put maximum distance between intimidating physical presence of crazy daddy and small helpless childhood bodies. Daily solving this problem does prepare Art 'n Els to excel in high school geometry class. Not surprisingly, ellipses, trapezoids and parallelo-grams become Art's fav geometric figures as they are distortions of more perfect figures, symbols of how Art perceives his life is profoundly *skewed* from normality. In terms of fashion, this penchant for imperfect forms carries over into Art's ill-developed sense of *couture.* Dirty blue jeans, a T-shirt under a tweed sport coat is as formal as young Art gets. Later, his attitude toward his dress and grooming will take dramatic reversal. Els gives him *Collected Writings of Ralph Waldo Emerson* for Christmas. After reading Emerson's remarks that "the sense of being well-dressed gives a feeling of inward tranquillity which religion is powerless to bestow," Art immediately ceases his transcendental meditation lessons and obtains a Neiman-Marcus credit card. At 25, he is born-again into a brave new world of tasteful clothes and inner peace. Art lives with contradictory feelings: hates capitalism, loves consuming. In late 1990s Canadian theorist Arthur Kroker identifies this psychic mechanism, terming it "spasm" and defining it as "The state of living with absolutely contradictory feelings all the time, and loving it."

Mind you, up to this point in his young life Art is still a virgin! Within weeks of his transformation, Art manages to seduce (or be seduced by, one can't be sure) one Kiki de Montparnasse, ex-hooker (it be said she can stare her way through seven pairs of leather pants) with impossibly beautiful legs, dogwood white teeth, eyelids perpetually at half-mast over ice-blue-orbs, all born on aerodynamic bone-structure born-again as 1970s-era feminist artist residing in large loft in Venice, California. Meets her at First Annual Dada Prom held in old warehouse in East L.A. She gets his attention with lips parted generously, holding out promise of erotic encounter so strange that it might jump species barrier. She sports Marie Antoinette wig over her shaved head, carrying well-thumbed paperback copy of Salvador Dali's *Hidden Faces,* and declaring: "Both capitalism and communism are powerless before omnipotence of Desire." According to Kiki, politics, like astrology, is totally spurious system of explanation. "My genes have guaranteed," she boasts, "I should never in my life commit an act of Marx." When Art starts to object she stands arms akimbo and adds: "You take for granted that politics, a sort of racket, is the be-all and end-all of life, and you have never taken notice of love or mystery as they appear in the world." What she's into is creative *weirdness: "Kraft durch Unheimlichkeit,* Strength through Weirdness, is my motto," she asserts as she reaches into her erotic fur-covered/lined purse cum vagina and pulls out big dildo shaped like a long black rat and tickles Art's bearded chin with this weird instrument of pleasure (this is only for male's benefit, she uses geisha device, *rin no tama,* ball-suspended in-liquid-within-ball). Art swoons. She's big fan of Venetian poet Giorgio Baffo.

"You just gotta read Baffo-the-Obscene," Kiki urges, "that famous syphilitic whom one can esteem as the greatest Priapean poet who ever lived and who was at the same time one of the most lyric poets of the eighteenth century. Say, ya know. You'd make a good *monachino.*" She gets off correct nod 'n smile, rather ghoulish in effect, as though she just looked up from pinching a baby. Art's face silently asks, *A what?* "A seducer of nuns, she replies. "Why, you're so . . . innocent. Sweet. You could have sex with them and they would still feel their they're virgins!"

"Thanks."

"Just joking." But she isn't; senses Art is still virgin territory.

Something is Crook in Middlebrook

"Hey, ya wanna see some videos of my performance work or maybe see a trashy Warhol film?"

"Sure." They exchange phone numbers.

For their first date, Kiki insists on seeing Andy Warhol's film *Kiss,* irrefutable epic of kisses, compendium of 13 osculations juxtaposing 2 orbicularis oris muscles in state of contraction against 2 other such muscles during continuous run of 100 feet of film (running time about 3 minutes each kiss). Overstimulated, they return to Kiki's place. In this "flesh back" we find Art luxuriating on Kiki's king-size water bed. Casually notices paperback book on Art Deco night stand, *Get Obsessed and Then Let Go,* and solved *New York Times* crossword puzzle, but none of the words jibe with clues given.

At first he is self-conscious due to odd-shaped birth mark on his left hip and hernia operation scar on his left side. She recounts case of California fruit fly, *dropsophila pseudo obscura*, whose breeding habits show that female fruit fly prefers males with rare markings over fruit flies with statistically average markings. "I'm like those female fruit flies," she coos. At first she's on top in reversed position where her shoulder blades become an expressive human face. Soon they be immersed in polymorphous perversity 'n systematic derangement of senses. His insides feel like some crazy million atoms of soft blue. *I wanted to give my soul to you Kiki*, reflects Art years later. Fact: it's an interesting statement in a grammatical sense in its use of the perfect tense, placing desire in the past; the past is the verb tense you can never fully trust as it relies so much on memory.

Then blindfolds, then masks, then mirrored shades—so they can see each reflected in each other's eyes—topped with colored wigs—she wears blue, he red—followed by edible erotic lingerie; interlocked limbs, tongues and sexual organs, rippling and throbbing in mysterious rhythm abound. Ho! Sex removed from marriage and reproduction, removed as far as possible from Puritanical strictures of his childhood Catholicity. They make love four times before Art leaves around 3 a.m. Once he's hooked on this ex-hooker, she gradually, over several months, moves their relationship to wonky heights of imagination, teaching Art new perversion Salvador Dali terms "cledalism" (Pau calls it *amour-voyance*) whereby things are taken to such an extreme, our lovers attain" torridgasm" (Kiki's term) without touching one another, by purely mental means. Conceptual sex, at first novel, rapidly becomes boring. Yes, as a conceptual artist he prefers dematerialization of artwork, but not dematerialization of Art's sex work. Ho, no! He desires full body contact. "You keep watching me as if I'm something you were just about to eat, damn it. Don'tcha know delayed gratification is what distinguishes us from printed circuits?"

Speaking about eating. Forgot to mention that this art-tart cooks up god-awful food (e.g., *veau engagé*) in battered and blackened cookware, serving her fare on horribly funky dinnerware; spoons and forks—black and twisted—appear to be survivors from old A-bomb test. To add injury to insult, Hispanic gang members hanging around environs of Kiki's place regularly smash driver's side window on Art's little green Honda 600 coupe; he tires of driving home on Freeway at wee hours with damp, cold wind slapping his face all way back to his live-in hillside studio, only to have to file insurance forms (in triplicate) day after.

Something is *Crook* in Middlebrook

Frustrated, pacing his studio, biting his nails, Art eventually breaks off with this touchless automatic wonder. But not after rationally assessing his situation. Pulling out his black, hardcover journal, he turns to a fresh page and methodically lists his assessment of pros 'n cons of their relationship:

PRO	**CON**
- gorgeous, weird, sexy girl	- She likes cledalism
- alive to the world and its quirky opportunities	- I desire elegant cuisine to precede real physical sex play, but Kiki just can't provide necessary touch and aesthetic satisfaction
- her words always wind up the the way it feels to wake up wide awake	
- makes plurilinguistic puns: refers to *camarones* (shrimp) as *cabrones,* calls brothels *lechería*	- Bad mornings after - apolitical
- has a great name	- name's a rip-off

Cons out-number pros. Ergo, *quod erat demonstrandum*. Art opts out of his first passionate relationship for indeterminate period of celibacy: "Like some wines our love could neither mature nor travel," he tells me. Only memorabilia he keeps to remind him of this bohemian fling is one very bad, oddball poem she mails him after he breaks off their relationship:

Flesh-Back
by Kiki de Montparnasse

A straw-colored hope sometimes glimmers/ in the back-rooms of cafés, when/ one sun-ray's enough to light up the gold in the beer/ and everyone there turns like an avid flower toward the flesh-flash of sky fallen on asphalt,/ oh old mirror of benzine/ where the long-haired urchin you once were in another life/ will come back to stamp with his vengeful foot/ shit shit and again shit/ at unstressed provincial eternity./ Yes. Ya, it's half past sick of the cock./ Time to go.

And so hot meal of romance be cooled by dull gravy of common sense.

8.7   Much to his amazement, Art see her one more time, few years hence, on TV documentary on Skinhead couples. Ho! She's changed her name *again*: to Varicella Zoster (born Miltonella Westenra to pedantic Milton scholar at Carnegie Mellon U.). Once a beautiful body and personality to burn (when Art knew her) now evilly lovely wife of Freder Zoster. Once all sweetness, now adamantine, heartless cruelty (she'll put the pox on you); once pure as driven snow, now steeped in voluptuous wantonness; once destined for pulpy suburbs of marriage, now hardened by loveless encounters with scores of low-life. Now sports gaunt Goth look: hair dyed black and center-parted, so it seems two opposing forces meet and with bristling difficulty contend. Black lipstick, mascara like a burglar's eye-mask, numerous piercing, black-laced Stolzenik Seg boots, black micro-mini skirt, and black T-shirt with handgun emblazoned in white and light grey on front. Interviewer probes her addiction to collecting souvenir shotglasses and anything related to clowns. Instead of ejaculations "damn!" or "shit!" she prefers "zunk!" According to her shrink, Varicella subject to mood swings characteristic of mild cyclothymic disorder.

Her husband lives in body hammered out of raw experience, things suffered 'n done to extreme limits. Temperature inside his head be always feverish. Left eye is hard to find beneath deep sag of its lid; lower rim of iris be visible, shut off in corner. That eye twists away from his nose, with brow straight 'n tilted upward. Raised seam of scar tissue traverses lid. Makes him look like man with a history. He has a history. There are evening streaks in white of that eye, sense of blood sun. Eye has kind of autonomy, a personality of its own, giving this Skinhead splitness, an unsettling alternative self. Surely, things have happened in his life. They call him Freek; not for his looks so much as fact that at early age, in reform school, he demonstrates visual acuity for design 'n draftsmanship.

But I digress. Back to Art's guardly duties.

8.8   Art turns back on his Motorola walkie-talkie. Calls into Security that he's now off break. Straightens his tie. Polishes his badge. Jauntily walks back into clatter 'n hum of gaggle of gawking tourists. To counter brain-numbing boredom, for remainder of his shift Art ungoops that weird ear of his, scans assiduously, then hovers around anyone he hears speaking with southern accent. Wants to make 'em subtly uncomfortable with his intimidating presence, slowly walk in front of them when they are looking at a painting, let guard chatter from his walkie-talkie annoy them. Listen in on their naive comments about art. *And if it's a Texas accent, I'll find something to bust 'em for, by gar!* he wickedly muses, rubbing his hands together in gleeful anticipation. But Art's real animosity be reserved for Daevid Ruinart (pronounced "Day-vee' Roon'-arr"), museum's photography curator, whose penchant to turn conceptual photographic artworks enlisting *the dumb snapshot* as document into poster art for modernist formalism always irked Art. When Ruinart installs show co-opting aesthetic subversiveness of Ed Ruscha's conceptual photobooks, Art sends him that notorious little postcard: *Instead of Writing a Review of Your Show I Filled Out This Form.* Ho! So it is in these dark basement galleries that Art plays martinet guard to perfection: chasing visitors out with his severe prohibitions, even playing at being a docent to unsuspecting visitors so he can pan Ruinart's ruinously-conceived exhibitions.

Ho! Shame on you Art! You seem to have temporarily foregone your solemn oath to Larry B. as mild-mannered fellow to aim at spreading friendliness to all.

As if to punish him for his nastiness, fate sees to it that youthful teenage visitor to Museum comes into Art's purview. Ho! Youth who could be clone of his long-dead buddy, Charles Hillary Hayduck. Art's knees get weak. His throat tenses, his mouth goes dry. His blood pressure rises. "Chuck," as all his school buddies call him, is for ever painful memory. Poor Chuck. Chuck the shy guy in high school. Chuck the closeted homosexual in a Catholic environment. Over his high school year book photo he scrawls: "Dissatis-faction with the flesh does not leave a man relieved of his passions." Chuck the brilliant math whiz raised by ignorant low-class slobs who can't appreciate his genius (so high a mental metabolism as his alters things by merely seeing them afresh). Chuck, who to get out of his fist-punctured parents' house, occupies room he builds in family garage. He proceeds to cover walls of his snuggery not with evidence of physical violence, but floor-to-ceiling cut-outs of comic strips *B.C.* and *The Wizard of Id.* Chuck who turns teenage Art onto music of Bob Dylan. He is incapable of doing anything in moderation. Chuck whose quips (like "Fission, fusion. The human race is one great Nuclear Family") and generosity (despite his poverty) earns him the moniker: "Santa Claus of the Atomic Age." Chuck who gets Art to think about how way one speaks does project a unique, rebellious self (e.g., he refers to his bicycle as "that which rolls," to wind as "that which blows," to his cock as "that which sprays," and so forth). And such phrases be delivered by Chuck with no inflection or nuance and equal stress on every syllable. A nutcracker, if it could talk, would do no differently. Chuck the gentle drafted war-protestor. After high school, he majors in math at UCLA, but drops out to become long-haired pot-smoking hippy after his academic advisor writes up following report: "His imagination is wild and extravagant, and escapes incessantly from every restraint of reason and taste, and in the course of its vagaries, leaves a tract of thought as incoherent and eccentric, as is the course of a meteor through the sky."

Chuck then ekes out meager living selling large, juicy strawberries at a corner fruit stand. Drafted at nineteen, commits suicide six months later while on leave rather than become cannon fodder in unjust war. (Art suspects shame over his homosexuality contributing factor.) Runs long garden hose from exhaust pipe into passenger compartment, gasses himself in his mother's white 1964 Chevy station wagon day before reporting for rigors of jungle training. Pens final cryptic note, pins it to his beige Nehru shirt: "The Monoxide Kid says: 'The person who kills is not the same as the person who is killed.' Amen." Art upsets Chuck's family when, on strength of this death-bed testimony, he does suggest police treat Chuck's death as special species of homicide. "The bad Chuck killed the good Chuck," Art insists.

Els last person to see him alive; she reports to Art after funeral: "He wore the low color of fear on his face. It's yellow, just like they say—yellow, sallow, sow-like, big-pored. Worst affected were the concavities beneath his eyes, where the muck had gathered in two dark stains, like scabs. The eyes themselves (once moist, gland-bright, almost fizzy) were the eyes of a trap-ped interior being, living inside Chuck and staring into the distance, to see if it would ever be safe to come out."

Thanks to Chuck's parents' anti-intellectualism, Art inherits his buddy's large book collection. Therein, in well-thumbed copy of Marcus Aurel-ius's *Meditations,* Chuck underlines following bit of Stoic wisdom: <u>Nothing happens to any man that he is not formed by nature to bear</u>. In margin Chuck crudely draws hand with upraised middle finny and scribbles nearby in red ink:

Stoic this up yer ass!

But there is deeper reason than Chuck chucking his life that gets Art so flustered. It brings to mind his own bouts with suicidal feelings. From

166

early age Art suffers from vertigo when at heights. But fear not really about heights *per se*, but about fear that he will be drawn to ecstatically hurl himself off such heights. He is simultaneously morbidly drawn to and physically repulsed by dangerous precipices. Creeps to building's roof edge or nature's rocky ledge, sticks head over precipice and goes into deep reverie. Once he stares entranced for an hour looking over long drop into enticing river canyon when hiking in California's magnificent High Sierras with his crazy daddy. He vividly imagines over 'n over doing elegant swan dive over edge, wind rushing frenetically past his ears as he approaches absolute certainty of rocky bottom; he sees his corpse in slow motion flattening into bloody lump on big breast-shaped boulder beneath, his flesh mingling ecstatically, slowly with granite crystals. Most intimate method of studying geology yet devised!

8.9　　More recently, Art tries putting himself into shoes of poor souls who jump from World Trade Center shortly after airliners ram it. Tries to be super empathic, to imagine what that long, dizzy fall to oblivion felt like, what people may have been thinking as they tumbled downward. Were they calm in their final moments? Did any of them yell "Geronimo!" as they jumped? Did they prefer to fall head first or feet first? Did they notice air temperature while falling? Did they keep their eyes open or closed? Did any people piss or shit their pants? Did any person attempt a wireless phone call on the way down? Were those who held hands as they jumped more comforted in their final moments than those who did not? Was person who fell onto Irish Catholic Fire Department chaplain, killing him, Jewish, Protestant, or Catholic? And so on.

Suffering pangs of Krokerian "spasm," Art finds desire for such gravitational release *both* pleasurable *and* horrible to contemplate. Later, true to his Catholic upbringing, feels guilty for entertaining such desire. Upon seeing this young man in gallery, all this psychic shit busts through Art's mental flood gates. So internally distracted does our hero become by this torrent of memories and emotions, he overlooks obvious violations of Museum Policy by small curious child held in young mother's arms who thinks all sculpture within reach are dignified residents in high-class petting zoo.

8.91　　Eventually calming down, Art saunters toward Museum's back stairs where vast Georgia O'Keefe *Sky Clouds* canvas floats, dominating what seems to be several stories of empty light. Notices matronly visitor with cute child in tow. Tiny girl looks at painting once, runs delightedly to landing, keeps on looking. Sensing something's about to happen, Art ungoops ear, aims her way:

WHO DREW IT? she whispers.

GEORGIA O'KEEFE, mother replies.

A pause from the awed daughter then, **I NEED TO TALK TO HER.**

Jeeze, that child is making a wholly unconscious but quite basic assumption (an awfully wrong one) about people and the work they do. She was erroneously assuming that the glory she saw in the work reflected a glory in its maker, muses Art-the-disillusioned critic. *Aw hell, I used to think that way—before becoming a convert to the philosophy of Posthopelessness.*

Fact: Posthopelessness—inspired by writings of George Bataille and William S. Burroughs—was first adumbrated by one Sean Buckelew and is condition where hopelessness is understood as given fact; yet this lack of hope leads not to nihilism, but to a life-affirming possibility that within the context of doomed society, or doomed world, new possibilities for bodily liberation are possible, even inevitable.

8.92   Simultaneously, in local elementary school, Boettcher Brats be in study hall where peers accord them Master Trickster status due to winter school prank: placing pink snowwoman, endowed with big boobs and crowd of soapless Brillo pads for pubic hair, so as to greet students and teachers returning from Christmas break. Today Brats be ignoring three R's in favor of listing all possible secondary qualities of that valued childhood entity: COOKIES:

Brat #1	Brat #2
Flakey	Gooey
Cakey	Mushy
Crunchy	Smooth
Firm	Too . . .
Flat	Not enough . . .
Chewy	Small
Strong	Large
Soft	Spicy
Crispy	Sour
Hard	Colorful
Sweet	Hefty
Chunky	Fluffy
Bland	Buttery
Thick	Thin
Flavorful	Moist
Dense	Plain
Tasteful	Soggy

Can you add to their list?

__________   __________

__________   __________

__________   __________

__________   __________

__________   __________

__________   __________

Good a place as any to either turn the page or close the book.

9.0

Six months after divorce from Art during which she recites optimistic mantra: "When the dear disappear, there are others waiting near." So no surprise that Brittany sits dead center in her *new* lover's loft in red bean bag chair resting on concrete floor painted battleship grey. Large windows behind her reveal Chicago skyline over which there is tumultuous, billowing shapes of gray tumbling through vaults of pink sunset with black rain clouds sailing overhead like an armada. Opposite, outside their loft's thick door, in dim, long hallway, sits chill of long-entombed air. Is there a doctor in the house? Writer, E. L. Doctorow, observes that "memory is in the ontological sense another reality" and Brittany (Timmy Maulstick simply calls her "Knee") can confirm this. "Knee" has open on her lap her well-thumbed diary, complete with snapshots she's taken, diary spanning years of her relationship with Art. She snaps last umber-and-beige half-moon of marzipan between her lips, sucks her thumb clean, randomly pages through her entries. If we watch closely, we will see "Knee's" movements of soul pass like shadows of clouds on plain swept by winds of regret, amusement, irritation, and other, less decipherable sensations. Under calendar date of her first date with Arthur S. Middlebrook, she reads:

> *This curious man, he seems to have an abiding satisfaction given to individuals who are more than a match for the life they have chosen for themselves. He's so well-spoken, insightful. Has a fabulous vocabulary. He said when I talk my "lepidopterous palms fold and unfold." He refused to play the thirteenth hole in miniature golf; says he suffers muchly from Triskaidekaphobia, fear of thirteen. I've given him my number which, luckily, doesn't have a one or a three in it. . . .*

A 4 x 5-inch snapshot of Art and Brittany is Elmer-glued into place under this entry. It depicts two youths standing side-by-side at a miniature golf hole display, mini-windmill on hole twelve, each holds a putter. Large smile on Art's face (has he just won the game?), Brittany forces a smile. Four months later she adds to her musings:

> *Arty sits so close that I begin to feel as if proximity were a concept to which I had previously been a stranger. All melted, my legs feel like cotton, my heart sunk between my thighs and raging as if inside a nest of red ants. He smells of fresh strawberries. I love how he tilts his head back and takes a long pull at his Sapporo beer bottle while eating sushi, his Adams apple rising and falling, the sparse light brown stubble on his throat moving like reeds lying on*

water. . . . Picnicking at the beach, I love to watch the sun span him, its warmth, lulling his shoulder and hair and sometimes, then, his mind goes quite blank except for a look that says: 'I want another Gin Rickey.' And when we kiss, it's a treasure cave of teeth (he calls it his 'sensual geode') inches from my tongue. God, he's so romantic. He tells me I use my senses 'like an artist uses colors to make a pretty picture'. Saw his rock 'n gem collection today. He showed me a queer, heterogeneous, solid substance, so oddly shaped, so whimsically put together by Mother Nature. An aggregate, he said. Very impressive, but not my cup of tea. . . .

Eight months later, this entry:

Love renews all faces and customs and ideals and leaves the bars of the prison shining. His name is Arthur (he likes to use the German pronunciation which doesn't use "th" as a digraph, but separates the sounds as "Art-hur") and in very classy restaurants when the worrisome-browed waiter asks if he wants tap or bottled water with gas, he opts (to the amazement of all) for holy water! God bless him! . . . While conversing with him today, I have a distinct recollection of frequently compressing my lips, putting my forefinger to the side of my nose, and making use of gesticulations and grimaces common to people who, at ease in their armchairs, meditate upon matters of intricacy or importance. This is a good sign. . . . [skips several pages, reads on] A thunder-summer afternoon. Shadows wander in from the corners of his bedroom. We lay spread on his bed, spread like soft butter on warm toast, our bodies trickling gratefully into the folds of the blankets. Happy, in love, I shed a tear, which is the purest of my destinies.

A much later entry reads:

I awoke at eight. It seemed like I emerged from the depths of slumber which had lasted for days. That happens to me sometimes after heavy fatigue and great mental strain, but this resulted only after a vehement evening of disagreements with Arthur over two things: 1) that perversion is justified—no demanded—by our environment that is now totally manmade, totally without a biology; and 2) his penchant for postmodern citation rooted in his belief that the phrases in his brain had been there long before he had; they were ready-made. So he's always got a little notebook with him into which he's constantly jotting down jokes, puns, snippets of overhead conversations, whole passages copped from novels, popular and esoteric. Likes, nay loves, to do what he calls "playin' jarism." Wholesale plagiarism. Poaching in the field of culture. Says everything has already been written or photographed. One only needs, he says, to reshuffle all the crap out there already. Beat writer Billy Burroughs knew this, he claims. I thought it was bullshit! So upset did I become, I had to go outdoors to get away from him; there I found a noiseless world under the lowering sky. The rain had stopped falling. Then suddenly the cloud lifted from me, if not from the sky. My blood seemed to run naturally through my veins again. I experienced the change of mood which a woman feels sometimes when her whole being is clarified by love. . . .

Yet another observation several weeks later:

If I'm reasonably intelligent, Art is unreasonably intelligent. His aesthetic and politics are postmodern, very liberal, radical even. Anarchistic. Talks about raising the black flag of anarchism. . . . Tonight Art showed up at my place with a large 4-topping pizza and wearing a T-shirt on which was emblazoned a schematic of a two-story house; on the second floor we see a toilet with sewer line connecting to a TV set on the floor below; caption under it reads: "TV—same old shit."

A pasted-in photo verifies this statement. Yet another entry, most extensive:

His facade is dropping. One night he opened up his heart and dumped all of it on the table—the noisy jangling parts, the quiet papery parts—just like the opening up his wallet and spilling everything out. About time, we've been seeing each other for a year now. Sometimes he can be sooo wonderful, so romantic. He cites writer Delmore Schwartz on "the infinite task of the human heart." He imagines a Loving Brotherhood attempting to make the planet a place where it is safe for people to love each other. So bookish. The bookcases he's ordered arrived and he took it as a sacred joy. So witty. He once said that "graffiti is the longing of the soot-choked urban heart for the sun life of the tropics." So perceptive. He makes a distinction between "simple Catholicity" and "profound Catholicity." Most Catholics fall into the former, he says, but Art's now-dead daddy fits the latter. For the uninitiated, he says, there's an easy way to make the distinction: Does this person lift up the padded kneeler so as to kneel painfully on the bare floor in Church or not? If so, then you probably have a

Something is *Crook* in Middlebrook

"profound Catholic" on your hands—er—floor. This is a sign of other religious intensities, of course. Like saints' statues and holy cards in every room of your home and an unshakeable belief that charges of sexual abuse by priests is a fraud, a plot wrought by Protestants. Other times, whoa! Once he said my neck was too thick for turtlenecks. Another instance. We were in his car at a stop light watching school girls in their short-hemmed uniforms crossing in front of us (from St. Camillus de Lellis high school for recalcitrant Catholic girls, named after the patron saint of repentant youth) and he up and says: "I've always imagined such girls do not keep themselves scrupulously clean; like, their thighs probably smell of urine!" As if she overheard this remark, one of the girls, a Comic-book pretty blond, scratches her butt then lifts her spunky heroine-ish left arm (not the right, which she uses to dip into holy water) over her head and from her clenched fist she extends her middle digit upwards at us. Or the time we were dining with my rad feminist girl friend, Miranda. Why he up and says: "Why do women have cunts? . . . So that men will talk to them." I suppose he meant it ironically, as an example of male sexism. But I find it hard to tell when he's sincere and when he's being facetious. Schizzy, he swings pendulously between these two positions so often. Just like he can be totally sensitized to the verbal one day, then to the visual the next. He wants to be a writer one day, a visual artist the next. Figures that as an art critic he can split the difference. Upbeat one day, downbeat the next. Like crazy cross-wiring in his brain. Fact that he often reverses numbers or paired terms seems to confirm a type of mild dyslexia. Ambimentalous, to coin a term.

When dusk comes (this time of year) lights be already on in all apartments. Hovering in Channel Five's News Jet-Telecopter outside Timmy and Brittany's building, one would spy several floors of action (simultaneously) like those voyeuristic scenes in Hitchcock's *Rear Window*: Brittany's still Buddha-seated in bean bag chair, three floors above a woman playing her piano (she's been matter-of-factly promiscuous all her life, yet believes herself to be lonely spinsterish-drab who works all day lecturing 'n marking papers); one floor below her, in identical spot, elderly woman waters her potted plant (she is calm and if we were to hear her sing, we'd find her voice to be beautiful). Below her bronze-skinned, testosterone-proud young man talks angrily on his phone (which reminds me: Art pays Boetther Brats to scratch out Timmy Maulstick's name out of every Chicago phonebook they can get their mini-mitts on); if we were to have camera in hand and zoom in on that young man we'd notice constantly scratches himself. Suffering neck-to-toes case of psoriasis? Hives? Ho! It's full-scale border rebellion. Skin as our border with external reality. Hispanic, be he itchin' for a New World Border? Several floors down a cleaning crew is prepping bare apartment for new tenant, former occupant having mysteriously croaked of Bangutot, that sudden-death syndrome haunting Asian men. One floor above, activist poet stares out window, unconsciously rubbing his left arm where large bruise obtained during street clash with police hides under his shirt. He might be recalling those days when, dressed in dashikis upon which were pinned peace medals, he always wore his black bushy hair in an Isro.

Brittany's finnies move quickly, advancing her some fifty pages ahead in her diary:

> *Heated political discussion at Cosi's tonight. Art orders vanilla latte, I mocha. Art's wearing leather. Concerning official state visit by some puffy-faced South American dictator to Washington, Art, pounding his chest, declaims while staring at my cleavage: "Shit Brit, my President embraces somber sociopaths wearing medals of murder on their chests!" Later in line for Joan Baez tickets his lucid eyes rolled over my body like two stones—cool, indifferent, yet somehow lustful.*

"Knee" lets her long finnies lightly stroke diary page with her green-inked entries and recalls: *Once Art said to me, "Language is something that almost isn't there." He's right.* She glances to her right at a pile of opened mail. Sees flyer from Amway Corporation. CEO is pictured with quote underneath his image: "I AM the Way. Buy Amway." Brittany suddenly remembers she needs to re-order a supply of FLUSH-AMWAY, Amway's premier drain-clog opener. Her desperate clients can't get it fast enough. Chicago's old buildings—ah, those sclerotic lead pipes—are plum opportunities for plumbers. And Brittany hates plumbers. In Chicago all electrical lines must be run through pipes. Boon to unions. More moola for them plumbers. They are up there on her "shit-list" that includes: feral children, fascists, hermits, street people, gamblers, forest-wardens, permanent invalids, recluses, autistics, road tramps, and all those sensory deprived. Last one to visit their distressed pipes with rotating snake has close-set eyes, color of dark plums and wears floppy chino slacks torn down one leg 'n belted with piece of clothesline that displays crack in his ass when he bows to his work; on his large feet he wears dirty white Stan Smith tennis sneakers, no socks; his couture is topped off by stained and greasy workshirt. Sits cross-legged on their floor before their stopped up kitchen drainpipe and just stares for several minutes before getting to down to business. Surprisingly, he dons medical workers face mask and rubber gloves, just like heart surgeon preparing to rod patient's carotid. Everyone's into hygiene now. Everyone's health-paranoid. Showing some ill-suppressed emotion, he mentions to Brittany something about "puzzlin' evidence" and that "our liberal media failed to mention that nine out of eleven plumbers working in those Twin Towers were killed on nine/eleven. They just ran plum outta luck," he says, coloring draining from his face. Putting down a book of poetry she's been reading, Brittany replies: "Those dead are a sleight and a fade. We fall like flowering plums." "Knee" closes, then quickly randomly pops opens her diary, practicing what Art prescribes: "Aleatory for what ails ya!" Entry there reads:

Something is *Crook* in Middlebrook

Arthur had me in stitches today. He always makes me laugh. He told about his teenage transgressions contra Ma Bell, his adventures in bugging people over the telephone. Its seems he and his high school buddy, Mike, each adopted a nom de téléphone. Skinny Art chose "Nick Ptroika," while chubby Mike went by "Falco Quichili." For several years they terrorized the suburban clients of Ma Bell. What a hoot! Said he 'n Mike drove frustrated victims to disconnect their numbers. Meticulously they kept track. After only six months, Art alone had over thirty disconnects to his credit They'd call 'n pretend to be old war buddies, or warn wives of supposedly unfaithful hubbies, or send five tow trucks to same goddamn corner, or get people whistling over the phone to test the decibel levels for a supposed phone repair man 'n tell 'em they'd receive a package of bird seed for their trouble, or leave a myriad of wacky messages, completely filling up answer machines of businesses with odd names like Della's Doll Hospital, Soo Way Kitchen, Wishy-Washy Laundry.

Yep, you name it—they did it. Some years later Art would mention to Al Schmerbauch that he'd be a millionaire today if he'd had the moxey to put together that TV show, "Crank Yankers," wherein puppets visualize for an audience crank phone calls similar to those he and Mike perpetrated.

Brittany pages to diary entry for their last anniversary celebration prior to Art's destructive brain event:

Art took me to Trio, a four-star restaurant in Evanston. He wore his tux, I my fav black dress. It annoyed me that Art lustfully stared at the hostess's cleavage (she had on a short, tight, low-cut black dress). The lights in the main dining room were too bright, so we asked to be moved on an adjacent, dimly lit, dining area. The ten-course dégustation was accompanied with a flight of wine—it was scrumptious! For starters, Iranian Osetra Caviar in a glass tube hollow on each end; one sucks it up; and Tempura of Rock Shrimp; these were paired with Iron Horse Brut LD champagne from Sonoma County, California. The very yeasty bubbly was the best champagne I've ever had. This was followed by a Purée of Chestnuts and Salsify wrapped in bread with shellfish, Meyer lemon, and parsley glass. The wine accompaniment for this was a delicate white, Pojer and Sandri Palai Müller Thurgau from the Dolomite region in Italy. Next came Poached Elysian Fields Farm Lamb with chanterelle mushrooms, coffee, and catmint flavorings, then Atlantic Monk Fish Tail with Perigord black truffles, radicchio, saucisson de Paris à l'ail. The red wine matched with these courses was Umathum Zweigelt from Burgenland, Austria. It had a great nose and superior, complex *flavors. Then some hot bread rolls helped clear our mouths for further taste stimulation. Next came North Dakota Goose foie gras, which was matched to a muscular, hearty red wine, Barbera d'Asti In Pectore from the Piedmont region of Italy. Three exquisite desserts formed a delightful dénouement: Rutabaga Sponge with wildflower honey sorbet, mustard, and mascarpone (yum!), then Effervescent Apamate Chocolate with persimmon, star anise, and toasted yogurt (wow!) and, finally, a Huckleberry served on a tripod (very unusual!). These sweets were paired with two dessert wines: Vinhos Barbeito Special Reserve Bual Madeira (the best I've had) followed by Château de Montifaud Pineau des Charentes. We got drunk, so the $636.00 bill didn't hurt as much as I thought it would. Had to walk off our buzz in the late evening chill until we could drive home safely. Fantastic evening. I felt so close to Art. He sure knows his cuisine and wines! He can quote that French gourmand, Brillat-Savarin, from memory. But, curiously, he remarked that he wished he could hear his food as well as taste and see it. What's that all about?*

Brittany sits back in bean bag chair. Brushes her hair back with one sweeping gesture. Looks up at ceiling, then back down to that last sentence in her diary. Audible sound of her sighing. *Strange that he should've had this fantasy prior to his cerebral event and the advent of his super-hearing,* she muses. *I never made the connection before. Now I wonder . . . My god! I almost forgot,* recalls Brittany. *Art used to smoke Indonesia kreteks when writing, and we often dined at one wonderful Indonesian restaurant near our house many years ago. Wait there's a diary entry for that!* She flips to frontmost entries. *It's somewhere in here, I know.* Finds it. Settles back and reads:

Special evening together. Art's delighted for an Indonesian restaurant, Tanjung Sari, has just opened near our home. Went there early. No other diners yet. Exotic art on their walls. Shadow puppets. Art says their food is a border cuisine, mixture of Dutch and indigenous influences as Indonesia was a Dutch colony once. For his personality adjustment, Art starts with arak bumbu, *a rice liqueur in which ginger, garlic pepper, honey, lime and other herbs and spices are woven into a perilously strong concoction. Art follows his cocktail with* nasi goreng *(fried rice) and* kerupuks *(shrimp chips), washing it all down with* es kelapa muda *(rose and coconut drink). I order their* satay *and* sayur asam *(veggies with tamarind sauce), and that weird drink called* es teler *(a mix of tropical fruits). Art says he loves the feel of the names of their cuisine in his mouth as much as the taste. I loved to see him eat with such relish! As we eat, my mind turns to the fact I'm beginning to see how passionate my hubby is for all variations of fried rice: Chinese, Thai, Korean, Vietnamese, Indian, or Indonesian.*

Something is *Crook* in Middlebrook

Each one has its unique merits and demerits, he says. When I point this culinary propensity of his out, he says something about fried rice being an aggregate, a whole composed of disparate parts, like some rocks he's been reading about in an old geology text book. He loves the diversity of flavors that attack his taste buds as he eats this fare. But I never like my food to mix ingredients like that. Just the taste of chicken mixing with beef or pork is enough to gag me. He says this marks a fundamental difference between us, a symptom of deeper differences. Even metaphysical differences! He says that cooking is complex chemistry, that a chef makes dishes much like Mother Earth makes her rocks and gems.

Big surprise. One expects traditional gamelon music here, but they're playing a Punk Rock tape as we eat. Art says it's a band called "The Dead Salamanders." That those dead salamanders must be Plethodontidae, or lungless, salamanders judging by the quality of their singing voices. God, he's always sooo witty! He goes on to inform me that the world's largest salamander—growing to some ten feet long and over two hundred pounds, the Ora, also known as the Komodo Dragon—is found on two islands in Indonesia. The species was discovered by a downed pilot during WWI who washed up on shore. Of course, nobody believed him at first. Would you? I'm gullible. And Art takes advantage of that alot. Hell, never sure when he's pulling my leg or not. Is he serious when he says there is a plot of extreme Republicans to institute fascism in our dear USA by 2020, or that we could balance the budget by having the American flag exclusively licensed to Walt Disney? . . .

9.1   Year prior to Art's brain event and divorce from Brittany. Except for TV's blizzard of images 'n blather—language that everyone understands only because understanding is both assumed and irrelevant—extreme quiet reigns under season's pale blue dome; things travel without obstruction; density of unwilled signals arrive from unknown transmitters defining contour of instant, like sound distant of chainsaw gas-powered arriving weak and tired at Mr. And Mrs. Arthur Middlebrook's brick bungalow. Keen, constant, implacable wind combs Chicago beneath motionless winter sun; cold seems to have power of shrinking one's face; you feel it in salt-whitened streets; you hear it in peculiar dense whooshing noise of passenger jets overhead. Yes, it's fuckin' freezing—an extraordinary zero degree Fahrenheit before wind-chill—combined with weatherman's exaggerated claim (he's wearing a cerise blazer): "This weather event is the worst in fifty-nine years." Weather as history. Now it's snowing, big, almost weightless crystals falling in clumps and covering ground with layer of pulverized white frost; frozen puddles stand out on road like cameo portraits. It is by way of inclement weather (or bad smog days) that our world promotes illusion of coherence by slipping every experience of moment into one atmospheric envelope. Art keeps hearing somebody's tires spinning on snow. Outside, Brittany struggles to hike back

Something is *Crook* in Middlebrook

from local White Hen convenience store, experiencing feeling of blizzard as walking through one long moment about to vanish, marked with shallow pencil strokes, circles, erasures. Random lines seem to add up to pattern and anything that looks like a pattern breaks down on scrutiny into random lines. Or pattern and randomness side-by-side with no relation to one another.

Snuggled down in his basement studio, oblivious to Brit's travail, directly beneath Brittany's home office stuffed with her Amway supplies, Art snuggles into his mother's home-knit lamb's wool sweater and dreams of sufficient warmth to melt snow; illusion of Spring so strong it feels like real projection in time. This mental Spring jack-in-the-box ups writerly inspiration for start of art history essay destined for Summer issue of prestigious *College Art Association Bulletin*:

In the Sonnenstein asylum high above the Elbe a solitary and unrecognized experimenter practices the apo-tropaic techniques that twelve years later would win fame and a public for the Zurich Dadaists in the Café Voltaire. He wishes to trace the sounding of hearts and loins. . . .

Snug basement site of reveries and research, pedanticism and prolific writing (also cries and conflict between our ill-fated couple). Why just yesterday our paunchy art critic e-mails off six-page review of "The American Lawn" show held at Canadian Centre for Architecture to Canadian art rag, *Parachute*. Art's take on show is largely positive, yet he laments lack of odoriferous whiff of new mown grass (which he always associates with his grandfather's mowing thick, green Wisconsin summer lawn):

Our suspicions that the museum experience can never truly simulate the real thing are confirmed, however: the fragrance that is so much a part of the "lawn experience" is missing. This is characteristic of the olfactory intolerance, the inodorateness, of the anosmic white cube of the proverbial modernist gallery space. It only reaffirms the politics of the pristine. . . . This show does confirm my belief that things build up something like "significance" without themselves having any.

Art prefers basement or attic spaces for his creative work, work in which he taps into both his left/right brain, male/female aspects of his personality, as well as his penchant for sound and smell. Art's psychic history can be narrated through architectural spaces he occupies—sees, smells, hears —sites of personal and social knowledge retrieved through memory traces that echo in Art's *vas bene clausum*. In that wonky interior space called Art's mind: bedrooms are coded feminine, dens masculine; photography darkrooms are feminine, photography studios masculine; lapidary studios are feminine, geology labs masculine; garages are bisexual, kitchens are coded gay; attics and basements are androgynous. Hence, for Art, both his cockloft (above) and dome-home's basement (below) are magic crucibles where his

Something is *Crook* in Middlebrook

feminine half (anima) shakes hands with his masculine half (animus) and he feels complete.

He traces this wondrous coupling to early childhood experiences in spacious attic and dim cellar in his mother's parents' home in Northern Wisconsin. Therein, during summer vacations, shy young Art delights in smell of his grandfather's cut lawn and revels in discovering magic of certain domestic spaces. It is in attics and basements where he becomes aware of his uniqueness, of his difference from others, where he feels wholly safe and safely whole. He becomes acutely aware of how muffled sounds of family conversations are subtly modified by his presence either above or below his clan's living room. He delights in vastly aromatopia of smells wafting about in these spaces. In attic: pungent mothballs, decaying leather and paper, a warm mustiness of dust. In basement: heavy odor of damp, moldy, coal-potatoes-drying clothes inflected with whiff of his grandmother's perfume.

Anticipating his later interest in photography, he notices marked differences in lighting in these places: dim bulb in attic casts sharp, deep shadows, accentuating outlines of innumerable boxes, broken perambulators, couture hailing from Flapper era, moribund radios, rusty fishing tackle, stacks of folded hand-made quilts; meanwhile, in basement sunlight punches through small windows set at ground level, splashing Rembrandt-lighting onto curious objects surviving from another era: wringer-style clothes washer, ancient zinc wash tubs, a clothesline hung with his grandmother's old whale-bone corsets, his grandfather's threadbare long-johns, an old hand-worn ax leaning against ax-punished stump used to split wood, a copper coal carrier tub, and dusty wooden shelves stuffed with jellied fruits, baskets of potatoes, stacks of Lava soap bars, jars of nails, screws, and fasteners of every shape and size. A delightful dank dungeon accessed by hops down rubber-covered wooden stairs, Art's small feet resonating on those steps like finnies on piano keys. Oh, that sound! It lends a peculiar color to that space and signals our little spelunker's descent into dimness to avoid dreaded daddy and welcome avid daydreams stimulated by this *mise-en-scent* of odd odors. Climbing onto a stool, peeping out those basement windows, Art (paradoxically) withdraws from our actually-existing world. Instinctively he knows this space, identified with solitude, is creative.

As shy, nerdy teenager with excessive pimples, he starts to photograph this murky place where curious objects dramatically leap out as sunlight bathes them, where precious memories leap out as thought, in turn, bathes them. Later, as adult, Art revisits this place of organic habits during delirious, delicious, bouts of skull-time. Aye! He performs topoanalysis, unlocking time compressed into that space. Ho! As Frenchy *philosophe* Gaston Bachelard does intuit: memories do be motionless, and more securely they be fixed in space, sounder they do be. Here memory and perception exchange functions. Images be produced through cooperation between real and unreal. *In toto,* Art's grandparents' house—from rationality of its attic down to irrationality of its basement—constitutes body of images that gives Arthur S. Middlebrook (if one professes modernism) *proofs* or (if one professes postmodernism) *illusions* of psychic stability. As Art (playin' jarism) professes to Al during shared summer supper on his back deck: "Ah, that house, Al … that house of those lovely dank, dim summers of my childhood."

Something is *Crook* in Middlebrook

Digression necessary to explain why only spaces wherein Art can exercise his creative impulse are either high-up or sunk-below. When he 'n Brittany buy their brick Chicago bungalow, bitter turf war breaks out as to who will occupy large, finished basement.

"Not *you* buster! Where'll I put my Amway crap? I need space."

"Not *you* sister! Where'll I write? I need inspiration."

So bitter does conflict become, compromise need to be worked out in couples' therapy. Fifth floor of Garland Building in Loop, room 512. Art sits nervously in large, dark brown leather chair, Brittany on leather sofa, sobs. Therapist, who reminds Brittany of actor Spaulding Gray, helps them work out mutual agreement. According to terms, Brittany gets to have sofa 'n coffee table, storage shelf 'n small magazine rack adjacent to Art's work table 'n computer equipment. Her section's walls are to be painted light green, his yellow. For two weeks this agreement holds. But gradually, imperceptibly, Art launches campaign to encroach on Brit's territory.

At first, old rubber mouse pads replace elegant coasters on coffee table. His favorite pen appears where hers once was. Next, Art's Japanese ceramic sake set sends Brit's delicate China tea set upstairs. Thereafter, his journal replaces her diary. Weeks follow, then stacks of his opened mail materializes where her stacks of her unopened mail once sat. Pictures of his family take front 'n center to hers. Copies of *Playboy* chase away copies of *Playgirl.* Following month, *Artforum* magazine and pedantic art theory books supplant Brittany's issues of *Vogue* and *Cosmopolitan.* Later, his odd-ball knickknacks defeat her cute knickknacks. Another month passes until his pee-stained BVDs replace her punctured pantyhose. In final offensive, his collection of vintage golf putters edges out her Amway inventory. After slow nine month gestation, basement reborn as Art's own intimate space.

One sad day his wife has *dual-sense epiphany*. Her eyes register that Art has painted what was once her green section to match his original yellow section. Her eyes take hold Art's and don't let go, as hot 'n hard 'n punishing as pair of torches. Standing, arms akimbo, she silently boils: *Yellow? Not green? Yellow!* She sniffs. Olfactory sense detects *pungent loci*, confirms visual evidence: sour smell of Art's dirty undergarments edges out sweet perfume odor of her intimate apparel. It suddenly dawns on our much abused Brittany: *Shit! I've been ousted! Foiled again. How in hell did he pull this off? I feel like that proverbial complacent lobster-in-the-pot bein' gradually cooked, heated to boiling degree by slow degree.* In protest, Brittany leaves acerbic ditty on little pink Post-It note on Art's computer screen. No longer will Art 'n Brittany's quarrels go up and burn out like bits of paper, leaving nothing but a feather of ash, a laugh in bed in the dark.

```
Art, Loving you thus, and hating you so,
my heart is torn in two. Crucified 'n
mortified.
        — Brit.
```

Something is *Crook* in Middlebrook

9.2   Why has your Author jumbled up the chronology? Time-honored strategy keeps Reader off-balance. Hell, all good writers of writerly texts do it. What better way to discourage middle-brow audience who likes flow that obeys every curve of the river!

This writerly wisdom comes from Art's sister, Els. After critiquing Art's writing. Brother 'n sister have agreement: Art teaches Els finer points of photography, Els teaches Art subversive modes of writing, textual theft. To be word criminal, learn by example. "Here's Artaud. Read him. Here's Gertrude Stein. Read her. Here's William Burroughs. Try to read him. Unlock your word hoard, expand it. Blessed are the greedy for words, for they shall have vocabulary; use words like *plangently* and *gormless.* Pepper your scribbles with stretch-words like *floccinaucinihilipilification* (it means the estimation of something as worthless). Remember, he who filches from someone a good word steals that which now enriches him, and leaves the other none the poorer."

Els seems to hear words from inside them; once amazes Art with her linguistic analysis of *mac-adam-iz-ation*: "It's made up of Celtic plus Hebrew plus Greek plus Latin." Another time she informed him: "There are, by the *O.E.D. VI*'s count, nineteen nonarchaic synonyms for *unresponsive*, of which nine are Latinate and four Saxonic." Always sensitive to energies at work in language, she reads poet Wallace Stevens aloud to him, selections from *Notes toward a Supreme Fiction,* a section entitled "It Must Be Abstract." She reveals to him how Stevens's words work: "The sonorities of 'purple . . . umber . . . slumber . . . autumn . . . umber' that Stevens chooses are playfully repetitive in their ridicule." She encourages him to violate norms: "Ya wanna become a real denizen of the logosphere? Use source material. Experiment with theft 'n plagiarism in any form that occurs to you. Recall the time-honored Cento, an aggregate poem culled from shards of other poems. Rewrite someone else's writing. Fuck with someone's writing, maybe someone formidable. Or try writing a short story or novel beginning with this sentence: *The floor boards hummed and tickled shod feet with the work of the hidden hypocaust.* . . . The writer is like a parrot, accepting language as something received. One is spoken. Read your Roland Barthes! . . . Arty, instead of a traditional *Bildungsroman*, you might embark on a novel that is a *Ludicakadroman.* Hey, if Fielding can call *Tom Jones* 'prosai-comi-epic writing,' I can coin a term for the pedantry of academic writing put in collision with the belly laughs of carnival; that is, a text spread-eagled between loftiness and lowliness, developing a writing that aggregates the styles of Rabelais, Kant, Joyce, Miller, and Vonnegut. Remember, 'In the Beginning was the Word, now there's nothing but the Quote.' Borrowing? Yes! From Natchez to Mobile. From the base, the sublime, from the low to the high, do take your ore. Hey, we are all little mimics, as Wordsworth noted: *As if his whole vocation/Were endless imitation.* A text, a novel, is made of multiple writings, drawn from many cultures and entering into mutual relations of dialogue, parody, contestation. This multiplicity is focused at the point of reception, The Reader. A text's unity lies in its destination. Now as for endings: at the back of the book should be a set of sealed envelopes in various colors. Each would be clearly marked on the outside: Traditional Happy Ending; Traditional Unhappy Ending; Traditional Half-and-Half Ending; *Deus ex Machina*; Modernist Arbitrary Ending; End of the World Ending; Cliffhanger Ending; Dream Ending; Opaque Ending; Surrealist Ending; and so on. The birth of The Reader, my dear bro', results in the death of The Author. Ya grok?"

"I grok," acknowledges Art, always all ears when it comes to honing evermore subtle skills of ludic inauthenticity, plagiaristic innovation.

"Oh, ya 'n one more thing . . . use a lot of *parentheses*, bro', very postmodern." Els returns to working on her unpublished parody of Southern novels, *Stirring's Still,* wherein her protagonist wanders in chapter three in boozy stupor near his illegal still. In a voice low in register, a breath of cool sand pouring, with lilt that gives it music, Els runs a sentence by her bro': "Weary of (vainly) milking his apparatus (hidden) in those remains, he moves (on) through the woods resigned to (not) knowing where he is (or) how he got there (or) where he is going (or) how to get back to whence he knew (not) how he came."

Thanks to her motherly literary advice, Art nicknames his sister "Parent(ha)Sis."

9.3   10 a.m. Bang Ho's radio blares on:

> *The world is changing, customs and habits vary nowadays, tastes are evolving: in our day and age a new concept of life has taken over, with a quite different scale of values: to become your real, total self call upon our services! We will immediately point out to you your most distinctive individual trait. Don't forget . . . upholding the brilliant future of our exemplary type of society will be the best way of ensuring that your own future will be a brilliant one.*

While inside Windy City office of officious Feds, our notorious Alderman "Pronto" Pietro (you remember him, right?) fond of obscure pronouncements 'n elliptical allusions, embellishing simple

remarks with such ornate imagery that you soon get lost trying to understand him (a necessary trait for political life) uses language as instrument of locomotion: darting, feinting, circling, disappearing, suddenly reappearing in a different spot—is exercising his rhetorical skills on one very frustrated F.B.I. agent trying to question him under auspices of Feds' Silver Shovel corruption investigation. Simultaneously courting 'n shunning, he's burning F.B.I eyeballs (and trying to up ante on ex-gov politicorruptian Rod Blagojevich's *basse couture*) with his stunning Sunderland pink jogging out-fit. "I'm in da pink!" Pietro boasts to media. *This is a test of the system, this is only a test.*

Was *that* Bang Ho's radio spewing italics or The-Author-of-These-Words?

10.0

Chicago sky, dark and forbidding, lets out stentorian boom and cries violent tears. It's an April thunderstorm simply yet tastefully staged outside Art's sliding glass deck doors. Spill-off fills gutters, falling off low rooftops in thick streams, pouring into drains so eagerly that air from sewers bubbles out of iron grills. Branches on trees blow so vigorously that chance stirring of them has high probability some may coincide with a sign gesture comprehensible to a deaf mute (you can be sure Al is working on calculating exact probability of such an event).

Across street, Peven Pogacnic sits at home at his 1950s yellow melamine, black tube-legged kitchen table near large window permitting flood of photons to crowd around his unresponsive eyes. He's cleaning his photographic equipment: interior of his Leica M-2 has just been sprayed with noisy blast of compressed air from can; now he lovingly wipes his latest purchase—extreme wide-angle 21mm f/4 Super Angulon lens which covers 92 degrees field of view—with soft Lens Wipes impregnated with glass-cleaning fluid. Noreen wipes dust off her chicken collection with one hand while extinguishing her cigarette in other into ashtray overflowing like vent of Vesuvius. So far she's been unsuccessful in getting Peven to purchase 12 million megapixel digital camera.

What Peven doesn't tell his wife, can't even start to explain to her, is his special attachment to traditional photographic equipment and craft of conventional photographic methods. Only another photographer from "those old wet lab days" would grok it. Oh that alchemy of transmuting latent image into visible image! The delight of working with light meter and Ansel Adam's Zone System. Peven's whole being responds to sharp smells of sinus-clearing hypo bath, odd slippery feeling of Dektol print developer on hands, those proud marks of chemical stained finnies, that funny foamy bath for cutting water spots on drying negatives. Why even just holding stack of 35mm slides in hand, manipulating them distractedly like stack of poker chips, gives deep pleasure. Prior to onset of his blindness, Peven loves thumbing shiny, crisp pages of his 1942 hard cover edition of *The Leica Manual*, enjoys memorizing which Wratten filter to use to obtain proper rendition of tones with black-and-white film, delights in calculating hyperfocal distance for different f/stops, and determining flash exposure based on film's guide number, as well as proper exposure compensation for long time exposures or for bellow extensions on close-up shots. Then there is sheer chemical joy of discovering "C-76," that is, pushing Kodak Panatomic-X ASA 25 film to ASA 125 by putting Crone Antifogging Additive (Benzotriazole) into Kodak's conventional D-76 film developer to get super-fine grain coupled with better emulsion speed. Or sheer delight in using new words, like slowly pronouncing those developing agents "Elon" and "Hydroquinone," or those Kodak papers "Azo" and "Velox." Many of these pleasures are, for Peven, associated with more pleasant days when he was still sighted, so all harder for him to give them up. Yes, all these erotics of conventional photography are disappearing in a honk 'n a flash in our digital age. (Peven here anticipates thesis of photographer Jeff Wall's

Something is Crook in Middlebrook

1989 essay "Photography and Liquid Intelligence.") As Roo once succinctly observes, "Shit, Pev. Now ya don't even have ta get drunk ta get pixellated."

Peven gently fits his shiny new Super Angulon lens on his Leica. Although useless to Peven, he slips accessory wide-angle viewer into shoe on of top camera. Looks through viewer as if he *could* see; *imagines* 92 degrees of lateral view. *I'll bet this lens covers nearly complete kitchen area.* He then loads up new roll of Afgachrome RSX II. This ASA 200 film gives fine grain, superb color saturation, and excellent sharpness of detail. Not that Peven can appreciate this. How he wishes he could *see* his images. Noreen's translations are wonderful, but language can do just so much. She can't accurately describe differing grain structures, subtle casts of tone and color, degrees of focus, hair-splitting compositional details, and so forth. Besides, Pev's getting heap suspicious that Noreen is fudging her translations, making scenes recorded more tantalizingly erotic or better composed than they actually are. And he's right. Yep, it's Saturday morning in Chicago and Peven feels he's been edged to edge of a world where black pages lift and fall.

10.1 The Bowmanville Bistro. Sawdust strewn on floor, decorative spittoons. Place empty but for Pau, his help, Art 'n Al, and one very thin CTA worker in orange overalls sporting dim, blood-shot eyes, two-day stubble, reddish blond, darker than hair on his head with fingernails yellowish 'n thick.

This *garçon de café* sits before his vegetarian breakfast special—"The Font of Youth," mushroom and bell pepper omelette with Fontina cheese—cup of hot java in hand, shoulders hunched in way that indicates special depth of solitude, like figure in Ed Hopper painting. Looks dumbly out window harvesting some deep furrow in his mind where wise counsels propagate; could we say he has dimly glimpsed difference between his 'authentic self' and his 'social role'?

Behind counter radio spouts old-time rock 'n roll. On television, muted, crowd of vestmented white people—what looks like The Mormon Tabernacle Choir—dumbly work their mouths as if eating invisible food. Two young women step in, so amazingly fresh 'n undamaged; they gingerly sit down, removing their shades in unison. Given menus by Deena clad in sneakers and retro getup that recalls that homely dress worn by Timmy's mother in original TV series "Lassie." Ho! There be low flame in her eyes and sports neighborly smile turned up till it could roast meat; asks what they want, chewing gum mechanically, waiting.

Lift 'n fall, lift 'n fall. Pau D'Arco strokes his *menton fuyant* ("fleeing chin") whilst wielding his spatula over hot greasy grill, back to his customers. So doesn't notice odd man in fire pink pants staring at him from sidewalk. That back, that wall of flesh, has a mighty physiognomy and expression all its own. When he turns to his customers, bright white of his chef's apron suggests a *tabula rasa*, bare canvas on which that day's Pollock-like painterly splatters of sauces gradually accumulate.

Something is *Crook* in Middlebrook

French Canadian by birth, Pau's claims to fame are three in number: 1) Olympic contender in archery during the 1970s; 2) studies martial arts in Japan; and 3) this *bon viveur* makes two of Art's fav French dishes: *l'omelette à la baveuse* (under-cooked omelette) and *la poularde en demi-deuil* (chicken, half in mourning) so named because truffles are carefully inserted just beneath transparent skin, offsetting golden hue of *la poularde* with flecks of somber black; a dish accompanied by delightful *mosaïque de légumes*, a stylish mélange of zucchini, carrots, artichokes, and asparagus bound with puréed fresh herbs. All these delights are served on square tables covered with *mâchon* (Left Bank vernacular for checkered oil-cloth). Ah, for Pau taste is a kiss that our mouth gives itself through intermediary of tasty foods.

Art (with Tig in tow) 'n Al do be performing their usual Saturday breakfast ritual. Al is jotting weird equations on his napkin:

> 2 arms + 1 brick + 1 window + dash
> of radical politics + 1 short
> temper = 1 broken window

Not to be outwitted, Art—Tig's bulk spilling off either side of his lap—follows suit:

> 1 female body + 2 male hands + 1 weird
> ear + 1 waterbed + 2 bees wax candles
> + 1 scented hot massage oil container +
> 2 glasses of Frangelico liqueur + 1 deluxe
> annotated edition of *"The Kama Sutra"* + 1
> stick of incense + 1 New Age music CD +
> organdy petticoat + fishnet stockings = XXX

Scrubbing down grill, Pau's body suddenly becomes re-entry vehicle for long-forgotten childhood jingle penetrating thick atmosphere of his Canadian anxiety. Ho! He might be wittily playing off famous reference Marx copped from *Hamlet* when comparing persistent impulse to revolt to that *old mole*, when he lustily burst forth with: *"Il y a dans la Lune/ Trois petits taupes de taverne,/ Qui mangent des prunes/ En buvant du vin . . ."*

"What's that your singing, Pau?" inquires Art, petting Tig's ugly head.

"*Quel*? Oh. Ah, *rien,* notzing."

"Oh ya? What's a *taupe de taverne*? asks Al as if quizzing a reluctant student.

"Eat ez zee Frenchly word for tavern moles, *mon amis. Un petit* ditty about folks like you two, regular patrons, *n'est pas*?"

"Well said, old mole! Talking about moles I am lead by metonymy to think of tunnels," asserts Al. "Have you heard about the supposedly secret tunnel city beneath Tokyo?"

"*Non*!"

Something is Crook in Middlebrook

"Nope."

"Japanese journalist, Shun Akiba, has recently written a book, *Imperial City Tokyo: Secret of a Hidden Underground Network*. Despite the book going into its fifth edition, he's been shunned by all the mass media."

"Maybe something to do with his name," wittily observes Art with a smirk on his face. "People taking his name literally."

"Ya, ya." Al brushes Art's silliness off, grin and frown contesting for suzerainty of his face. Grin wins.

"Sitting on the Ginza subway from Suehirocho to Kanda, he says you can see many mysterious tunnels leading off from the main track, but no such routes are shown on any maps. On the Ginza line, the first basement level is closed off, for official use only. Go to the toilet in basement level two and, he claims, there's a door to basement level one, but the door is locked. Weird stuff. Remnants of Cold War paranoia."

"Hey, that James Bond movie, *You Only Live Twice*, showed such a tunnel system as used by the Head of Japanese Security. Remember?" adds Art.

"Shit, ya. I *do* recall that! 'Bond-san' falls down a slippery slide and into the den of an overly polite . . ."

"That's it. He's then shown an underground rail system with this guy's private train waiting."

"*Sacré bleu*! Zee best way to keep something secret eez to put eat out front, put eat into zee fictional movie. Zee crafty strategy of concealment like zhat utilized *en* Monsieur Poe's tale of zee *Purloined Letter*!"

Pau sits down. Pulls out small sketchbook. Starts working over surface with stub of a pencil. Several minutes pass. No one speaks.

"Watcha doin' Pau?" says Art finally.

"Sketching, eat relaxes *moi*."

"Let us see," urges Al.

"Eat is zee attempt at getting zee essence of Deena's fear. Her eyes, zhey are so, how you say, *expressive, n'est pas*?" Tips his book so our two tavern moles can see his efforts.

"Not too shabby, Pau; sensitively limned," observes Art, squinting, leaning across table for a better view. "Why didn't you pursue your visual talents? You obviously have a sharp eye, a sensitive soul, a . . ."

"Zee *raison*? *Moi*, I was not, *moi* talent was not, taken seriously by *moi* parents nor by zee teachers. *Par les sept enfers de Landaire*! Bad mirrors, *mes amis*! Zhey never say to little Pau, 'You have talent.' *Mais, non.* Zhey play into *et* confirm *moi* insecurities. Zhat ez why *moi* do join zee Québecois-Separatists, to prove myself capable despite zee parents' negative shit. So only now do zhis chefly persona start to develop zee confidence in his draughtsmanshiply skills. Zee good mirror, Dee, she's been encouraging *moi* greatly." Pau runs his finny tips across his yellowing teeth, tasting his nail-quicks, a mix of arrogance and insecurity. "Have to look forward to *moi* retirement, *mes amis, et* zhose days of *leisure* ahead. Need zee, how you say, hobby. *N'est pas*?" Pau raises his bent arm to his brow. Performs a complicated, orchestral sniff.

"Talking about leisure," interjects Al, "in our New World Order today, work—and that includes *both* consumption and production—dominates life."

"In fact," adds Art, "such work *is* the new leisure. People seem to really only find fulfillment these days in their work. When they do take vacation, they take their laptops along and keep in daily touch with their employer."

"*Et*, by gar, zee true poetry of zee *nouvelle* millennium? Eat ez zee meaningless violence." He sighs and Art can hear distant seagulls falling through Pau's lungs.

"You know what writer J.G. Ballard has one of his characters say in his dark novel *Super-Cannes*? . . . Why that the Adolf Hitlers and Pol Pots of the future won't walk out of the desert, but will emerge from shopping malls and corporate business parks!"

"As long as zhey don't emerge from zee Bowmanville, heh?"

Al laughs.

Art doesn't. He catches deeper, disturbing meaning in Pau's remark. Recalls how quickly loving utopian schemes go awry, become excuses for US versus THEM, for new killing fields. Happy dreams turning to sad dreams. *How did author Martin Amis put it? Oh ya . . . 'Swing low in your weep ship, with your tear scans and your sob probes . . .' or something like that . . . and you can tune into sad, sad dreams.*

Oh how Art just *lives* for words, his words, other people's words. Words that are gems 'n gems that evoke wonderful words. Secret passion? Art wants to chair new academic venue, Department of Literary Gems, to encourage cross-disciplinary academic adventures between geology and *belles lettres,* with an emphasis on phenomenon of *aggregates.*

Take that mineral *arkose*, a sandstone rich in quartz and feldspar. A detrital sedimentary rock (as textbooks say) formed from accumulation of minerals and rocks derived from erosion of previously existing rocks or from weathered products of these rocks. That means it's an aggregate formed by appropriation, willy-nilly scavenging from other rocks. *Arkose* is a plagiarized rock. A geological intertextuality that accurately describes Art's personal mental geology. He's *arkose*. Mentally living off a detrital economy fueled by aesthetic erosions from zillions of texts. His head a hodgepodge of disparate citations from that vast repertoire culled from reading some four books per week for some fifty years. He thinks back to an event. Most often that event is a *book*. Most people remember their lives as an aggregate of lived experiences, like when they met their spouses, etcetera. Art recalls his life as an aggregate of excavations and narrations, stories of places and characters loved or despised. Words or rocks adored. Gems (written or dug up) are more vivid to Art and than, say, his wedding day. Ho! When Art (a confirmed *eidetiker*) reminisces, he sees in his engram drive-in slide show of precise pages of text complete with all his underlining 'n marginal gloss. In green fountain pen ink. In red ballpoint. In black felt-tip. Whole illustrations are rendered in perfect detail. For instance, here Art annotates a passage from Browning pertaining to an aggregate word:

> 92   LANGUAGE MADE PLAIN
>
> of bound forms or ' helper morphemes ' but strictly limited to one free form only. This would make words of ' John ' (one free form), ' John's ' (one free form and one bound form), ' its ' (the same), ' his ' (two bound forms adding up to one free form). It would not, however, make words of compounds like ' penknife ', ' manhole-cover ' or German *Geheimestaatspolizei* (' Secret-state-police ' or ' Gestapo '). There would have to be a new term, such as ' word-compound ', to cover these and the following fantastic verb coined by Robert Browning :
>
> > ' While treading down rose and ranunculus,   } *great!*
> > You Tommy-make-room-for-your-uncle us. '

Or take those perfect images of gorgeous guts of rocks split—geodes—each crystal defined. Like in that spectacular crystal-crammed rock he and Larry Binacka dig up during their youthful excursion to Hauser Geode Beds in Coachella Valley near Blythe, California.

Art recalls little detail about their camping at Coon Hollow Campgrounds or their adventures hoofing it in with packs to that marvelous repository of hollow rocks. But that rock's interior, its craggy texture and blue 'n white hues, is forever available in photographic detail during Art's bouts of skull-time.

When did that rock disappear from my collection, Art idly wonders. *Oh yes . . . my* parapapanoid *pappy, his mind marooned on its own planet, thought it was an alien communication device (all those crystals!) spying on us so he smashed it to smithereens with a sledge hammer one day. After clobbering said rock, he turns his head skyward watching two rumbling jets climb towards a shared apex, trailing their thin contrails. They pass; no contact. Strange, feral, look in my father's eyes.*

Art's poor pappy! He will admit to possibility he suffers from: cancer or muscular dystrophy or Ebola or Lassa Fever or rat-borne hantavirus or toxic shock syndrome or antibiotic-resistant staphylococcus—but *never* from mental illness. Closest he comes to 'fessin' up? Once, on Art's twenty-first birthday, while cutting his son's cake, his father confesses: "Words. Words fail me. Why? Won't someone tell me." Maybe why Art takes up writing, drops photography.

Trying to make words *not* fail, not fail *him* like they did his daddy. Art starts paging through dictionary, eyes glued to those words sitting at page top: syzygy, crapulent, posterity, smegma, toiletry, dystopia, dentrifice, bastinado, penumbra, portmanteau, and quonking. (This last term is mediaspeak for extraneous sounds picked by any microphone; it's now suffered by Art when he ungoops his weird ear.) Art tries writing fiction. Exercise his word-mysticism. Play with schizophrenic writing. Alas, his prose is too diagonal 'n mood-warped. Difficult to subject to caseation. His first novel's octuple time scheme and its rotating crew of sixteen unreliable narrators is bit too much for any publisher, for any audience beyond those pedantic dons haunting academia. Myriad of rejections sway like loose harpoons from

Something is *Crook* in Middlebrook

nucleus of his writerly soul. Reluctantly, after a day of huge personal recriminations accompanied by slicing small, painful paper cuts into his forearm, he goes back to reviewing.

While he still was working on his novel, when asked what he does, Art replies: "I ply, sir, the scrivener's trade." After he begins reviewing again, what he says is simply: "I write. I'm a writer." Ho! Does enjoy constructing a metacommentary hovering over 'n above visual or verbal text under review. Likes textual parasitism. Claims review is sort of verbal translation of what's reviewed. In one early review published in a San Pedro, California area throw-away weekly newspaper, *The Stevedore*, Art wittily engages with Marcel Duchamp's famous Dadaist installation, *11 Rue Larrey*, wherein a door services two door frames so that this paradoxical door is simultaneously open *and* closed. "Duchamp gives forth a harsh knock on the door of Aristotlean either/or logic," writes Art at the beginning of this review. "Instead of asking for one's mama," continues Art, "this installation finds us calling for our Dada." Yes, whole review is clever sublimation of Art's dealings with his paranoid papa's bent logic. Art's life seems to hinge on such a door. A door opens (he's born) and it closes (he's abused son of a *parapapanoid*). A door opens (his enhanced hearing) and it closes (his once smooth gait gone). A door closes (his marriage) and it opens (meeting Una).

Ding-a-ling tinkle of bell on bistro's door. In saunters new, but regular, customer Pau calls "Geek Girl *avec* zee *eau-de-nil* eyes, zee taste for nootropics, *et* she eez *trés tape a'loeil*." She's probably older than she looks. Hair in tight Protestant bun. Art swears he can, when she rearranges her bun, hear her "squeaky clean" hair running through her red ink-stained finnies. Sports baggy jeans 'n commodious sweat shirt, immaculate except for small areas burned away by dripping solder (not by cigarette ash). White tennis shoes, bruised from too many tumblings in old clothes dryer, completes uniform. Faint whiff of fabric softener and old books trails her. Confesses to Pau once, "I'm an anxious neurotic—I don't bite my nails but I don't know why I don't bite my nails." If this be movie, audience be chortling by now. Orders glass of fresh squeezed O. J., dissolves Piracetam pill therein, then does bee-line for The Knowledge Machine, coin-operated concession popular with Pau's peers. Sits squarely on its weary 'n worn bicycle seat, adjusts it downward, cleans smudges off her thick glasses with crisp new dollar bill, inserts 50 cents, grabs handle bars with her allergy-puffed mitts, places stubby index finny at ready to tap out correct answers on keypad. Kick-starts machine's video Question Screen; rousing Chinese New Year's level of racket interrupted by short pedantic citations from world's most revered dons announces machine's begrudging acknowledgment of its new challenger. Licking her lips, Geek Girl starts pedaling toward that ultimate goal of GENUINE GENIUS (15,000 points):

WHAT WOULD GET LEIBNITZ DROOLING OVER HIS PILL JAR?
   a) Isle of Mull in mid-March
   b) Subscription to *Playboy*
   c) Very advanced copy of Gilbert Ryle's *The Concept of Mind*
   d) Cultivating an ethic of fitting response
Greek Girl hits "a."   BUZZ (correct). 100 points.

Something is *Crook* in Middlebrook

THE RHETORIC OF CLEANLINESS IS CLOSEST TO:
    a) The rhetoric of deliciousness
    b) Tony Shaloub's heart
    c) The Information Age
    d) Global capitalism

Greek Girl selects "a."   BUZZ (correct). 150 points.

IF A TASK WAS "INFRA DIG," YOU'D PERFORM IT:
    a) Quickly
    b) Slowly
    c) Unwillingly
    d) As beneath one's dignity

Greek Girl punches "c."   BUZZ-BUZZ (incorrect). Minus 50 points.

EUSTACHIAN IS:
    a) The tube running from nose to ear drum
    b) A three-man group hailing from around the U.S.A. that blends touch-and-go beat structures, melded with warm obtrusive melodies and cackling, child-like expressionism
    c) Having the qualities of a narrow tunnel, e.g., his mind is positively *eustachian*
    d) All the above

Geek Girl punches "d"   BUZZ (correct). 200 points.

THE FRENCH IDIOMATIC EXPRESSION *AVOIR LES IDÉES AU-DESSUS DE SA GARE* MEANS:
    a) To entertain ideas beyond one's station in life
    b) To fart
    c) To adhere to the dominant ideology
    d) To light up a cigar over your host's objections

Geek Girl punches "b"   BUZZ (correct). 225 points.

WHAT HAS FOUR WHEELS AND FLIES?
    a) A Korean War vintage C-119 troop transport
    b) A paraplegic pilot
    c) A child's red wagon loaded with manure
    d) A gay caballero carrying two bicycles

Geek Girl punches "d"   BUZZ (correct). 325 points.

"She's on a roll tonight," whispers Al, jerking his thumb toward Geek Girl who sits astride bicycle in pompous indifference to our huddled crew.

Geek Girl is pedaling her way toward GENIUS status. Over 10,000 points logged so far as series of single BUZZES report her success. Glance at screen of The Knowledge Machine indicates she's now working her way up scale of difficulty in section labeled ODDITIES OF FILMIC HISTORY.

Something is *Crook* in Middlebrook

10.2   "*Merde. J'ai mal au coeur.* For all we know, *mes amis,* zhis *femme* ez zee eyes 'n ears of zee Department of Homeland Security checking up on us. Paranoid thought does evoke Proustian involuntary memory of Pau's martial arts training in Hiroshima some twenty years ago (and yes, he's seen Alain Resnais' film *Hiroshima Mon Amour* some twenty times). In his inner-eye, "Dai Ichi" (as his Jewish-Japanese Krav Maga self-defense instructor dubbed him, meaning "Number One") is perusing a Japanese Krav Maga mag while on way to his martial arts lesson, surrounded by rubber-stamped school kids in their blue 'n white uniforms, crammed like maki rolls into public transport.

Much to utter astonishment of his customers, Pau suddenly grunts ferociously, starts practicing some choice Krav Maga moves. "*Mes amis,* observe." Puts Al into vicious head lock, grabs Al's wrist tightly.

"By Odin, Pau!" yells Al, gasping, eyes bulging like tiny balloons. Gentle pressure of diaphragm and contraction of intercostal muscles and Al starts to emit a little air, scrupulously controlled; he slightly tightens some membranes in his throat so that column of air forces membranes to vibrate; meanwhile, number of minute movements, especially of his tongue, cause center of vibration to spread sideways across tongue, move suddenly forward, concentrate just back of upper teeth, and then cease; with cessation of this voiced sound, column of air hisses against upper teeth and gums, and is suddenly and momentarily stopped by a flip of his tongue. His tongue strikes roof of mouth with portion just back from tip, and spreads so that whole column of air is suddenly dammed up and then released; all this is done with muscles of his throat trying to relax under strain of Pau's headlock. When little explosion of air takes place, everything stops at once and Al's vocalic apparatus utters these words: "Odin be fucked, my wrist!"

"Al, zhis ez zee Jewish, not Scandinavian, defense technique. Zee famous Hungarian Jew, Imrich Sde-Or, develops zee street fighting discipline called Krav Maga to contend *avec* zee anti-Semitic gangs *en* mid-thirties Budapest. Zhis *bon homme* (known affectionately as 'Imi') does develop zee techniques more fully while *en* zee new State of Israel after zee tumult of war. Trains all zee Israeli military *en* his techniques. *Moi*, I just want to get *moi* frogly mitts on one of zhose Hollowcaustic Kids . . . ," growls Pau.

"Well, don't practice on *me*, Pau! High probably you've put my neck out of whack."

"Hey, Al," chides Art, "he's just acting on a whim, by chance. Simple demonstration of chance over necessity, pal."

"*Touché*!" exclaims Pau, smile cutting friendly slash ear-to-ear, causing him to release Al. Al vigorously rubs his chafed neck. Pau stands in graceful *repoussé.*

Just as Dürer and Leonardo sought inspiration in "the ultimate law of proportion," and Cézanne believed that "everything in nature is modeled on the sphere, the cone and the cylinder," while Braque thought only the cube made sense, Alfred Schmerbauch casts his fate to chance and (as Al puts it) "spontaneous illumination." In lectures to his students, our pot-bellied professor proclaims: "No one is equal before the law, whereas all are equal before the cold equations of chance, since it is arbitrary; in gaming—poker, dice, and so forth—the distribution of opportunities is equal, because it is that of chance. Casinos today are the last outposts of democracy!"

Yes, if Leonardo—for inspiration—perused ancient art and architecture, Al peruses French biologist Jacques Monod's *Chance and Necessity: An Essay on the Natural Philosophy of Modern Biology* (1971). Al underlines following passage in said book:

> The ancient covenant is in pieces; man knows at last that he is alone in the universe's unfeeling immensity, out of which he emerged only by chance. His destiny is nowhere spelled out, nor is his duty. The kingdom above or the darkness below; it is for him to choose.

10.3   Choice? Why Pau always selects *Uni* at his fav Sushi joint, raw sea urchin, whose exotic, amniotic flavors evoke the dark, deep ocean. "It gives *moi* zee urge *en amour*, *mes amis*." Little wonder Pau has been known to publically chant (to upbeat tune of Bob Seger's "Old Time Rock and Roll") his gustatory love of such:

> Gimme zhat bonafide *Uni* roll,
> Zhat grade-B style of sushi just soothes *moi* soul.
> I take *non* interest *en* zee filets of sole, *non.*
> *Moi, je désire* my bonafide *Uni* roll.
> Into *moi* salivating mouth *non* need to cajole.

Choice? Why did Larry Binacka decide to devote his life to an as-yet-unpublished tome titled *Great Bores of the Modern World*? Started in college. "From the beginning," youthful Larry explains to Art, "humankind experienced states of boredom, but no one has approached the matter front 'n center as a subject in its own right!" Larry elucidates certain obvious types: political, philosophical, ideological, educational, therapeutic bores. Later Larry works up to others frequently overlooked: innovative bores, for instance.

Choice? Why does Una decide to wear her trouser suit of yellow alligator skin with hair hidden in black raffia toque today, and *not* her creme cloche hat with Gatsby gown, or her lurex blouse, bobby sox 'n teenager's flared tartan skirt?

Choice? There is *too* many choices available to Art for inclusion in his ever incrementally increasing telling tome titled: *My Cabezal Emporium of Sonic Knowledge (and Taste).* Therein, Art records most interesting of sounds (and tastes) his *ear*-ly warning system serves up to him.

"It's a *databasso continuo*," Art once explains to Al, "wherein sonic shocks are not merely noted—like, **I GOTS DA HATE, HONKEY, HANDS OFFA MY DIFFERENCE!**—but classified (like rocks) into *qualities*: dull, sharp, nasally, pingy, blowiferous, whizzing, clangy, fizzy, buzzy, sizzley, sweet, angry, annoying, head-splitting, etcetera; into *ethical modalities*: racist, sexist, moronic, authoritative, antagonistic, hype, hyperbole, astute, pedantic; into *sources* such as flesh: pie-hole (and the qualities of sounds emanating therefrom: consonants, vowels, implosives, glottal, trills), bung-hole (farts 'n sharts), fists, feet, finnies, tummy; or metals: tin, iron, aluminum, bronze; plastics: non- and biodegradable, hard and soft; chemical: combustatory, acid-eating, gurgly, bubbly; and nature: wind, thunder, water, birds, dogs, squirrels, . . . well you get the idea. Ho! Then I match each sound with its synaesthetic accompaniment (sweet, bitter, salty, metallic, etcetera); sometimes vice versa, as when I do happily hear the mellifluous sound of angelic angels singing song while savoring Chicago's *Wunderkind* chef Grant Achatz's Ultimate PB&J [peeled grape coated in peanut butter, wrapped in micro-thin toasted brioche then sprayed with vaporized lavender] at his culinary Ultima Thule, Alinea. Ya grok?"

10.4   Choice? Motionless in center of ear-shaped bed, strands of blonde hair caught like seductive child's in her mouth, Una tries to get her lover to drink guarana taurine beer—"Homeslice, it mimics the world, concentrates the given, luminous, radiant, velvety, profound . . ."—but Art refuses. Later follows up by leaving pleading message after Art's answer machine blares: HO! THIS IS ART, CALL ME SOONEST. Then one morning after night of aural sex she even tries pressing herself naked against his full-length mirror, face turned in, leaving fogged marks of face, hands, breasts, 'n thighs and—with arched glance—and *promises* to do this each morning-after if he will just try that brew. No luck. *Nada. Nein. Non.* Mellowpoignantgraveferocious does Una's emotional trajectory fly in response to Art's stubborn stubborness.

Crazy Art. He gets pleasure out of seeing spaces between food items in his fridge get larger 'n better defined; once confesses to Una, "I feel a little towards my books as I do towards the fridge, that I have to manage these as well, prioritize, determine which book is likely to give me the thing I need most at a given moment; but unlike the fridge, I like to be surrounded by an excess of books." And when it comes to eating toast, Art prefers using spoon or fork, as touch of toast repulses him. His finnies *prefer* to touch books:

Something is *Crook* in Middlebrook

"Shit man, do the miraculous math! *Two* finnies are *for* books." Books. For relaxation, Art chooses to read wonky meta-fiction *in alphabetical order* by author—Abish, Barth, Coover, Doctorow, and so on—writerly stuff requiring analytical thought, stuff that most people's pat answer to is: "That sucks!" Fact: gets this idea from some Reality TV show where fifteen sons of a dead man's test-tube line up to bob for apples, retrieving them in alphabetical order: Granny Smiths, Gravensteins, Golden and Red Delicious, Galas, Jonathans, Gigis, and Romes. Now Art's up to the G's on his list. Confesses getting penchant for such arcane reading material from college buddies: "My friends were either super-intellectuals or potheads who, in many cases, were the same. Ho! They'd learned to think beyond the level of a simpleton, ya grok?"

Speeding El train rattles past dome-home, passengers aboard with look of menagerie-bored animals, just as UPS delivers *Amazon.com*-ordered book to Art's "Sphere-of-Influence" (Noreen's disparaging term for Art's dome). Jubilant, opens package to find anxiously awaited copy of *My Landlady the Lobotomist* by Chicago author Eckhard Gerdes. Ho! Discovers pagely paper is super-duper good thumbing stock: when thumb 'n index finnies be dry 'n clean their purchase on thick pages does return excellent sound-effects to soothe agitated weird ear 'n gives synaesthetic taste of Cosi's coffee laced with absinthe. Fact: odd digital habit proves Art's hand is faster than the word. Ungoops ear, opens slim hardcover, thumbs loudly, slowly turning to "Chapter One—Mrs. Lardenswill's Boarding House" and, with eyes-wide, eyeballs text detailing idiosyncratic hobby that surely trumps his own collection of Famous Paintings' Pigment Scrapings:

> *She* [Mrs. Lardenswill] *keeps jars of frontal lobes in form-aldehyde on shelves throughout the house. Each jar is labeled not with the name of the donor, as one might suspect, but the peculiar ailment that led to the donor's selection for "the procedure." Alongside the jars predictably labeled "uncontrollable rage" and "advanced psychosis" are a few surprising ones: "bad taste," "irritable bowel syndrome," and "annoying laugh," for example. But my favorite is the one that reads "bad table manners."*

Too bad she doesn't have wonky frontal lobes of my parapapanoid, he thinks, thumbing thick paper even more maniacally.

Something is *Crook* in Middlebrook

11.0

Sun is now above horizon, lifting steadily as if on a pulley; flattish clouds, pink and purple on top and golden underneath, stand still in sky around it. On Lake Michigan waves are waving, up down up down. Lakeshore Drive is filling with commuters; traffic jam developing around where knee-capped jogger was just mugged. Stunning sunrise reflects off tall Loop office buildings, looking like magnificent crystals that Art studies in his geology classes. In shuffle of street you see the visible: countless odd pairings, all colors, all ages, all sexes, queens and knaves, jacks and tens in clubs and diamonds, swords and coins, walking round hand-in-hand. You see dull-faced young woman, stodged out on booze or glands, taking leaning weight of her elderly companion, or man with misangled legs like broken dividers. You see punk girl of seventeen, who does resemble mad parrot with or without her two black eyes, on arm of security guard not quite old enough to be her father. Visible is huge political billboard for local elections; invisible are radio waves carrying deceptive rap from uptight neo-con radio talk show hosts with their appeal to a populace frightened by rapid change, their eroding economic

and patriarchal status. Like people in sinking boat, they grab onto what they can for buoyancy. They prefer world as sketched in harsh Republican black 'n white as opposed to subtle Democratic greys. Yep, Monday morning. Chicago twangs in its Spring ozone, girding itself for fires of July and riot heat of August. Ache of first smell of Spring's first grass, so green it's acoustic. At night Art hears homeless voices out over flat rooftops.

Art pulls out his blue, yellow, and black CTA transit card and gets in line behind attractive girl with long brown hair in dark blue coat. Ungoops ear and listens to her soft hair brush against fabric. Feels himself get excited by this auditory *frottage.* Eventually he gets his turn to stuff his card in slit that debits exactly $2.00 fare. Up escalator (it's working today!) with gaggle of Yuppies in Spring colors, stands on platform looking bored like everyone else as he awaits next Brown Line train to Loop. **SSSSSSSSSSSSSSSRRRRRRRR EEEEEEEEEEEECHHHHHH**, train comes rasping to halt alongside impatient crowd. Bawling, static-plagued P.A. system announces stop: **WESTERN!**

Push 'n shove, shove 'n push. Art notices among panting elite in stuffed car a clarinet-tube-of-a-guy to whom untowardness of times be given human form and perversity of a hatmaker given to wear on his *cabeza* soft, brown hat with plaited cord, an instrument which resembles guitar that might perhaps have plaited its strings together to make a girdle. Suddenly, in middle of some minor arrangements between enterprising passengers and consenting passengeresses and of bleating tremolos from one covetous seated rider, ludicrous cacophony breaks out in which fury of double bass be blended with irritation of trumpet and jitters of bassoon. Then, after sigh, silence, pause and double pause, there rings forth triumphant melody of button in process of going up an octave as it be ripped off his coat by irrate cane-carrying elder who demands (rightfully) a seat.

Art goops ear and resigns himself to standing on snaking Brown Line where during morning commute even rest requires energy. EL commuters are basically good people. They save gas, don't pollute our environment. Some read books, improving their minds. But many tune out by pinching their heads between Sony Walkman earphones. Too many more are simply engrossed by their own private struggles and so lack conversation or a courteous word.

To pass time, Art's mind recycles possible test questions and answers for forthcoming quiz in Geology: *Question: Mica-schist alternating with gneiss, granitic and amphibological zones with granular limestone forms what substance? Answer: Marble, of course. . . . Question: What is the Svecofennian Domain? Answer: It is a 1.9 Ga old metamorphic terrain composed of volcanic-sedimentary schist and magmatite gneiss belts, intruded by granitoids. Svecofennian meta-sedimentary carbonate rocks, marbles, come from four areas: Norrlammala and Nummi-Pusula are situated in the Uusimaa Belt, southwestern Finland, and Rummukka and Ukonkangas in the Virtasalmi district, southeastern Finland.*

On the elevated, we float above the city, thinks Art. *Above heated debates carried out in everything from English and German to Polish to Pakistani. Above crazies chattering to all and no one. Above green-coated meter maids dropping parking tickets on hoods of cars like orange flower petals. Above cops hassling gatherings of black youth. Above colliding cabs. Above whale-sized CTA buses swimming through gutters, wagging their articulated extensions and spewing black froth. Above dare-devil bike-messengers zipping around stalled traffic. All the while my mind is full of pictures of Britney Spears half naked, car commercials showing people driving SUVs the size of houses without the least regard for life and limb, happy little songs about the wonders of Fast Food and images of attractive people competing to marry a millionaire. My country is full of anorexic girls with bad bleach jobs, thousands of people dying in car accidents, sick, obese children and adults killing themselves slowly with prepackaged processed people snacks. Jeez, the traumatic events, creeping crises, and social crises—all interrelated —seem . . .*

As EL passes DePaul Catholic University, Art recalls how at myriad of universities he's taught at over many years, he is generally viewed as (to quote one typical evaluation) "an intolerable goofball." At a west coast Lutheran University, he is publicly humiliated by Dean Emma Schwarzkopf (a big, ruddy, fleshy thing, with huge chilled face as thick as an over-ripe sweet red pepper) for drinking from a Coke bottle during their Twentieth Annual Soren Kierkegaard Luncheon.

Shit. After all I did for that college, founding their photo department and getting all the darkroom equipment donated, the only chair the WASP administrators offer me is the electric chair! Hell, most of those people are so uptight you could sharpen your pencil in their sphincter muscle. Others are small-time tyrants, toy ogres, Scandinavian trolls, who control their classes with demented screams in some crazy nonstop pedagogical opera. The only faculty member I even start to relate to (oddly, his first name is Battle) wears tango dancer's shoes and walks in curious stride, each step forward a dig —only the toes were involved, the heels were on their own. His movement is not grotesque, but curiously expressive. I find myself gradually sympathizing with his eccentricities for he exhibits a wonky bipolar mixture of hold-tight delicacy and flyaway brutality that, at the time, unconsciously reminds me of my dead, dearly departed, daddy. This bipolarity is reflected in one glaring element of decor. In Professor Battle Swenson's faculty office, over a small table on which always lay a copy of Rousseau's Reveries of a Solitary Walker, *hangs a large reproduction of a famous painting depicting Judith holding the head of Holofernes by the hair, his mouth open, her eyes turned to heaven as if she's a natural chaste beauty, even though she just committed a most brutal murder. One aspect of his physiognomic decor I can't forget is his powerful forehead: it all came down to that bristling overhang of a super-orbital ridge intersecting the straight line of his nose and matching the tight parallels of his lips—it gave him the look of a Nordic king bent on conquest. . . . Funny, the only thing* verbal *about him I can recall is his famous dictum: "A thought-murder a day, keeps the psychiatrist away." And I, at the time, thought* that *very profound*! *Battle becomes really embattled when his eldest son, driving drunk from an excess of mead, kills himself and Dean Schwarz-kopf's only daughter while returning from a date with her to Solvang, a Scandinavian theme town an hour's drive north of the University. Life can be so cruel.*

11.1   "Wabash 'n Adams!" bellows forth prerecorded station call. Breaks Art's reverie. He stands up. Adjusts strap on his large carrying bag. His exit is next. He lines up with his fellow passengers all looking like paratroopers preparing to jump. Doors open. Geronimo! Art flings his body through parting doors, exiting into warmer spring chill in which one could smell first signs of secret summer slowly slipping northward. Slips expertly into jostling, bustling crowd where keeping a rhythm and one's temper are rules for success. An enormously obese woman precedes him down stairs to street level. Standing on corner, Art looks left. Clear. Steps out into Wabash. KATHUNK-THUD. Art's abruptly hit by a red jersey-clad bike-messenger zooming around corner, going wrong way up this one-way street. Luckily, Art's substantial carrying bag slung over his right shoulder takes worst of blow. Cushions him like an airbag from THE GRINCH. At least that's *le nom de bicyclette* painted in black cursive on bright yellow frame that has just ignominiously knocked him down into damn dirty gutter.

There is an exhalation in a collision that is almost seductive, muses messenger, who daily partakes of such bumps 'n grinds and (no surprise here) is avidly reading J. G. Ballard's bizarre novel, *Crash*. Months ago this brave twenties-something biker asked himself *Is this a job or a suicide mission?* and opted to leave it all up to fate. Had he known Alfred Schmer-bauch, he'd been privy to probabilities: that an average biker can expect to have a serious accident every two thousand fifty miles; and high probability of fatal accident by fifteen thousand five hundred miles. This svelte biker's therapist had it all figured though: "Tavis, you want to be maimed, punished for the failure you think—based on your mother's bourgeois expectations —you've made of your life."

Something is *Crook* in Middlebrook

In defense Tavis countered, "The bicycle courier is a direct descendant of the cowboys and the gauchos. Their prestige traced to the matador. His bicycle is directly linked to the matador's *muleta*. The bulls are larger and motorized. He attempts daring passes with the *muleta*. Each pass is pure artistry. It is bravado and skilled deception all at once."

Man with ridiculously big sideburns and a gut helps Art to his feet.

"Thanks," grins Art, trying to hide his pain.

Biker—with face so drenched with luminescence it looks like he'd just come back from long vacation in the Milky Way—is clad in navy blue helmet, black cycling skullcap, bulbous eye shields, red jersey, tan cargo shorts over black winter tights and racing shoes shielded by neoprene spats. His belt buckle looks like a coin slot and reads: "5 cents. Insert coin. Unzip. Shake well. Guaranteed action. Internal use only." He easily picks up his two frames, one fleshy, one metallic. "Tavis Gulley. I'm . . . Well, I almost went on to say 'Glad to run into you,' ha-ha!" he extends a powerful, gloved hand toward Art. He has square eyes, thin lids cropped low from hard times and hopeless situations.

"Glad you can find it funny," retorts Art, miffed, rubbing his left bruised buttock where it came into surprised contact with curb cement; he ignores Tavis's peace offering.

Awkward silence between these two randomly chosen urbanites is broken by barely understandable electronic squawk from Tavis's battered walkie-talkie: *Boss, I'm sitting on a pair of southbound rags, an MTA/Cock, and I got a Monkey on my back that needs a rear-end. Is that a 10-4? . . . 10-4. Call me with the teeth on. Over and out.*

"Now don't get too upset," coos Tavis. "Neither of us is hurt, much. Say fellow, don't let your anger fester under a thin veneer of impolite language," he says trying to calm an angered Art. "Why I'm just an information mercenary, hired to pedal a little bit peace of mind to the corporate world—and, with my blood 'n fire, that's just what I do."

"Well, I . . ." Squawk of radio interrupts Art's reply.

Wavy Gravy, Number thirty-three, thanks for your help. Big Dave, get out of Dodge. . . . Yo, I copy that. I'm outta Dodge. . . . 10-4.

Across intersection is female cop directing traffic. Her back to northwest corner, she missed witnessing accident. But now her curiosity is up. Art can see in her eyes cocky comfort of a Doberman Pinscher guarding an estate.

"Hey. Look," pleads Tavis. "Just give a swift kick in the ass or take a whack at my bike and we can both go our separate ways." In supplication, he bends over his bike frame, offering either his *derrière* or his bike's *derailleur* to Art's itchy-footed decision. Clever tactic. Gesture of contrition wins over Art's sympathy. Remembering he's supposed to exemplify idealistic utopian values, frown turns to gracious smile. Art gently taps THE GRINCH on its *derailleur* with his shoe tip. "There. . . . All's forgiven." Art pulls out an anti-capitalist GRATUITOUS GIFT card with a spanking-fresh twenty dollar bill paper-clipped to it.

Something is *Crook* in Middlebrook

"Hey, wow! Thanks man!" Tavis peruses card. "I swear! Another activist. Ya, man. Glad ta meetcha!" Extends his hand, his bare finnies poking through fingerless gloves. This time Art firmly grasps those powerful digits.

"You've got a challenging job," antes up Art.

"Whoa! I can twist Madison Ave. into a runway 'n penetrate a crowd like it was a puff o' smoke," he boasts, holding up his right index finny and blowing on it as if it was a smoking gun. "But ya gotta eat constantly on his job. For instance, an apple lasts about thirty minutes in my system, working its way straight through my pores like I'm a screen door." Scratching his bike-seat sore ass, he goes on to tell Art about his bike rides with Critical Mass, an anti-car activist group, about his analysis of urban, corporate America. Art's impressed. "What's that white shit drippin' outta yer ear there?"

"Oh . . . ah . . . got this ear problem. Hear stuff much much too well. Without the goop, I audit the grass bendin' 'n snappin' beneath my feet. Rubber soles on cement register like beats on a bass drum."

"Heap weirderoo." Shakes his narrow head, narrowed even more by his closely cropped hair.

Number Thirty-nine, what your 20? Tavis? Call in. I've got crap dying all over this board. Get your package onward, baby!

"Hey, gotta fly. . ." Grabs his radio and yells, "Sit tight control. I'm north, shy of five from Wack 'n rollin'. 10-4?"

10-4 Thirty-nine. Stop filing your fingernails. Hubba-hubba.

"Ya know that ridin' this bike through the city is like—a real rush—fallin' through crosstown traffic like a skydiver with my own horizontal brand o' gravity. Fun, but tough. By tonight I'm gonna be *bonked*, lookin' like a corpse that has just dug itself out of a cafeteria's salad bar."

"Bye-bye," says Art, waving as Tavis puts muscle to pedal.

Pumping with all his might in his tight, crotch-padded biking shorts, Tav accelerates until Wabash visually becomes a long, narrow hallway, his environs a series of positive and negative signals. *Halle-fuckin'-lujah! I'm swimming toward emptiness*, he muses Zen-ecstatically.

11.2 Excerpt from Tavis's *A Biker's Journal*:

Raining today. Out buying a new machine. I passed my hand with unintended tenderness across the saddle. Inexplicably it reminded me of a human face, not by any simple resemblance of shape or feature but by some association of textures, some incomprehensible familiarity at the fingertips. . . . I knew that I liked this bicycle more than I had ever liked any other, better even than I had liked some people with two legs. . . . Riding in the city, that sensation of perspective: In front of your eyes it is high noon, but day seems to be breaking at the end of every street.

Something is *Crook* in Middlebrook

Still. Watching Tavis's red jersey (sweat stains peering out from beneath his armpits like a brace of obscene jokes) disappear down Wabash. Standing on corner, Art looks about him; looks at all those high-rises; drinks in urban cacophony. Muses. *Elevators, like expressways, subways, and jumbo jets, they all help merge constant motion with constant stillness. . . . Hey, that was . . . well . . . kinda profound!* At times Art even surprises himself. Art urges his bulk into full stature and commands his wobbly legs walk forward toward those twin lions guarding Museum's entrance and his morning donuts 'n java with Mala, his testy but tasty workmate. On either side of him people either stare at his weird ear tattoo or look quizzically, wondering if Bob Hoskins is in their midst.

11.3   "*Huá,* you're early *Profe!* What's wrong, *ese*?" She delivers this with velocity at once velvet-smooth 'n razor-sharp.

"Mornin' Mala. What's wrong? Bumps 'n grinds, that's what. As you see," says Art, limping-limping around Museum's break room, brushing lint off his guard uniform.

"*Sí, you're* double limping, *ese*." Mala sips coffee, gives Art double scrutiny.

"Brush with a hasty bike messenger and an immovable curb. A real howitzer kind of guy on a snazzy yellow contraption. Shot from guns. A blur of red jersey and suddenly my arse is kissing the curb." Art rubs his tender left buttock. "Now I'm limping with *both* legs, shit."

"*Sí.* Those Mercuries on wheels can be dangerous to us urban foot soldiers," she nods in sympathy. "My Uncle Pedro was hit from behind so hard by one speed demon riding a Cannondale bike that he was propelled backward onto his *cabeza,* turning his brain to *berza cortada*, chopped cabbage; permanent brain damage. He's riding an electric wheelchair now. Once sharp, he's now dull. Once gentle, he's now a crabby shit. Once steady as a rock, now he suffers periodic epileptic fits. *El Monstruo* is what his wife calls him. Sued the messenger *compañía* that *hombre descuidado* worked for right into Chapter Eleven though. At least his wife can afford to live *con mucho gusto* in Ensenada, that Cinderella of the Pacific, with *mucho* settlement money. So *you*, *mi bato*, were *afortunado*, lucky."

"What gallery do they have you in today?" asks Art, changing painful topic, noticing she smells of burnt tortilla 'n newly sliced chiles.

"Regenstein Hall."

"Oh, the new show 'Seurat and the Making of *La Grand Jatte*'."

"*Sí.* I get to listen to *mucho gringos* ooh 'n aah over Seurat's tiny dots asking what's the point of pointillism or pointing out how closely they resemble digital pixels."

"Hey, don't knock it. More interesting than my assignment—the kids area—the Kraft Education Center. Again."

"Ah . . . screaming *niños.*"

"Yep. Someone up there doesn't like me."

Something is *Crook* in Middlebrook

BBBZZZZZZZ goes annoying shift-change buzzer.

"*Andale!* Our shift is on!" yells Mala, taking last gulp of java, wiping her mouth.

11.4   Bright sky is torn by contrails in various stages of dissolution, some way up, as solid-looking as pipe-cleaners, others like white stockings, discarded, flung in air, or light bedding after beautysleep, others like breakers on inconceivably distant shore. Employee time-clock on loading dock reads: big hand is on 12, little hand on 5. With polysemic screams of little children still echoing in his mind, Art painfully changes back into his civies, starts to limp homeward along with the shimmyers, jaywalkers, 'n darters. Mala Gradecido pegs him on his way past clock and out employee's side entrance, "*Hola* Arty! Survive the sandbox?"

"*Blessed Benimming!* Mala, someday I'll have to write a taxonomy of kid's screams. I mean people have studied the screeches of chimps, right? Written profound treatises on *homo ludens*, yes? But we've been wholly lax in detailing the divers range of squeals 'n squawks of our little *homo quiritatens*."

"How's your rump?"

"Getting very stiff 'n I'm fighting a headache too."

"Well . . . *buenas noches.*"

"G'night." Exhausted tone in Art's reply bespeaks longanimity with which he bore his suffering this day.

Good thing Art's ear goop was firmly screwed into his auditory canal. Once it wasn't in firmly enough and when a small Scandinavian baby let loose with maximum decibels within a yard of Art's left ear, a bicuspid on his left side shattered. Luckily, oral surgery needed was covered on his HMO policy. As Art steps out onto Monroe Street, facing tortured steel of Frank Gehry's Millennium Park bandshell, he sees in dimming daylight Loop rush hour in full log jam. Cars moving as slow as old horse 'n buggy of hundred years previous. Once he mentions to Al that our City of Big Shoulders should muscle in more lanes of traffic to handle this problem. "Al, the movement of traffic is just as essential to the life of the city as the movement of blood is to the life of the body."

But Al takes issue with that solution. He astutely recalls Braess's Paradox. "Art, in 1968 Dr. Dietrich Braess theorized that adding extra travel lanes for regular traffic may actually *increase* congestion because, given the extra room, drivers will pass more often and try to move more quickly, result-ing in numbers of cars trying to get ahead of one another, fighting to take the same traffic opportunities. Ergo, high probability that final result turns from a small delay into a humongous thirty-minute backup."

Then he sees it,. A bike messenger charging like a ram into Monroe and Michigan intersection. Way too fast to stop. Black SUV pulls out unexpectedly to wiggle around a shy yellow VW Golf. Biker in multicolored Lycra, sporting a thick red beard, leans forward on his handlebars until his back tire is drawn up off road; he stops pedaling and plants fixed back tire on asphalt, dragging it through carefully managed skid as SUV passes only a few feet from him. *Whew! Close call.*

Art does wheeling left-face, slow-gimps his way west on Monroe to EL station at Wabash. People stare at him. If this were film, aerial view would show Art wobbling through uniformity of rush-hour crowd to accompaniment of Lalo Schiffrin's tune "Rampage of the Driver Ants" from his film score for *The Hellstrom Chronicle*. Art is sad victim of a double-defect: his innate gimp and this new bike-induced limp. Once he gets to base of EL stop has to do all those steps up to platform. Ho! Effort sends dull aches through his left gluteals. *Now I know what it must feel like to be ninety.*

Once on platform, Art takes his mind off his pain by imaginatively turning noisy crowd milling about waiting for Green and Brown Line trains into perverse updated version of Hieronymous Bosch, say canvas titled *The Garden of Transportational Delights.* Conversely, when he confronts original Bosch canvases on his job in Museum, he ungoops weird ear, aims it directly at artwork, and imagines what sounds would emanate from those over-manned chaotic tangles of Lowlanders.

Finally northbound train arrives. Art squeezes into metal container. Feels as if he's being processed like some kind of food stuff. No seats available. Stands with his weight on right leg all way up snaking path to his stop. To pass time, he reads. For Art, reading means being transported elsewhere; it is, for Art, a setting up secret scene, place he can enter 'n leave as he pleases; it be utopian creation of recesses of shadow 'n night within an urban existence subject to technocratic transparency. It all starts as little Art's way to dodge surveillance of his paranoid pappy. Simply put, reading for Art is, as he once tells Al, "a retreat from *them.*" Art glances up to see one of *them:* man facing him holds up *Chicago Sun-Times* with headline, BUSH FOILS GREENS BID FOR CLEANER AIR.

11.5   If this were film, camera from high angle would show elevated train Art's riding on has coaches graphically painted in yellow-green and metallic blue calligraphies that howl without raising their voices and streak through city to advertise some event or product. As train moves west past dancing graphics whose fleeting apparitions are accompanied by rumble 'n electric sparks of train wheels on track, we would see immediately below "Pronto" Pietro's large black limo cross directly under said train, edging south on Dearborn Avenue. Pleasure for audience in seeing two diametrically opposed characters's paths nearly intersect—neither aware of it—while camera captures this conjunction of opposites in stunning visual moment *sans* narration. Such a scene affirms to audience that their knowledge exceeds that of novel's characters.

Thank you for riding the Brown Line train number 6201. This is Western, Western. Exit here for Lincoln Square, that Taste of Europe, announces distorted pre-recorded message over cheap speakers in coach. Door pops open. Art exits train. Walks out past a gaggle of panhandlers, eastward past Lothar Speer's huge wall mural of a bucolic European scene, then jogs left up Lincoln Avenue past Dergerberg Dojo where Brats hang out, past Selmarie Bakery. On his way through Giddings Plaza he sees usual gathering

Something is **Crook** in Middlebrook

of mazophilous German émigrés inhabiting park benches, admiring breasts of female pedestrians and occasionally rehashing yet another anti-Semitic joke. Streets still littered with paper cups, dirty napkins, plastic beer mugs, plastic cutlery, and little German flags left over from Sunday's celebration of Hitler's birthday sponsored by local German businesses. Smell of stale beer and sour sauerkraut stimulates Art to decide to eat dinner at Brauhaus German Restaurant. Cheap drinks; reasonably priced chow; wenches with generous cleavage serving *homo schnappiens*. As he opens restaurant's heavy wooden door door—over which small sign reads: *SCHMECKT WIE DAHEIM* (TASTES JUST LIKE AT HOME)—Art leaves early evening Spring chill for warmth of hearty fun 'n food. His nose be hit with delightful, pungent smells, 3/4-time roar of an oompah band knocks on his ears, and his eyes spy drunk patrons tipping precariously from tall stools or vigorously colliding large beer steins over their table of food. Large German woman, poor prickly soul with German accent and charmless restaurant charm that makes him think of a cash register, seats him with menu at small wooden table tucked into dim, wood-paneled corner. Blond waitress in Bavarian garb and barely audible over music takes his order. Starts with a double Berliner cocktail accompanying liver dumpling soup. Then big boot of Weissbier to savor with his main dish of sauerbraten. Very moist Black Forest cake for dessert with Kümmel (Henry Miller's fav apéritif) to settle his tummy.

While he sips his Berliner, Art scans playful crowd. Some middle-aged couples, more than a bit tipsy, are arrayed in circle doing The Chicken Dance played by The Innsbruck Dossers. When music starts, hands be held out front, opened and closed like a chicken beak, four times. Then thumbs are put in armpits and one's wings be flapped, four times. Next arms and hands placed like tail feathers of chicken and one wiggles down to floor, four times. Finally, one takes hands of those in on either side and turns in circle. When dizzy one reverses turn. Repeat. As dance comes to an end, woman at far end of bar topples off her stool without anyone paying notice. Drink still firmly in hand, she brushes off her dress and remounts her ersatz leather steed, continuing conversation without missing a beat. Other barflies underscore conversation with highly theatrical, apodictic gestures, beer bottle in right hand, left hand acting out one-armed, left-handed roles. *It might be a good ploy to tie the right hands of all drama students behind their backs for a year at the start of their training*, Art speculates as he spies on these locals.

During past visits here, Art ungoops, eavesdrops on whispered confidences. Ho! One time overhears table of four burly men, murmuring with marked German accents and peppered with *ja ja*, ja ja, enthuse over Hitler's *economic* policies; another time he tunes in anti-Semitic jokes concocted by three matrons; at another time he is privy to heated discussion about how best to sanitize Lincoln Square area of undesirables by table full of concerned local entrepreneurs chewing on their expensive cigars. This evening he keeps his ear goop stuffed tightly in. *Who needs that shit*, he thinks. *Besides, the band is too loud to distinguish conversations easily.*

While sipping thoughtfully of his caraway-flavored Kümmel, he notices cock-smiled insurance salesman at bar, that very same huffy stuffed shirt Art literally ran into on Lincoln Avenue near here few months back, back-slapping some mustachioed muscle beside him and giving him that false smile that swept country about fifteen years ago (to achieve it, you draw your upper lip away from your teeth, while looking at your interlocutor with charm). Can't mistake that drowsy pinch around his eyes, same as you see in certain leading men or Euro-jetslime. Has voluble tongue, indiscriminate and inexhaustible sociability. Never confesses to headaches or overactive bladder. Even though he now wears blue blazer with discreet buttons, instead of that dusty-white silver suit color of underside of moth wings dying in a holy light. Tonight his whole aura screams: *yacht*. He's so incredibly good-looking that when he hits the street courting couples snarl with lust 'n reach out to steady each other. But if you press his wife on it, she'll confess he has some small, unpleasant hole in his nature through which he sometimes creeps forth in his entirety.

This shit guy makes me think of loud cologne and urinals, muses Art as he tries to restrain himself from yanking out goop and turning his form-idable ear in guy's direction. *I don't want to be privy to more racist blather or another encomium to entrepreneurship.* To no avail. He's too curious. Art removes goop, cups hand over ear to focus its angle of attack, and tunes in.

AH, THE MAD AGILITY OF COMPOUND DECEIT! WE RAISE THE POOR BASTARD'S PREMIUM EVEN THOUGH THE ACCIDENT WASN'T HIS FAULT. I'M MEAN THE GUY WAS SITTING DEAD STILL AT A RED LIGHT WHEN THE OTHER VEHICLE PLOWED INTO HIM. THAT'S SMART MONEY. AND IF THE GUY COM-PLAINS, WHY WE THREATEN CANCELLATION. HE KNOWS HE'LL PAY THROUGH THE NOSE AT ANOTHER COMPANY WHO'LL PUT HIM ON HIGH RISK FOR A YEAR OR TWO. SO HE STAYS WITH US AND WE COLLECT BIG TIME. I LOVE FREE ENTERPRISE, DON'T YOU? AMERICA IS A LAND WITH SUCCESS IN ITS OZONE, A NEW WORLD FOR THE GO-GETTERS AND NEW-BOOMERS, A LAND WHERE FORTUNE GRINS AND MAKES THE TRIPLE-RING SIGN.

Art regoops ear. Blood be boiling. Recalls Al's observation that, "High probability that all classes are criminal today. We live in an age of equality." Returns to eating his cake. By time Art licks last bit of frosting from his fork, booze has worked its magic. He's forgotten insurance salesman. He feels no pain. *Soft bed here I come!* Flags waitress down. Pays check. A bit woozy, he performs mincing steps toward exit and experiences that thrilling moment when crisp, clear Spring evening air goes up his nose, past his deviated sep-tum. Sensation lights up Edenic daydream which briefly caroms around his boozy brain: *Ah, it's a serene evening, refreshing air, sky clear, flowers ex-hale fragrances! Beams of declining sun, whose mild splendor repose on summit of mountain, sheds glow of ruddy light over its green declivity and on multicolored jerseys of bicyclists pumping up a snaking road to summit; no sound heard, save murmurs of four fountains and reeds and voices of bikers cajoling to each other from different stages along a windy mountain road.*

Something is *Crook* in Middlebrook

11.6   While Art be thinking his thoughts, thought it be only fair to relate simultaneous event inside Pogacnic's domicile: Frozen-faced Noreen stares fiercely at TV screen as she clicks through cable channels rapid as lizard scaling a wall. Her pig eyes have glassy-hungry look of a child rushing through channels certain that something special is waiting. She's looking for anything Prada, Dior, Gucci, Nautica, Armani, Baccarat or Yves Saint Lauren—luxuries way beyond her pocket book whose images always gets her into what she calls "THE MOOD." Her tense mouth, disguised by midnight-plum lipstick, glossy as plastic, suffers from recent collagen injection gone bad that leaves hard little grimacing worms bracketing her mouth, just beneath skin, and at corner of her pig eyes are faint red lines like burst capillaries. Ho! If we could tune into her interior sounds, we'd hear soft-rock-Bach Muzak like sound piped seductively into dressing rooms. Wants to remain desirable to Peven. She belongs to Gottlieb Health Club, if only she had time to drop by. Despite her age and husband's blindness, Noreen doesn't want her looks to slip too far down the scale of respectability. Tonight she only sees two commercials, one for Calvin Klein, other for Shanghai Tang. Bare minimum for excitement needed. Noreen turns off her wide-screen LCD and retires briefly to her boudoir, returning reeking of some Wal Mart brand perfume, chemicals guaranteed to trump photo chemicals keeping Pev in his darkroom. Now sitting on couch together, Noreen reads to Peven from her old leather-bound diary with ulterior motive being to arouse ol' Pev into getting carpet burned knees on their hi-lo carpet.

"You were on leave, remember? First time I saw you since January first. You had recently sent me a letter from Fort Dix in which you'd passionately declared: 'Nory, your words deep within my heart are sculptured.' It says here, darling, that (I quote): 'Pevy called on me at the boarding house and in my room our lips met for the first time since New Year's Eve. I threw myself upon his prone body, pressing hard—hard—exquisite possibilities —then the door bell rang . . . damn Aunty B. keeping tabs on me again. The mood was broken but next morning, under the brilliant blue of winter day sky, Pevy resolved to do a portrait which would reveal *everything*—something of the delight of our present life. And so it came about that I bundled up and went outside to pose, leaning against a whitewashed wall—lips quivering— nostrils dilating—eyes dancing with delight. Pevy drew close, kissed me; a tear rolled down my cheek and began to freeze. And then he captured the moment—I think he announced grandly *f/eight at a tenth-of-a-second with a K-1 yellow filter—panchromatic film*. How brutally mechanical and calculated it sounds—yet really how spontaneous and genuine it was. The moment of mutual emotion was recorded on the silver film. We passed from the glare of the sun on white walls into Pevy's darkened room—my skin and somber nipples were revealed beneath a black nightie, which I slowly drew aside. We made love and my orgasm felt like a hundred glimmering goldfish expelled through the hole in an aquarium.' Pretty hot stuff, huh, Pevy?"

If this be film, camera would pan to blazing fire in fireplace seen through two wine glasses filled with Castello Banfi Brunello di Montalcino, Riserva Poggio All'Oro, 1997, while *The Carpenter's Level*, a four-CD anthology of mellowest Karen Carpenter songs (guaranteed to put a couple's respective bubbles back to center) provides background music. Camera-eye then turns back to gaze at furnishings and all that "cheerful clutter" (Noreen's term, not mine); one word enters us viewers' *cabeza*: quaint. Antiques, collectibles, *stuff*. Scratches, chips, and cracks. Hodgepodge of oldness that creates state of generic *pastness*. Soon Noreen's chicken collection be in sharp focus: inventoried and displayed cute escapees from innumerable flea markets and overpriced antique shoppes—some bought on e-Bay. Collection now worth $5000.00 'n change. *Styles die, only kitsch survives*, we silently, astutely observe. Camera dollies into cozy kitchen where over an Elmira Stove Works self-cleaning black antique-styled oven and matching rétro-styled dishwasher there be Amish hand-painted wooden sign edged in rendition of red roses tautologically declaring: FRIENDS ARE FRIENDLY. Refrigerator sports gaggle of decorative magnets purchased at oodles of antique stores Noreen frequents over past twenty odd years. *High probability you can tell a lot about a person from their fridge magnets*, we think. We can't help noticing how Noreen delights in conjoining harmony of opposites: placing ultra-feminine stuff next to unpolished and coarse items—pink ribbon tied around twig chair, china cup resting on roughhewn beam, dried flowers spilling out of rusty camp coffeepot, etcetera—with hi-lo carpeting running as *basso continuo* underneath it all.

 Blessed Benimming! thinks Art upon first visit to Pogacnic's domicile. Think most of us would be in agreement.

11.7   While Pev 'n Noreen romance, taste of beer bursts into Rusk's mouth in one big belch, proving he's once again ignored Dee's dictum: *Temper and intemperance tempt, so refuse da booze.* His face blurred in its angles by day's growth of beard, he reclines in his bath, rubber pillow behind his head, watching passing car headlights move across bathroom wall. Dark stain seems to leak from his mouth onto his chin, a shadow that is a blue tan from spending too much time in bars. Alcohol be leaving him in concentric waves. Paradise now to lie in steaming bath forever, right temperature eternally provided. Centuries might pass. Bathroom smells of stale cigarette smoke. Sound of children at play drift in as Roo shuffles his bare toes against taps, slithers lower into water. Only sound in house be Brats watching "Invader Zim" on Nickelodeon. Dee's working at Pau's Bistro. He stares upwards until his neck aches, his eyes swim. What thoughts Roo can muster—things like, *Isn't it funny that six drinks can sometimes do what five cannot?*—slide past frothing 'n bubbling, threadbare tricks of a shallow mind. Beats his fist against head to stop such thoughts—to his surprise it works. As he floats brown beer bottle down his bath, towards soap-dish, his thinking detours to recall pleasurable late-afternoon rendezvous at his fav watering hole on corner of Montrose and Lincoln, The Teddy-Bear Club (formerly The Glass Crutch), an establishment made famous by famous painter Benny Ronson's famous oil painting.

 As always on Sunday one can hear remote (not so remote for Art though) sounds of neighborhood people home from work, doing things they want to do that still-and-all-aren't making them happy. Air of lazy tinker-

At the Teddy-Bear Club (o/c, 6 ft. x 5 ft, 1995) Benjamin A. Ronson

ing, bored family visiting reigns over bright background of existence until afternoon cloudburst: rain runs down gutters with vomiting noise. When sky is clear and through departing cloudbanks early-rising moon be bone-white, Roo strolls to his home-away-from-home, noticing each crack in stonework along way looks like some surgical operation. While walking, visible world does graze his skin from its deep distance. If Roo be philosophical like Art, he might wonder: "What is it that holds perpetual fission of instants together?" If Roo be smart like Al, he'd have answered: "Habit holds things together and so does a sentence."

Roo be aware of certain liquid pulse of anticipation for sound of ice wheezing 'n popping in glasses, that spongy effect of alcohol. Along Lincoln Square's after-school pavement, girls tote their breasts like revolvers as ogling male youths lean against shop-fronts with hungry, vacant faces, wearing short jackets, tight jeans, 'n pointed shoes. Roo turns corner at high-speed gait, leaning into the turn; bursts through large green door and under Club's signature sign (large, bloated, pissing teddy-bear dubbed "FlowBear") as gust of wind blows piece of paper behind him, circling, performing drunken dance. Club's plush carpet swallows Roo's footsteps and he hears that soft farmyard noise of canned music that plays background to awful sonic concussion of drunken conversations that's so comforting; ambient soft bar-light creates world that seems better than home-not-so-sweet-home. British Bob-the-bar-keep (hailing from East Anglian village of Huguenot-Malherbe) spinsterish-like runs fluttering hands over glass mugs like some old maid with her china—nods at Roo-the-Regular, his glance holding affection; over bar sign reads: THINK GLOBALLY DRINK LOCALLY.

Roo plops onto barstool next to guy with two eyes just like you 'n me, but most of time you can't tell if he's using them to look with. He's not asleep but he's not quite awake either. He just exists. Who is he? One "Fluffy" Mahoney—moniker refers to his wallet full of pubic hairs—who is always reprimanding bartender, Brit Bob: "Yer glasses are thick 'n da whiskey thin!" Today "Fluffy" be snookered, carrying on about "da total éclair of da shunned dat's s'posed ta occur over Scotland today." Bored, Roo looks up at familiar teddy-bear memorabilia: in between two large jolly plush teddy bears sporting huge colored ribbons tied around their necks spies that curious, old, and oddly framed ad claiming: DUREX GOSSAMER SENSITOL LUBRICATED IS THE ONLY HOPE FOR INDIA. As his left hand fingers piece of tire-marking chalk in his pocket, Roo's right goes thumbs up to signal British Bob for his usual stein of ruby red Bishop's Finger imported from Kent, England. Place is already crowded: lighters being flicked; smiles spread over faces like jam; beer spilled in frothing continents over bartop. Constellation of bar regulars be forming, a decisive moment like film moment when relative positions of characters within virtual depths of image is more compelling than anything they might have to say.

Sign, The Teddy-Bear Club

Art once accompanies Roo here to watch his scotch swirl like smoke in a liquid sky in a glass, while enjoying Kip's Kalypso Kings's libidinous performance (Kip, jowly, ash-skinned, once sang back-up for Jimmy Buffett), observing: "Ah, Roo, con-

Something is *Crook* in Middlebrook

versation here 'twixt 'n 'tween men and women sounds like a musical conversation between an oboe and a harp." Roo glances down bar—sees men in stylized yawns with arms raised, men staring into dead space—waves at Happy "Hap" Huntington Blank, boozy womanizer whose mute, expressionless, but attentive face belies another mind acrobatically multi-tracking at high energy: logical reason, image-making, cataloguing and matching, analysis, memory search, language formation, and reverie be whizzing separately yet with a collective entity that's unified by his perennial alcoholic odor. He sits next to woman with cheeks rouged bright pink, wearing fuchsia pants 'n lemon yellow shirt; hair be greasy white platinum, like smoke from a green fire. She at the bar the way flies and mice might be, localized, seeing and knowing nothing but whatever her scanted nature allows. Her gaze has abridged quality, it isn't reaching either wall or window. Yep, she seems as deep as a dime. Her drink—some weird Rum concoction called Wrack 'n Ruin —be at that stage in life of a drink when you take that last bland sip and fade into rueful introspection, somewhere between self-pity and self-accusation.

Little balm of intellectualizing creeps into Roo's face—as if he might cry out, "A government is a criminal enterprise!"—then slowly drains away as he spies a pyknic figure, squat Hispanic woman on stool near him wearing marmalade-colored pants suit, who goggles like goldfish waiting for someone to throw her an ant's egg. Good-looking (angle of her nose 'n width of her jaw seem impossibly delicious) and unhappy (dark bronze without sparkle, mouth almost too indifferent to be sensuous, eyes so dark it looks like she's wearing sunglasses inside her head, forehead be a cloudy blank you could skate across). She moves slightly, revealing ink stain on one finny, her lipstick be smudged like badly applied crayon.

Roo develops sudden spurt of interior laughter. He comes here as much for the odd clientele as the beer. He's seen her here alot—albeit usually draped in white percale dress with mameluke sleeves—and has dubbed her "Olivia y Pineapple" for she's either sipping a Dirty Martini or a Blue Hawaiian with wedge of pineapple jammed in it. Roo notices she draws her nose over pineapple slice, smelling its tropical aroma (that certain acid juiciness within purely yellow spectrum with slightest notes of green 'n sugar). Slowly sipping her libation, her mind is always shooting out of present moment through frictionless gate of memory, that fast diode of imagination. This gives her look a look of challenging suspicion that makes her look dumb. Shunned as an outsider, she survives by making herself more unknown; turns her isolation into mystery to which only she knows trivial solution. British Bob thinks her well-kept secret is that she sings with poise and fluency of a professional but *only in absolute secrecy*. And twice Roo's overhead her complain to British Bob (who stares into the daylong narrows of his bartenderly detachment): 1) "Everyone's childhood is a plate that gets huge gobs of indigestible stuff and leaky gravy heaped on it;" and, 2) "Everyone knows and no one cares." Words say life sucks, but tone of voice says it doesn't matter. Twice Roo's noticed she avidly thumbs well-thumbed paperback copy of Evelyn Waugh's *Ronald Knox*, memory carrying her hand swiftly across page as if flying into grooves of something already traced there. Looking title up on Internet, Roo discovers it's biography of Right Reverend Ronald Arbuthnott Knox, heap famous Catholic convert.

Something is *Crook* in Middlebrook

Enormous multiplicity of the moment, as always; every instant an explosion of perception made manageable by habit of not paying attention, even when our broad world lays a present moment against our senses, small 'n sharp. In this instance that sharp 'n small prick be in guise of another barfly. Recognizing Roo as a regular, nudges him, covertly pointing to Olivia while conspiratorially whispering: "Dude, up on the latest current event?" Has to repeat himself twice before Roo gives his best I-haven't-had-my-booze-yet blank stare, wary of what Art once told him: "Beware of conversational erasure, the one who's talking often vacuums out the one who's listening. Ya grok?" Roo's head goes back on its stem with little cock to one side, eyes narrowed as if he has no idea what this guy's saying. Some robust fullness of self fills his body while Roo's interlocutor's bodily presence be so negligible as to be experienced as a tiring vacuum. Somewhere in background laughter, loud 'n often. Sounds like happiness; but it just might be Happy "Hap" Huntington Blank with another outlandish story about his badly synchronized mutt "Bah-Wah" whose bark 'n barking motions never jive. Retort from giggling bar buddy Hank Wattle (fuzzy brown haircut, wobbly oversize head 'n a game leg): "And if *he* was a *she* ya would've named 'er Bah Bah Wah Wah, right?"

"No?!" continues barfly to Roo, eyebrows arching in surprise. Round cheeks, bright eyes give him quick endearing look of an eager forest animal. "Such a sensation at St. Sappho's when *she* lapsed," tugs his thumb in Olivia's direction. "Rumor has it she found a currant in her communion wafer. Tossed all her religious readings into St. Sappho's large green dumpster, I hear." Leans back, breathing heavily. Satisfied. His search for sequence successful.

"Well," observes Roo in a statement that is as close as he'll ever come to being philosophical, "God laughs 'n snaps his finnies . . . da only thing fer a man or woman ta do is ta imitate God 'n snap da finnies too."

As he awaits his ruddy bitter beer, over sound of pool balls chattering like teeth on chilly day, Roo overhears some crypo-beat (fraudulent rebel whose anger is not strictly on the level, clad in grey T-shirt that screams in large black Helvetica MAYNARD G. KREBS LIVES) admonishing his drinking companion: "Blast it! You're one of those people who measure success by the *number* of copies sold. It might surprise you my friend to find out that *some* writers, *moi* included, are too good to be published!" Pissed, dude replies: "And *you* . . . well . . . they shouldn't let you into a bar without training wheels!" This guy's face has kind of starved intensity, seeming to change shape as though under water. His more prosperous-looking interlocutor puts hand to mouth and starts to bite his nails, nipping each finny in turn. This guy's face has kind of starved intensity, seeming to change shape as though under water. His more prosperous-looking interlocutor puts hand to mouth and starts to bite his nails, nipping each finny in turn.

Two gay men pass behind Roo, close enough for him to pick up a passing comment by one of them: "So we're *doing* a German play . . . and it's rather your line of country I should think deary, all about incest in the early days of aviation."

"I thought you'd be *doing* that one on King Richard who, on his way to the Crusades, did penance for sodomy."

Something is *Crook* in Middlebrook

Roo stares at himself in bar's mirror, pretending drunkness he hoped to achieve over the next hour and half; slowly moves head about, scrutinizing his chin, focusing on what he calls "myscar," a scar that originates in Gulf War incident he oft recalls: "It was da time some crazy sergeant threw a grenade at my CO; he was killed out right; thought I was a gonner too, unconscious fer days."

Brit Bob finally puts Roo's drink before him. Leans in toward his fav customer and asks in his British accent: "Mate, do you know what *subreption* is?" Bob is always making these bartenderish riddles, either delighting or pissing off his customers—it comes with the job.

"Fuck, do I look like I'm some kinda Arthurine scholar?" replies he making disparaging reference to Arthur S. Middlebrook. "It sounds like some-thin' da Brats would be pullin' off, huh?"

"It means, and I quote, 'To obtain something by misrepresentation.' It's what our so-called civilization does, holding carrots before us so we'll work our butts off. Do you know what it wants in exchange for a house, a car, a larger house, two cars, a flat-screen TV in every room?

"Nope."

Moving even closer. "It wants our lives," he whispers. "Working for what? For a better world? For a merry-go-round of more production?" Brit Bob looks Roo directly in his sad eyes, making our Beer-bibber feel slightly uncomfortable, for Bob has that cruelty of insight which knows no scruple. "They are so damn busy working," he continues, "they haven't the time to be unhappy; so busy watching the telly 'n driving round in cars, they haven't the time to think."

Roo's eyes feel like hot ashes. Puts out hand knotted with veins and picks up his glass. Takes one healthy swig of that unhealthy brew, suds sticking to his nose tip. Feels the cool-down. Returns Bob's gaze and replies: "Have I told you 'bout Dee 'n I's famous kitchen debate 'bout da dilemma of da underwear—slit in da front (Fruit o' da Loom) versus none (Calvin Klein)?" Ah yes, Dear Reader, this is the fug of normality, where Roo *should* be!

11.8 While Beer-bibber imbibes, wind picks up in Chicagoland. Until he moves from California to Illinois, Art never hears phrase "wind-chill" pro-nounced on TV. Over stimulated (dare we use the term "scared"?) by invisible din, Tig digs salamanderly deeper into dirt under deck, digging with demented joyfulness—like young dog—digging through true, stupid eternity of matter building itself up out of eroding matter. Tig digs into that shallow instant a furrow that *feels* to salamander like eternity. Two stories above, Art sits in cockloft watching agonized twisting of trees, blocking sound therefrom with ear goop. With look of someone who punishes others and himself with his intelligence, he grows philosophical: *Reality's thin core always kills us when we pass through it, yet we paddle around in its astonishing bath of effects from beginning to end.* Absent-mindedly twists ear goop in left ear. Next his restless mind takes his thoughts to how lucky he is to have gotten through childhood without growing up, then to Una, recalling those moments when little balm of intellectualizing silently creeps into her face and gentle pulsation in curve of blue vein beneath skin of her right temple becomes almost as fast as throbbing in Tig's throat when he lies motionless on rock in sun. Finally, to that double fantasy of marriage as one breathtaking aural safari with Una between breakfast table and ear-shaped bed. Recalls scene that appears full 'n lustrous in his imagination as if tipped in by an artful hand: Una lowers her gaze like small, spent sun, but then offers her mouth strong as sun at its zenith and declaims, "Arty, you're my homeslice! I am your comfort, so breathe with me, let me bring comfort, breathe with me, say yes, then say yes, I am the sea that rolls over you, I am the green and your comfort, lie with me, lie *with* me, but never lie *to* me." Words that be accompanied by scent of her perfume which be, he remembers, like knife blades, so acute his senses; feels each molecule of smell, one atom of air, against his stretched eardrum. He wanted to unplug, recalls. So now abruptly does pull out white ear goop 'n gingerly toe-turns swivel-stool toward Pogacnic's domicile.

In superficial, all important sense, Pogacnic's help create local nebula of existence in Art's universe. At first sound waves arrive all at once in clotted bunches due to wind's all important ability to splice elements. But after prying out small particle of goop that resisted initially evacuation and applying concentrated beam of attention, he catches in his aural net Noreen doing one of her finest photo-interpretations of latest batch of slides Pev shoots at The Teddy-Bear Club:

SHE'S AS TALL 'N SLILM 'N SHALLOW AS THE FEMALE LEAD IN A DUMB-BLONDE JOKE. IS THIS YOUNG GIRL'S LOOK ACTUALLY A PRIVATE CONTEMPLATIVE EXPRESSION, OR A SLACK-FACED DAYDREAMY ONE? DOES IT CONCEAL THOUGHT OR MIGHT IT CONCEAL THE LACK OF THOUGHT? IS IT A KIND OF MEDITATIVE INTELLIGENCE, THE BEGINNINGS OF A PARTICULAR AESTHETIC AND EMOTIONAL DETACHMENT FROM THE WORLD AROUND HER, OR IS IT ABOUT SOME GENTLE, EASILY OVERLOOKED INTELLECTUAL DEFICIENCY? DOES IT INVITE THESE SORTS OF QUERIES, OR IS THAT LOOK MORE CONCERNED WITH PLAIN EQUILIBRIUM, A NEW PERSPECTIVE ON THE BATHROOM AND TOILET SEAT IN WHICH SHE FINDS HERSELF FIRMLY ENSCONCED ... MY GOD, PEVY, YOU SNUCK INTO A LADIES ROOM!? GEEZE . . .

Fact: Noreen be heap good talker, tells stories well, with many shadings, surges of emotion or laughter, digressions. When Noreen talks her face fills screen of intimate space. Too bad Peven can't see it. So Pev conflicted: is happy-in-the-moment when Noreen verbally translates his images and at same time *out* of that moment in an unhappy way.

Art shifts his cone of listening 180 degrees; attaches toilet paper roll to narrow that focus more—one of variety

Art's Earcup

of such prostheses—and aims super-sensitive apparatus at Alfred Schmerbauch's bitty brick bungalow. Does hear faint grumbling, cooing, throat clearing, finger-snapping, cursing, laughter, flatulence mixed with dashes of barely perceptible scratchy pen-on-paper sounds. Like astute sonar operator who can discern mysterious sounds of the sea, Art can say with high degree of certainty—yes!—that Al is grading students' exams.

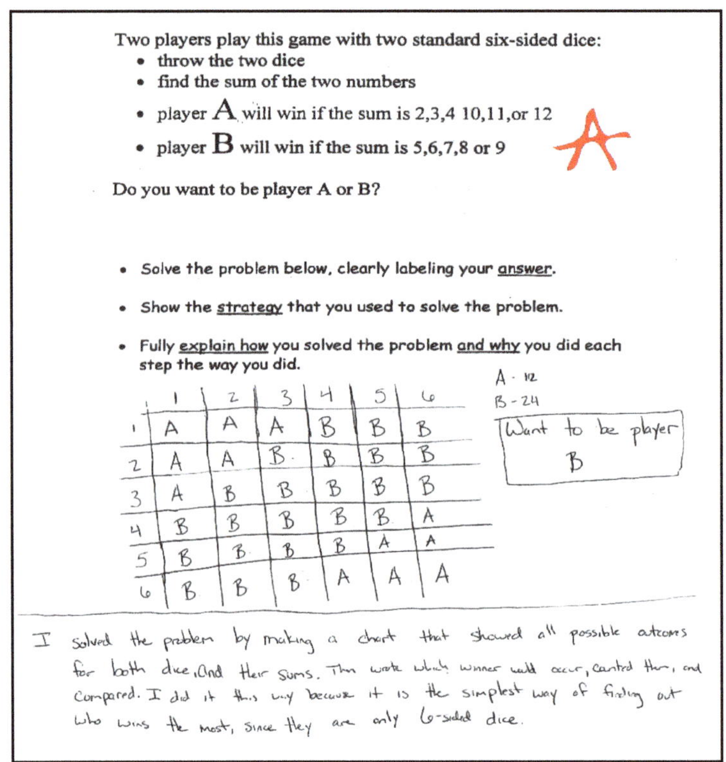

If this were film, camera would swoop in through Al's kitchen window, linger lovingly over Al lingering over exam at round wooden kitchen table, zoom into his face which would seem to embody geometry of totally alien obsessions, then resume zoom into frame-filling close-up of student's graded paper.

11.9   Excerpt from Art's Ear-Journal (titled *Herd This, Heard That*):

Sunday, Oct. 3rd. *Three o'crap in da morning 'n I'm wipin' me arse, mourning da turd, wipin' sleep out o' me eyes. Outside on street, over-imbibed buddy o' Dee 'n Roo's start-kicks "Rice-A-Roni" (a motorcycle cobbled together from Japanese 'n Italian parts) 'n revs 'er up unforgivingly. A nutso* placido domingo, señors! *Me bedroom be poorly placed.* Q.E.D.

12.0

Faint shiver at nape of his neck, organic warning somewhere above his diaphragm, change in temperature 'n in tempo of his consciousness. Art still sits immobile on his swivelling barstool up in his cockloft listening post. Two hours beyond midnight. In between spurts of emergency vehicle sirens, weird ear picks up faint female voice, due south by compass:

I AINT TELL MY MOMMA ON WARDINE AND REGINALD AND MOMMA AND ROY TONY. MY MOMMA SCARED OF ROY TONY. ROY TONY KILL COLUMBUS EPPS (YA KNOW, DA BROTHER WE USTA CALL 'MISTER BOUNCETY-BOUNCE' 'CAUSE O' HIS MOODS) OVER FOUR YEARS GONE, IN THE ROBERT TAYLOR PROJECT, FOR LOVE. BUT I KNOW REGINALD TELL. REGINALD SAY HE GONE DIE BEFORE WARDINE. MOMMA BEAT WARDINE AGAIN. HE SAY HE TAKE HIS SELF UP TO ROY TONY AND SAY HIM TO NOT MESS WITH WARDINE OR BREATHE BY HER MATTRESS AT [unintelligible]**. HE SAY HE TAKE HIS SELF ON DOWN TO THE PLAYGROUND AT THE PROJECT WHERE ROY TONY DO BUSINESS AND HE GO TO ROY TONY MAN-TO-MAN AND HE MAKE ROY TONY MAKE IT ALL RIGHT. BUT I THINK ROY TONY KILL REGINALD IF REGINALD GO. I THINK ROY TONY GONE KILL REGINALD AND THEN BEAT WARDINE TO DEATH WITH A HANGER. AND THEN SHIT NOBODY KNOW EXCEPT ME. AND I AM GONE HAVE A CHILD.**

Words send deep sorrow to invade Art's heart, as vast boundary of night rushes in from pre-history to exact present moment at 186,355 miles per second. Waxing gibbous moon looks at him so kindly. Battalion of storm clouds like clotted intestines be blowing high overhead, in 'n out of moon's ghastly light. Stars scatter in front of window like urinating soldiers. If this were film, camera would slowly, slowly pan back outside dome-home revealing lit interior scene recalling silence and melancholy of Ed Hopper's famous painting, *Nighthawks*. And musical accompaniment? Most apropos would be one of Mahler's most moving songs, *"Ich bin der Welt abhanden gekommen,"* with its flute and English horn, its theme of poetical withdrawal from world's everyday turmoil based on Friedrich Rückert's poetry.

Angles of his body in chair and his head and neck indicate he's too tired to sleep. Too much booze. On top of blow-out at Brauhaus, Pau gives Art two bottles of Napa Valley Singer Cellars's "The Song, 2005" (72 per cent Cabernet and 28 per cent Merlot) and tempts Art with his winsome wine review: "Zhis *vin* from zee Napa area has zee classic 'Rutherford dust' aroma; plums *et* zee green tea flavor opens later into zee ripe cherry fruit. Smooth black cherry flavors evolve into layers of blackberries, cocoa, *et* zee leathery finish with mouth-coating firm tannins. Zhis *vin* she be zee good balance of fruit, fine acid, integrated oak *et* alcohol—*c'est magnifique!*" Art polished off both bottles. This fruit-of-the-vine settles bet between he 'n Pau over one of their many Scrabble matches. Art (surprise, surprise?) always finds words easily, especially esoteric one's like ACROSTIC (by adding on to TIC) or ZEUGMA. Later in their hard-fought wordy agon, incorporating M and H that were first letters of two words going down, Art starts from first red square in top row and goes all way past second, making AMPHIBOLY. Twenty-one times nine, plus fifty-point bonus for playing all seven of his letters: two hundred and thirty-nine points in single play! "*Par les sept enfers de Landaire!*" yells Pau.

With swimming eyes he stares into dark sky, dark except for few restless small clouds floating at very great height. They look like loose 'n foamy bundles of reddish light (reflection from massive city's lights) drifting in cold, pale cosmic space. Suddenly, a flickering and glimmering appears here 'n there in still, glittering network of stars. As if usually invisible threads of net were suddenly leaping into flame. Like hurled stones, glowing 'n guttering, few stars fall slantwise across sky, one here, two there, few more here. Falling stars. A cosmic autumn with withered leaves from tree of heaven flinging themselves into void. A noiseless dispersal? Art wants to know if Una's corruption of a line of Dante's is correct when she calls his weird ear: "*L'orecchio che sente il sole e l'altre stelle*" (The ear that hears the sun and the other stars). So ungoops his weird ear and aims it at this uncanny celestial display. Frightful concentration on his face. Tries to filter out ambient city noise. *Damn EL and delivery trucks.* For brief second or two he thinks he hears faint fizz-zip like vastly speeded up recording of Alka Seltzer tab fizzing madly in water. Ho! Experiences slight taste of tooth-scratched gem. *Tastes like moonstone, also known as* albite*, a plagioclase feldspar that is easily scratched,* he pedantically muses. *Is it only I alone who have created this experience, or is it objective reality?* Letting his overactive imagination loose, he fancies his ear getting larger 'n larger as his cockloft seat turns into center of a vast net of associations where he comes to know everything, everything far beyond even what he could learn in institutions of learning. Knowledge would pour in on him who sits at this center as water runs to valley and hare to cabbage. By virtue of his ear 'n mind power he would unite all wonderful gifts 'n abilities within himself, using them at will. Everything would be steeped in new meaning, full of it as bread dough is of yeast. He would discover that way-of-ways giving sacredness 'n meaning to life.

12.1   Mystical musing abruptly terminated as something penetrates almost violently into his senses: house trembling, ear aching from some orotund voice. He stiffens into stone. At first his eyes blankly stare down Giddings Avenue. Nothing. Then he sees it. A big old blue Chicago street-sweeper, loudly protesting its late-night labor, angrily heading up his street. As he's often told Al, sense impressions are deeper soil for growing memories than best systems and analytical methods. Bombastic noise from sweeper sets Art into reveries. It's like gazing from a warm, cozy room out into broad, rain-soaked, war-torn fields, into his irrevocable past, a limbo of memory where bitter fragments of his past await redemption. Yes, our hero is doing skull-time. As Al once prophesied, "The *ear*-ly bird gets the worm." Now that worm is again digging into dank soil of his past.

Violated Portrait of Art's Papa

Like Proustian cookie dipped in tea, orotund voice of street-sweeper recalls brash, pompous, prolix, voice of his petulant *para-papanoid* as it painfully pricks little Art's ears. Piques Art? More than that. He experiences it as violation, auditory rape that often leaves taste of unpitted stale prunes in his mouth and his body stiff as stone. If sounds were to leave marks on one's body, little Art would've been perfect poster boy for child abuse. During father's psychotic rants daddy inverts words in sentence, then that of letters in word, then that of sentences, then that of words in sentence and that of letters in word. Exhausts all mathematical permutations. Fact: Al once told Art: "It would've been better perhaps had your dad modeled his speech upon the square root of minus two."During these tirades —father's voice be instrument of most terrible pertinaciousness—this Flogitious Father stands, then sits, then kneels; moves to 'n fro, from door to window, window to door, from breakfast nook to stove, from stove back to breakfast nook, from little Art's bed to fireplace to bed, to door and back. When his overbearing, *parapapanoid* so loses it, goes into howlin' fantods, little Art shuts down all systems. (Wouldn't you?) Turns to granite (where Art gets his geological propensities?). Or mewls. Later, as teeny teenager, enveloped by blind rage over daffy daddy, pimply Art envisions KAAABLAM-

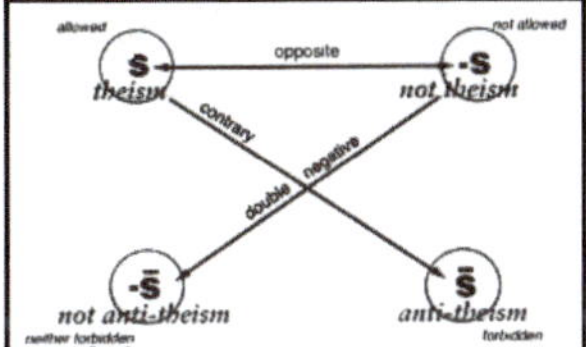

KAABLAM shooting this domestic despot with 4-barrel derringer loaded with dum-dums (best way to approach father be from behind John Booth-like, or so says famous *pater familias* pundit, D.D. Barthelme; moreover, Lacanian psychoanalyst would point out gun's four barrels figures semiotician Agirdas J. Greimas's famous theoretical shot-in-the-dark: The Semiotic Rectangle). Inspired by over-the-top *faux* violence of Sam Peckinpah's violent film, *The Wild Bunch,* Art envisions classic gunplay scenario as Hollywood version of his patricidal rage: multiple bullet hits, fountains of blood, slow-motion gore, daffy daddy bitterly flying hither 'n thither. Very very very satisfying.

12.2   In his youth Art's sense of peace unstable, visible one moment, gone next. Sometimes near as candle carried in hand, sometimes as remote as star in wintry sky. Bipolarity marching in tune with unpredictable mood swings of his *parapapanoid*. Can we blame him for developing passionate interest in utopias and their converse, dystopias? For in his heart each man carries some lost Paradise, some ruined world of submerged continents to which he wishes to return. So adolescent Art dreams his "Lavoo-Vahna," his ideal society:

bereft of that mind virus, established religion, and that toxic germ, arbitrary authority (both were incarnate in his daffy daddy), 'n where cultural poaching, "playin' jarism," is heap rampant (what today Art would characterize as "life in the trope-picks"). So middle-aged Art puts conch shell, Moana, to weird ear from which pours extraordinary confusion of sounds, immense ocean lapping all beaches of our world, roar 'n whistle of giant rollers, singing in undertow;, storms 'n typhonic winds boiling sea into maelstrom, then calming down into gentle amplitude.

Later, under influence of radical college prof, "Red" Rudy Acuña, Art will see fit to remove mass media, automobiles, and professionalized sports from his utopic vision. Rudy makes big impression on undergraduate Art when he tells his class: "We have made a wholly false definition of democracy as the freedom to buy and sell goods and to perpetuate the ideology of commerce. Unfortunately, we now understand democracy as just another *ideology*. Instead, we should see that democracy is an *ideal*. As an *ideology,* democracy differs little from Stalinism, both treat the individual as a means and not as an end. As an *ideal*, democracy treats individual as an end."

So Art dreams. Library of our dreams is language. Words are more than thought. They constitute a kind of reality in relation to thought. Language devours existence; existence feeds it. Humanity is a compost heap on which language germinates, grows, and flowers. After reading in his college linguistics class provocative Sapir-Whorf Hypothesis that language strongly shapes how we experience and construct our world, Art envisions his ideal society inventing artificial language akin to Esperanto so as to wipe ideological slate clean, so to speak. Moreover, Art intuits that speech means that one be not alone, our supposed "I" does not exist in isolated, chemically pure form. Through language there is always in each of us relationship with others (language as Bactine soothing 'n healing wound of our separations). Fact: such intuitions supported by Russian theorist Mikhail Bakhtin's dialogic theory, so Art will direct his enmity toward ossified, official discourses of society as being merely mass autism, as a mask for ideology that aims at monologue not dialogue. In totalitarian state, language seeks to drain first person pronoun of all its particularity, substituting group-thought. Yevgeny Zamyatin's famous dystopian novel, *We,* probes such.

A twelve-year-old boy who writes poetry, loves poetry, provides himself with what life cannot offer him. An eighteen-year-boy who writes utopias provides himself with what life does not offer him. The same boy who writes dystopias protests what life under capitalism does offer him. Books blossom in solitude, make us believe in freedom. Ho! A taste of that freedom comes to Art during his freshman English composition class when he is assigned to write a utopian or dystopian fantasy for term paper after his instructor read in class excerpts from Ernst Bloch's three-volume foray into the "not-yet," *The Principle of Hope*.

Art's daddy, his *parapapanoid,* be one scorching hot sun, a constant, merciless high noon. Everything intense, like when watching sports. Has up to three TVs and a radio on to cover several games at once. Yells loudly, empties house of Art, Els, and their mother. Ergo, Art hates sports. No surprise then when Art shocks his college mentor when he limns dystopian America (dubbed *SportsAmerika*) wherein mass media be all-pervasive.

Something is *Crook* in Middlebrook

Televised sports make up 80 per cent of all programming; ergo, all politicos are media personalities. Newscasters are drawn from arena of sports announcers. Coaches viewed as therapists. This thirty-page fabulation, banged out on Art's candy-apple red Smith-Corona, opens with heap profound sociological insight: "We do not know and conceivably can never know how an event at 2:00 p.m. in the upper right quadrant of Utopia is tied to the disappearance of a cultural species at 9:00 a.m. in the middle of Nostalgia." In this novelette, our newly elected "Coach" (title replaces former designation of "President") is Gym "Roarin' " Windrip. TV-image is of massive head with hands that seem carved from granite; tip of hat reveals baldness of a Verlaine that shines forth like fluorescing globe. Charismatic, when rises to speak, "[h]e bends forward his masterful head, like squared-off projectile, package full of good gunpowder, epitome of the cubic will of the State." (SA, P.32) Installed in office by landslide election, he be "Denver Broncos's winningest coach." Those great legislative bodies, House and Senate, be imagined by Art as arrayed with bleachers complete with manic vendors hawking drink and junk food (Coors 'n Twinkies preferred). Lobbyists be sketched as bubbly cheerleaders. And each state of our glorious Union has its mascot represented on legislative floor (Illinois has Chief Illiniwek, Mississippi has Stepin Fetchit). Votes in these assemblies are tallied on huge stadium score boards. After legislative sessions, "political-players" are given steam baths and vigorous massages. Years later, Art will say life imitates art when Ronnie Reagan makes it to White House, Jesse Ventura becomes governor, and former coach Mike Ditka be asked to run for a Republican Senate seat.

On sunny California day, March 20th, Art finishes this prescient tract; designates it "Hythlo Day," after Raphael Hythloday, protagonist in Sir Thomas More's famous book *Utopia*. Thereafter, he and his sister, Els, yearly celebrate Hythlo Day with an ice cream cake from Baskin-Robbins. Thereafter, he writes political diatribes for college paper under pseudonym of E.P.C.O.T. Fitzgerald. In one tongue-in-cheek *feuilleton,* Art adumbrates a new "Divided States of America" as solution to bitter political rancor between Left and Right; therein, each state would be autonomous and feature specific ideological bent: a state where Communism is practiced, a state where Fascism is the rule, state where Jim Crow Laws are in effect and citizens are required to carry Uzis and be proficient in survival techniques, a theocratic state where repair manuals would feature prayers to fix item in question, all-Jewish state, state populated by artists, aesthetes, and collectors, state wholly populated by elderly, etcetera. State for every kind of commitment 'n crazy. Federal level of government would be empowered only to organize disaster relief or raise Armed Forces for mutual protection.

As thoughts of these past sojourns into imaginative worlds simmer in Art's skull, he slowly comes to realization how consistent has been his desire for more just society, that they arose as response to his damaging upbringing and exposure to those monologic discourses inherent in family, church, society—institutions some term "Ideological State Apparatuses." For a new society to emerge, Art realizes, these institutions need to be critiqued, maybe abandoned, certainly radically changed. Heterogeneous language games need to replace our monologic master discourse. Global cooperation, rather than U.S. mandated empire. His eye catches student artwork he purchased at last School of the Art Institute's MFA show, conceptual piece depicting large Photo-Realist painting of one of those throwaway cameras. Camera jacket declaims: "Made in China with film from Italy or Germany." *Shit. The film itself accretes from more places on the map than emulsion can cover,* thinks Art. *Silver halides, metal salts, dye couplers, bleach fixatives, ingredients gathered from Russia, Arizona, Brazil, and underwater seabeds, before being decanted in the former DDR. Camera in a pouch, the true multinational: trees from the Pacific Northwest and the southwestern coastal plain. Straw and recovered wood scrap from Canada. Synthetic adhesive from Korea. Bauxite from Australia, Jamaica, Guinea. Oil from the Gulf of Mexico or North Sea Rent Blend, turned to plastic in the Republic of China before being shipped to its mortal enemies on the Mainland for molding. Cinnabar from Spain. Nickel and titanium from South Africa. Flash elements stamped in Malaysia, electronics in Singapore. Design and color transfers drawn up in New York. Assembled and shipped from that address in California by a merchant fleet beyond description, completing the most heavily choreographed conference in existence. . . . Malaysia? . . .*

Art's thoughts detour to Aldous Huxley's utopian novel *Island,* on how influential it was on him and youth of his generation, what with its conception of Pala, an ideal society situated in Malaysia and rooted in best of Western and Eastern thought. Inhabited by gentle people who love within context of vastly extended families, employing ecologically sound practices, and exemplifying dialogue and community. In Pala there is but one newspaper, but on it is panel of editors representing half dozen different parties and interests. Each of them gets his allotted space for comment and criticism. Thus, readers are in position to compare these arguments and make up their own minds. But, horrors, even that community appears doomed to subjection by greedy capitalist neighbors out to exploit its natural resources. *Huxley doesn't lull us, but keeps us aware of those always pervasive forces of reaction 'n exploitation. God . . . what would ol' Huxley say about our society today? He'd be amused, amused to death, I'll bet.*

12.3   Like diver decompressing on way to surface Art gradually emerges from skull-time. Eventually, he turns gaze back up into that chill night sky. Meteor shower no longer graces heavens with its fireworks. But moist studs of the stars, the seated stars, do seize onto space-time. Below, noisy streetsweeper be, judging from diminished sound, about a mile distant. Yet polyrhythmic and polyphonic movement of its progress evident. Art stretches. Yawns. His mind races through tidbits of adventures he's had like film editor reeling through scenes. *It might make a good book.*

Hops off his swivel stool and, sensing he can now sleep soundly, traipses to bedroom. Turns toward dresser. Looks at himself in oval mirror. Sees spittin' image of actor Bob Hoskins. Recognizes that most limited of all specialists: well-rounded man (pun intended). Sees face that be synergistic, constant struggle and cooperation between static and changeable aspects. Runs hands over his balding pate. Smiles. Turns to his right. Notices left ear is continuing to enlarge as time goes by. *A grotesque body; a body in the act of becoming. I'm creating another body! A body intertextually linked to other bodies through the intimacy of sound.* He flops down in his ear-shaped bed. Before tired triumphance passes over his face, we might glimpse thereon (if this were film close-up and we were very astute) a blending of activity, hesitations, laziness, brilliant utopias, of philosophical aspirations, and vague enthusiasms mixed with certain instincts towards a renaissance. He's forgotten to get undressed. No one sees him slip into delicious dreamful slumber in this unanimous night.

Dreams: Walkers of city travel at different speeds, their steps handwriting of personal mobility. In milling of crowd is choking of class relations, interruption of speed, and machine. Art sees himself speeding down car-jammed, noise-filled Chicago thoroughfare, weaving dangerously in 'n out of traffic, on tandem bike steered by wild-eyed Tavis Gulley. At stop-light Art glances left 'n notices his reflection superimposed in glass covering of an Armani Exchange ad 'n it's merging with sepia-toned photo of male model until both of them are melded together 'n it's hard to turn away; except for sound of Tavis's beeper going off city suddenly goes quiet, air crackling not with static but with something else, something less; cabs lumber by silently, someone dressed exactly like Art crosses street in front of them. Looking up, Art sees labradorescent true-noon sky; stares wondering, childlike, at Chicago's staunch high-rises; gazes at Lake Michigan with its glitter-sizzle 'n proton play of jet-skis on its surface—lake, lake like an explosion, in last split-second before it explodes.

Inexplicably (this is a dream!) it's now about seven o'clock, late afternoon hour that rub-a-dubs up against edges of Spring evening—not exactly twilight, with violet gloom that word conjures up, nor sunset with its frets of rose 'n gold, but time of darkening greenery 'n feverish sweetness, when stale afternoon air somehow manages to refresh itself 'n electric lights going on one by one suggest excitement 'n splendor beyond their modest wattage. Art's on tippy-top Chicago's fastigium—Sears (now Willis) Tower —overseeing snarled city set firmly fit inside our Coca-Donald Society, looking top-o'-building triumphant as architect Howard Roark in final seconds of King Vidor's film of *The Fountainhead*.

Ah . . . vertical intoxication! City spires jut up at me, spearing me in the side. I breathe the land of my city; the 'scrapers that darken as they rocket skyward conduct telluric currents that appeal to the modern gaps between my nerves. The city is knowledge in every form, molecules in every combination—raw data.

His weird ear be dangerously ungooped, vulnerable to different powers and sub-powers, high altitude 'n low. Both enchanted and repelled by hot inexhaustible variety 'n radiance of life-sounds rising to meet him: voices raucous, low, full, pleading, vulgar, sharp, cutting, jovial, harmonious, commanding, harrowing, seductive, explosive or irritated, a virago's, a virgin's, an overbearing father's, a passionate, imperious lover's, shouting out dreary obstinacy of true passion; a maternal, sisterly, counseling, pious, infantile, rasping, insolent, egalitarian voice, a team player's voice, a voice of encouragement, of destructiveness or caresses, an ironic or aggressive or cynical voice, an old alcoholic's cat mewling in the gutter, denying the arrival of spring; a voice that is vile, veiled, velvety, noble, high-pitched, servile, majestic, ample, sick, affronted, undercut by bird twitters and street cries reflecting off walls, a piercing, plaintive voice, asking questions and saying come here, an alarming voice, broken, sobbing. A din which shakes Art in his skin till his solar plexus vibrates, legs tremble, and rush of carbonation felt at base of skull.. In a shower of fire and in a lightning of enthusiasm, Art muses: *Yep. . . . This is my America. Flesh of the Multitude . . . Simply to stay sane is an achievement.* A screaming comes across mid-morning Chicago sky. It has happened before, but there is nothing to compare it to now. An ending that's a new beginning. *Where Now? Who Now? When Now?*

12.4   6 a.m. Bang Ho's Bakelite radio's old tubes do brighten up, anode 'n cathode beaming 'n blaring:

> *We still have clouds, we still have some fog north of the city along the lakeshore, but, uh, during the afternoon the sky can brighten, the sun can peek on through, temperatures get on up into the sixties. A couple of showers and maybe a thunderstorm this evening, and the weekend to follow look pretty good, at least partly sunny. . . .*

Art remains pensive.

— IT'S OVER, KINDA —

IN MEMORIAM

Just prior to this manuscript going to press, Art's friend (and by now, hopefully yours too) Pau D'Arco was found dead in a garbage can behind his bistro from a bullet (.380 ACP) tap-to-the-*tête*. Speculation is that sunny-dispositioned Pau's shady past with the Québecois-Separatist Left may have been a factor, but we must not forget that damned elusive Pimpernel —Paladin—is still on the job.

Pau's will began with this request: "Champagne for my real friends; real pain for my sham friends." It's unclear whether the word "pain" was meant to be French (bread) or English. As per that Last Will and Testament, Pau's body was poached in white wine, stock, olive oil, vinegar, aromatic vegetables, herbs, garlic, and slices of lemon for twenty-four hours and displayed *en Aspic* on a bed of lettuce leaves in his own establishment. Black napkins and tablecloths graced The Bowmanville Bistro. Deena served her famous "Love Omelette" (hearts of artichoke, hearts of palm).

Attending were: Deena Boettcher who (in French too mangled to translate here) offered the eulogy; Rusk Boettcher gave out his loudest belch yet and passed around jorums of homemade Belgian Ale; Al Schmerbauch read a litany of statistics on gun violence; Arthur S. Middlebrook offered up a bad pun: "When customers, delighted with their foodly fare, asked Pau for more, little did he grok *he'd* get *mort*." Guided by Noreen Pogacnic, the event was photographed for posterity by Peven.

—J. R. H.

Q & A:
An Auto-Interview with James Hugunin

The Setting: A storefront studio west of Chicago's Loop. Outside a man is swearing fine-sounding swearwords at a small yellow motorcar of Italian extraction, the same having joined its bumper to another bumper, the two bumpers intertangling like dueling interlocutors.

Question: Let's have a little talk. *[Cheshire cat smile.]*

Answer: I don't like little talks. *[Finger tapping kitchen table; frowns]*

Question: Then let's call it an interview.

Answer: Okay, but interviews are work and work is the opiate of the people. *[Eyes squint, eyebrows raise.]*

Question: That sounds like antagonistic cooperation?

Answer: At least it's cooperation. *[Blows nose.]*

Question: Your wacky postmodern text has been praised as exhibiting: "coruscating wit" and "penetrating social observation," but why bother writing about this specific, quirky fellow, Arthur Middlebrook? *[Picks his nose.]* Why not focus on yourself? Might it be because you see something of your own self in him? Through him do you probe your Self?

Answer: *[Wiping nose with his handkie.]* Ah, the old innerworld of the outerworld of the innerworld stuff! . . . I once took a seminar, "Becoming a Mundus Novian: Salutary Self-Expression and the Paradox of the Me," wherein we were told people write autobiographies to redeem the past and transform every 'It was' into an 'I wanted it thus!' and, moreover, that if there is, among all words, one that is inauthentic, then surely it is the word "authentic." Our seminar leader had us memorize this mantra: 'These actions, in which we now engage, do not denote what would be denoted by those actions which these actions denote'." There is no autobiography without biography. We make our lives, though often hermetically, out of the lives of others. The thing that's between us is fascination, and the fascination resides in our being alike. When Art and I met, our eyes locked and someone threw away the key. It was a sudden beating of brains, with all the charge and intimate grate of rubbed balloons. Maybe that had to do with the fact that with his sharp intelligence and impatience with trivialities, he was (like me) one of those men with whom others find it difficult to relax. Moreover, we are both serious 'foodies.' so I could relate when he talked of Pau's preparation of *filet aux moelles*—a filet with a bone marrow and Madeira sauce—registering synaesthetically like a fat organ chord in a tall church, hitting him hard: "Jim there's the base note (the beef), there's the middle note (the marrow), and there's the treble (the Madeira in the sauce)."

Something is *Crook* in Middlebrook

Sensing our similarities, well, it emptied our lungs! I make Art and Art makes me. We are mutually defining. We mirror each other in interesting ways. We are both "Caulbearers," born with the amniotic sac wrapped around us. Supposed to be good luck. After the fruits of our collaboration was complete, I commissioned one of my students to do Art's portrait as a pastiche of Alexei Jawlensky's German Expressionist style.

Let me use the Lacanian conception of The Mirror Stage to elucidate our relationship. Lacan postulates that the child at about six months *misrecognizes* itself in front of a mirror, seeing (and introjecting) an ideal unified self when, in fact, the infant has not yet developed such a command over its own body. Well, Art *is* that Lacanian mirror set before me, except this particular mirror is a carnival fun-house mirror that selectively distorts as it reflects. For instance, Art suffers that enlarged left ear and is fairly plump. He has a gimpy left leg. Art looks much like actor Bob Hoskins and I've been told if I was heavier I'd be a stunt double for that actor. Instead of being a child introjecting that mirror-image ideal, I've reversed the equation, *projecting* a distorted image of myself into print that may be more accurate psychologically as a representation than the idealized mirror-image self I've constructed my subjectivity around since I was a toddler. As Art would say, "Ya grok?" *[Cheshire cat smile.]*

Question: Interesting idea. So where does all that textual poaching come from and to what purpose? Do you want folks to say—as they do of Malcolm Lowry—"Oh! How *original* he is in his lack of originality?" How do you define a plagiarist? Poststructural genius or ingenious pragmatist? *[A challenging demeanor settles on his face.]*

Answer: Your "come from" is ambiguous. If you mean where do all the citations come from, well, they're so diverse and range over hundreds of texts read and assimilated. I'm a Robert Heinecken but who uses words rather than images. Too many to cite accurately. Besides, the point is to challenge the fetish of authorship and intellectual property.

Question: Like Walter Benjamin wanted to write a book made up entirely of quotations in order to purge all bourgeois subjectivity and allow the self to be a vehicle for the expression of "objective culture tendencies?" *[Strokes his beard, his eyes chasing each other like bugs round his face.]* It seems we have here an anthology held together by earnestness, yes?

Answer: Yes, what James Joyce called "that neverperfect everplanned." But if you mean where did my propensity for such appropriation originate, I'll need to also drop a big name in French theory, "an intelligence without bounds," as Roger Chartier called him.

Question: Who? Roland Barthes? *[Raises his eyebrows dramatically.]*

Answer: Close. Barthes *is* important to my thinking on intertextuality, the already-written, quotation, and on the replacement of the genius-notion of the *auteur* with that of the *bricoleur* who cobbles together texts from pre-existing texts. And sure, a variety of reader-response theories have been influential on me in terms of how readers *co-produce* the meaning of the text, not being simply injected with the author's intentions. But I have also drawn much from Michel de Certeau's two volume tome, *The Practice of Everyday Life*. I first read him in 1986, the year he died. His concept of . . .

Question: Poaching? I already read your citation from "Sore Toe" (as I like to call him) on your dedication page. *[Rubs index finger over front tooth.]*

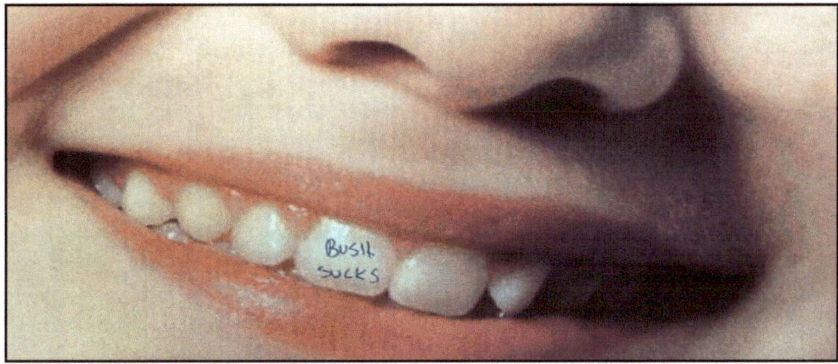

Photo by Lew Koch

Answer: Yes. He details "poaching" as an active consumption of cultural texts by the average person. Graffiti is one very basic example (see violated ad above). But more importantly, this concept subverts the staid academic notion of the expert reader as well as textual determinism, that the value of something is inherent in the thing itself and that it takes ample pedagogic preparation to interpret them. We assimilate texts (which are a tissue of other texts) and make of them what we can, even as they make us, become us. The most obvious case in point is fandom: fan cultures are not just bodies of enthusiastic readers, they are plunderers who are also active cultural producers. I'm a fan of diverse writings creatively combining those texts, making myself, playing with who I am. *[Clears his throat.]*

Question: The form of audience rewriting known as "filking" comes to mind here. Filk songs about TV programs, characters, and so forth. Fandom, the realm of creative appropriation pit against what they term "Mundania," the realm of lagging imaginations. *[Wiggles his ears.]*

Answer: Yes. This book is the result of an analogous plundering and rewriting. Reader-reception theorists talk about a virtual space or reserve, a distanciation inherent in the act of reading, that works to set up sites of pleasure or solace that fosters ironic detachment from the world imposed on the reader. What is captured in *Something is Crook in Middlebrook* in an attempt to give concrete expression to how we readers actually read texts, how we *impertinent* readers give personal meaning to texts encountered throughout our lives. How we are a tissue of texts that we weave from multifarious texts. What writers have written are here read and reread into a text (a production-in-use we might call it) that is then, of course, reread yet again by those who acquire it. Recall that this text was further redacted down from two earlier, larger texts as well. So at this level of extreme hypertextuality it *is*

Something is **Crook** in Middlebrook

possible—contra Brice Parain [see Prologue, p. x]—to be both a scholar *and* a knockabout comedian. *Voilà*! *[Tosses his arms upward.]*

Question: What was the most peculiar incident or issues you encountered in being Mr. Middlebrook's hired pen? *[Runs tongue over lips.]*

Answer: Well there were two, actually. First, in my prologue I mentioned Art wanted me to restrict the number of chapters, or parts, to twelve as Jean-Luc Godard had done in his film *Vivre Sa Vie.* It later occurred to me that that number also matched Christ's Passion, the Twelve Stations of the Cross! He got testy when I pressed on that. His Catholic upbringing is a touchy subject. Moreover, his comments about wanting to prove French philosopher Brice

Nana and Brice Parain

Parain wrong might have been motivated by the fact that in that Godard film—in episode nine, to be precise—the director's character, Nana—played by Godard's wife—sits in a café discussing the nature of language with Parain. Something about there is no going straight at the truth. Now I don't think that's a coincidence do you? *[Rubs neck with left hand.]*

Question: Hmmm. *[Eyes roll upward.]* As Al Schmerbauch might put it, there's a high probability you're right. What was the other incident?

 Answer: Well, secondly, when I complained this project would take years, he countered by admitting to the unfortunate habit of writing too quickly. I recall him saying: "Jim, your sloth will cancel out my bad habits: words come out of me like exhaust from an automobile, and if the vehicle eventually reaches its destination, the exhaust has by then dissipated. You can counter Peven Pogacnic's dicey dictum: 'A metaphor should take no longer to develop than a Polaroid.' Ya grok?" But much worse was his suggestion of, as he put it, "funhousing" the text.

Question: And that is? *[Scratches chin.]*

Answer: Having the writing translated into Russian by one undergraduate and then back into English again by another. To discourage him, I said the text *already* read like it was a bad translation and to "funhouse" the text might re-correct, might tame, the damn thing back into the zone of the normal. *That* scared him off.

Question: I find it important that the context for Art's adventures is the City of Chicago: its groans, screams, shots, sirens, rattles, clanks, curses, quips, confidences, and so forth. Like Saul Bellow wrote, "I heard the voice of the city." Any observations on that?

Answer: Pau D'Arco might mention that city, *cité* in French, is indistinguishable from *cité*, the French past participle of *citer*, 'to cite,' 'to quote.' Art's house is 'sited' in Chicago and passages in this text are 'cited' from a wide variety of sources. Moreover, like language, the city is change, uncertainty, instability. The city has its passages lined with text, the text here is lined with its passages.

Question: *[Chuckles and nods knowingly.]* About your ending, I registered that you end your text by copping the beginning of Thomas Pynchon's *Gravity's Rainbow*, but what is that reference to 'flesh of the Multitude'? Sounds kind of Whitmanesque.

Answer: *[Hikes left eyebrow.]* Michael Hardt and Antonio Negri's term for what is always excessive with respect to the value that capital can extract from the workers because capital can never capture all of life; it is a kind of *extimate* (to borrow a term from Jacques Lacan) element at the heart of capital. It retains revolutionary potential. Like hiccups.

Question: *[Licks finger, thumbs through his notes.]* Ah . . . hiccups?

Answer: Everything is different when you have hiccups. *[Remains thoughtful as if suddenly sunken in a strange subworld peopled with muddy, unknown forms.]* Hiccups reminds one that the act of speech does not take place in a void of purely formal relations: it is not a hermetic act but an *event* in the world. Art's weird ear experiences his aural environment, hiccups included, as a mélange of Orphic utterances in which world and word are brought forward as a phenomenological presence, a Life-World. *[Shuffles to his refrigerator, pulls out a superb bottle of Drouhin Chablis 2006 along with a gaggle of shucked raw Belon oysters. Silence; he is about to have a gastronomic experience thanks to Pau D'Arco. As the fork nears his mouth, his eyes and ears seem to have blanked out; all is concentrated in the power of taste. There follows a stage when the critical faculties are gathering, the head is bent, eyes wander, lips and tongue are working over the evidence. At last comes the climactic moment of judgment, upon which may hang the mood of the meal and with it who knows what devious changes in the course of this narrative. Starts to hiccup.]*

— The End —